The Modern A

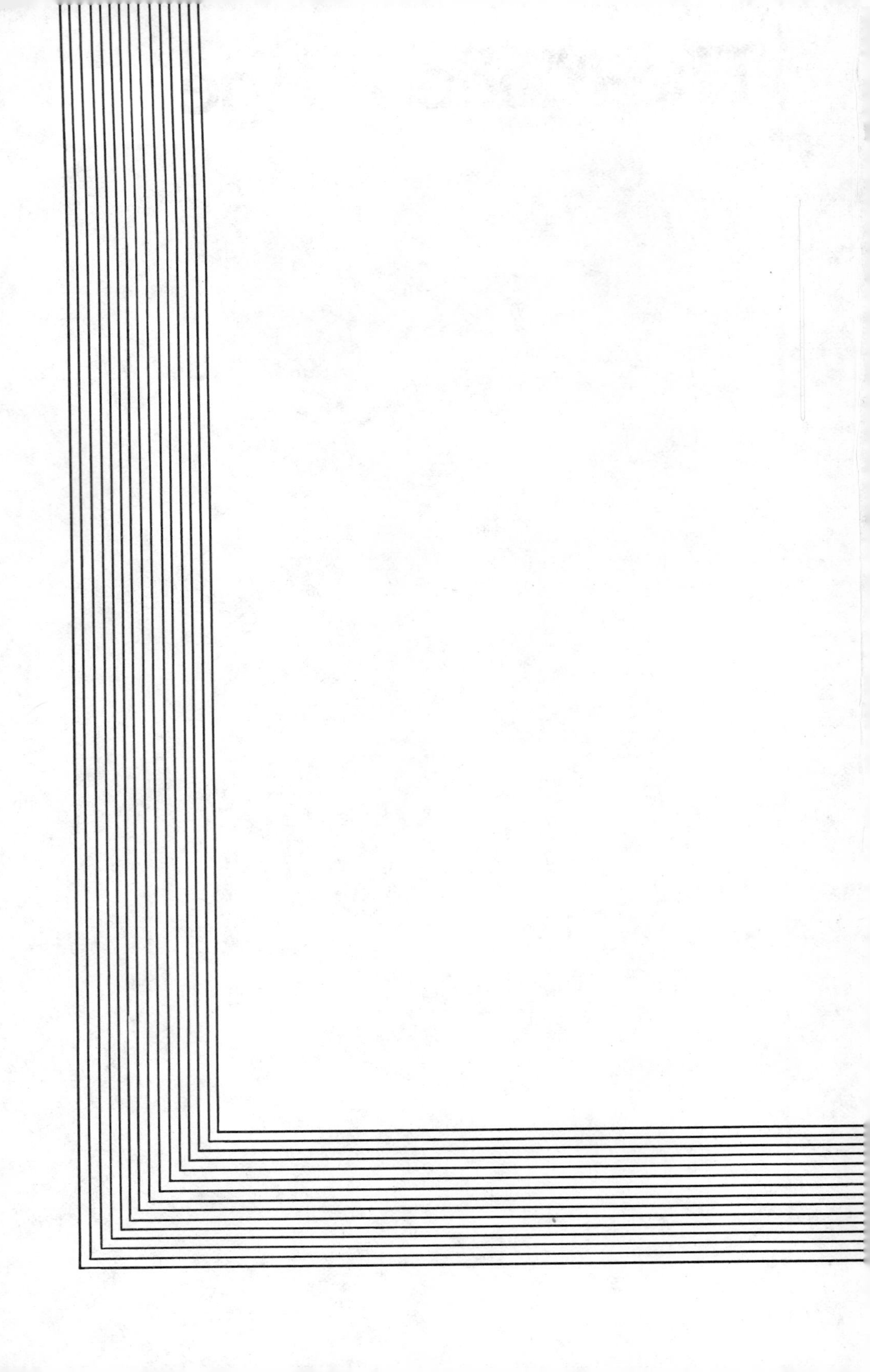

The Modern Age Literature

FOURTH EDITION

Leonard Lief
Herbert H. Lehman College
of The City University of New York

James F. Light
Southern Illinois University
at Carbondale

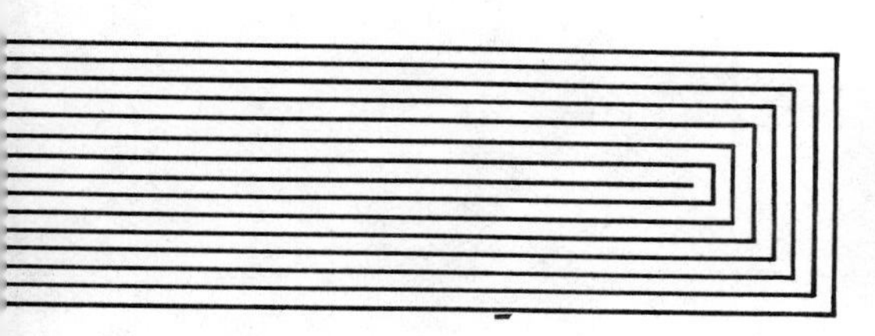

Holt, Rinehart and Winston
New York Chicago
San Francisco Dallas
Montreal Toronto

Library of Congress Cataloging in Publication Data

Lief, Leonard, comp.
The modern age.

Includes index.
1. American literature—20th century. 2. English literature—20th century. 3. American literature—19th century. 4. English literature—19th century. I. Light, James F., joint author. II. Title.
PS535.5.L5 1981 820'.8 80–24102

ISBN 0–03–055616–3

Printed in the United States of America
Published simultaneously in Canada
1 2 3 4 059 9 8 7 6 5 4 3 2 1

Preface

The fourth edition of *The Modern Age* is designed, as were the earlier editions, for use in first-year English and literature courses that require examples of expository writing as well as of fiction, poetry, and drama. The success of the earlier editions continues to maintain our belief in the appeal and the usefulness of a text that attempts, as we said earlier, "to provide a coherent intellectual adventure by illuminating some of the primary events and dilemmas of Anglo-American civilization of the recent past as these have been pondered by important writers." In order to achieve depth and focus we have confined our selections (with the exception of those by Marx, Engels, and Freud) to the work of Anglo-American writers.

Like the earlier editions of *The Modern Age*, the present edition is divided into three chronological segments. As in the third edition, the shortest division is the first ("Influential Voices") and the largest unit is the third ("Under the Volcano"). Through these proportions we have attempted to suggest some important aspects of the recent past but have stressed the variety and excitement of contemporary Anglo-American life and literature, particularly the shifting social, sexual, political, and ethnic relationships that absorb modern consciousness.

The basic emphasis of the text is historical, but an alternative table of contents has been provided for instructors who prefer to organize their courses around literary genres. In this alternative table, the expository sections are divided, somewhat arbitrarily, into exposition and argument; the selections categorized under exposition progress from essays that depend heavily on narration and description to essays that concentrate on ideas, while the argumentative selections progress from relatively objective arguments to arguments that are made emotionally, as well as intellectually, persuasive by the use of narration, description, and imaginative devices. The drama selections have been divided into tragedy and comedy, though with some awareness that the tragedies at times blend into tragicomedy and the comedies occasionally seem closer to comitragedy than to pure comedy. The fiction selections have been organized on the general principle of progression from the basically realistic and traditional to the symbolic, impressionistic, and experimental. The poetry selections have been divided into three major groups—narrative and dramatic poetry; lyric poetry; and poetry of wit and satire—but for teaching purposes a few special poetry forms have also been categorized.

As those who have used previous editions of *The Modern Age* will be aware, this use of genre as the basis for an alternative table of contents differs from the alternative thematic table of contents in earlier editions. The reason for this change is that the editors are persuaded by their more recent experiences in the classroom, as well as by the comments of a number of competent reviewers, that the genre table is at the present time more useful for teaching purposes than is the thematic division. Whatever the approach, however, we believe each selection speaks to the present generation, all the more so because numerous selections illuminate specific events (such as the assassination of Malcolm X) that are part of the living past, or depict (like "Tin Lizzie") people or movements that changed forever the quality of Anglo-American life. What we are today is a result of what we were yesterday. Accordingly, the selections in *The Modern Age* illuminate the continuity of past and present.

The selections also emphasize the dilemmas of our own times—our relationship to our fellow human beings, to our state, to our God (or gods), to our increasingly urban, mechanized environment, and to the world community fraught with wars and the terrifying question of destruction or survival. In addition, the selections manifest the influence of three intellectual giants of the modern era—Charles Darwin, Karl Marx, and Sigmund Freud—because no understanding of the present can pretend to intelligence without an awareness of their pervasive influence. Finally, as expressions of the human spirit, the selections capture the eternal joys, agonies, and aspirations of youth. Topics with which students identify and to which they most often respond—sex, love, marriage, rebellion, alienation—are fully represented.

In this fourth edition of *The Modern Age* we have eliminated a number of selections that seem less pertinent today than when they were included, and we have continued to exclude selections that, whatever their literary merit, have failed empirically the test of the classroom. We continue to believe, however, that there is a place in the college classroom for literature above the elementary level, and in that faith we have resisted the temptation to exclude a number of selections—among them those by Marx, Darwin, Freud, Eliot, and Faulkner—that we have been advised are too difficult for college students of the eighties. On the other hand it seems clear that the verbal ability of many college students has declined considerably over the last decade (a fact implied by the continuing deterioration of college verbal aptitude test scores) and that there is justice in the implied criticism in one reviewer's comment upon the third edition of *The Modern Age*: "It is telling that in section three there are approximately 53 pages of exposition and approximately 100 pages of poetry." For that reason we have expanded the expository section of *The Modern Age*, trying to choose essays of varying degrees of difficulty in concepts and language that might be helpful in the teaching of expository writing, and have added one essay with a variety of footnote forms to serve as an example of the footnoted paper. In addition, we have given greater representation to innovators of contemporary fiction by the inclusion of such artists as E. L. Doctorow, William Gass, and Robert Coover; have added a number of contemporary poets, from Robert Penn Warren (born in 1905) to Dave Smith (born in 1942); and have added three plays, one of them, *Death of a Salesman*, the play that many critics would claim to be Arthur Miller's major creation, and another, *The Hairy Ape*, the play that seems most effectively to dramatize Eugene O'Neill's tormented vision of man as a creature forever doomed to dangle between heaven and earth and never to be wholly suited to either sphere.

An *Instructor's Manual* is available. The manual may be obtained through a local Holt representative or by writing to the English Editor, College Department, Holt, Rinehart and Winston, 383 Madison Avenue, New York, NY 10017.

We are pleased to thank Richard S. Beal for his advice and Emita Hill, Herbert H. Lehman College, The City University of New York, for her editorial suggestions. We wish also to express our gratitude to the following readers of the manuscript for their valuable suggestions and constructive criticism: Arthur Croutier, Manchester Community College; Sheila Ewing, Purdue University; William Geyer, Augustana College; Robert Lorenzi, Camden County College; Susan Porterfield, Northern Illinois University; Philip W. Sawyer, Northern Illinois University.

L.L.
J.F.L.

Contents

2 The Long Armistice: 1918-1939

Exposition and Argument 150

Fiction 192

Drama 251

Poetry 315

3 Under the Volcano: 1939-1981

Poetry 619

Genre Contents

Exposition and Argument

Exposition

Argument

Fiction

Drama

Comedy

Tragedy

Poetry

Narrative and Dramatic Poetry

The Dramatic Monologue: A Special Form of Narrative Poetry

Lyric Poetry

The Sonnet: A Special Form of Lyric Poetry

The Elegy: A Special Form of Lyric Poetry

Poetry of Wit and Satire

Photograph of Astronaut Edwin E. Aldrin, Jr., NASA.

Influential Voices

1848–1917

Introduction

One might argue that the modern age begins with Nicolaus Copernicus, the sixteenth-century astronomer whose observations led him to believe that the sun, rather than the earth, was the center of the planetary system. His observations shook the medieval faith that the heavens had been created expressly for God's creature, man. Since Copernicus, scientific observation has continued to reveal man's insignificance. In an ever-expanding universe of awesome forces, it is hard to believe that man, once the center of creation, is more than a cosmic accident. For that reason, man's need to matter in his world is now largely unsatisfied, and few men today really believe that they are numbered among God's best beloved.

One might also argue that the modern age begins in the late nineteenth and early twentieth century, with the invention of wireless telegraphy and the airplane, both of which in their multitudinous evolution shrank the world's dimensions in time and space. Through such inventions the earth became a chain of nations, truly one mutually interdependent planet, and even the moon and stars became the neighbors of man. Although the reality of jet propulsion, as well as the swift transmission of sights and sounds over vast distances, brought poetic visions of brotherhood to some people, it brought nightmares of catastrophic destruction to others.

Without doubt the earth as it shrank became more endangered, and for that reason some people would argue that the modern age begins with the first atomic bomb, which exploded in Alamogordo, New Mexico, on July 16, 1945. The two subsequent explosions over Hiroshima and Nagasaki, which killed 152,000 and injured thousands more, haunt modern man with the horror of mass annihilation. Although everyday life continues in America, Russia, and China, the modern age might well be called the age of terror, and that fear recurs periodically in such episodes as the nuclear near-catastrophe of Three Mile Island, Pennsylvania.

Whatever its beginning, the modern age reflects the part of the past that has molded people toward thinking and writing as they do today. Among the influential voices that shaped and pervaded the thought of the present are those of Karl Marx and Friedrich Engels, who in 1848 stated the principles of "Scientific Socialism" (or Communism) in *The Communist Manifesto*. There they posited an economic interpretation of history, proclaimed the necessity of class struggle, and asserted the inevitable revolution of the proletariat against the capitalists. Their manifesto to the workers of the world—"unite; you have nothing to lose but your chains"—inspired such later proclamations as that of the American communist and labor hero, Joe Hill, who, before his execution, pleaded of his followers: "Don't mourn for me. Organize!"

Another nineteenth-century thinker, Charles Darwin, with the publication of his *On the Origin of the Species* (1859), precipitated a long debate between religion and science. After Darwin such religious men as Gerard Manley Hopkins could cling to the concept of God's grandeur, but Darwin's doctrine of evolution and the survival of the fittest led many thinking men to despair; led them to feel, as Thomas Hardy put it, "God-forgotten"; and led them to seek a viable faith—such as that implied in Matthew Arnold's cry in "Dover Beach," "Ah, love, let us be true to one another"—to replace the lost God of their fathers. Nietzsche's statement "God is dead" only affirmed the conviction of less learned men. Similarly, Stephen Crane's declaration in "The Open Boat" of man's insignificance in a world where chance, not justice, determines who survives and who does not, anticipated, long before the theories of existentialist philosophy became formalized, the absurdity of man's condition in a universe he neither made nor understands. Even to the common existentialist credo that man should matter, at least to himself, and therefore must act as if his choices have meaning, Crane gave one answer through the "supplicant" in "The Open Boat," who pleads, "Yes, but I love myself." To that solipsism nature answers by silence: "A high cold star on a winter's night is the word he feels that she says to him." Modern men and women still struggle to retain moral convictions in a universe that on the weight of considerable objective evidence seems governed less by absolute ethical law than by haphazard accident or by the "natural" law of brute force.

Other forces for change moved relentlessly onward in nineteenth-century England and America. Although imperialism reached its peak in the nineteenth century (see Kipling's poem "The White Man's Burden"), it also began to find opponents who hastened its relentless decline in the latter part of that century. Kipling mourned the decline of the British Empire in "Recessional" ("Lo, all our pomp of yesterday/ Is one with Nineveh and Tyre"), and Henry David Thoreau in his essay "Civil Disobedience" vehemently protested not only the immorality of force and violence in general but also the imperialistic exploitation that he felt dominated the Mexican-American War. Despite modern people's heightened consciousness of one world and the mutual problems its citizens must solve, nations persist in greed and violence, and young men keep, as did the poet Wilfred Owen in World War I, their tragic rendezvous with death.

Late-nineteenth and early-twentieth-century writers in England and America also sought emancipation from puritan morality and conventional artistic forms. George Bernard Shaw, a lifelong advocate of socialism and an iconoclast and dramatist, satirized the hypocrisy of alleged Christians and the "morality" of the ruling class. Walt Whitman may not have sought to destroy institutions, or so he claimed, but in his identification with democracy and the common man, and in the "barbaric yawp" of his poetry (the raw "free verse" that was to revolutionize twentieth-century poetry), Whitman belongs to the modern age as much as Allen Ginsberg, the guru of contemporary poetry. Rudyard Kipling shed poetic conventions for colloquial diction and realism. Robert Browning's variations in the dramatic monologue and Gerard Manley Hopkins' innovations in metrics and language expanded the boundaries of poetic form for future artistic exploration. Thomas Hardy and Stephen Crane, anticipating mid-century poets, presented in vivid images, ironic contrasts, and startling comparisons the universe as absurd. The familiar meters of the poetry of Matthew Arnold and A. E. Housman belie the modernity of their knowledge: that while old values and standards are dying, no new ones take their place. The complex wit, wordplay, half-rhymes, and stunning conceits of Emily Dickinson foreshadow by half a century T. S. Eliot's formulation of the objective correlative and MacLeish's dictum that a poem "should not mean, but be."

Though Victorian compromises and gentility lingered into the twentieth century, novelists as well as poets assaulted the artistic preconceptions and genteel sensibilities of their readers. Because they offended Victorian notions of decency, the works of D. H. Lawrence were originally banned. Even more daring than his linguistic innovation was his exploration of the Freudian unconscious, his revolt against rationalism, and his exaltation of the mystical. He dramatized the secret urges, agonies, and joys that attend the discovery and the loss of love. A contemporary of D. H. Lawrence, though without his desire to deify the mysteries of sex, was Katherine

Mansfield, who utilized stream-of-consciousness techniques to illuminate, much in the mode of the Russian Chekhov, perceptive insights in the lives of English men, women, and children. Perhaps the greatest creative emancipator of our time, however, was the Irishman James Joyce. In his short stories he captured the "epiphanies" (moments that blindingly reveal inward truths) that modern writers desperately strive to conceive and illuminate. With his weapons of "silence, exile, and cunning" he made his life a symbolic dedication to art. His novel *Ulysses* (written between 1914 and 1921 and first published in Paris in its complete form in 1922) gained immediate notoriety for its "obscenity" and "blasphemy." It was banned in the United States until 1933 but has steadily gained fame. *Ulysses* in its stream-of-consciousness technique, its multiple levels of meaning, its erudition and evocative wordplay (especially its puns in a variety of languages), its labyrinthian structure, and its dramatization of the trials of a representative modern man (the outcast Irish Jew, Leopold Bloom) in a representative modern city (Dublin) on a single day (June 16, 1904) taught innumerable writers some of the ways to enter the modern age in literature.

The spirit of innovations that has characterized the modern age bequeaths to artists today the freedom to be bound by nothing but the expressive needs of their material. Writers may dispense not only with rhyme and meter, chapters and verses, heroes and villains, but with conventional spelling, punctuation, even syntax. The need to be new in order to be modern may compel them to risk obscenity and narrow their audience by the demands they make. It is likely, however, that the artist of genuine merit, like James Joyce, will be clarified, not obscured by time.

Exposition and Argument

Charles Darwin (1809–1882)

Natural Selection

How will the struggle for existence . . . act in regard to variation? Can the principle of selection, which we have seen is so potent in the hands of man, apply under nature? I think we shall see that it can act most efficiently. Let the endless number of slight variations and individual differences occurring in our domestic productions, and, in a lesser degree, in those under nature, be borne in mind; as well as the strength of the hereditary tendency. Under domestication, it may be truly said that the whole organization becomes in some degree plastic. But the variability, which we almost universally meet with in our domestic productions, is not directly produced, as Hooker and Asa Gray have well remarked, by man; he can neither originate varieties, nor prevent their occurrency; he can preserve and accumulate such as do occur. Unintentionally he exposes organic beings to new and changing conditions of life, and variability ensues; but similar changes of conditions might and do occur under nature. Let it also be borne in mind how infinitely complex and close-fitting are the mutual relations of all organic beings to each other and to their physical conditions of life; and consequently what infinitely varied diversities of structure might be of use to each being under changing conditions of life. Can it, then, be thought improbable, seeing that variations useful to man have undoubtedly occurred, that other variations useful in some way to each being in the great and complex battle of life, should occur in the course of many successive generations? If such do occur, can we doubt (remembering that many more individuals are born than can possibly survive) that individuals having any advantage, however, slight, over others, would have the best chance of surviving and procreating their kind? On the other hand, we may feel sure that any variation in the least degree injurious would be rigidly destroyed. This preservation of favourable individual differences and variations, and the destruction of those which are injurious, I have called Natural Selection, or the Survival of the Fittest. Variations neither useful nor injurious would not be affected by natural selection, and would be left either a fluctuating element, as perhaps we see in certain polymorphic species, or would ultimately become fixed, owing to the nature of the organism and the nature of the conditions.

Several writers have misapprehended or objected to the term Natural Selec-

From *On the Origin of Species*, 1859.

tion. Some have even imagined that natural selection induces variability, whereas it implies only the preservation of such variations as arise and are beneficial to the being under its conditions of life. No one objects to agriculturists speaking of the potent effects of man's selection; and in this case the individual differences given by nature, which man for some object selects, must of necessity first occur. Others have objected that the term selection implies conscious choice in the animals which become modified; and it has even been urged that, as plants have no volition, natural selection is not applicable to them! In the literal sense of the word, no doubt, natural selection is a false term; but who ever objected to chemists speaking of the elective affinities of the various elements?—and yet an acid cannot strictly be said to elect the base with which it in preference combines. It has been said that I speak of natural selection as an active power or Deity; but who objects to an author speaking of the attraction of gravity as ruling the movements of the planets? Every one knows what is meant and is implied by such metaphorical expressions; and they are almost necessary for brevity. So again it is difficult to avoid personifying the word Nature; but I mean by Nature, only the aggregate action and product of many natural laws, and by laws the sequence of events as ascertained by us. With a little familiarity such superficial objections will be forgotten.

We shall best understand the probable course of natural selection by taking the case of a country undergoing some slight physical change, for instance, of climate. The proportional numbers of its inhabitants will almost immediately undergo a change, and some species will probably become extinct. We may conclude, from what we have seen of the intimate and complex manner in which the inhabitants of each country are bound together, that any change in the numerical proportions of the inhabitants, independently of the change of climate itself, would seriously affect the others. If the country were open on its borders, new forms would certainly immigrate, and this would likewise seriously disturb the relations of some of the former inhabitants. Let it be remembered how powerful the influence of a single introduced tree or mammal has been shown to be. But in the case of an island, or of a country partly surrounded by barriers, into which new and better adapted forms could not freely enter, we should then have places in the economy of nature which would assuredly be better filled up, if some of the original inhabitants were in some manner modified; for, had the area been open to immigration, these same places would have been seized on by intruders. In such cases, slight modifications, which in any way favored the individuals of any species, by better adapting them to their altered conditions, would tend to be preserved; and natural selection would have free scope for the work of improvement.

We have good reason to believe . . . that changes in the conditions of life give a tendency to increased variability; and in the foregoing cases the conditions have changed, and this would manifestly be favourable to natural selection, by affording a better chance of the occurrence of profitable variations. Unless such occur, natural selection can do nothing. Under the term of "variations," it must never be forgotten that mere individual differences are included. As man can produce a great result with his domestic animals and plants by adding up in any given direction individual differences, so could natural selection, but far more easily from having incomparably longer time for action. Nor do I believe that any great physical change, as of climate, or any unusual degree of isolation to check immigration, is necessary in order that new and unoccupied places should be left, for natural selection to fill up by improving some of the varying inhabitants. For as all the inhabitants of each country are struggling together with nicely balanced forces, extremely slight modifications in the structure or habits of one species would often give it an advantage over others; and still further modifications of the same kind would often still further increase the advantage, as long as the species continued under the same conditions of life and profited by similar means of subsistence and defence. No country can be named in which all the native inhabitants are now so perfectly adapted to each other and to the physical conditions under which they live, that none of them could be still better adapted or improved; for in all countries, the natives have been so far conquered by naturalised productions, that they have allowed some foreigners to take firm possession of the land. And as foreigners have thus in every country beaten some of the natives, we may safely conclude that the natives might have been modified with advantage, so as to have better resisted the intruders.

As man can produce, and certainly has produced, a great result by his methodical and unconscious means of selection, what may not natural selection effect? Man can act only on external and visible characters: Nature, if I may be allowed to personify the nature preservation of survival of the fittest, cares nothing for appearances, except in so far as they are useful to any being. She can act on every internal organ, on every shade of constitutional difference, on the whole machinery of life. Man selects only for his own good: Nature only for that of the being which she tends. Every selected character is fully exercised by her, as is implied by the fact of their selection. Man keeps the natives of many climates in the same country; he seldom exercises each selected character in some peculiar and fitting manner; he feeds a long- and a short-beaked pigeon on the same food; he does not exercise a long-backed or long-legged quadruped in any peculiar manner; he exposes sheep with long and short wool to the same climate. He does not allow the most vigorous males to struggle for the females. He does not rigidly destroy all inferior animals, but protects during each varying season, as far as lies in his power, all his productions. He often begins his selection by some half-monstrous form; or at least by some modification prominent enough to catch the eye or to be plainly useful to him. Under nature, the slightest differences of structure or constitution may well turn the nicely balanced scale in the struggle for life, and so be preserved. How fleeting are the wishes and efforts of man! how short his time! and consequently how poor will be his results, compared with those accumulated by Nature during whole geological periods! Can we wonder, then, that Nature's productions should be far "truer" in character than man's productions; that they should be infinitely better adapted to the most complex conditions of life, and should plainly bear the stamp of far higher workmanship?

It may metaphorically be said that natural selection is daily and hourly scrutinising, throughout the world, the slightest variations; rejecting those that are bad, preserving and adding up all that are good; silently and insensibly working, *whenever and wherever opportunity offers*, at the improvement of each organic being in relation to its organic and inorganic conditions of life. We see nothing of these slow changes in progress, until the hand of time has marked the lapse of ages, and then so imperfect is our view into long-past geological ages, that we see only that the forms of life are now different from what they formerly were. . . .

Karl Marx (1818–1883) and
Friedrich Engels (1820–1895)

The Communist Manifesto

A spectre is haunting Europe, the spectre of Communism. All the powers of old Europe have entered into a holy alliance to exorcise this spectre; Pope and Czar, Metternich and Guizot, French Radicals and German police-spies.

Where is the party in opposition that has not been decried as communistic by its opponents in power? Where is the Opposition that has not hurled back the branding reproach of Communism, against the more advanced opposition parties, as well as against its reactionary adversaries?

Two things result from this fact:

1. Communism is already acknowledged by all European powers to be itself a power.
2. It is high time that Communists should openly, in the face of the whole world, publish their views, their aims, their tendencies, and meet this nursery tale of the spectre of Communism with a manifesto of the party itself.

To this end, Communists of various nationalities have assembled in London, and sketched the following manifesto, to be published in the English, French, German, Italian, Flemish, and Danish languages.

I. BOURGEOIS AND PROLETARIANS

The history of all hitherto existing society is the history of class struggles.

Freeman and slave, patrician and plebeian, lord and serf, guild-master and journeyman, in a word, oppressor and oppressed, stood in constant opposition to one another, carried on an uninterrupted, now hidden, now open fight, a fight that each time ended either in a revolutionary reconstitution of society at large, or in the common ruin of the contending classes.

In the earlier epochs of history, we find almost everywhere a complicated arrangement of society into various orders, a manifold gradation of social rank. In ancient Rome we have patricians, knights, plebeians, slaves; in the Middle Ages, feudal lords, vassals, guild-masters, journeymen, apprentices, serfs; in almost all of these classes, again, subordinate gradations.

The modern bourgeois society that has sprouted from the ruins of feudal society has not done away with class antagonisms. It has but established new classes, new conditions of oppression, new forms of struggle in place of the old ones.

Our epoch, the epoch of the bourgeoisie, possesses, however, this distinctive feature; it has simplified the class antagonisms. Society as a whole is more and more splitting up into two great hostile camps, into two great classes directly facing each other: Bourgeoisie and Proletariat.

• • •

In proportion as the bourgeoisie, i.e., capital, is developed, in the same proportion is the proletariat, the modern working-class, developed, a class of laborers, who live only so long as they find work, and who find work only so long as their labor increases capital. These laborers, who must sell themselves piecemeal, are a commodity, like every other article of commerce, and are consequently exposed to all the vicissitudes of competition, to all the fluctuations of the market.

Owing to the extensive use of machinery and to division of labor, the work of the proletarians has lost all individual character, and, consequently, all charm for the workman. He becomes an appendage of the machine, and it is only the most simple, most monotonous, and most easily acquired knack that is required of him. Hence, the cost of production of a workman is restricted, almost entirely, to the means of subsistence that he requires for his maintenance, and for the propagation of his race. But the price of a commodity, and also of labor, is equal to its cost of production. In proportion, therefore, as the repulsiveness of the work increases, the wage decreases. Nay more, in proportion as the use of machinery and division of labor increases, in the same proportion the burden of toil also increases, whether by prolongation of the working hours, by increase of the work enacted in a given time, or by increased speed of the machinery, etc.

Modern industry has converted the little workshop of the patriarchal master into the great factory of the industrial capitalist. Masses of laborers, crowded into the factory, are organized like soldiers. As privates of the industrial army they are placed under the command of a perfect hierarchy of officers and sergeants. Not only are they the slaves of the bourgeois class, and of the bourgeois State, they are daily and hourly enslaved by the machine, by the overlooker, and, above all, by the individual bourgeois manufacturer himself. The more openly this despotism proclaims gain to be its end and aim, the more petty, the more hateful and the more embittering it is.

The less the skill and exertion or strength implied in manual labor, in other words, the more modern industry becomes developed, the more is the labor of men superseded by that of women. Differences of age and sex have no longer any distinctive social validity for the working class. All are instruments of labor, more or less expensive to use, according to their age and sex.

No sooner is the exploitation of the laborer by the manufacturer, so far at an end, and he receives his wages in cash, than he is set upon by the other portions of the bourgeoisie, the landlord, the shopkeeper, the pawnbroker, etc.

The lower strata of the middle class, the small tradespeople, shopkeepers, and retired tradesmen generally, the handicraftsmen and peasants, all these sink gradually into the proletariat, partly because their diminutive capital does not suffice for the scale on which Modern Industry is carried on, and is swamped in the competition with the large capitalists, partly because their specialized skill is rendered worthless by new methods of production. Thus the proletariat is recruited from all classes of the population.

• • •

Of all the classes that stand face to face with the bourgeoisie today, the proletariat alone is a really revolutionary class. The other classes decay and finally disappear in the face of modern industry; the proletariat is its special and essential product.

The lower middle-class, the small manufacturer, the shopkeeper, the artisan, the peasant, all these fight against the bourgeoisie, to save from extinction their existence as fractions of the middle class. They are, therefore, not revolutionary, but conservative. Nay more, they are reactionary, for they try to roll back the wheel of history. If by chance they are revolutionary, they are so, only in view of their impending transfer into the proletariat; they thus defend not their present, but their future interests, they desert their own standpoint to place themselves at that of the proletariat.

The "dangerous class," the social scum, that passively rotting mass thrown off by the lowest layers of old society, may, here and there, be swept into the movement by a proletarian revolution; its conditions of life, however, prepare it far more for the part of a bribed tool of reactionary intrigue.

In the conditions of the proletariat, those of old society at large are already virtually swamped. The proletarian is without property; his relation to his wife and children has no longer anything in common with the bourgeois family relations; modern industrial labor, modern subjection to capital, the same in England as in France, in America as in Germany, has stripped him of every trace of national character. Law, morality, religion, are to him so many bourgeois prejudices, behind which lurk in ambush just as many bourgeois interests. All the preceding classes that got the upper hand sought to fortify their already acquired status by subjecting society at large to their conditions of appropriation. The proletarians cannot become masters of the productive forces of society, except by abolishing their own previous mode of appropriation, and thereby also every other previous mode of appropriation. They have nothing of their own to secure and to fortify; their mission is to destroy all previous securities for, and insurances of, individual property.

All previous historical movements were movements of minorities, or in the interest of minorities. The proletarian movement is the self-conscious, independent movement of the immense majority, in the interest of the immense majority. The proletariat, the lowest stratum of our present society, cannot stir, cannot raise itself up, without the whole superincumbent strata of official society being sprung into the air.

Though not in substance, yet in form, the struggle of the proletariat with the bourgeoisie is at first a national struggle. The proletariat of each country must first of all settle matters with its bourgeoisie. In depicting the most general phases of the development of the proletariat, we traced the more or less veiled civil war, raging within existing society, up to the point where the war breaks out into open revolution, and where the violent overthrow of the bourgeoisie, lays the foundation for the sway of the proletariat.

Hitherto, every form of society has been based, as we have already seen, on the antagonism of oppressing and oppressed classes. But in order to oppress a class, certain conditions must be assured to it under which it can, at least, continue its slavish existence. The serf, in the period of serfdom, raised himself to membership in the commune, just as the petty bourgeois, under the yoke of feudal absolution, managed to develop into a bourgeois. The modern laborer, on the contrary, instead of rising with the progress of industry, sinks deeper and deeper below the conditions of existence of his own class. He becomes a pauper, and pauperism develops more rapidly than population and wealth. And here it becomes evident that the bourgeoisie is unfit any longer to be the ruling class in society, and to impose its conditions of existence upon society, as and overriding law. It is unfit to rule, because it is incompetent to assure an existence to its slave within his slavery, because it cannot help letting him sink into such a state that it has to feed him. Society can no longer live under this bourgeoisie, in other words, its existence is no longer compatible with society. The essential condition for the existence, and for the sway of the bourgeois class, is the formation and augmentation of capital; the condition for capital is wage-labor. Wage-labor rests exclusively on competition between the laborers. The advance of industry, whose involuntary promoter is the bourgeoisie, replaces the isolation of the laborers, due to competition, by their involuntary combination, due to association. The development of Modern Industry therefore cuts from under its feet the very foundation on which the bourgeoisie produces and appropriates products. What the bourgeoisie therefore produces, above all, are its own grave-diggers. Its fall and the victory of the proletariat are equally inevitable.

II. PROLETARIANS AND COMMUNISTS

In what relation do the Communists stand to the proletarians as a whole?

The Communists do not form a separate party opposed to other working-class parties.

They have no interests separate and apart from those of the proletariat as a whole.

They do not set up any sectarian principles of their own, by which to shape and mould the proletarian movement.

The communists are distinguished from the other working-class parties by this only: 1. In the national struggles of the proletarians of the different countries they point out and bring to the front the common interests of the entire proletariat independently of all nationality. 2. In the various stages of development which the struggle of the working class against the bourgeoisie has to pass through, they always and everywhere represent the interests of the movement as a whole.

The Communists, therefore, are on the one hand practically the most advanced and resolute section of the working-class parties of every country, that section which pushes forward all others; on the other hand, theoretically, they have over the great mass of the proletariat the advantage of clearly understanding the line of march, the conditions, and the ultimate general results of the proletarian movement.

The immediate aim of the Communists is the same as that of all the other proletarian parties: formation of the proletariat into a class, overthrow of the bourgeois supremacy, conquest of political power by the proletariat.

The theoretical conclusions of the Communists are in no way based on ideas or principles that have been invented, or discovered, by this or that would-be universal reformer.

They merely express, in general terms, actual relations springing from an existing class struggle, from an historical movement going on under our very eyes. The abolition of existing property relations is not at all a distinctive feature of Communism. All property relations in the past have continually been subject to historical change consequent upon the change in historical conditions.

• • •

You are horrified at our intending to do away with private property. But in your existing society, private property is already done away with for nine-tenths of the population; its existence for the few is solely due to its non-existence in the hands of those nine-tenths. You reproach us, therefore, with intending to do away with a form of property, the necessary condition for whose existence is the non-existence of any property for the immense majority of society. In a word, you reproach us with intending to do away with your property. Precisely so; that is just what we intend.

• • •

The selfish misconception that induces you to transform into eternal laws of nature and of reason, the social forms springing from your present mode of production and form of property, historical relations that rise and disappear in the progress of production, this misconception you share with every ruling class that has preceded you. What you see clearly in the case of ancient property, what you admit in the case of feudal property, you are of course forbidden to admit in the case of your own bourgeois form of property.

Abolition of the family! Even the most radical flare up at this infamous proposal of the Communists.

On what foundation is the present family, the bourgeois family, based? On capital, on private gain. In its completely developed form this family exists only among the bourgeoisie. But this state of things finds its complement in the practical absence of the family among the proletarians, and in public prostitution.

The bourgeois family will vanish as a matter of course when its complement vanishes, and both will vanish with the vanishing of capital.

Do you charge us with wanting to stop the exploitation of children by their parents? To this crime we plead guilty.

But, you will say, we destroy the most hallowed of relations, when we replace home education by social. And your education! Is not that also social, and determined by the social conditions under which you educate, by the intervention, direct or indirect, of society by means of school, etc.? The Communists have not invented the intervention of society in education; they do but seek to alter the character of that intervention, and to rescue education from the influence of the ruling class.

The bourgeois clap-trap about the family and education, about the hallowed co-relation of parent and child, becomes all the more disgusting, the more, by the action of Modern Industry, all family ties among the proletarians are torn asunder, and their children transformed into simple articles of commerce and instruments of labor.

But you Communists would introduce community of women, screams the whole bourgeoisie in chorus. The bourgeois sees in his wife a mere instrument of production. He hears that the instruments of production are to be exploited in common, and, naturally, can come to no other conclusion than that the lot of being common to all will likewise fall to the women.

He has not even a suspicion that the real point aimed at is to do away with the status of women as the mere instruments of production in society. For the rest, nothing is more ridiculous than the virtuous indignation of our bourgeois at the community of women which, they pretend, is to be openly and officially established by the Communists. The Communists have no need to introduce community of women; it has existed almost from time immemorial.

Our bourgeois, not content with having the wives and daughters of their proletarians at their disposal, not to speak of the common prostitutes, take the greatest pleasure in seducing each others' wives. Bourgeois marriage is in reality a system of wives in common and thus, at the most, what the Communists might possibly be reproached with, is that they desire to introduce, in substitution for a hypocritically concealed, an openly legalized community of women. For the rest, it is self-evident that the abolition of the present system of production must bring with it the abolition of the community of women springing from that system, i.e., of prostitution both public and private.

The Communists are further reproached with desiring to abolish countries and nationalities.

The working men have no country. We cannot take from them what they have not got. Since the proletariat must first of all acquire political supremacy, must rise to be the leading class of the nation, must constitute itself the nation, it is, so far, itself national, though not in the bourgeois sense of the word.

The national differences and antagonisms between peoples are daily more and more vanishing, owing to the development of the bourgeoisie, to freedom of commerce, to the world-market, to uniformity in the mode of production and in the conditions of life corresponding thereto.

The supremacy of the proletariat will cause them to vanish still faster. United action, of the leading civilized countries at least, is one of the first conditions for the emancipation of the proletariat.

In proportion as the exploitation of

one individual by another is put an end to, the exploitation of one nation by another will also be put an end to. In proportion as the antagonism between classes within the nation vanishes, the hostility of one nation to another will come to an end.

The charges against Communism made from a religious, a philosophical, and generally, from an ideological standpoint, are not deserving of serious examination.

Does it require deep intuition to comprehend that man's ideas, views, and conceptions, in one word, man's consciousness, changes with every change in the conditions of his material existence, in his social relations and in his social life?

What else does the history of ideas prove, than that intellectual production changes in character in proportion as material production is changed? The ruling ideas of each age have ever been the ideas of its ruling class.

When people speak of ideas that revolutionize society, they do but express the fact, that within the old society, the elements of a new one have been created, and that the dissolution of the old ideas keeps even pace with the dissolution of the old conditions of existence.

When the ancient world was in its last throes, the ancient religions were overcome by Christianity. When Christian ideas succumbed in the 18th century to rationalist ideas, feudal society fought its death battle with the then revolutionary bourgeoisie. The ideas of religious liberty and freedom of conscience, merely gave expression to the sway of free competition within the domain of knowledge. "Undoubtedly," it will be said, "religious, moral, philosophical and juridical ideas have been modified in the course of historical development. But religion, morality, philosophy, political science, and law, constantly survived this change.

"There are, besides, eternal truths, such as Freedom, Justice, etc., that are common to all states of society. But Communism abolishes eternal truths, it abolishes all religion, and all morality, instead of constituting them on a new basis; it therefore acts in contradiction to all past historical experience."

What does this accusation reduce itself to? The history of all past society has consisted in the development of class antagonisms, antagonisms that assumed different forms at different epochs.

But whatever form they may have taken, one fact is common to all past ages, viz., the exploitation of one part of society by the other. No wonder, then, that the social consciousness of past ages, despite all the multiplicity and variety it displays, moves within certain common forms, or general ideas, with the total disappearance of class antagonisms.

The Communist revolution is the most radical rupture with traditional property relations; no wonder its development involves the most radical rupture with the traditional ideas of all of the bourgeoisie. But let us have done with the bourgeois objections to Communism.

We have seen above, that the first step in the revolution by the working class, is to raise the proletariat to the position of ruling class, to win the battle of democracy.

The proletariat will use its political supremacy to wrest, by degrees, all capital from the bourgeoisie, to centralize all instruments of production in the hands of the State, i.e., of the proletariat organized as the ruling class, and to increase the total of productive forces as rapidly as possible.

Of course, in the beginning, this cannot be effected except by means of despotic inroads on the rights of property, and on the conditions of bourgeois production; by means of measures, therefore, which appear economically insufficient and untenable, but which, in the course of the movement, outstrip themselves, necessitate further inroads upon the old social order, and are unavoidable as a means of entirely revolutionizing the mode of production.

These measures will of course be different in different countries.

Nevertheless in the most advanced countries the following will be found pretty generally applicable:

1. Abolition of property in land and application of all rents of land to public purposes.
2. A heavy progressive or graduated income tax.
3. Abolition of all right of inheritance.
4. Confiscation of property of emigrants and rebels.
5. Centralization of credit in the hands of the State, by means of a national bank with State capital and an exclusive monopoly.
6. Centralization of the means of communication and transport in the hands of the State.
7. Extension of factories and instruments of production owned by the State; the bringing into cultivation of waste lands, and the improvement of the soil generally in accordance with a common plan.
8. Equal liability of all to labor. Establishment of industrial armies, especially for agriculture.
9. Combination of agriculture with manufacturing industries; gradual abolition of the distinction between town and country, by a more equitable distribution of population over the country.
10. Free education for all children in public schools. Abolition of children's factory labor in its present form. Combination of education with industrial production, etc., etc.

When, in the course of development, class distinctions have disappeared, and all production has been concentrated in the hands of a vast association of the whole nation, the public power will lose its political character. Political power, properly so called, is merely the organized power of one class for oppressing another. If the proletariat during its contest with the bourgeoisie is compelled, by the force of circumstances, to organize itself as a class, if, by means of a revolution, it makes itself the ruling class, and, as such, sweeps away by force the old conditions of production, then it will, along with these conditions, have swept away the conditions for the existence of class antagonisms, and of classes generally, and will thereby have abolished its own supremacy as a class.

In place of the old bourgeois society, with its classes and class antagonisms, we shall have an association, in which the free development of each is the condition for the free development of all. . . .

Henry David Thoreau (1817–1862)

Civil Disobedience

I heartily accept the motto,—"The government is best which governs least"; and I should like to see it acted up to more rapidly and systematically. Carried out, it finally amounts to this, which also I believe,—"That government is best which governs not at all"; and when men are prepared for it, that will be the kind of government which they will have. Government is at best but an expedient; but most governments are usually, and all governments are sometimes, inexpedient. The objections which have been brought against a standing army, and they are many and weighty, and deserve to prevail, may also at last be brought against a standing government. The standing army is only an arm of the standing government. The government itself, which is only the mode which the people have chosen to execute their will, is equally liable to be abused and perverted before the people can act through it. Witness the present Mexican war, the work of comparatively a few individuals using the standing government as their tool; for, in the outset, the people would not have consented to this measure.

This American government,—what is it but a tradition, though a recent one, endeavoring to transmit itself unimpaired to posterity, but each instant losing some of its integrity? It has not the vitality and force of a single living man; for a single man can bend it to his will. It is a sort of wooden gun to the people themselves. But it is not the less necessary for this; for the people must have some complicated machinery or other, and hear its din, to satisfy that idea of government which they have. Governments show thus how successfully men can be imposed on, even impose on themselves, for their own advantage. It is excellent, we must all allow. Yet this government never of itself furthered any enterprise, but by the alacrity with which it got out of its way. *It* does not keep the country free. *It* does not settle the West. *It* does not educate. The character inherent in the American people has done all that has been accomplished; and it would have done somewhat more, if the government had not sometimes got in its way. For government is an expedient by which men would fain succeed in letting one another alone; and, as has been said, when it is most expedient, the governed are most let alone by it. Trade and commerce, if they were not made of india-rubber, would never manage to bounce over the obstacles which legislators are continually putting in their way; and, if one were to judge these men wholly by the effects of their actions and not partly by their intentions, they would deserve to be classed and punished with those mischievous persons who put obstructions on the railroads.

But, to speak practically and as a citizen, unlike those who call themselves no-government men, I ask for, not at once no government, but *at once* a better government. Let every man make known what kind of government would command his respect, and that will be one step toward obtaining it.

After all, the practical reason why, when the power is once in the hands of the people, a majority are permitted, and for a long period continue, to rule is not because they are most likely to be in the right, nor because this seems fairest to the minority, but because they are physically the strongest. But a government in which the majority rule in all cases cannot be based on justice, even as far as men understand it. Can there not be a government in which majorities do not virtually decide right and wrong, but conscience?—in which majorities decide only those questions to which the rule of expediency is applicable? Must the citizen ever for a moment, or in the least degree, resign his conscience to the legislator? Why has every man a conscience, then? I think that we should be men first, and subjects afterward. It is not desirable to cultivate a respect for the law, so much as for the right. The only obligation which I have a right to assume is to do at any time what I think right. It is truly enough said that a corporation has no conscience; but a corporation of conscientious men is a corporation *with* a conscience. Law never made men a whit more just; and, by means of their respect for it, even the well-disposed are daily made the agents of injustice. A common and natural result of an undue respect for law is, that you may see a file of soldiers, colonel, captain, corporal, privates, powder-monkeys, and all, marching in admirable order over hill and dale to the wars, against their wills, ay, against their common sense and consciences, which makes it very steep marching indeed, and produces a palpitation of the heart. They have no doubt that it is a damnable business in which they are concerned; they are all peaceably inclined. Now, what are they? Men at all? or small movable forts and magazines, at the service of some unscrupulous man in power? Visit the Navy-Yard, and behold a marine, such a man as an American government can make, or such as it can make a man with its black arts,—a mere shadow and reminiscence of humanity, a man laid out alive and standing, and already, as one may say, buried under arms with funeral accompaniments, though it may be,—

> "Not a drum was heard, not a funeral note,
> As his corpse to the rampart we hurried;
> Not a soldier discharged his farewell shot
> O'er the grave where our hero we buried."

The mass of men serve the state thus, not as men mainly, but as machines, with their bodies. They are the standing army, and the militia, jailers, constables, *posse comitatus,* etc. In most cases there is no free exercise whatever of the judgment or of the moral sense; but they put themselves on a level with wood and earth and stones; and wooden men can perhaps be manufactured that will serve the purpose as well. Such command no more respect than men of straw or a lump of dirt. They have the same sort of worth only as horses and dogs. Yet such as these even are commonly esteemed good citizens. Others—as most legislators, politicians, lawyers, ministers, and office-holders—serve the state chiefly with their heads; and, as they rarely make any moral distinctions, they are as likely to serve the devil, without *intending* it, as God. A very few,—as heroes, patriots, martyrs, reformers in the great sense, and *men*—serve the state with their consciences also, and so necessarily resist it for the most part; and they are commonly treated as enemies by it. A wise man will only be useful as a man, and will not submit to be "clay," and "stop a hole to keep the wind away," but leave that office to his dust at least:—

> "I am too high-born to be propertied,
> To be a secondary at control,
> Or useful serving-man and instrument
> To any sovereign state throughout the world."

He who gives himself entirely to his fellow-men appears to them useless and selfish; but he who gives himself partially to them is pronounced a benefactor and philanthropist.

How does it become a man to behave toward this American government today? I answer, that he cannot without disgrace be associated with it. I cannot for an instant recognize that political organization as *my* government which is the *slave's* government also. . . .

Unjust laws exist: shall we be content to obey them, or shall we endeavor to amend them, and obey them until we have succeeded, or shall we transgress them at once? Men generally, under such a government as this, think that they ought to wait until they have persuaded the majority to alter them. They think that, if they should resist, the remedy would be worse than the evil. But it is the fault of the government itself that the remedy *is* worse than the evil. *It* makes it worse. Why is it not more apt to anticipate and provide for reform? Why does it not cherish its wise minority? Why does it cry and resist before it is hurt? Why does it not encourage its citizens to be on the alert to point out its faults, and *do* better than it would have them? Why does it always crucify

Christ, and excommunicate Copernicus and Luther, and pronounce Washington and Franklin rebels?

One would think, that a deliberate and practical denial of its authority was the only offense never contemplated by government; else, why has it not assigned its definite, its suitable and proportionate penalty? If a man who has no property refuses but once to earn nine shillings for the State, he is put in prison for a period unlimited by any law that I know, and determined only by the discretion of those who placed him there; but if he should steal ninety times nine shillings from the State, he is soon permitted to go at large again.

If the injustice is part of the necessary friction of the machine of government, let it go, let it go: perchance it will wear smooth,—certainly the machine will wear out. If the injustice has a spring, or a pulley, or a rope, or a crank, exclusively for itself, then perhaps you may consider whether the remedy will not be worse than the evil, but if it is of such a nature that it requires you to be the agent of injustice to another, then, I say, break the law. Let your life be a counter friction to stop the machine. What I have to do is to see, at any rate, that I do not lend myself to the wrong which I condemn.

As for adopting the ways which the State has provided for remedying the evil, I know not of such ways. They take too much time, and a man's life will be gone. I have other affairs to attend to. I came into this world, not chiefly to make this a good place to live in, but to live in it, be it good or bad. A man has not everything to do, but something; and because he cannot do *everything,* it is not necessary that he should do *something* wrong. It is not my business to be petitioning the Governor or the Legislature any more than it is theirs to petition me; and if they should not hear my petition, what should I do then? But in this case the State has provided no way: its very Constitution is the evil. This may seem to be harsh and stubborn and unconciliatory; but it is to treat with the utmost kindness and consideration the only spirit that can appreciate or deserve it. So is all change for the better, like birth and death, which convulse the body.

I do not hesitate to say, that those who call themselves Abolitionists should at once effectually withdraw their support, both in person and property, from the government of Massachusetts, and not wait till they constitute a majority of one, before they suffer the right to prevail through them. I think that it is enough if they have God on their side, without waiting for that other one. Moreover, any man more right than his neighbors constitutes a majority of one already.

I meet this American government, or its representative, the State government, directly, and face to face, once a year—no more—in the person of its tax-gatherer; this is the only mode in which a man situated as I am necessarily meets it; and it then says distinctly, Recognize me; and the simplest, the most effectual, and, in the present posture of affairs, the indispensablest mode of treating with it on this head, of expressing your little satisfaction with and love for it, is to deny it then. My civil neighbor, the tax-gatherer, is the very man I have to deal with,—for it is, after all, with men and not with parchment that I quarrel,—and he has voluntarily chosen to be an agent of the government. How shall he ever know well what he is and does as an officer of the government, or as a man, until he is obligated to consider whether he shall treat me, his neighbor, for whom he has respect, as a neighbor and well-disposed man, or as a maniac and disturber of the peace, and see if he can get over this obstruction to his neighborliness without a ruder and more impetuous thought or speech corresponding with his action. I know this well, that if one thousand, if one hundred, if ten men whom I could name,—if ten *honest* men only,—ay, if *one* HONEST man, in this State of Massachusetts, *ceasing to hold slaves,* were actually to withdraw from this copartnership, and be locked up in the county jail therefor, it would be the abolition of slavery in America. For it matters not how much the beginning may seem to be: what is once well done is done forever. But we love better to talk about it: that we say is our mission. Reform keeps many scores of newspapers in its service, but not one man. If my esteemed neighbor, the State's ambassador, who will devote his days to the settlement of the question of human rights in the Council Chamber, instead of being threatened with the prisons of Carolina, were to sit down the prisoner of Massachusetts, that State which is so anxious to foist the sin of slavery upon her sister,—though at present she can discover only an act of inhospitality to be the ground of a quarrel with her,—the Legislature would not wholly waive the subject the following winter.

Under a government which imprisons and unjustly, the true place for a just man is also a prison. The proper place to-day, the only place which Massachusetts has provided for her freer and less desponding spirits, is in her prisons, to be put out and locked out of the State by her own act, as they have already put themselves out by their principles. It is there that the fugitive slave, and the Mexican prisoner on parole, and the Indian come to plead the wrongs of his race should find them; on that separate, but more free and honorable ground, where the State places those who are not *with* her, but *against* her,—the only house in a slave State in which a free man can abide with honor. If any think that their influence would be lost there, and their voices no longer afflict the ear of the State, that they would not be as an enemy within its walls, they do not know by how much truth is stronger than error, nor how much more eloquently and effectively he can combat injustice who has experienced a little in his own person. Cast your whole vote, not a strip of paper merely, but your whole influence. A minority is powerless while it conforms to the majority; it is not even a minority then; but it is irresistible when it clogs by its whole weight. If the alternative is to keep all just men in prison, or give up war and slavery, the State will not hesitate which to choose. If a thousand men were not to pay their tax-bill this year, that would not be a violent and bloody measure, as it would be to pay them, and enable the State to commit violence and shed innocent blood. This is, in fact, the definition of a peaceable revolution, if any such is possible. If the tax-gatherer, or any other public officer, asks me, as one has done, "But what shall I do?" my answer is, "If you really wish to do anything, resign your office." When the subject has refused allegiance, and the officer has resigned his office, then the revolution is accomplished. But even suppose blood should flow. Is there not a sort of blood shed when the conscience is wounded? Through this wound a man's real manhood and immortality flow out, and he bleeds to an everlasting death. I see this blood flowing now.

I have contemplated the imprisonment of the offender, rather than the seizure of his goods,—though both will serve the same purpose,—because they who assert the purest right, and consequently are most dangerous to a corrupt State, commonly have not spent much time in accumulating property. To such the State renders comparatively small service, and a slight tax is wont to appear exorbitant, particularly if they are obliged to earn it by a special labor with their hands. If there were one who lived wholly without the use of money, the State itself would hesitate to demand it of him. But the rich man—not to make any invidious comparison—is always sold to the institution which makes him rich. Absolutely speaking, the more money, the less virtue; for money comes between a man and his objects, and obtains them for him; and it was certainly no great virtue to obtain it. It puts to rest many questions which he would otherwise be taxed to answer; while the only new question which it puts is the hard but superfluous one, how to spend it. Thus his moral ground is taken from under his feet. The opportunities of living are diminished in proportion as what are called the "means" are increased. The best thing a man can do for his culture when he is rich is to endeavor to carry out those schemes which he entertained when he was poor. Christ answered the Herodians according to their condition. "Show me the tribute-money," said he;—and took one penny out of his pocket;—if you use money which has the image of Caesar on it and which he has made current and valuable, that is, *if you are men of the State,* and gladly enjoy the advantages of Caesar's government, then pay him back some of his own when he demands it. "Render therefore to Caesar that which is Caesar's, and to God those things which are God's"—leaving them no wiser than before as to which was which; for they did not wish to know.

When I converse with the freest of my neighbors, I perceive that, whatever they may say about the magnitude and seriousness of the question, and their regard for the public tranquillity, the long and the short of the matter is, that they cannot spare the protection of the existing government, and they dread the consequences to their property and families of disobedience to it. For my own part, I should not like to think that I ever rely on the protection of the State. But, if I deny the authority of the State when it presents its tax-bill, it will soon take and waste all my property, and so harass me and my children without end. This is hard. This makes it impossible for a man to live h and at the same time comforta outward respects. It will not be worth the while to accumulate property; that would be sure to go again. You must hire or squat somewhere, and raise but a small crop, and eat that soon. You must live within yourself, and depend upon yourself always tucked up and ready for a start, and not have many affairs. A man may grow rich in Turkey even, if he will be in all respects a good subject of the Turkish government. Confucius said: "If a state is governed by the principles of reason, poverty and misery are subjects of shame; if a state is not governed by the principles of reason, riches and honors are the subjects of shame." No: until I want the protection of Massachusetts to be extended to me in some distant Southern port, where my liberty is endangered, or until I am bent solely on building up an estate at home by peaceful enterprise, I can afford to refuse allegiance to Massachusetts, and her right to my property and life. It costs me less in every sense to incur the penalty of disobedience to the State than it would to obey. I should feel as if I were worth less in that case.

Some years ago, the State met me in behalf of the Church, and commanded me to pay a certain sum toward the support of a clergyman whose preaching my father attended, but never I myself. "Pay," it said, "or be locked up in the jail." I declined to pay. But, unfortunately, another man saw fit to pay it. I did not see why the schoolmaster should be taxed to support the priest, and not the priest the schoolmaster; for I was not the State's schoolmaster, but I supported myself by voluntary subscription. I did not see why the lyceum should not present its tax-bill, and have the State to back its demand, as well as the Church. However, at the request of the selectmen, I condescended to make some such statement as this in writing:—"Know all men by these presents, that I, Henry Thoreau, do not wish to be regarded as a member of any incorporated society which I have not joined." This I gave to the town clerk; and he has it. The State, having thus learned that I did not wish to be regarded as a member of that church, has never made a like demand on me since; though it said that it must adhere to its original presumption that time. If I had known how to name them, I should then have signed off in detail from all the societies which I never signed on to; but I did not know where to find a complete list.

I have paid no poll-tax for six years. I was put into a jail once on this account, for one night; and, as I stood considering the walls of solid stone, two or three feet thick, the door of wood and iron, a foot thick, and the iron grating which strained the light, I could not help being struck with the foolishness of that institution which treated me as if I were mere flesh and blood and bones, to be locked up. I wondered that it should have concluded at length that this was the best use it could put me to, and had never thought to avail itself of my services in some way. I saw that, if there was a wall of stone between me and my townsmen, there was a still more difficult one to climb or break through before they could get to be as free as I was. I did not for a moment feel confined, and the walls seemed a great waste of stone and mortar. I felt as if I alone of all my townsmen had paid my tax. They plainly did not know how to treat me, but behaved like persons who are underbred. In every threat and in every compliment there was a blunder; for they thought that my chief desire was to stand the other side of that stone wall. I could not but smile to see how industriously they locked the door on my meditations, which followed them out again without let or hindrance, and *they* were really all that was dangerous. As they could not reach me, they had resolved to punish my body; just as boys, if they cannot come at some person against whom they have a spite, will abuse his dog. I saw that the State was half-witted, that it was timid as a lone woman with her silver spoons, and that it did not know its friends from its foes, and I lost all my remaining respect for it, and pitied it.

Thus the State never intentionally confronts a man's sense, intellectual or moral, but only his body, his senses. It is not armed with superior wit or honesty, but with superior physical strength. I was not born to be forced. I will breathe after my own fashion. Let us see who is the strongest. What force has a multitude? They only can force me who obey a higher law than I. They force me to become like themselves. I do not hear of *men* being *forced* to live this way or that by masses of men. What sort of life were that to live? When I meet a government which says to me, "Your money or your life," why should I be in haste to give it my money? It may be in a great strait, and not know what to do: I cannot help that. It must help itself; do as I do. It is not worth the while to snivel about it. I am not responsible for the successful working of the machinery of society. I am not the son of the engineer. I perceive that, when an acorn and a chestnut fall side by side, the one does not remain inert to make way for the other, but both obey their own laws, and spring and grow and flourish as best they can, till one, perchance, overshadows and destroys the other. If a plant cannot live according to its nature, it dies; and so a man.

The night in prison was novel and interesting enough. The prisoners in their shirt-sleeves were enjoying a chat and the evening air in the doorway, when I entered. But the jailer said, "Come, boys, it is time to lock up;" and so they dispersed, and I heard the sound of their steps returning into the hollow apartments. My room-mate was introduced to me by the jailer as "a first-rate fellow and a clever man." When the door was locked, he showed me where to hang my hat, and how he managed matters there. The rooms were whitewashed once a month; and this one, at least, was the whitest, most simply furnished, and probably the neatest apartment in the town. He naturally wanted to know where I came from, and what brought me there; and, when I had told him, I asked him in my turn how he came there, presuming him to be an honest man, of course; and, as the world goes, I believe he was. "Why," said he, "they accuse me of burning a barn: but I never did it." As near as I could discover, he had probably gone to bed in a barn when drunk, and smoked his pipe there; and so a barn was burnt. He had the reputation of being a clever man, had been there some three months waiting for his trial to come on, and would have to wait as much longer; but he was quite domesticated and contented, since he got his board for nothing, and thought that he was well treated.

He occupied one window, and I the other; and I saw that if one stayed there long, his principal business would be to look out the window. I had soon read all the tracts that were left there, and examined where former prisoners had broken out, and where a grate had been sawed off, and heard the history of the various occupants of that room; for I found that even here there was a history and a gossip which never circulated beyond the walls of the jail. Probably this is the only house in the town where verses are composed, which are afterward printed in circular form, but not published. I was shown quite a long list of verses which were composed by some young men who had been detected in an attempt to escape, who avenged themselves by singing them.

I pumped my fellow-prisoner as dry as I could, for fear I should never see him again; but at length he showed me which was my bed, and left me to blow out the lamp.

It was like traveling into a far country, such as I had never expected to behold, to lie there for one night. It seemed to me that I never had heard the town clock strike before, nor the evening sounds of the village; for we slept with the windows open, which were inside the grating. It was to see my native village in the light of the Middle Ages, and our Concord was turned into a Rhine stream, and visions of knights and castles passed before me. They were the voices of old burghers that I heard in the streets. I was an involuntary spectator and auditor of whatever was done and said in the kitchen of the adjacent village-inn,—a wholly new and rare experience to me. It was a closer view of my native town. I was fairly inside of it. I never had seen its institutions before. This is one of the peculiar institutions; for it is a shire town. I began to comprehend what its inhabitants were about.

In the morning, our breakfasts were put through the hole in the door, in small oblong-square tin pans, made to fit, and holding a pint of chocolate, with brown bread, and an iron spoon. When they called for the vessels again, I was green enough to return what bread I had left; but my comrade seized it, and said that I should lay that up for lunch or dinner. Soon after he was let out to work at haying in a neighboring field, whither he went every day, and would not be back till noon; so he bade me good-day, saying that he doubted if he should see me again.

When I came out of prison,—for some one interfered, and paid that tax,—I did not perceive that great changes had taken place on the common, such as he observed who went in a youth and emerged a tottering and gray-headed man; and yet a change had to my eyes come over the scene,—the town, and State, and country,—greater than any that mere time could effect. I saw yet more distinctly the State in which I lived. I saw to what extent the people among whom I lived could be trusted as good neighbors and friends; that their friendship was for summer weather only; that they did not greatly propose to do right; that they were a distinct race from me by their prejudices and superstitions, as the Chinamen and Malays are; that in their sacrifices to humanity they ran no risks, not even to their property; that after all they were not so noble but they treated the thief as he had treated them, and hoped, by a certain outward observance and a few prayers, and by walking in a particular straight though useless path from time to time, to save their souls. This may be to judge my neighbors harshly; for I believe that many of them are not aware that they have such an institution as the jail in their village.

It was formerly the custom in our village, when a poor debtor came out of jail, for his acquaintances to salute him, looking through their fingers, which were crossed to represent the grating of a jail window, "How do ye do?" My neighbors did not thus salute me, but first looked at me, and then at one another, as if I had returned from a long journey. I was put into jail as I was going to the shoemaker's to get a shoe which was mended. When I was let out the next morning, I proceeded to finish my errand, and, having put on my mended shoe, joined a huckleberry party, who were impatient to put themselves under my conduct; and in half an hour,—for the horse was soon tackled,—was in the midst of a huckleberry field, on one of our highest hills, two miles off, and then the State was nowhere to be seen.

This is the whole history of "My Prisons."

I have never declined paying the highway tax, because I am as desirous of being a good neighbor as I am of being a bad subject; and as for supporting schools, I am doing my part to educate my fellow countrymen now. It is for no particular item in the tax-bill that I refuse to pay it. I simply wish to refuse allegiance to the State, to withdraw and stand aloof from it effectually. I do not care to trace the course of my dollar, if I could, till it buys a man or a musket to shoot one with,—the dollar is innocent,—but I am concerned to trace the effects of my allegiance. In fact, I quietly declare war with the State, after my fashion, though I will still make what use and get what advantage of her I can, as is usual in such cases.

If others pay the tax which is demanded for me, from a sympathy with the State, they do but what they have already done in their own case, or rather they abet injustice to a greater extent than the State requires. If they pay the tax from a mistaken interest in the individual taxed, to save his property, or prevent his going to jail, it is because they have not considered wisely how far they let their private feelings interfere with the public good.

This, then, is my position at present. But one cannot be too much on his guard in such a case, lest his action be biased by obstinacy or an undue regard for the opinions of men. Let him see that he does only what belongs to himself and to the hour.

I think sometimes, Why, this people mean well, they are only ignorant; they would do better if they knew how: why give your neighbors this pain to treat you as they are not inclined to? But I think again, This is no reason why I should do as they do, or permit others to suffer much greater pain of a different kind. Again, I sometimes say to myself, When many millions of men, without heat, without ill will, without personal feeling of any kind, demand of you a few shillings only, without the possibility, such is their constitution, of retracting or altering their present demand, and without the possibility, on your side, of appeal to any other millions, why expose yourself to this overwhelming brute force? You do not resist cold and hunger, the winds and the waves, thus obstinately; you quietly submit to a thousand similar necessities. You do not put your head into the fire. But just in proportion as I regard this as not wholly a brute force, but partly a human force, and consider that I have relations to those millions as to so many millions of men, and not of mere brute or inanimate things, I see that appeal is possible, first and instantaneously, from them to the Maker of them, and, secondly, from them to themselves. But if I put my head deliberately into the fire, there is no appeal to fire or to the Maker of fire, and I have only myself to blame. If I could convince myself that I have any right to be satisfied with men as they are, and to treat them accordingly, and not according, in some respects, to my requisitions and expectations of what they and I ought to be, then, like a good Mussulman and fatalist, I should endeavor to be satisfied with things as they are, and say it is the will of God. And, above all, there is this difference between resisting this and a purely brute or natural force, that I can resist this with some effect; but I cannot expect, like Orpheus, to change the nature of the rocks and trees and beasts.

I do not wish to quarrel with any man or nation. I do not wish to split hairs, to make fine distinctions, or set myself up as better than any neighbors. I seek rather, I may say, even an excuse for conforming to the laws of the land. I am but too ready to conform to them. Indeed, I have reason to suspect myself on this head; and each year, as the tax-gatherer comes round, I find myself disposed to review the acts and position of the general and State governments, and the spirit of the people, to discover a pretext for conformity.

> "We must affect our country as our parents,
> And if at any time we alienate
> Our love or industry from doing it honor,
> We must respect effects and teach the soul
> Matter of conscience and religion,
> And not desire of rule or benefit."

I believe that the State will soon be able to take all my work of this sort out of my hands, and then I shall be no better a patriot than my fellow-countrymen. Seen from a lower point of view, the Constitution, with all its faults, is very good; the law and the courts are very respectable; even this State and this American government are, in many respects, very admirable, and rare things, to be thankful for, such as a great many have described them; but seen from a point of view a little higher, they are what I have described them; seen from a higher still, and the highest, who shall say what they are, or that they are worth looking at or thinking of at all?

However, the government does not concern me much, and I shall bestow the fewest possible thoughts on it. It is not many moments that I live under a government, even in this world. If a man is thought-free, fancy-free, imagination-free, that which *is not* never for a long time appearing *to be* to him, unwise rulers or reformers cannot fatally interrupt him.

I know that most men think differently from myself; but those whose lives are by profession devoted to the study of these or kindred subjects content me as little as any. Statesmen and legislators, standing so completely within the institution, never distinctly and nakedly behold it. They speak of moving society, but have no resting-place without it. They may be men of a certain experience and discrimination, and have no doubt invented ingenious and even useful systems, for which we sincerely thank them; but all their wit and usefulness lie within certain not very wide limits. They are wont to forget that the world is not governed by policy and expediency. Webster never goes behind government, and so cannot speak with authority about it. His words are wisdom to those legislators who contemplate no essential reform in the existing government; but for thinkers, and those who legislate for all time, he never once glances at the subject. I know of those whose serene and wise speculations on this theme would soon reveal the limits of his mind's range and hospitality. Yet, compared with the cheap professions of most reformers, and the still cheaper wisdom and eloquence of politicians in general, his are almost the only sensible and valuable words, and we thank Heaven for him. Comparatively, he is always strong, original, and, above all, practical. Still, his quality is not wisdom, but prudence. The lawyer's truth is not Truth, but consistency or a consistent expediency. Truth is always in harmony with herself, and is not concerned chiefly to reveal the justice that may consist with wrong-doing. He well deserves to be called, as he has been called, the Defender of the Constitution. There are really no blows to be given by him but defensive ones. He is not a leader, but a follower. His leaders are the men of '87. "I have never made an effort," he says, "and never propose to make an effort; I have never countenanced an effort, and never mean to countenance an effort, to disturb the arrangement as originally made, by which the various States came into the Union." Still thinking of the sanction which the Constitution gives to slavery, he says, "Because it was a part of the original compact,—let it stand." Notwithstanding his special acuteness and ability, he is unable to take a fact out of its merely political relations, and behold it as it lies absolutely to be disposed of by the intellect,—what, for instance, it behooves a man to do here in America to-day with regard to slavery,—but ventures, or is driven, to make some such desperate answer as the following, while professing to speak absolutely, and as a private man,— from which what new and singular code of social duties might be inferred? "The manner," says he, "in which the governments of those States where slavery exists are to regulate it is for their own consideration, under their responsibility to their constituents, to the general laws of propriety, humanity, and justice, and to God. Associations formed elsewhere, springing from a feeling of humanity, or any other cause, have nothing whatever to do with it. They have never received any encouragement from me, and they never will."

They who know of no purer sources of truth, who have traced up its stream no higher, stand, and wisely stand, by the Bible and the Consitution, and drink at it there with reverence and humility; but they who behold where it comes trickling into this lake or that pool, gird up their loins once more, and continue their pilgrimage toward its fountain-head.

No man with a genius for legislation has appeared in America. They are rare in the history of the world. There are orators, politicians, and eloquent men, by the thousands; but the speaker has not yet opened his mouth to speak who is capable of settling the much-vexed questions of the day. We love eloquence for its own sake, and not for any truth which it may utter, or any heroism it may inspire. Our legislators have not yet learned the comparative value of free trade and of freedom, of union, and of rectitude, to a nation. They have no genius or talent for comparatively humble questions of taxation and finance, commerce and manufactures and agriculture. If we were left solely to the wordy wit of legislators in Congress for our guidance, uncorrected by the seasonable experience and the effectual complaints of the people, America would not long retain her rank among the nations. For eighteen hundred years, though perchance I have no right to say it, the New Testament has been written; yet where is the legislator who has wisdom and practical talent enough to avail himself of the light which it sheds on the science of legislation?

The authority of government, even such as I am willing to submit to,—for I will cheerfully obey those who know and can do better than I, and in many things even those who neither know nor can do so well,—is still an impure one: to be strictly just, it must have the sanction and consent of the governed. It can have no pure right over my person and property but what I concede to it. The progress from an absolute to a limited monarchy, from a limited monarchy to a democracy, is a progress toward a true respect for the individual. Even the Chinese philosopher was wise enough to regard the individual as the basis of the empire. Is a democracy, such as we know it, the last improvement possible in government? Is it not possible to take a step further towards recognizing and organizing the rights of man? There will never be a really free and enlightened State until the State comes to recognize the individual as a higher and independent power, from which all its own power and authority are derived, and treats him accordingly. I please myself with imagining a State at last which can afford to be just to all men, and to treat the individual with respect as a neighbor; which even would not think it inconsistent with its own repose if a few were to live aloof from it, not meddling with it, nor embraced by it, who fulfilled all the duties of neighbors and fellow-men. A State which bore this kind of fruit, and suffered it to drop off as fast as it ripened, would prepare the way for a still more perfect and glorious State, which also I have imagined, but not yet anywhere seen.

Thomas Henry Huxley (1825–1895)

The Method of Scientific Investigation

The method of scientific investigation is nothing but the expression of the necessary mode of working of the human mind. It is simply the mode at which all phenomena are reasoned about, rendered precise and exact. There is no more difference, but there is just the same kind of difference, between the mental operations of a man of science and those of an ordinary person as there is between the operations and methods of a baker or of a butcher weighing out his goods in common scales and the operations of a chemist in performing a difficult and complex analysis by means of his balance and finely graduated weights. It is not that the action of the scales in the one case and the balance in the other differ in the principles of their construction or manner of working; but the beam of one is set on an infinitely finer axis than the other and of course turns by the addition of a much smaller weight.

You will understand this better, perhaps, if I give you some familiar example. You have all heard it repeated, I dare say, that men of science work by means of induction and deduction, and that by the help of these operations they, in a sort of sense, wring from nature certain other things which are called natural laws and causes, and that out of these, by some cunning skill of their own, they build up hypotheses and theories. And it is imagined by many that the operations of the common mind can be by no means compared with these processes and that they have to be acquired by a sort of special apprenticeship to the craft. To hear all these large words you would think that the mind of a man of science must be constituted differently from that of his fellow men; but if you will not be frightened by terms, you will discover that you are quite wrong and that all these terrible apparatus are being used by yourselves every day and every hour of your lives.

There is a well-known incident in one of Molière's plays where the author makes the hero express unbounded delight on being told that he had been talking prose during the whole of his life. In the same way I trust that you will take comfort and be delighted with yourselves on the discovery that you have been acting on the principles of inductive and deductive philosophy during the same period. Probably there is not one here who has not in the course of the day had occasion to set in motion a complex train of reasoning of the very same kind, though differing of course in degree, as that which a scientific man goes through in tracing the causes of natural phenomena.

A very trivial circumstance will serve to exemplify this. Suppose you go into a fruiterer's shop, wanting an apple. You take up one, and on biting it you find it is sour; you look at it and see that it is hard and green. You take up another one, and that too is hard, green, and sour. The shopman offers you a third; but before biting it you examine it and find that it is hard and green, and you immediately say that you will not have it, as it must be sour like those that you have already tried.

Nothing can be more simple than what you think, but if you will take the trouble to analyze and trace out into its logical elements what has been done by the mind, you will be greatly surprised. In the first place you have performed the operation of induction. You found that in two experiences hardness and greenness in apples go together with sourness. It was so in the first case, and it was confirmed by the second. True, it is a very small basis, but still it is enough to make an induction from; you generalize the facts, and you expect to find sourness in apples where you get hardness and greenness. You found upon that a general law that all hard and green apples are sour; and that, so far as it goes, is a perfect induction. Well, having got your natural law in this way, when you are offered another apple which you find is hard and green, you say, "All hard and green apples are sour; this apple is hard and green; therefore this apple is sour." That train of reasoning is what logicians call a syllogism and has all its various parts and terms—its major premise, its minor premise, and its conclusion. And by the help of further reasoning, which if drawn out would have to be exhibited in two or three other syllogisms, you arrive at your final determination, "I will not have that apple." So that, you see, you have, in the first place, established a law by induction, and upon that you have founded a deduction and reasoned out the special conclusion of the particular case. Well now suppose, having got your law that at some time afterwards you are discussing the qualities of apples with a friend. You will say to him, "It is a very curious thing, but I find that all hard and green apples are sour!" Your friend says to you, "But how do you know that?" You at once reply, "Oh, because I have tried them over and over again and have always found them to be so." Well, if we were talking science instead of common sense, we should call that an experimental verification. And if still opposed you go further and say, "I have heard from the people in Somersetshire and Devonshire, where a large number of apples are grown, that they have observed the same thing. It is also found to be the case in Normandy and in North America. In short, I find it to be the universal experience of mankind wherever attention has been directed to the subject." Whereupon, your friend, unless he is a very unreasonable man, agrees with you and is convinced that you are quite right in the conclusion you have drawn. He believes, although perhaps he does not know he believes it, that the more extensive verifications are, that the more frequently experiments have been made and results of the same kind arrived at, that the more varied the conditions under which the same results have been attained the more certain is the ultimate conclusion, and he disputes the question no further. He sees that the experiment has been tried under all sorts of conditions as to time, place, and people with the same result; and he says with you, therefore, that the law you have laid down must be a good one and he must believe it.

In science we do the same thing: the philosopher exercises precisely the same faculties, though in a much more delicate manner. In scientific inquiry it becomes a matter of duty to expose a supposed law to every possible kind of verification, and to take care, moreover, that this is done intentionally and not left to mere accident as in the case of the apples. And in science, as in common life, our confidence in a law is in exact proportion to the absence of variation in the result of our experimental verifications. For instance, if you let go your grasp of an article you may have in your hand, it will immediately fall to the ground. That is a very common verification of one of the best established laws of nature, that of gravitation. The method by which men of science established the existence of that law is exactly the same as that by which we have established the trivial proposition about the sourness of hard and green apples. But we believe it in such an extensive, thorough, and unhesitating manner because the universal experience of mankind verifies it, and we can verify it ourselves at any time; and that is the strongest possible foundation on which any natural law can rest.

So much by way of proof that the method of establishing laws in science is exactly the same as that pursued in common life. Let us now turn to another matter (though really it is but another phase of the same question), and that is the method by which from the relations of certain phenomena we prove that some stand in the position of causes towards the others.

I want to put the case clearly before you, and I will therefore show you what I mean by another familiar example. I will suppose that one of you, on coming down in the morning to the parlor of your house, finds that a teapot and some spoons which had been left in the room on the previous evening are gone; the window is open, and you observe the mark of a dirty hand on the windowframe; and perhaps, in addition to that, you notice the impress of a hobnailed shoe on the gravel outside. All these phenomena have struck your attention instantly, and before two seconds have passed you say, "Oh, somebody has broken open the window, entered the room, and run off with the spoons and the teapot!" That speech is out of your mouth in a moment. And you will probably add, "I know there has; I am quite sure of it." You mean to say exactly what you know; but in reality what you have said has been the expression of what is, in all essential particulars, an hypothesis. You do not *know* it at all; it is nothing but an hypothesis rapidly framed in your own mind! And it is an hypothesis founded on a long train of inductions and deductions.

What are those inductions and deductions, and how have you got at this hypothesis? You have observed, in the first place, that the window is open; but by a train of reasoning involving many inductions and deductions, you have probably arrived long before at the general law—and a very good one it is—that windows do not open of themselves; and you therefore conclude that something has opened the window. A second general law that you have arrived at in the same way is that teapots and spoons do not go out of a window spontaneously, and you are satisfied that, as they are not now where you left them; they have been removed. In the third place, you look at the marks on the window and the shoe marks outside, and you say that in all previous experience the former kind of mark has never been produced by anything else but the hand of a human being; and the same experience shows that no other animal but man at present wears shoes with hobnails on them such as would produce the marks in the gravel. I do not know, even if we could discover any of those "missing links" that are talked about, that they would help us to any other conclusion! At any rate the law which states our present experience is strong enough for my present purpose. You next reach the conclusion that as these kinds of marks have not been left by any other animal than man, or are liable to be formed in any other way than by a man's hand and shoe, the marks in question have been formed by a man in that way. You have, further, a general law founded on observation and experience, and that too is, I am sorry to say, a very universal and unimpeachable one—that some men are thieves; and you assume at once from all these premises—and that is what constitutes your hypothesis—that the man who made the marks outside and on the window sill opened the window, got into the room, and stole your teapot and spoons. You have now arrived at a *vera causa;* you have assumed a cause which it is plain is competent to produce all the phenomena you have observed. You can explain all these phenomena only by the hypothesis of a thief. But that is an hypothetical conclusion of the practice of which you have no absolute proof at all, it is only rendered highly probable by a series of inductive and deductive reasonings.

I suppose your first action, assuming that you are a man of ordinary common sense and that you have established this hypothesis to your own satisfaction, will very likely be to go off for the police and set them on the track of the burglar with the view to the recovery of your property. But just as you are starting with this object, some person comes in and on learning what you are about says, "My good friend, you are going on a great deal too fast. How do you know that the man who really made the marks took the spoons? It might have been a monkey that took them, and the man may have merely looked in afterwards." You would probably reply, "Well, that is all very well, but you see it is contrary to all experience of the way teapots and spoons are abstracted; so that, at any rate, your hypothesis is less probable than mine." While you are talking the thing over in this way, another friend arrives, one of that good kind of people that I was talking of a little while ago.

And he might say, "Oh, my dear sir, you are certainly going on a great deal too fast. You are most presumptuous. You admit that all these occurrences took place when you were fast asleep, at a time when you could not possibly have known anything about what was taking place. How do you know that the laws of nature are not suspended during the night? It may be that there has been some kind of supernatural interference in this case." In point of fact, he declares that your hypothesis is one of which you cannot at all demonstrate the truth and that you are by no means sure that the laws of nature are the same when you are asleep as when you are awake.

Well, now, you cannot at the moment answer that kind of reasoning. You feel that your worthy friend has you somewhat at a disadvantage. You will feel perfectly convinced in your own mind, however, that you are quite right, and you will say to him, "My good friend, I can only be guided by the natural probabilities of the case, and if you will be kind enough to stand aside and permit me to pass I will go and fetch the police." Well, we will suppose that your journey is successful and that by good luck you meet with a policeman; that eventually the burglar is found with your property on his person and the marks correspond to his hand and to his boots. Probably any jury would consider those facts a very good experimental verification of your hypothesis touching the cause of the abnormal phenomena observed in your parlor, and would act accordingly.

Now, in this suppositious case I have taken phenomena of a very common kind in order that you might see what are the different steps in an ordinary process of reasoning, if you will only take the trouble to analyze it carefully. All the operations I have described, you will see, are involved in the mind of any man of sense in leading him to a conclusion as to the course he should take in order to make good a robbery and punish the offender. I say that you are led, in that case, to your conclusion by exactly the same train of reasoning as that which a man of science pursues when he is endeavoring to discover the origin and laws of the most occult phenomena. The process is, and always must be, the same; and precisely the same mode of reasoning was employed by Newton and Laplace in their endeavors to discover and define the causes of the movements of the heavenly bodies as you with your own common sense would employ to detect a burglar. The only difference is that, the nature of the inquiry being more abstruse, every step has to be most carefully watched so that there may not be a single crack or flaw in your hypothesis. A flaw or crack in many of the hypotheses of daily life may be of little or no moment as affecting the general correctness of the conclusions at which we may arrive; but in a scientific inquiry a fallacy, great or small, is always of importance and is sure to be in the long run constantly productive of mischievous if not fatal results.

Do not allow yourselves to be misled by the common notion that any hypothesis is untrustworthy simply because it is an hypothesis. It is often urged in respect to some scientific conclusion that, after all, it is only an hypothesis. But what more have we to guide us in nine-tenths of the most important affairs of daily life than hypotheses, and often very ill-based ones? So that in science, where the evidence of an hypothesis is subjected to the most rigid examination, we may rightly pursue the same course. You may have hypotheses and hypotheses. A man may say, if he likes, that the moon is made of green cheese; that is an hypothesis. But another man, who has devoted a great deal of time and attention to the subject and availed himself of the most powerful telescopes and the results of the observations of others, declares that in his opinion it is probably composed of materials very similar to those of which our own earth is made up; and that is also only an hypothesis. But I need not tell you that there is an enormous difference in the value of the two hypotheses. That one which is based on sound scientific knowledge is sure to have a corresponding value; and that which is a mere hasty random guess is likely to have but little value. Every great step in our progress in discovering causes has been made in exactly the same way as that which I have detailed to you. A person observing the occurrence of certain facts and phenomena asks, naturally enough, what kind of operation known to occur in nature applied to the particular case, will unravel and explain the mystery. Hence you have the scientific hypothesis; and its value will be proportionate to the care and completeness with which its basis has been tested and verified. It is in these matters as in the commonest affairs of practical life: the guess of the fool will be folly, while the guess of the wise man will contain wisdom. In all cases you see that the value of the result depends on the patience and faithfulness with which the investigator applies to his hypothesis every possible kind of verification.

Fiction

Stephen Crane (1871–1900)

The Open Boat

A Tale Intended to be after the Fact: Being the Experience of Four Men from the Sunk Steamer "COMMODORE"

I

None of them knew the color of the sky. Their eyes glanced level, and were fastened upon the waves that swept toward them. These waves were of the hue of slate, save for the tops, which were of foaming white, and all of the men knew the colors of the sea. The horizon narrowed and widened, and dipped and rose, and at all times its edge was jagged with waves that seemed thrust up in points like rocks.

Many a man ought to have a bathtub larger than the boat which here rode upon the sea. These waves were most wrongfully and barbarously abrupt and tall, and each froth-top was a problem in small-boat navigation.

The cook squatted in the bottom, and looked with both eyes at the six inches of gunwale which separated him from the ocean. His sleeves were rolled over his fat forearms, and the two flaps of his unbuttoned vest dangled as he bent to bail out the boat. Often he said, "Gawd! that was a narrow clip." As he remarked it he invariably gazed eastward over the broken sea.

The oiler, steering with one of the two oars in the boat, sometimes raised himself suddenly to keep clear of water that swirled in over the stern. It was a thin little oar, and it seemed often ready to snap.

The correspondent, pulling at the other oar, watched the waves and wondered why he was there.

The injured captain, lying in the bow, was at this time buried in that profound dejection and indifference which comes, temporarily at least, to even the bravest and most enduring when, willy-nilly, the firm fails, the army loses, the ship goes down. The mind of the master of a vessel is rooted deep in the timbers of her, though he command for a day or a decade; and this captain had on him the stern impression of a scene in the grays of dawn of seven turned faces, and later a stump of a topmast with a white ball on it, that slashed to and fro at the waves, went low and lower, and down. Thereafter there was something strange in his voice. Although steady, it was deep with mourning, and a quality beyond oration or tears.

"Keep'er a little more south, Billie," said he.

"A little more south, sir," said the oiler in the stern.

A seat in this boat was not unlike a seat upon a bucking broncho, and by the same token a broncho is not much smaller. The craft pranced and reared and plunged like an animal. As each wave came, and she rose for it, she seemed like a horse making at a fence outrageously high. The manner of her scramble over these walls of water is a mystic thing, and, moreover, at the top of them were ordinarily these problems in white water, the foam racing down from the summit of each wave requiring a new leap, and a leap from the air. Then, after scornfully bumping a crest, she would slide and race and splash down a long incline, and arrive bobbing and nodding in front of the next menace.

A singular disadvantage of the sea lies in the fact that after successfully surmounting one wave you discover that there is another behind it just as important and just as nervously anxious to do something effective in the way of swamping boats. In a ten-foot dinghy one can get an idea of the resources of the sea in the line of waves that is not probable to the average experience, which is never at sea in a dinghy. As each slaty wall of water approached, it shut all else from the view of the men in the boat, and it was not difficult to imagine that this particular wave was the final outburst of the ocean, the last effort of the grim water. There was a terrible grace in the move of the waves, and they came in silence, save for the snarling of the crests.

In the wan light the faces of the men must have been gray. Their eyes must have glinted in strange ways as they gazed steadily astern. Viewed from a balcony, the whole thing would, doubtless, have been weirdly picturesque. But the men in the boat had no time to see it, and if they had had leisure, there were other things to occupy their minds. The sun swung steadily up the sky, and they knew it was broad day because the color of the sea changed from slate to emerald-green streaked with amber lights, and the foam was like tumbling snow. The process of the breaking day was unknown to them. They were aware only of the effect upon the color of the waves that rolled toward them.

In disjointed sentences the cook and the correspondent argued as to the difference between a life-saving station and a house of refuge. The cook had said: "There's a house of refuge just north of the Mosquito Inlet Light, and as soon as they see us they'll come off in their boat and pick us up."

"As soon as who sees us?" said the correspondent.

"The crew," said the cook.

"Houses of refuge don't have crews," said the correspondent. "As I understand them, they are only places where clothes and grub are stored for the benefit of shipwrecked people. They don't carry crews."

"Oh, yes, they do," said the cook.

"No, they don't," said the correspondent.

"Well, we're not there yet, anyhow," said the oiler, in the stern.

"Well," said the cook, "perhaps it's not a house of refuge that I'm thinking of as being near Mosquito Inlet Light; perhaps it's a life-saving station."

"We're not there yet," said the oiler in the stern.

II

As the boat bounced from the top of each wave the wind tore through the hair of the hatless men, and as the craft plopped her stern down again the spray splashed past them. The crest of each of these waves was a hill, from the top of which the men surveyed for a moment a broad tumultuous expanse, shining and wind-riven. It was probably splendid, it was probably glorious, this play of the free sea, wild with lights of emerald and white and amber.

"Bully good thing it's an on-shore wind," said the cook. "If not, where would we be? Wouldn't have a show."

"That's right," said the correspondent.

The busy oiler nodded his assent.

Then the captain, in the bow, chuckled in a way that expressed humor, contempt, tragedy, all in one. "Do you think we've got much of a show now, boys?" said he.

Whereupon the three were silent, save for a trifle of hemming and hawing. To express any particular optimism at this time they felt to be childish and stupid, but they all doubtless possessed this sense of the situation in their minds. A young man thinks doggedly at such times. On the other hand, the ethics of their condition was decidedly against any open suggestion of hopelessness. So they were silent.

"Oh, well," said the captain, soothing his children, "we'll get ashore all right."

But there was that in his tone which made them think; so the oiler quoth, "Yes! if this wind holds."

The cook was bailing. "Yes! if we don't catch hell in the surf."

Canton flannel gulls flew near and far. Sometimes they sat down on the sea, near patches of brown seaweed that rolled over the waves with a movement like carpets on a line in a gale. The birds sat comfortably in groups, and they were envied by some in the dinghy, for the wrath of the sea was no more to them than it was to a covey of prairie chickens a thousand miles inland. Often they came very close and stared at the men with black bead-like eyes. At these times they were uncanny and sinister in their unblinking scrutiny, and the men hooted angrily at them, telling them to be gone. One came, and evidently decided to alight on the top of the captain's head. The bird flew parallel to the boat and did not circle, but made short sidelong jumps in the air in chicken fashion. His black eyes were wistfully fixed upon the captain's head. "Ugly brute," said the oiler to the bird. "You look as if you were made with a jackknife." The cook and the correspondent swore darkly at the creature. The captain naturally wished to knock it away with the end of the heavy painter, but he did not dare do it, because anything resembling an emphatic gesture would have capsized this freighted boat; and so, with his open hand, the captain gently and carefully waved the gull away. After it had been discouraged from the pursuit the captain breathed easier on account of his hair, and others breathed easier because the bird struck their minds at this time as being somehow gruesome and ominous.

In the meantime the oiler and the correspondent rowed; and also they rowed. They sat together in the same seat, and each rowed an oar. Then the oiler took both oars; then the correspondent took both oars, then the oiler; then the correspondent. They rowed and they rowed. The very ticklish part of the business was when the time came for the reclining one in the stern to take his turn at the oars. By the very last star of truth, it is easier to steal eggs from under a hen than it was to change seats in the dinghy. First the man in the stern slid his hand along the thwart and moved with care, as if he were of Sèvres. Then the man in the rowing-seat slid his hand along the other thwart. It was all done with the most extraordinary care. As the two sidled past each other, the whole party kept watchful eyes on the coming wave, and the captain cried: "Look out, now! Steady, there!"

The brown mats of seaweed that appeared from time to time were like islands, bits of earth. They were travelling, apparently, neither one way nor the other. They were, to all intents, stationary. They informed the men in the boat that it was making progress slowly toward the land.

The captain, rearing cautiously in the bow after the dinghy soared on a great swell, said that he had seen the lighthouse at Mosquito Inlet. Presently the cook remarked that he had seen it. The correspondent was at the oars then, and for some reason he too wished to look at the lighthouse; but his back was toward the far shore, and the waves were important, and for some time he could not seize an opportunity to turn his head. But at last there came a wave more gentle than the others, and when at the crest of it he swiftly scoured the western horizon.

"See it?" said the captain.

"No," said the correspondent, slowly; "I didn't see anything."

"Look again," said the captain. He pointed. "It's exactly in that direction."

At the top of another wave the correspondent did as he was bid, and this time his eyes chanced on a small, still thing on the edge of the swaying horizon. It was precisely like the point of a pin. It took an anxious eye to find a lighthouse so tiny.

"Think we'll make it, Captain?"

"If this wind holds and the boat don't swamp, we can't do much else," said the captain.

The little boat, lifted by each towering sea and splashed viciously by the crests, made progress that in the absence of seaweed was not apparent to those in her. She seemed just a wee thing wallowing, miraculously top up, at the mercy of five oceans. Occasionally a great spread of water, like white flames, swarmed into her.

"Bail her, cook," said the captain, serenely.

"All right, Captain," said the cheerful cook.

III

It would be difficult to describe the subtle brotherhood of men that was here established on the seas. No one said that it was so. No one mentioned it. But it dwelt in the boat, and each man felt it warm him. They were a captain, an oiler, a cook, and a correspondent, and they were friends—friends in a more curiously iron-bound degree than may be common. The hurt captain, lying against the water-jar in the bow, spoke always in a low voice and calmly; but he could never command a more ready and swiftly obedient crew than the motley three of the dinghy. It was more than a mere recognition of what was best for the common safety. There was surely in it a quality that was personal and heart-felt. And after this devotion to the commander of the boat, there was this comradeship, that the correspondent, for instance, who had been taught to be cynical of men, knew even at the time was the best experience of his life. But no one said that it was so. No one mentioned it.

"I wish we had a sail," remarked the captain. "We might try my overcoat on the end of an oar, and give you two boys a chance to rest." So the cook and the correspondent held the mast and spread wide the overcoat; the oiler steered; and the little boat made good way with her new rig. Sometimes the oiler had to scull sharply to keep a sea from breaking into the boat, but otherwise sailing was a success.

Meanwhile the lighthouse had been growing slowly larger. It had now almost assumed color, and appeared like a little gray shadow on the sky. The man at the oars could not be prevented from turning his head rather often to try for a glimpse of this little gray shadow.

At last, from the top of each wave, the men in the tossing boat could see land. Even as the lighthouse was an upright shadow on the sky, this land seemed but a long black shadow on the sea. It certainly was thinner than paper. "We must be about opposite New Smyrna," said the cook, who had coasted this shore often in schooners. "Captain, by the way, I believe they abandoned that life-saving station there about a year ago."

"Did they?" said the captain.

The wind slowly died away. The cook and the correspondent were not now obliged to slave in order to hold high the oar. But the waves continued their old impetuous swooping at the dinghy, and the little craft, no longer under way, struggled woundily over them. The oiler or the correspondent took the oars again.

Shipwrecks are *apropos* of nothing. If men could only train for them and have them occur when the men had reached pink condition, there would be less drowning at sea. Of the four in the dinghy none had slept any time worth mentioning for two days and two nights previous to embarking in the dinghy, and in the excitement of clambering about the deck of a foundering ship they had also forgotten to eat heartily.

For these reasons, and for others, neither the oiler nor the correspondent was fond of rowing at this time. The correspondent wondered ingenuously how in the name of all that was sane could there be people who thought it amusing to row a boat. It was not an amusement; it was a diabolical punishment, and even a genius of mental aberrations could never conclude that it was anything but a horror to the muscles and a crime against the back. He mentioned to the boat in general how the amusement of rowing struck him, and the weary-faced oiler smiled in full sympathy. Previously to the foundering, by the way, the oiler had worked a double watch in the engineroom of the ship.

"Take her easy now, boys," said the captain. "Don't spend yourselves. If we have to run a surf you'll need all your strength, because we'll sure have to swim for it. Take your time."

Slowly the land arose from the sea. From a black line it became a line of black and a line of white—trees and sand. Finally the captain said that he could make out a house on the shore. "That's the house of refuge, sure," said the cook. "They'll see us before long, and come out after us."

The distant lighthouse reared high. "The keeper ought to be able to make us out now, if he's looking through a glass," said the captain. "He'll notify the life-saving people."

"None of those other boats could have got ashore to give word of this wreck," said the oiler, in a low voice, "else the lifeboat would be out hunting us."

Slowly and beautifully the land loomed out of the sea. The wind came again. It had veered from the northeast to the southeast. Finally a new sound struck the ears of the men in the boat. It was the low thunder of the surf on the shore. "We'll never be able to make the lighthouse now," said the captain. "Swing her head a little more north, Billie."

"A little more north, sir," said the oiler.

Whereupon the little boat turned her nose once more down the wind, and all but the oarsman watched the shore grow. Under the influence of this expansion doubt and direful apprehension were leaving the minds of the men. The management of the boat was still most absorbing, but it could not prevent a quiet cheerfulness. In an hour, perhaps, they would be ashore.

Their backbones had become thoroughly used to balancing in the boat, and they now rode this wild colt of a dinghy like circus men. The correspondent thought that he had been drenched to the skin, but happening to feel in the top pocket of his coat, he found therein eight cigars. Four of them were soaked with sea-water; four were perfectly scatheless. After a search, somebody produced three dry matches; and thereupon the four waifs rode impudently in their little boat and, with an assurance of an impending rescue shining in their eyes, puffed at the big cigars, and judged well and ill of all men. Everybody took a drink of water.

IV

"Cook," remarked the captain, "there don't seem to be any signs of life about your house of refuge."

"No," replied the cook. "Funny they don't see us!"

A broad stretch of lowly coast lay before the eyes of the men. It was of low dunes topped with dark vegetation. The roar of the surf was plain, and sometimes they could see the white lip of waves as it spun up the beach. A tiny house was blocked out black upon the sky. Southward, the slim lighthouse lifted its little gray length.

Tide, wind, and waves were swinging the dinghy northward. "Funny they don't see us," said the men.

The surf's roar was here dulled, but its tone was nevertheless thunderous and mighty. As the boat swam over the great rollers the men sat listening to this roar. "We'll swamp sure," said everybody.

It is fair to say here that there was not a life-saving station within twenty miles in either direction; but the men did not know this fact, and in consequence they made dark and opprobrious remarks concerning the eyesight of the nation's lifesavers. Four scowling men sat in the dinghy and surpassed records in the invention of epithets.

"Funny they don't see us."

The light-heartedness of a former time had completely faded. To their sharpened minds it was easy to conjure pictures of all kinds of incompetency and blindness and, indeed, cowardice. There was the shore of the populous land, and it was bitter and bitter to them that from it came no sign.

"Well," said the captain, ultimately, "I suppose we'll have to make a try for ourselves. If we stay out here too long, we'll none of us have strength left to swim after the boat swamps."

And so the oiler, who was at the oars, turned the boat straight for the shore. There was a sudden tightening of muscles. There was some thinking.

"If we don't all get ashore," said the captain—"if we don't all get ashore, I suppose you fellows know where to send news of my finish?"

They then briefly exchanged some addresses and admonitions. As for the reflections of the men, there was a great deal of rage in them. Perchance they might be formulated thus: "If I am going to be drowned—if I am going to be drowned—if I am going to be drowned, why, in the name of the seven mad gods who rule the sea, was I allowed to come thus far and contemplate sand and trees? Was I brought here merely to have my nose dragged away as I was about to nibble the sacred cheese of life? It is preposterous. If this old ninny-woman, Fate, cannot do better than this, she should be deprived of the management of men's fortunes. She is an old hen who knows not her intention. If she has decided to drown me, why did she not do it in the beginning and save me all this trouble? The whole affair is absurd. . . . But no; she cannot mean to drown me. She dare not drown me. She cannot drown me. Not after all this work." Afterward the man might have had an impulse to shake his fist at the clouds. "Just you drown me, now, and then hear what I call you!"

The billows that came at this time were more formidable. They seemed always just about to break and roll over the little boat in a turmoil of foam. There was a preparatory and long growl in the speech of them. No mind unused to the sea would have concluded that the dinghy could ascend these sheer heights in time. The shore was still afar. The oiler was a wily surfman. "Boys," he said swiftly, "she won't live three minutes more, and we're too far out to swim. Shall I take her to sea again, Captain!"

"Yes; go ahead!" said the captain.

This oiler, by a series of quick miracles and fast and steady oarsmanship, turned the boat in the middle of the surf and took her safely to sea again.

There was a considerable silence as the boat bumped over the furrowed sea to deeper water. Then somebody in gloom spoke: "Well, anyhow, they must have seen us from the shore by now."

The gulls went in slanting flight up the wind toward the gray, desolate east. A squall, marked by dinghy clouds and clouds brick-red, like smoke from a burning building, appeared from the southeast.

"What do you think of those life-saving people? Ain't they peaches?"

"Funny they haven't seen us."

"Maybe they think we're out here for sport! Maybe they think we're fishin'. Maybe they think we're damned fools."

It was a long afternoon. A changed tide tried to force them southward, but wind and wave said northward. Far ahead, where coast-line, sea, and sky formed their mighty angle, there were little dots which seemed to indicate a city on the shore.

"St. Augustine?"

The captain shook his head. "Too near Mosquito Inlet."

And the oiler rowed, and then the correspondent rowed; then the oiler rowed. It was a weary business. The human back can become the seat of more aches and pains than are registered in books for the composite anatomy of a regiment. It is a limited area, but it can become the theater of innumerable muscular conflicts, tangles, wrenches, knots, and other comforts.

"Did you ever like to row, Billie?" asked the correspondent.

"No," said the oiler; "hang it!"

When one exchanged the rowing-seat for a place in the bottom of the boat, he suffered a bodily depression that caused him to be careless of everything save an obligation to wiggle one finger. There was cold sea-water swashing to and fro in the boat, and he lay in it. His head, pillowed on a thwart, was within an inch of the swirl of a wave-crest, and sometimes a particularly obstreperous sea came inboard and drenched him once more. But these matters did not annoy him. It is almost certain that if the boat had capsized he would have tumbled comfortably out upon the ocean as if he felt sure that it was a great soft mattress.

"Look! There's a man on the shore!"

"Where?"

"There! See 'im? See 'im!"

"Yes, sure! He's walking along."

"Now he's stopped. Look! He's facing us!"

"He's waving at us!"

"So he is! By thunder!"

"Ah, now we're all right! Now we're all right! There'll be a boat out here for us in half an hour."

"He's going on. He's running. He's going up to that house there."

The remote beach seemed lower than the sea, and it required a searching glance to discern the little black figure. The captain saw a floating stick, and they rowed to it. A bath towel was by some weird chance in the boat, and, tying this on the stick, the captain waved it. The oarsman did not dare turn his head, so he was obliged to ask questions.

"What's he doing now!"

"He's standing still again. He's looking, I think. . . . There he goes again—toward the house. . . . Now he's stopped again."

"Is he waving at us?"

"No, not now; he was, though."

"Look! There comes another man!"

"He's running."

"Look at him go, would you!"

"Why, he's on a bicycle. Now he's met the other man. They're both waving at us. Look!"

"There comes something up the beach."

"What the devil is that thing?"

"Why, it looks like a boat."

"Why, certainly, it's a boat."

"No; it's on wheels."

"Yes, so it is. Well, that must be the life-boat. They drag them along shore on a wagon."

"That's the life-boat, sure."

"No, by God, it's—it's an omnibus."

"I tell you it's a life-boat."

"It is not! It's an omnibus. I can see it plain. See? One of these big hotel omnibuses."

"By thunder, you're right. It's an omnibus, sure as fate. What do you suppose they are doing with an omnibus? Maybe they are going around collecting the life-crew, hey?"

"That's it, likely. Look! There's a fellow waving a little black flag. He's standing on the steps of the omnibus. There come those other two fellows. Now they're all talking together. Look at the fellow with the flag. Maybe he ain't waving it!"

"That ain't a flag, is it? That's his coat. Why, certainly, that's his coat."

"So it is; it's his coat. He's taken it off and is waving it around his head. But would you look at him swing it!"

"Oh, say, there isn't any life-saving station there. That's just a winter-resort hotel omnibus that has brought over some of the boarders to see us drown."

"What's that idiot with the coat mean? What's he signaling, anyhow?"

"It looks as if he were trying to tell us to go north. There must be a life-saving station up there."

"No; he thinks we're fishing. Just giving us a merry hand. See? Ah, there, Willie!"

"Well, I wish I could make something out of those signals. What do you suppose he means?"

"He don't mean anything; he's just playing."

"Well, if he'd signal us to try the surf again, or to go to sea and wait, or go north, or go south, or go to hell, there would be some reason in it. But look at him! He just stands there and keeps his coat revolving like a wheel. The ass!"

"There come more people."

"Now there's quite a mob. Look! Isn't that a boat?"

"Where? Oh, I see where you mean. No, that's no boat."

"That fellow is still waving his coat."

"He must think we like to see him do that. Why don't he quit it! It don't mean anything."

"I don't know. I think he is trying to make us go south. It must be that there's a life-saving station there somewhere."

"Say, he ain't tired yet. Look at 'im wave!"

"Wonder how long he can keep that up. He's been revolving his coat ever since he caught sight of us. He's an idiot. Why aren't they getting men to bring a boat out? A fishing-boat—one of those big yawls—could come out here all right. Why don't he do something?"

"Oh, it's all right now."

"They'll have a boat out here for us in less than no time, now that they've seen us."

A faint yellow tone came into the sky over the low land. The shadows on the sea slowly deepened. The wind bore coldness with it, and the men began to shiver.

"Holy smoke!" said one, allowing his voice to express his impious mood, "if we keep on monkeying out here! If we've got to flounder out here all night!"

"Oh, we'll never have to stay here all night! Don't you worry. They've seen us now, and it won't be long before they'll come chasing out after us."

The shore grew dusky. The man waving a coat blended gradually into this gloom, and it swallowed in the same manner the omnibus and the group of people. The spray, when it dashed uproariously over the side, made the voyagers shrink and swear like men who were being branded.

"I'd like to catch the chump who waved the coat. I feel like socking him one, just for luck."

"Why? What did he do?"

"Oh, nothing, but then he seemed so damned cheerful."

In the meantime the oiler rowed, and then the corresponpondent rowed, and then the oiler rowed. Gray-faced and bowed forward, they mechanically, turn by turn, plied the leaden oars. The form of the lighthouse had vanished from the southern horizon, but finally a pale star appeared, just lifting from the sea. The streaked saffron in the west passed before the all-merging darkness, and the sea to the east was black. The land had vanished, and was expressed only by the low and drear thunder of the surf.

"If I am going to be drowned—if I am going to be drowned—if I am going to be drowned, why, in the name of the seven mad gods who rule the sea, was I allowed to come thus far and contemplate sand and trees? Was I brought here merely to have my nose dragged away as I was about to nibble the sacred cheese of life?"

The patient captain, drooped over the water-jar, was sometimes obliged to speak to the oarsman.

"Keep her head up! Keep her head up!"

"Keep her head up, sir." The voices were weary and low.

This was surely a quiet evening. All save the oarsman lay heavily and listlessly in the boat's bottom. As for him, his eyes were just capable of noting the tall black waves that swept forward in a most sinister silence, save for an occasional subdued growl of a crest.

The cook's head was on a thwart, and he looked without interest at the water under his nose. He was deep in other scenes. Finally he spoke. "Billie," he murmured, dreamfully, "what kind of pie do you like best?"

V

"Pie!" said the oiler and the correspondent, agitatedly. "Don't talk about those things, blast you!"

"Well," said the cook, "I was just thinking about ham sandwiches, and—"

A night on the sea in an open boat is a long night. As darkness settled finally, the shine of the light, lifting from the sea in the south, changed to full gold. On the northern horizon a new light appeared, a small bluish gleam on the edge of the waters. These two lights were the furniture of the world. Otherwise there was nothing but waves.

Two men huddled in the stern, and distances were so magnificent in the dinghy that the rower was enabled to keep his feet pretty warm by thrusting them under his companions. Their legs indeed extended far under the rowing-seat until they touched the feet of the captain forward. Sometimes, despite the efforts of the third oarsman, a wave came piling into the boat, an icy wave of the night, and the chilling water soaked them anew. They would twist their bodies for a moment and groan, and sleep the dead sleep once more, while the water in the boat gurgled about them as the craft rocked.

The plan of the oiler and the correspondent was for one to row until he lost the ability, and then arouse the other from his sea-water couch in the bottom of the boat.

The oiler plied the oars until his head drooped forward and the overpowering sleep blinded him; and he rowed yet afterward. Then he touched a man in the bottom of the boat, and called his name. "Will you spell me for a little while?" he said meekly.

"Sure, Billie," said the correspondent, awaking and dragging himself to a sitting position. They exchanged places carefully, and the oiler, cuddling down in the sea-water at the cook's side, seemed to go to sleep instantly.

The particular violence of the sea had ceased. The waves came without snarling. The obligation of the man at the oars was to keep the boat headed so that the tilt of the rollers would not capsize her, and to preserve her from filling when the crests rushed past. The black waves were silent and hard to be seen in the darkness. Often one was almost upon the boat before the oarsman was aware.

In a low voice the correspondent addressed the captain. He was not sure that the captain was awake, although this iron man seemed to be always awake. "Captain, shall I keep her making for the light north, sir?"

The same steady voice answered him. "Yes. Keep it about two points off the port bow."

The cook had tied a life-belt around himself in order to get even the warmth which this clumsy cork contrivance could donate, and he seemed almost stove-like when a rower, whose teeth invariably chattered wildly as soon as he ceased his labor, dropped down to sleep.

The correspondent, as he rowed, looked down at the two men sleeping underfoot. The cook's arm was around the oiler's shoulders, and, with their fragmentary clothing and haggard faces, they were the babes of the sea—a grotesque rendering of the old babes in the wood.

Later he must have grown stupid at his work, for suddenly there was a growling of water, and a crest came with a roar and a swash into the boat, and it was a wonder that it did not set the cook afloat in his life-belt. The cook continued to sleep, but the oiler sat up, blinking his eyes and shaking with the new cold.

"Oh, I'm awfully sorry, Billie," said the correspondent, contritely.

"That's all right, old boy," said the oiler, and lay down again and was asleep.

Presently it seemed that even the captain dozed, and the correspondent thought that he was the one man afloat on all the ocean. The wind had a voice as it came over the waves, and it was sadder than the end.

There was a long, loud swishing astern of the boat, and a gleaming trail of phosphorescence, like blue flame, was furrowed on the black waters. It might have been made by a monstrous knife.

Then there came a stillness, while the correspondent breathed with open mouth and looked at the sea.

Suddenly there was another swish and another long flash of bluish light, and this time it was alongside the boat, and might almost have been reached with an oar. The correspondent saw an enormous fin speed like a shadow through the water, hurling the crystalline spray and leaving the long glowing trail.

The correspondent looked over his shoulder at the captain. His face was hidden, and he seemed to be asleep. He looked at the babes of the sea. They certainly were sleep. So, being bereft of sympathy, he leaned a little way to one side and swore softly into the sea.

But the thing did not then leave the vicinity of the boat. Ahead or astern, on one side or the other, at intervals long or short, fled the long sparkling streak, and there was to be heard the *whirroo* of the dark fin. The speed and power of the thing was greatly to be admired. It cut the water like a gigantic and keen projectile.

The presence of this biding thing did not affect the man with the same horror that it would if he had been a picnicker. He simply looked at the sea dully and swore in an undertone.

Nevertheless, it is true that he did not wish to be alone with the thing. He wished one of his companions to awake by chance and keep him company with it. But the captain hung motionless over the water-jar, and the oiler and the cook in the bottom of the boat were plunged in slumber.

VI

"If I am going to be drowned—if I am going to be drowned—if I am going to be drowned, why, in the name of the seven mad gods who rule the sea, was I allowed to come thus far and contemplate sand and trees?"

During this dismal night, it may be remarked that a man would conclude that it was really the intention of the seven mad gods to drown him, despite the abominable injustice of it. For it was certainly an abominable injustice to drown a man who had worked so hard, so hard. The man felt it would be a crime most unnatural. Other people had drowned at sea since galleys swarmed with painted sails, but still—

When it occurs to a man that nature does not regard him as important, and that she feels she would not maim the universe by disposing of him, he at first wishes to throw bricks at the temple, and he hates deeply the fact that there are no bricks and no temples. Any visible expression of nature would surely be pelleted with his jeers.

Then, if there be no tangible thing to hoot, he feels, perhaps, the desire to confront a personification and indulge in pleas, bowed to one knee, and with hands supplicant, saying, "Yes, but I love myself.

A high cold star on a winter's night is the word he feels that she says to him. Thereafter he knows the pathos of his situation.

The men in the dinghy had not discussed these matters, but each had, no doubt, reflected upon them in silence and according to his mind. There was seldom any expression upon their faces save the general one of complete weariness. Speech was devoted to the business of the boat.

To chime the notes of his emotion, a verse mysteriously entered the correspondent's head. He had even forgotten that he had forgotten this verse, but it suddenly was in his mind.

> A soldier of the Legion lay dying in Algiers;
> There was lack of women's nursing, there was dearth of woman's tears;!
> But a comrade stood beside him, and he took that comrade's hand,
> And he said, "I never more shall see my own, my native land."

In his childhood the correspondent had been made acquainted with the fact that a soldier of the Legion lay dying in Algiers, but he had never regarded it as important. Myriads of his schoolfellows had informed him of the soldier's plight, but the dinning had naturally ended by making him perfectly indifferent. He had never considered it his affair that a soldier of the Legion lay dying in Algiers, nor had it appeared to him as a matter for sorrow. It was less to him than the breaking of a pencil's point.

Now, however, it quaintly came to him as a human, living thing. It was no longer merely a picture of a few throes in the breast of a poet, meanwhile drinking tea and warming his feet at the grate; it was an actuality—stern, mournful, and fine.

The correspondent plainly saw the soldier. He lay on the sand with his feet out straight and still. While his pale left hand was upon his chest in an attempt to thwart the going of his life, the blood came between his fingers. In the far Algerian distance, a city of low square forms was set against a sky that was faint with the last sunset hues. The correspondent, plying the oars and dreaming of the slow and slower movements of the lips of the soldier, was moved by a profound and perfectly impersonal comprehension. He was sorry for the soldier of the Legion who lay dying in Algiers.

The thing which had followed the boat and waited had evidently grown bored at the delay. There was no longer to be heard the slash of the cutwater, and there was no longer the flame of the long trail. The light in the north still glimmered, but it was apparently no nearer to the boat. Sometimes the boom of the surf rang in the correspondent's ears, and he turned the craft seaward then and rowed harder. Southward, some one had evidently built a watch-fire on the beach. It was too low and too far to be seen, but it made a shimmering, roseate reflection upon the bluff in back of it, and this could be discerned from the boat. The wind came stronger, and sometimes a wave suddenly raged out like a mountain-cat, and there was to be seen the sheen and sparkle of a broken crest.

The captain, in the bow, moved on his water-jar and sat erect. "Pretty long night," he observed to the correspondent. He looked at the shore. "Those life-saving people take their time."

"Did you see that shark playing around?"

"Yes, I saw him. He was a big fellow, all right."

"Wish I had known you were awake."

Later the correspondent spoke into the bottom of the boat. "Billie!" There was a slow and gradual disentanglement. "Billie, will you spell me?"

"Sure," said the oiler.

As soon as the correspondent touched the cold, comfortable sea-water in the bottom of the boat and had huddled close to the cook's life-belt he was deep in sleep, despite the fact that his teeth played all the popular airs. This sleep was so good to him that it was a moment before he heard a voice call his name in a tone that demonstrated the last stages of exhaustion. "Will you spell me?"

"Sure, Billie."

The light in the north had mysteriously vanished, but the correspondent took his course from the wide-awake captain.

Later in the night they took the boat farther out to sea, and the captain directed the cook to take one oar at the stern and keep the boat facing the seas. He was to call out if he should hear the thunder of the surf. This plan enabled the oiler and the correspondent to get respite together. "We'll give those boys a chance to get into shape again," said the captain. They curled down and, after a few preliminary chatterings and trembles, slept once more the dead sleep. Neither knew they had bequeathed to the cook the company of another shark, or perhaps the same shark.

As the boat caroused on the waves, spray occasionally bumped over the side and gave them a fresh soaking, but this had no power to break their repose. The ominous slash of the wind and the water affected them as it would have affected mummies.

"Boys," said the cook, with the notes of every reluctance in his voice, "she's drifted in pretty close. I guess one of you had better take her to sea again." The correspondent, aroused, heard the crash of the toppled crests.

As he was rowing, the captain gave him some whiskey-and-water, and this steadied the chills out of him. "If I ever get ashore and anybody shows me even a photograph of an oar—"

At last there was a short conversation.

"Billie! . . . Billie, will you spell me?"

"Sure," said the oiler.

VII

When the correspondent again opened his eyes, the sea and the sky were each of the gray hue of the dawning. Later, carmine and gold was painted upon the waters. The morning appeared finally, in its splendor, with a sky of pure blue, and the sunlight flamed on the tips of the waves.

On the distant dunes were set many little black cottages, and a tall white windmill reared above them. No man, nor dog, nor bicycle appeared on the beach. The cottages might have formed a deserted village.

The voyagers scanned the shore. A conference was held in the boat. "Well," said the captain, "if no help is coming, we might better try a run through the surf right away. If we stay out here much longer we will be too weak to do anything for ourselves at all." The others silently acquiesced in this reasoning. The boat was headed for the beach. The correspondent wondered if none ever ascended the tall wind-tower, and if then they never looked seaward. This tower was a giant, standing with its back to the plight of the ants. It represented in a degree, to the correspondent, the serenity of nature amid the struggles of the individual—nature in the wind, and nature in the vision of men. She did not seem cruel to him then, nor beneficent, nor treacherous, nor wise. But she was indifferent, flatly indifferent. It is, perhaps, plausible that a man in this situation, impressed with the unconcern of the universe, should see the innumerable flaws of his life, and have them taste wickedly in his mind, and wish for another chance. A distinction between right and wrong seems absurdly clear to him, then, in this new ignorance of the grave-edge, and he understands that if he were given another opportunity he would mend his conduct and his words, and be better and brighter during an introduction or at a tea.

"Now, boys," said the captain, "she is going to swamp sure. All we can do is to work her in as far as possible, and then when she swamps, pile out and scramble for the beach. Keep cool now, and don't jump until she swamps sure."

The oiler took the oars. Over his shoulders he scanned the surf. "Captain," he said, "I think I'd better bring her about and keep her head-on to the seas and back her in."

"All right, Billie," said the captain. "Back her in." The oiler swung the boat then, and, seated in the stern, the cook and the correspondent were obliged to look over their shoulders to contemplate the lonely and indifferent shore.

The monstrous inshore rollers heaved the boat high until the men were again enabled to see the white sheets of water scudding up the slanted beach. "We won't get in very close," said the captain. Each time a man could wrest his attention from the rollers, he turned his glance toward the shore, and in the expression of the eyes during this contemplation there was a singular quality. The correspondent, observing the others, knew that they were not afraid, but the full meaning of their glances was shrouded.

As for himself, he was too tired to grapple fundamentally with the fact. He tried to coerce his mind into thinking of it, but the mind was dominated at this time by the muscles, and the muscles said they did not care. It merely occurred to him that if he should drown it would be a shame.

There were no hurried words, no pallor, no plain agitation. The men simply looked at the shore. "Now, remember to get well clear of the boat when you jump," said the captain.

Seaward the crest of a roller suddenly fell with a thunderous crash, and the long white comber came roaring down upon the boat.

"Steady now," said the captain. The men were silent. They turned their eyes from the shore to the comber and waited. The boat slid up the incline, leaped at the furious top, bounced over it, and swung down the long back of the wave. Some water had been shipped, and the cook bailed it out.

But the next crest crashed also. The tumbling, boiling flood of white water caught the boat and whirled it almost perpendicular. Water swarmed in from all sides. The correspondent had his hands on the gunwale at this time, and when the water entered at that place he swiftly withdrew his fingers, as if he objected to wetting them.

The little boat, drunken with this weight of water, reeled and snuggled deeper into the sea.

"Bail her out, cook! Bail her out!" said the captain.

"All right, Captain," said the cook.

"Now boys, the next one will do for us sure," said the oiler. "Mind to jump clear of the boat."

The third wave moved forward, huge, furious, implacable. It fairly swallowed the dinghy, and almost simultaneously the men tumbled into the sea. A piece of life-belt had lain in the bottom of the boat, and as the correspondent went overboard he held this to his chest with his left hand.

The January water was icy, and he reflected immediately that it was colder than he had expected to find it off the coast of Florida. This appeared to his dazed mind as a fact important enough to be noted at the time. The coldness of the water was sad; it was tragic. This fact was somehow mixed and confused with his opinion of his own situation, so that it seemed almost a proper reason for tears. The water was cold.

When he came to the surface he was conscious of little but the noisy water. Afterward he saw his companions in the sea. The oiler was ahead in the race. He was swimming strongly and rapidly. Off to the correspondent's left, the cook's great white and corked back bulged out of the water, and in the rear the captain was hanging with his one good hand to the keel of the overturned dinghy.

There is a certain immovable quality to a shore, and the correspondent wondered at it amid the confusion of the sea.

It seemed also very attractive; but the correspondent knew that it was a long journey, and he paddled leisurely. The piece of life-preserver lay under him, and sometimes he whirled down the incline of a wave as if he were on a handsled.

But finally he arrived at a place in the sea where travel was beset with difficulty. He did not pause swimming to inquire what manner of current had caught him, but there his progress ceased. The shore was set before him like a bit of scenery on a stage, and he looked at it and understood with his eyes each detail of it.

As the cook passed, much farther to the left, the captain was calling to him, "Turn over on your back, cook! Turn over on your back and use the oar."

"All right, sir." The cook turned on his back, and, paddling with an oar, went ahead as if he were a canoe.

Presently the boat also passed to the left of the correspondent, with the captain clinging with one hand to the keel. He would have appeared like a man raising himself to look over a board fence if it were not for the extraordinary gymnastics of the boat. The correspondent marveled that the captain could still hold to it.

They passed on nearer to shore—the oiler, the cook, the captain—and following them went the water-jar, bouncing gaily over the seas.

The correspondent remained in the grip of this strange new enemy, a current. The shore, with its white slope of sand and its green bluff topped with little silent cottages, was spread like a picture before him. It was very near to him then, but he was impressed as one who, in a gallery, looks at a scene from Brittany or Algiers.

He thought: "I am going to drown? Can it be possible? Can it be possible? Can it be possible?" Perhaps an individual must consider his own death to be the final phenomenon of nature.

But later a wave perhaps whirled him out of this small deadly current, for he found suddenly that he could again make progress toward the shore. Later still he was aware that the captain, clinging with one hand to the keel of the dinghy, had his face turned away from the shore and toward him, and was calling his name. "Come to the boat! Come to the boat!"

In his struggle to reach the captain and the boat, he reflected that when one gets properly wearied drowning must really be a comfortable arrangement—a cessation of hostilities accompanied by a large degree of relief; and he was glad of it, for the main thing in his mind for some moments had been horror of the temporary agony; he did not wish to be hurt.

Presently he saw a man running along the short. He was undressing with most remarkable speed. Coat, trousers, shirt, everything flew magically off him.

"Come to the boat!" called the captain.

"All right, Captain." As the correspondent paddled, he saw the captain let himself down to bottom and leave the boat. Then the correspondent performed his one little marvel of the voyage. A large wave caught him and flung him with ease and supreme speed completely over the boat and far beyond it. It struck him even then as an event in gymnastics and a true miracle of the sea. An overturned boat in the surf is not a plaything to a swimming man.

The correspondent arrived in water that reached only to his waist, but his condition did not enable him to stand for more than a moment. Each wave knocked him into a heap, and the undertow pulled at him.

Then he saw the man who had been running and undressing, and undressing and running, come bounding into the water. He dragged ashore the cook, and then waded toward the captain; but the captain waved him away and sent him to the correspondent. He was naked—naked as a tree in winter; but a halo was about his head, and he shone like a saint. He gave a strong pull, and a long drag, and a bully heave at the correspondent's hand. The correspondent, schooled in the minor formulae, said, "Thanks, old man." But suddenly the man cried, "What's that?" He pointed a swift finger. The correspondent said, "Go."

In the shallows, face downward, lay the oiler. His forehead touched sand that was periodically, between each wave, clear of the sea.

The correspondent did not know all that transpired afterward. When he achieved safe ground he fell, striking the sand with each particular part of his body. It was as if he had dropped from a roof, but the thud was grateful to him.

It seemed that instantly the beach was populated with men with blankets, clothes, and flasks, and women with coffee-pots and all the remedies sacred to their minds. The welcome of the land to the men from the sea was warm and generous; but a still and dripping shape was carried slowly up the beach, and the land's welcome for it could only be the different and sinister hospitality of the grave.

When it came night, the white waves paced to and fro and the moonlight, and the wind brought the sound of the great sea's voice to the men on the shore, and they felt that they could then be interpreters.

James Joyce (1882–1941)

Araby

North Richmond Street, being blind, was a quiet street except at the hour when the Christian Brothers School set the boys free. An uninhabited house of two storeys stood at the blind end, detached from its neighbors in a square ground. The other houses of the street, conscious of decent lives within them, gazed at one another with brown imperturbable faces.

The former tenant of our house, a priest, had died in the back drawing-room. Air, musty from having been long enclosed, hung in all the rooms, and the waste room behind the kitchen was littered with old useless papers. Among these I found a few paper-covered books, the pages of which were curled and damp: *The Abbott*, By Walter Scott, *The Devout Communicant* and *The Memoirs of Vidocq.* I liked the last best because its leaves were yellow. The wild garden behind the house contained a central apple-tree and a few straggling bushes under one of which I found the late tenant's rusty bicycle-pump. He had been a very charitable priest; in his will he had left all his money to institutions and the furniture of his house to his sister.

When the short days of winter came dusk fell before we had well eaten our dinners. When we met in the street the houses had grown sombre. The space of sky above us was the colour of ever-changing violet and towards it the lamps of the street lifted their feeble lanterns. The cold air stung us and we played till our bodies glowed. Our shouts echoed in the silent street. The career of our play brought us through the dark muddy lanes behind the houses where we ran the gauntlet of the rough tribes from the cottages, to the back doors of the dark dripping gardens where odours arose from the ashpits, to the dark odorous stables where a coachman smoothed and combed the horse or shook music from the buckled harness. When we returned to the street light from the kitchen windows had filled the areas. If my uncle was seen turning the corner we hid in the shadow until we had seen him safely housed. Or if Mangan's sister came out on the doorstep to call her brother in to his tea we watched her from our shadow peer up and down the street. We waited to see whether she would remain or go in and, if she remained, we left our shadow and walked up to Mangan's steps resignedly. She was waiting for us, her figure defined by the light from the half-opened door. Her brother always teased her before he obeyed and I stood by the railings looking at her. Her dress swung as she moved her body and the soft rope of her hair tossed from side to side.

Every morning I lay on the floor in the front parlour watching her door. The blind was pulled down to within an inch of the sash so that I could not be seen. When she came out on the doorstep my heart leaped. I ran to the hall, seized my books and followed her. I kept her brown figure always in my eye and, when we came near the point at which our ways diverged, I quickened my pace and passed her. This happened morning after morning. I had never spoken to her, except for a few casual words, and yet her name was like a summons to all my foolish blood.

Her image accompanied me even in places the most hostile to romance. On Saturday evenings when my aunt went marketing I had to go to carry some of the parcels. We walked through the flaring streets, jostled by drunken men and bargaining women, amid the curses of labourers, the shrill litanies of shop-boys who stood on guard by the barrels of pigs' cheeks, the nasal chanting of street-singers, who sang a *come-all-you* about O'Donovan Rossa, or a ballad about the troubles in our native land. These noises converged in a single sensation of life for me: I imagined that I bore my chalice safely through a throng of foes. Her name sprang to my lips at moments in strange prayers and praises which I myself did not understand. My eyes were often full of tears (I could not tell why) and at times a flood from my heart seemed to pour itself out into my bosom. I thought little of the future. I did not know whether I would ever speak to her or not or, if I spoke to her, how I could tell her of my confused adoration. But my body was like a harp and her words and gestures were like fingers running upon the wires.

One evening I went into the back drawing-room in which the priest had died. It was a dark rainy evening and there was no sound in the house. Through one of the broken panes I heard the rain impinge upon the earth, the fine incessant needles of water playing in the sodden beds. Some distant lamp or lighted window gleamed below me. I was thankful that I could see so little. All my senses seemed to desire to veil themselves and, feeling that I was about to slip from them, I pressed the palms of my hands together until they trembled, murmuring: *"O love! O love!"* many times.

At last she spoke to me. When she addressed the first words to me I was so confused that I did not know what to answer. She asked me was I going to *Araby*. I forgot whether I answered yes or no. It would be a splendid bazaar, she said; she would love to go.

"And why can't you?" I asked.

While she spoke she turned a silver bracelet round and round her wrist. She could not go, she said, because there would be a retreat that week in her convent. Her brother and two other boys were fighting for their caps and I was alone at the railings. She held one of the spikes, bowing her head toward me. The light from the lamp opposite our door caught the white curve of her neck, lit up her hair that rested there and, falling, lit up the hand upon the railing. It fell over one side of her dress and caught the white border of a petticoat, just visible as she stood at ease.

"It's well for you," she said.

"If I go," I said, "I will bring you something."

What innumerable follies laid waste my waking and sleeping thoughts after that evening! I wished to annihilate the tedious intervening days. I chafed against the work of school. At night in my bedroom and by day in the classroom her image came between me and the page I strove to read. The syllables of the word *Araby* were called to me through the silence in which my soul luxuriated and cast an Eastern enchantment over me. I asked for leave to go to the bazaar on Saturday night. My aunt was surprised and hoped it was not some Freemason affair. I answered few questions in class. I watched my master's face pass from amiability to sternness; he hoped I was not beginning to idle. I could not call my wandering thoughts together. I had hardly any patience with the serious work of life which, now that it stood between me and my desire, seemed to me child's play, ugly monotonous child's play.

On Saturday morning I reminded my uncle that I wished to go to the bazaar in the evening. He was fussing at the hallstand, looking for the hat-brush, and answered me curtly:

"Yes, boy, I know."

As he was in the hall I could not go into the front parlour and lie at the window. I left the house in bad humour and walked slowly towards the school. The air was pitilessly raw and already my heart misgave me.

When I came home to dinner my uncle had not yet been home. Still it was early. I sat staring at the clock for some time and, when its ticking began to irritate me, I left the room. I mounted the staircase and gained the upper part of the house. The high cold empty gloomy rooms liberated me and I went from room to room singing. From the front window I saw my companions playing below in the street. Their cries reached me weakened and indistinct and, leaning my forehead against the cool glass, I looked over at the dark house where she lived. I may have stood there for an hour, seeing nothing but the brown-clad figure cast by my imagination, touched discreetly by the lamplight at the curved neck, at the hand upon the railings and at the border below the dress.

When I came downstairs again I found Mrs. Mercer sitting at the fire. She was an old garrulous woman, a pawnbroker's widow, who collected used stamps for some pious purpose. I had to endure the gossip of the tea-table. The meal was prolonged beyond an hour and still my uncle did not come. Mrs. Mercer stood up to go: she was sorry she couldn't wait any longer, but it was after eight o'clock and she did not like to be out late, as the night air was bad for her. When she had gone I began to walk up and down the room, clenching my fists. My aunt said:

"I'm afraid you may put off your bazaar for this night of Our Lord."

At nine o'clock I heard my uncle's latchkey in the halldoor. I heard him talking to himself and heard the hallstand rocking when it had received the weight of his overcoat. I could interpret these signs. When he was midway through his dinner I asked him to give me the money to go to the bazaar. He had forgotten.

"The people are in bed and after their first sleep now," he said.

I did not smile. My aunt said to him energetically:

"Can't you give him the money and let him go? You've kept him late enough as it is."

My uncle said he was very sorry he had forgotten. He said he believed in the old saying: "All work and no play makes Jack a dull boy." He asked me where I was going and, when I had told him a second time he asked me did I know *The Arab's Farewell to his Steed.* When I left the kitchen he was about to recite the opening lines of the piece to my aunt.

I held a florin tightly in my hand as I strode down Buckingham Street towards the station. The sight of the streets thronged with buyers and glaring with gas recalled to me the purpose of my journey. I took my seat in a third-class carriage of a deserted train. After an intolerable delay the train moved out of the station slowly. It crept onward among ruinous houses and over the twinkling river. At Westland Row Station a crowd of people pressed to the carriage doors; but the porters moved them back, saying that it was a special train for the bazaar. I remained alone in the bare carriage. In a few minutes the train drew up beside an improvised wooden platform. I passed out on to the road and saw by the lighted dial of a clock that it was ten minutes to ten. In front of me was a large building which displayed the magical name.

I could not find any sixpenny entrance and, fearing that the bazaar would be closed, I passed in quickly through a turnstile, handing a shilling to a weary-looking man. I found myself in a big hall girdled at half its height by a gallery. Nearly all the stalls were closed and the greater part of the hall was in darkness. I recognised a silence like that which pervades a church after a service. I walked into the centre of the bazaar timidly. A few people were gathered about the stalls which were still open. Before a curtain, over which the words *Café Chantant* were written in coloured lamps, two men were counting money on a salver. I listened to the fall of the coins.

Remembering with difficulty why I had come I went over to one of the stalls and examined porcelain vases and flowered tea-sets. At the door of the stall a young lady was talking and laughing with two young gentlemen. I remarked their English accents and listened vaguely to their conversation.

"O, I never said such a thing!"

"O, but you did!"

"O, but I didn't!"

"Didn't she say that?"

"Yes. I heard her."

"O, there's a . . . fib!"

Observing me the young lady came over and asked me did I wish to buy anything. The tone of her voice was not encouraging; she seemed to have spoken to me out of a sense of duty. I looked humbly at the great jars that stood like eastern guards at either side of the dark entrance to the stall and murmured:

"No, thank you."

The young lady changed the position of one of the vases and went back to the two young men. They began to talk of the same subject. Once or twice the young lady glanced at me over her shoulder.

I lingered before her stall, though I knew my stay was useless, to make my interest in her wares seem the more real. Then I turned away slowly and walked down the middle of the bazaar. I allowed the two pennies to fall against the sixpence in my pocket. I heard a voice call from one end of the gallery that the light was out. The upper part of the hall was now completely dark.

Gazing up into the darkness I saw myself as a creature driven and derided by vanity; and my eyes burned with anguish and anger.

D. H. Lawrence (1885–1930)

The Horse Dealer's Daughter

"Well, Mabel, and what are you going to do with yourself?" asked Joe, with foolish flippancy. He felt quite safe himself. Without listening for an answer, he turned aside, worked a grain of tobacco to the tip of his tongue, and spat it out. He did not care about anything, since he felt safe himself.

The three brothers and the sister sat round the desolate breakfast table, attempting some sort of desultory consultation. The morning's post had given the final tap to the family fortune, and all was over. The dreary dining-room itself, with its heavy mahogany furniture, looked as if it were waiting to be done away with.

But the consultation amounted to nothing. There was a strange air of ineffectuality about the three men, as they sprawled at table, smoking and reflecting vaguely on their own condition. The girl was alone, a rather short, sullen-looking young woman of twenty-seven. She did not share the same life as her brothers. She would have been good-looking, save for the impassive fixity of her face, "bull-dog," as her brothers called it.

There was a confused tramping of horses' feet outside. The three men all sprawled round in their chairs to watch. Beyond the dark holly-bushes that separated the strip of lawn from the highroad, they could see a cavalcade of shire horses swinging out of their own yard, being taken for exercise. This was the last time. These were the last horses that would go through their hands. The young men watched with critical, callous look. They were all frightened at the collapse of their lives, and the sense of disaster in which they were involved left them no inner freedom.

Yet they were three fine, well-set fellows enough. Joe, the eldest, was a man of thirty-three, broad and handsome in a hot, flushed way. His face was red, he twisted his black moustache over a thick finger, his eyes were shallow and restless. He had a sensual way of uncovering his teeth when he laughed, and his bearing was stupid. Now he watched the horses with a glazed look of helplessness in his eyes, a certain stupor of downfall.

The great draught-horses swung past. They were tied head to tail, four of them, and they heaved along to where a lane branched off from the highroad, planting their great hoofs floutingly in the fine black mud, swinging their great rounded haunches sumptuously, and trotting a few sudden steps as they were led into the lane, round the corner. Every movement showed a massive, slumbrous strength, and a stupidity which held them in subjection. The groom at the head looked back, jerking the leading rope. And the cavalcade moved out of sight up the lane, the tail of the last horse, bobbed up tight and stiff, held out taut from the swinging great haunches as they rocked behind the hedges in a motion like sleep.

Joe watched with glazed hopeless eyes. The horses were almost like his own body to him. He felt he was done for now. Luckily he was engaged to a woman as old as himself, and therefore her father, who was steward of a neighbouring estate, would provide him with a job. He would marry and go into harness. His life was over, he would be a subject animal now.

He turned uneasily aside, the retreating steps of the horses echoing in his ears. Then, with foolish restlessness, he reached for the scraps of bacon-rind from the plates, and making a faint whistling sound, flung them to the terrier that lay against the fender. He watched the dog swallow them, and waited till the creature looked into his eyes. Then a faint grin came on his face, and in a high, foolish voice he said:

"You won't get much more bacon, shall you, you little bitch?"

The dog faintly and dismally wagged its tail, then lowered its haunches, circled round, and lay down again.

There was another helpless silence at the table. Joe sprawled uneasily in his seat, not willing to go till the family conclave was dissolved. Fred Henry, the second brother, was erect, clean-limbed, alert. He had watched the passing of the horses with more sang-froid. If he was an animal, like Joe, he was an animal which controls, not one which is controlled. He was master of any horse, and he carried himself with a well-tempered air of mastery. But he was not master of the situations of life. He pushed his coarse brown moustache upwards, off his lip, and glanced irritably at his sister, who sat impassive and inscrutable.

"You'll go and stop with Lucy for a bit, shan't you?" he asked. The girl did not answer.

"I don't see what else you can do," persisted Fred Henry.

"Go as a skivvy," Joe interpolated laconically.

The girl did not move a muscle.

"If I was her, I should go in for training for a nurse," said Malcolm, the youngest of them all. He was the baby of the family, a young man of twenty-two, with a fresh, jaunty *museau.*

But Mabel did not take any notice of him. They had talked at her and round her for so many years, that she hardly heard them at all.

The marble clock on the mantelpiece softly chimed the half-hour, the dog rose uneasily from the hearthrug and looked at the party at the breakfast table. But still they sat on in inffectual conclave.

"Oh, all right," said Joe suddenly, apropos of nothing. "I'll get a move on."

He pushed back his chair, straddled his knees with a downward jerk, to get them free, in horsey fashion, and went to the fire. Still he did not go out of the room; he was curious to know what the others would do or say. He began to charge his pipe, looking down at the dog and saying, in a high, affected voice:

"Going wi' me? Going wi' me are ter? Tha'rt goin' further tha that counts on just now, dost hear?"

The dog faintly wagged its tail, the man struck out his jaw and covered his pipe with his hands, and puffed intently, losing himself in the tobacco, looking down all the while at the dog with an absent brown eye. The dog looked up at him in mournful distrust. Joe stood with his knees stuck out, in real horsey fashion.

"Have you had a letter from Lucy?" Fred Henry asked of his sister.

"Last week," came the neutral reply.

"And what does she say?"

There was no answer.

"Does she *ask* you to go and stop there?" persisted Fred Henry.

"She says I can if I like."

"Well, then, you'd better. Tell her you'll come on Monday."

This was received in silence.

"That's what you'll do then, is it?" said Fred Henry, in some exasperation.

But she made no answer. There was a silence of futility and irritation in the room. Malcolm grinned fatuously.

"You'll have to make up your mind between now and next Wednesday," said Joe loudly, "or else find yourself lodgings on the kerbstone."

The face of the young woman darkened, but she sat on immutable.

"Here's Jack Fergusson!" exclaimed Malcolm, who was looking aimlessly out of the window.

"Where?" exclaimed Joe, loudly.

"Just gone past."

"Coming in?"

Malcolm craned his neck to see the gate.

"Yes," he said.

There was a silence. Mabel sat on like one condemned, at the head of the table. Then a whistle was heard from the kitchen. The dog got up and barked sharply. Joe opened the door and shouted:

"Come on."

After a moment a young man entered. He was muffled up in overcoat and a purple woollen scarf, and his tweed cap, which he did not remove, was pulled down on his head. He was of medium height, his face was rather long and pale, his eyes looked tired.

"Hello, Jack! Well, Jack!" exclaimed Malcolm and Joe. Fred Henry merely said, "Jack."

"What's doing?" asked the newcomer, evidently addressing Fred Henry.

"Same. We've got to be out by Wednesday. Got a cold?"

"I have—got it bad, too."

"Why don't you stop in?"

"*Me* stop in? Why I can't stand on my legs, perhaps I shall have a chance." The young man spoke huskily. He had a slight Scotch accent.

"It's a knock-out, isn't it," said Joe, boisterously, "if a doctor goes round croaking with a cold. Looks bad for the patients, doesn't it?"

The young doctor looked at him slowly.

"Anything the matter with *you*, then?" he asked sarcastically.

"Not as I know of. Damn your eyes, I hope not. Why?"

"I thought you were very concerned about the patients, wondered if you might be one yourself."

"Damn it, no, I've never been patient to no flaming doctor, and hope I never shall be," returned Joe.

At this point Mabel rose from the table, and they all seemed to become aware of her existence. She began putting the dishes together. The young doctor looked at her, but did not address her. He had not greeted her. She went out of the room with the tray, her face impassive and unchanged.

"When are you off then, all of you?" asked the doctor.

"I'm catching the eleven-forty," replied Malcolm. "Are you goin' down wi' th' trap, Joe?"

"Yes, I've told you I'm going down wi' th' trap, haven't I?"

"We'd better be getting her in then. So long, Jack, if I don't see you before I go," said Malcolm, shaking hands.

He went out, followed by Joe, who seemed to have his tail between his legs.

"Well, this is the devil's own," exclaimed the doctor, when he was left alone with Fred Henry. "Going before Wednesday, are you?"

"That's the orders," replied the other.

"Where, to Northampton?"

"That's it."

"The devil!" exclaimed Ferguson, with quiet chagrin.

And there was silence between the two.

"All settled up, are you?" asked Fergusson.

"About."

There was another pause.

"Well, I shall miss yer, Freddy, boy," said the young doctor.

"And I shall miss thee, Jack," returned the other.

"Miss you like hell," mused the doctor.

Fred Henry turned aside. There was nothing to say. Mabel came in again, to finish clearing the table.

"What are *you* going to do, then, Miss Pervin?" asked Fergusson. "Going to your sister's, are you?"

Mabel looked at him with her steady, dangerous eyes, that always made him uncomfortable, unsettling his superficial ease.

"No," she said.

"Well, what in the name of fortune *are* you going to do? Say what you mean to do," cried Fred Henry, with futile intensity.

But she only averted her head, and continued her work. She folded the white table-cloth, and put on the chenille cloth.

"The sulkiest bitch that ever trod!" muttered her brother.

But she finished her task with perfectly impassive face, the young doctor watching her interestedly all the while. Then she went out.

Fred Henry stared after her, clenching his lips, his blue eyes fixing in sharp antagonism, as he made a grimace of sour exasperation.

"You could bray her into bits, and that's all you'd get out of her," he said in a small, narrowed tone.

The doctor smiled faintly.

"What's she *going* to do, then?" he asked.

"Strike me if *I* know!" returned the other.

There was a pause. Then the doctor stirred.

"I'll be seeing you to-night, shall I?" he said to his friend.

"Ay—where's it to be? Are we going over to Jessdale?"

"I don't know. I've got a cold on me. I'll come round to the Moon and Stars, anyway."

"Let Lizzie and May miss their night for once, eh?"

"That's it—if I feel as I do now."

"All's one—"

The two young men went through the passage and down to the back door together. The house was large, but it was servantless now, and desolate. At the back was a small bricked house-yard, and beyond that a big square, gravelled fine and red, and having stables on two sides. Sloping, dank, winter-dark fields stretched away on the open sides.

But the stables were empty. Joseph Pervin, the father of the family, had been a man of no education, who had become a fairly large horse dealer. The stables had been full of horses, there was a great turmoil and come-and-go of horses and of dealers and grooms. Then the kitchen was full of servants. But of late things had declined. The old man had married a second time, to retrieve his fortunes. Now he was dead and everything was gone to the dogs, there was nothing but debt and threatening.

For months, Mabel had been servantless in the big house, keeping the home together in penury for her ineffectual brothers. She had kept house for ten years. But previously it was with unstinted means. Then, however brutal and coarse everything was, the sense of oney had kept her proud, confident. The men might be foulmouthed, the women in the kitchen might have bad reputations, her brothers might have illegitimate children. But so long as there was money, the girl felt herself established, and brutally proud, reserved.

No company came to the house, save dealers and coarse men. Mabel had no associates of her own sex, after her sister went away. But she did not mind. She went regularly to church, she attended to her father. And she lived in the memory of her mother, who had died when she was fourteen, and whom she had loved. She had loved her father, too, in a different way, depending upon him, and feeling secure in him, until at the age of fifty-four he married again. And then she had set hard against him. Now he had died and left them all hopelessly in debt.

She had suffered badly during the period of poverty. Nothing, however, could shake the curious sullen, animal pride that dominated each member of the family. Now, for Mabel, the end had come. Still she would not cast about her. She would follow her own way just the same. She would always hold the keys of her own situation. Mindless and persistent, she endured from day to day. Why should she think? Why should she answer anybody? It was enough that this was the end, and there was no way out. She need not pass any more darkly along the main street of the small town, avoiding every eye. She need not demean herself any more going into the shops and buying the cheapest food. This was at an end. She thought of nobody, not even of herself. Mindless and persistent, she seemed in a sort of ecstasy to be coming nearer to her fulfillment, her own glorification, approaching her dead mother, who was glorified.

In the afternoon she took a little bag, with shears and sponge and a small scrubbing brush, and went out. It was a grey, wintery day, with saddened, dark green fields and an atmosphere blackened by the smoke of foundries not far off. She went quickly, darkly along the causeway, heeding nobody, through the town to the churchyard.

There she always felt secure, as if no one could see her, although as a matter of fact she was exposed to the stare of every one who passed along under the churchyard wall. Nevertheless, once under the shadow of the great looming church, among the graves, she felt immune from the world, reserved within the thick churchyard wall as in another country.

Carefully she clipped the grass from the grave, and arranged the pinky white, small chrysanthemums in the tin cross. When this was done, she took an empty jar from a neighbouring grave, brought water, and carefully, most scrupulously sponged the marble headstone and the coping-stone.

It gave her sincere satisfaction to do this. She felt in immediate contact with the world of her mother. She took minute pains, went through the park in a state bordering on pure happiness, as if in performing this task she came into a subtle, intimate connection with her mother. For the life she followed here in the world was far less real than the world of death she inherited from her mother.

The doctor's house was just by the Church. Fergusson, being a mere hired assistant, was slave to the country-side. As he hurried now to attend to the outpatients in the surgery, glancing across the grave yard with his quick eye, he saw the girl at her task at the grave. She seemed so intent and remote, it was like looking into another world. Some mystical element was touched in him. He slowed down as he walked, watching her as if spell-bound.

She lifted her eyes, feeling him looking. Their eyes met. And each looked away again at once, each feeling, in some way, found out by the other. He lifted his cap and passed on down the road. There remained distinct in his consciousness, like a vision, the memory of her face, lifted from the tombstone in the churchyard, and looking at him with slow, large, portentous eyes. It *was* portentous, her face. It seemed to mesmerize him. There was a heavy power in her eyes which laid hold of his whole being, as if he had drunk some powerful drug. He had been feeling weak and done before. Now the life came back into him, he felt delivered from his own fretted, daily self.

He finished his duties at the surgery as quickly as might be, hastily filling up the bottle of the waiting people with cheap drugs. Then, in perpetual haste, he set off again to visit several cases in another part of his round, before tea-time. At all times he preferred to walk if he could, but particularly when he was not well. He fancied the motion restored him.

The afternoon was falling. It was grey, deadened, and wintry, with a slow, moist, heavy coldness sinking in and deadening all the faculties. But why should he think or notice? He hastily climbed the hill and turned across the dark green fields, following the black cinder-track. In the distance, across a shallow dip in the country, the small town was clustered like smouldering ash, a tower, a spire, a heap of low, raw, extinct houses. And on the nearest fringe of the town, sloping into the dip, was Oldmeadow, the Pervins' house. He could see the stables and the out-buildings distinctly, as they lay towards him on the slope. Well, he would not go there many more times! Another resource would be lost to him, another place gone: the only company he cared for in the alien, ugly little town he was losing. Nothing but work, drudgery, constant hastening from dwelling to dwelling among the colliers and the iron-workers. It wore him out, but at the same time he had a craving for it. It was a stimulant to him to be in the homes of the working people, moving as it were through the innermost body of their life. His nerves were excited and gratified. He could come so near, into the very lives of the rough, inarticulate, powerfully emotional men and women. He grumbled, he said he hated the hellish hole. But as a matter of fact it excited him, the contact with the rough, strongly-feeling people was a stimulant applied direct to his nerves.

Below Oldmeadow, in the green, shallow, soddened hollow of fields, lay a square, deep pond. Roving across the landscape, the doctor's quick eye detected a figure in black passing through the gate of the field, down towards the pond. He looked again. It would be Mabel Pervin. His mind suddenly became alive and attentive.

Why was she going down there? He pulled up on the path on the slope above, and stood staring. He could just make sure of the small black figure moving in the hollow of the failing day. He seemed to see her in the midst of such obscurity, that he was like a clairvoyant, seeing rather with the mind's eye than with ordinary sight. Yet he could see her positively enough, whilst he kept his eye attentive. He felt, if he looked away from her, in the thick, ugly falling dusk, he would lose her altogether.

He followed her minutely as she moved, direct and intent, like something transmitted rather than stirring in voluntary activity, straight down the field towards the pond. There she stood on the bank for a moment. She never raised her head. Then she waded slowly into the water.

He stood motionless as the small black figure walked slowly and deliberately towards the centre of the pond, very slowly, gradually moving deeper into the motionless water, and still moving forward as the water got up to her breast. Then he could see her no more in the dusk of the dead afternoon.

"There!" he exclaimed. "Would you believe it?"

And he hastened straight down, running over the wet, soddened fields, pushing through the hedges, down into the depression of callous wintry obscurity. It took him several minutes to come to the pond. He stood on the bank, breathing heavily. He could see nothing. His eyes seemed to penetrate the dead water. Yes, perhaps that was the dark shadow of her black clothing beneath the surface of the water.

He slowly ventured into the pond. The bottom was deep, soft clay, he sank in, and the water clasped dead cold round his legs. As he stirred he could smell the cold, rotten clay that fouled up into the water. It was objectionable in his lungs. Still, repelled and yet not heeding, he moved deeper into the pond. The cold water rose over his thighs, over his loins, upon his abdomen. The lower part of his body was all sunk in the hideous cold element. And the bottom was so deeply soft and uncertain he was afraid of pitching with his mouth underneath. He could not swim, and was afraid.

He crouched a little, spreading his hands under the water and moving them round, trying to feel for her. The dead cold pond swayed upon his chest. He moved again, a little deeper, and again, with his hands underneath, he felt all around under the water. And he touched her clothing. But it evaded his fingers. He made a desperate effort to grasp it.

And so doing he lost his balance and went under, horribly, suffocating in the foul earthy water, struggling madly for a few moments. At last, after what seemed an eternity, he got his footing, rose again into the air and looked around. He gasped, and knew he was in the world. Then he looked at the water. She had risen near him. He grasped her clothing, and drawing her nearer, turned to take his way to land again.

He went very slowly, carefully, absorbed in the slow progress. He rose higher, climbing out of the pond. The water was now only about his legs; he was thankful, full of relief to be out of the clutches of the pond. He lifted her and staggered on to the bank, out of the horror of wet, grey clay.

He laid her down on the bank. She was quite unconscious and running with water. He made the water come from her mouth, he worked to restore her. He did not have to work very long before he could feel the breathing begin again in her; she was breathing naturally. He worked a little longer. He could feel her live beneath his hands; she was coming back. He wiped her face, wrapped her in his overcoat, looked round into the dim, dark grey world, then lifted her and staggered down the bank and across the fields.

It seemed an unthinkably long way, and his burden so heavy he felt he would never get to the house. But at last he was in the stable-yard, and then in the houseyard. He opened the door and went into the house. In the kitchen he laid her down on the hearthrug, and called. The house was empty. But the fire was burning in the grate.

Then again he kneeled to attend to her. She was breathing regularly, her eyes were wide open and as if conscious, but there seemed something missing in her look. She was conscious in herself, but unconscious of her surroundings.

He ran upstairs, took blankets from a bed, and put them before the fire to warm. Then he removed her saturated, earthy-smelling clothing, rubbed her dry with a towel, and wrapped her naked in the blankets. Then he went into the dining-room, to look for spirits. There was a little whisky. He drank a gulp himself, and put some into her mouth.

The effect was instantaneous. She looked full into his face, as if she had been seeing him for some time, and yet had only just become conscious of him.

"Dr. Fergusson?" she said.

"What?" he answered.

He was divesting himself of his coat, intending to find some dry clothing upstairs. He could not bear the smell of the dead, clayey water, and he was mortally afraid of his own health.

"What did I do?" she asked.

"Walked into the pond," he replied. He had begun to shudder like one sick, and could hardly attend to her. Her eyes remained full on him, he seemed to be going dark in his mind, looking back at her helplessly. The shuddering became quieter in him, his life came back in him, dark and unknowing, but strong again.

"Was I out of my mind?" she asked, while her eyes were fixed on him all the time.

"Maybe, for the moment," he replied. He felt quiet, because his strength had come back. The strange fretful strain had left him.

"Am I out of my mind now?" she asked.

"Are you?" he reflected a moment. "No," he answered truthfully, "I don't see that you are." He turned his face aside. He was afraid now, because he felt dazed, and felt dimly that her power was stronger than his, in this issue. And she continued to look at him fixedly all the time. "Can you tell me where I shall find some dry things to put on?" he asked.

"Did you dive into the pond for me?" she asked.

"No," he answered. "I walked in. But I went in overhead as well."

There was silence for a moment. He hesitated. He very much wanted to go upstairs to get into dry clothing. But there was another desire in him. And she seemed to hold him. His will seemed to have gone to sleep, and left him, standing there slack before her. But he felt warm inside himself. He did not shudder at all, though his clothes were sodden on him.

"Why did you?" she asked.

"Because I didn't want you to do such a foolish thing," he said.

"It wasn't foolish," she said, still gazing at him as she lay on the floor, with a sofa cushion under her head. "It was the right thing to do. *I* knew best, then."

"I'll go and shift these wet things," he said. But still he had not the power to move out of her presence, until she sent him. It was as if she had the life of his body in her hands, and he could not extricate himself. Or perhaps he did not want to.

Suddenly she sat up. Then she became aware of her own immediate condition. She felt the blankets about her, she knew her own limbs. For a moment it seemed as if her reason were going. She looked round, with wild eye, as if seeking something. He stood still with fear. She saw her clothing lying scattered.

"Who undressed me?" she asked, her eyes resting full and inevitable on his face.

"I did," he replied, "to bring you round."

For some moments she sat and gazed at him awfully, her lips parted.

"Do you love me, then?" she asked.

He only stood and stared at her, fascinated. His soul seemed to melt.

She shuffled forward on her knees, and put her arms round him, round his legs, and he stood there, pressing her breasts against his knees and thighs, clutching him with strange, convulsive certainty, pressing his thighs against her, drawing him to her face, her throat, as she looked up at him with flaring, humble eyes of transfiguration, triumphant in first possession.

"You love me," she murmured, in strange transport, yearning and triumphant and confident. "You love me. I know you love me, I know."

And she was passionately kissing his knees, through the wet clothing, passionately and indiscriminately kissing his knees, his legs, as if unaware of everything.

He looked down at the tangled wet hair, the wild, bare, animal shoulders. He was amazed, bewildered, and afraid. He had never thought of loving her. He had never wanted to love her. When he rescued her and restored her, he was a doctor, and she was a patient. He had had no single personal thought of her. Nay, this introduction of the personal element was very distasteful to him, a violation of his professional honour. It was horrible to have her there embracing his knees. It was horrible. He revolted from it, violently. And yet—and yet—he had not the power to break away.

She looked at him again, with the same supplication of powerful love, and the same transcendent, frightening light of triumph. In view of the delicate flame which seemed to come from her face like a light, he was powerless. And yet he had never intended to love her. He had never intended. And something stubborn in him could not give way.

"You love me," she repeated, in a murmur of deep, rhapsodic assurance. "You love me."

Her hands were drawing him, drawing him down to her. He was afraid, even a little horrified. For he had, really, no intention of loving her. Yet her hands were drawing him towards her. He put out his hand quickly to steady himself, and grasped her bare shoulder. A flame seemed to burn the hand that grasped her soft shoulder. He had no intention of loving her; his whole will was against his yielding. It was horrible. And yet wonderful was the touch of her shoulders, beautiful the shining of her face. Was she perhaps mad? He had a horror of yielding to her. Yet something in him ached also.

He had been staring away at the door, away from her. But his hand remained on her shoulder. She had gone suddenly very still. He looked down at her. Her eyes were now wide with fear, with doubt, the light was dying from her face, a shadow of terrible greyness was returning. He could not bear the touch of her eyes' question upon him, and the look of death behind the question.

With an inward groan he gave way. and let his heart yield towards her. A sudden gentle smile came on his face. And her eyes, which never left his face, slowly, slowly filled with tears. He watched the strange water rise in her eyes, like some slow fountain coming up. And his heart seemed to burn and melt away in his breast.

He could not bear to look at her any more. He dropped on his knees and caught her head with his arms and pressed her face against his throat. She was very still. His heart, which seemed to have broken, was burning with a kind of agony in his breast. And he felt her slow, hot tears wetting his throat. But he could not move.

He felt the hot tears wet his neck and the hollows of his neck, and he remained motionless, suspended through one of man's eternities. Only now it had become indispensable to him to have her face pressed close to him; he could never let her go again. He could never let her head go away from the close clutch of his arm. He wanted to remain like that for ever, with his heart hurting him in a pain that was also life to him. Without knowing, he was looking down on her damp, soft brown hair.

Then, as it were suddenly, he smelt the horrid stagnant smell of that water. And at the same moment she drew away from him and looked at him. Her eyes were wistful and unfathomable. He was afraid of them, and he fell to kissing her, not knowing what he was doing. He wanted her eyes not to have that terrible, wistful, unfathomable look.

When she turned her face to him again, a faint delicate flush was glowing, and there was again dawning that terrible shining of joy in her eyes, which really terrified him, and yet which he now wanted to see, because he feared the look of doubt still more.

"You love me?" she said, rather faltering.

"Yes." The word cost him a painful effort. Not because it wasn't true. But because it was too newly true, the *saying* seemed to tear open again his newly-torn heart. And he hardly wanted it to be true, even now.

She lifted her face to him, and he bent forward and kissed her on the mouth, gently, with the one kiss that is an eternal pledge. And as he kissed her his heart strained again in his breast. He never intended to love her. But now it was over. He had crossed over the gulf to her, and all that he had left behind had shrivelled and become void.

After the kiss, her eyes again slowly filled with tears. She sat still, away from him, with her face drooped aside, and her hands folded in her lap. The tears fell very slowly. There was complete silence. He too sat there motionless and silent on the hearthrug. The strange pain of his heart that was broken seemed to consume him. That he should love her? That this was love! That he should be ripped open in this way! Him, a doctor! How they would all jeer if they knew! It was agony to him to think they might know.

In the curious naked pain of the thought he looked again to her. She was sitting there drooped into a muse. He saw a tear fall, and his heart flared hot. He saw for the first time that one of her shoulders was quite uncovered, one arm bare, he could see one of her small breasts; dimly, because it had become almost dark in the room.

"Why are you crying!" he asked, in an altered voice.

She looked up at him, and behind her tears the consciousness of her situation for the first time brought a dark look of shame to her eyes.

"I'm not crying, really," she said, watching him half frightened.

He reached his hand, and softly closed it on her bare arm.

"I love you! I love you!" he said in a soft, low vibrating voice, unlike himself.

She shrank, and dropped her head. The soft, penetrating grip of his hand on her arm distressed her. She looked up at him.

"I want to go," she said. "I want to go and get you some dry things."

"Why?" he said. "I'm all right."

"But I want to go," she said. "And I want you to change your things."

He released her arm, and she wrapped herself in the blanket, looking at him rather frightened. And still she did not rise.

"Kiss me," she said wistfully.

He kissed her, but briefly, half in anger.

Then, after a second, she rose nervously, all mixed up in the blanket. He watched her in her confusion, as she tried to extricate herself and wrap herself up so that she could walk. He watched her relentlessly, as she knew. And as she went, the blanket trailing, and as he saw a glimpse of her feet and her white leg, he tried to remember her as she was when he had wrapped her in the blanket. But then he didn't want to remember, because she had been nothing to him then, and his nature revolted from remembering her as she was when she was nothing to him.

A tumbling, muffled noise from within the dark house startled him. Then he heard her voice:—"There are clothes." He rose and went to the foot of the stairs, and gathered up the garments she had thrown down. Then he came back to the fire, to rub himself down and dress. He grinned at his own appearance when he had finished.

The fire was sinking, so he put on coal. The house was now quite dark, save for the light of a streetlamp that shone in faintly from beyond the holly trees. He lit the gas with matches he found on the mantlepiece. Then he emptied the pockets of his own clothes, and threw all his wet things in a heap into the scullery. After which he gathered up her sodden clothes, gently, and put them in a separate heap on the copper-top in the scullery.

It was six o'clock on the clock. His own watch had stopped. He ought to go back to the surgery. He waited, and still she did not come down. So he went to the foot of the stairs and called:

"I shall have to go."

Almost immediately he heard her coming down. She had on her best dress of black voile, and her hair was tidy, but still damp. She looked at him—and in spite of herself, smiled.

"I don't like you in those clothes," she said.

"Do I look a sight?" he answered.

They were shy of one another.

"I'll make you some tea," she said.

"No, I must go."

"Must you?" And she looked at him again with the wide, strained, doubtful eyes. And again, from the pain of his breast, he knew how he loved her. He went and bent to kiss her, gently, passionately, with his heart's painful kiss.

"And my hair smells so horrible," she murmured in distraction. "And I'm so awful, I'm so awful! Oh, no, I'm too awful." And she broke into bitter, heartbroken sobbing. "You can't want to love me, I'm horrible."

"Don't be silly, don't be silly," he said, trying to comfort her, kissing her, holding her in his arms. "I want you, I want to marry you, we're going to be married, quickly, quickly—tomorrow if I can."

But she only sobbed terribly, and cried:

"I feel awful, I feel awful, I feel I'm horrible to you."

"No, I want you, I want you," was all he answered, blindly, with that terrible intonation which frightened her almost more than her horror lest he should *not* want her.

Katherine Mansfield (1888–1923)

Bliss

Although Bertha Young was thirty she still had moments like this when she wanted to run instead of walk, to take dancing steps on and off the pavement, to bowl a hoop, to throw something up in the air and catch it again, or to stand still and laugh at—nothing—at nothing, simply.

What can you do if you are thirty and, turning the corner of your own street, you are overcome, suddenly, by a feeling of bliss—absolute bliss!—as though you'd suddenly swallowed a bright piece of that late afternoon sun and it burned in your bosom, sending out a little shower of sparks into every particle, into every finger and toe? . . .

Oh, is there no way you can express it without being "drunk and disorderly"? How idiotic civilization is! Why be given a body if you have to keep it shut up in a case like a rare, rare fiddle?

"No, that about the fiddle is not quite what I mean," she thought, running up the steps and feeling in her bag for the key—she'd forgotten it, as usual—and rattling the letter-box. "It's not what I mean, because— Thank you, Mary"—she went into the hall. "Is nurse back?"

"Yes, M'm."

"And has the fruit come?"

"Yes, M'm. Everything's come."

"Bring the fruit up to the dining-room, will you? I'll arrange it before I go upstairs."

It was dusky in the dining-room and quite chilly. But all the same Bertha threw off her coat; she could not bear the tight clasp of it another moment, and the cold air fell on her arms.

But in her bosom there was still that bright glowing place—that shower of little sparks coming from it. It was almost unbearable. She hardly dared to breathe for fear of fanning it higher, and yet she breathed deeply, deeply. She hardly dared to look into the cold mirror—but she did look, and it gave her back a woman, radiant, with smiling, trembling lips, with big, dark eyes and an air of listening, waiting for something . . . divine to happen . . . that she knew must happen . . . infallibly.

Mary brought in the fruit on a tray and with it a glass bowl, and a blue dish, very lovely, with a strange sheen on it as though it had been dipped in milk.

"Shall I turn on the light, M'm?"

"No, thank you. I can see quite well."

There were tangerines and apples stained with strawberry pink. Some yellow pears, smooth as silk, some white grapes covered with a silver bloom and a big cluster of purple ones. These last she had bought to tone in with the new dining-room carpet. Yes, that did sound rather far-fetched and absurd, but it was really why she had bought them. She had thought in the shop: "I must have some purple ones to bring the carpet up to the table." And it had seemed quite sense at the time.

When she had finished with them and had made two pyramids of these bright round shapes, she stood away from the table to get the effects—and it really was most curious. For the dark table seemed to melt into the dusky light and the glass dish and the blue bowl to float in the air. This, of course in her present mood, was so incredibly beautiful. . . . She began to laugh.

"No, no. I'm getting hysterical." And she seized her bag and coat and ran upstairs to the nursery.

Nurse sat at a low table giving Little B her supper after her bath. The baby had on a white flannel gown and a blue woollen jacket, and her dark, fine hair was brushed up into a funny little peak. She looked up when she saw her mother and began to jump.

"Now, my lovely, eat it up like a good girl," said Nurse, setting her lips in a way that Bertha knew, and that meant she had come into the nursery at another wrong moment.

"Has she been good, Nanny?"

"She's been a little sweet all the afternoon," whispered Nanny. "We went to the park and I sat down on a chair and took her out of the pram and a big dog came along and put its head on my knee and she clutched its ear, tugged it. Oh, you should have seen her."

Bertha wanted to ask if it wasn't rather dangerous to let her clutch at a strange dog's ear. But she did not dare to. She stood watching them, her hands by her side, like the poor little girl in front of the rich little girl with the doll.

The baby looked up at her again, stared, and then smiled so charmingly that Bertha couldn't help crying:

"Oh, Nanny, do let me finish giving her her supper while you put the bath things away."

"Well, M'm, she oughtn't to be changed hands while she's eating," said Nanny, still whispering. "It unsettles her; it's very likely to upset her."

How absurd it was. Why have a baby if it has to be kept—not in a case like a rare, rare fiddle—but in another woman's arms?

"Oh, I must!" said she.

Very offended, Nanny handed her over.

"Now, don't excite her after her supper. You know you do, M'm. And I have such a time with her after!"

Thank heaven! Nanny went out of the room with the bath towels.

"Now I've got you to myself, my little precious," said Bertha, as the baby leaned against her.

She ate delightfully, holding up her lips for the spoon and then waving her hands. Sometimes she wouldn't let the spoon go; and sometimes, just as Bertha had filled it, she waved it away to the four winds.

When the soup was finished Bertha turned round to the fire.

"You're nice—you're very nice!" said she, kissing her warm baby. "I'm fond of you. I like you."

And, indeed, she loved Little B so much—her neck as she bent forward, her exquisite toes as they shone transparent in firelight—that all her feeling of bliss came back again, and again she didn't know how to express it—what to do with it.

"You're wanted on the telephone," said Nanny, coming back in triumph and seizing *her* Little B.

Down she flew. It was Harry.

"Oh, is that you, Ber? Look here. I'll be late. I'll take a taxi and come along as quickly as I can, but get dinner put back ten minutes—will you? All right?"

"Yes, perfectly. Oh, Harry!"

"Yes?"

What had she to say? She'd nothing to say. She only wanted to get in touch with him for a moment. She couldn't absurdly cry: "Hasn't it been a divine day!"

"What is it?" rapped out the little voice.

"Nothing. *Entendu*," said Bertha, and hung up the receiver, thinking how more than idiotic civilization was.

They had people coming to dinner. The Norman Knights—a very sound couple—he was about to start a theatre, and she was awfully keen on interior decoration, a young man, Eddie Warren, who had just published a little book of poems, and whom everybody was asking to dine, and a "find" of Bertha's called Pearl Fulton. What Miss Fulton did, Bertha didn't know. They had met at the club and Bertha had fallen in love with her, as she always did fall in love with beautiful women who had something strange about them.

The provoking thing was that, though they had been about together and met a number of times, and really talked, Bertha couldn't yet make her out. Up to a certain point Miss Fulton was rarely, wonderfully frank, but the certain point was there, and beyond that she would not go.

Was there anything beyond it? Harry said "No." Voted her dullish, and "cold like all blond women, with a touch, perhaps, of anæmia of the brain." But Bertha wouldn't agree with him: not yet, at any rate.

"No, the way she has of sitting her head a little on one side, and smiling, has something behind it, Harry, and I must find out what that something is."

"Most likely it's a good stomach," answered Harry.

He made a point of catching Bertha's heels with replies of that kind . . . "liver frozen, my dear girl," or "pure flatulence," or "kidney disease," . . . and so on. For some strange reason Bertha liked this, and almost admired it in him very much.

She went into the drawing-room and lighted the fire; then, picking up the cushions, one by one, that Mary had disposed so carefully, she threw them back on to the chairs and the couches. That made all the difference; the room came alive at once. As she was about to throw the last one she surprised herself by suddenly hugging it to her, passionately, passionately. But it did not put out the fire in her bosom. Oh, on the contrary!

The windows of the drawing-room opened on to a balcony overlooking the garden. At the far end, against the wall, there was a tall, slender pear tree in fullest, richest bloom; it stood perfect as though becalmed against the jade-green sky. Bertha couldn't help feeling, even from this distance, that it had not a single bud or a faded petal. Down below, in the garden beds, the red and yellow tulips, heavy with flowers, seemed to lean upon the dusk. A grey cat, dragging its belly, crept across the lawn, and a black one, its shadow, trailed after. The sight of them, so intent and so quick, gave Bertha a curious shiver.

"What creepy things cats are!" she

stammered, and she turned away from the window and began walking up and down. . . .

How strong the jonquils smelled in the warm room. Too strong? Oh, no. And yet, as though overcome, she flung down on a couch and pressed her hands to her eyes.

"I'm too happy—too happy!" she murmured.

And she seemed to see on her eyelids the lovely pear tree with its wide open blossoms as a symbol of her own life.

Really—really—she had everything. She was young. Harry and she were as much in love as ever, and they got on together splendidly and were really good pals. She had an adorable baby. They didn't have to worry about money. They had this absolutely satisfactory house and garden. And friends—modern, thrilling friends, writers and painters and poets or people keen on social questions—just the kind of friends they wanted. And then there were books, and there was music, and she had found a wonderful little dressmaker, and they were going abroad in the summer, and their new cook made the most superb omelettes. . . .

"I'm absurd. Absurd!" she sat up; but she felt quite dizzy, quite drunk. It must have been the spring.

Yes, it was the spring. Now she was so tired she could not drag herself upstairs to dress.

A white dress, a string of jade beads, green shoes and stockings. It wasn't intentional. She had thought of this scheme hours before she stood at the drawing-room window.

Her petals rustled softly into the hall, and she kissed Mrs. Norman Knight, who was taking off the most amusing orange coat with a procession of black monkeys round the hem and up the fronts.

". . . Why! Why! Why is the middle-class so stodgy—so utterly without a sense of humour! My dear, it's only by a fluke that I am here at all—Norman being the protective fluke. For my darling monkeys so upset the train that it rose to a man and simply ate me with its eyes. Didn't laugh—wasn't amused—that I should have loved. No, just stared—and bored me through and through."

"But the cream of it was," said Norman, pressing a large tortoise-shell-rimmed monocle into his eye, "you don't mind me telling this, Face, do you?" (In their home and among their friends they called each other Face and Mug.) "The cream of it was when she, being full fed, turned to the woman beside her and said: 'Haven't you ever seen a monkey before?' "

"Oh, yes!" Mrs. Norman Knight joined in the laughter. "Wasn't that too absolutely creamy?"

And a funnier thing still was that now her coat was off she did look like a very intelligent monkey—who had even made that yellow silk dress out of scraped banana skins. And her amber earrings; they were like little dangling nuts.

"This is a sad, sad fall!" said Mug, pausing in front of Little B's perambulator. "When the perambulator comes into the hall—" and he waved the rest of the quotation away.

The bell rang. It was lean, pale Eddie Warren (as usual) in a state of acute distress.

"It *is* the right house, *isn't* it?" he pleaded.

"Oh, I think so—I hope so," said Bertha brightly.

"I have had such a *dreadful* experience with a taxi-man; he was *most* sinister. I couldn't get him to *stop.* The *more* I knocked and called the *faster* he went. And *in* the moonlight this *bizarre* figure with the *flattened* head *crouching* over the *lit-tle* wheel. . . ."

He shuddered, taking off an immense white silk scarf. Bertha noticed that his socks were white, too—most charming.

"But how dreadful!" she cried.

"Yes, it really was," said Eddie, following her into the drawing-room. "I saw myself *driving* through Eternity in a *timeless* taxi."

He knew the Norman Knights. In fact, he was going to write a play for N. K. when the theatre scheme came off.

"Well, Warren, how's the play?" said Norman Knight, dropping his monocle and giving his eye a moment in which to rise to the surface before it was screwed down again.

And Mrs. Norman Knight: "Oh, Mr. Warren, what happy socks!"

"I *am* so glad you like them," said he, staring at his feet. "They seem to have got so *much* whiter since the moon rose." And he turned his lean sorrowful face to Bertha. "There *is* a moon, you know."

She wanted to cry: "I am sure there is—often—often!"

He really was a most attractive person. But so was Face, crouched before the fire in her banana skins, and so was Mug, smoking a cigarette and saying as he flicked the ash: "Why doth the bridegroom tarry?"

"There he is, now."

Bang went the front door open and shut. Harry shouted: "Hullo, you people. Down in five minutes." And they heard him swarm up the stairs. Bertha couldn't help smiling; she knew how he loved doing things at high pressure. What, after all, did an extra five minutes matter? But he would pretend to himself that they mattered beyond measure. And then he would make a great point of coming into the drawing-room, extravagantly cool and collected.

Harry had such a zest for life. Oh, how she appreciated it in him. And his passion for fighting—for seeking in everything that came up against him another test of his power and of his courage—that, too, she understood. Even when it made him just occasionally, to other people, who didn't know him well, a little ridiculous perhaps. . . . For there were moments when he rushed into battle where no battle was. . . . She talked and laughed and positively forgot until he had come in (just as she had imagined) that Pearl Fulton had not turned up.

"I wonder if Miss Fulton has forgotten?"

"I expect so," said Harry. "Is she on the 'phone?"

"Ah! There's a taxi now." And Bertha smiled with that little air of proprietorship that she always assumed while her women finds were new and mysterious. "She lives in taxis."

"She'll run to fat if she does," said Harry coolly, ringing the bell for dinner. "Frightful danger for blond women."

"Harry—don't," warned Bertha, laughing up at him.

Came another tiny moment, while they waited, laughing and talking, just a trifle too much at their ease, a trifle too unaware. And then Miss Fulton, all in silver, with a silver fillet binding her pale blond hair, came in smiling, her head a little on one side.

"Am I late?"

"No, not at all," said Bertha. "Come along." And she took her arm and they moved into the dining-room.

What was there in the touch of that cool arm that could fan—fan—start blazing—blazing—the fire of bliss that Bertha did not know what to do with?

Miss Fulton did not look at her; but then she seldom did look at people directly. Her heavy eyelids lay upon her eyes and the strange half smile came and went upon her lips as though she lived by listening rather than seeing. But Bertha knew, suddenly, as if the longest, most intimate look had passed between them—as if they had said to each other: "You, too?"—that Pearl Fulton, stirring the beautiful red soup in the grey plate, was feeling just what she was feeling.

And the others? Face and Mug, Eddie and Harry, their spoons rising and falling—dabbing their lips with their napkins, crumbling bread, fiddling with the forks and glasses and talking.

"I met her at the Alpha show—the weirdest little person. She'd not only cut off her hair, but she seemed to have taken a dreadfully good snip off her legs and arms and her neck and her poor little nose as well."

"Isn't she very *liée* with Michael Oat?"

"The man who wrote *Love in False Teeth?*"

"He wants to write a play for me. One act. One man. Decides to commit suicide. Gives all the reasons why he should and why he shouldn't. And just as he has made up his mind either to do it or not to do it—curtain. Not half a bad idea."

"What's he going to call it—'Stomach Trouble'?"

"I *think* I've come across the *same* idea in a lit-tle French review, *quite* unknown in England."

No, they didn't share it. They were dears—dears—and she loved having them there, at her table, and giving them delicious food and wine. In fact, she longed to tell them how delightful they were, and what a decorative group they made, how they seemed to set one another off and how they reminded her of a play by Tchekof!

Harry was enjoying his dinner. It was part of his—well, not his nature, exactly, and certainly not his pose—his—something or other—to talk about food and to glory in his "shameless passion for the white flesh of the lobster" and "the green of pistachio ices—green and cold like the eyelids of Egyptian dancers."

When he looked up at her and said: "Bertha, this is a very admirable *soufflée!*" she almost could have wept with child-like pleasure.

Oh, why did she feel so tender towards the whole world tonight? Everything was good—was right. All that happened seemed to fill again her brimming cup of bliss.

And still, in the back of her mind, there was the pear tree. It would be silver now, in the light of poor dear Eddie's moon, silver as Miss Fulton, who sat there turning a tangerine in her slender fingers that were so pale a light seemed to come from them.

What she simply couldn't make out—what was miraculous—was how she should have guessed Miss Fulton's mood so exactly and so instantly. For she never doubted for a moment that she was right, and yet what had she to go on? Less than nothing.

"I believe this does happen very, very rarely between women. Never between men," thought Bertha. "But while I am making the coffee in the drawing-room perhaps she will 'give a sign.' "

What she meant by that she did not know, and what would happen after that she could not imagine.

While she thought like this she saw herself talking and laughing. She had to talk because of her desire to laugh.

"I must laugh or die."

But when she noticed Face's little habit of tucking something down the front of her bodice—as if she kept a tiny, secret board of nuts there, too—Bertha had to dig her nails into her hands—so as not to laugh too much.

It was over at last. And: "Come and see my new coffee machine," said Bertha.

"We only have a new coffee machine once a fortnight," said Harry. Face took her arm this time; Miss Fulton bent her head and followed after.

The fire had died down in the drawing-room to a red, flickering "nest of baby phœnixes," said Face.

"Don't turn up the light for a moment. It is so lovely." And down she crouched by the fire again. She was always cold . . . "without her little red flannel jacket, of course," thought Bertha.

At that moment Miss Fulton "gave the sign."

"Have you a garden?" said the cool, sleepy voice.

This was so exquisite on her part that all Bertha could do was to obey. She crossed the room, pulled the curtains apart, and opened those long windows.

"There!" she breathed.

And the two women stood side by side looking at the slender, flowering tree. Although it was so still it seemed, like the flame of a candle, to stretch up, to point, to quiver in the bright air, to grow taller and taller as they gazed—almost to touch the rim of the round, silver moon.

How long did they stand there? Both, as it were, caught in that circle of unearthly light, understanding each other perfectly, creatures of another world, and wondering what they were to do in this one with all this blissful treasure that burned in their bosoms and dropped, in silver flowers, from their hair and hands?

For ever—for a moment? And did Miss Fulton murmur: "Yes. Just *that*." Or did Bertha dream it?

Then the light was snapped on and Face made the coffee and Harry said: "My dear Mrs. Knight, don't ask me about my baby. I never see her. I shan't feel the slightest interest in her until she has a lover," and Mug took his eye out of the conservatory for a moment and then put it under glass again and Eddie Warren drank his coffee and set down the cup with a face of anguish as though he had drunk and seen the spider.

"What I want to do is to give the young men a show. I believe London is simply teeming with first-chop, unwritten plays. What I want to say to 'em is: 'Here's the theatre. Fire ahead.' "

"You know, my dear, I am going to decorate a room for the Jacob Nathans. Oh, I am so tempted to do a fried-fish scheme, with the backs of the chairs shaped like frying pans and lovely chip potatoes embroidered all over the curtains."

"The trouble with our young writing men is that they are still too romantic. You can't put out to sea without being seasick and wanting a basin. Well, why won't they have the courage of those basins?"

"A *dreadful* poem about a *girl* who was *violated* by a beggar *without* a nose in a lit-tle wood. . . ."

Miss Fulton sank into the lowest, deepest chair and Harry handed round the cigarettes.

From the way he stood in front of her shaking the silver box and saying abruptly: "Egyptian? Turkish? Virginian? They're all mixed up," Bertha realized that she not only bored him; he really disliked her. And she decided from the way Miss Fulton said: "No, thank you, I won't smoke," that she felt it, too, and was hurt.

"Oh, Harry, don't dislike her. You are quite wrong about her. She's wonderful, wonderful. And, besides, how can you feel so differently about someone who means so much to me. I shall try to tell you when we are in bed tonight what has been happening. What she and I have shared."

At those last words something strange and almost terrifying darted into Bertha's mind. And this something blind and smiling whispered to her: "Soon these people will go. The house will be quiet—quiet. The lights will be out. And you and he will be alone together in the dark room—the warm bed. . . ."

She jumped up from her chair and ran over to the piano.

"What a pity someone does not play!" she cried. "What a pity somebody does not play."

For the first time in her life Bertha Young desired her husband.

Oh, she'd loved him—she'd been in love with him, of course, in every other way, but just not in that way. And, equally, of course, she'd understood that he was different. They'd discussed it so often. It had worried her dreadfully at first to find that she was so cold, but after a time it had not seemed to matter. They were so frank with each other—such good pals. That was the best of being modern.

But now—ardently! ardently! The word ached in her ardent body! Was this what that feeling of bliss had been leading up to? But then—then—

"My dear," said Mrs. Norman Knight, "you know our shame. We are the victims of time and train. We live in Hampstead. It's been so nice."

"I'll come with you into the hall,"

said Bertha. "I loved having you. But you must not miss the last train. That's so awful, isn't it?"

"Have a whisky, Knight, before you go?" called Harry.

"No, thanks, old chap."

Bertha squeezed his hand for that as she shook it.

"Good night, good-bye," she cried from the top step, feeling that this self of hers was taking leave of them for ever.

When she got back into the drawing-room the others were on the move.

". . . Then you can come part of the way in my taxi."

"I shall be *so* thankful *not* to have to face *another* drive *alone* after my *dreadful* experience."

"You can get a taxi at the rank just at the end of the street. You won't have to walk more than a few yards."

"That's a comfort. I'll go and put on my coat."

Miss Fulton moved towards the hall and Bertha was following when Harry almost pushed past.

"Let me help you."

Bertha knew that he was repenting his rudeness—she let him go. What a boy he was in some ways—so impulsive—so—simple.

And Eddie and she were left by the fire.

"I *wonder* if you have seen Bilks' *new* poem called *Table d'Hôte*," said Eddie softly. "It's *so* wonderful. In the last Anthology. Have you got a copy? I'd *so* like to *show* it to you. It begins with an *incredibly* beautiful line: 'Why Must it Always be Tomato Soup?' "

"Yes," said Bertha. And she moved noiselessly to a table opposite the drawing-room door and Eddie glided noiselessly after her. She picked up the little book and gave it to him; they had not made a sound.

While he looked it up she turned her head towards the hall. And she saw . . . Harry with Miss Fulton's coat in his arms and Miss Fulton with her back turned to him and her head bent. He tossed the coat away, put his hands on her shoulders and turned her violently to him. His lips said: "I adore you," and Miss Fulton laid her moonbeam fingers on his cheeks and smiled her sleepy smile. Harry's nostrils quivered; his lips curled back in a hideous grin while he whispered: "Tomorrow," and with her eyelids Miss Fulton said: "Yes."

"Here it is," said Eddie. " 'Why Must it Always be Tomato Soup?' It's so *deeply* true, don't you feel? Tomato soup is so *dreadfully* eternal."

"If you prefer," said Harry's voice, very loud, from the hall, "I can phone you a cab to come to the door."

"Oh, no. It's not necessary," said Miss Fulton, and she came up to Bertha and gave her the slender fingers to hold.

"Good-bye. Thank you so much."

"Good-bye," said Bertha.

Miss Fulton held her hand a moment longer.

"Your lovely pear tree!" she murmured.

And then she was gone, with Eddie following, like the black cat following the grey cat.

"I'll shut up shop," said Harry, extravagantly cool and collected.

"Your lovely pear tree—pear tree—pear tree!"

Bertha simply ran over to the long windows.

"Oh, what is going to happen now?" she cried.

But the pear tree was as lovely as ever and as full of flower and as still.

Drama

George Bernard Shaw (1856–1950)

Major Barbara

CHARACTERS

SIR ANDREW UNDERSHAFT

LADY BRITOMART UNDERSHAFT, *his wife*

BARBARA, *his elder daughter, a Major in the Salvation Army*

SARAH, *his younger daughter*

STEPHEN, *his son*

ADOLPHUS CUSINS, *a professor of Greek in love with Barbara*

CHARLES LOMAX, *young-man-about-town engaged to Sarah*

MORRISON, *Lady Britomart's butler*

BRONTERRE O'BRIEN ["Snobby"] PRICE, *a cobbler-carpenter down on his luck*

MRS ROMOLA ["Rummy"] MITCHENS, *a worn-out lady who relies on the Salvation Army worker*

JENNY HILL, *a young Salvation Army worker*

PETER SHIRLEY, *an unemployed coal-broker*

BILL WALKER, *a bully*

MRS BAINES, *Commissioner in the Salvation Army*

BILTON, *a foreman at Perivale St. Andrews*

The action of the play occurs within several days in January, 1906.

ACT I *The Library of Lady Britomart's house in Wilton Crescent, fashionable London suburb.*

ACT II *The yard of the Salvation Army shelter in West Ham, an industrial suburb in London's East End.*

ACT III *The library in Lady Britomart's house; a parapet overlooking Perivale St. Andrews, a region in Middlesex northwest of London.*

Act I

It is after dinner in January 1906, in the library in LADY BRITOMART UNDERSHAFT'S *house in Wilton Crescent. A large and comfortable settee is in the middle of the room, upholstered in dark leather. A person sitting on it {it is vacant at present} would have, on his right,* LADY BRITOMART'S *writing-table, with the lady herself busy at it; a smaller writing-table behind him on his left; the door behind him on* LADY BRITO-

MART'S *side; and a window with a window-seat directly on his left. Near the window is an armchair.*

LADY BRITOMART *is a women of fifty or thereabouts, well dressed and yet careless of her dress, well bred and quite reckless of her breeding, well mannered and yet appallingly outspoken and indifferent to the opinion of her interlocutors, amiable and yet peremptory, arbitrary, and high-tempered to the last bearable degree, and withal a very typical managing matron of the upper class, treated as a naughty child until she grew into a scolding mother, and finally settling down with plenty of practical ability and worldly experience, limited in the oddest way with domestic and class limitations, conceiving the universe exactly as if it were a large house in Wilton Crescent, though handling her corner of it very effectively on the assumption, and being quite enlightened and liberal as to the books in the library, the pictures on the wall, the music in the portfolios, and the articles in the papers.*

Her son, STEPHEN, *comes in. He is a gravely correct young man under 25, taking himself very seriously, but still in some awe of his mother, from childish habit and bachelor shyness rather than from any weakness of character.*

STEPHEN: What's the matter?

LADY BRITOMART: Presently, Stephen. [STEPHEN *submissively walks to the settee and sits down. He takes up a liberal weekly called* The Speaker]

LADY BRITOMART: Don't begin to read, Stephen. I shall require all your attention.

STEPHEN: It was only while I was waiting—

LADY BRITOMART: Don't make excuses, Stephen. *[He puts down* The Speaker] Now! *[She finishes her writing, rises; and comes to the settee]* I have not kept you waiting very long, I think.

STEPHEN: Not at all, mother.

LADY BRITOMART: Bring me my cushion. *[He takes the cushion from the chair at the desk and arranges it for her as she sits down on the settee]* Sit down. *[He sits down and fingers his tie nervously]* Don't fiddle with your tie, Stephen: there is nothing the matter with it.

STEPHEN: I beg your pardon. *[He fiddles with his watch chain instead]*

LADY BRITOMART: Now are you attending to me, Stephen?

STEPHEN: Of course, mother.

LADY BRITOMART: No: it's not of course. I want something much more than your everyday matter-of-course attention. I am going to speak to you very seriously, Stephen. I wish you to let that chain alone.

STEPHEN: *[Hastily relinquishing the chain]* Have I done anything to annoy you, mother? If so, it was quite unintentional.

LADY BRITOMART: *[Astonished]* Nonsense! *[With some remorse]* My poor boy, did you think I was angry with you?

STEPHEN: What is it, then, mother? You are making me very uneasy.

LADY BRITOMART: *[Squaring herself at him rather aggressively]* Stephen: may I ask how soon you intend to realize that you are a grown-up man, and that I am only a woman?

STEPHEN: *[Amazed]* Only a—

LADY BRITOMART: Don't repeat my words, please: it is a most aggravating habit. You must learn to face life seriously, Stephen. I really cannot bear the whole burden of our family affairs any longer. You must advise me: you must assume the responsibility.

STEPHEN: I!

LADY BRITOMART: Yes, you, of course. You were twenty-four last June. You've been at Harrow and Cambridge. You've been to India and Japan. You must know a lot of things, now; unless you have wasted your time most scandalously. Well, advise me.

STEPHEN: *[Much perplexed]* You

know I have never interfered in the household—

LADY BRITOMART: No: I should think not. I don't want you to order the dinner.

STEPHEN: I mean in our family affairs.

LADY BRITOMART: Well, you must interfere now; for they are getting quite beyond me.

STEPHEN: *[Troubled]* I have thought sometimes that perhaps I ought; but really, mother, I know so little about them; and what I do know is so pain ful—it is so impossible to mention some things to you—*[He stops, ashamed]*

LADY BRITOMART: I suppose you mean your father.

STEPHEN: *[Almost inaudibly]* Yes.

LADY BRITOMART: My dear: we can't go on all our lives not mentioning him. Of course you were quite right not to open the subject until I asked you to; but you are old enough now to be taken into my confidence, and to help me to deal with him about the girls.

STEPHEN: But the girls are all right. They are engaged.

LADY BRITOMART: *[Complacently]* Yes. I have made a very good match for Sarah. Charles Lomax will be a millionaire at thirty-five. But that is ten years ahead; and in the meantime his trustees cannot under the terms of his father's will allow him more than £800 a year.

STEPHEN: But the will says also that if he increases his income by his own exertions, they may double the increase.

LADY BRITOMART: Charles Lomax's exertions are much more likely to decrease his income than to increase it. Sarah will have to find at least another £800 a year for the next ten years; and even then they will be as poor as church mice. And what about Barbara? I thought Barbara was going to make the most brilliant career of all of you. And what does she do? Joins the Salvation Army; discharges her maid; lives on a pound a week; and walks in one evening with a professor of Greek whom she has picked up in the street, and who pretends to be a Salvationist, and actually plays the big drum for her in public because he has fallen head over ears in love with her.

STEPHEN: I was certainly rather taken aback when I heard they were engaged. Cusins is a very nice fellow, certainly: nobody would ever guess that he was born in Australia; but—

LADY BRITOMART: Oh, Adolphus Cusins will make a very good husband. After all, nobody can say a word against Greek: it stamps a man at once as an educated gentleman. And my family, thank Heaven, is not a pigheaded Tory one. We are Whigs, and believe in liberty. Let snobbish people say what they please: Barbara shall marry, not the man they like, but the man *I* like.

STEPHEN: Of course I was thinking only of his income. However, he is not likely to be extravagant.

LADY BRITOMART: Don't be too sure of that, Stephen. I know your quiet, simple, refined, poetic people like Adolphus—quite content with the best of everything! They cost more than your extravagant people, who are always as mean as they are second rate. No: Barbara will need at least £2000 a year. You see it means two additional households. Besides, my dear, you must marry soon. I don't approve of the present fashion of philandering bachelors and late marriages; and I am trying to arrange something for you.

STEPHEN: It's very good of you, mother; but perhaps I had better arrange that for myself.

LADY BRITOMART: Nonsense! you are much too young to begin match-making: you would be taken in by some pretty little nobody. Of course I don't mean that you are not to be consulted: you know that as well as I do. [STEPHEN *closes his lips and is silent*] Now don't sulk, Stephen.

STEPHEN: I am not sulking, mother. What has all this got to do with—with—with my father?

LADY BRITOMART: My dear Stephen:

where is the money to come from? It is easy enough for you and the other children to live on my income as long as we are in the same house; but I can't keep four families in four separate houses. You know how poor my father is: he has barely seven thousand a year now; and really, if he were not the Earl of Stevenage, he would have to give up society. He can do nothing for us. He says, naturally enough, that it is absurd that he should be asked to provide for the children of a man who is rolling in money. You see, Stephen, your father must be fabulously wealthy, because there is always a war going on somewhere.

STEPHEN: You need not remind me of that, mother. I have hardly ever opened a newspaper in my life without seeing our name in it. The Undershaft torpedo! The Undershaft quick firers! The Undershaft ten inch! The Undershaft disappearing rampart gun! The Undershaft submarine! and now the Undershaft aerial battleship! At Harrow they called me the Woolwich Infant. At Cambridge it was the same. A little brute at King's who was always trying to get up revivals, spoilt my Bible—your first birthday present to me—by writing under my name, "Son and heir to Undershaft and Lazarus, Death and Destruction Dealers: address, Christendom and Judea." But that was not so bad as the way I was kowtowed to everywhere because my father was making millions by selling cannons.

LADY BRITOMART: It is not only the cannons, but the war loans that Lazarus arranges under cover of giving credit for the cannons. You know, Stephen, it's perfectly scandalous. Those two men, Andrew Undershaft and Lazarus, positively have Europe under their thumbs. That is why your father is able to behave as he does. He is above the law. Do you think Bismarck or Gladstone or Disraeli could have openly defied every social and moral obligation all their lives as your father has? They simply wouldn't have dared. I asked Gladstone to take it up. I asked *The Times* to take it up. I asked the Lord Chamberlain to take it up. But it was just like asking them to declare war on the Sultan. They wouldn't. They said they couldn't touch him. I believe they were afraid.

STEPHEN: What could they do? He does not actually break the law.

LADY BRITOMART: Not break the law! He is always breaking the law. He broke the law when he was born: his parents were not married.

STEPHEN: Mother! Is that true?

LADY BRITOMART: Of course it's true: that was why we separated.

STEPHEN: He married without letting you know this!

LADY BRITOMART: *{Rather taken aback by this inference}* Oh no. To do Andrew justice, that was not the sort of thing he did. Besides, you know the Undershaft motto: Unashamed. Everybody knew.

STEPHEN: But you said that was why you separated.

LADY BRITOMART: Yes, because he was not content with being a foundling himself: he wanted to disinherit you for another foundling. That was what I couldn't stand.

STEPHEN: *{Ashamed}* Do you mean for—for—for—

LADY BRITOMART: Don't stammer, Stephen. Speak distinctly.

STEPHEN: But this is so frightful to me, mother. To have to speak to you about such things!

LADY BRITOMART: It's not pleasant for me, either, especially if you are still so childish that you must make it worse by a display of embarrassment. It is only in the middle classes, Stephen, that people get into a state of dumb helpless horror when they find that there are wicked people in the world. In our class, we have to decide what is to be done with wicked people; and nothing should disturb our self-possession. Now ask your question properly.

STEPHEN: Mother: you have no consideration for me. For Heaven's sake either treat me as a child, as you always do, and tell me nothing at all; or tell me everything and let me take it as best I can.

LADY BRITOMART: Treat you as a child! What do you mean? It is most unkind and ungrateful of you to say such a thing. You know I have never treated any of you as children. I have always made you my companions and friends, and allowed you perfect freedom to do and say whatever you liked, so long as you liked what I could approve of.

STEPHEN: *{Desperately}* I daresay we have been the very imperfect children of a very perfect mother; but I do beg of you to let me alone for once, and tell me about this horrible business of my father wanting to set me aside for another son.

LADY BRITOMART: *{Amazed}* Another son! I never said anything of the kind. I never dreamt of such a thing. This is what comes of interrupting me.

STEPHEN: But you said—

LADY BRITOMART: *{Cutting him short}* Now be a good boy, Stephen, and listen to me patiently. The Undershafts are descended from a foundling in the parish of St Andrew Undershaft in the city. That was long ago, in the reign of James the First. Well, this foundling was adopted by an armorer and gunmaker. In the course of time the foundling succeeded to the business; and from some notion of gratitude, or some vow or something, he adopted another foundling, and left the business to him. And that foundling did the same. Ever since that, the cannon business has always been left to an adopted foundling named Andrew Undershaft.

STEPHEN: But did they never marry? Were there no legitimate sons?

LADY BRITOMART: Oh yes: they married just as your father did; and they were rich enough to buy land for their own children and leave them well provided for. But they always adopted and trained some foundling to succeed them in the business; and of course they always quarreled with their wives furiously over it. Your father was adopted in that way; and he pretends to consider himself bound to keep up the tradition and adopt somebody to leave the business to. Of course I was not going to stand that. There may have been some reason for it when the Undershafts could only marry women in their own class, whose sons were not fit to govern great estates. But there could be no excuse for passing over my son.

STEPHEN: *{Dubiously}* I am afraid I should make a poor hand of managing a cannon foundry.

LADY BRITOMART: Nonsense! you could easily get a manager and pay him a salary.

STEPHEN: My father evidently had no great opinion of my capacity.

LADY BRITOMART: Stuff, child! you were only a baby: it had nothing to do with your capacity. Andrew did it on principle, just as he did every perverse and wicked thing on principle. When my father remonstrated, Andrew actually told him to his face that history tells us of only two successful institutions: one the Undershaft firm, and the other the Roman Empire under the Antonines. That was because the Antonine emperors all adopted their successors. Such rubbish! The Stevenages are as good as the Antonines, I hope; and you are a Stevenage. But that was Andrew all over. There you have the man! Always clever and unanswerable when he was defending nonsense and wickedness: always awkward and sullen when he had to behave sensibly and decently.

STEPHEN: Then it was on my account that your home life was broken up, mother. I am sorry.

LADY BRITOMART: Well, dear, there were other differences. I really cannot bear an immoral man. I am not a Pharisee, I hope; and I should not have minded his merely doing wrong things: we are none of us perfect. But your father didn't exactly do wrong things: he said them and thought them: that was what was so dreadful. He really had a sort of religion of wrongness. Just as one doesn't mind men practicing immorality so long as they own that they are in the wrong by preaching morality; so I couldn't forgive Andrew for preaching immorality while he practiced morality. You would all have grown up without principles, without any knowledge of right and wrong, if he had been in the house. You know, my dear, your father was a very attractive man in some ways. Children did not dislike him; and he took advantage of it to put the wickedest ideas into their heads, and make them quite unmanageable. I did not dislike him myself: very far from it; but nothing can bridge over moral disagreement.

STEPHEN: All this simply bewilders me, mother. People may differ about matters of opinion, or even about religion; but how can they differ about right and wrong? Right is right; and wrong is wrong; and if a man cannot distinguish them properly, he is either a fool or a rascal: that's all.

LADY BRITOMART: *{Touched}* That's my own boy! *{She pats his cheek}* Your father never could answer that: he used to laugh and get out of it under cover of some affectionate nonsense. And now that you understand the situation, what do you advise me to do?

STEPHEN: Well, what can you do?

LADY BRITOMART: I must get the money somehow.

STEPHEN: We cannot take money from him. I had rather go and live in some cheap place like Bedford Square or even Hampstead than take a farthing of his money.

LADY BRITOMART: But after all, Stephen, our present income comes from Andrew.

STEPHEN: *{Shocked}* I never knew that.

LADY BRITOMART: Well, you surely didn't suppose your grandfather had anything to give me. The Stevenages could not do everything for you. We gave you social position. Andrew had to contribute something. He had a very good bargain, I think.

STEPHEN: *{Bitterly}* We are utterly dependent on him and his cannons, then?

LADY BRITOMART: Certainly not: the money is settled. But he provided it. So you see it is not a question of taking money from him or not: it is simply a question of how much. I don't want any more for myself.

STEPHEN: Nor do I.

LADY BRITOMART: But Sarah does; and Barbara does. That is, Charles Lomax and Adolphus Cusins will cost them more. So I must put my pride in my pocket and ask for it, I suppose. That is your advise, Stephen, is it not?

STEPHEN: No.

LADY BRITOMART: *{Sharply}* Stephen!

STEPHEN: Of course if you are determined—

LADY BRITOMART: I am not determined: I ask your advice; and I am waiting for it. I will not have all the responsibility thrown on my shoulders.

STEPHEN: *{Obstinately}* I would die sooner than ask him for another penny.

LADY BRITOMART: *{Resignedly}* You mean that *I* must ask him. Very well, Stephen: it shall be as you wish. You will be glad to know that your grandfather concurs. But he thinks I ought to ask Andrew to come here and see the girls. After all he must have some natural affection for them.

STEPHEN: Ask him here! ! !

LADY BRITOMART: Do not repeat my words, Stephen. Where else can I ask him?

STEPHEN: I never expected you to ask him at all.

LADY BRITOMART: Now don't tease, Stephen. Come! you see that it is necessary that he should pay us a visit, don't you?

STEPHEN: *{Reluctantly}* I suppose so, if the girls cannot do without his money.

LADY BRITOMART: Thank you, Stephen: I knew you would give me the right advice when it was properly explained to you. I have asked your father to come this evening. [STEPHEN *bounds from his seat*] Don't jump, Stephen: it fidgets me.

STEPHEN: [*In utter consternation*] Do you mean to say that my father is coming here to-night—that he may be here at any moment?

LADY BRITOMART: [*Looking at her watch*] I said nine. [*He gasps. She rises*] Ring the bell, please. [STEPHEN *goes to the smaller writing table; presses a button on it; and sits at it with his elbows on the table and his head in his hands, outwitted and overwhelmed*] It is ten minutes to nine yet; and I have to prepare the girls. I asked Charles Lomax and Adolphus to dinner on purpose that they might be here. Andrew had better see them in case he should cherish any delusions as to their being capable of supporting their wives. [*The butler enters:* LADY BRITOMART *goes behind the settee to speak to him*] Morrison: go up to the drawing-room and tell everybody to come down here at once. [MORRISON *withdraws.* LADY BRITOMART *turns to* STEPHEN] Now remember, Stephen: I shall need all your countenance and authority. [*He rises and tries to recover some vestige of these attributes*] Give me a chair, dear. [*He pushes a chair forward from the wall to where she stands, near the smaller writing table. She sits down; and he goes to the armchair, into which he throws himself*] I don't know how Barbara will take it. Ever since they made her a major in the Salvation Army she has developed a propensity to have her own way and order people about which quite cows me sometimes. It's not ladylike: I'm sure I don't know where she picked it up. Anyhow, Barbara shan't bully me; but still it's just as well that your father should be here before she has time to refuse to meet him or make a fuss. Don't look nervous, Stephen: it will only encourage Barbara to make difficulties. *I* am nervous enough, goodness knows; but I don't shew it.

[SARAH *and* BARBARA *come in with their respective young men,* CHARLES LOMAX *and* ADOLPHUS CUSINS. SARAH *is slender, bored, and mundane.* BARBARA *is robuster, jollier, much more energetic.* SARAH *is fashionably dressed:* BARBARA *is in Salvation Army uniform.* LOMAX, *a young man about town, is like many other young men about town. He is afflicted with a frivolous sense of humor which plunges him at the most inopportune moments into paroxysms of imperfectly suppressed laughter.* CUSINS *is a spectacled student, slight, thin haired, and sweet voiced, with a more complex form of* LOMAX'*s complaint. His sense of humor is intellectual and subtle, and is complicated by an appalling temper. The life-long struggle of a benevolent temperament and a high conscience against impulses of inhuman ridicule and fierce impatience has set up a chronic strain which has visibly wrecked his constitution. He is a most implacable, determined, tenacious, intolerant person who by mere force of character presents himself as—and indeed actually is—considerate, gentle, explanatory, even mild and apologetic, capable possibly of murder, but not of cruelty or coarseness. By the operation of some instinct which is not merciful enough to blind him with the illusions of love, he is obstinately bent on marrying* BARBARA. LOMAX *likes* SARAH *and thinks it will be rather a lark to marry her. Consequently he has not attempted to resist* LADY BRITOMART'*s arrangements to that end.*

All four look as if they had been having a good deal of fun in the drawing room. The girls enter first, leaving the swains outside. SARAH *comes to the settee.* BARBARA *comes in after her and stops at the door*]

BARBARA: Are Cholly and Dolly to come in?

LADY BRITOMART: [*Forcibly*] Barbara: I will not have Charles called Cholly: the vulgarity of it positively makes me ill.

BARBARA: It's all right, mother: Cholly is quite correct nowadays. Are they to come in?

LADY BRITOMART: Yes, if they will behave themselves.

BARBARA: *[Through the door]* Come in, Dolly; and behave yourself. [BARBARA *comes to her mother's writing table.* CUSINS *enters smiling, and wanders towards* LADY BRITOMART]

SARAH: *[Calling]* Come in, Cholly. [LOMAX *enters, controlling his features very imperfectly, and places himself vaguely between* SARAH *and* BARBARA]

LADY BRITOMART: *[Peremptorily]* Sit down, all of you. *[They sit.* CUSINS *crosses to the window and seats himself there.* LOMAX *takes a chair.* BARBARA *sits at the writing table and* SARAH *on the settee]* I don't in the least know what you are laughing at, Adolphus. I am surprised at you, though I expected nothing better from Charles Lomax.

CUSINS: *[In a remarkably gentle voice]* Barbara has been trying to teach me the West Ham Salvation March.

LADY BRITOMART: I see nothing to laugh at in that; nor should you if you are really converted.

CUSINS: *[Sweetly]* You were not present. It was really funny, I believe.

LOMAX: Ripping.

LADY BRITOMART: Be quiet, Charles. Now listen to me, children. Your father is coming here this evening. *[General stupefaction.* LOMAX, SARAH, *and* BARBARA *rise:* SARAH *scared, and* BARBARA *amused and expectant]*

LOMAX: *[Remonstrating]* Oh I say!

LADY BRITOMART: You are not called on to say anything, Charles.

SARAH: Are you serious, mother?

LADY BRITOMART: Of course I am serious. It is on your account, Sarah, and also on Charles's. *[Silence.* SARAH *sits, with a shrug.* CHARLES *looks painfully unworthy]* I hope you are not going to object, Barbara.

BARBARA: I! why should I? My father has a soul to be saved like anybody else. He's quite welcome as far as I am concerned. *[She sits on the table, and softly whistles "Onward, Christian Soldiers"]*

LOMAX: *[Still remonstrant]* But really, don't you know! Oh I say!

LADY BRITOMART: *[Frigidly]* What do you wish to convey, Charles?

LOMAX: Well, you must admit that this is a bit thick.

LADY BRITOMART: *[Turning with ominous suavity to* CUSINS] Adolphus: you are a professor of Greek. Can you translate Charles Lomax's remarks into reputable English for us?

CUSINS: *[Cautiously]* If I may say so, Lady Brit, I think Charles has rather happily expressed what we all feel. Homer, speaking to Autolycus, uses the same phrase. πυκινὸν δόμον ἐλθεῖν means a bit thick.

LOMAX: *[Handsomely]* Not that I mind, you know, if Sarah don't *[He sits]*

LADY BRITOMART: *[Crushingly]* Thank you. Have I your permission, Adolphus, to invite my own husband to my own house?

CUSINS: *[Gallantly]* You have my unhesitating support in everything you do.

LADY BRITOMART: Tush! Sarah: have you nothing to say?

SARAH: Do you mean that he is coming regularly to live here?

LADY BRITOMART: Certainly not. The spare room is ready for him if he likes to stay for a day or two and see a little more of you; but there are limits.

SARAH: Well, he can't eat us, I suppose. *I* don't mind.

LOMAX: *[Chuckling]* I wonder how the old man will take it.

LADY BRITOMART: Much as the old woman will, no doubt, Charles.

LOMAX: *[Abashed]* I didn't mean—at least—

LADY BRITOMART: You didn't think, Charles. You never do; and the result is you never mean anything. And now please attend to me, children. Your father will be quite a stranger to us.

LOMAX: I suppose he hasn't seen Sarah since she was a little kid.

LADY BRITOMART: Not since she was a little kid, Charles, as you express it with that elegance of diction and refinement of thought that seem never to desert you. Accordingly—er— *(Impatiently)* Now I have forgotten what I was going to say. That comes of your provoking me to be sarcastic, Charles. Adolphus: will you kindly tell me where I was.

CUSINS: *(Sweetly)* You were saying that as Mr. Undershaft has not seen his children since they were babies, he will form his opinion of the way you have brought them up from their behavior tonight, and that therefore you wish us all to be particularly careful to conduct ourselves well, especially Charles.

LADY BRITOMART: *(With emphatic approval)* Precisely.

LOMAX: Look here, Dolly: Lady Brit didn't say that.

LADY BRITOMART: *(Vehemently)* I did, Charles. Adolphus's recollection is perfectly correct. It is most important that you should be good; and I do beg you for once not to pair off into opposite corners and giggle and whisper while I am speaking to your father.

BARBARA: All right, mother. We'll do you credit. *(She comes off the table, and sits in her chair with ladylike elegance)*

LADY BRITOMART: Remember Charles, that Sarah will want to feel proud of you instead of ashamed of you.

LOMAX: Oh I say! there's nothing to be exactly proud of, don't you know.

LADY BRITOMART: Well, try and look as if there was. [MORRISON, *pale and dismayed, breaks into the room in unconcealed disorder)*

MORRISON: Might I speak a word to you, my lady?

LADY BRITOMART: Nonsense! Shew him up.

MORRISON: Yes, my lady. *(He goes)*

LOMAX: Does Morrison know who it is?

LADY BRITOMART: Of course. Morrison has always been with us.

LOMAX: It must be a regular corker for him, don't you know.

LADY BRITOMART: Is this a moment to get on my nerves, Charles, with your outrageous expressions?

LOMAX: But this is something out of the ordinary, really—

MORRISON: *(At the door)* The—er—Mr. Undershaft. *(He retreats in confusion.* ANDREW UNDERSHAFT *comes in. All rise.* LADY BRITOMART *meets him in the middle of the room behind the settee.*

ANDREW *is, on the surface a stoutish, easy-going elderly man, with kindly patient manners, and an engaging simplicity of character. But he has a watchful, deliberate, waiting, listening face, and formidable reserves of power, both bodily and mental, in his capacious chest and long head. His gentleness is partly that of a strong man who has learnt by experience that his natural grip hurts ordinary people unless he handles them very carefully, and partly the mellowness of age and success. He is also a little shy in his present very delicate situation)*

LADY BRITOMART: Good evening, Andrew.

UNDERSHAFT: How do'ye do, my dear.

LADY BRITOMART: You look a good deal older.

UNDERSHAFT: *(Apologetically)* I am somewhat older. *(Taking her hand with a touch of courtship)* Time has stood still with you.

LADY BRITOMART: *(Throwing away his hand)* Rubbish! This is your family.

UNDERSHAFT: *(Surprised)* Is it so large? I am sorry to say my memory is failing very badly in some things. *(He offers his hand with paternal kindness to* LOMAX]

LOMAX: *(Jerkily shaking his hand)* Ahdedoo.

UNDERSHAFT: I can see you are my eldest. I am very glad to meet you again, my boy.

LOMAX: *(Remonstrating)* No, but look here don't you know—*(Overcome)* Oh I say!

LADY BRITOMART: *(Recovering from momentary speechlessness)* Andrew: do you mean to say that you don't remember how many children you have?

UNDERSHAFT: Well, I am afraid I—They have grown so much—er. Am I making any ridiculous mistake? I may as well confess: I recollect only one son. But so many things have happened since, of course—er—

LADY BRITOMART: *{Decisively}* Andrew: you are talking nonsense. Of course you have only one son.

UNDERSHAFT: Perhaps you will be good enough to introduce me, my dear.

LADY BRITOMART: That is Charles Lomax, who is engaged to Sarah.

UNDERSHAFT: My dear sir, I beg your pardon.

LOMAX: Notatall. Delighted, I assure you.

LADY BRITOMART: This is Stephen.

UNDERSHAFT: *{Bowing}* Happy to make your acquaintance, Mr. Stephen. Then *{Going to* CUSINS] you must be my son. *{Taking* CUSINS' *hands in his}* How are you, my young friend? *{To* LADY BRITOMART] He is very like you, my love.

CUSINS: You flatter me, Mr. Undershaft. My name is Cusins: engaged to Barbara. *{Very explicitly}* That is Major Barbara Undershaft, of the Salvation Army. That is Sarah, your second daughter. This is Stephen Undershaft, your son.

UNDERSHAFT: My dear Stephen, I beg your pardon.

STEPHEN: Not at all.

UNDERSHAFT: Mr. Cusins: I am indebted to you for explaining so precisely. *{Turning to* SARAH] Barbara, my dear—

SARAH: *{Prompting him}* Sarah.

UNDERSHAFT: Sarah, of course. *{They shake hands. He goes over to* BARBARA] Barbara—I am right this time, I hope.

BARBARA: Quite right. *{They shake hands}*

LADY BRITOMART: *{Resuming command}* Sit down, all of you. Sit down, Andrew. *{She comes forward and sits on the settee.* CUSINS *also brings his chair forward on her left.* BARBARA *and* STEPHEN *resume their seats.* LOMAX *gives his chair to* SARAH *and goes for another}*

UNDERSHAFT: Thank you, my love.

LOMAX: *{Conversationally, as he brings a chair forward between the writing table and the settee, and offers it to* UNDERSHAFT] Takes you some time to find out exactly where you are, don't it?

UNDERSHAFT: *{Accepting the chair, but remaining standing}* That is not what embarrasses me, Mr. Lomax. My difficulty is that if I play the part of a father, I shall produce the effect of an intrusive stranger; and if I play the part of a discreet stranger, I may appear a callous father.

LADY BRITOMART: There is no need for you to play any part at all, Andrew. You had much better be sincere and natural.

UNDERSHAFT: *{Submissively}* Yes, my dear: I daresay that will be best. *{He sits down comfortably}* Well, here I am. Now what can I do for you all?

LADY BRITOMART: You need not do anything, Andrew. You are one of the family. You can sit with us and enjoy yourself. *{A painfully conscious pause.* BARBARA *makes a face at* LOMAX, *whose too long suppressed mirth immediately explodes in agonized neighings}*

LADY BRITOMART: *{Outraged}* Charles Lomax: if you can behave yourself, behave yourself. If not, leave the room.

LOMAX: I'm awfully sorry, Lady Brit; but really, you know, upon my soul! *{He sits on the settee between* LADY BRITOMART *and* UNDERSHAFT, *quite overcome}*

BARBARA: Why don't you laugh if you want to, Cholly? It's good for your inside.

LADY BRITOMART: Barbara: you have had the education of a lady. Please let your father see that; and don't talk like a street girl.

UNDERSHAFT: Never mind me, my dear. As you know, I am not a gentleman; and I was never educated.

LOMAX: *{Encouragingly}* Nobody'd know it, I assure you. You look all right, you know.

CUSINS: Let me advise you to study Greek, Mr. Undershaft. Greek scholars are privileged men. Few of them know Greek; and none of them know anything else; but their position is unchallengeable. Other languages are the qualifications of waiters and commercial travellers: Greek is to a man of position what the hallmark is to silver.

BARBARA: Dolly: don't be insincere. Cholly: fetch your concertina and play something for us.

LOMAX: *{Jumps up eagerly, but checks himself to remark doubtfully to* UNDERSHAFT] Perhaps that sort of thing isn't in your line, eh?

UNDERSHAFT: I am particularly fond of music.

LOMAX: *{Delighted}* Are you? Then I'll get it. *{He goes upstairs for the instrument}*

UNDERSHAFT: Do you play, Barbara?

BARBARA: Only the tambourine. But Cholly's teaching me the concertina.

UNDERSHAFT: Is Cholly also a member of the Salvation Army?

BARBARA: No: he says it's bad form to be a dissenter. But I don't despair of Cholly. I made him come yesterday to a meeting at the dock gates, and take the collection in his hat.

UNDERSHAFT: *{Looks whimsically at his wife}*!!

LADY BRITOMART: It is not my doing, Andrew. Barbara is old enough to take her own way. She has no father to advise her.

BARBARA: Oh yes she has. There are no orphans in the Salvation Army.

UNDERSHAFT: Your father there has a great many children and plenty of experience, eh?

BARBARA: *{Looking at him with quick interest and nodding}* Just so. How did you come to understand that? [LOMAX *is heard at the door trying the concertina}*

LADY BRITOMART: Come in, Charles. Play us something at once.

LOMAX: Righto! *{He sits down in his former place, and preludes}*

UNDERSHAFT: One moment, Mr. Lomax, I am rather interested in the Salvation Army. Its motto might be my own: Blood and Fire.

LOMAX: *{Shocked}* But not your sort of blood and fire, you know.

UNDERSHAFT: My sort of blood cleanses: my sort of fire purifies.

BARBARA: So do ours. Come down tomorrow to my shelter—the West Ham shelter—and see what we're doing. We're going to march to a great meeting in the Assembly Hall at Mile End. Come and see the shelter and then march with us: it will do you a lot of good. Can you play anything?

UNDERSHAFT: In my youth I earned pennies, and even shillings occasionally, in the streets and in public house parlors by my natural talent for stepdancing. Later on, I became a member of the Undershaft orchestral society, and performed passably on the tenor trombone.

LOMAX: *{Scandalized—putting down the concertina}* Oh I say!

BARBARA: Many a sinner has played himself into heaven on the trombone, thanks to the Army.

LOMAX: *{To* BARBARA, *still rather shocked}* Yes; but what about the cannon business, don't you know? *{To* UNDERSHAFT] Getting into heaven is not exactly in your line, is it?

LADY BRITOMART: Charles ! ! !

LOMAX: Well; but it stands to reason, don't it? The cannon business may be necessary and all that: we can't get on without cannons; but it isn't right, you know. On the other hand, there may be a certain amount of tosh about the Salvation Army—I belong to the Established Church myself—but still you can't deny that it's religion; and you can't go against religion, can you? At least unless you're downright immoral, don't you know.

UNDERSHAFT: You hardly appreciate my position, Mr. Lomax—

LOMAX: *{Hastily}* I'm not saying anything against you personally—

UNDERSHAFT: Quite so, quite so. But consider for a moment. Here I am, a profiteer in mutilation and murder. I find myself in a specially amiable humor just now because, this morning, down at the foundry, we blew twenty-seven dummy soldiers into fragments with a gun which formerly destroyed only thirteen.

LOMAX: *{Leniently}* Well, the more destructive war becomes, the sooner it will be abolished, eh?

UNDERSHAFT: Not at all. The more destructive war becomes, the more fascinating we find it. No, Mr. Lomax: I am obliged to you for making the usual excuse for my trade; but I am not ashamed of it. I am not one of those men who keep their morals and their business in watertight compartments. All the spare money my trade rivals spend on hospitals, cathedrals, and other receptacles for conscience money, I devote to experiments and researches in improved methods of destroying life and property. I have always done so; and I always shall. Therefore your Christmas card moralities of peace on earth and goodwill among men are of no use to me. Your Christianity, which enjoins you to resist not evil, and to turn the other cheek, would make me a bankrupt. My morality—my religion—must have a place for cannons and torpedoes in it.

STEPHEN: *{Coldly—almost sullenly}* You speak as if there were half a dozen moralities and religions to choose from, instead of one true morality and one true religion.

UNDERSHAFT: For me there is only one true morality; but it might not fit you, as you do not manufacture aerial battleships. There is only one true morality for every man; but every man has not the same true morality.

LOMAX: *{Overtaxed}* Would you mind saying that again? I didn't quite follow it.

CUSINS: It's quite simple. As Euripides says, one man's meat is another man's poison morally as well as physically.

UNDERSHAFT: Precisely.

LOMAX: Oh, that. Yes, yes, yes. True. True.

STEPHEN: In other words, some men are honest and some are scoundrels.

BARBARA: Bosh. There are no scoundrels.

UNDERSHAFT: Indeed? Are there any good men?

BARBARA: No. Not one. There are neither good men nor scoundrels: there are just children of one Father; and the sooner they stop calling one another names the better. You needn't talk to me: I know them. I've had scores of them through my hands: scoundrels, criminals, infidels, philanthropists, missionaries, county councillors, all sorts. They're all just the same sort of sinner; and there's the same salvation ready for them all.

UNDERSHAFT: May I ask have you ever saved a maker of cannons?

BARBARA: No. Will you let me try?

UNDERSHAFT: Well, I will make a bargain with you. If I go to see you tomorrow in your Salvation Shelter, will you come the day after to see me in my cannon works?

BARBARA: Take care. I may end in your giving up the cannons for the sake of the Salvation Army.

UNDERSHAFT: Are you sure it will not end in your giving up the Salvation Army for the sake of cannons?

BARBARA: I will take my chance of that.

UNDERSHAFT: And I will take my chance of the other. *{They shake hands on it}* Where is your shelter?

BARBARA. In West Ham. At the sign of the cross. Ask anybody in Canning Town. Where are your works?

UNDERSHAFT: In Perivale St Andrews. At the sign of the sword. Ask anybody in Europe.

LOMAX: Hadn't I better play something?

BARBARA: Yes. Give us "Onward, Christian Soldiers."

LOMAX: Well, that's rather a strong order to begin with, don't you know.

Suppose I sing "Thou're passing hence, my brother." It's much the same tune.

BARBARA: It's too melancholy. You get saved, Cholly; and you'll pass hence, my brother, without making such a fuss about it.

LADY BRITOMART: Really, Barbara, you go on as if religion were a pleasant subject. Do have some sense of propriety.

UNDERSHAFT: I do not find it an unpleasant subject, my dear. It is the only one that capable people really care for.

LADY BRITOMART: *[Looking at her watch]* Well, if you are determined to have it, I insist on having it in a proper and respectable way. Charles: ring for prayers. *[General amazement.* STEPHEN *rises in dismay]*

LOMAX: *[Rising]* Oh I say!

UNDERSHAFT: *[Rising]* I am afraid I must be going.

LADY BRITOMART: You cannot go now, Andrew: it would be most improper. Sit down. What will the servants think?

UNDERSHAFT: My dear: I have conscientious scruples. May I suggest a compromise? If Barbara will conduct a little service in the drawing room, with Mr. Lomax as organist, I will attend it willingly. I will even take part, if a trombone can be procured.

LADY BRITOMART: Don't mock, Andrew.

UNDERSHAFT: *[Shocked—to* BARBARA] You don't think I am mocking, my love, I hope.

BARBARA: No, of course not; and it wouldn't matter if you were: half the Army came to their first meeting for a lark. *[Rising]* Come along. *[She throws her arm around her father and sweeps him out, calling to the others from the threshold]* Come, Dolly. Come, Cholly. [CUSINS *rises]*

LADY BRITOMART: I will not be disobeyed by everybody. Adolphus: sit down. *[He does not]* Charles: you may go. You are not fit for prayers: you cannot keep your contenance.

LOMAX: Oh I say! *[He goes out]*

LADY BRITOMART: *[Continuing]* But you, Adolphus, can behave yourself if you choose to. I insist on your staying.

CUSINS: My dear Lady Brit: there are things in the family prayer book that I couldn't bear to hear you say.

LADY BRITOMART: What things, pray?

CUSINS: Well, you would have to say before all the servants that we have done things we ought not to have done, and left undone things we ought to have done, and that there is no health in us. I cannot bear to hear you doing yourself such an injustice, and Barbara such an injustice. As for myself, I flatly deny it: I have done my best. I shouldn't dare to marry Barbara—I couldn't look you in the face—if it were true. So I must go to the drawing room.

LADY BRITOMART: *[Offended]* Well, go. *[He starts for the door]* And remember this, Adolphus *[He turns to listen]* I have a strong suspicion that you went to the Salvation Army to worship Barbara and nothing else. And I quite appreciate the clever way in which you systematically humbug me. I have found you out. Take care Barbara doesn't. That's all.

CUSINS: *[With unruffled sweetness]* Don't tell on me. *[He steals out]*

LADY BRITOMART: Sarah: if you want to go, go. Anything's better than to sit there as if you wished you were a thousand miles away.

SARAH: *[Languidly]* Very well, mamma. *[She goes]* [LADY BRITOMART, *with a sudden flounce, gives way to a little gust of tears]*

STEPHEN: *[Going to her]* Mother: what's the matter?

LADY BRITOMART: *[Swishing away her tears with her handkerchief]* Nothing, Foolishness. You can go with him, too, if you like, and leave me with the servants.

STEPHEN: Oh, you mustn't think that, mother. I—I don't like him.

LADY BRITOMART: The others do. That is the injustice of a woman's lot.

A woman has to bring up her children; and that means to restrain them, to deny them things they want, to set them tasks, to punish them when they do wrong, to do all the unpleasant things. And then the father, who has nothing to do but pet them and spoil them, comes in when all her work is done and steals their affection from her.

STEPHEN: He has not stolen our affection from you. It is only curiosity.

LADY BRITOMART: *{Violently}* I won't be consoled, Stephen. There is nothing the matter with me. *{She rises and goes towards the door}*

STEPHEN: Where are you going, mother?

LADY BRITOMART: To the drawing room, of course. *{She goes out. "Onward, Christian Soldiers," on the concertina, with tambourine accompaniment, is heard when the door opens}* Are you coming, Stephen?

STEPHEN: No. Certainly not. *{She goes. He sits down on the settee, with compressed lips and an expression of strong dislike}*

END OF ACT I

Act II

The yard of the West Ham shelter of the Salvation Army is a cold place on a January morning. The building itself, an old warehouse, is newly whitewashed. Its gabled end projects into the yard in the middle, with a door on the ground floor, and another in the loft above it without any balcony or ladder, but with a pulley rigged over it for hoisting sacks. Those who come from this central gable end into the yard have the gateway leading to the street on their left, with a stone horsetrough just beyond it, and, on the right, a penthouse shielding a table from the weather. There are forms at the table; and on them are seated a man and a woman, both much down on their luck, finishing a meal of bread (one thick slice each, with margarine and golden syrup) and diluted milk.

The man, a workman out of employment, is young, agile, a talker, a poser, sharp enough to be capable of anything in reason except honesty or altruistic considerations of any kind. The woman is a commonplace old bundle of poverty and hard-worn humanity. She looks sixty and probably is forty-five. If they were rich people, gloved and muffed and well wrapped up in furs and overcoats, they would be numbed and miserable; for it is a grindingly cold, raw, January day; and a glance at the background of grimy warehouses and leaden sky visible over the whitewashed walls of the yard would drive any idle rich person straight to the Mediterranean. But these two, being no more troubled with visions of the Mediterranean than of the moon, and being compelled to keep more of their clothes in the pawnshop, and less on their persons, in winter than in summer, are not depressed by the cold: rather are they stung into vivacity, to which their meal has just now given an almost jolly turn. The man takes a pull at his mug, and then gets up and moves about the yard with his hands deep in his pockets, occasionally breaking into a stepdance.

THE WOMAN: Feel better arter your meal, sir?

THE MAN: No. Call that a meal! Good enough for you, p'raps; but wot is it to me, an intelligent workin' man?

THE WOMAN: Workin' man! Wot are you?

THE MAN: Painter.

THE WOMAN: *{Skeptically}* Yus, I dessay.

THE MAN: Yus, you dessay! I know. Every loafer that can't do nothink calls 'isself a painter. Well, I'm a real painter: grainer, finisher, thirty-eight bob a week when I can get it.

THE WOMAN: Then why don't you go and get it?

THE MAN: I'll tell you why. Fust: I'm intelligent—fffff! it's rotten cold here *{He dances a step or two}*—yes; intelligent beyond the station o' life into which it has pleased the capitalists to call me; and they don't like a man that sees through 'em. Second, an intelligent bein' needs a doo share of 'appiness; so I drink somethink cruel when I get the chawnce. Third, I stand by my class and do as little as I can so's to leave 'arf the job for me fellow workers. Fourth, I'm fly enough to know wot's inside the law and wot's outside it; and inside it I do as the capitalists do: pinch wot I can lay me 'ands on. In a proper state of society I am sober, industrious, and honest: in Rome, so to speak, I do as the Romans do. Wot's the consequence? When trade is bad—and it's rotten bad just now—and the employers 'az to sack 'arf their men, they generally start on me.

THE WOMAN: What's your name?

THE MAN: Price. Bronterre O'Brien Price. Usually called Snobby Price, for short.

THE WOMAN: Snobby's a carpenter, ain't it? You said you was a painter.

PRICE: Not that kind of snob, but the genteel sort. I'm too uppish, owing to my intelligence, and my father being a Chartist and a reading, thinking man: a stationer, too. I'm none of your common hewers of wood and drawers of water; and don't you forget it. *{He returns to his seat at the table, and takes up his mug}* Wot's your name?

THE WOMAN: Rummy Mitchens, sir.

PRICE: *{Quaffing the remains of his milk to her}* Your 'elth, Miss Mitchens.

RUMMY: *{Correcting him}* Missis Mitchens.

PRICE: Wot! Oh Rummy, Rummy! Respectable married woman, Rummy, gittin' rescued by the Salvation Army by pretendin' to be a bad un. Same old game!

RUMMY: What am I to do? I can't starve. Them Salvation lasses is dear good girls; but the better you are, the worse they likes to think you were before they rescued you. Why shouldn't they 'av a bit o' credit, poor loves? they're worn to rags by their work. And where would they get the money to rescue us if we was to let on we're no worse than other people? You know what ladies and gentlemen are.

PRICE: Thievin' swine! Wish I 'ad their job, Rummy, all the same. Wot does Rummy stand for? Pet name p'raps?

RUMMY: Short for Romola.

PRICE: For wot!?

RUMMY: Romola. It was out of a new book. Somebody me mother wanted me to grow up like.

PRICE: We're companions in misfortune, Rummy. Both of us got names that nobody cawn't pronounce. Consequently I'm Snobby and you're Rummy because Bill and Sally wasn't good enough for our parents. Such is life!

RUMMY: Who saved you, Mr. Price? Was it Major Barbara?

PRICE: No: I come here on my own. I'm goin' to be Bronterre O'Brien Price, the converted painter. I know wot they like. I'll tell 'em how I blasphemed and gambled and wopped my poor old mother—

RUMMY: *{Shocked}* Used you to beat your mother?

PRICE: Not likely. She used to beat me. No matter: you come and listen to the converted painter, and you'll hear how she was a pious woman that taught me me prayers at 'er knee, an' how I used to come home drunk and drag her out o' bed be 'er snow-white 'airs, an' lam into 'er with the poker.

RUMMY: That's what's so unfair to us women. Your confessions is just as big lies as ours: you don't tell what you really done no more than us; but you men can tell your lies right out at the meetin's and be made much of for it; while the sort o' confessions we 'az to make 'az to be whispered to one lady at a time. It ain't right, spite of all their piety.

PRICE: Right! Do you s'pose the Army'd be allowed if it went and did right? Not much. It combs our 'air and makes us good little blokes to be robbed and put upon. But I'll play the game as good as any of 'em. I'll see somebody struck by lightnin', or hear a voice sayin' "Snobby Price: where will you spend eternity?" I'll 'ave a time of it, I tell you.

RUMMY: You won't be let drink, though.

PRICE: I'll take it out in gorspellin', then. I don't want to drink if I can get fun enough any other way. [JENNY HILL, *a pale, overwrought, pretty Salvation lass of eighteen, comes in through the yard gate, leading* PETER SHIRLEY, *a half hardened, half worn-out elderly man, weak with hunger*]

JENNY: [*Supporting him*] Come! pluck up. I'll get you something to eat. You'll be all right then.

PRICE: [*Rising and hurrying officiously to take the old man off* JENNY'S *hands*] Poor old man! Cheer up, brother: you'll find rest and peace and 'appiness 'ere. Hurry up with the food, miss: 'e's fair done. (JENNY *hurries into the shelter*] 'Ere, buck up, daddy! she's fetchin' y'a thick slice o' bread'n treacle, an' a mug o' skyblue. [*He seats him at the corner of the table*]

RUMMY: [*Gaily*] Keep up your old 'art! Never say die!

SHIRLEY: I'm not an old man. I'm only forty-six. I'm as good as ever I was. The grey patch come in my hair before I was thirty. All it wants is three pennorth o' hair dye: am I to be turned on the streets to starve for it? Holy God! I've worked ten to twelve hours a day since I was thirteen, and paid my way all through; and now am I to be thrown into the gutter and my job given to a young man that can do it no better than me because I've black hair that goes white at the first change?

PRICE: [*Cheerfully*] No good jawrin' about it. You're only a jumped-up, jerked-off, 'orspittle-turned-out incurable of a ole workin' man: who cares about you? Eh? Make the thievin' swine give you a meal: they've stole many a one from you. Get a bit o' your own back. [JENNY *returns with the usual meal*] There you are, brother. Awsk a blessin' an' tuck that into you.

SHIRLEY: [*Looking at it ravenously but not touching it, and crying like a child*] I never took anything before.

JENNY: [*Petting him*] Come, come! the Lord sends it to you: he wasn't above taking bread from his friends; and why should you be? Besides, when we find you a job you can pay us for it if you like.

SHIRLEY: [*Eagerly*] Yes, yes: that's true. I can pay you back: it's only a loan. [*Shivering*] Oh Lord! oh Lord! [*He turns to the table and attacks the meal ravenously*]

JENNY: Well, Rummy, are you more comfortable now?

RUMMY: God bless you, lovey! you've fed my body and saved my soul, haven't you? [JENNY, *touched, kisses her*] Sit down and rest a bit: you must be ready to drop.

JENNY: I've been going hard since morning. But there's more work than we can do. I mustn't stop.

RUMMY: Try a prayer for just two minutes. You'll work all the better after.

JENNY: [*Her eyes lighting up*] Oh isn't it wonderful how a few minutes prayer revives you! I was quite lightheaded at twelve o'clock, I was so tired; but Major Barbara just sent me to pray for five minutes; and I was able to go on as if I had only just begun. *{To* PRICE] Did you have a piece of bread?

PRICE: *{With unction}* Yes, miss; but I've got the piece that I value more; and that's the peace that passeth hall hannerstennin.

RUMMY: *{Fervently}* Glory Hallelujah! (BILL WALKER, *a rough customer of about 25, appears at the yard gate and looks malevolently at* JENNY]

JENNY: That makes me so happy. When you say that, I feel wicked for loitering here. I must get to work again. *{She is hurrying to the shelter, when the newcomer moves quickly up to the door and intercepts her. His manner is so threatening that she retreats as he comes at her truculently, driving her down the yard}*

BILL: Aw knaow you. You're the one that took aw'y maw girl. You're the one that set 'er agen me. Well, I'm gowin' to 'ev 'er aht. Not that Aw care a carse for 'er or you: see? But Aw'll let 'er knaow; and Aw'll let you knaow. Aw'm gowin' to give her a doin' that'll teach 'er to cat aw'y from me. Nah in wiv you and tell 'er to cam aht afore Aw cam in and kick 'er aht. Tell 'er Bill Walker wants 'er. She'll knaow wot thet means; and if she keeps me witin' it'll be worse. You stop to jawr beck at me; and Aw'll stawt on you: d'ye 'eah? There's your w'y. In you gow. *{He takes her by the arm and slings her towards the door of the shelter. She falls on her hand and knee.* RUMMY *helps her up again}*

PRICE: *{Rising, and venturing irresolutely towards* BILL] Easy there, mate. She ain't doin' you no 'arm.

BILL: 'Oo are you callin' mite? *{Standing over him threateningly}* Youre gowin' to stend up for 'er, aw yer? Put ap your 'ends.

RUMMY: *{Running indignantly to him to scold him}* Oh, you great brute —*{He instantly swings his left hand back against her face. She screams and reels back to the trough, where she sits down, covering her bruised face with her hands and rocking herself and moaning with pain}*

JENNY: *{Going to her}* Oh, God forgive you! How could you strike an old woman like that?

BILL: *{Seizing her by the hair so violently that she also screams, and tearing her away from the old woman}* You Gawd forgimme again and Aw'll Gawd forgive you one on the jawr thet'll stop you pryin' for a week. *{Holding her and turning fiercely on* PRICE] 'Ev you ennything to s'y agen it?

PRICE: *{Intimidated}* No, matey: she ain't anything to do with me.

BILL: Good job for you! Aw'd pat two meals into you and fawt you with one finger arter, you stawved cur. *{To* JENNY] Nah are you gowin' to fetch aht Mog Ebbijem; or em Aw to knock your fice off you and fetch her meself?

JENNY: *{Writhing in his grasp}* Oh, please, someone go in and tell Major Barbara— *{She screams again as he wrenches her head down; and* PRICE *and* RUMMY *flee into the shelter}*

BILL: You want to gow in and tell your Mijor of me, do you?

JENNY: Oh, please, don't drag my hair. Let me go.

BILL: Do you or down't you? *{She stifles a scream}* Yus or nao?

JENNY: God give me strength—

BILL: *{Striking her with his fist in the face}* Gow an' shaow her thet, and tell her if she wants one lawk it to cam and interfere with me. [JENNY, *crying with pain, goes into the shed. He goes to the form and addresses the old man}* 'Eah: finish your mess; and git aht o' maw w'y.

SHIRLEY: *{Springing up and facing him fiercely, with the mug in his hand}* You take a liberty with me, and I'll smash you over the face with the mug and cut your eye out. Ain't you satisfied —young whelps like you—with takin' the bread out o' the mouths of your elders that have brought you up and slaved for you, but you must come shovin' and cheekin' and bullyin' in here, where the bread o' charity is sickenin' in our stummicks?

BILL: *{Contemptuously, but backing a little}* Wot good are you, you aold palsy mag? Wot good are you?

SHIRLEY: As good as you and better. I'll do a day's work agen you or any fat young soaker of your age. Go and take my job at Horrockses, where I worked for ten year. They want young men there: they can't afford to keep men over forty-five. They're very sorry—give you a character and happy to help you to get anything suited to your years—sure a steady man won't be long out of a job. Well, let 'em try you. They'll find the differ. What do you know? Not as much as how to beeyave yourself—layin' your dirty fist across the mouth of a respectable woman!

BILL: Downt provowk me to l'ye it acrost yours: d'ye 'eah?

SHIRLEY: *{With blighting contempt}* Yes: you like an old man to hit, don't you, when you've finished with the women. I ain't seen you hit a young one yet.

BILL: *{Stung}* You loy, you aold soup-kitchener, you. There was a yang menn 'eah. Did aw offer to 'itt him or did Aw not?

SHIRLEY: Was he starvin' or was he not? Was he a man or only a crosseyed thief an' a loafer? Would you hit my son-in-law's brother?

BILL: 'Oo's 'ee?

SHIRLEY: Todger Fairmile o' Balls Pond. Him that won £20 off the Japanese wrastler at the music hall by standin' out 17 minutes 4 seconds agen him.

BILL: *{Sullenly}* Aw'm nao music 'awl wrastler. Ken he box?

SHIRLEY: Yes: an' you can't.

BILL: Wot! Aw cawn't, cawn't Aw? Wot's they you s'y? *{Threatening him}*

SHIRLEY: *{Not budging an inch}* Will you box Todger Fairmile if I put him on to you? Say the word.

BILL: *{Subsiding with a slouch}* Aw'll stend ap to enny menn alawv, if he was ten Todger Fairmawls. But Aw down't set ap to be a perfeshnal.

SHIRLEY: *{Looking down on him with unfathomable disdain}* You box! Slap an old woman with the back o' your hand! You hadn't even the sense to hit her where a magistrate couldn't see the mark of it, you silly young lump of conceit and ignorance. Hit a girl in the jaw an on'y make her cry! If Todger Fairmile'd done it, she wouldn't 'a got up inside o' ten minutes, no more than you would if he got on to you. Yah! I'd set about you myself if I had a week's feedin' in me instead o' two months' starvation. *{He turns his back on him and sits down moodily at the table}*

BILL: *{Following him and stooping over him to drive the taunt in}* You loy! you've the bread and treacle in you that you cam 'eah to beg.

SHIRLEY: *{Bursting into tears}* Oh God! it's true: I'm only an old pauper on the scrap heap. *{Furiously}* But you'll come to it yourself; and then you'll know. You'll come to it sooner than a teetotaller like me, fillin' yourself with gin at this hour o' the mornin!

BILL: Aw'm nao gin drinker, you oald lawr; bat wen Aw want to give my girl a bloomin' good' awdin' Aw lawk to 'ev a bit o' devil in me: see? An' 'eah Aw emm, talking to a rotten aold blawter like you stead o' given' 'er wot for. *{Working himself into a rage}* Aw'm gowin' in there to fetch her aht. *{He makes vengefully for the shelter door}*

SHIRLEY: You're goin' to the station on a stretcher, more likely; and they'll take the gin and the devil out of you there when they get you inside. You mind what you're about: the major here is the Earl o' Stevenage's granddaughter.

BILL: *{Checked}* Garn!

SHIRLEY: You'll see.

BILL: *{His resolution oozing}* Well, Aw ain't dan nathin' to 'er.

SHIRLEY: S'pose she said you did! who'd believe you?

BILL: *{Very uneasy, skulking back to the corner of the penthouse}* Gawd! there's no jastice in this cantry. To think wot them people can do! Aw'm as good as 'er.

SHIRLEY: Tell her so. It's just what a fool like you would do. [BARBARA, *brisk and businesslike, comes from the shelter with a note book, and addresses herself to* SHIRLEY. BILL, *cowed, sits down in the corner on a form, and turns his back on them}*

BARBARA: Good morning.

SHIRLEY: *{Standing up and taking off his hat}* Good morning, miss.

BARBARA: Sit down: make yourself at home. *{He hesitates; but she puts a friendly hand on his shoulder and makes him obey}* Now then! since you've made friends with us, we want to know all about you. Names and addresses and trades.

SHIRLEY: Peter Shirley. Fitter. Chucked out two months ago because I was too old.

BARBARA: *{Not at all surprised}* You'd pass still. Why didn't you dye your hair?

SHIRLEY: I did. Me age come out at a coroner's inquest on me daughter.

BARBARA: Steady?

SHIRLEY: Teetotaller. Never out of a job before. Good worker. And sent to the knackers like an old orse!

BARBARA: No matter: if you did your part God will do his.

SHIRLEY: *{Suddenly stubborn}* My religion's no concern of anybody but myself.

BARBARA: *{Guessing}* *I* know. Secularist?

SHIRLEY: *{Hotly}* Did I offer to deny it?

BARBARA: Why should you? My own father's a Secularist, I think. Our Father —*yours* and mine—fulfils himself in many ways; and I daresay he knew what he was about when he made a Secularist of you. So buck up, Peter! we can always find a job for a steady man like you. [SHIRLEY, *disarmed and a little bewildered, touches his hat. She turns from him to* BILL] What's your name?

BILL: *{Insolently}* Wot's thet to you?

BARBARA: *{Calmly making a note}* Afraid to give his name. Any trade?

BILL: 'Oo's afride to give 'is nime? *{Doggedly, with a sense of heroically defying the House of Lords in the person of Lord Stevenage}* If you want to bring a chawge agen me, bring it. *{She waits, unruffled}* Moy nime's Bill Walker.

BARBARA: *{As if the name were familiar: trying to remember how}* Bill Walker? *{Recollecting}* Oh, I know: you're the man that Jenny Hill was praying for inside just now. *{She enters his name in her note book}*

BILL: 'Oo's Jenny 'ill? And wot call 'as she to pr'y for me?

BARBARA: I don't know. Perhaps it was you that cut her lip.

BILL: *{Defiantly}* Yus, it was me that cat her lip. Aw ain't afride o' you.

BARBARA: How could you be, since you're not afraid of God? You're a brave man, Mr Walker. It takes some pluck to do our work here; but none of us dare lift our hand against a girl like that, for fear of her father in heaven.

BILL: *{Suddenly}* I want nan o' your kentin' jawr. I spowse you think Aw cam 'eah to beg from you, like this demmiged lot 'eah. Not me. Aw down't want your bread and scripe and ketlep. Aw don't b'live in your Gawd, no more than you do yourself.

BARBARA: *{Sunnily apologetic and ladylike, as on a new footing with him}* Oh, I beg your pardon for putting your name down, Mr Walker. I didn't understand. I'll strike it out.

BILL: *{Taking this as a slight, and deeply wounded by it}* 'Eah! you let maw nime alown. Ain't it good enaff to be in your book?

BARBARA: *{Considering}* Well, you see, there's no use putting down your name unless I can do something for you, is there? What's your trade?

BILL: *{Still smarting}* Thets nao concern o' yours.

BARBARA: Just so. *{Very businesslike}* I'll put you down as *{Writing}* the man who—struck—poor little Jenny Hill—in the mouth.

BILL: *{Rising threateningly}* See 'eah. Awve 'ed enaff o' this.

BARBARA: *{Quite sunny and fearless}* What did you come to us for?

BILL: Aw cam for maw gel, see? Aw came to tike her aht o' this and to brike 'er jawr for 'er.

BARBARA: *{Complacently}* You see I was right about your trade. [BILL, *on the point of retorting furiously, finds himself, to his great shame and terror, in danger of crying instead. He sits down again suddenly}* What's her name?

BILL: *{Dogged}* 'Er nime's Mog Ebbijem: thet's wot her nime is.

BARBARA: Mog Habbijam! Oh, she's gone to Canning Town, to our barracks there.

BILL: *{Fortified by his resentment of* MOG's *perfidy}* Is she? *{Vindictively}* Then Aw'm gowin' to Kennintahn arter her. *{He crosses to the gate; hesitates; finally comes back at* BARBARA] Are you loyin' to me to git shat o' me?

BARBARA: I don't want to get shut of you. I want to keep you here and save your soul. You'd better stay: you're going to have a bad time today, Bill.

BILL: 'Oo's gowin to give it to me? You, p'reps?

BARBARA: Someone you don't believe in. But you'll be glad afterwards.

BILL: *{Slinking off}* Aw'll gow to Kennintahn to be aht o' reach o' your tangue. *{Suddenly turning on her with intense malice}* And if Aw down't fawnd Mog there, Aw'll cam back and do two years for you, s'elp me Gawd if Aw downt!

BARBARA: *{A shade kindlier, if possible}* It's no use, Bill. She's got another bloke.

BILL: Wot!

BARBARA: One of her own converts. He fell in love with her when he saw her with her soul saved, and her face clean, and her hair washed.

BILL: *{Surprised}* Wottud she wash it for, the carroty slat? It's red.

BARBARA: It's quite lovely now, because she wears a new look in her eyes with it. It's a pity you're too late. The new bloke has put your nose out of joint, Bill.

BILL: Aw'll put his nowse aht o' joint for him. Not that Aw care a carse for 'er, mawnd thet. But Aw'll teach her to drop me as if Aw was dirt. And Aw'll teach him to meddle with maw judy. Wots 'iz bleedin' nime?

BARBARA: Sergeant Todger Fairmile.

SHIRLEY: *{Rising with grim joy}* I'll go with him, miss. I want to see them two meet. I'll take him to the infirmary when it's over.

BILL: *{To* SHIRLEY, *with undissembled misgiving}* Is thet 'im you was speakin' on?

SHIRLEY: That's him.

BILL: 'Im that wrastled in the music 'awl?

SHIRLEY: The competitions at the National Sportin' Club was worth nigh a hundred a year to him. He's gev 'em up now for religion; so he's a bit fresh for want of the exercise he was accustomed to. He'll be glad to see you. Come along.

BILL: Wot's 'is wight?

SHIRLEY: Thirteen four. [BILL's *last hope expires}*

BARBARA: Go and talk to him, Bill. He'll convert you.

SHIRLEY: He'll convert your head into a mashed potato.

BILL: *{Sullenly}* Aw ain't afride of 'im. Aw ain't afride of ennybody. Bat 'e can lick me. She's dan me. *{He sits down moodily on the edge of the horse trough}*

SHIRLEY: You ain't goin'. I thought not. *{He resumes his seat}*

BARBARA: *{Calling}* Jenny!

JENNY: *{Appearing at the shelter door with a plaster on the corner of her mouth}* Yes, Major.

BARBARA: Send Rummy Mitchens out to clear away here.

JENNY: I think she's afraid.

BARBARA: *{Her resemblance to her mother flashing out for a moment}* Nonsense! she must do as she's told.

JENNY: *{Calling into the shelter}* Rummy: the Major says you must come. [JENNY *comes to* BARBARA, *purposely keeping on the side next* BILL, *lest he should suppose that she shrank from him or bore malice}*

BARBARA: Poor little Jenny! Are you tired? *{Looking at the wounded cheek}* Does it hurt?

JENNY: No: it's all right now. It was nothing.

BARBARA: *{Critically}* It was as hard as he could hit, I expect. Poor Bill! You don't feel angry with him, do you?

JENNY: Oh no, no, no: indeed I don't, Major, bless his poor heart! [BARBARA *kisses her; and she runs away merrily into the shelter.* BILL *writhes with an agonizing return of his new and alarming symptoms, but says nothing.* RUMMY MITCHENS *comes from the shelter}*

BARBARA: *{Going to meet* RUMMY] Now Rummy, bustle. Take in those mugs and plates to be washed; and throw the crumbs about for the birds. [RUMMY *takes the three plates and mugs; but* SHIRLEY *takes back his mug from her, as there is still some milk left in it}*

RUMMY: There ain't any crumbs. This ain't a time to waste good bread on birds.

PRICE: *{Appearing at the shelter door}* Gentleman come to see the shelter, Major. Says he's your father.

BARBARA: All right. Coming [SNOBBY *goes back into the shelter, followed by* BARBARA]

RUMMY: *{Stealing across to* BILL *and addressing him in a subdued voice, but with intense conviction}* I'd 'av the lor of you, you flat eared pignosed potwalloper, if she'd let me. You're no gentleman, to hit a lady in the face. [BILL, *with greater things moving in him, takes no notice}*

SHIRLEY: *{Following her}* Here! in with you and don't get yourself into more trouble by talking.

RUMMY: *{With hauteur}* I ain't 'ad the pleasure o' being hintroduced to you, as I can remember. *{She goes into the shelter with the plates}*

SHIRLEY: That's the—

BILL: *{Savagely}* Downt you talk to me, d'ye 'eah? You lea' me alown, or Aw'll do you a mischief. Aw'm not dirt under your feet, ennywy.

SHIRLEY: *{Calmly}* Don't you be afeerd. You ain't such prime company that you need expect to be sought after. *{He is about to go into the shelter when* BARBARA *comes out, with* UNDERSHAFT *on her right}*

BARBARA: Oh, there you are, Mr Shirley! *{Between them}* This is my father: I told you he was a Secularist, didn't I? Perhaps you'll be able to comfort one another.

UNDERSHAFT: *{Startled}* A Secularist! Not the least in the world: on the contrary, a confirmed mystic.

BARBARA: Sorry, I'm sure. By the way, papa, what is your religion? in case I have to introduce you again.

UNDERSHAFT: My religion? Well, my dear, I am a Millionaire. That is my religion.

BARBARA: Then I'm afraid you and Mr Shirley won't be able to comfort one another after all. You're not a Millionnaire, are you, Peter?

SHIRLEY: No; and proud of it.

UNDERSHAFT: *{Gravely}* Poverty, my friend, is not a thing to be proud of.

SHIRLEY: *{Angrily}* Who made your millions for you? Me and my like. What's kep' us poor? Keepin' you rich. I wouldn't have your conscience, not for all your income.

UNDERSHAFT: I wouldn't have your

income, not for all your conscience, Mr Shirley. *{He goes to the penthouse and sits down on a form}*

BARBARA: *{Stopping* SHIRLEY *adroitly as he is about to retort}* You wouldn't think he was my father, would you, Peter? Will you go into the shelter and lend the lasses a hand for a while: we're worked off our feet.

SHIRLEY: *{Bitterly}* Yes: I'm in their debt for a meal, ain't I?

BARBARA: Oh, not because you're in their debt, but for love of them, Peter, for love of them. *{He cannot understand, and is rather scandalized}* There! don't stare at me. In with you; and give that conscience of yours a holiday. *{Bustling him into the shelter}*

SHIRLEY: *{As he goes in}* Ah! it's a pity you never was trained to use your reason, miss. You'd have been a very taking lecturer on Secularism. [BARBARA *turns to her father}*

UNDERSHAFT: Never mind me, my dear. Go about your work; and let me watch it for a while.

BARBARA: All right.

UNDERSHAFT: For instance, what's the matter with that outpatient over there?

BARBARA: *{Looking at* BILL, *whose attitude has never changed, and whose expression of brooding wrath has deepened}* Oh, we shall cure him in no time. Just watch. *{She goes over to* BILL *and waits. He glances up at her and casts his eyes down again, uneasy, but grimmer than ever}* It would be nice to just stamp on Mog Habbijam's face, wouldn't it, Bill?

BILL: *{Starting up from the trough in consternation}* It's a loy: Aw never said so. *{She shakes her head}* 'Oo taold you wot was in moy mawnd?

BARBARA: Only your new friend.

BILL: Wot new friend?

BARBARA: The devil, Bill. When he gets round people they get miserable, just like you.

BILL: *{With a heartbreaking attempt at devil-may-care cheerfulness}* Aw ain't miserable. *{He sits down again, and stretches his legs in an attempt to seem indifferent}*

BARBARA: Well, if you're happy, why don't you look happy, as we do?

BILL: *{His legs curling back in spite of him}* Aw'm 'eppy enaff, Aw tell you. Woy cawn't you lea' me alown? Wot 'ev I dan to you? Aw ain't smashed your fice, 'ev Aw?

BARBARA: *{Softly: wooing his soul}* It's not me that's getting at you, Bill.

BILL: 'Oo else is it?

BARBARA: Somebody that doesn't intend you to smash women's faces, I suppose. Somebody or something that wants to make a man of you.

BILL: *{Blustering}* Mike a menn o' me! Ain't Aw a menn? eh? 'Oo sez Aw'm not a menn?

BARBARA: There's a man in you somewhere, I suppose. But why did he let you hit poor little Jenny Hill? That wasn't very manly of him, was it?

BILL: *{Tormented}* 'Ev dan wiv it, Aw tell you. Chack it. Aw'm sick o' your Jenny 'Ill and 'er silly little fice.

BARBARA: Then why do you keep thinking about it? Why does it keep coming up against you in your mind? You're not getting converted, are you?

BILL: *{With conviction}* Not ME. Not lawkly.

BARBARA: That's right, Bill. Hold out against it. Put out your strength. Don't let's get you cheap. Todger Fairmile said he wrestled for three nights against his salvation harder than he ever wrestled with the Jap at the music hall. He gave in to the Jap when his arm was going to break. But he didn't give in to his salvation until his heart was going to break. Perhaps you'll escape that. You havn't any heart, have you?

BILL: Wot d'ye mean? Woy ain't Aw got a 'awt the sime as ennybody else?

BARBARA: A man with a heart wouldn't have bashed poor little Jenny's face, would he?

BILL: *[Almost crying]* Ow, will you lea' me alown? 'Ev Aw ever offered to meddle with you, that you cam neggin' and provowkin' me lawk this? *[He writhes convulsively from his eyes to his toes]*

BARBARA: *[With a steady soothing hand on his arm and a gentle voice that never lets go]* It's your soul that's hurting you, Bill, and not me. We've been through it all ourselves. Come with us, Bill. *[He looks wildly round]* To brave manhood on earth and eternal glory in heaven. *[He is on the point of breaking down]* Come. *[A drum is heard in the shelter; and* BILL, *with a gasp, escapes from the spell as* BARBARA *turns quickly.* ADOLPHUS *enters from the shelter with a big drum]* Oh! there you are, Dolly. Let me introduce a new friend of mine, Mr Bill Walker. This is my bloke, Bill: Mr Cusins. [CUSINS *salutes with his drumstick]*

BILL: Gowing to merry 'im?

BARBARA: Yes.

BILL: *[Fervently]* Gawd 'elp 'im! Gaw-aw-aw-awd 'elp 'im!

BARBARA: Why? Do you think he won't be happy with me?

BILL: Awve aony 'ed to stend it for a mawnin': 'e'll 'ev to stend it for a lawftawn.

CUSINS: That is a frightful reflection, Mr Walker. But I can't tear myself away from her.

BILL: Well, Aw ken. *[To* BARBARA] 'Eah! do you knaow where Aw'm gowin' to, and wot Aw'm gowin' to do?

BARBARA: Yes: you're going to heaven; and you're coming back here before the week's out to tell me so.

BILL: You loy. Aw'm gowin to Kennintahn, to spit in Todger Fairmawl's eye. Aw beshed Jenny 'Ill's fice; an nar Aw'll git me aown fice beshed and cam beck and shaow it to 'er. 'Ee'll 'itt me 'ardern Aw 'itt 'er. That'll mike us square. *[To* ADOLPHUS] Is that fair or is it not? You're a genlm'n: you oughter knaow.

BARBARA: Two black eyes won't make one white one, Bill.

BILL: Aw didn't awst you. Cawnt you never keep your mahth shat? Oy awst the genlm'n.

CUSINS: *[Reflectively]* Yes: I think you're right, Mr Walker. Yes: I should do it. It's curious: it's exactly what an ancient Greek would have done.

BARBARA: But what good will it do?

CUSINS: Well, it will give Mr Fairmile some exercise; and it will satisfy Mr Walker's soul.

BILL: Rot! there ain't nao sach a thing as a saoul. Ah kin you tell wevver Aw've a saoul or not? You never seen it.

BARBARA: I've seen it hurting you when you went against it.

BILL: *[With compressed aggravation]* If you was maw gel and took the word aht o' me mahth lawk thet, Aw'd give you sathink you'd feel 'urtin, Aw would. *[To* ADOLPHUS] You tike maw tip, mite. Stop 'er jawr; or you'll doy afoah your tawm. *[With intense expression]* Wore aht: thet's you'll be: wore aht. *[He goes away through the gate]*

CUSINS: *[Looking after him]* I wonder!

BARBARA: Dolly! *[Indignant, in her mother's manner]*

CUSINS: Yes, my dear, it's very wearing to be in love with you. If it lasts, I quite think I shall die young.

BARBARA: Should you mind?

CUSINS: Not at all. *[He is suddenly softened, and kisses her over the drum, evidently not for the first time, as people cannot kiss over a big drum without practice.* UNDERSHAFT *coughs]*

BARBARA: It's all right, papa, we've not forgotten you. Dolly: explain the place to papa: I havn't time. *[She goes busily into the shelter.* UNDERSHAFT *and* ADOLPHUS *now have the yard to themselves.* UNDERSHAFT, *seated on a form, and still keenly attentive, looks hard at* ADOLPHUS. ADOLPHUS *looks hard at him]*

UNDERSHAFT: I fancy you guess something of what is in my mind, Mr Cusins. [CUSINS *flourishes his drumsticks as if in the act of beating a lively rataplan, but makes no sound*] Exactly so. But suppose Barbara finds you out!

CUSINS: You know, I do not admit that I am imposing on Barbara. I am quite genuinely interested in the views of the Salvation Army. The fact is, I am a sort of collector of religions; and the curious thing is that I find I can believe them all. By the way, have you any religion?

UNDERSHAFT: Yes.

CUSINS: Anything out of the common?

UNDERSHAFT: Only that there are two things necessary to Salvation.

CUSINS: [*Disappointed, but polite*] Ah, the Church Catechism. Charles Lomax also belongs to the Established Church.

UNDERSHAFT: The two things are—

CUSINS: Baptism and—

UNDERSHAFT: No. Money and gunpowder.

CUSINS: [*Surprised, but interested*] That is the general opinion of our governing classes. The novelty is in hearing any man confess it.

UNDERSHAFT: Just so.

CUSINS: Excuse me: is there any place in your religion for honor, justice, truth, love, mercy and so forth?

UNDERSHAFT: Yes: they are the graces and luxuries of a rich, strong, and safe life.

CUSINS: Suppose one is forced to choose between them and money or gunpowder?

UNDERSHAFT: Choose money and gunpowder; for without enough of both you cannot afford the others.

CUSINS: That is your religion?

UNDERSHAFT: Yes. [*The cadence of this reply makes a full close in the conversation.* CUSINS *twists his face dubiously and contemplates* UNDERSHAFT. UNDERSHAFT *contemplates him*]

CUSINS: Barbara won't stand that. You will have to choose between your religion and Barbara.

UNDERSHAFT: So will you, my friend. She will find out that that drum of yours is hollow.

CUSINS: Father Undershaft: you are mistaken: I am a sincere Salvationist. You do not understand the Salvation Army. It is the army of joy, of love, of courage: it has banished the fear and remorse and despair of the old hell-ridden evangelical sects: it marches to fight the devil with trumpet and drum, with music and dancing, with banner and palm, as becomes a sally from heaven by its happy garrison. It picks the waster out of the public house and makes a man of him: it finds a worm wriggling in a back kitchen, and lo! a woman! Men and women of rank too, sons and daughters of the Highest. It takes the poor professor of Greek, the most artificial and self-suppressed of human creatures, from his meal of roots, and lets loose the rhapsodist in him; reveals the true worship of Dionysos to him; sends him down the public street drumming dithyrambs. [*He plays a thundering flourish on the drum*]

UNDERSHAFT: You will alarm the shelter.

CUSINS: Oh, they are accustomed to these sudden ecstasies of piety. However, if the drum worries you—[*He pockets the drumsticks; unhooks the drum; and stands it on the ground opposite the gateway*]

UNDERSHAFT: Thank you.

CUSINS: You remember what Euripides says about your money and gunpowder?

UNDERSHAFT: No.

CUSINS: [*Declaiming*]

One and another
In money and guns may outpass his brother;
And men in their millions float and flow

And seethe with a million hopes as leaven;
And they win their will; or they miss their will;
And their hopes are dead or are pined for still;
But whoe'er can know
As the long days go
That to live is happy, has found his heaven.

My translation: what do you think of it?

UNDERSHAFT: I think, my friend, that if you wish to know, as the long days go, that to live is happy, you must first acquire money enough for a decent life, and power enough to be your own master.

CUSINS: You are damnably discouraging. *{He resumes his declamation}*

Is it so hard a thing to see
That the spirit of God—whate'er it be—
The law that abides and changes not, ages long,
The Eternal and Nature-born: these things be strong?
What else is Wisdom? What of Man's endeavor,
Or God's high grace so lovely and so great?
To stand from fear set free? to breathe and wait?
To hold a hand uplifted over Fate?
And shall not Barbara be loved for ever?

UNDERSHAFT: Euripides mentions Barbara, does he?

CUSINS: It is a fair translation. The word means Loveliness.

UNDERSHAFT: May I ask—as Barbara's father—how much a year she is to be loved for ever on?

CUSINS: As Barbara's father, that is more your affair than mine. I can feed her by teaching Greek: that is about all.

UNDERSHAFT: Do you consider it a good match for her?

CUSINS: *{With polite obstinacy}* Mr Undershaft: I am in many ways a weak, timid, ineffectual person; and my health is far from satisfactory. But whenever I feel that I must have anything, I get it, sooner or later. I feel that way about Barbara. I don't like marriage: I feel intensely afraid of it; and I don't know what I shall do with Barbara or what she will do with me. But I feel that I and nobody else must marry her. Please regard that as settled—Not that I wish to be arbitrary; but why should I waste your time in discussing what is inevitable?

UNDERSHAFT: You mean that you will stick at nothing: not even the conversion of the Salvation Army to the worship of Dionysos.

CUSINS: The business of the Salvation Army is to save, not to wrangle about the name of the pathfinder. Dionysos or another: what does it matter?

UNDERSHAFT: *{Rising and approaching him}* Professor Cusins: you are a young man after my own heart.

CUSINS: Mr Undershaft: you are, as far as I am able to gather, a most infernal old rascal; but you appeal very strongly to my sense of ironic humor. [UNDERSHAFT *mutely offers his hand. They shake}*

UNDERSHAFT: *{Suddenly concentrating himself}* And now to business.

CUSINS: Pardon me. We were discussing religion. Why go back to such an uninteresting and unimportant subject as business?

UNDERSHAFT: Religion is our business at present, because it is through religion alone that we can win Barbara.

CUSINS: Have you, too, fallen in love with Barbara?

UNDERSHAFT: Yes, with a father's love.

CUSINS: A father's love for a grown-up daughter is the most dangerous of all infatuations. I apologize for mentioning my own pale, coy, mistrustful fancy in the same breath with it.

UNDERSHAFT: Keep to the point. We have to win her; and we are neither of us Methodists.

CUSINS: That doesn't matter. The power Barbara wields here—the power that wields Barbara herself—is not Calvinism, not Presbyterianism, not Methodism—

UNDERSHAFT: Not Greek Paganism either, eh?

CUSINS: I admit that. Barbara is quite original in her religion.

UNDERSHAFT: *{Triumphantly}* Aha! Barbara Undershaft would be. Her inspiration comes from within herself.

CUSINS: How do you suppose it got there?

UNDERSHAFT: *{In towering excitement}* It is the Undershaft inheritance. I shall hand on my torch to my daughter. She shall make my converts and preach my gospel—

CUSINS: What! Money and gunpowder!

UNDERSHAFT: Yes, money and gunpowder; freedom and power; command of life and command of death.

CUSINS: *{Urbanely: trying to bring him down to earth}* This is extremely interesting, Mr Undershaft. Of course you know that you are mad.

UNDERSHAFT: *{With redoubled force}* And you?

CUSINS: Oh, mad as a hatter. You are welcome to my secret since I have discovered yours. But I am astonished. Can a madman make cannons?

UNDERSHAFT: Would anyone else than a madman make them? And now *{With surging energy}* question for question. Can a sane man translate Euripides?

CUSINS: No.

UNDERSHAFT: *{Seizing him by the shoulder}* Can a sane woman make a man of a waster or a woman of a worm?

CUSINS: *{Reeling before the storm}* Father Colossus—Mammoth Millionaire—

UNDERSHAFT: *{Pressing him}* Are there two mad people or three in this Salvation shelter to-day?

CUSINS: You mean Barbara is as mad as we are?

UNDERSHAFT: *{Pushing him lightly off and resuming his equanimity suddenly and completely}* Pooh, Professor! let us call things by their proper names. I am a millionaire; you are a poet; Barbara is a savior of souls. What have we three to do with the common mob of slaves and idolators? *{He sits down with a shrug of contempt for the mob}*

CUSINS: Take care! Barbara is in love with the common people. So am I. Have you never felt the romance of that love?

UNDERSHAFT: *{Cold and sardonic}* Have you ever been in love with Poverty, like St Francis? Have you ever been in love with Dirt, like St Simeon? Have you ever been in love with disease and suffering, like our nurses and philanthropists? Such passions are not virtues, but the most unnatural of all the vices. This love of the common people may please an earl's granddaughter and a university professor; but I have been a common man and a poor man; and it has no romance for me. Leave it to the poor to pretend that poverty is a blessing: leave it to the coward to make a religion of his cowardice by preaching humility: we know better than that. We three must stand together above the common people: how else can we help their children to climb up beside us? Barbara must belong to us, not to the Salvation Army.

CUSINS: Well, I can only say that if you think you will get her away from the Salvation Army by talking to her as you have been talking to me, you don't know Barbara.

UNDERSHAFT: My friend: I never ask for what I can buy.

CUSINS: *{In a white fury}* Do I understand you to imply that you can buy Barbara?

UNDERSHAFT: No; but I can buy the Salvation Army.

CUSINS: Quite impossible.

UNDERSHAFT: You shall see. All religious organizations exist by selling themselves to the rich.

CUSINS: Not the Army. That is the Church of the poor.

UNDERSHAFT: All the more reason for buying it.

CUSINS: I don't think you quite know what the Army does for the poor.

UNDERSHAFT: Oh, yes, I do. It draws their teeth: that is enough for me—as a man of business—

CUSINS: Nonsense! It makes them sober—

UNDERSHAFT: I prefer sober workmen. The profits are larger.

CUSINS: —honest—

UNDERSHAFT: Honest workmen are the most economical.

CUSINS: —attached to their homes—

UNDERSHAFT: So much the better: they will put up with anything sooner than change their shop.

CUSINS: —happy—

UNDERSHAFT: An invaluable safeguard against revolution.

CUSINS: —unselfish—

UNDERSHAFT: Indifferent to their own interests, which suits me exactly.

CUSINS: —with their thoughts on heavenly things—

UNDERSHAFT: *{Rising}* And not on Trade Unionism nor Socialism. Excellent.

CUSINS: *{Revolted}* You really are an infernal old rascal.

UNDERSHAFT: *{Indicating* PETER SHIRLEY, *who has just come from the shelter and strolled dejectedly down the yard between them}* And this is an honest man!

SHIRLEY: Yes; and what 'av I got by it? *{He passes on bitterly and sits on the form, in the corner of the penthouse.* SNOBBY PRICE, *beaming sanctimoniously, and* JENNY HILL, *with a tambourine full of coppers, come from the shelter and go to the drum, on which* JENNY *begins to count the money}*

UNDERSHAFT: *{Replying to* SHIRLEY] Oh, your employers must have got a good deal by it from first to last. *{He sits on the table, with one foot on the side form.* CUSINS, *overwhelmed, sits down on the same form nearer the shelter.* BARBARA *comes from the shelter to the middle of the yard. She is excited and a little overwrought}*

BARBARA: We've just had a splendid experience meeting at the other gate in Cripp's Lane. I've hardly ever seen them so much moved as they were by your confession, Mr Price.

PRICE: I could almost be glad of my past wickedness if I could believe that it would 'elp to keep hathers stright.

BARBARA: So it will, Snobby. How much, Jenny?

JENNY: Four and tenpence, Major.

BARBARA: Oh, Snobby, if you had given your poor mother just one more kick, we should have got the whole five shillings!

PRICE: If she heard you say that, Miss, she'd be sorry I didn't. But I'm glad. Oh what a joy it will be to her when she hears I'm saved!

UNDERSHAFT: Shall I contribute the odd twopence, Barbara? The millionaire's mite, eh? *{He takes a couple of pennies from his pocket}*

BARBARA: How did you make that twopence?

UNDERSHAFT: As usual. By selling cannons, torpedoes, submarines, and my new patent Grand Duke hand grenade.

BARBARA: Put it back in your pocket. You can't buy your Salvation here for twopence: you must work it out.

UNDERSHAFT: Is twopence not enough? I can afford a little more, if you press me.

BARBARA: Two million millions would not be enough. There is bad blood on your hands; and nothing but good blood can cleanse them. Money is no use. Take it away. *{She turns to* CUSINS] Dolly: you must write another letter for me to the papers. *{He makes a wry face}* Yes: I know you don't like it; but it must be done. The starvation this winter is beating us: everybody is unemployed. The General says we must close this shelter if we can't get more money. I force the collections at the meetings until I am ashamed: don't I, Snobby?

PRICE: It's a fair treat to see you work it, Miss. The way you got them up from three-and-six to four-and-ten with that hymn, penny by penny and verse by verse, was a caution. Not a Cheap Jack on Mile End Waste could touch you at it.

BARBARA: Yes; but I wish we could do without it. I am getting at last to think more of the collection than of the people's souls. And what are those hatfuls of pence and halfpence? We want thousands! tens of thousands! hundreds of thousands! I want to convert people, not to be always begging for the Army in a way I'd die sooner than beg for myself.

UNDERSHAFT: *{In profound irony}* Genuine unselfishness is capable of anything, my dear.

BARBARA: *{Unsuspectingly, as she turns away to take the money from the drum and put it in a cash bag she carries}* Yes, isn't it? [UNDERSHAFT *looks sardonically at* CUSINS]

CUSINS: *{Aside to* UNDERSHAFT] Mephistopheles! Machiavelli!

BARBARA: *{Tears coming into her eyes as she ties the bag and pockets it}* How are we to feed them? I can't talk religion to a man with bodily hunger in his eyes. *{Almost breaking down}* It's frightful.

JENNY: *{Running to her}* Major, dear—

BARBARA: *{Rebounding}* No: don't comfort me. It will be all right. We shall get the money.

UNDERSHAFT: How?

JENNY: By praying for it, of course. Mrs Baines says she prayed for it last night; and she has never prayed for it in vain: never once. *{She goes to the gate and looks out into the street}*

BARBARA: *{Who has dried her eyes and regained her composure}* By the way, dad, Mrs Baines has come to march with us to our big meeting this afternoon; and she is very anxious to meet you, for some reason or other. Perhaps she'll convert you.

UNDERSHAFT: I shall be delighted, my dear.

JENNY: *{At the gate: excitedly}* Major! Major! here's that man back again.

BARBARA: What man?

JENNY: The man that hit me. Oh, I hope he's coming back to join us. [BILL WALKER, *with frost on his packet, comes through the gate, his hands deep in his pockets and his chin sunk between his shoulders, like a cleaned-out gambler. He halts between* BARBARA *and the drum}*

BARBARA: Hullo, Bill! Back already!

BILL: *{Nagging at her}* Bin talkin' ever sence, 'ev you?

BARBARA: Pretty nearly. Well, has Todger paid you out for poor Jenny's jaw?

BILL: Nao 'e ain't.

BARBARA: I thought your jacket looked a bit snowy.

BILL: Sao it is snaowy. You want to knaow where the snaow cam from, down't you?

BARBARA: Yes.

BILL: Well, it cam from orf the grahnd in Pawkinses Corner in Kennintahn. It got rabbed orf be maw shaoulders: see?

BARBARA: Pity you didn't rub some off with your knees, Bill! That would have done you a lot of good.

BILL: *{With sour mirthless humor}* Aw was savin' anather menn's knees at the tawm. 'E was kneelin' on moy 'ed, 'e was.

JENNY: Who was kneeling on your head?

BILL: Todger was. 'E was pryin' for me: pryin' camfortable wiv me as a cawpet. Sow was Mog. Sao was the aol bloomin' meetin'. Mog she sez "Ow Lawd brike is stabborn sperrit; bat down't 'urt is dear 'art." Thet was wot she said. "Down't 'urt is dear 'art"! An 'er blowk—thirteen stun four!—kneelin' wiv all is wight on me. Fanny, ain't it?

JENNY: Oh no. We're so sorry, Mr Walker.

BARBARA: *{Enjoying it frankly}* Nonsense! of course it's funny. Served you right, Bill! You must have done something to him first.

BILL: *{Doggedly}* Aw did wot Aw said Aw'd do. Aw spit in 'is eye. 'E looks ap at the skoy and sez, "Ow that Aw should be fahnd worthy to be spit upon for the gospel's sike!" 'e sez; an Mog sez "Gloary 'Allelloolier"; an' then 'e called me Braddher, and dahned me as if Aw was a kid and 'e was me mather worshin' me a Setterda nawt. Aw 'ednt jast nao shaow wiv 'im at all. 'Arf the street pr'yed; and the tather 'arf larfed fit to split theirselves. *{To* BARBARA] There! are you sattisfawd nah?

BARBARA: *{Her eyes dancing}* Wish I'd been there, Bill.

BILL: Yus: you'd 'a got in a hextra bit 'o talk on me, wouldn't you?

JENNY: I'm so sorry, Mr Walker.

BILL: *{Fiercely}* Down't you gow bein' sorry for me: you've no call. Listen 'eah. Aw browk your pawr.

JENNY: No, it didn't hurt me: indeed it didn't, except for a moment. It was only that I was frightened.

BILL: Aw down't want to be forgive be you, or be ennybody. Wot Aw did Aw'll p'y for. Aw trawd to gat me aown jawr browk to settisfaw you—

JENNY: *{Distressed}* Oh no—

BILL: *{Impatiently}* Tell y' Aw did: cawnt you listen to wot's bein' taold you? All Aw got be it was being mide a sawt of in the pablic street for me pines. Well, if Aw cawnt settisfaw you one wy, Aw ken anather. Listen 'eah! Aw 'ed two quid sived agen the frost; an Aw've a pahnd of it left. A mite o' mawn last week 'ed words with the judy 'e's gowin to merry. 'E give 'er wotfor; and 'e's bin fawnd fifteen bob. 'E 'ed a rawt to 'itt 'er cause they was gowin to be merrid; but Aw 'ednt nao rawt to 'itt you; sao put anather fawv bob on an cal it a pahnd's worth. *{He produces a sovereign}* 'Eahs the manney. Tike it; and let's 'ev no more o' your forgivin' an' pryin' and your Mijor jawrin' me. Let wot dan be dan an' pide for; and let there be a end of it.

JENNY: Oh, I couldn't take it, Mr Walker. But if you would give a shilling or two to poor Rummy Mitchens! you really did hurt her; and she's old.

BILL: *{Contemptuously}* Not lawkly. Aw'd give her anather as soon as look at 'er. Let her 'ev the lawr o' me as she threatened! She ain't forgiven me: not mach. Wot Aw dan to 'er is not on me mawnd—wot she *{Indicating* BARBARA] mawt call on me conscience—no more than stickin' a pig. It's this Christian gime o' yours that Aw wown't 'ev pl'yed agen me: this bloomin' forgivin' an neggin' an jawrin' that mikes a menn thet sore that 'iz lawf's a burden to 'im. Aw wown't 'ev it, Aw tell you! sao tike your manney and stop thraowin' your silly beshed fice hap agen me.

JENNY: Major: may I take a little of it for the Army?

BARBARA: No: the Army is not to be bought. We want your soul, Bill; and we'll take nothing less.

BILL: *{Bitterly}* Aw knaow. Me an' maw few shillin's is not good enaff for you. You're a earl's grendorter, you are. Nathink less than a 'andered pahnd for you.

UNDERSHAFT: Come, Barbara! you could do a great deal of good with a hundred pounds. If you will set this gentleman's mind at ease by taking his pound, I will give the other ninety-nine. [BILL, *dazed by such opulence, instinctively touches his cap}*

BARBARA: Oh, you're too extravagant, papa. Bill offers twenty pieces of silver. All you need offer is the other ten. That will make the standard price to buy anybody who's for sale. I'm not; and the Army's not. *{To* BILL] You'll never have another quiet moment, Bill, until you come around to us. You can't stand out against your salvation.

BILL: *{Sullenly}* Aw cawnt stend aht agen music 'awl wrastlers and awtful tangued women. Aw've offered to p'y. Aw can do no more. Tike it or leave it. There it is. *{He throws the sovereign on the drum, and sits down on the horse trough. The coin fascinates* SNOBBY PRICE, *who takes an early opportunity of dropping his cap on it.* MRS BAINES *comes from the shelter. She is dressed as a Salvation Army Commissioner. She is an earnest looking woman of about forty, with a caressing, urgent voice, and an appealing manner}*

BARBARA: This is my father, Mrs Baines. [UNDERSHAFT *comes from the table, taking his hat off with marked civility}* Try what you can do with him. He won't listen to me, because he remembers what a fool I was when I was a baby. *{She leaves them together and chats with* JENNY]

MRS BAINES: Have you been shewn over the shelter, Mr Undershaft? You know the work we're doing, of course.

UNDERSHAFT: *{Very civilly}* The whole nation knows it, Mrs Baines.

MRS BAINES: No, sir: the whole nation does not know it, or we should not be crippled as we are for want of money to carry our work through the length and breadth of the land. Let me tell you that there would have been rioting this winter in London but for us.

UNDERSHAFT: You really think so?

MRS BAINES: I know it. I remember 1886, when you rich gentlemen hardened your hearts against the cry of the poor. They broke the windows of your clubs in Pall Mall.

UNDERSHAFT: *{Gleaming with approval of their method}* And the Mansion House Fund went up the next day from thirty thousand pounds to seventy-nine thousand! I remember quite well.

MRS BAINES: Well, won't you help me to get at the people? They won't break windows then. Come here, Price. Let me shew you to this gentleman. [PRICE *comes to be inspected}* Do you remember the window breaking?

PRICE: My ole father thought it was the revolution, ma'am.

MRS BAINES: Would you break windows now?

PRICE: Oh no ma'am. The windows of 'eaven 'av bin opened to me. I know now that the rich man is a sinner like myself.

RUMMY: *{Appearing above at the loft door}* Snobby Price!

SNOBBY: Wot is it?

RUMMY: Your mother's askin' for you at the other gate in Crippses Lane. She's heard about your confession. [PRICE *turns pale}*

MRS BAINES: Go, Mr Price; and pray with her.

JENNY: You can go through the shelter, Snobby.

PRICE: *{To* MRS BAINES] I couldn't face her now, ma'am, with all the weight of my sins fresh on me. Tell her she'll find her son at 'ome, waitin' for her in prayer. *{He skulks off through the gate, incidentally stealing the sovereign on his way out by picking up his cap from the drum}*

MRS BAINES: *{With swimming eyes}* You see how we take the anger and bitterness against you out of their hearts, Mr Undershaft.

UNDERSHAFT: It is certainly most convenient and gratifying to all large employers of labor, Mrs Baines.

MRS BAINES: Barbara: Jenny: I have good news: most wonderful news. [JENNY *runs to her}* My prayers have been answered. I told you they would, Jenny, didn't I?

JENNY: Yes, yes.

BARBARA: *{Moving nearer to the drum}* Have we got money enough to keep the shelter open?

MRS BAINES: I hope we shall have enough to keep all the shelters open. Lord Saxmundham has promised us five thousand pounds—

BARBARA: Hooray!

JENNY: Glory!

MRS BAINES: —if—

BARBARA: "If!" If what?

MRS BAINES: —if five other gentlemen will give a thousand each to make it up to ten thousand.

BARBARA: Who is Lord Saxmundham? I never heard of him.

UNDERSHAFT: *{Who has pricked up his ears at the peer's name, and is now watching* BARBARA *curiously}* A new creation my dear. You have heard of Sir Horace Bodger?

BARBARA: Bodger! Do you mean the distiller? Bodger's whisky!

UNDERSHAFT: That is the man. He is one of the greatest of our public benefactors. He restored the cathedral at Hakington. They made him a baronet for that. He gave half a million to the funds of his party: they made him a baron for that.

SHIRLEY: What will they give him for the five thousand?

UNDERSHAFT: There is nothing left to give him. So the five thousand, I should think, is to save his soul.

MRS BAINES: Heaven grant it may! Oh Mr Undershaft, you have some very rich friends. Can't you help us towards the other five thousand? We are going to hold a great meeting this afternoon at the Assembly Hall in the Mile End Road. If I could only announce that one gentleman had come forward to support Lord Saxmundham, others would follow. Don't you know somebody? couldn't you? wouldn't you? *{Her eyes fill with tears}* oh, think of those poor people, Mr Undershaft: think of how much it means to them, and how little to a great man like you.

UNDERSHAFT: *{Sardonically gallant}* Mrs Baines: you are irresistible. I can't disappoint you; and I can't deny myself the satisfaction of making Bodger pay up. You shall have your five thousand pounds.

MRS BAINES: Thank God!

UNDERSHAFT: You don't thank me?

MRS BAINES: Oh sir, don't try to be cynical: don't be ashamed of being a good man. The Lord will bless you abundantly; and our prayers will be like a strong fortification round you all the days of your life. *{With a touch of caution}* You will let me have the cheque to shew at the meeting, won't you? Jenny: go in and fetch a pen and ink. [JENNY *runs to the shelter door}*

UNDERSHAFT: Do not disturb Miss Hill: I have a fountain pen. [JENNY *halts. He sits at the table and writes the cheque.* CUSINS *rises to make room for him. They all watch him silently}*

BILL: *{Cynically, aside to* BARBARA, *his voice and accent horribly debased}* Wot prawce Selvytion nah?

BARBARA: Stop. [UNDERSHAFT *stops writing: they all turn to her in surprise}* Mrs Baines: are you really going to take this money?

MRS BAINES: *{Astonished}* Why not, dear?

BARBARA: Why not! Do you know what my father is? Have you forgotten that Lord Saxmundham is Bodger the whisky man? Do you remember how we implored the County Council to stop him from writing Bodger's whisky in letters of fire against the sky; so that the poor drink-ruined creatures on the Embankment would not wake up from their snatches of sleep without being reminded of their deadly thirst by that wicked sky sign? Do you know that the worst thing I have had to fight here is not the devil, but Bodger, Bodger, Bodger, with his whisky, his distilleries, and his tied houses? Are you going to make our shelter another tied house for him, and ask me to keep it?

BILL: Rotten dranken whisky it is too.

MRS BAINES: Dear Barbara: Lord Saxmundham has a soul to be saved like any of us. If heaven has found the way to make a good use of his money, are we to set ourselves up against the answer to our prayers?

BARBARA: I know he has a soul to be saved. Let him come down here; and I'll do my best to help him to his salvation. But he wants to send his cheque down to buy us, and go on being as wicked as ever.

UNDERSHAFT: *{With a reasonable-*

ness which CUSINS *alone perceives to be ironical}* My dear Barbara: alcohol is a very necessary article. It heals the sick—

BARBARA: It does nothing of the sort.

UNDERSHAFT: Well, it assists the doctor: that is perhaps a less questionable way of putting it. It makes life bearable to millions of people who could not endure their existence if they were quite sober. It enables Parliament to do things at eleven at night that no sane person would do at eleven in the morning. Is it Bodger's fault that this inestimable gift is deplorably abused by less than one per cent of the poor? *{He turns again to the table; signs the cheque; and crosses it}*

MRS BAINES: Barbara: will there be less drinking or more if all those poor souls we are saving come tomorrow and find the doors of our shelters shut in their faces? Lord Saxmundham gives us the money to stop drinking—to take his own business from him.

CUSINS: *{Impishly}* Pure self-sacrifice on Bodger's part, clearly! Bless dear Bodger! [BARBARA *almost breaks down as Adolphus, too, fails her}*

UNDERSHAFT: *{Tearing out the cheque and pocketing the book as he rises and goes past* CUSINS *to* MRS BAINES] I also, Mrs Baines, may claim a little disinterestedness. Think of my business; think of the widows and orphans! the men and lads torn to pieces with shrapnel and poisoned with lyddite! [MRS BAINES *shrinks; but he goes on remorselessly}* the oceans of blood, not one drop of which is shed in a really just cause! the ravaged crops! the peaceful peasants forced, women and men, to till their fields under the fire of opposing armies on pain of starvation! the bad blood of the fierce little cowards at home who egg on others to fight for the gratification of their national vanity! All this makes money for me: I am never richer, never busier than when the papers are full of it. Well, it is your work to preach peace on earth and goodwill to men. [MRS BAINES's *face lights up again}* Every convert you make is a vote against war. *{Her lips move in prayer}* Yet I give you this money to help you to hasten my own commercial ruin. *{He gives her the cheque}*

CUSINS: *{Mounting the form in an ecstasy of mischief}* The millennium will be inaugurated by the unselfishness of Undershaft and Bodger. Oh be joyful! *{He takes the drumsticks from his pocket and flourishes them}*

MRS BAINES: *{Taking the cheque}* The longer I live the more proof I see that there is an Infinite Goodness that turns everything to the work of salvation sooner or later. Who would have thought that any good could have come out of war and drink? And yet their profits are brought today to the feet of salvation to do its blessed work. *{She is affected to tears}*

JENNY: *{Running to* MRS BAINES *and throwing her arms around her}* Oh dear! how blessed, how glorious it all is!

CUSINS: *{In a convulsion of irony}* Let us seize this unspeakable moment. Let us march to the great meeting at once. Excuse me just an instant. *{He rushes into the shelter.* JENNY *takes her tambourine from the drum head}*

MRS BAINES: Mr Undershaft: have you ever seen a thousand people fall on their knees with one impulse and pray? Come with us to the meeting. Barbara shall tell them that the Army is saved, and saved through you.

CUSINS: *{Returning impetuously from the shelter with a flag and a trombone, and coming between* MRS BAINES *and* UNDERSHAFT] You will carry the flag down the first street, Mrs Baines. *{He gives her the flag}* Mr Undershaft is a gifted trombonist: he shall intone an Olympian diapason to the West Ham Salvation March. *{Aside to* UNDERSHAFT, *as he forces the trombone on him}* Blow, Machiavelli, blow.

UNDERSHAFT: *{Aside to him, as he takes the trombone}* The trumpet in Zion! [CUSINS *rushes to the drum, which he takes up and puts on.* UNDERSHAFT *continues aloud}* I will do my best. I could vamp a bass if I knew the tune.

CUSINS: It is a wedding chorus from one of Donizetti's operas; but we have converted it. We convert everything to good here, including Bodger. You remember the chorus. "For thee immense rejoicing—*immenso giubilo—immenso giubilo.*" *{With drum obligato}* Rum tum ti tum tum, tum tum ti ta—

BARBARA: Dolly: you are breaking my heart.

CUSINS: What is a broken heart more or less here? Dionysos Undershaft has descended. I am possessed.

MRS BAINES: Come, Barbara: I must have my dear Major to carry the flag with me.

JENNY: Yes, yes, Major darling. [CUSINS *snatches the tambourine out of* JENNY's *hand and mutely offers it to* BARBARA]

BARBARA: *{Coming forward a little as she puts the offer behind her with a shudder, whilst* CUSINS *recklessly tosses the tambourine back to* JENNY *and goes to the gate}* I can't come.

JENNY: Not come!

MRS BAINES: *{With tears in her eyes}* Barbara: do you think I am wrong to take the money?

BARBARA: *{Impulsively going to her and kissing her}* No, no: God help you, dear, you must: you are saving the Army. Go; and may you have a great meeting!

JENNY: But aren't you coming?

BARBARA: No. *{She begins taking off the silver S brooch from her collar}*

MRS BAINES: Barbara: what are you doing?

JENNY: Why are you taking your badge off? You can't be going to leave us, Major.

BARBARA: *{Quietly}* Father: come here.

UNDERSHAFT: *{Coming to her}* My dear! *{Seeing that she is going to pin the badge on his collar, he retreats to the penthouse in some alarm}*

BARBARA: *{Following him}* Don't be frightened. *{She pins the badge on and steps back towards the table, shewing him to the others}* There! It's not much for £5000, is it?

MRS BAINES: Barbara: if you won't come and pray with us, promise me you will pray for us.

BARBARA: I can't pray now. Perhaps I shall never pray again.

MRS BAINES: Barbara!

JENNY: Major!

BARBARA: *{Almost delirious}* I can't bear any more. Quick march!

CUSINS: *{Calling to the procession in the street outside}* Off we go. Play up, there! *Immenso giubilo. {He gives the time with his drum; and the band strikes up the march, which rapidly becomes more distant as the procession moves briskly away}*

MRS BAINES: I must go, dear. You're overworked: you will be all right tomorrow. We'll never lose you. Now Jenny: step out with the old flag. Blood and Fire! *{She marches out through the gate with her flag}*

JENNY: Glory Hallelujah! *{Flourishing her tambourine and marching}*

UNDERSHAFT: *{To* CUSINS, *as he marches out past him easing the slide of his trombone}* "My ducats and my daughter"!

BARBARA: Drunkenness and Murder! My God: why hast thou forsaken me? *{She sinks on the form with her face buried in her hands. The march passes away into silence.* BILL WALKER *steals across to her}*

BILL: *{Taunting}* Wot prawce selvytion nah?

SHIRLEY: Don't you hit her when she's down.

BILL: She 'itt me wen aw wiz dahn. Waw shouldn't Aw git a bit o' me aown beck?

BARBARA: *{Raising her head}* I didn't take your money, Bill. *{She crosses the yard to the gate and turns her back on the two men to hide her face from them}*

BILL: *{Sneering after her}* Naow, it warn't enaff for you. *{Turning to the drum, he misses the money}* 'Ellow! If you ain't took it sammun else 'ez. Were's it gorn? Bly me if Jenny 'ill didn't tike it arter all!

RUMMY: *{Screaming at him from the*

loft} You lie, you dirty blackguard! Snobby Price pinched it off the drum when he took up his cap. I was up here all the time an see 'im do it.

BILL: Wot! Stowl maw money! Waw didn't you call thief on him, you silly aold macker you?

RUMMY: To serve you aht for 'ittin me acrost the face. It's cost y'pahnd, that 'az *{Raising a paean of squalid triumph}* I done you. I'm even with you. I've 'ad it aht o'y—[BILL *snatches up* SHIRLEY'S *mug and hurls it at her. She slams the loft door and vanishes. The mug smashes against the door and falls in fragments}*

BILL: *{Beginning to chuckle}* Tell us, aol menn, wot o'clock this mawnin' was it wen 'im as they call Snobby Prawce was sived?

BARBARA: *{Turning to him more composedly, and the unspoiled sweetness}* About half past twelve, Bill. And he pinched your pound at a quarter to two. *I* know. Well, you can't afford to lose it. I'll send it to you.

BILL: *{His voice and accent suddenly improving}* Not if Aw wiz to stawve for it. Aw ain't to be bought.

SHIRLEY: Ain't you? You'd sell yourself to the devil for a pint o' beer; only there ain't no devil to make the offer.

BILL: *{Unashamed}* Sao Aw would, mite, and often 'ev, cheerful. But she cawn't baw me. *{Approaching* BARBARA] You wanted maw saoul, did you? Well, you ain't got it.

BARBARA: I nearly got it, Bill. But we've sold it back to you for ten thousand pounds.

SHIRLEY: And dear at the money!

BARBARA: No, Peter: it was worth more than money.

BILL: *{Salvationproof}* It's nao good: you cawn't get rahnd me nah. Aw down't b'lieve in it; and Aw've seen tod'y that Aw was rawt. *{Going}* Sao long, aol soup-kitchener! Ta, ta, Mijor Earl's Grendorter! *{Turning at the gate}* Wot prawce selvytion nah? Snobby Prawce! Ha! Ha!

BARBARA: *{Offering her hand}* Goodbye, Bill.

BILL: *{Taken aback, half plucks his cap off; then shoves it on again defiantly}* Git aht. [BARBARA *drops her hand, discouraged. He has a twinge of remorse}* But thet's aw rawt, you knaow. Nathink pasn'l. Naow mellice. Sao long, Judy. *{He goes}*

BARBARA: No malice. So long, Bill.

SHIRLEY: *{Shaking his head}* You make too much of him, Miss, in your innocence.

BARBARA: *{Going to him}* Peter: I'm like you now. Cleaned out, and lost my job.

SHIRLEY: You've youth and hope. That's two better than me.

BARBARA: I'll get you a job, Peter. That's hope for you: the youth will have to be enough for me. *{She counts her money}* I have just enough left for two teas at Lockharts, a Rowton doss for you, and my tram and bus home. *{He frowns and rises with offended pride. She takes his arm}* Don't be proud, Peter: it's sharing between friends. And promise me you'll talk to me and not let me cry. *{She draws him towards the gate}*

SHIRLEY: Well, I'm not accustomed to talk to the like of you—

BARBARA: *{Urgently}* Yes, yes: you must talk to me. Tell me about Tom Paine's books and Bradlaugh's lectures. Come along.

SHIRLEY: Ah, if you would only read Tom Paine in the proper spirit, Miss! *{They go out through the gate together}*

END OF ACT II

Act III

Next day after lunch LADY BRITOMART *is writing in the library in Wilton Crescent.* SARAH *is reading in the armchair near the window.* BARBARA, *in ordinary fashion-*

able dress, pale and brooding, is on the settee. CHARLES LOMAX *enters. He starts on seeing* BARBARA *fashionably attired and in low spirits.*

LOMAX: You've left off your uniform! [BARBARA *says nothing; but an expression of pain passes over her face*]

LADY BRITOMART: [*warning him in low tones to be careful*] Charles!

LOMAX: [*Much concerned, coming behind the settee and bending sympathetically over* BARBARA] I'm awfully sorry, Barbara. You know I helped you all I could with the concertina and so forth. [*Momentously*] Still, I have never shut my eyes to the fact that there is a certain amount of tosh about the Salvation Army. Now the claims of the Church of England—

LADY BRITOMART: That's enough, Charles. Speak of something suited to your mental capacity.

LOMAX: *But surely the Church of England is suited to all our capacities.*

BARBARA: [*Pressing his hand*] Thank you for your sympathy, Cholly. Now go and spoon with Sarah.

LOMAX: [*Dragging a chair from the writing table and seating himself affectionately by* SARAH's *side*] How is my ownest today?

SARAH: I wish you wouldn't tell Cholly to do things, Barbara. He always comes straight and does them. Cholly: we're going to the works this afternoon.

LOMAX: What works?

SARAH: The cannon works.

LOMAX: What? Your governor's shop!

SARAH: Yes.

LOMAX: Oh I say! [CUSINS *enters in poor condition. He also starts visibly when he sees* BARBARA *without her uniform*]

BARBARA: I expected you this morning, Dolly. Didn't you guess that?

CUSINS: [*Sitting down beside her*] I'm sorry. I have only just breakfasted.

SARAH: But we've just finished lunch.

BARBARA: Have you had one of your bad nights?

CUSINS: No: I had rather a good night: in fact, one of the most remarkable nights I have ever passed.

BARBARA: The meeting?

CUSINS: No: after the meeting.

LADY BRITOMART: You should have gone to bed after the meeting. What were you doing?

CUSINS: Drinking.

LADY BRITOMART: Adolphus!
SARAH: Dolly!
BARBARA: Dolly!
LOMAX: Oh I say!

LADY BRITOMART: What were you drinking, may I ask?

CUSINS: A most devilish kind of Spanish burgundy, warranted free from added alcohol: a Temperance burgundy in fact. Its richness in natural alcohol made any addition superfluous.

BARBARA: Are you joking, Dolly?

CUSINS: [*Patiently*] No. I have been making a night of it with the nominal head of this household: that is all.

LADY BRITOMART: Andrew made you drunk!

CUSINS: No: he only provided the wine. I think it was Dionysos who made me drunk. [*To* BARBARA] I told you I was possessed.

LADY BRITOMART: You're not sober yet. Go home to bed at once.

CUSINS: I have never before ventured to reproach you, Lady Brit; but how could you marry the Prince of Darkness?

LADY BRITOMART: It was much more excusable to marry him than to get drunk with him. That is a new accomplishment of Andrew's, by the way. He usen't to drink.

CUSINS: He doesn't now. He only sat there and completed the wreck of my moral basis, the rout of my convictions, the purchase of my soul. He cares for you, Barbara. That is what makes him so dangerous to me.

BARBARA: That has nothing to do with it, Dolly. There are larger loves and diviner dreams than the fireside ones. You know that, don't you?

CUSINS: Yes: that is our understanding. I know it. I hold to it. Unless he can win me on that holier ground he may amuse me for a while; but he can get no deeper hold, strong as he is.

BARBARA: Keep to that; and the end will be right. Now tell me what happened at the meeting?

CUSINS: It was an amazing meeting. Mrs Baines almost died of emotion. Jenny Hill simply gibbered with hysteria. The Prince of Darkness played his trombone like a madman: its brazen roarings were like the laughter of the damned. 117 conversions took place then and there. They prayed with the most touching sincerity and gratitude for Bodger, and for the anonymous donor of the £5000. Your father would not let his name be given.

LOMAX: That was rather fine of the old man, you know. Most chaps would have wanted the advertisement.

CUSINS: He said the charitable institutions would be down on him like kites on a battle field if he gave his name.

LADY BRITOMART: That's Andrew all over. He never does a proper thing without giving an improper reason for it.

CUSINS: He convinced me that I have all my life been doing improper things for proper reasons.

LADY BRITOMART: Adolphus: now that Barbara has left the Salvation Army, you had better leave it too. I will not have you playing that drum in the streets.

CUSINS: Your orders are already obeyed, Lady Brit.

BARBARA: Dolly: were you ever really in earnest about it? Would you have joined if you had never seen me?

CUSINS: *{Disingenuously}* Well—er—well, possibly, as a collector of religions—

LOMAX: *{Cunningly}* Not as a drummer, though, you know. You are a very clearheaded brainy chap, Dolly; and it must have been apparent to you that there is a certain amount of tosh about—

LADY BRITOMART: Charles: if you must drivel, drivel like a grown-up man and not like a schoolboy.

LOMAX: *{Out of countenance}* Well, drivel is drivel, don't you know, whatever a man's age.

LADY BRITOMART: In good society in England, Charles, men drivel at all ages by repeating silly formulas with an air of wisdom. Schoolboys make their own formulas out of slang, like you. When they reach your age, and get political private secretaryships and things of that sort, they drop slang and get their formulas out of *The Spectator* or *The Times*. You had better confine yourself to *The Times*. You will find that there is a certain amount of tosh about *The Times*; but at least its language is reputable.

LOMAX: *{Overwhelmed}* You are so awfully strong-minded, Lady Brit—

LADY BRITOMART: Rubbish! [MORRISON *comes in}* What is it?

MORRISON: If you please, my lady, Mr Undershaft has just drove up to the door.

LADY BRITOMART: Well, let him in. [MORRISON *hesitates}* What's the matter with you?

MORRISON: Shall I announce him, my lady; or is he at home here, so to speak, my lady?

LADY BRITOMART: Announce him.

MORRISON: Thank you, my lady. You won't mind my asking, I hope. The occasion is in a manner of speaking new to me.

LADY BRITOMART: Quite right. Go and let him in.

MORRISON: Thank you, my lady. *{He withdraws}*

LADY BRITOMART: Children: go and get ready. [SARAH *and* BARBARA *go upstairs for their out-of-door wraps}* Charles: go and tell Stephen to come down here in five minutes: you will find him in the drawing room. [CHARLES *goes}* Adolphus: tell them to send round the carriage in about fifteen minutes. [ADOLPHUS *goes}*

MORRISON: *{At the door}* Mr Undershaft. [UNDERSHAFT *comes in.* MORRISON *goes out*]

UNDERSHAFT: Alone! How fortunate!

LADY BRITOMART: *(Rising)* Don't be sentimental, Andrew. Sit down. *(She sits on the settee: he sits down beside her, on her left. She comes to the point before he has time to breathe)* Sarah must have £800 a year until Charles Lomax comes into his property. Barbara will need more, and need it permanently, because Adolphus hasn't any property.

UNDERSHAFT: *(Resignedly)* Yes, my dear: I will see to it. Anything else? for yourself, for instance?

LADY BRITOMART: I want to talk to you about Stephen.

UNDERSHAFT: *(Rather wearily)* Don't, my dear. Stephen doesn't interest me.

LADY BRITOMART: He does interest me. He is our son.

UNDERSHAFT: Do you really think so? He has induced us to bring him into the world; but he chose his parents very incongruously, I think. I see nothing of myself in him, and less of you.

LADY BRITOMART: Andrew: Stephen is an excellent son, and a most steady, capable, highminded young man. You are simply trying to find an excuse for disinheriting him.

UNDERSHAFT: My dear Biddy: the Undershaft tradition disinherits him. It would be dishonest of me to leave the cannon foundry to my son.

LADY BRITOMART: It would be most unnatural and improper of you to leave it to anyone else, Andrew. Do you suppose this wicked and immoral tradition can be kept up for ever? Do you pretend that Stephen could not carry on the foundry just as well as all the other sons of the big business houses?

UNDERSHAFT: Yes: he could learn the office routine without understanding the business, like all the other sons; and the firm would go on by its own momentum until the real Undershaft—probably an Italian or a German—would invent a new method and cut him out.

LADY BRITOMART: There is nothing that any Italian or German could do that Stephen could not do. And Stephen at least has breeding.

UNDERSHAFT: The son of a foundling! Nonsense!

LADY BRITOMART: My son, Andrew! And even you may have good blood in your veins for all you know.

UNDERSHAFT: True. Probably I have. That is another argument in favor of a foundling.

LADY BRITOMART: Andrew: don't be aggravating. And don't be wicked. At present you are both.

UNDERSHAFT: This conversation is part of the Undershaft tradition, Biddy. Every Undershaft's wife has treated him to it ever since the house was founded. It is mere waste of breath. If the tradition be ever broken it will be for an abler man than Stephen.

LADY BRITOMART: *(Pouting)* Then go away.

UNDERSHAFT: *(Deprecatory)* Go away!

LADY BRITOMART: Yes: go away. If you will do nothing for Stephen, you are not wanted here. Go to your foundling, whoever he is; and look after him.

UNDERSHAFT: The fact is, Biddy—

LADY BRITOMART: Don't call me Biddy. I don't call you Andy.

UNDERSHAFT: I will not call my wife Britomart: it is not good sense. Seriously, my love, the Undershaft tradition has landed me in a difficulty. I am getting on in years; and my partner Lazarus has at last made a stand and insisted that the succession must be settled one way or the other; and of course he is quite right. You see, I haven't found a fit successor yet.

LADY BRITOMART: *(Obstinately)* There is Stephen.

UNDERSHAFT: That's just it: all the foundlings I can find are exactly like Stephen.

LADY BRITOMART: Andrew!

UNDERSHAFT: I want a man with no relations and no schooling: that is, a man who would be out of the running altogether if he were not a strong man. And I can't find him. Every blessed foundling nowadays is snapped up in his infancy by Bernardo homes or School Board officers, or Boards of Guardians; and if he shews the least ability, he is fastened on by schoolmasters; trained to win scholarships like a racehorse; crammed with secondhand ideas; drilled and disciplined in docility and what they call good taste; and lamed for life so that he is fit for nothing but teaching. If you want to keep the foundry in the family, you had better find an eligible foundling and marry him to Barbara.

LADY BRITOMART: Ah! Barbara! Your pet! You would sacrifice Stephen to Barbara.

UNDERSHAFT: Cheerfully. And you, my dear, would boil Barbara to make soup for Stephen.

LADY BRITOMART: Andrew: this is not a question of our likings and dislikings: it is a question of duty. It is your duty to make Stephen your successor.

UNDERSHAFT: Just as much as it is your duty to submit to your husband. Come, Biddy! these tricks of the governing class are of no use with me. I am one of the governing class myself; and it is waste of time giving tracts to a missionary. I have the power in this matter; and I am not to be humbugged into using it for your purposes.

LADY BRITOMART: Andrew: you can talk my head off; but you can't change wrong into right. And your tie is all on one side. Put it straight.

UNDERSHAFT: *{Disconcerted}* It won't stay unless it's pinned—*{He fumbles at it with childish grimaces.* STEPHEN *comes in}*

STEPHEN: *{At the door}* I beg your pardon. *{About to retire}*

LADY BRITOMART: No: come in, Stephen. [STEPHEN *comes forward to his mother's writing table}*

UNDERSHAFT: *{Not very cordially}* Good afternoon.

STEPHEN: *{Coldly}* Good afternoon.

UNDERSHAFT: *{To* LADY BRITOMART] He knows all about the tradition, I suppose?

LADY BRITOMART: Yes. *{To* STEPHEN] It is what I told you last night, Stephen.

UNDERSHAFT: *{Sulkily}* I understand you want to come into the cannon business.

STEPHEN: *I* go into trade! Certainly not.

UNDERSHAFT: *{Opening his eyes, greatly eased in mind and manner}* Oh! in that case—

LADY BRITOMART: Cannons are not trade, Stephen. They are enterprise.

STEPHEN: I have no intention of becoming a man of business in any sense. I have no capacity for business and no taste for it. I intend to devote myself to politics.

UNDERSHAFT: *{Rising}* My dear boy: this is an immense relief to me. And I trust it may prove an equally good thing for the country. I was afraid you would consider yourself disparaged and slighted. *{He moves towards* STEPHEN *as if to shake hands with him}*

LADY BRITOMART: *{Rising and interposing}* Stephen: I cannot allow you to throw away an enormous property like this.

STEPHEN: *{Stiffly}* Mother: there must be an end of treating me as a child, if you please. [LADY BRITOMART *recoils, deeply wounded by his tone}* Until last night I did not take your attitude seriously, because I did not think you meant it seriously. But I find now that you left me in the dark as to matters which you should have explained to me years ago. I am extremely hurt and offended. Any further discussion of my intentions had better take place with my father, as between one man and another.

LADY BRITOMART: Stephen! *{She sits*

down again, her eyes filling with tears}

UNDERSHAFT: *{With grave compassion}* You see, my dear, it is only the big men who can be treated as children.

STEPHEN: I am sorry, mother, that you have forced me—

UNDERSHAFT: *{Stopping him}* Yes, yes, yes, yes: that's all right, Stephen. She won't interfere with you any more: your independence is achieved: you have won your watchkey. Don't rub it in; and above all, don't apologize. *{He resumes his seat}* Now what about your future, as between one man and another—I beg your pardon, Biddy: as between two men and a woman.

LADY BRITOMART: *{Who has pulled herself together strongly}* I quite understand, Stephen. By all means go your own way if you feel strong enough. [STEPHEN *sits down magisterially in the chair at the writing table with an air of affirming his majority}*

UNDERSHAFT: It is settled that you do not ask for the succession to the cannon business.

STEPHEN: I hope it is settled that I repudiate the cannon business.

UNDERSHAFT: Come, come! don't be so devilishly sulky: it's boyish. Freedom should be generous. Besides, I owe you a fair start in life in exchange for disinheriting you. You can't become prime minister all at once. Haven't you a turn for something? What about literature, art, and so forth?

STEPHEN: I have nothing of the artist about me, either in faculty or character, thank Heaven!

UNDERSHAFT: A philosopher, perhaps? Eh?

STEPHEN: I make no such ridiculous pretension.

UNDERSHAFT: Just so. Well, there is the army, the navy, the Church, the Bar. The Bar requires some ability. What about the Bar?

STEPHEN: I have not studied law. And I am afraid I have not the necessary push—I believe that is the name barristers give to their vulgarity—for success in pleading.

UNDERSHAFT: Rather a difficult case, Stephen. Hardly anything left but the stage, is there? [STEPHEN *makes an impatient movement}* Well, come! is there anything you know or care for?

STEPHEN: *{Rising and looking at him steadily}* I know the difference between right and wrong.

UNDERSHAFT: *{Hugely tickled}* You don't say so! What! no capacity for business, no knowledge of law, no sympathy with art, no pretension to philosophy; only a simple knowledge of the secret that has puzzled all the philosophers, baffled all the lawyers, muddled all the men of business, and ruined most of the artists: the secret of right and wrong. Why, man, you're a genius, a master of masters, a god! At twenty-four, too!

STEPHEN: *{Keeping his temper with difficulty}* You are pleased to be facetious. I pretend to nothing more than any honorable English gentleman claims as his birthright. *{He sits down angrily}*

UNDERSHAFT: Oh, that's everybody's birthright. Look at poor little Jenny Hill, the Salvation lassie! She would think you were laughing at her if you asked her to stand up in the street and teach grammar or geography or mathematics or even drawing room dancing; but it never occurs to her to doubt that she can teach morals and religion. You are all alike, you respectable people. You can't tell me the bursting strain of a ten-inch gun, which is a very simple matter; but you all think you can tell me the bursting strain of a man under temptation. You daren't handle high explosives; but you're all ready to handle honesty and truth and justice and the whole duty of man, and kill one another at that game. What a country! What a world!

LADY BRITOMART: *{Uneasily}* What do you think he had better do, Andrew?

UNDERSHAFT: Oh, just what he wants to do. He knows nothing and he thinks he knows everything. That points clearly to a political career. Get him a private secretaryship to someone who can get him an Under Secretaryship; and then leave him alone. He will find his natural and proper place in the end on the Treasury Bench.

STEPHEN: *{Springing up again}* I am sorry, sir, that you force me to forget the respect due to you as my father. I am an Englishman and I will not hear the Government of my country insulted. *{He thrusts his hands in his pockets, and walks angrily across to the window}*

UNDERSHAFT: *{With a touch of brutality}* The government of your country! *I* am the government of your country: I, and Lazarus. Do you suppose that you and half a dozen amateurs like you, sitting in a row in that foolish gabble shop, can govern Undershaft and Lazarus? No, my friend: you will do what pays us. You will make war when it suits us, and keep peace when it doesn't. You will find out that trade requires certain measures when we have decided on those measures. When I want anything to keep my dividends up, you will discover that my want is a national need. When other people want something to keep my dividends down, you will call out the police and military. And in return you shall have the support and applause of my newspapers, and the delight of imagining that you are a great statesman. Government of your country! Be off with you, my boy, and play with your caucuses and leading articles and historic parties and great leaders and burning questions and the rest of your toys. *I* am going back to my counting house to pay the piper and call the tune.

STEPHEN: *{Actually smiling, and putting his hand on his father's shoulder with indulgent patronage}* Really, my dear father, it is impossible to be angry with you. You don't know how absurd all this sounds to me. You are very properly proud of having been industrious enough to make money; and it is greatly to your credit that you have made so much of it. But it has kept you in circles where you are valued for your money and deferred to for it, instead of in the doubtless very old-fashioned and behind-the-times public school and university where I formed my habits of mind. It is natural for you to think that money governs England; but you must allow me to think I know better.

UNDERSHAFT: And what does govern England, pray?

STEPHEN: Character, father, character.

UNDERSHAFT: Whose character? Yours or mine?

STEPHEN: Neither yours nor mine, father, but the best elements in the English national character.

UNDERSHAFT: Stephen: I've found your profession for you. You're a born journalist. I'll start you with a hightoned weekly review. There! *{Before* STEPHEN *can reply* SARAH, BARBARA, LOMAX, *and* CUSINS *come in ready for walking.* BARBARA *crosses the room to the window and looks out.* CUSINS *drifts amiably to the armchair.* LOMAX *remains near the door, whilst* SARAH *comes to her mother.*

STEPHEN *goes to the smaller writing table and busies himself with his letters}*

SARAH: Go and get ready, mamma: the carriage is waiting. [LADY BRITOMART *leaves the room}*

UNDERSHAFT: *{To* SARAH] Good day, my dear. Good afternoon, Mr Lomax.

LOMAX: *{Vaguely}* Ahdedoo.

UNDERSHAFT: *{To* CUSINS] Quite well after last night, Euripides, eh?

CUSINS: As well as can be expected.

UNDERSHAFT: That's right. *{To* BARBARA] So you are coming to see my death and devastation factory, Barbara?

BARBARA: *{At the window}* You came yesterday to see my salvation factory. I promised you a return visit.

LOMAX: *{Coming forward between* SARAH *and* UNDERSHAFT] You'll find it awfully interesting. I've been through the Woolwich Arsenal; and it gives you a ripping feeling of security, you know, to think of the lot of beggars we could kill if it came to fighting. *{To* UNDERSHAFT, *with sudden solemnity}* Still, it must be rather an awful reflection for you, from the religious point of view as it were. You're getting on, you know, and all that.

SARAH: You don't mind Cholly's imbecility, papa, do you?

LOMAX: *{Much taken aback}* Oh I say!

UNDERSHAFT: Mr Lomax looks at the matter in a very proper spirit, my dear.

LOMAX: Just so. That's all I meant, I assure you.

SARAH: Are you coming, Stephen?

STEPHEN: Well, I am rather busy—er— *{Magnanimously}* Oh well, yes: I'll come. That is, if there is room for me.

UNDERSHAFT: I can take two with me in a little motor I am experimenting with for field use. You won't mind its being rather unfashionable. It's not painted yet; but it's bullet proof.

LOMAX: *{Appalled at the prospect of confronting Wilton Crescent in an unpainted motor}* Oh I say!

SARAH: The carriage for me, thank you. Barbara doesn't mind what she's seen in.

LOMAX: I say, Dolly old chap: do you really mind the car being a guy? Because of course if you do I'll go in it. Still—

CUSINS: I prefer it.

LOMAX: Thanks awfully, old man. Come, my ownest. *{He hurries out to secure his seat in the carriage.* SARAH *follows him}*

CUSINS: *{Moodily walking across to* LADY BRITOMART's *writing table}* Why are we two coming to this Works Department of Hell? that is what I ask myself.

BARBARA: I have always thought of it as a sort of pit where lost creatures with blackened faces stirred up smoky fires and were driven and tormented by my father. Is it like that, dad?

UNDERSHAFT: *{Scandalized}* My dear! It is a spotlessly clean and beautiful hillside town.

CUSINS: With a Methodist chapel? Oh do say there's a Methodist chapel.

UNDERSHAFT: There are two: a Primitive one and a sophisticated one. There is even an Ethical Society; but it is not much patronized, as my men are all strongly religious. In the High Explosives Sheds they object to the presence of Agnostics as unsafe.

CUSINS: And yet they don't object to you!

BARBARA: Do they obey all your orders?

UNDERSHAFT: I never give them any orders. When I speak to one of them it is "Well, Jones, is the baby doing well? and has Mrs Jones made a good recovery?" "Nicely, thank you, sir." And that's all.

CUSINS: But Jones has to be kept in order. How do you maintain discipline among your men?

UNDERSHAFT: I don't. They do. You see, the one thing Jones won't stand is any rebellion from the man under him, or any assertion of social equality between the wife of the man with 4 shillings a week less than himself, and Mrs Jones! Of course they all rebel against me, theoretically. Practically, every man of them keeps the man just below him in his place. I never meddle with them. I never bully them. I don't even bully Lazarus. I say that certain things are to be done; but I don't order anybody to do them. I don't say, mind you, that there is no ordering about and snubbing and even bullying. The men snub the boys and order them about; the carmen snub the sweepers; the artisans snub the unskilled laborers; the foremen drive and bully both the laborers and artisans; the assistant engineers find fault with the foremen; the chief engineers drop on the assistants; the departmental managers worry the chiefs; and the clerks have tall hats and hymnbooks and keep up the social tone by refusing to associate on equal terms with anybody. The result is a colossal profit, which comes to me.

CUSINS: *{Revolted}* You really are a —well, what I was saying yesterday.

BARBARA: What was he saying yesterday?

UNDERSHAFT: Never mind, my dear.

He thinks I have made you unhappy. Have I?

BARBARA: Do you think I can be happy in this vulgar silly dress? I! who have worn the uniform. Do you understand what you have done to me? Yesterday I had a man's soul in my hand. I set him in the way of life with his face to salvation. But when we took your money he turned back to drunkenness and derision. *{With intense conviction}* I will never forgive you that. If I had a child, and you destroyed its body with your explosives—if you murdered Dolly with your horrible guns—I could forgive you if my forgiveness would open the gates of heaven to you. But to take a human soul from me, and turn it into the soul of a wolf! that is worse than any murder.

UNDERSHAFT: Does my daughter despair so easily? Can you strike a man to the heart and leave no mark on him?

BARBARA: *{Her face lighting up}* Oh, you are right: he can never be lost now: where was my faith?

CUSINS: Oh, clever clever devil!

BARBARA: You may be a devil; but God speaks through you sometimes. *{She takes her father's hands and kisses them}* You have given me back my happiness: I feel it deep down now, though my spirit is troubled.

UNDERSHAFT: You have learnt something. That always feels at first as if you had lost something.

BARBARA: Well, take me to the factory of death; and let me learn something more. There must be some truth or other behind all this frightful irony. Come, Dolly. *{She goes out}*

CUSINS: My guardian angel! *{To* UNDERSHAFT] Avaunt! *{He follows* BARBARA]

STEPHEN: *{Quietly, at the writing table}* You must not mind Cusins, father. He is a very amiable good fellow; but he is a Greek scholar and naturally a little eccentric.

UNDERSHAFT: Ah, quite so. Thank you, Stephen. Thank you. *{He goes out.* STEPHEN *smiles patronizingly; buttons his coat responsibly; and crosses the room to the door.* LADY BRITOMART, *dressed for out-of-doors, opens it before he reaches it. She looks around for the others; looks at* STEPHEN; *and turns to go without a word}*

STEPHEN: *{Embarrassed}* Mother—

LADY BRITOMART: Don't be apologetic, Stephen. And don't forget that you have outgrown your mother. *{he goes out}*

{Perivale St Andrews lies between two Middlesex hills, half climbing the northern one. It is an almost smokeless town of white walls, roofs of narrow green slates or red tiles, tall trees, domes, campaniles, and slender chimney shafts, beautifully situated and beautiful in itself. The best view of it is obtained from the crest of a slope about half a mile to the east, where the high explosives are dealt with. The foundry lies hidden in the depths between, the tops of its chimneys sprouting like huge skittles into the middle distance. Across the crest runs an emplacement of concrete, with a firestep, and a parapet which suggests a fortification, because there is a huge cannon of the obsolete Woolwich Infant pattern peering across it at the town. The cannon is mounted on an experimental gun carriage: possibly the original model of the Undershaft disappearing rampart gun alluded to by Stephen. The firestep, being a convenient place to sit, is furnished here and there with straw disc cushions; and at one place there is the additional luxury of a fur rug.

BARBARA *is standing on the firestep, looking over the parapet towards the town. On her right is the cannon; on her left the end of a shed raised on piles, with a ladder of three or four steps up to the door, which opens outwards and has a little wooden landing at the threshold, with a fire bucket in the corner of the landing. Several dummy soldiers more or less mutilated, with straw protruding from their gashes, have been shoved out of the way under the landing. A few others are nearly upright against the shed; and one has fallen forward and lies, like a grotesque corpse, on the emplacement. The parapet stops short of the shed, leaving a gap which is the beginning of the path down the hill through the foundry to the town. The rug is on the firestep near this gap. Down on the emplacement behind the cannon is a trolley carrying a huge conical bombshell with a red band painted on it. Further to the right is the door of an office, which, like the sheds, is of the lightest possible construction.* CUSINS *arrives by the path from the town}*

BARBARA: Well?

CUSINS: Not a ray of hope. Everything perfect! wonderful! real! It only needs a cathedral to be a heavenly city instead of a hellish one.

BARBARA: Have you found out whether they have done anything for old Peter Shirley?

CUSINS: They have found him a job as gatekeeper and timekeeper. He's frightfully miserable. He calls the timekeeping brainwork, and says he isn't used to it; and his gate lodge is so splendid that he's ashamed to use the rooms, and skulks in the scullery.

BARBARA: Poor Peter! {STEPHEN *arrives from the town. He carries a field-glass}*

STEPHEN: *{Enthusiastically}* Have you two seen the place? Why did you leave us?

CUSINS: I wanted to see everything I was not intended to see; and Barbara wanted to make the men talk.

STEPHEN: Have you found anything discreditable?

CUSINS: No. They call him Dandy Andy and are proud of his being a cunning old rascal; but it's all horribly, frightfully, immorally, unanswerably perfect. {SARAH *arrives}*

SARAH: Heavens! what a place! *{She crosses to the trolley}* Did you see the nursing home! *{She sits down on the shell}*

STEPHEN: Did you see the libraries and schools?

SARAH: Did you see the ball room and the banqueting chamber in the Town Hall?

STEPHEN: Have you gone into the insurance fund, the pension fund, the building society, the various applications of cooperation!? {UNDERSHAFT *comes from the office, with a sheaf of telegrams in his hand}*

UNDERSHAFT: Well, have you seen everything? I'm sorry I was called away. *{Indicating the telegrams}* Good news from Manchuria.

STEPHEN: Another Japanese victory?

UNDERSHAFT: Oh, I don't know. Which side wins does not concern us here. No: the good news is that the aerial battleship is a tremendous success. At the first trial it has wiped out a fort with three hundred soldiers in it.

CUSINS: *{From the platform}* Dummy *soldiers?*

UNDERSHAFT: *{Striding across to* STEPHEN *and kicking the prostrate dummy brutally out of his way}* No: the real thing. {CUSINS *and* BARBARA *exchange glances. Then* CUSINS *sits on the step and buries his face in his hands.* BARBARA *gravely lays her hand on his shoulder. He looks up at her in whimsical desperation}*

UNDERSHAFT: Well, Stephen, what do you think of the place?

STEPHEN: Oh, magnificent. A perfect triumph of modern industry. Frankly, my dear father, I have been a fool: I had no idea of what it all meant: of the wonderful forethought, the power of organization, the administrative capacity, the financial genius, the colossal capital it represents. I have been repeating to myself as I came through your streets "Peace hath her victories no less renowned than War." I have only one misgiving about it all.

UNDERSHAFT: Out with it.

STEPHEN: Well, I cannot help thinking that all this provision for every want of your workmen may sap their independence and weaken their sense of responsibility. And greatly as we enjoyed our tea at that splendid restaurant —how they gave us all that luxury and cake and jam and cream for threepence I really cannot imagine!—still you must remember that restaurants break up home life. Look at the continent, for instance! Are you sure so much pampering is really good for the men's characters?

UNDERSHAFT: Well you see, my dear boy, when you are organizing civilization you have to make up your mind whether trouble and anxiety are good things or not. If you decide that they are, then, I take it, you simply don't organize civilization; and there you are, with trouble and anxiety enough to make us all angels! But if you decide the other way, you may as well go through with it. However, Stephen, our characters are safe here. A sufficient dose of anxiety is always provided by the fact that we may be blown to smithereens at any moment.

SARAH: By the way, papa, where do you make the explosives?

UNDERSHAFT: In separate little sheds, like that one. When one of them blows up, it costs very little; and only the people quite close to it are killed. [STEPHEN, *who is quite close to it, looks at it rather scaredly, and moves away quickly to the cannon. At the same moment the door of the shed is thrown abruptly open; and a foreman in overalls and list slippers comes out on the little landing and holds the door for* LOMAX, *who appears in the doorway*}

LOMAX: {*With studied coolness*} My good fellow: you needn't get into a state of nerves. Nothing's going to happen to you; and I suppose it wouldn't be the end of the world if anything did. A little bit of British pluck is what you want, old chap. {*He descends and strolls across to* SARAH]

UNDERSHAFT: {*To the foreman*} Anything wrong, Bilton?

BILTON: {*With ironic calm*} Gentleman walked into the high explosives shed and lit a cigaret, sir: that's all.

UNDERSHAFT: Ah, quite so. {*Going over to* LOMAX] Do you happen to remember what you did with the match?

LOMAX: Oh come! I'm not a fool. I took jolly good care to blow it out before I chucked it away.

BILTON: The top of it was red hot inside, sir.

LOMAX: Well, suppose it was! I didn't chuck it into any of your messes.

UNDERSHAFT: Think no more of it, Mr Lomax. By the way, would you mind lending me your matches?

LOMAX: {*Offering his box*} Certainly.

UNDERSHAFT: Thanks. {*He pockets the matches*}

LOMAX: {*Lecturing to the company generally*} You know, these high explosives don't go off like gunpowder, except when they're in a gun. When they're spread loose, you can put a match to them without the least risk: they just burn quietly like a bit of paper. {*Warming to the scientific interest of the subject*} Did you know that, Undershaft? Have you ever tried?

UNDERSHAFT: Not on a large scale, Mr Lomax. Bilton will give you a sample of gun cotton when you are leaving if you ask him. You can exeperiment with it at home. [BILTON *looks puzzled*}

SARAH: Bilton will do nothing of the sort, papa. I suppose it's your business to blow up the Russians and Japs; but you might really stop short of blowing up poor Cholly. [BILTON *gives it up and retires into the shed*}

LOMAX: My ownest, there is no danger. {*He sits beside her on the shell;* LADY BRITOMART *arrives from the town with a bouquet*}

LADY BRITOMART: {*Impetuously*} Andrew: you shouldn't have let me see this place.

UNDERSHAFT: Why, my dear?

LADY BRITOMART: Never mind why: you shouldn't have: that's all. To think of all that {*Indicating the town*} being yours! and that you have kept it to yourself all these years!

UNDERSHAFT: It does not belong to me. I belong to it. It is the Undershaft inheritance.

LADY BRITOMART: It is not. Your ridiculous cannons and that noisy banging foundry may be the Undershaft inheritance; but all that plate and linen, all that furniture and those houses and orchards and gardens belong to us. They belong to me: they are not a man's business. I won't give them up. You must be out of your senses to throw them all away; and if you persist in such folly, I will call in a doctor.

UNDERSHAFT: *{Stooping to smell the bouquet}* Where did you get the flowers my dear?

LADY BRITOMART: Your men presented them to me on your William Morris Labor Church.

CUSINS: Oh! It needed only that. A Labor Church! *{He mounts the firestep distractedly, and leans with his elbows on the parapet, turning his back to them}*

LADY BRITOMART: Yes, with Morris's words in mosaic letters ten feet high round the dome. NO MAN IS GOOD ENOUGH TO BE ANOTHER MAN'S MASTER. The cynicism of it!

UNDERSHAFT: It shocked the men at first, I am afraid. But now they take no more notice of it than of the ten commandments in church.

LADY BRITOMART: Andrew: you are trying to put me off the subject of the inheritance by profane jokes. Well, you shan't. I don't ask it any longer for Stephen: he has inherited far too much of your perversity to be fit for it. But Barbara has rights as well as Stephen. Why should not Adolphus succeed to the inheritance? I could manage the town for him; and he can look after the cannons, if they are really necessary.

UNDERSHAFT: I should ask nothing better if Adolphus were a foundling. He is exactly the sort of new blood that is wanted in English business, But he's not a foundling; and there's an end of it. *{He makes for the office door}*

CUSINS: *{Turning to them}* Not quite. *{They all turn and stare at him}* I think— Mind! I am not committing myself in any way as to my future course —but I think the foundling difficulty can be got over. *{He jumps down to the emplacement}*

UNDERSHAFT: *{Coming back to him}* What do you mean?

CUSINS: Well, I have something to say which is in the nature of a confession.

SARAH:
LADY BRITOMART:
BARBARA:
STEPHEN:
} Confession!

LOMAX: Oh I say!

CUSINS: Yes, a confession. Listen, all. Until I met Barbara I thought myself in the main an honorable, truthful man, because I wanted the approval of my conscience more than I wanted anything else. But the moment I saw Barbara, I wanted her far more than the approval of my conscience.

LADY BRITOMART: Adolphus!

CUSINS: It is true. You accused me yourself, Lady Brit, of joining the Army to worship Barbara; and so I did. She bought my soul like a flower at a street corner; but she bought it for herself.

UNDERSHAFT: What! Not for Dionysos or another?

CUSINS: Dionysos and all the others are in herself. I adored what was divine in her, and was therefore a true worshipper. But I was romantic about her too. I thought she was a woman of the people, and that a marriage with a professor of Greek would be far beyond the wildest social ambitions of her rank.

LADY BRITOMART: Adolphus!!

CUSINS: When I learnt the horrible truth—

LADY BRITOMART: What do you mean by the horrible truth, pray?

CUSINS: That she was enormously rich; that her grandfather was an earl; that her father was the Prince of Darkness—

UNDERSHAFT: Chut!

CUSINS: —and that I was only an

adventurer trying to catch a rich wife, then I stooped to deceive her about my birth.

BARBARA: *{Rising}* Dolly!

LADY BRITOMART: Your birth! Now Adolphus, don't dare to make up a wicked story for the sake of these wretched cannons. Remember: I have seen photographs of your parents; and the Agent General for South Western Australia knows them personally and has assured me that they are most respectable married people.

CUSINS: So they are in Australia; but here they are outcasts. Their marriage is legal in Australia, but not in England. My mother is my father's deceased wife's sister; and in this island I am consequently a foundling. *{Sensation}*

BARBARA: Silly! *{She climbs to the cannon, and leans, listening, in the angle it makes with the parapet}*

CUSINS: Is the subterfuge good enough, Machiavelli?

UNDERSHAFT: *{Thoughtfully}* Biddy: this may be a way out of the difficulty.

LADY BRITOMART: Stuff! A man can't make cannons any the better for being his own cousin instead of his proper self. *{She sits down on the rug with a bounce that expresses her downright contempt for their casuistry}*

UNDERSHAFT: *{To* CUSINS] You are an educated man. That is against the tradition.

CUSINS: Once in ten thousand times it happens that the schoolboy is a born master of what they try to teach him. Greek has not destroyed my mind: it has nourished it. Besides, I did not learn it at an English public school.

UNDERSHAFT: Hm! Well, I cannot afford to be too particular: you have cornered the foundling market. Let it pass. You are eligible, Euripides: you are eligible.

BARBARA: Dolly: yesterday morning, when Stephen told us all about the tradition, you became very silent; and you have been strange and excited ever since. Were you thinking about your birth then?

CUSINS: When the finger of Destiny suddenly points at a man in the middle of his breakfast, it makes him thoughtful.

UNDERSHAFT: Aha! You have had your eye on the business, my young friend, have you?

CUSINS: Take care! There is an abyss of moral horror between me and your accursed aerial battleships.

UNDERSHAFT: Never mind the abyss for the present. Let us settle the practical details and leave your final decision open. You know that you will have to change your name. Do you object to that?

CUSINS: Would any man named Adolphus—any man called Dolly!—object to be called something else?

UNDERSHAFT: Good. Now, as to money! I propose to treat you handsomely from the beginning. You shall start at a thousand a year.

CUSINS: *{With sudden heat, his spectacles twinkling with mischief}* A thousand! You dare offer a miserable thousand to the son-in-law of a millionaire! No, by Heavens, Machiavelli! you shall not cheat me. You cannot do without me; and I can do without you. I must have two thousand five hundred a year for two years. At the end of that time, if I am a failure, I go. But if I am a success, and stay on, you must give me the other five thousand.

UNDERSHAFT: What other five thousand?

CUSINS: To make the two years up to five thousand a year. The two thousand five hundred is only half pay in case I should turn out a failure. The third year I must have ten per cent of the profits.

UNDERSHAFT: *{Taken aback}* Ten per cent! Why, man, do you know what my profits are?

CUSINS: Enormous, I hope: otherwise I shall require twenty-five per cent.

UNDERSHAFT: But, Mr Cusins, this is a serious matter of business. You are not bringing any capital into the concern.

CUSINS: What! no capital! Is my

mastery of Greek no capital? Is my access to the subtlest thought, the loftiest poetry yet attained by humanity, no capital? My character! my intellect! my life! my career! what Barbara calls my soul! are these no capital? Say another word; and I double my salary.

UNDERSHAFT: Be reasonable—

CUSINS: *{Peremptorily}* Mr Undershaft: you have my terms. Take them or leave them.

UNDERSHAFT: *{Recovering himself}* Very well. I note your terms; and I offer you half.

CUSINS: *{Disgustedly}* Half!

UNDERSHAFT: *{Firmly}* Half.

CUSINS: You call yourself a gentleman; and you offer me half!!

UNDERSHAFT: I do not call myself a gentleman; but I offer you half.

CUSINS: This to your future partner! your successor! your son-in-law!

BARBARA: You are selling your own soul, Dolly, not mine. Leave me out of the bargain, please.

UNDERSHAFT: Come! I will go a step further for Barbara's sake. I will give you three fifths; but this is my last word.

CUSINS: Done!

LOMAX: Done in the eye! Why, *I* get only eight hundred, you know.

CUSINS: By the way, Mac, I am a classical scholar, not an arithmetical one. Is three fifths more than half or less?

UNDERSHAFT: More, of course.

CUSINS: I would have taken two hundred and fifty. How you can succeed in business when you are willing to pay all that money to a University don who is obviously not worth a junior clerk's wages!—well! What will Lazarus say?

UNDERSHAFT: Lazarus is a gentle romantic Jew who cares for nothing but string quartets and stalls at fashionable theatres. He will be blamed for your rapacity in money matters, poor fellow! as he has hitherto been blamed for mine. You are a shark of the first order, Euripides. So much the better for the firm!

BARBARA: Is the bargain closed, Dolly? Does your soul belong to him now?

CUSINS: No: the price is settled: that is all. The real tug of war is still to come. What about the moral question?

LADY BRITOMART: There is no moral question in the matter at all, Adolphus. You must simply sell cannons and weapons to people whose cause is right and just, and refuse them to foreigners and criminals.

UNDERSHAFT: *{Determinedly}* No: none of that. You must keep the true faith of an Armorer, or you don't come in here.

CUSINS: What on earth is the true faith of an Armorer?

UNDERSHAFT: To give arms to all men who offer an honest price for them, without respect of persons or principles: to aristocrat and republican, to Nihilist and Tsar, to Capitalist and Socialist, to Protestant and Catholic, to burglar and policeman, to black man, white man and yellow man, to all sorts and conditions, all nationalities, all faiths, all follies, all causes and all crimes. The first Undershaft wrote up in his shop IF GOD GAVE THE HAND, LET NOT MAN WITHHOLD THE SWORD. The second wrote up ALL HAVE THE RIGHT TO FIGHT: NONE HAVE THE RIGHT TO JUDGE. The third wrote up TO MAN THE WEAPON: TO HEAVEN THE VICTORY. The fourth had no literary turn; so he did not write up anything; but he sold cannons to Napoleon under the nose of George the Third. The fifth wrote up PEACE SHALL NOT PREVAIL SAVE WITH A SWORD IN HER HAND. The sixth, my master, was the best of all. He wrote up NOTHING IS EVER DONE IN THIS WORLD UNTIL MEN ARE PREPARED TO KILL ONE ANOTHER IF IT IS NOT DONE. After that, there was nothing left for the seventh to say. So he wrote up, simply UNASHAMED.

CUSINS: My good Machiavelli, I shall certainly write something up on the wall; only as I shall write it in Greek, you won't be able to read it. But as to your Armorer's faith, if I take my neck out of the noose of my own morality I am not going to put it into the noose of yours. I shall sell cannons to whom I please and refuse them to whom I please. So there!

UNDERSHAFT: From the moment when you become Andrew Undershaft, you will never do as you please again. Don't come here lusting for power, young man.

CUSINS: If power were my aim I should not come here for it. You have no power.

UNDERSHAFT: None of my own, certainly.

CUSINS: I have more power than you, more will. Yo do not drive this place; it drives you. And what drives the place?

UNDERSHAFT: *{Enigmatically}* A will of which I am a part.

BARBARA: *{Startled}* Father! Do you know what you are saying; or are you laying a snare for my soul?

CUSINS: Don't listen to his metaphysics, Barbara. The place is driven by the most rascally part of society, the money hunters, the pleasure hunters, the military promotion hunters; and he is their slave.

UNDERSHAFT: Not necessarily. Remember the Armorer's Faith. I will take an order from a good man as cheerfully as from a bad one. If you good people prefer teaching and shirking to buying my weapons and fighting the rascals, don't blame me. I cannot make courage and conviction. Bah! you tire me, Euripides, with your morality mongering. Ask Barbara: she understands. *{He suddenly reaches up and takes* BARBARA's *hands, looking powerfully into her eyes}* Tell him, my love, what power really means.

BARBARA: *{Hypnotized}* Before I joined the Salvation Army, I was in my own power; and the consequence was that I never knew what to do with myself. When I joined it, I had not time enough for all the things I had to do.

UNDERSHAFT: *{Approvingly}* Just so. And why was that, do you suppose?

BARBARA: Yesterday I should have said, because I was in the power of God. *{She resumes her self-possession, withdrawing her hands from his with a power equal to his own}* But you came and shewed me that I was in the power of Bodger and Undershaft. Today I feel —oh! how can I put it into words? Sarah: do you remember the earthquake at Cannes, when we were little children? —how little the surprise of the first shock mattered compared to the dread and horror of waiting for the second? That is how I feel in this place today. I stood on the rock I thought eternal; and without a word of warning it reeled and crumbled under me. I was safe with an infinite wisdom watching me, an army marching to Salvation with me; and in a moment, at a stroke of your pen in a cheque book, I stood alone; and the heavens were empty. That was the first shock of the earthquake: I am waiting for the second.

UNDERSHAFT: Come, come, my daughter! don't make too much of your little tinpot tragedy. What do we do here when we spend years of work and thought and thousands of pounds of solid cash on a new gun or an aerial battle ship that turns out just a hairbreadth wrong after all? Scrap it. Scrap it without wasting another hour or another pound on it. Well, you have made for yourself something that you call a morality or a religion or what not. It doesn't fit the facts. Well, scrap it. Scrap it and get one that does fit. That is what is wrong with the world at present. It scraps its obsolete steam engines and dynamos; but it won't scrap its old prejudices and its old moralities and its old religions and its old political constitutions. What's the result? In machinery it does very well; but in morals and religion and politics it is working at a loss that brings it nearer bankruptcy every year. Don't persist in that folly. If your old religion broke down yesterday, get a newer and a better one for tomorrow.

BARBARA: Oh how gladly I would

take a better one to my soul! But you offer me a worse one. *{Turning on him with sudden vehemence}* Justify yourself: shew me some light through the darkness of this dreadful place, with its beautifully clean workshops, and respectable workmen, and model homes.

UNDERSHAFT: Cleanliness and respectability do not need justification, Barbara; they justify themselves. I see no darkness here, no dreadfulness. In your Salvation shelter I saw poverty, misery, cold and hunger. You gave them bread and treacle and dreams of heaven. I give them thirty shilling a week to twelve thousand a a year. They find their own dreams; but I look after the drainage.

BARBARA: And their souls?

UNDERSHAFT: I save their souls just as I saved yours.

BARBARA: *{Revolted}* You saved my soul! What do you mean?

UNDERSHAFT: I fed you and clothed you and housed you. I took care that you should have money enough to live handsomely—more than enough; so that you could be wasteful, careless, generous. That saved your soul from the seven deadly sins.

BARBARA: *{Bewildered}* The seven deadly sins!

UNDERSHAFT: Yes, the deadly seven. *{Counting on his fingers}* Food, clothing, firing, rent, taxes, respectability and children. Nothing can lift those seven millstones from Man's neck but money; and the spirit cannot soar until the millstones are lifted. I lifted them from your spirit. I enabled Barbara to become Major Barbara; and I saved her from the crime of poverty.

CUSINS: Do you call poverty a crime?

UNDERSHAFT: The worst of crimes. All the other crimes are virtues beside it: all the other dishonors are chivalry itself by comparison. Poverty blights whole cities; spreads horrible pestilences; strikes dead the very souls of all who come within sight, sound or smell of it. What you call crime is nothing: a murder here and a theft there, a blow now and a curse then: what do they matter? they are only the accidents and illnesses of life: there are not fifty genuine professional criminals in London. But there are millions of poor people, abject people, dirty people, ill fed, ill clothed people. They poison us morally and physically: they kill the happiness of society: they force us to do away with our own liberties and to organize unnatural cruelties for fear they should rise against us and drag us down into their abyss. Only fools fear crime: we all fear poverty. Pah! *{Turning on* BARBARA*]* you talk of your half-saved ruffian in West Ham: you accuse me of dragging his soul back to perdition. Well, bring him to me here; and I will drag his soul back again to salvation for you. Not by words and dreams; but by thirty-eight shilling a week, a sound house in a handsome street, and a permanent job. In three weeks he will have a fancy waistcoat; in three months a tall hat and a chapel sitting; before the end of the year he will shake hands with a duchess at a Primrose League meeting, and join the Conservative Party.

BARBARA: And will he be the better for that?

UNDERSHAFT: You know he will. Don't be a hypocrite, Barbara. He will be better fed, better housed, better clothed, better behaved; and his children will be pounds heavier and bigger. That will be better than an American cloth mattress in a shelter, chopping firewood, eating bread and treacle, and being forced to kneel down from time to time to thank heaven for it: knee drill, I think you call it. It is cheap work converting starving men with a Bible in one hand and a slice of bread in the other. I will undertake to convert West Ham to Mahometanism on the same terms. Try your hand on my men: their souls are hungry because their bodies are full.

BARBARA: And leave the east end to starve?

UNDERSHAFT: *{His energetic tone*

dropping into one of bitter and brooding remembrance} I was an east ender. I moralized and starved until one day I swore that I would be a full-fed free man at all costs—that nothing should stop me except a bullet, neither reason nor morals nor the lives of other men. I said "Thou shalt starve ere I starve"; and with that word I became free and great. I was a dangerous man until I had my will: now I am a useful, beneficient, kindly person. That is the history of most self-made millionaires, I fancy. When it is the history of every Englishman we shall have an England worth living in.

LADY BRITOMART: Stop making speeches, Andrew. This is not the place for them.

UNDERSHAFT: *{Punctured}* My dear: I have no other means of conveying my ideas.

LADY BRITOMART: Your ideas are nonsense. You got on because you were selfish and unscrupulous.

UNDERSHAFT: Not at all. I had the strongest scruples about poverty and starvation. Your moralists are quite unscrupulous about both: they make virtues of them. I had rather be a thief than a pauper. I had rather been a murderer than a slave. I don't want to be either; but if you force the alternative on me, then, by Heaven, I'll choose the braver and more moral one. I hate poverty and slavery worse than any other crimes whatsoever. And let me tell you this. Poverty and slavery have stood up for centuries to your sermons and leading articles: they will not stand up to my machine guns. Don't preach at them: don't reason with them. Kill them.

BARBARA: Killing. Is that your remedy for everything?

UNDERSHAFT: It is the final test of conviction, the only lever strong enough to overturn a social system, the only way of saying Must. Let six hundred and seventy fools loose in the streets; and three policemen can scatter them. But huddle them together in a certain house in Westminster; and let them go through certain ceremonies and call themselves certain names until at last they get the courage to kill; and your six hundred and seventy fools become a government. Your pious mob fills up ballot papers and imagines it is governing its masters; but the ballot paper that really governs is the paper that has a bullet wrapped up in it.

CUSINS: That is perhaps why, like most intelligent people, I never vote.

UNDERSHAFT: Vote! Bah! When you vote, you only change the names of the cabinet. When you shoot, you pull down governments, inaugurate new epochs, abolish old orders and set up new. Is that historically true, Mr Learned Man, or is it not?

CUSINS: It is historically true. I loathe to having to admit it. I repudiate your sentiments. I abhor your nature. I defy you in every possible way. Still, it is true. But it ought not to be true.

UNDERSHAFT: Ought! ought! ought! ought! ought! Are you going to spend your life saying ought, like the rest of our moralists? Turn your oughts into shalls, man. Come and make explosives with me. Whatever can blow men up can blow society up. The history of the world is the history of those who had courage enough to embrace this truth. Have you the courage to embrace it, Barbara?

LADY BRITOMART: Barbara, I positively forbid you to listen to your father's abominable wickedness. And you, Adolphus, ought to know better than to go about saying that wrong things are true. What does it matter whether they are true if they are wrong?

UNDERSHAFT: What does it matter whether they are wrong if they are true?

LADY BRITOMART: *{Rising}* Children: come home instantly. Andrew: I am exceedingly sorry I allowed you to call on us. You are wickeder than ever. Come at once.

BARBARA: *{Shaking her head}* It's no

use running away from wicked people, mamma.

LADY BRITOMART: It is every use. It shews your disapprobation of them.

BARBARA: It does not save them.

LADY BRITOMART: I can see that you are going to disobey me. Sarah: are you coming home or are you not?

SARAH: I daresay it's very wicked of papa to make cannons; but I don't think I shall cut him on that account.

LOMAX: *{Pouring oil on the troubled waters}* The fact is, you know, there is a certain amount of tosh about this notion of wickedness. It doesn't work. You must look at the facts. Not that I would say a word in favor of anything wrong; but then, you see, all sorts of chaps are always doing all sorts of things; and we have to fit them in somehow, don't you know. What I mean is that you can't go cutting everybody; and that's about what it comes to. *{Their rapt attention to his eloquence makes him nervous}* Perhaps I don't make myself clear.

LADY BRITOMART: You are lucidity itself, Charles. Because Andrew is successful and has plenty of money to give to Sarah, you will flatter him and encourage him in his wickedness.

LOMAX: *{Unruffled}* Well, where the carcase is, there will the eagles be gathered, don't you know. *{To* UNDERSHAFT] Eh? What?

UNDERSHAFT: Precisely. By the way, may I call you Charles?

LOMAX: Delighted. Cholly is the usual ticket.

UNDERSHAFT: *{To* LADY BRITOMART] Biddy—

LADY BRITOMART: *{Violently}* Don't dare call me Biddy. Charles Lomax: you are a fool. Adolphus Cusins: you are a Jesuit. Stephen: you are a prig. Barbara: you are a lunatic. Andrew: you are a vulgar tradesman. Now you all know my opinion; and my conscience is clear, at all events. *{She sits down with a vehemence that the rug fortunately softens}*

UNDERSHAFT: My dear: you are the incarnation of morality. *{She snorts}* Your conscience is clear and your duty done when you have called everybody names. Come, Euripides! it is getting late; and we all want to go home. Make up your mind.

CUSINS: Understand this, you old demon—

LADY BRITOMART: Adolphus!

UNDERSHAFT: Let him alone, Biddy. Proceed, Euripides.

CUSINS: You have me in a horrible dilemma. I want Barbara.

UNDERSHAFT: Like all young men, you greatly exaggerate the difference between one young woman and another.

BARBARA: Quite true, Dolly.

CUSINS: I also want to avoid being a rascal.

UNDERSHAFT: *{With biting contempt}* You lust for personal righteousness, for self-approval, for what you call a good conscience, for what Barbara calls salvation, for what I call patronizing people who are not so lucky as yourself.

CUSINS: I do not: all the poet in me recoils from being a good man. But there are things in me that I must reckon with. Pity—

UNDERSHAFT: Pity! The scavenger of misery.

CUSINS: Well, love.

UNDERSHAFT: I know. You love the needy and the outcast: you love the oppressed races, the negro, the Indian ryot, the underdog everywhere. Do you love the Japanese? Do you love the French? Do you love the English?

CUSINS: No. Every true Englishman detests the English. We are the wickedest nation on earth; and our success is a moral horror.

UNDERSHAFT: That is what comes of your gospel of love, is it?

CUSINS: May I not love even my father-in-law?

UNDERSHAFT: Who wants your love, man? By what right do you take the liberty of offering it to me? I will have your due heed and respect, or I will kill you. But your love! Damn your impertinence!

CUSINS: *{Grinning}* I may not be able to control my affections, Mac.

UNDERSHAFT: You are fencing, Euripides. You are weakening: your grip is slipping. Come! try your last weapon. Pity and love have broken in your hand: forgiveness is still left.

CUSINS: No: forgiveness is a beggar's refuge. I am with you there: we must pay our debts.

UNDERSHAFT: Well said. Come! you will suit me. Remember the words of Plato.

CUSINS: *{Starting}* Plato! You dare quote Plato to me!

UNDERSHAFT: Plato says, my friend, that society cannot be saved until either the Professors of Greek take to making gunpowder, or else the makers of gunpowder become Professors of Greek.

CUSINS: Oh, tempter, cunning tempter!

UNDERSHAFT: Come! choose, man, choose.

CUSINS: But perhaps Barbara will not marry me if I make the wrong choice.

BARBARA: Perhaps not.

CUSINS: *{Desperately perplexed}* You hear!

BARBARA: Father: do you love nobody?

UNDERSHAFT: I love my best friend.

LADY BRITOMART: And who is that, pray?

UNDERSHAFT: My bravest enemy. That is the man who keeps me up to the mark.

CUSINS: You know, the creature is really a sort of poet in his way. Suppose he is a great man, after all!

UNDERSHAFT: Suppose you stop talking and make up your mind, my young friend.

CUSINS: But you are driving me against my nature. I hate war.

UNDERSHAFT: Hatred is the coward's revenge for being intimidated. Dare you make war on war? Here are the means: my friend Mr Lomax is sitting on them.

LOMAX: *Springing up}* Oh I say! You don't mean that this thing is loaded, do you? My ownest: come off it.

SARAH: *{Sitting placidly on the shell}* If I am to be blown up, the more thoroughly it is done the better. Don't fuss, Cholly.

LOMAX: *{To* UNDERSHAFT, *strongly remonstrant}* Your own daughter, you know.

UNDERSHAFT: So I see. *{To* CUSINS] well, my friend, may we expect you here at six tomorrow morning?

CUSINS: *{Firmly}* Not on any account. I will see the whole establishment blown up with its own dynamite before I will get up at five. My hours are healthy, rational hours: eleven to five.

UNDERSHAFT: Come when you please: before a week you will come at six and stay until I turn you out for the sake of your health. *{Calling}* Bilton! *{He turns to* LADY BRITOMART, *who rises}* My dear: let us leave these two young people to themselves for a moment. [BILTON *comes from the shed}* I am going to take you through the gun cotton shed.

BILTON: *{Barring the way}* You can't take anything explosive in here, sir.

LADY BRITOMART: What do you mean? Are you alluding to me?

BILTON: *{Unmoved}* No, ma'am. Mr Undershaft has the other gentleman's matches in his pocket.

LADY BRITOMART: *{Abruptly}* Oh! I beg your pardon. *{She goes into the shed}*

UNDERSHAFT: Quite right, Bilton, quite right: here you are. *{He gives* BILTON *the box of matches}* Come, Stephen. Come, Charles. Bring Sarah. *{He passes into the shed.* BILTON *opens the box and deliberately drops the matches into the fire-bucket}*

LOMAX: Oh I say! [BILTON *stolidly hands him the empty box}* Infernal nonsense! Pure scientific ignorance! *{He goes in}*

SARAH: Am I all right, Bilton?

BILTON: You'll have to put on list slippers, miss: that's all. We've got 'em inside. *{She goes in}*

STEPHEN: *{Very seriously to* CUSINS] Dolly, old fellow, think. Think before you decide. Do you feel that you are a sufficiently practical man? It is a huge undertaking, an enormous responsibility. All this mass of business will be Greek to you.

CUSINS: Oh, I think it will be much less difficult than Greek.

STEPHEN: Well, I just want to say this before I leave you to yourselves. Don't let anything I have said about right and wrong prejudice you against this great chance in life. I have satisfied myself that the business is one of the highest character and a credit to our country. *{Emotionally}* I am very proud of my father. I— *{Unable to proceed, he presses* CUSINS' *hand and goes hastily into the shed, followed by* BILTON. BARBARA *and* CUSINS, *left alone together, look at one another silently}*

CUSINS: Barbara: I am going to accept this offer.

BARBARA: I thought you would.

CUSINS: You understand, don't you, that I had to decide without consulting you. If I had thrown the burden of the choice on you, you would sooner or later have despised me for it.

BARBARA: Yes: I did not want you to sell your soul for me any more than for this inheritance.

CUSINS: It is not the sale of my soul that troubles me: I have sold it too often to care about that. I have sold it for a professorship. I have sold it for an income. I have sold it to escape being imprisoned for refusing to pay taxes for hangmen's ropes and unjust wars and things that I abhor. What is all human conduct but the daily and hourly sale of our souls for trifles? What I am now selling it for is neither money nor position nor comfort, but for reality and for power.

BARBARA: You know that you will have no power, and that he has none.

CUSINS: I know. It is not for myself alone. I want to make power for the world.

BARBARA: I want to make power for the world too; but it must be spiritual power.

CUSINS: I think all power is spiritual: these cannons will not go off by themselves. I have tried to make spiritual power by teaching Greek. But the world can never be really touched by a dead language and a dead civilization. The people must have power; and the people cannot have Greek. Now the power that is made here can be wielded by all men.

BARBARA: Power to burn women's houses down and kill their sons and tear their husbands to pieces.

CUSINS: You cannot have power for good without having power for evil too. Even mother's milk nourishes murderers as well as heroes. This power which only tears men's bodies to pieces has never been so horribly abused as the intellectual power, the imaginative power, the poetic, religious power that can enslave men's souls. As a teacher of Greek I gave the intellectual man weapons against the common man. I now want to give the common man weapons against the intellectual man. I love the common people. I want to arm them against the lawyers, the doctors, the priests, the literary men, the professors, the artists, and the politicians, who, once in authority, are more disastrous and tyrannical than all the fools, rascals, and imposters. I want a power simple enough for common man to use, yet strong enough to force the intellectual oligarchy to use its genius for the general good.

BARBARA: Is there no higher power than that? *{Pointing to the shell}*

CUSINS: Yes; but that power can destroy the higher powers just as a tiger can destroy a man: therefore Man must master that power first. I admitted this when the Turks and Greeks were last at war. My best pupil went out to fight for Hellas. My parting gift to him was not a copy of Plato's *Republic*, but a revolver and a hundred Undershaft cartridges. The blood of every Turk he shot—if he shot any—is on my head as well as on Undershaft's. That act committed me to this place for ever. Your father's challenge has beaten me. Dare I make war on war? I dare. I must. I will. And now, is it all over between us?

BARBARA: *{Touched by his evident dread of her answer}* Silly baby Dolly! How could it be!

CUSINS: *{Overjoyed}* Then you—you—you— Oh for my drum! *{He flourishes imaginary drumsticks}*

BARBARA: *{Angered by his levity}* Take care, Dolly, take care. Oh, if only I could get away from you and from father and from it all! if I could have the wings of a dove and fly away to heaven!

CUSINS: And leave me!

BARBARA: Yes, you, and all the other naughty mischievous children of men. But I can't. I was happy in the Salvation Army for a moment. I escaped from the world into a paradise of enthusiasm and prayer and soul saving; but the moment our money ran short, it all came back to Bodger: it was he who saved our people: he, and the Prince of Darkness, my papa. Undershaft and Bodger: their hands stretch everywhere: when we feed a starving fellow creature: it is with their bread, because there is no other bread; when we tend the sick, it is in the hospitals they endow; if we turn from the churches they build, we must kneel on the stones of the streets they pave. As long as that lasts, there is no getting away from them. Turning our backs on Bodger and Undershaft is turning our backs on life.

CUSINS: I though you were determined to turn your back on the wicked side of life.

BARBARA: There is no wicked side: life is all one. And I never wanted to shirk my share in whatever evil must be endured, whether it be sin or suffering. I wish I could cure you of middle-class ideas, Dolly.

CUSINS: *{Gasping}* Middle cl—! A snub! A social snub to me; from the daughter of a foundling!

BARBARA: That is why I have no class, Dolly: I come straight out of the heart of the whole people. If I were middle-class I should turn my back on my father's business; and we should both live in an artistic drawing room, with you reading the reviews in one corner, and I in the other at the piano, playing Schumann: both very superior persons, and neither of us a bit of use. Sooner than that, I would sweep out the guncotton shed, or be one of Bodger's barmaids. Do you know what would have happened if you had refused papa's offer?

CUSINS: I wonder!

BARBARA: I should have given you up and married the man who accepted it. After all, my dear old mother has more sense than any of you. I felt like her when I saw this place—felt that I must have it—that never, never, never, could I let it go; only she thought it was the houses and the kitchen ranges and the linen and china, when it was really all the human souls to be saved: not weak souls in starved bodies, sobbing with gratitude for a scrap of bread and treacle, but fullfed, quarrelsome, snobbish, uppish creatures, all standing on their little rights and dignities, and thinking that my father ought to be greatly obliged to them for making so much money for him—and so he ought. That is where salvation is really wanted. My father shall never throw it in my teeth again that my converts were bribed with bread. *{She is transfigured}* I have got rid of the bribe of bread. I have got rid of the bribe of heaven. Let God's work be done for its own sake: the work he had to create us to do because it cannot be done except by living men and women. When I die, let him be in my debt, not I in him; and let me forgive him as becomes a woman of my rank.

CUSINS: Then the way of life lies through the factory of death?

BARBARA: Yes, through the raising of hell to heaven and of man to God, through the unveiling of an eternal light in the Valley of The Shadow. *{Seizing him with both hands}* Oh, did you think my courage would never come back? did you believe that I was a deserter? that I, who have stood in the streets, and taken my people to my heart, and talked of the holiest and greatest things with them, could ever turn back and chatter foolishly to fashionable people about nothing in a drawing room? Never, never, never, never: Major Barbara will die with colors. Oh! and I have my dear little Dolly boy still; and he has found me my place and my work. Glory Hallelujah! *{She kisses him}*

CUSINS: My dearest: consider my delicate health. I cannot stand as much happiness as you can.

BARBARA: Yes: it is not easy work being in love with me, is it? But it's good for you. *{She runs to the shed, and calls, childlike}* Mamma! Mamma! [BILTON *comes out of the shed, followed by* UNDERSHAFT] I want mamma.

UNDERSHAFT: She is taking off her list slippers, dear. *{He passes on to* CUSINS] Well? What does she say?

CUSINS: She has gone right up into the skies.

LADY BRITOMART: *{Coming from the shed and stopping on the steps, obstructing* SARAH, *who follows with* LOMAX. BARBARA *clutches like a baby at her mother's skirt}* Barbara: when will you learn to be independent and to act and think for yourself? I know as well as possible what that cry of "Mamma, Mamma," means. Always running to me!

SARAH: *{Touching* LADY BRITOMART'S *ribs with her finger tips and imitating a bicycle horn}* Pip! pip!

LADY BRITOMART: *{Highly indignant}* How dare you say Pip! pip! to me, Sarah? You are both very naughty children. What do you want, Barbara?

BARBARA: I want a house in the village to live in with Dolly. *{Dragging at the skirt}* Come and tell me which one to take.

UNDERSHAFT: *{To* CUSINS] Six o'clock tomorrow morning, Euripides.

CURTAIN

Drawing by Lorenz;

Poetry

Robert Browning (1812–1889)

My Last Duchess

That's my last Duchess painted on the wall,
Looking as if she were alive. I call
That piece a wonder, now; Frà Pandolf's hands
Worked busily a day, and there she stands.
Will 't please you sit and look at her? I said
"Frà Pandolf" by design, for never read
Strangers like you that pictured countenance,
The depth and passion of its earnest glance,
But to myself they turned (since none puts by
The curtain I have drawn for you, but I) 10
And seemed as they would ask me, if they durst,
How such a glance came there; so, not the first
Are you to turn and ask thus. Sir, 'twas not
Her husband's presence only, called that spot
Of joy into the Duchess' cheek; perhaps
Frà Pandolf chanced to say, "Her mantle laps
Over my lady's wrist too much," or "Paint
Must never hope to reproduce the faint
Half-flush that dies along her throat." Such stuff
Was courtesy, she thought, and cause enough 20
For calling up that spot of joy. She had
A heart—how shall I say?—too soon made glad,
Too easily impressed; she liked whate'er
She looked on, and her looks went everywhere.
Sir, 'twas all one! My favor at her breast,
The dropping of the daylight in the West,
The bough of cherries some officious fool
Broke in the orchard for her, the white mule
She rode with round the terrace—all and each
Would draw from her alike that approving speech, 30
Or blush, at least. She thanked men—good! but thanked
Somehow—I know not how—as if she ranked
My gift of a nine-hundred-years-old name
With anybody's gift. Who'd stoop to blame
This sort of trifling? Even had you skill
In speech—which I have not—to make your will

Quite clear to such an one, and say, "Just this
Or that in you disgusts me; here you miss,
Or there exceed the mark"—and if she let
Herself be lessoned so, nor plainly set 40
Her wits to yours, forsooth, and made excuse—
E'en then would be some stooping; and I choose
Never to stoop. Oh, sir, she smiled, no doubt,
Whene'er I passed her; but who passed without
Much the same smile? This grew; I gave commands;
Then all smiles stopped together. There she stands
As if alive. Will 't please you rise? We'll meet
The company below, then. I repeat,
The Count your master's known munificence
Is ample warrant that no just pretense 50
Of mine for dowry will be disallowed;
Though his fair daughter's self, as I avowed
At starting, is my object. Nay, we'll go
Together down, sir. Notice Neptune, though,
Taming a sea-horse, thought a rarity,
Which Claus of Innsbruck cast in bronze for me!

Walt Whitman (1819–1892)

I Hear It Was Charged Against Me

I hear it was charged against me that I sought to destroy institutions,
But really I am neither for or against institutions,
(What indeed have I in common with them? or what with the destruction of them?)
Only I will establish in the Mannahatta and in every city of these States inland and seaboard,
And in the fields and woods, and above every keel little or large that dents the water, 5
Without edifices or rules or trustees or any argument,
The institution of the dear love of comrades.

The Commonplace

The commonplace I sing;
How cheap is health! how cheap nobility!
Abstinence, no falsehood, no gluttony, lust;
The open air I sing, freedom, toleration,
(Take here the mainest lesson—less from books—less from the schools,) 5
The common day and night—the common earth and waters,
Your farm—your work, trade, occupation,
The democratic wisdom underneath, like solid ground for all.

When I Heard the Learn'd Astronomer

When I heard the learn'd astronomer,
When the proofs, the figures, were ranged in columns before me,
When I was shown the charts and diagrams, to add, divide, and measure them,
When I sitting heard the astronomer where he lectured with much applause in the lecture-room,
How soon unaccountable I became tired and sick, 5
Till rising and gliding out I wander'd off by myself,
In the mystical moist night-air, and from time to time,
Look'd up in perfect silence at the stars.

A Sight in Camp in the Daybreak Gray and Dim

A sight in camp in the daybreak gray and dim,
As from my tent I emerge so early sleepless,
As slow I walk in the cool fresh air the path near by the hospital tent,
Three forms I see on stretchers lying, brought out there untended lying,
Over each the blanket spread, ample brownish woolen blanket, 5
Gray and heavy blanket, folding, covering all.

Curious I halt and silent stand,
Then with light fingers I from the face of the nearest the first just lift the blanket;
Who are you elderly man so gaunt and grim, with well-gray'd hair, and flesh all sunken about the eyes?
Who are you my dear comrade? 10

Then to the second I step—and who are you my child and darling?
Who are you sweet boy with cheeks yet blooming?

Then to the third—a face nor child nor old, very calm, as of beautiful yellow-white ivory;
Young man I think I know you—I think this face is the face of Christ himself,
Dead and divine and brother of all, and here again he lies. 15

A Noiseless Patient Spider

A noiseless patient spider,
I mark'd where on a little promontory it stood isolated,
Mark'd how to explore the vacant vast surrounding,
It launch'd forth filament, filament, filament out of itself,
Ever unreeling them, ever tirelessly speeding them. 5

And you O my soul where you stand,
Surrounded, detached, in measureless oceans of space,

Ceaselessly musing, venturing, throwing, seeking the spheres to connect them,
Till the bridge you will need be form'd, till the ductile anchor hold,
Till the gossamer thread you fling catch somewhere, O my soul. 10

Matthew Arnold (1822–1888)

Dover Beach

The sea is calm to-night.
The tide is full, the moon lies fair
Upon the straits;—on the French coast the light
Gleams and is gone; the cliffs of England stand
Glimmering and vast, out in the tranquil bay. 5

Come to the window, sweet is the night-air!
Only, from the long line of spray
Where the sea meets the moon-blanch'd land,
Listen, you hear the grating roar
Of pebbles which the waves draw back, and fling, 10
At their return, up the high strand,
Begin, and cease, and then again begin,
With tremulous cadence slow, and bring
The eternal note of sadness in.

Sophocles long ago 15
Heard it on the Ægean, and it brought
Into his mind the turbid ebb and flow,
Of human misery; we
Find also in the sound a thought,
Hearing it by this distant northern sea. 20

The Sea of Faith
Was once, too, at the full, and round earth's shore
Lay like the folds of a bright girdle furl'd.
But now I only hear
Its melancholy, long, withdrawing roar, 25
Retreating, to the breath
Of the night-wind, down the vast edges drear
And naked shingles of the world.

Ah, love, let us be true
To one another! for the world, which seems 30
To lie before us like a land of dreams,
So various, so beautiful, so new,
Hath really neither joy, nor love, nor light,
Nor certitude, nor peace, nor help for pain;
And we are here as on a darkling plain 35
Swept with confused alarms of struggle and flight,
Where ignorant armies clash by night.

Emily Dickinson (1830–1886)

I Like to See It Lap the Miles

I like to see it lap the miles,
And lick the valleys up,
And stop to feed itself at tanks;
And then, prodigious, step

Around a pile of mountains, 5
And, supercilious, peer
In shanties by the sides of roads;
And then a quarry pare

To fit its sides, and crawl between,
Complaining all the while 10
In horrid, hooting stanza;
Then chase itself down hill

And neigh like Boanerges;
Then, punctual as a star,
Stop—docile and omnipotent— 15
At its own stable door.

Because I Could Not Stop for Death

Because I could not stop for Death,
He kindly stopped for me;
The carriage held but just ourselves
And Immortality.

We slowly drove, he knew no haste, 5
And I had put away
My labor, and my leisure too,
For his civility.

We passed the school where children
played,
Their lessons scarcely done; 10
We passed the fields of gazing grain,
We passed the setting sun.

We paused before a house that seemed
A swelling on the ground;
The roof was scarcely visible, 15
The cornice but a mound.

Since then 'tis centuries; but each
Feels shorter than the day
I first surmised the horses' heads
Were toward eternity. 20

What Soft, Cherubic Creatures

What soft, cherubic creatures
These gentlewomen are!
One would as soon assault a plush
Or violate a star.

Such dimity convictions, 5
A horror so refined
Of freckled human nature,
Of Deity ashamed,—

It's such a common glory,
A fisherman's degree! 10
Redemption, brittle lady,
Be so ashamed of thee.

I Taste a Liquor Never Brewed

I taste a liquor never brewed,
From tankards scooped in pearl;
Not all the vats upon the Rhine
Yield such an alcohol!

Inebriate of air am I, 5
And debauchee of dew,
Reeling, through endless summer days,
From inns of molten blue.

When landlords turn the drunken bee
Out of the foxlove's door, 10
When butterflies renounce their drams,
I shall but drink the more!

Till seraphs swing their snowy hats,
And saints to windows run,
To see the little tippler 15
Leaning against the sun!

A Narrow Fellow in the Grass

A narrow fellow in the grass
Occasionally rides;
You may have met him,—did you not?
His notice sudden is.

The grass divides as with a comb, 5
A spotted shaft is seen;
And then it closes at your feet
And opens further on.

He likes a boggy acre,
A floor too cool for corn, 10
Yet when a boy, and barefoot,
I more than once, at morn,

Have passed, I thought, a whip-lash
Unbraiding in the sun,—
When, stooping to secure it, 15
It wrinkled, and was gone.

Several of nature's people
I know, and they know me;
I feel for them a transport
Of cordiality; 20

But never met this fellow,
Attended or alone,
Without a tighter breathing,
And zero at the bone.

Thomas Hardy (1840–1928)

God-Forgotten

I towered far, and lo! I stood within
The presence of the Lord Most High,
Sent thither by the sons of Earth, to win
Some answer to their cry.

—"The Earth, sayest thou? The Human race? 5
By Me created? Sad its lot?
Nay: I have no remembrance of such place:
Such world I fashioned not."—

—"O Lord, forgive me when I say
Thou spakest the word that made it all."— 10
"The Earth of men—let them bethink me. . . . Yea!
I dimly do recall

"Some tiny sphere I built long back
(Mid millions of such shapes of mine)
So named . . . It perished, surely—not a wrack 15
Remaining, or a sign?

"It lost my interest from the first,
My aims therefore succeeding ill;
Haply it died of doing as it durst?"—
"Lord, it existeth still."— 20

"Dark, then, its life! For not a cry
Of aught it bears do I now hear;
Of its own act the threads were snapt whereby
Its plaints had reached mine ear.

"It used to ask for gifts of good, 25
Till came its severance, self-entailed,
When sudden silence on that side ensued,
And has till now prevailed.

"All other orbs have kept in touch;
Their voicings reach me speedily: 30
Thy people took upon them overmuch
In sundering them from me!

"And it is strange—though sad enough—
Earth's race should think that one whose call
Frames, daily, shining spheres of flawless stuff 35
Must heed their tainted ball! . . .

"But sayest it is by pangs distraught,
And strife, and silent suffering?—
Sore grieved am I that injury should be wrought
Even on so poor a thing! 40

"Thou shouldst have learnt that *Not to Mend*
For Me could mean but *Not to Know:*
Hence, Messengers! and straightway put an end
To what men undergo." . . .

Homing at dawn, I thought to see 45
One of the Messengers standing by.
—Oh, childish thought! . . . Yet often it comes to me
When trouble hovers nigh.

The Darkling Thrush

I leant upon a coppice gate
  When Frost was specter-gray,
And Winter's dregs made desolate
  The weakening eye of day.
The tangled bine-stems scored the
    sky 5
  Like strings of broken lyres,
And all mankind that haunted nigh
  Had sought their household fires.

The land's sharp features seemed to be
  The Century's corpse outleant, 10
His crypt the cloudy canopy,
  The wind his death-lament.
The ancient pulse of germ and birth
  Was shrunken hard and dry,
And every spirit upon earth 15
  Seemed fervorless as I.

At once a voice arose among
  The bleak twigs overhead
In a fullhearted evensong
  Of joy illimited; 20
An aged thrush, frail, gaunt, and small,
  In blast-beruffled plume,
Had chosen thus to fling his soul
  Upon the growing gloom.

So little cause for carolings 25
  Of such ecstatic sound
Was written on terrestrial things
  Afar or nigh around,
That I could think there trembled
    through
His happy good-night air 30
Some blessed Hope, whereof he knew
  And I was unaware.

The Convergence of the Twain
(Lines on the Loss of the "Titanic")

    In a solitude of the sea
    Deep from human vanity,
And the Pride of Life that planned her, stilly couches she.

    Steel chambers, late the pyres
    Of her salamandrine fires, 5
Cold currents thrid, and turn to rhythmic tidal lyres.

    Over the mirrors meant
    To glass the opulent
The sea worm crawls—grotesque, slimed, dumb, indifferent.

    Jewels in joy designed 10
    To ravish the sensuous mind
Lie lightless, all their sparkles bleared and black and blind.

    Dim moon-eyed fishes near
    Gaze at the gilded gear
And query: "What does this vaingloriousness down here?" . . . 15

    Well: while was fashioning
    This creature of cleaving wing,
The Immanent Will that stirs and urges everything

Prepared a sinister mate
For her—so gaily great— 20
A Shape of Ice, for the time far and dissociate.

And as the smart ship grew
In stature, grace, and hue,
In shadowy silent distance grew the Iceberg too.

Alien they seemed to be: 25
No mortal eye could see
The intimate welding of their later history,

Or sign that they were bent
By paths coincident
On being anon twin halves of one august event, 30

Till the Spinner of the Years
Said "Now!" And each one hears,
And consummation comes, and jars two hemispheres.

In Time of "The Breaking of Nations"

1

Only a man harrowing clods
In a slow silent walk
With an old horse that stumbles and nods
Half asleep as they stalk.

2

Only thin smoke without flame 5
From the heaps of couch-grass;
Yet this will go onward the same
Though Dynasties pass.

3

Yonder a maid and her wight
Come whispering by; 10
War's annals will cloud into night
Ere their story die.

Gerard Manley Hopkins (1844–1889) 

God's Grandeur

The world is charged with the grandeur of God.
  It will flame out, like shining from shook foil;
  It gathers to a greatness, like the ooze of oil
Crushed. Why do men then now not reck his rod? 4
Generations have trod, have trod, have trod;
  And all is seared with trade; bleared, smeared with toil; ,
  And wears man's smudge and shares man's smell: the soil
Is bare now, nor can foot feel, being shod. 8

And for all this, nature is never spent;
  There lives the dearest freshness deep down things;
And though the last lights off the black West went
  Oh, morning, at the brown brink eastward, springs—
Because the Holy Ghost over the bent
  World broods with warm breast and with ah! bright wings. 14

Pied Beauty

Glory be to God for dappled things—
  For skies of couple-color as a brinded cow;
    For rose-moles all in stipple upon trout that swim;
Fresh-firecoal chestnut-falls; finches' wings;
  Landscape plotted and pieced—fold, fallow, and plow; 5
    And all trádes, their gear and tackle and trim.
All things counter, original, spare, strange;
  Whatever is fickle, freckled (who knows how?)
    With swift, slow; sweet, sour; adazzle, dim;
He fathers-forth whose beauty is past change: 10
          Praise him.

The Windhover
To Christ Our Lord

I caught this morning morning's minion, king-
 dom of daylight's dauphin, dapple-dawn-drawn Falcon, in his riding
 Of the rolling level underneath him steady air, and striding
High there, how he rung upon the rein of a wimpling wing
In his ecstasy! then off, off forth on swing,
 As a skate's heel sweeps smooth on a bow-bend: the hurl and gliding
 Rebuffed the big wind. My heart in hiding
Stirred for a bird,—the achieve of, the mastery of the thing! 7

Brute beauty and valor and act, oh, air, pride, plume, here
 Buckle! and the fire that breaks from thee then, a billion
Times told lovelier, more dangerous, O my chevalier!

 No wonder of it: shéer plód makes plow down sillion
Shine, and blue-bleak embers, ah my dear,
 Fall, gall themselves, and gash gold-vermilion. 13

A. E. Housman (1859–1936)

Loveliest of Trees

Loveliest of trees, the cherry now
Is hung with bloom along the bough,
And stands about the woodland ride
Wearing white for Eastertide.

Now, of my threescore years and ten, 5
Twenty will not come again,
And take from seventy springs a score,
It only leaves me fifty more.

And since to look at things in bloom
Fifty springs are little room, 10
About the woodlands I will go
To see the cherry hung with snow.

) an Athlete Dying Young

The time you won your town the race
We chaired you through the
    marketplace;
Man and boy stood cheering by,
And home we brought you shoulder-
    high.

To-day, the road all runners come, 5
Shoulder-high we bring you home,
And set you at your threshold down,
Townsman of a stiller town.

Smart lad, to slip betimes away
From fields where glory does not
    stay 10
And early though the laurel grows
It withers quicker than the rose.

Eyes the shady night has shut
Cannot see the record cut,
And silence sounds no worse than
    cheers 15
After earth has stopped the ears.

Now you will not swell the rout
Of lads that wore their honours out,
Runners whom renown outran
And the name died before the man. 20

So set, before its echoes fade,
The fleet foot on the sill of shade,
And hold to the low lintel up
The still-defended challenge-cup.

And round that early-laurelled head 25
Will flock to gaze the strengthless dead,
And find unwithered on its curls
The garland briefer than a girl's.

Terence, This Is Stupid Stuff

'Terence, this is stupid stuff:
You eat your victuals fast enough;
There can't be much amiss, 'tis clear,
To see the rate you drink your beer.
But oh, good Lord, the verse you
    make, 5
It gives a chap the belly-ache.
The cow, the old cow, she is dead;
It sleeps well, the horned head:
We poor lads, 'tis our turn now
To hear such tunes as killed the
    cow. 10
Pretty friendship 'tis to rhyme
Your friends to death before their time
Moping melancholy mad:
Come, pipe a tune to dance to, lad.'
  Why, if 'tis dancing you would
    be, 15
There's brisker pipes than poetry.
Say, for what were hop-yards meant,
Or why was Burton built on Trent?
Oh many a peer of England brews
Livelier liquor than the Muse, 20
And malt does more than Milton can
To justify God's ways to man.
Ale, man, ale's the stuff to drink
For fellows whom it hurts to think:
Look into the pewter pot 25
To see the world as the world's not.
And faith, 'tis pleasant till 'tis past:
The mischief is that 'twill not last.
Oh I have been to Ludlow fair
And left my necktie God knows
    where, 30
And carried half-way home, or near,
Pints and quarts of Ludlow beer:
Then the world seemed none so bad,
And I myself a sterling lad;
And down in lovely muck I've lain, 35
Happy till I woke again.
Then I saw the morning sky:
Heigho, the tale was all a lie;

The world, it was the old world yet,
I was I, my things were wet, 40
And nothing now remained to do
But begin the game anew.
Therefore, since the world has still
Much good, but much less good than ill,
And while the sun and moon
endure 45
Luck's a chance, but trouble's sure,
I'd face it as a wise man would,
And train for ill and not for good.
'Tis true, the stuff I bring for sale
Is not so brisk a brew as ale: 50
Out of a stem that scored the hand
I wrung it in a weary land.
But take it: if the smack is sour,
The better for the embittered hour;
It should do good to heart and head 55
When your soul is in my soul's stead;
And I will friend you, if I may,
In the dark and cloudy day.

There was a king reigned in the East:
There, when kings will sit to feast, 60
They get their fill before they think
With poisoned meat and poisoned
drink.
He gathered all that springs to birth
From the many-venomed earth;
First a little, thence to more, 65
He sampled all her killing store;
And easy, smiling, seasoned sound,
Sate the king when healths went round.
They put arsenic in his meat
And stared aghast to watch him eat; 70
They poured strychnine in his cup
And shook to see him drink it up:
They shook, they stared as white's their
shirt:
Them it was their poison hurt.
—I tell the tale that I heard told. 75
Mithridates, he died old.

Rudyard Kipling (1865–1936)

Tommy

I went into a public-'ouse to get a pint o' beer,
The publican 'e up an' sez, "We serve no red-coats here."
The girls be'ind the bar they laughed an' giggled fit to die,
I outs into the street again, an' to myself sez I:
O it's Tommy this, an' Tommy that, an' "Tommy go away"; 5
But it's "Thank you, Mister Atkins," when the band begins to play,
The band begins to play, my boys, the band begins to play,
O it's "Thank you, Mister Atkins," when the band begins to play.

I went into a theatre as sober as could be,
They give a drunk civilian room, but 'adn't none for me; 10
They sent me to the gallery or round the music-'alls,
But when it comes to fightin', Lord! they'll shove me in the stalls.
For it's Tommy this, and Tommy that, an' "Tommy wait outside";
But it's "Special train for Atkins," when the trooper's on the tide,
The troopships on the tide, my boys, etc. 15

O makin' mock o' uniforms that guard you while you sleep
Is cheaper than them uniforms, an' they're starvation cheap;
An' hustlin' drunken sodgers when they're goin' large a bit
Is five times better business than paradin' in full kit.
    Then it's Tommy this, and Tommy that, an' "Tommy 'ow's yer soul?" 20
    But it's "Thin red lines of 'eroes" when the drums begin to roll,
    The drums begin to roll, my boys, etc.

We aren't no thin red 'eroes, nor we aren't no blackguards too,
But single men in barricks, most remarkable like you;
An' if sometimes our conduck isn't all your fancy paints, 25
Why, single men in barricks don't grow into plaster saints.
    While it's Tommy this, and Tommy that, an' "Tommy fall be'ind";
    But it's "Please to walk in front, sir," when there's trouble in the wind,
    There's trouble in the wind, my boys, etc.

You talk o' better food for us an' schools, an' fires, an' all: 30
We'll wait for extra rations if you treat us rational.
Don't mess about the cook-room slops, but prove it to our face
The Widow's uniform is not the soldier-man's disgrace.
    But it's Tommy this, an' Tommy that, an' "Chuck him out, the brute!"
    But it's "Saviour of 'is country" when the guns begin to shoot; 35
    An' it's Tommy this, an' Tommy that, an' anything you please;
    An' Tommy ain't a bloomin' fool—you bet that Tommy sees!

Recessional

God of our fathers, known of old,
  Lord of our far-flung battle-line,
Beneath whose awful hand we hold
  Dominion over palm and pine—
Lord God of Hosts, be with us yet, 5
Lest we forget—lest we forget!

The tumult and the shouting dies;
  The captains and the kings depart:
Still stands Thine ancient sacrifice,
  An humble and a contrite heart. 10
Lord God of Hosts, be with us yet,
Lest we forget—lest we forget!

Far-called, our navies melt away;
  On dune and headland sinks the fire:
Lo, all our pomp of yesterday 15
  Is one with Nineveh and Tyre!
Judge of the Nations, spare us yet,
Lest we forget—lest we forget!

If, drunk with sight of power, we loose
  Wild tongues that have not Thee in awe, 20
Such boastings as the Gentiles use,
  Or lesser breeds without the Law—
Lord God of Hosts, be with us yet,
Lest we forget—lest we forget!

For heathen heart that puts her trust 25
  In reeking tube and iron shard,
All valiant dust that builds on dust,
  And, guarding, calls not Thee to guard
For frantic boast and foolish word—
Thy Mercy on Thy People, Lord! 30

The White Man's Burden

Take up the White Man's burden—
Send forth the best ye breed—
Go bind your sons to exile
To serve your captives' need;

To wait in heavy harness, 5
On fluttered folk and wild—
Your new-caught, sullen peoples,
Half-devil and half-child.

Take up the White Man's burden—
In patience to abide, 10
To veil the threat of terror
An check the show of pride;
By open speech and simple,
An hundred times made plain,
To seek another's profit, 15
And work another's gain.

Take up the White Man's burden—
The savage wars of peace—
Fill full the mouth of Famine
And bid the sickness cease; 20
And when your goal is nearest
The end for others sought,
Watch Sloth and heathen Folly
Bring all your hope to nought.

Take up the White Man's burden— 25
No tawdry rule of kings,
But toil of serf and sweeper—
The tale of common things.
The ports ye shall not enter,
The roads ye shall not tread, 30
Go make them with your living,
And mark them with your dead.

Take up the White Man's burden—
And reap his old reward:
The blame of those ye better, 35
The hate of those ye guard—
The cry of hosts ye humor
(Ah, slowly!) toward the light:—
"Why brought ye us from bondage,
Our loved Egyptian night?" 40

Take up the White Man's burden—
Ye dare not stoop to less—
Nor call too loud on Freedom
To cloak your weariness;
By all ye cry or whisper, 45
By all ye leave or do,
The silent sullen peoples
Shall weigh your Gods and you.

Take up the White Man's burden—
Have done with childish days— 50
The lightly proffered laurel,
The easy, ungrudged praise.
Come now, to search your manhood
Through all the thankless years,
Cold, edged with dear-bought
wisdom, 55
The judgment of your peers!

Edwin Arlington Robinson (1869–1935)

Richard Cory

Whenever Richard Cory went down town,
We people on the pavement looked at him:
He was a gentleman from sole to crown,
Clean favored, and imperially slim.

And he was aways quietly arrayed, 5
And he was always human when he talked;
But still he fluttered pulses when he said,
"Good-morning," and he glittered when he walked.

And he was rich,—yes, richer than a king,—
And admirably schooled in every grace: 10
In fine, we thought that he was everything
To make us wish that we were in his place.

So on we worked, and waited for the light,
And went without the meat, and cursed the bread;
And Richard Cory, one calm summer night, 15
Went home and put a bullet through his head.

Stephen Crane (1871–1900)

A Man Said to the Universe

A man said to the universe:
"Sir, I exist!"
"However," replied the universe,
"The fact has not created in me
A sense of obligation." 5

The Trees in the Garden Rained Flowers

The trees in the garden rained flowers.
Children ran there joyously.
They gathered the flowers
Each to himself.
Now there were some 5
Who gathered great heaps—
Having opportunity and skill—
Until, behold, only chance blossoms
Remained for the feeble,
Then a little spindling tutor 10
Ran importantly to the father, crying:
"Pray, come hither!

See this unjust thing in your garden!"
But when the father had surveyed,
He admonished the tutor: 15
"Not so, small sage!
This thing is just.
For, look you,
Are not they who possess the flowers
Stronger, bolder, shrewder 20
Than they who have none?
Why should the strong—
The beautiful strong—
Why should they not have the flowers?"
Upon reflection, the tutor bowed to the ground, 25
"My Lord," he said,
"The stars are displaced
By this towering wisdom."

God Fashioned the Ship of the World Carefully

God fashioned the ship of the world carefully.
With the infinite skill of an All-Master
Made He the hull and the sails,
Held He the rudder
Ready for adjustment. 5
Erect stood He, scanning His work proudly.
Then—at fateful time—a wrong called,
And God turned, heeding.
Lo, the ship, at this opportunity, slipped slyly,
Making cunning noiseless travel down the ways, 10
So that, for ever rudderless, it went upon the seas
Going ridiculous voyages,
Making quaint progress,
Turning as with serious purpose
Before stupid winds. 15
And there were many in the sky
Who laughed at this thing.

Do Not Weep, Maiden, for War Is Kind

Do not weep, maiden, for war is kind.
Because your lover threw wild hands toward the sky
And the affrighted steed ran on alone,
Do not weep.
War is kind. 5

Hoarse, booming drums of the regiment,
Little souls who thirst for fight,
These men were born to drill and die.
The unexplained glory flies above them,
Great is the battle-god, great, and his kingdom— 10
A field where a thousand corpses lie.

Do not weep, babe, for war is kind.
Because your father tumbled in the yellow trenches,
Raged at his breast, gulped and died, 15
Do not weep.
War is kind.

Swift blazing flag of the regiment,
Eagle with crest of red and gold,
These men were born to drill and die. 20
Point for them the virtue of slaughter,
Make plain to them the excellence of killing
And a field where a thousand corpses lie.

Mother whose heart hung humble as a button
On the bright splendid shroud of your son, 25
Do not weep.
War is kind.

Wilfred Owen (1893–1918)

Arms and the Boy

Let the boy try along this bayonet-blade
How cold steel is, and keen with hunger of blood;
Blue with all malice, like a madman's flash;
And thinly drawn with famishing for flesh.

Lend him to stroke these blind, blunt bullet-heads 5
Which long to nuzzle in the heart of lads,
Or give him cartridges of fine zinc teeth,
Sharp with the sharpness of grief and death.

For his teeth seem for laughing round an apple.
There lurk no claws behind his fingers supple; 10
And god will grow no talons at his heels,
Nor antlers through the thickness of his curls.

Anthem for Doomed Youth

What passing-bells for these who die as
cattle?
Only the monstrous anger of the guns.
Only the stuttering rifles' rapid rattle
Can patter out their hasty orisons.
No mockeries for them; no prayers nor
bells, 5
Nor any voice of mourning save the
choirs,—
The shrill, demented choirs of wailing
shells;
And bugles calling for them from sad
shires.

What candles may be held to speed
them all?
Not in the hands of boys, but in their
eyes 10
Shall shine the holy glimmers of goodbyes.
The pallor of girls' brows shall be their
pall;
Their flowers the tenderness of patient
minds,
And each slow dusk a drawing-down of
blinds.

Greater Love

Red lips are not so red
As the stained stones kissed by the
English dead.
Kindness of wooed and wooer
Seems shame to their love pure.
O Love, your eyes lose lure 5
When I behold eyes blinded in my
stead!

Your slender attitude
Trembles not exquisite like limbs
knife-skewed,
Rolling and rolling there
Where God seems not to care; 10
Till the fierce love they bear
Cramps them in death's extreme
decrepitude.

Your voice sings not so soft,—
Though even as wind murmuring
through raftered loft,—
Your dear voice is not clear, 15
Gentle, and evening clear,
As theirs whom none now hear
Now earth has stopped their piteous
mouths that coughed.

Heart, you were never hot,
Nor large, nor full like hearts made
great with shot; 20
And though your hand be pale,
Paler are all which trail
Your cross through flame and hail:
Weep, you may weep, for you may
touch them not.

Dulce et Decorum Est

Bent double, like old beggars under sacks,
Knock-kneed, coughing like hags, we cursed through sludge,
Till on the haunting flares we turned our backs
And towards our distant rest began to trudge. 5
Men marched asleep. Many had lost their boots
But limped on, blood-shod. All went lame; all blind;
Drunk with fatigue; deaf even to the hoots
Of tired, outstripped Five-Nines that dropped behind.

Gas! GAS! Quick, boys!—An ecstasy of fumbling,
Fitting the clumsy helmets just in time; 10
But someone still was yelling out and stumbling
And flound'ring like a man in fire or lime . . .
Dim, through the misty panes and thick green light,
As under a green sea, I saw him drowning.

In all my dreams, before my helpless sight, 15
He plunges at me, guttering, choking, drowning.

If in some smothering dreams you too could pace
Behind the wagon that we flung him in,
And watch the white eyes writhing in his face,
His hanging face, like a devil's sick of sin; 20
If you could hear, at every jolt, the blood
Come gargling from the froth-corrupted lungs,
Obscene as cancer, bitter as the cud
Of vile, incurable sores on innocent tongues,—
My friend, you would not tell with such high zest 25
To children ardent for some desperate glory,
The old Lie: Dulce et decorum est
Pro patria mori.

"The trouble with you boys to-day is you have no imagination!"
"Well, girlie, nowadays we don't need imagination."

John Held, Jr. "Flapper." Culver Pictures.

The Long Armistice

1918–1939

Introduction

The Long Armistice between November 11, 1918 and November 1, 1939 was turbulent. The idealistic hopes of Woodrow Wilson, who dreamt of making peace with honor, soon lapsed into the disillusioned conviction that World War I had been fought less to save the world for democracy than to increase corporate profits. That despair was deepened by the implications of Freudian and behavioristic psychology, which suggested that man was at the mercy of drives he could neither understand nor control, and by some interpretations of the new physics, which seemed to imply, by the law of entropy, that the earth's supply of available energy was limited and the universe was inevitably doomed. The stock market crash of 1929 lent credence to Marx's economic predictions, and the Great Depression lured many men to envision a political system that might provide greater security than capitalistic democracy.

The prospect of a second world war grew ever more certain. The seeds for that conflict were planted in innumerable ways: in the division of the spoils of war at the Treaty of Versailles in 1919; in the American isolationism that led Congress, in 1919, to reject membership in the League of Nations; in the irresponsible boom and bust psychology of the 1920's; in the diminution of the British Empire; in the territorial ambitions of Japan, Italy, and Germany which spawned aggression respectively in China, Ethiopia, and Europe; in the Nazi violence against Jews and other minority groups; and in the Spanish Civil War, the dress rehearsal for World War II. By the time Neville Chamberlain, the British prime minister, flew to Munich in March, 1939, to make his futile attempt to appease Hitler—a trip from which Chamberlain returned with the ironic promise of "peace in our time"—the Long Armistice was nearly over.

Economic and political changes were vast. The Bolshevist Revolution of 1917, inspired by the doctrines of Karl Marx, established a communist state, abolished most private property, and proclaimed the Soviet Union the international champion of the labor class. After the death of Lenin in 1924, Joseph Stalin substituted personal dictatorship for the "dictatorship of the proletariat" and intense nationalism for the goal of international revolution. He demanded immense sacrifice and absolute obedience of all Soviet citizens. The purges of the 1930s, in which Stalin "liquidated" every vestige of opposition to his authority, revealed the potential of the modern totalitarian state to control every aspect of its citizens' lives. Though Stalinist tyranny disillusioned some Marxists, others in England, America, and elsewhere continued to look to Russia for leadership in the class struggle.

In Germany, Adolph Hitler returned from World War I with an Iron Cross for bravery and a fanatic dream to unify and glorify the German fatherland. The skillful demagogue, Hitler founded the National Socialist (or Nazi) Party and captured power in Germany by terror and propaganda. With the aid of his brown-shirted storm troops he intimidated opposition, and after the blood purges of 1934 proclaimed himself "Der Fuehrer" and prescribed "Heil Hitler" as the official German salutation. His doctrine of racial differences extolled the supremacy of Aryan peoples—the master race—and demanded the extermination or subordination of inferior "races." The "final solution" of the Jewish question was to be accomplished in such notorious death camps as Dachau and Auschwitz. His messianic purpose was not contained within German boundaries. Ostensibly in quest of "lebensraum," German forces invaded and conquered the Rhineland in 1936, Austria in 1938, and Czechoslovakia in the same year—conquests that England and France were too weak or intimidated to oppose. Hitler's alliance with the Italian dictator, Benito Mussolini, was made explicit by cooperative efforts, from 1936 till 1939, to assist General Francisco Franco, the rebel leader in the Spanish war, and was consolidated in 1939 by the Berlin-Rome Axis (later to include Tokyo). With the Russo-German nonaggression pact of August 9, 1939, Hitler secured Russian neutrality, and, on September 1, he ordered the invasion of Poland. Chamberlain's dream of "peace in our time" had lasted less than six months.

In America, the interim between the wars began with the dreams of President Woodrow Wilson and ended with the pragmatism of President Franklin Delano Roosevelt. On November 11, 1918 when the war ended, Wilson proclaimed that "everything for which America fought has been accomplished," but in the light of history that affirmation is more pathetic than ironic. The American Congress refused to approve the work of the "four old men" who dominated the peace conference of 1919 at Versailles, and Congress firmly rejected membership in the League of Nations. By its actions, the Congress derided Wilson's declaration: "We cannot turn back. We can only go forward, with lifted eyes and freshened spirit, to follow the vision." His declaration reflected the idealism and illusions with which the War had been fought. Soon, however, such utopian slogans of Wilson as "A war to end war" were replaced by the kind of cynicism that Hemingway expressed in *A Farewell to Arms* in 1929: "I was always embarrassed by the words *sacred, glorious, sacrifice* and the expression *in vain*. . . . I had seen nothing sacred, and the things that were glorious had no glory and the sacrifices were like the stockyards at Chicago if nothing was done with the meat except to bury it."

From Wilson's aspirations and the vainglory of foreign intervention, America was lured by Warren Harding's promise of "a full dinner pail" to elect a president who promised, in his inaugural address, nothing more venturesome than a "return to normalcy." The Roaring Twenties, the Jazz Age, the Big Boom, and the Lost Generation are epithets applied to the postwar decade, a period of material prosperity, monetary inflation, restless morality, governmental ineptness and corruption, reckless lawlessness (stimulated in part by the folly of prohibition), extreme philistinism, and intellectual disillusionment. The "new" jazz, cacophonous and savage to older ears, blared everywhere, and new dances such as the Charleston and the Black Bottom replaced the waltz. Henry Ford's Tin Lizzie filled the highways and altered living habits, and movies, radio, and organized sport became national passions. "Flappers" and "bob-haired bandits" talked a great deal about sex and its prophet Dr. Freud, bound their breasts tightly in an effort to become just one of the boys, and asserted their newfound sophistication by cursing, drinking, and smoking. Everywhere young people were rootless and restless. Many of them would have agreed with Amory Blaine, the hero of F. Scott Fitzgerald's novel *This Side of Paradise*, that they had "grown up to find all Gods dead, all wars fought, all faiths in man shaken. . . ."

The period ended with a bang on Black Thursday, October 24, 1929, the day the stock market crashed. Its plunge ushered in the Great Depression. General Electric, a typical blue-chip stock, fell from a high of 396¼ on September 3, 1929 to 197¼ on November 13, 1929 to 34 in 1936. Although the Depression was worldwide, it was most severe in America. Banks failed; unemployment spread; hunger and starvation were common; bewilderment and fear bred murmurs of chaos and communism. The unkempt veterans, the Bonus Army of 1932, marching on Washington to plead for a veteran's bonus, seemed a portent of imminent revolution.

If the name of President Woodrow Wilson dominated the early part of the period, and if the collapse of his utopian dreams into a carnival of sensuous, restless escapism reflected the intellectual disillusionment of the twenties, the name of Franklin Delano Roosevelt dominated the period from 1930 until the beginning of World War II. With his election as president in 1932, Roosevelt promised a "New Deal"; he and a "Brain Trust" of intellectuals set about shuffling the cards. It was about time, for the Depression had left Americans of all classes bewildered by a catastrophe they could not comprehend. Traditional authority had been weakened. Paternal status had been undermined by unemployment, and free enterprise had been reduced to a set of economic imponderables. Business leaders were as confused as their employees. Charles N. Schwab, a United States Steel tycoon, confessed: "I'm afraid, every man is afraid. I don't know, we don't know, whether the values we have are going to be real next month or not." As Robert and Helen Lynd concluded in their study of the average town, which they dubbed Middletown: ". . . the great knife of the Depression had cut down impartially through the entire population cleaving open lives and hopes of rich as well as poor. . . . it has approached in its elemental shock the primary experience of birth and death."

Instead of merely promising, like his predecessor Herbert Hoover, that prosperity was "just around the corner," Roosevelt acted; and although the projects of the New Deal—such as the TVA, CWA, WPA, CCC, and the NYA—did not solve all economic ills, they gave hope to millions of Americans and may well have averted revolution. Although he avoided the dictatorial course of Stalin, Hitler, and Mussolini, Roosevelt greatly expanded the powers of the federal government. *Laissez-faire* had proved an insufficient guarantor of prosperities; since Roosevelt's administration governmental regulation of private enterprise has increased rather than disappeared.

In America, as in England, the internal problems posed by the Depression were so extreme that most national leaders (England's Winston Churchill was a notable exception) were reluctant to face the unspeakable horrors of the German regime and the threat of the Nazi military juggernaut. That terror loomed over the thirties, and its images—of Nazi troops, goose-stepping in ostentatious parade, of the black Nazi insignia and the rigid Nazi salute, of the balcony harangues of Der Fuehrer as he roared "Only force rules . . . force is the first law"—remain etched in the modern consciousness.

The literature of the period reflects its moods and contradictions. Although William Butler Yeats in "A Prayer for My Daughter" looked to the stability and order of an earlier time, and although Robert Frost used traditional poetic forms, simple diction, and spoken language rhythms to paint rural scenes and to suggest personal and universal religious tensions, most writers of the twenties were radically experimental. A poetic renaissance began in 1912 with the founding in America of Harriet Monroe's *Poetry: A Magazine of Verse*; among its contributors were a group of Imagists, with whom Ezra Pound and Carl Sandburg were originally associated. The Imagists strove to evoke emotional response to verbal images. In seeking to liberate poetry from its traditional form and subject matter, they often abandoned meter and rhyme in favor of more natural rhythms; they sought the simplicity and naturalness of real speech and everyday life; they relied on imaginative association rather than conventional syntax; and they insisted on the freedom to go beyond typically "poetic" subjects.

Many writers in the twenties, preoccupied with the physical and psychic wounds left by World War I, created poetically a sterile, loveless, godless wasteland, where shell-shocked creatures clung to a precarious mental balance and stoically stifled their fears. Ernest Hemingway deifies stoicism in a world where, as he wrote his friend F. Scott Fitzgerald, "we are all bitched from the start." In the simple diction and deliberate understatement of "In Another Country" he reveals his suspicion of complex ideas and dramatizes, through the actions and reactions of two wounded soldiers, the "grammar" of courage by the actions of one who knows the language well—but still cannot "resign" himself—and another who has yet to grasp the total grammar but is slowly learning it in his bones. Hemingway's suspicion of the intellect, like that of D. H. Lawrence and E. E. Cummings, implies a postwar disillusionment with the rational and the scientific. In both style and attitude, Hemingway became a model for his contemporaries.

T. S. Eliot, an intellectual aristocrat unlike Hemingway, dictated poetic sensibility in the postwar decade. Like his creature, J. Alfred Prufrock, Eliot was bored by the triviality of polite society and offended by the crudities of "men in shirt sleeves." In his view, man was not a tragic hero but a pathetic fool, dead, yet yearning to be born. That awareness Eliot raised to a metaphor of the human condition in "The Hollow Men": the hollow men desire to pray, to believe, but can only begin, never complete, an act of devotion. Paralyzed by indecision, they engage in empty rituals: "Here we go round the prickly pear/At five o'clock in the morning."

Perhaps even more important than his ideas, however, were Eliot's poetic strategies. The indirection and obscurity of his poetry (much like that of his early teacher Ezra Pound) anticipate much of modern poetry. Eliot's sophistication and intellectualism, his recondite and at times private allusions, his dry wit and omnipresent irony, his contrast of this brass age with an earlier golden one, his complex symbolism, his psychological leaps (which result in the lack of logical transitions so common in his poetry), and his disgust with the vulgarity of modern man and his milieu —all these qualities were so overwhelming that not until the late 1950s did there begin to be a serious revolt against the "tryanny" of Eliot's influence.

Save for the furor aroused by the trial and execution of two poor anarchists, Sacco and Vanzetti, the twenties was a time more concerned with individual problems—especially spiritual emptiness—than with practical politics or social justice. The Great Depression, however, lured many writers to preach radical ideology in such lyrical phrases as those of Stephen Spender's "The Express," or in such challenges as that of John Dos Passos (in his trilogy *USA*): "all right we are two nations." And always, in the late thirties, the stench of the Nazi concentration camps pervaded the air, not only throughout Germany, but in England and America. In his long poem "Autumn Journal" Louis MacNeice captures the despair and paralysis of those months in 1939 when the world waited to reap the whirlwind sown by clever, greedy, and irresponsible men.

With the thirties the mood of artistic experimentation declined. Instead of looking inward, most artists looked outward, and what they saw led them at times to mawkish sentimentality (as in the popular song "Brother, Can You Spare a Dime") and at others to cry out for social reform. Though the influence of Freud did not diminish greatly, Marx became the dominant prophet of the age. To assert their artistic independence, artists were often content to proclaim, in conventional forms, the rottenness of the capitalistic system, and innumerable writers created propagandistic novels with such titles as those of Jack Conroy's "The Disinherited" (a powerful cry for the union of the oppressed against their capitalistic exploiters) and "A World to Win" (inspired by the concluding peroration of *The Communist Manifesto*: "Workers of the World unite; you have nothing to lose but your chains; you have a world to win!"). Eugene O'Neill in *The Hairy Ape* dramatized in part the conflict between the exploiters and the exploited of society, even though he eventually concluded that the needs of his hairy ape to belong to something were greater than could be realized by any social panacea. More explicitly Stephen Spender, in his revolutionary poetic "manifesto" entitled "The Express," foresaw a new social system—"new eras of wild happiness"—created from modern ideas and modern machinery. These, he felt, would transform the present religious and social fabric of society (Calvinistic, Catholic, and Capitalist), and would destroy the conventions of past romantic literary modes much as the socialistic express does: "Ah, like a comet through flames she moves entranced/Wrapt in her music no bird song, no, nor bough/Breaking with honey buds, shall ever equal." That day of reckoning William Faulkner also foresaw. In "Delta Autumn" he dramatizes the sins and the guilt of past generations, both in their treatment of blacks and in their thoughtless exploitation of the land, and he implies the necessity of new, more cooperative, and more Christian modes of life and thought. By such protest many writers outraged conventional society but soothed their own indignation. The painter Rivera, who so offended Nelson Rockefeller by questioning the right of wealth to dictate the terms of art (and of whom E. B. White writes in "I Paint What I See"), was a common phenomenon among artists in the thirties.

Though there is little doubt that the period between the wars is split at the beginning of the Great Depression, some artistic obsessions cover the entire era. Throughout the period creative writers reflect the theories of the subconscious posed by Freud and dramatize the ideas of behaviorist psychologists such as John Watson, which seem to reduce men to mere fleshly machines responding automatically to appropriate stimuli. In the course of his career Freud gradually emphasized the use of dreams and the free association of ideas as methods of psychiatric analysis. Constantly he explored man's subconscious fears and fantasies with the consequent conflicts between id, ego, and superego (concepts effectively dramatized in such a story as Graham Greene's "The Basement Room") and insistently he stated the importance of sexual drives (especially repressed sexual urges) in the understanding of personality and its malformation (sexual urges that Sherwood Anderson explored in numerous stories such as "Seeds"). Among the numerous theories of Freud that have become folklore, none have become more widespread than those of the oedipal and electra complex, and much of modern literature dramatizes such concepts. Because of the influence of such men as Freud and Watson, many of the characters in the fiction and the drama of the times seem grotesques, to use a favorite word of Sherwood Anderson, who, like Mildred in *The Hairy Ape* or Prufrock in "The Love Song of J. Alfred Prufrock," have become so completely artificial that they have completely lost touch with the world of natural beauty or simple reality.

Almost as omnipresent is the fascination with, and the fear of, the machines by which man continued to transform his environment and social habits. The distaste with which E. M. Forster in "The Machine Stops" contemplated the progress of man toward sluggish, loveless dehumanization under the tyranny of the machine is paralleled by Stephen Vincent Benét's satire in "Nightmare Number Three." In Benét's poem, the human narrator dreams, after the revolt and victory of the machines, "Oh, it's going to be jake./There won't be so much real difference—honest, there won't—." But Benét knew there would be. And we are today increasingly finding out the quality of the difference.

Exposition and Argument

Sigmund Freud (1856–1940)

from The Interpretation of Dreams

According to my already extensive experience, parents play a leading part in the infantile psychology of all persons who subsequently become psychoneurotics. Falling in love with one parent and hating the other forms part of the permanent stock of the psychic impulses which arise in early childhood, and are of such importance as the material of the subsequent neurosis. But I do not believe that psychoneurotics are to be sharply distinguished in this respect from other persons who remain normal—that is, I do not believe that they are capable of creating something absolutely new and peculiar to themselves. It is far more probable—and this is confirmed by incidental observations of normal children—that in their amorous or hostile attitude toward their parents, psychoneurotics do not more than reveal to us, by magnification, something that occurs less markedly and intensively in the minds of the majority of children. Antiquity has furnished us with legendary matter which corroborates this belief, and the profound and universal validity of the old legends is explicable only by an equally universal validity of the above-mentioned hypothesis of infantile psychology.

I am referring to the legend of King Oedipus and the *Oedipus Rex* of Sophocles. Oedipus, the son of Laius, king of Thebes, and Jocasta, is exposed as a suckling, because an oracle had informed the father that his son, who was still unborn, would be his murderer. He is rescued, and grows up as a king's son at a foreign court, until, being uncertain of his origin he, too, consults the oracle, and is warned to avoid his native place, for he is destined to become the murderer of his father and the husband of his mother. On the road leading away from his supposed home he meets King Laius, and in a sudden quarrel strikes him dead. He comes to Thebes, where he solves the riddle of the Sphinx, who is barring the way to the city, whereupon he is elected king by the grateful Thebans, and is rewarded with the hand of Jocasta. He reigns for many years in peace and honour, and begets two sons and two daughters upon his unknown mother, until at last a plague breaks out—which causes the Thebans to consult the oracle anew. Here Sophocles' tragedy begins. The messengers bring the reply that the plague will stop as soon as the murderer of Laius is driven from the country. But where is he?

"Where shall be found,
Faint, and hard to be known, the trace
of the ancient guilt?"

The action of the play consists simply in the disclosure, approached step by step and artistically delayed (and comparable to the work of a psychoanalysis) that Oedipus himself is the murderer of Laius, and that he is the son of the murdered man and Jocasta. Shocked by the abominable crime which he has unwittingly committed, Oedipus blinds himself, and departs from his native city. The prophecy of the oracle has been fulfilled. . . .

If the *Oedipus Rex* is capable of moving a modern reader or playgoer no less powerfully than it moved the contemporary Greeks, the only possible explanation is that the effect of the Greek tragedy does not depend upon the conflict between fate and human will, but upon the peculiar nature of the material by which this conflict is revealed. There must be a voice within us which is prepared to acknowledge the compelling power of fate in the *Oedipus* . . . And there actually is a motive in the story of King Oedipus which explains the verdict of this inner voice. His fate moves us only because it might have been our own, because the oracle laid upon us before our birth the very curse which rested upon him. It may be that we were all destined to direct our first sexual impulses toward our mothers, and our first impulses of hatred and violence toward our fathers; our dreams convince us that we were. King Oedipus, who slew his father Laius and wedded his mother Jocasta, is nothing more or less than a wish-fulfillment —the fulfilment of the wish of our childhood. But we, more fortunate than he, in so far as we have not become psychoneurotics, have since our childhood succeeded in withdrawing our sexual impulses from our mothers, and in forgetting our jealousy of our fathers. We recoil from the person for whom this primitive wish of our childhood has been fulfilled with all the force of the repression which these wishes have undergone in our minds since childhood. As the poet brings the guilt of Oedipus to light by his investigation, he forces us to become aware of our inner selves, in which the same impulses are still extant, even though they are suppressed. The antithesis with which the chorus departs:—

". . . Behold this is Oedipus,
Who unravelled the great riddle, and
was first in power,
Whose fortune all the townsmen
praised and envied:
See in what dread adversity he sank!"

—this admonition touches us and our own pride, us who since the years of our childhood have grown so wise and so powerful in our own estimation. Like Oedipus, we live in ignorance of the desires that offend morality, the desires that nature has forced upon us and after their unveiling we may well prefer to avert our gaze from the scenes of our childhood.

In the very text of Sophocles' tragedy there is an unmistakable reference to the fact that the Oedipus legend had its source in dream-material of immemorial antiquity, the content of which was the painful disturbance of the child's relations to its parents caused by the first impulses of sexuality. Jocasta comforts Oedipus,—who is not yet enlightened, but is troubled by the recollection of the oracle—by an allusion, to a dream which is often dreamed, though it cannot, in her opinion, mean anything:—

"For many a man hath seen himself in
dreams
His mother's mate, but he who gives
no heed
To suchlike matters bears the easier
life . . ."

Another of the great poetic tragedies, Shakespeare's Hamlet, is rooted in the same soil as *Oedipus Rex.* But the whole difference in the psychic life of the two widely separated periods of civilization, and the progress, during the course of time, of repression in the emotional life of humanity, is manifested in the differing treatment of the same material. In *Oedipus Rex* the basic wish-phantasy of the child is brought to light and realized as it is in dreams; in Hamlet it remains repressed, and we learn of its existence—as we discover the relevant facts in a neurosis—only through the inhibitory effects which proceed from it . . . The play is based upon Hamlet's hesitation in accomplishing the task of revenge assigned to him; the text does not give the cause or the motive of this hesitation, nor have the manifold attempts at interpretation succeeded in doing so. According to the still prevailing conception, a conception for which Goethe was first responsible, Hamlet represents the type of man whose active energy is paralysed by excessive intellectual activity: "Sicklied o'er with the pale cast of thought." According to another conception, the poet has endeavoured to portray a morbid, irresolute character, on the verge of neurasthenia. The plot of the drama, however, shows us that Hamlet is by no means intended to appear as a character wholly incapable of action. On two separate occasions we see him assert himself: once in a sudden outburst of rage, when he stabs the eavesdropper behind the arras, and on the other occasion when he deliberately, and even craftily, with the complete unscrupulousness of a prince of the Renaissance, sends the two courtiers to the death which was intended for himself. What is it, then, that inhibits him in accomplishing the task which his father's ghost has laid upon him? Here the explanation offers itself that it is the peculiar nature of this task. Hamlet is able to do anything but take vengeance upon the man who did away with his father and has taken his father's place with his mother—the man who shows him in realization the repressed desires of his own childhood. The loathing which should have driven him to revenge is thus replaced by self-reproach, by conscientious scruples, which tell him that he himself is no better than the murderer whom he is required to punish. I have here translated into consciousness what had to remain unconscious in the mind of the hero; if anyone wishes to call Hamlet an hysterical subject I cannot but admit that this is the deduction to be drawn from my interpretation. The sexual aversion which Hamlet expresses in conversation with Ophelia is perfectly consistent with this deduction—the same sexual aversion during the next few years was increasingly to take possession of the poet's soul, until it found its supreme utterance in *Timon of Athens*. It can, of course, be only the poet's own psychology with which we are confronted in *Hamlet*; and in a work on Shakespeare by Georg Brandes (1896) I find the statement that the drama was composed immediately after the death of Shakespeare's father (1601)—that is to say, when he was still mourning his loss, and during a revival, as we may fairly assume, of his own childish feelings in respect of his father. It is known, too, that Shakespeare's son, who died in childhood, bore the name of Hamnet (identical with Hamlet). . . .

John Dos Passos (1896–1970)

Tin Lizzie

"Mr. Ford the automobileer," the feature-writer wrote in 1900,

"Mr. Ford the automobileer began by giving his steed three or four sharp jerks with the lever at the righthand side of the seat; that is, he pulled the level up and down sharply in order, as he said, to mix air with gasoline and drive the charge into the exploding cylinder. . . . Mr. Ford slipped a small electric switch handle and there followed a puff, puff, puff. . . . The puffing of the machine assumed a higher key. She was flying along about eight miles an hour. The ruts in the road were deep, but the machine certainly went with a dreamlike smoothness. There was none of the bumping common even to a streetcar. . . . By this time the boulevard had been reached, and the automobileer, letting a lever fall a little, let her out. Whiz! She picked up speed with infinite rapidity. As she ran on there was a clattering behind, the new noise of the automobile."

For twenty years or more,

ever since he'd left his father's farm when he was sixteen to get a job in a Detroit machineshop, Henry Ford had been nuts about machinery. First it was watches, then he designed a steamtractor, then he built a horseless carriage with an engine adapted from the Otto gas-engine he'd read about in *The World of Science*, then a mechanical buggy with a onecylinder fourcyle motor, that would run forward but not back;

at last, in ninetyeight, he felt he was far enough along to risk throwing up his job with the Detroit Edison Company, where he'd worked his way up from night fireman to chief engineer, to put all his time into working on a new gasoline engine,

(in the late eighties he'd met Edison at a meeting of electriclight employees in Atlantic City. He'd gone up to Edison after Edison had delivered an address and asked him if he thought gasoline was practical as a motor fuel. Edison had said yes. If Edison said it, it was true. Edison was the great admiration of Henry Ford's life);

and in driving his mechanical buggy, sitting there at the lever jauntily dressed in a tightbuttoned jacket and a high collar and a derby hat, back and forth over the level illpaved streets of Detroit,

scaring the big brewery horses and the skinny trotting horses and the sleek-rumped pacers with the motor's loud explosions,

looking for men scatterbrained enough to invest money in a factory for building automobiles.

He was the eldest son of an Irish immigrant who during the Civil War had married the daughter of a prosperous Pennsylvania Dutch farmer and settled down to farming near Dearborn in Wayne County, Michigan;

like plenty of other Americans, young Henry grew up hating the endless slogging through the mud about the chores, the hauling and pitching manure, the kerosene lamps to clean, the irk and sweat and solitude of the farm.

He was a slender, active youngster, a good skater, clever with his hands; what he liked was to tend the machinery and let the others do the heavy work. His mother had told him not to drink, smoke, gamble or go into debt, and he never did.

When he was in his early twenties his father tried to get him back from

From *The Big Money*, third volume of the *USA* trilogy, by John Dos Passos, copyright by John Dos Passos 1936 and 1964; published by Houghton Mifflin Company.

Detroit, where he was working as mechanic and repairman for the Drydock Engine Company that built engines for steamboats, by giving him forty acres of land.

Young Henry built himself an uptodate square white dwelling-house with a false mansard roof and married and settled down on the farm,

but he let the hired men do the farming;

he bought himself a buzzsaw and rented a stationary engine and cut the timber off the woodlots.

He was a thrifty young man who never drank or smoked or gambled or coveted his neighbor's wife, but he couldn't stand living on the farm.

He moved to Detroit, and in the brick barn behind his house tinkered for years in his spare time with a mechanical buggy that would be light enough to run over the clayey wagonroads of Wayne County, Michigan.

By 1900 he had a practicable car to promote.

He was forty years old before the Ford Motor Company was started and production began to move.

Speed was the first thing the early automobile manufacturers went after. Races advertised the makes of cars.

Henry Ford himself hung up several records at the track at Grosse Pointe and on the ice on Lake St. Clair. In his 999 he did the mile in thirtynine and fourfifths seconds.

But it had always been his custom to hire others to do the heavy work. The speed he was busy with was speed in production, the records were records in efficient output. He hired Barney Oldfield, a stunt bicyclerider from Salt Lake City, to do the racing for him.

Henry Ford had ideas about other things than the designing of motors, carburetors, magnetos, jigs and fixtures, punches and dies; he had ideas about sales,

that the big money was in economical quantity production, quick turnover, cheap interchangeable easilyreplaced standardized parts;

it wasn't until 1909, after years of arguing with his partners, that Ford put out the first Model T.

Henry Ford was right.

That season he sold more than ten thousand tin lizzies, ten years later he was selling almost a million a year.

In these years the Taylor Plan was stirring up plantmanagers and manufacturers all over the country. Efficiency was the word. The same ingenuity that went into improving the performance of a machine could go into improving the performance of the workmen producing the machine.

In 1913 they established the assemblyline at Ford's. That season the profits were something like twentyfive million dollars, but they had trouble in keeping the men on the job, machinists didn't seem to like it at Ford's.

Henry Ford had ideas about other things than production.

He was the largest automobile manufacturer in the world; he paid high wages; maybe if the steady workers thought they were getting a cut (a very small cut) in the profits, it would give trained men an inducement to stick to their jobs,

wellpaid workers might save enough money to buy a tin lizzie; the first day Ford's announced that cleancut properly-married American workers who wanted jobs had a chance to make five bucks a day (of course it turned out that there were strings to it; always there were strings to it)

such an enormous crowd waited outside the Highland Park plant

all through the zero January night

that there was a riot when the gates were opened; cops broke heads, jobhunters threw bricks; property, Henry

Ford's own property, was destroyed. The company dicks had to turn on the fire-hose to beat back the crowd.

The American Plan; automotive prosperity seeping down from above; it turned out there were strings to it.

But that five dollars a day

paid to good, clean American workmen

who didn't drink or smoke cigarettes or read or think,

and who didn't commit adultery

and whose wives didn't take in boarders,

made America once more the Yukon of the sweated workers of the world;

made all the tin lizzies and the automotive age, and incidentally,

made Henry Ford, the automobileer, the admirer of Edison, the birdlover,

the great American of his time.

But Henry Ford had ideas about other things beside assemblylines and the livinghabits of his employees. He was full of ideas. Instead of going to the city to make his fortune, here was a country boy who'd made his fortune by bringing the city out to the farm. The precepts he'd learned out of McGuffey's Reader, his mother's prejudices and preconceptions, he had preserved clean and unworn as freshprinted bills in the safe in a bank.

He wanted people to know about his ideas, so he bought the *Dearborn Independent* and started a campaign against cigarettesmoking.

When war broke out in Europe, he had ideas about that too. (Suspicion of armymen and soldiering were part of the midwest farm tradition, like thrift, stickativeness, temperance and sharp practice in money matters.) Any intelligent American mechanic could see that if the Europeans hadn't been a lot of ignorant underpaid foreigners who drank, smoked, were loose about women and wasteful in their methods of production, the war could never have happened.

When Rosika Schwimmer broke through the stockade of secretaries and servicemen who surrounded Henry Ford and suggested to him that he could stop the war,

he said sure they'd hire a ship and go over and get the boys out of the trenches by Christmas.

He hired a steamboat, the *Oscar II*, and filled it up with pacifists and social-workers,

to go over to explain to the princelings of Europe

that what they were doing was vicious and silly.

It wasn't his fault that Poor Richard's commonsense no longer rules the world and that most of the pacifists were nuts,

goofy with headlines.

When William Jennings Bryan went over to Hoboken to see him off, somebody handed William Jennings Bryan a squirrel in a cage; William Jennings Bryan made a speech with the squirrel under his arm. Henry Ford threw American Beauty roses to the crowd. The band played *I Didn't Raise My Boy to Be a Soldier*. Practical jokers let loose more squirrels. An eloping couple was married by a platoon of ministers in the saloon, and Mr. Zero, the flophouse humanitarian who reached the dock too late to sail,

dove into the North River and swam after the boat.

The *Oscar II* was described as a floating Chautauqua; Henry Ford said it felt like a middlewestern village, but by the time they reached Christiansand in Norway, the reporters had kidded him so that he had gotten cold feet and gone to bed. The world was too crazy outside of Wayne County, Michigan. Mrs. Ford and the management sent an Episcopal dean after him who brought him home under wraps, and the pacifists had to speechify without him.

Two years later Ford's was manufacturing munitions, Eagle boats; Henry Ford was planning oneman tanks, and oneman submarines like the one tried out in the Revolutionary War. He announced to the press that he'd turn over his war profits to the government,

but there's no record that he ever did.

One thing he brought back from his trip

was the Protocols of the Elders of Zion.

He started a campaign to enlighten the world in the *Dearborn Independent*; the Jews were why the world wasn't like Wayne County, Michigan, in the old horse and buggy days;

the Jews had started the war. Bolshevism, Darwinism, Marxism, Nietzsche, short skirts and lipstick. They were behind Wall Street and the international bankers, and the whiteslave traffic and the movies and the Supreme Court and ragtime and the illegal liquor business.

Henry Ford denounced the Jews and ran for senator and sued the *Chicago Tribune* for libel,

and was the laughingstock of the kept metropolitan press;

but when the metropolitan bankers tried to horn in on his business

he thoroughly outsmarted them.

In 1918 he had borrowed on notes to buy out his minority stockholders for the picayune sum of seventyfive million dollars.

In February, 1920, he needed cash to pay off some of these notes that were coming due. A banker is supposed to have called on him and offered him every facility if the bankers' representative could be made a member of the board of directors. Henry Ford handed the banker his hat,

and went about raising the money in his own way:

he shipped every car and part he had in his plant to his dealers and demanded immediate cash payment. Let the other fellow do the borrowing had always been a cardinal principle. He shut down production and canceled all orders from the supplyfirms. Many dealers were ruined, many supplyfirms failed, but when he reopened his plant,

he owned it absolutely,

the way a man owns an unmortgaged farm with the taxes paid up.

In 1922 there started the Ford boom for President (high wages, waterpower, industry scattered to the small towns) that was skillfully pricked behind the scenes

by another crackerbarrel philosopher, Calvin Coolidge,

but in 1922 Henry Ford sold one million three hundred and thirtytwo thousand two hundred and nine tin lizzies; he was the richest man in the world.

Good roads had followed the narrow ruts made in the mud by the Model T. The great automotive boom was on. At Ford's production was improving all the time; less waste, more spotters, straw-bosses, stoolpigeons (fifteen minutes for lunch, three minutes to go to the toilet, the Taylorized speedup everywhere, reach under, adjust washer, screw down bolt, shove in cotterpin, reachunder adjustwasher, screwdown bolt, reachunderadjustscrewdownreachunderadjust until every ounce of life was sucked off into production and at night the workmen went home grey shaking husks).

Ford owned every detail of the process from the ore in the hills until the car rolled off the end of the assemblyline under its own power, the plants were rationalized to the last tenthousandth of an inch as measured by the Johansen scale;

in 1926 the production cycle was reduced to eightyone hours from the

ore in the mine to the finished salable car proceeding under its own power,
but the Model T was obsolete.

New Era prosperity and the American Plan
(there were strings to it, always there were strings to it)
had killed Tin Lizzie
Ford's was just one of many automobile plants.
When the stockmarket bubble burst,
Mr. Ford the crackerbarrel philosopher said jubilantly,
"I told you so.
Serves you right for gambling and getting in debt.
The country is sound."
But when the country on cracked shoes, in frayed trousers, belts tightened over hollow bellies,
idle hands cracked and chapped with the cold of that coldest March day of 1932,
started marching from Detroit to Dearborn, asking for work and the American Plan, all they could think of at Ford's was machineguns.
The country was sound, but they mowed the marchers down.
They shot four of them dead.

Henry Ford was an old man
is a passionate antiquarian,
(lives besieged on his father's farm embedded in an estate of thousands of millionaire acres, protected by an army of servicemen, secretaries, secret agents, dicks under orders of an English exprizefighter,
always afraid of the feet in broken shoes on the roads, afraid the gangs will kidnap his grandchildren,
that a crank will shoot him,
that Change and the idle hands out of work will break through the gates and the high fences;
protected by a private army against
the new America of starved children and hollow bellies and cracked shoes stamping on souplines,
that has swallowed up the old thrifty farmlands
of Wayne County, Michigan,
as if they had never been).
Henry Ford as an old man
is a passionate antiquarian.
He rebuilt his father's farmhouse and put it back exactly in the state he remembered it in as a boy. He built a village of museums for buggies, sleighs, coaches, old plows, waterwheels, obsolete models of motorcars. He scoured the country for fiddlers to play oldfashioned squaredances.
Even old taverns he bought and put back into their original shape, as well as Thomas Edison's early laboratories.
When he bought the Wayside Inn near Sudbury, Massachusetts, he had the new highway where the newmodel cars roared and slithered and hissed oilily past *(the new noise of the automobile)*,

moved away from the door,
put back the old bad road,
so that everything might be
the way it used to be,
in the days of horses and buggies.

George Orwell (1903–1950)

Shooting an Elephant

In Moulmein, in Lower Burma, I was hated by large numbers of people—the only time in my life that I have been important enough for this to happen to me. I was sub-divisional police officer of the town, and in an aimless, petty kind of way anti-European feeling was very bitter. No one had the guts to raise a riot, but if a European woman went through the bazaars alone somebody would probably spit betel juice over her dress. As a police officer I was an obvious target and was baited whenever it seemed safe to do so. When a nimble Burman tripped me up on the football field and the referee (another Burman) looked the other way, the crowd yelled with hideous laughter. This happened more than once. In the end the sneering yellow faces of young men that met me everywhere, the insults hooted after me when I was at a safe distance, got badly on my nerves. The young Buddhist priests were the worst of all. There were several thousands of them in the town and none of them seemed to have anything to do except stand on street corners and jeer at Europeans.

All this was perplexing and upsetting. For at that time I had already made up my mind that imperialism was an evil thing and the sooner I chucked up my job and got out of it the better. Theoretically—and secretly, of course—I was all for the Burmese and all against their oppressors, the British. As for the job I was doing, I hated it more bitterly than I can perhaps make clear. In a job like that you see the dirty work of Empire at close quarters. The wretched prisoners huddling in the stinking cages of the lock-ups, the grey, cowed faces of the long-term convicts, the scarred buttocks of the men who had been flogged with bamboos—all these oppressed me with an intolerable sense of guilt. But I could get nothing into perspective. I was young and ill-educated and I had had to think out my problems in the utter silence that is imposed on every Englishman in the East. I did not even know that the British Empire is dying, still less did I know that it is a great deal better than the younger empires that are going to supplant it. All I knew was that I was stuck between my hatred of the empire I served and my rage against the evil-spirited little beasts who tried to make my job impossible. With one part of my mind I thought of the British Raj as an unbreakable tyranny, as something clamped down, in *saecula saeculorum*, upon the will of prostrate peoples; with another part I thought that the greatest joy in the world would be to drive a bayonet into a Buddhist priest's guts. Feelings like these are the normal by-products of imperialism; ask any Anglo-Indian official, if you can catch him off duty.

One day something happened which in a roundabout way was enlightening. It was a tiny incident in itself, but it gave me a better glimpse than I had had before of the real nature of imperialism—the real motives for which despotic governments act. Early one morning the sub-inspector at a police station the other end of the town rang me up on the 'phone and said that an elephant was ravaging the bazaar. Would I please come and do something about it? I did not know what I could do, but I wanted to see what was happening and I got on to a pony and started out. I took my rifle, an old .44 Winchester and much too small to kill an elephant, but I thought the noise might be useful *in terrorem.* Various Burmans stopped me on the way and told me about the elephant's doings. It was not, of course, a wild elephant, but a tame one which had gone "must." It had been chained up, as tame elephants always are when their attack of "must" is due, but on the previous night it had broken its chain and escaped. Its mahout, the only person who could manage it when it was in that state, had set out in pursuit, but had taken the wrong direction and was now twelve hours' journey away, and in the morning the elephant had suddenly reappeared in the town. The Burmese population had no weapons and were quite helpless against it. It had already destroyed somebody's bamboo hut, killed a cow and raided some fruit-stalls and devoured the stock; also it had met the municipal rubbish van and, when the driver jumped out and took to his heels, had turned the van over and inflicted violences upon it.

The Burmese sub-inspector and some Indian constables were waiting for me in the quarter where the elephant had been seen. It was a very poor quarter, a labyrinth of squalid bamboo huts, thatched with palm-leaf, winding all over a steep hillside. I remember that it was a cloudy, stuffy morning at the beginning of the rains. We began questioning the people as to where the elephant had gone and, as usual, failed to get any definite information. That is invariably the case in the East, a story always sounds clear enough at a distance, but the nearer you get to the scene of events the vaguer it becomes. Some of the people said that the elephant had gone in one direction, some said that he had gone in another, some professed not even to have heard of any elephant. I had almost made up my mind that the whole story was a pack of lies, when we heard yells a little distance away. There was a loud, scandalized cry of "Go away, child! Go away this instant!" and an old woman with a switch in her hand came round the corner of a hut, violently shooing away a crowd of naked children. Some more women followed, clicking their tongues and exclaiming; evidently there was something that the children ought not to have seen. I rounded the hut and saw a man's dead body sprawling in the mud. He was an Indian, a black Dravidian coolie, almost naked, and he could not have been dead many minutes. The people said that the elephant had come suddenly upon him round the corner of the hut, caught him with its trunk, put its foot on his back and ground him into the earth. This was the rainy season and the ground was soft, and his face had scored a trench a foot deep and a couple of yards long. He was lying on his belly with arms crucified and head sharply twisted to one side. His face was coated with mud, the eyes wide open, the teeth bared and grinning with an expression of unendurable agony. (Never tell me, by the way, that the dead look peaceful. Most of the corpses I have seen looked devilish.) The friction of the great beast's foot had stripped the skin from his back as neatly as one skins a rabbit. As soon as I saw the dead man I sent an orderly to a friend's house nearby to borrow an elephant rifle. I had already sent back the pony, not wanting it to go mad with fright and throw me if it smelt the elephant.

The orderly came back in a few minutes with a rifle and five cartridges, and meanwhile some Burmans had arrived and told us that the elephant was in the paddy fields below, only a few hundred yards away. As I started forward practically the whole population of the quarter flocked out of the houses and followed me. They had seen the rifle and were all shouting excitedly that I was going to shoot the elephant. They had not shown much interest in the elephant when he was merely ravaging their homes, but it was different now that he was going to be shot. It was a bit of fun to them, as it would be to an English crowd; besides they wanted the meat. It made me vaguely uneasy. I had no intention of shooting the elephant—I had merely sent for the rifle to defend myself if necessary—and it is always unnerving to have a crowd following you. I marched down the hill, looking and feeling a fool, with the rifle over my shoulder and an ever-growing army of people jostling at my heels. At the bottom, when you got away from the huts, there was a metalled road and beyond that a miry waste of paddy fields a thousand yards across, not yet ploughed but soggy from the first rains and dotted with coarse grass. The elephant was standing eight yards from the road, his left side towards us. He took not the slightest notice of the crowd's approach. He was tearing up bunches of grass, beating them against his knees to clean them and stuffing them into his mouth.

I had halted on the road. As soon as I saw the elephant I knew with perfect certainty that I ought not to shoot him. It is a serious matter to shoot a working elephant—it is comparable to destroying a huge and costly piece of machinery—and obviously one ought not to do it if it can possibly be avoided. And at that distance, peacefully eating, the elephant looked no more dangerous than a cow. I thought then and I think now that his attack of "must" was already passing off; in which case he would merely wander harmlessly about until the mahout came back and caught him. Moreover, I did not in the least want to shoot him. I decided that I would watch him for a little while to make sure that he did not turn savage again, and then go home.

But at that moment I glanced round at the crowd that had followed me. It was an immense crowd, two thousand at the least and growing every minute. It blocked the road for a long distance on either side. I looked at the sea of yellow faces above the garish clothes—faces all happy and excited over this bit of fun, all certain that the elephant was going to be shot. They were watching me as they would watch a conjurer about to perform a trick. They did not like me, but with the magical rifle in my hands I was momentarily worth watching. And suddenly I realized that I should have to shoot the elephant after all. The people expected it of me and I had got to do it; I could feel their two thousand wills pressing me forward, irresistibly. And it was at this moment, as I stood there with the rifle in my hands, that I first grasped the hollowness, the futility of the white man's dominion in the East. Here was I, the white man with his gun, standing in front of the unarmed native crowd—seemingly the leading actor of the piece; but in reality I was only an absurd puppet pushed to and fro by the will of those yellow faces behind. I perceived in this moment that when the white man turns tyrant it is his own freedom that he destroys. He becomes a sort of hollow, posing dummy, the conventionalized figure of a sahib. For it is the condition of his rule that he shall spend his life in trying to impress the "natives," and so in every crisis he has got to do what the "natives" expect of him. He wears a mask; and his face grows to fit it. I had got to shoot the elephant. I had committed myself to doing it when I sent for the rifle. A sahib has got to act like a sahib; he has got to appear resolute, to know his own mind and do definite things. To come all that way, rifle in hand, with two thousand people marching at my heels, and then to trail feebly away, having done nothing—no, that was impossible. The crowd would laugh at me. And my whole life, every white man's life in the East, was one long struggle not to be laughed at.

But I did not want to shoot the elephant. I watched him beating his bunch of grass against his knees, with that preoccupied grandmotherly air that elephants have. It seemed to me that it would be murder to shoot him. At that age I was not squeamish about killing animals, but I had never shot an elephant and never wanted to. (Somehow it always seems worse to kill a *large* animal.) Besides, there was the beast's owner to be considered. Alive, the elephant was worth at least a hundred pounds; dead, he would only be worth the value of his tusks, five pounds, possibly. But I had got to act quickly. I turned to some experienced-looking Burmans who had been there when we arrived, and asked them how the elephant had been behaving. They all said the same thing: he took no notice of you if you left him alone, but he might charge if you went too close to him.

It was perfectly clear to me what I ought to do. I ought to walk up to within, say, twenty-five yards of the elephant and test his behavior. If he charged, I could shoot; if he took no notice of me, it would be safe to leave him until the mahout came back. But also I knew that I was going to do no such thing. I was a poor shot with a rifle and the ground was soft mud into which one would sink at every step. If the elephant charged and I missed him, I should have about as much chance as a toad under a steam-roller. But even then I was not thinking particularly of my own skin, only of the watchful yellow faces behind. For at that moment, with the crowd watching me, I was not afraid in the ordinary sense, as I would have been if I had been alone. A white man mustn't be frightened in front of "natives"; and so, in general, he isn't frightened. The sole thought in my mind was that if anything went wrong those two thousand Burmans would see me pursued, caught, trampled on and reduced to a grinning corpse like that Indian up the hill. And if that happened it was quite probable that some of them would laugh. That would never do. There was only one alternative. I shoved the cartridges into the magazine and lay down on the road to get a better aim.

The crowd grew very still, and a deep, low, happy sigh, as of people who see the theatre curtain go up at last, breathed from innumerable throats. They were going to have their bit of fun after all. The rifle was a beautiful German thing with cross-hair sights. I did not then know that in shooting an elephant one would shoot to cut an imaginary bar running from ear-hole to ear-hole. I ought, therefore, as the elephant was sideways on, to have aimed straight at his ear-hole; actually I aimed several inches in front of this, thinking the brain would be further forward.

When I pulled the trigger I did not hear the bang or feel the kick—one never does when a shot goes home—but I heard the devilish roar of glee that went up from the crowd. In that instant, in too short a time, one would have thought, even for the bullet to get there, a mysterious, terrible change had come over the elephant. He neither stirred nor fell, but every line of his body had altered. He looked suddenly stricken, shrunken, immensely old, as though the frightful impact of the bullet had paralysed him without knocking him down. At last, after what seemed a long time—it might have been five seconds, I dare say—he sagged flabbily to his knees. His mouth slobbered. An enormous senility seemed to have settled upon him. One could have imagined him thousands of years old. I fired again into the same spot. At the second shot he did not collapse but climbed with desperate slowness to his feet and stood weakly upright, with legs sagging and head drooping. I fired a third time. That was the shot that did for him. You could see the agony of it jolt his whole body and knock the last remnant of strength from his legs. But in falling he seemed for a moment to rise, for as his hind legs collapsed beneath him he seemed to tower upward like a huge rock toppling, his trunk reaching skywards like a tree. He trumpeted, for the first and only time. And then down he came, his belly towards me, with a crash that seemed to shake the ground even where I lay.

I got up. The Burmans were already racing past me across the mud. It was obvious that the elephant would never rise again, but he was not dead. He was breathing very rhythmically with long rattling gasps, his great mound of a side painfully rising and falling. His mouth was wide open—I could see far down into caverns of pale pink throat. I waited a long time for him to die, but his breathing did not weaken. Finally I fired my two remaining shots into the spot where I thought his heart must be. The thick blood welled out of him like red velvet, but still he did not die. His body did not even jerk when the shots hit him, the tortured breathing continued without a pause. He was dying, very slowly and in great agony, but in some world remote from me where not even a bullet could damage him further. I felt that I had got to put an end to that dreadful noise. It seemed dreadful to see the great beast lying there, powerless to move and yet powerless to die, and not even to be able to finish him. I sent back for my small rifle and poured shot after shot into his heart and down his throat. They seemed to make no impression. The tortured gasps continued as steadily as the ticking of a clock.

In the end I could not stand it any longer and went away. I heard later that it took him half an hour to die. Burmans were bringing dahs and baskets even before I left, and I was told they had stripped his body almost to the bones by the afternoon.

Afterwards, of course, there were endless discussions about the shooting of the elephant. The owner was furious, but he was only an Indian and could do nothing. Besides, legally I had done the right thing, for a mad elephant has to be killed, like a mad dog, if its owner fails to control it. Among the Europeans opinion was divided. The older men said I was right, the younger men said it was a damn shame to shoot an elephant for killing a coolie, because an elephant was worth more than any damn Coringhee coolie. And afterwards I was very glad that the coolie had been killed; it put me legally in the right and it gave me a sufficient pretext for shooting the elephant. I often wondered whether any of the others grasped that I had done it solely to avoid looking a fool.

Politics and the English Language

Most people who bother with the matter at all would admit that the English language is in a bad way, but it is generally assumed that we cannot by conscious action do anything about it. Our civilization is decadent and our language—so the argument runs—must inevitably share in the general collapse. It follows that any struggle against the abuse of language is a sentimental archaism, like preferring candles to electric light or hansom cabs to aeroplanes. Underneath this lies the half-conscious belief that language is a natural growth and not an instrument which we shape for our own purposes.

Now, it is clear that the decline of a language must ultimately have political and economic causes: it is not due simply to the bad influence of this or that individual writer. But an effect can become a cause, reinforcing the original cause and producing the same effect in an intensified form, and so on indefinitely. A man may take to drink because he feels himself to be a failure, and then fail all the more completely because he drinks. It is rather the same thing that is happening to the English language. It becomes ugly and inaccurate because our thoughts are foolish, but the slovenliness of our language makes it easier for us to have foolish thoughts. The point is that the process is reversible. Modern English, especially written English, is full of bad habits which spread by imitation and which can be avoided if one is willing to take the necessary trouble. If one gets rid of these habits one can think more clearly, and to think clearly is a necessary first step towards political regeneration: so that the fight against bad English is not frivolous and is not the exclusive concern of professional writers. I will come back to this presently, and I hope that by that time the meaning of what I have said here will have become clearer. Meanwhile, here are five specimens of the English language as it is now habitually written.

These five passages have not been picked out because they are especially bad—I could have quoted far worse if I had chosen—but because they illustrate various of the mental vices from which we now suffer. They are a little below the average, but are fairly representative samples. I number them so that I can refer back to them when necessary:

(1) I am not, indeed, sure whether it is not true to say that the Milton who once seemed not unlike a seventeenth-century Shelley had not become, out of an experience ever more bitter in each year, more alien *{sic}* to the founder of that Jesuit sect which nothing could induce him to tolerate.

Professor Harold Laski
(Essay in *Freedom of Expression*).

(2) Above all, we cannot play ducks and drakes with a native battery of idioms which prescribes such egregious collocations of vocables as the Basic *put up with* for *tolerate* or *put at a loss* for *bewilder*.

Professor Lancelot Hogben
(*Interglossa*).

(3) On the one side we have the free personality: by definition it is not neurotic, for it has neither conflict nor dream. Its desires, such as they are, are transparent, for they are just what institutional approval keeps in the forefront of consciousness; another institutional pattern would alter their number and intensity; there is little in them that is natural, irreducible, or culturally dangerous. But *on the other side,* the social bond itself is nothing but the mutual reflection of these self-secure integrities. Recall the definition of love. Is not this the very picture of a small academic? Where is there a place in this hall of mirrors for either personality or fraternity?

Essay on psychology in *Politics*
(New York).

(4) All the "best people" from the gentlemen's clubs, and all the frantic fascist captains, united in common hatred of Socialism and bestial horror of the rising tide of the mass revolutionary movement, have turned to acts of provocation, to foul incendiarism, to medieval legends of poisoned wells, to legalize their own destruction of proletarian organizations, and rouse the agitated petty-bourgeoisie to chauvinistic fervor on behalf of the fight against the revolutionary way out of the crisis.

Communist pamphlet.

(5) If a new spirit *is* to be infused into this old country, there is one thorny and contentious reform which must be tackled, and that is the human-

ization and galvanization of the B.B.C. Timidity here will bespeak canker and atrophy of the soul. The heart of Britain may be sound and of strong beat, for instance, but the British lion's roar at present is like that of Bottom in Shakespeare's *Midsummer Night's Dream*—as gentle as any sucking dove. A virile new Britain cannot continue indefinitely to be traduced in the eyes or rather ears, of the world by the effete languors of Langham Place, brazenly masquerading as "standard English." When the Voice of Britain is heard at nine o'clock, better far and infinitely less ludicrous to hear aitches honestly dropped than the present priggish, inflated, inhibited, schoolma'amish arch braying of blameless bashful mewing maidens!

Letter in *Tribune*

Each of these passages has faults of its own, but, quite apart from avoidable ugliness, two qualities are common to all of them. The first is staleness of imagery; the other is lack of precision. The writer either has a meaning and cannot express it, or he inadvertently says something else, or he is almost indifferent as to whether his words mean anything or not. This mixture of vagueness and sheer incompetence is the most marked characteristic of modern English prose, and especially of any kind of political writing. As soon as certain topics are raised, the concrete melts into the abstract and no one seems able to think of turns of speech that are not hackneyed: prose consists less and less of *words* chosen for the sake of their meaning, and more and more of *phrases* tacked together like the sections of a prefabricated hen-house. I list below, with notes and examples, various of the tricks by means of which the work of prose-construction is habitually dodged:

Dying metaphors. A newly invented metaphor assists thought by evoking a visual image, while on the other hand a metaphor which is technically "dead" (e.g. *iron resolution*) has in effect reverted to being an ordinary word and can generally be used without loss of vividness. But in between these two classes there is a huge dump of worn-out metaphors which have lost all evocative power and are merely used because they save people the trouble of inventing phrases for themselves. Examples are: *Ring the changes on, take up the cudgels for, toe the line, ride roughshod over, stand shoulder to shoulder with, play into the hands of, no axe to grind, grist to the mill, fishing in troubled waters, on the order of the day, Achilles' heel, swan song, hotbed.* Many of these are used without knowledge of their meaning (what is a "rift," for instance?), and incompatible metaphors are frequently mixed, a sure sign that the writer is not interested in what he is saying. Some metaphors now current have been twisted out of their original meaning without those who use them even being aware of the fact. For example, *toe the line* is sometimes written *tow the line.* Another example is *the hammer and the anvil,* now always used with the implication that the anvil gets the worst of it. In real life it is always the anvil that breaks the hammer, never the other way about: a writer who stopped to think what he was saying would be aware of this, and would avoid perverting the original phrase.

Operators or *verbal false limbs.* These save the trouble of picking out appropriate verbs and nouns, and at the same time pad each sentence with extra syllables which give it an appearance of symmetry. Characteristic phrases are *render inoperative, militate against, make contact with, be subjected to, give rise to, give grounds for, have the effect of, play a leading part* (*role*) *in, make itself felt, take effect, exhibit a tendency to, serve the purpose of, etc., etc.* The keynote is the elimination of simple verbs. Instead of being a single word, such as *break, stop, spoil, mend, kill,* a verb becomes a *phrase*, made up of a noun or adjective tacked on to some general-purposes verb such as *prove, serve, form, play, render*. In addition, the passive voice is wherever possible used in preference to the active, and noun constructions are used instead of gerunds (*by examination of* instead of *by examining*). The range of verbs is further cut down by means of the *-ize* and *de-* formations, and the banal statements are given an appearance of profundity by means of the *not un-* formation. Simple conjunctions and prepositions are replaced by such phrases as *with respect to, having regard to, the fact that, by dint of, in view of, in the interests of, on the hypothesis that*; and the ends of sentences are saved by anticlimax by such resounding common-places as *greatly to be desired, cannot be left out of account, a development to be expected in the near future, deserving of serious consideration, brought to a satisfactory conclusion*, and so on and so forth.

Pretentious diction. Words like *phenomenon, element, individual* (as noun), *objective, categorical, effective, virtual, basic, primary, promote, constitute exhibit, exploit, utilize, eliminate, liquidate*, are used to dress up simple statement and give an air of scientific impartiality to biased judgments. Adjectives like *epoch-making, epic, historic, unforgettable, triumphant, age-old, inevitable, inexorable, veritable,* are used to dignify the sordid processes of international politics, while writing that aims at glorifying war usually takes on an archaic color, its characteristic words being: *realm, throne, chariot, mailed fist, trident, sword, shield, buckler, banner, jackboot, clarion.* Foreign words and expressions such as *cul de sac, ancien régime, deus ex machina, mutatis mutandis, status quo, gleichschaltung, weltanschauung*, are used to give an air of culture and elegance. Except for the useful abbreviations *i.e., e.g.,* and *etc.*, there is no real need for any of the hundreds of foreign phrases now current in English. Bad writers, and especially scientific, political and sociological writers, are nearly always haunted by the notion that Latin or Greek words are grander than Saxon ones, and unnecessary words like *expedite, ameliorate, predict, extraneous, deracinated, clandestine, subaqueous* and hundreds of others constantly gain ground from their Anglo-Saxon opposite numbers.[1] The jargon peculiar to Marxist writing (*hyena, hangman, cannibal, petty bourgeois, these gentry, lacquey, flunkey, mad dog, White Guard,* etc.) consists largely of words and phrases translated from Russian, German or French; but the normal way of coining a new word is to use a Latin or Greek root with the appropriate affix and, where necessary, the size formation. It is often easier to make up words of this kind (*deregionalize, impermissible, extramarital, non-fragmentary* and so forth) than to think up the English words that will cover one's meaning. The result, in general, is an increase in slovenliness and vagueness.

Meaningless words. In certain kinds of writing, particularly in art criticism and literary criticism, it is normal to come across long passages which are almost completely lacking in meaning.[2] Words like *romantic, plastic, values, human, dead, sentimental, natural, vitality*, as used in art criticism, are

[1] An interesting illustration of this is the way in which the English flower names which were in use till very recently are being ousted by Greek ones, *snapdragon* becoming *antirrhinum, forget-me-not* becoming *myositis*, etc. It is hard to see any practical reason for this change of fashion: it is probably due to an instinctive turning-away from the more homely word and a vague feeling that the Greek word is scientific.

[2] Example: "Comforts catholicity of perception and image, strangly Whitmanesque in range, almost the exact opposite in aesthetic compulsion, continues to evoke that trembling atmospheric accumulative hinting at a cruel, an inexorably serene timelessness. . . . Wrey Gardiner scores by aiming at simple bull's-eyes with precision. Only they are not so simple, and through this contented sadness runs more than the surface bitter-sweet of resignation." (*Poetry Quarterly.*)

strictly meaningless, in the sense that they not only do not point to any discoverable object, but are hardly ever expected to do so by the reader. When one critic writes, "The outstanding feature of Mr. X's work is its living quality," while another writes, "The immediately striking thing about Mr. X's work is its peculiar deadness," the reader accepts this as a simple difference of opinion. If words like *black* and *white* were involved, instead of the jargon words *dead* and *living*, he would see at once that language was being used in an improper way. Many political words are similarly abused. The word *Fascism* has now no meaning except in so far as it signifies "something not desirable." The words *democracy, socialism, freedom, patriotic, realistic, justice,* have each of them several different meanings which cannot be reconciled with one another. In the case of a word like *democracy*, not only is there no agreed definition, but the attempt to make one is resisted from all sides. It is almost universally felt that when we call a country democratic we are praising it: consequently the defenders of every kind of régime claim that it is a democracy, and fear that they might have to stop using the word if it were tied down to any one meaning. Words of this kind are often used in a consciously dishonest way. That is, the person who uses them has his own private definition, but allows his hearer to think he means something quite different. Statements like *Marshal Pétain was a true patriot, The Soviet Press is the freest in the world, The Catholic Church is opposed to persecution,* are almost always made with intent to deceive. Other words used in variable meanings, in most cases more or less dishonestly, are: *class, totalitarian, science, progressive, reactionary, bourgeois, equality*. . .

Now that I have made this catalogue of swindles and perversions, let me give another example of the kind of writing that they lead to. This time it must of its nature be an imaginary one. I am going to translate a passage of good English into modern English of the worst sort. Here is a well-known verse from *Ecclesiastes*:

> I returned and saw under the sun, that the race is not to the swift, nor the battle to the strong, neither yet bread to the wise, nor yet riches to men of understanding, nor yet favour to men of skill; but time and chance happeneth to them all.

Here it is in modern English:

> Objective considerations of contemporary phenomena compels the conclusion that success or failure in competition activities exhibits no tendency to be commensurate with innate capacity, but that a considerable element of the unpredictable must invariably be taken into account.

This is a parody, but not a very gross one. Exhibit (3), above, for instance, contains several patches of the same kind of English. It will be seen that I have not made a full translation. The beginning and ending of the sentence follow the original meaning fairly closely, but in the middle the concrete illustrations—race, battle, bread—dissolve into the vague phrase "success or failure in competitive activities." This had to be so, because no modern writer of the kind I am discussing—no one capable of using phrases like "objective consideration of contemporary phenomena"—would ever tabulate his thoughts in that precise and detailed way. The whole tendency of modern prose is away from *concreteness.* Now analyse these two sentences a little more closely. The first contains forty-nine words but only sixty syllables, and all its words are those of everyday life. The second contains thirty-eight words of ninety syllables: eighteen of its words are from Latin roots, and one from Greek. The first sentence contains six vivid images, and only one phrase ("time and chance") that could be called vague. The second contains not a single fresh, arresting phrase, and in spite of its ninety syllables it gives only a shortened version of the meaning contained in the first. Yet without a doubt it is the second kind of sentence that is gaining ground in modern English. I do not want to exaggerate. This kind of writing is not yet universal, and outcrops of simplicity will occur here and there in the worst-written page. Still, if you or I were told to write a few lines on the uncertainty of human fortunes, we should probably come much nearer to my imaginary sentence than to the one from *Ecclesiastes*.

As I have tried to show, modern writing at its worst does not consist in picking out words for the sake of their meaning and inventing images in order to make the meaning clearer. It consists in gumming together long strips of words which have already been set in order by someone else, and making the results presentable by sheer humbug. The attraction of this way of writing is that it is easy. It is easier—even quicker, once you have the habit—to say *In my opinion it is not an unjustifiable assumption that* than to say *I think*. If you use ready-made phrases, you not only don't have to hunt about for words; you also don't have to bother with the rhythms of your sentences, since these phrases are generally so arranged as to be more or less euphonious. When you are composing in a hurry—when you are dictating to a stenographer, for instance, or making a public speech—it is natural to fall into a pretentious, Latinized style. Tags like *a consideration which we should do well to bear in mind* or *a conclusion to which all of us would readily assent* will save many a sentence from coming down with a bump. By using stale metaphors, similes and idioms, you save much mental effort, at the cost of leaving your meaning vague, not only for your reader but for yourself. This is the significance of mixed metaphors. The sole aim of a metaphor is to call up a visual image. When these images clash—as in *The Fascist octopus has sung its swan song, the jackboot is thrown into the melting pot*—it can be taken as certain that the writer is not seeing a mental image of the objects he is naming; in other words he is not really thinking. Look again at the examples I gave at the beginning of this essay. Professor Laski (1) uses five negatives in fifty-three words. One of these is superfluous, making nonsense of the whole passage, and in addition there is the slip *alien* for akin, making further nonsense, and several avoidable pieces of clumsiness which increase the general vagueness. Professor Hogben (2) plays ducks and drakes with a battery which is able to write prescriptions, and, while disapproving of the everyday phrase *put up with*, is unwilling to look *egregious* up in the dictionary and see what it means; (3), if one takes an uncharitable attitude towards it, is simply meaningless: probably one could work out its intended meaning by reading the whole of the article in which it occurs. In (4), the writer knows more or less what he wants to say, but an accumulation of stale phrases chokes him like tea leaves blocking a sink. In (5), words and meaning have almost parted company. People who write in this manner usually have a general emotional meaning—they dislike one thing and want to express solidarity with another—but they are not interested in the detail of what they are saying. A scrupulous writer, in every sentence that he writes, will ask himself at least four questions, thus: What am I trying to say? What words will express it? What image or idiom will make it clearer? Is this image fresh enough to have an effect? And he will probably ask himself two more: Could I put it more shortly? Have I said anything that is avoidably ugly? But you are not obliged to go to all this trouble. You can shirk it by simply throwing your mind open and letting the ready-made phrases come crowding in. They will construct your sentences for you—even think your thoughts for you, to a certain extent—and at need they will perform the important service of partially concealing your meaning even from yourself. It is at this point that the special connection between politics and the debasement of language becomes clear.

In our time it is broadly true that political writing is bad writing. Where it is not true, it will generally be found that the writer is some kind of rebel, expressing his private opinions and not a "party line." Orthodoxy, of whatever color, seems to demand a lifeless, imitative style. The political dialects to be found in pamphlets, leading articles, manifestos, White Papers and the speeches of under-secretaries do, of course, vary from party to party, but they are all alike in that one almost never finds in them a fresh, vivid, home-made turn of speech. When one watches some tired hack on the platform mechanically repeating the familiar phrases —*bestial atrocities, iron heel, blood-stained tyranny, free peoples of the world, stand shoulder to shoulder*—one often has a curious feeling that one is not watching a live human being but some kind of dummy: a feeling which suddenly becomes stronger at moments when the light catches the speaker's spectacles and turns them into blank discs which seem to have no eyes behind them. And this is not altogether fanciful. A speaker who uses that kind of phraseology has gone some distance towards turning himself into a machine. The appropriate noises are coming out of his larynx, but his brain is not involved as it would be if he were choosing his words for himself. If the speech he is making is one that he is accustomed to make over and over again, he may be almost unconscious of what he is saying, as one is when one utters the responses in church. And this reduced state of consciousness, if not indispensable, is at any rate favorable to political conformity.

In our time, political speech and writing are largely the defence of the indefensible. Things like the continuance of British rule in India, the Russian purges and deportations, the dropping of the atom bombs on Japan, can indeed be defended, but only by arguments which are too brutal for most people to face, and which do not square with the professed aims of political parties. Thus political language has to consist largely of euphemism, question-begging and sheer cloudy vagueness. Defenceless villages are bombarded from the air, the inhabitants driven out into the countryside, the cattle machine-gunned, the huts set on fire with incendiary bullets: this is called *pacification*. Millions of peasants are robbed of their farms and sent trudging along the roads with no more than they can carry: this is called *transfer of population* or *rectification of frontiers*. People are imprisoned for years without trial, or shot in the back of the neck or sent to die of scurvy in Arctic lumber camps: this is called *elimination of unreliable elements*. Such phraseology is needed if one wants to name things without calling up mental pictures of them. Consider for instance some comfortable English professor defending Russian totalitarianism. He cannot say outright, "I believe in killing off your opponents when you can get good results by doing so." Probably, therefore, he will say something like this:

> While freely conceding that the Soviet regime exhibits certain features which the humanitarian may be inclined to deplore, we must, I think, agree that a certain curtailment of the right to political opposition is an unavoidable concomitant of transitional periods, and that the rigors which the Russian people have been called upon to undergo have been amply justified in the sphere of concrete achievement.

The inflated style is itself a kind of euphemism. A mass of Latin words falls upon the facts like soft snow, blurring the outlines and covering up all the details. The great enemy of clear language is insincerity. When there is a gap between one's real and one's declared aims, one turns as it were instinctively to long words and exhausted idioms, like a cuttlefish squirting out ink. In our age there is no such thing as "keeping out of politics." All issues are political issues, and politics itself is a mass of lies, evasions, folly, hatred and schizophrenia. When the general atmosphere is bad, language must suffer. I should expect to find—this is a guess which I have not sufficient knowledge to verify—that the German, Russian and Italian languages have all deteriorated in the last ten or fifteen years, as a result of dictatorship.

But if thought corrupts language, language can also corrupt thought. A bad usage can spread by tradition and imitation, even among people who should and do know better. The debased language that I have been discussing is in some ways very convenient. Phrases like *a not unjustifiable assumption, leaves much to be desired, would serve no good purpose, a consideration which we should do well to bear in mind,* are a continuous temptation, a packet of aspirins always at one's elbow. Look back through this essay, and for certain you will find that I have again and again committed the very faults I am protesting against. By this morning's post I have received a pamphlet dealing with conditions in Germany. The author tells me that he "felt impelled" to write it. I open it at random, and here is almost the first sentence that I see: "[The Allies] have an opportunity not only of achieving a radical transformation of Germany's social and political structure in such a way as to avoid a nationalistic reaction in Germany itself, but at the same time of laying the foundations of a co-operative and unified Europe." You see, he "feels impelled" to write—feels, presumably, that he has something new to say—and yet his words, like cavalry horses answering the bugle, group themselves automatically into the familiar dreary pattern. This invasion of one's mind by ready-made phrases (*lay the foundations, achieve a radical transformation*) can only be prevented if one is constantly on guard against them, and every such phrase anaesthetizes a portion of one's brain.

I said earlier that the decadence of our language is probably curable. Those who deny this would argue, if they produced an argument at all, that language merely reflects existing social conditions, and that we cannot influence its development by any direct tinkering with words and constructions. So far as the general tone or spirit of a language goes, this may be true, but it is not true in detail. Silly words and expressions have often disappeared, not through any evolutionary process but owing to the conscious action of a minority. Two recent examples were *explore every avenue* and *leave no stone unturned,* which were killed by the jeers of a few journalists. There is a long list of flyblown metaphors which could similarly be got rid of if enough people would interest themselves in the job; and it should also be possible to laugh the *not un-* formation out of existence,[3] to reduce the amount of Latin and Greek in the average sentence, to drive out foreign phrases and strayed scientific words, and, in general, to make pretentiousness unfashionable. But all these are minor points. The defence of the English language implies more than

[3] One can cure oneself of the *not un-* formation by memorizing this sentence: *A not unblack dog was chasing a not unsmall rabbit across a not ungreen field.*

this, and perhaps it is best to start by saying what it does *not* imply.

To begin with it has nothing to do with archaism, with the salvaging of obsolete words and turns of speech, or with the setting up of a "standard English" which must never be departed from. On the contrary, it is especially concerned with the scrapping of every word or idiom which has outworn its usefulness. It has nothing to do with correct grammar and syntax, which are of no importance so long as one makes one's meaning clear, or with the avoidance of Americanisms, or with having what is called a "good prose style." On the other hand it is not concerned with faked simplicity and the attempt to make written English colloquial. Nor does it even imply in every case preferring the Saxon word to the Latin one, though it does imply using the fewest and shortest words that will cover one's meaning. What is above all needed is to let the meaning choose the word, and not the other way about. In prose, the worst thing one can do with words is to surrender to them. When you think of a concrete object, you think wordlessly, and then, if you want to describe the thing you have been visualizing you probably hunt about till you find the exact words that seem to fit it. When you think of something abstract you are more inclined to use words from the start, and unless you make a conscious effort to prevent it, the existing dialect will come rushing in and do the job for you, at the expense of blurring or even changing your meaning. Probably it is better to put off using words as long as possible and get one's meaning as clear as one can through pictures or sensations. Afterwards one can choose—not simply *accept*—the phrases that will best cover the meaning, and then switch round and decide what impression one's words are likely to make on another person. This last effort of the mind cuts out all stale or mixed images, all prefabricated phrases, needless repetitions, and humbug and vagueness generally. But one can often be in doubt about the effect of a word or a phrase, and one needs rules that one can rely on when instinct fails. I think the following rules will cover most cases:

(i) Never use a metaphor, simile or other figure of speech which you are used to seeing in print.

(ii) Never use a long word where a short one will do.

(iii) If it is possible to cut a word out, always cut it out.

(iv) Never use the passive where you can use the active.

(v) Never use a foreign phrase, a scientific word or a jargon word if you can think of an everyday English equivalent.

(vi) Break any of these rules sooner than say anything outright barbarous.

These rules sound elementary, and so they are, but they demand a deep change of attitude in anyone who has grown used to writing in the style now fashionable. One could keep all of them and still write bad English, but one could not write the kind of stuff that I quoted in those five specimens at the beginning of this article.

I have not here been considering the literary use of language, but merely language as an instrument of expressing and not for concealing or preventing thought. Stuart Chase and others have come near to claiming that all abstract words are meaningless, and have used this as a pretext for advocating a kind of political quietism. Since you don't know what Fascism is, how can you struggle against Fascism? One need not swallow such absurdities as this, but one ought to recognize that the present political chaos is connected with the decay of language, and that one can probably bring about some improvement by starting at the verbal end. If you simplify your English, you are freed from the worst follies of orthodoxy. You cannot speak any of the necessary dialects, and when you make a stupid remark its stupidity will be obvious, even to yourself. Political language—and with variations this is true of all political parties, from Conservatives to Anarchists—is designed to make lies sound truthful and murder respectable, and to give an appearance of solidity to pure wind. One cannot change this all in a moment, but one can at least change one's own habits, and from time to time one can even, if one jeers loudly enough, send some worn-out and useless phrase—some *jackboot, Achilles' heel, hotbed, melting pot, acid test, veritable inferno* or other lump of verbal refuse—into the dustbin where it belongs.

Loren C. Eiseley (1907–1979)

The Bird and the Machine

I suppose their little bones have years ago been lost among the stones and winds of those high glacial pastures. I suppose their feathers blew eventually into the piles of tumbleweed beneath the straggling cattle fences and rotted there in the mountain snows, along with dead steers and all the other things that drift to an end in the corners of the wire. I do not quite know why I should be thinking of birds over the *New York Times* at breakfast, nor particularly of the birds of my youth half a continent away. It is a funny thing what the brain will do with memories and how it will treasure them and finally bring them into odd juxtapositions with other things, as though it wanted to make a design, or get some meaning out of them, whether you want it or not, or even see it.

It used to seem marvelous to me, but I read now that there are machines, that can do these things in a small way, machines that can crawl about like animals, and that it may not be long now until they do more things—maybe even make themselves—I saw that piece in the *Times* just now—and then they will, maybe—well, who knows—but you read about it more and more with no one making any protest, and already they can add better than we and reach up and hear things through the dark and finger the guns over the night sky.

This is the new world that I read about at breakfast. This is the world that confronts me in my biological books and journals, until there are times when I sit quietly in my chair and try to hear the little purr of the cogs in my head and the tubes flaring and dying as the messages go through them and the circuits snap shut or open. This is the great age, make no mistake about it; the robot has been born somewhat appropriately along with the atom bomb, and the brain they say now is just another type of more complicated feedback system. The engineers have its basic principles worked out; it's mechanical, you know; nothing to get superstitious about; and man can always improve on nature once he gets the idea. Well, he's got it all right and that's why, I guess, that I sit here in my chair, with the article crunched in my hand, remembering those two birds and that blue mountain sunlight. There is another magazine title on my desk that reads "Machines Are Getting Smarter Every Day." I don't deny it, but I'll stick with the birds. It's life I believe in, not machines.

Maybe you don't believe there is any difference. A skeleton is all joints and pulleys, I'll admit. And when man was in his simpler stages of machine building in the eighteenth century, he quickly saw the resemblances. "What," wrote Hobbes, "is the heart but a spring, and the nerves so many springs, and the joints but so many wheels, giving motion to the whole body?" Tinkering about in their shops it was inevitable in the end that men would see the world as a huge machine "subdivided into an infinite number of lesser machines."

The idea took on with a vengeance. Little automatons toured the country—dolls controlled by clockwork. Clocks described as little worlds were taken on tours by their designers. They were made up of moving figures, shifting scenes, and other remarkable devices. The life of the cell was unknown. Man, whether he was conceived as possessing a soul or not, moved and jerked about like these tiny puppets. A human being thought of himself in terms of his own tools and implements. He had been fashioned like the puppets he produced and was only a more clever model made by a great designer.

Then in the nineteenth century, the cell was discovered, and the single machine in its turn was found to be the product of millions of infinitesimal machines—the cells. Now, finally, the cell itself dissolves away into an abstract chemical machine—and that into some intangible, inexpressible flow of energy. The secret seems to lurk all about, the wheels get smaller and smaller, and they turn more rapidly, but when you try to seize it the life is gone—and so, it is popular to say, the life was never there in the first place. The wheels and the cogs are the secret and we can make them better in time—machines that will run faster and more accurately than real mice to cheese.

I have no doubt it can be done, though a mouse harvesting seeds on an autumn thistle is to me a fine sight and more complicated, I think, in his multiform activity, than a machine "mouse" running a maze. Also, I like to think of the possible shape of the future brooding in mice, just as it brooded once in a rather ordinary mousy insectivore who became a man. It leaves a nice fine indeterminate sense of wonder that even an electronic brain hasn't got, because you know perfectly well that if the electronic brain changes it will be because of something man has done to it. But what man will do to himself he doesn't really know. A certain scale of time and a ghostly intangible thing called change are ticking in him. Powers and potentialities like the oak in the seed, or a red and awful ruin. Either way, it's impressive; and the mouse has it, too—or those birds, I'll never forget those birds, though I learned the lesson of time first of all. I was young then and left alone in a great desert—part of an expedition that had scattered its men over several hundred miles in order to carry on research more effectively. I learned there that time is a series of planes existing superficially in the same universe. The tempo is a human illusion, a subjective clock ticking in our kind of protoplasm.

As the long months passed, I began to live on the slower planes and to observe more readily what passed for life there. I sauntered, I passed more and more slowly up and down the canyons in the dry baking heat of midsummer. I slumbered for long hours in the shade of huge brown boulders that had gathered in tilted companies out on the flats. I had forgotten the world of men and the world had forgotten me. Now and then I found a skull in the canyons and these justified my remaining there. I took a serene cold interest in these discoveries. I had come, like many a naturalist before me, to view life with a wary and subdued attention. I had grown to take pleasure in the divested bone.

I sat once on a high ridge that fell away before me into a waste of sand dunes. I sat through hours of a long afternoon. Finally glancing by my boot an indistinct configuration caught my eye. It was a coiled rattlesnake, a big one. How long he had sat with me I do not know. I had not frightened him. We were both locked in the sleep-walking tempo of the earlier world, baking in the same high air and sunshine. Perhaps he had been there when I came. He slept on as I left, his coils, so ill discerned by me, dissolving once more among the stones and gravel from which I had barely made him out.

Another time, I got on a higher ridge, among some tough little wind-warped pines half covered over with sand in a basin-like depression that caught everything carried by the air up to those heights. There were a few thin bones of birds, some cracked shells of indeterminable age, and the knotty fingers of pine roots bulged out of shape from their long and agonizing grasp upon the crevices of the rock. I lay under the pines in the sparse shade and went to sleep once more.

It grew cold finally, for autumn was in the air by then, and the few things that lived thereabouts were sinking down into an even chillier scale of time. In the moments between sleeping and waking I saw the roots about me and slowly, slowly, a foot in what seemed many centuries, I moved by sleep-stiffened hands over the scaling bark and lifted my numbed face after the vanishing sun. I was a great awkward thing of knots and aching limbs, trapped up there in some long patient endurance that involved the necessity of putting living fingers into rock and by slow, aching expansion bursting those rocks asunder. I suppose, so thin and slow was the time of my pulse by then, that I might have stayed on to drift still deeper into the lower cadences of the frost, or the crystalline life that glisters pebbles or shines in a snow flake, or dreams in the meteoric iron between the worlds.

It was a dim descent but time was present in it. Somewhere far down in that scale the notion struck me that one might come the other way. Not many months thereafter, I joined some colleagues heading higher into a remote windy tableland where huge bones were reputed to protrude like boulders from the turf. I had drowsed with reptiles and moved with the century-long pulse of trees; now, lethargically, I was climbing back up some invisible ladder of quickening hours. There had been talk of birds in connection with my duties. Birds are intense, fast-living creatures—reptiles, I suppose one might say—that have escaped out of the heavy sleep of time, transformed fairy creatures dancing over sunlit meadows. It is a youthful fancy, no doubt, but because of something that happened up there among the escarpments of that range, it remains with me a life-long impression. I can never bear to see a bird imprisoned.

We came into that valley through the trailing mists of a spring night. It was a place that looked as though it might never have known the foot of man, but our scouts had been ahead of us and we knew all about the abandoned cabin of stone that lay far up on one hillside. It had been built in the land rush of the last century and then lost to the cattlemen again as the marginal soils failed to take to the plow.

There were spots like this all over that country. Lost graves marked by unlettered stones and old corroding rim-fire cartridge cases lying where somebody had made a stand among the boulders that rimmed the valley. They are all that remain of the range wars; the men are under the stones now. I could see our cavalcade winding in and out through the mist below us: torches, and lights reflected on collecting tins, and the far-off bumping of a loose dinosaur thigh bone in the bottom of a trailer. I stood on a rock a moment looking down and thinking what it cost in money and equipment to capture the past.

We had, in addition, instructions to lay hands on the present. The word had come through to get them alive, birds, reptiles, anything. A zoo somewhere abroad needed restocking. It was one of those reciprocal matters in which science involves itself. Maybe our museum needed a stray ostrich egg and this was the payoff. Anyhow, my job was to help capture some birds and that was why I was there before the trucks.

The cabin had not been occupied for years. We intended to clean it out and live in it, but there were holes in the roof and the birds had come in and were roosting in the rafters. You could depend on it in a place like this where everything blew away and even a bird needed some place out of the weather and away from coyotes. A cabin going back to nature in a wild place draws them till they come in, listening at the eaves, I imagine, pecking softly among the shingles till they find a hole and then suddenly the place is theirs and man is forgotten.

Sometimes of late years I find myself thinking the most beautiful sight in the world might be the birds taking over New York after the last man has run away to the hills. I will never live to see it, of course, but I know just how it will sound because I've lived up high and I know the sort of watch birds keep on us. I've listened to sparrows tapping tentatively on the tin of the air conditioners when they thought no one was listening, and I know how other birds test the vibrations that come up to them through the television aerials.

"Is he gone?" they ask, and the vibrations come up from below, "not yet, not yet."

Well, to come back, I got the door open softly and I had the spotlight all ready to turn on and blind whatever birds were there so they couldn't see to get out through the roof. I had a short piece of ladder to put against the far wall where there was a shelf on which I expected to make the biggest haul. I had all the information I needed just like any skilled assassin. I pushed the door open with the hinges only squeaking a little after the oil was put on them. A bird or so stirred—I could hear them—but nothing flew and there was a faint starshine through the holes in the roof.

I padded across the floor, got the ladder up, and the light ready, and slithered up the ladder till my head and arms were over the shelf. Everything was dark as pitch except for the starlight at a little place back of the shelf near the eaves. With the light to blind them, they'd never make it. I had them. I reached my arm carefully over in order to be ready to seize whatever was there and I put the flash on the edge of the shelf where it would stand by itself when I turned it on. That way I'd be able to use both hands.

Everything worked perfectly except for one detail—I didn't know what kind of birds were there. I never thought about it all and it wouldn't have mattered if I had. My orders were to get something interesting. I snapped on the flash and sure enough there was a great beating and feathers flying, but instead of my having them, they, or rather he, had me. He had my hand, that is, and for a small hawk not much bigger than my fist he was doing all right. I heard him give one short metallic cry when the light went on and my hand descended on the bird beside him; after that he was busy with his claws and his beak was sunk in my thumb. In the struggle I knocked the lamp over on the shelf and his mate got her sight back and whisked neatly through the hole in the roof, and off among the stars outside. It all happened in fifteen seconds and you might think I would have fallen down the ladder, but no, I had a professional assassin's reputation to keep up and the bird, of course, made the mistake of thinking the hand was the enemy and not the eyes behind it. He chewed my thumb up pretty effectively and lacerated my hand with his claws, but in the end I got him, having two hands to work with.

He was a sparrow hawk and a fine young male in the prime of life. I was sorry not to catch the pair of them, but as I dripped blood and folded his wings carefully, holding him by the back so he couldn't strike again, I had to admit the two of them might have been a little more than I could have handled under the circumstances. The little fellow had saved his mate by diverting me, and that was that. He was born to it, and made no outcry now, resting in my hand hopelessly, but peering toward me in the shadows behind the lamp with a fierce, almost indifferent glance. He neither gave nor expected mercy and something out of the air passed from him to me, stirring a faint embarrassment.

I quit looking into that eye and managed to get my huge carcass with its fist full of prey back down the ladder. I put the bird in a box too small to allow him to injure himself by struggle and walked out to welcome the arriving trucks. It had been a long day and camp was still to make in the darkness. In the morning that bird would be just another episode. He would go back with the bones in the truck to a small cage in a city where he would spend the rest of his life. And a good thing, too. I sucked my aching thumb and spat out some blood. An assassin has to get used to these things. I had a professional reputation to keep up.

In the morning with the change that comes on suddenly in that high country, the mist that had hovered below us in the valley was gone. The sky was a deep blue and one could see for miles over the high outcroppings of stone. I was up early and brought the box in which the little hawk was imprisoned out onto the grass where I was building a cage. A wind as cool as a mountain spring ran over the grass and stirred my hair. It was a fine day to be alive. I looked up and all around and at the hole in the cabin roof out of which the other little hawk had fled. There was no sign of her anywhere that I could see.

"Probably in the next county by now," I thought cynically, but before beginning work I decided I'd have a look at my last night's capture.

Secretively, I looked again all around the camp and up and down and opened the box. I got him right out in my hand with his wings folded properly and I was careful not to startle him. He lay limp in my grasp and I could feel his heart pound under the feathers but he only looked beyond me and up.

I saw him look that last look away beyond me into a sky so full of light that I could not follow his gaze. The little breeze flowed over me again, and nearby a mountain aspen shook all its tiny leaves. I suppose I must have had an idea about then of what I was going to do, but I never let it come up into consciousness. I just reached over and laid the hawk on the grass.

He lay there a long minute without

hope, unmoving, his eyes still fixed on that blue vault above him. It must have been that he already was so far away in heart that he never felt the release from my hand. He never even stood. He just lay with his breast against the grass and my eye upon him.

In the next second after that long minute he was gone. Like a flicker of light, he had vanished with my eyes full on him, but without actually seeing even a premonitory wing beat. He was gone straight into that towering emptiness of light and crystal that my eyes could scarcely bear to penetrate. For another long moment there was silence. I could not see him. The light was too intense. Then from far up somewhere a cry came ringing down.

I was young then and had seen little of the world, but when I heard that cry my heart turned over. It was not the cry of the hawk I had captured; for, by shifting my position against the sun, I was now seeing further up. Straight out of the sun's eye, where she must have been soaring restlessly above us for untold hours, hurtled his mate. And from far up, ringing from peak to peak of the summits over us, came a cry of such unutterable and ecstatic joy that it sounds down across the years and tingles among the cups on my quiet breakfast table.

I saw them both now. He was rising fast to meet her. They met in a great soaring gyre that turned to a whirling circle and a dance of wings. Once more, just once, their two voices, joined in a harsh wild medley of question and response, struck and echoed against the pinnacles of the valley. Then they were gone forever somewhere into those upper regions beyond the eyes of men.

I am older now, and sleep less, and have seen most of what there is to see and am not very impressed any more, I suppose, by anything. "What Next in the Attributes of Machines?" my morning headline runs. "It Might be the Power to Reproduce Themselves."

I lay the paper down and across my mind a phrase floats insinuatingly: "It does not seem that there is anything in the construction, constituents, or behavior of the human being which it is essentially impossible for science to duplicate and synthesize. On the other hand . . ."

All over the city the cogs in the hard, bright mechanisms have begun to turn. Figures move through computers, names are spelled out, a thoughtful machine selects the fingerprints of a wanted criminal from an array of thousands. In the laboratory an electronic mouse runs swiftly through a maze toward the cheese it can neither taste nor enjoy. On the second run it does better than a living mouse.

"On the other hand . . ." Ah, my mind takes up, on the other hand the machine does not bleed, ache, hang for hours in the empty sky in a torment of hope to learn the fate of another machine, nor does it cry out with joy nor dance in the air with the fierce passion of a bird. Far off, over a distance greater than space, that remote cry from the heart of heaven makes a faint buzzing among my breakfast dishes and passes on and away.

Rollo May (1909–)

from Love and Will
Paradoxes of Sex and Love

Sexual intercourse is the human counterpart of the cosmic process.
—Proverb of Ancient China

A patient brought in the following dream: "I am in bed with my wife, and between us is my accountant. He is going to have intercourse with her. My feeling about this is odd—only that somehow it seemed appropriate."
—Reported by Dr. John Schimel

There are four kinds of love in Western tradition. One is *sex*, or what we call lust, libido. The second is *eros*, the drive of love to procreate or create—the urge, as the Greeks put it, toward higher forms of being and relationship. A third is *philia*, or friendship, brotherly love. The fourth is *agape*, or *caritas* as the Latins called it, the love which is devoted to the welfare of the other, the prototype of which is the love of God for man. Every human experience of authentic love is a blending, in varying proportions, of these four.

We begin with sex not only because that is where our society begins but also because that is where every man's biological existence begins as well. Each of us owes his being to the fact that at some moment in history a man and a woman leapt the gap, in T. S. Eliot's words, "between the desire and the spasm." Regardless of how much sex may be banalized in our society, it still remains the power of procreation, the drive which perpetuates the race, the source at once of the human being's most intense pleasure and his most pervasive anxiety. It can, in its daimonic form, hurl the individual into sloughs of despond, and, when allied with eros, it can lift him out of his despondency into orbits of ecstasy.

The ancients took sex, or lust, for granted just as they took death for granted. It is only in the contemporary age that we have succeeded, on a fairly broad scale, in singling out sex for our chief concern and have required it to carry the weight of all four forms of love. Regardless of Freud's overextension of sexual phenomena as such—in which he is but the voice of the struggle of thesis and antithesis of modern history—it remains true that sexuality is basic to the ongoing power of the race and surely has the *importance* Freud gave it, if not the *extension*. Trivialize sex in our novels and dramas as we will, or defend ourselves from its power by cynicism and playing it cool as we wish, sexual passion remains ready at any moment to catch us off guard and prove that it is still the *mysterium tremendum*.

But as soon as we look at the relation of sex and love in our time, we find ourselves immediately caught up in a whirlpool of contradictions. Let us, therefore, get our bearings by beginning with a brief phenomenological sketch of the strange paradoxes which surround sex in our society.

SEXUAL WILDERNESS

In Victorian times, when the denial of sexual impulses, feelings, and drives was the mode and one would not talk about sex in polite company, an aura of sanctifying repulsiveness surrounded the whole topic. Males and females dealt with each other as though neither possessed sexual organs. William James, that redoubtable crusader who was far ahead of his time on every other topic, treated sex with the polite aversion characteristic of the turn of the century. In the whole two volumes of his epoch-making *Principles of Psychology*, only one page is devoted to sex, at the end of which he adds, "These details are a little unpleasant to discuss. . . ."[1] But William Blake's warning a century before Victorianism, that "He who desires but acts not, breeds pestilence," was amply demonstrated by the later psychotherapists. Freud, a Victorian who did look at sex, was right in his description of the morass of neurotic symptoms which resulted from cutting off so vital a part of the human body and the self.

Then, in the 1920's, a radical change occurred almost overnight. The belief became a militant dogma in liberal circles that the opposite of repression—namely, sex education, freedom of talking, feeling, and expression—would have healthy effects, and obviously constituted the only stand for the enlightened person. In an amazingly short period following World War I, we shifted from acting as though sex did not exist at all to being obsessed with it. We now placed more emphasis on sex than any society since that of ancient Rome, and some scholars believe we are more preoccupied with sex than any other people in all of history. Today, far from not talking about sex, we might well seem, to a visitor from Mars dropping into Times Square, to have no other topic of communication.

And this is not solely an American obsession. Across the ocean in England, for example, "from bishops to biologists, everyone is in on the act." A perceptive front-page article in *The Times Literary Supplement*, London, goes on to point to the "whole turgid flood of post-Kinsey utilitarianism and post-Chatterley moral uplift. Open any newspaper, any day (Sunday in particular), and the odds are you will find some pundit treating the public to his views on contraception, abortion, adultery, obscene publications, homosexuality between consenting adults or (if all else fails) contemporary moral patterns among our adolescents."[2]

Partly as a result of this radical shift, many therapists today rarely see patients who exhibit repression of sex in the manner of Freud's pre-World War I hysterical patients. In fact, we find in the people who come for help just the opposite: a great deal of talk about sex, a great deal of sexual activity, practically no one complaining of cultural prohibitions over going to bed as often or with as many partners as one wishes. But what our patients do complain of is lack of feeling and passion. "The curious thing about this ferment of discussion is how little anyone seems to be *enjoying* emancipation."[3] So much sex and so little meaning or even fun in it!

Where the Victorian didn't want anyone to know that he or she had sexual feelings, we are ashamed if we do not. Before 1910, if you called a lady "sexy" she would be insulted; nowadays, she prizes the compliment and rewards you by turning her charms in your direction. Our patients often have the problems of frigidity and impotence, but the strange and poignant thing we observe is how desperately they struggle not to let anyone find out they don't feel sexually. The Victorian nice man or woman was guilty if he or she did experience sex; now we are guilty if we *don't*.

One paradox, therefore, is that en-

[1] William James, *Principles of Psychology* (New York, Dover Publications, 1950; originally published by Henry Holt, 1890), II, p. 439.

[2] *Atlas*, November, 1965, p. 302. Reprinted from *The Times Literary Supplement*, London.

[3] *Ibid.*

lightenment has not solved the sexual problems in our culture. To be sure, there are important positive results of the new enlightenment, chiefly in increased freedom for the individual. Most external problems are eased: sexual knowledge can be bought in any bookstore, contraception is available everywhere except in Boston where it is still believed, as the English countess averred on her wedding night, that sex is "too good for the common people." Couples can, without guilt and generally without squeamishness, discuss their sexual relationship and undertake to make it more mutually gratifying and meaningful. Let these gains not be underestimated. External social anxiety and guilt have lessened; dull would be the man who did not rejoice in this.

But *internal* anxiety and guilt have increased. And in some ways these are more morbid, harder to handle, and impose a heavier burden upon the individual than external anxiety and guilt.

The challenge a woman used to face from men was simple and direct—would she or would she not go to bed?—a direct issue of how she stood vis-à-vis cultural mores. But the question men ask now is no longer, "Will she or won't she?" but "Can she or can't she?" The challenge is shifted to the woman's personal adequacy, namely, her own capacity to have the vaunted orgasm—which should resemble a *grand mal* seizure. Though we might agree that the second question places the problem of sexual decision more where it should be, we cannot overlook the fact that the first question is much easier for the person to handle. In my practice, one woman was afraid to go to bed for fear that the man "won't find me very good at making love." Another was afraid because "I don't even know how to do it," assuming that her lover would hold this against her. Another was scared to death of the second marriage for fear that she wouldn't be able to have the orgasm as she had not in her first. Often the woman's hesitation is formulated as, "He won't like me well enough to come back again."

In past decades you could blame society's strict mores and preserve your own self-esteem by telling yourself what you did or didn't do was society's fault and not yours. And this would give you some time in which to decide what you do want to do, or to let yourself grow into a decision. But when the question is simply how you can perform, your own sense of adequacy and self-esteem is called immediately into question, and the whole weight of the encounter is shifted inward to how you can meet the test.

College students, in their fights with college authorities about hours girls are to be permitted in the men's rooms, are curiously blind to the fact that rules are often a boon. Rules give the student time to find himself. He has the leeway to consider a way of behaving without being committed before he is ready, to try on for size, to venture into relationships tentatively—which is part of any growing up. Better to have the lack of commitment direct and open rather than to go into sexual relations under pressure—doing violence to his feelings by having physical commitment without psychological. He may flout the rules; but at least they give some structure to be flouted. My point is true whether he obeys the rule or not. Many contemporary students, understandably anxious because of their new sexual freedom, repress this anxiety ("one should *like* freedom") and then compensate for the additional anxiety the repression gives them by attacking the parietal authorities for not giving them more freedom!

What we did not see in our shortsighted liberalism in sex was that throwing the individual into an unbounded and empty sea of free choice does not in itself give freedom, but is more apt to increase inner conflict. The sexual freedom to which we were devoted fell short of being fully human.

In the arts, we have also been discovering what an illusion it was to believe that mere freedom would solve our problem. Consider, for example, the drama. In an article entitled "Is Sex Kaput?," Howard Taubman, former drama critic of *The New York Times*, summarized what we have all observed in drama after drama: "Engaging in sex was like setting out to shop on a dull afternoon; desire had nothing to do with it and even curiosity was faint."[4] Consider also the novel. In the "revolt against the Victorians," writes Leon Edel, "the extremists have had their day. Thus far they have impoverished the novel rather than enriched it."[5] Edel perceptively brings out the crucial point that in sheer realistic "enlightenment" there has occurred a *dehumanization* of sex in fiction. There are "sexual encounters in Zola," he insists, "which have more truth in them than any D. H. Lawrence described—and also more humanity."[6]

The battle against censorship and for freedom of expression surely was a great battle to win, but has it not become a new straitjacket? The writers, both novelists and dramatists, "would rather hock their typewriters than turn in a manuscript without the obligatory scenes of unsparing anatomical documentation of their characters' sexual behavior. . . ."[7] Our "dogmatic enlightenment" is self-defeating: it ends up destroying the very sexual passion it set out to protect. In the great tide of realistic chronicling, we forgot, on the stage and in the novel and even in psychotherapy, that imagination is the life-blood of eros, and that realism is neither sexual nor erotic. Indeed, there is nothing *less* sexy than sheer nakedness, as a random hour at any nudist camp will prove. It requires the infusion of the imagination (which I shall later call intentionality) to transmute physiology and anatomy into *interpersonal* experience—into art, into passion, into eros in a million forms which has the power to shake or charm us.

Could it not be that an "enlightenment" which reduces itself to sheer realistic detail is itself an escape from the anxiety involved in the relation of human imagination to erotic passion?

SALVATION THROUGH TECHNIQUE

A second paradox is that *the new emphasis on technique in sex and love-making backfires*. It often occurs to me that there is an inverse relationship between the number of how-to-do-it books perused by a person or rolling off the presses in a society and the amount of sexual passion or even pleasure experienced by the persons involved. Certainly nothing is wrong with technique as such, in playing golf or acting or making love. But the emphasis beyond a certain point on technique in sex makes for a mechanistic attitude toward love-making, and goes along with alienation, feelings of loneliness, and depersonalization.

One aspect of the alienation is that the lover, with his age-old art, tends to be superseded by the computer operator with his modern efficiency. Couples place great emphasis on bookkeeping and timetables in their love-making—a practice confirmed and standardized by Kinsey. If they fall behind schedule they become anxious and feel impelled to go to bed whether they want to or not. My colleague, Dr. John Schimel, observes, "My patients have endured stoically, or without noticing, remark-

[4] Howard Taubman, "Is Sex Kaput?," *The New York Times*, sect. 2, January 17, 1965.

[5] Leon Edel, "Sex and the Novel," *The New York Times*, sect. 7, pt. I, November 1, 1964.

[6] *Ibid.*

[7] See Taubman.

ably destructive treatment at the hands of their spouses, but they have experienced falling behind in the sexual timetable as a loss of love."[8] The man feels he is somehow losing his masculine status if he does not perform up to schedule, and the woman that she has lost her feminine attractiveness if too long a period goes by without the man at least making a pass at her. The phrase "between men," which women use about their affairs, similarly suggests a gap in time like the *entr'acte*. Elaborate accounting- and ledger-book lists—how often this week have we made love? did he (or she) pay the right amount of attention to me during the evening? was the foreplay long enough?—make one wonder how the spontaneity of this most spontaneous act can possibly survive. The computer hovers in the stage wings of the drama of love-making the way Freud said one's parents used to.

It is not surprising then, in this preoccupation with techniques, that the questions typically asked about an act of love-making are not, Was there passion or meaning or pleasure in the act? but, How well did I perform?[9] Take, for example, what Cyril Connolly calls "the tyranny of the orgasm," and the preoccupation with achieving a simultaneous orgasm, which is another aspect of the alienation. I confess that when people talk about the "apocalyptic orgasm," I find myself wondering, Why do they have to try so hard? What abyss of self-doubt, what inner void of loneliness, are they trying to cover up by this great concern with grandiose effects?

Even the sexologists, whose attitude is generally the more sex the merrier, are raising their eyebrows these days about the anxious overemphasis on achieving the orgasm and the great importance attached to "satisfying" the partner. A man makes a point of asking the woman if she "made it," or if she is "all right," or uses some other euphemism for an experience for which obviously no euphemism is possible. We men are reminded by Simone de Beauvoir and other women who try to interpret the love act that this is the last thing in the world a woman wants to be asked at that moment. Furthermore, the technical preoccupation robs the woman of exactly what she wants most of all, physically and emotionally, namely the man's spontaneous abandon at the moment of climax. This abandon gives her whatever thrill or ecstasy she and the experience are capable of. When we cut through all the rigmarole about roles and performance, what still remains is how amazingly important the sheer fact of intimacy of relationship is—the meeting, the growing closeness with the excitement of not knowing where it will lead, the assertion of the self, and the giving of the self—in making a sexual encounter memorable. Is it not this intimacy that makes us return to the event in memory again and again when we need to be warmed by whatever hearths life makes available?

It is a strange thing in our society that what goes into building a relationship—the sharing of tastes, fantasies, dreams, hopes for the future, and fears from the past—seems to make people more shy and vulnerable than going to bed with each other. They are more wary of the tenderness that goes with

[8] John L. Schimel, "Ideology and Sexual Practices," *Sexual Behavior and the Law*, ed. Ralph Slovenko (Springfield, Ill., Charles C. Thomas, 1965), pp. 195, 197.

[9] Sometimes a woman patient will report to me, in the course of describing how a man tried to seduce her, that he cites as part of his seduction line how efficient a lover he is, and he promises to perform the act eminently satisfactorily for her. (Imagine Mozart's Don Giovanni offering such an argument!) In fairness to elemental human nature, I must add that as far as I can remember, the women reported that this "advance billing" did not add to the seducers' chances of success.

psychological and spiritual nakedness than they are of the physical nakedness in sexual intimacy.

THE NEW PURITANISM

The third paradox is that our highly vaunted sexual freedom has turned out to be a new form of puritanism. I spell it with a small "p" because I do not wish to confuse this with the original Puritanism. That, as in the passion of Hester and Dimmesdale in Hawthorne's *The Scarlet Letter*, was a very different thing.[10] I refer to puritanism as it came down via our Victorian grandparents and became allied with industrialism and emotional and moral compartmentalization.

I define this puritanism as consisting of three elements. First, *a state of alienation from the body*. Second, *the separation of emotion from reason*. And third, *the use of the body as a machine.*

In our new puritanism, bad health is equated with sin.[11] Sin used to mean giving in to one's sexual desires; it now means not having full sexual expression. Our contemporary puritan holds that it is immoral *not* to express your libido. Apparently this is true on both sides of the ocean: "There are few more depressing sights," the London *Times Literary Supplement* writes, "than a progressive intellectual determined to end up in bed with someone from a sense of moral duty. . . . There is no more high-minded puritan in the world than your modern advocate of salvation through properly

[10] That the actual Puritans in the sixteenth and seventeenth centuries were a different breed from those who represented the deteriorated forms in our century can be seen in a number of sources. Roland H. Bainton in the chapter "Puritanism and the Modern Period," of his book *What Christianity Says About Sex, Love and Marriage* (New York, Reflection Books, Association Press, 1957), writes "The Puritan ideal for the relations of man and wife was summed up in the words, 'a tender respectiveness.'" He quotes Thomas Hooker: "The man whose heart is endeared to the woman he loves, he dreams of her in the night, hath her in his eye and apprehension when he awakes, museth on her as he sits at table, walks with her when he travels and parlies with her in each place he comes." Ronald Mushat Frye, in a thoughtful paper, "The Teachings of Classical Puritanism on Conjugal Love," *Studies from the Renaissance*, II (1955), submits conclusive evidence that classical Puritanism inculcated a view of sexual life in marriage as the "Crown of all our bliss," "Founded in Reason, Loyal, Just, and Pure" (p. 149). He believes that "the fact remains that the education of England in a more liberal view of married love in the sixteenth and early seventeenth centuries was in large part the work of that party within English Protestantism which is called Puritan" (p. 149). The Puritans were against lust and acting on physical attraction outside of marriage, but they as strongly believed in the sexual side of marriage and believed it the duty of all people to keep this alive all their lives. It was a later confusion which associated them with the asceticism of continence in marriage. Frye states, "In the course of a wide reading of Puritan and other Protestant writers in the sixteenth and early seventeenth centuries, I have found nothing but opposition to this type of ascetic 'perfection'" (p. 152).

One has only to look carefully at the New England churches built by the Puritans and in the Puritan heritage to see the great refinement and dignity of form which surely implies a passionate attitude toward life. They had the dignity of controlled passion, which may have made possible an actual living with passion in contrast to our present pattern of expressing and dispersing all passion. The deterioration of Puritanism into our modern secular attitudes was caused by the confluence of three trends: industrialism, Victorian emotional compartmentalization, and the secularization of all religious attitudes. The first introduced the specific mechanical model; the second introduced the emotional dishonesty which Freud analyzed so well; and the third took away the depth-dimensions of religion and made the concerns how one "behaved" in such matters as smoking, drinking, and sex in the superficial forms which we are attacking above. (For a view of the delightful love letters between husband and wife in this period, see the two-volume biography of John Adams by Page Smith. See also the writings on the Puritans by Perry Miller.)

[11] This formulation was originally suggested to me by Dr. Ludwig Lefebre.

directed passion. . . ."[12] A woman used to be guilty if she went to bed with a man; now she feels vaguely guilty if after a certain number of dates she still refrains; her sin is "morbid repression," refusing to "give." And the partner, who is always completely enlightened (or at least pretends to be) refuses to allay her guilt by getting overtly angry at her (if she could fight him on the issue, the conflict would be a lot easier for her). But he stands broadmindedly by, ready at the end of every date to undertake a crusade to assist her out of her fallen state. And this, of course, makes her "no" all the more guilt-producing for her.

This all means, of course, that people not only have to learn to perform sexually but have to make sure, at the same time, that they can do so without letting themselves go in passion or unseemly commitment—the latter of which may be interpreted as exerting an unhealthy demand upon the partner. *The Victorian person sought to have love without falling into sex; the modern person seeks to have sex without falling into love....*

FREUD AND PURITANISM

How Freudian psychoanalysis was intertwined with both the new sexual libertarianism and puritanism is a fascinating story. Social critics at cocktail parties tend to credit Freud with being the prime mover of, or at least the prime spokesman for, the new sexual freedom. But what they do not see is that Freud and psychoanalysis reflected and expressed the new puritanism in both its positive and negative forms.

The psychoanalytic puritanism is positive in its emphasis on rigorous honesty and cerebral rectitude, as exemplified in Freud himself. It is negative in its providing a new system by which the body and self can be viewed, rightly or wrongly, as a mechanism for gratification by way of "sexual objects." The tendency in psychoanalysis to speak of sex as a "need" in the sense of a tension to be reduced plays into this puritanism.

We thus have to explore this problem to see how the new sexual values in our society were given a curious twist as they were rationalized psychoanalytically. "Psychoanalysis is Calvinism in Bermuda shorts," pungently stated Dr. C. Macfie Campbell, president of the American Psychiatric Association in 1936–37, discussing the philosophical aspects of psychoanalysis. The aphorism is only half true, but that half is significant. Freud himself was an excellent example of a puritan in the positive sense in his strength of character, control of his passions, and compulsive work. Freud greatly admired Oliver Cromwell, the Puritan commander, and named a son after him. Philip Rieff, in his study *Freud: The Mind of the Moralist*, points out that this "affinity for militant puritanism was not uncommon among secular Jewish intellectuals, and indicates a certain preferred character type, starched with independence and cerebral rectitude rather than a particular belief or doctrine."[13] In his ascetic work habits, Freud shows one of the most significant aspects of puritanism, namely the use of *science as a monastery*. His compulsive industry was rigorously devoted to achieving his scientific goals, which transcended everything else in life (and, one might add, life itself) and for which he sublimated his passion in a quite real rather than figurative sense.

Freud himself had a very limited sexual life. His own sexual expression be-

[12] *Atlas*, November, 1965, p. 302.

[13] Philip Rieff, *Freud: The Mind of the Moralist* (New York, Viking Press, 1959), quoted in James A. Knight's "Calvinism and Psychoanalysis: A Comparative Study," *Pastoral Psychology*, December, 1963, p. 10.

gan late, around thirty, and subsided early, around forty, so his biographer Ernest Jones tells us. At forty-one, Freud wrote to his friend Wilhelm Fliess complaining of his depressed moods, and added, "Also sexual excitation is of no more use to a person like me." Another incident points to the fact that around this age his sexual life had more or less ended. Freud reports in *The Interpretation of Dreams* that at one time, in his forties, he felt physically attracted to a young woman and reached out half-voluntarily and touched her. He comments on how surprised he was that he was "still" able to find the possibility for such attraction in him.[14]

Freud believed in the control and channeling of sexuality, and was convinced that this had specific value both for cultural development and for one's own character. In 1883, during his prolonged engagement to Martha Bernays, the young Freud wrote to his future wife:

> . . . it is neither pleasant nor edifying to watch the masses amusing themselves; we at least don't have much taste for it. . . . I remember something that occurred to me while watching a performance of *Carmen*: the mob gives vent to its appetites, and we deprive ourselves. We deprive ourselves in order to maintain our integrity, we economize in our health, our capacity for enjoyment, our emotions; we save ourselves for something, not knowing for what. And this constant suppression of natural instincts gives us the quality of refinement. . . . And the extreme case of people like ourselves who chain themselves together for life and death, who deprive themselves and pine for years so as to remain faithful, who probably wouldn't survive a catastrophe that robbed them of their beloved. . . .[15]

The basis of Freud's doctrine of sublimation lies in this belief that libido exists in a certain quantity in the individual, that you can deprive yourself, "economize" emotionally in one way to increase your enjoyment in another, and that if you spend your libido in direct sexuality you will not have it for utilization, for example, in artistic creation. In a positive statement of appreciation of Freud's work, Paul Tillich nevertheless remarks that the "concept of sublimation is Freud's most puritanical belief. . . .[16]

MOTIVES OF THE PROBLEM

In my function as a supervisory analyst at two analytic institutes, I supervise one case of each of six psychiatrists or psychologists who are in training to become analysts. I cite the six patients of these young analysts both because I know a good deal about them by now and also because, since they are not my parents, I can see them with a more objective perspective. Each one of these patients goes to bed without ostensible shame or guilt—and generally with different partners. The women—four of the six patients—all state that they don't feel much in the sex act. The motives of two of the women for going to bed seem to be to hang on to the man and

[14] Knight, p. 11.

[15] Cf. Marcus, *The Other Victorians*, pp. 146–147. Freud's letter goes on: "Our whole conduct of life presupposes that we are protected from the direst poverty and that the possibility exists of being able to free ourselves increasingly from social ills. The poor people, the masses, could not survive without their thick skins and their easy-going ways. Why should they scorn the pleasures of the moment when no other awaits them? The poor are too helpless, too exposed, to behave like us. When I see the people indulging themselves, disregarding all sense of moderation, I invariably think that this is their compensation for being a helpless target for all the taxes, epidemics, sickness, and evils of social institutions."

[16] Paul. Tillich, in a speech, "Psychoanalysis and Existentialism," given at the Conference of the American Association of Existential Psychology and Psychiatry, February, 1962.

to live up to the standard that sexual intercourse is "what you do" at a certain stage. The third woman has the particular motive of generosity: she sees going to bed as something nice you give a man—and she makes tremendous demands upon him to take care of her in return. The fourth woman seems the only one who does experience some real sexual lust, beyond which her motives are a combination of generosity to and anger at the man ("I'll *force* him to give me pleasure!"). The two male patients were originally impotent, and now, though able to have intercourse, have intermittent trouble with potency. But the outstanding fact is they never report getting much of a "bang" out of their sexual intercourse. Their chief motive for engaging in sex seems to be to demonstrate their masculinity. The specific purpose of one of the men, indeed, seems more to tell his analyst about his previous night's adventure, fair or poor as it may have been, in a kind of backstage interchange of confidence between men, than to enjoy the love-making itself.

Let us now pursue our inquiry on a deeper level by asking, What are the underlying motives in these patterns? What drives people toward the contemporary compulsive preoccupation with sex in place of their previous compulsive denial of it?

The struggle to prove one's identity is obviously a central motive—an aim present in women as well as men, as Betty Friedan in *The Feminine Mystique* made clear. This has helped spawn the idea of *egalitarianism* of the sexes and the *interchangeability* of the sexual roles. Egalitarianism is clung to at the price of denying not only biological differences—which are basic, to say the least—between men and women, but emotional differences from which come much of the delight of the sexual act. The self-contradiction here is that the compulsive need to prove you are identical with your partner means that you repress your own unique sensibilities—and this is exactly what undermines your own sense of identity. This contradiction contributes to the tendency in our society for us to become machines even in bed.

Another motive is the individual's hope to overcome his own solitariness. Allied with this is the desperate endeavor to escape feelings of emptiness and the threat of apathy: partners pant and quiver hoping to find an answering quiver in someone else's body just to prove that their own is not dead; they seek a responding, a longing in the other to prove their own feelings are alive. Out of an ancient conceit, this is called love.

One often gets the impression, amid the male's flexing of sexual prowess, that men are in training to become sexual athletes. But what is the great prize of the game? Not only men, but women struggle to prove their sexual power—they too must keep up to the timetable, must show passion, and have the vaunted orgasm. Now it is well accepted in psychotherapeutic circles that, dynamically, the overconcern with potency is generally a compensation for feelings of impotence.

The use of sex to prove potency in all these different realms has led to the increasing emphasis on technical performance. And here we observe another curiously self-defeating pattern. It is that the excessive concern with technical performance in sex is actually correlated with the reduction of sexual feeling. The techniques of achieving this approach the ludicrous: one is that an anesthetic ointment is applied to the penis before intercourse. Thus feeling less, the man is able to postpone his orgasm longer. I have learned from colleagues that the prescribing of this anesthetic "remedy" for premature ejaculation is not unusual. "One male patient," records Dr. Schimel, "was desperate about his 'premature ejaculations,' even though these ejaculations took place after periods of penetration of ten minutes or more. A neighbor who was a urologist recommended an anesthetic ointment to be used prior to intercourse. This patient expressed complete satisfaction with the solution and was very grateful to the urologist."[17] Entirely willing to give up any pleasure of his own, he sought only to prove himself a competent male.

A patient of mine reported that he had gone to a physician with the problem of premature ejaculation, and that such an anesthetic ointment had been prescribed. My surprise, like Dr. Schimel's, was particularly over the fact that the patient had accepted this solution with no questions and no conflicts. Didn't the remedy fit the necessary bill, didn't it help him turn in a better performance? But by the time that young man got to me, he was impotent in every way imaginable, even to the point of being unable to handle such scarcely ladylike behavior on the part of his wife as her taking off her shoe while they were driving and beating him over the head with it. By all means the man was impotent in this hideous caricature of a marriage. And his penis, before it was drugged senseless, seemed to be the only character with enough "sense" to have the appropriate intention, namely to get out as quickly as possible.

Making one's self *feel less* in order to *perform better!* This is a symbol, as macabre as it is vivid, of the vicious circle in which so much of our culture is caught. The more one must demonstrate his potency, the more he treats sexual intercourse—this most intimate and personal of all acts—as a performance to be judged by exterior requirements, the more he then views himself as a machine to be turned on, adjusted, and steered, and the less feeling he has for either himself or his partner; and the less feeling, the more he loses genuine sexual appetite and ability. The upshot of this self-defeating pattern is that, in the long run, *the lover who is most efficient will also be the one who is impotent.*

A poignant note comes into our discussion when we remind ourselves that this excessive concern for "satisfying" the partner is an expression, however perverted, of a sound and basic element in the sexual act: the pleasure and experience of self-affirmation in being able to *give* to the partner. The man is often deeply grateful toward the woman who lets herself be gratified by him—lets him give her an orgasm, to use the phrase that is often the symbol for this experience. This is a point midway between lust and tenderness, between sex and agapé—and it partakes of both. Many a male cannot feel his own identity either as a man or a person in our culture until he is able to gratify a woman. The very structure of human interpersonal relations is such that the sexual act does not achieve its full pleasure or meaning if the man and woman cannot feel they are able to gratify the other. And it is the inability to experience this pleasure at the gratification of the other which often underlies the exploitative sexuality of the rape type and the compulsive sexuality of the Don Juan seduction type. Don Juan has to perform the act over and over again because he remains forever unsatisfied, quite despite the fact that he is entirely potent and has a technically good orgasm.

Now the problem is not the desire and need to satisfy the partner as such, but the fact that this need is interpreted by the persons in the sexual act in only a technical sense—giving physical sensation. What is omitted even from our very vocabulary (and thus the words may sound "square" as I say them here) is the experience of giving feelings, sharing fantasies, offering the inner psychic richness that normally takes a little

[17] Schimel, p. 198.

time and enables sensation to transcend itself in emotion and emotion to transcend itself in tenderness and sometimes love.

It is not surprising that contemporary trends toward the mechanization of sex have much to do with the problem of impotence. The distinguishing characteristic of the machine is that it can go through all the *motions* but it never *feels*. A knowledgeable medical student, one of whose reasons for coming into analysis was his sexual impotence, had a revealing dream. He was asking me in the dream to put a pipe in his head that would go down through his body and come out at the other end of his penis. He was confident in the dream that the pipe would constitute an admirably strong erection. What was entirely missing in this intelligent scion of our sophisticated times was any understanding at all that *what he conceived of as his solution was exactly the cause of his problem*, namely the image of himself as a "screwing machine." His symbol is remarkably graphic: the brain, the intellect, is included, but true symbol of our alienated age, his shrewd system bypasses entirely the seats of emotions, the thalamus, the heart and lungs, even the stomach. Direct route from head to penis —but what is lost is the heart![18]

I do not have statistics on hand concerning the present incidence of impotence in comparison with past periods, nor does anyone else so far as I have been able to discover. But my impression is that impotence is increasing these days despite (or is it because of) the unrestrained freedom on all sides. All therapists seem to agree that more men are coming to them with that problem —though whether this represents a real increase in the prevalence of sexual impotence or merely a greater awareness and ability to talk about it cannot be definitely answered. Obviously, it is one of those topics on which meaningful statistics are almost impossible to get. The fact that the book dealing with impotence and frigidity, *Human Sexual Response*, clung near the top of the best-seller lists for so many months, expensive and turgidly written as it was, would seem to be plenty of evidence of the urge of men to get help on impotence. Whatever the reason, it is becoming harder for the young man as well as the old to take "yes" for an answer.

To see the curious ways the new puritanism shows itself, you have only to open an issue of *Playboy*, that redoubtable journal reputedly sold mainly to college students and clergymen. You discover the naked girls with silicated breasts side by side with the articles by reputable authors, and you conclude on first blush that the magazine is certainly on the side of the new enlightenment. But as you look more closely you see a strange expression in these photographed girls: detached, mechanical, uninviting, vacuous—the typical schizoid personality in the negative sense of that term. You discover that they are not "sexy" at all but that *Playboy* has only shifted the fig leaf from the genitals to the face. You read the letters to the editor and find the first, entitled "Playboy Priest," telling of a priest who "lectures on Hefner's philosophy to audiences of young people and numerous members of the clergy," that "true Christian ethics and morality are not incompatible with Hefner's philosophy," and—written with enthusiastic approbation—that "most clergymen in their fashionable parsonages live more like playboys than ascetics."[19] You find another letter entitled "Jesus was a playboy," since he loved Mary Magdalene, good food, and

[18] Leopold Caligor and Rollo May, in *Dreams and Symbols* (New York, Basic Books, 1968), p. 108*n*, similarly maintain that today's patients, as a whole, seem to be preoccupied with the head and genitals in their dreams and leave out the heart.

[19] *Playboy*, April, 1957.

good grooming, and castigated the Pharisees. And you wonder why all this religious justification and why people, if they are going to be "liberated," can't just enjoy their liberation?

Whether one takes the cynical view that letters to the editor are "planted," or the more generous one that these examples are selected from hundreds of letters, it amounts to the same thing. An image of a type of American male is being presented—a suave, detached, self-assured bachelor, who regards the girl as a "Playboy accessory" like items in his fashionable dress. You note also that *Playboy* carries no advertising for trusses, bald heads, or anything that would detract from this image. You discover that the good articles (which, frankly, can be bought by an editor who wants to hire an assistant with taste and pay the requisite amount of money) give authority to this male image.[20] Harvey Cox concludes that *Playboy* is basically antisexual, and that it is the "latest and slickest episode in man's continuing refusal to be human." He believes "the whole phenomenon of which *Playboy* is only a part vividly illustrates the awful fact of the new kind of tyranny."[21] The poet-sociologist Calvin Herton, discussing *Playboy* in connection with the fashion and entertainment world, calls it the new sexual fascism.[22]

Playboy has indeed caught on to something significant in American society: Cox believes it to be "the repressed fear of involvement with women."[23] I go farther and hold that it, as an example of the new puritanism, gets its dynamic from a repressed anxiety in American men that underlies even the fear of involvement. This is the repressed anxiety about impotence. Everything in the magazine is beautifully concocted to bolster the *illusion of potency* without ever putting it to the test or challenge at all. Noninvolvement (like playing it cool) is elevated into the ideal model for the Playboy. This is possible because the illusion is air-tight, ministering as it does to men fearful for their potency, and capitalizing on this anxiety. The character of the illusion is shown further in the fact that the readership of *Playboy* drops off significantly after the age of thirty, when men cannot escape dealing with real women. This illusion is illustrated by the fact that Hefner himself, a former Sunday-school teacher and son of devout Methodists, practically never goes outside his large establishment in North Chicago. Ensconced there, he carries on his work surrounded by his bunnies and amidst his non-alcoholic bacchanals on Pepsi-Cola.

THE REVOLT AGAINST SEX

With the confusion of motives in sex that we have noted above—almost every motive being present in the act except the desire to make love—it is no wonder that there is a diminution of feeling and that passion has lessened almost to the vanishing point. This diminution of

[20] These articles by notable people can be biased, as was Timothy Leary's famous interview which *Playboy* used broadly in its advertising, holding that LSD makes possible a "hundred orgasms" for the woman, and that "an LSD session that doesn't involve an ultimate merger isn't really complete." Actually, LSD seemingly temporarily "turns off" the sexual functions. This interview inspired a rejoinder from a writer who is an authority on both LSD and sex, Dr. R. E. L. Masters, who wrote, "Such claims about LSD effects are not only false, they are dangerous. . . . That occasional rare cases might support some of his claims, I don't doubt; but he suggests that he is describing the rule, not the exception, and that is altogether false" (mimeographed letter, privately circulated).

[21] "*Playboy's* Doctrine of the Male," in *Christianity and Crisis*, XXI/6, April 17, 1961, unpaged.

[22] Discussion in symposium on sex, Michigan State University, February, 1969.

[23] *Ibid.*

feeling takes the form of a kind of anesthesia (now with no need of ointment) in people who can perform the mechanical aspects of the sexual act very well. We are becoming used to the plaint from the couch or patient's chair that "We made love, but I didn't feel anything." Again, the poets tell us the same things as our patients. T. S. Eliot writes in *The Waste Land* that after "lovely woman stoops to folly," and the carbuncular clerk who seduced her at tea leaves,

> She turns and looks a moment in the glass,
> Hardly aware of her departed lover;
> Her brain allows one half-formed thought to pass;
> "Well now that's done: and I'm glad it's over."
> When lovely woman stoops to folly and
> Paces about her room again, alone,
> She smoothes her hair with automatic hand,
> And puts a record on the gramophone.
> (III:249–256)

Sex is the "last frontier," David Riesman meaningfully phrases it in *The Lonely Crowd.* Gerald Sykes, in the same vein, remarks, "In a world gone grey with market reports, time studies, tax regulations and path lab analyses, the rebel finds sex to be the one green thing."[24] It is surely true that the zest, adventure, and trying out of one's strength, the discovering of vast and exciting new areas of feeling and experience in one's self and in one's relations to others, and the validation of the self that goes with these are indeed "frontier experiences." They are rightly and normally present in sexuality as part of the psychosocial development of every person. Sex in our society did, in fact, have this power for several decades after the 1920's, when almost every other activity was becoming "other-directed," jaded, emptied of zest and adventure. But for various reasons—one of them being that sex by itself had to carry the weight for the validation of the personality in practically all other realms as well—the frontier freshness, newness, and challenge become more and more lost.

For we are now living in the post-Riesman age, and are experiencing the long-run implications of Riesman's "other-directed" behavior, the radar-reflected way of life. The last frontier has become a teeming Las Vegas and no frontier at all. Young people can no longer get a bootlegged feeling of personal identity out of revolting in sexuality since there is nothing there to revolt against. Studies of drug addiction among young people report them as saying that the revolt against parents, the social "kick of feeling their own oats" which they used to get from sex, they now have to get from drugs. One such study indicates that students express a "certain boredom with sex, while drugs are synonymous with excitement, curiosity, forbidden adventure, and society's abounding permissiveness."[25]

[24] Gerald Sykes, *The Cool Millennium* (New York, 1967).

[25] A survey of students on three college campuses in the New York/New Jersey area conducted by Dr. Sylvia Hertz, chairman of the Essex County Council on Drug Addiction, reported in *The New York Times* on November 26, 1967, that "The use of drugs has become so prominent, that it has relegated sex to second place."

As sex began to lose its power as the arena of proving one's individuality by rebellion and merged with the use of drugs as the new frontier, both then became related to the preoccupation with acts of violence. Efforts crop up anachronistically here and there to use sex as the vehicle for revolt against society. When I was speaking at a college in California, my student chauffeur to the campus told me that there was a society at the college dedicated, as its name indicates, to "Sex Unlimited." I remarked that I hadn't noticed anybody in California trying to limit sex, so what did this society do? He answered that the previous week, the total membership (which turned out to be six or seven students) got undressed at noon and, naked, jumped into the goldfish pool in the center of the campus. The city police then came and hiked them off to jail. My response was that if one wanted to get arrested, that was a good way to do it, but I couldn't see that the experience had a thing in the world to do with sex.

It no longer sounds new when we discover that for many young people what used to be called love-making is now experienced as a futile "panting palm to palm," in Aldous Huxley's predictive phrase; that they tell us that it is hard for them to understand what the poets were talking about, and that we should so often hear the disappointed refrain, "We went to bed but it wasn't any good."

Nothing to revolt against, did I say? Well, there is obviously one thing left to revolt against, and that is sex itself. The frontier, the establishing of identity, the validation of the self can be, and not infrequently does become for some people, a revolt against sexuality entirely. I am certainly not advocating this. What I wish to indicate is that the very revolt against sex—this modern Lysistrata in robot's dress—is rumbling at the gates of our cities or, if not rumbling, at least hovering. The sexual revolution comes finally back on itself not with a bang but a whimper.

Thus it is not surprising that, as sex becomes more machinelike, with passion irrelevant and then even pleasure diminishing, the problem has come full circle. And we find, *mirabile dictu*, a progression from an *anesthetic* attitude to an *antiseptic* one. Sexual contact itself then tends to get put on the shelf and to be avoided. This is another and surely least constructive aspect of the new puritanism: it returns, finally, to a new asceticism. This is said graphically in a charming limerick that seems to have sprung up on some sophisticated campus:

The word has come down from the
Dean
That with the aid of the teaching
machine,
King Oedipus Rex
Could have learned about sex
Without ever touching the Queen.

Marshall McLuhan, among others, welcomes this revolt against sex. "Sex as we now think of it may soon be dead," write McLuhan and Leonard. "Sexual concepts, ideals and practices already are being altered almost beyond recognition. . . . The foldout playmate in *Playboy* magazine—she of outsize breast and buttocks, pictured in sharp detail—signals the death throes of a departing age."[26] McLuhan and Leonard then go on to predict that eros will not be lost in the new sexless age but diffused, and that all life will be more erotic than now seems possible.

This last reassurance would be comforting indeed to believe. But as usual, McLuhan's penetrating insights into *present* phenomena are unfortunately placed in a framework of history—"pretribalism" with its so-called lessened distinction between male and female—which has no factual basis at all.[27] And he gives us no evidence whatever for his optimistic prediction that new eros, rather than apathy, will succeed the demise of *vive la difference*. Indeed, there are amazing confusions in this article arising from McLuhan's and Leonard's worship of the new electric age. In likening Twiggy to an X-ray as against Sophia Loren to a Rubens, they ask, "And what does an X-ray of a woman

[26] Marshall McLuhan and George G. Leonard, "The Future of Sex," *Look Magazine*, July 25, 1967, p. 58. The article makes a significant point with respect to the polls about sex: "When survey-takers 'prove' that there is no sexual revolution among our young people by showing that the frequency of sexual intercourse has not greatly increased, they are missing the point completely. Indeed, the frequency of intercourse may decrease in the future *because of* a real revolution in attitudes toward, feelings about and uses of sex, especially concerning the roles of male and female" (p. 57).

[27] Not being an anthropologist, I conferred with Ashley Montague on this point. The judgment was expressed orally to me.

reveal? Not a realistic picture, but a deep, involving image. Not a specialized female, but a *human being*."[28] Well! An X-ray actually reveals not a human being at all but a depersonalized, fragmentized segment of bone or tissue which can be read only by a highly specialized technician and from which we could never in a thousand years recognize a human being or any man or woman we know, let alone one we love. Such a "reassuring" view of the future is frightening and depressing in the extreme.

And may I not be permitted to prefer Sophia Loren over Twiggy for an idle erotic daydream without being read out of the New Society?

Our future is taken more seriously by the participants in the discussion on this topic at the Center for the Study of Democratic Institutions at Santa Barbara. Their report, called "The A-Sexual Society," frankly faces the fact that "we are hurtling into, not a bisexual or a multi-sexual, but an a-sexual society: the boys grow long hair and the girls wear pants. . . . Romance will disappear; in fact, it has almost disappeared now. . . . Given the guaranteed Annual Income and The Pill, will women choose to marry? Why should they?"[29] Mrs. Eleanor Garth, a participant in the discussion and writer of the report, goes on to point out the radical change that may well occur in having and rearing children. "What of the time when the fertilized ovum can be implanted in the womb of a mercenary, and one's progeny selected from a sperm-bank? Will the lady choose to reproduce her husband, if there still are such things? . . . No problems, no jealousy, no love-transference. . . . And what of the children, incubated under glass? . . . Will communal love develop the human qualities that we assume emerge from the present rearing of children? Will women under these conditions lose the survival drive and become as death-oriented as the present generation of American men? . . . I don't raise the question in advocacy," she adds, "I consider some of the possibilities horrifying."[30]

Mrs. Garth and her colleagues at the Center recognize that the real issue underlying this revolution is not what one does with sexual organs and sexual functions per se, but what happens to man's humanity. "What disturbs me is the real possibility of the disappearance of our humane, life-giving qualities with the speed of developments in the life sciences, and the fact that no one seems to be discussing the alternative possibilities for good and evil in these developments."[31]

The purpose of our discussion in this book is precisely to raise the questions of the alternative possibilities for good and evil—that is, the destruction or the enhancement of the qualities which constitute man's "humane, life-giving qualities."

[28] McLuhan and Leonard, p. 58. The words are italicized by McLuhan and Leonard.

[29] Eleanor Garth, "The A-Sexual Society," *Center Diary*, published by the Center for the Study of Democratic Institutions, 15, November–December, 1966, p. 43.

[30] *Ibid.*

[31] *Ibid.*

Fiction

Sherwood Anderson (1876–1941)

Seeds

He was a small man with a beard and was very nervous. I remember how the cords of his neck were drawn taut.

For years he had been trying to cure people of illness by the method called psychoanalysis. The idea was the passion of his life. "I came here because I am tired," he said dejectedly. "My body is not tired but something inside me is old and worn-out. I want joy. For a few days or weeks I would like to forget men and women and the influences that make them the sick things they are."

There is a note that comes into the human voice by which you may know real weariness. It comes when one has been trying with all his heart and soul to think his way along some difficult road of thought. Of a sudden he finds himself unable to go on. Something within him stops. A tiny explosion takes place. He bursts into words and talks, perhaps foolishly. Little side currents of his nature he didn't know were there run out and get themselves expressed. It is at such times that a man boasts, uses big words, makes a fool of himself in general.

And so it was the doctor became shrill. He jumped up from the steps where he had been sitting, talking, and walked about. "You come from the West. You have kept away from people. You have preserved yourself—damn you! I haven't—" His voice had indeed become shrill. "I have entered into lives. I have gone beneath the surface of the lives of men and women. Women especially I have studied—our own women, here in America."

"You have loved them?" I suggested.

"Yes," he said. "Yes—you are right there. I have done that. It is the only way I can get at things. I have to try to love. You see how that is? It's the only way. Love must be the beginning of things with me."

I began to sense the depths of his weariness. "We will go swim in the lake," I urged.

"I don't want to swim or do any damn plodding thing. I want to run and shout," he declared. "For a while, for a few hours, I want to be like a dead leaf blown by the winds over these hills. I have one desire and one only—to free myself."

We walked in a dusty country road. I wanted him to know that I thought I understood, so I put the case in my own way.

When he stopped and stared at me I talked. "You are no more and no better than myself," I declared. "You are a dog that has rolled in offal, and because you are not quite a dog you do not like the smell of your own hide."

In turn my voice became shrill. "You blind fool," I cried impatiently. "Men like you are fools. You cannot go along that road. It is given to no man to venture far along the road of lives."

I became passionately in earnest. "The illness you pretend to cure is the universal illness," I said. "The thing you want to do cannot be done. Fool—do you expect love to be understood?"

We stood in the road and looked at each other. The suggestion of a sneer played about the corners of his mouth. He put a hand on my shoulder and shook me. "How smart we are—how aptly we put things!"

He spat the words out and then turned and walked a little away. "You think you understand, but you don't understand," he cried. "What you say can't be done can be done. You're a liar. You cannot be so definite without missing something vague and fine. You miss the whole point. The lives of people are like young trees in a forest. They are being choked by climbing vines. The vines are old thoughts and beliefs planted by dead men. I am myself covered by crawling creeping vines that choke me."

He laughed bitterly. "And that's why I want to run and play," he said. "I want to be a leaf blown by the wind over hills. I want to die and be born again, and I am only a tree covered with vines and slowly dying. I am, you see, weary and want to be made clean. I am an amateur venturing timidly into lives," he concluded. "I am weary and want to be made clean. I am covered by creeping crawling things."

A woman from Iowa came here to Chicago and took a room in a house on the west-side. She was about twenty-seven years old and ostensibly she came to the city to study advanced methods for teaching music.

A certain young man also lived in the west-side house. His room faced a long hall on the second floor of the house and the one taken by the woman was across the hall facing his room.

In regard to the young man—there is something very sweet in his nature. He is a painter but I have often wished he would decide to become a writer. He tells things with understanding and he does not paint brilliantly.

And so the woman from Iowa lived in the west-side house and came home from the city in the evening. She looked like a thousand other women one sees in the streets every day. The only thing that at all made her stand out among the women in the crowds was that she was a little lame. Her right foot was slightly deformed and she walked with a limp. For three months she lived in the house—where she was the only woman except the landlady—and then a feeling in regard to her began to grow up among the men of the house.

The men all said the same thing concerning her. When they met in the hallway at the front of the house they stopped, laughed and whispered. "She wants a lover," they said and winked. "She may not know it but a lover is what she needs." One knowing Chicago and Chicago men would think that an easy want to be satisfied. I laughed when my friend—whose name is LeRoy—told me the story, but he did not laugh. He shook his head. "It wasn't so easy," he said. "There would be no story were the matter that simple."

LeRoy tried to explain. "Whenever a man approached her she became alarmed," he said. Men kept smiling and speaking to her. They invited her to dinner and to the theatre, but nothing would induce her to walk in the streets with a man. She never went into the streets at night. When a man stopped and tried to talk with her in the hallway she turned her eyes to the floor and then ran into her room. Once a young drygoods clerk who lived there induced her to sit with him on the steps before the house.

He was a sentimental fellow and took hold of her hand. When she began to cry he was alarmed and arose. He put a hand on her shoulder and tried to explain, but under the touch of his fingers, her whole body shook with terror.

Don't touch me," she cried, "don't let your hands touch me!" She began to scream and people passing in the streets stopped to listen. The drygoods clerk was alarmed and ran upstairs to his own room. He bolted the door and stood listening. "It is a trick," he declared in a trembling voice. "She is trying to make trouble. I did nothing to her. It was an accident and anyway what's the matter? I only touched her arm with my fingers."

Perhaps a dozen times LeRoy has spoken to me of the experience of the Iowa woman in the west-side house. The men there began to hate her. Although she would have nothing to do with them she would not let them alone. In a hundred ways she continually invited approaches that when made she repelled. When she stood naked in the bathroom facing the hallway where the men passed up and down she left the door slightly ajar. There was a couch in the living room downstairs, and when men were present she would sometimes enter and without saying a word throw herself down before them. On the couch she lay with lips drawn slightly apart. Her eyes stared at the ceiling. Her whole physical being seemed to be waiting for something. The sense of her filled the room. The men standing about pretended not to see. They talked loudly. Embarrassment took possession of them and one by one they crept quietly away.

One evening the woman was ordered to leave the house. Someone, perhaps the drygoods clerk, had talked to the landlady and she acted at once. "If you leave tonight I shall like it that much better," LeRoy heard the elder woman's voice saying. She stood in the hallway before the Iowa woman's room. The landlady's voice rang through the house.

LeRoy the painter is tall and lean and his life has been spent in devotion to ideas. The passions of his brain have consumed the passions of his body. His income is small and he has not married. Perhaps he has never had a sweetheart. He is not without physical desire but he is not primarily concerned with desire.

On the evening when the Iowa woman was ordered to leave the west-side house, she waited until she thought the landlady had gone downstairs, and then went into LeRoy's room. It was about eight o'clock and he sat by a window reading a book. The woman did not knock but opened the door. She said nothing but ran across the floor and knelt at his feet. LeRoy said that her twisted foot made her run like a wounded bird, that her eyes were burning and that her breath came in little gasps. "Take me," she said, putting her face down upon his knees and trembling violently. "Take me quickly. There must be a beginning to things. I can't stand the waiting. You must take me at once."

You may be quite sure LeRoy was perplexed by all this. From what he has said I gathered that until that evening he had hardly noticed the woman. I suppose that of all the men in the house he had been the most indifferent to her. In the room something happened. The landlady followed the woman when she ran to LeRoy, and the two women confronted him. The woman from Iowa knelt trembling and frightened at his feet. The landlady was indignant. LeRoy acted on impulse. An inspiration came to him. Putting his hand on the kneeling woman's shoulder he shook her violently. "Now behave yourself," he said quickly. "I will keep my promise." He turned to the landlady and smiled. "We have been engaged to be married," he said. "We have quarreled. She came here to be near me. She has been unwell and excited. I will take her away. Please don't let yourself be annoyed. I will take her away."

When the woman and LeRoy got out of the house she stopped weeping and put her hand into his. Her fears had all gone away. He found a room for her in another house and then went with her into a park and sat on a bench.

Everything LeRoy has told me concerning this woman strengthens my belief in what I said to the man that day in the mountains. You cannot venture along the road of lives. On the bench he and the woman talked until midnight and he saw and talked with her many times later. Nothing came of it. She went back, I suppose, to her place in the West.

In the place from which she had come the woman had been a teacher of music. She was one of four sisters, all engaged in the same sort of work and, LeRoy says, all quiet capable women. Their father had died when the eldest girl was not yet ten, and five years later the mother died also. The girls had a house and a garden.

In the nature of things I cannot know what the lives of the women were like but of this one may be quite certain—they talked only of women's affairs, thought only of women's affairs. No one of them ever had a lover. For years no man came near the house.

Of them all only the youngest, the one who came to Chicago, was visibly affected by the utterly feminine quality of their lives. It did something to her. All day and every day she taught music to young girls and then went home to the women. When she was twenty-five she began to think and to dream of men. During the day and through the evening she talked with women of women's affairs, and all the time she wanted desperately to be loved by a man. She went to Chicago with that hope in mind. LeRoy explained her attitude in the matter and her strange behavior in the west-side house by saying she had thought too much and acted too little. "The life force within her became decentralized," he declared. "What she wanted she could not achieve. The living force within could not find expression. When it could not get expressed in one way it took another. Sex spread itself out over her body. It permeated the very fibre of her being. At the last she was sex personified, sex become condensed and impersonal. Certain words, the touch of a man's hand, sometimes even the sight of a man passing in the street did something to her."

Yesterday I saw LeRoy and he talked to me again of the woman and her strange and terrible fate.

We walked in the park by the lake. As we went along the figure of the woman kept coming into my mind. An idea came to me.

"You might have been her lover," I said. "That was possible. She was not afraid of you."

LeRoy stopped. Like the doctor who was so sure of his ability to walk into lives he grew angry and scolded. For a moment he stared at me and then a rather odd thing happened. Words said by the other man in the dusty road in the hills came to LeRoy's lips and were said over again. The suggestion of a sneer played about the corners of his mouth. "How smart we are. How aptly we put things," he said.

The voice of the young man who walked with me in the park by the lake in the city became shrill. I sensed the weariness in him. Then he laughed and said quietly and softly, "It isn't so simple. By being sure of yourself you are in danger of losing all of the romance of life. You miss the whole point. Nothing in life can be settled so definitely. The woman—you see—was like a young tree choked by a climbing vine. The thing that wrapped her about had shut out the light. She was as grotesque as many trees in the forest are grotesque. Her problem was such a difficult one that thinking of it has changed the whole current of my life. At first I was like you. I was quite sure. I thought I would be her lover and settle the matter."

LeRoy turned and walked a little away. Then he came back and took hold of my arm. A passionate earnestness took possession of him. His voice trembled. "She needed a lover, yes, the men in the house were quite right about that," he said. "She needed a lover and at the same time a lover was not what she needed. The need of a lover was, after all, a quite secondary thing. She needed to be loved, to be long and quietly and patiently loved. To be sure she is grotesque, but then all the people in the world are grotesque. We all need to be loved. What would cure her would cure the rest of us also. The disease she had is, you see, universal. We all want to be loved and the world has no plan for creating our lovers."

LeRoy's voice dropped and he walked beside me in silence. We turned away from the lake and walked under trees. I looked closely at him. The cords of his neck were drawn taut. "I have seen under the shell of life and I am afraid," he mused. "I am myself like the woman. I am covered with creeping crawling vine-like things. I cannot be a lover. I am not subtle or patient enough. I am paying old debts. Old thoughts and beliefs—seeds planted by dead men—spring up in my soul and choke me."

For a long time we walked and LeRoy talked, voicing the thoughts that came into his mind. I listened in silence. His mind struck upon the refrain voiced by the man in the mountains. "I would like to be a dead dry thing," he muttered looking at the leaves scattered over the grass. "I would like to be a leaf blown away by the wind." He looked up and his eyes turned to where among the trees we could see the lake in the distance. "I am weary and want to be made clean. I am a man covered by creeping crawling things. I would like to be dead and blown by the wind over limitless waters," he said. "I want more than anything else in the world to be clean."

E. M. Forster (1879–1970)

The Machine Stops

PART I: THE AIR-SHIP

Imagine, if you can, a small room, hexagonal in shape, like the cell of a bee. It is lighted neither by window nor by lamp, yet it is filled with a soft radiance. There are no apertures for ventilation, yet the air is fresh. There are no musical instruments, and yet, at the moment that my meditation opens, this room is throbbing with melodious sounds. An arm-chair is in the center, by its side a reading-desk—that is all the furniture. And in the arm-chair there sits a swaddled lump of flesh—a woman, about five feet high, with a face as white as a fungus. It is to her that the little room belongs.

An electric bell rang.

The woman touched a switch and the music was silent.

"I suppose I must see who it is," she thought, and set her chair in motion. The chair, like the music, was worked by machinery, and it rolled her to the other side of the room, where the bell still rang importunately.

"Who is it?" she called. Her voice was irritable, for she had been interrupted often since the music began. She knew several thousand people; in certain directions human intercourse had advanced enormously.

But when she listened into the receiver, her white face wrinkled into smiles, and she said:

"Very well. Let us talk, I will isolate myself. I do not expect anything important will happen for the next five minutes—for I can give you fully five minutes, Kuno. Then I must deliver my lecture on 'Music during the Australian Period.' "

She touched the isolation knob, so that no one else could speak to her. Then she touched the lighting apparatus, and the little room was plunged into darkness.

"Be quick!" she called, her irritation returning. "Be quick, Kuno; here I am in the dark wasting my time."

But it was fully fifteen seconds before the round plate that she held in her hands began to glow. A faint blue light shot across it, darkening to purple, and presently she could see the image of her son, who lived on the other side of the earth, and he could see her.

"Kuno, how slow you are."

He smiled gravely.

"I really believe you enjoy dawdling."

"I have called you before, mother, but you were always busy or isolated. I have something particular to say."

"What it is, dearest boy? Be quick. Why could you not send it by pneumatic post?"

"Because I prefer saying such a thing. I want—"

"Well?"

"I want you to come and see me."

Vashti watched his face in the blue plate.

"But I can see you!" she exclaimed. "What more do you want?"

"I want to see you not through the Machine," said Kuno. "I want to speak to you not through the wearisome Machine."

"Oh, hush!" said his mother, vaguely shocked. "You mustn't say anything against the Machine."

"Why not?"

"One mustn't."

"You talk as if a god had made the Machine," cried the other. "I believe that you pray to it when you are unhappy. Men made it, do not forget that. Great men, but men. The Machine is much, but it is not everything. I see something like you in this plate, but I do not see you. I hear something like you through this telephone, but I do not hear you. That is why I want you to come. Come and stop with me. Pay me a visit, so that we can meet face to face, and talk about the hopes that are in my mind."

She replied that she could scarcely spare the time for a visit.

"The air-ship barely takes two days to fly between me and you."

"I dislike air-ships."

"Why?"

"I dislike seeing the horrible brown earth, and the sea, and the stars when it is dark. I get no ideas in an air-ship."

"I do not get them anywhere else."

"What kind of ideas can the air give you?"

He paused for an instant.

"Do you not know four big stars that form an oblong, and three stars close together in the middle of the oblong, and hanging from these stars, three other stars?"

"No, I do not. I dislike the stars. But did they give you an idea? How interesting; tell me."

"I had an idea that they were like a man."

"I do not understand."

"The four big stars are the man's shoulders and his knees. The three stars in the middle are his belts that men wore once, and the three stars hanging are like a sword."

"A sword?"

"Men carried swords about with them, to kill animals and other men."

"It does not strike me as a very good idea, but it is certainly original. When did it come to you first?"

"In the air-ship—" He broke off, and she fancied that he looked sad. She could not be sure, for the Machine did not transmit nuances of expression. It only gave a general idea of people—an idea that was good enough for all practical purposes, Vashti thought. The imponderable bloom, declared by a discredited philosophy to be the actual essence of intercourse, was rightly ignored by the Machine, just as the imponderable bloom of the grape was ignored by the manufacturers of artificial fruit. Something "good enough" had long since been accepted by our race.

"The truth is," he continued, "that I want to see these stars again. They are curious stars. I want to see them not from the air-ship, but from the surface of the earth, as our ancestors did, thousands of years ago. I want to visit the surface of the earth."

She was shocked again.

"Mother you must come, if only to explain to me what is the harm of visiting the surface of the earth."

"No harm," she replied, controlling herself. "But no advantage. The surface of the earth is only dust and mud, no life remains on it, and you would need a respirator, or the cold of the outer air would kill you. One dies immediately in the outer air."

"I know; of course I shall take all precautions."

"And besides—"

"Well?"

She considered, and chose her words with care. Her son had a queer temper, and she wished to dissuade him from the expedition.

"It is contrary to the spirit of the age," she asserted.

"Do you mean by that, contrary to the Machine?"

"In a sense, but—"

His image in the blue plate faded.

"Kuno!"

He had isolated himself.

For a moment Vashti felt lonely.

Then she generated the light, and the sight of her room, flooded with radiance and studded with electric buttons and switches everywhere—buttons to call for food, for music, for clothing. There was the hotbath button, by pressure of which a basin of (imitation) marble rose out of the floor, filled to the brim with a warm deodorized liquid. There was the cold-bath button. There was the button that produced literature. And there were of course the buttons by which she communicated with her friends. The room, though it contained nothing, was in touch with all that she cared for in the world.

Vashti's next move was to turn off the isolation-switch and all the accumulations of the last three minutes burst upon her. The room was filled with the noise of bells, and speaking-tubes. What was the new food like? Could she recommend it? Had she had any ideas lately? Might one tell her one's own ideas? Would she make an engagement to visit the public nurseries at an early date?—say this day month.

To most of these questions she replied with irritation—a growing quality in that accelerated age. She said that the new food was horrible. That she could not visit the public nurseries through press of engagements. That she had no ideas of her own but had just been told one—that four stars and three in the middle were like a man: She doubted there was much in it. Then she switched off her correspondents, for it was time to deliver her lecture on Australian music.

The clumsy system of public gatherings had been long since abandoned; neither Vashti nor her audience stirred from their rooms. Seated in her armchair she spoke, while they in their armchairs heard her, fairly well, and saw her, fairly well. She opened with a humorous account of music in the pre-Mongolian epoch, and went on to describe the great outburst of song that followed the Chinese conquest. Remote and primeval as were the methods of I-San-So and the Brisbane school, she yet felt (she said) that study of them might repay the musician of today; they had freshness; they had, above all, ideas.

Her lecture, which lasted ten minutes, was well received, and at its conclusion she and many of her audience listened to a lecture on the sea; there were ideas to be got from the sea; the speaker had donned a respirator and visited it lately. Then she fed, talked to many friends, had a bath, talked again, and summoned her bed.

The bed was not to her liking. It was too large, and she had a feeling for a small bed. Complaint was useless, for beds were of the same dimension all over the world, and to have had an alternative size would have involved vast alterations in the Machine. Vashti isolated herself—it was necessary, for neither day nor night existed under the ground—and reviewed all that had happened since she had summoned the bed last. Ideas? Scarcely any. Events—was Kuno's invitation an event?

By her side, on the little reading-desk, was a survival from the ages of litter—one book. This was the Book of the Machine. In it were instructions against every possible contingency. If she was hot or cold or dyspeptic or at loss for a word, she went to the Book, and it told her which button to press. The Central Committee published it. In accordance with a growing habit, it was richly bound.

Sitting up in the bed, she took it reverently in her hands. She glanced round the glowing room as if some one might be watching her. Then, half ashamed, half joyful, she murmured, "O Machine! O Machine!" and raised the volume to her lips. Thrice she kissed it, thrice inclined her head, thrice she felt the delirium of acquiescence. Her ritual performed, she turned to page 1367, which gave the times of the departure of the air-ships from the island in the southern hemisphere, under whose soil she lived, to the island in the northern hemisphere, whereunder lived her son.

She thought, "I have not the time."

She made the room dark and slept; she awoke and made the room light; she ate and exchanged ideas with her friends, and listened to music and attended lectures; she made the room dark and slept. Above her, beneath her, and around her, the Machine hummed eternally; she did not notice the noise, for she had been born with it in her ears. The earth, carrying her, hummed as it sped through silence, turning her now to the invisible sun, now to the invisible stars. She awoke and made the room light.

"Kuno!"

"I will not talk to you," he answered, "until you come."

"Have you been on the surface of the earth since we spoke last?"

His image faded.

Again she consulted the Book. She became very nervous and lay back in her chair palpitating. Think of her as without teeth or hair. Presently she directed the chair to the wall, and pressed an unfamiliar button. The wall swung apart slowly. Through the opening she saw a tunnel that curved slightly, so that its goal was not visible. Should she go to see her son, here was the beginning of the journey.

Of course she knew all about the communication-system. There was nothing mysterious in it. She would summon a car and it would fly with her down the tunnel until it reached the lift that communicated with the air-ship station: the system had been in use for many, many years, long before the universal establishment of the Machine. And of course she had studied the civilization that had immediately preceded her own—the civilization that had mistaken the functions of the system, and had used it for bringing people to things, instead of for bringing things to people. Those funny old days, when men went for change of air instead of changing the air in their rooms! And yet—she was frightened of the tunnel: she had not seen it since her last child was born. It curved—but not quite as brilliant as a lecturer had suggested. Vashti was seized with the terrors of direct experience. She shrank back into the room, and the wall closed up again.

"Kuno," she said, "I cannot come to see you. I am not well."

Immediately an enormous apparatus fell on to her out of the ceiling, a thermometer was automatically inserted between her lips, a stethoscope was automatically laid upon her heart. She lay powerless. Cool pads soothed her forehead. Kuno had telegraphed to her doctor.

So the human passions still blundered up and down in the Machine. Vashti drank the medicine that the doctor projected into her mouth, and the machinery retired into the ceiling. The voice of Kuno was heard asking how she felt.

"Better." Then with irritation: "But why do you not come to me instead?"

"Because I cannot leave this place."

"Why?"

"Because, any moment, something tremendous may happen."

"Have you been on the surface of the earth yet?"

"Not yet."

"Then what is it?"

"I will not tell you through the Machine."

She resumed her life.

But she thought of Kuno as a baby, his birth, his removal to the public nurseries, her one visit to him there, his visits to her—visits which stopped when the Machine had assigned him a room on the other side of the earth. "Parents, duties of," said the Book of the Machine, "cease at the moment of birth. P. 422327483." True, but there was something special about Kuno—indeed there had been something special about all her children—and, after all, she must brave the journey if he desired it. And "something tremendous might happen." What did he mean? The nonsense of a youthful man, no doubt, but she must go. Again she pressed the unfamiliar button, again the wall swung back, and she saw the tunnel that curved out of sight. Clasping the Book, she rose, tottered onto the platform, and summoned the car. Her room closed behind her: the journey to the northern hemisphere had begun.

Of course it was perfectly easy. The car approached and in it she found armchairs exactly liked her own. When she signaled, it stopped, and she tottered into the lift. One other passenger was in the lift, the first fellow creature she had seen face to face for months. Few traveled in these days, for, thanks to the advance of science, the earth was exactly alike all over. Rapid intercourse, from which the previous civilization had hoped so much, had ended by defeating itself. What was the good of going to Pekin when it was just like Shrewsbury? Why return to Shrewsbury when it would be just like Pekin? Men seldom moved their bodies; all unrest was concentrated in the soul.

The air-ship service was a relic from the former age. It was kept up, because it was easier to keep it up than to stop it or to diminish it, but it now far exceeded the wants of the population. Vessel after vessel would rise from the vomitories of Rye or of Christchurch (I use the antique names), would sail into the crowded sky, and would draw up at the wharves of the south—empty. So nicely adjusted was the system, so independent of meteorology, that the sky, whether calm or cloudy, resembled a vast kaleidoscope whereon the same patterns periodically recurred. The ship on which Vashti sailed started now at sunset, now at dawn. But always, as it passed above Rheims, it would neighbor the ship that served between Helsingfors and the Brazils, and every third time it surmounted the Alps, the fleet of Palermo would cross its track behind. Night and day, wind and storm, tide and earthquake, impeded man no longer. He had harnessed Leviathan. All the old literature, with its praise of Nature, and its fear of Nature, rang false as the prattle of a child.

Yet as Vashti saw the vast flank of the ship, stained with exposure to the outer air, her horror of direct experience returned. It was not quite like the air-ship in the cinematophote. For one thing it smelt—not strongly or unpleasantly, but it did smell, and with her eyes shut she should have known that a new thing was close to her. Then she had to walk to it from the lift, had to submit to glances from the other passengers. The man in front dropped his Book—no great matter, but it disquieted them all. In the rooms, if the Book was dropped, the floor raised it mechanically, but the gangway to the air-ship was not so prepared, and the sacred volume lay motionless. They stopped—the thing was unforeseen—and the man, instead of picking up his property, felt the muscles of his arm to see how they had failed him. Then someone actually said with direct utterance: "We shall be late"—and they trooped on board, Vashti treading on the pages as she did so.

Inside, her anxiety increased. The arrangements were old-fashioned and rough. There was even a female attendant, to whom she would have to announce her wants during the voyage. Of course a revolving platform ran the length of the boat, but she was expected to walk from it to her cabin. Some cabins were better than others, and she did not get the best. She thought the attendant had been unfair, and spasms of rage shook her. The glass valves had closed, she could not go back. She saw, at the end of the vestibule, the lift in which she had ascended going quietly up and down, empty. Beneath those corridors of shining tiles were rooms, tier below tier, reaching far into the earth, and in each room there sat a human being, eating, or sleeping, or producing ideas. And buried deep in the hive was her own room. Vashti was afraid.

"O Machine! O Machine!" she murmured, and caressed her Book, and was comforted.

Then the sides of the vestibule seemed to melt together, as do the passages that we see in dreams, the life vanished, the Book that had been dropped slid to the left and vanished, polished tiles rushed by like a stream of water, there was a slight jar, and the air-ship, issuing from its tunnel, soared above the waters of a tropical ocean.

It was night. For a moment she saw the coast of Sumatra edged by the phosphorescence of waves, and crowned by light-houses, still sending forth their disregarded beams. They also vanished, and only the stars distracted her. They were not motionless, but swayed to and fro above her head, thronging out of one sky-light into another, as if the universe and not the air-ship was careening. And, as often happens on clear nights, they seemed now to be in perspective, now on a plane; now piled tier beyond tier into the infinite heavens, now concealing infinity, a roof limiting for ever the visions of men. In either case they seemed intolerable. "Are we to travel in the dark?" called the passengers angrily, and the attendant, who had been careless, generated the light, and pulled down the blinds of pliable metal. When the air-ships had been built, the desire to look direct at things still lingered in the world. Hence the extraordinary number of skylights and windows, and the proportionate discomfort to those who were civilized and refined. Even in Vashti's cabin one star peeped through a flaw in the blind, and after a few hours' uneasy slumber, she was disturbed by an unfamiliar glow, which was the dawn.

Quick as the ship had sped westwards, the earth had rolled eastwards quicker still, and had dragged back Vashti and her companions towards the sun. Science could prolong the night, but only for a little, and those high hopes of neutralizing the earth's diurnal revolution had passed, together with hopes that were possibly higher. To "keep pace with the sun," or even to outstrip it, had been the aim of the civilization preceding this. Racing aeroplanes had been built for the purpose, capable of enormous speed, and steered by the greatest intellects of the epoch. Round the globe they went, round and round, westward, westward, round and round, amidst humanity's applause. In vain. The globe went eastward quicker still, horrible accidents occurred, and the Committee of the Machine, at the time rising into prominence, declared the pursuit illegal, unmechanical, and punishable by Homelessness.

Of Homelessness more will be said later.

Doubtless the Committee was right. Yet the attempt to "defeat the sun" aroused the last common interest that our race experienced about the heavenly bodies, or indeed about anything. It was the last time that men were compacted by thinking of a power outside the world. The sun had conquered, yet it was the end of his spiritual dominion. Dawn, midday, twilight, the zodiacal path, touched neither men's lives nor their hearts, and science retreated into the ground, to concentrate herself upon problems that she was certain of solving.

So when Vashti found her cabin invaded by a rosy finger of light, she was annoyed, and tried to adjust the blind. But the blind flew up altogether, and she saw through the skylight small pink clouds, swaying against a background of blue, and as the sun crept higher, its radiance entered direct, brimming down the wall, like a golden sea. It rose and fell with the air-ship's motion, just as waves rise and fall, but it advanced steadily as a tide advances. Unless she was careful, it would strike her face. A spasm of horror shook her and she rang for the attendant. The attendant too was horrified, but she could do nothing; it was not her place to mend the blind. She could only suggest that the lady should change her cabin, which she accordingly prepared to do.

People were almost exactly alike all over the world, but the attendant of the air-ship, perhaps owing to her exceptional duties, had grown a little out of the common. She had often to address passengers with direct speech, and this had given her a certain roughness and originality of manner. When Vashti swerved away from the sunbeams with a cry, she behaved barbarically—she put out her hand to steady her.

"How dare you!" exclaimed the passenger. "You forget yourself!"

The woman was confused, and apologized for not having let her fall. People never touched one another. The custom had become obsolete, owing to the Machine.

"Where are we now?" asked Vashti haughtily.

"We are over Asia," said the attendant, anxious to be polite.

"Asia?"

"You must excuse my common way of speaking. I have got into the habit of calling places over which I pass by their unmechanical names."

"Oh, I remember Asia. The Mongols came from it."

"Beneath us, in the open air, stood a city that was once called Simla."

"Have you ever heard of the Mongols and of the Brisbane school?"

"No."

"Brisbane also stood in the open air."

"Those mountains to the right—let me show you them." She pushed back a metal blind. The main chain of the Himalayas was revealed. "They were once called the Roof of the World, those mountains."

"What a foolish name!"

"You must remember that, before the dawn of civilization, they seemed to be an impenetrable wall that touched the stars. It was supposed that no one but the gods could exist above their summits. How we have advanced, thanks to the Machine!"

"How we have advanced, thanks to the Machine!" said Vashti.

"How we have advanced, thanks to the Machine!" echoed the passenger who had dropped his Book the night before, and who was standing in the passage.

"And that white stuff in the cracks?—what is it?"

"I have forgotten its name."

"Cover the window, please. These mountains give me no ideas."

The northern aspect of the Himalayas was in deep shadow: on the Indian slope the sun had just prevailed. The forests had been destroyed during the literature epoch for the purpose of making newspaper-pulp, but the snows were awakening to their morning glory, and clouds still hung on the breasts of Kinchinjunga. In the plain were seen the ruins of cities, with diminished rivers creeping by their walls, and by the sides of these were sometimes the signs of vomitories, marking the cities of today. Over the whole prospect air-ships rushed, crossing and intercrossing with incredible aplomb, and rising nonchalantly when they desired to escape the perturbations of the lower atmosphere and to traverse the Roof of the World.

"We have indeed advanced, thanks to the Machine," repeated the attendant, and hid the Himalayas behind a metal blind.

The day dragged wearily forward. The passengers sat each in his cabin, avoiding one another with an almost physical repulsion and longing to be once more under the surface of the earth. There were eight or ten of them, mostly young males, sent out from the public nurseries to inhabit the rooms of those who had died in various parts of the earth. The man who had dropped his Book was on the homeward journey. He had been sent to Sumatra for the purpose of propagating the race. Vashti alone was traveling by her private will.

At midday she took a second glance at the earth. The air-ship was crossing another range of mountains, but she could see little, owing to clouds. Masses of black rock hovered below her, and merged indistinctly into gray. Their shapes were fantastic; one of them resembled a prostrate man.

"No ideas here," murmured Vashti, and hid the Caucasus behind a metal blind.

In the evening she looked again. They were crossing a golden sea, in which lay many small islands and one peninsula.

She repeated, "No ideas here," and hid Greece behind a metal blind.

PART II: THE MENDING APPARATUS

By a vestibule, by a lift, by a tubular railway, by a platform, by a sliding door—by reversing all the steps of her departure did Vashti arrive at her son's room, which exactly resembled her own. She might well declare that the visit was superfluous. The buttons, the knobs, the reading-desk with the Book, the temperature, the atmosphere, the illumination—all were exactly the same. And if Kuno himself, flesh of her flesh, stood close beside her at last, what profit was there in that? She was too well-bred to shake him by the hand.

Averting her eyes, she spoke as follows:

"Here I am. I have had the most terrible journey and greatly retarded the development of my soul. It is not worth it, Kuno, it is not worth it. My time is too precious. The sunlight almost touched me, and I have met with the rudest people. I can only stop a few minutes. Say what you want to say, and then I must return."

"I have been threatened with Homelessness, and I could not tell you such a thing through the Machine."

Homelessness means death. The victim is exposed to the air, which kills him.

"I have been outside since I spoke to you last. The tremendous thing has happened, and they have discovered me."

"But why shouldn't you go outside!" she exclaimed. "It is perfectly legal, perfectly mechanical, to visit the surface of the earth. I have lately been to a lecture on the sea; there is no objection to that; one simply summons a respirator and gets an Egression-permit. It is not the kind of thing that spiritually-minded people do, and I begged you not to do it, but there is no legal objection to it."

"I did not get an Egression-permit."

"Then how did you get out?"

"I found out a way of my own."

The phrase conveyed no meaning to her, and he had to repeat it.

"A way of your own?" she whispered. "But that would be wrong."

"Why?"

The question shocked her beyond measure.

"You are beginning to worship the Machine," he said coldly. "You think it irreligious of me to have found out a way of my own. It was just what the Committee thought, when they threatened me with Homelessness."

At this she grew angry. "I worship nothing!" she cried. "I am most advanced. I don't think you irreligious, for there is no such thing as religion left. All the fear and the superstition that existed once have been destroyed by the Machine. I only meant that to find out a way of your own was—Besides, there is no new way out."

"So it is always supposed."

"Except through the vomitories, for which one must have an Egression-permit, it is impossible to get out. The Book says so."

"Well, the Book's wrong, for I have been out on my feet."

For Kuno was possessed of a certain physical strength.

By these days it was a demerit to be muscular. Each infant was examined at birth, and all who promised undue strength were destroyed. Humanitarians may protest, but it would have been no true kindness to let an athlete live; he would never have been happy in that state of life to which the Machine had called him; he would have yearned for trees to climb, rivers to bathe in, meadows and hills against which he might measure his body. Man must be adapted to his surroundings, must he not? In the dawn of the world our weakly must be exposed on Mount Taygetus, in its twilight our strong will suffer Euthanasia, that the Machine may progress, that the Machine may progress, that the Machine may progress eternally.

"You know that we have lost the sense of space. We say 'space is annihilated,' but we have annihilated not space, but the sense thereof. We have lost a part of ourselves. I determined to recover it, and I began by walking up and down the platform of the railway outside my room. Up and down, until I was tired, and so did recapture the meaning of 'Near' and 'Far.' 'Near' is a place to which I can get quickly *on my feet*, not a place to which the train or the air-ship will take me quickly. 'Far' is a place to which I cannot get quickly on my feet; the vomitory is 'far,' though I could be there in thirty-eight seconds by summoning the train. Man is the measure. That was my first lesson. Man's feet are the measure for distance, his hands are the measure for ownership, his body is the measure for all that is lovable and desirable and strong. Then I went further: it was then that I called to you for the first time, and you would not come.

"This city, as you know, is built deep beneath the surface of the earth, with only the vomitories protruding. Having paced the platform outside my own room, I took the lift to the next platform and paced that also, and so with each in turn, until I came to the topmost, above which begins the earth. All the platforms were exactly alike, and all that I gained by visiting them was to develop my sense of space and my muscles. I think I should have been content with this—it is not a little thing—but as I walked and brooded, it occurred to me that our cities had been built in the days when men still breathed the outer air and that there had been ventilation shafts for the workmen. I could think of nothing but these ventilation shafts. Had they been destroyed by all the food-tubes and medicine-tubes and music-tubes that the Machine had evolved lately? Or did traces of them remain? One thing was certain. If I came upon them anywhere, it would be in the railway-tunnels of the topmost story. Everywhere else, all space was accounted for.

"I am telling my story quickly, but don't think that I was not a coward or that your answers never depressed me. It is not the proper thing, it is not mechanical, it is not decent to walk along a railway-tunnel. I did not fear that I might tread upon a live rail and be killed. I feared something far more intangible—doing what was not contemplated by the Machine. Then I said to myself, 'Man is the measure,' and I went, and after many visits I found an opening.

"The tunnels, of course, were lighted. Everything is light, artificial light; darkness is the exception. So when I saw a black gap in the tiles, I knew that it was an exception, and rejoiced. I put in my arm—I could put in no more at first—and waved it round and round in ecstasy. I loosened another tile, and put in my head, and shouted into the darkness: 'I am coming, I shall do it yet,' and my voice reverberated down endless passages. I seemed to hear the spirits of those dead workmen who had returned each evening to the starlight and to their wives, and all the generations who had lived in the open air called back to me, 'You will do it yet, you are coming.' "

He paused, and, absurd as he was, his last words moved her. For Kuno had lately asked to be a father, and his request had been refused by the Committee. His was not a type that the Machine desired to hand on.

"Then a train passed. It brushed by me, but I thrust my head and arms into the hole. I had done enough for one day, so I crawled back to the platform, went down in the lift, and summoned my bed. Ah, what dreams! And again I called you, and again you refused."

She shook her head and said:

"Don't. Don't talk of these terrible things. You make me miserable. You are throwing civilization away."

"But I had got back the sense of space and a man cannot rest then. I determined to get in at the hole and climb the shaft. And so I exercised my arms. Day after day I went through ridiculous movements, until my flesh ached, and I could hang by my hands and hold the pillow of my bed outstretched for many minutes. Then I summoned a respirator, and started.

"It was easy at first. The mortar had somehow rotted, and I soon pushed some more tiles in, and clambered after them into the darkness, and the spirits of the dead comforted me. I don't know what I mean by that. I just say what I felt. I felt, for the first time, that a protest had been lodged against corruption, and that even as the dead were comforting me, so I was comforting the unborn. I felt that humanity existed, and that it existed without clothes. How can I possibly explain this? It was naked, humanity seemed naked, and all these tubes and buttons and machineries neither came into the world with us, nor will they follow us out, nor do they matter supremely while we are here. Had I been strong, I would have torn off every garment I had, and gone out into the outer air unswaddled. But this is not for me, nor perhaps for my generation. I climbed with my respirator and my hygienic clothes and my dietetic tabloids! Better thus than not at all.

"There was a ladder, made of some primeval metal. The light from the railway fell upon its lowest rungs, and I saw that it led straight upwards out of the rubble at the bottom of the shaft. Perhaps our ancestors ran up and down it a dozen times daily, in their building. As I climbed, the rough edges cut through my gloves so that my hands bled. The light helped me for a little, and then came darkness and, worse still, silence which pierced my ears like a sword. The Machine hums! Did you know that? Its hum penetrates our blood, and may even guide our thoughts. Who knows! I was getting beyond its power. Then I thought: 'This silence means that I am doing wrong.' But I heard voices in the silence, and again they strengthened me." He laughed. "I had need of them. The next moment I cracked my head against something."

She sighed.

"I had reached one of those pneumatic stoppers that defend us from the outer air. You may have noticed them on the air-ship. Pitch dark, my feet on the rungs of an invisible ladder, my hands cut; I cannot explain how I lived through this part, but the voices still comforted me, and I felt for fastenings. The stopper, I suppose, was about eight feet across. I passed my hand over it as far as I could reach. It was perfectly smooth. I felt it almost to the center. Not quite to the center, for my arm was too short. Then the voice said: 'Jump. It is worth it. There may be a handle in the center, and you may catch hold of it and so come to us your own way. And if there is no handle so that you may fall and are dashed to pieces—it is still worth it; you will still come to us your own way.' So I jumped. There was a handle, and—"

He paused. Tears gathered in his mother's eyes. She knew that he was fated. If he did not die today he would die tomorrow. There was not room for such a person in the world. And with her pity disgust mingled. She was ashamed at having borne such a son, she who had always been so respectable and so full of ideas. Was he really the little boy to whom she had taught the use of his stops and buttons, and to whom she had given his first lessons in the Book? The very hair that disfigured his lip showed that he was reverting to some savage type. On atavism the Machine can have no mercy.

"There was a handle, and I did catch it. I hung tranced over the darkness and heard the hum of these workings as the last whisper in a dying dream. All the things I had cared about and all the people I had spoken to through tubes appeared infinitely little. Meanwhile the handle revolved. My weight had set something in motion and I spun slowly, and then—

"I cannot describe it. I was lying with my face to the sunshine. Blood poured from my nose and ears and I heard a tremendous roaring. The stopper, with me clinging to it, had simply been blown out of the earth, and the air that we make down here was escaping through the vent into the air above. It burst up like a fountain. I crawled back to it—for the upper air hurts—and, as it were, I took great sips from the edge. My respirator had flown goodness knows where, my clothes were torn. I just lay with my lips close to the hole, and I sipped until the bleeding stopped. You can imagine nothing so curious. This hollow in the grass—I will speak of it in a minute,—the sun shining into it, not brilliantly but through marbled clouds,—the peace, the nonchalance, the sense of space, and, brushing my cheek, the roaring fountain of our artificial air! Soon I spied my respirator, bobbing up and down in the current high above my head, and higher still were many air-ships. But no one ever looks out of air-ships, and in my case they could not have picked me up. There I was, stranded. The sun shone a little way down the shaft, and revealed the topmost rung of the ladder, but it was hopeless trying to reach it. I should either have been tossed up again by the escape, or else have fallen in, and died. I could only lie on the grass, sipping and sipping, and from time to time glancing around me.

"I knew that I was in Wessex, for I had taken care to go to a lecture on the subject before starting. Wessex lies above the room in which we are talking now. It was once an important state. Its kings held all the southern coast from the Andredswald to Cornwall, while the Wansdyke protected them on the north, running over the high ground. The lecturer was only concerned with the rise of Wessex, so I do not know how long it remained an international power, nor would the knowledge have assisted me. To tell the truth I could do nothing but laugh, during this part. There was I, with a pneumatic stopper by my side and a respirator bobbing over my head, imprisoned, all three of us, in a grass-grown hollow that was edged with fern."

Then he grew grave again.

"Lucky for me that it was a hollow. For the air began to fall back into it and to fill it as water fills a bowl. I could crawl about. Presently I stood. I breathed a mixture, in which the air that hurts predominated whenever I tried to climb the sides. This was not so bad. I had not lost my tabloids and remained ridiculously cheerful, and as for the Machine, I forgot about it altogether. My one aim now was to get to the top, where the ferns were, and to view whatever objects lay beyond.

"I rushed the slope. The new air was still too bitter for me and I came rolling back, after a momentary vision of something gray. The sun grew very feeble, and I remembered that he was in Scorpio—I had been to a lecture on that too. If the sun is in Scorpio and you are in Wessex, it means that you must be as quick as you can, or it will get too dark. (This is the first bit of useful information I have ever got from a lecture, and I expect it will be the last.) It made me try frantically to breathe the new air, and to advance as far as I dared out of my pond. The hollow filled so slowly. At times I thought that my fountain played with less vigor. My respirator seemed to dance nearer the earth; the roar was decreasing."

He broke off.

"I don't think this is interesting you. The rest will interest you even less. There are no ideas in it, and I wish that I had not troubled you to come. We are too different, mother."

She told him to continue.

"It was evening before I climbed the bank. The sun had very nearly slipped out of the sky by this time, and I could not get a good view. You, who have just crossed the Roof of the World, will not want to hear an account of the little hills that I saw—low colorless hills. But to me they were living and the turf that covered them was a skin, under which their muscles rippled, and I felt that those hills had called with incalculable force to men in the past, and that men had loved them. Now they sleep—perhaps forever. They commune with humanity in dreams. Happy the man, happy the woman, who awakes the hills of Wessex. For though they sleep, they will never die."

His voice rose passionately.

"Cannot you see, cannot all your lecturers see, that it is we who are dying, and that down here the only thing that really lives is the Machine? We created the Machine, to do our will, but we cannot make it do our will now. It has robbed us of the sense of space and of the sense of touch, it has blurred every human relation and narrowed down love to a carnal act, it has paralyzed our bodies and our wills, and now it compels us to worship it. The Machine develops—but not to our goal. We only exist as the blood corpuscles that course through its arteries, and if it could work without us, it would let us die. Oh, I have no remedy—or, at least, only one—to tell men again and again that I have seen the hills of Wessex as Aelfrid saw them when he overthrew the Danes.

"So the sun set. I forgot to mention that a belt of mist lay between my hill and other hills, and that it was the color of pearl."

He broke off for the second time.

"Go on. Nothing that you say can distress me now. I am hardened."

"I had meant to tell you the rest, but I cannot: I know that I cannot: goodby."

Vashti stood irresolute. All her nerves were tingling with his blasphemies. But she was also inquisitive.

"This is unfair," she complained. "You have called me across the world to hear your story, and hear it I will. Tell me—as briefly as possible, for this is a disastrous waste of time—tell me how you returned to civilization."

"Oh,—that!" he said, starting. "You would like to hear about civilization. Certainly. Had I got to where my respirator fell down?"

"No—but I understand everything now. You put on your respirator, and managed to walk along the surface of the earth to a vomitory, and there your conduct was reported to the Central Committee."

"By no means."

He passed his hand over his forehead, as if dispelling some strong impression. Then, resuming his narrative, he warmed to it again.

"My respirator fell about sunset. I had mentioned that the fountain seemed feebler, had I not?"

"Yes."

"About sunset, it let the respirator fall. As I said, I had entirely forgotten about the Machine, and I paid no great attention at the time, being occupied with other things. I had my pool of air, into which I could dip when the outer keenness became intolerable, and which would possibly remain for days, provided that no wind sprang up to disperse it. Not until it was too late, did I realize what the stoppage of the escape implied. You see—the gap in the tunnel had been mended; the Mending Apparatus, the Mending Apparatus, was after me.

"One other warning I had, but I neglected it. The sky at night was clearer than it had been in the day, and the moon, which was about half the sky behind the sun, shone into the dell at moments quite brightly. I was in my usual place—on the boundary between the two atmospheres—when I thought I saw something dark move across the bottom on the dell, and vanish into the shaft. In my folly, I ran down. I bent over and listened, and I thought I heard a faint scraping noise in the depths.

"At this—but it was too late—I took alarm. I determined to put on my respirator and to walk right out of the dell. But my respirator had gone. I knew exactly where it had fallen—between the stopper and the aperture—and I could even feel the mark that it had made in the turf. It had gone, and I realized that something evil was at work, and I had better escape to the other air, and, if I must die, die running towards the cloud that had been the color of a pearl. I never started. Out of the shaft—it is too horrible. A worm, a long white worm, had crawled out of the shaft and was gliding over the moonlit grass.

"I screamed. I did everything that I should not have done, I stamped upon the creature instead of flying from it, and it fought. The worm let me run all over the dell, but edged up my leg as I ran. 'Help!' I cried. (That part is too awful. It belongs to the part that you will never know.) 'Help!' I cried. (Why cannot we suffer in silence?) 'Help!' I cried. Then my feet were wound together, I fell, I was dragged away from the dear ferns and the living hills, and past the great metal stopper (I can tell you this part), and I thought it might save me again if I caught hold of the handle. It also was enwrapped, it also. Oh, the whole dell was full of the things. They were searching it in all directions, they were denuding it, and the white snouts of others peeped out of the hole, ready if needed. Everything that could be moved they brought—brushwood, bundles of fern, everything, and down we all went intertwined into hell. The last things that I saw, ere the stopper closed after us, were certain stars, and I felt that a man of my sort lived in the sky. For I did fight, I fought till the very end, and it was only my head hitting against the ladder that quieted me. I woke up in this room. The worms had vanished. I was surrounded by artificial air, artificial light, artificial peace, and my friends were calling to me down speaking-tubes to know whether I had come across any new ideas lately."

Here his story ended. Discussion of it was impossible, and Vashti turned to go.

"It will end in Homelessness," she said quietly.

"I wish it would," retorted Kuno.

"The Machine has been most merciful."

"I prefer the mercy of God."

"By that superstitious phrase, do you mean that you could live in the outer air?"

"Yes."

"Have you ever seen, round the vomitories, the bones of those who were extruded after the Great Rebellion?"

"Yes."

"They were left where they perished for our edification. A few crawled away, but they perished, too—who can doubt it? And so with the Homeless of our own day. The surface of the earth supports life no longer."

"Indeed."

"Ferns and a little grass may survive, but all higher forms have perished. Has any air-ship detected them?"

"No."

"Has any lecturer dealt with them?"

"No."

"Then why this obstinacy?"

"Because I have seen them," he exploded.

"Seen *what?*"

"Because I have seen her in the twilight—because she came to my help when I called—because she, too, was entangled by the worms, and, luckier than I, was killed by one of them piercing her throat."

He was mad. Vashti departed, nor, in the troubles that followed, did she ever see his face again.

PART III: THE HOMELESS

During the years that followed Kuno's escapade, two important developments took place in the Machine. On the surface they were revolutionary, but in either case men's minds had been prepared beforehand, and they did but express tendencies that were latent already.

The first of these was the abolition of respirators.

Advanced thinkers, like Vashti, had

always held it foolish to visit the surface of the earth. Air-ships might be necessary, but what was the good of going out for mere curiosity and crawling along for a mile or two in a terrestrial motor? The habit was vulgar and perhaps faintly improper; it was unproductive of ideas, and had no connection with the habits that really mattered. So respirators were abolished, and with them, of course, the terrestrial motors, and except for a few lecturers, who complained that they were debarred access to their subject-matter, the development was accepted quietly. Those who still wanted to know what the earth was like had after all only to listen to some gramophone, or to look into some cinematophote. And even the lecturers acquiesced when they found that a lecture on the sea was none the less stimulating when compiled out of other lectures that had already been delivered on the same subject. "Beware of first-hand ideas!" exclaimed one of the most advanced of them. "First-hand ideas do not really exist. They are but the physical impressions produced by love and fear, and on this gross foundation who could erect a philosophy? Let your ideas be second-hand, and if possible tenth-hand, for then they will be far removed from that disturbing element—direct observation. Do not learn anything about this subject of mine—the French Revolution. Learn instead what I think that Enichamon thought Urizen thought Gutch thought Ho-Yung thought Chi-Bo-Sing thought Lafcadio Hearn thought Carlyle thought Mirabeau said about the French Revolution. Through the medium of these eight great minds, the blood that was shed at Paris and the windows that were broken at Versailles will be clarified to an idea which you may employ most profitably in your daily lives. But be sure that the intermediates are many and varied, for in history one authority exists to counteract another. Urizen must counteract the skepticism of Ho-Yung and Enicharmon, I must myself counteract the impetuosity of Gutch. You who listen to me are in a better position to judge about the French Revolution than I am. Your descendants will be even in a better position than you, for they will learn what you think I think, and yet another intermediate will be added to the chain. And in time"—his voice rose—"there will come a generation that has got beyond facts, beyond impressions, a generation absolutely colorless, a generation

seraphically free
From taint of personality,

which will see the French Revolution not as it happened, nor as they would like it to have happened, but as it would have happened, had it taken place in the days of the Machine."

Tremendous applause greeted this lecture, which did but voice a feeling already latent in the minds of men—a feeling that terrestrial facts must be ignored, and that the abolition of respirators was a positive gain. It was even suggested that air-ships should be abolished too. This was not done, because air-ships had somehow worked themselves into the Machine's system. But year by year they were used less, and mentioned less by thoughtful men.

The second great development was the re-establishment of religion.

This, too, had been voiced in the celebrated lecture. No one could mistake the reverent tone in which the peroration had concluded, and it awakened a responsive echo in the heart of each. Those who had long worshiped silently, now began to talk. They described the strange feeling of peace that came over them when they handled the Book of the Machine, the pleasure that it was to repeat certain numerals out of it, however little meaning those numerals conveyed to the outward ear, the ecstasy of touching a button, however unimportant, or of ringing an electric bell, however superfluously.

"The Machine," they exclaimed, "feeds us and clothes us and houses us; through it we speak to one another, through it we see one another, in it we have our being. The Machine is the friend of ideas and the enemy of superstition: the Machine omnipotent, eternal; blessed is the Machine." And before long this allocution was printed on the first page of the Book, and in subsequent editions the ritual swelled into a complicated system of praise and prayer. The word "religion" was sedulously avoided, and in theory the Machine was still the creation and the implement of man. But in practice all, save a few retrogrades, worshiped it as divine. Nor was it worshiped in unity. One believer would be chiefly impressed by the blue optic plates, through which he saw other believers; another by the Mending Apparatus, which sinful Kuno had compared to worms; another by the lifts, another by the Book. And each would pray to this or to that, and ask it to intercede for him with the Machine as a whole. Persecution—that also was present. It did not break out, for reasons that will be set forward shortly. But it was latent, and all who did not accept the minimum known as "undenominational Mechanism" lived in danger of Homelessness, which means death, as we know.

To attribute these two great developments to the Central Committee, is to take a very narrow view of civilization. The Central Committee announced the developments, it is true, but they were no more the cause of them than were the kings of the imperialistic period the cause of war. Rather did they yield to some invincible pressure, which came no one knew whither, and which, when gratified, was succeeded by some new pressure equally invincible. To such a state of affairs it is convenient to give the name of progress. No one confessed the Machine was out of hand. Year by year it was served with increased efficiency and decreased intelligence. The better a man knew his own duties upon it, the less he understood the duties of his neighbor, and in all the world there was not one who understood the monster as a whole. Those master brains had perished. They had left full directions, it is true, and their successors had each of them mastered a portion of those directions. But Humanity, in its desire for comfort, had over-reached itself. It had exploited the riches of nature too far. Quietly and complacently, it was sinking into decadence, and progress had come to mean the progress of the Machine.

As for Vashti, her life went peacefully forward until the final disaster. She made her room dark and slept; she awoke and made the room light. She lectured and attended lectures. She exchanged ideas with her innumerable friends and believed she was growing more spiritual. At times a friend was granted Euthanasia, and left his or her room for the homelessness that is beyond all human conception. Vashti did not much mind. After an unsuccessful lecture, she would sometimes ask for Euthanasia herself. But the death-rate was not permitted to exceed the birth-rate, and the Machine had hitherto refused it to her.

The troubles began quietly, long before she was conscious of them.

One day she was astonished at receiving a message from her son. They never communicated, having nothing in common, and she had only heard indirectly that he was still alive, and had been transferred from the northern hemisphere, where he had behaved so mischievously, to the southern—indeed, to a room not far from her own.

"Does he want me to visit him?" she thought. "Never again, never. And I have not the time."

No, it was madness of another kind.

He refused to visualize his face upon the blue plate, and speaking out of the darkness with solemnity said:

"The Machine stops."

"What do you say?"

"The Machine is stopping. I know it, I know the signs."

She burst into a peal of laughter. He heard her and was angry, and they spoke no more.

"Can you imagine anything more absurd?" she cried to a friend. "A man who was my son believes that the Machine is stopping. It would be impious if it was not mad."

"The Machine is stopping?" her friend replied. "What does that mean? The phrase conveys nothing to me."

"Nor to me."

"He does not refer, I suppose, to the trouble there has been lately with the music?"

"Oh, no, of course not. Let us talk about music."

"Have you complained to the authorities?"

"Yes, and they say it wants mending, and referred me to the Committee of the Mending Apparatus. I complained of those curious gasping sighs that disfigure the symphonies of the Brisbane school. They sound like someone in pain. The Committee of the Mending Apparatus say that it shall be remedied shortly."

Obscurely worried, she resumed her life. For one thing, the defect in the music irritated her. For another thing, she could not forget Kuno's speech. If he had known that the music was out of repair—he could not know it, for he detested music—if he had known that it was wrong, "the Machine stops" was exactly the venomous sort of remark he would have made. Of course he had made it at a venture, but the coincidence annoyed her, and she spoke with some petulance to the Committee of the Mending Apparatus.

They replied, as before, that the defect would be set right shortly.

"Shortly! At once!" she retorted. "Why should I be worried by imperfect music? Things are always put right at once. If you do not mend it at once, I shall complain to the Central Committee."

"No personal complaints are received by the Central Committee," the Committee of the Mending Apparatus replied.

"Through whom am I to make my complaint, then?"

"Through us."

"I complain then."

"Your complaint shall be forwarded in its turn."

"Have others complained?"

This question was unmechanical, and the Committee of the Mending Apparatus refused to answer it.

"It is too bad!" she exclaimed to another of her friends. "There never was such an unfortunate woman as myself. I can never be sure of my music now. It gets worse and worse each time I summon it."

"I too have my troubles," the friend replied. "Sometimes my ideas are interrupted by a slight jarring noise."

"What is it?"

"I do not know whether it is inside my head, or inside the wall."

"Complain, in either case."

"I have complained, and my complaint will be forwarded in its turn to the Central Committee."

Time passed, and they resented the defects no longer. The defects had not been remedied, but the human tissues in the latter day had become so subservient, that they readily adapted themselves to every caprice of the Machine. The sigh at the crisis of the Brisbane symphony no longer irritated Vashti; she accepted it as part of the melody. The jarring noise, whether in the head or in the wall, was no longer resented by her friend. And so with the moldy artificial fruit, so with the bath water that began to stink, so with the defective rhymes that the poetry machine had taken to emit. All were bitterly complained of at first, and then acquiesced in and forgotten. Things went from bad to worse unchallenged.

It was otherwise with the failure of the sleeping apparatus. That was a more serious stoppage. There came a day when over the whole world—in Sumatra, in Wessex, in the innumerable cities of Courland and Brazil—the beds, when summoned by their tired owners, failed to appear. It may seem a ludicrous matter, but from it we may date the collapse of humanity. The Committee responsible for the failure was assailed by complainants, whom it referred, as usual, to the Committee of the Mending Apparatus, who in its turn assured them that their complaints would be forwarded to the Central Committee. But the discontent grew, for mankind was not yet sufficiently adaptable to do without sleeping.

"Someone is meddling with the Machine—" they began.

"Someone is trying to make himself king, to reintroduce the personal element."

"Punish that man with Homelessness."

"To the rescue! Avenge the Machine! Avenge the Machine!"

"War! Kill the man!"

But the Committee of the Mending Apparatus now came forward, and allayed the panic with well-chosen words. It confessed that the Mending Apparatus was itself in need of repair.

The effect of this frank confession was admirable.

"Of course," said a famous lecturer—he of the French Revolution, who gilded each new decay with splendor—"of course we shall not press our complaints now. The Mending Apparatus has treated us so well in the past that we all sympathize with it, and will wait patiently for its recovery. In its own good time it will resume its duties. Meanwhile let us do without our beds, our tabloids, our other little wants. Such, I feel sure, would be the wish of the Machine."

Thousands of miles away his audience applauded. The Machine still linked them. Under the sea, beneath the roots of the mountains, ran the wires through which they saw and heard, the enormous eyes and ears that were their heritage, and the hum of many workings clothed their thoughts in one garment of subserviency. Only the old and the sick remained ungrateful, for it was rumored that Euthanasia, too, was out of order, and that pain had reappeared among men.

It became difficult to read. A blight entered the atmosphere and dulled its luminosity. At times Vashti could scarcely see across her room. The air, too, was foul. Loud were the complaints, impotent the remedies, heroic the tone of the lecturer as he cried: "Courage, courage! What matter so long as the Machine goes on? To it the darkness and the light are one." And though things improved again after a time, the old brilliancy was never recaptured, and humanity never recovered from its entrance into twilight. There was an hysterical talk of "measures," of "provisional dictatorship," and the inhabitants of Sumatra were asked to familiarize themselves with the workings of the central power station, the said power station being situated in France. But for the most part panic reigned, and men spent their strength praying to their Books, tangible proofs of the Machine's omnipotence. There were gradations of terror—at times came rumors of hope—the Mending Apparatus was almost mended—the enemies of the Machine had been got under—new "nerve-centers" were evolving, which would do the work even more magnificently than before. But there came a day when, without the slightest warning, without any previous hint of feebleness, the entire communication-system broke down, all over the world, and the world, as they understood it, ended.

Vashti was lecturing at the time and her earlier remarks had been punctuated with applause. As she proceeded the audience became silent, and at the conclusion there was no sound. Somewhat displeased, she called to a friend who was a specialist in sympathy. No sound: doubtless the friend was sleeping. And so with the next friend whom she tried to summon, and so with the next, until she remembered Kuno's cryptic remark, "The Machine stops."

The phrase still conveyed nothing. If Eternity was stopping it would of course be set going shortly.

For example, there was still a little light and air—the atmosphere had improved a few hours previously. There was still the Book, and while there was the Book there was security.

Then she broke down, for with the cessation of activity came an unexpected terror—silence.

She had never known silence, and the coming of it nearly killed her—it did kill many thousands of people outright. Ever since her birth she had been surrounded by the steady hum. It was to the ear what artificial air was to the lungs, and agonizing pains shot across her head. And scarcely knowing what she did, she stumbled forward and pressed the unfamiliar button, the one that opened the door of her cell.

Now the door of the cell worked on a simple hinge of its own. It was not connected with the central power station, dying far away in France. It opened, rousing immoderate hopes in Vashti, for she thought that the Machine had been mended. It opened, and she saw the dim tunnel that curved far away towards freedom. One look, and then she shrank back. For the tunnel was full of people—she was almost the last in that city to have taken alarm.

People at any time repelled her, and these were nightmares from her worst dreams. People were crawling about, people were screaming, whimpering, gasping for breath, touching each other, vanishing in the dark, and ever and anon being pushed off the platform onto the live rail. Some were fighting round the electric bells, trying to summon trains which could not be summoned. Others were yelling for Euthanasia or for respirators, or blaspheming the Machine. Others stood at the doors of their cells fearing, like herself, either to stop in them or to leave them. And behind all the uproar was silence—the silence which is the voice of the earth and of the generations who have gone.

No—it was worse than solitude. She closed the door again and sat down to wait for the end. The disintegration went on, accompanied by horrible cracks and rumbling. The valves that restrained the Medical Apparatus must have been weakened, for it ruptured and hung hideously from the ceiling. The floor heaved and fell and flung her from her chair. A tube oozed towards her serpent fashion. And at last the final horror approached—light began to ebb, and she knew that civilizations' long day was closing.

She whirled round, praying to be saved from this, at any rate, kissing the Book, pressing button after button. The uproar outside was increasing, and even penetrated the wall. Slowly the brilliancy of her cell was dimmed, the reflections faded from her metal switches. Now she could not see the reading-stand, now not the Book, though she held it in her hand. Light followed the flight of sound, air was following light, and the original void returned to the cavern from which it had been so long excluded. Vashti continued to whirl, like the devotees of an earlier religion, screaming, praying, striking at the buttons with bleeding hands.

It was thus that she opened her prison and escaped—escaped in the spirit: at least so it seems to me, ere my meditation closes. That she escapes in the body—I cannot perceive that. She struck, by chance, the switch that released the door, and the rush of foul air on her skin, the loud throbbing whispers in her ears, told her that she was facing the tunnel again, and that tremendous platform on which she had seen men fighting. They were not fighting now. Only the whispers remained,

Cartoon by Colos, *The New York Times*, January 11, 1971. © by The New York Times Company. Reprinted by permission.

and the little whimpering groans. They were dying by hundreds out in the dark.

She burst into tears.

Tears answered her.

They wept for humanity, those two, not for themselves. They could not bear that this should be the end. Ere silence was completed their hearts were opened, and they knew what had been important on the earth. Man, the flower of all flesh, the noblest of all creatures visible, man who had once made god in his image, and had mirrored his strength on the constellations, beautiful naked man was dying, strangled in the garments that he had woven. Century after century had he toiled, and here was his reward. Truly the garment had seemed heavenly at first, shot with the colors of culture, sewn with the threads of self-denial. And heavenly it had been so long as it was a garment and no more, so long as man could shed it at will and live by the essence that is his soul, and the essence, equally divine, that is his body. The sin against the body—it was for that they wept in chief; the centuries of wrong against the muscles and nerves, and those five portals by which we can alone apprehend—glozing it over with talk of evolution, until the body was white pap, the home of ideas as colorless, last sloshy stirrings of a spirit that had grasped the stars.

"Where are you?" she sobbed.

His voice in the darkness said, "Here."

"Is there any hope, Kuno?"

"None for us."

"Where are you?"

She crawled towards him over the bodies of the dead. His blood spurted over her hands.

"Quicker," he gasped, "I'm dying—but we touch, we talk, not through the Machine."

He kissed her.

"We have come back to our own. We die, but we have recaptured life, as it was in Wessex, when Aelfrid overthrew the Danes. We know what they know outside, they who dwelt in the cloud that is the color of a pearl."

"But, Kuno, is it true? Are there still men on the surface of the earth? Is this—this tunnel, this poisoned darkness—really not the end?"

He replied:

"I have seen them, spoken to them, loved them. They are hiding in the mist and the ferns until our civilization stops. Today they are the Homeless—tomorrow—"

"Oh, tomorrow—some fool will start the Machine again, tomorrow."

"Never," said Kuno, "never. Humanity has learnt its lesson."

As he spoke, the whole city was broken like a honey-comb. An air-ship had sailed in through the vomitory into a ruined wharf. It crashed downwards, exploding as it went, rending gallery after gallery with its wings of steel. For a moment they saw the nations of the dead, and, before they joined them, scraps of the untainted sky.

William Faulkner (1897–1962)

Delta Autumn

Soon now they would enter the Delta. The sensation was familiar to him. It had been renewed like this each last week in November for more than fifty years—the last hill, at the foot of which the rich unbroken alluvial flatness began as the sea began at the base of its cliffs, dissolving away beneath the unhurried November rain as the sea itself would dissolve away.

At first they had come in wagons: the guns, the bedding, the dogs, the food, the whisky, the keen heart-lifting anticipation of hunting; the young men who could drive all night and all the following day in the cold rain and pitch a camp in the rain and sleep in the wet blankets and rise at daylight the next morning and hunt. There had been bear then. A man shot a doe or a fawn as quickly as he did a buck, and in the afternoons they shot wild turkey with pistols to test their stalking skill and markmanship, feeding all but the breast to the dogs. But that time was gone now. Now they went in cars, driving faster and faster each year because the roads were better and they had farther and farther to drive, the territory in which game still existed drawing yearly inward as his life was drawing inward, until now he was the last of those who had once made the journey in wagons without feeling it and now those who accompanied him were the sons and grandsons of the men who had ridden for twenty-four hours in the rain or sleet behind the steaming mules. They called him 'Uncle Ike' now, and he no longer told anyone how near eighty he actually was because he knew as well as they did that he no longer had any business making such expeditions, even by car.

In fact, each time now, on that first night in camp, lying aching and sleepless in the harsh blankets, his blood only faintly warmed by the single thin whisky-and-water which he allowed himself, he would tell himself that this would be his last. But he would stand that trip—he still shot almost as well as he ever had, still killed almost as much of the game he saw as he ever killed; he no longer even knew how many deer had fallen before his gun—and the fierce long heat of the next summer would renew him. Then November would come again, and again in the car with two of the sons of his old companions, whom he had taught not only how to distinguish between the prints left by a buck or a doe but between the sound they made in moving, he would look ahead past the jerking arc of the windshield wiper and see the land flatten suddenly and swoop, dissolving away beneath the rain as the sea itself would dissolve, and he would say, "Well, boys, there it is again."

This time though, he didn't have time to speak. The driver of the car stopped it, slamming it to a skidding halt on the greasy pavement without warning, actually flinging the two passengers forward until they caught themselves with their braced hands against the dash. "What the hell, Roth!" the man in the middle said. "Cant you whistle first when you do that? Hurt you, Uncle Ike?"

"No," the old man said. "What's the matter?" The driver didn't answer. Still leaning forward, the old man looked sharply past the face of the man between them, at the face of his kinsman. It was the youngest face of them all, aquiline, saturnine, a little ruthless, the face of his ancestor too, tempered a little, altered a little, staring sombrely through the streaming windshield across which the twin wipers flicked and flicked.

"I didn't intend to come back in here this time," he said suddenly and harshly.

"You said that back in Jefferson last week," the old man said. "Then you changed your mind. Have you changed it again? This aint a very good time to——"

"Oh, Roth's coming," the man in the middle said. His name was Legate. He seemed to be speaking to no one, as he was looking at neither of them. "If it was just a buck he was coming all this distance for, now. But he's got a doe in here. Of course a old man like Uncle Ike cant be interested in no doe, not one that walks on two legs—when she's standing up, that is. Pretty light-colored too. The one he was after them nights last fall when he said he was coon-hunting, Uncle Ike. The one I figured maybe he was still running when he was gone all that month last January. But of course a old man like Uncle Ike aint got no interest in nothing like that." He chortled, still looking at no one, not completely jeering.

"What?" the old man said. "What's that?" But he had not even so much as glanced at Legate. He was still watching his kinsman's face. The eyes behind the spectacles were the blurred eyes of an old man, but they were quite sharp too; eyes which could still see a gun-barrel and what ran beyond it as well as any of them could. He was remembering himself now: how last year, during the final stage by motor boat in to where they camped, a box of food had been lost overboard and how on the next day his kinsman had gone back to the nearest town for supplies and had been gone overnight. And when he did return, something had happened to him. He would go into the woods with his rifle each dawn when the others went, but the old man, watching him, knew that he was not hunting. "All right," he said. "Take me and Will on to shelter where we can wait for the truck, and you can go on back."

"I'm going in," the other said harshly, "Dont worry. Because this will be the last of it."

"The last of deer hunting, or of doe hunting?" Legate said. This time the old man paid no attention to him even by speech. He still watched the young man's savage and brooding face.

"Why?" he said.

"After Hitler gets through with it? Or Smith or Jones or Roosevelt or Willkie or whatever he will call himself in this country?"

"We'll stop him in this country," Legate said. "Even if he calls himself George Washington."

"How?" Edmonds said. "By singing God bless America in bars at midnight and wearing dime-store flags in our lapels?"

"So that's what's worrying you," the old man said. "I aint noticed this country being short of defenders yet, when it needed them. You did some of it yourself twenty-odd years ago, before you were a grown man even. This country is a little mite stronger than any one man or group of men, outside of it or even inside of it either. I reckon, when the time comes and some of you have done got tired of hollering we are whipped if we dont go to war and some more are hollering we are whipped if we do, it will cope with one Austrian paper-hanger, no matter what he will be calling himself. My pappy and some other better men than any of them you named tried once to tear it in two with a war, and they failed."

"And what have you got left?" the other said. "Half the people without jobs and half the factories closed by strikes. Half the people on public dole that wont work and half that couldn't work even if they would. Too much cotton and corn and hogs, and not enough for people to eat and wear. The country full of people to tell a man how he cant raise his own cotton whether he will or wont, and Sally Rand with a sergeant's stripes and not even the fan couldn't fill the army rolls. Too much not-butter and not even the guns——"

"We got a deer camp—if we ever get to it," Legate said. "Not to mention does."

"It's a good time to mention does," the old man said. "Does and fawns both. The only fighting anywhere that ever had anything of God's blessing on it has been when men fought to protect does and fawns. If it's going to come to fighting, that's a good thing to mention and remember too."

"Haven't you discovered in—how many years more than seventy is it?—that women and children are one thing there's never any scarcity of?" Edmonds said.

"Maybe that's why all I am worrying about right now is that ten miles of river we still have got to run before we can make camp," the old man said. "So let's get on."

They went on. Soon they were going fast again, as Edmonds always drove, consulting neither of them about the speed just as he had given neither of them any warning when he slammed the car to stop. The old man relaxed again. He watched, as he did each recurrent November while more than sixty of them passed, the land which he had seen change. At first there had been only the old towns along the River and the old towns along the hills, from each of which the planters with their gangs of slaves and then of hired laborers had wrested from the impenetrable jungle of water-standing cane and cypress, gum and holly and oak and ash, cotton patches which as the years passed became fields and then plantations. The paths made by deer and bear became roads and then highways, with towns in turn springing up along them and along the rivers Tallahatchie and Sunflower which joined and became the Yazoo, the River of the Dead of the Choctaws—the thick, slow, black, unsunned streams almost without current, which once each year ceased to flow at all and then reversed, spreading, drowning the rich land and subsiding again, leaving it still richer.

Most of that was gone now. Now a man drove two hundred miles from Jefferson before he found wilderness to hunt in. Now the land lay open from the cradling hills on the East to the rampart of levee on the West, standing horseman-tall with cotton for the world's looms—the rich black land, imponderable and vast, fecund up to the very doorsteps of the negroes who worked it and of the white men who owned it; which exhausted the hunting life of a dog in one year, the working life of a mule in five and of a man in twenty—the land in which neon flashed past them from the little countless towns and countless shining this-year's automobiles sped past them on the broad plumb-ruled highways, yet in which the only permanent mark of man's occupation seemed to be the tremendous gins, constructed in sections of sheet iron and in a week's time though they were, since no man, millionaire though he be, would build more than a roof and walls to shelter the camping equipment he lived from when he knew that once each ten years or so his house would be flooded to the second storey and all within it ruined; —the land across which there came now no scream of panther but instead the long hooting of locomotives: trains of incredible length and drawn by a single engine, since there was no gradient anywhere and no elevation save those raised by forgotten aboriginal hands as refuges from the yearly water and used by their Indian successors to sepulchre their fathers' bones, and all that remained of that old time were the Indian names on the little towns and usually pertaining to water—Aluschaskuna, Tillatoba, Homochitto, Yazoo.

By early afternoon, they were on water. At the last little Indian-named town at the end of pavement they waited until the other car and the two trucks—the one carrying the bedding and tents and food, the other the horses —overtook them. They left the concrete and, after another mile or so, the gravel too. In caravan they ground on through the ceaselessly dissolving afternoon, with skid-chains on the wheels now, lurching and splashing and sliding among the ruts, until presently it seemed to him that the retrograde of his remembering had gained an inverse velocity from their own slow progress, that the land had retreated not in minutes from the last spread of gravel but in years, decades, back toward what it had been when he first knew it: the road they now followed once more the ancient pathway of bear and deer, the diminishing fields they now passed once more scooped punily and terrifically by axe and saw and mule-drawn plow from the wilderness' flank, out of the brooding and immemorial tangle, in place of ruthless mile-wide parallelograms wrought by ditching the dyking machinery.

They reached the river landing and unloaded, the horses to go overland down stream to a point opposite the camp and swim the river, themselves and the bedding and food and dogs and guns in the motor launch. It was himself, though no horseman, no farmer, not even a countryman save by his distant birth and boyhood, who coaxed and soothed the two horses, drawing them by his own single frail hand until, backing, filling, trembling a little, they surged, halted, then sprang scrambling down from the truck, possessing no affinity for them as creatures, beasts, but being merely insulated by his years and time from the corruption of steel and oiled moving parts which tainted the others.

Then, his old hammer double gun which was only twelve years younger than he standing between his knees, he watched even the last puny marks of man—cabin, clearing, the small and irregular fields which a year ago were jungle and in which the skeleton stalks of this year's cotton stood almost as tall and rank as the old cane had stood, as if man had had to marry his planting to the wilderness in order to conquer it —fall away and vanish. The twin banks marched with wilderness as he remembered it—the tangle of brier and cane impenetrable even to sight twenty feet away, the tall tremendous soaring of oak and gum and ash and hickory which had rung to no axe save the hunter's, had echoed to no machinery save the beat of oldtime steam boats traversing it or to the snarling of launches like their own of people going into it to dwell for a week or two weeks because it was still wilderness. There was some of it left, although now it was two hundred miles from Jefferson when once it had been thirty. He had watched it, not being conquered, destroyed, so much as retreating since its purpose was served now and its time an outmoded time, retreating southward through this inverted-apex, this ▽-shaped section of earth between hills and River until what was left of it seemed now to be gathered and for the time arrested in one tremendous density of brooding and inscrutable impenetrability at the ultimate funneling tip.

They reached the site of their last-year's camp with still two hours left of light. "You go on over under that driest tree and set down," Legate told him. "—if you can find it. Me and these other young boys will do this." He did neither. He was not tired yet. That would come later. *Maybe it wont come at all this time*, he thought, as he had thought at this point each November for the last five or six of them. *Maybe I will go out on stand in the morning too;* knowing that he would not, not even if he took the advice and sat down under the driest shelter and did nothing until camp was made and supper cooked. Because it would not be the fatigue. It would be because he would not sleep tonight but would lie instead wakeful and peaceful on the cot amid the tent-filling snoring and the rain's whisper as he always did on the first night in camp; peaceful, without regret or fretting, telling himself that was all right too, who didn't have so many of them left as to waste one sleeping.

In his slicker he directed the unloading of the boat—the tents, the stove, bedding, the food for themselves and the dogs until there should be meat in camp. He sent two of the negroes to cut firewood; he had the cook-tent raised and the stove up and a fire going and supper cooking while the big tent was still being staked down. Then in the beginning of dusk he crossed in the boat to where the horses waited, backing and snorting at the water. He took the lead-ropes and with no more weight than that and his voice, he drew them down into the water and held them beside the boat with only their heads above the surface, as though they actually were suspended from his frail and strengthless old man's hands, while the boat recrossed and each horse in turn lay prone in the shallows, panting and trembling, its eyes rolling in the dusk, until the same weightless hand and unraised voice gathered it surging upward, splashing and thrashing up the bank.

Then the meal was ready. The last of light was gone now save the thin stain of it snared somewhere between the river's surface and the rain. He had the single glass of thin whisky-and-water, then, standing in the churned mud beneath the stretched tarpaulin, he said grace over the fried slabs of pork, the hot soft shapeless bread, the canned beans and molasses and coffee in iron plates and cups,—the town food, brought along with them—then covered himself again, the others following. "Eat," he said. "Eat it all up. I dont want a piece of town meat in camp after breakfast tomorrow. Then you boys will hunt. You'll have to. When I first started hunting in this bottom sixty years ago with old General Compson and Major de Spain and Roth's grandfather and Will Legate's too, Major de Spain wouldn't allow but two pieces of foreign grub in his camp. That was one side of pork and one ham of beef. And not to eat for the first supper and breakfast neither. It was to save until along toward the end of camp when everybody was so sick of bear meat and coon and venison that we couldn't even look at it."

"I thought Uncle Ike was going to say the pork and beef was for the dogs," Legate said, chewing. "But that's right; I remember. You just shot the dogs a mess of wild turkey every evening when they got tired of deer guts."

"Times are different now," another said. "There was game here then."

"Yes," the old man said quietly. "There was game here then."

"Besides, they shot does then too," Legate said. "As it is now, we aint got but one doe-hunter in——"

"And better men hunted it," Edmonds said. He stood at the end of the rough plank table, eating rapidly and steadily as the others ate. But again the old man looked sharply across at the sullen, handsome, brooding face which appeared now darker and more sullen still in the light of the smoky lantern. "Go on. Say it."

"I didn't say that," the old man said. "There are good men everywhere, at all times. Most men are. Some are just unlucky, because most men are a little better than their circumstances give them a chance to be. And I've known some that even the circumstances couldn't stop."

"Well, I wouldn't say—" Legate said.

"So you've lived almost eighty years," Edmonds said. "And that's what you finally learned about the other animals you lived among. I suppose the question to ask you is, where have you been all the time you were dead?"

There was a silence; for the instant even Legate's jaw stopped chewing while he gaped at Edmonds. "Well, by God, Roth—" the third speaker said. But it was the old man who spoke, his voice still peaceful and untroubled and merely grave:

"Maybe so," he said. "But if being what you call alive would have learned me any different, I reckon I'm satisfied, wherever it was I've been."

"Well, I wouldn't say that Roth—" Legate said.

The third speaker was still leaning forward a little over the table looking at Edmonds. "Meaning that it's only because folks happen to be watching him that a man behaves at all," he said. "Is that it?"

"Yes," Edmonds said. "A man in a blue coat, with a badge on it watching him. Maybe just the badge."

"I deny that," the old man said. "I dont——"

The other two paid no attention to him. Even Legate was listening to them for the moment, his mouth still full of food and still open a little, his knife with another lump of something balanced on the tip of the blade arrested halfway to his mouth. "I'm glad I dont have your opinion of folks," the third speaker said. "I take it you include yourself."

"I see," Edmonds said. "You prefer Uncle Ike's opinion of circumstances. All right. Who makes the circumstances?"

"Luck," the third said. "Chance. Happen-so. I see what you are getting at. But that's just what Uncle Ike said: that now and then, maybe most of the time, man is a little better than the net result of his and his neighbors' doings, when he gets the chance to be."

This time Legate swallowed first. He was not to be stopped this time. "Well, I wouldn't say that Roth Edmonds can hunt one doe every day and night for two weeks and was a poor hunter or a unlucky one neither. A man that still have the same doe left to hunt on again next year——"

"Have some meat," the man next to him said.

"—aint so unlucky—What?" Legate said.

"Have some meat." The other offered the dish.

"I got some," Legate said.

"Have some more," the third speaker said. "You and Roth Edmonds both.

Have a heap of it. Clapping your jaws together that way with nothing to break the shock." Someone chortled. Then they all laughed, with relief, the tension broken. But the old man was speaking, even into the laughter, in that peaceful and still untroubled voice:

"I still believe. I see proof everywhere. I grant that man made a heap of his circumstances, him and his living neighbors between them. He even inherited some of them already made, already almost ruined even. A while ago Henry Wyatt there said how there used to be more game here. There was. So much that we even killed does. I seem to remember Will Legate mentioning that too—" Someone laughed, a single guffaw, stillborn. It ceased and they all listened, gravely, looking down at their plates. Edmonds was drinking his coffee, sullen, brooding, inattentive.

"Some folks still kill does," Wyatt said. "There wont be just one buck hanging in this bottom tomorrow night without any head to fit it."

"I didn't say all men," the old man said. "I said most men. And not just because there is a man with a badge to watch us. We probably wont even see him unless maybe he will stop here about noon tomorrow and eat dinner with us and check our licenses——"

"We dont kill does because if we did kill does in a few years there wouldn't even be any bucks left to kill, Uncle Ike," Wyatt said.

"According to Roth yonder, that's one thing we wont never have to worry about," the old man said. "He said on the way here this morning that does and fawns—I believe he said women and children—are two things this world aint ever lacked. But that aint all of it," he said. "That's just the mind's reason a man has to give himself because the heart dont always have time to bother with thinking up words that fit together. God created man and He created the world for him to live in and I reckon He created the kind of world He would have wanted to live in if He had been a man—the ground to walk on, the big woods, the trees and the water, and the game to live in it. And maybe He didn't put the desire to hunt and kill game in man but I reckon He knew it was going to be there, that man was going to teach it to himself, since he wasn't quite God himself yet——"

"When will he be?" Wyatt said.

"I think that every man and woman, at the instant when it dont even matter whether they marry or not, I think that whether they marry then or afterward or dont never, at that instant the two of them together were God."

"Then there are some Gods in this world I wouldn't want to touch, and with a damn long stick," Edmonds said. He set his coffee cup down and looked at Wyatt. "And that includes myself, if that's what you want to know. I'm going to bed." He was gone. There was a general movement among the others. But it ceased and they stood again about the table, not looking at the old man, apparently held there yet by his quiet and peaceful voice as the heads of the swimming horses had been held above the water by his weightless hand. The three negroes—the cook and his helper and old Isham—were sitting quietly in the entrance of the kitchen tent, listening too, the three faces dark and motionless and musing.

"He put them both here: man, and the game he would follow and kill, foreknowing it. I believe He said, 'So be it.' I reckon He even foreknew the end. But He said, 'I will give him his chance. I will give him warning and foreknowledge too, along with the desire to follow and the power to slay. The woods and fields he ravages and the game he devastates will be the consequence and signature of his crime and guilt, and his punishment.'—Bed time," he said. His voice and inflection did not change at all. "Breakfast at four o'clock, Isham. We want meat on the ground by sunup time."

There was a good fire in the sheet-iron heater; the tent was warm and was beginning to dry out, except for the mud underfoot. Edmonds was already rolled into his blankets, motionless, his face to the wall. Isham had made up his bed too—the strong, battered iron cot, the stained mattress which was not quite soft enough, the worn, often-washed blankets which as the years passed were less and less warm enough. But the tent was warm; presently, when the kitchen was cleaned up and readied for breakfast, the young negro would come in to lie down before the heater, where he could be roused to put fresh wood into it from time to time. And then, he knew now he would not sleep tonight anyway; he no longer needed to tell himself that perhaps he would. But it was all right now. The day was ended now and night faced him, but alarmless, empty of fret. *Maybe I came for this*, he thought: *Not to hunt, but for this. I would come anyway, even if only to go back home tomorrow.* Wearing only his bagging woolen underwear, his spectacles folded away in the worn case beneath the pillow where he could reach them readily and his lean body fitted easily into the old worn groove of mattress and his eyes closed while the others undressed and went to bed and the last of the sporadic talking died into snoring. Then he opened his eyes and lay peaceful and quiet as a child, looking up at the motionless belly of rain-murmured canvas upon which the glow of the heater was dying slowly away and would fade still further until the young negro, lying on two planks before it, would sit up and stoke it and lie back down again.

They had a house once. That was sixty years ago, when the Big Bottom was only thirty miles from Jefferson and old Major de Spain, who had been his father's cavalry commander in '61 and '2 and '3 and '4, and his cousin (his older brother; his father too) had taken him into the woods for the first time. Old Sam Fathers was alive then, born in slavery, son of a Negro slave and a Chickasaw chief, who had taught him how to shoot, not only when to shoot but when not to; such a November dawn as tomorrow would be and the old man led him straight to the great cypress and he had known the buck would pass exactly there because there was something running in Sam Fathers' veins which ran in the veins of the buck too, and they stood there against the tremendous trunk, the old man of seventy and the boy of twelve, and there was nothing save the dawn until suddenly the buck was there, smoke-colored out of nothing, magnificent with speed: and Sam Fathers said, 'Now. Shoot quick and shoot slow:' and the gun levelled rapidly without haste and crashed and he walked to the buck lying still intact and still in the shape of that magnificent speed and bled it with Sam's knife and Sam dipped his hands into the hot blood and marked his face forever while he stood trying not to tremble, humbly and with pride too though the boy of twelve had been unable to phrase it then: *I slew you; my bearing must not shame your quitting life. My conduct forever onward must become your death*; marking him for that and for more than that: that day and himself and McCaslin juxtaposed not against the wilderness but against the tamed land, the old wrong and shame itself, in repudiation and denial at least of the land and the wrong and shame even if he couldn't cure the wrong and eradicate the shame, who at fourteen when he learned of it had believed he could do both when he became competent and when at twenty-one he became competent he knew that he could do neither but at least he could repudiate the wrong and shame, at least in principle, and at least the land itself in fact, for his son at least: and did, thought he had: then (married then) in a rented cubicle in a back-street stock-traders' boarding-house, the first and last time he ever saw her naked body, himself and his wife juxtaposed in their turn against that same land, that same wrong and shame from whose regret and grief he would at least save and free his son and, saving and freeing his son, lost him. They had the house then. That roof, the two weeks of each November which they spent under it, had become his home. Although since that time they had lived during the two fall weeks in tents and not always in the same place two years in succession and now his companions were the sons and even the grandsons of them with whom he had lived in the house and for almost fifty years now the house itself had not even existed, the conviction, the sense and feeling of home, had been merely transferred into the canvas. He owned a house in Jefferson, a good house though small, where he had had a wife and lived with her and lost her, ay, lost her even though he had lost her in the rented cubicle before he and his old clever dipsomaniac partner had finished the house for them to move into it: but lost her, because she loved him. But women hope for so much. They never live too long to still believe that anything within the scope of their passionate wanting is likewise within the range of their passionate hope: and it was still kept for him by his dead wife's widowed niece and her children and he was comfortable in it, his wants and needs and even the small trying harmless crochets of an old man looked after by blood at least related to the blood which he had elected out of all the earth to cherish. But he spent the time within those walls waiting for November, because even this tent with its muddy floor and the bed which was not wide enough nor soft enough nor even warm enough, was his home and these men, some of whom he only saw during these two November weeks and not one of whom even bore any name he used to know—De Spain and Compson and Ewell and Hogganbeck—were more his kin than any. Because this was his land——

The shadow of the youngest negro loomed. It soared, blotting the heater's dying glow from the ceiling, the wood billets thumping into the iron maw until the glow, the flame, leaped high and bright across the canvas. But the negro's shadow still remained, by its length and breadth, standing, since it covered most of the ceiling, until after a moment he raised himself on one elbow to look. It was not the negro, it was his kinsman; when he spoke the other turned sharp against the red firelight the sullen and ruthless profile.

"Nothing," Edmonds said. "Go on back to sleep."

"Since Will Legate mentioned it," McCaslin said, "I remember you had some trouble sleeping in here last fall too. Only you called it coon-hunting then. Or was it Will Legate called it that?" The other didn't answer. Then he turned and went back to his bed. McCaslin, still propped on his elbow, watched until the other's shadow sank down the wall and vanished, became one with the mass of sleeping shadows. "That's right," he said. "Try to get some sleep. We must have meat in camp tomorrow. You can do all the setting up you want to after that." He lay down again, his hands crossed again on his breast, watching the glow of the heater on the canvas ceiling. It was steady again now, the fresh wood accepted, being assimilated; soon it would begin to fade again, taking with it the last echo of that sudden upflare of a young man's passion and unrest. Let him lie awake for a little while, he thought; he will lie still some day for a long time without even dissatisfaction to disturb him. And lying awake here, in these surroundings, would soothe him if anything could, if anything could soothe a man just forty years old. Yes, he thought; forty years old or thirty, or even the trembling and sleepless ardor of a boy; already the tent, the rain-murmured canvas globe, was once more filled with it. He lay on his back, his eyes closed, his breathing quiet and peaceful as a child's, listening to it—that silence which was never silence but was myriad. He could almost see it, tremendous, primeval, looming, musing downward upon this puny evanescent clutter of human sojourn which after a single brief week would vanish and in another week would be completely healed, traceless in the unmarked solitude. Because it was his land, although he had never owned a foot of it. He had never wanted to, not even after he saw plain its ultimate doom, watching it retreat year by year before the onslaught of axe and saw and log-lines and then dynamite and tractor plows, because it belonged to no man. It belonged to all; they had only to use it well, humbly and with pride. Then suddenly he knew why he had never wanted to own any of it, arrest at least that much of what people called progress, measure his longevity at least against that much of its ultimate fate. It was because there was just exactly enough of it. He seemed to see the two of them—himself and the wilderness—as coevals, his own span as a hunter, a woodsman not contemporary with his first breath but transmitted to him, assumed by him gladly, humbly, with joy and pride, from that old Major de Spain and that old Sam Fathers who had taught him to hunt, the two spans running out together, not toward oblivion, nothingness, but into a dimension free of both time and space where once more the untreed land warped and wrung to mathematical squares of rank cotton for the frantic old-world people to turn into shells to shoot at one another, would find ample room for both—the names, the faces of the old men he had known and loved and for a little while outlived, moving again among the shades of tall unaxed trees and sightless brakes where the wild strong immortal game ran forever before the tireless belling immortal hounds, falling and rising phoenix-like to the soundless guns.

He had been asleep. The lantern was lighted now. Outside in the darkness the oldest negro, Isham, was beating a spoon against the bottom of a tin pan and crying, "Raise up and get yo foa clock coffy. Raise up and get yo foa clock coffy," and the tent was full of low talk and of men dressing, and Legate's voice, repeating: "Get out of here now and let Uncle Ike sleep. If you wake him up, he'll go out with us. And he aint got any business in the woods this morning."

So he didn't move. He lay with his eyes closed, his breathing gentle and peaceful, and heard them one by one leave the tent. He listened to the breakfast sounds from the table beneath the tarpaulin and heard them depart—the horses, the dogs, the last voice until it died away and there was only the sounds of the negroes clearing breakfast away. After a while he might possibly even hear the first faint clear cry of the first hound ring through the wet woods from where the buck had bedded, then he would go back to sleep again—The tent-flap swung in and fell. Something jarred sharply against the end of the cot and a hand grasped his knee through the blanket before he could open his eyes. It was Edmonds, carrying a shotgun in place of his rifle. He spoke in a harsh, rapid voice:

"Sorry to wake you. There will be a——"

"I was awake," McCaslin said. "Are you going to shoot that shotgun today?"

"You just told me last night you want meat," Edmonds said. "There will be a——"

"Since when did you start having trouble getting meat with your rifle?"

"All right," the other said, with that harsh, restrained, furious impatience. Then McCaslin saw in his hand a thick oblong: an envelope. "There will be a message here some time this morning, looking for me. Maybe it wont come. If it does, give the messenger this and tell h—say I said No."

"A what?" McCaslin said. "Tell who?" He half rose onto his elbow as Edmonds jerked the envelope onto the blanket, already turning toward the entrance, the envelope striking solid and heavy and without noise and already sliding from the bed until McCaslin caught it, divining by feel through the paper as instantaneously and conclusively as if he had opened the envelope and looked, the thick sheaf of banknotes. "Wait," he said. "Wait:"—more than the blood kinsman, more even than the senior in years, so that the other paused, the canvas lifted, looking back, and McCaslin saw that outside it was already day. "Tell her No," he said. "Tell her." They stared at one another—the old face, wan, sleep-raddled above the tumbled bed, the dark and sullen younger one at once furious and cold. "Will Legate was right. This is what you called coon-hunting. And now this." He didn't raise the envelope. He made no motion, no gesture to indicate it. "What did you promise her that you haven't the courage to face her and retract?"

"Nothing!" the other said. "Nothing! This is all of it. Tell her I said No." He was gone. The tent flap lifted on an inwaft of faint light and the constant murmur of rain, and fell again, leaving the old man still half-raised onto one elbow, the envelope clutched in the other shaking hand. Afterward it seemed to him that he had begun to hear the approaching boat almost immediately, before the other could have got out of sight even. It seemed to him that there had been no interval whatever: the tent flap falling on the same out-waft of faint and rain-filled light like the suspiration and expiration of the same breath and then in the next second lifted again—the mounting snarl of the outboard engine, increasing, nearer and nearer and louder and louder then cut short off, ceasing with the absolute instantaneity of a blown-out candle, into the lap and plop of water under the bows as the skiff slid in to the bank, the youngest negro, the youth, raising the tent flap beyond which for that instant he saw the boat—a small skiff with a negro man sitting in the stern beside the up-slanted motor—then the woman entering, in a man's hat and a man's slicker and rubber boots, carrying the blanket-swaddled bundle on one arm and holding the edge of the unbuttoned raincoat over it with the other hand: and bringing something else, something intangible, an effluvium which he knew he would recognise in a moment because Isham had already told him, warned him, by sending the young negro to the tent to announce the visitor instead of coming himself, the flap falling at last on the young negro and they were alone—the face indistinct and as yet only young and with dark eyes, queerly colorless but not ill and not that of a country woman despite the garments she wore, looking down at him where he sat upright on the cot now, clutching the envelope, about him and the twisted blankets huddled about his hips.

"Is that his?" he cried. "Dont lie to me!"

"Yes," she said. "He's gone."

"Yes. He's gone. You wont jump him here. Not this time. I dont reckon even you expected that. He left you this. Here." He fumbled at the envelope. It was not to pick it up, because it was still in his hand; he had never put it down. It was as if he had to fumble somehow to co-ordinate physically his heretofore obedient hand with what his brain was commanding of it, as if he had never performed such an action before, extending the envelope at last, saying again, "Here. Take it. Take it:" until he became aware of her eyes, or not the eyes so much as the look, the regard fixed now on his face with that immersed contemplation, that bottomless and intent candor, of a child. If she had ever seen either the envelope or his movement to extend it, she did not show it.

"You're Uncle Isaac," she said.

"Yes," he said. "But never mind that. Here. Take it. He said to tell you No." She looked at the envelope, then she took it. It was sealed and bore no superscription. Nevertheless, even after she glanced at the front of it, he watched her hold it in the one free hand and tear the corner off with her teeth and manage to rip it open and tilt the neat sheaf of bound notes onto the blanket without even glancing at them and look into the empty envelope and take the edge between her teeth and tear it completely open before she crumpled and dropped it.

"That's just money," she said.

"What did you expect? What else did you expect? You have known him long enough or at least often enough to have got that child, and you dont know him any better than that?"

"Not very often. Not very long. Just that week here last fall, and in January he sent for me and we went West, to New Mexico. We were there six weeks, where I could at least sleep in the same apartment where I cooked for him and looked after his clothes—"

"But not marriage," he said. "Not marriage. He didn't promise you that. Dont lie to me. He didn't have to."

"No. He didn't have to. I didn't ask him to. I knew what I was doing. I knew that to begin with, long before honor I imagine he called it told him the time had come to tell me in so many words what his code I suppose he would call it would forbid him forever to do. And we agreed. Then we agreed again before he left New Mexico, to make sure. That that would be all of it. I believed him. No, I dont mean that; I mean I believed myself. I wasn't even listening to him anymore by then because by that time it had been a long time since he had had anything else to tell me for me to have to hear. By then I wasn't even listening enough to ask him to please stop talking. I was listening to myself. And I believed it. I must have believed it. I dont see how I could have helped but believe it, because he was gone then as we had agreed and he didn't write as we had agreed, just the money came to the bank in Vicksburg in my name but coming from nobody as we had agreed. So I must have believed it. I even wrote him last month to make sure again and the letter came back unopened and I was sure. So I left the hospital and rented myself a room to live in until the deer season opened so I could make sure myself and I was waiting beside the road yesterday when your car passed and he saw me and so I was sure."

"Then what do you want?" he said. "What do you want? What do you expect?"

"Yes," she said. And while he glared at her, his white hair awry from the pillow and his eyes, lacking the spectacles to focus them, blurred and irisless and apparently pupilless, he saw again that grave, intent, speculative and detached fixity like a child watching him. "His great great—Wait a minute.—great great *great* grandfather was your grandfather. McCaslin. Only it got to be Edmonds. Only it got to be more than that. Your cousin McCaslin was there that day when your father and Uncle Buddy won Tennie from Mr. Beauchamp for the one that had no name but Terrel so you called him Tomey's Terrel, to marry. But after that it got to be Edmonds." She regarded him, almost peacefully, with that unwinking and heatless fixity—the dark wide bottomless eyes in the face's dead and toneless pallor which to the old man looked anything but dead, but young and incredibly and even ineradicably alive—as though she were not only not looking at anything, she was not even speaking to anyone but herself. "I would have made a man of him. He's not a man yet. You spoiled him. You, and Uncle Lucas and Aunt Mollie. But mostly you."

"Me?" he said. "Me?"

"Yes. When you gave to his grandfather that land which didn't belong to him, not even half of it by will or even law."

"And never mind that too," he said. "Never mind that too. You," he said. "You sound like you have been to college even. You sound almost like a Northerner even, not like the draggle-tailed women of these Delta peckerwoods. Yet you meet a man on the street one afternoon just because a box of groceries happened to fall out of a boat. And a month later you go off with him and live with him until he got a child on you: and then, by your own statement, you sat there while he took his hat and said goodbye and walked out. Even a Delta peckerwood would look after even a draggle-tail better than that. Haven't you got any folks at all?"

"Yes," she said. "I was living with one of them. My aunt, in Vicksburg. I came to live with her two years ago when my father died; we lived in Indianapolis then. But I got a job, teaching school here in Aluschaskuna, because my aunt was a widow, with a big family, taking in washing to sup——"

"Took in what?" he said. "Took in washing?" He sprang, still seated even, flinging himself backward onto one arm, awry-haired, glaring. Now he understood what it was she had brought into the tent with her, what old Isham had already told him by sending the youth to bring her in to him—the pale lips, the skin pallid and dead-looking yet not ill, the dark and tragic and foreknowing eyes. *Maybe in a thousand or two thousand years in America,* he thought. *But not now! Not now!* He cried, not loud, in a voice of amazement, pity, and outrage: "You're a nigger!"

"Yes," she said. "James Beauchamp—you called him Tennie's Jim though he had a name—was my grandfather. I said you were Uncle Isaac."

"And he knows?"

"No," she said. "What good would that have done?"

"But you did," he cried. "But you did. Then what do you expect here?"

"Nothing."

"Then why did you come here? You said you were waiting in Aluschaskuna yesterday and he saw you. Why did you come this morning?"

"I'm going back North. Back home. My cousin brought me up the day before yesterday in his boat. He's going to take me on to Leland to get the train."

"Then go," he said. Then he cried again in that thin not loud and grieving voice: "Get out of here! I can do nothing for you! Cant nobody do nothing for you!" She moved; she was not looking at him again, toward the entrance. "Wait," he said. She paused again, obediently still, turning. He took up the sheaf of banknotes and laid it on the blanket at the foot of the cot and drew his hand back beneath the blanket. "There," he said.

Now she looked at the money, for the first time, one brief blank glance, then away again. "I dont need it. He gave me money last winter. Besides the money he sent to Vicksburg. Provided. Honor and code too. That was all arranged."

"Take it," he said. His voice began to rise again, but he stopped it. "Take it out of my tent." She came back to the cot and took up the money; whereupon once more he said, "Wait:" although she had not turned, still stooping, and he put out his hand. But, sitting, he could not complete the reach until she moved her hand, the single hand which held the money, until he touched it. He didn't grasp it, he merely touched it—the gnarled, bloodless, bone-light bone-dry old man's fingers touching for a second the smooth young flesh where the strong old blood ran after its long lost journey back to home. "Tennie's

Jim," he said. "Tennie's Jim." He drew the hand back beneath the blanket again: he said harshly now: "It's a boy, I reckon. They usually are, except that one that was its own mother too."

"Yes," she said. "It's a boy." She stood for a moment longer, looking at him. Just for an instant her free hand moved as though she were about to lift the edge of the raincoat away from the child's face. But she did not. She turned again when once more he said Wait and moved beneath the blanket.

"Turn your back," he said. "I am going to get up. I aint got my pants on." Then he could not get up. He sat in the huddled blanket, shaking, while again she turned and looked down at him in dark interrogation. "There," he said harshly, in the thin and shaking old man's voice. "On the nail there. The tent-pole."

"What?" she said.

"The horn!" he said harshly. "The horn." She went and got it, thrust the money into the slicker's side pocket as if it were a rag, a soiled handkerchief, and lifted down the horn, the one which General Compson had left him in his will, covered with the unbroken skin from a buck's shank and bound with silver.

"What?" she said.

"It's his. Take it."

"Oh," she said. "Yes. Thank you."

"Yes," he said, harshly, rapidly, but not so harsh now and soon not harsh at all but just rapid, urgent, until he knew that his voice was running away with him and he had neither intended it nor could stop it: "That's right. Go back North. Marry: a man in your own race. That's the only salvation for you—for a while yet, maybe a long while yet. We will have to wait. Marry a black man. You are young, handsome, almost white; you could find a black man who would see in you what it was you saw in him, who would ask nothing of you and expect less and get even still less than that, if it's revenge you want. Then you will forget all this, forget it ever happened, that he ever existed—" until he could stop it at last and did, sitting there in his huddle of blankets during the instant when, without moving at all, she blazed silently down at him. Then that was gone too. She stood in the gleaming and still dripping slicker, looking quietly down at him from under the sodden hat.

"Old man," she said, "have you lived so long and forgotten so much that you dont remember anything you ever knew or felt or even heard about love?"

Then she was gone too. The waft of light and the murmur of the constant rain flowed into the tent and then out again as the flap fell. Lying back once more, trembling, panting, the blanket huddled to his chin and his hands crossed on his breast, he listened to the pop and snarl, the mounting then fading whine of the motor until it died away and once again the tent held only silence and the sound of rain. And cold too: he lay shaking faintly and steadily in it, rigid save for the shaking. This Delta, he thought: This Delta. *This land which man has deswamped and denuded and derivered in two generations so that white men can own plantations and commute every night to Memphis and black men own plantations and ride in jim crow cars to Chicago to live in millionaires' mansions on Lakeshore Drive, where white men rent farms and live like niggers and niggers crop on shares and live like animals, where cotton is planted and grows man-tall in the very cracks of the sidewalks, and usury and mortgage and bankruptcy and measureless wealth, Chinese and African and Aryan and Jew, all breed and spawn together until no man has time to say which one is which nor cares.* . . . No wonder the ruined woods I used to know dont cry for retribution! he thought: The people who have destroyed it will accomplish its revenge.

The tent flap jerked rapidly in and fell. He did not move save to turn his head and open his eyes. It was Legate. He went quickly to Edmonds' bed and stooped, rummaging hurriedly among the still-tumbled blankets.

"What is it?" he said.

"Looking for Roth's knife," Legate said. "I come back to get a horse. We got a deer on the ground." He rose, the knife in his hand, and hurried toward the entrance.

"Who killed it?" McCaslin said. "Was it Roth?"

"Yes," Legate said, raising the flap.

"Wait," McCaslin said. He moved, suddenly, onto his elbow. "What was it?" Legate paused for an instant beneath the lifted flap. He did not look back.

"Just a deer, Uncle Ike," he said impatiently. "Nothing extra." He was gone; again the flap fell behind him, wafting out of the tent again the faint light and the constant and grieving rain. McCaslin lay back down, the blanket once more drawn to his chin, his crossed hands once more weightless on his breast in the empty tent.

"It was a doe," he said.

Ernest Hemingway (1898–1961)

In Another Country

In the fall the war was always there, but we did not go to it any more. It was cold in the fall in Milan and the dark came very early. Then the electric lights came on, and it was pleasant along the streets looking in the windows. There was much game hanging outside the shops, and the snow powdered in the fur of the foxes and the wind blew their tails. The deer hung stiff and heavy and empty, and small birds blew in the wind and the wind turned their feathers. It was a cold fall and the wind came down from the mountains.

We were all at the hospital every afternoon, and there were different ways of walking across the town through the dusk to the hospital. Two of the ways were alongside canals, but they were long. Always, though, you crossed a bridge across a canal to enter the hospital. There was a choice of three bridges. On one of them a woman sold roasted chestnuts. It was warm, standing in front of her charcoal fire, and the chestnuts were warm afterward in your pocket. The hospital was very old and very beautiful, and you entered through a gate on the other side. There were usually funerals starting from the courtyard. Beyond the old hospital were the new brick pavilions, and there we met every afternoon and were all very polite and interested in what was the matter, and sat in the machines that were to make so much difference.

The doctor came up to the machine where I was sitting and said: "What did you like best to do before the war? Did you practise a sport?"

I said: "Yes, football."

"Good," he said. "You will be able to play football again better than ever."

My knee did not bend and the leg dropped straight from the knee to the ankle without a calf, and the machine was to bend the knee and make it move as in riding a tricycle. But it did not bend yet, and instead the machine lurched when it came to the bending part. The doctor said: "That will all pass. You are a fortunate young man. You will play football again like a champion."

In the next machine was a major who had a little hand like a baby's. He winked at me when the doctor examined his hand, which was between two leather straps that bounced up and down and flapped the stiff fingers, and said: "And will I too play football, captain-doctor?" He had been a very great fencer, and before the war the greatest fencer in Italy.

The doctor went to his office in a back room and brought a photograph which showed a hand that had been withered almost as small as the major's, before it had taken a machine course, and after was a little larger. The major held the photograph with his good hand and looked at it very carefully. "A wound?" he asked.

"An industrial accident," the doctor said.

"Very interesting, very interesting," the major said, and handed it back to the doctor.

"You have confidence?"

"No," said the major.

There were three boys who came each day who were about the same age I was. They were all three from Milan, and one of them was to be a lawyer, and one was to be a painter, and one had intended to be a soldier, and after we were finished with the machines, sometimes we walked back together to the Café Cova, which was next door to the Scala. We walked the short way through the communist quarter because we were four together. The people hated us because we were officers, and from a wine-shop some one called out, "A basso gli ufficiali!" as we passed. Another boy who walked with us sometimes and made us five wore a black silk handkerchief across his face because he had no nose then and his face was to be rebuilt. He had gone out to the front from the military academy and been wounded within an hour after he had gone into the front line for the first time. They rebuilt his face, but he came from a very old family and they could never get the nose exactly right. He went to South America and worked in a bank. But this was a long time ago, and then we did not any of us know how it was going to be afterward. We only knew then that there was always the war, but that we were not going to it any more.

We all had the same medals, except the boy with the black silk bandage across his face, and he had not been at the front long enough to get any medals. The tall boy with a very pale face who was to be a lawyer had been a lieutenant of Arditi and had three medals of the sort we each had only one of. He had lived a very long time with death and was a little detached. We were all a little detached, and there was nothing that held us together except that we met every afternoon at the hospital. Although, as we walked to the Cova through the tough part of town, walking in the dark, with light and singing coming out of the wine-shops, and sometimes having to walk into the street when the men and women would crowd together on the sidewalk so that we would have had to jostle them to get by, we felt held together by there being something that had happened that they, the people who disliked us, did not understand.

We ourselves all understood the Cova, where it was rich and warm and not too brightly lighted, and noisy and smoky at certain hours, and there were always girls at the tables and the illustrated papers on a rack on the wall. The girls at the Cova were very patriotic, and I found that the most patriotic people in Italy were the café girls—and I believe they are still patriotic.

The boys at first were very polite about my medals and asked me what I had done to get them. I showed them the papers, which were written in very beautiful language and full of *fratellanza* and *abnegazione*, but which really said, with the adjectives removed, that I had been given the medals because I was an American. After that their manner changed a little toward me, although I was their friend against outsiders. I was a friend, but I was never really one of them after they had read the citations, because it had been different with them and they had done very different things to get their medals. I had been wounded, it was true; but we all knew that being wounded, after all, was really an accident. I was never ashamed of the ribbons, though, and sometimes, after the cocktail hour, I would imagine myself having done all the things they had done to get their medals; but walking home at night through the empty streets with the cold wind and all the shops closed, trying to keep near the street lights, I knew that I would never have done such things, and I was very much afraid to die, and often lay in bed at night by myself, afraid to die and wondering how I would be when I went back to the front again.

The three with the medals were like hunting-hawks; and I was not a hawk, although I might seem a hawk to those who had never hunted; they, the three, knew better and so we drifted apart. But I stayed good friends with the boy who had been wounded his first day at the front, because he would never know now how he would have turned out; so he could never be accepted either, and I liked him because I thought perhaps he would not have turned out to be a hawk either.

The major, who had been the great fencer, did not believe in bravery, and spent much time while we sat in the machines correcting my grammar. He had complimented me on how I spoke Italian, and we talked together very easily. One day I had said that Italian seemed such an easy language to me that I could not take a great interest in it; everything was so easy to say. "Ah, yes," the major said. "Why, then, do you not take up the use of grammar?" So we took up the use of grammar, and soon Italian was such a difficult language that I was afraid to talk to him until I had the grammar straight in my mind.

The major came very regularly to the hospital. I do not think he ever missed a day, although I am sure he did not believe in the machines. There was a time when none of us believed in the machines, and one day the major said it was all nonsense. The machines were new then and it was we who were to prove them. It was an idiotic idea, he said, "a theory, like another." I had not learned my grammar, and he said I was a stupid impossible disgrace, and he was a fool to have bothered with me. He was a small man and he sat straight up in his chair with his right hand thrust into the machine and looked straight ahead at the wall while the straps thumped up and down with his fingers in them.

"What will you do when the war is over if it is over?" he asked me. "Speak grammatically!"

"I will go to the States."

"Are you married?"

"No, but I hope to be."

"The more of a fool you are," he said. He seemed very angry. "A man must not marry."

"Why, Signor Maggiore?"

"Don't call me 'Signor Maggiore.' "

"Why must not a man marry?"

"He cannot marry. He cannot marry," he said angrily. "If he is to lose everything, he should not place himself in a position to lose that. He should not place himself in a position to lose. He should find things he cannot lose."

He spoke very angrily and bitterly, and looked straight ahead while he talked.

"But why should he necessarily lose it?"

"He'll lose it," the major said. He was

looking at the wall. Then he looked down at the machine and jerked his little hand out from between the straps and slapped it hard against his thigh. "He'll lose it," he almost shouted. "Don't argue with me!" Then he called to the attendant who ran the machines. "Come and turn this damned thing off."

He went back into the other room for the light treatment and the massage. Then I heard him ask the doctor if he might use his telephone and he shut the door. When he came back into the room, I was sitting in another machine. He was wearing his cape and had his cap on, and he came directly toward my machine and put his arm on my shoulder.

"I am so sorry," he said, and patted me on the shoulder with his good hand. "I would not be rude. My wife has just died. You must forgive me."

"Oh—" I said, feeling sick for him. "I am *so* sorry."

He stood there biting his lower lip. "It is very difficult," he said. "I cannot resign myself."

He looked straight past me and out through the window. Then he began to cry. "I am utterly unable to resign myself," he said and choked. And then crying, his head up looking at nothing, carrying himself straight and soldierly, with tears on both his cheeks and biting his lips, he walked past the machines and out the door.

The doctor told me that the major's wife, who was very young and whom he had not married until he was definitely invalided out of the war, had died of pneumonia. She had been sick only a few days. No one expected her to die. The major did not come to the hospital for three days Then he came at the usual hour, wearing a black band on the sleeve of his uniform. When he came back, there were large framed photographs around the wall, of all sorts of wounds before and after they had been cured by the machines. In front of the machine the major used were three photographs of hands like his that were completely restored. I do not know where the doctor got them. I always understood we were the first to use the machines. The photographs did not make much difference to the major because he only looked out of the window.

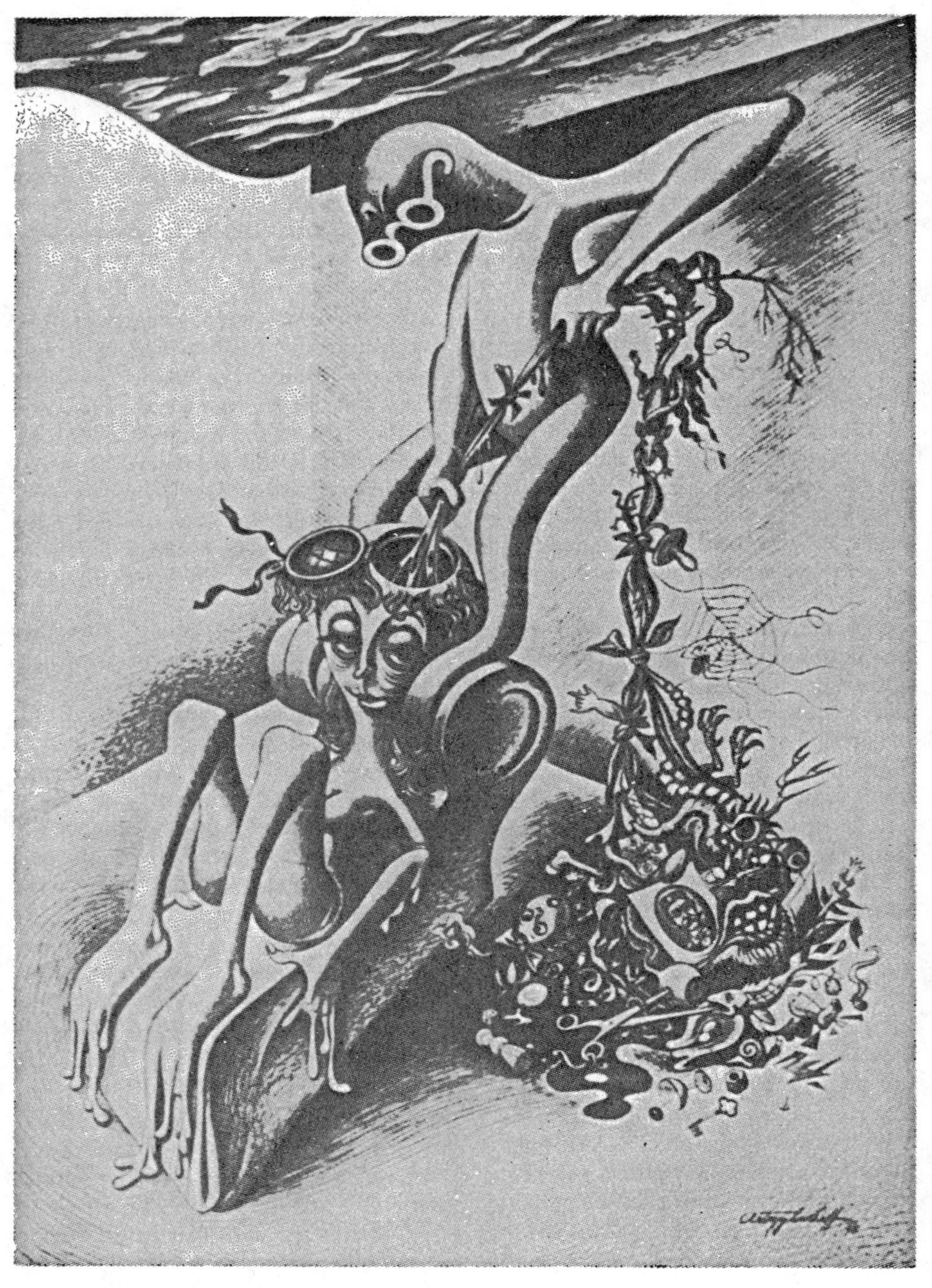

"We are getting to the bottom of it."

Graham Greene (1904–   )

The Basement Room

1

When the front door had shut them out and the butler Baines had turned back into the dark heavy hall, Philip began to live. He stood in front of the nursery door, listening until he heard the engine of the taxi die out along the street. His parents were gone for a fortnight's holiday; he was "between nurses," one dismissed and the other not arrived; he was alone in the great Belgravia house with Baines and Mrs. Baines.

He could go anywhere, even through the green baize door to the pantry or down the stairs to the basement living-room. He felt a stranger in his home because he could go into any room and all the rooms were empty.

You could only guess who had once occupied them: the rack of pipes in the smoking-room beside the elephant tusks, the carved wood tobacco jar; in the bedroom the pink hangings and pale perfumes and the three-quarter finished jars of cream which Mrs. Baines had not yet cleared away; the high glaze on the never-opened piano in the drawing-room, the china clock, the silly little tables and the silver: but here Mrs. Baines was already busy, pulling down the curtains, covering the chairs in dust-sheets.

"Be off out of here, Master Philip," and she looked at him with her hateful peevish eyes, while she moved round, getting everything in order, meticulous and loveless and doing her duty.

Philip Lane went downstairs and pushed at the baize door; he looked into the pantry, but Baines was not there, then he set foot for the first time on the stairs to the basement. Again he had the sense: this is life. All his seven nursery years vibrated with the strange, the new experience. His crowded busy brain was like a city which feels the earth tremble at a distant earthquake shock. He was apprehensive, but he was happier than he had ever been. Everything was more important than before.

Baines was reading a newspaper in his shirtsleeves. He said: "Come in, Phil, and make yourself at home. Wait a moment and I'll do the honours," and going to a white cleaned cupboard he brought out a bottle of ginger-beer and half a Dundee cake. "Half-past eleven in the morning," Baines said. "It's opening time, my boy," and he cut the cake and poured out the ginger-beer. He was more genial than Philip had ever known him, more at his ease, a man in his own home.

"Shall I call Mrs. Baines?" Philip asked, and he was glad when Baines said no. She was busy. She liked to be busy, so why interfere with her pleasure?

"A spot of drink at half-past eleven," Baines said, pouring himself out a glass of ginger-beer, "gives an appetite for chop and does no man any harm."

"A chop?" Philip asked.

"Old Coasters," Baines said, "call all food chop."

"But it's not a chop?"

"Well, it might be, you know, cooked with palm oil. And then some paw-paw to follow."

Philip looked out of the basement window at the dry stone yard, the ash-can and the legs going up and down beyond the railings.

"Was it hot there?"

"Ah, you never felt such heat. Not a nice heat, mind, like you get in the park on a day like this. Wet," Baines said, "corruption." He cut himself a slice of cake. "Smelling of rot," Baines said, rolling his eyes round the small basement room, from clean cupboard to clean cupboard, the sense of bareness, of nowhere to hide a man's secrets. With an air of regret for something lost he took a long draught of ginger-beer.

"Why did father live out there?"

"It was his job," Baines said, "same as this is mine now. And it was mine then too. It was a man's job. You wouldn't believe it now, but I've had forty niggers under me, doing what I told them to."

"Why did you leave?"

"I married Mrs. Baines."

Philip took the slice of Dundee cake in his hand and munched it round the room. He felt very old, independent and judicial; he was aware that Baines was talking to him as man to man. He never called him Master Philip as Mrs. Baines did, who was servile when she was not authoritative.

Baines had seen the world; he had seen beyond the railings, beyond the tired legs of typists, the Pimlico parade to and from Victoria. He sat there over his ginger pop with the resigned dignity of an exile; Baines didn't complain; he had chosen his fate; and if his fate was Mrs. Baines he had only himself to blame.

But today, because the house was almost empty and Mrs. Baines was upstairs and there was nothing to do, he allowed himself a little acidity.

"I'd go back tomorrow if I had the chance."

"Did you ever shoot a nigger?"

"I never had any call to shoot," Baines said. "Of course I carried a gun. But you didn't need to treat them bad. That just made them stupid. Why," Baines said, bowing his thin grey hair with embarrassment over the ginger pop, "I loved some of those damned niggers. I couldn't help loving them. There they'd be, laughing, holding hands; they liked to touch each other; it made them feel fine to know the other fellow was round.

"It didn't mean anything we could understand; two of them would go about all day without loosing hold, grown men; but it wasn't love; it didn't mean anything we could understand."

"Eating between meals," Mrs. Baines said. "What would your mother say, Master Philip?"

She came down the steep stairs to the basement, her hands full of pots of cream and salve, tubes of grease and paste. "You oughtn't to encourage him, Baines," she said, sitting down in a wicker armchair and screwing up her small ill-humoured eyes at the Coty lipstick, Pond's cream, the Leichner rouge and Cyclax powder and Elizabeth Arden astringent.

She threw them one by one into the wastepaper basket. She saved only the cold cream. "Telling the boy stories," she said. "Go along to the nursery, Master Philip, while I get lunch."

Philip climbed the stairs to the baize door. He heard Mrs. Baines's voice like the voice in a nightmare when the small Price light has gutted in the saucer and the curtains move; it was sharp and shrill and full of malice, louder than people ought to speak, exposed.

"Sick to death of your ways, Baines, spoiling the boy. Time you did some work about the house," but he couldn't hear what Baines said in reply. He pushed open the baize door, came up like a small earth animal in his grey flannel shorts into a wash of sunlight on a parquet floor, the gleam of mirrors dusted and polished and beautified by Mrs. Baines.

Something broke downstairs, and Philip sadly mounted the stairs to the nursery. He pitied Baines; it occurred to him how happily they could live together in the empty house if Mrs. Baines were called away. He didn't want to play with his Meccano sets; he wouldn't take out his train or his soldiers; he sat at the table with his chin on his hands: this is life; and suddenly he felt responsible for Baines, as if he were the master of the house and Baines an ageing servant who deserved to be cared for. There was not much one could do; he decided at least to be good.

He was not surprised when Mrs. Baines was agreeable at lunch; he was used to her changes. Now it was "another helping of meat, Master Philip," or "Master Philip, a little more of this nice pudding." It was a pudding he liked, Queen's pudding with a perfect meringue, but he wouldn't eat a second helping lest she might count that a victory. She was the kind of woman who thought that any injustice could be counterbalanced by something good to eat.

She was sour, but she liked making sweet things; one never had to complain of a lack of jam or plums; she ate well herself and added soft sugar to the meringue and the strawberry jam. The half light through the basement window set the motes moving above her pale hair like dust as she sifted the sugar, and Baines crouched over his plate saying nothing.

Again Philip felt responsibility. Baines had looked forward to this, and Baines was disappointed: everything was being spoilt. The sensation of disappointment was one which Philip could share; knowing nothing of love or jealousy or passion, he could understand better than anyone this grief, something hoped for not happening, something promised not fulfilled, something exciting turning dull. "Baines," he said, "will you take me for a walk this afternoon?"

"No," Mrs. Baines said, "no. That he won't. Not with all the silver to clean."

"There's a fortnight to do it in," Baines said.

"Work first, pleasure afterwards." Mrs. Baines helped herself to some more meringue.

Baines suddenly put down his spoon and fork and pushed his plate away, "Blast," he said.

"Temper," Mrs. Baines said softly, "temper. Don't you go breaking any more things, Baines, and I won't have you swearing in front of the boy. Master Philip, if you've finished you can get down." She skinned the rest of the meringue off the pudding.

"I want to go for a walk," Philip said.

"You'll go and have a rest."

"I will go for a walk."

"Master Philip," Mrs. Baines said. She got up from the table, leaving her meringue unfinished, and came towards him, thin, menacing, dusty in the basement room. "Master Philip, you do as you're told." She took him by the arm and squeezed it gently; she watched him with a joyless passionate glitter and above her head the feet of the typists trudged back to the Victoria offices after the lunch interval.

"Why shouldn't I go for a walk?" But he weakened; he was scared and ashamed of being scared. This was life; a strange passion he couldn't understand moving in the basement room. He saw a small pile of broken glass swept into a corner by the wastepaper basket. He looked to Baines for help and only intercepted hate; and sad hopeless hate of something behind bars.

"Why shouldn't I?" he repeated.

"Master Philip," Mrs. Baines said, "you've got to do as you're told. You mustn't think just because your father's away there's nobody here to—"

"You wouldn't dare," Philip cried, and was startled by Baines's low interjection, "There's nothing she wouldn't dare."

"I hate you," Philip said to Mrs. Baines. He pulled away from her and ran to the door, but she was there before him; she was old, but she was quick.

"Master Philip," she said, "you'll say you're sorry." She stood in front of the door quivering with excitement. "What would your father do if he heard you say that?"

She put a hand out to seize him, dry and white with constant soda, the nails cut to the quick, but he backed away and put the table between them, and suddenly to his surprise she smiled; she became again as servile as she had been arrogant. "Get along with you, Master Philip," she said with glee. "I see I'm going to have my hands full till your father and mother come back."

She left the door unguarded and when he passed her she slapped him playfully. "I've got too much to do today to trouble about you. I haven't covered half the chairs," and suddenly even the upper part of the house became unbearable to him as he thought of Mrs. Baines moving round shrouding the sofas, laying out the dust-sheets.

So he wouldn't go upstairs to get his cap but walked straight out across the shining hall into the street, and again, as he looked this way and looked that way, it was life he was in the middle of.

2

It was the pink sugar cakes in the window on a paper doily, the ham, the slab of mauve sausage, the wasps driving like small torpedoes across the pane that caught Philip's attention. His feet were tired by pavements; he had been afraid to cross the road, had simply walked first in one direction, then in the other. He was nearly home now; the square was at the end of the street; this was a shabby outpost of Pimlico, and he smudged the pane with his nose, looking for sweets, and saw between the cakes and ham a different Baines. He hardly recognized the bulbous eyes, the bald forehead. It was a happy, bold and buccaneering Baines, even though it was, when you looked closer, a desperate Baines.

Philip had never seen the girl. He remembered Baines had a niece and he thought that this might be her. She was thin and drawn, and she wore a white mackintosh; she meant nothing to Philip; she belonged to a world about which he knew nothing at all. He couldn't make up stories about her, as he could make them up about withered Sir Hubert Reed, the Permanent Secretary, about Mrs. Wince-Dudley who came up once a year from Penstanley in Suffolk with a green umbrella and an enormous black handbag, as he could make them up about the upper servants in all the houses where he went to tea and games. She just didn't belong; he thought of mermaids and Undine; but she didn't belong there either, nor to the adventures of Emil, nor to the Bastables. She sat there looking at an iced pink cake in the detachment and mystery of the completely disinherited, looking at the half-used pots of powder which Baines had set out on the marble-topped table between them.

Baines was urging, hoping, entreating, commanding, and the girl looked at the tea and the china pots and cried. Baines passed his handkerchief across the table, but she wouldn't wipe her eyes; she screwed it in her palm and let the tears run down, wouldn't do anything, wouldn't speak, would only put up a silent despairing resistance to what she dreaded and wanted and refused to listen to at any price. The two brains battled over the tea-cups loving each other, and there came to Philip outside, beyond the ham and wasps and dusty Pimlico pane, a confused indication of the struggle.

He was inquisitive and he didn't understand and he wanted to know. He went and stood in the doorway to see better, he was less sheltered than he had ever been; other people's lives for the first time touched and pressed and moulded. He would never escape that scene. In a week he had forgotten it, but it conditioned his career, the long austerity of his life; when he was dying he said: "Who is she?"

Baines had won; he was cocky and the girl was happy. She wiped her face, she opened a pot of powder, and their fingers touched across the table. It occurred to Philip that it would be amusing to imitate Mrs. Baines's voice and call "Baines" to him from the door.

It shrivelled them; you couldn't describe it in any other way; it made them smaller, they weren't happy any more and they weren't bold. Baines was the first to recover and trace the voice, but that didn't make things as they were. The sawdust was spilled out of the afternoon; nothing you did could mend it, and Philip was scared. "I didn't mean. . ." He wanted to say that he loved Baines, that he had only wanted to laugh at Mrs. Baines. But he had discovered that you couldn't laugh at Mrs. Baines. She wasn't Sir Hubert Reed, who used steel nibs and carried a pen-wiper in his pocket; she wasn't Mrs. Wince-Dudley; she was darkness when the night-light went out in a draught; she was the frozen blocks of earth he had seen one winter in a graveyard when someone said, "They need an electric drill"; she was the flowers gone bad and smelling in the little closet room at Penstanley. There was nothing to laugh about. You had to endure her when she was there and forget about her quickly when she was away, suppress the thought of her, ram it down deep.

Baines said, "It's only Phil," beckoned him in and gave him the pink iced cake the girl hadn't eaten, but the afternoon was broken, the cake was like dry bread in the throat. The girl left them at once; she even forgot to take the powder; like a small blunt icicle in her white mackintosh she stood in the doorway with her back to them, then melted into the afternoon.

"Who is she?" Philip asked. "Is she your niece?"

"Oh, yes," Baines said, "that's who she is; she's my niece," and poured the last drops of water on to the coarse black leaves in the teapot.

"May as well have another cup," Baines said.

"The cup that cheers," he said hopelessly, watching the bitter black fluid drain out of the spout.

"Have a glass of ginger pop, Phil?"

"I'm sorry. I'm sorry, Baines."

"It's not your fault, Phil. Why, I could believe it wasn't you at all, but her. She creeps in everywhere." He fished two leaves out of his cup and laid them on the back of his hand, a thin soft flake and a hard stalk. He beat them with his hand: "Today," and the stalk detached itself, "tomorrow, Wednesday, Thursday, Friday, Saturday, Sunday," but the flake wouldn't come, stayed where it was, drying under his blows, with a resistance you wouldn't believe it to possess. "The tough one wins," Baines said.

He got up and paid the bill and out they went into the street. Baines said, "I don't ask you to say what isn't true. But you needn't mention to Mrs. Baines you met us here."

"Of course not," Philip said, and catching something of Sir Hubert Reed's manner, "I understand, Baines." But he didn't understand a thing; he was caught up in other people's darkness.

"It was stupid," Baines said. "So near home, but I hadn't time to think, you see. I'd got to see her."

"Of course, Baines."

"I haven't time to spare," Baines said. "I'm not young. I've got to see that she's all right."

"Of course you have, Baines."

"Mrs. Baines will get it out of you if she can."

"You can trust me, Baines," Philip said in a dry important Reed voice; and then, "Look out. She's at the window watching." And there indeed she was, looking up at them, between the lace curtains, from the basement room, speculating. "Need we go in, Baines?" Philip asked, cold lying heavy on his stomach like too much pudding; he clutched Baines's arm.

"Careful," Baines said softly, "careful."

"But need we go in, Baines? It's early. Take me for a walk in the park."

"Better not."

"But I'm frightened, Baines."

"You haven't any cause," Baines said. "Nothing's going to hurt you. You just run along upstairs to the nursery. I'll go down by the area and talk to Mrs. Baines." But even he stood hesitating at the top of the stone steps pretending not to see her, where she watched between the curtains. "In at the front door, Phil, and up the stairs."

Philip didn't linger in the hall; he ran, slithering on the parquet Mrs. Baines had polished, to the stairs. Through the drawing-room doorway on the first floor he saw the draped chairs; even the china clock on the mantel was covered like a canary's cage; as he passed it, it chimed the hour, muffled and secret under the duster. On the nursery table he found his supper laid out: a glass of milk and a piece of bread and butter, a sweet biscuit, and a little cold Queen's pudding without the meringue. He had no appetite; he strained his ears for Mrs. Baines's coming, for the sound of voices, but the basement held its secrets; the green baize door shut off that world. He drank the milk and ate the biscuit, but he didn't touch the rest, and presently he could hear the soft precise footfalls of Mrs. Baines on the stairs: she was a good servant, she walked softly; she was a determined woman, she walked precisely.

But she wasn't angry when she came in; she was ingratiating as she opened the night nursery door—"Did you have a good walk, Master Philip?"—pulled down the blinds, laid out his pyjamas, came back to clear his supper. "I'm glad Baines found you. Your mother wouldn't have liked your being out alone." She examined the tray. "Not much appetite, have you, Master Philip? Why don't you try a little of this nice pudding? I'll bring you up some more jam for it."

"No, no, thank you, Mrs. Baines," Philip said.

"You ought to eat more," Mrs. Baines said. She sniffed round the room like a dog. "You didn't take any pots out of the wastepaper basket in the kitchen, did you, Master Philip?"

"No," Philip said.

"Of course you wouldn't. I just wanted to make sure." She patted his shoulder and her fingers flashed to his lapel; she picked off a tiny crumb of pink sugar. "Oh, Master Philip," she said, "that's why you haven't any appetite. You've been buying sweet cakes. That's not what your pocket money's for."

"But I didn't," Philip said. "I didn't."

She tasted the sugar with the tip of her tongue.

"Don't tell lies to me, Master Philip. I won't stand for it any more than your father would."

"I didn't, I didn't," Philip said. "They gave it me. I mean Baines," but she had pounced on the word "they." She had got what she wanted; there was no doubt about that, even when you didn't know what it was she wanted. Philip was angry and miserable and disappointed because he hadn't kept Baines's secret. Baines oughtn't to have trusted him; grown-up people should keep their own secrets, and yet here was Mrs. Baines immediately entrusting him with another.

"Let me tickle your palm and see if you can keep a secret." But he put his hand behind him; he wouldn't be touched. "It's a secret between us, Master Philip, that I know all about them. I suppose she was having tea with him," she speculated.

"Why shouldn't she?" he said, the responsibility for Baines weighing on his spirit, the idea that he had got to keep her secret when he hadn't kept Baines's making him miserable with the unfairness of life. "She was nice."

"She was nice, was she?" Mrs. Baines said in a bitter voice he wasn't used to.

"And she's his niece."

"So that's what he said," Mrs. Baines struck softly back at him like the clock under the duster. She tried to be jocular. "The old scoundrel. Don't you tell him I know, Master Philip." She stood very still between the table and the door, thinking very hard, planning something. "Promise you won't tell. I'll give you that Meccano set, Master Philip. . . ."

He turned his back on her; he wouldn't promise, but he wouldn't tell. He would have nothing to do with their secrets, the responsibilities they were determined to lay on him. He was only anxious to forget. He had received already a larger dose of life than he had bargained for, and he was scared. "A 2A Meccano set, Master Philip." He never opened his Meccano set again, never built anything, never created anything, died, the old dilettante, sixty years later with nothing to show rather than preserve the memory of Mrs. Baines's malicious voice saying good night, her soft determined footfalls on the stairs to the basement, going down, going down.

3

The sun poured in between the curtains and Baines was beating a tattoo on the water-can. "Glory, glory," Baines said. He sat down on the end of the bed and said, "I beg to announce that Mrs. Baines has been called away. Her mother's dying. She won't be back till tomorrow."

"Why did you wake me up so early?" Philip said. He watched Baines with uneasiness; he wasn't going to be drawn in; he'd learnt his lesson. It wasn't right for a man of Baines's age to be so merry. It made a grown person human in the same way that you were human. For if a grown-up could behave so childishly, you were liable to find yourself in their world. It was enough that it came at you in dreams: the witch at the corner, the man with a knife. So "It's very early," he complained, even though he loved Baines, even though he couldn't help being glad that Baines was happy. He was divided by the fear and the attraction of life.

"I want to make this a long day," Baines said. "This is the best time." He pulled the curtains back. "It's a bit misty. The cat's been out all night. There she is, sniffing round the area. They haven't taken in any milk at 59. Emma's shaking out the mats at 63." He said, "This was what I used to think about on the Coast: somebody shaking mats and the cat coming home. I can see it today," Baines said, "just as if I was still in Africa. Most days you don't notice what you've got. It's a good life if you don't weaken." He put a penny on the washstand. "When you've dressed, Phil, run and get a *Mail* from the barrow at the corner. I'll be cooking the sausages."

"Sausages?"

"Sausages," Baines said. "We're going to celebrate today. A fair bust." He celebrated at breakfast, reckless, cracking jokes, unaccountably merry and nervous. It was going to be a long, long day, he kept on coming back to that: for years he had waited for a long day, he had sweated in the damp Coast heat, changed shirts, gone down with fever, lain between the blankets and sweated, all in the hope of this long day, that cat sniffing round the area, a bit of mist, the mats beaten at 63. He propped the *Mail* in front of the coffeepot and read pieces aloud. He said, "Cora Down's been married for the fourth time." He was amused, but it wasn't his idea of a long day. His long day was the Park, watching the riders in the Row, seeing Sir Arthur Stillwater pass beyond the rails ("He dined with us once in Bo; up from Freetown; he was governor there"), lunch at the Corner House for Philip's sake (he'd have preferred himself a glass of stout and some oysters at the York bar), the Zoo, the long bus ride home in the last summer light: the leaves in the Green Park were beginning to turn and the motors nuzzled out of Berkeley Street with the low sun gently glowing on their wind-screens. Baines envied no one, not Cora Down, or Sir Arthur Stillwater, or Lord Sandale, who came out on to the steps of the Army and Navy and then went back again because he hadn't got anything to do and might as well look at another paper. "I said don't let me see you touch that black again." Baines had led a man's life; everyone on top of the bus pricked their ears when he told Philip all about it.

"Would you have shot him?" Philip asked, and Baines put his head back and tilted his dark respectable man-servant's hat to a better angle as the bus swerved round the artillery memorial.

"I wouldn't have thought twice about it. I'd have shot to kill," he boasted, and the bowed figure went by, the steel helmet, the heavy cloak, the downturned rifle and the folded hands.

"Have you got the revolver?"

"Of course I've got it," Baines said. "Don't I need it with all the burglaries there've been?" This was the Baines whom Philip loved: not Baines singing and carefree, but Baines responsible, Baines behind barriers, living his man's life.

All the buses streamed out from Victoria like a convoy of aeroplanes to bring Baines home with honour. "Forty blacks under me," and there waiting near the area steps was the proper conventional reward, love at lighting-up time.

"It's your niece," Philip said, recognizing the white mackintosh, but not the happy sleepy face. She frightened him like an unlucky number; he nearly told Baines what Mrs. Baines had said; but he didn't want to bother, he wanted to leave things alone.

"Why, so it is," Baines said. "I shouldn't wonder if she was going to have a bite of supper with us." But he said they'd play a game, pretend they didn't know her, slip down the area steps, "and here," Baines said, "we are," lay the table, put out the cold sausages, a bottle of beer, a bottle of ginger pop, a flagon of harvest burgundy. "Everyone his own drink," Baines said. "Run upstairs, Phil, and see if there's been a post."

Philip didn't like the empty house at dusk before the lights went on. He hurried. He wanted to be back with Baines. The hall lay there in quiet and shadow prepared to show him something he didn't want to see. Some letters rustled down and someone knocked. "Open in the name of the Republic." The tumbrils rolled, the head bobbed in the bloody basket. Knock, knock, and the postman's footsteps going away. Philip gathered the letters. The slit in the door was like the grating in a jeweller's window. He remembered the policeman he had seen peer through. He had said to his nurse, "What's he doing?" and when she said, "He's seeing if everything's all right," his brain immediately filled with images of all that might be wrong. He ran to the baize door and the stairs. The girl was already there and Baines was kissing her. She leant breathless against the dresser.

"This is Emmy, Phil."

"There's a letter for you, Baines."

"Emmy," Baines said, "it's from her." But he wouldn't open it. "You bet she's coming back."

"We'll have supper, anyway," Emmy said. "She can't harm that."

"You don't know her," Baines said. "Nothing's safe. Damn it," he said, "I was a man once," and he opened the letter.

"Can I start?" Philip asked, but Baines didn't hear; he presented in his stillness and attention an example of the importance grown-up people attached to the written word: you had to write your thanks, not wait and speak them, as if letters couldn't lie. But Philip knew better than that, sprawling his thanks across a page to Aunt Alice who had given him a doll he was too old for. Letters could lie all right, but they made the lie permanent: they lay as evidence against you; they made you meaner than the spoken word.

"She's not coming back till tomorrow night," Baines said. He opened the bottles, he pulled up the chairs, he kissed Emmy again against the dresser.

"You oughtn't to," Emmy said, "with the boy here."

"He's got to learn," Baines said, "like the rest of us," and he helped Philip to three sausages. He only took one himself; he said he wasn't hungry; but when Emmy said she wasn't hungry either he stood over her and made her eat. He was timid and rough with her; he made her drink the harvest burgundy because he said she needed building up; he wouldn't take no for an answer, but when he touched her his hands were light and clumsy too, as if he were afraid to damage something delicate and didn't know how to handle anything so light.

"This is better than milk and biscuits, eh?"

"Yes," Philip said, but he was scared, scared for Baines as much as for himself. He couldn't help wondering at every bite, at every draught of the ginger pop, what Mrs. Baines would say if she ever learnt of this meal; he couldn't imagine it, there was a depth of bitterness and rage in Mrs. Baines you couldn't sound. He said, "She won't be coming back tonight?" but you could tell by the way they immediately understood him that she wasn't really away at all; she was there in the basement with them, driving them to longer drinks and louder talk, biding her time for the right cutting word. Baines wasn't really happy; he was only watching happiness from close to instead of from far away.

"No," he said, "she'll not be back till late tomorrow." He couldn't keep his eyes off happiness; he'd played around as much as other men, he kept on reverting to the Coast as if to excuse himself for his innocence; he wouldn't have been so innocent if he'd lived his life in London, so innocent when it came to tenderness. "If it was you, Emmy," he said, looking at the white dresser, the scrubbed chairs, "this'd be like a home." Already the room was not quite so harsh; there was a little dust in corners, the silver needed a final polish, the morning's paper lay untidily on a chair. "You'd better go to bed, Phil; it's been a long day."

They didn't leave him to find his own way up through the dark shrouded house; they went with him, turning on lights, touching each other's fingers on the switches; floor after floor they drove the night back; they spoke softly among the covered chairs; they watched him undress, they didn't make him wash or clean his teeth, they saw him into bed and lit his night-light and left his door ajar. He could hear their voices on the stairs, friendly like the guests he heard at dinner-parties when they moved down the hall, saying good night. They belonged; wherever they were they made a home. He heard a door open and a clock strike, he heard their voices for a long while, so that he felt they were not far away and he was safe. The voices didn't dwindle, they simply went out, and he could be sure that they were still somewhere not far from him, silent together in one of the many empty rooms, growing sleepy together as he grew sleepy after the long day.

He had just time to sigh faintly with satisfaction, because this too perhaps had been life, before he slept and the inevitable terrors of sleep came round him: a man with a tricolour hat beat at the door on His Majesty's service, a bleeding head lay on the kitchen table in a basket, and the Siberian wolves crept closer. He was bound hand and foot and couldn't move; they leapt round him breathing heavily; he opened his eyes and Mrs. Baines was there, her gray untidy hair in threads over his face, her black hat askew. A loose hairpin fell on pillow and one musty thread brushed his mouth. "Where are they?" she whispered. "Where are they?"

4

Philip watched her in terror. Mrs. Baines was out of breath as if she had been searching all the empty rooms, looking under loose covers.

With her untidy grey hair and her black dress buttoned to her throat, her gloves of black cotton, she was so like the witches of his dreams that he didn't dare to speak. There was a stale smell in her breath.

"She's here," Mrs. Baines said; "you can't deny she's here." Her face was simultaneously marked with cruelty and misery; she wanted to "do things" to people, but she suffered all the time. It would have done her good to scream, but she daren't do that: it would warn them. She came ingratiatingly back to the bed where Philip lay rigid on his back and whispered, "I haven't forgotten the Meccano set. You shall have it tomorrow, Master Philip. We've got secrets together, haven't we? Just tell me where they are."

He couldn't speak. Fear held him as firmly as any nightmare. She said, "Tell Mrs. Baines, Master Philip. You love your Mrs. Baines, don't you?" That was too much; he couldn't speak; but he could move his mouth in terrified denial, wince away from her dusty image.

She whispered, coming closer to him, "Such deceit. I'll tell your father. I'll settle with you myself when I've found them. You'll smart; I'll see you smart." Then immediately she was still, listening. A board had creaked on the floor below, and a moment later, while she stooped listening above his bed, there came the whispers of two people who were happy and sleepy together after a long day. The night-light stood beside the mirror and Mrs. Baines could see bitterly there her own reflection, misery and cruelty wavering in the glass, age and dust and nothing to hope for. She sobbed without tears, a dry, breathless sound; but her cruelty was a kind of pride which kept her going; it was her best quality, she would have been merely pitiable without it. She went out of the door on tiptoe, feeling her way across the landing, going so softly down the stairs that no one behind a shut door could hear her. Then there was complete silence again; Philip could move; he raised his knees; he sat up in bed; he wanted to die. It wasn't fair, the walls were down again between his world and theirs; but this time it was something worse than merriment that the grown people made him share; a passion moved in the house he recognized but could not understand.

It wasn't fair, but he owed Baines everything: the Zoo, the ginger pop, the bus ride home. Even the supper called on his loyalty. But he was frightened; he was touching something he touched in dreams: the bleeding head, the wolves, the knock, knock, knock. Life fell on him with savagery; you couldn't blame him if he never faced it again in sixty years. He got out of bed, carefully from habit put on his bedroom slippers, and tiptoed to the door: it wasn't quite dark on the landing below because the curtains had been taken down for the cleaners and the light from the street came in through the tall windows. Mrs. Baines had her hand on the glass doorknob; she was very carefully turning it; he screamed: "Baines, Baines."

Mrs. Baines turned and saw him cowering in his pyjamas by the banister; he was helpless, more helpless even than Baines, and cruelty grew at the sight of him and drove her up the stairs. The nightmare was on him again and he couldn't move; he hadn't any more courage left for ever; he'd spent it all, had been allowed no time to let it grow, no years of gradual hardening; he couldn't even scream.

But the first cry had brought Baines out of the best spare bedroom and he moved quicker than Mrs. Baines. She hadn't reached the top of the stairs before he'd caught her round the waist. She drove her black cotton gloves at his face and he bit her hand. He hadn't time to think, he fought her savagely like a stranger, but she fought back with knowledgeable hate. She was going to teach them all and it didn't really matter whom she began with; they had all deceived her; but the old image in the glass was by her side, telling her she must be dignified, she wasn't young enough to yield her dignity; she could beat his face, but she mustn't bite; she could push, but she mustn't kick.

Age and dust and nothing to hope for were her handicaps. She went over the banisters in a flurry of black clothes and fell into the hall; she lay before the front door like a sack of coals which should have gone down the area into the basement. Philip saw; Emmy saw; she sat down suddenly in the doorway of the best spare bedroom with her eyes open as if she were too tired to stand any longer. Baines went slowly down into the hall.

It wasn't hard for Philip to escape; they'd forgotten him completely; he went down the back, the servants' stairs, because Mrs. Baines was in the hall; he didn't understand what she was doing lying there; like the startling pictures in a book no one had read to him, the things he didn't understand terrified him. The whole house had been turned over to the grown-up world; he wasn't safe in the night nursery; their passions had flooded it. The only thing he could do was to get away, by the back stair, and up through the area, and never come back. You didn't think of the cold, of the need of food and sleep; for an hour it would seem quite possible to escape from people for ever.

He was wearing pyjamas and bedroom slippers when he came up into the square, but there was no one to see him. It was that hour of the evening in a residential district when everyone is at the theatre or at home. He climbed over the iron railings into the little garden: the plane-trees spread their large pale palms between him and the sky. It might have been an illimitable forest into which he had escaped. He crouched behind a trunk and the wolves retreated; it seemed to him between the little iron seat and the tree-trunk that no one would ever find him again. A kind of embittered happiness and self-pity made him cry; he was lost; there wouldn't be any more secrets to keep; he surrendered responsibility once and for all. Let grown-up people keep to their world and he would keep to his, safe in the small garden between the plane-trees. "In the lost childhood of Judas Christ was betrayed"; you could almost see the small unformed face hardening into the deep dilettante selfishness of age.

Presently the door of 48 opened and Baines looked this way and that; then he signalled with his hand and Emmy came; it was as if they were only just in time for a train, they hadn't a chance of saying good-bye; she went quickly by, like a face at a window swept past the platform, pale and unhappy and not wanting to go. Baines went in again and shut the door; the light was lit in the basement, and a policeman walked round the square, looking into the areas. You could tell how many families were at home by the lights behind the first-floor curtains.

Philip explored the garden: it didn't

take long: a twenty-yard square of bushes and plane-trees, two iron seats and a gravel path, a padlocked gate at either end, a scuffle of old leaves. But he couldn't stay: something stirred in the bushes and two illuminated eyes peered out at him like a Siberian wolf, and he thought how terrible it would be if Mrs. Baines found him there. He'd have no time to climb the railings; she'd seize him from behind.

He left the square at the unfashionable end and was immediately among the fish-and-chip shops, the little stationers selling Bagatelle, among the accommodation addresses and the dingy hotels with open doors. There were few people about because the pubs were open, but a blowsy woman carrying a parcel called out to him across the street and the commissionaire outside a cinema would have stopped him if he hadn't crossed the road. He went deeper: you could go farther and lose yourself more completely here than among the plane-trees. On the fringe of the square he was in danger of being stopped and taken back: it was obvious where he belonged: but as he went deeper he lost the marks of his origin. It was a warm night: any child in those free-living parts might be expected to play truant from bed. He found a kind of camaraderie even among grown-up people; he might have been a neighbour's child as he went quickly by, but they weren't going to tell on him, they'd been young once themselves. He picked up a protective coating of dust from the pavements, of smuts from the trains which passed along the backs in a spray of fire. Once he was caught in a knot of children running away from something or somebody, laughing as they ran; he was whirled with them round a turning and abandoned, with sticky fruit-drop in his hand.

He couldn't have been more lost; but he hadn't the stamina to keep on. At first he feared that someone would stop him; after an hour he hoped that someone would. He couldn't find his way back, and in any case he was afraid of arriving home alone; he was afraid of Mrs. Baines, more afraid than he had ever been. Baines was his friend, but something had happened which gave Mrs. Baines all the power. He began to loiter on purpose to be noticed, but no one noticed him. Families were having a last breather on the doorsteps, the refuse bins had been put out and bits of cabbage stalks soiled his slippers. The air was full of voices, but he was cut off; these people were strangers and would always now be strangers; they were marked by Mrs. Baines and he shied away from them into a deep class-consciousness. He had been afraid of policemen, but now he wanted one to take him home; even Mrs. Baines could do nothing against a policeman. He sidled past a constable who was directing traffic, but he was too busy to pay him any attention. Philip sat down against a wall and cried.

It hadn't occurred to him that that was the easiest way, that all you had to do was to surrender, to show you were beaten and accept kindness. . . . It was lavished on him at once by two women and a pawnbroker. Another policeman appeared, a young man with a sharp incredulous face. He looked as if he noted everything he saw in pocket-books and drew conclusions. A woman offered to see Philip home, but he didn't trust her: she wasn't a match for Mrs. Baines immobile in the hall. He wouldn't give his address; he said he was afraid to go home. He had his way; he got his protection. "I'll take him to the station," the policeman said, and holding him awkwardly by the hand (he wasn't married; he had his career to make) he led him round the corner, up the stone stairs into the little bare overheated room where Justice waited.

5

Justice waited behind a wooden counter

on a high stool; it wore a heavy moustache; it was kindly and had six children ("three of them nippers like yourself"); it wasn't really interested in Philip, but it pretended to be, it wrote the address down and sent a constable to fetch a glass of milk. But the young constable was interested; he had a nose for things.

"Your home's on the telephone, I suppose," Justice said. "We'll ring them up and say you are safe. They'll fetch you very soon. What's your name, sonny?"

"Philip."

"Your other name."

"I haven't got another name." He didn't want to be fetched; he wanted to be taken home by someone who would impress even Mrs. Baines. The constable watched him, watched the way he drank the milk, watched him when he winced away from questions.

"What made you run away? Playing truant, eh?"

"I don't know."

"You oughtn't do it, young fellow. Think how anxious your father and mother will be."

"They are away."

"Well, your nurse."

"I haven't got one."

"Who looks after you, then?" That question went home. Philip saw Mrs. Baines coming up the stairs at him, the heap of black cotton in the hall. He began to cry.

"Now, now, now," the sergeant said. He didn't know what to do; he wished his wife were with him; even a policewoman might have been useful.

"Don't you think it's funny," the constable said, "that there hasn't been an inquiry?"

"They think he's tucked up in bed."

"You are scared, aren't you?" the constable said. "What scared you?"

"I don't know."

"Somebody hurt you?"

"No."

"He's had bad dreams," the sergeant said. "Thought the house was on fire, I expect. I've brought up six of them. Rose is due back. She'll take him home."

"I want to go home with you," Philip said; he tried to smile at the constable, but the deceit was immature and unsuccessful.

"I'd better go," the constable said. "There may be something wrong."

"Nonsense," the sergeant said. "It's a woman's job. Tact is what you need. Here's Rose. Pull up your stockings, Rose. You're a disgrace to the Force. I've got a job of work for you." Rose shambled in: black cotton stockings drooping over her boots, a gawky Girl Guide manner, a hoarse hostile voice. "More tarts, I suppose."

"No, you've got to see this young man home." She looked at him owlishly.

"I won't go with her," Philip said. He began to cry again. "I don't like her."

"More of that womanly charm, Rose," the sergeant said. The telephone rang on his desk. He lifted the receiver. "What? What's that?" he said. "Number 48? You've got a doctor?" He put his hand over the telephone mouth. "No wonder this nipper wasn't reported," he said. "They've been too busy. An accident. Woman slipped on the stairs."

"Serious?" the constable asked. The sergeant mouthed at him; you didn't mention the word death before a child (didn't he know? he had six of them), you made noises in the throat, you grimaced, a complicated shorthand for a word of only five letters anyway.

"You'd better go, after all," he said, "and make a report. The doctor's there."

Rose shambled from the stove; pink apply-dapply cheeks, loose stockings. She stuck her hands behind her. Her large morgue-like mouth was full of blackened teeth. "You told me to take him and now just because something interesting . . . I don't expect justice from a man . . ."

"Who's at the house?" the constable asked.

"The butler."

"You don't think," the constable said, "he saw . . ."

"Trust me," the sergeant said. "I've brought up six. I know 'em through and through. You can't teach me anything about children."

"He seemed scared about something."

"Dreams," the sergeant said.

"What name?"

"Baines."

"This Mr. Baines," the constable said to Philip, "you like him, eh? He's good to you?" They were trying to get something out of him; he was suspicious of the whole roomful of them; he said "yes" without conviction because he was afraid at any moment of more responsibilities, more secrets.

"And Mrs. Baines?"

"Yes."

They consulted together by the desk; Rose was hoarsely aggrieved; she was like a female impersonator, she bore her womanhood with an unnatural emphasis even while she scorned it in her creased stockings and her weather-exposed face. The charcoal shifted in the stove; the room was overheated in the mild late summer evening. A notice on the wall described a body found in the Thames, or rather the body's clothes: wool vest, wool pants, wool shirt with blue stripes, size ten boots, blue serge suit worn at the elbows, fifteen and a half celluloid collar. They couldn't find anything to say about the body, except its measurements, it was just an ordinary body.

"Come along," the constable said. He was interested, he was glad to be going, but he couldn't help being embarrassed by his company, a small boy in pyjamas. His nose smelt something, he didn't know what, but he smarted at the sight of the amusement they caused: the pubs had closed and the streets were full again of men making as long a day of it as they could. He hurried through the less frequented streets, chose the darker pavements, wouldn't loiter, and Philip wanted more and more to loiter, pulling at his hand, dragging with his feet. He dreaded the sight of Mrs. Baines waiting in the hall: he knew now that she was dead. The sergeant's mouthings had conveyed that; but she wasn't buried, she wasn't out of sight; he was going to see a dead person in the hall when the door opened.

The light was on in the basement, and to his relief the constable made for the area steps. Perhaps he wouldn't have to see Mrs. Baines at all. The constable knocked on the door because it was too dark to see the bell, and Baines answered. He stood there in the doorway of the neat bright basement room and you could see the sad complacent plausible sentence he had prepared wither at the sight of Philip; he hadn't expected Philip to return like that in the policeman's company. He had to begin thinking all over again; he wasn't a deceptive man; if it hadn't been for Emmy he would have been quite ready to let the truth lead him where it would.

"Mr. Baines?" the constable asked.

He nodded; he hadn't found the right words; he was daunted by the shrewd knowing face, the sudden appearance of Philip there.

"This little boy from here?"

"Yes," Baines said. Philip could tell that there was a message he was trying to convey, but he shut his mind to it. He loved Baines, but Baines had involved him in secrets, in fears he didn't understand. The glowing morning thought "This is life" had become under Baines's tutelage the repugnant memory "That was life": the musty hair across the mouth, the breathless cruel tortured inquiry "Where are they?," the heap of black cotton tipped into the hall. That was what happened when you loved: you got involved; and Philip extricated himself from life, from love, from Baines with a merciless egotism.

There had been things between them, but he laid them low, as a retreating army cuts the wires, destroys the bridges. In the abandoned country you may leave much that is dear—a morning in the Park—an ice at a corner house, sausages for supper—but more is concerned in the retreat than temporary losses. There are old people who, as the tractors wheel away, implore to be taken, but you can't risk the rearguard for their sake: a whole prolonged retreat from life, from care, from human relationships is involved.

"The doctor's here," Baines said. He nodded at the door, moistened his mouth, kept his eyes on Philip, begging for something like a dog you can't understand. "There's nothing to be done. She slipped on these stone basement stairs. I was in here. I heard her fall." He wouldn't look at the notebook, at the constable's tiny spidery writing which got a terrible lot on one page.

"Did the boy see anything?"

"He can't have done. I thought he was in bed. Hadn't he better go up? It's a shocking thing. Oh," Baines said, losing control, "it's a shocking thing for a child."

"She's through there?" the constable asked.

"I haven't moved her an inch," Baines said.

"He better then—"

"Go up the area and through the hall," Baines said and again he begged dumbly like a dog: one more secret, keep this secret, do this for old Baines, he won't ask another.

"Come along," the constable said. "I'll see you up to bed. You're a gentleman; you must come in the proper way through the front door like the master should. Or will you go along with him, Mr. Baines, while I see the doctor?"

"Yes," Baines said, "I'll go." He came across the room to Philip, begging, begging, all the way with his soft old stupid expression: this is Baines, the old Coaster; what about a palm-oil chop, eh?; a man's life; forty niggers; never used a gun; I tell you I couldn't help loving them: it wasn't what we call love, nothing we could understand. The messages flickered out from the last posts at the border, imploring, beseeching, reminding: this is your old friend Baines; what about an eleven's; a glass of ginger pop won't do you any harm; sausages; a long day. But the wires were cut, the messages just faded out into the enormous vacancy of the neat scrubbed room in which there had never been a place where a man could hide his secrets.

"Come along, Phil, it's bedtime. We'll just go up the steps . . ." Tap, tap, tap, at the telegraph; you may get through, you can't tell, somebody may mend the right wire. "And in at the front door."

"No," Philip said, "no. I won't go. You can't make me go. I'll fight. I won't see her."

The constable turned on them quickly. "What's that? Why won't you go?"

"She's in the hall," Philip said. "I know she's in the hall. And she's dead. I won't see her."

"You moved her then?" the constable said to Baines. "All the way down here? You've been lying, eh? That means you had to tidy up. . . . Were you alone?"

"Emmy," Philip said, "Emmy." He wasn't going to keep any more secrets: he was going to finish once and for all with everything, with Baines and Mrs. Baines and the grown-up life beyond him; it wasn't his business and never, never again, he decided, would he share their confidences and companionship. "It was all Emmy's fault," he protested with a quaver which reminded Baines that after all he was only a child; it had been hopeless to expect help there; he was a child; he didn't understand what it all meant; he couldn't read this shorthand of terror; he'd had a long day and he was tired out. You could see him dropping asleep where he stood against the dresser, dropping back into the comfortable nursery peace. You couldn't blame him. When he woke in the morning, he'd hardly remember a thing.

"Out with it," the constable said, addressing Baines with professional ferocity, "who is she?" just as the old man sixty years later startled his secretary, his only watcher, asking, "Who is she? Who is she?" dropping lower and lower into death, passing on the way perhaps the image of Baines: Baines hopeless, Baines letting his head drop, Baines "coming clean."

Drama

Eugene O'Neill (1887–1953)

The Hairy Ape

A Comedy of Ancient and Modern Life in Eight Scenes

CHARACTERS

ROBERT SMITH, "YANK"
PADDY
LONG
MILDRED DOUGLAS
HER AUNT
SECOND ENGINEER
A GUARD
A SECRETARY OF AN ORGANIZATION

Stokers, Ladies, Gentlemen, etc.

SCENES

Scene I: The firemen's forecastle of an ocean liner an hour after sailing from New York.
Scene II: Section of promenade deck, two days out—morning
Scene III: The stokehole. A few minutes later.
Scene IV: Same as Scene I. Half an hour later.
Scene V: Fifth Avenue, New York. Three weeks later.
Scene VI: An island near the city. The next night.
Scene VII: In the city. About a month later.
Scene VIII: In the city. Twilight of the next day.

SCENE ONE

The firemen's forecastle of a transatlantic liner an hour after sailing from New York for the voyage across. Tiers of narrow, steel bunks, three deep, on all sides. An entrance in rear. Benches on the floor before the bunks. The room is crowded with men, shouting, cursing, laughing, singing—a confused, inchoate uproar swelling into a sort of unity, a meaning—the bewildered, furious, baffled defiance of a beast in a cage. Nearly all the men are drunk. Many bottles are passed from hand to hand. All are dressed in dungaree pants, heavy ugly shoes. Some wear singlets, but the majority are stripped to the waist.

The treatment of this scene, or of any other scene in the play, should by no means be naturalistic. The effect sought after is a cramped space in the bowels of a ship, imprisoned by white steel. The lines of bunks, the uprights supporting them, cross each other like the steel framework of a cage. The ceiling crushes down upon the men's heads. They cannot stand upright. This accentuates the natural stooping posture which shoveling coal and the resultant over-development of back and shoulder muscles have given them. The men themselves should resemble those pictures in which the appearance of Neanderthal Man is guessed at. All are hairy-chested, with long arms of tremendous power, and low, receding brows above their small, fierce, resentful eyes. All the civilized white races are represented, but except for the slight differentiation in color of hair, skin, eyes, all these men are alike.

The curtain rises on a tumult of sound. YANK *is seated in the foreground. He seems broader, fiercer, more truculent, more powerful, more sure of himself than the rest. They respect his superior strength—the grudging respect of fear. Then, too, he represents to them a self-expression, the very last word in what they are, their most highly developed individual.*

VOICES: Gif me trink dere, you!
'Ave a wet!
Salute!
Gesundheit!
Skoal!
Drunk as a lord, God stiffen you!
Here's how!
Luck!
Pass back that bottle, damn you!
Pourin' it down his neck!
Ho, Froggy! Where the devil have you been?
La Touraine.
I hit him smash in yaw, py Gott!
Jenkins—the First—he's a rotten swine—
And the coppers nabbed him —and I run—
I like peer better. It don't pig head gif you.
A slut, I'm sayin'! She robbed me aslape—
To hell with 'em all!
You're a bloody liar!
Say dot again! *{Commotion. Two men about to fight are pulled apart}.*
No scrappin' now!
Tonight—
See who's the best man!
Bloody Dutchman!
Tonight on the for'ard square.
I'll bet on Dutchy.
He packa da wallop, I tella you!
Shut up, Wop!
No fightin', mates. We're all chums, ain't we?
{A voice starts bawling a song}.

"Beer, beer, glorious beer!
Fill yourselves right up to here."

YANK. *{For the first time seeming to take notice of the uproar about him, turns around threateningly—in a tone of contemptuous authority}* Choke off dat noise! Where d'yuh get dat beer stuff? Beer, hell! Beer's for goils—and Dutchmen. Me for somep'n wit a kick to it! Gimmie a drink, one of youse guys. *{Several bottles are eagerly offered. He takes a tremendous gulp at one of them; then, keeping the bottle in his hand, glares belligerently at the owner, who hastens to acquiesce in this robbery by saying}* All righto, Yank. Keep it and have another. [YANK *contemptuously turns his back on the crowd again. For a second there is an embarrassed silence. Then—}*

VOICES: We must be passing the Hook.
She's beginning to roll to it.
Six days in hell—and then Southampton.
Py Yesus, I vish somepody take my first vatch for me!
Gittin' seasick, Square-head?
Drink up and forget it!
What's in your bottle?
Gin.
Dot's nigger trink.

Absinthe? It's doped. You'll go off your chump, Froggy.
Cochon!
Whisky, that's the ticket!
Where's Paddy?
Going asleep.
Sing us that whisky song, Paddy.

{They all turn to an old, wizened Irishman who is dozing, very drunk, on the benches forward. His face is extremely monkey-like with all the sad, patient pathos of that animal in his small eyes}.

Singa da song, Caruso Pat!
He's gettin old. The drink is too much for him.
He's too drunk.

PADDY: [*Blinking about him, starts to his feet resentfully, swaying, holding on to the edge of a bunk*} I'm never too drunk to sing. 'Tis only when I'm dead to the world I'd be wishful to sing at all. *{With a sort of sad contempt}* "Whisky Johnny," ye want? A chanty, ye want? Now that's a queer wish from the ugly like of you, God help you. But no matther. *{He starts to sing in a thin, nasal, doleful tone}:*

Oh, whisky is the life of man!
Whisky! O Johnny! *{They all join in on this}.*
Oh, whisky is the life of man!
Whisky for my Johnny! *{Again chorus}.*

Oh, whisky drove my old man mad!
Whisky! O Johnny!
Oh, whisky drove my old man mad!
Whisky for my Johnny!

YANK: *{Again turning around scornfully}* Aw hell! Nix on dat old sailing ship stuff! All dat bull's dead, see? And you're dead, too, yuh damned old Harp, on'y yuh don't know it. Take it easy, see. Give us a rest. Nix on de loud noise. *{With a cynical grin}* Can't youse see I'm tryin' to t'ink?

ALL: *{Repeating the word after him as one with the same cynical amused mockery}* Think! *{ The chorused word has a brazen metallic quality as if their throats were phonograph horns. It is followed by a general uproar of hard, barking laughter}.*

VOICES: Don't be cracking your head wit ut, Yank.
You get headache, py yingo!
One thing about it—it rhymes with drink!
Ha, ha, ha!
Drink, don't think!
Drink, don't think!
Drink, don't think!

{A whole chorus of voices has taken up this refrain, stamping on the floor, pounding on the benches with fists}.

YANK: *{Taking a gulp from his bottle—good-naturedly}* Aw right. Can de noise. I got yuh de foist time. *{The uproar subsides. A very drunken sentimental tenor begins to sing}:*

"Far away in Canada,
Far across the sea,
There's a lass who fondly waits
Making a home for me—"

YANK: *{Fiercely contemptuous}* Shut up, yuh lousy boob! Where d'yuh get dat tripe? Home? Home, hell! I'll make a home for yuh! I'll knock yuh dead. Home! T'hell wit home! Where d'yuh get dat tripe? Dis is home, see? What d'yuh want wit home? *{Proudly}* I runned away from mine when I was a kid. On'y too glad to beat it, dat was me. Home was lickings for me, dat's all. But yuh can bet your shoit no one ain't never licked me since! Wanter try it, any of youse? Huh! I guess not. *{In a more placated but still contemptuous tone}* Goils waitin' for yuh, huh? Aw, hell! Dat's all tripe. Dey don't wait for no one. Dey'd double-cross yuh for a nickel. Dey're all tarts, get me? Treat 'em rough, dat's me. To hell wit 'em. Tarts, dat's what, de whole bunch of 'em.

LONG: *{Very drunk, jumps on a bench excitedly, gesticulating with a bottle in his hand}* Listen 'ere, Comrades! Yank 'ere is right. 'E say this 'ere stinkin' ship is our 'ome. And 'e says as 'ome is 'ell. And 'e's right! This is 'ell.

We lives in 'ell, Comrades—and right enough we'll die in it. *{Raging}* And who's ter blame, I arsks yer? We ain't. We wasn't born this rotten way. All men is born free and ekal. That's in the bleedin' Bible, maties. But what d'they care for the Bible—them lazy, bloated swine what travels first cabin? Them's the ones. They dragged us down 'til we're on'y wage slaves in the bowels of a bloody ship, sweatin', burnin' up, eatin' coal dust! Hit's them's ter blame—the damned Capitalist clarss! *{There had been a gradual murmur of contemptuous resentment rising among the men until now he is interrupted by a storm of catcalls, hisses, boos, hard laughter}.*

VOICES: Turn it off!
Shut up!
Sit down!
Closa da face!
Tamn fool! *{Etc.}.*

YANK: *{Standing up and glaring at* LONG] Sit down before I knock yuh down! [LONG *makes haste to efface himself.* YANK *goes on contemptuously}* De Bible, huh? De Cap'tlist class, huh? Aw nix on dat Salvation Army-Socialist bull. Git a soapbox! Hire a hall! Come and be saved, huh? Jerk us to Jesus, huh? Aw g'wan! I've listened to lots of guys like you, see. Yuh're all wrong. Wanter know what I t'ink? Yuh ain't no good for no one. Yuh're de bunk. Yuh ain't got no noive, get me? Yuh're yellow, dat's what. Yellow, dat's you. Say! What's dem slobs in de foist cabin got to do with us? We're better men dan dey are, ain't we? Sure! One of us guys could clean up de whole mob wit one mit. Put one of 'em down here for one watch in de stokehole, what'd happen? Dey'd carry him off on a stretcher. Dem boids don't amount to nothin'. Dey're just baggage. Who makes dis old tub run? Ain't it us guys? Well den, we belong, don't we? We belong and dey don't. Dat's all. *{A loud chorus of approval.* YANK *goes on}* As for dis bein' hell—aw, nuts! Yuh lost your noive, dat's what. Dis is a man's job, get me? It belongs. It runs dis tub. No stiffs need apply. But yuh're a stiff, see? Yuh're yellow, dat's you.

VOICES: *{With a great hard pride in them}*
Righto!
A man's job!
Talk is cheap, Long.
He never could hold up his end.
Divil take him!
Yank's right. We make it go.
Py Gott, Yank say right ting!
We don't need no one cryin' over us.
Makin' speeches.
Throw him out!
Yellow!
Chuck him overboard!
I'll break his jaw for him!
{They crowd around LONG *threateningly}.*

YANK. *{Half good-natured again—contemptuously}* Aw, take it easy. Leave him alone. He ain't woith a punch. Drink up. Here's how, whoever owns dis. *{He takes a long swallow from his bottle. All drink with him. In a flash all is hilarious amiability again, back-slapping, loud talk, etc.}.*

PADDY: *{Who has been sitting in a blinking, melancholy daze—suddenly cries out in a voice full of old sorrow}* We belong to this, you're saying? We make the ship to go, you're saying? Yerra then, that Almighty God have pity on us! *{His voice runs into the wail of a keen, he rocks back and forth on his bench. The men stare at him, startled and impressed in spite of themselves}* Oh, to be back in the fine days of my youth, ochone! Oh, there was fine beautiful ships them days—clippers wid tall masts touching the sky—fine strong men in them—men that was sons of the sea as if 'twas the mother that bore them. Oh, the clean skins of them, and the clear eyes, the straight backs and full chests of them! Brave men they was, and bold men surely! We'd be sailing out, bound down round the Horn maybe. We'd be making sail in the dawn, with a fair breeze, singing a chanty song wid no care to it. And astern the land would be sinking low and dying out, but we'd give it no heed but a laugh, and never a look behind. For the day that was, was enough, for we was free men—and I'm thinking 'tis only slaves do be giving heed to the day that's gone or the day to come—until they're old like me. *{With a sort of religious exaltation}* Oh, to be scudding south again wid the power of the Trade Wind driving her on steady through the nights and the days! Full sail on her! Nights and days! Nights when the foam of the wake would be flaming wid fire, when the sky'd be blazing and winking wid stars. Or the full of the moon maybe. Then you'd see her driving through the gray night, her sails stretching aloft all silver and white, not a sound on the deck, the lot of us dreaming dreams, till you'd believe 'twas no real ship at all you was on but a ghost ship like the *Flying Dutchman* they say does be roaming the seas forevermore, widout touching a port. And there was the days, too. A warm sun on the clean decks. Sun warming the blood of you, and wind over the miles of shiny green ocean like strong drink to your lungs. Work—aye, hard work—but who'd mind that at all? Sure, you worked under the sky and 'twas work wid skill and daring to it. And wid the day done, in the dog watch, smoking me pipe at ease, the lookout would be raising land maybe, and we'd see the mountains of South Americy wid the red fire of the setting sun painting their white tops and the clouds floating by them! *{His tone of exaltation ceases. He goes on mournfully}* Yerra, what's the use of talking? 'Tis a dead man's whisper. *{To* YANK *resentfully}* 'Twas them days men belonged to ships, not now. 'Twas them days a ship was part of the sea, and a man was part of a ship, and the sea joined all together and made it one. *{Scornfully}* Is it one wid this you'd be, Yank—black smoke from the funnels smudging the sea, smudging the decks—the bloody engines pounding and throbbing and shaking—wid divil a sight of sun or a breath of clean air—choking our lungs wid coal dust—breaking our backs and hearts in the hell of the stokehole—feeding the bloody furnace—feeding our lives along wid the coal, I'm thinking—caged in by steel from a sight of the sky like bloody apes in the Zoo! *{With a harsh laugh}* Ho-ho, divil mend you! Is it to belong to that you're wishing? Is it a flesh and blood wheel of the engines you'd be?

YANK: *{Who has been listening with a contemptuous sneer, barks out the answer}* Sure ting! Dat's me. What about it?

PADDY: *{As if to himself—with great sorrow}* Me time is past due. That a great wave wid sun in the heart of it may sweep me over the side sometime I'd be dreaming of the days that's gone!

YANK: Aw, yuh crazy Mick! *{He springs to his feet and advances on* PADDY *threateningly—then stops, fighting some queer struggle within himself—lets his hands fall to his side—contemptuously}* Aw, take it easy. Yuh're aw right, at dat. Yuh're bugs, dat's all—nutty as a cuckoo. All dat tripe yuh been pullin'— Aw, dat's all right. On'y it's dead, get me? Yuh don't belong no more, see. Yuh don't get de stuff. Yuh're too old. *{Disgustedly}* But aw say, come up for air onct in a while, can't yuh? See what's happened since yuh croaked. *{He suddenly bursts forth vehemently, growing more and more excited}* Say! Sure I meant it! What de hell— Say, lemme talk! Hey! Hey, you old Harp! Hey, youse guys! Say, listen to me—wait a moment—I gotter talk, see. I belong and he don't. He's dead but I'm livin'. Listen to me! Sure I'm part of de engines! Why de hell not! Dey move, don't they. Dey're speed, ain't dey? Dey smash trou, don't dey? Twenty-five knots a hour! Dat's goin' some! Dat's new stuff! Dat belongs! But him, he's too old. He gets dizzy. Say, listen. All dat crazy tripe about nights and days; all dat crazy tripe about stars and moons; all dat crazy tripe about suns and winds, fresh air and de rest of it—Aw hell, dat's all a dope dream! Hittin' de pipe of de past, dat's what he's doin'. He's old and don't belong no more. But me, I'm young! I'm in de pink! I move wit it! It, get me! I mean de ting dat's de guts of all dis. It ploughs trou all de tripe he's been sayin'. It blows dat up! It knocks dat dead! It slams dat offen de face of de oith! It, get me! De engines and de coal and de smoke and all de rest of it! He can't breathe and swallow coal dust, but I kin, see? Dat's fresh air for me! Dat's food for me! I'm new, get me? Hell in de stokehole? Sure! It takes a man to work in hell. Hell, sure, dat's my fav-rite climate. I eat it up! I git fat on it! It's me makes it hot! It's me makes it roar! It's me makes it move! Sure, on'y for me everything stops. It all goes dead, get me? De noise and smoke and all de engines movin' de woild, dey stop. Dere ain't nothin' no more. Dat's what I'm sayin'. Everyting else dat makes de woild move, somep'n makes it move. It can't move witout somep'n else, see? Den yuh get down to me. I'm at de bottom, get me! Dere ain't nothin' foither. I'm de end! I'm de start! I start somep'n and de woild moves! It—dat's me!—de new dat's moiderin' de old! I'm de ting in coal that makes it boin; I'm steam and oil for de engines; I'm de ting in noise dat makes yuh hear it; I'm smoke and express trains and steamers and factory whistles; I'm de ting in gold dat makes it money! And I'm what makes iron into steel! Steel, dat stands for de whole ting! And I'm steel—steel—steel! I'm de muscles in steel, de punch behind it! *[As he says this he pounds his fist against the steel bunks. All the men, roused to a pitch of frenzied self-glorification by his speech, do likewise. There is a deafening metallic roar, through which* YANK'S *voice can be heard bellowing]* Slaves, hell! We run de whole woiks. All de rich guys dat tink dey're somep'n, dey ain't nothin'! Dey don't belong. But us guys, we're in de move, we're at de bottom, de whole ting is us! [PADDY *from the start of* YANK'S *speech has been taking one gulp after another from his bottle, at first frightenedly, as if he were afraid to listen, then desperately, as if to drown his senses, but finally has achieved complete indifferent, even amused, drunkenness.* YANK *sees his lips moving. He quells the uproar with a shout]* Hey, youse guys, take it easy! Wait a moment! De nutty Harp is sayin' somep'n.

PADDY: *[Is heard now—throws his head back with a mocking burst of laughter]* Ho-ho-ho-ho-ho—

YANK: *[Drawing back his fist, with a snarl]* Aw! Look out who yuh're givin' the bark!

PADDY: *[Begins to sing the "Miller of Dee" with enormous good nature]*.

"I care for nobody, no, not I,
And nobody cares for me."

YANK: *[Good-natured himself in a flash, interrupts* PADDY *with a slap on the bare back like a report]* Dat's de stuff! Now yuh're gettin' wise to somep'n. Care for nobody, dat's de dope! To hell wit 'em all! And nix on nobody else carin'. I kin care for myself, get me! *[Eight bells sound, muffled, vibrating through the steel walls as if some enormous brazen gong were imbedded in the heart of the ship. All the men jump up mechanically, file through the door silently close upon each other's heels in what is very like a prisoners' lockstep.* YANK *slaps* PADDY *on the back]* Our watch, yuh old Harp! *[Mockingly]* Come on down in hell. Eat up de coal dust. Drink in de heat. It's it, see! Act like yuh liked it, yuh better—or croak yuhself.

PADDY: *[With jovial defiance]* To the divil wid it! I'll not report this watch. Let thim log me and be damned. I'm no slave the like of you. I'll be sittin' here at me ease, and drinking, and thinking, and dreaming dreams.

YANK: *{Contemptuously}* Tinkin' and dreamin', what'll that get yuh? What's tinkin' got to do wit it? We move, don't we? Speed, ain't it? Fog, dat's all you stand for. But we drive trou dat, don't we? We split dat up and smash trou—twenty-five knots a hour! *{Turns his back on* PADDY *scornfully}* Aw, yuh make me sick! Yuh don't belong! *{He strides out the door in rear.* PADDY *hums to himself, blinking drowsily}*

CURTAIN

SCENE TWO

Two days out. A section of the promenade deck. MILDRED DOUGLAS *and her aunt are discovered reclining in deck chairs. The former is a girl of twenty, slender, delicate, with a pale, pretty face marred by a self-conscious expression of disdainful superiority. She looks fretful, nervous and discontented, bored by her own anemia. Her aunt is a pompous and proud—and fat—old lady. She is a type even to the point of a double chin and lorgnettes. She is dressed pretentiously, as if afraid her face alone would never indicate her position in life.* MILDRED *is dressed all in white.*

The impression to be conveyed by this scene is one of the beautiful, vivid life of the sea all about—sunshine on the deck in a great flood, the fresh sea wind blowing across it. In the midst of this, these two incongruous, artificial figures, inert and disharmonious, the elder like a gray lump of dough touched up with rouge, the younger looking as if the vitality of her stock had been sapped before she was conceived, so that she is the expression not of its life energy but merely of the artificialities that energy had won for itself in the spending.

MILDRED: *{Looking up with affected dreaminess}* How the black smoke swirls back against the sky! Is it not beautiful?

AUNT: *{Without looking up}* I dislike smoke of any kind.

MILDRED: My great-grandmother smoked a pipe—a clay pipe.

AUNT: *{Ruffling}* Vulgar!

MILDRED: She was too distant a relative to be vulgar. Time mellows pipes.

AUNT: *{Pretending boredom but irritated}* Did the sociology you took up at college teach you that—to play the ghoul on every possible occasion, excavating old bones? Why not let your great-grandmother rest in her grave?

MILDRED: *{Dreamily}* With her pipe beside her—puffing in Paradise.

AUNT: *{With spite}* Yes, you are a natural born ghoul. You are even getting to look like one, my dear.

MILDRED: *{In a passionless tone}* I detest you, Aunt. *{Looking at her critically}* Do you know what you remind me of? Of a cold pork pudding against a background of linoleum tablecloth in the kitchen of a—but the possibilities are wearisome. *{She closes her eyes}.*

AUNT: *{With a bitter laugh}* Merci for your candor. But since I am and must be your chaperon—in appearance, at least—let us patch up some sort of armed truce. For my part you are quite free to indulge any pose of eccentricity that beguiles you—as long as you observe the amenities—

MILDRED: *{Drawling}* The inanities?

AUNT: *{Going on as if she hadn't heard}* After exhausting the morbid thrills of social service work on New York's East Side—how they must have hated you, by the way, the poor that you made so much poorer in their own eyes!—you are now bent on making your slumming international. Well, I hope Whitechapel will provide the needed nerve tonic. Do not ask me to chaperon you there, however. I told your father I would not. I loathe deformity. We will hire an army of detectives and you may investigate everything—they allow you to see.

MILDRED: *{Protesting with a trace of genuine earnestness}* Please do not mock at my attempts to discover how the other half lives. Give me credit for some sort of groping sincerity in that at least. I would like to help them. I would like to be some use in the world. Is it my fault I don't know how? I would like to be sincere, to touch life somewhere. *{With weary bitterness}* But I'm afraid I have neither the vitality nor integrity. All that was burnt out in our stock before I was born. Grandfather's blast furnaces, flaming to the sky, melting steel, making millions—then father keeping those home fires burning, making more millions—and little me at the tail-end of it all. I'm a waste product in the Bessemer process—like the millions. Or rather, I inherit the acquired trait of the by-product, wealth, but none of the energy, none of the strength of the steel that made it. I am sired by gold and damned by it, as they say at the race track—damned in more ways than one. *{She laughs mirthlessly}*.

AUNT: *{Unimpressed—superciliously}* You seem to be going in for sincerity today. It isn't becoming to you, really—except as an obvious pose. Be as artificial as you are, I advise. There's a sort of sincerity in that, you know. And, after all, you must confess you like that better.

MILDRED: *{Again affected and bored}* Yes, I suppose I do. Pardon me for my outburst. When a leopard complains of its spots, it must sound rather grotesque. *{In a mocking tone}* Purr, little leopard. Purr, scratch, tear, kill, gorge yourself and be happy—only stay in the jungle where your spots are camouflage. In a cage they make you conspicuous.

AUNT: I don't know what you are talking about.

MILDRED: It would be rude to talk about anything to you. Let's just talk. *{She looks at her wrist watch}* Well, thank goodness, it's about time for them to come for me. That ought to give me a new thrill, Aunt.

AUNT: *{Affectedly troubled}* You don't mean to say you're really going? The dirt—the heat must be frightful—

MILDRED: Grandfather started as a puddler. I should have inherited an immunity to heat that would make a salamander shiver. It will be fun to put it to the test.

AUNT: But don't you have to have the captain's—or someone's—permission to visit the stokehole?

MILDRED: *{With a triumphant smile}* I have it—both his and the chief engineer's. Oh, they didn't want to at first, in spite of my social service credentials. They didn't seem a bit anxious that I should investigate how the other half lives and works on a ship. So I had to tell them that my father, the president of Nazareth Steel, chairman of the board of directors of this line, had told me it would be all right.

AUNT: He didn't.

MILDRED: How naïve age makes one! But I said he did, Aunt. I even said he had given me a letter to them—which I had lost. And they were afraid to take the chance that I might be lying. *{Excitedly}* So it's ho! for the stokehole. The second engineer is to escort me. *{Looking at her watch again}* It's time. And here he comes, I think. *{The* SECOND ENGINEER *enters. He is a husky, fine-looking man of thirty-five or so. He stops before the two and tips his cap, visibly embarrassed and ill-at-ease}*.

SECOND ENGINEER: Miss Douglas?

MILDRED: Yes. *{Throwing off her rugs and getting to her feet}* Are we ready to start?

SECOND ENGINEER: In just a second, ma'am. I'm waiting for the Fourth. He's coming along.

MILDRED: *{With a scornful smile}* You don't care to shoulder this responsibility alone, is that it?

SECOND ENGINEER: *{Forcing a smile}* Two are better than one. *{Disturbed by* *her eyes, glances out to sea—blurts out}* A fine day we're having.

MILDRED: Is it?

SECOND ENGINEER: A nice warm breeze—

MILDRED: It feels cold to me.

SECOND ENGINEER: But it's hot enough in the sun—

MILDRED: Not hot enough for me. I don't like Nature. I was never athletic.

SECOND ENGINEER: *{Forcing a smile}* Well, you'll find it hot enough where you're going.

MILDRED: Do you mean hell?

SECOND ENGINEER: *{Flabbergasted, decides to laugh}* Ho-ho! No, I mean the stokehole.

MILDRED: My grandfather was a puddler. He played with boiling steel.

SECOND ENGINEER: *{All at sea—uneasily}* Is that so? Hum, you'll excuse me, ma'am, but are you intending to wear that dress?

MILDRED: Why not?

SECOND ENGINEER: You'll likely rub against oil and dirt. It can't be helped.

MILDRED: It doesn't matter. I have lots of white dresses.

SECOND ENGINEER: I have an old coat you might throw over—

MILDRED: I have fifty dresses like this. I will throw this one into the sea when I come back. That ought to wash it clean, don't you think?

SECOND ENGINEER: *{Doggedly}* There's ladders to climb down that are none too clean—and dark alleyways—

MILDRED: I will wear this very dress and none other.

SECOND ENGINEER: No offense meant. It's none of my business. I was only warning you—

MILDRED: Warning? That sounds thrilling.

SECOND ENGINEER: *{Looking down the deck—with a sigh of relief}* There's the Fourth now. He's waiting for us. If you'll come—

MILDRED: Go on. I'll follow you. *{He goes.* MILDRED *turns a mocking smile on her aunt}* An oaf—but a handsome, virile oaf.

AUNT: *{Scornfully}* Poser!

MILDRED: Take care. He said there were dark alleyways—

AUNT: *{In the same tone}* Poser!

MILDRED: *{Biting her lips angrily}* You are right. But would that my millions were not so anemically chaste!

AUNT: Yes, for a fresh pose I have no doubt you would drag the name of Douglas in the gutter!

MILDRED: From which it sprang. Good-by, Aunt. Don't pray too hard that I may fall into the fiery furnace.

AUNT: Poser!

MILDRED: *{Viciously}* Old hag! *{She slaps her aunt insultingly across the face and walks off, laughing gaily}.*

AUNT: *{Screams after her}* I said poser!

CURTAIN

SCENE THREE

The stokehole. In the rear, the dimly outlined bulks of the furnaces and boilers. High overhead one hanging electric bulb sheds just enough light through the murky air laden with coal dust to pile up masses of shadows everywhere. A line of men, stripped to the waist, is before the furnace doors. They bend over, looking neither to right nor left, handling their shovels as if they were part of their bodies, with a strange, awkward, swinging rhythm. They use the shovels to throw open the furnace doors. Then from these fiery round holes in the black a flood of terrific light and heat pours full upon the men who are outlined in silhouette in the crouching, inhuman attitudes of chained gorillas. The men shovel with a rhythmic motion, swinging as on a pivot from the coal which lies in heaps on the floor behind to hurl it into the flaming mouths before them. There is a tumult of noise—the brazen clang of the furnace doors as they are flung open or slammed shut, the grating, teeth-gritting grind of steel against steel, of crunching coal. This clash of sounds stuns one's ears with its rending dissonance. But there is order in it, rhythm, a mechanical regulated recurrence, a tempo. And rising above all, making the air hum with the quiver of liberated energy, the roar of leaping flames in the furnaces, the monotonous throbbing beat of the engines.

As the curtain rises, the furnace doors are shut. The men are taking a breathing spell. One or two are arranging the coal behind them, pulling it into more accessible heaps. The others can be dimly made out leaning on their shovels in relaxed attitudes of exhaustion.

PADDY: *{From somewhere in the line plaintively}* Yerra, will this divil's own watch nivir end? Me back is broke. I'm destroyed entirely.

YANK: *{From the center of the line—with exuberant scorn}* Aw, yuh make me sick! Lie down and croak, why don't yuh? Always beefin', dat's you! Say, dis is a cinch! Dis was made for me! It's my meat, get me! *{A whistle is blown—a thin, shrill note from somewhere overhead in the darkness.* YANK *curses without resentment}* Dere's de damn engineer crackin' de whip. He tinks we're loafin'.

PADDY: *{Vindictively}* God stiffen him!

YANK: *{In an exultant tone of command}* Come on, youse guys! Git into de game! She's gittin' hungry! Pile some grub in her. Trow it into her belly! Come on now, all of youse! Open her up! *{At this last all the men, who have followed his movements of getting into position, throw open their furnace doors with a deafening clang. The fiery light floods over their shoulders as they bend round for the coal. Rivulets of sooty sweat have traced maps on their backs. The enlarged muscles form bunches of high light and shadow}.*

YANK: *{Chanting a count as he shovels without seeming effort}* One—two—tree— *{His voice rising exultantly in the joy of battle}* Dat's de stuff! Let her have it! All togedder now! Sling it into her! Let her ride! Shoot de piece now! Call de toin on her! Drive her into it! Feel her move! Watch her smoke! Speed, dat's her middle name! Give her coal, youse guys! Coal, dat's her booze! Drink it up, baby! Let's see yuh sprint! Dig in and gain a lap! Dere she go-o-es. *{This last in the chanting formula of the gallery gods at the six-day bike race. He slams his furnace door shut. The others do likewise with as much unison as their wearied bodies will permit. The effect is of one fiery eye after another being blotted out with a series of accompanying bangs}.*

PADDY: *{Groaning}* Me back is broke. I'm bate out—bate— *{There is a pause. Then the inexorable whistle sounds again from the dim regions above the electric light. There is a growl of cursing rage from all sides}.*

YANK: *{Shaking his fist upward—contemptuously}* Take it easy dere, you! Who d'yuh tink's runnin' dis game, me or you? When I git ready, we move. Not before! When I git ready, get me!

VOICES: *{Approvingly}*
That's the stuff!
Yank tal him, py golly!
Yank ain't affeerd.
Goot poy, Yank!
Give him hell!
Tell 'im 'e's a bloody swine!
Bloody slave-driver!

YANK: *{Contemptuously}* He ain't got no noive. He's yellow, get me? All de engineers is yellow. Dey got streaks a mile wide. Aw, to hell wit him! Let's move, youse guys. We had a rest. Come on, she needs it! Give her pep! It ain't for him. Him and his whistle, dey don't belong. But we belong, see! We gotter feed de baby! Come on! *{He turns and flings his furnace door open. They all* *follow his lead. At this instant the* SECOND *and* FOURTH ENGINEERS *enter from the darkness on the left with* MILDRED *between them. She starts, turns paler, her pose is crumbling, she shivers with fright in spite of the blazing heat, but forces herself to leave the* ENGINEERS *and take a few steps nearer the men. She is right behind* YANK. *All this happens quickly while the men have their backs turned}.*

YANK: Come on, youse guys! *{He is turning to get coal when the whistle sounds again in a peremptory, irritating note. This drives* YANK *into a sudden fury. While the other men have turned full around and stopped, dumbfounded by the spectacle of* MILDRED *standing there in her white dress,* YANK *does not turn far enough to see her. Besides, his head is thrown back, he blinks upward through the murk trying to find the owner of the whistle, he brandishes his shovel murderously over his head in one hand, pounding on his chest, gorilla-like, with the other, shouting}* Toin off dat whistle! Come down outa dere, yuh yellow, brass-buttoned, Belfast bum, yuh! Come down and I'll knock yer brains out! Yuh lousy, stinkin', yellow mut of a Catholic-moiderin' bastard! Come down and I'll moider yuh! Pullin' dat whistle on me, huh? I'll show yuh! I'll crash yer skull in! I'll drive yet teet' down yer troat! I'll slam yer nose trou de back of yer head! I'll cut yer guts out for a nickel, yuh lousy boob, yuh dirty, crummy, muck-eatin' son of a— *{Suddenly he becomes conscious of all the other men staring at something directly behind his back. He whirls defensively with a snarling, murderous growl, crouching to spring, his lips drawn back over his teeth, his small eyes gleaming ferociously. He sees* MILDRED, *like a white apparition in the full light from the open furnace doors. He glares into her eyes, turned to stone. As for her, during his speech she has listened, paralyzed with horror, terror, her whole personality crushed, beaten in, collapsed, by the terrific impact of this unknown, abysmal brutality, naked and shameless. As she looks at his gorilla face, as his eyes bore into hers, she utters a low, choking cry and shrinks away from him, putting both hands up before her eyes to shut out the sight of his face, to protect her own. This startles* YANK *to a reaction. His mouth falls open, his eyes grow bewildered}.*

MILDRED: *{About to faint—to the* ENGINEERS, *who now have her one by each arm—whimperingly}* Take me away! Oh, the filthy beast! *{She faints. They carry her quickly back, disappearing in the darkness at the left, rear. An iron door clangs shut. Rage and bewildered fury rush back on* YANK. *He feels himself insulted in some unknown fashion in the very heart of his pride. He roars}* God damn yuh! *{And hurls his shovel after them at the door which has just closed. It hits the steel bulkhead with a clang and falls clattering on the steel floor. From overhead the whistle sounds again in a long, angry, insistent command}.*

CURTAIN

SCENE FOUR

The firemen's forecastle. YANK'S *watch has just come off duty and had dinner. Their faces and bodies shine from a soap and water scrubbing but around their eyes, where a hasty dousing does not touch, the coal dust sticks like black make-up, giving them a queer, sinister expression.* YANK *has not washed either face or body. He stands out in contrast to them, a blackened brooding figure. He is seated forward on a bench in the exact attitude of Rodin's "The Thinker." The others, most of them smoking pipes, are staring at* YANK *half-apprehensively, as if fearing an outburst; half-amusedly, as if they saw a joke somewhere that tickled them.*

VOICES: He ain't ate nothin'.
Py golly, a fallar gat to gat grub in him.
Divil a lie.
Yank feeda da fire, no feeda da face.
Ha-ha.
He ain't even washed hisself.
He's forgot.
Hey, Yank, you forgot to wash.

YANK: *{Sullenly}* Forgot nothin'! To hell wit washin'.

VOICES: It'll stick to you.
It'll get under your skin.
Give yer the bleedin' itch, that's wot.
It makes spots on you—like a leopard.
Like a piebald nigger, you mean.
Better wash up, Yank.
You sleep better.
Wash up, Yank.
Wash up! Wash up!

YANK: *{Resentfully}* Aw say, youse guys. Lemme alone. Can't youse see I'm tryin to tink?

ALL: *{Repeating the word after him as one with cynical mockery}* Think! *{The word has a brazen, metallic quality as if their throats were phonograph horns. It is followed by a chorus of hard, barking laughter}*.

YANK: *{Springing to his feet and glaring at them belligerently}* Yes, tink! Tink, dat's what I said! What about it? *{They are silent, puzzled by his sudden resentment at what used to be one of his jokes.* YANK *sits down again in the same attitude of "The Thinker"}*.

VOICES: Leave him alone.
He's got a grouch on.
Why wouldn't he?

PADDY: *{With a wink at the others}* Sure I know what's the matter. 'Tis aisy to see. He's fallen in love, I'm telling you.

ALL: *{Repeating the word after him as one with cynical mockery}* Love! *{The word has a brazen, metallic quality as if their throats were phonograph horns. It is followed by a chorus of hard, barking laughter}*.

YANK: *{With a contemptuous snort}* Love, hell! Hate, dat's what. I've fallen in hate, get me?

PADDY: *{Philosophically}* 'Twould take a wise man to tell one from the other. *{With a bitter, ironical scorn, increasing as he goes on}* But I'm telling you it's love that's in it. Sure what else but love for us poor bastes in the stokehole would be bringing a fine lady, dressed like a white quane, down a mile of ladders and steps to be havin' a look at us? *{A growl of anger goes up from all sides}*.

LONG: *{Jumping on a bench—hecticly}* Hinsultin' us! Hinsultin' us, the bloody cow! And them bloody engineers! What right 'as they got to be exhibitin' us 's if we was bleedin' monkeys in a menagerie? Did we sign for hinsults to our dignity as 'onest workers? Is that in the ship's articles? You kin bloody well bet it ain't! But I knows why they done it. I arsked a deck steward 'o she was and 'e told me. 'Er old man's a bleedin' millionaire, a bloody Capitalist! 'E's got enuf bloody gold to sink this bleedin' ship! 'E makes arf the bloody steel in the world! 'E owns this bloody boat! And you and me, Comrades, we're 'is slaves! And the skipper and mates and engineers, they're 'is slaves! And she's 'is bloody daughter and we're all 'er slaves, too! And she gives 'er orders as 'ow she wants to see the bloody animals below decks and down they takes 'er! *{There is a roar of rage from all sides}*.

YANK: *{Blinking at him bewilderedly}* Say! Wait a moment! Is all dat straight goods?

LONG: Straight as string! The bleedin' steward as waits on 'em, 'e told me about 'er. And what're we goin' ter do, I arsks yer? 'Ave we got ter swaller 'er hinsults like dogs? It ain't in the ship's articles. I tell yer we got a case. We kin go to law—

YANK: *{With abysmal contempt}* Hell! Law!

ALL: *{Repeating the word after him as one with cynical mockery}* Law! *{The word has a brazen metallic quality as if their throats were phonograph horns. It is followed by a chorus of hard, barking laughter}.*

LONG: *{Feeling the ground slipping from under his feet—desperately}* As voters and citizens we kin force the bloody governments—

YANK: *{With abysmal contempt}* Hell! Governments!

ALL: *{Repeating the word after him as one with cynical mockery}* Governments! *{The word has a brazen metallic quality as if their throats were phonograph horns. It is followed by a chorus of hard, barking laughter}.*

LONG: *{Hysterically}* We're free and equal in the sight of God—

YANK: *{With abysmal contempt}* Hell! God!

ALL: *{Repeating the word after him as one with cynical mockery}* God! *{The word has a brazen metallic quality as if their throats were phonograph horns. It is followed by a chorus of hard, barking laughter}.*

YANK: *{Witheringly}* Aw, join de Salvation Army!

ALL: Sit down! Shut up! Damn fool! Sea-lawyer! [LONG *slinks back out of sight}.*

PADDY: *{Continuing the trend of his thoughts as if he had never been interrupted—bitterly}* And there she was standing behind us, and the Second pointing at us like a man you'd hear in a circus would be saying: In this cage is a queerer kind of baboon than ever you'd find in darkest Africy. We roast them in their own sweat—and be damned if you won't hear some of thim saying they like it! *{He glances scornfully at* YANK].

YANK: *{With a bewildered uncertain growl}* Aw!

PADDY: And there was Yank roarin' curses and turning round wid his shovel to brain her—and she looked at him, and him at her—

YANK: *{Slowly}* She was all white. I tought she was a ghost. Sure.

PADDY: *{With heavy, biting sarcasm}* 'Twas love at first sight, divil a doubt of it! If you'd seen the endearin' look on her pale mug when she shriveled away with her hands over her eyes to shut out the sight of him! Sure, 'twas as if she'd seen a great hairy ape escaped from the Zoo!

YANK: *{Stung—with a growl of rage}* Aw!

PADDY: And the loving way Yank heaved his shovel at the skull of her, only she was out the door! *{A grin breaking over his face}* 'Twas touching, I'm telling you! It put the touch of home, swate home in the stokehole. *{There is a roar of laughter from all}.*

YANK: *{Glaring at* PADDY *menacingly}* Aw, choke dat off, see!

PADDY: *{Not heeding him—to the others}* And her grabbin' at the Second's arm for protection. *{With a grotesque imitation of a woman's voice}* Kiss me, Engineer dear, for it's dark down here and me old man's in Wall Street making money! Hug me tight, darlin', for I'm afeerd in the dark and me mother's on deck makin' eyes at the skipper! *{Another roar of laughter}.*

YANK: *{Threateningly}* Say! What yuh tryin' to do, kid me, yuh old Harp?

PADDY: Divil a bit! Ain't I wishin' myself you'd brained her?

YANK: *{Fiercely}* I'll brain her! I'll brain her yet, wait 'n' see! *{Coming over to* PADDY*—slowly}* Say, is dat what she called me—a hairy ape?

PADDY: She looked it at you if she didn't say the word itself.

YANK: *{Grinning horribly}* Hairy ape, huh? Sure! Dat's de way she looked at me, aw right. Hairy ape! So dat's me, huh? *{Bursting into rage—as if she were still in front of him}* Yuh skinny tart! Yuh white-faced bum, yuh! I'll show yuh who's a ape! *{Turning to the others, bewilderment seizing him again}*

Say, youse guys. I was bawlin' him out for pullin' de whistle on us. You heard me. And den I seen youse lookin' at somep'n and I thought he'd sneaked down to come up in back of me, and I hopped round to knock him dead wit de shovel. And dere she was wit de light on her! Christ, yuh coulda pushed me over with a finger! I was scared, get me? Sure! I thought she was a ghost, see? She was all in white like dey wrap around stiffs. You seen her. Kin yuh blame me? She didn't belong, dat's what. And den when I come to and seen it was a real skoit and seen de way she was lookin' at me—like Paddy said—Christ, I was sore, get me? I don't stand for dat stuff from nobody. And I flung de shovel—on'y she'd beat it. *(Furiously)* I wished it'd banged her! I wished it'd knocked her block off!

LONG: And be 'anged for murder or 'lectrocuted? She ain't bleedin' well worth it.

YANK: I don't give a damn what! I'd be square wit her, wouldn't I? Tink I wanter let her put somep'n over on me? Tink I'm goin' to let her git away wit dat stuff? Yuh don't know me! No one ain't never put nothin' over on me and got away wit it, see!—not dat kind of stuff—no guy and no skoit neither! I'll fix her! Maybe she'll come down again—

VOICE: No chance, Yank. You scared her out of a year's growth.

YANK: I scared her? Why de hell should I scare her? Who de hell is she? Ain't she de same as me? Hairy ape, huh? *(With his old confident bravado)* I'll show her I'm better'n her, if she on'y knew it. I belong and she don't, see! I move and she's dead! Twenty-five knots a hour, dat's me! Dat carries her but I make dat. She's on'y baggage. Sure! *(Again bewilderedly)* But, Christ, she was funny lookin'! Did yuh pipe her hands? White and skinny. Yuh could see de bones through 'em. And her mush, dat was dead white, too. And her eyes, dey was like dey'd seen a ghost. Me, dat was! Sure! Hairy ape! Ghost, huh? Look at dat arm! *(He extends his right arm, swelling out the great muscles)* I coulda took her wit dat, wit just my little finger even, and broke her in two. *(Again bewilderedly)* Say, who is dat skoit, huh? What is she? What's she come from? Who made her? Who give her de noive to look at me like dat? Dis ting's got my goat right. I don't get her. She's new to me. What does a skoit like her mean, huh? She don't belong, get me! I can't see her. *(With growing anger)* But one ting I'm wise to, aw right, aw right! Youse all kin bet your shoits I'll get even wit her. I'll show her if she tinks she— She grinds de organ and I'm on de string, huh? I'll fix her! Let her come down again and I'll fling her in de furnace! She'll move den! She won't shiver at nothin', den! Speed, dat'll be her! She'll belong den! *(He grins horribly)*.

PADDY: She'll never come. She's had her belly-full, I'm telling you. She'll be in bed now, I'm thinking, wid ten doctors and nurses feedin' her salts to clean the fear out of her.

YANK: *(Enraged)* Yuh tink I made her sick, too, do yuh? Just lookin' at me, huh? Hairy ape, huh? *(In a frenzy of rage)* I'll fix her! I'll tell her where to git off! She'll git down on her knees and take it back or I'll bust de face offen her! *(Shaking one fist upward and beating on his chest with the other)* I'll find yuh! I'm comin', d'yuh hear? I'll fix yuh, God damn yuh! *(He makes a rush for the door)*.

VOICES: Stop him!
He'll get shot!
He'll murder her!
Trip him up!
Hold him!
He's gone crazy!
Gott, he's strong!
Hold him down!
Look out for a kick!
Pin his arms!

(They have all piled on him and, after a fierce struggle, by sheer weight

of numbers have borne him to the floor just inside the door}.

PADDY: *{Who has remained detached}* Kape him down till he's cooled off. *{Scornfully}* Yerra, Yank, you're a great fool. Is it payin' attention at all you are to the like of that skinny sow widout one drop of rale blood in her?

YANK: *{Frenziedly, from the bottom of the heap}* She done me doit! She done me doit, didn't she? I'll git square wit her! I'll get her some way! Git offen me, youse guys! Lemme up! I'll show her who's a ape!

CURTAIN

SCENE FIVE

Three weeks later. A corner of Fifth Avenue in the Fifties on a fine Sunday morning. A general atmosphere of clean, well-tidied, wide street; a flood of mellow, tempered sunshine; gentle, genteel breezes. In the rear, the show windows of two shops, a jewelry establishment on the corner, a furrier's next to it. Here the adornments of extreme wealth are tantalizingly displayed. The jeweler's window is gaudy with glittering diamonds, emeralds, rubies, pearls, etc., fashioned in ornate tiaras, crowns, necklaces, collars, etc. From each piece hangs an enormous tag from which a dollar sign and numerals in intermittent electric lights wink out the incredible prices. The same in the furrier's. Rich furs of all varieties hang there bathed in a downpour of artificial light. The general effect is of a background of magnificence cheapened and made grotesque by commercialism, a background in tawdry disharmony with the clear light and sunshine on the street itself.

Up the side street YANK *and* LONG *come swaggering.* LONG *is dressed in shore clothes, wears a black Windsor tie, cloth cap.* YANK *is in his dirty dungarees. A fireman's cap with black peak is cocked defiantly on the side of his head. He has not shaved for days and around his fierce, resentful eyes—as around those of* LONG *to a lesser degree—the black smudge of coal dust still sticks like make-up. They hesitate and stand together at the corner, swaggering, looking about them with a forced, defiant contempt.*

LONG: *{Indicating it all with an oratorical gesture}* Well, 'ere we are. Fif' Avenoo. This 'ere's their bleedin' private lane, as yer might say. *{Bitterly}* We're trespassers 'ere. Proletarians keep orf the grass!

YANK: *{Dully}* I don't see no grass, yuh boob. *{Staring at the sidewalk}* Clean, ain't it? Yuh could eat a fried egg offen it. The white wings got some job sweepin' dis up. *{Looking up and down the avenue—surlily}* Where's all de white-collar stiffs yuh said was here—and de skoits—*her* kind?

LONG: In church, blarst 'em! Arskin' Jesus to give 'em more money.

YANK: Choich, huh? I useter go to choich onct—sure—when I was a kid. Me old man and woman, dey made me. Dey never went demselves, dough. Always got too big a head on Sunday mornin', dat was dem. *{With a grin}* Dey was scrappers for fair, bot' of dem. On Satiday nights when dey bot' got a skinful dey could put up a bout oughter been staged at de Garden. When dey got trough dere wasn't a chair or table wit a leg under it. Or else dey bot' jumped on me for somep'n. Dat was where I loined to take punishment. *{With a grin and a swagger}* I'm a chip offen de old block, get me?

LONG: Did yer old man follow the sea?

YANK: Naw. Worked along shore. I runned away when me old lady croaked wit de tremens. I helped at truckin' and in de market. Den I shipped in de stokehole. Sure. Dat belongs. De rest was nothin'. *{Looking around him}* I ain't never seen dis before. De Brooklyn waterfront, dat was where I was dragged up. *{Taking a deep breath}* Dis ain't so bad at dat, huh?

LONG: Not bad? Well, we pays for it wiv our bloody sweat, if yer wants to know!

YANK: *{With sudden angry disgust}* Aw, hell! I don't see no one, see—like her. All dis gives me a pain. It don't belong. Say, ain't dere a back room around dis dump? Let's go shoot a ball. All dis is too clean and quiet and dolled-up, get me! It gives me a pain.

LONG: Wait and yer'll bloody well see—

YANK: I don't wait for no one. I keep on de move. Say, what yuh drag me up here for, anyway? Tryin' to kid me, yuh simp, yuh?

LONG: Yer wants to get back at 'er don't yer? That's what yer been sayin' every bloomin' hour since she hinsulted yer.

YANK: *{Vehemently}* Sure ting I do! Didn't I try to get even wit her in Southampton? Didn't I sneak on de dock and wait for her by de gangplank? I was goin' to spit in her pale mug, see! Sure, right in her pop-eyes! Dat woulda made me even, see? But no chanct. Dere was a whole army of plainclothes bulls around. Dey spotted me and gimme de bum's rush. I never seen her. But I'll git square wit her yet, you watch! *{Furiously}* De lousy tart! She tinks she kin get away wit moider—but not wit me! I'll fix her! I'll tink of a way!

LONG: *{As disgusted as he dares to be}* Ain't that why I brought yer up 'ere —to show yer? Yer been lookin' at this 'ere 'ole affair wrong. Yer been actin' an' talkin' 's if it was all a bleedin' personal matter between yer and that bloody cow. I wants to convince yer she was on'y a representative of 'er clarss. I wants to awaken yer bloody clarss consciousness. Then yer'll see it's 'er clarss yer've got to fight, not 'er alone. There's a 'ole mob of 'em like 'er, Gawd blind 'em!

YANK: *{Spitting on his hands—belligerently}* De more de merrier when I gits started. Bring on de gang!

LONG: Yer'll see 'em in arf a mo', when that church lets out. *{He turns and sees the window display in the two stores for the first time}* Blimey! Look at that, will yer? *{They both walk back and stand looking in the jeweler's.* LONG *flies into a fury}* Just look at this 'ere bloomin' mess! Just look at it. Look at the bleedin' prices on 'em—more'n our 'ole bloody stokehole makes in ten voyages sweatin' in 'ell! And they—'er and 'er bloody clarss—buys 'em for toys to dangle on 'em! One of these 'ere would buy scoff for a starvin' family for a year!

YANK: Aw, cut de sob stuff! T' hell wit de starvin' family! Yuh'll be passin' de hat to me next. *{With naïve admiration}* Say, dem tings is pretty, huh? Bet yuh dey'd hock for a piece of change aw right. *{Then turning away, bored}* But, aw hell, what good are dey? Let her have 'em. Dey don't belong no more'n she does. *{With a gesture of sweeping the jewelers into oblivion}* All dat don't count, get me?

LONG: *{Who has moved to the furrier's—indignantly}* And I s'pose this 'ere don't count neither—skins of poor, 'armless animals slaughtered so as 'er and 'ers can keep their bleedin' noses warm!

YANK: *{Who has been staring at something inside—with queer excitement}* Take a slant at dat! Give it de once-over! Monkey fur—two t'ousand bucks! *{Bewilderedly}* Is dat straight goods—monkey fur? What de hell—?

LONG: *{Bitterly}* It's straight enuf. *{With grim humor}* They wouldn't bloody well pay that for a 'airy ape's skin—no, not for the 'ole livin' ape with all 'is 'ead, and body, and soul thrown in!

YANK: *{Clenching his fists, his face growing pale with rage as if the skin in the window were a personal insult}* Trowin' it up in my face! Christ! I'll fix her!

LONG: *{Excitedly}* Church is out. 'Ere they come, the bleedin' swine. *{After a glance at* YANK'S *lowering face—uneasily}* Easy goes, Comrade. Keep yer bloomin' temper. Remember force defeats itself. It ain't our weapon. We must impress our demands through peaceful means—the votes of the on-marching proletarians of the bloody world!

YANK: *{With abysmal contempt}* Votes, hell! Votes is a joke, see. Votes for women! Let dem do it!

LONG: *{Still more uneasily}* Calm, now. Treat 'em wiv the proper contempt. Observe the bleedin' parasites but 'old yer 'orses.

YANK: *{Angrily}* Git away from me! Yuh're yellow, dat's what. Force, dat's me! De punch, dat's me every time, see! *{The crowd from church enter from the right, sauntering slowly and affectedly, their heads held stiffly up, looking neither to right nor left, talking in toneless, simpering voices. The women are rouged, calcimined, dyed, overdressed to the nth degree. The men are in Prince Alberts, high hats, spats, canes, etc. A procession of gaudy marionettes, yet with something of the relentless horror of Frankensteins in their detached, mechanical unawareness}.*

VOICES: Dear Doctor Caiaphas! He is so sincere!
What was the sermon? I dozed off.
About the radicals, my dear—and the false doctrines that are being preached.
We must organize a hundred per cent American bazaar.
And let everyone contribute one one-hundredth per cent of their income tax.
What an original idea!
We can devote the proceeds to rehabilitating the veil of the temple.
But that has been done so many times.

YANK: *{Glaring from one to the other of them—with an insulting snort of scorn}* Huh! Huh! *{Without seeming to see him, they make wide detours to avoid the spot where he stands in the middle of the sidewalk}.*

LONG: *{Frightenedly}* Keep yer bloomin' mouth shut, I tells yer.

YANK: *{Viciously}* G'wan! Tell it to Sweeney! *{He swaggers away and deliberately lurches into a top-hatted gentleman, then glares at him pugnaciously}* Say, who d'yuh tink yuh're bumpin'? Tink yuh own de oith?

GENTLEMAN: *{Coldly and affectedly}* I beg your pardon. *{He has not looked at* YANK *and passes on without a glance, leaving him bewildered}.*

LONG: *{Rushing up and grabbing* YANK'S *arm}* 'Ere! Come away! This wasn't what I meant. Yer'll 'ave the bloody coppers down on us.

YANK: *{Savagely—giving him a push that sends him sprawling}* G'wan!

LONG: *{Picks himself up—hysterically}* I'll pop orf then. This ain't what I meant. And whatever 'appens, yer can't blame me. *{He slinks off left}.*

YANK: T' hell wit youse! *{He approaches a lady—with a vicious grin and a smirking wink}* Hello, Kiddo. How's every little ting? Got anything on for tonight? I know an old boiler down to de docks we kin crawl into. *{The lady stalks by without a look, without a change of pace.* YANK *turns to others—insultingly}* Holy smokes, what a mug! Go hide yuhself before de horses shy at yuh. Gee, pipe de heine on dat one! Say, youse, yuh look like de stoin of a ferry-boat. Paint and powder! All dolled up to kill! Yuh look like stiffs laid out for de boneyard! Aw, g'wan, de lot of youse! Yuh give me de eye-ache. Yuh don't belong, get me! Look at me, why don't youse dare! I belong, dat's me! *{Pointing to a skyscraper across the street which is in process of construction—with bravado}* See dat building goin' up dere? See de steel work? Steel, dat's me! Youse guys live on it and tink yuh're somep'n. But I'm *in* it, see! I'm de hoistin' engine dat makes it go up! I'm it—de inside and bottom of it! Sure! I'm steel and steam and smoke and de rest of it! It moves—speed—twenty-five stories up—and me at de top and bottom—movin'! Youse simps don't move.

Yuh're on'y dolls I winds up to see 'm spin. Yuh're de garbage, get me—de leavins—de ashes we dump over de side! Now, what 'a' yuh gotta say? *{But as they seem neither to see nor hear him, he flies into a fury}* Bums! Pigs! Tarts! Bitches! *{He turns in a rage on the men, bumping viciously into them but not jarring them the least bit. Rather it is he who recoils after each collision. He keeps growling}* Git off de oith! G'wan, yuh bum! Look where yuh're goin', can't yuh? Git outa here! Fight, why don't yuh? Put up yer mits! Don't be a dog! Fight or I'll knock yuh dead! *{But, without seeming to see him, they all answer with mechanical affected politeness}:* I beg your pardon. *{Then at a cry from one of the women, they all scurry to the furrier's window}.*

THE WOMAN: *{Ecstatically, with a gasp of delight}* Monkey fur! *{The whole crowd of men and women chorus after her in the same tone of affected delight}* Monkey fur!

YANK: *{With a jerk of his head back on his shoulders, as if he had received a punch full in the face—raging}* I see yuh, all in white! I see yuh, yuh white-faced tart, yuh! Hairy ape, huh? I'll hairy ape yuh! *{He bends down and grips at the street curbing as if to pluck it out and hurl it. Foiled in this, snarling with passion, he leaps to the lamp-post on the corner and tries to pull it up for a club. Just at that moment a bus is heard rumbling up. A fat, high-hatted, spatted gentleman runs out from the side street. He calls out plaintively}:* Bus! Bus! Stop there! *{and runs full tilt into the bending, straining* YANK, *who is bowled off his balance}.*

YANK: *{Seeing a fight—with a roar of joy as he springs to his feet}* At last! Bus, huh? I'll bust yuh! *{He lets drive a terrific swing, his fist landing full on the fat gentleman's face. But the gentleman stands unmoved as if nothing had happened}.*

GENTLEMAN: I beg your pardon. *{Then irritably}* You have made me lose my bus. *{He claps his hands and begins to scream}:* Officer! Officer! *{Many police whistles shrill out on the instant and a whole platoon of policemen rush in on* YANK *from all sides. He tries to fight but is clubbed to the pavement and fallen upon. The crowd at the window have not moved or noticed this disturbance. The clanging gong of the patrol wagon approaches with a clamoring din}.*

CURTAIN

SCENE SIX

Night of the following day. A row of cells in the prison on Blackwells Island. The cells extend back diagonally from right front to left rear. They do not stop, but disappear in the dark background as if they ran on, numberless, into infinity. One electric bulb from the low ceiling of the narrow corridor sheds its light through the heavy steel bars of the cell at the extreme front and reveals part of the interior. YANK *can be seen within, crouched on the edge of his cot in the attitude of Rodin's "The Thinker." His face is spotted with black and blue bruises. A blood-stained bandage is wrapped around his head.*

YANK: *{Suddenly starting as if awakening from a dream, reaches out and shakes the bars—aloud to himself, wonderingly}* Steel. Dis is de Zoo, huh? *{A burst of hard, barking laughter comes from the unseen occupants of the cells, runs back down the tier, and abruptly ceases}.*

VOICES: *{Mockingly}* The Zoo?
That's a new name for this coop—a damn good name!
Steel, eh? You said a mouth-

ful. This is the old iron house.
Who is that boob talkin'?
He's the bloke they brung in out of his head. The bulls had beat him up fierce.

YANK: *(Dully)* I musta been dreamin'. I thought I was in a cage at de Zoo—but de apes don't talk, do dey?

VOICES: *(With mocking laughter)*
You're in a cage aw right.
A coop!
A pen!
A sty!
A kennel! *(Hard laughter—a pause)*.
Say, guy! Who are you? No, never mind lying. What are you?
Yes, tell us your sad story. What's your game?
What did they jug yuh for?

YANK: *(Dully)* I was a fireman—stokin' on de liners. *(Then with sudden rage, rattling his cell bars)* I'm a hairy ape, get me? And I'll bust youse all in de jaw if yuh don't lay off kiddin' me.

VOICES: Huh! You're a hard boiled duck, ain't you!
When you spit, it bounces! *(Laughter)*.
Aw, can it. He's a regular guy. Ain't you?
What did he say he was—a ape?

YANK: *(Defiantly)* Sure ting! Ain't dat what youse all are—apes? *(A silence. Then a furious rattling of bars from down the corridor)*.

A VOICE: *(Thick with rage)* I'll show yuh who's a ape, yuh bum!

VOICES: Ssshh! Nix!
Can de noise!
Piano!
You'll have the guard down on us!

YANK: *(Scornfully)* De guard? Yuh mean de keeper, don't yuh? *(Angry exclamations from all the cells)*.

VOICE: *(Placatingly)* Aw, don't pay no attention to him. He's off his nut from the beatin'-up he got. Say, you guy! We're waitin' to hear what they landed you for—or ain't yuh tellin'?

YANK: Sure, I'll tell youse. Sure! Why de hell not? On'y—youse won't get me. Nobody gets me but me, see? I started to tell de Judge and all he says was: "Toity days to tink it over." Tink it over! Christ, dat's all I been doin' for weeks! *(After a pause)* I was tryin' to git even wit someone, see?—someone dat done me doit.

VOICES: *(Cynically)* De old stuff, I bet. Your goil, huh?
Give yuh the double-cross, huh?
That's them every time!
Did yuh beat up de odder guy?

YANK: *(Disgustedly)* Aw, yuh're all wrong! Sure dere was a skoit in it—but not what youse mean, not dat old tripe. Dis was a new kind of skoit. She was dolled up all in white—in de stokehole. I tought she was a ghost. Sure. *(A pause)*.

VOICES: *(Whispering)* Gee, he's still nutty.
Let him rave. It's fun listen-in'.

YANK: *(Unheeding—groping in his thoughts)* Her hands—dey was skinny and white like dey wasn't real but painted on somep'n. Dere was a million miles from me to her—twenty-five knots a hour. She was like some dead ting de cat brung in. Sure, dat's what. She didn't belong. She belonged in de window of a toy store, or on de top of a garbage can, see! Sure! *(He breaks out angrily)* But would yuh believe it, she had de noive to do me doit. She lamped me like she was seein' somep'n broke loose from de menagerie. Christ, yuh'd oughter seen her eyes! *(He rattles the bars of his cell furiously)* But I'll get back at her yet, you watch! And if I can't find her I'll take it out on de gang she runs wit. I'm wise to where dey hangs out now. I'll show her who belongs! I'll show her who's on de move and who ain't. You watch my smoke!

VOICES: *(Serious and joking)* Dat's

de talkin'!
Take her for all she's got!
What was this dame, anyway? Who was she, eh?

YANK: I dunno. First cabin stiff. Her old man's a millionaire, dey says—name of Douglas.

VOICES: Douglas? That's the president of the Steel Trust, I bet.
Sure. I seen his mug in de papers.
He's filthy with dough.

VOICE: Hey, feller, take a tip from me. If you want to get back at that dame, you better join the Wobblies. You'll get some action then.

YANK: Wobblies? What de hell's dat?

VOICE: Ain't you ever heard of the I. W .W.?

YANK: Naw. What is it?

VOICE: A gang of blokes—a tough gang. I been readin' about 'em today in the paper. The guard give me the *Sunday Times.* There's a long spiel about 'em. It's from a speech made in the Senate by a guy named Senator Queen. *{He is in the cell next to* YANK'S. *There is a rustling of paper}* Wait'll I see if I got light enough and I'll read you. Listen. *{He reads}:* "There is a menace existing in this country today which threatens the vitals of our fair Republic—as foul a menace against the very lifeblood of the American Eagle as was the foul conspiracy of Catiline against the eagles of ancient Rome!"

VOICE: *{Disgustedly}* Aw, hell! Tell him to salt de tail of dat eagle!

VOICE: *{Reading}:* "I refer to that devil's brew of rascals, jailbirds, murderers and cutthroats who libel all honest working men by calling themselves the Industrial Workers of the World; but in the light of their nefarious plots, I call them the Industrious *Wreckers* of the World!"

YANK: *{With vengeful satisfaction}* Wreckers, dat's de right dope! Dat belongs! Me for dem!

VOICE: Ssshh! *{Reading}:* "This fiendish organization is a foul ulcer on the fair body of our Democracy—"

VOICE: Democracy, hell! Give him the boid, fellers—the raspberry! *{They do}.*

VOICE: *Ssshh! {Reading}:* "Like Cato I say to this Senate, the I. W. W. must be destroyed! For they represent an ever-present dagger pointed at the heart of the greatest nation the world has ever known, where all men are born free and equal, with equal opportunities to all, where the Founding Fathers have guaranteed to each one happiness, where Truth, Honor, Liberty, Justice, and the Brotherhood of Man are a religion absorbed with one's mother's milk, taught at our father's knee, sealed, signed, and stamped upon in the glorious Constitution of these United States!" *{A perfect storm of hisses, catcalls, boos, and hard laughter}.*

VOICES: *{Scornfully}* Hurrah for de Fort' of July!
Pass de hat!
Liberty!
Justice!
Honor!
Opportunity!
Brotherhood!

ALL: *{With abysmal scorn}* Aw, hell!

VOICE: Give that Queen Senator guy the bark! All togedder now—one—two—tree— *{A terrific chorus of barking and yapping}.*

GUARD: *{From a distance}* Quiet there, youse—or I'll git the hose. *{The noise subsides}.*

YANK: *{With growling rage}* I'd like to catch dat senator guy alone for a second. I'd loin him some trute!

VOICE: Ssshh! Here's where he gits down to cases on the Wobblies. *{Reads}:* "They plot with fire in one hand and dynamite in the other. They stop not before murder to gain their ends, nor at the outraging of defenseless womanhood. They would tear down society, put the lowest scum in the seats of the mighty, turn Almighty God's revealed plan for the world topsy-turvy, and make of our sweet and lovely civilization a shambles, a desolation where man, God's masterpiece, would soon degenerate back to the ape!"

VOICE: *{To* YANK*}* Hey, you guy. There's your ape stuff again.

YANK: *{With a growl of fury}* I got him. So dey blow up tings, do dey? Dey turn tings round, do dey? Hey, lend me dat paper, will yuh?

VOICE: Sure. Give it to him. On'y keep it to yourself, see. We don't wanter listen to no more of that slop.

VOICE: Here you are. Hide it under your mattress.

YANK: *{Reaching out}* Tanks. I can't read much but I kin manage. *{He sits, the paper in the hand at his side, in the attitude of Rodin's "The Thinker." A pause. Several snores from down the corridor. Suddenly* YANK *jumps to his feet with a furious groan as if some appalling thought had crashed on him—bewilderedly}* Sure—her old man—president of de Steel Trust—makes half de steel in de world—steel—where I tought I belonged—drivin' trou—movin'—in dat—to make *her*—and cage me in for her to spit on! Christ! *{He shakes the bars of his cell door till the whole tier trembles. Irritated, protesting exclamations from those awakened or trying to get to sleep}* He made dis—dis cage! Steel! *It* don't belong, dat's what! Cages, cells, locks, bolts, bars—dat's what it means!—holdin' me down wit him at de top! But I'll drive trou! Fire, dat melts it! I'll be fire—under de heap—fire dat never goes out—hot as hell—breakin' out in de night—*{While he has been saying this last he has shaken his cell door to a clanging accompaniment. As he comes to the "breakin' out" he seizes one bar with both hands and, putting his two feet up against the others so that his position is parallel to the floor like a monkey's, he gives a great wrench backwards. The bar bends like a licorice stick under his tremendous strength. Just at this moment the* PRISON GUARD *rushes in, dragging a hose behind him}*.

GUARD: *{Angrily}* I'll loin youse bums to wake me up! *{Sees* YANK*}* Hello, it's you huh? Got the D. Ts., hey? Well, I'll cure 'em. I'll drown your snakes for yuh! *{Noticing the bar}* Hell, look at dat bar bended! On'y a bug is strong enough for dat!

YANK: *{Glaring at him}* Or a hairy ape, yuh big yellow bum! Look out! Here I come! *{He grabs another bar}*.

GUARD: *{Scared now—yelling off left}* Toin de hose on, Ben!—full pressure! And call de others—and a strait-jacket! *{The curtain is falling. As it hides* YANK *from view, there is a splattering smash as the stream of water hits the steel of* YANK'S *cell}*.

CURTAIN

SCENE SEVEN

Nearly a month later. An I. W. W. local near the waterfront, showing the interior of a front room on the ground floor, and the street outside. Moonlight on the narrow street, buildings massed in black shadow. The interior of the room, which is general assembly room, office, and reading room, resembles some dingy settlement boys' club. A desk and high stool are in one corner. A table with papers, stacks of pamphlets, chairs about it, is at center. The whole is decidedly cheap, banal, commonplace and unmysterious as a room could well be. The secretary is perched on the stool making entries in a large ledger. An eye shade casts his face into shadows. Eight or ten men, longshoremen, iron workers, and the like, are grouped about the table. Two are playing checkers. One is writing a letter. Most of them are smoking pipes. A big signboard is on the wall at the rear, "Industrial Workers of the World—Local No. 57.

YANK: *{Comes down the street outside. He is dressed as in Scene Five. He moves cautiously, mysteriously. He comes to a point opposite the door; tiptoes softly up to it, listens, is impressed by the silence within, knocks carefully, as if he were guessing at the password to some secret rite. Listens. No answer. Knocks again a bit louder. No answer. Knocks impatiently, much louder}.*

SECRETARY: *{Turning around on his stool}* What the hell is that—someone knocking? *{Shouts}:* Come in, why don't you? *{All the men in the room look up.* YANK *opens the door slowly, gingerly, as if afraid of an ambush. He looks around for secret doors, mystery, is taken aback by the commonplaceness of the room and the men in it, thinks he may have gotten in the wrong place, then sees the signboard on the wall and is reassured}.*

YANK: *{Blurts out}* Hello.

MEN: *{Reservedly}* Hello.

YANK: *{More easily}* I thought I'd bumped into de wrong dump.

SECRETARY: *{Scrutinizing him carefully}* Maybe you have. Are you a member?

YANK: Naw, not yet. Dat's what I come for—to join.

SECRETARY: That's easy. What's your job—longshore?

YANK: Naw, Fireman—stoker on de liners.

SECRETARY: *{With satisfaction}* Welcome to our city. Glad to know you people are waking up at last. We haven't got many members in your line.

YANKS Naw. Dey're all dead to de woild.

SECRETARY: Well, you can help to wake 'em. What's your name? I'll make out your card.

YANK: *{Confused}* Name? Lemme tink.

SECRETARY: *{Sharply}* Don't you know your own name?

YANK: Sure; but I been just Yank for so long—Bob, dat's it—Bob Smith.

SECRETARY: *{Writing}* Robert Smith. *{Fills out the rest of card}* Here you are. Cost you half a dollar.

YANK: Is dat all—four bits? Dat's easy. *{Gives the Secretary the money}.*

SECRETARY: *{Throwing it in drawer}* Thanks. Well, make yourself at home. No introduction needed. There's literature on the table. Take some of those pamphlets with you to distribute aboard ship. They may bring results. Sow the seed, only go about it right. Don't get caught and fired. We got plenty out of work. What we need is men who can hold their jobs—and work for us at the same time.

YANK: Sure. *{But he still stands, embarrassed and uneasy}.*

SECRETARY: *{Looking at him—curiously}* What did you knock for? Think we had a coon in uniform to open doors?

YANK: Naw. I tought it was locked—and dat yuh'd wanter give me the once-over trou a peep-hole or somep'n to see if I was right.

SECRETARY: *{Alert and suspicious but with an easy laugh}* Think we were running a crap game? That door is never locked. What put that in your nut?

YANK: *{With a knowing grin, convinced that this is all camouflage, a part of the secrecy}* Dis burg is full of bulls, ain't it?

SECRETARY: *{Sharply}* What have the cops got to do with us? We're breaking no laws.

YANK: *{With a knowing wink}* Sure. Youse wouldn't for woilds. Sure. I'm wise to dat.

SECRETARY: You seem to be wise to a lot of stuff none of us knows about.

YANK: *{With another wink}* Aw, dat's aw right, see. *{Then made a bit resentful by the suspicious glances from all sides}* Aw, can it! Youse needn't put me trou de toid degree. Can't youse see I belong? Sure! I'm reg'lar. I'll stick, get me? I'll shoot de woiks for youse. Dat's why I wanted to join in.

SECRETARY: *{Breezily, feeling him out}* That's the right spirit. Only are you sure you understand what you've joined? It's all plain and above board; still, some guys get a wrong slant on us. *{Sharply}* What's your notion of the purpose of the I. W. W.?

YANK: Aw, I know all about it.

SECRETARY: *{Sarcastically}* Well, give us some of your valuable information.

YANK: *{Cunningly}* I know enough not to speak outa my toin. *{Then resentfully again}* Aw, say! I'm reg'lar. I'm wise to de game. I know yuh got to watch your step wit a stranger. For all youse know, I might be a plain-clothes dick, or somep'n, dat's what you're tinkin', huh? Aw, forget it! I belong, see? Ask any guy down to de docks if I don't.

SECRETARY: Who said you didn't?

YANK: After I'm 'nitiated, I'll show yuh.

SECRETARY: *{Astounded}* Initiated? There's no initiation.

YANK: *{Disappointed}* Ain't there no password—no grip nor nothin'?

SECRETARY: What'd you think this is—the Elks—or the Black Hand?

YANK: De Elks, hell! De Black Hand, dey're a lot of yellow back-stickin' Ginees. Naw. Dis is a man's gang, ain't it?

SECRETARY: You said it! That's why we stand on our two feet in the open. We got no secrets.

YANK: *{Surprised but admiringly}* Yuh mean to say yuh always run wide open—like dis?

SECRETARY: Exactly.

YANK: Den yuh sure got your noive wit youse!

SECRETARY: *{Sharply}* Just what was it made you want to join us? Come out with that straight.

YANK: Yuh call me? Well, I got noive, too! Here's my hand. Yuh wanter blow tings up, don't yuh? Well, dat's me! I belong!

SECRETARY: *{With pretended carelessness}* You mean change the unequal conditions of society by legitimate direct action—or with dynamite?

YANK: Dynamite! Blow it offen de oith—steel—all de cages—all de factories, steamers, buildings, jails—de Steel Trust and all dat makes it go.

SECRETARY: So—that's your idea, eh? And did you have any special job in that line you wanted to propose to us? *{He makes a sign to the men, who get up cautiously one by one and group behind* YANK].

YANK: *{Boldly}* Sure, I'll come out wit it. I'll show youse I'm one of de gang. Dere's dat millionaire guy, Douglas—

SECRETARY: President of the Steel Trust, you mean? Do you want to assassinate him?

YANK: Naw, dat don't get yuh nothin'. I mean blow up de factory, de woiks, where he makes de steel. Dat's what I'm after—to blow up de steel, knock all de steel in de woild up to de moon. Dat'll fix tings! *{Eagerly, with a touch of bravado}* I'll do it by me lonesome! I'll show yuh! Tell me where his woiks is, how to git there, all de dope. Gimme de stuff, de old butter—and watch me do de rest! Watch de smoke and see it move! I don't give a damn if dey nab me—long as it's done! I'll soive life for it—and give 'em de laugh! *{Half to himself}* And I'll write her a letter and tell her de hairy ape done it. Dat'll square tings.

SECRETARY: *{Stepping away from* YANK] Very interesting. *{He gives a signal. The men, huskies all, throw themselves on* YANK *and before he knows it they have his legs and arms pinioned. But he is too flabbergasted to make a struggle, anyway. They feel him over for weapons}.*

MAN: No gat, no knife. Shall we give him what's what and put the boots to him?

SECRETARY: No. He isn't worth the trouble we'd get into. He's too stupid. *{He comes closer and laughs mockingly in* YANK'S *face}* Ho-ho! By God, this is the biggest joke they've put up on us yet. Hey, you Joke! Who sent you—

Burns or Pinkerton? No, by God, you're such a bonehead I'll bet you're in the Secret Service! Well, you dirty spy, you rotten agent provocator, you can go back and tell whatever skunk is paying you blood-money for betraying your brothers that he's wasting his coin. You couldn't catch a cold. And tell him that all he'll ever get on us, or ever has got, is just his own sneaking plots that he's framed up to put us in jail. We are what our manifesto says we are, neither more nor less—and we'll give him a copy of that any time he calls. And as for you— *{He glares scornfully at* YANK, *who is sunk in an oblivious stupor}* Oh, hell, what's the use of talking? You're a brainless ape.

YANK: *{Aroused by the word to fierce but futile struggle}* What's dat, yuh Sheeny bum, yuh!

SECRETARY: Throw him out boys. *{In spite of his struggles, this is done with gusto and éclat. Propelled by several parting kicks,* YANK *lands sprawling in the middle of the narrow cobbled street. With a growl he starts to get up and storm the closed door, but stops bewildered by the confusion in his brain, pathetically impotent. He sits there, brooding, in as near to the attitude of Rodin's "Thinker" as he can get in his position}.*

YANK: *{Bitterly}* So dem boids don't tink I belong, neider. Aw, to hell wit 'em! Dey're in de wrong pew—de same old bull—soap-boxes and Salvation Army—no guts! Cut out an hour offen de job a day and make me happy! Gimmie a dollar more a day and make me happy! Tree square a day, and cauliflowers in de front yard—ekal rights—a woman and kids—a lousy vote—and I'm all fixed for Jesus, huh? Aw, hell! What does dat get yuh? Dis ting's in your inside, but it ain't your belly. Feedin' your face—sinkers and coffee—dat don't touch it. It's way down—at de bottom. Yuh can't grab it, and yuh can't stop it. It moves, and everything moves. It stops and de whole woild stops. Dat's me now—I don't tick, see?—I'm a busted Ingersoll, dat's what. Steel was me, and I owned de woild. Now I ain't steel, and de woild owns me. Aw, hell! I can't see—it's all dark, get me? It's all wrong! *{He turns a bitter mocking face up like an ape gibbering at the moon}* Say, youse up dere, Man in de Moon, yuh look so wise, gimme de answer, huh? Slip me de inside dope, de information right from de stable—where do I get off at, huh?

A POLICEMAN: *{Who has come up the street in time to hear this last—with grim humor}.* You'll get off at the station, you boob, if you don't get up out of that and keep movin'.

YANK: *{Looking up at him—with a hard, bitter laugh}* Sure! Lock me up! Put me in a cage Dat's de on'y answer yuh know. G'wan, lock me up!

POLICEMAN: What you been doin'?

YANK: Enuf to gimme life for! I was born, see? Sure, dat's de charge. Write it in de blotter. I was born, get me!

POLICEMAN: *{Jocosely}* God pity your old woman! *{Then matter-of-fact}* But I've no time for kidding. You're soused. I'd run you in but it's too long a walk to the station. Come on now, get up, or I'll fan your ears with this club. Beat it now! *{He hauls* YANK *to his feet}.*

YANK: *{In a vague mocking tone}* Say, where do I go from here?

POLICEMAN: *{Giving him a push—with a grin, indifferently}* Go to hell.

CURTAIN

SCENE EIGHT

Twilight of the next day. The monkey house at the Zoo. One spot of clear gray light falls on the front of one cage so that the interior can be seen. The other cages are vague, shrouded in shadow from which chatterings pitched in a conversational tone can be heard. On the one cage a sign from which the word "gorilla" stands out.

The gigantic animal himself is seen squatting on his haunches on a bench in much the same attitude as Rodin's "Thinker." YANK *enters from the left. Immediately a chorus of angry chattering and screeching breaks out. The gorilla turns his eyes but makes no sound or move.*

YANK: *{With a hard, bitter laugh}* Welcome to your city, huh? Hail, hail, de gang's all here! *{At the sound of his voice the chattering dies away into an attentive silence.* YANK *walks up to the gorilla's cage and, leaning over the railing, stares in at its occupant, who stares back at him, silent and motionless. There is a pause of dead stillness. Then* YANK *begins to talk in a friendly confidential tone, half-mockingly, but with a deep undercurrent of sympathy}* Say, yuh're some hard-lookin' guy, ain't yuh? I seen lots of tough nuts dat de gang called gorillas, but yuh're de foist real one I ever seen. Some chest yuh got, and shoulders, and dem arms and mits! I bet yuh got a punch in eider fist dat'd knock 'em all silly! *{This with genuine admiration. The gorilla, as if he understood, stands upright, swelling out his chest and pounding on it with his fist.* YANK *grins sympathetically}* Sure, I get yuh. Yuh challenge de whole woild, huh? Yuh got what I was sayin' even if yuh muffed de woids. *{Then bitterness creeping in}* And why wouldn't yuh get me? Ain't we both members of de same club—de Hairy Apes? *{They stare at each other—a pause—then* YANK *goes on slowly and bitterly}* So yuh're what she seen when she looked at me, de white-faced tart! I was you to her, get me? On'y outa de cage—broke out —free to moider her, see? Sure! Dat's what she thought. She wasn't wise dat I was in a cage, too—worser'n yours— sure—a damn sight—'cause you got some chanct to bust loose—but me— *{He grows confused}* Aw, hell! It's all wrong, ain't it? *{A pause}* I s'pose yuh wanter know what I'm doin' here, huh? I been warmin' a bench down to de Battery—ever since last night. Sure. I seen de sun come up. Dat was pretty, too—all red and pink and green. I was lookin' at de skyscrapers—steel—and all de ships comin' in, sailin' out, all over de oith—and dey was steel, too. De sun was warm, dey wasn't no clouds, and dere was a breeze blowin'. Sure, it was great stuff. I got it aw right—what Paddy said about dat bein' de right dope —on'y I couldn't get *in* it, see? I couldn't belong in dat. It was over my head. And I kept tinkin'—and den I beat it up here to see what youse was like. And I waited till dey was all gone to git yuh alone. Say, how d'yuh feel sittin' in dat pen all de time, havin' to stand for 'em comin' and starin' at yuh —de white-faced, skinny tarts and de boobs what marry 'em—makin' fun of yuh, laughin' at yuh, gittin' scared of yuh—damn 'em! *{He pounds on the rail with his fist. The gorilla rattles the bars of his cage and snarls. All the other monkeys set up an angry chattering in the darkness.* YANK *goes on excitedly}* Sure! Dat's de way it hits me, too. On'y yuh're lucky, see? Yuh don't belong wit 'em and yuh know it. But me, I belong wit 'em—but I don't, see? Dey don't belong wit me, dat's what. Get me? Tinkin' is hard— *{He passes one hand across his forehead with a painful gesture. The gorilla growls impatiently.* YANK *goes on gropingly}* It's dis way, what I'm drivin' at. Youse can sit and dope dream in de past, green woods, de jungle and de rest of it. Den yuh belong and dey don't. Den yuh kin laugh at 'em, see? Yuh're de champ of de woild. But me— I ain't got no past to tink in, nor nothin' dat's comin', on'y what's now—and dat don't belong. Sure, you're de best off! Yuh can't tink, can yuh? Yuh can't talk neider. But I kin make a bluff at talkin' and tinkin'—a'most git away wit it— a'most!—and dat's where de joker comes in. *{He laughs}* I ain't on oith and I ain't in heaven, get me? I'm in de middle tryin' to separate 'em, takin' all de woist punches from bot' of 'em. Maybe dat's what dey call hell, huh? But you, yuh're at de bottom. You belong! Sure! Yuh're de on'y one in de woild dat does, yuh lucky stiff! *[The gorilla growls proudly]* And dat's why dey gotter put yuh in a cage, see? *[The gorilla roars angrily]* Sure! Yuh get me. It beats it when you try to tink it or talk it—it's way down—deep—behind—you 'n' me we feel it. Sure! Bot' members of dis club! *[He laughs—then in a savage tone]* What de hell! 'T' hell wit it! A little action, dat's our meat! Dat belongs! Knock 'em down and keep bustin' 'em till dey croaks yuh wit a gat—wit steel! Sure! Are yuh game? Dey've looked at youse, ain't dey—in a cage? Wanter git even? Wanter wind up like a sport 'stead of croakin' slow in dere? *[The gorilla roars an emphatic affirmative.* YANK *goes on with a sort of furious exaltation]* Sure! Yuh're reg'lar! Yuh'll stick to de finish! Me 'n' you, huh?—bot' members of this club! We'll put up one last star bout dat'll knock 'em offen deir seats! Dey'll have to make de cages stronger after we're trou! *[The gorilla is straining at his bars, growling, hopping from one foot to the other.* YANK *takes a jimmy from under his coat and forces the lock on the cage door. He throws this open]* Pardon from de governor! Step out and shake hands. I'll take yuh for a walk down Fif' Avenoo. We'll knock 'em offen de oith and croak wit de band playin'. Come on, Brother. *[The gorilla scrambles gingerly out of his cage. Goes to* YANK *and stands looking at him.* YANK *keeps his mocking tone—holds out his hand]* Shake—de secret grip of our order. *[Something, the tone of mockery, perhaps, suddenly enrages the animal. With a spring he wraps his huge arms around* YANK *in a murderous hug. There is a cracking snap of crushed ribs—a gasping cry, still mocking, from* YANK] Hey, I didn't say kiss me! *[The gorilla lets the crushed body slip to the floor; stands over it uncertainly, considering; then picks it up, throws it in the cage, shuts the door, and shuffles off menacingly into the darkness at left. A great uproar of frightened chattering and whimpering comes from the other cages. Then* YANK *moves, groaning, opening his eyes, and there is silence. He mutters painfully]* Say—dey oughter match him—wit Zybszko. He got me, aw right. I'm trou. Even him didn't tink I belonged. *[Then, with sudden passionate despair]* Christ, where do I get off at? Where do I fit in? *[Checking himself as suddenly]* Aw, what de hell! No squawkin', see! No quittin', get me! Croak wit your boots on! *[He grabs hold of the bars of the cage and hauls himself painfully to his feet—looks around him bewilderedly—forces a mocking laugh]* In de cage, huh? *[In the strident tones of a circus barker]* Ladies and gents, step forward and take a slant at de one and only— *[His voice weakening]*—one and original—Hairy Ape from de wilds of— *[He slips in a heap on the floor and dies. The monkeys set up a chattering, whimpering wail. And, perhaps, the Hairy Ape at last belongs]*.

Thornton Wilder (1897–1975)

The Skin of Our Teeth

CHARACTERS

(In the order of their appearance)

ANNOUNCER
SABINA
MR. FITZPATRICK
MRS. ANTROBUS
DINOSAUR
MAMMOTH
TELEGRAPH BOY
GLADYS
HENRY
MR. ANTROBUS
DOCTOR
PROFESSOR
JUDGE
HOMER
MISS E. MUSE
MISS T. MUSE
MISS M. MUSE
TWO USHERS
TWO DRUM MAJORETTES
FORTUNE TELLER
TWO CHAIR PUSHERS
SIX CONVEENERS
BROADCAST OFFICIALS
DEFEATED CANDIDATE
MR. TREMAYNE
HESTER
IVY
FRED BAILEY

ACT I. *Home, Excelsior, New Jersey.*

ACT II. *Atlantic City Boardwalk.*

ACT III. *Home, Excelsior, New Jersey.*

Act I

A projection screen in the middle of the curtain. The first lantern slide: the name of the theatre, and the words: NEWS EVENTS OF THE WORLD. An ANNOUNCER'S *voice is heard.*

ANNOUNCER: The management takes pleasure in bringing to you—The News Events of the World: *(Slide of the sun appearing above the horizon)*

Freeport, Long Island.

The sun rose this morning at 6:32 a.m. This gratifying event was first reported by Mrs. Dorothy Stetson of Free-

The Skin of Our Teeth: A Play in Three Acts from *Three Plays* by Thornton Wilder.

port, Long Island, who promptly telephoned the Mayor.

The Society for Affirming the End of the World at once went into a special session and postponed the arrival of that event for TWENTY-FOUR HOURS.

All honor to Mrs. Stetson for her public spirit.

New York City: *{Slide of the front doors of the theatre in which this play is playing; three cleaning* WOMEN *with mops and pails}*

The X Theatre. During the daily cleaning of this theatre a number of lost objects were collected as usual by Mesdames Simpson, Pateslewski, and Moriarty.

Among these objects found today was a wedding ring, inscribed: To Eva from Adam. Genesis II:18.

The ring will be restored to the owner or owners, if their credentials are satisfactory.

Tippehatchee, Vermont: *{Slide representing a glacier}*

The unprecedented cold weather of this summer has produced a condition that has not yet been satisfactorily explained. There is a report that a wall of ice is moving southward across these counties. The disruption of communications by the cold wave now crossing the country has rendered exact information difficult, but little credence is given to the rumor that the ice has pushed the Cathedral of Montreal as far as St. Albans, Vermont.

For further information see your daily papers.

Excelsior, New Jersey: *{Slide of a modest suburban home}*

The home of Mr. George Antrobus, the inventor of the wheel. The discovery of the wheel, following so closely on the discovery of the lever, has centered the attention of the country on Mr. Antrobus of this attractive suburban residence district. This is his home, a commodious seven-room house, conveniently situated near a public school, a Methodist church, and a firehouse; it is right handy to an A. and P. *{Slide of* MR. ANTROBUS *on his front steps, smiling and lifting his straw hat. He holds a wheel}*

Mr. Antrobus, himself. He comes of very old stock and has made his way up from next to nothing.

It is reported that he was once a gardener, but left that situation under circumstances that have been variously reported.

Mr. Antrobus is a veteran of foreign wars, and bears a number of scars, front and back. *{Slide of* MRS. ANTROBUS, *holding some roses}*

This is Mrs. Antrobus, the charming and gracious president of the Excelsior Mothers' Club.

Mrs. Antrobus is an excellent needlewoman; it is she who invented the apron on which so many interesting changes have been rung since. *{Slide of the* FAMILY *and* SABINA]

Here we see the Antrobuses with their two children, Henry and Gladys, and friend. The friend in the rear, is Lily Sabina, the maid.

I know we all want to congratulate this typical American family on its enterprise. We all wish Mr. Antrobus a successful future. Now the management takes you to the interior of this home for a brief visit.

{Curtain rises. Living room of a commuter's home. SABINA*—straw-blonde, overrouged—is standing by the window back center, a feather duster under her elbow}*

SABINA: Oh, oh, oh! Six o'clock and the master not home yet.

Pray God nothing serious has happened to him crossing the Hudson River. If anything happened to him, we would certainly be inconsolable and have to move into a less desirable residence district.

The fact is I don't know what'll become of us. Here it is the middle of August and the coldest day of the year. It's simply freezing; the dogs are sticking to the sidewalks; can anybody explain that? No.

But I'm not surprised. The whole world's at sixes and sevens, and why the house hasn't fallen down about our ears long ago is a miracle to me. *{A fragment of the right wall leans precariously over the stage.* SABINA *looks at it nervously and it slowly rights itself}*

Every night this same anxiety as to whether the master will get home safely: whether he'll bring home anything to eat. In the midst of life we are in the midst of death, a truer word was never said. *{The fragment of scenery flies up into the lofts.* SABINA *is struck dumb with surprise, shrugs her shoulders and starts dusting* MR. ANTROBUS' *chair, including the under side}*

Of course, Mr. Antrobus is a very fine man, an excellent husband and father, a pillar of the church, and has all the best interests of the community at heart. Of course, every muscle goes tight every time he passes a policeman; but what I think is that there are certain charges that ought not to be made, and I think I may add, ought not to be allowed to be made; we're all human; who isn't? *{She dusts* MRS. ANTROBUS' *rocking chair}*

Mrs. Antrobus is as fine a woman as you could hope to see. She lives only for her children; and if it would be any benefit to her children she'd see the rest of us stretched out dead at her feet without turning a hair,—that's the truth. If you want to know anything more about Mrs. Antrobus, just go and look at a tigress, and look hard.

As to the children—

Well, Henry Antrobus is a real, clean-cut American boy. He'll graduate from High School one of these days, if they make the alphabet any easier.—Henry, when he has a stone in his hand, has a perfect aim; he can hit anything from a bird to an older brother—Oh! I didn't mean to say that!—but it certainly was an unfortunate accident, and it was very hard getting the police out of the house.

Mr. and Mrs. Antrobus' daughter is named Gladys. She'll make some good man a good wife some day, if he'll just come down off the movie screen and ask her.

So here we are!

We've managed to survive for some time now, catch as catch can, the fat and the lean, and if the dinosaurs don't trample us to death, and if the grasshoppers don't eat up our garden, we'll all live to see better days, knock on wood.

Each new child that's born to the Antrobuses seems to them to be sufficient reason for the whole universe's being set in motion; and each new child that dies seems to them to have been spared a whole world of sorrow, and what the end of it will be is still very much an open question.

We've rattled along, hot and cold, for some time now—*{A portion of the wall above the door, right, flies up into the air and disappears}*—and my advice to you is not to inquire into why or whither, but just enjoy your ice cream while it's on your plate,—that's my philosophy.

Don't forget that a few years ago we came through the depression by the skin of our teeth! One more tight squeeze like that and where will we be? *{This is a cue line.* SABINA *looks angrily at the kitchen door and repeats:}* . . . we came through the depression by the skin of our teeth; one more tight squeeze like that and where will we be? *{Flustered, she looks through the opening in the right wall; then goes to the window and reopens the Act}*

Oh, oh, oh! Six o'clock and the master not home yet. Pray God nothing has happened to him crossing the Hudson. Here it is the middle of August and the coldest day of the year. It's simply freezing; the dogs are sticking. One more tight squeeze like that and where will we be?

VOICE: *{off stage}* Make up something! Invent something!

SABINA: Well . . . uh . . . this certainly is a fine American home . . . and —uh . . . everybody's very happy . . . and—uh . . . *(Suddenly flings pretense to the winds and coming downstage says with indignation:)*

I can't invent any words for this play, and I'm glad I can't. I hate this play and every word in it.

As for me, I don't understand a single word of it, anyway,—all about the troubles the human race has gone through, there's a subject for you.

Besides, the author hasn't made up his silly mind as to whether we're all living back in caves or in New Jersey today, and that's the way it is all the way through.

Oh—why can't we have plays like we used to have—*Peg o' My Heart*, and *Smilin' Thru*, and *The Bat*—good entertainment with a message you can take home with you?

I took this hateful job because I had to. For two years I've sat up in my room living on a sandwich and a cup of tea a day, waiting for better times in the theatre. And look at me now: I—I who've played *Rain* and *The Barretts of Wimpole Street* and *First Lady*—God in Heaven! *(The* STAGE MANAGER *puts his head out from the hole in the scenery)*

MR. FITZPATRICK: Miss Somerset!! Miss Somerset!

SABINA: Oh! Anyway!—nothing matters! It'll all be the same in a hundred years. *(Loudly)*

We came through the depression by the skin of our teeth,—that's true!—one more tight squeeze like that and where will we be? *(Enter* MRS. ANTROBUS, *a mother)*

MRS. ANTROBUS: Sabina, you've let the fire go out.

SABINA: *(In a lather)* One-thing-and-another; don't - know - whether - my - wits - are - upside - or - down; might - as - well - be - dead - as - alive - in - a - house - all - sixes - and - sevens. . . .

MRS. ANTROBUS: You've let the fire go out. Here it is the coldest day of the year right in the middle of August, and you've let the fire go out.

SABINA: Mrs. Antrobus, I'd like to give my two weeks' notice, Mrs. Antrobus. A girl like I can get a situation in a home where they're rich enough to have a fire in every room, Mrs. Antrobus, and a girl don't have to carry the responsibility of the whole house on her two shoulders. And a home without children, Mrs. Antrobus, because children are a thing only a parent can stand, and a truer word was never said; and a home, Mrs. Antrobus, where the master of the house don't pinch decent, self-respecting girls when he meets them in a dark corridor. I mention no names and make no charges. So you have my notice, Mrs. Antrobus. I hope that's perfectly clear.

MRS. ANTROBUS: You've let the fire go out!—Have you milked the mammoth?

SABINA: I don't understand a word of this play.—Yes, I've milked the mammoth.

MRS. ANTROBUS: Until Mr. Antrobus comes home we have no food and we have no fire. You'd better go over to the neighbors and borrow some fire.

SABINA: Mrs. Antrobus! I can't! I'd die on the way, you know I would. It's worse than January. The dogs are sticking to the sidewalks. I'd die.

MRS. ANTROBUS: Very well, I'll go.

SABINA: *(Even more distraught, coming forward and sinking on her knees)* You'd never come back alive; we'd all perish; if you weren't here, we'd just perish. How do we know Mr. Antrobus'll be back? We don't know. If you go out, I'll just kill myself.

MRS. ANTROBUS: Get up, Sabina.

SABINA: Every night it's the same thing. Will he come back safe, or won't he? Will we starve to death, or freeze to death, or boil to death or will we be killed by burglars? I don't know why we go on living. I don't know why we go on living at all. It's easier being dead. *(She flings her arms on the table and buries her head in them. In each of the succeed-*

ing speeches she flings her head up—and sometimes her hands—then quickly buries her head again}

MRS. ANTROBUS: The same thing! Always throwing up the sponge, Sabina. Always announcing your own death. But give you a new hat—or a plate of ice cream—or a ticket to the movies, and you want to live forever.

SABINA: You don't care whether we live or die; all you care about is those children. If it would be any benefit to them you'd be glad to see us all stretched out dead.

MRS. ANTROBUS: Well, maybe I would.

SABINA: And what do they care about? Themselves—that's all they care about. *{Shrilly}*

They make fun of you behind your back. Don't tell me: they're ashamed of you. Half the time, they pretend they're someone else's children. Little thanks you get from them.

MRS. ANTROBUS: I'm not asking for any thanks.

SABINA: And Mr. Antrobus—you don't understand *him.* All that work he does—trying to discover the alphabet and the multiplication table. Whenever he tries to learn anything you fight against it.

MRS. ANTROBUS: Oh, Sabina, I know you.

When Mr. Antrobus raped you home from your Sabine hills, he did it to insult me.

He did it for your pretty face, and to insult me.

You were the new wife, weren't you?

For a year or two you lay on your bed all day and polished the nails on your hands and feet.

You made puff-balls of the combings of your hair and you blew them up to the ceiling.

And I washed your underclothes and I made you chicken broths.

I bore children and between my very groans I stirred the cream that you'd put on your face.

But I knew you wouldn't last.

You didn't last.

SABINA: But it was I who encouraged Mr. Antrobus to make the alphabet. I'm sorry to say it, Mrs. Antrobus, but you're not a beautiful woman, and you can never know what a man could do if he tried. It's girls like I who inspire the multiplication table.

I'm sorry to say it, but you're not a beautiful woman, Mrs. Antrobus, and that's the God's truth.

MRS. ANTROBUS: And you didn't last—you sank to the kitchen. And what do you do there? *You let the fire go out!*

No wonder to you it seems easier being dead.

Reading and writing and counting on your fingers is all very well in their way,—but I keep the home going.

MRS. ANTROBUS: —There's that dinosaur on the front lawn again.—Shoo! Go away. Go away. *{The baby* DINOSAUR *puts his head in the window}*

DINOSAUR: It's cold.

MRS. ANTROBUS: You go around to the back of the house where you belong.

DINOSAUR: It's cold.

{The DINOSAUR *disappears.* MRS. ANTROBUS *goes calmly out.* SABINA *slowly raises her head and speaks to the audience. The central portion of the center wall rises, pauses, and disappears into the loft}*

SABINA: Now that you audience are listening to this, too, I understand it a little better.

I wish eleven o'clock were here; I don't want to be dragged through this whole play again. *{The* TELEGRAPH BOY *is seen entering along the back wall of the stage from the right. She catches sight of him and calls:}*

Mrs. Antrobus! Mrs. Antrobus! Help! There's a strange man coming to the house. He's coming up the walk, help! *{Enter* MRS. ANTROBUS *in alarm, but efficient}*

MRS. ANTROBUS: Help me quick! *{They barricade the door by piling the furniture against it}*

Who is it? What do you want?

TELEGRAPH BOY: A telegram for Mrs. Antrobus from Mr. Antrobus in the city.

SABINA: Are you sure, are you sure? Maybe it's just a trap!

MRS. ANTROBUS: I know his voice, Sabina. We can open the door. *{Enter the* TELEGRAPH BOY, *12 years old, in uniform. The* DINOSAUR *and* MAMMOTH *slip by him into the room and settle down front right}* I'm sorry we kept you waiting. We have to be careful, you know. *{To the* ANIMALS]

Hm! . . . Will you be quiet? *{They nod}*

Have you had your supper? *{They nod}*

Are you ready to come in? *{They nod}*

Young man, have you any fire with you? Then light the grate, will you? *{He nods, produces something like a briquet; and kneels by the imagined fireplace, footlights center. Pause}*

What are people saying about this cold weather? *{He makes a doubtful shrug with his shoulders}*

Sabina, take this stick and go and light the stove.

SABINA: Like I told you, Mrs. Antrobus; two weeks. That's the law. I hope that's perfectly clear. *{Exit}*

MRS. ANTROBUS: What about this cold weather?

TELEGRAPH BOY: *{Lowered eyes}* Of course, I don't know anything . . . but they say there's a wall of ice moving down from the North, that's what they say. We can't get Boston by telegraph, and they're burning pianos in Hartford.

. . . It moves everything in front of it, churches and post offices and city halls.

I live in Brooklyn myself.

MRS. ANTROBUS: What are people doing about it?

TELEGRAPH BOY: Well . . . uh . . . Talking, mostly.

Or just what you'd do a day in February.

There are some that are trying to go South and the roads are crowded; but you can't take old people and children very far in a cold like this.

MRS. ANTROBUS: —What's this telegram you have for me?

TELEGRAPH BOY: *{Fingertips to his forehead}*

If you wait just a minute; I've got to remember it. *{The* ANIMALS *have left their corner and are nosing him. Presently they take places on either side of him, leaning against his hips, like heraldic beasts}* This telegram was flashed from Murray Hill to University Heights! And then by puffs of smoke from University Heights to Staten Island.

And then by lantern from Staten Island to Plainfield, New Jersey. What hath God wrought! *{He clears his throat}*

"To Mrs. Antrobus, Excelsior, New Jersey:

My dear wife, will be an hour late. Busy day at the office.

Don't worry the children about the cold just keep them warm burn everything except Shakespeare." *{Pause}*

MRS. ANTROBUS: Men!—He knows I'd burn ten Shakespeares to prevent a child of mine from having one cold in the head. What does it say next? *{Enter* SABINA]

TELEGRAPH BOY: "Have made great discoveries today have separated em from en."

SABINA: I know what that is, that's the alphabet, yes it is. Mr. Antrobus is just the cleverest man. Why, when the alphabet's finished, we'll be able to tell the future and everything.

TELEGRAPH BOY: Then listen to this: "Ten tens make a hundred semi-colon consequences far-reaching." *{Watches for effect}*

MRS. ANTROBUS: The earth's turning to ice, and all he can do is to make up new numbers.

TELEGRAPH BOY: Well, Mrs. Antrobus, like the head man at our office said: a few more discoveries like that and we'll be worth freezing.

MRS. ANTROBUS: What does he say next?

TELEGRAPH BOY: I . . . I can't do this last part very well. *{He clears his* *throat and sings)*

"Happy w'dding ann'vers'ry to you, Happy ann'vers'ry to you—" *(The* ANIMALS *begin to howl soulfully;* SABINA *screams with pleasure)*

MRS. ANTROBUS: Dolly! Frederick! Be quiet.

TELEGRAPH BOY: *(Above the din)* "Happy w'dding ann'vers'ry, dear Eva; happy w'dding ann'vers'ry to you."

MRS. ANTROBUS: Is that in the telegram? Are they singing telegrams now? *(He nods)*

The earth's getting so silly no wonder the sun turns cold.

SABINA: Mrs. Antrobus, I want to take back the notice I gave you. Mrs. Antrobus, I don't want to leave a house that gets such interesting telegrams and I'm sorry for anything I said. I really am.

MRS. ANTROBUS: Young man, I'd like to give you something for all this trouble; Mr. Antrobus isn't home yet and I have no money and no food in the house—

TELEGRAPH BOY: Mrs. Antrobus . . . I don't like to . . . appear to . . . ask for anything, but . . .

MRS. ANTROBUS: What is it you'd like?

TELEGRAPH BOY: Do you happen to have an old needle you could spare? My wife just sits home all day thinking about needles.

SABINA: *(Shrilly)* We only got two in the house. Mrs. Antrobus, you know we only got two in the house.

MRS. ANTROBUS: *(After a look at* SABINA *taking a needle from her collar)* Why yes, I can spare this.

TELEGRAPH BOY: *(Lowered eyes)* Thank you, Mrs. Antrobus. Mrs. Antrobus, can I ask for something else? I have two sons of my own; if the cold gets worse, what should I do?

SABINA: I think we'll all perish, that's what I think. Cold like this in August is just the end of the whole world. *(Silence)*

MRS. ANTROBUS: I don't know. After all, what does one do about anything? Just keep as warm as you can. And don't let your wife and children see that you're worried.

TELEGRAPH BOY: Yes . . . Thank you, Mrs. Antrobus. Well, I'd better be going.—Oh, I forgot! There's one more sentence in the telegram. "Three cheers have invented the wheel."

MRS. ANTROBUS: A wheel? What's a wheel?

TELEGRAPH BOY: I don't know. That's what it said. The sign for it is like this. Well, goodbye. *(The* WOMEN *see him to the door, with goodbyes and injunctions to keep warm)*

SABINA: *(Apron to her eyes, wailing)* Mrs. Antrobus, it looks to me like all the nice men in the world are already married; I don't know why that is. *(Exit)*

MRS. ANTROBUS: *(Thoughtful; to the* ANIMALS*)* Do you ever remember hearing tell of any cold like this in August? *(The* ANIMALS *shake their heads)*

From your grandmothers or anyone? *(They shake their heads)*

Have you any suggestions? *(They shake their heads. She pulls her shawl around, goes to the front door and opening it an inch calls:)*

HENRY. GLADYS. CHILDREN. Come right in and get warm. No, no, when mamma says a thing she means it.

Henry! HENRY. Put down that stone. You know what happened last time. *(Shriek)*

HENRY! Put down that stone!

Gladys! Put down your dress! Try and be a lady. *(The* CHILDREN *bound in and dash to the fire. They take off their winter things and leave them in heaps on the floor)*

GLADYS: Mama, I'm hungry. Mama, why is it so cold?

HENRY: *(At the same time)* Mama, why doesn't it snow? Mama, when's supper ready?

Maybe, it'll snow and we can make snowballs.

GLADYS: Mama, it's so cold that in one

more minute I just couldn't of stood it.

MRS. ANTROBUS: Settle down, both of you, I want to talk to you. *{She draws up a hassock and sits front center over the orchestra pit before the imaginary fire. The* CHILDREN *stretch out on the floor, leaning against her lap. Tableau by Raphael. The* ANIMALS *edge up and complete the triangle}*

It's just a cold spell of some kind. Now listen to what I'm saying:

When your father comes home I want you to be extra quiet. He's had a hard day at the office and I don't know but what he may have one of his moods.

I just got a telegram from him very happy and excited, and you know what that means. Your father's temper's uneven; I guess you know that. *{Shriek}*

Henry! Henry!

Why—why can't you remember to keep your hair down over your forehead? You must keep that scar covered up. Don't you know that when your father sees it he loses all control over himself? He goes crazy. He wants to die. *{After a moment's despair she collects herself decisively, wets the hem of her apron in her mouth and starts polishing his forehead vigorously}*

Lift your head up. Stop squirming. Blessed me, sometimes I think that it's going away—and then there it is: just as red as ever.

HENRY: Mama, today at school two teachers forgot and called me by my old name. They forgot, Mama. You'd better write another letter to the principal, so that he'll tell them I've changed my name. Right out in class they called me: Cain.

MRS. ANTROBUS: *{Putting her hand on his mouth, too late; hoarsely}*

Don't say it. *{Polishing feverishly}*

If you're good they'll forget it. Henry, you didn't hit anyone . . . today, did you?

HENRY: Oh . . . no-o-o!

MRS. ANTROBUS: *{Still working, not looking at Gladys}* And, Gladys, I want you to be especially nice to your father tonight. You know what he calls you when you're good—his little angel, his little star. Keep your dress down like a little lady. And keep your voice nice and low. Gladys Antrobus. What's that red stuff you have on your face? *{Slaps her}*

You're a filthy detestable child! *{Rises in real, though temporary, repudiation and despair}*

Get away from me, both of you! I wish I'd never seen sight or sound of you. Let the cold come! I can't stand it. I don't want to go on. *{She walks away}*

GLADYS: *{Weeping}* All the girls at school do, Mama.

MRS. ANTROBUS: *{Shrieking}*

I'm through with you, that's all!—Sabina! Sabina!—Don't you know your father'd go crazy if he saw that paint on your face? Don't you know your father thinks you're perfect? Don't you know he couldn't live if he didn't think you were perfect?—Sabina! *{Enter* SABINA]

SABINA: Yes, Mrs. Antrobus!

MRS. ANTROBUS: Take this girl out into the kitchen and wash her face with the scrubbing brush.

MR. ANTROBUS: *{Outside, roaring}* "I've been working on the railroad, all the livelong day . . . etc." *{The* ANIMALS *start running around in circles, bellowing.* SABINA *rushes to the window}*

MRS. ANTROBUS: Sabina, what's that noise outside?

SABINA: Oh, it's a drunken tramp. It's a giant, Mrs. Antrobus. We'll all be killed in our beds, I know it!

MRS. ANTROBUS: Help me quick. Quick. Everybody. *{Again they stack all the furniture against the door.* MR. ANTROBUS *pounds and bellows}* Who is it? What do you want?—Sabina, have you any boiling water ready?—Who is it?

MR. ANTROBUS: Broken-down camel of a pig's snout, open this door.

MRS. ANTROBUS: God be praised! It's your father.—Just a minute, George!

—Sabina, clear the door, quick. Gladys, come here while I clean your nasty face!

MR. ANTROBUS: She-bitch of a goat's gizzard, I'll break every bone in your body. Let me in or I'll tear the whole house down.

MRS. ANTROBUS: Just a minute, George, something's the matter with the lock.

MR. ANTROBUS: Open the door or I'll tear your livers out. I'll smash your brains on the ceiling, and Devil take the hindmost.

MRS. ANTROBUS: Now you can open the door, Sabina. I'm ready. *{The door is flung open. Silence.* MR. ANTROBUS*—face of a Keystone Comedy Cop—stands there in fur cap and blanket. His arms are full of parcels, including a large stone wheel with a center in it. One hand carries a railroad man's lantern. Suddenly he bursts into joyous roar}*

MR. ANTROBUS: Well, how's the whole crooked family? *{Relief. Laughter. Tears. Jumping up and down.* ANIMALS *cavorting.* ANTROBUS *throws the parcels on the ground. Hurls his cap and blanket after them. Heroic embraces. Melee of* HUMANS *and* ANIMALS, SABINA *included}* I'll be scalded and tarred if a man can't get a little welcome when he comes home. Well, Maggie, you old gunny-sack, how's the broken down old weather hen?—Sabina, old fishbait, old skunkpot.—And the children,—how've the little smellers been?

GLADYS: Papa, Papa, Papa, Papa.

MR. ANTROBUS: How've they been, Maggie?

MRS. ANTROBUS: Well, I must say, they've been as good as gold. I haven't had to raise my voice once. I don't know what's the matter with them.

ANTROBUS: *{Kneeling before* GLADYS] Papa's little weasel, eh?—Sabina, there's some food for you.—Papa's little gopher?

GLADYS: *{Her arm around his neck}* Papa, you're always teasing me.

ANTROBUS: And Henry? Nothing rash today, I hope. Nothing rash?

HENRY: No, Papa.

ANTROBUS: *{Roaring}* Well that's good, that's good—I'll bet Sabina let the fire go out.

SABINA: Mr. Antrobus, I've given my notice. I'm leaving two weeks from today. I'm sorry, but I'm leaving.

ANTROBUS: *{Roar}* Well, if you leave now you'll freeze to death, so go and cook the dinner.

SABINA: Two weeks, that's the law. *{Exit}*

ANTROBUS: Did you get my telegram?

MRS. ANTROBUS: Yes.—What's a wheel? *{He indicates the wheel with a glance.* HENRY *is rolling it around the floor. Rapid, hoarse interchange:* MRS. ANTROBUS: *What does this cold weather mean? It's below freezing.* ANTROBUS: *Not before the children!* MRS. ANTROBUS: *Shouldn't we do something about it?—start off, move?* ANTROBUS: *Not before the children!!! He gives* HENRY *a sharp slap}*

HENRY: Papa, you hit me!

ANTROBUS: Well, remember it. That's to make you remember today. Today. The day the alphabet's finished; and the day that we *saw* the hundred—the hundred, the hundred, the hundred, the hundred, the hundred—there's no end to 'em.

I've had a day at the office!

Take a look at that wheel, Maggie—when I've got that to rights: you'll see a sight.

There's a reward there for all the walking you've done.

MRS. ANTROBUS: How do you mean?

ANTROBUS: *{On the hassock looking into the fire; with awe}* Maggie, we've reached the top of the wave. There's not much more to be done. We're there!

MRS. ANTROBUS: *{Cutting across his mood sharply}* And the ice?

ANTROBUS: The ice!

HENRY: *{Playing with the wheel}* Papa, you could put a chair on this.

ANTROBUS: *{Broodingly}* Ye-e-s, any

booby can fool with it now,—but I thought of it first.

MRS. ANTROBUS: Children, go out in the kitchen. I want to talk to your father alone. *{The* CHILDREN *go out.* ANTROBUS *has moved to his chair up left. He takes the goldfish bowl on his lap; pulls the canary cage down to the level of his face. Both the* ANIMALS *put their paws up on the arm of his chair.* MRS. ANTROBUS *faces him across the room, like a judge}*

MRS. ANTROBUS: Well?

ANTROBUS: *{Shortly}* It's cold.—How things been, eh? Keck, keck, keck.—And you, Millicent?

MRS. ANTROBUS: I know it's cold.

ANTROBUS: *{To the canary}* No spilling of sunflower seed, eh? No singing after lights-out, y'know what I mean?

MRS. ANTROBUS: You can try and prevent us freezing to death, can't you? You can do something? We can start moving. Or we can go on the animals' backs?

ANTROBUS: The best thing about animals is that they don't talk much.

MAMMOTH: It's cold.

ANTROBUS: Eh, eh, eh! Watch that!——By midnight we'd turn to ice. The roads are full of people now who can scarcely lift a foot from the ground. The grass out in front is like iron,—which reminds me, I have another needle for you.—The people up north—where are they?

Frozen . . . crushed. . . .

MRS. ANTROBUS: Is that what's going to happen to us?—Will you answer me?

ANTROBUS: I don't know. I don't know anything. Some say that the ice is going slower. Some say that it's stopped. The sun's growing cold. What can I do about that? Nothing we can do but burn everything in the house, and the fenceposts and the barn. Keep the fire going. When we have no more fire, we die.

MRS. ANTROBUS: Well, why didn't you say so in the first place? [MRS. ANTROBUS *is about to march off when she catches sight of two* REFUGEES, *men, who have appeared against the back wall of the theatre and who are soon joined by others}*

REFUGEES: Mr. Antrobus! Mr. Antrobus! Mr. An-nn-tro-bus!

MRS. ANTROBUS: Who's that? Who's that calling you?

ANTROBUS: *{Clearing his throat guiltily}* Hm—let me see. *{Two* REFUGEES *come up to the window}*

REFUGEE: Could we warm our hands for a moment, Mr. Antrobus. It's very cold, Mr. Antrobus.

ANOTHER REFUGEE: Mr. Antrobus, I wonder if you have a piece of bread or something that you could spare. *{Silence. They wait humbly.* MRS. ANTROBUS *stands rooted to the spot. Suddenly a knock at the door, then another hand knocking in short rapid blows}*

MRS. ANTROBUS: Who are these people? Why, they're all over the front yard. What have they come *here* for? *{Enter* SABINA]

SABINA: Mrs. Antrobus! There are some tramps knocking at the back door.

MRS. ANTROBUS: George, tell these people to go away. Tell them to move right along. I'll go and send them away from the back door. Sabina, come with me. *{She goes out energetically}*

ANTROBUS: Sabina! Stay here! I have something to say to you. *{He goes to the door and opens it a crack and talks through it}* Ladies and gentlemen! I'll have to ask you to wait a few minutes longer. It'll be all right . . . while you're waiting you might each one pull up a stake of the fence. We'll need them all for the fireplace. There'll be coffee and sandwiches in a moment. [SABINA *looks out door over his shoulder and suddenly extends her arm pointing, with a scream}*

SABINA: Mr. Antrobus, what's that??—that big white thing? Mr. Antrobus, it's ICE. It's ICE!!

ANTROBUS: Sabina, I want you to go in the kitchen and make a lot of coffee. Make a whole pail full.

SABINA: Pail full!!

ANTROBUS: *{With gesture}* And

sandwiches . . . piles of them . . . like this.

SABINA: Mr. An . . . !! *{Suddenly she drops the play, and says in her own person as* MISS SOMERSET, *with surprise}* Oh, *I* see what this part of the play means now! This means refugees. *{She starts to cross to the proscenium}*

Oh, I don't like it. I don't like it. *{She leans against the proscenium and bursts into tears}*

ANTROBUS: Miss Somerset! *{Voice of the* STAGE MANAGER*]* Miss Somerset!

SABINA: *{Energetically, to the audience}* Ladies and gentlemen! Don't take this play serious. The world's not coming to an end. You know it's not. People exaggerate! Most people really have enough to eat and a roof over their heads. Nobody actually starves—you can always eat grass or something. That ice-business—why, it was a long, long time ago. Besides they were only savages. Savages don't love their families—not like we do.

ANTROBUS *and* STAGE MANAGER: Miss Somerset!! *{There is renewed knocking at the door}*

SABINA: All right. I'll say the lines, but I won't think about the play. *{Enter* MRS. ANTROBUS*]*

SABINA: *{Parting thrust at the audience}* And I advise *you* not to think about the play, either. *{Exit* SABINA*]*

MRS. ANTROBUS: George, these tramps say that you asked them to come to the house. What does this mean? *{Knocking at the door}*

ANTROBUS: Just . . . uh . . . there are a few friends, Maggie, I met on the road. Real nice, real useful people. . . .

MRS. ANTROBUS: *{Back to the door}* Now don't you ask them in! George Antrobus, not another soul comes in here over my dead body.

ANTROBUS: Maggie, there's a doctor there. Never hurts to have a good doctor in the house. We've lost a peck of children, one way and another. You can never tell when a child's throat will get stopped up. What you and I have seen—!!! *{He puts his fingers on his throat and imitates diphtheria}*

MRS. ANTROBUS: Well, just one person then, the Doctor. The others can go right along the road.

ANTROBUS: Maggie, there's an old man, particular friend of mine.

MRS. ANTROBUS: I won't listen to you.

ANTROBUS: It was he that really started off the A.B.C.'s.

MRS. ANTROBUS: I don't care if he perishes. We can do without reading or writing. We can't do without food.

ANTROBUS: Then let the ice come!! Drink your coffee!! I don't want any coffee if I can't drink it with some good people.

MRS. ANTROBUS: Stop shouting. Who else is out there trying to push us off the cliff?

ANTROBUS: Well, there's the man . . . who makes all the laws. Judge Moses!

MRS. ANTROBUS: Judges can't help us now.

ANTROBUS: And if the ice melts? . . . and if we pull through? Have you and I been able to bring up Henry? What have we done?

MRS. ANTROBUS: Who are those old women?

ANTROBUS: *{Coughs}* Up in town there are nine sisters. There are three or four of them here. They're sort of music teachers . . . and one of them recites and one of them—

MRS. ANTROBUS: That's the end. A singing troupe! Well, take your choice, live or die. Starve your own children before your face.

ANTROBUS: *{Gently}* These people don't take much. They're used to starving.

They'll sleep on the floor.

Besides, Maggie, listen: no, listen:

Who've we got in the house, but Sabina? Sabina's always afraid the worst will happen. Whose spirits can she keep up? Maggie, these people never give up. They think they'll live and work forever.

MRS. ANTROBUS: *{Walks slowly to the middle of the room}*

All right, let them in. Let them in. You're master here. *{Softly}*—But these animals must go. Enough's enough. They'll soon be big enough to push the walls down, anyway. Take them away.

ANTROBUS: *{Sadly}* All right. The dinosaur and mammoth—! Come on, baby, come on Frederick. Come for a walk. That's a good little fellow.

DINOSAUR: It's cold.

ANTROBUS: Yes, nice cold fresh air. Bracing. *{He holds the door open and the* ANIMALS *go out. He beckons to his friends. The* REFUGEES *are typically elderly out-of-works from the streets of New York today.* JUDGE MOSES *wears a skull cap.* HOMER *is a blind beggar with a guitar. The seedy crowd shuffles in and waits humbly and expectantly.* ANTROBUS *introduces them to his wife who bows to each with a stately bend of her head}*

Make yourself at home, Maggie, this the doctor . . . m . . . Coffee'll be here in a minute. . . . Professor, this is my wife. . . . And: . . . Judge . . . Maggie, you know the Judge. *{An old blind man with a guitar}* Maggie, you know . . . you know Homer?—Come right in, Judge.—

Miss Muse—are some of your sisters here? Come right in. . . .

Miss E. Muse; Miss T. Muse, Miss M. Muse.

MRS. ANTROBUS: Please to meet you.

Just . . . make yourself comfortable. Supper'll be ready in a minute. *{She goes out, abruptly}*

ANTROBUS: Make yourself at home, friends. I'll be right back. *{He goes out.*

The REFUGEES *stare about them in awe. Presently several voices start whispering "Homer! Homer!" All take it up.* HOMER *strikes a chord or two on his guitar, then starts to speak:}*

HOMER: *Μῆνιν ἄειδε, θεὰ, Πηληϊάδεω Ἀχιλῆος, οὐλομένην, ἣ ηυρί' Ἀχαιοῖς ἄλγε' ἔθηκεν, πολλὰς δ' ἰφθίμους Ψυχὰς*—

{HOMER's *face shows he is lost in thought and memory and the words die away on his lips. The* REFUGEES *likewise nod in dreamy recollection. Soon the whisper "Moses, Moses!" goes around. An aged Jew parts his beard and recites dramatically:}*

MOSES:

בְּרֵאשִׁית בָּרָא אֱלֹהִים אֵת הַשָּׁמַיִם וְאֵת הָאָרֶץ׃
וְהָאָרֶץ הָיְתָה תֹהוּ וָבֹהוּ וְחֹשֶׁךְ עַל־פְּנֵי תְהוֹם
וְרוּחַ אֱלֹהִים מְרַחֶפֶת עַל־פְּנֵי הַמָּיִם׃

{The same dying away of the words takes place, and on the part of the REFUGEES *the same retreat into recollection. Some of them murmur, "Yes, yes."*

The mood is broken by the abrupt entrance of MR. *and* MRS. ANTROBUS *and* SABINA *bearing platters of sandwiches and a pail of coffee.* SABINA *stops and stares at the guests}*

MR. ANTROBUS: Sabina, pass the sandwiches.

SABINA: I thought I was working in a respectable house that had respectable guests. I'm giving my notice, Mr. Antrobus: two weeks, that's the law.

MR. ANTROBUS: Sabina! Pass the sandwiches.

SABINA: Two weeks, that's the law.

MR. ANTROBUS: There's the law. That's Moses.

SABINA: *{Stares}* The Ten Commandments — faugh!! — *{To Audience}* That's the worst line I've ever had to say on any stage.

ANTROBUS: I think the best thing to do is just not to stand on ceremony, but pass the sandwiches around from left to right.—Judge, help yourself to one of these.

MRS. ANTROBUS: The roads are crowded, I hear?

THE GUESTS: *{All talking at once}* Oh, ma'am, you can't imagine. . . . You can hardly put one foot before you . . . people are trampling one another. *{Sudden silence}*

MRS. ANTROBUS: Well, you know what I think it is,—I think it's sunspots!

THE GUESTS: *{Discreet hubbub}* Oh,

you're right, Mrs. Antrobus . . . that's what it is. . . . That's what I was saying the other day. *{Sudden silence}*

ANTROBUS: Well, I don't believe the whole world's going to turn to ice. *{All eyes are fixed on him, waiting}*

I can't believe it, Judge! Have we worked for nothing? Professor! Have we just failed in the whole thing?

MRS. ANTROBUS: It is certainly very strange—well fortunately on both sides of the family we come of very hearty stock.—Doctor, I want you to meet my children. They're eating their supper now. And of course I want them to meet you.

MISS M. MUSE: How many children have you, Mrs. Antrobus?

MRS. ANTROBUS: I have two,—a boy and a girl.

MOSES: *{Softly}* I understood you had two sons, Mrs. Antrobus. [MRS. ANTROBUS *in blind suffering; she walks toward the footlights}*

MRS. ANTROBUS: *{In a low voice}* Abel, Abel, my son, my son, Abel, my son, Abel, Abel my son. *{The* REFUGEES *move with a few steps toward her as though in comfort murmuring words in Greek, Hebrew, German, et cetera.*

A piercing shriek from the kitchen,— SABINA's *voice. All heads turn}*

ANTROBUS: What's that? [SABINA *enters, bursting with indignation, pulling on her gloves}*

SABINA: Mr. Antrobus—that son of yours, that boy Henry Antrobus—I don't stay in this house another moment!—He's not fit to live among respectable folks and that's a fact.

MRS. ANTROBUS: Don't say another word, Sabina. I'll be right back. *{Without waiting for an answer she goes past her into the kitchen}*

SABINA: Mrs. Antrobus, Henry has thrown a stone again and if he hasn't killed the boy that lives next door, I'm very much mistaken. He finished his supper and went out to play; and I heard such a fight; and then I saw it. I saw it with my own eyes. And it looked to me like stark murder. [MRS. ANTROBUS *appears at the kitchen door, shielding* HENRY *who follows her. When she steps aside, we see on* HENRY's *forehead a large ochre and scarlet scar in the shape of a C.* MR. ANTROBUS *starts toward him. A pause.* HENRY *is heard saying under his breath:}*

HENRY: He was going to take the wheel away from me. He started to throw a stone at me first.

MRS. ANTROBUS: George, it was just a boyish impulse. Remember how young he is. *{Louder, in an urgent wail}* George, he's only four thousand years old.

SABINA: And everything was going along so nicely! *{Silence.* ANTROBUS *goes back to the fireplace}*

ANTROBUS: Put out the fire! Put out all the fires. *{Violently}* No wonder the sun grows cold. *{He starts stamping on the fireplace}*

MRS. ANTROBUS: Doctor! Judge! Help me!—George, have you lost your mind?

ANTROBUS: There is no mind. We'll not try to live. *{To the guests}* Give it up. Give up trying. [MRS. ANTROBUS *seizes him}*

SABINA: Mr. Antrobus! I'm downright ashamed of you.

MRS. ANTROBUS: George, have some more coffee.—Gladys! Where's Gladys gone? [GLADYS *steps in, frightened}*

GLADYS: Here I am, mama.

MRS. ANTROBUS: Go upstairs and bring your father's slippers. How could you forget a thing like that, when you know how tired he is? [ANTROBUS *sits in his chair. He covers his face with his hands.* MRS. ANTROBUS *turns to the* REFUGEES:] Can't some of you sing? It's your business in life to sing, isn't it? Sabina! *{Several of the women clear their throats tentatively, and with frightened faces gather around* HOMER's *guitar. He establishes a few chords. Almost inaudibly they start singing, led by* SABINA. *"Jingle Bells."* MRS. ANTROBUS *continues to* ANTROBUS *in a low voice,* *while taking off his shoes:}* George, remember all the other times. When the volcanoes came right up in the front yard. And the time the grasshoppers ate every single leaf and blade of grass, and all the grain and spinach you'd grown with your own hands. And the summer there were earthquakes every night.

ANTROBUS: Henry! Henry! *{Puts his hand on his forehead}* Myself. All of us, we're covered with blood.

MRS. ANTROBUS: Then remember all the times you were pleased with him and when you were proud of yourself. —Henry! Henry! Come here and recite to your father the multiplication table that you do so nicely. {HENRY *kneels on one knee beside his father and starts whispering the multiplication table}*

HENRY: *{Finally}* Two times six is twelve; three times six is eighteen—I don't think I know the sixes. {*Enter* GLADYS *with the slippers.* MRS. ANTROBUS *makes stern gestures to her: Go in there and do your best. The* GUESTS *are now singing "Tenting Tonight."}*

GLADYS: *{Putting slippers on his feet}* Papa . . . Papa . . . I was very good in school today. Miss Conover said right out in class that if all the girls had as good manners as Gladys Antrobus, that the world would be a very different place to live in.

MRS. ANTROBUS: You recited a piece at assembly, didn't you? Recite it to your father.

GLADYS: Papa, do you want to hear what I recited in class? *{Fierce directional glance from her mother}* "THE STAR" by Henry Wadsworth LONGFELLOW.

MRS. ANTROBUS: Wait!!! The fire's going out. There isn't enough wood! Henry, go upstairs and bring down the chairs and start breaking up the beds. *{Exit* HENRY. *The singers return to "Jingle Bells," still very softly}*

GLADYS: Look, Papa, here's my report card. Lookit. Conduct A! Look, Papa. Papa, do you want to hear the Star, by Henry Wadsworth Longfellow? Papa, you're not mad at me, are you?—I know it'll get warmer. Soon it'll be just like spring, and we can go to a picnic at the Hibernian Picnic Grounds like you always like to do, don't you remember? Papa, just look at me once. *{Enter* HENRY *with some chairs}*

ANTROBUS: You recited in assembly, did you? *{She nods eagerly}* You didn't forget it?

GLADYS: No!!! I was perfect. *{Pause. Then* ANTROBUS *rises, goes to the front door and opens it. The* REFUGEES *draw back timidly; the song stops; he peers out of the door, then closes it}*

ANTROBUS: *{With decision, suddenly}* Build up the fire. It's cold. Build up the fire. We'll do what we can. Sabina, get some more wood. Come around the fire, everybody. At least the young ones may pull through. Henry, have you eaten something?

HENRY: Yes, papa.

ANTROBUS: Gladys, have you had some supper?

GLADYS: I ate in the kitchen, papa.

ANTROBUS: If you do come through this—what'll you be able to do? What do you know? Henry, did you take a good look at that wheel?

HENRY: Yes, papa.

ANTROBUS: *{Sitting down in his chair}* Six times two are—

HENRY: —twelve; six times three are eighteen; six times four are—Papa, it's hot and cold. It makes my head all funny. It makes me sleepy.

ANTROBUS: *{Gives him a cuff}* Wake up. I don't care if your head is sleepy. Six times four are twenty-four. Six times five are—

HENRY: Thirty. Papa!

ANTROBUS: Maggie, put something into Gladys' head on the chance she can use it.

MRS. ANTROBUS: What do you mean, George?

ANTROBUS: Six times six are thirty-six. Teach her the beginning of the Bible.

GLADYS: But, Mama, it's so cold and

close. [HENRY *has all but drowsed off. His father slaps him sharply and the lesson goes on*]

MRS. ANTROBUS: "In the beginning God created the heavens and the earth; and the earth was waste and void; and the darkness was upon the face of the deep—" [*The singing starts up again louder.* SABINA *has returned with wood*]

SABINA: [*After placing wood on the fireplace comes down to the footlights and addresses the audience:*] Will you please start handing up your chairs? We'll need everything for this fire. Save the human race.—Ushers, will you pass the chairs up here? Thank you.

HENRY: Six times nine are fifty-four; six times ten are sixty. [*In the back of the auditorium the sound of chairs being ripped up can be heard.* USHERS *rush down the aisles with chairs and hand them over*]

GLADYS: "And God called the light Day and the darkness he called Night."

SABINA: Pass up your chairs, everybody. Save the human race.

CURTAIN

Act II

Toward the end of the intermission, though with the houselights still up, lantern slide projections begin to appear on the curtain. Timetables for trains leaving Pennsylvania Station for Atlantic City. Advertisements of Atlantic City hotels, drugstores, churches, rug merchants; fortune tellers, Bingo parlors.

When the houselights go down, the voice of an ANNOUNCER *is heard.*

ANNOUNCER: The Management now brings you the News Events of the World. Atlantic City, New Jersey: [*Projection of a chrome postcard of the waterfront, trimmed in mica with the legend: FUN AT THE BEACH*] This great convention city is playing host this week to the anniversary convocation of that great fraternal order,—the Ancient and Honorable Order of Mammals, Subdivision Humans. This great fraternal, militant and burial society is celebrating on the Boardwalk, ladies and gentlemen, its six hundred thousandth Annual Convention.

It has just elected its president for the ensuing term,—[*Projection of* MR. *and* MRS. ANTROBUS *posed as they will be shown a few moments later*] Mr. George Antrobus of Excelsior, New Jersey. We show you President Antrobus and his gracious and charming wife, every inch a mammal. Mr. Antrobus has had a long and chequered career. Credit has been paid to him for many useful enterprises including the introduction of the lever, of the wheel and the brewing of beer. Credit has been also extended to President Antrobus's gracious and charming wife for many practical suggestions, including the hem, the gore, and the gusset; and the novelty of the year,—frying in oil. Before we show you Mr. Antrobus accepting the nomination, we have an important announcement to make. As many of you know, this great celebration of the Order of the Mammals has received delegations from the other rival Orders,—or shall we say: esteemed concurrent Orders: the WINGS, the FINS, the SHELLS, and so on. These Orders are holding their conventions also, in various parts of the world, and have sent representatives to our own, two of a kind.

Later in the day we will show you President Antrobus broadcasting his words of greeting and congratulation to the collected assemblies of the whole natural world.

Ladies and Gentlemen! We give you President Antrobus! [*The screen becomes a Transparency.* MR. ANTROBUS *stands beside a pedestal;* MRS. ANTROBUS *is seated wearing a corsage of orchids.* ANTROBUS *wears an untidy Prince Albert; spats; from a red rosette in his buttonhole hangs a fine long purple ribbon of honor. He wears a gay lodge hat,—something between a fez and a legionnaire's cap}*

ANTROBUS: Fellow-mammals, fellow-vertebrates, fellow-humans, I thank you. Little did my dear parents think,—when they told me to stand on my own two feet,—that I'd arrive at this place.

My friends, we have come a long way.

During this week of happy celebration it is perhaps not fitting that we dwell on some of the difficult times we have been through. The dinosaur is extinct—*{Applause}*—the ice has retreated; and the common cold is being pursued by every means within our power. [MRS. ANTROBUS *sneezes, laughs prettily, and murmurs: "I beg your pardon"}* In our memorial service yesterday we did honor to all our friends and relatives who are no longer with us, by reason of cold, earthquakes, plagues and . . . and . . . *{Coughs}* differences of opinion.

As our Bishop so ably said . . . uh . . . so ably said. . . .

MRS. ANTROBUS: *{Closed lips}* 'Gone, but not forgotten.'

ANTROBUS: 'They are gone, but not forgotten.'

I think I can say, I think I can prophesy with complete . . . uh . . . with complete. . . .

MRS. ANTROBUS: Confidence.

ANTROBUS: Thank you, my dear,—With complete lack of confidence, that a new day of security is about to dawn.

The watchword of the closing year was: Work. I give you the watchword for the future: Enjoy Yourselves.

MRS. ANTROBUS: George, sit down!

ANTROBUS: Before I close, however, I wish to answer one of those unjust and malicious accusations that were brought against me during this last electoral campaign.

Ladies and gentlemen, the charge was made that at various points in my career I leaned toward joining some of the rival orders,—that's a lie.

As I told reporters of the *Atlantic City Herald*, I do not deny that a few months before my birth I hesitated between . . . uh . . . between pinfeathers and gillbreathing,—and so did many of us here,—but for the last million years I have been viviparous, hairy and diaphragmatic. *{Applause. Cries of 'Good old Antrobus,' 'The Prince chap!' 'Georgie,' etc.}*

ANNOUNCER: Thank you. Thank you very much, Mr. Antrobus.

Now I know that our visitors will wish to hear a word from that gracious and charming mammal, Mrs. Antrobus, wife and mother,—Mrs. Antrobus! [MRS. ANTROBUS *rises, lays her program on her chair, bows and says:}*

MRS. ANTROBUS: Dear friends, I don't really think I should say anything. After all, it was my husband who was elected and not I. Perhaps, as president of the Women's Auxiliary Bed and Board Society,—I had some notes here, oh, yes, here they are:—I should give a short report from some of our committees that have been meeting in this beautiful city.

Perhaps it may interest you to know that it has at last been decided that the tomato is edible. Can you all hear me? The tomato *is* edible.

A delegate from across the sea reports that the thread woven by the silkworm gives a cloth . . . I have a sample of it here . . . can you see it? smooth, elastic. I should say that it's rather attractive,—though personally I prefer less shiny surfaces. Should the windows of a sleeping apartment be open or shut? I know all mothers will follow our debates on this matter with close interest. I am sorry to say that the most expert authorities have not yet decided. It does seem to me that the night air would be bound to be unhealthy for our children, but there are many distinguished authorities on both sides. Well, I could go on talking forever,—as Shakespeare says: a woman's work is seldom done; but I think I'd better join my husband in saying thank you, and sit down. Thank you. *(She sits down)*

ANNOUNCER: Oh, Mrs. Antrobus!

MRS. ANTROBUS: Yes?

ANNOUNCER: We understand that you are about to celebrate a wedding anniversary. I know our listeners would like to extend their felicitations and hear a few words from you on that subject.

MRS. ANTROBUS: I have been asked by this kind gentleman . . . yes, my friends, this Spring Mr. Antrobus and I will be celebrating our five thousandth wedding anniversary.

I don't know if I speak for my husband, but I can say that, as for me, I regret every moment of it. *(Laughter of confusion)* I beg your pardon. What I *mean* to say is that I do not regret one moment of it. I hope none of you catch my cold. We have two children. We've always had two children, though it hasn't always been the same two. But as I say, we have two fine children, and we're very grateful for that. Yes, Mr. Antrobus and I have been married five thousand years. Each wedding anniversary reminds me of the times when there were no weddings. We had to crusade for marriage. Perhaps there are some women within the sound of my voice who remember that crusade and those struggles; we fought for it, didn't we? We chained ourselves to lampposts and we made disturbances in the Senate,—anyway, at last we women got the ring.

A few men helped us, but I must say that most men blocked our way at every step: they said we were unfeminine.

I only bring up these unpleasant memories, because I see some signs of backsliding from that great victory.

Oh, my fellow mammals, keep hold of that.

My husband says that the watchword for the year is Enjoy Yourselves. I think that's very open to misunderstanding.

My watchword for the year is: Save the Family. It's held together for over five thousand years: Save it! Thank you.

ANNOUNCER: Thank you, Mrs. Antrobus. *(The transparency disappears)*

We had hoped to show you the Beauty Contest that took place here today.

President Antrobus, an experienced judge of pretty girls, gave the title of Miss Atlantic City 1942, to Miss Lily-Sabina Fairweather, charming hostess of our Boardwalk Bingo Parlor.

Unfortunately, however, our time is up, and I must take you to some views of the Convention City and conveeners,—enjoying themselves.

(A burst of music; the curtain rises. The Boardwalk. The audience is sitting in the ocean. An handrail of scarlet cord stretches across the front of the stage. A ramp—also with scarlet hand rail—descends to the right corner of the orchestra pit where a great scarlet beach umbrella or a cabana stands. Front and right stage left are benches facing the sea; attached to each bench is a street-lamp.

The only scenery is two cardboard cut-outs six feet high, representing shops at the back of the stage. Reading from left to right they are: SALT WATER TAFFY: FORTUNE TELLER; then the blank space; BINGO PARLOR; TURKISH BATH. They have practical doors, that of the Fortune Teller's being hung with bright gypsy curtains.

By the left proscenium and rising from the orchestra pit is the weather signal; it is like the mast of a ship with cross bars. From time to time black discs are hung on it to indicate the storm and hurricane warnings. Three roller chairs, pushed by melancholy NEGROES, *file by empty. Throughout the act they traverse the stage in both directions.*

From time to time, CONVEENERS, *dressed like* MR. ANTROBUS, *cross the stage. Some walk sedately by; others engage in inane horseplay. The old gypsy* FORTUNE TELLER *is seated at the door of her shop, smoking a corncob pipe.*

From the Bingo Parlor comes the voice of the CALLER]

BINGO CALLER: A-Nine; A-Nine. C-Twenty-six; C-Twenty-six. A-Four; A-Four, B-Twelve.

CHORUS: *[Back-stage]* Bingo!!! *[The front of the Bingo Parlor shudders, rises a few feet in the air and returns to the ground trembling]*

FORTUNE TELLER: *[Mechanically, to the unconscious back of a passerby, pointing with her pipe]* Bright's disease! Your partner's deceiving you in that Kansas City deal. You'll have six grandchildren. Avoid high places. *[She rises and shouts after another:]* Cirrhosis of the liver! [SABINA *appears at the door of the Bingo Parlor. She hugs about her a blue raincoat that almost conceals her red bathing suit. She tries to catch the* FORTUNE TELLER's *attention]*

SABINA: Ssssst! Esmeralda! Ssssst!

FORTUNE TELLER: Keck!

SABINA: Has President Antrobus come along yet?

FORTUNE TELLER: No, no, no. Get back there. Hide yourself.

SABINA: I'm afraid I'll miss him. Oh, Esmeralda, if I fail in this, I'll die; I know I'll die. President Antrobus!!! And I'll be his wife! If it's the last thing I'll do, I'll be Mrs. George Antrobus.—Esmeralda, tell me my future.

FORTUNE TELLER: Keck!

SABINA: All right, I'll tell *you* my future. *[Laughing dreamily and tracing it out with one finger on the palm of her hand]* I've won the Beauty Contest in Atlantic City,—well, I'll win the Beauty Contest of the whole world. I'll take President Antrobus away from that wife of his. Then I'll take every man away from his wife. I'll turn the whole earth upside down.

FORTUNE TELLER: Keck!

SABINA: When all those husbands just think about me they'll get dizzy. They'll faint in the streets. They'll have to lean against lampposts.—Esmeralda, who was Helen of Troy?

FORTUNE TELLER: *[Furiously]* Shut your foolish mouth. When Mr. Antrobus comes along you can see what you can do. Until then,—go away. [SABINA *laughs. As she returns to the door of her Bingo Parlor a group of* CONVEENERS *rush over and smother her with attentions: "Oh, Miss Lily, you know me. You've known me for years."]*

SABINA: Go away, boys, go away. I'm after bigger fry than you are.—Why, Mr. Simpson! How *dare* you!! I expect that even you nobodies must have girls to amuse you; but where you find them and what you do with them, is of absolutely no interest to me. *[Exit. The* CONVEENERS *squeal with pleasure and stumble in after her.*

The FORTUNE TELLER *rises, puts her pipe down on the stool, unfurls her voluminous skirts, gives a sharp wrench to her bodice and strolls toward the audience, swinging her hips like a young woman]*

FORTUNE TELLER: I tell the future. Keck. Nothing easier. Everybody's future is in their face. Nothing easier.

But who can tell your past,—eh? Nobody!

Your youth,—where did it go? It slipped away while you weren't looking. While you were asleep. While you were drunk? Puh! You're like our friends, Mr. and Mrs. Antrobus; you lie awake nights trying to know your past. What did it mean? What was it trying to say to you?

Think! Think! Split your heads. I can't tell the past and neither can you. If anybody tries to tell you the past, take my word for it, they're charlatans! Charlatans! But I can tell the future. *[She suddenly barks at a passing chair-pusher]* Apoplexy! *[She returns to the audience]* Nobody listens.—Keck! I see a face among you now—I won't embarrass him by pointing him out, but, listen, it may be you: Next year the watchsprings inside you will crumple up. Death by regret,—Type Y. It's in the corners of your mouth. You'll decide that you should have lived for pleasure, but that you missed it. Death by regret,—Type Y. . . . Avoid mirrors. You'll try to be angry,—but no!—no anger. *[Far forward, confidentially]* And now what's the immediate future of our friends, the Antrobuses? Oh, you've seen it as well as I have, keck,—that dizziness of the head; that Great Man dizziness? The inventor of beer and gunpowder. The sudden fits of temper and then the long stretches of inertia? "I'm a sultan; let my slave-girls fan me?"

You know as well as I what's coming. Rain. Rain. Rain in floods. The deluge. But first you'll see shameful things—shameful things. Some of you will be saying: "Let him drown. He's not worth saving. Give the whole thing up." I can see it in your faces. But you're wrong. Keep your doubts and despairs to yourselves.

Again there'll be the narrow escape. The survival of a handful. From destruction,—total destruction. *[She points sweeping with her hand to the stage]*

Even of the animals, a few will be saved: two of a kind, male and female, two of a kind. *[The heads of* CONVEENERS *appear about the stage and in the orchestra pit, jeering at her]*

CONVEENERS: Charlatan! Madam Kill-Joy! Mrs. Jeremiah! Charlatan!

FORTUNE TELLER: And *you!* Mark my words before it's too late. Where'll *you* be?

CONVEENERS: The croaking raven. Old dust and ashes. Rags, bottles, sacks.

FORTUNE TELLER: Yes, stick out your tongues. You can't stick your tongues out far enough to lick the death-sweat from your foreheads.

It's too late to work now—bail out the flood with your soup spoons. You've had your chance and you've lost.

CONVEENERS: Enjoy yourselves!!! *[They disappear. The* FORTUNE TELLER *looks off left and puts her finger on her lips]*

FORTUNE TELLER: They're coming—the Antrobuses. Keck. Your hope. Your despair. Your selves. *[Enter from the left,* MR. *and* MRS. ANTROBUS *and* GLADYS*]*

MRS. ANTROBUS: Gladys Antrobus, stick your stummick in.

GLADYS: But it's easier this way.

MRS. ANTROBUS: Well, it's too bad the new president has such a clumsy daughter, that's all I can say. Try and be a lady.

FORTUNE TELLER: Aijah! That's been said a hundred billion times.

MRS. ANTROBUS: Goodness! Where's Henry? He was here just a minute ago. Henry! *[Sudden violent stir. A roller-chair appears from the left. About it are dancing in great excitement* HENRY *and a* NEGRO CHAIR-PUSHER*]*

HENRY: *[Slingshot in hand]* I'll put your eye out. I'll make you yell, like you never yelled before.

NEGRO: *[At the same time]* Now, I warns you. I warns you. If you make me mad, you'll get hurt.

ANTROBUS: Henry! What is this? Put down that slingshot.

MRS. ANTROBUS: *[At the same time]* Henry! HENRY! Behave yourself.

FORTUNE TELLER: That's right, young man. There are too many people in the world as it is. Everybody's in the way, except one's self.

HENRY: All I wanted to do was—have some fun.

NEGRO: Nobody can't touch my chair, nobody, without I allow 'em to. You get clean away from me and you get away fast. *[He pushes his chair off, muttering]*

ANTROBUS: What were you doing, Henry?

HENRY: Everybody's always getting mad. Everybody's always trying to push you around. I'll make him sorry for this; I'll make him sorry.

ANTROBUS: Give me that slingshot.

HENRY: I won't. I'm sorry I came to this place. I wish I weren't here. I wish I weren't anywhere.

MRS. ANTROBUS: Now, Henry, don't get so excited about nothing. I declare I don't know what we're going to do with you. Put your slingshot in your pocket, and don't try to take hold of things that don't belong to you.

ANTROBUS: After this you can stay home. I wash my hands of you.

MRS. ANTROBUS: Come now, let's forget all about it. Everybody take a good breath of that sea air and calm down. *{A passing* CONVEENER *bows to* ANTROBUS *who nods to him}* Who was that you spoke to, George?

ANTROBUS: Nobody, Maggie. Just the candidate who ran against me in the election.

MRS. ANTROBUS: The man who ran against you in the election!! *{She turns and waves her umbrella after the disappearing* CONVEENER*]* My husband didn't speak to you and he never will speak to you.

ANTROBUS: Now, Maggie.

MRS. ANTROBUS: After those lies you told about him in your speeches! Lies, that's what they were.

GLADYS AND HENRY: Mama, everybody's looking at you. Everybody's laughing at you.

MRS. ANTROBUS: If you must know, my husband's a SAINT, a downright SAINT, and you're not fit to speak to him on the street.

ANTROBUS: Now, Maggie, now, Maggie, that's enough of that.

MRS. ANTROBUS: George Antrobus, you're a perfect worm. If you won't stand up for yourself, I will.

GLADYS: Mama, you just act awful in public.

MRS. ANTROBUS: *{Laughing}* Well, I must say I enjoyed it. I feel better. Wish his wife had been there to hear it. Children, what do you want to do?

GLADYS: Papa, can we ride in one of those chairs? Mama, I want to ride in one of those chairs.

MRS. ANTROBUS: No, sir. If you're tired you just sit where you are. We have no money to spend on foolishness.

ANTROBUS: I guess we have money enough for a thing like that. It's one of the things you do at Atlantic City.

MRS. ANTROBUS: Oh, we have? I tell you it's a miracle my children have shoes to stand up in. I didn't think I'd ever live to see them pushed around in chairs.

ANTROBUS: We're on a vacation, aren't we? We have a right to some treats, I guess. Maggie, some day you're going to drive me crazy.

MRS. ANTROBUS: All right, go. I'll just sit here and laugh at you. And you can give me my dollar right in my hand. Mark my words, a rainy day is coming. There's a rainy day ahead of us: I feel it in my bones. Go on, throw your money around. I can starve. I've starved before. I know how. *{A* CONVEENER *puts his head through Turkish Bath window, and says with raised eyebrows:}*

CONVEENER: Hello, George. How are ya? I see where you brought the WHOLE family along.

MRS. ANTROBUS: And what do you mean by that? [CONVEENER *withdraws head and closes window}*

ANTROBUS: Maggie, I tell you there's a limit to what I can stand. God's Heaven, haven't I worked *enough?* Don't I get *any* vacation? Can't I even give my children so much as a ride in a roller-chair?

MRS. ANTROBUS: *{Putting out her hand for raindrops}* Anyway, it's going to rain very soon and you have your broadcast to make.

ANTROBUS: Now, Maggie, I warn you. A man can stand a family only just so long. I'm warning you. *{Enter* SABINA *from the Bingo-Parlor. She wears a flounced red silk bathing suit, 1905. Red stockings, shoes, parasol. She bows demurely to* ANTROBUS *and starts down the ramp.* ANTROBUS *and the children stare at her.* ANTROBUS *bows gallantly}*

MRS. ANTROBUS: Why, George Antrobus, how can you say such a thing! You have the best family in the world.

ANTROBUS: Good morning, Miss Fairweather. [SABINA *finally disappears behind the beach umbrella or in a cabana in the orchestra pit}*

MRS. ANTROBUS: Who on earth was that you spoke to George?

ANTROBUS: *{Complacent; mock-modest}* Hm . . . m . . . Just a . . . solambaka keray.

MRS. ANTROBUS: What? I can't understand you.

GLADYS: Mama, wasn't she beautiful?

HENRY: Papa, introduce her to me.

MRS. ANTROBUS: Children, will you be quiet while I ask your father a simple question?—Who did you say it was, George?

ANTROBUS: Why-uh . . . a friend of mine. Very nice refined girl.

MRS. ANTROBUS: I'm waiting.

ANTROBUS: Maggie, that's the girl I gave the prize to in the beauty contest,—that's Miss Atlantic City 1942.

MRS. ANTROBUS: Hm! She looked like Sabina to me.

HENRY: *{At the railing}* Mama, the lifeguard knows her, too. Mama, he knows her well.

ANTROBUS: Henry, come here.—She's a very nice girl in every way and the sole support of her aged mother.

MRS. ANTROBUS: So was Sabina, so was Sabina; and it took a wall of ice to open your eyes about Sabina.—Henry, come over and sit down on this bench.

ANTROBUS: She's a very different matter from Sabina. Miss Fairweather is a college graduate, Phi Beta Kappa.

MRS. ANTROBUS: Henry, you sit here by mama. Gladys—

ANTROBUS: *{Sitting}* Reduced circumstances have required her taking a position as hostess in a Bingo Parlor; but there isn't a girl with higher principles in the country.

MRS. ANTROBUS: Well, let's not talk about it.—Henry, I haven't seen a whale yet.

ANTROBUS: She speaks seven languages and has more culture in her little finger than you've acquired in a lifetime.

MRS. ANTROBUS: *{Assumed amiability}* All right, all right, George. I'm glad to know there are such superior girls in the Bingo Parlors.—Henry, what's that? *{Pointing at the storm signal, which has one black disk}*

HENRY: What is it, Papa?

ANTROBUS: What? Oh, that's the storm signal. One of those black disks means bad weather; two means storm; three means hurricane; and four means the end of the world. *{As they watch it a second black disk rolls into place}*

MRS. ANTROBUS: Goodness! I'm going this very minute to buy you all some raincoats.

GLADYS: *{Putting her cheek against her father's shoulder}* Mama, don't go yet. I like sitting this way. And the ocean coming in and coming in. Papa, don't you like it?

MRS. ANTROBUS: Well, there's only one thing I lack to make me a perfectly happy woman: I'd like to see a whale.

HENRY: Mama, we saw two. Right out there. They're delegates to the convention. I'll find you one.

GLADYS: Papa, ask me something. Ask me a question.

ANTROBUS: Well . . . how big's the ocean?

GLADYS: Papa, you're teasing me. It's—three-hundred and sixty million square-miles — and — it — covers — three-fourths — of — the — earth's — surface — and — its — deepest-place — is — five — and — a — half — miles — deep — and — its — average — depth — is — twelve-thousand-feet. No, Papa, ask me something hard, real hard.

MRS. ANTROBUS: *{Rising}* Now I'm going off to buy those raincoats. I think that bad weather's going to get worse and worse. I hope it doesn't come before your broadcast. I should think we have about an hour or so.

HENRY: I hope it comes and zzzzzz everything before it. I hope it—

MRS. ANTROBUS: Henry!—George, I think . . . maybe, it's one of those storms that are just as bad on land as on the sea. When you're just as safe and safer in a good stout boat.

HENRY: There's a boat out at the end of the pier.

MRS. ANTROBUS: Well, keep your eye

on it. George, you shut your eyes and get a good rest before the broadcast.

ANTROBUS: Thundering Judas, do I have to be told when to open and shut my eyes? Go and buy your raincoats.

MRS ANTROBUS: Now, children, you have ten minutes to walk around. Ten minutes. And Henry: control yourself. Gladys, stick by your brother and don't get lost. *{They run off}*

MRS. ANTROBUS: Will you be all right, George? {CONVEENERS *suddenly stick their heads out of the Bingo Parlor and Salt Water Taffy store, and voices rise from the orchestra pit}*

CONVEENERS: George, Geo-r-r-rge! George! Leave the old hen-coop at home, George. Do-mes-ticated Georgie!

MRS. ANTROBUS: *{Shaking her umbrella}* Low common oafs! That's what they are. Guess a man has a right to bring his wife to a convention, if he wants to. *{She starts off}* What's the matter with a family, I'd like to know. What else have they got to offer? *{Exit.* ANTROBUS *has closed his eyes. The* FORTUNE TELLER *comes out of her shop and goes over to the left proscenium. She leans against it watching* SABINA *quizzically}*

FORTUNE TELLER: Heh! Here she comes!

SABINA: *{Loud whisper}* What's he doing?

FORTUNE TELLER: Oh, he's ready for you. Bite your lips, dear, take a long breath and come on up.

SABINA: I'm nervous. My whole future depends on this. I'm nervous.

FORTUNE TELLER: Don't be a fool. What more could you want? He's forty-five. His head's a little dizzy. He's just been elected president. He's never known any other woman than his wife. Whenever he looks at her he realizes that she knows every foolish thing he's ever done.

SABINA: *{Still whispering}* I don't know why it is, but every time I start one of these I'm nervous. *{The* FORTUNE TELLER *stands in the center of the stage watching the following:}*

FORTUNE TELLER: You make me tired.

SABINA: First tell me my fortune. *{The* FORTUNE TELLER *laughs drily and makes the gesture of brushing away a nonsensical question.* SABINA *coughs and says:}* Oh, Mr. Antrobus,—dare I speak to you for a moment?

ANTROBUS: What?—Oh, certainly, certainly, Miss Fairweather.

SABINA: Mr. Antrobus . . . I've been so unhappy. I've wanted . . . I've wanted to make sure that you don't think that I'm the kind of girl who goes out for beauty contests.

FORTUNE TELLER: That's the way!

ANTROBUS: Oh, I understand. I understand perfectly.

FORTUNE TELLER: Give it a little more. Lean on it.

SABINA: I knew you would. My mother said to me this morning: Lily, she said, that fine Mr. Antrobus gave you the prize because he saw at once that you weren't the kind of girl who'd go in for a thing like that. But, honestly, Mr. Antrobus, in this world, honestly, a good girl doesn't know where to turn.

FORTUNE TELLER: Now you've gone too far.

ANTROBUS: My dear Miss Fairweather!

SABINA: You wouldn't know how hard it is. With that lovely wife and daughter you have. Oh, I think Mrs. Antrobus is the finest woman I ever saw. I wish I were like her.

ANTROBUS: There, there. There's . . . uh . . . room for all kinds of people in the world, Miss Fairweather.

SABINA: How wonderful of you to say that. How generous!—Mr. Antrobus, have you a moment free? . . . I'm afraid I may be a little conspicuous here . . . could you come down, for just a moment, to my beach cabana . . . ?

ANTROBUS: Why-uh . . . yes, certainly . . . for a moment . . . just for a moment.

SABINA: There's a deck chair there. Because: you know you *do* look tired.

Just this morning my mother said to me: Lily, she said, I hope Mr. Antrobus is getting a good rest. His fine strong face has deep lines in it. Now isn't it true, Mr. Antrobus: you work too hard?

FORTUNE TELLER: Bingo! *{She goes into her shop}*

SABINA: Now you will just stretch out. No, I shan't say a word, not a word. I shall just sit there,—privileged. That's what I am.

ANTROBUS: *{Taking her hand}* Miss Fairweather . . . you'll . . . spoil me.

SABINA: Just a moment. I have something I wish to say to the audience.— Ladies and gentlemen. I'm not going to play this particular scene tonight. It's just a short scene and we're going to skip it. But I'll tell you what takes place and then we can continue the play from there on. Now in this scene—

ANTROBUS: *{Between his teeth}* But, Miss Somerset!

SABINA: I'm sorry. I'm sorry. But I have to skip it. In this scene, I talk to Mr. Antrobus, and at the end of it he decides to leave his wife, get a divorce at Reno and marry me. That's all.

ANTROBUS: Fitz!—Fitz!

SABINA: So that now I've told you we can jump to the end of it,—where you say: *{Enter in fury* MR. FITZPATRICK, *the stage manager}*

MR. FITZPATRICK: Miss Somerset, we insist on your playing this scene.

SABINA: I'm sorry, Mr. Fitzpatrick, but I can't and I won't. I've told the audience all they need to know and now we can go on. *{Other* ACTORS *begin to appear on the stage, listening}*

MR. FITZPATRICK: And *why* can't you play it?

SABINA: Because there are some lines in that scene that would hurt some people's feelings and I don't think the theatre is a place where people's feelings ought to be hurt.

MR. FITZPATRICK: Miss Somerset, you can pack up your things and go home. I shall call the understudy and I shall report you to Equity.

SABINA: I sent the understudy up to the corner for a cup of coffee and if Equity tries to penalize me I'll drag the case right up to the Supreme Court. Now listen, everybody, there's no need to get excited.

MR. FITZPATRICK *and* ANTROBUS: Why can't you play it . . . what's the matter with the scene?

SABINA: Well, if you must know, I have a personal guest in the audience tonight. Her life hasn't been exactly a happy one. I wouldn't have my friend hear some of these lines for the whole world. I don't suppose it occurred to the author that some other women might have gone through the experience of losing their husbands like this. Wild horses wouldn't drag from me the details of my friend's life, but . . . well, they'd been married twenty years, and before he got rich, why, she'd done the washing and everything.

MR. FITZPATRICK: Miss Somerset, your friend will forgive you. We must play this scene.

SABINA: Nothing, nothing will make me say some of those lines . . . about "a man outgrows a wife every seven years" and . . . and that one about "the Mohammedans being the only people who looked the subject square in the face." Nothing.

MR. FITZPATRICK: Miss Somerset! Go to your dressing room. I'll *read* your lines.

SABINA: Now everybody's nerves are on edge.

MR. ANTROBUS: Skip the scene. {MR. FITZPATRICK *and the other* ACTORS *go off}*

SABINA: Thank you. I knew you'd understand. We'll do just what I said. So Mr. Antrobus is going to divorce his wife and marry me. Mr. Antrobus, you say: "It won't be easy to lay all this before my wife." *{The* ACTORS *withdraw.* ANTROBUS *walks about, his hand to his forehead muttering:}*

ANTROBUS: Wait a minute. I can't get back into it as easily as all that.

"My wife is a very obstinate woman." Hm . . . then you say . . . hm . . . Miss Fairweather, I mean Lily, it won't be easy to lay all this before my wife. It'll hurt her feelings a little.

SABINA: Listen, George: *other* people haven't got feelings. Not in the same way that we have,—we who are presidents like you and prize-winners like me. Listen, other people haven't got feelings; they just imagine they have. Within two weeks they go back to playing bridge and going to the movies.

Listen, dear: everybody in the world except a few people like you and me are just people of straw. Most people have no insides at all. Now that you're president you'll see that. Listen, darling, there's a kind of secret society at the top of the world,—like you and me,—that know this. The world was made for us. What's life anyway? Except for two things, pleasure and power, what is life? Boredom! Foolishness. You know it is. Except for those two things, life's nau-se-at-ing. So,—come here! *{She moves close. They kiss}* So.

Now when your wife comes, it's really very simple; just tell her.

ANTROBUS: Lily, Lily: you're a wonderful woman.

SABINA: Of course I am. *{They enter the cabana and it hides them from view. Distant roll of thunder. A third black disk appears on the weather signal. Distant thunder is heard.* MRS. ANTROBUS *appears carrying parcels. She looks about, seats herself on the bench left, and fans herself with her handkerchief. Enter* GLADYS *right, followed by two* CONVEENERS. *She is wearing red stockings}*

MRS. ANTROBUS: Gladys!

GLADYS: Mama, here I am.

MRS. ANTROBUS: Gladys Antrobus!!! Where did you get those dreadful things?

GLADYS: Wha-a-t? Papa liked the color.

MRS. ANTROBUS: You go back to the hotel this minute!

GLADYS: I won't. I won't. Papa liked the color.

MRS. ANTROBUS: All right. All right. You stay here. I've a good mind to let your father see you that way. You stay right here.

GLADYS: I . . . don't want to stay if . . . if you don't think he'd like it.

MRS. ANTROBUS: Oh . . . it's all one to me. I don't care what happens. I don't care if the biggest storm in the whole world comes. Let it come. *{She folds her hands}* Where's your brother?

GLADYS: *{In a small voice}* He'll be here.

MRS. ANTROBUS: Will he? Well, let him get into trouble. I don't care. I don't know where your father is, I'm sure. *{Laughter from the cabana}*

GLADYS: *{Leaning over the rail}* I think he's . . . Mama, he's talking to the lady in the red dress.

MRS. ANTROBUS: Is that so? *{Pause}* We'll wait till he's through. Sit down here beside me and stop fidgeting . . . what are you crying about? *{Distant thunder. She covers* GLADYS'S *stockings with a raincoat}*

GLADYS: You don't like my stockings. *{Two* CONVEENERS *rush in with a microphone on a standard and various paraphernalia. The* FORTUNE TELLER *appears at the door of her shop. Other characters gradually gather}*

BROADCAST OFFICIAL: Mrs. Antrobus! Thank God we've found you at last. Where's Mr. Antrobus? We've been hunting everywhere for him. It's about time for the broadcast to the conventions of the world.

MRS. ANTROBUS: *{Calm}* I expect he'll be here in a minute.

BROADCAST OFFICIAL: Mrs. Antrobus, if he doesn't show up in time, I hope you will consent to broadcast in his place. It's the most important broadcast of the year. [SABINA *enters from cabana followed by* ANTROBUS*}*

MRS. ANTROBUS: No, I shan't. I haven't one single thing to say.

BROADCAST OFFICIAL: Then won't you help us find him, Mrs. Antrobus? A storm's coming up. A hurricane. A deluge!

SECOND CONVEENER: *{Who has sighted* ANTROBUS *over the rail}* Joe! Joe! Here he is.

BROADCAST OFFICIAL: In the name of God, Mr. Antrobus, you're on the air in five minutes. Will you kindly please come and test the instrument? That's all we ask. If you just please begin the alphabet slowly. [ANTROBUS, *with set face, comes ponderously up the ramp. He stops at the point where his waist is level with the stage and speaks authoritatively to the* OFFICIALS]

ANTROBUS: I'll be ready when the time comes. Until then, move away. Go away. I have something I wish to say to my wife.

BROADCAST OFFICIAL: *{Whimpering}* Mr. Antrobus! This is the most important broadcast of the year. *{The* OFFICIALS *withdraw to the edge of the stage.* SABINA *glides up the ramp behind* ANTROBUS]

SABINA: *{Whispering}* Don't let her argue. Remember arguments have nothing to do with it.

ANTROBUS: Maggie, I'm moving out of the hotel. In fact, I'm moving out of everything. For good. I'm going to marry Miss Fairweather. I shall provide generously for you and the children. In a few years you'll be able to see that it's all for the best. That's all I have to say.

BROADCAST OFFICIAL: Mr. Antrobus! I hope you'll be ready. This is the most important broadcast of the year.

GLADYS: What did Papa say, Mama? I didn't hear what Papa said.

BINGO ANNOUNCER: A—nine; A—nine. D—forty-two; D—forty-two. C—thirty; C—thirty. B—seventeen; B—seventeen. C—forty; C—forty.

CHORUS: Bingo!!

BROADCAST OFFICIAL: Mr. Antrobus. All we want to do is test your voice with the alphabet.

ANTROBUS: Go away. Clear out.

MRS. ANTROBUS: *{Composedly with lowered eyes}* George, I can't talk to you until you wipe those silly red marks off your face.

ANTROBUS: I think there's nothing to talk about. I've said what I have to say.

SABINA: Splendid!!

ANTROBUS: You're a fine woman, Maggie, but . . . but a man has his own life to lead in the world.

MRS. ANTROBUS: Well, after living with you for five thousand years I guess I have a right to a word or two, haven't I?

ANTROBUS: *{To* SABINA] What can I answer to that?

SABINA: Tell her conversation would only hurt her feelings. It's-kinder-in-the-long-run-to-do-it-short-and-quick.

ANTROBUS: I want to spare your feelings in every way I can, Maggie.

BROADCAST OFFICIAL: Mr. Antrobus, the hurricane signal's gone up. We could begin right now.

MRS. ANTROBUS: *{Calmly, almost dreamily}* I didn't marry you because you were perfect. I didn't even marry you because I loved you. I married you because you gave me a promise.

{She takes off her ring and looks at it}

That promise made up for your faults. And the promise I gave you made up for mine. Two imperfect people got married and it was the promise that made the marriage.

ANTROBUS: Maggie, . . . I was only nineteen.

MRS. ANTROBUS: *{She puts her ring back on her finger}* And when our children were growing up, it wasn't a house that protected them; and it wasn't our love, that protected them—it was that promise.

And when that promise is broken—this can happen! *{With a sweep of the hand she removes the raincoat from* GLADYS'S *stockings}*

ANTROBUS: *{Stretches out his arm, apoplectic}* Gladys!! Have you gone crazy? Has everyone gone crazy? *{Turning on* SABINA] You did this. You gave them to her.

SABINA: I never said a word to her.

ANTROBUS: *{To* GLADYS] You go back to the hotel and take those horrible things off.

GLADYS: *{Pert}* Before I go, I've got something to tell you,—it's about Henry.

MRS. ANTROBUS: *{Claps her hands peremptorily}* Stop your noise,—I'm taking her back to the hotel, George. Before I go I have a letter. . . . I have a message to throw into the ocean. *{Fumbling in her handbag}* Where is the plagued thing? Here it is. *{She flings something—invisible to us—far over the heads of the audience to the back of the auditorium}* It's a bottle. And in the bottle's a letter. And in the letter is written all the things that a woman knows.

It's never been told to any man and it's never been told to any woman, and if it finds its destination, a new time will come. We're not what books and plays say we are. We're not what advertisements say we are. We're not in the movies and we're not on the radio.

We're not what you're all told and what you think we are: We're ourselves. And if any man can find one of us he'll learn why the whole universe was set in motion. And if any man harm any one of us, his soul—the only soul he's got—had better be at the bottom of that ocean,—and that's the only way to put it. Gladys, come here. We're going back to the hotel. *{She drags* GLADYS *firmly off by the hand, but* GLADYS *breaks away and comes down to speak to her father}*

SABINA: Such goings-on. Don't give it a minute's thought.

GLADYS: Anyway, I think you ought to know that Henry hit a man with a stone. He hit one of those colored men that push the chairs and the man's very sick. Henry ran away and hid and some policemen are looking for him very hard. And I don't care a bit if you don't want to have anything to do with mama and me, because I'll never like you again and I hope nobody ever likes you again,—so there! *{She runs off.* ANTROBUS *starts after her}*

ANTROBUS: I . . . I have to go and see what I can do about this.

SABINA: You stay right here. Don't you go now while you're excited. Gracious sakes, all these things will be forgotten in a hundred years. Come, now, you're on the air. Just say anything,—it doesn't matter what. Just a lot of birds and fishes and things.

BROADCAST OFFICIAL: Thank you, Miss Fairweather. Thank you very much. Ready, Mr. Antrobus.

ANTROBUS: *{Touching the microphone}* What is it, what is it? Who am I talking to?

BROADCAST OFFICIAL: Why, Mr. Antrobus! To our order and to all the other orders.

ANTROBUS: *{Raising his head}* What are all those birds doing?

BROADCAST OFFICIAL: Those are just a few of the birds. Those are the delegates to our convention,—two of a kind.

ANTROBUS: *{Pointing into the audience}* Look at the water. Look at them all. Those fishes jumping. The children should see this!—There's Maggie's whales!! Here are your whales, Maggie!!

BROADCAST OFFICIAL: I hope you're ready, Mr. Antrobus.

ANTROBUS: And look on the beach! You didn't tell me these would be here!

SABINA: Yes, George. Those are the animals.

BROADCAST OFFICIAL: *{Busy with the apparatus}* Yes, Mr. Antrobus, those are the vertebrates. We hope the lion will have a word to say when you're through. Step right up, Mr. Antrobus, we're ready. We'll just have time before the storm. *{Pause. In a hoarse whisper:}* They're waiting. *{It has grown dark. Soon after he speaks a high whistling noise begins. Strange veering lights start whirling about the stage. The other characters disappear from the stage}*

ANTROBUS: Friends. Cousins. Four score and ten billion years ago our forefather brought forth upon this planet the spark of life,—*(He is drowned out by thunder. When the thunder stops the* FORTUNE TELLER *is seen standing beside him)*

FORTUNE TELLER: Antrobus, there's not a minute to be lost. Don't you see the four disks on the weather signal? Take your family into that boat at the end of the pier.

ANTROBUS: My family? I have no family. Maggie! Maggie! They won't come.

FORTUNE TELLER: They'll come.—Antrobus! Take these animals into that boat with you. All of them,—two of each kind.

SABINA: George, what's the matter with you? This is just a storm like any other storm.

ANTROBUS: Maggie!

SABINA: Stay with me, we'll go . . . *(Losing conviction)* This is just another thunderstorm,—isn't it? Isn't it?

ANTROBUS: Maggie!!! [MRS. ANTROBUS *appears beside him with* GLADYS]

MRS. ANTROBUS: *(Matter-of-fact)* Here I am and here's Gladys.

ANTROBUS: Where've you been? Where have you been? Quick, we're going into that boat out there.

MRS. ANTROBUS: I know we are. But I haven't found Henry. *(She wanders off into the darkness calling "Henry!")*

SABINA: *(Low urgent babbling, only occasionally raising her voice)* I don't believe it. I don't believe it's anything at all. I've seen hundreds of storms like this.

FORTUNE TELLER: There's no time to lose. Go. Push the animals along before you. Start a new world. Begin again.

SABINA: Esmeralda! George! Tell me,—is it really serious?

ANTROBUS: *(Suddenly very busy)* Elephants first. Gently, gently.—Look where you're going.

GLADYS: *(Leaning over the ramp and striking an animal on the back)* Stop it or you'll be left behind!

ANTROBUS: Is the Kangaroo there? *There* you are! Take those turtles in your pouch, will you? *(To some other animals, pointing to his shoulder)* Here! You jump up here. You'll be trampled on.

GLADYS: *(To her father, pointing below)* Papa, look,—the snakes!

MRS. ANTROBUS: I can't find Henry. Hen-ry!

ANTROBUS: Go along. Go along. Climb on their backs.—Wolves! Jackals—whatever you are,—tend to your own business!

GLADYS: *(Pointing, tenderly)* Papa,—look.

SABINA: Mr. Antrobus—take me with you. Don't leave me here. I'll work. I'll help. I'll do anything. [THREE CONVEENERS *cross the stage, marching with a banner)*

CONVEENERS: George! What are you scared of?—George! Fellas, it looks like rain.—"Maggie, where's my umbrella?"—George, setting up for Barnum and Bailey.

ANTROBUS: *(Again catching his wife's hand)* Come on now, Maggie,—the pier's going to break any minute.

MRS. ANTROBUS: I'm not going a step without Henry. Henry!

GLADYS: *(On the ramp)* Mama! Papa! Hurry. The pier's cracking, Mama. It's going to break.

MRS. ANTROBUS: Henry! Cain! CAIN! [HENRY *dashes into the stage and joins his mother)*

HENRY: Here I am, Mama.

MRS. ANTROBUS: Thank God!—now come quick.

HENRY: I didn't think you wanted me.

MRS. ANTROBUS: Quick! *(She pushes him down before her into the aisle)*

SABINA: *(All the* ANTROBUSES *are now in the theatre aisle.* SABINA *stands at the top of the ramp)* Mrs. Antrobus, take me. Don't you remember me? I'll work. I'll help. Don't leave me here!

MRS. ANTROBUS: *(Impatiently, but as though it were of no importance)* Yes, yes. There's a lot of work to be done. Only hurry.

FORTUNE TELLER: *(Now dominating*

the stage. To SABINA *with a grim smile}* Yes, go—back to the kitchen with you.

SABINA: *{Half-down the ramp. To* FORTUNE TELLER} I don't know why my life's always being interrupted—just when everything's going fine!! *{She dashes up the aisle. Now the* CONVEENERS *emerge doing a serpentine dance on the stage. They jeer at the* FORTUNE TELLER}

CONVEENERS: Get a canoe—there's not a minute to be lost! Tell me my future, Mrs. Croaker.

FORTUNE TELLER: Paddle in the water, boys—enjoy yourselves.

VOICE FROM THE BINGO PARLOR: A-nine; A-nine. C-Twenty-four. C-Twenty-four.

CONVEENERS: Rags, bottles, and sacks.

FORTUNE TELLER: Go back and climb on your roofs. Put rags in the cracks under your doors.—Nothing will keep out the flood. You've had your chance. You've had your day. You've failed. You've lost.

VOICE FROM THE BINGO PARLOR: B-fifteen. B-Fifteen.

FORTUNE TELLER: *{Shading her eyes and looking out to sea}* They're safe. George Antrobus! Think it over! A new world to make—think it over!

CURTAIN

Act III

Just before the curtain rises, two sounds are heard from the stage: a cracked bugle call.

The curtain rises on almost total darkness. Almost all the flats composing the walls of MR. ANTROBUS'S *house, as of Act I, are up, but they lean helter-skelter against one another, leaving irregular gaps. Among the flats missing are two in the back wall, leaving the frames of the window and door crazily out of line. Off stage, back right, some red Roman fire is burning. The bugle call is repeated. Enter* SABINA *through the tilted door. She is dressed as a Napoleonic camp follower, "la fille du regiment," in begrimed reds and blues.*

SABINA: Mrs. Antrobus! Gladys! Where are you?

The war's over. The war's over. You can come out. The peace treaty's been signed.

Where are they?—Hmph! Are they dead, too? Mrs. Annnntrobus! Glaaaadus! Mr. Antrobus'll be here this afternoon. I just saw him downtown. Huuuurry and put things in order. He says that now that the war's over we'll all have to settle down and be perfect. *{Enter* MR. FITZPATRICK, *the stage manager, followed by the whole company, who stand waiting at the edges of the stage.* MR. FITZPATRICK *tries to interrupt* SABINA}

MR. FITZPATRICK: Miss Somerset, we have to stop a moment.

SABINA: They may be hiding out in the back—

MR. FITZPATRICK: Miss Somerset! We have to stop a moment.

SABINA: What's the matter?

MR. FITZPATRICK: There's an explanation we have to make to the audience.—Lights, please. *{To the actor who plays* MR. ANTROBUS,} Will you explain the matter to the audience? *{The lights go up. We now see that a balcony or elevated runway has been erected at the back of the stage, back of the wall of the Antrobus house. From its extreme right and left ends ladder-like steps descend to the floor of the stage}*

ANTROBUS: Ladies and gentlemen, an unfortunate accident has taken place back stage. Perhaps I should say *another* unfortunate accident.

SABINA: I'm sorry. I'm sorry.

ANTROBUS: The management feels, in fact, we all feel that you are due an apology. And now we have to ask your indulgence for the most serious mishap of all. Seven of our actors have . . . have been taken ill. Apparently, it was something they ate. I'm not exactly clear what happened. *{All the* ACTORS *start to talk at once.* ANTROBUS *raises his hand}* Now, now—not all at once. Fitz, do you know what it was?

MR. FITZPATRICK: Why, it's perfectly clear. These seven actors had dinner together, and they ate something that disagreed with them.

SABINA: Disagreed with them!!! They have ptomaine poisoning. They're in Bellevue Hospital this very minute in agony. They're having their stomachs pumped out this very minute, in perfect agony.

ANTROBUS: Fortunately, we've just heard they'll all recover.

SABINA: It'll be a miracle if they do, a downright miracle. It was the lemon meringue pie.

ACTORS: It was the fish . . . it was the canned tomatoes . . . it was the fish.

SABINA: It was the lemon meringue pie. I saw it with my own eyes; it had blue mould all over the bottom of it.

ANTROBUS: Whatever it was, they're in no condition to take part in this performance. Naturally, we haven't enough understudies to fill all those roles; but we do have a number of splendid volunteers who have kindly consented to help us out. These friends have watched our rehearsals, and they assure me that they know the lines and the business very well. Let me introduce them to you—my dresser, Mr. Tremayne,—himself a distinguished Shakespearean actor for many years; our wardrobe mistress, Hester; Miss Somerset's maid, Ivy; and Fred Bailey, captain of the ushers in this theatre. *{These persons bow modestly.* IVY *and* HESTER *are colored girls}*

Now this scene takes place near the end of the act. And I'm sorry to say we'll need a short rehearsal, just a short run-through. And as some of it takes place in the auditorium, we'll have to keep the curtain up. Those of you who wish can go out in the lobby and smoke some more. The rest of you can listen to us, or . . . or just talk quietly among yourselves, as you choose. Thank you. Now will you take it over, Mr. Fitzpatrick?

MR. FITZPATRICK: Thank you.—Now for those of you who are listening perhaps I should explain that at the end of this act, the men have come back from the War and the family's settled down in the house. And the author wants to show the hours of the night passing by over their heads, and the planets crossing the sky . . . uh . . . over their heads. And he says—this is hard to explain—that each of the hours of the night is a philosopher, or a great thinker. Eleven o'clock, for instance, is Aristotle. And nine o'clock is Spinoza. Like that. I don't suppose it means anything. It's just a kind of poetic effect.

SABINA: Not mean anything! Why, it certainly does. Twelve o'clock goes by saying those wonderful things. I think it means that when people are asleep they have all those lovely thoughts, much better than when they're awake.

IVY: Excuse me, I think it means,—excuse me, Mr. Fitzpatrick—

SABINA: What were you going to say, Ivy?

IVY: Mr. Fitzpatrick, you let my father come to a rehearsal; and my father's a Baptist minister, and he said that the author meant that—just like the hours and stars go by over our heads at night, in the same way the ideas and thoughts of the great men are in the air around us all the time and they're working on us, even when we don't know it.

MR. FITZPATRICK: Well, well, maybe that's it. Thank you, Ivy. Anyway,—the hours of the night are philosophers. My friends, are you ready? Ivy, can you be eleven o'clock? "This good estate of the mind possessing its object in energy we call divine." Aristotle.

IVY: Yes, sir. I know that and I know twelve o'clock and I know nine o'clock.

MR. FITZPATRICK: Twelve o'clock? Mr. Tremayne, the Bible.

TREMAYNE: Yes.

MR. FITZPATRICK: Ten o'clock? Hester,—Plato? *{She nods eagerly}* Nine o'clock, Spinoza,—Fred?

BAILEY: Yes, sir. [FRED BAILEY *picks up a great gilded cardboard numeral IX and starts up the steps to the platform.* MR. FITZPATRICK *strikes his forehead}*

MR. FITZPATRICK: The planets!! We forgot all about the planets.

SABINA: O my God! The planets! Are they sick too? [ACTORS *nod}*

MR. FITZPATRICK: Ladies and gentlemen, the planets are singers. Of course, we can't replace them, so you'll have to imagine them singing in this scene. Saturn sings from the orchestra pit down here. The Moon is way up there. And Mars with a red lantern in his hand, stands in the aisle over there—Tz-tz-tz. It's too bad; it all makes a very fine effect. However! Ready—nine o'clock: Spinoza.

BAILEY: *{Walking slowly across the balcony, left to right}* "After experience had taught me that the common occurrences of daily life are vain and futile—"

FITZPATRICK: Louder, Fred, "And I saw that all the objects of my desire and fear—"

BAILEY: "And I saw that all the objects of my desire and fear were in themselves nothing good nor bad save insofar as the mind was affected by them—"

FITZPATRICK: Do you know the rest? All right. Ten o'clock. Hester. Plato.

HESTER: "Then tell me, O Critias, how will a man choose the ruler that shall rule over him? Will he not—"

FITZPATRICK: Thank you. Skip to the end, Hester.

HESTER: ". . . can be multiplied a thousand fold in its effects among the citizens."

FITZPATRICK: Thank you.—Aristotle, Ivy?

IVY: "This good estate of the mind possessing its object in energy we call divine. This we mortals have occasionally and it is this energy which is pleasantest and best. But God has it always. It is wonderful in us; but in Him how much more wonderful."

FITZPATRICK: Midnight. Midnight, Mr. Tremayne. That's right,—you've done it before.—All right, everybody. You know what you have to do.—Lower the curtain. House lights up. Act Three of THE SKIN OF OUR TEETH. *{As the curtain descends he is heard saying:}* You volunteers, just wear what you have on. Don't try to put on the costumes today. *{House lights go down. The Act begins again. The Bugle call. Curtain rises. Enter* SABINA]

SABINA: Mrs. Antrobus! Gladys! Where are you?

The war's over.—You've heard all this—*{She gabbles the main points}*

Where — are — they? Are — they — dead, too, et cetera.

I — just — saw — Mr. — Antrobus — down town, et cetera. *{Slowing up:}* He says that now that the war's over we'll all have to settle down and be perfect. They may be hiding out in the back somewhere. Mrs. An-tro-bus. *{She wanders off. It has grown lighter. A trapdoor is cautiously raised and* MRS. ANTROBUS *emerges waist-high and listens. She is disheveled and worn; she wears a tattered dress and a shawl half covers her head. She talks down through the trapdoor}*

MRS. ANTROBUS: It's getting light. There's still something burning over there—Newark, or Jersey City. What? Yes, I could swear I heard someone moving about up here. But I can't see anybody. I say: I can't see anybody. *{She starts to move about the stage.* GLADYS' *head appears at the trapdoor. She is holding a* BABY]

GLADYS: Oh, Mama. Be careful.

MRS. ANTROBUS: Now, Gladys, you stay out of sight.

GLADY: Well, let me stay here just a minute. I want the baby to get some of this fresh air.

MRS. ANTROBUS: All right, but keep your eyes open. I'll see what I can find. I'll have a good hot plate of soup for you before you can say Jack Robinson. Gladys Antrobus! Do you know what I think I see? There's old Mr. Hawkins sweeping the sidewalk in front of his A. and P. store. Sweeping it with a broom. Why, he must have gone crazy, like the others! I see some other people moving about, too.

GLADYS: Mama, come back, come back. [MRS. ANTROBUS *returns to the trapdoor and listens*]

MRS. ANTROBUS: Gladys, there's something in the air. Everybody's movement's sort of different. I see some women walking right out in the middle of the street.

SABINA'S VOICE: Mrs. An-tro-bus!

MRS. ANTROBUS AND GLADYS: What's that?!!

SABINA'S VOICE: Glaaaadys! Mrs. Antro-bus! [*Enter* SABINA]

MRS. ANTROBUS: Gladys, that's Sabina's voice as sure as I live.—Sabina! Sabina!—Are you *alive?!!*

SABINA: Of course, I'm alive. How've you girls been?—*Don't try and kiss me.* I never want to kiss another human being as long as I live. Sh-sh, there's nothing to get emotional about. Pull yourself together, the war's over. Take a deep breath,—the war's over.

MRS. ANTROBUS: The war's over!! I don't believe you. I don't believe you. I can't believe you.

GLADYS: Mama!

SABINA: Who's that?

MRS. ANTROBUS: That's Gladys and her baby. I don't believe you. Gladys, Sabina says the war's over. Oh, Sabina.

SABINA: [*Leaning over the* BABY] Goodness! Are there any babies left in the world! Can it see? And can it cry and everything?

GLADYS: Yes, he can. He notices everything very well.

SABINA: Where on earth did you get it? Oh, I won't ask.—Lord, I've lived all these seven years around camp and I've forgotten how to behave.—Now we've got to think about the men coming home.—Mrs. Antrobus, go and wash your face, I'm ashamed of you. Put your best clothes on. Mr. Antrobus'll be here this afternoon. I just saw him downtown.

MRS. ANTROBUS AND GLADYS: He's alive!! He'll be here!! Sabina, you're not joking?

MRS. ANTROBUS: And Henry?

SABINA: [*dryly*] Yes, Henry's alive, too, that's what they say. Now don't stop to talk. Get yourself fixed up. Gladys, you look terrible. Have you any decent clothes? [SABINA *has pushed them toward the trapdoor*]

MRS. ANTROBUS: [*Half down*] Yes, I've something to wear just for this very day. But, Sabina,—who won the war?

SABINA: Don't stop now,—just wash your face. [*A whistle sounds in the distance*] Oh, my God, what's that silly little noise?

MRS. ANTROBUS: Why, it sounds like . . . it sounds like what used to be the noon whistle at the shoe-polish factory. [*Exit*]

SABINA: That's what it is. Seems to me like peacetime's coming along pretty fast—shoe polish!

GLADYS: [*Half down*] Sabina, how soon after peacetime begins does the milkman start coming to the door?

SABINA: As soon as he catches a cow. Give him time to catch a cow, dear. [*Exit* GLADYS. SABINA *walks about a moment, thinking*] Shoe polish! My, I'd forgotten what peacetime was like. [*She shakes her head, then sits down by the trapdoor and starts talking down the hole*] Mrs. Antrobus, guess what I saw Mr. Antrobus doing this morning at dawn. He was tacking up a piece of paper on the door of the Town Hall. You'll die when you hear: it was a recipe for grass soup, for a grass soup that doesn't give you the diarrhea. Mr. Antrobus is still thinking up new things.—He told me to give you his love. He's got all sorts of ideas for peacetime, he says. No more laziness and idiocy, he says. And oh, yes! Where are his books? What? Well, pass them up. The first thing he wants to see are his books. He says if you've burnt those books, or if the rats have eaten them, he says it isn't worthwhile starting over again. Everybody's going to be beautiful, he says, and diligent, and very intelligent. *{A hand reaches up with two volumes}* What language is that? Pu-u-gh,—mold! And he's got such plans for you, Mrs. Antrobus. You're going to study history and algebra—and so are Gladys and I—and philosophy. You should hear him talk: *{Taking two more volumes}* Well, these are in English, anyway.—To hear him talk, seems like he expects you to be a combination, Mrs. Antrobus, of a saint and a college professor, and a dancehall hostess, if you know what I mean. *{Two more volumes}* Ugh. German! *{She is lying on the floor; one elbow bent, her cheek on her hand, meditatively}* Yes, peace will be here before we know it. In a week or two we'll be asking the Perkinses in for a quiet evening of bridge. We'll turn on the radio and hear how to be big successes with a new toothpaste. We'll trot down to the movies and see how girls with wax faces live—all *that* will begin again. Oh, Mrs. Antrobus, God forgive me but I enjoyed the war. Everybody's at their best in wartime. I'm sorry it's over. And, oh, I forgot! Mr. Antrobus sent you another message —can you hear me?—*{Enter* HENRY, *blackened and sullen. He is wearing torn overalls, but has one gaudy admiral's epaulette hanging by a thread from his right shoulder, and there are vestiges of gold and scarlet braid running down his left trouser leg. He stands listening}* Listen! Henry's never to put foot in this house again, he says. He'll kill Henry on sight, if he sees him.

You don't know about Henry??? Well, where have you been? What? Well, Henry rose right to the top. Top of *what?* Listen, I'm telling you. Henry rose from corporal to captain, to major, to general.—I don't know how to say it, but the enemy is *Henry;* Henry *is* the enemy. Everybody knows that.

HENRY: He'll kill me, will he?

SABINA: Who are you? I'm not afraid of you. The war's over.

HENRY: I'll kill him so fast. I've spent seven years trying to find him; the others I killed were just substitutes.

SABINA: Goodness! It's Henry!—*{He makes an angry gesture}* Oh, I'm not afraid of you. The war's over, Henry Antrobus, and you're not any more important than any other unemployed. You go away and hide yourself, until we calm your father down.

HENRY: The first thing to do is to burn up those old books; it's the ideas he gets out of those old books that . . . that makes the whole world so you can't live in it. *{He reels forward and starts kicking the books about, but suddenly falls down in a sitting position}*

SABINA: You leave those books alone!! Mr. Antrobus is looking forward to them a-special.—Gracious sakes, Henry, you're so tired you can't stand up. Your mother and sister'll be here in a minute and we'll think what to do about you.

HENRY: What did they ever care about me?

SABINA: There's that old whine again. All you people think you're not loved enough, nobody loves you. Well, you start being lovable and we'll love you.

HENRY: *{Outraged}* I don't want anybody to love me.

SABINA: Then stop talking about it all the time.

HENRY: I *never* talk about it. The last thing I want is anybody to pay any attention to me.

SABINA: I can hear it behind every word you say.

HENRY: I want everybody to hate me.

SABINA: Yes, you've decided that's second best, but it's still the same thing. —Mrs. Antrobus! Henry's here. He's so tired he can't stand up. [MRS. ANTROBUS *and* GLADYS, *with her* BABY, *emerge. They are dressed as in Act I.* MRS. ANTROBUS *carries some objects in her apron, and* GLADYS *has a blanket over her shoulder}*

MRS. ANTROBUS AND GLADYS: Henry! Henry! Henry!

HENRY: *{Glaring at them}* Have you anything to eat?

MRS. ANTROBUS: Yes, I have, Henry. I've been saving it for this very day,—two good baked potatoes. No! Henry! one of them's for your father. Henry!! Give me that other potato back this minute. [SABINA *sidles up behind him and snatches the other potato away}*

SABINA: He's so dog-tired he doesn't know what he's doing.

MRS. ANTROBUS: Now you just rest there, Henry, until I can get your room ready. Eat that potato good and slow, so you can get all the nourishment out of it.

HENRY: You all might as well know right now that I haven't come back here to live.

MRS. ANTROBUS: Sh. . . . I'll put this coat over you. Your room's hardly damaged at all. Your football trophies are a little tarnished, but Sabina and I will polish them up tomorrow.

HENRY: Did you hear me? I don't live here. I don't belong to anybody.

MRS. ANTROBUS: Why, how can you say a thing like that! You certainly do belong right here. Where else would you want to go? Your forehead's feverish, Henry, seems to me. You'd better give me that gun, Henry. You won't need that any more.

GLADYS: *{Whispering}* Look, he's fallen asleep already, with his potato half-chewed.

SABINA: Puh! The terror of the world.

MRS. ANTROBUS: Sabina, you mind your own business, and start putting the room to rights. [HENRY *has turned his face to the back of the sofa.* MRS. ANTROBUS *gingerly puts the revolver in her apron pocket, then helps* SABINA. SABINA *has found a rope hanging from the ceiling. Grunting, she hangs all her weight on it, and as she pulls the walls begin to move into their right places.* MRS. ANTROBUS *brings the overturned tables, chairs and hassock into the positions of Act I}*

SABINA: That's all we do—always beginning again! Over and over again. Always beginning again. *{She pulls on the rope and part of the wall moves into place. She stops. Meditatively:}* How do we know that it'll be any better than before? Why do we go on pretending? Some day the whole earth's going to have to turn cold anyway, and until that time all these other things'll be happening again: it will be more wars and more walls of ice and floods and earthquakes.

MRS. ANTROBUS: Sabina!! Stop arguing and go on with your work.

SABINA: All right. I'll go on just out of *habit,* but I won't believe in it.

MRS. ANTROBUS: *{Aroused}* Now, Sabina. I've let you talk long enough. I don't want to hear any more of it. Do I have to explain to you what everybody knows,—everybody who keeps a home going? Do I have to say to you what nobody should ever *have* to say, because they can read it in each other's eyes?

Now listen to me: [MRS. ANTROBUS *takes hold of the rope}* I could live for seventy years in a cellar and make soup out of grass and bark, without doubting that this world has a work to do and will do it.

Do you hear me?

SABINA: *{Frightened}* Yes, Mrs. Antrobus.

MRS. ANTROBUS: Sabina, do you see this house,—216 Cedar Street,—do you see it?

SABINA: Yes, Mrs. Antrobus.

MRS. ANTROBUS: Well, just to have known this house is to have seen the idea of what we can do someday if we keep our wits about us. Too many people have suffered and died for my children for us to start reneging now. So we'll start putting this house to rights. Now, Sabina, go and see what you can do in the kitchen.

SABINA: Kitchen! Why is it that however far I go away, I always find myself back in the kitchen? *{Exit}*

MRS. ANTROBUS: *{Still thinking over her last speech, relaxes and says with a reminiscent smile:}* Goodness gracious, wouldn't you know that my father was a parson? It was just like I heard his own voice speaking and he's been dead five thousand years. There! I've gone and almost waked Henry up.

HENRY: *{Talking in his sleep, indistinctly}* Fellows . . . what have they done for us? . . . Blocked our way at every step. Kept everything in their own hands. And you've stood it. When are you going to wake up?

MRS. ANTROBUS: Sh, Henry. Go to sleep. Go to sleep. Go to sleep.—Well, that looks better. Now let's go and help Sabina.

GLADYS: Mama, I'm going out into the backyard and hold the baby right up in the air. And show him that we don't have to be afraid any more. *{Exit* GLADYS *to the kitchen.* MRS. ANTROBUS *glances at* HENRY, *exits into kitchen.* HENRY *thrashes about in his sleep. Enter* ANTROBUS, *his arms full of bundles, chewing the end of a carrot. He has a slight limp. Over the suit of Act I he is wearing an overcoat too long for him, its skirts trailing on the ground. He lets his bundles fall and stands looking about. Presently his attention is fixed on* HENRY, *whose words grow clearer}*

HENRY: All right! What have you got to lose? What have they done for us? That's right—nothing. Tear everything down. I don't care what you smash. We'll begin again and we'll show 'em. *{*ANTROBUS *takes out his revolver and holds it pointing downwards. With his back towards the audience he moves toward the footlights.* HENRY'S *voice grows louder and he wakes with a start. They stare at one another. Then* HENRY *sits up quickly. Throughout the following scene* HENRY *is played, not as a misunderstood or misguided young man, but as a representation of strong unreconciled evil}* All right! Do something. *{Pause}* Don't think I'm afraid of you, either. All right, do what you were going to do. Do it. *{Furiously}* Shoot me, I tell you. You don't have to think I'm any relation of yours. I haven't got any father or any mother, or brothers or sisters. And I don't want any. And what's more I haven't got anybody over me; and I never will have. I'm alone, and that's all I want to be: alone. So you can shoot me.

ANTROBUS: You're the last person I wanted to see. The sight of you dries up all my plans and hopes. I wish I were back at war still, because it's easier to fight you than to live with you. War's a pleasure—do you hear me?—War's a pleasure compared to what faces us now: trying to build up a peacetime with you in the middle of it. *{*ANTROBUS *walks up to the window}*

HENRY: I'm not going to be a part of any peacetime of yours. I'm going a long way from here and make my own world that's fit for a man to live in. Where a man can be free, and have a chance, and do what he wants to do in his own way.

ANTROBUS: *{His attention arrested; thoughtfully. He throws the gun out of the window and turns with hope}* . . . Henry, let's try again.

HENRY: Try what? Living *here?*—Speaking polite downtown to all the old men like you? Standing like a sheep at the street corner until the red light turns to green? Being a good boy and a good sheep, like all the stinking ideas you get out of your books? Oh, no. I'll make a world, and I'll show you.

ANTROBUS: *{Hard}* How can you make a world for people to live in, unless you've first put order in yourself? Mark my words: I shall continue fighting you until my last breath as long as you mix up your idea of liberty with your idea of hogging everything for yourself. I shall have no pity on you. I shall pursue you to the far corners of the earth. You and I want the same thing;

but until you think of it as something that everyone has a right to, you are my deadly enemy and I will destroy you.—I hear your mother's voice in the kitchen. Have you seen her?

HENRY: I have no mother. Get it into your head. I don't belong here. I have nothing to do here. I have no home.

ANTROBUS: Then why did you come here? With the whole world to choose from, why did you come to this one place: 216 Cedar Street, Excelsior, New Jersey. . . . Well?

HENRY: What if I did? What if I wanted to look at it once more, to see if—

ANTROBUS: Oh, you're related, all right—When your mother comes in you must behave yourself. Do you hear me?

HENRY: *{Wildly}* What is this?—*must behave* yourself. Don't you say *must* to me.

ANTROBUS: Quiet! *{Enter* MRS ANTROBUS *and* SABINA]

HENRY: Nobody can say *must* to me. All my life everybody's been crossing me,—everybody, everything, all of you. I'm going to be free, even if I have to kill half the world for it. Right now, too. Let me get my hands on his throat. I'll show him. *{He advances toward* ANTROBUS. *Suddenly,* SABINA *jumps between them and calls out in her own person:}*

SABINA: Stop! Stop! Don't play this scene. You know what happened last night. Stop the play. *{The men fall back, panting.* HENRY *covers his face with his hands}* Last night you almost strangled him. You became a regular savage. Stop it!

HENRY: It's true. I'm sorry. I don't know what comes over me. I have nothing against him personally. I respect him very much . . . I . . . I admire him. But something comes over me. It's like I become fifteen years old again. I . . . I . . . listen; my own father used to whip me and lock me up every Saturday night. I never had enough to eat. He never let me have enough money to buy decent clothes. I was ashamed to go downtown. I never could go to the dances. My father and my uncle put rules in the way of everything I wanted to do. They tried to prevent my living at all.—I'm sorry. I'm sorry.

MRS. ANTROBUS: *{Quickly}* No, go on. Finish what you were saying. Say it all.

HENRY: In this scene it's as though I were back in High School again. It's like I had some big emptiness inside me,—the emptiness of being hated and blocked at every turn. And the emptiness fills up with the one thought that you have to strike and fight and kill. Listen, it's as though you have to kill somebody else so as not to end up killing yourself.

SABINA: That's not true. I knew your father and your uncle and your mother. You imagined all that. Why, they did everything they could for you. How can you say things like that? They didn't lock you up.

HENRY: They did. They did. They wished I hadn't been born.

SABINA: That's not true.

ANTROBUS: *{In his own person, with self-condemnation, but cold and proud}* Wait a minute. I have something to say, too. It's not wholly his fault that he wants to strangle me in this scene. It's my fault, too. He wouldn't feel that way unless there were something in me that reminded him of all that. He talks about an emptiness. Well, there's an emptiness in me, too. Yes,—work, work, work,—that's all I do. I've ceased to *live.* No wonder he feels that anger coming over him.

MRS. ANTROBUS: There! At least you've said it.

SABINA: We're all just as wicked as we can be, and that's the God's truth.

MRS. ANTROBUS: *{Nods a moment, then comes forward; quietly:}* Come. Come and put your head under some cold water.

SABINA: *{In a whisper}* I'll go with him. I've known him a long while. You have to go on with the play. Come with me. [HENRY *starts out with* SABINA, *but turns at the exit and says to* ANTROBUS:]

HENRY: Thanks. Thanks for what you said. I'll be all right tomorrow. I won't lose control in that place. I promise. *{Exeunt* HENRY *and* SABINA. ANTROBUS *starts toward the front door, fastens it.* MRS. ANTROBUS *goes up stage and places the chair close to table}*

MRS. ANTROBUS: George, do I see you limping?

ANTROBUS: Yes, a little. My old wound from the other war started smarting again. I can manage.

MRS. ANTROBUS: *{Looking out of the window}* Some lights are coming on,—the first in seven years. People are walking up and down looking at them. Over in Hawkins' open lot they've built a bonfire to celebrate the peace. They're dancing around it like scarecrows.

ANTROBUS: A bonfire! As though they hadn't seen enough things burning.—Maggie,—the dog died?

MRS. ANTROBUS: Oh, yes. Long ago. There are no dogs left in Excelsior.—You're back again! All these years. I gave up counting on letters. The few that arrived were anywhere from six months to a year late.

ANTROBUS: Yes, the ocean's full of letters, along with the other things.

MRS. ANTROBUS: George, sit down, you're tired.

ANTROBUS: No, you sit down. I'm tired but I'm restless. *{Suddenly, as she comes forward:}* Maggie! I've lost it. I've lost it.

MRS. ANTROBUS: What, George? What have you lost?

ANTROBUS: The most important thing of all: The desire to begin again, to start building.

MRS. ANTROBUS: *{Sitting in the chair right of the table}* Well, it will come back.

ANTROBUS: *{At the window}* I've lost it. This minute I feel like all those people dancing around the bonfire—just relief. Just the desire to settle down; to slip into the old grooves and keep the neighbors from walking over my lawn.—Hm. But during the war,—in the middle of all that blood and dirt and hot and cold—every day and night, I'd have moments, Maggie, when I *saw* the things that we could do when it was over. When you're at war you think about a better life; when you're at peace you think about a more comfortable one. I've lost it. I feel sick and tired.

MRS. ANTROBUS: Listen! The baby's crying.

I hear Gladys talking. Probably she's quieting Henry again. George, while Gladys and I were living here—like moles, like rats, and when we were at our wits' end to save the baby's life—the only thought we clung to was that you were going to bring something good out of this suffering. In the night, in the dark, we'd whisper about it, starving and sick.—Oh, George, you'll have to get it back again. Think! What else kept us alive all these years? Even now, it's not comfort we want. We can suffer whatever's necessary; only give us back that promise. *{Enter* SABINA *with a lighted lamp. She is dressed as in Act I}*

SABINA: Mrs. Antrobus . . .

MRS. ANTROBUS: Yes, Sabina?

SABINA: Will you need me?

MRS. ANTROBUS: No, Sabina, you can go to bed.

SABINA: Mrs. Antrobus, if it's all right with you, I'd like to go to the bonfire and celebrate seeing the war's over. And, Mrs. Antrobus, they've opened the Gem Movie Theatre and they're giving away a hand-painted soup tureen to every lady, and I thought one of us ought to go.

ANTROBUS: Well, Sabina, I haven't any money. I haven't seen any money for quite a while.

SABINA: Oh, you don't need money.

They're taking anything you can give them. And I have some . . . some . . . Mrs. Antrobus, promise you won't tell anyone. It's a little against the law. But I'll give you some, too.

ANTROBUS: What is it?

SABINA: I'll give you some, too. Yesterday I picked up a lot of . . . of beefcubes! {MRS. ANTROBUS *turns and says calmly:}*

MRS. ANTROBUS: But, Sabina, you know you ought to give that in to the Center downtown. They know who needs them most.

SABINA: *{Outburst}* Mrs. Antrobus, I didn't make this war. I didn't ask for it. And, in my opinion, after anybody's gone through what we've gone through, they have a right to grab what they can find. You're a very nice man, Mr. Antrobus, but you'd have got on better in the world if you'd realized that dog-eat-dog was the rule in the beginning and always will be. And most of all now. *{In tears}* Oh, the world's an awful place, and you know it is. I used to think something could be down about it; but I know better now. I hate it. I hate it. *{She comes forward slowly and brings six cubes from the bag}* All right. All right. You can have them.

ANTROBUS: Thank you, Sabina.

SABINA: Can I have . . . can I have one to go to the movies? {ANTROBUS *in silence gives her one}* Thank you.

ANTROBUS: Good night, Sabina.

SABINA: Mr. Antrobus, don't mind what I say. I'm just an ordinary girl, you know what I mean, I'm just an ordinary girl. But you're a bright man, you're a very bright man, and of course you invented the alphabet and the wheel, and, my God, a lot of things . . . and if you've got any other plans, my God, don't let me upset them. Only every now and then I've got to go to the movies. I mean my nerves can't stand it. But if you have any ideas about improving the crazy old world, I'm really with you. I really am. Because it's . . . it's . . . Good night. *{She goes out.* ANTROBUS *starts laughing softly with exhilaration}*

ANTROBUS: Now I remember what three things always went together when I was able to see things most clearly: three things. Three things: *{He points to where* SABINA *has gone out}* The voice of the people in their confusion and their need. And the thought of you and the children and this house. . . . And . . . Maggie! I didn't dare ask you: my books! They haven't been lost, have they?

MRS. ANTROBUS: No. There are some of them right here. Kind of tattered.

ANTROBUS: Yes.—Remember, Maggie, we almost lost them once before? And when we finally did collect a few torn copies out of old cellars they ran in everyone's head like a fever. They as good as rebuilt the world. *{Pauses, book in hand, and looks up}* Oh, I've never forgotten for long at a time that living is struggle. I know that every good and excellent thing in the world stands moment by moment on the razor-edge of danger and must be fought for—whether it's a field, or a home, or a country. All I ask is the chance to build new worlds and God has always given us that. And has given us *{Opening the book}* voices to guide us; and the memory of our mistakes to warn us. Maggie, you and I will remember in peacetime all the resolves that were so clear to us in the days of war. We've come a long way. We've learned. We're learning. And the steps of our journey are marked for us here. *{He stands by the table turning the leaves of a book}* Sometimes out there in the war,—standing all night on a hill—I'd try and remember some of the words in these books. Parts of them and phrases would come back to me. And after a while I used to give names to the hours of the night. *{He sits, hunting for a passage in the book}* Nine o'clock I used to call Spinoza. Where is it: "After experience had taught me—" *{The back* *wall has disappeared, revealing the platform.* FRED BAILEY *carrying his numeral has started from left to right.* MRS. ANTROBUS *sits by the table sewing}*

BAILEY: "After experience had taught me that the common occurrences of daily life are vain and futile; and I saw that all the objects of my desire and fear were in themselves nothing good nor bad save insofar as the mind was affected by them; I at length determined to search out whether there was something truly good and communicable to man." *{Almost without break* HESTER, *carrying a large Roman numeral ten, starts crossing the platform.* GLADYS *appears at the kitchen door and moves towards her mother's chair}*

HESTER: "Then tell me, O Critias, how will a man choose the ruler that shall rule over him? Will he not choose a man who has first established order in himself, knowing that any decision that has its spring from anger or pride or vanity can be multiplied a thousand fold in its effects upon the citizens?" {HESTER *disappears and* IVY, *as eleven o'clock starts speaking}*

IVY: "This good estate of the mind possessing its object in energy we call divine. This we mortals have occasionally and it is this energy which is pleasantest and best. But God has it always. It is wonderful in us; but in Him how much more wonderful." *{As* MR. TREMAYNE *starts to speak,* HENRY *appears at the edge of the scene, brooding and unreconciled, but present}*

TREMAYNE: "In the beginning, God created the Heavens and the earth; And the Earth was waste and void; And the darkness was upon the face of the deep. And the Lord said let there be light and there was light." *{Sudden black-out and silence, except for the last strokes of the midnight bell. Then just as suddenly the lights go up, and* SABINA *is standing at the window, as at the opening of the play}*

SABINA: Oh, oh, oh. Six o'clock and the master not home yet. Pray God nothing serious has happened to him crossing the Hudson River. But I wouldn't be surprised. The whole world's at sixes and sevens, and why the house hasn't fallen down about our ears long ago is a miracle to me. *{She comes down to the footlights}*

This is where you came in. We have to go on for ages and ages yet.

You go home.

The end of this play isn't written yet.

Mr. and Mrs. Antrobus! Their heads are full of plans and they're as confident as the first day they began,—and they told me to tell you: good night.

Poetry

William Butler Yeats (1865–1939)

A Prayer for My Daughter

Once more the storm is howling, and half hid
Under this cradle-hood and coverlid
My child sleeps on. There is no obstacle
But Gregory's wood and one bare hill
Whereby the haystack and roof-leveling wind 5
Bred on the Atlantic, can be stayed;
And for an hour I have walked and prayed
Because of the great gloom that is in my mind.

I have walked and prayed for this young child an hour
And heard the sea-wind scream upon the tower, 10
And under the arches of the bridge, and scream
In the elms above the flooded stream;
Imagining in excited reverie
That the future years had come,
Dancing to a frenzied drum, 15
Out of the murderous innocence of the sea.

May she be granted beauty, and yet not
Beauty to make a stranger's eye distraught,
Or hers before a looking-glass, for such,
Being made beautiful overmuch, 20
Consider beauty a sufficient end,
Lose natural kindness and maybe
The heart-revealing intimacy
That chooses right, and never find a friend.

Helen being chosen found life flat and dull 25
And later had much trouble from a fool,
While the great Queen, that rose out of the spray,
Being fatherless could have her way
Yet chose a bandy-legged smith for man.
It's certain that fine women eat 30
A crazy salad with their meat
Whereby the Horn of Plenty is undone.

In courtesy I'd have her chiefly learned;
Hearts are not had as a gift but hearts are earned
By those that are not entirely beautiful; 35
Yet many, that have played the fool
For beauty's very self, has charm made wise,
And many a poor man that has roved,
Loved and thought himself beloved,
From a glad kindness cannot take his eyes. 40

May she become a flourishing hidden
  tree
That all her thoughts may like the
  linnet be,
And have no business but dispensing
  round
Their magnanimities of sound,
Nor but in merriment begin a chase, 45
Nor but in merriment a quarrel.
Oh, may she live like some green laurel
Rooted in one dear perpetual place.

My mind, because the minds that I have
  loved,
The sort of beauty that I have
approved, 50
Prosper but little, has dried up of late,
Yet knows that to be choked with hate
May well be of all evil chances chief.
If there's no hatred in a mind
Assault and battery of the wind 55
Can never tear the linnet from the leaf.

An intellectual hatred is the worst,
So let her think opinions are accursed.
Have I not seen the loveliest woman
  born
Out of the mouth of Plenty's horn, 60
Because of her opinionated mind
Barter that horn and every good
By quiet natures understood
For an old bellows full of angry wind?

Considering that, all hatred driven
  hence, 65
The soul recovers radical innocence
And learns at last that it is self-
  delighting,
Self-appeasing, self-affrighting,
And that its own sweet will is Heaven's
  will;
She can, though every face should
  scowl 70
And every windy quarter howl
Or every bellows burst, be happy still.

And may her bridegroom bring her to
  a house
Where all's accustomed, ceremonious;
For arrogance and hatred are the
  wares 75
Peddled in the thoroughfares.
How but in custom and in ceremony
Are innocence and beauty born?
Ceremony's a name for the rich horn,
And custom for the spreading laurel
  tree. 80

The Second Coming

Turning and turning in the widening
  gyre
The falcon cannot hear the falconer;
Things fall apart; the centre cannot
  hold;
Mere anarchy is loosed upon the world,
The blood-dimmed tide is loosed, and
  everywhere 5
The ceremony of innocence is drowned;
The best lack all conviction, while the
  worst
Are full of passionate intensity.
Surely some revelation is at hand;
Surely the Second Coming is at
  hand: 10
The Second Coming! Hardly are those
  words out
When a vast image out of *Spiritus
  Mundi*
Troubles my sight: somewhere in sands
  of the desert
A shape with lion body and the head of
  a man,
A gaze blank and pitiless as the sun, 15
Is moving its slow thighs, while all
  about it
Reel shadows of the indignant desert
  birds.
The darkness drops again; but now I
  know

That twenty centuries of stony sleep
Were vexed to nightmare by a rocking
cradle, 20
And what rough beast, its hour come
round at last,
Slouches towards Bethlehem to be
born?

The Leaders of the Crowd

They must to keep their certainty
accuse
All that are different of a base intent;
Pull down established honor; hawk for
news
Whatever their loose phantasy invent
And murmur it with bated breath, as
though 5
The abounding gutter had been Helicon
Or calumny is a song. How can they
know
Truth flourishes where the student's
lamp has shone,
And there alone, that have no solitude?
So the crowd come they care not what
may come. 10
They have loud music, hope every day
renewed
And heartier loves; that lamp is from
the tomb.

Easter 1916

I have met them at close of day
Coming with vivid faces
From counter or desk among grey
Eighteenth-century houses.
I have passed with a nod of the head 5
Or polite meaningless words,
Or have lingered awhile and said
Polite meaningless words,
And thought before I had done
Of a mocking tale or a gibe 10
To please a companion
Around the fire at the club,
Being certain that they and I
But lived where motley is worn:
All changed, changed utterly: 15
A terrible beauty is born.
That woman's days were spent
In ignorant good will,
Her nights in argument
Until her voice grew shrill. 20
What voice more sweet than hers
When, young and beautiful,
She rode to harriers?
This man had kept a school
And rode our winged horse; 25
This other his helper and friend
Was coming into his force;
He might have won fame in the end,
So sensitive his nature seemed,
So daring and sweet his thought. 30
The other man I had dreamed
A drunken, vainglorious lout.
He had done most bitter wrong
To some who are near my heart,
Yet I number him in the song; 35
He, too, had resigned his part
In the casual comedy;
He, too, has been changed in his turn,
Transformed utterly:
A terrible beauty is born. 40

Hearts with one purpose alone
Through summer and winter seem
Enchanted to a stone
To trouble the living stream.
The horse that comes from the road, 45

The rider, the birds that range
From cloud to tumbling cloud,
Minute by minute they change;
A shadow of cloud on the stream
Changes minute by minute; 50
A horse-hoof slides on the brim,
And a horse splashes within it;
The long-legged moor-hens dive,
And hens to moor-cocks call;
Minute by minute they live: 55
The stone's in the midst of all.
Too long a sacrifice
Can make a stone of the heart.
O when may it suffice?
That is Heaven's part, our part 60
To mutter name upon name,
As a mother names her child
When sleep at last has come
On limbs that had run wild.
Was it but nightfall? 65
No, no, not night but death;
Was it needless death after all?
For England may keep faith
For all that is done and said.
We know their dreams; enough 70
To know they dreamed and are dead;
And what if excess of love
Bewildered them till they died?
I write it out in verse—
MacDonagh and MacBride 75
And Connolly and Pearse
Now and in time to be,
Wherever green is worn,
Are changed, changed utterly:
A terrible beauty is born. 80

Sailing to Byzantium

I

That is no country for old men. The young
In one another's arms, birds in the trees,
—Those dying generations—at their song,
The salmon-falls, the mackerel-crowded seas,
Fish, flesh, or fowl, command all summer long 5
Whatever is begotten, born, and dies.
Caught in that sensual music all neglect
Monuments of unageing intellect.

II

An agèd man is but a paltry thing,
A tattered coat upon a stick, unless 10
Soul clap its hands and sing, and louder sing
For every tatter in its mortal dress,
Nor is there singing school but studying
Monuments of its own magnificence;
And therefore I have sailed the seas and come 15
To the holy city of Byzantium.

III

O sages standing in God's holy fire
As in the gold mosaic of a wall,

Come from the holy fire, perne in a gyre,
And be the singing-masters of my soul. 20
Consume my heart away; sick with desire
And fastened to a dying animal
It knows not what it is; and gather me
Into the artifice of eternity.

IV

Once out of nature I shall never take 25
My bodily form from any natural thing,
But such a form as Grecian goldsmiths make
Of hammered gold and gold enamelling
To keep a drowsy Emperor awake;
Or set upon a golden bough to sing 30
To lords and ladies of Byzantium
Of what is past, or passing, or to come.

Robert Frost (1874–1963)

The Tuft of Flowers

I went to turn the grass once after one
Who mowed it in the dew before the sun.

The dew was gone that made his blade so keen
Before I came to view the leveled scene.

I looked for him behind an isle of trees; 5
I listened for his whetstone on the breeze.

But he had gone his way, the grass all mown,
And I must be, as he had been—alone,

"As all must be," I said within my heart,
"Whether they work together or apart." 10

But as I said it, swift there passed me by
On noiseless wing a bewildered butterfly,

Seeking with memories grown dim o'er night
Some resting flower of yesterday's delight.

And once I marked his flight go round and round, 15
As where some flower lay withering on the ground.

And then he flew as far as eye could see,
And then on tremulous wing came back to me.

I thought of questions that have no reply,
And would have turned to toss the grass to dry; 20

But he turned first, and led my eye to look
At a tall tuft of flowers beside a brook,

A leaping tongue of bloom the scythe had spared
Beside a reedy brook the scythe had bared.

The mower in the dew had loved them thus, 25
By leaving them to flourish, not for us,

Nor yet to draw one thought of ours to him,
But from sheer morning gladness at the brim.

The butterfly and I had lit upon,
Nevertheless, a message from the dawn, 30

That made me hear the wakening birds around,
And hear his long scythe whispering to the ground,

And feel a spirit kindred to my own;
So that henceforth I worked no more alone;

But glad with him, I worked as with his aid, 35
And weary, sought at noon with him the shade;

And dreaming, as it were, held brotherly speech
With one whose thought I had not hoped to reach

"Men work together," I told him from the heart,
"Whether they work together or apart." 40

The Star-Splitter

"You know Orion always comes up sideways.
Throwing a leg up over our fence of mountains,
And rising on his hands, he looks in on me
Busy outdoors by lantern-light with something
I should have done by daylight, and indeed, 5
After the ground is frozen, I should have done
Before it froze, and a gust flings a handful

Of waste leaves at my smoky lantern chimney
To make fun of my way of doing things,
Or else fun of Orion's having caught me. 10
Has a man, I should like to ask, no rights
These forces are obliged to pay respect to?"
So Brad McLaughlin mingled reckless talk
Of heavenly stars with hugger-mugger farming,
Till having failed at hugger-mugger farming, 15
He burned his house down for the first insurance
And spent the proceeds on a telescope
To satisfy a life-long curiosity
About our place among the infinities.

"What do you want with one of those blame things?" 20
I asked him well beforehand. "Don't you get one!"
"Don't call it blamed; there isn't anything
More blameless in the sense of being less
A weapon in our human fight," he said.
"I'll have one if I sell my farm to buy it." 25
There where he moved the rocks to plough the ground
And ploughed between the rocks he couldn't move,
Few farms changed hands; so rather than spend years
Trying to sell his farm and then not selling,
He burned his house down for the fire insurance 30
And bought the telescope with what it came to.
He had been heard to say by several:
"The best thing that we're put here for's to see;
The strongest thing that's given us to see with's
A telescope. Someone in every town 35
Seems to me owes it to the town to keep one.
In Littleton it may as well be me."
After such loose talk it was no surprise
When he did what he did and burned his house down.

Mean laughter went about town that day 40
To let him know we weren't the least imposed on,
And he could wait—we'd see to him tomorrow.
But the first thing next morning we reflected
If one by one we counted people out
For the least sin, it wouldn't take us long 45
To get so we had no one left to live with.
For to be social is to be forgiving.
Our thief, the one who does our stealing from us,
We don't cut off from coming to church suppers,
But what we miss we go to him and ask for. 50
He promptly gives it back, that is if still
Uneaten, unworn out, or undisposed of.
It wouldn't do to be too hard on Brad
About his telescope. Beyond the age
Of being given one for Christmas gift, 55
He had to take the best way he knew how

To find himself in one. Well, all we said was
He took a strange thing to be roguish over.
Some sympathy was wasted on the house, 60
A good old-timer dating back along;
But a house isn't sentient; the house
Didn't feel anything. And if it did,
Why not regard it as a sacrifice,
And an old-fashioned sacrifice by fire, 65
Instead of a new-fashioned one at auction?
Out of a house and so out of a farm
At one stroke (of a match), Brad had to turn
To earn a living on the Concord railroad,
As under-ticket-agent at a station 70
Where his job, when he wasn't selling tickets,
Was setting out up track and down, not plants
As on a farm, but planets, evening stars
That varied in their hue from red to green.

He got a good glass for six hundred dollars. 75
His new job gave him leisure for star-gazing.
Often he bid me come and have a look
Up the brass barrel, velvet black inside,
At a star quaking in the other end.
I recollect a night of broken clouds 80
And underfoot snow melted down to ice,
And melting further in the wind to mud.
Bradford and I had out the telescope.
We spread our two legs as we spread its three,
Pointed our thoughts the way we pointed it, 85
And standing at our leisure till the day broke,
Said some of the best things we ever said.
That telescope was christened the Star-splitter,
Because it didn't do a thing but split
A star in two or three the way you split 90
A globule of quicksilver in your hand
With one stroke of your finger in the middle.
It's a star splitter if there ever was one
And ought to do some good if splitting stars
'Sa thing to be compared with splitting wood.

We've looked and looked, but after all where are we? 95
Do we know any better where we are,
And how it stands between the night tonight
And a man with a smoky lantern chimney?
How different from the way it ever stood?

Acquainted with the Night

I have been one acquainted with the night.
I have walked out in rain—and back in rain.
I have walked the furthest city light.
I have looked down the saddest city lane.
I have passed by the watchman on his beat 5
And dropped my eyes, unwilling to explain.

I have stood still and stopped the sound of feet
When far away an interrupted cry
Came over houses from another street,

But not to call me back or say goodbye; 10
And further still at an unearthly height,
One luminary clock against the sky
Proclaimed the time was neither wrong nor right.
I have been one acquainted with the night.

Two Tramps in Mud Time
or, A Full-time Interest

Out of the mud two strangers came
And caught me splitting wood in the yard.
And one of them put me off my aim
By hailing cheerily "Hit them hard!"
I knew pretty well what he had in mind: 5
He wanted to take my job for pay.

Good blocks of oak it was I split,
As large around as the chopping block;
And every piece I squarely hit
Fell splinterless as a cloven rock. 10
The blows that a life of self-control
Spares to strike for the common good
That day, giving a loose to my soul,
I spent on the unimportant wood.

The sun was warm but the wind was chill. 15
You know how it is with an April day
When the sun is out and the wind is still,
You're one month on in the middle of May.
But if you so much as dare to speak,
A cloud comes over the sunlit arch, 20
A wind comes off a frozen peak,
And you're two months back in the middle of March.

A bluebird comes tenderly up to alight
And turns to the wind to unruffle a plume
His song so pitched as not to excite 25
A single flower as yet to bloom.
It is snowing a flake: and he half knew
Winter was only playing possum.
Except in color he isn't blue.
But he wouldn't advise a thing to blossom. 30

The water for which we may have to look
In summertime with a witching-wand,
In every wheelrut's now a brook,
In every print of a hoof a pond.
Be glad of water, but don't forget 35
The lurking frost in the earth beneath
That will steal forth after the sun is set
And show on the water its crystal teeth.

The time when most I loved my task
These two must make me love it
 more 40
By coming with what they came to ask.
You'd think I never had felt before
The weight of an axe-head poised aloft,
The grip on earth of outspread feet.
The life of muscles rocking soft 45
And smooth and moist in vernal heat.

Out of the woods two hulking tramps
(From sleeping God knows where last
 night,
But not long since in the lumber
 camps).
They thought all chopping was theirs of
right. 50
Men of the woods and lumberjacks,
They judged me by their appropriate
 tool.
Except as a fellow handled an axe,
They had no way of knowing a fool.

Nothing on either side was said. 55
They knew they had but to stay their
 stay
And all their logic would fill my head:
As that I had no right to play
With what was another man's work for
 gain.
My right might be love but theirs was
 need. 60
And where the two exist in twain
Theirs was the better right—agreed.

But yield who will to their separation,
My object in living is to unite
My avocation and my vocation 65
As my two eyes make one in sight.
Only where love and need are one,
And the work is play for mortal stakes,
Is the deed ever really done
For Heaven and the future's sakes. 70

Departmental
or, The End of My Ant Jerry

An ant on the tablecloth
Ran into a dormant moth
Of many times her size.
He showed not the least surprise.
His business wasn't with such. 5
He gave it scarcely a touch,
And was off on his duty run.
Yet if he encountered one
Of the hive's inquiry squad
Whose work is to find out God 10
And the nature of time and space,
He would put him on to the case.
Ants are a curious race;
One crossing with hurried tread
The body of one of their dead 15
Isn't given a moment's arrest—
Seems not even impressed.
But he no doubt reports to any
With whom he crosses antennae,
And they no doubt report 20
To the higher up at court.
Then word goes forth in Formic:
"Death's come to Jerry McCormic,
Our selfless forager Jerry.
Will the special Janizary 25
Whose office it is to bury
The dead of the commissary
Go bring him home to his people.
Lay him in state on a sepal.
Wrap him for shroud in a petal. 30
Embalm him with ichor of nettle.
This is the word of your Queen."
And presently on the scene
Appears a solemn mortician;
And taking formal position 35
With feelers calmly atwiddle,
Seizes the dead by the middle,
And heaving him high in air
Carries him out of there.
No one stands around to stare. 40
It is nobody else's affair.

It couldn't be called ungentle.
But how thoroughly departmental.

The White-Tailed Hornet

The white-tailed hornet lives in a balloon
That floats against the ceiling of the woodshed.
The exit he comes out at like a bullet
Is like the pupil of a pointed gun.
And having power to change his aim in flight, 5
He comes out more unerring than a bullet.
Verse could be written on the certainty
With which he penetrates my best defense
Of whirling hands and arms about the head
To stab me in the sneeze-nerve of a nostril. 10
Such is the instinct of it I allow.
Yet how about the insect certainty
That in the neighborhood of home and children
Is such an execrable judge of motives
As not to recognize in me the exception 15
I like to think I am in everything—
One who would never hang above a bookcase
His Japanese crepe-paper globe for trophy?
He stung me first and stung me afterward.
He rolled me off the field head over heels 20
And would not listen to my explanations.

That's when I went as visitor to his house.
As visitor at my house he is better.
Hawking for flies about the kitchen door,
In at one door perhaps and out another, 25
Trust him then not to put you in the wrong.
He won't misunderstand your freest movements.
Let him light on your skin unless you mind
So many prickly grappling feet at once.
He's after the domesticated fly 30
To feed his thumping grubs as big as he is.
Here he is at his best, but even here—
I watched him where he swooped, he pounced, he struck;
But what he found he had was just a nailhead.
He struck a second time. Another nailhead. 35
"Those are just nailheads. Those are fastened down."
Then disconcerted and not unannoyed,
He stooped and struck a little huckleberry
The way a player curls around a football.
"Wrong shape, wrong color, and wrong scent," I said. 40
The huckleberry rolled him on his head.
At last it was a fly. He shot and missed;
And the fly circled round him in derision.
But for the fly he might have made me think
He had been at his poetry, comparing 45
Nailhead with fly and fly with huckleberry:
How like a fly, how very like a fly.

But the real fly he missed would never do;
The missed fly made me dangerously skeptic.

Won't this whole instinct matter bear revision? 50
Won't almost any theory bear revision?
To err is human, not to, animal.
Or so we pay the compliment to instinct,
Only too liberal of our compliment.
That really takes away instead of gives. 55
Or worship, humor, conscientiousness
Went long since to the dogs under the table.
And served us right for having instituted
Downward comparisons. As long on earth
As our comparisons were stoutly upward 60
With gods and angels, we were men at least,
But little lower than the gods and angels.
But once comparisons were yielded downward,
Once we began to see our images
Reflected in the mud and even dust, 65
'Twas disillusion upon disillusion.
We were lost piecemeal to the animals,
Like people thrown out to delay the wolves.
Nothing but fallibility was left us,
And this day's work made even that seem doubtful. 70

There Are Roughly Zones

We sit indoors and talk of the cold outside.
And every gust that gathers strength and heaves
Is a threat to the house. But the house has long been tried.
We think of the tree. If it never again has leaves,
We'll know, we say, that this was the night it died. 5
It is very far north, we admit, to have brought the peach.
What comes over a man, is it soul or mind—
That to no limits and bounds he can stay confined?
You would say his ambition was to extend the reach
Clear to the Arctic of every living kind. 10
Why is his nature forever so hard to teach
That though there is no fixed line between wrong and right,
There are roughly zones whose laws must be obeyed?
There is nothing much we can do for the tree tonight,
But we can't help feeling more than a little betrayed 15
That the northwest wind should rise to such a height
Just when the cold went down so many below.
The tree has no leaves and may never have them again.
We must wait till some months hence in the spring to know.
But if it is destined never again to grow, 20
It can blame this limitless trait in the hearts of men.

Design

I found a dimpled spider, fat and white,
On a white heal-all, holding up a moth
Like a white piece of rigid satin cloth—
Assorted characters of death and blight
Mixed ready to begin the morning right, 5
Like the ingredients of a witches' broth—
A snow-drop spider, a flower like a froth,
And dead wings carried like a paper kite.

What had the flower to do with being white,
The wayside blue and innocent heal-all? 10
What brought the kindred spider to that height,
Then steered the white moth thither in the night?
What but design of darkness to appall?—
If design govern in a thing so small.

Carl Sandburg (1878–1967)

To a Contemporary Bunkshooter

You come along . . . tearing your shirt . . . yelling about Jesus.
Where do you get that stuff?
What do you know about Jesus?
Jesus had a way of talking soft and outside of a few bankers and higher-ups among the con men of Jerusalem everybody liked to have this Jesus around because he never made any fake passes and everything he said went and he helped the sick and gave the people hope.
You come along squirting words at us, shaking your fist and call us all damn fools so fierce the froth slobbers over your lips . . . always blabbing we're all going to hell straight off and you know all about it. 5

I've read Jesus' words. I know what he said. You don't throw any scare into me. I've got your number. I know how much you know about Jesus.
He never came near clean people or dirty people but they felt cleaner because he came along. It was your crowd of bankers and business men and lawyers hired the sluggers and murderers who put Jesus out of the running.
I say the same bunch backing you nailed the nails into the hands of this Jesus of Nazareth. He had lined up against him the same crooks and strong-arm men now lined up with you paying your way.

This Jesus was good to look at, smelled good, listened good. He threw out something fresh and beautiful from the skin of his body and the touch of his hands whereever he passed along.
You slimy bunkshooter, you put a smut on every human blossom in reach of your rotten breath belching about hell-fire and hiccupping about this Man who lived a clean life in Galilee. 10

When are you going to quit making the carpenters build emergency hospitals for women and girls driven crazy with wrecked nerves from your gibberish about Jesus?—I put it to you again: Where do you get that stuff? What do you know about Jesus?

Go ahead and bust all the chairs you want to. Smash a whole wagon-load of furniture at every performance. Turn sixty somersaults and stand on your nutty head. If it wasn't for the way you scare the women and kids I'd feel sorry for you and pass the hat.
I like to watch a good four-flusher work, but not when he starts people puking and calling for the doctors.
I like a man that's got nerve and can pull off a great original performance, but you—you're only a bug-house pedlar of secondhand gospel—you're only shoving out a phoney imitation of the goods this Jesus wanted free as air and sunlight.

You tell people living in shanties Jesus is going to fix it up all right with them by giving them mansions in the skies after they're dead and the worms have eaten 'em. 15
You tell $6 a week department store girls all they need is Jesus; you take a steel trust wop, dead without having lived, grey and shrunken at forty years of age, and you tell him to look at Jesus on the cross and he'll be all right.
You tell poor people they don't need any more money on pay day and even if it's fierce to be out of a job, Jesus'll fix that up all right, all right—all they gotta do is take Jesus the way you say.
I'm telling you Jesus wouldn't stand for the stuff you're handing out. Jesus played it different. The bankers and lawyers of Jerusalem got their sluggers and murderers to go after Jesus just because Jesus wouldn't play their game. He didn't sit in with the big thieves.

I don't want a lot of gab from a bunkshooter in my religion.
I won't take my religion from any man who never works except with his mouth and never cherishes any memory except the face of the woman on the American silver dollar. 20
I ask you to come through and show me where you're pouring out the blood of your life.
I've been to this suburb of Jerusalem they call Golgotha, where they nailed Him, and I know if the story is straight it was real blood ran from His hands and the nailholes, and it was real blood spurted in red drops where the spear of the Roman soldier rammed in between the ribs of this Jesus of Nazareth.

D. H. Lawrence (1885–1930)

Wedding Morn

The morning breaks like pomegranate
In a shining crack of red;
Ah, when tomorrow the dawn comes late
Whitening across the bed
It will find me at the marriage gate 5
And waiting while light is shed
On him who is sleeping satiate
With a sunk, unconscious head.

And when the dawn comes creeping in,
Cautiously I shall raise 10
Myself to watch the daylight win
On my first of days,
As it shows him sleeping a sleep he got
With me, as under my gaze
He grows distinct, and I see his hot 15
Face freed of the wavering blaze.

Then I shall know which image of God
My man is made toward;
And I shall see my sleeping rod
Or my life's reward; 20

And I shall count the stamp and worth
Of the man I've accepted as mine,
Shall see an image of heaven or of earth
On his minted metal shine.

Oh, I long to see him sleep 25
In my power utterly;
So I shall know what I have to keep . . .
I long to see
My love, that spinning coin, laid still
And plain at the side of me 30
For me to reckon—for surely he will
Be wealth of life to me.

And then he will be mine, he will lie
Revealed to me;
Patent and open beneath my eye 35
He will sleep of me;
He will lie negligent, resign
His truth to me, and I
Shall watch the dawn light up for me
This fate of mine. 40

And as I watch the wan light shine
On his sleep that is filled of me,
On his brow where the curved wisps clot and twine
Carelessly,

On his lips where the light breaths come and go 45
Unconsciously,
On his limbs in sleep at last laid low
Helplessly,
I shall weep, oh, I shall weep, I know
For joy or for misery. 50

Love on the Farm

What large, dark hands are those at the window
Grasping in the golden light
Which weaves its way through the evening wind
At my heart's delight?

Ah, only the leaves! But in the west 5
I see a redness suddenly come
Into the evening's anxious breast—
'Tis the wound of love goes home!

The woodbine creeps abroad 10
Calling low to her lover:
The sun-lit flirt who all the day
Has poised above her lips in play
And stolen kisses, shallow and gay
Of pollen, now has gone away—
She woos the moth with her sweet, low word; 15
And when above her his moth-wings hover
Then her bright breast she will uncover
And yield her honey-drop to her lover.

Into the yellow, evening glow
Saunters a man from the farm below; 20
Leans, and looks in at the low-built shed
Where the swallow has hung her marriage bed.
The bird lies warm against the wall.
She glances quick her startled eyes
Towards him, then she turns away 25
Her small head, making warm display
Of red upon the throat. Her terrors sway
Her out of the nest's warm, busy ball,
Whose plaintive cry is heard as she flies
In one blue stoop from out the sties 30
Into the twilight's empty hall.
Oh, water-hen, beside the rushes,
Hide your quaintly scarlet blushes,
Still your quick tail, lie still as dead,
Till the distance folds over his ominous tread! 35

The rabbit presses back her ears,
Turns back her liquid, anguished eyes
And crouches low; then with wild spring
Spurts from the terror of his oncoming;
To be choked back, the wire ring 40
Her frantic effort throttling:
Piteous brown ball of quivering fears!
Ah, soon in his large, hard hand she dies,

Yet calm and kindly are his eyes
And ready to open in brown surprise 45
Should I not answer to his talk
Or should he my tears surmise.

I hear his hand on the latch, and rise from my chair
Watching the door open; he flashes bare
His strong teeth in a smile, and flashes his eyes 50
In a smile like triumph upon me; then careless-wise
He flings the rabbit soft on the table board
And comes toward me: he! the uplifted sword
Of his hand against my bosom! and oh, the broad
Blade of his glance that asks me to applaud 55
His coming! With his hand he turns my face to him
And caresses me with his fingers that still smell grim
Of rabbit's fur! God, I am caught in a snare!
I know not what fine wire is round my throat;
I only know I let him finger there 60
My pulse of life, and let him nose like a stoat
Who sniffs with joy before he drinks the blood.

And down his mouth comes to my mouth! and down
His bright dark eyes come over me, like a hood
Upon my mind! his lips meet mine, and a flood 65
Of sweet fire sweeps across me, so I drown
Against him, die, and find death good.

Snake

A snake came to my water-trough
On a hot, hot day, and I in pyjamas for the heat,
To drink there.

In the deep, strange-scented shade of the great dark carob tree 5
I came down the steps with my pitcher
And must wait, must stand and wait, for there he was at the trough before me.

He reached down from a fissure in the earth-wall in the gloom
And trailed his yellow-brown slackness soft-bellied down, over the edge of the stone trough
And rested his throat upon the stone bottom,
And where the water had dripped from the tap, in a small clearness, 10
He sipped with his straight mouth
Softly drank through his straight gums, into his slack long body,
Silently.

Someone was before me at my water-trough,
And I, like a second-comer, waiting. 15

He lifted his head from his drinking, as cattle do,
And looked at me vaguely, as drinking cattle do,
And flicked his two-forked tongue from his lips, and mused a moment,

And stooped and drank a little more,
Being earth-brown, earth-golden from the burning bowels of the earth 20
On the day of Sicilian July, with Etna smoking.

The voice of my education said to me
He must be killed,
For in Sicily the black black snakes are innocent, the gold are venomous.

And voices in me said, If you were a man, 25
You would take a stick and break him now, and finish him off.

But must I confess how I liked him,
How glad I was he had come like a guest in quiet, to drink at my water-trough
And depart peaceful, pacified, and thankless
Into the burning bowels of this earth? 30

Was it cowardice, that I dared not kill him?
Was it perversity, that I longed to talk to him?
Was it humility, to feel so honoured?
I felt so honoured.

And yet those voices: 35
If you were not afraid, you would kill him!

And truly I was afraid, I was most afraid,
But even so, honoured still more
That he should seek my hospitality
From out the dark door of the secret earth. 40

He drank enough
And lifted his head, dreamily, as one who has drunken,

And flickered his tongue like a forked night on the air, so black,
Seeming to lick his lips,
And looked around like a god unseeing, into the air, 45

And slowly turned his head,
And slowly, very slowly, as if thrice adream
Proceeded to draw his slow length curving round
And climb again the broken bank of my wall-face.

And as he put his head into that dreadful hole, 50
And as he slowly drew up, snake-easing his shoulders, and entered further,
A sort of horror, a sort of protest against his withdrawing into that horrible
black hole,
Deliberately going into the blackness, and slowly drawing himself after,
Overcame me now his back was turned.

I looked round, I put down my pitcher, 55
I picked up a clumsy log
And threw it at the water-trough with a clatter.

I think it did not hit him;
But suddenly that part of him that was left behind convulsed in undignified
haste,
Writhed like lightning, and was gone 60
Into the black hole, the earth-lipped fissure in the wall-front
At which, in the intense still noon, I stared with fascination.

And immediately I regretted it.
I thought how paltry, how vulgar, what a mean act!
I despised myself and the voices of my accused human education. 65
And I thought of the albatross,
And I wished he would come back, my snake.

For he seemed to me again like a king,
Like a king in exile, uncrowned in the underworld,
Now due to be crowned again. 70
And so, I missed my chance with one of the lords
Of life.
And I have something to expiate:
A pettiness.

Wallace Stevens (1879–1955)

The Snow Man

One must have a mind of winter
To regard the frost and the boughs
Of the pine-trees crusted with snow;

And have been cold a long time
To behold the junipers shagged with
ice, 5
The spruces rough in the distant glitter
Of the January sun; and not to think
Of any misery in the sound of the wind,
In the sound of a few leaves,

Which is the sound of the land 10
Full of the same wind
That is blowing in the same bare place

For the listener, who listens in the
snow,
And, nothing himself, beholds
Nothing that is not there and the
nothing that is. 15

The Emperor of Ice-Cream

Call the roller of big cigars,
The muscular one, and bid him whip
In kitchen cups concupiscent curds.
Let the wenches dawdle in such dress
As they are used to wear, and let the boys 5
Bring flowers in last month's newspapers.
Let be be finale of seem.
The only emperor is the emperor of ice-cream.

Take from the dresser of deal,
Lacking the three glass knobs, that sheet 10
On which she embroidered fantails once
And spread it so as to cover her face.
If her horny feet protrude, they come
To show how cold she is, and dumb.
Let the lamp affix its beam. 15
The only emperor is the emperor of ice-cream.

Anecdote of the Jar

I placed a jar in Tennessee,
And round it was, upon a hill.
It made the slovenly wilderness
Surround that hill.

The wilderness rose up to it, 5
And sprawled around, no longer wild.
The jar was round upon the ground
And tall and of a port in air.

It took dominion everywhere.
The jar was gray and bare. 10
It did not give of bird or brush,
Like nothing else in Tennessee.

William Carlos Williams (1883–1963)

Tract

I will teach you my townspeople
how to perform a funeral
for you have it over a troop
of artists—
unless one should scour the world— 5
you have the ground sense necessary.

See! the hearse leads.
I begin with a design for a hearse.
For Christ's sake not black—
nor white either—and not polished! 10
Let it be weathered—like a farm wagon—
with gilt wheels (this could be
applied fresh at small expense)
or no wheels at all:
a rough day to drag over the ground. 15

Knock the glass out!
My God—glass, my townspeople!
For what purpose? Is it for the dead
to look out or for us to see 20

how well he is housed or to see
the flowers or the lack of them—
or what?
To keep the rain and snow from him?
He will have a heavier rain soon:
pebbles and dirt and what not. 25
Let there be no glass—
and no upholstery, phew!
and no little brass rollers
and small easy wheels on the bottom—
my townspeople what are you thinking
of? 30

A rough plain hearse then
with gilt wheels and no top at all.
On this the coffin lies
by its own weight.

No wreaths please—35
especially no hot house flowers.
Some common memento is better,
something he prized and is known by:
his old clothes—a few books perhaps—
God knows what! You realize 40
how we are about these things
my townspeople—
something will be found—anything
even flowers if he had come to that.
So much for the hearse. 45

For heaven's sake though see to the
driver!
Take off the silk hat! In fact
that's no place at all for him—
up there unceremoniously
dragging our friend out to his own
dignity! 50
Bring him down—bring him down!
Low and inconspicuous! I'd not have
him ride
on the wagon at all—damn him—
the undertaker's understrapper!

Let him hold the reins 55
and walk at the side
and inconspicuously too!

Then briefly as to yourselves:
Walk behind—as they do in France,
seventh class, or if you ride 60
Hell take curtains! Go with some show
of inconvenience; sit openly—
to the weather as to grief.
Or do you think you can shut grief in?
What—from us? We who have
perhaps 65
nothing to lose? Share with us
share with us—it will be money
in your pockets.
Go now
I think you are ready. 70

The Red Wheelbarrow

so much depends
upon

a red wheel
barrow

glazed with rain 5
water

beside the white
chickens.

The Yachts

contend in a sea which the land partly encloses
shielding them from the too heavy blows
of an ungoverned ocean which when it chooses

tortures the biggest hulls, the best man knows
to pit against its beatings, and sinks them pitilessly.
Mothlike in mists, scintillant in the minute

brilliance of cloudless days, with broad bellying sails
they glide to the wind tossing green water
from their sharp prows while over them the crew crawls

ant like, solicitously grooming them, releasing,
making fast as they turn, lean far over and having
caught the wind again, side by side, head for the mark.

In a well guarded arena of open water surrounded by
lesser and greater craft which, sycophant, lumbering
and flittering follow them, they appear youthful, rare

as the light of a happy eye, live with the grace
of all that in the mind is feckless, free and
naturally to be desired. Now the sea which holds them

is moody, lapping their glossy sides, as if feeling
for some slightest flaw but fails completely.
Today no race. Then the wind comes again. The yachts

move, jockeying for a start, the signal is set and they
are off. Now the waves strike at them but they are too
well made, they slip through, though they take in canvas.

Arms with hands grasping seek to clutch at the prows.
Bodies thrown recklessly in the way are cut aside.
It is a sea of faces about them in agony, in despair

until the horror of the race dawns staggering the mind,
the whole sea becoming entanglement of water bodies
lost to the world bearing what they cannot hold. Broken,

beaten, desolate, reaching from the dead to be taken up
they cry out, failing, failing! their cries rising
in waves still as the skillful yachts pass over.

Ezra Pound (1885–1972)

Portrait d'une Femme

Your mind and you are our Sargasso
  Sea,
London has swept about you this score
  years
And bright ships left you this or that in
  fee:
Ideas, old gossip, oddments of all things,
Strange spars of knowledge and
  dimmed wares of price. 5
Great minds have sought you—lacking
  someone else.
You have been second always. Tragical?
No. You preferred it to the usual thing:
One dull man, dulling and uxorious,
One average mind—with one thought
  less, each year. 10
Oh, you are patient, I have seen you sit
Hours, where something might have
  floated up.
And now you pay one. Yes, you richly
  pay.
You are a person of some interest, one
  comes to you
And takes strange gain away: 15
Trophies fished up; some curious
  suggestion;
Fact that leads nowhere; and a tale or
  two,
Pregnant with mandrakes, or with
  something else
That might prove useful and yet never
  proves,
That never fits a corner or shows
  use, 20
Or finds its hours upon the loom of
  days:
The tarnished, gaudy, wonderful old
  work;
Idols and ambergris and rare inlays,
These are your riches, your great store; and yet
For all this sea-hoard of deciduous
  things, 25
Strange woods half sodden, and new
  brighter stuff:
In the slow float of differing light and
  deep,
No! there is nothing! In the whole and
  all,
Nothing that's quite your own.
      Yet this is you. 30

Robinson Jeffers (1887–1962)

The Purse-Seine

Our sardine fishermen work at night in the dark of the moon; day-light or moonlight
They could not tell where to spread the net, unable to see the phosphorescence of
  the shoals of fish.
They work northward from Monterey, coasting Santa Cruz; off New Year's Point
  or off Pigeon Point
The look-out man will see some lakes of milk-color light on the sea's night-purple;
  he points, and the helmsman

Turns the dark prow, the motorboat circles the gleaming shoal and drifts out her seine-net. They close the circle 5
And purse the bottom of the net, then with great labor haul it in.

I cannot tell you
How beautiful the scene is, and a little terrible, then, when the crowded fish
Know they are caught, and wildly beat from one wall to the other of their closing destiny the phosphorescent
Water to a pool of flame, each beautiful slender body sheeted with flame, like a live rocket 10
A comet's tail wake of clear yellow flame; while outside the narrowing
Floats and cordage of the net great sea-lions come up to watch, sighing in the dark; the vast walls of night
Stand erect to the stars.

Lately I was looking from a night mountain-top
On a wide city, the colored splendor, galaxies of light: how could I help but recall the seine-net 15
Gathering the luminous fish? I cannot tell you how beautiful the city appeared, and a little terrible.
I thought, We have geared the machines and locked all together into interdependence; we have built the great cities; now
There is no escape. We have gathered vast populations incapable of free survival, insulated
From the strong earth, each person in himself helpless, on all dependent. The circle is closed, and the net 20
Is being hauled in. They hardly feel the cords drawing, yet they shine already. The inevitable mass-disasters
Will not come in our time nor in our children's, but we and our children
Must watch the net draw narrower, government take all powers—or revolution, and the new government
Take more than all, add to kept bodies kept souls—or anarchy, the mass-disasters.

These things are Progress; 25
Do you marvel our verse is troubled or frowning, while it keeps its reason? Or it lets go, lets the mood flow
In the manner of the recent young men into mere hysteria, splintered gleams, crackled laughter. But they are quite wrong.
There is no reason for amazement; surely one always knew that cultures decay, and life's end is death.

May-June 1940

Foreseen for so many years: these evils, this monstrous violence, these massive agonies: no easier to bear.
We saw them with slow stone strides approach, everyone saw them; we closed our eyes against them, we looked
And they had come nearer. We ate and drank and slept, they came nearer. Sometimes we laughed, they were nearer. Now
They are here. And now a blind man foresees what follows them: Degradation, famine, recovery and so forth, and the
Epidemic manias: but not enough death to serve us, not enough death. It would be better for men 5
To be few and live far apart, where none could infect another; then slowly the sanity of field and mountain
And the cold ocean and glittering stars might enter their minds.
Another
dream, another dream.
We shall have to accept certain limitations
In future, and abandon some humane dreams; only hard-minded, sleepless and realistic, can ride this rock-slide 10
To new fields down the dark mountain; and we shall have to perceive that these insanities are normal;
We shall have to perceive that battle is a burning flower or like a huge music, and the dive-bomber's screaming orgasm
As beautiful as other passions; and that death and life are not serious alternatives. One has known all these things
For many years: there is greater and darker to know
In the next hundred. 15

And why do you cry, my dear, why do you cry?
It is all in the whirling circles of time.
If millions are born millions must die,
If England goes down and Germany goes up
The stronger dog will still be on top, 20
All in the turning of time.
If civilization goes down, that
Would be an event to contemplate.
It will not be in our time, alas, my dear,
It will not be in our time. 25

Thomas Stearns Eliot (1888–1965)

The Love Song of J. Alfred Prufrock

S'io credesse che mia riposta fosse
A persona che mai tornasse al mondo,
Questa fiamma staria senza piu scosse.
Ma perciocche giammai di questo fondo
Non torno vivo alcun, s'i'odo il vero,
Senza tema d'infamia ti rispondo[1]

Let us go then, you and I,
When the evening is spread out against the sky
Like a patient etherised upon a table;
Let us go, through certain half-deserted streets, 5
The muttering retreats
Of restless nights in one-night cheap hotels
And sawdust restaurants with oyster-shells:
Streets that follow like a tedious argument
Of insidious intent
To lead you to an overwhelming question . . . 10
Oh, do not ask, "What is it?"
Let us go and make our visit.
In the room the women come and go
Talking of Michelangelo.

The yellow fog that rubs its back upon the window-panes, 15
The yellow smoke that rubs its muzzle on the window-panes
Licked its tongue into the corners of the evening,
Lingered upon the pools that stand in drains,
Let fall upon its back the soot that falls from chimneys,
Slipped by the terrace, made a sudden leap, 20
And seeing that it was a soft October night,
Curled once about the house, and fell asleep.

And indeed there will be time
For the yellow smoke that slides along the street,
Rubbing its back upon the window-panes; 25
There will be time, there will be time
To prepare a face to meet the faces that you meet;
There will be time to murder and create,
And time for all the works and days of hands
That lift and drop a question on your plate; 30
Time for you and time for me,
And time yet for a hundred indecisions,
And for a hundred visions and revisions,
Before the taking of a toast and tea.

In the room the women come and go 35
Talking of Michelangelo.

And indeed there will be time
To wonder, "Do I dare?" and, "Do I dare?"
Time to turn back and descend the stair,

[1] *Epigraph:* "If I thought my answer were to one who ever could return to the world, this flame should shake no more; but since no one did ever return alive from this depth, if what I hear be true, without fear of infamy I answer thee." (Dante, *Inferno*, XXVII, 61–66)

With a bald spot in the middle of my
hair— 40
(They will say: "How his hair is
growing thin!")
My morning coat, my collar mounting
firmly to the chin,
My necktie rich and modest, but
asserted by a simple pin—
(They will say: "But how his arms and
legs are thin!")
Do I dare 45
Disturb the universe?
In a minute there is time
For decisions and revisions which a
minute will reverse.

For I have known them all already,
known them all:
Have known the evenings, mornings,
afternoons, 50
I have measured out my life with coffee
spoons;
I know the voices dying with a dying
fall
Beneath the music from a farther room.
So how should I presume?

And I have known the eyes already,
known them all— 55
The eyes that fix you in a formulated
phrase,
And when I am formulated, sprawling
on a pin,
When I am pinned and wriggling on
the wall,
Then how should I begin
To spit out all the butt-ends of my days
and ways? 60
And how should I presume?

And I have known the arms already,
known them all—
Arms that are braceleted and white and
bare
(But in the lamplight, downed with
light brown hair!)
Is it perfume from a dress 65
That makes me so digress?
Arms that lie along a table, or wrap
about a shawl.

And should I then presume?
And how should I begin?
. . .
Shall I say, I have gone at dusk through
narrow streets 70
And watched the smoke that rises from
the pipes
Of lonely men in shirt-sleeves, leaning
out of windows? . . .

I should have been a pair of ragged
claws
Scuttling across the floors of silent seas.
. . .
And the afternoon, the evening, sleeps
so peacefully! 75
Smoothed by long fingers,
Asleep . . . tired . . . or it malingers,
Stretched on the floor, here beside you
and me.
Should I, after tea and cakes and ices,
Have the strength to force the moment
to its crisis? 80
But though I have wept and fasted,
wept and prayed,
Though I have seen my head (grown
slightly bald) brought in upon a
platter,
I am no prophet—and here's no great
matter;
I have seen the moment of my greatness
flicker,
And I have seen the eternal Footman
hold my coat, and snicker 85
And in short, I was afraid.

And would it have been worth it,
after all,
After the cups, the marmalade, the tea,
Among the porcelain, among some talk
of you and me,
Would it have been worth while, 90
To have bitten off the matter with a
smile,
To have squeezed the universe into a
ball
To roll it toward some overwhelming
question,
To say: "I am Lazarus, come from the
dead,

Come back to tell you all, I shall tell
you all"— 95
If one, settling a pillow by her head,
Should say: "That is not what I meant
at all.
That is not it, at all."

And would it have been worth it,
after all,
Would it have been worth while, 100
After the sunsets and the dooryards and
the sprinkled streets,
After the novels, after the teacups, after
the skirts that trail along the
floor—
And this, and so much more?—
It is impossible to say just what I mean!
But as if a magic lantern threw the
nerves in patterns on a screen: 105
Would it have been worth while
If one, settling a pillow or throwing off
a shawl,
And turning toward the window, should
say:
"That is not it at all,
That is not what I meant, at all." 110

. . .

No! I am not Prince Hamlet, nor was
meant to be:
Am an attendant lord, one that will do
To swell a progress, start a scene or two,
Advise the prince; no doubt, an easy
tool,
Deferential, glad to be of use, 115
Politic, cautious, and meticulous;
Full of high sentence, but a bit obtuse;
At times, indeed, almost ridiculous—
Almost, at times, the Fool.

I grow old. . . . I grow old . . . 120
I shall wear the bottoms of my trousers
rolled.

Shall I part my hair behind? Do I
dare to eat a peach?
I shall wear white flannel trousers, and
walk upon the beach.
I have heard the mermaids singing, each
to each.

I do not think that they will sing to
me. 125
I have seen them riding seaward on
the waves
Combing the white hair of the waves
blown back
When the wind blows the water white
and black.
We have lingered in the chambers of
the sea
By sea-girls wreathed with seaweed red
and brown 130
Till human voices wake us, and we
drown.

The Hollow Men

Mistah Kurtz—he dead.
A penny for the Old Guy.

I

We are the hollow men
We are the stuffed men
Leaning together
Headpiece filled with straw. Alas!
Our dried voices, when 5
We whisper together
Are quiet and meaningless
As wind in dry grass
Or rats' feet over broken glass
In our dry cellar 10
Shape without form, shade without
colour,
Paralysed force, gesture without
motion;

Those who have crossed
With direct eyes, to death's other
Kingdom
Remember us—if at all—not as lost 15
Violent souls, but only
As the hollow men
The stuffed men.

II

Eyes I dare not meet in dreams
In death's dream kingdom 20
These do not appear:
There, the eyes are
Sunlight on a broken column
There, is a tree swinging
And voices are 25
In the wind's singing
More distant and more solemn
Than a fading star.
Let me be no nearer
In death's dream kingdom 30
Let me also wear
Such deliberate disguises
Rat's coat, crowskin, crossed staves
In a field
Behaving as the wind behaves 35
No nearer—

Not that final meeting
In the twilight kingdom.

III

This is the dead land
This is cactus land 40
Here the stone images
Are raised, here they receive
The supplication of a dead man's hand
Under the twinkle of a fading star.

Is it like this 45
In death's other kingdom
Waking alone
At the hour when we are
Trembling with tenderness
Lips that would kiss 50
Form prayers to broken stone

IV

The eyes are not here
There are no eyes here
In this valley of dying stars
In this hollow valley 55
This broken jaw of our lost kingdoms.

In this last of meeting places
We grope together
And avoid speech
Gathered on this beach of the tumid
river. 60

Sightless, unless
The eyes reappear
As the perpetual star
Multifoliate rose
Of death's twilight kingdom 65
The hope only
Of empty men.

V

Here we go round the prickly pear
Prickly pear prickly pear
Here we go round the prickly pear 70
At five o'clock in the morning.

Between the idea
And the reality
Between the motion
And the act 75
Falls the Shadow
For Thine is the Kingdom

Between the conception
And the creation
Between the emotion 80
And the response
Falls the Shadow
Life is very long

Between the desire
And the spasm 85
Between the potency
And the existence
Between the essence
And the descent
Falls the Shadow 90
For Thine is the Kingdom

For Thine is
Life is
For Thine is the

This is the way the world ends 95
This is the way the world ends
This is the way the world ends
Not with a bang but a whimper.

John Crowe Ransom (1888–1974)

Bells for John Whiteside's Daughter

There was such speed in her little body,
And such lightness in her footfall,
It is no wonder that her brown study
Astonishes us all.

Her wars were bruited in our high window. 5
We looked among orchard trees and beyond,
Where she took arms against her shadow,
Or harried unto the pond

The lazy geese, like a snow cloud
Dripping their snow on the green grass, 10
Tricking and stopping, sleepy and proud,
Who cried in goose, Alas,

For the tireless heart within the little
Lady with rod that made them rise
From their noon apple-dreams, and scuttle 15
Goose-fashion under the skies!

But now go the bells, and we are ready;
In one house we are sternly stopped
To say we are vexed at her brown study, 20
Lying so primly propped.

Edna St. Vincent Millay (1892–1950)

Justice Denied in Massachusetts

Let us abandon then our gardens and go home
And sit in the sitting-room.
Shall the larkspur blossom or the corn grow under this cloud?
Sour to the fruitful seed
Is the cold earth under this cloud, 5
Fostering quack and weed, we have marched upon but cannot conquer;
We have bent the blades of our hoes against the stalks of them.
Let us go home, and sit in the sitting-room.
Not in our day
Shall the cloud go over and the sun rise as before, 10
Beneficient upon us
Out of the glittering bay,
And the warm winds be blown inward from the sea
Moving the blades of corn
With a peaceful sound. 15
Forlorn, forlorn,
Stands the blue hay-rack by the empty mow.
And the petals drop to the ground,
Leaving the tree unfruited.
The sun that warmed our stooping backs and withered the weed uprooted— 20
We shall not feel it again.
We shall die in darkness, and be buried in the rain.

What from the splendid dead
We have inherited—
Furrows sweet to the grain, and the weed subdued— 25
See now the slug and the mildew plunder.
Evil does overwhelm
The larkspur and the corn;
We have seen them go under.

Let us sit here, sit still, 30
Here in the sitting-room until we die;
At the step of Death on the walk, rise and go;
Leaving to our children's children this beautiful doorway,
And this elm,
And a blighted earth to till 35
With a broken hoe.

What Lips My Lips Have Kissed

What lips my lips have kissed, and where, and why,
I have forgotten, and what arms have lain
Under my head till morning; but the rain
Is full of ghosts tonight, that tap and sigh
Upon the glass and listen for reply; 5
And in my heart there stirs a quiet pain
For unremembered lads that not again
Will turn to me at midnight with a cry.
Thus in the winter stands the lonely tree,
Nor knows what birds have vanished one by one, 10
Yet knows its boughs more silent than before:
I cannot say what loves have come and gone;
I only know that summer sang in me
A little while, that in me sings no more.

Archibald MacLeish (1892–   )

Memorial Rain

Ambassador Puser the ambassador
Reminds himself in French, felicitous tongue,
What these (young men no longer) lie here for
In rows that once, and somewhere else, were young . . .

All night in Brussels the wind had tugged at my door: 5
I had heard the wind at my door and the trees strung
Taut, and to me who had never been before
In that country it was a strange wind, blowing
Steadily, stiffening the walls, the floor,
The roof of my room. I had not slept for knowing 10
He too, dead, was a stranger in that land
And felt beneath the earth in the wind's flowing
A tightening of roots and would not understand,
Remembering lake winds in Illinois,
That strange wind. I had felt his bones in the sand 15
Listening.

. . . Reflects that these enjoy
Their country's gratitude, that deep repose,
That peace no pain can break, no hurts destroy,
That rest, that sleep . . . 20

At Ghent the wind rose.
There was a smell of rain and a heavy drag
Of wind in the hedges but not as the wind blows
Over fresh water when the waves lag
Foaming and the willows huddle and it will rain; 25
I felt him waiting.

. . . Indicates the flag
Which (may he say) enisles in Flanders' plain
This little field these happy, happy dead
Have made America . . .

In the ripe grain
The wind coiled glistening, darted, fled,
Dragging its heavy body: at Waereghem 30
The wind coiled in the grass above his head:
Waiting—listening . . .

. . . Dedicates to them
This earth their bones have hallowed, this last gift
A grateful country . . .

Under the dry grass stem 35
The words are blurred, are thickened, the words sift
Confused by the rasp of the wind, by the thin grating
Of ants under the grass, the minute shift
And tumble of dusty sand separating
From dusty sand. The roots of the grass strain, 40
Tighten, the earth is rigid, waits—he is waiting—

And suddenly, and all at once, the rain!

The living scatter, they run into houses, the wind
Is trampled under the rain, shakes free, is again
Trampled. The rain gathers, running in thinned 45
Spurts of water that ravel in the dry sand,
Seeping into the sand under the grass roots, seeping
Between cracked boards to the bones of a clenched hand:
The earth relaxes, loosens; he is sleeping,
He rests, he is quiet, he sleeps in a strange land. 50

E. E. Cummings (1894–1962)

Poem, or Beauty Hurts Mr. Vinal

take it from me kiddo
believe me
my country, 'tis of
you, land of the Cluett
Shirt Boston Garter and Spearmint 5
Girl With The Wrigley Eyes (of you
land of the Arrow Ide
and Earl &
Wilson
Collars) of you i 10
sing: land of Abraham Lincoln and Lydia E. Pinkham,
land above all of Just Add Hot Water And Serve—
from every B.V.D.

let freedom ring

amen. i do however protest, anent the un 15
-spontaneous and otherwise scented merde which
greets one (Everywhere Why) as divine poesy per
that and this radically defunct periodical. i would

suggest that certain ideas gestures
rhymes, like Gillette Razor Blades 20
having been used and reused
to the mystical moment of dullness emphatically are
Not To Be Resharpened. (Case in point

if we are to believe these gently O sweetly
melancholy trillers amid the thrillers 25
these crepuscular violinists among my and your
skyscrapers—Helen & Cleopatra were Just Too Lovely,
The Snail's On The Thorn enter Morn and God's
In His andsoforth

do you get me?)according 30
to such supposedly indigenous
throstles Art is O World O Life
a formula: example, Turn Your Shirttails Into
Drawers and If It Isn't An Eastman It Isn't A
Kodak therefore my friends let 35

us now sing each and all fortissimo A-
mer
i

ca, I
love, 40
You. And there're a
hun-dred-mil-lion-oth-ers, like
all of you successfully if
delicately gelded (or spaded)
gentlemen (and ladies)—pretty 45
littleliverpill-
hearted-Nujolneeding-There's-A-Reason
americans (who tensetendoned and with
upward vacant eyes, painfully
perpetually crouched, quivering, upon the 50
sternly allotted sandpile
—how silently
emit a tiny violetflavored nuisance: Odor?

ono.
comes out like a ribbon lies flat on the brush 55

La Guerre

I

the bigness of cannon
is skillful,

but i have seen
death's clever enormous voice
which hides in a fragility 5
of poppies. . . .

i say that sometimes
on these long talkative animals
are laid fists of huger silence

I have seen all the silence 10
filled with vivid noiseless boys

at Roupy
i have seen
between barrages,

the night utter ripe unspeaking girls. 15

II

O sweet spontaneous
earth how often have
the
doting
fingers of 20
prurient philosophers pinched
and
poked

thee
, has the naughty thumb 25
of science prodded
thy
beauty .how
often have the religions taken
thee upon their scraggy knees 30
squeezing and

buffeting thee that thou mightest conceive
gods

(but
true 35

to the incomparable
couch of death thy
rhythmic
lover

thou answerest 40

them only with
spring)

Portrait VIII

Buffalo Bill's
defunct
who used to
ride a watersmooth-silver
stallion 5
and break onetwothreefourfive pigeonsjustlikethat
Jesus
he was a handsome man
and what i want to know is
how do you like your blueeyed boy
Mister death.

Pity This Busy Monster, Manunkind

pity this busy monster, manunkind,

not. Progress is a comfortable disease:
your victim (death and life safely
beyond)

plays with the bigness of his littleness
—electrons deify one razorblade 5
into a mountainrange; lenses extend

unwish through curving wherewhen till
unwish
returns on its unself.

A world of made
is not a world of born—pity poor
flesh 10

and trees,poor stars and stones,but
never this
fine specimen of hypermagical

ultraomnipotence. We doctors know

a hopeless case if—listen: there's a hell
of a good universe next door; let's
go 15

Next to of Course God

"next to of course god america i
love you land of the pilgrims' and so forth oh
say can you see by the dawn's early my
country 'tis of centuries come and go
and are no more what of it we should worry 5
in every language even deafanddumb
thy sons acclaim your glorious name by gorry
by jingo by gee by gosh by gum
why talk of beauty what could be more beautiful than these heroic happy dead 10
who rushed like lions to the roaring slaughter
they did not stop to think they died instead
then shall the voice of liberty be mute?"

He spoke. And drank rapidly a glass of water.

My Father Moved Through Dooms of Love

my father moved through dooms of love
through sames of am through haves of give,
singing each morning out of each night
my father moved through depths of height

this motionless forgetful where 5
turned at his glance to shining here;
that if (so timid air is firm)
under his eyes would stir and squirm

newly as from unburied which
floats the first who, his april touch 10
drove sleeping selves to swarm their fates
woke dreamers to their ghostly roots

and should some why completely weep
my father's fingers brought her sleep:
vainly no smallest voice might cry 15
for he could feel the mountains grow.

Lifting the valleys of the sea
my father moved through griefs of joy;
praising a forehead called the moon
singing desire into begin 20

joy was his song and joy so pure
a heart of star by him could steer
and pure so now and now so yes
the wrists of twilight would rejoice

keen as midsummer's keen beyond 25
conceiving mind of sun will stand,
so strictly (over utmost him
so hugely) stood my father's dream

his flesh was flesh his blood was blood:
no hungry man but wished him food; 30
no cripple wouldn't creep one mile
uphill to only see him smile.

Scorning the pomp of must and shall
my father moved through dooms of feel;
his anger was as right as rain 35
his pity was as green as grain

septembering arms of year extend
less humbly wealth to foe and friend
than he to foolish and to wise
offered immeasurable is 40

proudly and (by octobering flame
beckoned) as earth will downward climb,
so naked for immortal work
his shoulders marched against the dark

his sorrow was as true as bread: 45
no liar looked him in the head;
if every friend became his foe
he'd laugh and build a world with snow.

My father moved through theys of we,
singing each new leaf out of each
tree 50
(and every child was sure that spring
danced when she heard my father sing)

then let men kill which cannot share,
let blood and flesh be mud and mire,
scheming images,passion willed, 55
freedom a drug that's bought and sold

giving to steal and cruel kind,
a heart to fear,to doubt a mind,
to differ a disease of same,
conform the pinnacle of am 60

though dull were all we taste as bright,
bitter all utterly things sweet,
maggoty minus and dumb death
all we inherit,all bequeath

and nothing quite so least as truth 65
—i say though hate were why men
breathe—
because my father lived his soul
love is the whole and more than all

Stephen Vincent Benét (1898–1943)

Nightmare Number Three

We had expected everything but revolt
And I kind of wonder myself when they started thinking—
But there's no dice in that now.
I've heard fellows say
They must have planned it for years and maybe they did. 5
Looking back, you can find little incidents here and there,
Like the concrete-mixer in Jersey eating the wop
Or the roto press that printed "Fiddle-dee-dee!"
In a three-color process all over Senator Sloop,
Just as he was making a speech. The thing about that 10
Was, how could it walk upstairs? But it was upstairs,
Clicking and mumbling in the Senate Chamber.
They had to knock out the wall to take it away
And the wrecking-crew said it grinned.
It was only the best 15
Machines, of course, the superhuman machines,
The ones we'd built to be better than flesh and bone,
But the cars were in it, of course . . .
and they hunted us
Like rabbits through the cramped streets on that Bloody Monday, 20
The Madison Avenue busses leading the charge.
The busses were pretty bad—but I'll not forget
The smash of glass when the Dusenberg left the show-room

And pinned three brokers to the Racquet Club steps
Or the long howl of the horns when they saw men run, 25
When they saw them looking for holes in the solid ground . . .

I guess they were tired of being ridden in
And stopped and started by pygmies for silly ends,
Of wrapping cheap cigarettes and bad chocolate bars 30
Collecting nickels and waving platinum hair
And letting six million people live in a town.
I guess it was that. I guess they got tired of us
And the whole smell of human hands.
But it was a shock 35
To climb sixteen flights of stairs to Art Zuckow's office
(Nobody took the elevators twice)
And find him strangled to death in a nest of telephones,

The octopus-tendrils waving over his head,
And a sort of quiet humming filling the air . . . 40
Do they eat? . . . There was red . . . But I did not stop to look.
I don't know yet how I got to the roof in time
And it's lonely, here on the roof.
For a while, I thought
That window-cleaner would make it, and keep me company. 45
But they got him with his own hoist at the sixteenth floor
And dragged him in, with a squeal.
You see, they cooperate. Well, we taught them that
And it's fair enough, I suppose. You see, we built them.
We taught them to think for themselves. 50
It was bound to come. You can see it was bound to come.

And it won't be so bad, in the country. I hate to think
Of the reapers, running wild in the Kansas fields,
And the transport planes like hawks on a chickenyard,
But the horses might help. We might make a deal with the horses. 55
At least, you've more chance, out there.
And they need us, too.
They're bound to realize that when they once calm down.
They'll need oil and spare parts and adjustments and tuning up.
Slaves? Well, in a way, you know, we were slaves before. 60
There won't be so much real difference—honest, there won't.
(I wish I hadn't looked into that beauty-parlor
And seen what was happening there.
But those are female machines and a bit high-strung.)
Oh, settle down. We'll arrange it. We'll compromise. 65
It wouldn't make sense to wipe out the whole human race.
Why, I bet if I went to my old Plymouth now
(Of course you'd have to do it the tactful way)
And said, "Look here! Who got you the swell French horn?" 70
He wouldn't turn me over to those police cars;
At least I don't think he would.

Oh, it's going to be jake.
There won't be so much real difference—honest, there won't—
And I'd go down in a minute and take my chance—
I'm a good American and I always liked them— 75
Except for one small detail that bothers me
And that's the food proposition. Because, you see,
The concrete-mixer may have made a mistake,
And it looks like just high spirits.
But, if it's got so they like the flavor . . . well . . . 80

Hart Crane (1899–1932)

Chaplinesque

We make our meek adjustments,
Contented with such random consolations
As the wind deposits
In slithered and too ample pockets.

For we can still love the world, who find 5
A famished kitten on the step, and know
Recesses for it from the fury of the street,
Or warm torn elbow coverts.

We will sidestep, and to the final smirk
Dally the doom of that inevitable thumb 10
That slowly chafes its puckered index toward us,
Facing the dull squint with what innocence
And what surprise!

And yet these fine collapses are not lies
More than the pirouettes of any pliant cane; 15
Our obsequies are, in a way, no enterprise.
We can evade you, and all else but the heart:
What blame to us if the heart live on.

The game enforces smirks; but we have seen
The moon in lonely alleys make 20
A grail of laughter of an empty ash can,
And through all sound of gaiety and quest
Have heard a kitten in the wilderness.

The River
(from The Bridge)

Stick your patent name on a signboard
brother—all over—going west—young man
Tintex—Japalac—Certain-teed Overalls ads
and lands sakes! under the new playbill ripped
in the guaranteed corner—see Bert Williams what? 5
Minstrels when you steal a chicken just
save me the wing, for if it isn't
Erie it ain't for miles around a
Mazda—and the telegrapic night coming on Thomas

a Ediford—and whistling down the tracks 10
a headlight rushing with the sound—can you
imagine—while an EXPRESS makes time like
SCIENCE—COMMERCE and the HOLYGHOST
RADIO ROARS IN EVERY HOME WE HAVE THE NORTHPOLE
WALLSTREET AND VIRGINBIRTH WITHOUT STONES OR 15
WIRES OR EVEN RUNNING brooks connecting ears
and no more sermon windows flashing roar
Breathtaking—as you like it . . . eh?

So the 20th Century—so
whizzed the Limited—roared by and left 20
three men, still hungry on the tracks, ploddingly
watching the tail lights wizen and converge,
slipping gimleted and neatly out of sight.
The last bear, shot drinking in the Dakotas,
Loped under wires that span the mountain stream. 25
Keen instruments, strung to a vast precision
Bind town to town and dream to ticking dream.
But some men take their liquor slow—and count—
Though they'll confess no rosary nor clue—
The river's minute by the far brook's year. 30
Under a world of whistles, wires and steam
Caboose-like they go ruminating through
Ohio, Indiana—blind baggage—
To Cheyenne tagging . . . Maybe Kalamazoo.

Time's renderings, time's blendings they construe 35
As final reckonings of fire and snow;
Strange bird-wit, like the elemental gist
Of unwalled winds they offer, singing low
My Old Kentucky Home and *Casey Jones,*
Some Sunny Day. I heard a road-gang chanting so. 40
And afterwards, who had a colt's eyes—one said,
"Jesus! Oh I remember watermelon days!" And sped
High in a cloud of merriment, recalled
"—And when my Aunt Sally Simpson smiled," he drawled—
"It was almost Louisiana, long ago." 45

"There's no place like Booneville though, Buddy,"
One said, excising a last burr from his vest,
"—For early trouting." Then peering in the can,
"—But I kept on the tracks." Possessed, resigned,
He trod the fire down pensively and grinned,
Spreading dry shingles of a beard . . . 50

Behind
My father's cannery works I used to see
Rail-squatters ranged in nomad raillery,
The ancient men—wifeless or runaway 55
Hobo-trekkers that forever search
An empire wilderness of freight and rails.
Each seemed a child, like me, on a loose perch,
Holding to childhood like some termless play.
John, Jake, or Charley, hopping the slow freight 60
—Memphis to Tallahassee—riding the rods,
Blind fists of nothing, humpty-dumpty clods.

Yet they touch something like a key perhaps.
From pole to pole across the hills, the states
—They know a body under the wide rain; 65
Youngsters with eyes like fjords, old reprobates
With racetrack jargon,—dotting immensity
They lurk across her, knowing her yonder breast
Snow-silvered, sumac-stained or smoky blue,
Is past the valley-sleepers, south or west. 70
—As I have trod the rumorous midnight, too.

And past the circuit of the lamp's thin flame
(O Nights that brought me to her body bare!)
Have dreamed beyond the print that bound her name.
Trains sounding the long blizzards out—I heard 75
Wail into distances I knew were hers.
Papooses crying on the wind's long mane
Screamed redskin dynasties that fled the brain,
—Dead echoes! But I knew her body there
Time like a serpent down her shoulder dark, 80
And space, an eagle's wing, laid on her hair.

Under the Ozarks, domed by Iron Mountain,
The old gods of the rain lie wrapped in pools
Where eyeless fish curvet a sunken fountain
And re-descend with corn from querulous crows. 85
Such pilferings make up their timeless eatage,
Propitiate them for their timber torn
By iron, iron—always the iron dealt cleavage!
They doze now, below axe and powder horn.

And Pullman breakfasters glide glistening steel 90
From tunnel into field—iron strides the dew—
Straddles the hill, a dance of wheel on wheel.
You have a half-hour's wait at Siskiyou,

Or stay the night and take the next train through.
Southward, near Cairo passing, you can see 95
The Ohio merging,—borne down Tennessee;
And if it's summer and the sun's in dusk
Maybe the breeze will lift the River's musk
—As though the waters breathed that you might know
Memphis Johnny, Steamboat Bill, Missouri Joe. 100

Oh, lean from the window, if the train slows down,
As though you touched hands with some ancient clown,
—A little while gaze absently below
And hum *Deep River* with them while they go.

Yes, turn again and sniff once more—look see, 105
O Sheriff, Brakeman and Authority—
Hitch up your pants and crunch another quid,
For you, too, feed the River timelessly.
And few evade full measure of their fate;
Always they smile out eerily what they seem. 110
I could believe he joked at heaven's gate—
Dan Midland—jolted from the cold brake-beam.

Down, down—born pioneers in time's despite,
Grimed tributaries to an ancient flow—
They win no frontier by their wayward plight, 115
But drift in stillness, as from Jordan's brow.

You will not hear it as the sea; even stone
Is not more hushed by gravity . . . But slow,
As loth to take more tribute—sliding prone
Like one whose eyes were buried long ago 120

The River, spreading, flows—and spends your dream.
What are you, lost within this tideless spell?
You are your father's father, and the stream—
A liquid theme that floating niggers swell.

Damp tonnage and alluvial march of days— 125
Nights turbid, vascular with silted shale
And roots surrendered down of moraine clays:
The Mississippi drinks the farthest dale.

O quarrying passion, undertowed sunlight!
The basalt surface drags a jungle grace 130
Ochreous and lynx-barred in lengthening might;
Patience! and you shall reach the biding place!

Over De Soto's bones the freighted floors
Throb past the City storied of three thrones.
Down two more turns the Mississippi pours 135
(Anon tall ironsides up from salt lagoons)

And flows within itself, heaps itself free.
All fades but one thin skyline 'round . . . Ahead
No embrace opens but the stinging sea;
The River lifts itself from its long bed. 140

Poised wholly on its dream, a mustard glow,
Tortured with history, its one will—flow!
—The Passion spreads in wide tongues, choked and slow,
Meeting the Gulf, hosannas silently below.

E. B. White (1899–)

I Paint What I See

A Ballad of Artistic Integrity

"What do you paint, when you paint a wall?"
Said John D.'s grandson Nelson.
"Do you paint just anything there at all?
"Will there be any doves, or a tree in fall?
"Or a hunting scene, like an English hall?" 5

"I paint what I see," said Rivera.

"What are the colors you use when you paint?"
Said John D.'s grandson Nelson.
"Do you use any red in the beard of a saint?
"If you do, is it terribly red, or faint? 10
"Do you use any blue? Is it Prussian?"

"I paint what I paint," said Rivera.

"Whose is that head that I see on my wall?"
Said John D.'s grandson Nelson.
"Is it anyone's head whom we know, at all? 15
"A Rensselaer, or a Saltonstall?
"Is it Franklin D.? Is it Mordaunt Hall?
"Or is it the head of a Russian?"

"I paint what I think," said Rivera.

"I paint what I paint, I paint what I see, 20
"I paint what I think," said Rivera,
"And the thing that is dearest in life to me

"In a bourgeois hall is Integrity;
"However . . .
"I'll take out a couple of people drinkin' 25
"And put in a picture of Abraham Lincoln,
"I could even give you McCormick's reaper
"And still not make my art much cheaper.
"But the head of Lenin has got to stay
"Or my friends will give me the bird today 30
"The bird, the bird, forever."

"It's not good taste in a man like me,"
Said John D.'s grandson Nelson,
"To question an artist's integrity
"Or mention a practical thing like a fee, 35
"But I know what I like to a large degree
"Though art I hate to hamper;
"For twenty-one thousand conservative bucks

"You painted a radical. I say shucks,
"I never could rent the offices— 40
"The capitalistic offices.
"For this, as you know, is a public hall
"And people want doves, or a tree in fall,
"And though your art I dislike to hamper,
"I owe a *little* to God and Gramper, 45
"And after all,
"It's *my* wall . . ."

"We'll see if it is," said Rivera.

Kenneth Fearing (1902–1961)

American Rhapsody (2)

First you bit your fingernails. And then you comb your hair again. And then you wait. And wait.
(They say, you know, that first you lie. And then you steal, they say. And then, they say, you kill.)

Then the doorbell rings. Then Peg drops in. And Bill. And Jane. And Doc.
And first you talk, and smoke, and hear the news and have a drink. Then you walk down the stairs.
And you dine, then, and go to a show after that, perhaps, and after that a night spot, and after that come home again, and climb the stairs again, and again go to bed. 5

But first Peg argues, and Doc replies. First you dance the same dance and you drink the same drink you always drank before.
And the piano builds a roof of notes above the world.
And the trumpet weaves a dome of music through space. And the drum makes a ceiling over space and time and night.
And then the table-wit. And then the check. Then home again to bed.
But first, the stairs 10
And do you now, baby, as you climb the stairs, do you still feel as you felt back there?
Do you feel again as you felt this morning? And the night before? And then the night before that?

(They say, you know, that first you hear voices. And then you have visions, they say. Then, they say, you kick and scream and rave.)
Or do you feel: What is one more night in a lifetime of nights?
What is one more death, or friendship, or divorce out of two, or three? Or four? Or five? 15
One more face among so many, many faces, one more life among so many million lives?

But first, baby, as you climb and count the stairs (and they total the same) did you, sometime or somewhere, have a different idea?
Is this, baby, what you were born to feel, and do, and be?

Countee Cullen (1903–1946)

Yet Do I Marvel

I doubt not God is good, well-meaning, kind,
And did He stoop to quibble could tell why
The little buried mole continues blind,
Why flesh that mirrors Him must some day die,
Make plain the reason tortured Tantalus
Is baited by the fickle fruit, declare
If merely brute caprice dooms Sisyphus
To struggle up a never-ending stair.
Inscrutable His ways are, and immune
To catechism by a mind too strewn
With petty cares to slightly understand
What awful brain compels His awful hand.
Yet do I marvel at this curious thing:
To make a poet black, and bid him sing!

Heritage

(For Harold Jackman)

What is Africa to me:
Copper sun or scarlet sea,
Jungle star or jungle track,
Strong bronzed men, or regal black
Women from whose loins I sprang
When the birds of Eden sang?
One three centuries removed
From the scenes his fathers loved,
Spicy grove, cinnamon tree,
What is Africa to me?

So I lie, who all day long
Want no sound except the song
Sung by wild barbaric birds
Goading massive jungle herds,
Juggernauts of flesh that pass
Trampling tall defiant grass
Where young forest lovers lie,
Plighting troth beneath the sky.
So I lie, who always hear,
Though I cram against my ear
Both my thumbs, and keep them there,
Great drums throbbing through the air.
So I lie, whose fount of pride,
Dear distress, and joy allied,
Is my somber flesh and skin,
With the dark blood dammed within
Like great pulsing tides of wine
That, I fear, must burst the fine
Channels of the chafing net
Where they surge and foam and fret.

Africa? A book one thumbs
Listlessly, till slumber comes.
Unremembered are her bats
Circling through the night, her cats
Crouching in the river reeds,
Stalking gentle flesh that feeds
By the river brink; no more
Does the bugle-throated roar
Cry that monarch claws have leapt
From the scabbards where they slept.
Silver snakes that once a year
Doff the lovely coats you wear,

Seek no covert in your fear
Lest a mortal eye should see;
What's your nakedness to me?
Here no leprous flowers rear
Fierce corollas in the air;
Here no bodies sleek and wet,
Dripping mingled rain and sweat,
Tread the savage measures of
Jungle boys and girls in love.
What is last year's snow to me,
Last year's anything? The tree

Budding yearly must forget
How its past arose or set—
Bough and blossom, flower, fruit,
Even what shy bird with mute
Wonder at her travail there,
Meekly labored in its hair.
One three centuries removed
From the scenes his father loved,
Spicy grove, cinnamon tree,
What is Africa to me?

So I lie, who find no peace
Night or day, no slight release
From the unremittant beat
Made by cruel padded feet
Walking through my body's street.
Up and down they go, and back,
Treading out a jungle track.
So I lie, who never quite
Safely sleep from rain at night—
I can never rest at all
When the rain begins to fall;
Like a soul gone mad with pain
I must match its weird refrain;
Ever must I twist and squirm,
Writhing like a baited worm,
While its primal measures drip
Through my body, crying, "Strip!
Doff this new exuberance.
Come and dance the Lover's Dance!"
In an old remembered way
Rain works on me night and day.
Quaint, outlandish heathen gods
Black men fashion out of rods,
Clay, and brittle bits of stone,
In a likeness like their own,
My conversion came high-priced;
I belong to Jesus Christ,
Preacher of humility;
Heathen gods are naught to me.

Father, Son, and Holy Ghost,
So I make an idle boast;
Jesus of the twice-turned cheek,
Lamb of God, although I speak
With my mouth thus, in my heart,
Do I play a double part.
Ever at Thy glowing altar
Must my heart grow sick and falter,
Wishing He I served were black,
Thinking then it would not lack
Precedent of pain to guide it,
Let who would or might deride it;
Surely then this flesh would know
Yours had borne a kindred woe.
Lord, I fashion dark gods, too,
Daring even to give You
Dark despairing features where,
Crowned with dark rebellious hair,
Patience waves just so much as
Mortal grief compels, while touches
Quick and hot, of anger, rise
To smitten cheek and weary eyes.
Lord, forgive me if my need
Sometimes shapes a human creed.

All day long and all night through,
One thing only must I do:
Quench my pride and cool my blood,
Lest I perish in the flood.
Lest a hidden ember set
Timber that I thought was wet
Burning like the dryest flax,
Melting like the nearest wax,
Lest the grave restore its dead.
Not yet has my heart or head
In the least way realized
They and I are civilized.

C. Day Lewis (1904–1972)

Newsreel

Enter the dream-house, brothers and sisters, leaving
Your debts asleep, your history at the door:
This is the home for heroes, and this loving
Darkness a fur you can afford.

Fish in their tank electrically heated 5
Nose without envy the glass wall: for them
Clerk, spy, nurse, killer, prince, the great and the defeated,
Move in a mute day-deam.

Bathed in this common source, you gape incurious
At what your active hours have willed— 10
Sleep-walking on that silver wall, the furious
Sick shapes and pregnant fancies of your world.

There is the mayor opening the oyster season:
A society wedding: the autumn hats look well:
An old crock's race, and a politician 15
In fishing-waders to prove that all is well.

Oh, look at the warplanes! Sreaming hysteric treble
In the long power-dive, like gannets they fall steep.
But what are they to trouble—
These silver shadows to trouble your watery, womb-deep sleep? 20

See the big guns, rising, groping, erected
To plant death in your world's soft womb,
Fire-bud, smoke-blossom, iron seed projected—
Are these exotics? They will grow nearer home:

Grow nearer home—and out of the dream-house stumbling 25
One night into a strangling air and the flung
Rags of children and thunder of stone niagaras tumbling,
You'll know you slept too long.

Robert Penn Warren (1905–)

Original Sin: A Short Story

Nodding, its great head rattling like a gourd,
And locks like seaweed strung on the stinking stone,
The nightmare stumbles past, and you have heard
It fumble your door before it whimpers and is gone:
It acts like the old hound that used to snuffle your door and moan. 5

You thought you had lost it when you left Omaha.
For it seemed connected then with your grandpa, who
Had a wen on his forehead and sat on the veranda
To finger the precious protuberance, as was his habit to do,
Which glinted in sun like rough garnet or the rich old brain bulging through. 10

But you met it in Harvard Yard as the historic steeple
Was confirming the midnight with its hideous racket,
And you wondered how it had come, for it stood so imbecile,
With empty hands, humble, and surely nothing in pocket:
Riding the rods, perhaps—or Grandpa's will paid the ticket. 15

You were almost kindly then, in your first homesickness,
As it tortured its stiff face to speak, but scarcely mewed.
Since then you have outlived all your homesickness.
But have met it in many another distempered latitude:
Oh, nothing is lost, ever lost! at last you understood. 20

It never came in the quantum glare of sun
To shame you before your friends, and had nothing to do
With your public experience or private reformation:
But it thought no bed too narrow—it stood with lips askew
And shook its great head sadly like the abstract Jew. 25

Never met you in the lyric arsenical meadow
When children call and your heart goes stone in the bosom—
At the orchard anguish never, nor ovoid horror,
Which is furred like a peach or avid like the delicious plum.
It takes no part in your classic prudence or fondled axiom. 30

Not there when you exclaimed: "Hope is betrayed by
Disastrous glory of sea-capes, sun-torment of whitecaps
—There must be a new innocence for us to be stayed by."
But there it stood, after all the timetables, all the maps,
In the crepuscular clutter of *always, always,* or *perhaps.* 35

You have moved often and rarely left an address,
And hear of the deaths of friends with a sly pleasure,

A sense of cleansing and hope which blooms from distress;
But it has not died, it comes, its hand childish, unsure,
Clutching the bribe of chocolate or a toy you used to treasure. 40

It tries the lock; you hear, but simply drowse:
There is nothing remarkable in that sound at the door.
Later you hear it wander the dark house
Like a mother who rises at night to seek a childhood picture;
Or it goes to the backyard and stands like an old horse cold in the pasture. 45

Speleology

At the foot of the cliff, where the great ledge thrusts, the cave
Debouches, soil level and rank where the stream once
Had come boiling forth, and now, from alluvial earth,
The last of the old virgin forest rises to cliff height.
And at noon twilight reigns. No one comes there. 5

I must have been six when first I found the cave mouth
Under ledges moss-green, and moss-green inner darkness.
Each summer I came, and in twilight peered in, crept farther,
Till one summer all I could see was the gray blotch
Of light far behind. Ran back. Didn't want to be dead. 10

By twelve, I was bolder. Besides, now had me a flashlight.
And all night before couldn't sleep. Then daylight. Then breakfast.
The cave wandered on, roof lower and lower except
Where chambers of darkness rose and stalactites stabbed
To the heart of the light I held. Then lower again. 15

I cut off the light. Knew darkness and depth and no Time.
Felt the cave cricket move up an arm. Switched the light back on,
And saw the lone life there, the cave cricket pale
On white and velvety stone. I thought: *They are blind.*
Crept on, light on. Heard faintly, below, a silken 20

And whispering rustle. Like what? Like water. And swung
The light to one side, and saw. I had crawled on a ledge
Under which, far down, far below now, the water yet channelled
And sang to itself, and answered my high light with swollen
White bursts of bubble. Light out, I lay there, unmoving. 25

Lulled in a sound like song in dream, knowing
I dared not move in that darkness so absolute,
I thought: *This is me.* Thought: *Who am I?* And felt
My heart beat to the pulse of darkness and earth, and thought
How it would be to be here forever, my heart, 30

In its beat, part of all. Suppose I stayed there, part of all?
But I woke with a scream. Had I dozed? Scarcely, I managed
To grab the flashlight as it fell. Turned it on, and
Once more looked down the slow slicing of limestone where
Water winked, in bubbles like fish eyes, and song was a terror. 35

I never came back. But years later, past dream, have lain
In dark and heard the depth of interminable song,
And laid hand to heart, and once again thought: *This is me.*
And thought: *Who am I*? And with hand on heart have wondered
What it would be like to be, after all, part of all. 40

Louis MacNeice (1907–1963)

from Autumn Journal, 1938

Conferences, adjournments, ultimatums,
  Flights in the air, castles in the air,
The autopsy of treaties, dynamite under the bridges,
  The end of *laissez faire.*
After the warm days the rain comes pimpling 5
  The paving stones with white
And with the rain the national conscience, creeping,
  Seeping through the night.
And in the sodden park on Sunday protest
  Meetings assemble not, as so often, now 10
Merely to advertise some patent panacea
  But simply to avow
The need to hold the ditch; a bare avowal
  That may perhaps imply
Death at the doors in a week but perhaps in the long run 15
  Exposure of the lie.
Think of a number, double it, treble it, square it,
  And sponge it out
And repeat *ad lib.* and mark the slate with crosses;
  There is no time to doubt 20
If the puzzle really has an answer. Hitler yells on the wireless,
  The night is damp and still
And I hear dull blows on wood outside my window;
  They are cutting down the trees on Primrose Hill.
The wood is white like the roast flesh of chicken, 25
  Each tree falling like a closing fan;
No more looking at the view from seats beneath the branches,
  Everything is going to plan;

They want the crest of this hill for anti-aircraft,
  The guns will take the view 30
And searchlights probe the heavens for bacilli
  With narrow wands of blue.
And the rain came on as I watched the territorials
  Sawing and chopping and pulling on ropes like a team
In a village tug-of-war; and I found my dog had vanished 35
  And thought 'This is the end of the old regime,'
But found the police had got her at St. John's Wood station
  And fetched her in the rain and went for a cup
Of coffee to an all-night shelter and heard a taxi-driver
  Say 'It turns me up 40
When I see them soldiers in lorries'—rumble of tumbrils
  Drums in the trees
Breaking the eardrums of the ravished dryads—
  Its turns me up; a coffee, please.
And as I go out I see a windshield-wiper 45
  In an empty car
Wiping away like mad and I feel astounded
  That things have gone so far.
And I come back here to my flat and wonder whether
  From now on I need take 50
The trouble to go out choosing stuff for curtains
  As I don't know anyone to make
Curtains quickly. Rather one should quickly
  Stop the cracks for gas or dig a trench
And take one's paltry measures against the coming 55
  Of the unknown *Uebermensch.*
But one—meaning I—is bored, am bored, the issue
  Involving principle but bound in fact
To squander principle in panic and self-deception—
  Accessories after the act, 60
So that all we foresee is rivers in spate spouting
  With drowning hands
And men like dead frogs floating till the rivers
  Lose themselves in the sands.
And we who have been brought up to think of 'Gallant Belgium' 65
  As so much blague
Are now preparing again to essay good through evil
  For the sake of Prague;
And must, we suppose, become uncritical, vindictive,
  And must, in order to beat 70
The enemy, model ourselves upon the enemy,
  A howling radio for our paraclete.
The night continues wet, the axe keeps falling,
  The hill grows bald and bleak
No longer one of the sights of London but maybe 75
  We shall have fireworks here by this day week.

W. H. Auden (1907–1973)

In Memory of Sigmund Freud

When there are so many we shall have to mourn,
When grief has been made so public, and exposed
    To the critique of a whole epoch
    The frailty of our conscience and anguish,

Of whom shall we speak? For every day they die — 5
Among us, those who were doing us some good,
    And knew it was never enough but
    Hoped to improve a little by living.

Such was this doctor: still at eighty he wished
To think of our life, from whose unruliness — 10
    So many plausible young futures
    With threats or flattery ask obedience.

But his wish was denied him; he closed his eyes
Upon that last picture common to us all,
    Of problems like relatives standing — 15
    Puzzled and jealous about our dying.

For about him at the very end were still
Those he had studied, the nervous and the nights,
    And shades that still waited to enter
    The bright circle of his recognition — 20

Turned elsewhere with their disappointment as he
Was taken away from his old interest
    To go back to the earth in London,
    An important Jew who died in exile.

Only Hate was happy, hoping to augment — 25
His practice now, and his shabby clientele
    Who think they can be cured by killing
    And covering the gardens with ashes.

They are still alive but in a world he changed
Simply by looking back with no false regrets; — 30
    All that he did was to remember
    Like the old and be honest like children.

He wasn't clever at all: he merely told
The unhappy Present to recite the Past
Like a poetry lesson till sooner
Or later it faltered at the line where 35

Long ago the accusations had begun,
And suddenly knew by whom it had been judged,
How rich life had been and how silly,
And was life-forgiven and most humble. 40

Able to approach the Future as a friend
Without a wardrobe of excuses, without
A set mask of rectitude or an
Embarrassing over-familiar gesture.

No wonder the ancient cultures of conceit 45
In his technique of unsettlement foresaw
The fall of princes, the collapse of
Their lucrative patterns of frustration.

If he succeeded, why, the Generalised Life
Would become impossible, the monolith 50
Of State be broken and prevented
The co-operation of avengers.

Of course they called on God: but he went his way,
Down among the Lost People like Dante, down
To the stinking fosse where the injured 55
Lead the ugly life of the rejected.

And showed us what evil is: not as we thought
Deeds that must be punished, but our lack of faith,
Or dishonest mood of denial,
The concupiscence of the oppressor. 60

And if something of the autocratic pose,
The paternal strictness he distrusted, still
Clung to his utterance and features,
It was a protective imitation

For one who lived among enemies so long; 65
If often he was wrong and at times absurd,
To us he is no more a person
Now but a whole climate of opinion,

Under whom we conduct our differing lives:
Like weather he can only hinder or help, 70
The proud can still be proud but find it
A little harder, and the tyrant tries

To make him do but doesn't care for him much.
He quietly surrounds all our habits of growth;
He extends, till the tired in even 75
The remotest most miserable duchy

Have felt the change in their bones and are cheered,
And the child unlucky in his little State,
        Some hearth where freedom is excluded,
        A hive whose honey is fear and worry, 80

Feels calmer now and somehow assured of escape;
While as they lie in the grass of our neglect,
        So many long-forgotten objects
        Revealed by his undiscouraged shining

Are returned to us and made precious again; 85
Games we had thought we must drop as we grew up,
        Little noises we dared not laugh at,
        Faces we made when no one was looking.

But he wishes us more than this: to be free
Is often to be lonely; he would unite 90
        The unequal moieties fractured
        By our own well-meaning sense of justice.

Would restore to the larger the wit and will
The smaller possesses but can only use
        For arid disputes, would give back to 95
        The son the mother's richness of feeling.

But he would have us remember most of all
To be enthusiastic over the night
        Not only for the sense of wonder
        It alone has to offer, but also 100

Because it needs our love: for with sad eyes
Its delectable creatures look up and beg
        Us dumbly to ask them to follow;
        They are exiles who long for the future

That lies in our power. They too would rejoice 105
If allowed to serve enlightenment like him,
        Even to bear our cry of "Judas,"
        As he did and all must bear who serve it.

One rational voice is dumb: over a grave
The household of Impulse mourns one dearly loved. 110
        Sad is Eros, builder of cities,
        And weeping anarchic Aphrodite.

Herman Melville

Towards the end he sailed into an extraordinary mildness,
And anchored in his home and reached his wife
And rode within the harbour of her hand,
And went across each morning to an office
As though his occupation were another island. 5

Goodness existed: that was the new knowledge.
His terror had to blow itself quite out
To let him see it; but it was the gale had blown him
Past the Cape Horn of sensible success
Which cries: "This rock is Eden. Shipwreck here." 10

But deafened him with thunder and confused with lightning:
—The maniac hero hunting like a jewel
The rare ambiguous monster that had maimed his sex,
Hatred for hatred ending in a scream,
The unexplained survivor breaking off the nightmare— 15
All that was intricate and false; the truth was simple.

Evil is unspectacular and always human,
And shares our bed and eats at our own table,
And we are introduced to Goodness every day,
Even in drawing-rooms among a crowd of faults; 20
He has a name like Billy and is almost perfect
But wears a stammer like a decoration:
And every time they meet the same thing has to happen;
It is the Evil that is helpless like a lover
And has to pick a quarrel and succeeds, 25
And both are openly destroyed before our eyes.

For now he was awake and knew
No one is ever spared except in dreams;
But there was something else the nightmare had distorted—
Even the punishment was human and a form of love: 30
The howling storm had been his father's presence
And all the time he had been carried on his father's breast.

Who now had set him gently down and left him.
He stood upon the narrow balcony and listened:
And all the stars above him sang as in his childhood 35
"All, all is vanity," but it was not the same;
For now the words descended like the calm of mountains—
—Nathaniel had been shy because his love was selfish—
But now he cried in exultation and surrender
"The Godhead is broken like bread. We are the pieces." 40

And sat down at his desk and wrote a story.

Voltaire at Ferney

Perfectly happy now, he looked at his estate.
An exile making watches glanced up as he passed
And went on working; where a hospital was rising fast,
A joiner touched his cap; an agent came to tell
Some of the trees he'd planted were progressing well. 5
The white alps glittered. It was summer. He was very great.

Far off in Paris where his enemies
Whispered that he was wicked, in an upright chair
A blind old woman longed for death and letters. He would write,
"Nothing is better than life." But was it? Yes, the fight 10
Against the false and the unfair
Was always worth it. So was gardening. Civilize.

Cajoling, scolding, screaming, cleverest of them all,
He'd had the other children in a holy war
Against the infamous grown-ups; and, like a child, been sly 15
And humble, when there was occasion for
The two-faced answer or the plain protective lie,
But, patient like a peasant, waited for their fall.

And never doubted, like D'Alembert, he would win:
Only Pascal was a great enemy, the rest 20
Were rats already poisoned; there was much, though, to be done,
And only himself to count upon.
Dear Diderot was dull but did his best;
Rousseau, he'd always known, would blubber and give in.

Night fell and made him think of women: Lust 25
Was one of the great teachers; Pascal was a fool.
How Emilie had loved astronomy and bed;
Pimpette had loved him too, like scandal; he was glad.
He'd done his share of weeping for Jerusalem: As a rule,
It was the pleasure-haters who became unjust. 30

Yet, like a sentinel, he could not sleep. The night was full of wrong,
Earthquakes and executions: Soon he would be dead,
And still all over Europe stood the horrible nurses
Itching to boil their children. Only his verses
Perhaps could stop them: He must go on working: Overhead, 35
The uncomplaining stars composed their lucid song.

Who's Who

A shilling life will give you all the facts:
How Father beat him, how he ran away,
What were the struggles of his youth,
what acts
Made him the greatest figure of his day:
Of how he fought, fished, hunted,
worked all night, 5
Though giddy, climbed new mountains;
named a sea:
Some of the last researchers even write
Love made him weep his pints like you
and me.

With all his honours on, he sighed for
one
Who, say astonished critics, lived at
home; 10
Did little jobs about the house with skill
And nothing else; could whistle; would
sit still
Or potter round the garden; answered
some
Of his long marvellous letters but kept
none.

Musée des Beaux Arts

About suffering they were never wrong,
The Old Masters: how well they understood
Its human position; how it takes place
While someone else is eating or opening a window or just walking dully along;
How, when the aged are reverently, passionately waiting 5
For the miraculous birth, there always must be
Children who did not specially want it to happen, skating
On a pond at the edge of the wood:
They never forgot
That even the dreadful martyrdom must run its course 10
Anyhow in a corner, some untidy spot
Where the dogs go on with their doggy life and the torturer's horse
Scratches its innocent behind on a tree.

In Brueghel's *Icarus,* for instance: how everything turns away
Quite leisurely from the disaster; the ploughman may 15
Have heard the splash, the forsaken cry,
But for him it was not an important failure; the sun shone
As it had to on the white legs disappearing into the green
Water; and the expensive delicate ship that must have seen
Something amazing, a boy falling out of the sky, 20
Had somewhere to get to and sailed calmly on.

Drawing by Chas. Addams; © 1975 The New Yorker Magazine, Inc.

The Unknown Citizen

(To JS/07/M/378
This Marble Monument
Is Erected by the State)

He was found by the Bureau of Statistics to be
One against whom there was no official complaint,
And all the reports on his conduct agree
That, in the modern sense of an old-fashioned word, he was a saint,
For in everything he did he served the Greater Community. 5
Except for the War till the day he retired
He worked in a factory and never got fired,
But satisfied his employers, Fudge Motors Inc.
Yet he wasn't a scab or odd in his views,
For his Union reports that he paid his dues, 10
(Our report on his Union shows it was sound)
And our Social Psychology workers found
That he was popular with his mates and liked a drink.
The Press are convinced that he bought a paper every day
And that his reactions to advertisements were normal in every way. 15
Policies taken out in his name prove that he was fully insured,
And his Health-card shows he was once in hospital but left it cured.
Both Producers Research and High-Grade Living declare
He was fully sensible to the advantages of the Instalment Plan
And had everything necessary to the Modern Man, 20
A phonograph, a radio, a car and a frigidaire.
Our researchers into Public Opinion are content
That he held the proper opinions for the time of year;
When there was peace, he was for peace; when there was war, he went.
He was married and added five children to the population, 25
Which our Eugenist says was the right number for a parent of his generation,
And our teachers report that he never interfered with their education.
Was he free? Was he happy? The question is absurd:
Had anything been wrong, we should certainly have heard.

Stephen Spender (1909–   )

The Express

After the first powerful plain manifesto
The black statement of pistons, without more fuss
But gliding like a queen, she leaves the station.
Without bowing and with restrained unconcern
She passes the houses which humbly crowd outside, 5
The gasworks and at last the heavy page
Of death, printed by gravestones in the cemetery.
Beyond the town there lies the open country
Where, gathering speed, she acquires mystery,
The luminous self-possession of ships on ocean. 10
It is now she begins to sing—at first quite low
Then loud, and at last with a jazzy madness—
The song of her whistle screaming at curves,
Of deafening tunnels, brakes, innumerable bolts.
And always light, aerial, underneath 15
Goes the elate meter of her wheels.
Steaming through metal landscape on her lines
She plunges new eras of wild happiness
Where speed throws up strange shapes, broad curves
And parallels clean like the steel of guns. 20
At last, further than Edinburgh or Rome,
Beyond the crest of the world, she reaches night
Where only a low streamline brightness
Of phosphorus on the tossing hills is white.
Ah, like a comet through flames she moves entranced 25
Wrapt in her music no bird song, no, nor bough
Breaking with honey buds, shall ever equal.

Ultima Ratio Regum

The guns spell money's ultimate reason
In letters of lead on the spring hillside.
But the boy lying dead under the olive trees
Was too young and too silly
To have been notable to their important eye. 5
He was a better target for a kiss.

When he lived, tall factory hooters never summoned him.
Nor did restaurant plate-glass doors revolve to wave him in.
His name never appeared in the papers.
The world maintained its traditional wall 10
Round the dead with their gold sunk deep as a well,
Whilst his life, intangible as a Stock Exchange rumour, drifted outside.

O too lightly he threw down his cap
One day when the breeze threw petals from the trees.
The unflowering wall sprouted with guns, 15
Machine-gun anger quickly scythed the grasses;
Flags and leaves fell from hands and branches;
The tweed cap rotted in the nettles.

Consider his life which was valueless
In terms of employment, hotel ledgers, news files. 20
Consider. One bullet in ten thousand kills a man.
Ask. Was so much expenditure justified
On the death of one so young and so silly
Lying under the olive trees, O world, O death?

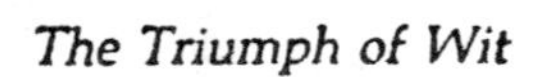

The Triumph of Wit

Boris Artzybasheff. Reproduced by permission of the estate of Boris Artzybasheff.

Under the Volcano 1939–1981

Introduction

The year 1939 was a memorable one. John Steinbeck published *The Grapes of Wrath* and thus dramatized the human tragedy of the Great Depression in America. The Daughters of the American Revolution refused to allow the great black singer Marian Anderson to give a concert in Washington's Constitution Hall, and though Miss Anderson sang, on Easter Day, on the steps of the Lincoln Memorial, the atonement was hollow. Dr. Sigmund Freud died, and with his death scientists began to question the validity of his techniques and ideas, while the mass media began to popularize Freud's gospel in newspapers, movies, and ultimately television. Science and technology continued to transform the world: the first regular weekly North Atlantic air service was inaugurated; the first public television program was broadcast at the opening ceremonies of the New York World's Fair; and a letter from Albert Einstein to Franklin Delano Roosevelt noted: "Some recent work by E. Fermi and L. Szilard . . . leads me to expect that the element uranium may be turned into a new and important source of energy in the immediate future. . . . This new phenomenon would lead also to the construction of bombs."

In 1939 the Great Depression, in America and abroad, was coming to an end, but even so 17 percent of the American work force was unemployed (compared with 5 percent in 1960 and 9 percent in 1975). The average weekly wage for American production workers—those lucky enough to have a job—was $25; and of the 130 million American citizens in 1939, 126 million had incomes under $2,000. An advertisement in New York City for twelve female laboratory assistants, at an annual salary of $960.00, brought 239 early applicants willing to wait through a February night in hopes of an interview the next morning. The federal government announced its budget for 1939 as some 9 billion dollars (compared to a 1980 "austerity" budget of more than 13 billion dollars for New York City alone).

Abroad, Germany's quest for "lebensraum" met its first significant opposition in 1939: on September 1 the German Army marched into Poland and in so doing precipitated World War II. With its lightning, mechanized attacks—which gave the word *blitzkrieg* to the English language—the German army swiftly overran most of Western Europe. The allied troops were routed. Only England seemed to stand between Hitler and total victory, and the defeat of the French and English armies was not altered by the rhetoric of Winston Churchill's speech "Dunkirk," with its magnificent peroration:

> Even though large tracts of Europe and many old and famous states have fallen or may fall into the grip of the Gestapo and all the odious apparatus of Nazi rule, we shall not flag or fail. We shall go on to the end, we shall fight in France, we shall fight on the seas and oceans, we shall fight with growing confidence and growing strength in the air, we shall defend our island, whatever the cost may be, we shall fight on the beaches, we shall fight on the landing grounds, we shall fight in the fields and in the streets, we shall fight in the hills; we shall never surrender, and even if, which I do not for a moment believe, this island or a large part of it were subjugated and starving, then our Empire beyond the seas, armed and guarded by the British Fleet, would carry on the struggle, until, in God's good time, the New World, with all its power and might steps forth to the rescue and the liberation of the old.

From this point, the high-water mark of the Axis cause, Winston Churchill sustained English hope and courage through the Battle of Britain until the New World did begin to pour its men and resources into the struggle. The American entrance into the war, abetted by Hitler's fatal miscalculation when he marched on Russia, ultimately led to the defeat of Germany and Italy. The third Axis nation, Japan, surrendered only after atomic bombs devastated two of its major cities. Although much of the world rejoiced in the Allied victory, atomic bombs became synonymous with visions of doom, and since their use, the world has been poised between the hope of cooperation embodied in the United Nations Charter and the fear of universal destruction.

After 1945 the British accelerated their withdrawal from their former colonies and haltingly moved toward an economy regulated by socialist concepts of income redistribution but weakened economically by the escalating demands of labor. By 1975 England was suffering under an annual inflation rate of approximately 25 percent, and though the victory of the conservative Margaret Thatcher as Prime Minister in the latter seventies led to lower inflation, the discontent of labor under her tenure made the preservation of economic stability most precarious. As England's global influence shrank, that of America and Russia grew, a fact that occasionally led to "cold war" confrontation. One consequence was that the American suspicion of communism intensified in the forties and fifties. Demagogues like Senator Joseph McCarthy fabricated dark communist conspiracies and maligned private citizens and public servants indiscriminately. In some ways the "cold war" reached its climax during the presidency of John F. Kennedy, when Russia installed missile bases on Cuban soil and America threatened to retaliate. For a brief period the world toppled on the brink of nuclear confrontation. The very prospect, however, acted as a deterrent, and for a number of years the two great world powers, though politically unreconciled, achieved a limited "détente," most especially in economic and cultural ventures. Not until the Soviet invasion of Afghanistan was "détente" severely tested, but that aggression, added to the general turmoil within the Arabian world and then specific tensions generated by the war begun in 1980 between Iran and Iraq, resulted not only in the American reappraisal of its relations with Russia, but also in closer ties with China.

The "cold war" was further complicated by the emergence of China as a significant world force, and by the Vietnam war, which tested American power. During the war some called American actions in Vietnam "the arrogance of power," whereas others stressed American idealism. There is little doubt, however, that the American moral fiber, as well as its economic capabilities, were weakened in the struggle. Though the "peace" negotiated by Secretary of State Henry Kissinger was greeted with ambivalent emotions, strengthened by North Vietnam's total victory over the South after American withdrawal, one thing seems certain: America will not again enter lightly into such military adventures. That fact was shown by the patience with which America, and the Western World generally, responded to the militant rhetoric of the Islamic nations during the late seventies and early eighties. During that period the Iranian Shah Mohammed Riza Pahlevi, who may have been less than a humane ruler of his people but was always a staunch ally of America, was overthrown and replaced by the Moslem religious Ayatollah Ruhomial Khomeini. The rhetoric of the Ayatollah, who seemed to hold the West, and especially America, responsible for all the ills of the Islamic nations, inspired, at least in part, a band of radical Iranians to capture the American Embassy in Iran and to proclaim that the captured American diplomatic personnel would be held hostage—some even tried as spies—unless the Shah was returned to Iran for trial. This public humiliation of the United States, almost simultaneous with the aggressive actions of the Soviets in Afghanistan, led some people to contrast American "impotence" with Soviet "power," while others compared the two events in terms of American "civilization" contrasted to Russian "barbarism."

The tensions of the "cold war" eased throughout much of the seventies, but others remained. By 1975 six nations had exploded nuclear bombs and joined the proliferating nuclear club. In Ireland the political, social, and religious conflicts between Catholics and Protestants escalated into terror and violence, and British troops intervened to prevent civil war. Israel and the Arab states quarreled over the rights of the Palestinian refugees to a homeland and the territorial integrity of the Jewish state. Their contention erupted into intermittent political terrorism and then exploded into warfare. From partisan stances Russia and America attempted to mediate the apparently irreconcilable dispute. Under the impetus of the Yom Kippur war between Israel and the Arab states in 1973, a number of Arab members of the Organization of Petroleum Exporting Countries (OPEC) imposed an embargo on oil export to countries supporting Israel, and the success of that political weapon led the oil cartel later on to raise the price of oil drastically. The effectiveness of this action led other underdeveloped nations with essential natural resources such as copper and bauxite to aspire to similar cartels and profits. No cartel, however, came remotely close to the profitability and the power of that of the OPEC nations—a power so extreme that it led President Carter, shortly after his assumption of office in 1976, to proclaim that he planned to lead the American people in a battle—"the moral equivalent of war" —to lessen American dependence upon foreign energy sources. To any objective observer that war has yet to be won, and the cost of heating oil and gasoline continued to increase. By 1980 the cost of gasoline was well beyond a dollar, with projections of two dollars a gallon by the mid-eighties. One of the consequences of this increase was rapid inflation—in America the rate in 1979 was over 13 percent—and a steady erosion not only of confidence in the dollar abroad but of the worth of the dollar in America itself. Benjamin Franklin's moral that "A penny saved is a penny earned" seemed a mockery to both Americans and Europeans who found that their savings became ever less valuable in real purchasing power over the course of time.

During the sixties two other horrors, to some extent exacerbated by the Vietnam war, emerged clearly: drug abuse and increasing violence. What began as debate between proponents of legalized marijuana and those who demanded harsh penalties for its use was made academic by the widespread use of LSD, heroin, and other hard drugs. Though not peculiar to America, the drug problem is most intense there. In both England and America, however, the tolerance among the young of the use of drugs has led many of their elders to be skeptical of youthful idealism and morality. Statistics support, if not justify, the skepticism: between 1961 and 1975 the rate for all serious crimes in America has more than doubled; almost half of all arrests are of teenagers and young adults; and 44 percent of those arrested for murder are under the age of twenty-five, while 75 percent of those arrested for street crimes, excluding murder, are under twenty-five. Whatever accounts for these crimes, the streets of many large American cities have become canyons of fear largely deserted after dark; even though in the latter part of the seventies there was a modest abatement in major crime in a number of large American cities—and even a dramatic reduction, brought about apparently by increased representation of black policemen on the force, in Detroit—that decrease has not been significant enough to lead anyone of sane mind to desire to explore New York's Central Park after twilight.

In America, and to a lesser extent in England, the population explosion following World War II has led to demographic changes and innumerable modifications of standards and values. In 1950 there were 24 million Americans between the ages of fourteen and twenty-four; by 1960 that number had increased to 27 million and by 1970 to 44 million. There was also an increase in the number of the elderly, as well as an increase in life expectancy. From 1954 to 1968 the life expectancy of those aged 65 rose only two-tenths of a year, from 14.4 to 14.6, but by 1977 the life expectancy of those aged 65 had risen to an average 16.3 years — 13.9 years for males and 18.3 years for females. This increase in the numbers of the aged radically altered the proportion of the middle-aged (those between twenty-five and sixty-four) to the adolescent and young adult (those between fourteen and twenty-four) from three-to-one to two-to-one. Undoubtedly this demographic change, in part at least, has lessened parental authority and intensified the difficulty in the social assimilation of the young. Indicative of their defiance of tradition, many of the young in the sixties and early seventies adopted unconventional modes of dress —jeans, bangles, T-shirts, and long hair and headbands—that to them symbolized the difference in life-styles, as well as the generation gap, between the "establishment" and the "counterculture." By the latter part of the seventies, however, the desire for security, most especially for a decent job, led many young Americans not only to a more presentable appearance and more conventional dreams but also to more conservative political stances. In this they reflected, though possibly not to the same degree, the political convictions of their elders—a fact revealed by the increasing domination of American domestic and foreign policies by the conservative wings of both the Democratic and Republican parties, and especially dramatized by former Governor Ronald Reagan's capture of the 1980 Republican nomination for President.

Perhaps the greatest social revolution during the period between 1939 and 1980 was the modification of many sexual conventions. The availability of "the pill" and the changes in legal and moral attitudes toward abortion have enabled the young to accept premarital and extramarital sex with a casualness foreign to their elders, and the advancement of medical science has led to the reality of a human female egg being fertilized in a test tube, then implanted in the female womb and brought to term—a process that had by the late seventies occurred with enough frequency and success to lead to fantasies of human breeding farms, where well-to-do married couples could have their progeny brought to birth, through union of their own egg and sperm, without the dangers and complexities of pregnancy. Even before such heady possibilities, many women demanded equality with men in everything from employment opportunities to military obligations. The National Organization for Women (NOW) has challenged, both in the courts and on the streets, masculine prerogatives from bars to baseball. Between 1968 and 1978 the percentage of American women in the work force increased from 36.6 percent to 41.2 percent, but their salaries averaged only 60 percent of that of men. In 1980 the second United Nations' World Conference on Women, held in Copenhagen, served as an international forum for women to voice their claims for equal opportunities, equal respect, and equal justice. Though in America the Equal Rights Amendment to the Constitution still had not passed by 1980, militant American feminists used their political power and sophistication to place increasing pressure upon legislators in reluctant states such as Illinois.

In recent years England and America have been racked by racial conflict. Although in both countries laws ostensibly guarantee all races the same civil rights, it has been difficult to translate that legality into reality. Ironically, the murder of the Reverend Martin Luther King, Jr., whose entire life was a preachment against violence, set off in 1968 an orgy of looting and rioting in many American cities. In the nation's capital, where the disorder was the worst, federal troops patrolled the gates of the White House. For some people violation of the law has become rationalized into a mode of political protest. The Symbionese Liberation Army justified itself on "political" grounds when it kidnapped Patricia Hearst, forced her parents to provide more than a million dollars of food for the poor of California, and seduced her into not only bank robbery but also into her proclamation in 1974, "I am a soldier in the people's army." Similar political grounds in the late seventies led such blacks as the Reverend Jesse Jackson—though other black leaders disagree with him—to support the goals, if not the terrorist tactics, of the Palestine Liberation Organization. This support, which was defended as merely an extension of the Reverend Martin Luther King's advocacy of blacks reaching out to the Third World nations, has endangered, if not destroyed, the traditional alliance between blacks and Jews in defense of civil rights.

Whatever the justification for physical violence or political extremism, many American blacks, as well as other minorities, began to feel in the seventies attitudes similar to those expressed by Vernon E. Jordan, the President of the Urban League, when he stated that the seventies "turned out to be a decade of fighting desperately to hold on to what we had gotten in the sixties." This feeling was reinforced by certain realities. One was that median white American family income in 1979 was $16,740, while median black family income was $9,242. Another was the fact that 54.6 of American blacks in 1979 lived in metropolitan areas. Of these blacks, a considerable majority lived in impoverished neighborhoods of the inner cities, and their neighbors were more likely to be Hispanics than otherwise. The coexistence of these ethnic minorities—and one of the phenomena of the seventies in America was the vast surge of the Hispanic population in such cities as Los Angeles, Miami, and New York—seemed to justify, at least in part, the proclamation of one study that the "cities have been cast as reservations for the poor and despised minorities of our society."

Finally, for many conservative Americans the seventies was a traumatic period, not only because of the humiliation of Vietnam, Cambodia, and Iran, but also because of the ineptness, pettiness, corruption, and immorality at the heart of a federal government whose leaders, from the Attorney General to the Vice-President to the President himself, had ironically proclaimed their belief not only in probity but also in law and order. The peculations that drove one Vice-President from office, and the hypocrisy and mendacity that brought a President to resign under fear of impeachment, left many Americans disillusioned and enraged, wondering in what they could place their faith. In the Federal Bureau of Investigation—whose chief, J. Edgar Hoover, was rumored to have regaled American presidents with pornography? In the Central Intelligence Agency—with the rumors that it, with or without presidential knowledge and consent, might have plotted the assassination of foreign leaders such as Fidel Castro? In a born-again Christian with the unlikely name of Jimmy Carter? In themselves and their desires—the great "Me" of what the journalist Tom Wolfe called the "Me Decade"? In what? As the two final decades of the twentieth century began, with the stock market uncertain and only rising taxes sure, good bourgeois Americans could hardly be censured for inquiring into the worth of their values, as Robert Pirsig did in his volume *Zen and the Art of Motorcycle Maintenance*, or for feeling, as that staunch conservative William Butler Yeats had once put it, "Things fall apart; the centre cannot hold; mere anarchy is loosed upon the world . . ."

Much English and American literature after 1939 has been preoccupied with war and survival. Edith Sitwell and Richard Eberhart responded to the horrors of aerial bombardment and atomic sunrises. In Wales Dylan Thomas composed his poignant elegy refusing to mourn the fiery death of a London child. War seared the brains of the young and sensitive: the British poet Ted Hughes and his American wife Sylvia Plath saw the world as they do—full of savagery in nature and animalism in man, with violence everywhere—in part because of the horror they knew in youth.

In England the better poets after World War II (Thomas, Betjeman, Larkin) used unconventional forms in their art, though Thomas' work seems more impassioned than does the wry, intellectual poetry of Betjeman and Larkin. In America the struggle between the academic poets and the poets of the streets—the combat between what Robert Lowell has called "cooked" verse and "raw" verse—has gained critical attention for the former and large sales and great notoriety for the latter. The language, for instance, of Ginsberg's poem "Howl" brought indignant outcries at police precincts and academic teas alike. Other modern poets belong to what M. L. Rosenthal has called the "confessional" school (Plath, Roethke, Sexton). A number (Hall, Simpson, Wright) whose poetry is more "cooked" than that of the "Beat" poets have won by simplicity, directness, and social convictions a considerable audience.

Robert Hayden and Gwendolyn Brooks, black poets and mature artists, have consistently placed their art above revolutionary rhetoric and adolescent vulgarities. Other black artists have used their anger effectively in their work. The depths and width of American black rage have been revealed as fully in the explosion of black poetry—by such writers as Raymond R. Patterson, Imamu Amiri Baraka, Clarence Major, and Nikki Giovanni—as in the riots of Watts, Detroit, and Washington.

In fiction the spiritual malaise of modern times has perturbed innumerable writers. More and more Americans—and Englishmen too—have questioned not only suburban, bourgeois values but also national mores. The motif of helplessness has obsessed many modern writers. Even such an ultimately religious writer as Flannery O'Connor seems to proclaim, in her story "A Good Man Is Hard to Find," that we are all innocent but all victims, so that a casual choice of any kind may leave our lives at the mercy of some strange Misfit who does not know the crime for which he was sent to prison but does know that he is fated to be what he is, a murderer whose only pleasure is meanness, because "somewheres along the line I did something wrong . . ." Yet the modern writer's quest for identity, purpose, and meaning in life remains. Metaphorically, John Cheever suggests this search in "The Swimmer," by his image of a man swimming through the pools of suburbia, and through his life as well, while Donald Barthelme in "Me and Miss Mandible" sends a thirty-five-year-old man back to elementary school to learn the social lessons of conformity and hypocrisy he needs for survival. Whatever the image, the vision has less of hope than of despair.

Modern fiction often uses symbolic and allegorical implications and mysterious, dreamlike, surrealistic overtones. "The Swimmer" and "Me and Miss Mandible" go beyond the natural world and into the inward truth of the human heart, while James Alan McPherson, in his story "Of Cabbages and Kings," explores the tension in black men between brotherhood and separateness, between the rational and the irrational, in rhythms and images that evoke an underground world beyond logical understanding. Similarly, in her story "Where Are You Going, Where Have You Been?" Joyce Carol Oates fuses the conscious and subconscious knowledge of an insecure, adolescent girl into her weird initiation into the meaning of evil. In a real world where helplessness and fear are dominant emotions, the story reflects one vision of the nightmare of life today. Yet another strand of contemporary fiction is the innovative and experimental work produced by such writers as E. L. Doctorow, William Gass, and Robert Coover. Perhaps the most successful of these authors, at least in terms of a popular audience, is Doctorow; in such novels as *Ragtime* he wove historical figures like Henry Ford into the fabric of his work in hopes of fusing past and present realities into some timeless revelation of human stupidity, venality, and mystery—a device Doctorow defended when he commented of *Ragtime*: "The book gives the reader all sorts of facts—made-up facts, distorted facts—but I happen to think my representation of historical characters is true to the soul of them." The use of such techniques, at least as they involve living beings, became a matter of legality when a California psychologist, Paul Bindrim, contended that he was the model for a fictional character who was engaged in nude encounter therapy in the novel *Touching*, and the United States Supreme Court declined to review the judgment of a California court that Mr. Bindrim had been defamed.

Like the fiction and poetry, the drama since World War II echoes the despair and emptiness of contemporary life. Tennessee William's first important work was "The Glass Menagerie," a "memory" play that dramatizes with wit and pathos the contrast between the dreams of the characters and the Darwinian fact that the weak perish and the strong survive. Dominating the play are the emotions of betrayal and guilt—most especially dramatized at the end of the play as the fragile Laura's "candles" die out and leave the stage in darkness—but the play's allusions to violent conquest and its antireligious imagery extend the betrayal and the guilt into a universe "lit by lightning" that goes far beyond the dreary apartment in which the Wingfields exist.

Remarkably similar in concept and treatment to *The Glass Menagerie* is the only other undeniable masterpiece of American dramatic literature after World War II. That play, of course, is Arthur Miller's *Death of a Salesman.* Like *The Glass Menagerie, Death of a Salesman* is a memory play. Drenched in the theme of betrayal, the play totally lacks literal realism as it moves back and forth in time between the memories and the realities in the life and death of the salesman Willie Loman. Arthur Miller claimed that the play was a tragedy, though not in the classic sense of the fall of a great man from high to low estate, while other commentators of the time insisted that the dramatization of the memories and eventual suicide of a low man was more pathetic than tragic. Whatever the truth, the play is certainly a moving one, with overtones that proclaim the need of all men for a bit of respect and dignity, and asserts that Willie Loman's need to dream and his inability to find a dream worth the dreaming is a universal tragedy of mankind.

Quite a different play is *Play Without Words, I.* Written by the Irish-born playwright Samuel Beckett (who shifted between English and French in his writing but who wrote his most successful plays such as *Waiting for Godot* in French), this brief play is representative in its ideas and techniques of the most significant revolt of twentieth-century drama against the realistic theatre. This dramatic mode, often referred to as the Theatre of the Absurd, is international in its scope and is illuminated not only by the work of Samuel Beckett but also by the drama of such other artists as Ionesco, Genet, Ghelderode, Albee, and Pinter. Though the absurdists differ in their art, they generally agree in feeling that the individual is insignificant; that his strivings are usually both pathetic and comic; that his plight is identical to that of the mythological Sisyphus (who was doomed to roll a gigantic stone up a hill, only to have it roll back as he approached the peak of the hill); that his attempts at communication are futile; and that his death is merely a final act of absurdity. This kind of despair is implied in the action and images of *Act Without Words, I,* which strips to its barest essentials man's birth, thoughts, and foolish strivings until, at the end of the play, he is left on a bare stage to stare at his useless hands—and to wait. Though hardly comforting, Beckett's dramatizations of an irrational universe, in which man is a clown and life is a Punch and Judy show, have not only brought him the Nobel prize for literature but have become an enduring part of the vision of the modern age.

Exposition and Argument

Lewis Thomas (1913–   )

On Cloning a Human Being

It is now theoretically possible to re-create an identical creature from any animal or plant, from the DNA contained in the nucleus of any somatic cell. A single plant root-tip cell can be teased and seduced into conceiving a perfect copy of the whole plant; a frog's intestinal epithelial cell possesses the complete instructions needed for a new, same frog. If the technology were further advanced, you could do this with a human being, and there are now startled predictions all over the place that this will in fact be done, someday, in order to provide a version of immortality for carefully selected, especially valuable people.

The cloning of humans is on most of the lists of things to worry about from Science, along with behavior control, genetic engineering, transplanted heads, computer poetry, and the unrestrained growth of plastic flowers.

Cloning is the most dismaying of prospects, mandating as it does the elimination of sex with only a metaphoric elimination of death as compensation. It is almost no comfort to know that one's cloned, identical surrogate lives on, especially when the living will very likely involve edging one's real, now aging self off to the side, sooner or later. It is hard to imagine anything like filial affection or respect for a single, unmated nucleus; harder still to think of one's new, self-generated self as anything but an absolute, desolate orphan. Not to mention the complex interpersonal relationship involved in raising one's self from infancy, teaching the language, enforcing discipline, instilling good manners, and the like. How would you feel if you became an incorrigible juvenile delinquent by proxy, at the age of fifty-five?

The public questions are obvious. Who is to be selected, and on what qualifications? How to handle the risks of misused technology, such as self-determined cloning by the rich and powerful but socially objectionable, or the cloning by governments of dumb, docile masses for the world's work? What will be the effect on all the uncloned rest of us of human sameness? After all, we've accustomed ourselves through hundreds of millennia to the continual exhilaration of uniqueness; each of us is totally different, in a fundamental sense, from all the other four billion. Selfness is an essential fact of life. The thought of human nonselfness, precise sameness, is terrifying, when you think about it.

Well, don't think about it, because it isn't a probable possibility, not even as a long shot for the distant future, in my opinion. I agree that you might clone some people who would look amazingly like their parental cell donors, but the odds are that they'd be almost as different as you or me, and certainly more different than any of today's identical twins.

The time required for the experiment is only one of the problems, but a formidable one. Suppose you wanted to clone a prominent, spectacularly successful diplomat, to look after the Middle East problems of the distant future. You'd have to catch him and persuade him, probably not very hard to do, and extirpate a cell. But then you'd have to wait for him to grow up through embryonic life and then for at least forty years more, and you'd have to be sure all observers remained patient and unmeddlesome through his unpromising, ambiguous childhood and adolescence.

Moreover, you'd have to be sure of recreating his environment, perhaps down to the last detail. "Environment" is a word which really means people, so you'd have to do a lot more cloning than just the diplomat himself.

This is a very important part of the cloning problem, largely overlooked in our excitement about the cloned individual himself. You don't have to agree all the way with B. F. Skinner to acknowledge that the environment does make a difference, and when you examine what we really mean by the word "environment" it comes down to other human beings. We use euphemisms and jargon for this, like "social forces," "cultural influences," even Skinner's "verbal community," but what is meant is the dense crowd of nearby people who talk to, listen to, smile or frown at, give to, withhold from, nudge, push, caress, or flail out at the individual. No matter what the genome says, these people have a lot to do with shaping a character. Indeed, if all you had was the genome, and no people around, you'd grow a sort of vertebrate plant, nothing more.

So, to start with, you will undoubtedly need to clone the parents. No question about this. This means the diplomat is out, even in theory, since you couldn't have gotten cells from both his parents at the time when he was himself just recognizable as an early social treasure. You'd have to limit the list of clones to people already certified as sufficiently valuable for the effort, with both parents still alive. The parents would need cloning and, for consistency, their parents as well. I suppose you'd also need the usual informed-consent forms, filled out and signed, not easy to get if I know parents, even harder for grandparents.

But this is only the beginning. It is the whole family that really influences the way a person turns out, not just the parents, according to current psychiatric thinking. Clone the family.

Then what? The way each member of the family develops has already been determined by the environment set around him, and this environment is more people, people outside the family, schoolmates, acquaintances, lovers, enemies, car-pool partners, even, in special circumstances, peculiar strangers across the aisle on the subway. Find them, and clone them.

But there is no end to the protocol. Each of the outer contacts has his own surrounding family, and his and their outer contacts. Clone them all.

To do the thing properly, with any hope of ending up with a genuine duplicate of a single person, you really have no choice. You must clone the world, no less.

We are not ready for an experiment of this size, nor, I should think, are we willing. For one thing, it would mean replacing today's world by an entirely identical world to follow immediately, and this means no new, natural, spontaneous, random, chancy children. No children at all, except for the manufactured doubles of those now on the scene. Plus all those identical adults, including all of today's politicians, all seen double. It is too much to contemplate.

Moreover, when the whole experiment is finally finished, fifty years or so from now, how could you get a responsible scientific reading on the outcome? Somewhere in there would be the original clonee, probably lost and overlooked, now well into middle age, but everyone around him would be precise duplicates of today's everyone. It would be today's same world, filled to overflowing with duplicates of today's people and their same, duplicated problems, probably all resentful at having had to go through our whole thing all over, sore enough at the clonee to make endless trouble for him, if they found him.

And obviously, if the whole thing were done precisely right, they would still be casting about for ways to solve the problem of universal dissatisfaction, and sooner or later they'd surely begin to look around at each other, wondering who should be cloned for his special value to society, to get us out of all this. And so it would go, in regular cycles, perhaps forever.

I once lived through a period when I wondered what Hell could be like, and I stretched my imagination to try to think of a perpetual sort of damnation. I have to confess, I never thought of anything like this.

I have an alternative suggestion, if you're looking for a way out. Set cloning aside, and don't try it. Instead, go in the other direction. Look for ways to get mutations more quickly, new variety, different songs. Fiddle around, if you must fiddle, but never with ways to keep things the same, no matter who, not even yourself. Heaven, somewhere ahead, has got to be a change.

Daniel Lang (1915–   )

A Vapor Moving North-Northwest

A few moments after the underground nuclear blast known as Project Gnome went off, at noon on a Sunday last month [December 1961], in a flat and chilly stretch of desert southeast of Carlsbad, New Mexico, all of us who were watching the event from a mound of bulldozed earth four and a half miles due south of ground zero—some four hundred foreign observers, congressmen, government scientists, local citizens, photographers, and reporters—could tell that something had gone wrong. What gave us this impression was not the broad blanket of dust that the explosive—deep below in a formation of salt rock—had jolted out of the desert. Nor was it the bouncing we took—the result of a violent earth tremor that had been caused by the nuclear charge, which was one-fourth as powerful as the Hiroshima bomb. (In the immediate vicinity of the explosion, the desert leaped three feet, and it has yet to descend to its former level.) We had been told to expect these things. Rather, it was the sight of thick and steadily thickening white vapor at the scene of the firing that made us think that plans had miscarried. The vapor was puffing up through an elevator shaft that dropped twelve hundred feet to an eleven-hundred-foot tunnel, at the end of which the explosive, and also much of the project's experimental equipment, had been installed. As we watched the vapor slowly begin to spread, like ground fog, and, rising, vanish into the air, we knew we were witnessing something that we had been practically assured wouldn't happen—venting, or the accidental escape of radioactivity into the atmosphere. "The probability of the experiment venting is so low as to approach the impossible," the Atomic Energy Commission had stated in a comprehensive pamphlet it had published on Project Gnome. Indeed, at a briefing held the previous evening in Carlsbad, where Gnome's headquarters were located, one of the speakers had warned that the shot was just a small one and might well disappoint us as a spectacle. It was the excitement of its underlying idea that made it worthwhile for us to be at the proving ground, we had been told, for Project Gnome marked the opening of the Plowshare Program—a series of nuclear blasts whose purpose, as the name implied, was to turn the atom to peaceful ways. Any number of benefits, we were informed, could flow from these blasts: harbors might be carved out of wasteland in Alaska; oil might be dislodged from shale; abundant sources of water under great mountains might be freed; diamonds might be made out of ordinary carbon.

We were in no danger—the wind was blowing the vapor to the north-northwest of us—but the feeling seemed to take hold that this wasn't necessarily the Prophet Isaiah's day. Before the explosion, a gala mood had prevailed on our barren mound. Local ranchers, their big Stetsons bobbing, had heartily declared that it was a great day for these parts. The operators of nearby potash mines—the world's largest producers of this chemical—had agreed. Their wives, modishly clad, had greeted each other effusively. And Louis M. Whitlock, the manager of the Carlsbad Chamber of Commerce, had assured me, "This bomb is for the good of mankind, and we're for it," as we awaited the explosion. Representative Ben Franklin Jensen, of Iowa, a Republican member of the House Appropriations Committee, had also caught the proper spirit. "There are certain things you just have to spend money on, and Plowshare is one of them," he told me. The foreign visitors lent a certain glamour to the occasion. There was Professor Francis Perrin, for instance —a small, goateed man with elegant manners who is the High Commissioner of France's Commissariat à l'Energie Atomique. The science attaché of the Japanese Embassy was there, too—a young chemist named Dr. Seiichi Ishizaka. Chatting with him shortly before the venting, I had gathered that his government was of two minds about the wisdom of the day's explosion. "Japan is curious," he had told me, smiling politely. The bustle of the many journalists on the scene had added to the festive air. The local people had been fascinated by their activities, clustering around each time Dr. Edward Teller, the widely celebrated father of the H-bomb, who is also the father of Plowshare, posed for television crews. On the high-school platform in Carlsbad during the previous evening's briefing, he had, in response to a reporter's question, agreed that the Plowshare Program was "too little and too late," and had gone on to say, "Plowshare had to wait for permission from the Kremlin, which it is giving in a slightly ungracious manner."

Now, as the insidious gases continued to escape from the shaft, the gala mood faded. An A.E.C. official, speaking over a public-address system from a crudely constructed lectern, announced that all drivers should turn their cars around to facilitate a speedy retreat from the test area. An evacuation, he said, might be in order. A short while later—about half an hour after the detonation—the same official, a calm, affable man by the name of Richard G. Elliott, announced that, according to word from a control point a hundred yards forward, the venting had created a radioactive cloud, low and invisible, which was moving in the general direction of Carlsbad, twenty-three miles away to the northwest. The invisible cloud, which was being tracked by an Air Force helicopter equipped with radiation counters, was expected to miss the town, but it would pass over a section of the highway on which we had driven from Carlsbad. The state police had consequently been instructed to throw up a roadblock there. Until further notice, the only way to reach Carlsbad would be to head southeast and follow a detour of a hundred and fifty miles. Some spectators left at once to take this round-about route, figuring that they might as well get the trip over and done with, rather than face an indefinite delay. Some other spectators also departed hurriedly; they suspected the A.E.C. of being excessively cautious, and hoped to use the direct highway to Carlsbad before the police could organize their blockade. As things turned out, a few of these motorists did elude the police, only to be intercepted eventually in Carlsbad itself. Seven cars were found to be contaminated; the A.E.C. paid to have them washed down. Two of the passengers, according to the A.E.C., showed slight, easily removable, traces of radioactivity, one on his hand and the other on his clothing and hair. As for the cloud, the helicopter that had started tracking it had been forced to return to base when the craft's instruments showed that it was being contaminated. Another machine took its place, and the pilot of this kept the cloud under surveillance until darkness forced him to give up his mission; the cloud was then five miles north of a small town called Artesia, about sixty miles north-northwest of the test site; it had hovered briefly over the eastern edge of the town, and continued in its north-northwesterly path. At the time he took his leave of the cloud, the pilot reported, its radiation was diminishing steadily—a process attributable to nature, rather than to Gnome's artificers.

Fortunately, the countryside over which this gaseous debris was being wafted was only sparsely populated. In fact, this was one of the reasons the explosive had been set off in this particular area. In spite of the reassurances about venting in the pamphlet, the A.E.C. and its chief contractor for Plowshare—the University of California's Lawrence Radiation Laboratory, in Livermore, California—had had this eventuality very much in mind when they planned Gnome. Many precautions had been taken. The tunnel was packed with bags of salt and blocks of concrete, designed to arrest the spread of radioactivity. Wind patterns had been analyzed by the United States Weather Bureau during the entire week before the shot. The day's detonation had, in fact, been delayed four hours until the winds were considered to be blowing in a safe direction. Ranchers for five miles around had been evacuated, tactfully, by being asked to join the Gnome spectators; their cattle, less privileged, had simply been driven off to roam different pastures for the day—or for however long it might take the United States Public Health Service to certify the cleanliness of their familiar acres. The Federal Aviation Agency had been asked to order planes in the area to maintain a certain altitude until further notice. The dryness of the salt formation notwithstanding, the United States Geological Survey had made ground-water surveys of the surrounding area for six months before the shot and would continue to do so for at least a year afterward, in order to keep tabs on any underground movement of radioactive material. Seismic effects had also been anticipated. A special bill had been put through Congress to assure the potash industry of suitable indemnification in the event of damage. On the day of the detonation, no potash miners were on hand to chip at the rose-colored walls of their rough corridors. Nor were tourists permitted to explore the Carlsbad Caverns, thirty-four miles to the east of the detonation site. Acting on behalf of Project Gnome, the Coast and Geodetic Survey had placed a seismograph inside the Caverns. A member of the Caverns' staff—a naturalist from the National Park Service—was on hand to measure seismic effects in his own way; he watched to see if the blast would ripple one of the still, subterranean ponds that had been created over millennia, partly by drops of water from the cave's stalactites. (It didn't.) In retrospect, perhaps the most significant of all the precautions taken was the relatively last-minute reduction of the yield of the explosive from ten kilotons, as originally planned, to five kilotons. "Whoever made *that* decision, I'd like to shake his hand," an A.E.C. official told me the day after the shot.

Those of us who, like me, were waiting for the roadblock to be lifted, passed the time as best we could. We discussed our reactions to the blast for a while, but, oddly, this soon began to pall. Some of us wandered over to a chuck wagon that the A.E.C. had thoughtfully laid on, and bought ourselves coffee and sandwiches. Now and then, we heard new announcements, of varying interest, on the public-address system. One dealt with the far-flung network of seismic recording stations that had been organized by the Department of Defense. A colonel mounted the lectern to tell us that the network appeared to have functioned well. (He didn't know then that Gnome's seismic signal had been recorded in Scandinavia and Japan.) The firing, the colonel added, had taken place "at exactly one four-thousandth of a second after noon." Returning to the lectern, Elliott told us that, according to the instruments, the radiation at the bottom of the shaft now came to a million roentgens an hour, while on the ground at the top of the shaft the count was ten thousand roentgens an hour—twelve and a half times the lethal exposure for a healthy man.

After a while, some of us went and sat in our cars to read or doze or just get out of the cold. Those who didn't could stare at the shaft, from which vapor was still issuing, or, if they preferred, scan the desert, stubbled with tumbleweed and greasewood and cactus. Only the distant sight of a potash refinery relieved the terrain. Bluish-white smoke was pouring from its tall chimney, its furnace having been left unbanked on this day of days. The refinery lay due northwest, near the Carlsbad road, so I knew that the radioactive gases were bound to mingle with the vapors of the tall chimney. Like my fellow-spectators, though, I had no idea when that would come to pass.

The technical objectives of the day's blast, which were almost entirely in the hands of Livermore scientists, were well planned, it had been impressed on me in the course of the briefings before the shot. The central purpose was to see what happened when an atomic explosive was set off in a salt formation—what is called phenomenology. The Livermore people hadn't previously had a chance for such a test, their underground efforts thus far having been limited to military shots in the volcanic tuff of the Nevada test site—a substance that doesn't retain heat nearly as well as salt does. And heat was the key to much of what the researchers were seeking to learn. Gnome would enable them to carry out a heat-extraction experiment, for example—the general idea being to investigate the possibility of tapping for productive uses the inferno of superheated steam and other forms of energy that would result from the detonation. This energy, it was hoped, would be contained in a cavity in the salt that the explosive, low though its yield was, would create in about a tenth of a second. The cavity, if it didn't collapse, would be eggshaped and glowing, and it would be about a hundred and ten feet in diameter; six thousand tons of molten salt were expected to run down its sides and compose a pool thirty-five feet deep. The cavity would also be "mined," by remote control, for radioactive isotopes

—unstable atoms that are produced by a nuclear explosion, a fair percentage of which are valuable in scientific research, medical treatment, and industrial processes. (One of them, strontium 90, which is greatly feared in fallout, may someday be used in long-lived batteries to power unmanned weather stations in godforsaken regions, a Livermore expert told me.)

For pure researchers, it was thought, Gnome's most interesting data might be gained from the large number of neutrons—uncharged particles that are part of the atomic nucleus— that would be produced by the blast. In the instant of the explosion, I had been told, Gnome would release as many neutrons as a laboratory apparatus could release in several thousand years. So plentiful would they be, in fact, that only one out of ten million could be studied. Even so, much new light might be shed on such matters as the different velocities of neutrons and the interaction of these particles, which are usually emitted in bursts that last less than a hundred-millionth of a second, an interval of time that is known in scientific shoptalk as "a shake."

But these technical objectives of Project Gnome were only a part of the Plowshare Program, and the Plowshare Program was something more than a scientific enterprise—a fact that had become apparent in the days immediately preceding the desert shot, when Carlsbad had been rife with briefings, interviews, and informative handouts. The case for Plowshare, in the opinion of some of the foreign observers and other people I talked with, seemed to rest on a variety of grounds. I learned, for example, that the proposed series of blasts had been approved by the A.E.C. four years before, which raised the question of why they were being started at this particular time. Plowshare officials readily acknowledged that the complete answer certainly included the state of international affairs. Was Plowshare, then, a solid program or a passing, virtuous response to the Russian resumption of atmospheric testing? Perhaps Plowshare's name was partly to blame for this questioning attitude. "It sounds a little too much like magic," a foreign scientist remarked. "So many swords are being made just now."

In any event, a day or two before the shot, I discussed Plowshare in Carlsbad with two of its overseers, both of whom were strongly in favor of the program, as one would expect, but in a fairly thoughtful, unmagical way. One of them was John S. Kelly, a bespectacled, mild-mannered man of thirty-nine who is the director of the A.E.C.'s Division of Peaceful Nuclear Explosives. He saw Plowshare's explosives as scientific and engineering tools. It excited him, he said, to contemplate the excavation jobs that might be performed in the future, like blasting lakes out of the wilderness and breaking up ore deposits that could be leached out. Plowshare represented a continuation of the whole history of explosives, Kelly said. Certainly explosives could be harmful, he conceded, but on the other hand gunpowder had done away with the feudal system and TNT had made possible the mining of fossil fuels.

"But can we afford to guess wrong with nuclear explosives?" I asked. "Don't they represent an ultimate kind of energy?"

"Why not use them for our ultimate good?" Kelly replied.

For an undertaking concerned with the peaceful uses of the atom, I remarked, Plowshare appeared to have its ambiguities. The fissionable material and the equipment for the Gnome explosive, I mentioned, had been taken from our armaments stockpile; the explosive was being concealed from the public gaze, the same as a weapon is; men in uniform had come to Carlsbad for the shot, and were participating actively in its preparation; and among those prominently involved were people from Livermore, which was noted primarily as a center of weapons design.

Kelly was quick to grant that the line between the peaceful and the military sides of the atom was fuzzy. It would be nice, he said, if the two functions could be neatly demarcated, for in that case the Plowshare Program, living up to its name more fully, could have postponed the blasts until war was an obsolete institution. But that wasn't the way things were, in Kelly's view. "We may have to take our peaceful uses when we can," he said.

The other official I talked with was Dr. Gary H. Higgins, the director of the Plowshare Division of the Lawrence Radiation Laboratory. Higgins is a soft-spoken chemist of thirty-four, whose desk in his Carlsbad office was adorned, when I saw it, with a small ceramic gnome he had bought in a department store. Like Kelly, he believes that nuclear explosives have a great peacetime future. "Within five to fifteen years, they'll be basic to our industrial economy," he told me. "They'll help us get at raw materials we need for our growing population. It may take us time to make use of them. After all, forest husbandry developed only when the nation was practically deforested." He was delighted that the United States was moving ahead with Plowshare, but not, he told me, because it relieved him of his weapons duties at Livermore. The two kinds of work, he felt, were not pure opposites; there was a difference between weapons and war, he said, just as there was between a police force and murder. But whether an idea like Plowshare or an arms race was to dominate our lives in the years ahead was another matter. It depended, Higgins thought, on whether mankind could eventually achieve an immense self-consciousness. "It would not cater to the oversimplified images that religion and ethics tend to give us," Higgins said. "It would enable us to recognize our weaknesses. We'd know our motives for acting the way we do, and what else is it that counts but intent, whether shots are called Plowshare or something else?"

It was almost four hours after the detonation when I left the bulldozed mound in the desert. The roadblock hadn't yet been lifted, but to a number of us that didn't matter. We were chafing to get away, although not for any sensible reason I heard expressed. Perhaps the others felt, as I did, a sense of rebellion and indignation at being trapped by a mysterious, invisible antagonist. In the distance, the refinery's tall chimney continued to surrender its thick plume of smoke, giving no sign, of course, whether there had yet been any mingling with the radioactive cloud. Absurdly, I felt like going to the refinery to find out. Around us, shadows were beginning to fall on the desert, making it seem more limitless than ever, and underscoring our marooned condition.

At any rate, when a rancher who was among the spectators mentioned to some of us that certain back roads might bring one out on the Carlsbad highway three or four miles beyond the police blockade, I was off at once, in a car with two other men—Ken Fujisaki, a young correspondent for a Tokyo newspaper, the *Sankei Shimbun*, and David Perlman, a reporter for the San Francisco *Chronicle*. The rancher, who himself was in no hurry to leave, had said he hadn't used those particular back roads in fifteen years, but at the time this remark had struck us as irrelevant. Our immediate goals were a windmill and a gas well —two landmarks that, the rancher had said, might soon guide us on our way to Carlsbad.

"How would you like to spend two weeks in a fallout shelter?" Perlman, who was driving, asked me as he impatiently started the car.

After a ten-minute drive over a bumpy, rutted road, we were at the gas well. We were also at a dead end. As we were looking at each other in puzzlement, we heard the honk of a car horn behind us, and discovered that we had been leaders of men. Nine other cars had followed us to the dead end; we had been too intent on our flight from safety to notice them. One of the vehicles was a small orange government truck, and another was a sports car—a dirty, white Triumph whose driver wore goggles. Some of us got out of our cars, conferred ignorantly, and decided to go back and follow a dirt road that had intersected the one we were on. This road also came to a dead end. Backtracking, we tried another, and then another. The fourth ran parallel to a ranch fence, on the other side of which were cattle and horses. Beyond the field they were in we could see the Carlsbad highway, only a couple of miles off. The fence seemed to run on endlessly, leading nowhere. Our caravan halted, and a few of us climbed a stile to seek advice at the ranch. We found a young Mexican hand, who obligingly corralled the animals, and opened a gate into a muddy, reddish road that crossed the field. In no time we were on the highway to Carlsbad. To get there, we had gone east, north, west, and northeast. Now we passed the potash refinery, its tall stack still smoking. I looked at it as long as I could. No police intercepted us. When we reached the Project Gnome office in Carlsbad, we learned that the roadblock had been called off fifteen minutes after our departure. Perlman asked that he be gone over with a radiation counter. He proved to be fine, which meant the rest of us were.

When I arrived at my motel, the manager phoned me. He was a transplanted Englishman with whom I had made friends. Since I was leaving the next day, I thought perhaps he was calling to say goodbye, but it was Project Gnome that was on his mind.

"I'm sick in bed, you see, so *I'm* quite all right, but it's the staff—" he began. A guest, he said, had told the cashier in the restaurant not to touch the money of anyone who had been to the test. The cashier had become hysterical. Then a policeman had come and collected two other members of the staff to have them "counted" at the Gnome office; the two had been spectators at the shot and had been among those who eluded the roadblock.

"There's no need for any concern, is there?" the manager asked me uneasily. "I mean, those men out there know what they're doing, don't they?"

I could hear him breathing at the other end of the phone, waiting for my answer.

"Of course they do," I said. "Of course everything's all right."

Barry Commoner (1917–   )

Once and Future Fuel

Thus far, one of the most troublesome features of the effort to deal with the energy crisis might be called the reality problem. Is the frequently proclaimed shortage of energy real or contrived? Are the dangers of nuclear power genuine or imagined? Is solar energy a valid alternative, or is it only a beguiling possibility? The distinction between what is real and what is not has troubled not only the public's perception of the energy crisis but also the government's effort to do something about it. The Administration and Congress have produced elaborate plans for resolving the energy crisis, but they have had a great deal of difficulty in converting these abstractions into realities. Most of the campaigns in the "moral equivalent of war" that President Carter proclaimed when he announced the original National Energy Plan in 1977 have never materialized. The elaborate tax measures designed to encourage energy conservation by raising the price of fuel and of gas-guzzling cars died in Congress. The mandated switch of utility fuel from oil and natural gas to coal has been postponed. Even as simple an aim as storing emergency supplies of imported oil in abandoned salt mines has been difficult to achieve. (Although oil was deposited in the mines, it was unrecoverable for months after, because the necessary pumps were missing.)

Now there is a new energy plan. Shortly after emerging from his retreat at Camp David last July, Mr. Carter delivered a television address in which he once more exhorted his listeners to believe that "the energy crisis is real. . . . It is a clear and present danger to our nation." To deal with the crisis, he said, "I am tonight setting a clear goal for the energy policy of the United States. Beginning this moment, this nation will never use more foreign oil than we did in 1977. Never." To accomplish this goal, Mr. Carter proposed "the most massive peacetime commitment of funds and resources in our nation's history to develop America's own alternative sources of fuel." The funds that the Administration proposes to spend for this purpose are indeed enormous—about a hundred and forty billion dollars, almost two-thirds of it for the production of "synthetic fuels." The proposed eighty-eight-billion-dollar investment in synthetic fuels is about equal to the total assets (as of 1978) of the country's three largest oil companies (Exxon, Mobil, and Texaco), which represent nearly forty per cent of the assets of the eighteen major oil companies. Once again, the Administration has asked us to believe that a huge new energy undertaking can actually be put into effect, and once again the country is confronted with the gap between supposition and substance.

The emergence of synthetic fuels as the chief element in the national energy program is a sharp departure from earlier policies, for the energy sources that have until now preoccupied the Administration and Congress—oil, natural gas, coal, and uranium—are natural, rather than synthetic. In ordinary usage, there is a clear distinction between natural and synthetic materials. Natural materials are produced by processes that occur in nature without human intervention (that, in fact, often occurred long before people existed), while synthetic materials are man-made. Thus, penicillin, which is produced by certain fungi, is natural, while sulfanilamide, a man-made antibacterial drug, is synthetic; silk and iron ore are natural, while nylon and steel are synthetic. In the bill that the Administration has introduced to carry out Mr. Carter's new energy policy, however, this distinction is obliterated. The legislation defines synthetic fuels in this way:

> Synthetic fuel shall mean any liquid, gaseous, or solid hydrocarbon (including mixtures of coal and petroleum) which can be used as a substitute for supplies of petroleum or natural gas (and for any derivatives thereof) derived from domestic sources of:
>
> (A) coal, including lignite and peat;
>
> (B) shale;
>
> (C) tar sands, including those heavy oil resources which cannot technically or economically be produced using conventional or unconventional petroleum recovery techniques; and
>
> (D) biomass, which shall include timber, animal and timber waste, municipal and industrial waste, sewage, sludge, oceanic and terrestrial plants, and other organic matter.

This definition embraces not only synthetic crude oil made by chemically treating coal but also ethanol—ordinary, drinkable alcohol—which is the natural, biological product of yeast and other microörganisms when they ferment sugary fluids, whether the vintner's pressed grapes, the moonshiner's corn mash, or decaying fruit lying on the jungle floor. (All of these contain organic materials that are derived—in keeping with the legislative definition—not from crude oil or natural gas but from carbon dioxide, which the grapevine, the corn plant, or the tropical fruit tree converts to organic matter photosynthetically, by means of solar energy.)

The arbitrary inclusion of crude oil made chemically from coal and alcohol made biologically from sugar—the one truly synthetic and the other clearly natural by any definition other than the Congress's—under the same legislative umbrella is bound to cause trouble. The environmental and economic consequences of producing the two types of fuel are so different that they can hardly be dealt with successfully in the same legislative measure. The extreme chemical conditions in which truly synthetic fuels are produced yield a wide range of substances, many of them toxic or carcinogenic. The estimated cost, as of last July, of producing synthetic fuels (between twenty-five and fifty dollars per barrel) is so much higher than the price of imported natural crude oil (about eighteen dollars per barrel) that their entry into the fuel market is bound to intensify the worst symptom of the energy crisis—the escalating price of energy. The synthetic-fuel scheme would rely on private initiative to build the plants, with the government guaranteeing to buy the product at a set (and relatively high) price—financial protection that could be easily overwhelmed by the discovery of a serious technical deficiency during the construction of a plant. Yet much synthetic-fuel technology is still unproved, and is likely to become more expensive as needed improvements are made. For that reason, and because each plant is very costly (two billion dollars or more), the risk of financial failure is not only real but intimidating; it might be great enough to bankrupt all but the very largest corporations. In contrast, ethanol, a natural fuel, can be made from annually renewed crops by well-established, environmentally benign techniques that are likely to become less rather than more costly with experience. Ethanol plants can be operated economically on a rather small scale; the largest plants cost from fifty million to seventy-five million dollars each, and much smaller plants—costing from fifty thousand to a hundred thousand dollars each—may be equally efficient. Farmers' coöperatives are capable of financing the larger plants, and the smaller ones could be financed by single farmers or by small groups of them. So the risk and the financial consequences of failure are relatively small. Experience with the most important energy innovation introduced in recent decades—nuclear power—warns us that economic and environmental constraints are usually the main hindrance to converting an energy program into reality. The effort to translate the abstract aims of the new synthetic-fuel legislation into actual production of fuel is likely, therefore, to yield very different results when it is applied to two fuels that differ so much in their origins and in their environmental and economic impacts.

The aim of what has become known as the "synfuels" program is to substitute for the fuels now derived from imported oil alternatives that can be produced from domestic sources. Gasoline is an important candidate for substitution, because it is essential to the American economy, and because about half the amount we now use (a total of about a hundred and twenty billion gallons annually) is refined from imported oil. Gasoline is a hydrocarbon—that is, it consists of molecules in which carbon atoms, linked in chains or in closed rings, are associated with hydrogen atoms. Conventional crude oil is a mixture of many kinds of these molecules, ranging from small, lightweight ones that readily vaporize to the large ones found in the tarry residues that remain after the lighter constituents evaporate. Gasoline can be separated from this mixture by condensing the vapors that boil off the crude oil at a particular range of temperatures. Modern refineries can produce more gasoline hydrocarbons than occur naturally in crude oil by breaking up (in the industry's jargon, "cracking") some of the larger oil molecules or by joining smaller ones ("re-forming").

There are several optional ways of producing a substitute for ordinary gasoline which would conform to the terms of the proposed synfuels legislation. One way is to convert coal into synthetic crude oil and then refine gasoline from that. Another is to produce ethanol from agricultural crops, such as corn or sugar beets—or, for that matter, from food-processing wastes such as cannery scraps or the whey left over from cheesemaking. Ethanol is an effective automotive fuel. The engine of the old Model T Ford was designed to operate on ethanol, gasoline, or any mixture of the two. Modern car engines work quite well, and in some respects better than they do on pure gasoline, on a mixture of ten per cent ethanol in gasoline, or "gasohol." Automobile factories in Brazil, where ethanol produced from sugarcane is rapidly replacing gasoline, are planning to build engines that run on pure ethanol.

In theory, the process of converting coal into synthetic crude oil is simple. Since coal is made up chiefly of sheets of linked hexagonal rings of carbon atoms (the pattern made by the tiles on an old-fashioned bathroom floor is a good approximation of the molecular structure of coal), it can be converted into hydrocarbons, such as those in crude oil, by chemical reaction with hydrogen. The first practical process, developed by the German chemist Friedrich Bergius in 1911 and later improved on by I. G. Farben, was successful enough to supply eighty-five per cent of the gasoline used by the German Luftwaffe in the Second World War. Finely ground coal is mixed with oil produced by the process itself, and then heated to 900°F. or so in a high-pressure tank, where it reacts with hydrogen, which is itself obtained by treating coal with steam and oxygen. After solid and tarry materials are removed, there remains a kind of crude oil which can then be refined in the usual manner to yield gasoline.

Outlined in this way, the process seems simple, neat, and self-contained, but in practice it is rather complex and messy, and environmentally hazardous. A relatively small pilot plant, designed to hydrogenate about three hundred tons of coal per day, which was operated between 1952 and 1959 by the Union Carbide Chemicals Company, consisted of a half-dozen complex, multistory units, elaborately interconnected by a network of pipes, spread over a twenty-acre site at Institute, West Virginia. Although the main products included only two grades of synthetic oil, and coke, pitch, and ash, more than two hundred individual chemicals were identified in these products, most of them hydrocarbons. Unfortunately, these hydrocarbons included some extremely potent cancer-producing chemicals. Perhaps the most notorious carcinogenic hydrocarbon is 3,4-benzo(a)pyrene. Its effects were first noted by a celebrated English surgeon, Sir Percivall Pott, whose classic account, "Chirurgical Observations," published in 1775, showed that the high incidence of cancer of the scrotum among chimney sweeps was connected with their occupation—the first record of an environmental cancer. In 1933, a team of British chemists discovered that at least one of the cancer-inducing chemicals in the coal tar to which chimney sweeps were exposed was 3,4-benzo(a)pyrene, which thereby became the first identified chemical carcinogen.

Aware that the coal-hydrogenation products were likely to contain benzo-(a)pyrene, the medical staff of the West Virginia plant tested its several products by painting them on the shaved skin of white mice—a standard test for carcinogenicity. The plant's heavier oil products were found to be "highly carcinogenic," meaning that between forty and a hundred per cent of the treated animals developed skin cancers within a year. In the face of these results, the plant management established stringent hygiene procedures in order to protect workers from exposure to carcinogens. Also, engineers made a detailed survey of the occurrence of benzo(a)pyrene in the air in various parts of the plant. It was detected nearly everywhere; in a few places, the levels were several hundred times as great as those observed in typical industrial cities, where some benzo-(a)pyrene is released when coal or oil is burned. Despite the rigorous protective measures, by the time the plant closed, skin cancer had occurred among the plant's three hundred and fifty-nine workers at least sixteen times as frequently as it did among a comparable population of men not exposed to the plant environment.

Apart from these difficulties, a coal-liquefaction plant creates a number of other environmental hazards. Coal liquefaction uses several hundred gallons of water for every ton of coal processed; although four-fifths of the water is used for cooling, and could be recirculated, such a plant is nevertheless a serious drain on local water supplies. Coal-liquefaction plants emit coal dust, sulphur dioxide, nitrogen oxides, and carbon monoxide, all of which need to be controlled in order to avoid an unacceptable level of air pollution. Various toxic chemicals also occur in the plant's waste water, again requiring extensive environmental controls. Five to eight per cent of the original coal remains as ash, which must be carefully disposed of in order to avoid the release of toxic materials.

All this is mostly theory, because actual experience with the production of synthetic fuels from coal is very limited, and hardly approaches the huge scale that the new program would require. Although several pilot plants with a capacity of a few hundred tons of coal per day, such as the one in West Virginia, have been operated, there are as yet no full-scale coal-conversion plants—that is, plants with a capacity of about fifty thousand tons of coal per day—in operation in the United States. Eight or ten such plants would be needed to meet the Administration's minimum goal of producing about a million barrels of synthetic fuels per day from coal. On the basis of present technical experience, it is certainly possible to build plants capable of meeting that goal. But the same can be said of the government's plan to build nuclear power plants, which is, nevertheless, far from being realized (new orders for nuclear plants fell from thirty-four in 1973 to two in 1978), because of economic and environmental difficulties. If the synfuels scheme is to be realized, it needs to face the same test that has slowed the nuclear program: Can an actual full-sized plant operate economically, in a particular location, within the constraints of environmental requirements?

The Department of Energy has attempted to answer this question in a report ("Environmental Analysis of Synthetic Liquid Fuels," first published in July, 1979, and reprinted, apparently because of heavy demand, in August) based on the goal of producing a million barrels per day of synthetic liquid fuel, mostly from coal (oil shale is a lesser source). This is a relatively modest target; several of the bills introduced in

Congress propose to reach a figure five times as large as that by 1990. The chief virtue of the D.O.E. analysis is that it reduces the arbitrary legislative goals to some semblance of reality by considering a series of practical regulations. First, in order to avoid expensive transportation costs, a synfuel project must be situated where the coal is. Assuming that the plant must operate for twenty-five years in order to give a satisfactory return on the investment, and taking into account the minimum size of a cost-efficient plant, this consideration limits plants to counties that contain at least four hundred million tons of recoverable coal. According to the report, there are a hundred and fifty-nine such counties in the United States, of which twenty-two have coal deposits that are even larger—up to twelve hundred million tons. When environmental requirements —that the area have sufficient water and clean enough air (meaning sparse industrial and urban areas) to absorb the plant's effluents without exceeding environmental limits—are added, however, the suitable sites are reduced to forty-one counties, of which thirteen have the larger coal reserves. When another standard is applied—that the area should have a sufficient population (at least fifty thousand in the 1970 census) to support the heavy influx of people and new activities that a synfuel plant would bring, in order to avoid suffering the economic and social dislocations brought on by temporary boom towns—thirty-one of the forty-one sites become unacceptable, and all the larger coal deposits are eliminated.

The final step in reducing the synfuel scheme to reality is to specify the actual location of the feasible production sites. If the boom-town problem is ignored, twenty-seven of the forty-one feasible sites are in Western states, which supports the expectation, often voiced by legislators from that area, that the West would be heavily affected by the synfuels program. When the boom-town problem is taken into account, however, the picture changes drastically. All but one of the sites in the Western states—where, because the population is sparsely distributed, the entry of an intensive industry is likely to be very disruptive—then become infeasible. Of the remaining nine sites, six are in Illinois, two are in West Virginia, and one is in Pennsylvania.

The upshot of these considerations is that if present environmental constraints are taken into account, there are only ten sites in the country where coal-liquefaction plants could feasibly be constructed. The coal available at these sites (a total of about four billion tons) would probably yield about ten billion barrels of synthetic fuel, or about one million barrels per day—the minimum goal of a synfuels program. But the four billion tons would be exhausted in twenty-five years, and six of the ten plants would have to be built in Illinois.

By chance, Illinois is a place that could also quite readily produce ethanol made from grain and other crops—one of the natural substances that fit the Congress's curious definition of "synthetic fuels." Testing the feasibility of an ethanol-production program is fairly simple, since the compatibility of its component processes with environmental constraints is already established and the relevant economic issues are fairly well understood. To begin with, the source of the raw material that is used to produce ethanol is simply agricultural production: a process that is already widely carried out within the constraints of existing environmental regulations (although some agricultural technologies, such as the heavy use of pesticides and fertilizers, are probably insufficiently regulated as yet). Human experience with the next stage in ethanol production—fermentation of the crop mash—is even older than agriculture, for archeological evidence suggests that brews were prepared from wild grain and fruit before crops were cultivated. Fermentation is a natural biological process, and for that reason yields by-products that are readily accommodated in natural ecological cycles. Apart from ethanol, the process produces carbon dioxide and the unfermentable residue of the starting material. The residue is quite rich in protein, and is therefore a valuable livestock feed; used in that way, it readily enters the natural crop-livestock-manure-soil cycle that supports plant and animal life, which, with proper precautions, can be kept in ecological balance.

The final segment of the ethanol-production process—the distillation of concentrated ethanol from the fermentation mash—is also quite benign environmentally. A small amount of ethanol and other volatile materials may be emitted from the still, but these are easily recaptured by passing the vented fumes through a small water trap, from which the ethanol can be recovered. The residual grain is often dried, so it can be easily shipped as a livestock feed. This may involve using heat from the flue gas emitted by the boilers that fire the still. The boiler stacks can also be fitted with scrubbers, so that, according to a recent study made for the D.O.E., the emitted gases "will readily meet federal and state regulations for particulate and sulfur dioxide emissions."

Although there has been some argument over the economic feasibility of producing ethanol from grain at a cost competitive with the price of gasoline, that is being resolved by the continuing escalation of fuel prices. At a recent workshop on how to market gasohol, Thomas H. Finch, Jr., vice-president of the Finch Oil Company, of Fayetteville, North Carolina, reported that in that state (which does not exempt gasohol from state road taxes) gasohol costs the fuel distributor about ninety-two cents per gallon. Since gasohol is a substitute for unleaded premium gasoline, which sells at retail for about a dollar and five cents per gallon, the distributor and retailer can share a profit of only thirteen cents per gallon. As Mr. Finch pointed out, under these circumstances the sale of gasohol could compete with the sale of gasoline only if the present volume of gasohol sales—which is limited by the very small size of present ethanol-production facilities—was substantially increased. In states that exempt gasohol from road taxes, the profit margin is increased by as much as eight cents per gallon, so that profits there are economically competitive even at the present low volume. The exemption of gasohol from federal and some state taxes is a mixed blessing, however. Although such exemptions do make gasohol competitive in some states, they also allow the producers of ethanol to charge an unnecessarily high price for it (about a dollar and seventy-five cents per gallon, which, according to another D.O.E. report, could be reduced to between a dollar and five cents and a dollar and sixteen cents per gallon and still give the producers a suitable profit). A number of farm coöperatives are planning to build ethanol plants; when they begin to operate, the selling price is likely to fall sharply, and gasohol will become economically competitive all over the country. (Adding ethanol to low-grade gasoline raises the "octane value"—which determines engine combustion efficiency—to the point ordinarily attained by adding lead or other octane-boosters to the fuel. Gasohol derives about half its economic value from this octane-boosting effect.) As the price of gasoline continues to rise, gasohol will become an increasingly economic substitute for unleaded gasoline.

The question of how much ethanol the United States could produce from biological sources without interfering with food production has been in dispute. However, according to the latest government estimate (by the D.O.E.), ethanol production from grain and sugar crops could amount to about a hundred and forty-five million barrels per year.

This compares favorably with the projected 1990 estimate of synthetic-fuel production from coal (if environmental constraints are honored). Taking into account, as well, that ethanol production can be considerably increased by altering the present crop-growing pattern to one that can more effectively support the production of both food and energy, it would appear that ethanol production from crops could meet even the larger expectations of the synfuels program.

Thus, on technical grounds, the synfuels program, if it is enacted, could lead to a vast program for producing gasoline and other synthetic fuels from coal or to an at least equally large program for producing an effective gasoline substitute, ethanol, from agricultural crops. Curiously, the impact of the choice between these two ways of reducing our present dependence on imported oil would be felt largely in one state, Illinois. Through an accident of geography, most of that state is covered with soil that supports much of the crop production needed to establish an ethanol program, and beneath that soil are coal deposits that could support most of the synthetic-fuel production that is feasible if present environmental regulations are maintained. The scheme of producing truly synthetic fuels from coal would graft onto the state's economy a huge new but financially risky industry that would last only twenty-five years before the local coal deposits ran out. The alternative—producing ethanol from crops—would integrate the production of this fuel into the state's existing, well-established system of agriculture. Like agriculture itself, then, ethanol production would be a renewable source of solar energy; and, unlike nonrenewable fuels such as coal or oil or their synthetic products, the source of ethanol would not run out or, before then, escalate in cost. The coal-based synthetic-fuels program would be governed by the few very large industrial corporations that could cope with its inherent economic risks. The natural, ethanol program would be governed by considerably smaller, more numerous entrepreneurs—the farmers of Illinois. These are the very different realities that might emerge from Mr. Carter's as yet unrealized intention for the country to undertake "the most massive peacetime commitment of funds and resources in our nation's history to develop America's own alternative sources of fuel."

Elaine Morgan (1920–   )

from The Descent of Woman

The maternal relationship, then, seems to be offering less immediate biological reward to many women, largely because the environmental context is inimical to it.

But the opposite, surely, is true of her relations with the male. The actual performance of the sex act should be, and usually is, more pleasurable to her than it has been for her predecessors over a good many generations. She has been relieved of a good deal of the load of artificial and unnecessary shame and guilt associated with it, and the amount of attention concentrated recently on her own sensations and reactions and responses has been unprecedented. One might expect her to be overwhelmed with feelings of joyous gratitude for this. The whole relationship between men and women should by now be irradiated with a cordial new atmosphere of warmth and comradeship and mutual esteem.

In individual cases I have no doubt that this has happened. But only an optimist would maintain that the net result of recent developments has been to make men and women on the whole *like* each other any better than they did under earlier, less permissive regimes. There are plenty of signs that in many ways they have actually less liking and respect and admiration for one another than their great-grandparents had in the old days when in the words of the old cliché men were men and women were glad of it; and chastity had not been outmoded; and sex was so hedged around with taboos that, as Thurber wrote, "It got so that in speaking of birth and other natural phenomena, women seemed often to be discussing something else, such as the Sistine Madonna or the aurora borealis."

We don't want to go back there. A lot of cant has been swept away, and the areas of human experience that could not be spoken of have drastically shrunk, and this cannot be anything but a solid gain. The only advantage of the old system was that in essentials it had been in operation for a pretty long time; people were used to it and knew where they were, and what roles they had to play, and to nine people out of ten this is always a great comfort.

The roles they played were based upon a script constructed around a few basic axioms. One was that men were created dominant and would always remain so because of their superior strength and superior wisdom, and because it was the will of God. (Milton: "He for God only, she for God in him.") But in a secular and mechanical age Milton's God is out of date, muscle power seems to have less and less relevance, and even the male's superior wisdom is not the self-evident proposition that it once was.

Another axiom was the division of labor. Woman was unfit to face the harsh realities of economic life, so her place was in the kitchen and in the nursery. As long as there was no way out of this, most women adapted themselves to it very well, and took a pride in it, and the nuclear family (based from the beginning far more on division of labor than on sex) continued to cohere. Nowadays most women for some part of their lives face the harsh realities of economic life, and find them far from intolerable. They have also discovered that male dominance was not so much based on the fact that he had more muscles and more wisdom, but on the fact that as long as she stayed in the kitchen he had *all* of the money.

An even more venerable axiom going right back to the Garden of Eden was: "In sorrow shalt thou bring forth." It was one of the eternal rules that any act of sexual intercourse was likely to be (inside marriage) "blessed," or (outside it) "punished," by pregnancy. Now, new contraceptive methods, though still comparatively in their infancy, have set a light to this one. It is burning its way along a long fuse, but the evolutionary bomb at the end of it has not yet gone off.

With so many bastions of his dominant status skidding out from under him, man hung on tight to the one symbol nobody could take away from him. He still, by God, had his penis. However cool and efficient and economically independent a female might be, if he ever had any tremor of doubt that he was worth three of her, he had only to remind himself that underneath that elegant exterior was a nude female with all the usual sexual appendages. If he was driven to ask himself what the position of women ought to be, he could always—if only in his mind—come up with Stokely Carmichael's answer: "Prone." (I have never been quite clear whether Mr. Carmichael had a sexual prejudice against the "missionary position," or whether he just didn't know the difference between prone and supine, but it was obvious to everybody what he meant.)

This reaction of course is not typical of all men, or even of most men. Most well-adjusted men, especially intelligent ones, have on the whole welcomed the emancipation of women, if only because they have to spend at least part of their time in the company of women in nonsexual contexts—even the marital context is nonsexual for most of the twenty-four hours—and it is less boring to talk to women since they have acquired a few more topics of conversation.

However, I think the reaction is one factor contributing to the astonishing boom in sex and pornography. The urge isn't new; it was always there, but the recent wave of obsession with it in Western countries seems to be new, and the women's liberation complaint that females are being regarded more and more as "sexual objects" has a lot of truth in it.

Only a very small minority of women as yet are "complaining." Most of them are rejoicing. Sex is nice; being looked at and admired and talked about is very nice; and the keen competition to be the sexiest among the local sex objects is worth millions to the manufacturers of cosmetics, perfumes, eyelashes, miniskirts, hot pants, and the pill.

Reactions to all these phenomena are sharply divided. Some people see the new attitudes toward sex as a tremendous liberation of benevolent life-enhancing forces once cruelly held in chains by sour-faced puritans. It is regarded by others as a Gadarene rush away from all standards of decency and morality down a muddy slope into filth and debauchery. One side sees it as an emergence into sanity and sunshine; the other as the crumbling away of the very foundations of order and civilization.

These reactions are both slightly hysterical, and accompanied by acute manifestations of mutual aggression, fear, hatred, and moral indignation, with each side totally convinced it has a monopoly of the only really moral morality.

They hurl atrocity stories at one another. One side weeps for "the youth pined away with desire and the pale virgin shrouded in snow," couples trapped in impossible marriages, unmarried mothers pilloried by prejudice, children tortured with guilt and fear because they'd been told masturbation was deadly sin and led to epilepsy and dementia; homosexuals hounded and persecuted simply because they loved one another; Marie Stopes pelted with filth and threatened with arson.

The other side points to soaring figures of venereal diseases, abortion, and drug deaths; to shattered children of homes broken by adultery, desertion, and divorce; to schoolgirls promiscuous at eleven and pregnant at twelve; to cynical commercial exploitations of pornography and exhibitionism and perversion driving family entertainment out of cinemas and theaters.

It is very unlikely that the net effect on the total of human happiness will be as great as either side believes. Some things become easier with greater "permissiveness," others become harder. People are less likely now to be embarrassed when a man says he loves another man, which would once have been shocking: they are more likely now to be embarrassed if he says he loves his mother, which would once have been commendable. It is easier for a young girl to kiss a young man in public; but a recent inquiry revealed that in many areas she would be chary of walking about with her arms around the waist of another girl—though ladies in the novels of Jane Austen and Dickens and Tolstoy do it constantly with complete lack of inhibition—because now she has heard of lesbianism and it has taught her a new taboo.

Guilt and anxiety are not being dispersed, only attached to different situations. There is less shame attached to losing one's virginity too soon, and more attached to keeping it too long. It is less taboo to say "shit," and more taboo to say "nigger." There is less fear that you can be unbalanced by masturbation, but a new conviction that you can be unbalanced by abstention. Less obloquy attaches to sleeping with a girl without giving her a wedding ring; but to do it without giving her an orgasm is a newly patented way of lousing up your self-esteem and peace of mind.

Tolerance is not really being enlarged: it is moving its targets. The woman who cuts loose from an unpleasant husband because she cannot bear to live with him is praised where once she was condemned. But the woman who hangs on to a reluctant husband because she cannot bear to live without him is condemned where once she was praised. Anyone who succumbs to alcoholism meets with less censure and more compassion than formerly ("it's an illness, really . . . perfectly understandable, the pressures are too great . . ."), but anyone who succumbs to obesity gets short shrift ("no excuse for it these days . . . only needs a bit of will power . . . *other* people manage not to let themselves go. . . ."). The total number of moral attitudes struck, the difficulty of trying to conform to them, and the weight of social disapproval visited on those who fail vary hardly at all.

As for the obsession with sex itself, it is partly a by-product of affluence. Less and less time and attention needs to be given to the gratification of other physical needs, so this one is thrown into prominence. Even in primitive societies sexual activity is heightened at periods when the community is more than usually well stocked up, so that there is feasting and no need to go foraging for several days.

For people with boring jobs whose work only demands a small fraction of their mental capacity—and there are more of these every year—sex provides them with something interesting to think about; for people starved for love or a sense of identity it ensures that at least one person will pay them close attention for a while; for those who win the rat race it is a trophy and for those who lose it, a consolation prize.

The trouble is that sex as a pastime, when divorced from love, has one serious drawback. Like many forms of physical gratification, it is subject to a law of diminishing returns. To a hungry man any food is delicious; to a not very hungry man only delicious food is delicious; to a sated man no food is delicious. It is very frustrating for a man with the means and the opportunity to satisfy an appetite when he finds the appetite itself is failing him.

In some of its more extreme aspects the sexual revolution seems to have passed the point of campaigning for the liberation of a natural appetite, and reached the vomitorial stage of trying to reactivate an exhausted one.

Up to a point, as any biologist knows, it is possible to achieve this. When a given stimulus, on account of repeated applications, ceases to elicit a given response, it is possible to reawaken the response by increasing the stimulus. The foster parents of the cuckoo's chick work themselves to skin and bone to rear their enormous changeling and let their own go hungry, because a large gaping beak is a stronger stimulus than a small one. Many birds will show a preference for trying to hatch a larger-than-life egg; a male butterfly will get besotted over an artificial female with larger-than-life spots on her wings.

In terms of human sex this technique can be applied in various ways—cosmetic aids can supply redder lips, longer lashes, brighter hair, whiter teeth, larger breasts, or smaller waists as fashion may demand. There are, however, certain natural limits. Where the demand for increased stimulation centers on increased exposure it runs into a cul-de-sac, because you can't get nuder than nude. Once full frontal nakedness as a public spectacle has become another *déjà vu*, there is no further for it to go except into the nightmare of one cartoonist who drew a stripped striptease girl responding to the demand for more by gracefully, with an enticing smile, drawing out her entrails and displaying them to her avid audience.

Recently there have been some signs that the sex boom is running out of steam, and certainly in some areas it is encountering a vigorous backlash. Much of it has been due to a well-recognized syndrome known as "cultural shock." At least it is recognized by anthropologists, who know that primitive tribes have sometimes literally died of it. But at home many progressives, who are hotly indignant when ham-handed imperialists trample over the taboos of subject races, fail to see that their sexual iconoclasm is inflicting the same trauma on some of their fellow countrymen. This doesn't necessarily mean the process should be halted. It does mean it should be carried out non-aggressively, and the words "I believe you are shocked!" should be spoken not with derision but with concern, whether the shock was inflicted by defective electrical wiring or by a change in sexual mores.

How will all this finally affect the status of women? They will have some hard thinking to do and some careful adjustments to make if they are not to end up losers on the deal. Because what is happening is slackening of the rules. Some of them were bad rules; and I believe they will inevitably be replaced by new rules, because that is the nature of human society. Meanwhile, whenever you get a situation where the rules are temporarily suspended—as in the Wild West before the lawmen came—the effect is that the tough come to the top and the weakest go to the wall. And women, in the aggregate, are not the tougher sex.

Thus one effect is that there are rather fewer sexual problems for young men, as chastity gets outmoded; but a higher proportion of young women are faced with the still formidable crises of unsupported motherhood or abortion. Insofar as it is true that more men are content with casual sex and more women desire a permanent relationship, the males are now capturing the moral initiative; so that if a girl does want love and marriage, she can now sometimes be conned into actually feeling ashamed of wanting them, and denying with profuse apologies that she had any such unreasonable thought in her mind.

Males are capturing the hypochondriac initiative, too. In the old days it was the bride who had to be treated tenderly, with infinite tact and patience, if the relationship was to be a success. Now it is the groom whose delicate ego must be cosseted, because he has a more fragile piece of machinery there than was dreamed of in the old philosophy. To judge by the letters sent in to some male magazines, he spends half his life worrying because his ejaculations come too quickly or too infrequently or in highly specialized circumstances, just as mothers used to worry about similar aberrations in their babies' bowel movements, until Dr. Spock breezed along and posed the cosmic question: "So what?"

Despite all this there are some women's liberation types who are in the forefront of the sexual revolution and calling for more, on the grounds that marriage can be slavery, and sex is getting more democratic, or on the more general grounds that things have been so horrible up to now that they want to change everything. However, these are for the most part pretty tough babies who know they will survive even the most drastic upheavals. And even they don't find it too easy, because a sex-ridden society is always ready to resurrect the old slogan of "woman's place is on her back," and a man whose gaze is too avidly riveted on a woman's cleavage only gets irritated if he's asked to listen, really listen, to any words coming out of her mouth....

Up to a few generations ago the decline of sexual attractiveness was still not hard to take. The change of role from blushing bride to full-time mother happened in a few short busy years, and most women after the first nine or ten pregnancies would be uttering fervent prayers for the whole business to be over and done with. Even Queen Victoria, a loving wife if ever there was one, grew to feel strongly that one could have altogether too much of a good thing. There would be all the children to be absorbed in and worried about, and then the arrival of the grandchildren, and then good night.

The shape of our lives is vastly different now. The children are fewer. They need *economic* support for a longer period than ever; but the actual physical chore of supervising the average two-point-something offspring after they have reached school age is simply not enough to absorb the energies of their mother for the rest of her (greatly extended) active life. As for grandmotherhood, which used to mean a resurgence of importance in a new, pleasant and well-nigh indispensable role, it is not what it used to be, certainly in the West. In a society where sex is king and youth at a premium, a forty-two-year-old granny has mixed feelings about laying claim to the title, and with more mobile populations and the fragmentation of the extended family it is a relationship increasingly conducted at long distance via phone calls, and birthday cards, rather than in the chimney corner with fairy tales and lullabies.

The net result is that a girl who plumps joyously at sixteen for being "strictly a female female," with her eyelashes all in curl, and her sights trained on the "career" of marriage, embarks on adult life looking sexy, having fun, and with everything going for her. Anyone who approaches her then and says, "It's all very well being beautiful, but keep pegging away at your math because you may need it yet," or "What about equal pay?" is going to get a very short answer. She knows that youth's a stuff will not endure, her status is as high as a baboon's in full estrus, she's hell-bent on falling in love, and being fallen in love with, and living happily ever after. Nobody can blame her. It's the way she's been conditioned to think.

Around thirty-five or thirty-six she looks over her shopping list one week and sees, with a comic ruefulness, that it includes a couple of items like antiwrinkle cream and a new slightly more supportive foundation garment because a body stocking no longer quite fills the bill. Slowly, consciously or subconsciously, it gets borne in on her that from here on, for the strictly female female in a sex-obsessed society, the role gets tougher all the time.

This is where, in the more prosperous sections of society, all that famous neurosis begins to set in. If her husband is in the rat race she doesn't dare let up on looking sexy, because her husband's image suffers considerable damage if his wife isn't at least trying her best to be sexually attractive. It used to be okay if she was faithful and patient and competent, but now he has this thing about his virility, and the most sure-fire way of proving it is to have a woman in tow who makes the other chaps feel: "Boy, he's doing all right for himself there!" Moreover, marriage isn't as binding a bond as it used to be. If he feels she's seriously letting him down in this department, he's liable to look elsewhere for this status symbol, and possibly think about switching over in early middle age to a Mark II wife maybe ten or twelve years younger. Because the graph for a man doesn't follow the same curve. His status (sexual as well as social) depends to a much greater extent on factors that at thirty-five or forty are still on the upgrade—power, and knowhow, and money.

America is the place where these attitudes first appeared; they are not nearly as prevalent outside it. It is also the place where (no accident) women's liberation first began to make a real noise. And for most of the Western world, for good or ill, it seems to be the place the wind blows from where social changes of this kind are concerned. If they are, as they appear to be, consequences of increasing affluence and increasingly detaching the concept of sex from the concept of love, they are likely to spread.

"Matriarchy" is a word often applied to American life, but one of the best comments on this came from J. B. Priestley:

"If [American] women become aggressive, demanding, dictatorial, it is because they find themselves struggling to find satisfaction in a world that is not theirs. If they use sex as a weapon, it is because they so badly need a weapon. They are like the inhabitants of an occupied country. They are compelled to accept values and standards that are alien to their deepest nature. . . . A society in which a man takes his wife for a night out and they pay extra, out of their common stock of dollars, to see another woman undressing herself is a society in which the male has completely imposed his values." Woman "is compelled to appear not as her true self, but as the reflection of a man's immature, half-childish, half-adolescent fancies and dreams. Victorious woman forms a lasting relationship with a mature man. Defeated woman strips and teases." If these tendencies continue to spread we shall all be facing defeat.

No one can go on about a problem at the length I have been going on without raising the expectation that the last chapter will demand in ringing tones: "What then must we do to be saved?" and come up with a slick answer. Anyone who fails to do so may be accused of chickening out. I haven't got a slick answer, and I don't particularly mind being accused of chickening out. But since there are a few things I feel quite strongly we ought *not* to do, it might be a good idea to take a tentative stab at considering where we might go from here.

What we surely mustn't do is try to found a women's movement on a kind of pseudo-male bonding, alleging the whole male sex to be a ferocious leopard, and whipping up hatred against it. We mustn't do this for four good reasons.

1. In the words of Bertrand Russell: "To love is wise: to hate is foolish." Any damage it might do to the hated is nothing compared to the corrosive effect it has on the hater.

2. It is arrant nonsense to pretend that men are hateful. Not more than 2 or 3 percent of them are activated by malice against women. It's just that while things are in a state of flux they are just as confused about their role as we are about ours; most of them, if they see any advantage to be gained from the confusion, will attempt to cash in on it, and most women given the chance will do the same. It takes two to tango, and it takes two to make a woman into a sex object: at the time of going to press most women are highly flattered to be so regarded, and would be insulted if their efforts to look sexy weren't rewarded with precisely this "tribute." If some women feel

trapped by marriage, you can bet your bottom dollar that at least as many men feel trapped by it, and any woman feeling disenchanted by the status quo should pay heed to Thurber's heartfelt answer: "We're all disenchanted."

3. As a bonding mechanism it just won't work. Most women don't hallucinate that easily. You may raise the alarm and beat the drum, but when you point your finger at the enemy, most of them will say: "No, no, those aren't leopards. That's the postman, and that one is my son, and the one with the nice blue eyes is the one who was so kind to us last winter when there was all that snow." And they will be right.

4. Where a bonding mechanism doesn't work, more than half the steam that's been worked up gets diverted from the "enemy" and redirected against the "traitors." This we just can't afford. Most women have far too little self-confidence anyway, and when they start criticizing one another everything gets ten times worse. The nonworking wife gets on the defensive because she feels the working ones think she's turning into a vegetable; the working ones are on the defensive because they feel the full-time mothers think their kitchens are in a mess and their children neglected. Childless women write defensive letters to the papers, feeling they are being called selfish because they'd rather have their freedom and a new car or go on with their careers; mothers of five are on the defensive about the population problem. It is time we stopped all this nonsense.

The first of all the things women need to be liberated from is their chronic tendency to feelings (admitted, concealed, or aggressively overcompensated for) of guilt and inadequacy. A woman who feels bad because her house is in a mess is tempted to restore her self-esteem by sneering at her house-proud neighbor: but what on earth is wrong with being house-proud if that's what turns you on? Keeping a house beautiful is no more barren or "stultifying" a job than a professional gardener's keeping a garden beautiful.

Any attempt at "bonding" women into a cohort all facing one way is not only doomed to failure, but will result in undermining their self-esteem still further. . . .

Out with the hate bit, then. I admit to feeling uneasy on this account about Kate Millett's *Sexual Politics*, as well as a few other liberationist writings along the same lines. It's a highly intelligent book meticulously analyzing the pornographic fantasies incorporated in the works of some high-rating and best-selling male authors. But what is Kate Millett's book *for*? What it is saying to women seems to be something like: "This is what men really think of us. It's pretty loathsome and insulting stuff. We do right to hate them."

I doubt it. I doubt whether this kind of writing has anything to do with politics, or with anything at all in the real world. Without having met the gentleman I would hazard a bet that not even Mr. Norman Mailer actually moves around the United States committing brutal sexual attacks on casually encountered females. Surely this is dream stuff, male soap-opera, and the women in it are dolls, not people. And in their waking moments the men who write it must be aware of this truth and act on it; otherwise they would be certifiable.

Let us grant that men, or some men, have some of this stuff fuming around in the bottom of their minds. It's been left there from a very long time ago; it's a little surprising it hasn't evaporated yet. But it has no more "political" significance than Jack and the Beanstalk. It shouldn't be too hard to verify this, for some women likewise have masochistic fantasies, and doubtless they form pair bonds with "sadistic" dreamers and play bedroom games together, as dramatized by John Osborne in one of his plays. The sixty-four-thousand-dollar question is whether the "submissive" partner in these capers is necessarily any more likely on that account to give way in the cold light of dawn over the color of the new drawing-room carpet, or anything else she feels strongly about. And I suspect not. Any more than the jackbooted "governess"-type prostitute could flog an extra thousand dollars out of her kinky clients with her whip. Dream worlds have no effect on where the real power lies.

If we don't go for hate, what should we go for? Two or three objectives seem fairly clear. First, as for any other ex-subject population, greater self-respect. I remember watching Pierre Trudeau in a confrontation with a group of young females, and he addressed them as "girls." They informed him that they had recently attained their majority, and so were no longer girls. This shook him somewhat and he floundered for a minute looking for another polite euphemism for what they were. "Er—ladies?" he hazarded. "We are women," they said, as if they were proud of it. It was like the first time somebody said right out loud: "Black is beautiful."

Second, economic independence; because until every woman feels confident that she can at need support herself we will never quite eradicate the male suspicion that when we say, "I want love. I want a permanent relationship," we really mean, "I want a meal ticket. I want you to work and support me for the rest of my life." It needn't mean the end, for everybody, of the division-of-labor family. If a man wants a wife who will stay home and raise his children and finds a woman who wants to do just that, then that's fine; as long as he has paused to assure himself that it *is* what he wants and that like anything else it costs money; and as long as she has paused to ask herself the important question, "First I will raise our children—and *then what*?" Because the "then what" may last for forty years and she doesn't want it all to be anticlimax.

Third, the *certainty* of having no more children than she wants, and none at all if she doesn't want any. This is essential not only for women but for everybody, because every human being should have the inalienable right not to be born to a mother who doesn't want him. Once this is fully achieved it will be within the power of every woman to decide whether or not she wishes to have a child.

"Take what you want," said God in the old proverb, "and pay for it." If she wants this, one way or another she's got to pay for it, and it doesn't come cheap. She may do it by devoting a few years of her life to rearing it. She may do it by settling for at least a period of economic dependence (probably on a husband) while she's doing it. If she's very fiercely independent she may do it by settling for a period of comparative economic penury while she's doing it.

She may wish to have the child and get someone else to do most of the rearing, and this is fine if she's lucky enough to have sufficient capital or earning power or a rich enough husband. She has the right to shout and complain and move heaven and earth to try to get some public recognition that the job she's doing is important to society, and money should be expended on enabling her to do it better and more efficiently; and to combine with other women to set up play groups or anything else that will make things easier until such time as heaven and earth begin to listen to her. She has the right and duty to select a husband who also wants children, if she wants them herself; and to urge him to help her as far as he is able and willing.

What she will no longer have any right to do, once "accident" is altogether ruled out and every child is the result of conscious choice, is to give birth to it and then shortly afterward start raising the cry of "Will no one for Pete's sake come and take this kid off my back?" If we campaign for more efficient and foolproof contraception and free abortion on demand (as I believe we must), then we must face the moral consequence of this, which is that motherhood will be an option, not an imperative; that anyone who thinks the price too high needn't take up the option; and from that point on, where children are concerned, more inexorably than ever before, the buck stops here. On the distaff side. If we try to dodge that, we lose all credibility.

What about marriage? The more way-out liberationists seem to be hell-bent on destroying the institution. I can't quite see why there has to be a "policy" about this. When we're just getting loose of one lot of people laying down the law that we *must* get married, it's a bit rough to run head on into another lot telling us we mustn't. It is surely, as Oscar Wilde ruled about the tallness of aunts, a matter that a girl may be allowed to decide for herself.

Anyway, marriage is going to be with us for a long time yet. As Shulamith Firestone mourned: "Everybody debunks marriage, but everybody ends up married." And one of the most durable statements ever made about it was Dr. Johnson's: "Marriage is not commonly unhappy otherwise than as life is unhappy." It can sometimes be tough for two people of opposite sexes trying to live permanently at close quarters without driving each other up the wall. But it can be equally tough trying to do it with someone of the same sex, or with a child, or a parent, or a sibling, or a colleague; or with a succession of different partners; or with a commune (for the rate of failed communes is at least as high as the rate of failed marriages). And it can be toughest of all trying to live in an empty house or apartment quite alone.

Nor is there much fear that men, once sex is more freely available, will seriously seek to escape the "trap" of matrimony. Even on the physical level, there's nothing quite like having it on tap at home, without having to go out in all winds and weathers to chase after it. Besides, though they seldom admit it, their psychological need of a stable relationship is as great as ours, or greater. After studies carried out at the Mental Research Institute in Berkeley, California, a research group reported: "In accordance with the popular idea of marriage as a triumph for women and a defeat for men . . . we could expect to find those men who escaped marriage to be much better adjusted than those women who failed to marry. . . . The findings suggest the opposite. More single men are maladjusted than single women [as shown] particularly in indices of unhappiness, of severe neurotic tendencies and of antisocial tendencies."

So marriage (or something less legalistic but the same in essence) will certainly endure until the people who say it's a miserable institution can come up with a convincing answer to the question, "Compared to what?" I haven't been convinced by any of the answers yet.

But can marriage (or even sex) survive, once women have achieved equality and independence? The cichlid school of thought affects to have grave doubts about this. The cichlid is the fish that the "psychological castration" boys go on about. It appears that a female cichlid is incapable of mating with a male one unless he is aggressive, belligerent, and masterful; and a male cichlid is rendered impotent by a female who fails to put on a display of timorousness and subservience. Therefore, it is subtly implied, if women ever attain equality, then we will find to our horror that men are no longer men, and we will all heartily wish that we hadn't been so hasty.

What we are less often reminded of is that human beings are not fish, but mammals; that psychological castration is quite a common feature in many mammal societies also, but that in these cases the mechanism is totally different. In the vast majority of mammal species the only creature who can psychologically castrate a male mammal is *another* male mammal; and he does it quite simply by beating him in fair combat. This pattern is exemplified over and over again in studies of primate behavior, but the most classic and frequently quoted illustration of the process comes from cattle. There was this bull who was growing older and no longer able to service all the cows in the herd, so they brought in a couple of younger bulls to help him with the chore. He challenged them; he fought them; he defeated them. And not only were the defeated bulls psychologically castrated, but the victorious one had attained such an access of virility that he returned to his harem, serviced all his remaining wives, and snorted around for the rest of the season like Alexander looking for new worlds to conquer. Any man who insists on playing the cichlid game and complaining he's castrated because the little woman isn't being submissive enough shouldn't be surprised if she asks him what's going on at the office lately.

For the real answer to this we needn't go to the animal kingdom at all. In Soviet Russia, women have had economic equality for a long time now. Seventy-five percent of their doctors and teachers are women, and 58 percent of their technicians and a third of their engineers, and 63 percent of their economists, and nearly half their scientists and their lawyers, and all the women in all the jobs get equal pay. And while I have heard a lot of criticisms leveled in the West against the average Russian communist, I don't remember hearing anyone call him a sissy.

For a final speculative look into the future I would like to link together one of the earliest and one of the latest items in this history—Darwin, and the pill.

People have talked a good deal about the possible effects of the pill on society, and sexual relations, and the birth rate, and so on. There has been surprisingly little discussion about its possible genetic effects, and what there has been has been conducted mostly in 1984 terms, about the possibility of the state stepping in and stipulating which men and women should be allowed to breed and what type of citizen it wants to produce.

It is very unlikely to happen that way. Reproduction will continue to take place, as it has taken place since the days of the dinosaur and earlier, as a result of processes of natural selection. Only the pill will have thrown two monumental wrenches into the works. One thing it will mean is that the evolutionary effects of natural selection may in some directions be immeasurably speeded up. The other thing is that slightly different types of human beings will be "selected" as parents of the next generation.

Suppose that there is some genetic predisposition in certain women to be more favorably disposed than others to undertake the task of child-rearing. Such a predisposition has been treated in a previous chapter as a class and therefore a cultural difference, which to a great extent it probably is. But almost certainly there are also genetic factors involved. For instance, certain strains of poultry are more "maternally" inclined than others, and this tendency can be greatly increased by selective breeding. A farmer who has invested in an incubator, and doesn't want his hens to stop laying eggs in order to sit on a clutch of them, can breed out the "broodies" until he has eliminated this behavior pattern entirely. He could also do the opposite, if it were in his economic interest to do so.

Back in the jungle or the sea or the savannah, a woman who was deficient in maternal promptings would be less likely than the average to perpetuate her line. She would continue to produce infants but would have less interest in them, less patience with them, and tend to neglect them. More of them would die, and the ones who survived would be unlikely to become dominant and prolific, though some might be taken under the wing of other females and thrive. The mechanism would be weighted appreciably against this nonmaternal factor. It would not entirely die out, but its incidence would not increase.

In civilized society up to the last century the picture was different. Women who didn't want or like children continued to produce them quite prolifically because they fell in love, or because they wanted a home and security and marital status, and the children arrived as part of the package deal. The danger that they would actually die of neglect and starvation as a direct result of maternal indifference was less, and in the more prosperous sections of society where one woman produced the child and another woman reared it, it was nil. It was perfectly possible for a woman totally deficient in maternal promptings to produce a large, highly prosperous, and dominant line of progeny. Her kind would multiply, especially in the upper classes, and there is some reason to believe that it did: as with the poultry, the "broodies" were increasingly bred out.

But if we arrive at a situation where a woman can have sex and security without having children, where children are a handicap to her in pursuing the objectives more important to her, where nannies are a rare and terribly expensive luxury, and where demographers are plugging childlessness as a benefaction to humanity, such a woman is increasingly likely to have very few children or none. She will select herself out. It will not be a painfully slow and gradual business, as evolutionary processes have hitherto been, powered only by the fact that certain genetic factors make their inheritors marginally more or marginally less likely to survive. It could come down like a guillotine. If we lost the tradition that there is some "status" involved in being a mother—it is a tradition beginning to falter and has recently for the first time ever been coming under direct fire—then the only women to have children would be the ones who cordially wanted them. The others would wipe themselves out in a generation.

It may well be that one hundred and fifty years hence people will read with astonishment of our fears that the net effect of the pill would be to defeminize women. Their own females will all be descendants of grandmothers and great-grandmothers so fizzing with estrogen that a baby meant more to them than almost any other objective in life.

Any selective effect on the males would be far less instantaneous. The impetuous sexy Don Juan character who once careered around stamping his image over large areas of the countryside cannot do so from now on. He may still career, and his animal magnetism may prove as irresistible, but his likeness will not appear in the cradles for very much longer. Whether his type will die out depends on whether there is a hereditary element in his behavior, or whether it is purely a psychological aberration, and we cannot be quite sure about this.

In the past husbands have been selected for a variety of reasons. Physical attractiveness is one, and fairly adaptive since it presupposes at least a degree of health and fitness. Being

"They have this arrangement. He earns the money and she takes care of the house."

a "good provider" is another, also adaptive since it implies at least a degree of competence. In the aristocracy "breeding" has weighed heavily—genetically the worst bet of the lot since a noble name correlates neither with physical nor with mental viability. But the net genetic effect of all this in civilized society has been minimal, since unlike the gorilla and the baboon we have monogamy, and the prerogative of the "breeding male" is unknown. Fatherhood is not limited to the handsome, the intelligent, the noble, or the dominant, as long as nearly everybody in the end gets married and children "appear" as a consequence.

In future this may be slightly less true. The truly "proletarian" family (literally those for whom their children constitute their only wealth and for the female her only status) is on the way out, and the woman with the "lady's" attitude (that there are many other and easier ways of getting rewards out of life) is becoming the norm. In places where equality between the sexes has gone furthest, as for instance Moscow, the birth rate is going down fairly rapidly, not because of ecological exhortation by the state—the authorities are getting no joy out of the trend—but because more women have more options to choose from, and they make their own decisions on the matter.

Another tendency beginning to show itself in Russia and Scandinavia and other places is for girls of independent outlook to decide to have the baby without the husband. They obviously feel that the latter is a more bothersome thing to get saddled with than the former.

If both of these trends continue, then the process of husband-selecting might for the first time begin to have some genetic significance. The woman who decides to have a baby without a husband is making a cool and conscious choice anyway, and presumably doesn't select its father without thinking: "I should be well content if my child turned out to resemble him." And if, say, 15 percent of women decided in this way against marriage, the remaining 85 percent would have a wider choice and could afford to be more discriminating. Children are less likely to be the result of a woman's being "swept off her feet" by an excess of passion. She can afford to get swept off her feet with joyous abandon for a year or so and still wait, before cementing the bond with a couple of children, to see whether the partnership looks like settling down comfortably for a long run; and the qualifications for this are somewhat different. It calls for less of sexiness on the male's part and more of loving-kindness. Men who possess most of this quality will be the likeliest to perpetuate their kind and help to form their children's minds.

What it adds up to is that, with the advent of the pill, woman is beginning to get her finger on the genetic trigger. What she will do with it we cannot quite foresee. But it is a far cry from the bull who gets to be prolific just because he's tops at beating the daylights out of all the other bulls.

It may be that for Homo sapiens in the future, extreme manifestations of the behavior patterns of dominance and aggression will be evolutionarily at a discount; and if that happens he will begin to shed them as once, long ago, he shed his coat of fur.

He may feel a little odd for the first few millennia because he is less accustomed to living without them than we are; but he has passed through more violent vicissitudes than this and survived. He is the most miraculous of all the creatures God ever made or the earth ever spawned. All we need to do is hold out loving arms to him and say:

"Come on in. The water's lovely."

Robert M. Pirsig (1928–   )

from Zen and the Art of Motorcycle Maintenance: An Inquiry into Values

. . . Today now I want to take up the first phase of his journey into Quality, the nonmetaphysical phase, and this will be pleasant. It's nice to start journeys pleasantly, even when you know they won't end that way. Using his class notes as reference material I want to reconstruct the way in which Quality became a working concept for him in the teaching of rhetoric. His second phase, the metaphysical one, was tenuous and speculative, but this first phase, in which he simply taught rhetoric, was by all accounts solid and pragmatic and probably deserves to be judged on its own merits, independently of the second phase.

He'd been innovating extensively. He'd been having trouble with students who had nothing to say. At first he thought it was laziness but later it became apparent that it wasn't. They just couldn't think of anything to say.

One of them, a girl with strong-lensed glasses, wanted to write a five-hundred-word essay about the United States. He was used to the sinking feeling that comes from statements like this, and suggested without disparagement that she narrow it down to just Bozeman.

When the paper came due she didn't have it and was quite upset. She had tried and tried but she just couldn't think of anything to say.

He had already discussed her with her previous instructors and they'd confirmed his impressions of her. She was very serious, disciplined and hardworking, but extremely dull. Not a spark of creativity in her anywhere. Her eyes, behind the thick-lensed glasses, were the eyes of a drudge. She wasn't bluffing him, she really couldn't think of anything to say, and was upset by her inability to do as she was told.

It just stumped him. Now *he* couldn't think of anything to say. A silence occurred, and then a peculiar answer: "Narrow it down to the *main street* of Bozeman." It was a stroke of insight.

She nodded dutifully and went out. But just before her next class she came back in *real* distress, tears this time, distress that had obviously been there for a long time. She still couldn't think of anything to say, and couldn't understand why, if she couldn't think of anything about *all* of Bozeman, she should be able to think of something about just one street.

He was furious. "You're not *looking*!" he said. A memory came back of his own dismissal from the University for having *too much* to say. For every fact there is an *infinity* of hypotheses. The more you *look* the more you *see*. She really wasn't looking and yet somehow didn't understand this.

He told her angrily, "Narrow it down to the *front* of *one* building on the main street of Bozeman. The Opera House. Start with the upper left-hand brick."

Her eyes, behind the thick-lensed glasses, opened wide.

She came in the next class with a puzzled look and handed him a five-thousand-word essay on the front of the Opera House on the main street of Bozeman, Montana. "I sat in the hamburger stand across the street," she said, "and started writing about the first brick, and the second brick, and then by the third brick it all started to come and I couldn't stop. They thought I was crazy, and they kept kidding me, but here it all is. I don't understand it."

Neither did he, but on long walks

through the streets of town he thought about it and concluded she was evidently stopped with the same kind of blockage that had paralyzed him on his first day of teaching. She was blocked because she was trying to repeat, in her writing, things she had already heard, just as on the first day he had tried to repeat things he had already decided to say. She couldn't recall anything she had heard worth repeating. She was strangely unaware that she could look and see freshly for herself, as she wrote, without primary regard for what had been said before. The narrowing down to one brick destroyed the blockage because it was so obvious she *had* to do some original and direct seeing.

He experimented further. In one class he had everyone write all hour about the back of his thumb. Everyone gave him funny looks at the beginning of the hour, but everyone did it, and there wasn't a single complaint about "nothing to say."

In another class he changed the subject from the thumb to a coin, and got a full hour's writing from every student. In other classes it was the same. Some asked, "Do you have to write about both sides?" Once they got into the idea of seeing directly for themselves they also saw there was no limit to the amount they could say. It was a confidence-building assignment too, because what they wrote, even though seemingly trivial, was nevertheless their own thing, not a mimicking of someone else's. Classes where he used that coin exercise were always less balky and more interested.

As a result of his experiments he concluded that imitation was a real evil that had to be broken before real rhetoric teaching could begin. This imitation seemed to be an external compulsion. Little children didn't have it. It seemed to come later on, possibly as a result of school itself.

That sounded right, and the more he thought about it the more right it sounded. Schools teach you to imitate. If you don't imitate what the teacher wants you get a bad grade. Here, in college, it was more sophisticated, of course; you were supposed to imitate the teacher in such a way as to convince the teacher you were not imitating, but taking the essence of the instruction and going ahead with it on your own. That got you A's. Originality on the other hand could get you anything—from A to F. The whole grading system cautioned against it.

He discussed this with a professor of psychology who lived next door to him, an extremely imaginative teacher, who said, "Right. Eliminate the whole degree-and-grading system and then you'll get real education."

Phaedrus thought about this, and when weeks later a very bright student couldn't think of a subject for a term paper, it was still on his mind, so he gave it to her as a topic. She didn't like the topic at first, but agreed to take it anyway.

Within a week she was telling about it to everyone, and within two weeks had worked up a superb paper. The class she delivered it to didn't have the advantage of two weeks to think about the subject, however, and was quite hostile to the whole idea of eliminating grades and degrees. This didn't slow her down at all. Her tone took on an old-time religious fervor. She begged the other students to *listen*, to understand this was really *right*. "I'm not saying this for *him*," she said and glanced at Phaedrus. "It's for *you*."

Her pleading tone, her religious fervor, greatly impressed him, along with the fact that her college entrance examinations had placed her in the upper one percent of the class. During the next quarter, when teaching "persuasive writing," he chose this topic as a "demonstrator," a piece of persuasive writing he worked up by himself, day by day, in front of and with the help of the class.

He used the demonstrator to avoid talking in terms of principles of composition, all of which he had deep doubts about. He felt that by exposing classes to his own sentences as he made them, with all the misgivings and hang-ups and erasures, he would give a more honest picture of what writing was like than by spending class time picking nits in completed student work or holding up the completed work of masters for emulation. This time he developed the argument that the whole grading system and degree should be eliminated, and to make it something that truly involved the students in what they were hearing, he withheld all grades during the quarter. . . .

Phaedrus' argument for the abolition of the degree-and-grading system produced a nonplussed or negative reaction in all but a few students at first, since it seemed, on first judgment, to destroy the whole University system. One student laid it wide open when she said with complete candor, "Of course you can't eliminate the degree and grading system. After all, that's what we're here for."

She spoke the complete truth. The idea that the majority of students attend a university for an education independent of the degree and grades is a little hypocrisy everyone is happier not to expose. Occasionally some students do arrive for an education but rote and the mechanical nature of the institution soon converts them to a less idealistic attitude.

The demonstrator was an argument that elimination of grades and degrees would destroy this hypocrisy. Rather than deal with generalities it dealt with the specific career of an imaginary student who more or less typified what was found in the classroom, a student completely conditioned to work for a grade rather than for the knowledge the grade was supposed to represent.

Such a student, the demonstrator hypothesized, would go to his first class, get his first assignment and probably do it out of habit. He might go to his second and third as well. But eventually the novelty of the course would wear off and, because his academic life was not his only life, the pressure of other obligations or desires would create circumstances where he just would not be able to get an assignment in.

Since there was no degree or grading system he would incur no penalty for this. Subsequent lectures which presumed he'd completed the assignment might be a little more difficult to understand, however, and this difficulty, in turn, might weaken his interest to a point where the next assignment, which he would find quite hard, would also be dropped. Again no penalty.

In time his weaker and weaker understanding of what the lectures were about would make it more and more difficult for him to pay attention in class. Eventually he would see he wasn't learning much; and facing the continual pressure of outside obligations, he would stop studying, feel guilty about this and stop attending class. Again, no penalty would be attached.

But what had happened? The student, with no hard feelings on anybody's part, would have flunked himself out. Good! This is what should have happened. He wasn't there for a real education in the first place and had no real business there at all. A large amount of money and effort had been saved and there would be no stigma of failure and ruin to haunt him the rest of his life. No bridges had been burned.

The student's biggest problem was a slave mentality which had been built into him by years of carrot-and-whip grading, a mule mentality which said, "If you don't whip me, I won't work." He didn't get whipped. He didn't work. And the cart of civilization, which he supposedly was being trained to pull, was just going to have to creak along a little slower without him.

This is a tragedy, however, only if you presume that the cart of civilization, "the system," is pulled by mules. This is a common, vocational, "location" point of view, but it's not the Church attitude.

The Church attitude is that civilization, or "the system" or "society" or whatever you want to call it, is best served not by mules but by free men. The purpose of abolishing grades and degrees is not to punish mules or to get rid of them but to provide an environment in which that mule can turn into a free man.

The hypothetical student, still a mule, would drift around for a while. He would get another kind of education quite as valuable as the one he'd abandoned, in what used to be called the "school of hard knocks." Instead of wasting money and time as a high-status mule, he would now have to get a job as a low-status mule, maybe as a mechanic. Actually his *real* status would go up. He would be making a contribution for a change. Maybe that's what he would do for the rest of his life. Maybe he'd found his level. But don't count on it.

In time—six months; five years, perhaps—a change could easily begin to take place. He would become less and less satisfied with a kind of dumb, day-to-day shopwork. His creative intelligence, stifled by too much theory and too many grades in college, would now become reawakened by the boredom of the shop. Thousands of hours of frustrating mechanical problems would have made him more interested in machine design. He would like to design machinery himself. He'd think he could do a better job. He would try modifying a few engines, meet with success, look for more success, but feel blocked because he didn't have the theoretical information. He would discover that when before he felt stupid because of his lack of interest in theoretical information, he'd now find a brand of theoretical information which he'd have a lot of respect for, namely, mechanical engineering.

So he would come back to our degreeless and gradeless school, but with a difference. He'd no longer be a grade-motivated person. He'd be a knowledge-motivated person. He would need no external pushing to learn. His push would come from inside. He'd be a free man. He wouldn't need a lot of discipline to shape him up. In fact, if the instructors assigned him were slacking on the job he would be likely to shape *them* up by asking rude questions. He'd be there to learn something, would be paying to learn something and they'd better come up with it.

Motivation of this sort, once it catches hold, is a ferocious force, and in the gradeless, degreeless institution where our student would find himself, he wouldn't stop with rote engineering information. Physics and mathematics were going to come within his sphere of interest because he'd see he needed them. Metallurgy and electrical engineering would come up for attention. And, in the process of intellectual maturing that these abstract studies gave him, he would be likely to branch out into other theoretical areas that weren't directly related to machines but had become a part of a newer larger goal. This larger goal wouldn't be the imitation of education in Universities today, glossed over and concealed by grades and degrees that give the appearance of something happening when, in fact, almost nothing is going on. It would be the real thing.

Such was Phaedrus' demonstrator, his unpopular argument, and he worked on it all quarter long, building it up and modifying it, arguing for it, defending it. All quarter long papers would go back to the students with comments but no grades, although the grades were entered in a book.

As I said before, at first almost everyone was sort of nonplussed. The majority probably figured they were stuck with some idealist who thought removal of grades would make them happier and thus work harder, when it was obvious that without grades everyone would just loaf. Many of the students with A records in previous quarters were contemptuous and angry at first, but because of their acquired self-discipline went ahead and did the work anyway. The B students and high-C students missed some of the early assignments or turned in sloppy work. Many of the low-C and D students didn't even show up for class. At this time another teacher asked him what he was going to do about this lack of response.

"Outwait them," he said.

His lack of harshness puzzled the students at first, then made them suspicious. Some began to ask sarcastic questions. These received soft answers and the lectures and speeches proceeded as usual, except with no grades.

Then a hoped-for phenomenon began. During the third or fourth week some of the A students began to get nervous and started to turn in superb work and hang around after class with questions that fished for some indication as to how they were doing. The B and high-C students began to notice this and work a little and bring up the quality of their papers to a more usual level. The low C, D, and future F's began to show up for class just to see what was going on.

After midquarter an even more hoped-for phenomenon took place. The A-rated students lost their nervousness and became active participants in everything that went on with a friendliness that was uncommon in a grade-getting class. At this point the B and C students were in a panic, and turned in stuff that looked as though they'd spent hours of painstaking work on it. The D's and F's turned in satisfactory assignments.

In the final weeks of the quarter, a time when normally everyone knows what his grade will be and just sits back half asleep, Phaedrus was getting a kind of class participation that made other teachers take notice. The B's and C's had joined the A's in friendly free-for-all discussion that made the class seem like a successful party. Only the D's and F's sat frozen in their chairs, in a complete internal panic.

The phenomenon of relaxation and friendliness was explained later by a couple of students who told him, "A lot of us got together outside of class to try to figure out how to beat this system. Everyone decided the best way was just to figure you were going to fail and then go ahead and do what you could anyway. Then you start to relax. Otherwise you go out of your mind!"

The students added that once you got used to it it wasn't so bad, you were more interested in the subject matter, but repeated that it wasn't easy to get used to.

At the end of the quarter the students were asked to write an essay evaluating the system. None of them knew at the time of writing what his or her grade would be. Fifty-four percent opposed it. Thirty-seven percent favored it. Nine percent were neutral.

On the basis of one man, one vote, the system was very unpopular. The majority of students definitely wanted their grades as they went along. But when Phaedrus broke down the returns according to the grades that were in his book—and the grades were not out of line with grades predicted by previous classes and entrance evaluations—another story was told. The A students were 2 to 1 in favor of the system. The B and C students were evenly divided. And the D's and F's were *unanimously* opposed!

This surprising result supported a hunch he had had for a long time: that the brighter, more serious students were the *least* desirous of grades, possibly because they were more interested in the subject matter of the course, whereas the dull or lazy students were the *most* desirous of grades, possibly because grades told them if they were getting by. . . .

Phaedrus thought withholding grades was good, according to his notes, but he didn't give it scientific value. In a true experiment you keep constant every cause you can think of except one, and then see what the effects are of varying that one cause. In the classroom you can never do this. Student knowledge, student attitude, teacher attitude, all change from all kinds of causes which are uncontrollable and mostly unknowable. Also, the observer in this case is himself one of the causes and can never judge his effects without altering his effects. So he didn't attempt to draw any hard conclusions from all this, he just went ahead and did what he liked.

The movement from this to his enquiry into Quality took place because of a sinister aspect of grading that the withholding of grades exposed. Grades really cover up failure to teach. A bad instructor can go through an entire quarter leaving absolutely nothing memorable in the minds of his class, curve out the scores of an irrelevant test, and leave the impression that some have learned and some have not. But if the grades are removed the class is forced to wonder each day what it's *really* learning. The questions, What's being taught? What's the goal? How do the lectures and assignments accomplish the goal? become ominous. The removal of grades exposes a huge and frightening vacuum.

What was Phaedrus trying to do, anyway? This question became more and more imperative as he went on. The answer that had seemed right when he started now made less and less sense. He had wanted his students to become creative by deciding for themselves what was good writing instead of asking him all the time. The real purpose of withholding the grades was to force them to look within themselves, the only place they would ever get a really right answer.

But now this made no sense. If they already knew what was good and bad, there was no reason for them to take the course in the first place. The fact that they were there as students presumed they did *not* know what was good or bad. That was his job as instructor—to tell them what was good or bad. The whole idea of individual creativity and expression in the classroom was really basically opposed to the whole idea of the University.

For many of the students, this withholding created a Kafkaesque situation in which they saw they were to be punished for failure to do something but no one would tell them what they were supposed to do. They looked within themselves and saw nothing and looked at Phaedrus and saw nothing and just sat there helpless, not knowing what to do. The vacuum was deadly. One girl suffered a nervous breakdown. You cannot withhold grades and sit there and create a goalless vacuum. You have to provide some goal for a class to work toward that will fill that vacuum. This he wasn't doing.

He couldn't. He could think of no possible way he could tell them what they should work toward without falling back into the trap of authoritarian, didactic teaching. But how can you put on the blackboard the mysterious internal goal of each creative person?

The next quarter he dropped the whole idea and went back to regular grading, discouraged, confused, feeling he was right but somehow it had come out all wrong. When spontaneity and individuality and really good original stuff occurred in a classroom it was in spite of the instruction, not because of it. This seemed to make sense. He was ready to resign. Teaching dull conformity to hateful students wasn't what he wanted to do.

He'd heard that Reed College in Oregon withheld grades until graduation, and during the summer vacation he went there but was told the faculty was divided on the value of withholding grades and that no one was tremendously happy about the system. During the rest of the summer his mood became depressed and lazy. He and his wife camped a lot in those mountains. She asked why he was so silent all the time but he couldn't say why. He was just stopped. Waiting. For that missing seed crystal of thought that would suddenly solidify everything.

Tom Wolfe (1931–   )

The Me Decade and the Third Great Awakening

1. ME AND MY HEMORRHOIDS

The trainer said, "Take your finger off the repress button." Everybody was supposed to let go, let all the vile stuff come up and gush out. They even provided vomit bags, like the ones on a 747, in case you literally let it *gush out*! Then the trainer told everybody to think of "the one thing you would most like to eliminate from your life." And so what does our girl blurt over the microphone?

"Hemorrhoids!"

Just so!

That was how she ended up in her present state . . . stretched out on the wall-to-wall carpet of a banquet hall in the Ambassador Hotel in Los Angeles with her eyes closed and her face pressed into the stubble of the carpet, which is a thick commercial weave and feels like clothesbrush bristles against her face and smells a bit *high* from cleaning solvent. That was how she ended up lying here concentrating on her hemorrhoids.

Eyes shut! deep in her own space! her hemorrhoids! the grisly peanut—

Many others are stretched out on the carpet all around her; some 249 other souls, in fact. They're all strewn across the floor of the banquet hall with their eyes closed, just as she is. But, Christ, the others are concentrating on things that sound serious and deep when you talk about them. And how they had talked about them! They had all marched right up to the microphone and "shared," as the trainer called it. What did they want to eliminate from their lives? Why, they took their fingers right off the old repress button and told the whole room. My husband! my wife! my homosexuality! my inability to communicate, my self-hatred, self-destructiveness, craven fears, puling weaknesses, primordial horrors, premature ejaculation, impotence, frigidity, rigidity, subservience, laziness, alcoholism, major vices, minor vices, grim habits, twisted psyches, tortured souls—and then it had been her turn, and she had said, "Hemorrhoids."

You can imagine what that sounded like. That broke the place up. The trainer looked like a cocky little bastard up there on the podium, with his deep tan, white tennis shirt, and peach-colored sweater, a dynamic color combination, all very casual and spontaneous—after about two hours of trying on different outfits in front of a mirror, *that* kind of casual and spontaneous, if her guess was right. And yet she found him attractive. *Commanding* was the word. He probably wondered if she was playing the wiseacre, with her "hemorrhoids," but he rolled with it. Maybe she *was* being playful. Just looking at him made her feel mischievous. In any event, *hemorrhoids* was what had bubbled up into her brain.

Then the trainer had told them to stack their folding chairs in the back of the banquet hall and lie down on the floor and close their eyes and get deep into their own spaces and concentrate on that one item they wanted to get rid of most—and really feel it and let the feeling gush out.

So now she's lying here concentrating on her hemorrhoids. The strange thing is . . . it's no joke after all! She begins to feel her hemorrhoids in all their morbid presence. She can actually *feel* them. The sieges always began with her having the sensation that a peanut was caught in her anal sphincter. That meant a section of swollen varicose vein had pushed its way out of her intestines and was actually coming out of her bottom. It was as hard as a peanut and felt bigger and grislier than a peanut. Well —for God's sake!—in her daily life, even at work, *especially* at work, and she works for a movie distributor, her whole picture of herself was of her . . . *seductive physical presence.* She was not the most successful businesswoman in Los Angeles, but she was certainly successful enough, and quite in addition to that, she was . . . *the main sexual presence in the office.* When she walked into the office each morning, everyone, women as well as men, checked her out. She *knew* that. She could feel her sexual presence go through the place like an invisible chemical, like a hormone, a scent, a universal solvent.

The most beautiful moments came when she was in her office or in a conference room or at Mr. Chow's taking a meeting—nobody "had" meetings any more, they "took" them—with two or three men, men she had never met before or barely knew. The overt subject was, inevitably, eternally, "the deal." She always said there should be only one credit line up on the screen for any movie: "Deal by . . ." But the meeting would also have a subplot. The overt plot would be "The Deal." The subplot would be "The Men Get Turned On by Me." Pretty soon, even though the conversation had not strayed overtly from "the deal," the men would be swaying in unison like dune grass at the beach. And she was the wind, of course. And then one of the men would say something and smile and at the same time reach over and touch her . . . on top of the hand or on the side of the arm . . . as if it meant nothing . . . as if it were just a gesture for emphasis . . . *but, in fact, a man is usually deathly afraid of reaching out and touching a woman he doesn't know* . . . and she knew it meant she had hypnotized him sexually . . .

Well—for God's sake!—at just that sublime moment, likely as not, the goddamn peanut would be popping out of her tail! As she smiled sublimely at her conquest, she also had to sit in her chair lopsided, with one cheek of her buttocks higher than the other, as if she were about to crepitate, because it hurt to sit squarely on the peanut. If for any reason she had to stand up at the point and walk, she would have to walk as if her hip joints were rusted out, as if she were sixty-five years old, because a normal stride pressed the peanut, and the pain would start up, and the bleeding, too, very likely. Or if she couldn't get up and had to sit there for a while and keep her smile and her hot hormonal squinted eyes pinned on the men before her, the peanut would start itching or burning, and she would start double-tracking, as if her mind were a tape deck with two channels going at once. In one she's the sexual princess, the Circe, taking a meeting and clouding men's minds . . . and in the other she's a poor bitch who wants nothing more in this world than to go down the corridor to the ladies' room and get some Kleenex and some Vaseline and push the peanut back up into her intestines with her finger.

And even if she's able to get away and do that, she will spend the rest of that day and the next, and the next, with a *deep worry* in the back of her brain, the sort of worry that always stays on the edge of your consciousness, no matter how hard you think of something else. She will be wondering at all times what the next bowel movement will be like, how solid and compact the bolus will be, trying to think back and remember if she's had any milk, cream, chocolate, or any other binding substance in the last twenty-four hours, or any nuts or fibrous vegetables like broccoli. Is she really *in for it* this time—

The Sexual Princess! On the outside she has on her fireproof grin and her Fiorio scarf, as if to say she lives in a world of Sevilles and 450SL's and dinner last night at Dominick's, a movie business restaurant on Beverly Boulevard that's so exclusive, Dominick keeps his neon sign (*Dominick's*) turned off at night to make the wimps think it's closed, but *she* (Hi, Dominick!) can get a table—while inside her it's all the battle between the bolus and the peanut—

—and is it too late to leave the office and go get some mineral oil and let some of that vile glop roll down her gullet or get a refill on the softener tablets or eat some prunes or drink some coffee or do something else to avoid one of those horrible hard-clay boluses that will come grinding out of her, crushing the peanut and starting not only the bleeding but . . . *the pain!* . . . a horrible humiliating pain that feels like she's getting a paper cut in her anus, like the pain you feel when the edge of a piece of bond paper slices your finger, plus a horrible purple bloody varicose pressure, but lasting not for an instant, like a paper cut, but for an eternity, prolonged until the tears are rolling down her face as she sits in the cubicle, and she wants to cry out, to scream until it's over, to make the screams of fear, fury, and humiliation obliterate the pain. But someone would hear! No doubt they'd come bursting right into the ladies' room to save her! and feed and water their morbid curiosities! And what could she possibly say? And so she had simply held that feeling in all these years, with her eyes on fire and her entire pelvic saddle a great purple tub of pain. She had repressed the whole squalid horror of it—*the searing peanuts*—until now. The trainer had said, "Take your finger off the repress button!" Let it gush up and pour out!

And now, as she lies here on the floor of the banquet hall of the Ambassador Hotel with 249 other souls, she knows exactly what he meant. She can feel it *all*, all of the pain, and on top of the pain all the humiliation, and for the first time in her life she has permission from the Management, from herself and everyone around her, to let the feeling gush forth. So she starts moaning.

"Oooooooooooooooooooooooohhhhhhhhhhhhhhhhhh!" . . .

—which is not simply *her* scream any longer . . . but the world's! Each soul is concentrated on its own burning item—my husband! my wife! my homosexuality! my inability to communicate, my self-hatred, self-destruction, craven fears, puling weaknesses, primordial horrors, premature ejaculation, impotence, frigidity, rigidity, subservience, laziness, alcoholism, major vices, minor vices, grim habits, twisted psyches, tortured souls—and yet each unique item has been raised to a cosmic level and united with every other until there is but one piercing moment of release and liberation at last!—a whole world of anguish set free by—

My hemorrhoids.

"Me and My Hemorrhoids Star at the Ambassador" . . . during a three-day Erhard Seminars Training (est) course in the banquet hall. The truly odd part, however, is yet to come. In her experience lies the explanation of certain grand puzzles of the 1970's, a period that will come to be known as the Me Decade.

2. THE HOLY ROLL

In 1972 a farsighted caricaturist did this drawing of Teddy Kennedy, entitled "President Kennedy campaigning for reelection in 1980 . . . courting the so-called Awakened vote." The picture shows Kennedy ostentatiously wearing not only a crucifix but also (if one looks just above the cross) a pendant of the Bleeding Heart of Jesus. The crucifix is the symbol of Christianity in general, but the Bleeding Heart is the symbol of some of Christianity's most ecstatic, non-rational, holy-rolling cults. I should point out that the artist's prediction lacked certain refinements. For one thing, Kennedy may be campaigning to be President in 1980, but he is not terribly likely to be the incumbent. For another, the odd spectacle of politicians using ecstatic non-rational, holy-rolling religion in Presidential campaigning was to appear first not in 1980 but in 1976.

The two most popular new figures in the 1976 campaign, Jimmy Carter and Jerry Brown, are men who rose up from state politics . . . absolutely aglow with mystical religious streaks. Carter turned out to be an evangelical Baptist who had recently been "born again" and "saved," who had "accepted Jesus Christ as my personal Savior"—i.e., he was of the Missionary lectern-pounding Amen ten-finger C-major chord Sister-Martha-at-the-Yamaha-keyboard loblolly piney-woods Baptist faith in which the members of the congregation stand up and "give witness" and "share it, Brother" and "share it, Sister" and "praise God!" during the service.* Jerry Brown turned out to be the Zen Jesuit, a former Jesuit seminarian who went about like a hair-shirt Catholic monk, but one who happened to believe also in the Gautama Buddha, and who got off koans in an offhand but confident manner, even on political issues, as to how it is not the right answer that matters but the right question, and so forth.

Newspaper columnists and news-magazine writers continually referred to the two men's "enigmatic appeal." Which is to say, they couldn't explain it. Nevertheless, they tried. They theorized that the war in Vietnam, Watergate, the FBI and CIA scandals, had left the electorate shellshocked and disillusioned and that in their despair the citizens were groping no longer for specific remedies but for sheer faith, something, anything (even holy rolling), to believe in. This was in keeping with the current fashion of interpreting all new political phenomena in terms of recent disasters, frustrations, protest, the decline of civilization . . . the Grim Slide. But when *The New York Times* and CBS employed a polling organization to try to find out just what great gusher of "frustration" and "protest" Carter had hit, the results were baffling. A Harvard political scientist, William Schneider, concluded for the Los Angeles *Times* that "the Carter protest" was a new kind of protest, "a protest of good feelings." That was a new kind, sure enough: a protest that wasn't a protest.

In fact, both Carter and Brown had stumbled upon a fabulous terrain for which there are no words in current political language. A couple of politicians had finally wandered into the Me Decade.

3. HIM?—THE NEW MAN?

The saga of the Me Decade begins with one of those facts that are so big and so obvious (like the Big Dipper) no one ever comments on them any more. Namely: the thirty-year boom. Wartime spending in the United States in the 1940's touched off a boom that has continued for more than thirty years. It has pumped money into every class level of the population on a scale without parallel in any country in history. True,

* Carter is not, however, a member of the most down-home and ecstatic of the Baptist sects, which is a back-country branch known as the Primitive Baptist Church. In the Primitive Baptist churches men and women sit on different sides of the room, no musical instruments are allowed, and there is a good deal of foot-washing and other rituals drawn from passages in the Bible. The Progressive Primitives, another group, differ from the Primitives chiefly in that they allow a piano or organ in the church. The Missionary Baptists, Carter's branch, are a step up socially (not necessarily divinely) but would not be a safe bet for an ambitious member of an in-town country club. The In-town Baptists, found in communities of 25,000 or more, are too respectable, socially, to be called ecstatic and succeed in being almost as tame as the Episcopalians, Presbyterians, and Methodists.

nothing has solved the plight of those at the very bottom, the chronically unemployed of the slums. Nevertheless, in the city of Compton, California, it is possible for a family of four at the very lowest class level, which is known in America today as "on welfare," to draw an income of $8,000 a year entirely from public sources. This is more than most British newspaper columnists and Italian factory foremen make, even allowing for differences in living costs. In America truck drivers, mechanics, factory workers, policemen, firemen, and garbagemen make so much money—$15,000 to $20,000 (or more) per year is not uncommon—that the word "proletarian" can no longer be used in this country with a straight face. So one now says "lower middle class." One can't even call workingmen "blue collar" any longer. They all have on collars like Joe Namath's or Johnny Bench's or Walt Frazier's. They all have on $35 superstar Qiana sport shirts with elephant collars and 1940's Airbrush Wallpaper Flowers Buncha Grapes & Seashell designs all over them.

Well, my God, the old utopian socialists of the nineteenth century—such as Saint-Simon, Owen, Fourier, and Marx—*lived* for the day of the liberated workingman. They foresaw a day when industrialism (Saint-Simon coined the word) would give the common man the things he needed in order to realize his potential as a human being: surplus (discretionary) income, political freedom, free time (leisure), and freedom from grinding drudgery. Some of them, notably Owen and Fourier, thought all this might come to pass first in the United States. So they set up communes here: Owen's New Harmony commune in Indiana and thirty-four Fourier-style "phalanx" settlements—socialist communes, because the new freedom was supposed to be possible only under socialism. The old boys never dreamed that it would come to pass instead as the result of a Go-Getter Bourgeois business boom such as began in the U.S. in the 1940's. Nor would they have liked it if they had seen it. For one thing, the *homo novus*, the new man, the liberated man, the first common man in the history of the world with the much-dreamed-of combination of money, freedom, and free time—this American workingman—didn't *look* right. The Joe Namath–Johnny Bench–Walt Frazier superstar Qiana wallpaper sports shirts, for a start.

He didn't look right . . . and he wouldn't . . . *do right*! I can remember what brave plans visionary architects at Yale and Harvard still had for *the common man* in the early 1950's. (They actually used the term "the common man.") They had brought the utopian socialist dream forward into the twentieth century. They had things figured out for the workingman down to truly minute details, such as lamp switches. The new liberated workingman would live as the Cultivated Ascetic. He would be modeled on the B.A.-degree Greenwich Village bohemian of the late 1940's—dark wool Hudson Bay shirts, tweed jackets, flannel trousers, briarwood pipes, good books, sandals and simplicity—except that he would live in a Worker Housing project. All Yale and Harvard architects worshipped Bauhaus principles and had the Bauhaus vision of Worker Housing. The Bauhaus movement absolutely hypnotized American architects, once its leaders, such as Walter Gropius and Ludwig Mies van der Rohe, came to the United States from Germany in the 1930's. Worker Housing in America would have pure beige rooms, stripped, freed, purged of all moldings, cornices, and overhangs—which Gropius regarded as symbolic "crowns" and therefore loathsome. Worker Housing would be liberated from all wallpaper, "drapes," Wilton rugs with flowers on them, lamps with fringed shades and bases that looked like vases or Greek columns. It would be cleansed of all doilies, knickknacks, mantelpieces, headboards, and radiator covers. Radiator coils would be left bare as honest, abstract sculptural objects.

But somehow the workers, incurable slobs that they were, avoided Worker Housing, better known as "the projects," as if it had a smell. They were heading out instead to the suburbs—the *suburbs*!—to places like Islip, Long Island, and the San Fernando Valley of Los Angeles—and buying houses with clapboard siding and pitched roofs and shingles and gaslight-style front-porch lamps and mailboxes set up on top of lengths of stiffened chain that seemed to defy gravity, and all sorts of other unbelievably cut or antiquey touches, and they loaded these houses with "drapes" such as baffled all description and wall-to-wall carpet you could lose a shoe in, and they put barbecue pits and fish ponds with concrete cherubs urinating into them on the lawn out back, and they parked twenty-five-foot-long cars out front and Evinrude cruisers up on tow trailers in the carport just beyond the breezeway.*

By the 1960's the common man was also getting quite interested in this business of "realizing his potential as a human being." But once again he crossed everybody up! Once more he took his money and ran—determined to do-it-himself!

4. PLUGGING IN

In 1971 I made a lecture tour of Italy, talking (at the request of my Italian hosts) about "contemporary American life." Everywhere I went, from Turin to Palermo, Italian students were interested in just one question: Was it really true that young people in America, no older than themselves, actually left home and lived communally according to their own rules and created their own dress styles and vocabulary and had free sex and took dope? They were talking, of course, about the hippie or psychedelic movement that had begun flowering about 1965. What fascinated them the most, however, was the first item on the list: that the hippies *actually left home and lived communally according to their own rules.*

To Italian students this seemed positively amazing. Several of the students I met lived wild enough lives during daylight hours. They were in radical organizations and had fought pitched battles with police, *on the barricades*, as it were. But by 8:30 p.m., they were back home, obediently washing their hands before dinner with Mom and Dad and Buddy and Sis and the Maiden Aunt. When they left home for good, it was likely to be via the only admissible ticket: marriage. Unmarried sons of thirty-eight and thirty-nine would still be sitting around the same old table, morosely munching the gnocchi.

Meanwhile, ordinary people in America were breaking off from conventional society, from family, neighborhood, and community, and creating worlds of their own. This had no parallel in history, certainly considering the scale of it. The hippies were merely the most flamboyant example. The New Left students of the late 1960's were another. The New Lefters lived in communes much like the hippies' but with a slightly different emphasis. Dope, sex, nudity, costumes, and vocabulary became sym-

* Ignored or else held in contempt by working people, Bauhaus design eventually triumphed as a symbol of wealth and privilege, attuned chiefly to the tastes of businessmen's wives. For example, Mies's most famous piece of furniture design, the Barcelona chair, now sells for $1,680 and is available only through one's decorator. The high price is due in no small part to the chair's Worker Housing Honest Materials: stainless steel and leather. No chromed iron is allowed, and customers are refused if they want to have the chair upholstered in material of their own choice. Only leather is allowed, and only six shades of that: Seagram's Building Lobby Palomino, Monsanto Chemical Company Lobby Antelope, Arco Towers Pecan, Trans-America Building Ebony, Bank of America Building Walnut, and Architectural Digest Mink.

bols of defiance of bourgeois life. The costumery tended to be semi-military: non-com officers' shirts, combat boots, commando berets—worn in combination with blue jeans or a turtleneck jersey, however, to show that one wasn't a uniform freak.

That people so young could go off on their own, without taking jobs, and live a life completely of their own design—to Europeans it was astounding. That ordinary factory workers could go off to the suburbs and buy homes and create their own dream houses—this, too, was astounding. And yet the new life of old people in America in the 1960's was still more astounding. Throughout European history and in the United States up to the Second World War, old age was a time when you had to cling to your children or other kinfolk, and to their sufferance and mercy, if any. The Old Folks at Home happily mingling in the old manse with the generations that followed? The little ones learning at Grandpa's and Grandma's bony knees? These are largely the myths of nostalgia. The beloved old folks were often exiled to the attic or the outbuildings, and the servants brought them their meals. They were not considered decorative in the dining room or the parlor.

In the 1960's, old people in America began doing something that was more extraordinary than it ever seemed at the time. They cut through the whole dreary humiliation of old age by heading off to "retirement villages" and "leisure developments"—which quickly became Old Folks communes. Some of the old parties managed to take this to a somewhat psychedelic extreme. For example, the trailer caravaners. The caravaners were (and are) mainly retired couples who started off their Golden Years by doing the usual thing. They went to their children, Buddy and Sis, and gingerly suggested that now that Dad had retired, he and Mom might move in with one of them. They get the old "Uhh . . . sure"—plus a death-ray look. So the two old crocks depart and go out and buy what is the only form of prefabricated housing that has ever caught on in America: the house trailer, or mobile home. Usually the old pair would try to make the trailer look like a real house. They'd park it on a plot in a trailer park and put it up on blocks and put some latticework around the bottom to hide the axles and the wheel housings and put little awnings above the windows and a big one out over the door to create the impression of a breezeway. By and by, however, they would discover that there were people their age who actually moved off dead center with these things and went out into the world and *rolled.* At this point they would join a trailer caravan. And when the trailer caravans got rolling, you had a chance to see some of the most amazing sights of the modern American landscape . . . such as thirty, forty, fifty Airstream trailers, the ones that are silver and have rounded corners and ends and look like silver bullets . . . thirty, forty, fifty of these silver bullets in a line, in a caravan, hauling down the highway in the late afternoon with the sun at a low angle and exploding off the silver surfaces of the Airstreams until the whole convoy looks like some gigantic and improbable string of jewelry, each jewel ablaze with a highlight, rolling over the face of the earth—the million-volt, billion-horsepower bijoux of America!

The caravaners might start off taking the ordinary touring routes of the West, but they would soon get a taste for adventure and head for the badlands, through the glacier forests of the Northwest and down through western Mexico, not fat green chile relleno red jacaranda blossom mariachi band caballero sombrero Tourist Mexico but *western* Mexico, where the terrain is all skulls and bones and junk frito and hard-cheese mestizos hunkered down at the crossroads, glowering, and cows and armadillos by the side of the road on their backs with their bellies bloated and all four feet up in the air. The caravaners would get deeper and deeper into a life of sheer *trailering.* They would become experts at this twentieth-century nomad life. They would begin to look back on Buddy & Sis as sad conventional sorts whom they had left behind, poor turkeys who knew nothing of the initiations and rites of passage of trailering.

The mighty million-volt rites! Every now and then the caravan would have to seek out a trailer camp for a rest in the rush across the face of Western America, and in these camps you'd have to plug a power line from your trailer into the utility poles the camps provide, so as to be able to use the appliances in the trailer when your car engine wasn't generating electricity. In some of the older camps these poles were tricky to use. If you didn't plug your line in in just the right manner, with the right prong up and the right one down, you stood to get a hell of a shock, a feedback of what felt like about two thousand volts. So about dusk you might see the veterans sitting outside their trailers in aluminum-and-vinyl folding chairs, pretending to be just chewing the fat at sunset but in fact nudging one another and keeping everyone on the alert for what is about to happen when the rookie—the rheumy-eyed, gray-haired old Dad who, with Mom, has just joined the caravan—plugs into the malicious Troll Pole for the first time.

Old Dad tries to plug in, and of course he gets it wrong, tries to put the wrong prong in on top and the wrong one on the bottom, and—*bowwwwwww!*—he gets a thunderbolt jolt like Armageddon itself and does an inverted one-and-a-half gainer and lands on his back—and the veterans, men and women, just absolutely crack up, bawl, cry, laugh until they're turning inside out. And only after the last whoops and snorts have died down does it dawn on you that this poor wet rookie who plugged in wrong and has just done this involuntary Olympic diving maneuver and landed on his spine with his fingers smoking . . . is a gray-haired party seventy-two years old. But that's also the beauty of it! They always survive! They're initiates! hierophants of the caravan who have moved off dead center! Various deadly rheumatoid symptoms disappear, as if by magic! The Gerontoid Cowboys ride! deep into a new land and a new life they've created for themselves!

5. LEMON SESSIONS

It was remarkable enough that ordinary folks now had enough money to take it and run off and alter the circumstances of their lives and create new roles for themselves, such as Trailer Sailor. But simultaneously still others decided to go . . . *all the way.* They plunged straight toward what has become the alchemical dream of the Me Decade.

The old alchemical dream was changing base metals into gold. The new alchemical dream is: changing one's personality—remaking, remodeling, elevating, and polishing one's very *self* . . . and observing, studying, and doting on it. (Me!) This had always been an aristocratic luxury, confined throughout most of history to the life of the courts, since only the very wealthiest classes had the free time and the surplus income to dwell upon this sweetest and vainest of pastimes. It smacked so much of vanity, in fact, that the noble folk involved in it always took care to call it quite something else.

Much of the satisfaction well-born people got from what is known historically as the "chivalric tradition" was precisely that: dwelling upon *Me* and every delicious nuance of my conduct and personality. At Versailles, Louis XIV founded a school for girls called Saint-Cyr. At the time most schools for girls were in convents. Louis had quite something else in mind, a secular school that would develop womenfolk suitable for the superior *race guerrière* that he believed himself to be creating in France. Saint-Cyr was the forerunner for what was known up until a few years ago as *the finishing school.* And what was the *finishing school?* Why, a school in which the personality was to be shaped and buffed like a piece of high-class psychological cabinetry. For centuries most of upper-class college education in France and England has been fashioned in the same manner: with an eye toward sculpting the personality as carefully as the intellectual faculties.

At Yale the students on the outside have wondered for eighty years what went on inside the fabled secret senior societies, such as Skull & Bones. On Thursday nights one would see the secret-society members walking silently and single-file, in black flannel suits, white shirts, and black knit ties with gold pins on them, toward their great Greek Revival temples, buildings whose mystery was doubled by the fact that they had no windows. What in the name of God or Mammon went on in those thirty-odd Thursday nights during the senior years of these happy few? What went on was . . . *lemon sessions*!—a regularly scheduled series of the lemon sessions, just like the ones that occurred informally in girls' finishing schools.

In the girls' schools these lemon sessions tended to take place at random on nights when a dozen or so girls might end up in someone's dormitory room. One girl would become "it," and the others would rip into her personality, pulling it to pieces to analyze every defect . . . her spitefulness, her awkwardness, her bad breath, embarrassing clothes, ridiculous laugh, her suck-up fawning, latent lesbianism, or whatever. The poor creature might be reduced to tears. She might blurt out the most terrible confessions, hatreds, and primordial fears. But, it was presumed, she would be the stronger for it afterward. She would be on her way toward a new personality. Likewise, in the secret societies, they held lemon sessions for boys. Is masturbation your problem? Out with the truth, you ridiculous weenie! And Thursday night after Thursday night the awful truths would out, as he who was It stood up before them and answered the most horrible questions. Yes! I do it! I whack whack whack it! I'm *afraid* of women! I'm afraid of *you*! And I get my shirts at Rosenberg's instead of Press! (Oh, you dreary turkey, you wet smack, you little shit!) . . . But out of the fire and the heap of ashes would come a better man, a brother, of good blood and good bone, for the American *race guerrière.* And what was more . . . they loved it. No matter how dreary the soap opera, the star was *Me.*

By the mid-1960's this service, this luxury, had become available for one and all, i.e., the middle classes. Lemon Sessions Central was the Esalen Institute, a lodge perched on a cliff overlooking the Pacific in Big Sur, California. Esalen's specialty was lube jobs for the personality. Businessmen, businesswomen, housewives—anyone who could afford it, and by now many could—paid $220 a week to come to Esalen to learn about themselves and loosen themselves up and wiggle their fannies a bit, in keeping with methods developed by William S. Schutz and Frederick Perls. Fritz Perls, as he was known, was a remarkable figure, a psychologist who had a gray beard and went about in a blue terry-cloth jumpsuit and looked like a great blue grizzled father bear. His lemon sessions sprang not out of the Manly Virtues & Cold Showers Protestant Prep-School tradition of Yale but out of psychoanalysis. His sessions were a variety of the "marathon encounter."* He put the various candi-

* The real "marathons," in which the group stayed in the same room for twenty-four hours or longer, were developed by George R. Bach and Frederick Stroller of Los Angeles.

dates for personality change in groups, and they stayed together in close quarters day after day. They were encouraged to bare their own souls and to strip away one another's defensive façade. Everyone was to face his own emotions squarely for the first time.

Encounter sessions, particularly of the Schutz variety, were often wild events. Such aggression! such sobs! tears! moans, hysteria, vile recriminations, shocking revelations, such explosions of hostility between husbands and wives, such mudballs of profanity from previously mousy mommies and workadaddies, such redmad attacks! Only physical assault was prohibited. The encounter session became a standard approach in many other movements, such as Scientology, Arica, the Mel Lyman movement, Synanon, Daytop Village, and Primal Scream. Synanon had started out as a drug-rehabilitation program, but by the late 1960's the organization was recruiting "lay members," a lay member being someone who had never been addicted to heroin . . . but was ready for the lemon-session life.

Outsiders, hearing of these sessions, wondered what on earth their appeal was. Yet the appeal was simple enough. It is summed up in the notion: "Let's talk about *Me*." No matter whether you managed to renovate your personality through encounter sessions or not, you had finally focused your attention and your energies on the most fascinating subject on earth: *Me*. Not only that, you also put *Me* onstage before a live audience. The popular est movement has managed to do that with great refinement. Just imagine . . . *Me and My Hemorrhoids* . . . moving an entire hall to the most profound outpouring of emotion! Just imagine . . . *my life* becoming a drama with universal significance . . . analyzed, like Hamlet's, for what it signifies for the rest of mankind . . .

The encounter session—although it was not called that—was also a staple practice in psychedelic communes and, for that matter, in New Left communes. In fact, the analysis of the self, and of one another, was unceasing. But in these groups and at Esalen and in movements such as Arica there were two common assumptions that distinguished them from the aristocratic lemon sessions and personality *finishings* of yore. The first was: I, with the help of my brothers and sisters, must strip away all the shams and excess baggage of society and my upbringing in order to find the Real Me. Scientology uses the word "clear" to identify the state that one must strive for. But just what is that state? And what will the Real Me be like? It is at this point that the new movements tend to take on a religious or spiritual atmosphere. In one form or another they arrive at an axiom first propounded by the Gnostic Christians some eighteen hundred years ago: namely, that at the apex of every human soul there exists a spark of the light of God. In most mortals that spark is "asleep" (the Gnostic's word), all but smothered by the façades and general falseness of society. But those souls who are clear can find that spark within themselves and unite their souls with God's. And with that conviction comes the second assumption: there is an *other order* that actually reigns supreme in the world. Like the light of God itself, this *other order* is invisible to most mortals. But he who has dug himself out from under the junk heap of civilization can discover it .

And with that . . . the Me movements were about to turn *righteous*.

6. YOUNG FAITH, AGING GROUPIES

By the early 1970's so many of the Me movements had reached this Gnostic religious stage, they now amounted to a new religious wave. Synanon, Arica, and the Scientology movement had become religions. The much-publicized psychedelic or hippie communes of the 1960's, although no longer big items in the press, were spreading widely and becoming more and more frankly religious. The huge Steve Gaskin commune in the Tennessee scrublands was a prime example. A *New York Times* survey concluded that there were at least two thousand communes in the United States by 1970, barely five years after the idea first caught on in California. Both the Esalen-style and Primal Therapy or Primal Scream encounter movements were becoming progressively less psychoanalytical and more mystical in their approach. The Oriental "meditation" religions—which had existed in the United States mainly in the form of rather intellectual and bohemian zen and yoga circles—experienced a spectacular boom. Groups such as the Hare Krishna, the Sufi, and the Maharaj Ji communes began to discover that they could enroll thousands of new members and (in some cases) make small fortunes in real estate to finance the expansion. Many members of the New Left communes of the 1960's began to turn up in Me movements in the 1970's, including two of the celebrated "Chicago Eight." Rennie Davis became a follower of the Maharaj Ji, Jerry Rubin enrolled in both est and Arica. Barbara Garson—who with the help of her husband, Marvin, wrote the agitprop epic of the New Left, *MacBird*—would later observe, with considerable bitterness: "My husband, Marvin, forsook everything (me included) to find peace. For three years he wandered without shoes or money or glasses. Now he is in Israel with some glasses and possibly with some peace." And not just him, she said, but so many other New Lefters as well: "Some follow a guru, some are into primal scream, some seek a rest from the diaspora—a home in Zion." It is entirely possible that in the long run historians will regard the entire New Left experience as not so much a political as a religious episode wrapped in semi-military gear and guerrilla talk. . . .

Today it is precisely the most rational, intellectual, secularized, modernized, updated, relevant religions—all the brave, forward-looking Ethical Culture, Unitarian, and Swedenborgian movements of only yesterday—that are finished, gasping, breathing their last. What the Urban Young People want from religion is a little . . . *Hallelujah!* . . . and *talking in tongues!* . . . *Praise God!* Precisely that! In the most prestigious divinity schools today, Catholic, Presbyterian, and Episcopal, the avant-garde movement—the leading edge—is "charismatic Christianity" . . . featuring talking in tongues, ululalia, visions, holy-rolling, and other non-rational, even anti-rational, practices. Some of the most respectable old-line Protestant congregations, in the most placid suburban settings, have begun to split into the Charismatics and the Easter Christians ("All they care about is being seen in church on Easter"). The Easter Christians still usually control the main Sunday-morning service—but the Charismatics take over on Sunday evening and do the holy roll.

This curious development has breathed new life into the existing fundamentalists, theosophists, and older salvation seekers of all sorts. Ten years ago, if anyone of wealth, power, or renown had publicly "announced for Christ," people would have looked at him as if his nose had been eaten away by weevils. Today it happens regularly . . . Harold Hughes resigns from the U.S. Senate to become an evangelist . . . Jim Irwin, the astronaut, teams up with a Baptist evangelist in an organization called High Flight . . . singers like Pat Boone and Anita Bryant announce for Jesus . . . Charles Colson, the former hardballer of the Nixon Administration, announces for Jesus . . . The leading candidate for President of the United States, Jimmy Carter, announces for Jesus. O Jesus People.

7. ONLY ONE LIFE

In 1961 a copy writer named Shirley Polykoff was working for the Foote, Cone & Belding advertising agency on the Clairol hair-dye account when she came up with the line: "If I've only one life, let me live it as a blonde!" In a single slogan she had summed up what might be described as the secular side of the Me Decade. "If I've only one life, let me live it as a ———!" (You have only to fill in the blank.)

This formula accounts for much of the popularity of the women's liberation or feminist movement. "What does a woman want?" said Freud. Perhaps there are women who want to humble men or reduce their power or achieve equality or even superiority for themselves and their sisters. But for every one such woman, there are nine who simply want to *fill in the blank* as they see fit. If I've only one life, let me live it as . . . a free spirit!" (Instead of . . . a house slave: a cleaning woman, a cook, a nursemaid, a stationwagon hacker, and an occasional household sex aid.) But even that may be overstating it, because often the unconscious desire is nothing more than: *Let's talk about Me.* The great unexpected dividend of the feminist movement has been to elevate an ordinary status—woman, housewife—to the level of drama. One's very existence as a *woman* . . . as *Me* . . . becomes something all the world analyzes, agonizes over, draws cosmic conclusions from, or, in any event, takes seriously. Every woman becomes Emma Bovary, Cousin Bette, or Nora . . . or Erica Jong or Consuelo Saah Baehr.

Among men the formula becomes: "I'f I've only one life, let me live it as a . . . Casanova or a Henry VIII! (instead of a humdrum workadaddy, eternally faithful, except perhaps for a mean little skulking episode here and there, to a woman who now looks old enough to be your aunt and needs a shave or else has electrolysis lines above her upper lip, as well as atrophied calves, and is an embarrassment to be seen with when you take her on trips). The right to shuck overripe wives and take on fresh ones was once seen as the prerogative of kings only, and even then it was scandalous. In the 1950's and 1960's it began to be seen as the prerogative of the rich, the powerful, and the celebrated (Nelson Rockefeller, Henry Ford, and Show Business figures), although it retained the odor of scandal. Wife-shucking damaged Adlai Stevenson's chances of becoming President in 1952 and 1956 and Rockefeller's chances of becoming the Republican nominee in 1964 and 1968. Until the 1970's wife-shucking made it impossible for an astronaut to be chosen to go into space. Today, in the Me Decade, it becomes *normal behavior*, one of the factors that has pushed the divorce rate above 50 percent.

When Eugene McCarthy filled in the blank in 1972 and shucked his wife, it was hardly noticed. Likewise in the case of several astronauts. When Wayne Hays filled in the blank in 1976 and shucked his wife of thirty-eight years, it did not hurt his career in the slightest. Copulating with the girl in the office, however, was still regarded as scandalous. (Elizabeth Ray filled in the blank in another popular fashion: If I've only one life, let me live it as a . . . Celebrity!" As did Arthur Bremer, who kept a diary during his stalking of Nixon and, later, George Wallace . . . with an eye toward a book contract. Which he got.) Some wiseacre has remarked, supposedly with levity, that the federal government may in time have to create reservations for women over thirty-five, to take care of the swarms of shucked wives and widows. In fact, women in precisely those categories have begun setting up communes or "extended families" to provide one another support and companionship in a world without workadaddies. ("If I've only one life, why live it as an anachronism?")

Much of what is now known as the "sexual revolution" has consisted of both women and men filling in the blank this way: "If I've only one life, let me live it as . . . a Swinger!" (Instead of a frustrated, bored monogamist.) In "swinging," a husband and wife give each other license to copulate with other people. There are no statistics on the subject that mean anything, but I do know that it pops up in conversation today in the most unexpected corners of the country. It is an odd experience to be in De Kalb, Illinois, in the very corncrib of America, and have some conventional-looking housewife (not *housewife*, damn it!) come up to you and ask: "Is there much tripling going on in New York?"

"Tripling?"

Tripling turns out to be a practice, in De Kalb, anyway, in which a husband and wife invite a third party—male or female, but more often female—over for an evening of whatever, including polymorphous perversity, even the practices written of in the one-hand magazines, such as *Hustler*, all the things involving tubes and hoses and tourniquets and cups and double-jointed sailors.

One of the satisfactions of this sort of life, quite in addition to the groin spasms, is talk: *Let's talk about Me.* Sexual adventurers are given to the most relentless and deadly serious talk . . . about Me. They quickly succeed in placing themselves onstage in the sexual drama whose outlines were sketched by Freud and then elaborated by Wilhelm Reich. Men and women of all sorts, not merely swingers, are given just now to the most earnest sort of talk about the Sexual Me. A key drama of our own day is Ingmar Bergman's movie *Scenes from a Marriage.* In it we see a husband and wife who have good jobs and a well-furnished home but who are unable to "communicate"—to cite one of the signature words of the Me Decade. Then they begin to communicate, and thereupon their marriage breaks up and they start divorce proceedings. For the rest of the picture they communicate endlessly, with great candor, but the "relationship"—another signature word—remains doomed. Ironically, the lesson that people seem to draw from this movie has to do with . . . "the need to communicate." . . .

8. HOW YOU DO IT, MY BOYS!

We are now—in the Me Decade—seeing the upward roll (and not yet the crest, by any means) of the third great religious wave in American history, one that historians will very likely term the Third Great Awakening. Like the others it has begun in a flood of *ecstasy*, achieved through LSD and other psychedelics, orgy, dancing (the New Sufi and the Hare Krishna), meditation, and psychic frenzy (the marathon encounter). This third wave has built up from more diverse and exotic sources than the first two, from therapeutic movements as well as overtly religious movements, from hippies and students of "psi phenomena" and Flying Saucerites as well as from charismatic Christians. But other than that, what will historians say about it?

The historian Perry Miller credited the First Great Awakening with helping to pave the way for the American Revolution through its assault on the colonies' religious establishment and, thereby, on British colonial authority generally. The sociologist Thomas F. O'Dea credited the Second Great Awakening with creating the atmosphere of Christian asceticism (known as "bleak" on the East Coast) that swept through the Midwest and the West during the nineteenth century and helped make it possible to build communities in the face of great hardship. And the Third Great Awakening? Journalists—historians have not yet tackled the subject—have shown a morbid tendency to regard the various movements in this wave as "fascist." The hippie movement was often attacked as "fascist" in the late 1960's. Over the past year a barrage of articles has attacked the est movement and the "Moonies" (followers of the Rev. Sun Myung Moon) along the same lines.

Frankly, this tells us nothing except that journalists bring the same conventional Grim Slide concepts to every subject. The word "fascism" derives from the old Roman symbol of power and authority, the *fasces*, a bundle of sticks bound together by thongs (with an ax head protruding from one end). One by one the sticks would be easy to break. Bound together they are indestructible. Fascist ideology called for binding all classes, all levels, all elements of an entire nation together into a single organization with a single will.

The various movements of the current religious wave attempt very nearly the opposite. They begin with . . . "Let's talk about Me." They begin with the most delicious look inward; with considerable narcissism, in short. When the believers bind together into religions, it is always with a sense of splitting off from the rest of society. We, the enlightened (lit by the sparks at the apexes of our souls), hereby separate ourselves from the lost souls around us. Like all religions before them, they proselytize—but always promising the opposite of nationalism: a City of Light that is above it all. There is no ecumenical spirit within this Third Great Awakening. If anything, there is a spirit of schism. The contempt the various gurus and seers have for one another is breathtaking. One has only to ask, say, Oscar Ichazo of Arica about Carlos Castaneda or Werner Erhard of est to learn that Castaneda is a fake and Erhard is a shallow sloganeer. It's exhilarating!—to watch the faithful split off from one another to seek ever more perfect and refined crucibles in which to fan the Divine spark . . . and to *talk about Me.*

Whatever the Third Great Awakening amounts to, for better or for worse, will have to do with this unprecedented post-World War II American luxury: the luxury enjoyed by so many millions of middling folk, of dwelling upon the self. At first glance, Shirley Polykoff's slogan—"If I've only one life, let me live it as a blonde!"—seems like merely another example of a superficial and irritating rhetorical trope (*antanaclasis**) that now happens to be fashionable among advertising copy writers. But in fact the notion of "If I've only one life to live" challenges one of those assumptions of society that are so deep-rooted and ancient they have no name—they are simply lived by. In this case: man's age-old belief in serial immortality.

The husband and wife who sacrifice their own ambitions and their material assets in order to provide a "better future" for their children . . . the soldier who risks his life, or perhaps consciously sacrifices it, in battle . . . the man who devotes his life to some struggle for "his people" that cannot possibly be won in his lifetime . . . people (or most of them) who buy life insurance or leave wills . . . are people who conceive of themselves, however unconsciously, as part of a great biological stream. Just as something of their ancestors lives on in them, so will something of them live

* This figure of speech consists of repeating a word (or words with the same root) in such a way that the second usage has a different meaning from the first. "This is WINS, 1010 on your dial—New York wants to *know*, and we *know* it" (1. know = "find out"; 2. know = "realize" or "have the knowledge") . . . "We're American Airlines, *doing* what we *do* best" (1. doing = "performing"; 2. what we do = "our job") . . . "If you think refrigerators cost *too much*, maybe you're looking at *too much* refrigerator (1. cost; 2. size or complexity). The smart money *is* on Admiral (Admiral's italics)" . . . There is also an example of the *pun* in the WINS slogan and of *epanadiplosis* in the Admiral slogan (the ABBA pattern of *refrigerator . . . too much/too much refrigerator*).

on in their children . . . or in their people, their race, their community—for childless people, too, conduct their lives and try to arrange their post-mortem affairs with concern for how the great stream is going to flow on. Most people, historically, have *not* lived their lives as if thinking, "I have only one life to live." Instead, they have lived as if they are living their ancestors' lives and their offsprings' lives and perhaps their neighbors' lives as well. They have seen themselves as inseparable from the great tide of chromosomes of which they are created and which they pass on. The mere fact that you were only going to be here a short time and would be dead soon enough did not give you the license to try to climb out of the stream and change the natural order of things. The Chinese, in ancestor worship, have literally worshipped the great tide itself, and not any god or gods. For anyone to renounce the notion of serial-immortality, in the West or the East, has been to defy what seems like a law of nature. Hence the wicked feeling—the excitement!—of "If I've only one life, let me live it as a ———!" Fill in the blank, if you dare.

And now many dare it! In *Democracy in America* de Tocqueville (the inevitable and ubiquitous de Tocqueville) saw the American sense of equality itself as disrupting the stream, which he called "time's pattern": "Not only does democracy make each man forget his ancestors, it hides his descendants from him, and divides him from his contemporaries; it continually turns him back into himself, and threatens, at last, to enclose him entirely in the solitude of his own heart." A grim prospect to the good Alexis de T.—but what did he know about . . . *Let's talk about Me!*

De Tocqueville's idea of modern man lost "in the solitude of his own heart" has been brought forward into our time in such terminology as *alienation* (Marx), *anomie* (Durkheim), the *mass man* (Ortega y Gasset) and *the lonely crowd* (Riesman). The picture is always of a creature uprooted by industrialism, packed together in cities with people he doesn't know, helpless against massive economic and political shifts—in short, a creature like Charlie Chaplin in *Modern Times*, a helpless, bewildered, and dispirited slave of the machinery. This victim of modern times has always been a most appealing figure to intellectuals, artists, and architects. The poor devil so obviously needs *us* to be his Engineers of the Soul, to use a term popular in the Soviet Union in the 1920's. We will pygmalionize this sad lump of clay into a *homo novus*, a New Man, with a new philosophy, a new aesthetics, not to mention new Bauhaus housing and furniture.

But once the dreary little bastards started getting money in the 1940's, they did an astonishing thing—they took their money and ran! They did something only aristocrats (and intellectuals and artists) were supposed to do—they discovered and started doting on *Me*! They've created the greatest age of individualism in American history! All rules are broken! The prophets are out of business! Where the Third Great Awakening will lead—who can presume to say? One only knows that the great religious waves have a momentum all their own. Neither arguments nor policies nor acts of the legislature have been any match for them in the past. And this one has the mightiest, holiest roll of all, the beat that goes . . . *Me* . . . *Me* . . . *Me* . . . *Me* . . .

Dwight D. Eisenhower et al.

The Vietnamization of Vietman: An Oral Chronicle

YOU HAVE A ROW OF DOMINOES SET UP, YOU KNOCK OVER THE FIRST ONE, AND WHAT WILL HAPPEN TO THE LAST ONE IS THE CERTAINTY THAT IT WILL GO OVER VERY QUICKLY.

—President Dwight D. Eisenhower explaining "the falling domino principle" at a news conference, April 1954

MY SOLUTIONS? TELL THE VIETNAMESE THEY'VE GOT TO DRAW IN THEIR HORNS OR WE'RE GOING TO BOMB THEM BACK INTO THE STONE AGE.

—Gen. Curtis E. LeMay, Air Force Chief of Staff, May 1964

BUT WE ARE NOT ABOUT TO SEND AMERICAN BOYS NINE OR TEN THOUSAND MILES AWAY FROM HOME TO DO WHAT ASIAN BOYS OUGHT TO BE DOING FOR THEMSELVES.

—President Lyndon B. Johnson, Akron, Ohio, October 1964

COME HOME WITH THAT COONSKIN ON THE WALL.

—President Johnson to commanders at Cam Ranh Bay, October 1966

I SEE LIGHT AT THE END OF THE TUNNEL.

—Walt W. Rostow, President Johnson's national security adviser, in *Look*, December 1967

WE HAD TO DESTROY IT IN ORDER TO SAVE IT.

—American officer at Ben Tre after Tet attack, February 1968

IN THE PATRIOTIC STRUGGLE AGAINST U.S. AGGRESSION, WE SHALL HAVE INDEED TO UNDERGO MORE DIFFICULTIES AND SACRIFICES, BUT WE ARE SURE TO WIN TOTAL VICTORY. THIS IS AN ABSOLUTE CERTAINTY.

—The Last Testament of Ho Chi Minh, 1969

WE BELIEVE PEACE IS AT HAND.

—Henry A. Kissinger, President Richard M. Nixon's national security adviser, October 1972

THIS IS IT. EVERYBODY OUT.

—Word from the American embassy in Saigon to the last American evacuees from the city, April 30, 1975

Terror of War. Children flee from their village after South Vietnamese planes dropped Napalm on it by mistake during the Vietnamese war. *(Wide World Photos)*

Fiction

John Cheever (1912–   )

The Swimmer

It was one of those midsummer Sundays when everyone sits around saying: "I *drank* too much last night." You might have heard it whispered by the parishioners leaving church, heard it from the lips of the priest himself, struggling with his cassock in the *vestiarium,* heard it from the golf links and the tennis courts, heard it from the wild-life preserve where the leader of the Audubon group was suffering from a terrible hangover. "I *drank* too much," said Donald Westerhazy. "We all *drank* too much," said Lucinda Merill. "It must have been the wine," said Helen Westerhazy. "I *drank* too much of that claret."

This was at the edge of the Westerhazys' pool. The pool, fed by an artesian well with a high iron content, was a pale shade of green. It was a fine day. In the west there was a massive stand of cumulus cloud so like a city seen from a distance—from the bow of an approaching ship—that it might have had a name. Lisbon. Hackensack. The sun was hot. Neddy Merill sat by the green water, one hand in it, one around a glass of gin. He was a slender man—he seemed to have the especial slenderness of youth—and while he was far from young he had slid down his banister that morning and given the bronze backside of Aphrodite on the hall table a smack, as he jogged toward the smell of coffee in his dining room. He might have been compared to a summer's day, particularly the last hours of one, and while he lacked a tennis racket or a sail bag the impression was definitely one of youth, sport, and clement weather. He had been swimming, and now he was breathing deeply, stertorously as if he could gulp into his lungs the components of that moment, the heat of the sun, the intenseness of his pleasure. It all seemed to flow into his chest. His own house stood in Bullet Park, eight miles to the south, where his four beautiful daughters would have had their lunch and might be playing tennis. Then it occurred to him that by taking a dogleg to the southwest he could reach his home by water.

His life was not confining and the delight he took in this observation could not be explained by its suggestion of escape. He seemed to see, with a cartographer's eye, that string of swimming pools, that quasi-subterranean stream that curved across the country. He had made a discovery, a contribution to modern geography; he would name the stream Lucinda after his wife. He was not a practical joker nor was he a fool but he was determinedly original and had a vague and modest idea of himself as a legendary figure. The day was beautiful and it seemed to him that a long swim might enlarge and celebrate its beauty.

He took off a sweater that was hung over his shoulders and dove in. He had an inexplicable contempt for men who did not hurl themselves into pools. He swam a choppy crawl, breathing either with every stroke or every fourth stroke and counting somewhere well in the back of his mind the one-two one-two of a flutter kick. It was not a serviceable stroke for long distances but the domestication of swimming had saddled the sport with some customs and in his part of the world a crawl was customary. To be embraced and sustained by the light green water was less a pleasure, it seemed, than the resumption of a natural condition, and he would have liked to swim without trunks, but this was not possible, considering his project. He hoisted himself up on the far curb —he never used the ladder—and started across the lawn. When Lucinda asked where he was going he said he was going to swim home.

The only maps and charts he had to go by were remembered or imaginary but these were clear enough. First there were the Grahams, the Hammers, the Lears, the Howlands, and the Crosscups. He would cross Ditmar Street to the Bunkers and come, after a short portage, to the Levys, the Welchers; and the public pool in Lancaster. Then there were the Hallorans, the Sachses, the Biswangers, Shirley Adams, the Gilmartins, and the Clydes. The day was lovely, and that he lived in a world so generously supplied with water seemed like a clemency, a beneficence. His heart was high and he ran across the grass. Making his way home by an uncommon route gave him the feeling that he was a pilgrim, an explorer, a man with a destiny, and he knew that he would find friends all along the way; friends would line the banks of the Lucinda River.

He went through a hedge that separated the Westerhazys' land from the Grahams', walked under some flowering apple trees, passed the shed that housed their pump and filter, and came out at the Grahams' pool. "Why Neddy," Mrs. Graham said, "what a marvelous surprise. I've been trying to get you on the phone all morning. Here let me get you a drink." He saw then, like any explorer, that the hospitable customs and traditions of the natives would have to be handled with diplomacy if he was ever going to reach his destination. He did not want to mystify or seem rude to the Grahams nor did he have the time to linger there. He swam the length of their pool and joined them in the sun and was rescued, a few minutes later, by the arrival of two car-loads of friends from Connecticut. During the uproarious reunions he was able to slip away. He went down by the front of the Grahams' house, stepped over a thorny hedge, and crossed a vacant lot to the Hammers'. Mrs. Hammer, looking up from her roses, saw him swim by although she wasn't quite sure who it was. The Lears heard him splashing past the open windows of their living room. The Howlands and the Crosscups were away. After leaving the Howlands' he crossed Ditmar Street and started for the Bunkers', where he could hear, even at that distance, the noise of a party.

The water refracted the sound of voices and laughter and seemed to suspend it in midair. The Bunkers' pool was on a rise and he climbed some stairs to a terrace where twenty-five or thirty men and women were drinking. The only person in the water was Rusty Towers, who floated there on a rubber raft. Oh how bonny and lush were the banks of the Lucinda River! Prosperous men and women gathered by the sapphire-colored waters while caterer's men in white coats passed them cold gin. Overhead a red de Haviland trainer was circling around and around and around in the sky with something like the glee of a child in a swing. Ned felt a passing affection for the scene, a tenderness for the gathering, as if it was something he might touch. In the distance he heard thunder. As soon as Enid Bunker saw him she began to scream: "Oh look who's here! What a marvelous surprise! When Lucinda said that you couldn't come I thought I'd *die*." She made her way to him through the crowd, and when they had finished kissing she led him to the bar, a progress that was slowed by the fact that he stopped to kiss eight or ten other women and shake the hands of as many men. A smiling bartender he had seen at a hundred parties gave him a gin and tonic and he stood by the bar for a moment, anxious not to get stuck in any conversation that would delay his voyage. When he seemed about to be surrounded he dove in and swam close to the side to avoid colliding with Rusty's raft. At the far end of the pool he bypassed the Tomlinsons with a broad smile and jogged up the garden path. The gravel cut his feet but this was the only unpleasantness. The party was confined to the pool, and as he went toward the house he heard the brilliant, watery sound of voices fade, heard the noise of a radio from the Bunkers' kitchen, where someone was listening to a ballgame. Sunday afternoon. He made his way through the parked cars and down the grassy border of their driveway to Alewives' Lane. He did not want to be seen on the road in his bathing trunks but there was no traffic and he made the short distance to the Levys' driveway, marked with a private property sign and a green tube for the *New York Times*. All the doors and windows of the big house were open but there were no signs of life; not even a dog barked. He went around the side of the house to the pool and saw that the Levys had only recently left. Glasses and bottles and dishes of nuts were on a table at the deep end, where there was a bathhouse or gazebo, hung with Japanese lanterns. After swimming the pool he got himself a glass and poured a drink. It was his fourth or fifth drink and he had swum nearly half the length of the Lucinda River. He felt tired, clean, and pleased at that moment to be alone; pleased with everything.

It would storm. The stand of cumulus cloud—that city—had risen and darkened, and while he sat there he heard the percussiveness of thunder again. The de Haviland trainer was still circling overhead and it seemed to Ned that he could almost hear the pilot laugh with pleasure in the afternoon; but when there was another peal of thunder he took off for home. A train whistle blew and he wondered what time it had gotten to be. Four! Five? He thought of the provincial station at that hour, where a waiter, his tuxedo concealed by a raincoat, a dwarf with some flowers wrapped in newspaper, and a woman who had been crying would be waiting for the local. It was suddenly growing dark; it was that moment when the pin-headed birds seem to organize their song into some acute and knowledgeable recognition of the storm's approach. Then there was a fine noise of rushing water from the crown of an oak at his back, as if a spigot there had been turned. Then the noise of fountains came from the crowns of all the tall trees. Why did he love storms, what was the meaning of his excitement when the door sprang open and the rain wind fled rudely up the stairs, why had the simple task of shutting the windows of an old house seemed fitting and urgent, why did the first watery notes of a storm wind have for him the unmistakable sound of good news, cheer, glad tidings? Then there was an explosion, a smell of cordite, and rain lashed the Japanese lanterns that Mrs. Levy had bought in Kyoto the year before last, or was it the year before that?

He stayed in the Levys' gazebo until the storm had passed. The rain had cooled the air and he shivered. The force of the wind had stripped a maple of its red and yellow leaves and scattered them over the grass and the water. Since it was midsummer the tree must be blighted, and yet he felt a peculiar sadness at this sign of autumn. He braced his shoulders, emptied his glass, and started for the Welchers' pool. This meant crossing the Lindleys' riding ring and he was surprised to find it over-grown with grass and all the jumps dismantled. He wondered if the Lindleys had sold their horses or gone away for the summer and put them out to board. He seemed to remember having heard something about the Lindleys and their horses but the memory was unclear. On he went, barefoot through the wet grass, to the Welchers', where he found their pool was dry.

This breach in his chain of water disappointed him absurdly, and he felt like some explorer who seeks a torrential headwater and finds a dead stream. He was disappointed and mystified. It was common enough to go away for the summer but no one ever drained his pool. The Welchers had definitely gone away. The pool furniture was folded, stacked, and covered with a tarpaulin. The bathhouse was locked. All the windows of the house were shut, and when he went around to the driveway in front he saw a for-sale sign nailed to a tree. When had he last heard from the Welchers—when, that is, had he and Lucinda last regretted an invitation to dine with them. It seemed only a week or so ago. Was his memory failing or had he so disciplined it in the repression of unpleasant facts that he had damaged his sense of the truth? Then in the distance he heard the sound of a tennis game. This cheered him, cleared away all his apprehensions and let him regard the overcast sky and the cold air with indifference. This was the day that Neddy Merrill swam across the county. That was the day! He started off then for his most difficult portage.

Had you gone for a Sunday afternoon ride that day you might have seen him, close to naked, standing on the shoulders of route 424, waiting for a chance to cross. You might have wondered if he was the victim of foul play, had his car broken down, or was he merely a fool. Standing barefoot in the deposits of the highway—beer cans, rags, and blowout patches—exposed to all kinds of ridicule, he seemed pitiful. He had known when he started that this was a part of his journey—it had been on his maps—but confronted with the lines of traffic, worming through the summery light, he found himself unprepared. He was laughed at, jeered at, a beer can was thrown at him, and he had no dignity or humor to bring to the situation. He could have gone back, back to the Westerhazys', where Lucinda would still be sitting in the sun. He had signed nothing, vowed nothing, pledged nothing not even to himself. Why, believing as he did, that all human obduracy was susceptible to common sense, was he unable to turn back? Why was he determined to complete his journey even if it meant putting his life in danger? At what point had this prank, this joke, this piece of horseplay become serious? He could not go back, he could not even recall with any clearness the green water at the Westerhazys', the sense of inhaling the day's components, the friendly and relaxed voices saying that they had *drunk* too much. In the space of an hour, more or less, he had covered a distance that made his return impossible.

An old man, tooling down the highway at fifteen miles an hour, let him get to the middle of the road, where there was a grass divider. Here he was exposed to the ridicule of the northbound traffic, but after ten or fifteen minutes he was able to cross. From here he had only a short walk to the Recreation Center at the edge of the Village of Lancaster, where there were some handball courts and a public pool.

The effect of the water on voices, the illusion of brilliance and suspense, was the same here as it had been at the Bunkers' but the sounds here were louder, harsher, and more shrill, and as soon as he entered the crowded enclosure he was confronted with regimentation. "ALL SWIMMERS MUST TAKE A SHOWER BEFORE USING THE POOL. ALL SWIMMERS MUST USE THE FOOTBATH. ALL SWIMMERS MUST WEAR THEIR IDENTIFICATION DISKS." He took a shower, washed his feet in a cloudy and bitter solution and made his way to the edge of the water. It stank of chlorine and looked to him like a sink. A pair of lifeguards in a pair of towers blew police whistles at what seemed to be regular intervals and abused the swimmers through a public address system. Neddy remembered the sapphire water at the Bunkers' with longing and thought that he might contaminate himself—damage his own prosperousness and charm—by swimming in this murk, but he reminded himself that he was an explorer, a pilgrim, and that this was merely a stagnant bend in the Lucinda River. He dove, scowling with distaste, into the chlorine and had to swim with his head above water to avoid collisions, but even so he was bumped into, splashed and jostled. When he got to the shallow end both lifeguards were shouting at him; "Hey, you, you without the identification disk, get outa the water." He did, but they had no way of pursuing him and he went through the reek of suntan oil and chlorine out through the hurricane fence and passed the handball courts. By crossing the road he entered the wooded part of the Halloran estate. The woods were not cleared and the footing was treacherous and difficult until he reached the lawn and the clipped beech hedge that encircled their pool.

The Hallorans were friends, an elderly couple of enormous wealth who seemed to bask in the suspicion that they might be Communists. They were zealous reformers but they were not Communists, and yet when they were accused, as they sometimes were, of subversion, it seemed to gratify and excite them. Their beech hedge was yellow and he guessed this had been blighted like the Levys' maple. He called hullo, hullo, to warn the Hallorans of his approach, to palliate his invasion of their privacy. The Hallorans, for reasons that had never been explained to him, did not wear bathing suits. No explanations were in order, really. Their nakedness was a detail in their uncompromising zeal for reform and he stepped politely out of his trunks before he went through the opening in the hedge.

Mrs. Halloran, a stout woman with white hair and a serene face, was reading the *Times*. Mr. Halloran was taking beech leaves out of the water with a scoop. They seemed not surprised or displeased to see him. Their pool was perhaps the oldest in the county, a fieldstone rectangle, fed by a brook. It had no filter or pump and its waters were the opaque gold of the stream.

"I'm swimming across the county," Ned said.

"Why, I didn't know one could," exclaimed Mrs. Halloran.

"Well, I've made it from the Westerhazys'," Ned said. "That must be about four miles."

He left his trunks at the deep end, walked to the shallow end, and swam this stretch. As he was pulling himself out of the water he heard Mrs. Halloran say: "We've been *terribly* sorry to hear about all your misfortunes?" Neddy."

"My misfortunes?" Ned asked. "I don't know what you mean."

"Why, we heard that you'd sold the house and that your poor children . . ."

"I don't recall having sold the house," Ned said, "and the girls are at home."

"Yes," Mrs. Halloran sighed. "Yes . . ." Her voice filled the air with an unseasonable melancholy and Ned spoke briskly. "Thank you for the swim."

"Well, have a nice trip," said Mrs. Halloran.

Beyond the hedge he pulled on his trunks and fastened them. They were loose and he wondered if, during the space of an afternoon, he could have lost some weight. He was cold and he was tired and the naked Hallorans and their dark water had depressed him. The swim was too much for his strength but how could he have guessed this, sliding down the banister that morning and sitting in the Westerhazys' sun? His arms were lame. His legs felt rubbery and ached at the joints. The worst of it was the cold in his bones and the feeling that he might never be warm again. Leaves were falling down around him and he smelled woodsmoke on the wind. Who would be burning wood at this time of year?

He needed a drink. Whiskey would warm him, pick him up, carry him through the last of his journey, refresh his feeling that it was original and valorous to swim the county. Channel swimmers took brandy. He needed a stimulant. He crossed the lawn in front of the Hallorans' house and went down a little path to where they had built a house for their only daughter Helen and her husband Eric Sachs. The Sachses' pool was small and he found Helen and her husband there.

"Oh, *Neddy*," Helen said. "Did you lunch at Mother's?"

"Not *really*," Ned said. "I *did* stop to see your parents." This seemed to be explanation enough. "I'm terribly sorry to break in on you like this but I've taken a chill and I wonder if you'd give me a drink."

"Why, I'd *love* to," Helen said, "but there hasn't been anything in this house to drink since Eric's operation. That was three years ago."

Was he losing his memory, had his gift for concealing painful facts let him forget that he had sold his house, that his children were in trouble, and that his friend had been ill? His eyes slipped from Eric's face to his abdomen, where he saw three pale, sutured scars, two of them at least a foot long. Gone was his navel, and what, Neddy thought, would the roving hand, bed-checking one's gifts at 3 A.M. make of a belly with no navel, no link to birth, this breach in the succession?

"I'm sure you can get a drink at the Biswangers'," Helen said. "They're having an enormous do. You can hear it from here. Listen!"

She raised her head and from across the road, the lawns, the gardens, the woods, the fields, he heard again the brilliant noise of voices over water. "Well, I'll get wet," he said, still feeling that he had no freedom of choice about his means of travel. He dove into the Sachses' cold water and, gasping, close to drowning, made his way from one end of the pool to the other. "Lucinda and I want *terribly* to see you," he said over his shoulder, his face set toward the Biswangers'. "We're sorry it's been so long and we'll call you *very* soon."

He crossed some fields to the Biswangers' and the sounds of revelry there. They would be honored to give him a drink, they would be happy to give him a drink, they would in fact be lucky to give him a drink. The Biswangers invited him and Lucinda for dinner four times a year, six weeks in advance. They were always rebuffed and yet they continued to send out their invitations, unwilling to comprehend the rigid and undemocratic realities of their society. They were the sort of people who discussed the price of things at cocktails, exchanged market tips during dinner, and after dinner told dirty stories to mixed company. They did not belong to Neddy's set—they were not even on Lucinda's Christmas card list. He went toward their pool with feelings of indifference, charity, and some unease, since it seemed to be getting dark and these were the longest days of the year. The party when he joined it was noisy and large. Grace Biswanger was the kind of hostess who asked the optometrist, the veterinarian, the real-estate dealer and the dentist. No one was swimming and the twilight, reflected on the water of the pool, had a wintry gleam. There was a bar and he started for this. When Grace Biswanger saw him she came toward him, not affectionately as he had every right to expect, but bellicosely.

"Why, this party has everything," she said loudly, "including a gate crasher."

She could not deal him a social blow—there was no question about this and he did not flinch. "As a gate crasher," he asked politely, "do I rate a drink?"

"Suit yourself," she said. "You don't seem to pay much attention to invitations."

She turned her back on him and joined some guests, and he went to the bar and ordered a whiskey. The bartender served him but he served him rudely. His was a world in which the caterer's men kept the social score, and to be rebuffed by a part-time barkeep meant that he had suffered some loss of social esteem. Or perhaps the man was new and uninformed. Then he heard Grace at his back say: "They went for broke overnight—nothing but income —and he showed up drunk one Sunday and asked us to loan him five thousand dollars. . . ." She was always talking about money. It was worse than eating your peas off a knife. He dove into the pool, swam its length and went away.

The next pool on his list, the last but two, belonged to his old mistress, Shirley Adams. If he had suffered any injuries at the Biswangers' they would be cured here. Love—sexual roughhouse in fact—was the supreme elixir, the painkiller, the brightly colored pill that would put the spring back into his step, the joy of life in his heart. They had had an affair last week, last month, last year. He couldn't remember. It was he who had broken it off, his was the upper hand, and he stepped through the gate of the wall that surrounded her pool with nothing so considered as self-confidence. It seemed in a way to be his pool as the lover, particularly the illicit lover, enjoys the possessions of his mistress with an authority unknown to holy matrimony. She was there, her hair the color of brass, but her figure, at the edge of the lighted, cerulean water, excited in him no profound memories. It had been, he thought, a lighthearted affair, although she had wept when he broke it off. She seemed confused to see him and he wondered if she was still wounded. Would she, God forbid, weep again?

"What do you want?" she asked.

"I'm swimming across the county."

"Good Christ. Will you ever grow up?"

"What's the matter?"

"If you've come here for money," she said, "I won't give you another cent."

"You could give me a drink."

"I could but I won't. I'm not alone."

"Well, I'm on my way."

He dove in and swam the pool, but when he tried to haul himself up onto the curb he found that the strength in his arms and his shoulders had gone, and he paddled to the ladder and climbed out. Looking over his shoulder he saw, in the lighted bathhouse, a young man. Going out onto the dark lawn he smelled chrysanthemums or marigolds—some stubborn autumnal fragrance—on the night air, strong as gas. Looking overhead he saw that the stars had come out, but why should he seem to see Andromeda, Cepheus, and Cassiopeia? What had become of the constellations of midsummer? He began to cry.

It was probably the first time in his adult life that he had ever cried, certainly the first time in his life that he had ever felt so miserable, cold, tired, and bewildered. He could not understand the rudeness of the caterer's barkeep or the rudeness of a mistress who had come to him on her knees and showered his trousers with tears. He had swum too long, he had been immersed too long, and his nose and his throat were sore from the water. What he needed then was a drink, some company, and some clean dry clothes, and while he could have cut directly across the road to his home he went on to the Gilmartins' pool. Here, for the first time in his life, he did not dive but went down the steps into the icy water and swam a hobbled side stroke that he might have learned as a youth. He staggered with fatigue on his way to the Clydes' and paddled the length of their pool, stopping again and again with his hand on the curb to rest. He climbed up the ladder and wondered if he had the strength to get home. He had done what he wanted, he had swum the county, but he was so stupefied with exhaustion that his triumph seemed vague. Stooped, holding onto the gateposts for support, he turned up the driveway of his own house.

The place was dark. Was it so late that they had all gone to bed? Had Lucinda stayed at the Westerhazys' for supper? Had the girls joined her there or gone someplace else? Hadn't they agreed, as they usually did on Sunday, to regret all their invitations and stay at home? He tried the garage doors to see what cars were in but the doors were locked and rust came off the handles onto his hands. Going toward the house, he saw that the force of the thunderstorm had knocked one of the rain gutters loose. It hung down over the front door like an umbrella rib, but it could be fixed in the morning. The house was locked, and he thought that the stupid cook or the stupid maid must have locked the place up until he remembered that it had been some time since they had employed a maid or a cook. He shouted, pounded on the door, tried to force it with his shoulder, and then, looking in at the windows, saw that the place was empty.

Bernard Malamud (1914–   )

The Magic Barrel

Not long ago there lived in uptown New York, in a small, almost meager room, though crowded with books, Leo Finkle, a rabbinical student in the Yeshivah University. Finkle, after six years of study, was to be ordained in June and had been advised by an acquaintance that he might find it easier to win himself a congregation if he were married. Since he had no present prospects of marriage, after two tormented days of turning it over in his mind, he called in Pinye Salzman, a marriage broker whose two-line advertisement he had read in the *Forward*.

The matchmaker appeared one night

out of the dark fourth-floor hallway of the graystone rooming house where Finkle lived, grasping a black, strapped portfolio that had been worn thin with use. Salzman, who had been long in the business, was of slight but dignified build, wearing an old hat, and an overcoat too short and tight for him. He smelled frankly of fish, which he loved to eat, and although he was missing a few teeth, his presence was not displeasing, because of an amiable manner curiously contrasted with mournful eyes. His voice, his lips, his wisp of beard, his bony fingers were animated, but give him a moment of repose and his mild blue eyes revealed a depth of sadness, a characteristic that put Leo a little at ease although the situation, for him, was inherently tense.

He at once informed Salzman why he had asked him to come, explaining that his home was in Cleveland, and that but for his parents, who had married comparatively late in life, he was alone in the world. He had for six years devoted himself almost entirely to his studies, as a result of which, understandably, he had found himself without time for a social life and the company of young women. Therefore he thought it the better part of trial and error—of embarrassing fumbling—to call in an experienced person to advise him on these matters. He remarked in passing that the function of the marriage broker was ancient and honorable, highly approved in the Jewish community, because it made practical the necessary without hindering joy. Moreover, his own parents had been brought together by a matchmaker. They had made, if not a financially profitable marriage—since neither had possessed any worldly goods to speak of—at least a successful one in the sense of their everlasting devotion to each other. Salzman listened in embarrassed surprise, sensing a sort of apology. Later, however, he experienced a glow of pride in his work, an emotion that had left him years ago, and he heartily approved of Finkle.

The two went to their business. Leo had led Salzman to the only clear place in the room, a table near a window that overlooked the lamp-lit city. He seated himself at the matchmaker's side but facing him, attempting by an act of will to suppress the unpleasant tickle in his throat. Salzman eagerly unstrapped his portfolio and removed a loose rubber band from a thin packet of much-handled cards. As he flipped through them, a gesture and sound that physically hurt Leo, the student pretended not to see and gazed steadfastly out the window. Although it was still February, winter was on its last legs, signs of which he had for the first time in years begun to notice. He now observed the round white moon, moving high in the sky through a cloud menagerie, and watched with half-open mouth as it penetrated a huge hen, and dropped out of her like an egg laying itself. Salzman, though pretending through eyeglasses he had just slipped on, to be engaged in scanning the writing on the cards, stole occasional glances at the young man's distinguished face, noting with pleasure the long, severe scholar's nose, brown eyes heavy with learning, sensitive yet ascetic lips, and a certain, almost hollow quality of the dark cheeks. He gazed around at shelves upon shelves of books and let out a soft, contented sigh.

When Leo's eyes fell upon the cards, he counted six spread out in Salzman's hand.

"So few?" he asked in disappointment.

"You wouldn't believe me how much cards I got in my office," Salzman replied. "The drawers are already filled to the top, so I keep them now in a barrel, but is every girl good for a new rabbi?"

Leo blushed at this, regretting all he had revealed of himself in a curriculum vitae he had sent to Salzman. He had thought it best to acquaint him with his strict standards and specifications, but in having done so, felt he had told the marriage broker more than was absolutely necessary.

He hesitantly inquired, "Do you keep photographs of your clients on file?"

"First comes family, amount of dowry, also what kind promises," Salzman replied, unbuttoning his tight coat and settling himself in the chair. "After comes pictures, rabbi."

"Call me Mr. Finkle. I'm not yet a rabbi."

Salzman said he would, but instead called him doctor, which he changed to rabbi when Leo was not listening too attentively.

Salzman adjusted his horn-rimmed spectacles, gently cleared his throat and read in an eager voice the contents of the top card:

"Sophie P. Twenty four years. Widow one year. No children. Educated high school and two years college. Father promises eight thousand dollars. Has wonderful wholesale business. Also real estate. On the mother's side comes teachers, also one actor. Well known on Second Avenue."

Leo gazed up in surprise. "Did you say a widow?"

"A widow don't mean spoiled, rabbi. She lived with her husband maybe four months. He was a sick boy she made a mistake to marry him."

"Marrying a widow has never entered my mind."

"This is because you have no experience. A widow, especially if she is young and healthy like this girl, is a wonderful person to marry. She will be thankful to you the rest of her life. Believe me, if I was looking now for a bride, I would marry a widow."

Leo reflected, then shook his head.

Salzman hunched his shoulders in an almost imperceptible gesture of disappointment. He placed the card down on the wooden table and began to read another:

"Lily H. High school teacher. Regular. Not a substitute. Has savings and new Dodge car. Lived in Paris one year. Father is successful dentist thirty-five years. Interested in professional man. Well Americanized family. Wonderful opportunity.

"I knew her personally," said Salzman. "I wish you could see this girl. She is a doll. Also very intelligent. All day you could talk to her about books and theyater and what not. She also knows current events."

"I don't believe you mentioned her age?"

"Her age?" Salzman said, raising his brows. "Her age is thirty-two years."

Leo said after a while. "I'm afraid that seems a little too old."

Salzman let out a laugh. "So how old are you, rabbi?"

"Twenty-seven."

"So what is the difference, tell me, between twenty-seven and thirty-two? My own wife is seven years older than me. So what did I suffer?—Nothing. If Rothschild's a daughter wants to marry you, would you say on account her age, no?"

"Yes," Leo said dryly.

Salzman shook off the no in the yes. "Five years don't mean a thing. I give you my word that when you will live with her for one week you will forget her age. What does it mean five years—that she lived more and knows more than somebody who is younger? On this girl, God bless her, years are not wasted. Each one that it comes makes better the bargain."

"What subject does she teach in high school?"

"Languages. If you heard the way she speaks French, you will think it is music. I am in the business twenty-five years, and I recommend her with my whole heart. Believe me, I know what I'm talking, rabbi."

"What's on the next card?" Leo said abruptly.

Salzman reluctantly turned up the third card:

"Ruth K. Nineteen years. Honor student. Father offers thirteen thousand cash to the right bridegroom. He is a medical doctor. Stomach specialist with marvelous practice. Brother in law owns own garment business. Particular people."

Salzman looked as if he had read his trump card.

"Did you say nineteen?" Leo asked with interest.

"On the dot."

"Is she attractive?" He blushed. "Pretty?"

Salzman kissed his finger tips. "A little doll. On this I give you my word. Let me call the father tonight and you will see what means pretty."

But Leo was troubled. "You're sure she's that young?"

"This I am positive. The father will show you the birth certificate."

"Are you positive there isn't something wrong with her?" Leo insisted.

"Who says there is wrong?"

"I don't understand why an American girl her age should go to a marriage broker."

A smile spread over Salzman's face. "So for the same reason you went, she comes."

Leo flushed. "I am pressed for time."

Salzman, realizing he had been tactless, quickly explained. "The father came, not her. He wants she should have the best, so he looks around himself. When we will locate the right boy he will introduce him and encourage. This makes a better marriage than if a young girl without experience takes for herself. I don't have to tell you this."

"But don't you think this young girl believes in love?" Leo spoke uneasily.

Salzman was about to guffaw but caught himself and said soberly, "Love comes with the right person, not before."

Leo parted dry lips but did not speak. Noticing that Salzman had snatched a glance at the next card, he cleverly asked. "How is her health?"

"Perfect," Salzman said, breathing with difficulty. "Of course, she is a little lame on her right foot from an auto accident that it happened to her when she was twelve years, but nobody notices on account she is so brilliant and also beautiful."

Leo got up heavily and went to the window. He felt curiously bitter and up-braided himself for having called in the marriage broker. Finally, he shook his head.

"Why not?" Salzman persisted, the pitch of his voice rising.

"Because I detest stomach specialists."

"So what do you care what is his business? After you marry her do you need him? Who says he must come every Friday night in your house?"

Ashamed of the way the talk was going, Leo dismissed Salzman, who went home with heavy, melancholy eyes.

Though he had felt only relief at the marriage broker's departure, Leo was in low spirits the next day. He explained it as arising from Salzman's failure to produce a suitable bride for him. He did not care for his type of clientele. But when Leo found himself hesitating whether to seek out another matchmaker, one more polished than Pinye, he wondered if it could be—his protestations to the contrary, and although he honored his father and mother—that he did not, in essence, care for the matchmaking institution? This thought he quickly put out of mind yet found himself still upset. All day he ran around in the woods—missed an important appointment, forgot to give out his laundry, walked out of a Broadway cafeteria without paying and had to run back with the ticket in his hand; had even not recognized his landlady in the street when she passed with a friend and courteously called out, "A good evening to you, Doctor Finkle." By nightfall, however, he had regained sufficient calm to sink his nose into a book and there found peace from his thoughts.

Almost at once there came a knock on the door. Before Leo could say enter, Salzman, commercial cupid, was standing in the room. His face was gray and meager, his expression hungry, and he looked as if he would expire on his feet. Yet the marriage broker managed, by some trick of the muscles, to display a broad smile.

"So good evening. I am invited?"

Leo nodded, disturbed to see him again, yet unwilling to ask the man to leave.

Beaming still, Salzman laid his portfolio on the table. "Rabbi, I got for you tonight good news."

"I've asked you not to call me rabbi. I'm still a student."

"Your worries are finished. I have for you a first-class bride."

"Leave me in peace concerning this subject." Leo pretended lack of interest.

"The world will dance at your wedding."

"Please, Mr. Salzman, no more."

"But first must come back my strength," Salzman said weakly. He fumbled with the portfolio straps and took out of the leather case an oily paper bag, from which he extracted a hard, seeded roll and a small, smoked white fish. With a quick motion of his hand he stripped the fish out of its skin and began ravenously to chew. "All day in a rush," he muttered.

Leo watched him eat.

"A sliced tomato you have maybe?" Salzman hesitantly inquired.

"No."

The marriage broker shut his eyes and ate. When he had finished he carefully cleaned up the crumbs and rolled up the remains of the fish, in the paper bag. His spectacled eyes roamed the room until he discovered, amid some piles of books, a one-burner gas stove. Lifting his hat he humbly asked, "A glass tea you got, rabbi?"

Conscience-stricken, Leo rose and brewed the tea. He served it with a chunk of lemon and two cubes of lump sugar, delighting Salzman.

After he had drunk his tea, Salzman's strength and good spirits were restored. "So tell me, rabbi," he said amiably, "you considered some more the three clients I mentioned yesterday?"

"There was no need to consider."

"Why not?"

"None of them suits me."

"What then suits you?"

Leo let it pass because he could give only a confused answer.

Without waiting for a reply, Salzman asked, "You remember this girl I talked to you—the high school teacher?"

"Age thirty-two?"

But surprisingly, Salzman's face lit in a smile. "Age twenty-nine."

Leo shot him a look. "Reduced from thirty-two?"

"A mistake," Salzman avowed. "I talked today with the dentist. He took me to his safety deposit box and showed me the birth certificate. She was twenty-nine years last August. They made her a party in the mountains where she went for her vacation. When her father spoke to me the first time I forgot to write the age and I told you thirty-two, but now I remember this was a different client, a widow."

"The same one you told me about? I thought she was twenty-four?"

"A different. Am I responsible that the world is filled with widows?"

"No, but I'm not interested in them, nor for that matter, in school teachers."

Salzman pulled his clasped hands to his breast. Looking at the ceiling he devoutly exclaimed, "Yiddishe kinder, what can I say to somebody that he is not interested in high school teachers? So what then you are interested?"

Leo flushed but controlled himself.

"In what else will you be interested," Salzman went on, "if you not interested in this fine girl that she speaks four languages and has personally in the bank ten thousand dollars? Also her father guarantees further twelve thousand. Also she has a new car, wonderful clothes, talks on all subjects, and she will give you a first-class home and children. How near do we come in our life to paradise?"

"If she's so wonderful, why wasn't she married ten years ago?"

"Why?" said Salzman with a heavy laugh. "—Why? Because she is *partikiler.* This is why. She wants the *best.*"

Leo was silent, amused at how he had entangled himself. But Salzman had aroused his interest in Lily H., and he began seriously to consider calling on her. When the marriage broker observed how intently Leo's mind was at work on the facts he had supplied, he felt certain they would soon come to an agreement.

Late Saturday afternoon, conscious of Salzman, Leo Finkle walked with Lily Hirschorn along Riverside Drive. He walked briskly and erectly, wearing with distinction the black fedora he had that morning taken with trepidation out of the dusty hat box on his closet shelf, and the heavy black Saturday coat he had thoroughly whisked clean. Leo also owned a walking stick, a present from a distant relative, but quickly put temptation aside and did not use it. Lily, petite and not unpretty, had on something signifying the approach of spring. She was au courant, animatedly, with all sorts of subjects, and he weighed her words and found her surprisingly sound—score another for Salzman, whom he uneasily sensed to be somewhere around, hiding perhaps high in a tree along the street, flashing the lady signals with a pocket mirror; or perhaps a cloven-hoofed Pan, piping nuptial ditties as he danced his invisible way before them, strewing wild buds on the walk and purple grapes in their path, symbolizing fruit of a union, though there was of course still none.

Lily startled Leo by remarking, "I was thinking of Mr. Salzman, a curious figure, wouldn't you say?"

Not certain what to answer, he nodded.

She bravely went on, blushing, "I for one am grateful for his introducing us. Aren't you?"

He courteously replied, "I am."

"I mean," she said with a little laugh—and it was all in good taste, or at least gave the effect of being not in bad—"do you mind that we came together so?"

He was not displeased with her honesty, recognizing that she meant to set the relationship aright, and understanding that it took a certain amount of experience in life, and courage, to want to do it quite that way. One had to have some sort of past to make that kind of beginning.

He said that he did not mind. Salzman's function was traditional and honorable—valuable for what it might achieve, which, he pointed out, was frequently nothing.

Lily agreed with a sigh. They walked on for a while and she said after a long silence, again with a nervous laugh, "Would you mind if I asked you something a little bit personal? Frankly, I find the subject fascinating." Although Leo shrugged, she went on half embarrassedly, "How was it that you came to your calling? I mean was it a sudden passionate inspiration?"

Leo, after a time, slowly replied, "I was always interested in the Law."

"You saw revealed in it the presence of the Highest?"

He nodded and changed the subject. "I understand that you spent a little time in Paris, Miss Hirschorn?"

"Oh, did Mr. Salzman tell you, Rabbi Finkle?" Leo winced but she went on, "It was ages ago and almost forgotten. I remember I had to return for my sister's wedding."

And Lily would not be put off. "When," she asked in a trembly voice, "did you become enamored of God?"

He stared at her. Then it came to him that she was talking not about Leo Finkle, but of a total stranger, some mystical figure, perhaps even passionate prophet that Salzman had dreamed up for her—no relation to the living or dead. Leo trembled with rage and weakness. The trickster had obviously sold her a bill of goods, just as he had him, who'd expected to become acquainted with a young lady of twenty-nine, only to behold, the moment he laid eyes upon her strained and anxious face, a woman past thirty-five and aging rapidly. Only his self control had kept him this long in her presence.

"I am not," he said gravely, "a talented religious person," and in seeking words to go on, found himself possessed by shame and fear. "I think," he said in a strained manner, "that I came to God not because I loved Him, but because I did not."

This confession he spoke harshly because its unexpectedness shook him.

Lily wilted. Leo saw a profusion of loaves of bread go flying like ducks high over his head, not unlike the winged loaves by which he had counted himself to sleep last night. Mercifully, then, it snowed, which he would not put past Salzman's machinations.

He was infuriated with the marriage broker and swore he would throw him out of the room the minute he reappeared. But Salzman did not come that night, and when Leo's anger had subsided, an unaccountable despair grew in its place. At first he thought this was caused by his disappointment in Lily, but before long it became evident that he had involved himself with Salzman without a true knowledge of his own intent. He gradually realized—with an emptiness that seized him with six hands—that he had called in the broker to find him a bride because he was incapable of doing it himself. This terrifying insight he had derived as a result of his meeting and conversation with Lily Hirschorn. Her probing questions had somehow irritated him into revealing—to himself more than her—the true nature of his relationship to God, and from that it had come upon him, with shocking force, that apart from his parents, he had never loved anyone. Or perhaps it went the other way, that he did not love God so well as he might, because he had not loved man. It seemed to Leo that his whole life stood starkly revealed and he saw himself for the first time as he truly was—unloved and loveless. This bitter but somehow not fully unexpected revelation brought him to a point of panic, controlled only by extraordinary effort. He covered his face with his hands and cried.

The week that followed was the worst of his life. He did not eat and lost weight. His beard darkened and grew ragged. He stopped attending seminars and almost never opened a book. He seriously considered leaving the Yeshivah, although he was deeply troubled at the thought of the loss of all his years of study—saw them like pages torn from a book, strewn over the city—and at the devastating effect of this decision upon his parents. But he had lived without knowledge of himself, and never in the Five Books and all the Commentaries—mea culpa—had the truth been revealed to him. He did not know where to turn, and in all this desolating loneliness there was no *to whom*, although he often thought of Lily but not once could bring himself to go downstairs and make the call. He became touchy and irritable, especially with his landlady, who asked him all manner of personal questions; on the other hand, sensing his own disagreeableness, he waylaid her on the stairs and apologized abjectly, until mortified, she ran from him. Out of this, however, he drew the consolation that he was a Jew and that a Jew suffered. But gradually, as the long and terrible week drew to a close, he regained his composure and some idea of purpose in life: to go on as planned. Although he was imperfect, the ideal was not. As for his quest of a bride, the thought of continuing afflicted him with anxiety and heartburn, yet perhaps with this new knowledge of himself he would be more successful than in the past. Perhaps love would now come to him and a bride to that love. And for this sanctified seeking who needed a Salzman?

The marriage broker, a skeleton with haunted eyes, returned that very night. He looked, withal, the picture of frustrated expectancy—as if he had steadfastly waited the week at Miss Lily Hirschorn's side for a telephone call that never came.

Casually coughing, Salzman came immediately to the point: "So how did you like her?"

Leo's anger rose and he could not refrain from chiding the matchmaker: "Why did you lie to me, Salzman?"

Salzman's pale face went dead white, the world had snowed on him.

"Did you not state that she was twenty-nine?" Leo insisted.

"I give you my word—"

"She was thirty-five, if a day. *At least* thirty-five."

"Of this don't be too sure. Her father told me—"

"Never mind. The worst of it was that you lied to her."

"How did I lie to her, tell me?"

"You told her things about me that weren't true. You made me out to be more, consequently less than I am. She had in mind a totally different person, a sort of semi-mystical Wonder Rabbi."

"All I said, you was a religious man."

"I can imagine."

Salzman sighed. "This is my weakness that I have," he confessed. "My wife says to me I shouldn't be a salesman, but when I have two fine people that they would be wonderful to be married, I am so happy that I talk too much." He smiled wanly. "This is why Salzman is a poor man."

Leo's anger left him. "Well, Salzman, I'm afraid that's all."

The marriage broker fastened hungry eyes on him.

"You don't want any more a bride?"

"I do," said Leo, "but I have decided to seek her in a different way. I am no longer interested in an arranged marriage. To be frank, I now admit the necessity of premarital love. That is, I want to be in love with the one I marry."

"Love?" said Salzman, astounded. After a moment he remarked, "For us, our love is our life, not for the ladies. In the ghetto they—"

"I know, I know," said Leo. "I've thought of it often. Love, I have said to myself, should be a by-product of living and worship rather than its own end. Yet for myself I find it necessary to establish the level of my need and fulfill it."

Salzman shrugged but answered, "Listen, rabbi, if you want love, this I can find for you also. I have such beautiful clients that you will love them the minute your eyes will see them."

Leo smiled unhappily. "I'm afraid you don't understand."

But Salzman hastily unstrapped his portfolio and withdrew a manila packet from it.

"Pictures," he said, quickly laying the envelope on the table.

Leo called after him to take the pictures away, but as if on the wings of the wind, Salzman had disappeared.

March came. Leo had returned to his regular routine. Although he felt not quite himself yet—lacked energy—he was making plans for a more active social life. Of course it would cost something, but he was an expert in cutting corners; and when there were no corners left he would make circles rounder. All the while Salzman's pictures had lain on the table, gathering dust. Occasionally as Leo sat studying, or enjoying a cup of tea, his eyes fell on the manila envelope, but he never opened it.

The days went by and no social life to speak of developed with a member of the opposite sex—it was difficult, given the circumstances of his situation. One morning Leo toiled up the stairs to his room and stared out the window at the city. Although the day was bright his view of it was dark. For some time he watched the people in the street below hurrying along and then turned with a heavy heart to his little room. On the table was the packet. With a sudden relentless gesture he tore it open. For a half-hour he stood by the table in a state of excitement, examining the photographs of the ladies Salzman had included. Finally, with a deep sigh he put them down. There were six, of varying degrees of attractiveness, but look at them long enough and they all became Lily Hirschorn: all past their prime, all starved behind bright smiles, not a true personality in the lot. Life, despite their frantic yoohooings, had passed them by; they were pictures in a brief case that stank of fish. After a while, however, as Leo attempted to return the photographs into the envelope, he found in it another, a snapshot of the type taken by a machine for a quarter. He gazed at it a moment and let out a cry.

Her face deeply moved him. Why, he could at first not say. It gave him the impression of youth—spring flowers, yet age—a sense of having been used to the bone, wasted; this came from the eyes, which were hauntingly familiar, yet absolutely strange. He had a vivid impression that he had met her before, but try as he might he could not place her although he could almost recall her name, as if he had read it in her own handwriting. No, this couldn't be; he would have remembered her. It was not, he affirmed, that she had an extraordinary beauty—no, though her face was attractive enough; it was that *something* about her moved him. Feature for feature, even some of the ladies of the photographs could do better; but she leaped forth to his heart—had *lived,* or wanted to—more than just wanted, perhaps regretted how she had lived—had somehow deeply suffered: it could be seen in the depths of those reluctant eyes, and from the way the light enclosed and shone from her, and within her, opening realms of possibility: this was her own. Her he desired. His head ached and eyes narrowed with the intensity of his gazing, then as if an obscure fog had blown up in the mind, he experienced fear of her and was aware that he had received an impression, somehow, of evil. He shuddered, saying softly, it is thus with us all. Leo brewed some tea in a small pot and sat sipping it without sugar, to calm himself. But before he had finished drinking, again with excitement he examined the face and found it good: good for Leo Finkle. Only such a one could understand him and help him seek whatever he was seeking. She might, perhaps, love him. How she had happened to be among the discards in Salzman's barrel he could never guess, but he knew he must urgently go find her.

Leo rushed downstairs, grabbed up the Bronx telephone book, and searched for Salzman's home address. He was not listed, nor was his office. Neither was he in the Manhattan book. But Leo remembered having written down the address on a slip of paper after he had read Salzman's advertisement in the "personals" column of the *Forward.* He ran up to his room and tore through his papers, without luck. It was exasperating. Just when he needed the matchmaker he was nowhere to be found. Fortunately Leo remembered to look in his wallet. There on a card he found his name written and a Bronx address. No phone number was listed, the reason—Leo now recalled—he had originally communicated with Salzman by letter. He got on his coat, put a hat on over his skull cap and hurried to the subway station. All the way to the far end of the Bronx he sat on the edge of his seat. He was more than once tempted to take out the picture and see if the girl's face was as he remembered it, but he refrained, allowing the snapshot to remain in his inside coat pocket, content to have her so close. When the train pulled into the station he was waiting at the door and bolted out. He quickly located the street Salzman had advertised.

The building he sought was less than a block from the subway, but it was not an office building, nor even a loft, nor a store in which one could rent office space. It was a very old tenement house. Leo found Salzman's name in pencil on a soiled tag under the bell and climbed three dark flights to his apartment. When he knocked, the door was opened by a thin, asthmatic, gray-haired woman, in felt slippers.

"Yes?" she said, expecting nothing. She listened without listening. He could have sworn he had seen her, too, before but knew it was an illusion.

"Salzman—does he live here? Pinye Salzman," he said, "the matchmaker?"

She stared at him a long minute. "Of course."

He felt embarrassed. "Is he in?"

"No." Her mouth, though left open, offered nothing more.

"The matter is urgent. Can you tell me where his office is?"

"In the air." She pointed upward.

"You mean he has no office?" Leo asked.

"In his socks."

He peered into the apartment. It was sunless and dingy, one large room divided by a half-open curtain, beyond which he could see a sagging metal bed. The near side of the room was crowded with rickety chairs, old bureaus, a three-legged table, racks of cooking utensils, and all the apparatus of a kitchen. But there was no sign of Salzman or his magic barrel, probably also a figment of the imagination. An odor of frying fish made Leo weak to the knees.

"Where is he?" he insisted. "I've got to see your husband."

At length she answered, "So who knows where he is? Every time he thinks a new thought he runs to a different place. Go home, he will find you."

"Tell him Leo Finkle."

She gave no sign she had heard.

He walked downstairs, depressed.

But Salzman, breathless, stood waiting at his door.

Leo was astounded and overjoyed. "How did you get here before me?"

I rushed."

"Come inside."

They entered. Leo fixed tea, and a sardine sandwich for Salzman. As they were drinking he reached behind him for the packet of pictures and handed them to the marriage broker.

Salzman put down his glass and said expectantly, "You found somebody you like?"

"Not among these."

The marriage broker turned away.

"Here is the one I want." Leo held forth a snapshot.

Salzman slipped on his glasses and took the picture into his trembling hand. He turned ghastly and let out a groan.

"What's the matter?" cried Leo.

"Excuse me. Was an accident this one—wild, without shame. This is not a picture. She isn't for you."

Salzman frantically shoved the manila packet into his protfolio. He thrust the snapshot into his pocket and fled down the stairs.

Leo, after momentary paralysis, gave chase and cornered the marriage broker in the vestibule. The landlady made hysterical outcries but neither of them listened.

"Give me back the picture, Salzman."

"No." The pain in his eyes was terrible.

"Tell me who she is then."

"This I can't tell you. Excuse me."

He made to depart, but Leo, forgetting himself, seized the matchmaker by his tight coat and shook him frenziedly.

"Please," sighed Saltzman. *"Please."*

Leo ashamedly let him go. "Tell me who she is," he begged. "It's very important for me to know."

"She is not for you. She is a wild bride for a rabbi."

"What do you mean wild?"

"Like an animal. Like a dog. For her to be poor was a sin. This is why to me she is dead now."

"In God's name, what do you mean?"

Her I can't introduce to you," Salzman cried.

"Why are you so excited?"

"Why, he asks," Salzman said, bursting into tears. "This is my baby, my Stella, she should burn in hell."

Leo hurried up to bed and hid under the covers. Under the covers he thought his life through. Although he soon fell asleep he could not sleep her out of his mind. He woke, beating his breast. Though he prayed to be rid of her, his prayers went unanswered. Through days of torment he endlessly struggled not to love her; fearing success, he escaped it. He then concluded to convert her to goodness, himself to God. The idea alternately nauseated and exalted him.

He perhaps did not know he had come to a final decision until he encountered Salzman in a Broadway cafeteria. He was sitting alone at a rear table, sucking the bony remains of a fish. The marriage broker appeared haggard, and transparent to the point of vanishing.

Salzman looked up at first without recognizing him. Leo had grown a pointed beard and his eyes were weighted with wisdom.

"Salzman," he said, "love has at last come to my heart."

"Who can love from a picture?" mocked the marriage broker.

"It is not impossible."

"If you can love her, then you can love anybody. Let me show you some new clients that they just sent me their photographs. One is a little doll."

"Just her I want," Leo murmured.

"Don't be a fool, doctor. Don't bother with her."

"Put me in touch with her, Salzman," Leo said humbly. "Perhaps I can be of service."

Salzman had stopped eating and Leo understood with emotion that it was now arranged.

Leaving the cafeteria, he was, however, afflicted by a tormenting suspicion that Salzman had planned it all to happen this way.

Leo was informed by letter that she would meet him on a certain corner, and she was there one spring night, waiting under a street lamp. He appeared, carrying a small bouquet of violets and rosebuds. Stella stood by the lamp post, smoking. She wore white with red shoes, which fitted his expectations, although in a troubled moment he had imagined the dress red, and only the shoes white. She waited uneasily and shyly. From afar he saw that her eyes—clearly her father's—were filled with desperate innocence. He pictured, in her, his own redemption. Violins and lit candles revolved in the sky. Leo ran forward with flowers outthrust.

Around the corner, Salzman, leaning against a wall, chanted prayers for the dead.

E. L. Doctorow (1931–)
from Ragtime

Morgan's residence in New York City was No. 219 Madison Avenue, in Murray Hill, a stately brownstone on the northeast corner of 36th Street. Adjoining it was the white marble Morgan Library, which he had built to receive the thousands of books and art objects collected on his travels. It had been designed in the Italian Renaissance style by Charles McKim, a partner of Stanford White's. The marble blocks were fitted without mortar. A snowfall darker than the stones of the Library lay on the streets the day Henry Ford arrived for lunch. All the sounds of the city were muffled by the snow. A city policeman was stationed at the door of the residence. Across the street and on every corner of 36th and Madison small groups of men with their coat collars turned up stood staring at the great man's home.

Morgan had ordered a light lunch. They did not say much as they dined without other company on Chincoteagues, bisque of terrapin, a Montrachet, rack of lamb, a Château Latour, fresh tomatoes and endives, rhubarb pie in heavy cream, and coffee. The service was magical, two of Morgan's house staff making dishes appear and disappear with such self-effacement as to suggest no human agency. Ford ate well but he did not touch the wine. He finished before his host. He gazed frankly at the Morgan nose. He found a crumb on the tablecloth and deposited it in the saucer of his coffee cup. His fingers idly rubbed the gold plate.

At the conclusion of lunch Morgan indicated to Ford that he would like him to come to the Library. They walked out of the dining room and through a kind of dark public parlor where sat three or four men hoping to secure a few moments of Pierpont Morgan's time. These were his lawyers. They were there to advise him on his forthcoming appearance before the House Committee on Banking and Finance then sitting in Washington for the purpose of inquiring into the possibility that a money trust existed in the United States. Morgan waved the lawyers away as they rose upon sight of him. There was also in attendance an art dealer in a morning coat who had traveled from Rome expressly to see him. The dealer rose only to bow.

None of this display was lost on Ford. He was a man of homespun tastes but was not at all put off by what he recognized as an empire different only in style from his own. Morgan brought him to the great West Room of the Library. Here they took chairs on opposite sides of a fireplace that was as tall as a man. It was a good day for a fire, Morgan said. Ford agreed. Cigars were offered. Ford refused. He noticed the ceiling was gilded. The walls were covered in red silk damask. There were fancy paintings hanging behind glass in heavy frames—pictures of yellowish soulful-looking people with golden haloes. He guessed nobody had their pictures made in those days who wasn't a saint. There was a madonna and child. He ran his fingers along the arm of his chair of red plush.

Morgan let him take it all in. He puffed on his cigar. Finally he spoke. Ford, he said gruffly, I have no interest in acquiring your business or in sharing its profits. Nor am I associated with any of your competitors. Ford nodded.

I have to allow that is good news, he said, giving off a sly glance. Nevertheless, his host continued, I admire what you have done, and while I must have qualms about a motorcar in the hands of every mongoloid who happens to have a few hundred dollars to spend, I recognize that the future is yours. You're still a young man—fifty years or thereabouts?—and perhaps you understand as I cannot the need to separately mobilize the masses of men. I have spent my life in the coordination of capital resources and the harmonic combination of industries, but I have never considered the possibility that the employment of labor is in itself a harmonically unifying process apart from the enterprise in which it is enlisted. Let me ask you a question. Has it occurred to you that your assembly line is not merely a stroke of industrial genius but a projection of organic truth? After all, the interchangeability of parts is a rule of nature. Individuals participate in their species and in their genus. All mammals reproduce in the same way and share the same designs of self-nourishment, with digestive and circulatory systems that are recognizably the same, and they enjoy the same senses. Obviously this is not to say all mammals have interchangeable parts, as your automobiles. But shared design is what allows taxonomists to classify mammals as mammals. And within a species—man, for example—the rules of nature operate so that our individual differences occur on the basis of our similarity. So that individuation may be compared to a pyramid in that it is only achieved by the placement of the top stone.

Ford pondered this. Exceptin the Jews, he muttered. Morgan didn't think he had heard correctly. I beg your pardon, he said. The Jews, Ford said. They ain't like anyone else I know. There goes your theory up shits creek. He smiled.

Morgan was silent for some minutes. He smoked his cigar. The fire crackled. Gusts of snow blown by the wind gently spattered the Library windows. Morgan spoke again. From time to time, he said, I have retained scholars and scientists to assist me in my philosophical investigations in hopes of reaching some conclusions about this life that are not within the reach of the masses of men. I am proposing to share the fruits of my study. I do not think you can be so insolent as to believe your achievements are the result only of your own effort. Did you attribute your success in this manner, I would warn you, sir, of the terrible price to be paid. You would find yourself stranded on the edge of the world and see as no other man the emptiness of the firmament. Do you believe in God? That's my business, Ford said. Well and good, Morgan said, I would not expect any man of your intelligence to embrace such a common idea. You may need me more than you think. Suppose I could prove to you that there are universal patterns of order and repetition that give meaning to the activity of this planet. Suppose I could demonstrate that you yourself are an instrumentation in our modern age of trends in human identity that affirm the oldest wisdom in the world.

Abruptly Morgan stood and left the room. Ford turned in his chair and looked after him. In a moment the old man was in the doorway and beckoning to him with a vehement gesture. Ford followed him through the central hall of the Library to the East Room, whose high walls were covered with bookshelves. There were two upper tiers with promenades of frosted glass and polished brass balustrades so that any book could be easily removed from its place no matter how high. Morgan walked up to the far wall, pressed the spine of a certain book, and part of the shelving swung away to reveal a passageway through which a man could pass. If you please, he said to Ford, and following him into a small chamber he pressed a button that closed the door behind them.

This was an ordinary-sized room modestly appointed with a round polished table, two spindle-back chairs, and a cabinet with a glass top for the display of manuscripts. Morgan turned on a table lamp with a green metal lampshade. Nobody has ever joined me in this room before, he said. He turned on a floor lamp arranged to light the display cabinet. Come over here, sir, he said. Ford looked through the glass and saw an ancient parchment covered with Latin calligraphy. That, Morgan said, is a folio of one of the first Rosicrucian texts, *The Chemical Wedding of Christian Rosencrutz.* Do you know who the original Rosicrucians were, Mr. Ford? They were Christian alchemists of the Rhenish palatinate whose elector was Frederick V. We are talking about the early seventeenth century, sir. These great and good men promulgated the idea of an ongoing, beneficent magic available to certain men of every age for the collective use of mankind. The Latin for this is *prisca theologia,* secret wisdom. The odd thing is that this belief in a secret wisdom is not the Rosicrucians' alone. We know in London in the middle of the same century of the existence of a society called the Invisible College. Its members were reputed to be the very carriers of the beneficent magic I speak of. You of course do not know of the writings of Giordano Bruno, of which here is a specimen page in his own handwriting. My scholars have traced for me, like the best detectives, the existence of this idea and of various mysterious organizations to maintain it, in most of the Renaissance cultures, in medieval societies and in ancient Greece. I hope you are following this closely. The earliest recorded mention of special people born in each age to ease the sufferings of humankind with their *prisca theologia* comes to us through the Greek in the translated writings of the Egyptian priest Hermes Trismegistus. It is Hermes who gives the historical name to this occult knowledge. It is called the Hermetica. With his thick index finger Morgan thumped the glass above the last display piece in the cabinet, a fragment of pink stone upon which geometric scratchings were faintly visible. That, sir, may be a specimen of Hermes in the original cuneiform. And now let me ask you a question. Why do you suppose an idea which had currency in every age and civilization of mankind disappears in modern times? Because only in the age of science have these men and their wisdom dropped from view. I'll tell you why: The rise of mechanistic science, of Newton and Descartes, was a great conspiracy, a great devilish conspiracy to destroy our apprehension of reality and our awareness of the transcendentally gifted among us. But they are with us today nevertheless. They are with us in every age. They come back, you see? They come back!

Morgan was now florid with excitement. He directed Ford's attention to the furthermost corner of the room where in the shadow stood yet another furnishing, something rectangular that was covered with a gold velvet cloth. Morgan gripped the corner of the cloth in his fist, and staring with fierce proprietary triumph at his guest he pulled it away and dropped it to the floor. Ford inspected the item. It was a glass case sealed with lead. Within the case was a sarcophagus. He heard the old man's harsh panting breath. It was the only sound in the room. The sarcophagus was of alabaster. Topping it was a wooden effigy of the fellow who lay within. The effigy was painted in gold leaf, red ochre and blue. This, sir, said Morgan in a hoarse voice, is the coffin of a great Pharaoh. The Egyptian government and the entire archaeological community believe it resides in Cairo. Were my possession of it known, there would be an international uproar. It is literally beyond value. My private staff of Egyptologists has taken every scientific precaution to preserve it from the ravages of the air. Under the mask that you see is the mummy of the great Pharaoh of the Nineteenth Dynasty, Seti the First, recovered from the Temple of Karnak where it lay for over three thousand years. I will show it to you in due course. Let me now say only that I guarantee the visage of the great king will be of considerable interest to you.

Morgan had to recover his composure. He pulled back one of the chairs and sat down at the table. Slowly his breathing returned to normal. Ford had sat down across from him, and understanding the old man's physical difficulties, remained quiet and stared at his own shoes. The shoes, brown lace-ups, he had bought from the catalogue of L. L. Bean. They were good comfortable shoes. Mr. Ford, Pierpont Morgan said, I want you to be my guest on an expedition to Egypt. That is very much the place, sir. That is where it all begins. I have commissioned a steamer designed expressly for sailing the Nile. When she's ready, I want you to come with me. Will you do that? It will require no investment on your part. We must go to Luxor and Karnak. We must go to the Great Pyramid at Giza. There are so few of us, sir. My money has brought me to the door of certain crypts, the deciphering of sacred hieroglyphs. Why should we not satisfy ourselves of the truth of who we are and the eternal beneficent force which we incarnate?

Ford sat slightly hunched. His long hands lay over the wooden arms of his chair as if broken at the wrists. He considered everything that had been said. He looked at the sarcophagus. When he had satisfied himself that he understood, he nodded his head solemnly and replied as follows: If I understand you right, Mr. Morgan, you are talking about reincarnation. Well, let me tell you about that. As a youth I was faced with an awful crisis in my mental life when it came over me that I had no call to know what I knew. I had grit, all right, but I was an ordinary country boy who had suffered his McGuffey like the rest of them. Yet I knew how everything worked. I could look at something and tell you how it worked and probably show you how to make it work better. But I was no intellectual, you see, and I had no patience with the two-dollar words.

Morgan listened. He felt that he mustn't move.

Well then, Ford continued. I happened to pick up a little book. It was called *An Eastern Fakir's Eternal Wisdom*, published by the Franklin Novelty Company of Philadelphia, Pennsylvania. And in this book, which cost me just twenty-five cents, I found everything I needed to set my mind at rest. Reincarnation is the only belief I hold, Mr. Morgan. I explain my genius this way—some of us have just lived more times than others. So you see, what you have spent on scholars and traveled around the world to find, I already knew. And I'll tell you something, in thanks for the eats, I'm going to lend that book to you. Why, you don't have to fuss with all these Latiny things, he said waving his arm, you don't have to pick the garbage pails of Europe and build steamboats to sail the Nile just to find out something that you can get in the mail order for two bits!

The two men stared at each other. Morgan sat back in his chair. The blood drained from his face and his eyes lost their fierce light. When he spoke, it was with the weak voice of an old man. Mr. Ford, he said, if my ideas can survive their attachment to you, they will have met the ultimate test.

Nevertheless the crucial breakthrough had been made. About a year after this extraordinary meeting Morgan made his trip to Egypt. Although Ford did not go with him he had conceded the possibility of an awesome lineage. And together they had managed to found the most secret and exclusive club in America, The Pyramid, of which they were the only members. It endowed certain researches which persist to this day.

William Gass (1924–   )

Order of Insects

We certainly had no complaints about the house after all we had been through in the other place, but we hadn't lived there very long before I began to notice every morning the bodies of a large black bug spotted about the downstairs carpet; haphazardly, as earth worms must die on the street after a rain; looking when I first saw them like rolls of dark wool or pieces of mud from the children's shoes, or sometimes, if the drapes were pulled, so like ink stains or deep burns they terrified me, for I had been intimidated by that thick rug very early and the first week had walked over it wishing my bare feet would swallow my shoes. The shells were usually broken. Legs and other parts I couldn't then identify would be scattered near like flakes of rust. Occasionally I would find them on their backs, their quilted undersides showing orange, while beside them were smudges of dark-brown powder that had to be vacuumed carefully. We believed our cat had killed them. She was frequently sick during the night then—a rare thing for her—and we could think of no other reason. Overturned like that they looked pathetic even dead.

I could not imagine where the bugs had come from. I am terribly meticulous myself. The house was clean, the cupboards tight and orderly, and we never saw one alive. The other place had been infested with those flat brown fuzzy roaches, all wires and speed, and we'd seen *them* all right, frightened by the kitchen light, sifting through the baseboards and the floor's cracks; and in the pantry I had nearly closed my fingers on one before it fled, tossing its shadow across the starch like an image of the startle in my hand.

Dead, overturned, their three pairs of legs would be delicately drawn up and folded shyly over their stomachs. When they walked I suppose their forelegs were thrust out and then bent to draw the body up. I still wonder if they jumped. More than once I've seen our cat hook one of her claws under a shell and toss it in the air, crouching while the insect fell, feigning leaps—but there was daylight; the bug was dead; she was not really interested any more; and she would walk immediately away. That image takes the place of jumping. Even if I actually saw those two back pairs of legs unhinge, as they would have to if one leaped, I think I'd find the result unreal and mechanical, a poor try measured by that sudden, high, head-over-heels flight from our cat's paw. I could look it up, I guess, but it's no study for a woman . . . bugs.

At first I reacted as I should, bending over, wondering what in the world; yet even before I recognized them I'd withdrawn my hand, shuddering. Fierce, ugly, armored things: they used their shadows to seem large. The machine sucked them up while I looked the other way. I remember the sudden thrill of horror I had hearing one rattle up the wand. I was relieved that they were dead, of course, for I could never have killed one, and if they had been popped, alive, into the dust bag of the cleaner, I believe I would have had nightmares again as I did the time my husband fought the red ants in our kitchen. All night I lay awake thinking of the ants alive in the belly of the machine, and when toward morning I finally slept I found myself in the dreadful elastic tunnel of the suction tube where ahead of me I heard them: a hundred bodies rustling in the dirt.

I never think of their species as alive

but as comprised entirely by the dead ones on our carpet, all the new dead manufactured by the action of some mysterious spoor—perhaps that dust they sometimes lie in—carried in the air, solidified by night and shaped, from body into body, spontaneously, as maggots were before the age of science. I have a single book about insects, a little dated handbook in French which a good friend gave me as a joke—because of my garden, the quaintness of the plates, the fun of reading about worms in such an elegant tongue—and my bug has his picture there climbing the stem of an orchid. Beneath the picture is his name: *Periplaneta orientalis L. Ces répugnants insectes ne sont que trop communs dans les cuisines des vieilles habitations des villes, dans les magasins, entrepôts, boulangeries, brasseries, restaurants, dans la cale des navires, etc.*, the text begins. Nevertheless they are a new experience for me and I think that I am grateful for it now.

The picture didn't need to show me there were two, adult and nymph, for by that time I'd seen the bodies of both kinds. Nymph. My god the names we use. The one was dark, squat, ugly, sly. The other, slimmer, had hard sheath-like wings drawn over its back like another shell, and you could see delicate interwoven lines spun like fossil gauze across them. The nymph was a rich golden color deepening in its interstices to mahogany. Both had legs that looked under a glass like the canes of a rose, and the nymph's were sufficiently transparent in a good light you thought you saw its nerves merge and run like a jagged crack to each ultimate claw.

Tipped, their legs have fallen shut, and the more I look at them the less I believe my eyes. Corruption, in these bugs, is splendid. I've a collection now I keep in typewriter-ribbon tins, and though, in time, their bodies dry and the interior flesh decays, their features hold, as I suppose they held in life, an Egyptian determination, for their protective plates are strong and death must break bones to get in. Now that the heavy soul is gone, the case is light.

I suspect if we were as familiar with our bones as with our skin, we'd never bury dead but shrine them in their rooms, arranged as we might like to find them on a visit; and our enemies, if we could steal their bodies from the battle sites, would be museumed as they died, the steel still eloquent in their sides, their metal hats askew, the protective toes of their shoes unworn, and friend and enemy would be so wondrously historical that in a hundred years we'd find the jaws still hung for the same speech and all the parts we spent our life with tilted as they always were—rib cage, collar, skull—still repetitious, still defiant, angel light, still worthy of memorial and affection. After all, what does it mean to say that when our cat has bitten through the shell and put confusion in the pulp, the life goes out of them? Alas for us, I want to cry, our bones are secret, showing last, so we must love what perishes: the muscles and the waters and the fats.

Two prongs extend like daggers from the rear. I suppose I'll never know their function. That kind of knowledge doesn't take my interest. At first I had to screw my eyes down, and as I consider it now, the whole change, the recent alteration in my life, was the consequence of finally coming near to something. It was a self-mortifying act, I recall, a penalty I laid upon myself for the evil-tempered words I'd shouted at my children in the middle of the night. I felt instinctively the insects were infectious and their own disease, so when I knelt I held a handkerchief over the lower half of my face . . . saw only horror . . . turned, sick, masking my eyes . . . yet the worst of angers held me through the day: vague, searching, guilty, and ashamed.

After that I came near often; saw for the first time, the gold nymph's difference; put between the mandibles a tinted nail I'd let grow long; observed the movement of the jaws, the stalks of the antennae, the skull-shaped skull, the lines banding the abdomen, and found an intensity in the posture of the shell, even when tipped, like that in the gaze of Gauguin's natives' eyes. The dark plates glisten. They are wonderfully shaped; even the buttons of the compound eyes show a geometrical precision which prevents my earlier horror. It isn't possible to feel disgust toward such an order. Nevertheless, I reminded myself, a roach . . . and you a woman.

I no longer own my own imagination. I suppose they came up the drains or out of the registers. It may have been the rug they wanted. Crickets, too, I understand, will feed on wool. I used to rest by my husband . . . stiffly . . . waiting for silence to settle in the house, his sleep to come, and then the drama of their passage would take hold of me, possess me so completely that when I finally slept I merely passed from one dream to another without the slightest loss of vividness or continuity. Never alive, they came with punctures; their bodies formed little whorls of copperish dust which in the downstairs darkness I couldn't possibly have seen; and they were dead and upside down when they materialized, for it was in that moment that our cat, herself darkly invisible, leaped and brought her paws together on the true soul of the roach; a soul so static and intense, so immortally arranged, I felt, while I lay shell-like in our bed, turned inside out, driving my mind away, it was the same as the dark soul of the world itself—and it was this beautiful and terrifying feeling that took possession of me, finally, stiffened me like a rod beside my husband, played caesar to my dreams.

The weather drove them up, I think . . . moisture in the tubes of the house. The first I came on looked put together in Japan; broken, one leg bent under like a metal cinch; unwound. It rang inside the hollow of the wand like metal too; brightly, like a stream of pins. The clatter made me shiver. Well I always see what I fear. Anything my eyes have is transformed into a threatening object: mud, or stains, or burns, or if not these, then toys in unmendable metal pieces. Not fears to be afraid of. The ordinary fears of daily life. Healthy fears. Womanly, wifely, motherly ones: the children may point at the wretch with the hunch and speak in a voice he will hear; the cat has fleas again, they will get in the sofa; one's face looks smeared, it's because of the heat; is the burner on under the beans? the washing machine's obscure disease may reoccur, it rumbles on rinse and rattles on wash; my god it's already eleven o'clock; which one of you has lost a galosh? So it was amid the worries of our ordinary life I bent, innocent and improperly armed, over the bug that had come undone. Let me think back on the shock. . . . My hand would have fled from a burn with the same speed; anyone's death or injury would have weakened me as well; and I could have gone cold for a number of reasons, because I felt in motion in me my own murderous disease, for instance; but none could have produced the revulsion that dim recognition did, a reaction of my whole nature that flew ahead of understanding and made me withdraw like a spider.

I said I was innocent. Well I was not. Innocent. My god the names we use. What do we live with that's alive we haven't tamed—people like me?—even our houseplants breathe by our permission. All along I had the fear of what it was—something ugly and poisonous, deadly and terrible—the simple insect, worse and wilder than fire—and I should rather put my arms in the heart of a flame than in the darkness of a moist and webby hole. But the eye never ceases to change. When I examine my collection now it isn't any longer roaches I observe but gracious order, wholeness, and divinity. . . . My handkerchief, that time, was useless. . . . O my husband, they are a terrible disease.

The dark soul of the world . . . a phrase I should laugh at. The roach shell sickened me. And my jaw has broken open. I lie still, listening, but there is nothing to hear. Our cat is quiet. They pass through life to immortality between her paws.

Am I grateful now my terror has another object? From time to time I think so, but I feel as though I'd been entrusted with a kind of eastern mystery, sacred to a dreadful god, and I am full of the sense of my unworthiness and the clay of my vessel. So strange. It is the sewing machine that has the fearful claw. I live in a scatter of blocks and children's voices. The chores are my clock, and time is every other moment interrupted. I had always thought that love knew nothing of order and that life itself was turmoil and confusion. Let us leap, let us shout! I have leaped, and to my shame, I have wrestled. But this bug that I hold in my hand and know to be dead is beautiful, and there is a fierce joy in its composition that beggars every other, for its joy is the joy of stone, and it lives in its tomb like a lion.

I don't know which is more surprising: to find such order in a roach, or such ideas in a woman.

I could not shake my point of view, infected as it was, and I took up their study with a manly passion. I sought out spiders and gave them sanctuary; played host to worms of every kind; was generous to katydids and lacewings, aphids, ants and various grubs; pampered several sorts of beetle; looked after crickets; sheltered bees; aimed my husband's chemicals away from the grasshoppers, mosquitoes, moths, and flies. I have devoted hours to watching caterpillars feed. You can see the leaves they've eaten passing through them; their bodies thin and swell until the useless pulp is squeezed in perfect rounds from their rectal end; for caterpillars are a simple section of intestine, a decorated stalk of yearning muscle, and their whole being is enlisted in the effort of digestion. *Le tube digestif des Insectes est situé dans le grand axe de la cavité générale du corps . . . de la bouche vers l'anus . . . Le pharynx . . . L'œsophage . . . Le jabot . . . Le ventricule chylifique . . . Le rectum et l'iléon . . .* Yet when they crawl their curves conform to graceful laws.

My children ought to be delighted with me as my husband is, I am so diligent, it seems, on their behalf, but they have taken fright and do not care to pry or to collect. My hobby's given me a pair of dreadful eyes, and sometimes I fancy they start from my head; yet I see, perhaps, no differently than Galileo saw when he found in the pendulum its fixed intent. Nonetheless my body resists such knowledge. It wearies of its edge. And I cannot forget, even while I watch our moonvine blossoms opening, the simple principle of the bug. It is a squat black cockroach after all, such a bug as frightens housewives, and it's only come to chew on rented wool and find its death absurdly in the teeth of the renter's cat.

Strange. Absurd. I am the wife of the house. This point of view I tremble in is the point of view of a god, and I feel certain, somehow, that could I give myself entirely to it, were I not continuing a woman, I could disarm my life, find peace and order everywhere; and I lie by my husband and I touch his arm and consider the temptation. But I am a woman. I am not worthy. Then I want to cry O husband, husband, I am ill, for I have seen what I have seen. What should he do at that, poor man, starting up in the night from his sleep to such nonsense, but comfort me blindly and murmur dream, small snail, only dream, bad dream, as I do to the children. I could go away like the wise cicada who abandons its shell to move to other mischief. I could leave and let my bones play cards and spank the children. . . .

Peace. How can I think of such ludicrous things—beauty and peace, the dark soul of the world—for I am the wife of the house, concerned for the rug, tidy and punctual, surrounded by blocks.

Flannery O'Connor (1925–1964)

A Good Man Is Hard to Find

for Sally and Robert Fitzgerald

The dragon is by the side of the road, watching those who pass. Beware lest he devour you. We go to the father of souls, but it is necessary to pass by the dragon.

ST. CYRIL OF JERUSALEM

The grandmother didn't want to go to Florida. She wanted to visit some of her connections in east Tennessee and she was seizing at every chance to change Bailey's mind. Bailey was the son she lived with, her only boy. He was sitting on the edge of his chair at the table, bent over the orange sports section of the *Journal.* "Now look here, Bailey," she said, "see here, read this," and she stood with one hand on her thin hip and the other rattling the newspaper at his bald head. "Here this fellow that calls himself The Misfit is aloose from the Federal Pen and headed toward Florida and you read here what it says he did to these people. Just you read it. I wouldn't take my children in any direction with a criminal like that aloose in it. I couldn't answer to my conscience if I did."

Bailey didn't look up from his reading so she wheeled around then and faced the children's mother, a young woman in slacks, whose face was as broad and innocent as a cabbage and was tied around with a green headkerchief that had two points on the top like a rabbit's ears. She was sitting on the sofa, feeding the baby his apricots out of a jar. "The children have been to Florida before," the old lady said. "You all ought to take them somewhere else for a change so they would see different parts of the world and be broad. They never have been to east Tennessee."

The children's mother didn't seem to hear her but the eight-year-old boy, John Wesley, a stocky child with glasses, said, "If you don't want to go to Florida, why dontcha stay at home?" He and the little girl, June Star, were reading the funny papers on the floor.

"She wouldn't stay at home to be queen for a day," June Star said without raising her yellow head.

"Yes and what would you do if this fellow, the Misfit, caught you?" the grandmother asked.

"I'd smack his face," John Wesley said.

"She wouldn't stay at home for a million bucks," June Star said. "Afraid she'd miss something. She has to go everywhere we go."

"All right, Miss," the grandmother said. "Just remember that the next time you want me to curl your hair."

June Star said her hair was naturally curly.

The next morning the grandmother

was the first one in the car, ready to go. She had her big black valise that looked like the head of a hippopotamus in one corner, and underneath it she was hiding a basket with Pitty Sing, the cat, in it. She didn't intend for the cat to be left alone in the house for three days because he would miss her too much and she was afraid he might brush against one of the gas burners and accidentally asphyxiate himself. Her son, Bailey, didn't like to arrive at a motel with a cat.

She sat in the middle of the back seat with John Wesley and June Star on either side of her. Bailey and the children's mother and the baby sat in front and they left Atlanta at eight forty-five with the mileage on the car at 55890. The grandmother wrote this down because she thought it would be interesting to say how many miles they had been when they got back. It took them twenty minutes to reach the outskirts of the city.

The old lady settled herself comfortably, removing her white cotton gloves and putting them up with her purse on the shelf in front of the back window. The children's mother still had on slacks and still had her head tied up in a green kerchief, but the grandmother had on a navy blue straw sailor hat with a bunch of white violets on the brim and a navy blue dress with a small white dot in the print. Her collars and cuffs were white organdy trimmed with lace and at her neckline she had pinned a purple spray of cloth violets containing a sachet. In case of an accident, anyone seeing her dead on the highway would know at once that she was a lady.

She said she thought it was going to be a good day for driving, neither too hot nor too cold, and she cautioned Bailey that the speed limit was fifty-five miles an hour and that the patrolmen hid themselves behind billboards and small clumps of trees and sped out after you before you had a chance to slow down. She pointed out interesting details of the scenery: Stone Mountain; the blue granite that in some places came up to both sides of the highway; the brilliant red clay banks slightly streaked with purple; and the various crops that made rows of green lacework on the ground. The trees were full of silver-white sunlight and the meanest of them sparkled. The children were reading comic magazines and their mother had gone back to sleep.

"Let's go through Georgia fast so we won't have to look at it much," John Wesley said.

"If I were a little boy," said the grandmother, "I wouldn't talk about my native state that way. Tennessee has the mountains and Georgia has the hills."

"Tennessee is just a hillbilly dumping ground," John Wesley said, "and Georgia is a lousy state too."

"You said it," June Star said.

"In my time," said the grandmother, folding her thin veined fingers, "children were more respectful of their native states and their parents and everything else. People did right then. Oh look at the cute little pickaninny!" she said and pointed to a Negro child standing in the door of a shack. "Wouldn't that make a picture, now?" she asked and they all turned and looked at the little Negro out of the back window. He waved.

"He didn't have any britches on," June Star said.

"He probably didn't have any," the grandmother explained. "Little niggers in the country don't have things like we do. If I could paint, I'd paint that picture," she said.

The children exchanged comic books.

The grandmother offered to hold the baby and the children's mother passed him over the front seat to her. She set him on her knee and bounced him and told him about the things they were passing. She rolled her eyes and screwed up her mouth and stuck her leathery thin face into his smooth bland one. Occasionally he gave her a faraway smile. They passed a large cotton field with five or six graves fenced in the middle of it, like a small island. "Look at the graveyard!" the grandmother said, pointing it out. "That was the old family burying ground. That belonged to the plantation."

"Where's the plantation?" John Wesley asked.

"Gone With the Wind," said the grandmother. "Ha. Ha."

When the children finished all the comic books they had brought, they opened the lunch and ate it. The grandmother ate a peanut butter sandwich and an olive and would not let the children throw the box and the paper napkins out the window. When there was nothing else to do they played a game by choosing a cloud and making the other two guess what shape it suggested. John Wesley took one the shape of a cow and June Star guessed a cow and John Wesley said, no, an automobile, and June Star said he didn't play fair, and they began to slap each other over the grandmother.

The grandmother said she would tell them a story if they would keep quiet. When she told a story, she rolled her eyes and waved her head and was very dramatic. She said once when she was a maiden lady she had been courted by a Mr. Edgar Atkins Teagarden from Jasper, Georgia. She said he was a very good-looking man and a gentleman and that he brought her a watermelon every Saturday afternoon with his initials cut in it, E. A. T. Well, one Saturday, she said, Mr. Teagarden brought the watermelon and there was nobody at home and he left it on the front porch and returned in his buggy to Jasper, but she never got the watermelon, she said, because a nigger boy ate it when he saw the initials, E. A. T.! This story tickled John Wesley's funny bone and he giggled and giggled but June Star didn't think it was any good. She said she wouldn't marry a man that just brought her a watermelon on Saturday. The grandmother said she would have done well to marry Mr. Teagarden because he was a gentleman and had bought Coca-Cola stock when it first came out and that he had died only a few years ago, a very wealthy man.

They stopped at The Tower for barbecued sandwiches. The Tower was a part stucco and part wood filling station and dance hall set in a clearing outside of Timothy. A fat man named Red Sammy Butts ran it and there were signs stuck here and there on the building and for miles up and down the highway saying, TRY RED SAMMY'S FAMOUS BARBECUE. NONE LIKE FAMOUS RED SAMMY'S! RED SAM! THE FAT BOY WITH THE HAPPY LAUGH. A VETERAN! RED SAMMY'S YOUR MAN!

Red Sammy was lying on the bare ground outside The Tower with his head under a truck while a gray monkey about a foot high, chained to a small chinaberry tree, chattered nearby. The monkey sprang back into the tree and got on the highest limb as soon as he saw the children jump out of the car and run toward him.

Inside, The Tower was a long dark room with a counter at one end and tables at the other and dancing space in the middle. They all sat down at a board table next to the nickelodeon and Red Sam's wife, a tall burnt-brown woman with hair and eyes lighter than her skin, came and took their order. The children's mother put a dime in the machine and played "The Tennessee Waltz," and the grandmother said that tune always made her want to dance. She asked Bailey if he would like to dance but he only glared at her. He didn't have a naturally sunny disposition like she did and trips made him nervous. The grandmother's brown eyes were very bright. She swayed her head from side to side and pretended she was dancing in her chair. June Star said play something she could tap to so the children's mother put in another dime and played a fast number and June Star stepped out onto the dance floor and did her tap routine.

"Ain't she cute?" Red Sam's wife said, leaning over the counter. "Would you like to come be my little girl?"

"No I certainly wouldn't," June Star said. "I wouldn't live in a broken-down place like this for a million bucks!" and she ran back to the table.

"Ain't she cute?" the woman repeated, stretching her mouth politely.

"Aren't you ashamed?" hissed the grandmother.

Red Sam came in and told his wife to quit lounging on the counter and hurry up with these people's order. His khaki trousers reached just to his hip bones and his stomach hung over them like a sack of meal swaying under his shirt. He came over and sat down at a table nearby and let out a combination sigh and yodel. "You can't win," he said. "You can't win," and he wiped his sweating red face off with a gray handkerchief. "These days you don't know who to trust," he said. "Ain't that the truth?"

"People are certainly not nice like they used to be," said the grandmother.

"Two fellers come in here last week," Red Sammy said, "driving a Chrysler. It was a old beat-up car but it was a good one and these boys looked all right to me. Said they worked at the mill and you know I let them fellers charge the gas they bought? Now why did I do that?"

"Because you're a good man!" the grandmother said at once.

"Yes'm, I suppose so," Red Sam said as if he were struck with this answer.

His wife brought the orders, carrying the five plates all at once without a tray, two in each hand and one balanced on her arm. "It isn't a soul in this green world of God's that you can trust," she said. "And I don't count nobody out of that, not nobody," she repeated, looking at Red Sammy.

"Did you read about that criminal, The Misfit, that's escaped?" asked the grandmother.

"I wouldn't be a bit surprised if he didn't attact this place right here," said the woman. "If he hears about it being here, I wouldn't be none surprised to see him. If he hears it's two cent in the cash register, I wouldn't be a tall surprised if he . . ."

"That'll do," Red Sam said. "Go bring these people their Co'-Colas," and the woman went off to get the rest of the order.

"A good man is hard to find," Red Sammy said. "Everything is getting terrible. I remember the day you could go off and leave your screen door unlatched. Not no more."

He and the grandmother discussed better times. The old lady said that in her opinion Europe was entirely to blame for the way things were now. She said the way Europe acted you would think we were made of money and Red Sam said it was no use talking about it, she was exactly right. The children ran outside into the white sunlight and looked at the monkey in the lacy chinaberry tree. He was busy catching fleas on himself and biting each one carefully between his teeth as if it were a delicacy.

They drove off again into the hot afternoon. The grandmother took cat naps and woke up every few minutes with her own snoring. Outside of Toombsboro she woke up and recalled an old plantation that she had visited in this neighborhood once when she was a young lady. She said the house had six white columns across the front and that there was an avenue of oaks leading up to it and two little wooden trellis arbors on either side in front where you sat down with your suitor after a stroll in the garden. She recalled exactly which road to turn off to get to it. She knew that Bailey would not be willing to lose any time looking at an old house, but the more she talked about it, the more she wanted to see it once again and find out if the little twin arbors were still standing. "There was a secret panel in this house," she said craftily, not telling the truth but wishing that she were, "and the story went that all the family silver was hidden in it when Sherman came through but it was never found . . ."

"Hey!" John Wesley said. "Let's go see it! We'll find it! We'll poke all the woodwork and find it! Who lives there? Where do you turn off at? Hey Pop, can't we turn off there?"

"We never have seen a house with a secret panel!" June Star shrieked. "Let's go to the house with the secret panel! Hey Pop, can't we go see the house with the secret panel!"

"It's not far from here, I know," the grandmother said. "It wouldn't take over twenty minutes."

Bailey was looking straight ahead. His jaw was as rigid as a horseshoe. "No," he said.

The children began to yell and scream that they wanted to see the house with the secret panel. John Wesley kicked the back of the front seat and June Star hung over her mother's shoulder and whined desperately into her ear that they never had any fun even on their vacation, that they could never do what THEY wanted to do. The baby began to scream and John Wesley kicked the back of the seat so hard that his father could feel the blows in his kidney.

"All right!" he shouted and drew the car to a stop at the side of the road. "Will you all shut up? Will you all just shut up for one second? If you don't shut up, we won't go anywhere."

"It would be very educational for them," the grandmother murmured.

"All right," Bailey said, "but get this: this is the only time we're going to stop for anything like this. This is the one and only time."

"The dirt road that you have to turn down is about a mile back," the grandmother directed. "I marked it when we passed."

"A dirt road," Bailey groaned.

After they had turned around and were headed toward the dirt road, the grandmother recalled other points about the house, the beautiful glass over the front doorway and the candle-lamp in the hall. John Wesley said that the secret panel was probably in the fireplace.

"You can't go inside this house," Bailey said. "You don't know who lives there."

"While you all talk to the people in front, I'll run around behind and get in a window," John Wesley suggested.

"We'll all stay in the car," his mother said.

They turned onto the dirt road and the car raced roughly along in a swirl of pink dust. The grandmother recalled the times when there were no paved roads and thirty miles was a day's journey. The dirt road was hilly and there were sudden washes in it and sharp curves on dangerous embankments. All at once they would be on a hill, looking down over the blue tops of trees for miles around, then the next minute, they would be in a red depression with the dust-coated trees looking down on them.

"This place had better turn up in a minute," Bailey said, "or I'm going to turn around."

The road looked as if no one had traveled on it in months.

"It's not much farther," the grandmother said and just as she said it, a horrible thought came to her. The thought was so embarrassing that she turned red in the face and her eyes dilated and her feet jumped up, upsetting her valise in the corner. The instant the valise moved, the newspaper top she had over the basket under it rose with a snarl and Pitty Sing, the cat, sprang onto Bailey's shoulder.

The children were thrown to the floor and their mother, clutching the baby, was thrown out the door onto the ground; the old lady was thrown into the front seat. The car turned over once and landed right-side-up in a gulch off the side of the road. Bailey remained in the driver's seat with the cat—gray-striped with a broad white face and an orange nose—clinging to his neck like a caterpillar.

As soon as the children saw they could move their arms and legs, they scrambled out of the car, shouting, "We've had an ACCIDENT!" The grandmother was curled up under the dashboard, hoping she was injured so that Bailey's wrath would not come down on her all at once. The horrible thought she had had before the accident was that the house she had remembered so vividly was not in Georgia but in Tennessee.

Bailey removed the cat from his neck with both hands and flung it out the window against the side of a pine tree. Then he got out of the car and started looking for the children's mother. She was sitting against the side of the red gutted ditch, holding the screaming baby, but she only had a cut down her face and a broken shoulder. "We've had an ACCIDENT!" the children screamed in a frenzy of delight.

"But nobody's killed," June Star said with disappointment as the grandmother limped out of the car, her hat still pinned to her head but the broken front brim standing up at a jaunty angle and the violet spray hanging off the side. They all sat down in the ditch, except the children, to recover from the shock. They were all shaking.

"Maybe a car will come along," said the children's mother hoarsely.

"I believe I have injured an organ," said the grandmother, pressing her side, but no one answered her. Bailey's teeth were clattering. He had on a yellow sport shirt with bright blue parrots designed in it and his face was as yellow as the shirt. The grandmother decided that she would not mention that the house was in Tennessee.

The road was about ten feet above and they could see only the tops of the trees on the other side of it. Behind the ditch they were sitting in there were more woods, tall and dark and deep. In a few minutes they saw a car some distance away on top of a hill, coming slowly as if the occupants were watching them. The grandmother stood up and waved both arms dramatically to attract their attention. The car continued to come on slowly, disappeared around a bend and appeared again, moving even slower, on top of the hill they had gone over. It was a big black battered hearse-like automobile. There were three men in it.

It came to a stop just over them and for some minutes, the driver looked down with a steady expressionless gaze to where they were sitting, and didn't speak. Then he turned his head and muttered something to the other two and they got out. One was a fat boy in black trousers and a red sweat shirt with a silver stallion embossed on the front of it. He moved around on the right side of them and stood staring, his mouth partly open in a kind of loose grin. The other had on khaki pants and a blue striped coat and a gray hat pulled down very low, hiding most of his face. He came around slowly on the left side. Neither spoke.

The driver got out of the car and stood by the side of it, looking down at them. He was an older man than the other two. His hair was just beginning to gray and he wore silver-rimmed spectacles that gave him a scholarly look. He had a long creased face and didn't have on any shirt or undershirt. He had on blue jeans that were too tight for him and was holding a black hat and a gun. The two boys also had guns.

"We've had an ACCIDENT!" the children screamed.

The grandmother had the peculiar feeling that the bespectacled man was someone she knew. His face was as familiar to her as if she had known him all her life but she could not recall who he was. He moved away from the car and began to come down the embankment, placing his feet carefully so that he wouldn't slip. He had on tan and white shoes and no socks, and his ankles were red and thin. "Good afternoon," he said. "I see you all had you a little spill."

"We turned over twice!" said the grandmother.

"Oncet," he corrected. "We seen it happen. Try their car and see will it run, Hiram," he said quietly to the boy with the gray hat.

"What you got that gun for?" John Wesley asked. "Whatcha gonna do with that gun?"

"Lady," the man said to the children's mother, "would you mind calling them children to sit down by you? Children make me nervous. I want all you all to sit down right together there where you're at."

"What are you telling US what to do for?" June Star asked.

Behind them the line of woods gaped like a dark open mouth. "Come here," said their mother.

"Look here now," Bailey began suddenly, "we're in a predicament! We're in . . ."

The grandmother shrieked. She scrambled to her feet and stood staring. "You're The Misfit!" she said. "I recognized you at once!"

"Yes'm," the man said, smiling slightly as if he were pleased in spite of himself to be known, "but it would have been better for all of you, lady, if you hadn't of reckernized me."

Bailey turned his head sharply and said something to his mother that shocked even the children. The old lady began to cry and The Misfit reddened.

"Lady," he said, "don't you get upset. Sometimes a man says things he don't mean. I don't reckon he meant to talk to you thataway."

"You wouldn't shoot a lady, would you?" the grandmother said and removed a clean handkerchief from her cuff and began to slap at her eyes with it.

The Misfit pointed the toe of his shoe into the ground and made a little hole and then covered it up again. "I would hate to have to," he said.

"Listen," the grandmother almost screamed, "I know you're a good man. You don't look a bit like you have common blood. I know you must come from nice people!"

"Yes mam," he said, "finest people in the world." When he smiled he showed a row of strong white teeth. "God never made a finer woman than my mother and my daddy's heart was pure gold," he said. The boy with the red sweat shirt had come around behind them and was standing with his gun at his hip. The Misfit squatted down on the ground. "Watch them children, Bobby Lee," he said. "You know they make me nervous." He looked at the six of them huddled together in front of him and he seemed to be embarrassed as if he couldn't think of anything to say. "Ain't a cloud in the sky," he remarked, looking up at it. "Don't see no sun but don't see no cloud neither."

"Yes, it's a beautiful day," said the grandmother. "Listen," she said, "you shouldn't call yourself The Misfit because I know you're a good man at heart. I can just look at you and tell."

"Hush!" Bailey yelled. "Hush! Everybody shut up and let me handle this!" He was squatting in the position of a runner about to sprint forward but he didn't move.

"I pre-chate that, lady," The Misfit said and drew a little circle in the ground with the butt of his gun.

"It'll take a half a hour to fix this here car," Hiram called, looking over the raised hood of it.

"Well, first you and Bobby Lee get him and that little boy to step over yonder with you," The Misfit said, pointing to Bailey and John Wesley. "The boys want to ast you something," he said to Bailey. "Would you mind stepping back in them woods there with them?"

"Listen," Bailey began, "we're in a terrible predicament! Nobody realizes what this is," and his voice cracked. His eyes were as blue and intense as the parrots in his shirt and he remained perfectly still.

The grandmother reached up to adjust her hat brim as if she were going to the woods with him but it came off in her hand. She stood staring at it and after a second she let it fall on the ground. Hiram pulled Bailey up by the arm as if he were assisting an old man. John Wesley caught hold of his father's hand and Bobby Lee followed. They went off toward the woods and just as they reached the dark edge, Bailey turned and supporting himself against a gray naked pine trunk, he shouted, "I'll be back in a minute, Mamma, wait on me!"

"Come back this instant!" his mother shrilled but they all disappeared into the woods.

"Bailey Boy!" the grandmother called in a tragic voice but she found she was looking at The Misfit squatting on the ground in front of her. "I just know you're a good man," she said desperately. "You're not a bit common!"

"Nome, I ain't a good man," The Misfit said after a second as if he had considered her statement carefully, "but I ain't the worst in the world neither. My daddy said I was a different breed of dog from my brothers and sisters. 'You know,' Daddy said, 'it's some that can live their whole life out without asking about it and it's others has to know why it is, and this boy is one of the latters. He's going to be into everything!' " He put on his black hat and looked up suddenly and then away deep into the woods as if he were embarrassed again. "I'm sorry I don't have on a shirt before you ladies," he said, hunching his shoulders slightly. "We buried our clothes that we had on when we escaped and we're just making do until we can get better. We borrowed these from some folks we met," he explained.

"That's perfectly all right," the grandmother said. "Maybe Bailey has an extra shirt in his suitcase."

"I'll look and see terrectly," The Misfit said.

"Where are they taking him?" the children's mother screamed.

"Daddy was a card himself," The Misfit said. "You couldn't put anything over on him. He never got in trouble with the Authorities though. Just had the knack of handling them."

"You could be honest too if you'd only try," said the grandmother. "Think how wonderful it would be to settle down and live a comfortable life and not have to think about somebody chasing you all the time."

The Misfit kept scratching in the ground with the butt of his gun as if he were thinking about it. "Yes'm, somebody is always after you," he murmured.

The grandmother noticed how thin his shoulder blades were just behind his hat because she was standing up looking down on him. "Do you ever pray?" she asked.

He shook his head. All she saw was the black hat wiggle between his shoulder blades. "Nome," he said.

There was a pistol shot from the woods, followed closely by another. Then silence. The old lady's head jerked around. She could hear the wind move through the tree tops like a long satisfied insuck of breath. "Bailey Boy!" she called.

"I was a gospel singer for a while," The Misfit said. "I been most everything. Been in the arm service, both land and sea, at home and abroad, been twict married, been an undertaker, been with the railroads, plowed Mother Earth, been in a tornado, seen a man burnt alive oncet," and he looked up at the children's mother and the little girl who were sitting close together, their faces white and their eyes glassy; "I even seen a woman flogged," he said.

"Pray, pray," the grandmother began, "pray, pray . . ."

"I never was a bad boy that I remember of," The Misfit said in an almost dreamy voice, "but somewheres along the line I done something wrong and got sent to the penitentiary. I was buried alive," and he looked up and held her attention to him by a steady stare.

"That's when you should have started to pray," she said. "What did you do to get sent to the penitentiary that first time?"

"Turn to the right, it was a wall," The Misfit said, looking up again at the cloudless sky. "Turn to the left, it was a wall. Look up it was a ceiling, look down it was a floor. I forget what I done, lady. I set there and set there, trying to remember what it was I done and I ain't recalled it to this day. Oncet in a while, I would think it was coming to me, but it never come."

"Maybe they put you in by mistake," the old lady said vaguely.

"Nome," he said. "It wasn't no mistake. They had the papers on me."

"You must have stolen something," she said.

The Misfit sneered slightly. "Nobody had nothing I wanted," he said. "It was a head-doctor at the penitentiary said what I had done was kill my daddy but I known that for a lie. My daddy died in nineteen ought nineteen of the epidemic flu and I never had a thing to do with it. He was buried in the Mount Hopewell Baptist churchyard and you can go there and see for yourself."

"If you would pray," the old lady said, "Jesus would help you."

"That's right," The Misfit said.

"Well then, why don't you pray?" she asked trembling with delight suddenly.

"I don't want no hep," he said. "I'm doing all right by myself."

Bobby Lee and Hiram came ambling back from the woods. Bobby Lee was dragging a yellow shirt with bright blue parrots in it.

"Thow me that shirt, Bobby Lee," The Misfit said. The shirt came flying at him and landed on his shoulder and he put it on. The grandmother couldn't name what the shirt reminded her of. "No, lady," The Misfit said while he was buttoning it up, "I found out the crime don't matter. You can do one thing or you can do another, kill a man or take a tire off his car, because sooner or later you're going to forget what it was you done and just be punished for it."

The children's mother had begun to make heaving noises as if she couldn't get her breath. "Lady," he asked, "would you and that little girl like to step off yonder with Bobby Lee and Hiram and join your husband?"

"Yes, thank you" the mother said faintly. Her left arm dangled helplessly and she was holding the baby, who had gone to sleep, in the other. "Hep that lady up, Hiram," The Misfit said as she struggled to climb out of the ditch, "and Bobby Lee, you hold onto that little girl's hand."

"I don't want to hold hands with him," June Star said. "He reminds me of a pig."

The fat boy blushed and laughed and caught her by the arm and pulled her off into the woods after Hiram and her mother.

Alone with The Misfit, the grandmother found that she had lost her voice. There was not a cloud in the sky nor any sun. There was nothing around her but woods. She wanted to tell him that he must pray. She opened and closed her mouth several times before anything came out. Finally she found herself saying, "Jesus, Jesus," meaning, Jesus will help you, but the way she was saying it, it sounded as if she might be cursing.

"Yes'm," The Misfit said as if he agreed. "Jesus thown everything off balance. It was the same case with Him as with me except He hadn't committed any crime and they could prove I had committed one because they had the papers on me. Of course," he said, "they never shown me my papers. That's why I sign myself now. I said long ago, you get you a signature and sign everything you do and keep a copy of it. Then you'll know what you done and you can hold up the crime to the punishment and see do they match and in the end you'll have something to prove you ain't been treated right. I call myself The Misfit," he said, "because I can't make what all I done wrong fit what all I gone through in punishment."

There was a piercing scream from the woods, followed closely by a pistol report. "Does it seem right to you, lady, that one is punished a heap and another ain't punished at all?"

"Jesus!" the old lady cried. "You've got good blood! I know you wouldn't shoot a lady! I know you come from nice people! Pray! Jesus, you ought not to shoot a lady. I'll give you all the money I've got!"

"Lady," The Misfit said, looking beyond her far into the woods, "there never was a body that give the undertaker a tip."

There were two more pistol reports and the grandmother raised her head like a parched old turkey hen crying for water and called, "Bailey Boy, Bailey Boy!" as if her heart would break.

"Jesus was the only One that ever raised the dead," The Misfit continued, "and He shouldn't have done it. He thown everything off balance. If He did what He said, then it's nothing for you to do but thow away everything and follow Him, and if He didn't, then it's nothing for you to do but enjoy the few minutes you got left the best way you can—by killing somebody or burning down his house or doing some other meanness to him. No pleasure but meanness," he said and his voice had become almost a snarl.

"Maybe He didn't raise the dead," the old lady mumbled, not knowing what she was saying and feeling so dizzy that she sank down in the ditch with her legs twisted under her.

"I wasn't there so I can't say He didn't," The Misfit said. "I wisht I had of been there," he said, hitting the ground with his fist. "It ain't right I wasn't there because if I had of been there I would of known. Listen lady," he said in a high voice, "if I had of been there I would of known and I wouldn't be like I am now." His voice seemed about to crack and the grandmother's head cleared for an instant. She saw the man's face twisted close to her own as if he were going to cry and she murmured, "Why you're one of my babies. You're one of my own children!" She reached out and touched him on the shoulder. The Misfit sprang back as if a snake had bitten him and shot her three times through the chest. Then he put his gun down on the ground and took off his glasses and began to clean them.

Hiram and Bobby Lee returned from the woods and stood over the ditch, looking down at the grandmother who half sat and half lay in a puddle of blood with her legs crossed under her like a child's and her face smiling up at the cloudless sky.

Without his glasses, The Misfit's eyes were red-rimmed and pale and defenseless-looking. "Take her off and thow her where you thown the others," he said, picking up the cat that was rubbing itself against his leg.

"She was a talker, wasn't she?" Bobby Lee said, sliding down the ditch with a yodel.

"She would of been a good woman," The Misfit said, "if it had been somebody there to shoot her every minute of her life."

"Some fun!" Bobby Lee said.

"Shut up, Bobby Lee," The Misfit said. "It's no real pleasure in life."

Quenby and Ola, Swede and Carl

Robert Coover (1932–)

Night on the lake. A low cloud cover. The boat bobs silently, its motor for some reason dead. There's enough light in the far sky to see the obscure humps of islands a mile or two distant, but up close: nothing. There are islands in the intermediate distance, but their uncertain contours are more felt than seen. The same might be said, in fact, for the boat itself. From either end, the opposite end seems to melt into the blackness of the lake. It feels like it might rain.

° ° °

Imagine Quenby and Ola at the barbecue pit. Their faces pale in the gathering dusk. The silence after the sudden report broken only by the whine of mosquitos in the damp grass, a distant whistle. Quenby has apparently tried to turn Ola away, back toward the house, but Ola is staring back over her shoulder. What is she looking at, Swede or the cat? Can she even see either?

° ° °

In the bow sat Carl. Carl was from the city. He came north to the lake every summer for a week or two of fishing. Sometimes he came along with other guys, this year he came alone.

He always told himself he liked it up on the lake, liked to get away, that's what he told the fellows he worked with, too: get out of the old harness, he'd say. But he wasn't sure. Maybe he didn't like it. Just now, on a pitchblack lake with a stalled motor, miles from nowhere, cold and hungry and no fish to show for the long day, he was pretty sure he didn't like it.

° ° °

You know the islands are out there, not more than a couple hundred yards probably, because you've seen them in the daylight. All you can make out now is here and there the pale stroke of what is probably a birch trunk, but you know there are spruce and jack pines as well, and balsam firs and white cedars and Norway pines and even maples and tamaracks. Forests have collapsed upon forests on these islands.

° ° °

The old springs crush and grate like crashing limbs, exhausted trees, rocks tumbling into the bay, like the lake wind rattling through dry branches and pine needles. She is hot, wet, rich, softly spread. Needful. "Oh yes!" she whispers.

° ° °

Walking on the islands, you've noticed saxifrage and bellwort, clintonia, shinleaf, and stemless lady's slippers. Sioux country once upon a time, you've heard tell, and Algonquin, mostly Cree and Ojibwa. Such things you know. Or the names of the birds up here: like spruce grouse and whiskey jack and American three-toed woodpecker. Blue-headed vireo. Scarlet tanager. Useless information. Just now, anyway. You don't even know what makes that strange whistle that pierces the stillness now.

° ° °

"Say, what's that whistling sound, Swede? Sounds like a goddamn traffic whistle!" That was pretty funny, but Swede didn't laugh. Didn't say anything. "Some bird, I guess. Eh, Swede? Some goddamn bird."

"Squirrels," Swede said finally.

"Squirrels!" Carl was glad Swede had said something. At least he knew he was still back there. My Jesus, it was dark! He waited hopefully for another response from Swede, but it didn't come. "Learn something new every day."

° ° °

Ola, telling the story, laughed brightly. The others laughed with her. What had she seen that night? It didn't matter, it was long ago. There were more lemon pies and there were more cats. She enjoyed being at the center of attention and she told the story well, imitating her father's laconic ways delightfully. She strode longleggedly across the livingroom floor at the main house, gripping an imaginary cat, her face puckered in a comic scowl. Only her flowering breasts under the orange shirt, her young hips packed snugly in last year's bright white shorts, her soft girlish thighs, slender calves: these were not Swede's.

° ° °

She is an obscure teasing shape, now shattering the sheen of moonlight on the bay, now blending with it. Is she moving toward the shore, toward the house? No, she is in by the boats near the end of the docks, dipping in among shadows. You follow.

° ° °

By day, there is a heavy greenness, mostly the deep dense greens of pines and shadowed undergrowth, and glazed blues and the whiteness of rocks and driftwood. At night, there is only darkness. Branches scrape gently on the roof of the guests' lodge; sometimes squirrels scamper across it. There are bird calls, the burping of frogs, the rustle of porcupines and muskrats, and now and then what sounds like the crushing footfalls of deer. At times, there is the sound of wind or rain, waves snapping in the bay. But essentially a deep stillness prevails, a stillness and darkness unknown to the city. And often, from far out on the lake, miles out perhaps, yet clearly ringing as though just outside the door: the conversation of men in fishing boats.

° ° °

"Well, I guess you know your way around this lake pretty well. Eh, Swede?"

"Oh yah."

"Like the back of your hand, I guess." Carl felt somehow encouraged that Swede had answered him. That "oh yah" was Swede's trademark. He almost never talked, and when he did, it was usually just "oh yah." Up on the "oh," down on the "yah." Swede was bent down over the motor, but what was he looking at? Was he looking at the motor or was he looking back this way? It was hard to tell. "It all looks the same to me, just a lot of trees and water and sky, and now you can't even see that much. Those goddamn squirrels sure make a lot of noise, don't they?" Actually, they were probably miles away.

Carl sighed and cracked his knuckles. "Can you hunt ducks up here?" Maybe it was better up here in the fall or winter. Maybe he could get a group interested. Probably cold, though. It was cold enough right now. "Well, I suppose you can. Sure, hell, why not?"

° ° °

Quenby at the barbecue pit, grilling steaks. Thick T-bones, because he's back after two long weeks away. He has poured a glass of whiskey for himself, splashed a little water in it, mixed a more diluted one for Quenby. He hands her her drink and spreads himself into a lawnchair. Flames lick and snap at the steaks, and smoke from the burning fat billows up from the pit. Quenby wears pants, those relaxed faded bluejeans probably, and a soft leather jacket. The late evening sun gives a gentle rich glow to the leather. There is something solid and good about Quenby. Most women complain about hunting trips. Quenby bakes lemon pies to celebrate returns. Her full buttocks flex in the soft blue denim as, with tongs, she flips the steaks over. Imagine.

° ° °

Her hips jammed against the gunwales, your wet bodies sliding together, astonished, your lips meeting—you wonder at your madness, what an island can do to a man, what an island girl can do. Later, having crossed the bay again, returning to the rocks, you find your underwear is gone. Yes, here's the path, here's the very tree—but gone. A childish prank? But she was with you all the time. Down by the kennels, the dogs begin to yelp.

° ° °

Swede was a native of sorts. He and his wife Quenby lived year-round on an island up here on the lake. They operated a kind of small rustic lodge for men from the city who came up to fish and hunt. Swede took them out to the best places, Quenby cooked and kept the cabin up. They could take care of as many as eight at a time. They moved here years ago, shortly after marrying. Real natives, folks born and bred on the lake, are pretty rare; their 14-year-old daughter Ola is one of the few.

How far was it to Swede's island? This is a better question maybe than "Who is Swede?" but you are even less sure of the answer. You've been fishing all day and you haven't been paying much attention. No lights to be seen anywhere, and Swede always keeps a dock light burning, but you may be on the back side of his island, cut off from the light by the thick pines, only yards away from home, so to speak. Or maybe miles away. Most likely miles.

° ° °

Yes, goddamn it, it was going to rain. Carl sucked on a beer in the bow. Swede tinkered quietly with the motor in the stern.

What made a guy move up into these parts? Carl wondered. It was okay for maybe a week or two, but he couldn't see living up here all the time. Well, of course, if a man really loved to fish. Fish and hunt. If he didn't like the ratrace in the city, and so on. Must be a bitch for Swede's wife and kid, though. Carl knew his own wife would never stand still for the idea. And Swede was probably pretty hard on old Quenby. With Swede there were never two ways about it. That's the idea Carl got.

Carl tipped the can of beer back, drained it. Stale and warm. It disgusted him. He heaved the empty tin out into the darkness, heard it plunk somewhere on the black water. He couldn't see if it sank or not. It probably didn't sink. He'd have to piss again soon. Probably he should do it before they got moving again. He didn't mind pissing from the boat, in a way he even enjoyed it, he felt like part of things up here when he was pissing from a boat, but right now it seemed too quiet or something.

Then he got to worrying that maybe he shouldn't have thrown it out there on the water, that beercan, probably there was some law about it, and anyway you could get things like that caught in boat motors, couldn't you? Hell, maybe that was what was wrong with the goddamn motor now. He'd just shown his ignorance again probably. That was what he hated most about coming up here, showing his ignorance. In groups it wasn't so bad, they were all green and could joke about it, but Carl was all alone this trip. Never again.

° ° °

The Coleman lantern is lit. Her flesh glows in its eery light and the starched white linens are ominously alive with their thrashing shadows. She has brought clean towels; or perhaps some coffee, a book. Wouldn't look right to put out the lantern while she's down here, but its fierce gleam is disquieting. Pine boughs scratch the roof. The springs clatter and something scurries under the cabin. "Hurry!" she whispers.

° ° °

"Listen, Swede, you need some help?" Swede didn't reply, so Carl stood up in a kind of crouch and made a motion as though he were going to step back and give a hand. He could barely make Swede out back there. He stayed carefully in the middle of the boat. He wasn't completely stupid.

Swede grunted. Carl took it to mean he didn't want any help, so he sat down again. There was one more can of beer under his seat, but he didn't much care to drink it. His pants, he had noticed on rising and sitting, were damp, and he felt stiff and sore. It was late. The truth was, he didn't know the first goddamn thing about outboard motors anyway.

° ° °

There's this story about Swede. Ola liked to tell it and she told it well. About three years ago, when Ola was eleven, Swede had come back from a two-week hunting trip up north. For ducks. Ola, telling the story, would make a big thing about the beard he came back with and the jokes her mother made about it.

Quenby had welcomed Swede home with a big steak supper: thick T-bones, potatos wrapped in foil and baked in the coals, a heaped green salad. And lemon pie. Nothing in the world like Quenby's homemade lemon pie, and she'd baked it just for Swede. It was a great supper. Ola skipped most of the details, but one could imagine them. After supper, Swede said he'd bring in the pie and coffee.

In the kitchen, he discovered that Ola's cat had tracked through the pie. Right through the middle of it. It was riddled with cat tracks, and there was lemon pie all over the bench and floor. Daddy had been looking forward to that lemon pie for two weeks, Ola would say, and now it was full of cat tracks.

He picked up his gun from beside the back door, pulled some shells out of his pocket, and loaded it. He found the cat in the laundryroom with lemon pie still stuck to its paws and whiskers. He picked it up by the nape and carried it outside. It was getting dark, but you could still see plainly enough. At least against the sky.

He walked out past the barbecue pit. It was dark enough that the coals seemed to glow now. Just past the pit, he stopped. He swung his arm in a lazy arc and pitched the cat high in the air. Its four paws scrambled in space. He lifted the gun to his shoulder and blew the cat's head off. Her daddy was a good shot.

° ° °

Her mock pout, as she strides across the room, clutching the imaginary cat, makes you laugh. She needs a new pair of shorts. Last year they were loose on her, wrinkled where bunched at the waist, gaping around her small thighs. But she's grown, filled out a lot, as young girls her age do. When her shirt rides up over her waist, you notice that the zipper gapes in an open V above her hip bone. The white cloth is taut and glossy over her firm bottom; the only wrinkle is the almost painful crease between her legs.

° ° °

Carl scrubbed his beard. It was pretty bristly, but that was because it was still new. He could imagine what his wife would say. He'd kid his face into a serious frown and tell her, hell, he was figuring on keeping the beard permanently now. Well, he wouldn't, of course, he'd feel like an ass at the office with it on, he'd just say that to rile his wife a little. Though, damn it, he did enjoy the beard. He wished more guys where he worked wore beards. He liked to scratch the back of his hand and wrist with it.

"You want this last beer, Swede?" he asked. He didn't get an answer. Swede was awful quiet. He was a quiet type of guy. Reticent, that's how he is, thought Carl. "Maybe Quenby's baked a pie," he said, hoping he wasn't being too obvious. Sure was taking one helluva long time.

° ° °

He lifts the hem of his tee shirt off his hairy belly, up his chest, but she can't seem to wait for that—her thighs jerk up, her ankles lock behind his buttocks, and they crash to the bed, the old springs shrieking and thumping like a speeding subway, traffic at noon, arriving trains. His legs and buttocks, though pale and flabby, seem dark against the pure white spectacle of the starched sheets, the flushed glow of her full heaving body, there in the harsh blaze of the Coleman lantern. Strange, they should keep it burning. His short stiff beard scrubs the hollow of her throat, his broad hands knead her trembling flesh. She sighs, whimpers, pleads, as her body slaps rhythmically against his. "Yes!" she cries hoarsely.

You turn silently from the window. At the house, when you arrive, you find Ola washing dishes.

° ° °

What did Quenby talk about? Her garden probably, pie baking, the neighbors. About the wind that had come up one night while he'd been gone, and how she'd had to move some of the boats around. His two-week beard: looked like a darned broom, she said. He'd have to sleep down with the dogs if he didn't cut it off. Ola would giggle, imagining her daddy sleeping with the dogs. And, yes, Quenby would probably talk about Ola, about the things she'd done or said while he was away, what she was doing in sixth grade, about her pets and her friends and the ways she'd helped around the place.

Quenby at the barbecue pit, her full backside to him, turning the steaks, sipping the whiskey, talking about life on the island. Or maybe not talking at all. Just watching the steaks maybe. Ola inside setting the table. Or swimming down by the docks. A good thing here. The sun now an orangish ball over behind the pines. Water lapping at the dock and the boats, curling up on the shore, some minutes after a boat passes distantly. The flames and the smoke. Down at the kennels, the dogs were maybe making a ruckus. Maybe Ola's cat had wandered down there. The cat had a habit of teasing them outside their pen. The dogs had worked hard, they deserved a rest. Mentally, he gave the cat a boot in the ribs. He had already fed the dogs, but later he would take the steak bones down.

° ° °

Quenby's thighs brush together when she walks. In denim, they whistle; bare, they whisper. Not so, Ola's. Even with her knees together (they rarely are), there is space between her thighs. A pressure there, not of opening, but of awkwardness.

Perhaps, too, island born, her walk is different. Her mother's weight is settled solidly beneath her buttocks; she moves out from there, easily, calmly, weightlessly. Ola's center is still between her narrow shoulders, somewhere in the midst of her fine new breasts, and her quick astonished stride is guided by the tips of her hipbones, her knees, her toes. Quenby's thick black cushion is a rich locus of movement; her daughter still arches uneasily out and away from the strange outcropping of pale fur that peeks out now at the inner edges of the white shorts.

It is difficult for a man to be alone on a green island.

° ° °

Carl wished he had a cigarette. He'd started out with cigarettes, but he'd got all excited once when he hooked a goddamn fish, and they had all spilled out on the wet bottom of the boat. What was worse, the damn fish—a great northern, Swede had said—had broke his line and got away. My Jesus, the only strike he'd got all day, and he'd messed it up! Swede had caught two. Both bass. A poor day, all in all. Swede didn't smoke.

To tell the truth, even more than a cigarette, he wished he had a good stiff drink. A hot supper. A bed. Even that breezy empty lodge at Swede's with its stale piney smell and cold damp sheets and peculiar noises filled him with a terrific longing. Not to mention home, real home, the TV, friends over for bridge or poker, his own electric blanket.

"Sure is awful dark, ain't it?" Carl said "ain't" out of deference to Swede. Swede always said "ain't" and Carl liked to talk that way when he was up here. He liked to drink beer and say "ain't" and "he don't" and stomp heavily around with big boots on. He even found himself saying "oh yah!" sometimes, just like Swede did. Up on the "oh," down on the "yah." Carl wondered how it would go over back at the office. They might even get to know him by it. When he was dead, they'd say: "Well, just like good old Carl used to say: oh yah!"

° ° °

In his mind, he watched the ducks fall. He drank the whiskey and watched the steaks and listened to Quenby and watched the ducks fall. They didn't just plummet, they fluttered and flopped. Sometimes they did seem to plummet, but in his mind he saw the ones that kept trying to fly, kept trying to understand what the hell was happening. It was the rough flutter sound and the soft loose splash of the fall that made him like to hunt ducks.

° ° °

Swede, Quenby, Ola, Carl . . . Having a drink after supper, in the livingroom around the fireplace, though there's no fire in it. Ola's not drinking, of course. She's telling a story about her daddy and a cat. It is easy to laugh. She's a cute girl. Carl stretches. "Well, off to the sack, folks. Thanks for the terrific supper. See you in the morning, Swede." Quenby: "Swede or I'll bring you fresh towels, Carl. I forgot to put any this morning."

° ° °

You know what's going on out here, don't you? You're not that stupid. You know why the motor's gone dead, way out here, miles from nowhere. You know the reason for the silence. For the wait. Dragging it out. Making you feel it. After all, there was the missing underwear. Couldn't find it in the morning sunlight either.

But what could a man do? You remember the teasing buttocks as she dogpaddled away, the taste of her wet belly on the gunwales of the launch, the terrible splash when you fell. Awhile ago, you gave a tug on the stringer. You were hungry and you were half-tempted to paddle the boat to the nearest shore and cook up the two bass. The stringer felt oddly weighted. You had a sudden vision of a long cold body at the end of it, hooked through a cheek, eyes glazed over, childish limbs adrift. What do you do with a vision like that? You forget it. You try to.

° ° °

They go in to supper. He mixes a couple more drinks on the way. The whiskey plup-plup-plups out of the bottle. Outside, the sun is setting. Ola's cat rubs up against his leg. Probably contemplating the big feed when the ducks get cleaned. Brownnoser. He lifts one foot and scrubs the cat's ears with the toe of his boot. Deep-throated purr. He grins, carries the drinks in and sits down at the diningroom table.

Quenby talks about town gossip, Ola talks about school and Scouts, and he talks about shooting ducks. A pretty happy situation. He eats with enthusiasm. He tells how he got the first bird, and Ola explains about the Golden Gate Bridge, cross-pollination, and Tom Sawyer, things she's been reading in school.

He cleans his plate and piles on seconds and thirds of everything. Quenby smiles to see him eat. She warns him to save room for the pie, and he replies that he could put away a herd of elephants and still have space for ten pies. Ola laughs gaily at that. She sure has a nice laugh. Ungainly as she is just now, she's going to be a pretty girl, he decides. He drinks his whiskey off, announces he'll bring in the pie and coffee.

° ° °

How good it had felt. In spite of the musty odors, the rawness of the stiff sheets, the gaudy brilliance of the Coleman lantern, the anxious haste, the cool air teasing the hairs on your buttocks, the scamper of squirrels across the roof, the hurried by-passing of preliminaries (one astonishing kiss, then shirt and jacket and pants had dropped away in one nervous gesture, and down you'd gone, you in teeshirt and socks still): once it began, it was wonderful! Lunging recklessly into that steaming softness, your lonely hands hungering over her flesh, her heavy thighs kicking up and up, then slamming down behind your knees, hips rearing up off the sheets, her voice rasping: "Hurry!"—everything else forgotten, how good, how good!

And then she was gone. And you lay in your teeshirt and socks, staring half-dazed at the Coleman lantern, smoking a cigarette, thinking about tomorrow's fishing trip, idly sponging away your groin's dampness with your shorts. You stubbed out the cigarette, pulled on your khaki pants, scratchy on your bare and agitated skin, slipped out the door to urinate. The light leaking out your shuttered window caught your eye. You went to stand there, and through the broken shutter, you stared at the bed, the roughed-up sheets, watched yourself there. Well. Well. You pissed on the wall, staring up toward the main house, through the pines. Dimly, you could see Ola's head in the kitchen window.

You know. You know.

° ° °

"Listen, uh, Swede . . ."

"Yah?"

"Oh, nothing. I mean, well, what I started to say was, maybe I better start putting my shoulder to, you know, one of the paddles or whatever the hell you call them. I—well, unless you're sure you can get it—"

"Oh yah. I'm sure."

"Well . . ."

° ° °

Swede, Carl, Ola, Quenby . . . One or more may soon be dead. Swede or Carl, for example, in revenge or lust or self-defense. And if one or both of them do return to the island, what will they find there? Or perhaps Swede is long since dead, and Carl only imagines his presence. A man can imagine a lot of things, alone on a strange lake in a dark night.

° ° °

Carl, Quenby, Swede, Ola . . . Drinks in the livingroom. An after-dinner sleepiness on all of them. Except Ola. Wonderful supper. Nothing like fresh lake bass. And Quenby's lemon pie. "Did you ever hear about Daddy and the cat?" Ola asks. "No!" All smile. Ola perches forward on the hassock. "Well, Daddy had been away for two weeks . . ."

° ° °

Listen: alone, far from your wife, nobody even to play poker with, a man does foolish things sometimes. You're stretched out in your underwear on an uncomfortable bed in the middle of the night; for example, awakened perhaps by the footfalls of deer outside the cabin, or the whistle of squirrels, the cry of loons, unable now to sleep. You step out, barefoot, to urinate by the front wall of the lodge. There seems to be someone swimming down in the bay, over near the docks, across from the point here. No lights up at the main house, just the single dull bulb glittering as usual out on the far end of the dock, casting no light. A bright moon.

You pad quietly down toward the bay, away from the kennels, hoping the dogs don't wake. She is swimming this way. She reaches the rocks near the point here, pulls herself up on them, then stands shivering, her slender back to you, gazing out on the way she's come, out toward the boats and docks, heavy structures crouched in the moonglazed water. Pinpricks of bright moonlight sparkle on the crown of her head, her narrow shoulders and shoulderblades, the crest of her buttocks, her calves and heels.

Hardly thinking, you slip off your underwear, glance once at the house, then creep out on the rock beside her. "How's the water?" you whisper.

She huddles over her breasts, a little surprised, but smiles up at you. "It's better in than out," she says, her teeth chattering a little with the chill.

You stoop to conceal, in part, your burgeoning excitement, which you'd hoped against, and dip your fingers in the water. Is it cold? You hardly notice, for you are glancing back up now, past the hard cleft nub where fine droplets of water, catching the moonlight, bejewel the soft down, past the flat gleaming tummy and clutched elbows, at the young girl's dark shivering lips. She, too, seems self-conscious, for like you, she squats now, presenting you only her bony knees and shoulders, trembling, and her smile. "It's okay," you say," I have a daughter just your age." Which is pretty stupid.

° ° °

They were drifting between two black islands. Carl squinted and concentrated, but he couldn't see the shores, couldn't guess how far away the islands were. Didn't matter anyway. Nobody on them. "Hey, listen, Swede, you need a light? I think I still got some matches here if they're not wet—"

"No, sit down. Just be a moment . . ."

Well, hell, stop and think, goddamn it, you can't stick a lighted match around a gasoline motor. "Well, I just thought . . ." Carl wondered why Swede didn't carry a flashlight. My Jesus, a man lives up here on a lake all these years and doesn't know enough to take along a goddamn flashlight. Maybe he wasn't so bright, after all.

He wondered if Swede's wife wasn't worrying about them by now. Well, she was probably used to it. A nice woman, friendly, a good cook, probably pretty well built in her day, though not Carl's type really. A little too slack in the britches. Skinny little daughter, looked more like Swede. Filling out, though. Probably be a cute girl in a couple years. Carl got the idea vaguely that Quenby, Swede's wife, didn't really like it up here. Too lonely or something. Couldn't blame her.

He knew it was a screwy notion, but he kept wishing there was a goddamn neon light or something around. He fumbled under the seat for the other beer.

° ° °

"I asked Daddy why he shot my cat," she said. She stood at the opposite end of the livingroom, facing them, in her orange shirt and bright white shorts, thin legs apart. It was a sad question, but her lips were smiling, her small white teeth glittering gaily. She'd just imitated her daddy lobbing the cat up in the air and blowing its head off. " 'Well, honey, I gave it a sporting chance,' he said. 'I threw it up in the air, and if it'd flown away, I wouldn't have shot it!' " She joined in the general laughter, skipping awkwardly, girlishly, back to the group. It was a good story.

° ° °

She slips into the water without a word, and dogpaddles away, her narrow bottom bobbing in and out of sight. What the hell, the house is dark, the dogs silent: you drop into the water—wow! sudden breathtaking impact of the icy envelope! whoopee!—and follow her, a dark teasing shape rippling the moonlit surface.

You expect her to bend her course in toward the shore, toward the house, and, feeling suddenly exposed and naked and foolish in the middle of the bright bay, in spite of your hunger to see her again, out of the water, you pause, prepare to return to the point. But, no, she is in by the boats, near the end of the docks, disappearing into the wrap of shadows. You sink out of sight, swim underwater to the docks—a long stretch for a man your age—and find her there, holding onto the rope ladder of the launch her father uses for guiding large groups. The house is out of sight, caution out of mind.

She pulls herself up the ladder and you follow close behind, her legs brushing your face and shoulders. At the gunwales, she emerges into full moonlight, and as she bends forward to crawl into the launch, drugged by the fantasy of the moment, you leap up to kiss her glistening buttocks. In your throbbing mind is the foolish idea that, if she protests, you will make some joke about your beard.

° ° °

He punched the can and the beer exploded out. He ducked just in time, but got part of it in his ear. "Hey! Did I get you, Swede?" he laughed. Swede didn't say anything. Hell, it was silly even to ask. The beer had shot off over his shoulder, past the bow, the opposite direction from Swede. He had asked only out of habit. Because he didn't like the silence. He punched a second hole and put the can to his lips. All he got at first was foam. But by tipping the can almost straight up, he managed a couple swallows of beer. At first, he thought it tasted good, but a moment later, the flat warm yeasty taste sliming his mouth, he wondered why the hell he had opened it up. He considered dumping the rest of it in the lake. But, damn it, Swede would hear him and wonder why he was doing it. This time, though, he would remember and not throw the empty can away.

° ° °

Swede, Quenby, Carl, Ola . . . The story and the laughter and off to bed. The girl has omitted one detail from her story. After her daddy's shot, the cat had plummeted to the earth. But afterwards, there was a fluttering sound on the ground where it hit. Still, late at night, it caused her wonder. Branches scrape softly on the roof. Squirrels whistle and scamper. There is a rustling of beavers, foxes, skunks, and porcupines. A profound stillness, soon to be broken surely by rain. And, from far out on the lake, men in fishing boats, arguing, chattering, opening beercans. Telling stories.

Donald Barthelme (1933–)

Me and Miss Mandible

13 September

Miss Mandible wants to make love to me but she hesitates because I am officially a child; I am, according to the records, according to the gradebook on her desk, according to the card index in the principal's office, eleven years old. There is a misconception here, one that I haven't quite managed to get cleared up yet. I am in fact thirty-five, I've been in the Army, I am six feet one, I have hair in the appropriate places, my voice is a baritone, I know very well what to do with Miss Mandible if she ever makes up her mind.

In the meantime we are studying common fractions. I could, of course, answer all the questions, or at least most of them (there are things I don't remember). But I prefer to sit in this too-small seat with the desktop cramping my thighs and examine the life around me. There are thirty-two in the class, which is launched every morning with the pledge of allegiance to the flag. My own allegiance, at the moment, is divided between Miss Mandible and Sue Ann Brownly, who sits across the aisle from me all day long and is, like Miss Mandible, a fool for love. Of the two I prefer, today, Sue Ann; although between eleven and eleven and a half (she refuses to reveal her exact age) she is clearly a woman, with a woman's disguised aggression and woman's peculiar contradictions. Strangely neither she nor any of the other children seem to see any incongruity in my presence here.

15 September

Happily our geography text, which contains maps of all the principal landmasses of the world, is large enough to conceal my clandestine journal-keeping, accomplished in an ordinary black composition book. Every day I must wait until Geography to put down such thoughts as I may have had during the morning about my situation and my fellows. I have tried writing at other times and it does not work. Either the teacher is walking up and down the aisles (during this period, luckily, she sticks close to the map rack in the front of the room) or Bobby Vanderbilt, who sits behind me, is punching me in the kidneys and wanting to know what I am doing. Vanderbilt, I have found out from certain desultory conversations on the playground, is hung up on sports cars, a veteran consumer of *Road & Track.* This explains the continual roaring sounds which seem to emanate from his desk; he is reproducing a record album called *Sounds of Sebring.*

19 September

Only, I, at times (only at times), understand that somehow a mistake has been made, that I am in a place where I don't belong. It may be that Miss Mandible also knows this, at some level, but for reasons not fully understood by me she is going along with the game. When I was first assigned to this room I wanted to protest, the error seemed obvious, the stupidest principal could have seen it; but I have come to believe it was deliberate, that I have been betrayed again.

Now it seems to make little difference. This life-role is as interesting as my former life-role, which was that of a claims adjuster for the Great Northern Insurance Company, a position which compelled me to spend my time amid the debris of our civilization: rumpled fenders, roofless sheds, gutted warehouses, smashed arms and legs. After ten years of this one has a tendency to see the world as a vast junkyard, looking at a man and seeing only his (potentially) mangled parts, entering a house only to trace the path of the inevitable fire. Therefore when I was installed here, although I knew an error had been made, I countenanced it, I was shrewd; I was aware that there might well be some kind of advantage to be gained from what seemed a disaster. The role of The Adjuster teaches one much.

22 September

I am being solicited for the volleyball team. I decline, refusing to take unfair profit from my height.

23 September

Every morning the roll is called: Bestvina, Bokenfohr, Broan, Brownly, Cone, Coyle, Crecelius, Darin, Durbin, Geiger, Guiswite, Heckler, Jacobs, Kleinschmidt, Lay, Logan, Masei, Mitgang, Pfeilsticker. It is like the litany chanted in the dim miserable dawns of Texas by the cadre sergeant of our basic training company.

In the Army, too, I was ever so slightly awry. It took me a fantastically long time to realize what the others grasped almost at once: that much of what we were doing was absolutely pointless, to no purpose. I kept wondering why. Then something happened that proposed a new question. One day we were commanded to whitewash, from the ground to the topmost leaves, all of the trees in our training area. The corporal who relayed the order was nervous and apologetic. Later an off-duty captain sauntered by and watched us, white-splashed and totally weary, strung out among the freakish shapes we had created. He walked away swearing. I understood the principle (orders are orders), but I wondered: Who decides?

29 September

Sue Ann is a wonder. Yesterday she viciously kicked my ankle for not paying attention when she was attempting to pass me a note during History. It is swollen still. But Miss Mandible was watching me, there was nothing I could do. Oddly enough Sue Ann reminds me of the wife I had in my former role, while Miss Mandible seems to be a child. She watches me constantly, trying to keep sexual significance out of her look; I am afraid the other children have noticed. I have already heard, on that ghostly frequency that is the medium of classroom communication, the words "*Teacher's pet!*"

2 October

Sometimes I speculate on the exact nature of the conspiracy which brought me here. At times I believe it was instigated by my wife of former days, whose name was . . . I am only pretending to forget. I know her name very well, as well as I know the name of my former motor oil (Quaker State) or my old Army serial number (US 54109268). Her name was Brenda, and the conversation I recall best, the one which makes me suspicious now, took place on the day we parted. "You have the soul of a whore," I said on that occasion, stating nothing less than literal, unvarnished fact. "You," she replied, "are a pimp, a poop, and a child. I am leaving you forever and I trust that without me you will perish of your own inadequacies. Which are considerable."

I squirm in my seat at the memory of this conversation, and Sue Ann watches me with malign compassion. She has noticed the discrepancy between the size of my desk and my own size, but apparently sees it only as a token of my glamour, my dark man-of-the-worldness.

7 October

Once I tiptoed up to Miss Mandible's desk (when there was no one else in the room) and examined its surface. Miss Mandible is a clean-desk teacher, I discovered. There was nothing except her gradebook (the one in which I exist as a sixth-grader) and a text, which was open at a page headed *Making the Processes Meaningful*. I read: "Many pupils enjoy working fractions when they understand what they are doing. They have confidence in their ability to take the right steps, and to obtain correct answers. However, to give the subject full social significance, it is necessary that many realistic situations requiring the processes be found. Many interesting and lifelike problems involving the use of fractions should be solved . . ."

8 October

I am not irritated by the feeling of having been through all this before. Things are done differently now. The children, moreover, are in some ways different from those who accompanied me on my first voyage through the elementary schools: "*They have confidence in their ability to take the right steps and to obtain correct answers.*" This is surely true. When Bobby Vanberbilt, who sits behind me and has the great tactical advantage of being able to maneuver in my disproportionate shadow, wishes to bust a classmate in the mouth he first asks Miss Mandible to lower the blind, saying that the sun hurts his eyes. When she does so, *bip!* My generation would never have been able to con authority so easily.

13 October

It may be that on my first trip through the schools I was too much under the impression that what the authorities (who decides?) had ordained for me was right and proper, that I confused authority with life itself. My path was not particularly of my own choosing. My career stretched out in front of me like a paper chase, and my role was to pick up the clues. When I got out of school, the first time, I felt that this estimate was substantially correct, and eagerly entered the hunt. I found clues abundant: diplomas, membership cards, campaign buttons, a marriage license, insurance forms, discharge papers, tax returns, Certificates of Merit. They seemed to prove, at the very least, that I was *in the running.* But that was before my tragic mistake on the Mrs. Anton Bichek claim.

I misread a clue. Do not misunderstand me: it was a tragedy only from the point of view of the authorities. I conceived that it was my duty to obtain satisfaction for the injured, for this elderly lady (not even one of our policy-holders, but a claimant against Big Ben Transfer & Storage, Inc.) from the company. The settlement was $165,000; the claim, I still believe, was just. But without my encouragement Mrs. Bichek would never have had the self-love to prize her injury so highly. The company paid, but its faith in me, in my efficacy in the role, was broken. Henry Goodykind, the district manager, expressed this thought in a few not altogether unsympathetic words, and told me at the same time that I was to have a new role. The next thing I knew I was here, at Horace Greeley Elementary, under the lubricious eye of Miss Mandible.

17 October

Today we are to have a fire drill. I know this because I am a Fire Marshal, not only for our room but for the entire right wing of the second floor. This distinction, which was awarded shortly after my arrival, is interpreted by some as another mark of my somewhat dubious relations with our teacher. My armband, which is red and decorated with white felt letters reading FIRE, sits on the little shelf under my desk, next to the brown paper bag containing the lunch I carefully make for myself each morning. One of the advantages of packing my own lunch (I have no one to pack it for me) is that I am able to fill it with things I enjoy. The peanut butter sandwiches that my mother made in my former existence, many years ago, have been banished in favor of ham and cheese. I have found that my diet has mysteriously adjusted to my new situation; I no longer drink, for instance, and when I smoke, it is in the boys' john, like everybody else. When school is out I hardly smoke at all. It is only in the matter of sex that I feel my own true age; this is apparently something that, once learned, can never be forgotten. I live in fear that Miss Mandible will one day keep me after school, and when we are alone, create a compromising situation. To avoid this I have become a model pupil: another reason for the pronounced dislike I have encountered in certain quarters. But I cannot deny that I am singled by those long glances from the vicinity of the chalkboard; Miss Mandible is in many ways, notably about the bust, a very tasty piece.

24 October

There are isolated challenges to my largeness, to my dimly realized position in the class as Gulliver. Most of my classmates are polite about this matter, as they would be if I had only one eye, or wasted, metal-wrapped legs. I am viewed as a mutation of some sort but essentially a peer. However Harry Broan, whose father has made himself rich manufacturing the Broan Bathroom Vent (with which Harry is frequently reproached; he is always being asked how things are in Ventsville), today inquired if I wanted to fight. An interested group of his followers had gathered to observe this suicidal undertaking. I replied that I didn't feel quite up to it, for which he was obviously grateful. We are now friends forever. He has given me to understand privately that he can get me all the bathroom vents I will ever need, at a ridiculously modest figure.

25 October

"*Many interesting and lifelike problems involving the use of fractions should be solved . . .*" The theorists fail to realize that everything that is either interesting or lifelike in the classroom proceeds from what they would probably call interpersonal relations: Sue Ann Brownly kicking me in the ankle. How lifelike, how womanlike, is her tender solicitude after the deed! Her pride in my newly acquired limp is transparent; everyone knows that she has set her mark upon me, that it is a victory in her unequal struggle with Miss Mandible for my great, overgrown heart. Even Miss Mandible knows, and counters in perhaps the only way she can, with sarcasm. "Are you wounded, Joseph?" Conflagrations smolder behind her eyelids, yearning for the Fire Marshal clouds her eyes. I mumble that I have bumped my leg.

30 October

I return again and again to the problem of my future.

4 November

The underground circulating library has brought me a copy of *Movie—TV Secrets*, the multicolor cover blazoned with the headline. "Debbie's Date Insults Liz!" It is a gift from Frankie Randolph, a rather plain girl who until today has had not one word for me, passed on via Bobby Vanderbilt. I nod and smile over my shoulder in acknowledgment; Frankie hides her head under her desk. I have seen these magazines being passed around among the girls (sometimes one of the boys will condescend to inspect a particularly lurid cover). Miss Mandible confiscates them whenever she finds one. I leaf through *Movie—TV Secrets* and get an eyeful. "The exclusive picture on these pages isn't what it seems. We know how it looks and we know what the gossipers will do. So in the interests of a nice guy, we're publishing the facts first. Here's what really happened!" The picture shows a rising young movie idol in bed, pajama-ed and bleary-eyed, while an equally blowzy young woman looks startled beside him. I am happy to know that the picture is not really what it seems; it seems to be nothing less than divorce evidence.

What do these hipless eleven-year-olds think when they come across, in the same magazine, the full-page ad for Maurice de Paree, which features "Hip Helpers" or what appear to be padded rumps? ("A real undercover agent that adds appeal to those hips and derriere, both!") If they cannot decipher the language the illustrations leave nothing to the imagination. "Drive him frantic . . ." the copy continues. Perhaps this explains Bobby Vanderbilt's preoccupation with Lancias and Maseratis; it is a defense against being driven frantic.

Sue Ann has observed Frankie Randolph's overture, and catching my eye, she pulls from her satchel no less then seventeen of these magazines, thrusting them at me as if to prove that anything any of her rivals has to offer, she can top. I shuffle through them quickly, noting the broad editorial perspective:

"Debbie's Kids Are Crying"
"Eddie Asks Debbie. Will You . . .?"
"The Nightmares Liz Has About Eddie!"

"The Things Debbie Can Tell About Eddie"
"The Private Life of Eddie and Liz"
"Debbie Gets Her Man Back?"
"A New Life for Liz"
"Love Is a Tricky Affair"
"Eddie's Taylor-Made Love Nest"
"How Liz Made a Man of Eddie"
"Are They Planning to Live Together?"
"Isn't It Time to Stop Kicking Debbie Around?"
"Debbie's Dilemma"
"Eddie Becomes a Father Again"
"Is Debbie Planning to Re-wed?"
"Can Liz Fulfill Herself?"
"Why Debbie Is Sick of Hollywood"

Who are these people, Debbie, Eddie, Liz, and how did they get themselves in such a terrible predicament? Sue Ann knows, I am sure; it is obvious that she has been studying their history as a guide to what she may expect when she is suddenly freed from this drab, flat classroom.

I am angry and I shove the magazines back at her with not even a whisper of thanks.

5 November

The sixth grade at Horace Greeley Elementary is a furnace of love, love, love. Today it is raining, but inside the air is heavy and tense with passion. Sue Ann is absent; I suspect that yesterday's exchange has driven her to her bed. Guilt hangs about me. She is not responsible, I know, for what she reads, for the models proposed to her by a venal publishing industry; I should not have been so harsh. Perhaps it is only the flu.

Nowhere have I encountered an atmosphere as charged with aborted sexuality as this. Miss Mandible is helpless; nothing goes right today. Amos Darin has been found drawing a dirty picture in the cloakroom. Sad and inaccurate, it was offered not as a sign of something else but as an act of love in itself. It has excited even those who have not seen it, even those who saw but understood only that it was dirty. The room buzzes with imperfectly comprehended titillation. Amos stands by the door, waiting to be taken to the principal's office. He wavers between fear and enjoyment of his temporary celebrity. From time to time Miss Mandible looks at me reproachfully, as if blaming me for the uproar. But I did not create this atmosphere, I am caught in it like all the others.

8 November

Everything is promised my classmates and I, most of all the future. We accept the outrageous assurances without blinking.

9 November

I have finally found the nerve to petition for a larger desk. At recess I can hardly walk; my legs do not wish to uncoil themselves. Miss Mandible says she will take it up with the custodian. She is worried about the excellence of my themes. Have I, she asks, been receiving help? For an instant I am on the brink of telling her my story. Something, however, warns me not to attempt it. Here I am safe, I have a place; I do not wish to entrust myself once more to the whimsy of authority. I resolve to make my themes less excellent in the future.

11 November

A ruined marriage, a ruined adjusting career, a grim interlude in the Army when I was almost not a person. This is the sum of my existence to date, a dismal total. Small wonder that re-education seemed my only hope. It is clear even to me that I need reworking in some fundamental way. How efficient is the society that provides thus for the salvage of its clinkers!

Plucked from my unexamined life among other pleasant, desperate, money-making young Americans, thrown backward in space and time, I am beginning to understand how I went wrong, how we all go wrong. (Although this was far from the intention of those who sent me here; they require only that I *get right.*)

14 November

The distinction between children and adults, while probably useful for some purposes, is at bottom a specious one, I feel. There are only individual egos, crazy for love.

15 November

The custodian has informed Miss Mandible that our desks are all the correct size for sixth-graders, as specified by the Board of Estimate and furnished the schools by the Nu-Art Educational Supply Corporation of Englewood, California. He has pointed out that if the desk size is correct, then the pupil size must be incorrect. Miss Mandible, who has already arrived at this conclusion, refuses to press the matter further. I think I know why. An appeal to the administration might result in my removal from the class, in a transfer to some sort of setup for "exceptional children." This would be a disaster of the first magnitude. To sit in a room with child geniuses (or, more likely, children who are "retarded") would shrivel me in a week. Let my experience here be that of the common run, I say; let me be, please God, typical.

20 November

We read signs as promises. Miss Mandible understands by my great height, by my resonant vowels, that I will one day carry her off to bed. Sue Ann interprets these same signs to mean that I am unique among her male acquaintances, therefore most desirable, therefore her special property as is everything that is Most Desirable. If neither of these propositions work out then life has broken faith with them.

I myself, in my former existence, read the company motto ("Here to Help in Time of Need") as a description of the duty of the adjuster, drastically mislocating the company's deepest concerns. I believed that because I had obtained a wife who was made up of wife-signs (beauty, charm, softness, perfume, cookery) I had found love. Brenda, reading the same signs that have now misled Miss Mandible and Sue Ann Brownly, felt she had been promised that she would never be bored again. All of us, Miss Mandible, Sue Ann, myself, Brenda, Mr. Goodykind, still believe that the American flag betokens a kind of general righteousness.

But I say, looking about me in this incubator of future citizens, that signs are signs, and that some of them are lies. This is the great discovery of my time here.

23 November

It may be that my experience as a child will save me after all. If only I can remain quietly in this classroom, making my notes while Napoleon plods through Russia in the droning voice of Harry Broan, reading aloud from our History text. All of the mysteries that perplexed me as an adult have their origins here, and one by one I am numbering them, exposing their roots.

2 December

Miss Mandible will refuse to permit me to remain ungrown. Her hands rest on my shoulders too warmly, and for too long.

7 December

It is the pledges that this place makes to me, pledges that cannot be redeemed, that confuse me later and make me feel I am not *getting anywhere.* Everything is presented as the result of some knowable process; if I wish to arrive at four I get there by way of two and two. If I wish to burn Moscow the route I must travel has already been marked out by another visitor. If, like Bobby Vanderbilt, I yearn for the wheel of the Lancia 2.4-liter coupé, I have only to go through the appropriate process, that is, get the money. And if it is money itself that I desire, I have only to make it. All of these goals are equally beautiful in the sight of the Board of Estimate; the proof is all around us, in the no-nonsense ugliness of this steel and glass building, in the straightline matter-of-factness with which Miss Mandible handles some of our less reputable wars. Who points out that arrangements sometimes slip, that errors are made, that signs are misread? "*They have confidence in their ability to take the right steps and to obtain correct answers.*" I take the right steps, obtain correct answers, and my wife leaves me for another man.

8 December

My enlightenment is proceeding wonderfully.

9 December

Disaster once again. Tomorrow I am to be sent to a doctor, for observation. Sue Ann Brownly caught Miss Mandible and me in the cloakroom, during recess, and immediately threw a fit. For a moment I thought she was actually going to choke. She ran out of the room weeping, straight for the principal's office, certain now which of us was Debbie, which Eddie, which Liz. I am sorry to be the cause of her disillusionment, but I know that she will recover. Miss Mandible is ruined but fulfilled. Although she will be charged with contributing to the delinquency of a minor, she seems at peace; *her* promise has been kept. She knows now that everything she has been told about life, about America, is true.

I have tried to convince the school authorities that I am a minor only in a very special sense, that I am in fact mostly to blame—but it does no good. They are as dense as ever. My contemporaries are astounded that I present myself as anything other than an innocent victim. Like the Old Guard marching through the Russian drifts, the class marches to the conclusion that truth is punishment.

Bobby Vanderbilt has given me his copy of *Sounds of Sebring*, in farewell.

Woody Allen (1935–   )

The Whore of Mensa

One thing about being a private investigator, you've got to learn to go with your hunches. That's why when a quivering pat of butter named Word Babcock walked into my office and laid his cards on the table, I should have trusted the cold chill that shot up my spine.

"Kaiser?" he said. "Kaiser Lupowitz?"

"That's what it says on my license," I owned up.

"You've got to help me. I'm being blackmailed. Please!"

He was shaking like the lead singer in a rumba band. I pushed a glass across the desk top and a bottle of rye I keep handy for nonmedicinal purposes. "Suppose you relax and tell me all about it."

"You . . . you won't tell my wife?"

"Level with me, Word. I can't make any promises."

He tried pouring a drink, but you

could hear the clicking sound across the street, and most of the stuff wound up in his shoes.

"I'm a working guy," he said. "Mechanical maintenance. I build and service joy buzzers. You know—those little fun gimmicks that give people a shock when they shake hands?"

"So?"

"A lot of your executives like 'em. Particularly down on Wall Street."

"Get to the point."

"I'm on the road a lot. You know how it is—lonely. Oh, not what you're thinking. See, Kaiser, I'm basically an intellectual. Sure, a guy can meet all the bimbos he wants. But the really brainy women—they're not so easy to find on short notice."

"Keep talking."

"Well, I heard of this young girl. Eighteen years old. A Vassar student. For a price, she'll come over and discuss any subject—Proust, Yeats, anthropology. Exchange of ideas. You see what I'm driving at?"

"Not exactly."

"I mean, my wife is great, don't get me wrong. But she won't discuss Pound with me. Or Eliot. I didn't know that when I married her. See, I need a woman who's mentally stimulating, Kaiser. And I'm willing to pay for it. I don't want an involvement—I want a quick intellectual experience, then I want the girl to leave. Christ, Kaiser, I'm a happily married man."

"How long has this been going on?"

"Six months. Whenever I have that craving, I call Flossie. She's a madam, with a master's in comparative lit. She sends me over an intellectual, see?"

So he was one of those guys whose weakness was really bright women. I felt sorry for the poor sap. I figured there must be a lot of jokers in his position, who were starved for a little intellectual communication with the opposite sex and would pay through the nose for it.

"Now she's threatening to tell my wife," he said.

"Who is?"

"Flossie. They bugged the motel room. They got tapes of me discussing *The Waste Land* and *Styles of Radical Will*, and, well, really getting into some issues. They want ten grand or they go to Carla. Kaiser, you've got to help me! Carla would die if she knew she didn't turn me on up here."

The old call-girl racket. I had heard rumors that the boys at headquarters were on to something involving a group of educated women, but so far they were stymied.

"Get Flossie on the phone for me."

"What?"

"I'll take your case, Word. But I get fifty dollars a day, plus expenses. You'll have to repair a lot of joy buzzers."

"It won't be ten Gs' worth, I'm sure of that," he said with a grin, and picked up the phone and dialed a number. I took it from him and winked. I was beginning to like him.

Seconds later, a silky voice answered, and I told her what was on my mind. "I understand you can help me set up an hour of good chat," I said.

"Sure, honey. What do you have in mind?"

"I'd like to discuss Melville."

"*Moby Dick* or the shorter novels?"

"What's the difference?"

"The price. That's all. Symbolism's extra."

"What'll it run me?"

"Fifty, maybe a hundred for *Moby Dick*. You want a comparative discussion—Melville and Hawthorne? That could be arranged for a hundred."

"The dough's fine," I told her and gave her the number of a room at the Plaza.

"You want a blonde or a brunette?"

"Surprise me," I said, and hung up.

I shaved and grabbed some black coffee while I checked over the Monarch College Outline series. Hardly an hour had passed before there was a knock on my door. I opened it, and standing there was a young redhead who was packed into her slacks like two big scoops of vanilla ice cream.

"Hi, I'm Sherry."

They really knew how to appeal to your fantasies. Long straight hair, leather bag, silver earrings, no make-up.

"I'm surprised you weren't stopped, walking into the hotel dressed like that," I said. "The house dick can usually spot an intellectual."

"A five-spot cools him."

"Shall we begin?" I said, motioning her to the couch.

She lit a cigarette and got right to it. "I think we could start by approaching *Billy Budd* as Melville's justification of the ways of God to man, *n'est-ce pas?"*

"Interestingly, though, not in a Miltonian sense." I was bluffing. I wanted to see if she'd go for it.

"No. *Paradise Lost* lacked the substructure of pessimism." She did.

"Right, right. God, you're right," I murmured.

"I think Melville reaffirmed the virtues of innocence in a naïve yet sophisticated sense—don't you agree?"

I let her go on. She was barely nineteen years old, but already she had developed the hardened facility of the pseudo-intellectual. She rattled off her ideas glibly, but it was all mechanical. Whenever I offered an insight, she faked a response: "Oh, yes, Kaiser. Yes, baby, that's deep. A platonic comprehension of Christianity—why didn't I see it before?"

We talked for about an hour and then said she had to go. She stood up and I laid a C-note on her.

"Thanks, honey."

"There's plenty more where that came from."

"What are you trying to say?"

I had piqued her curiosity. She sat down again.

"Suppose I wanted to—have a party?" I said.

"Like what kind of party?"

"Suppose I wanted Noam Chomsky explained to me by two girls?"

"Oh, wow."

"If you'd rather forget it . . ."

"You'd have to speak with Flossie," she said. "It'd cost you."

Now was the time to tighten the screws. I flashed my private-investigator's badge and informed her it was a bust.

"What!"

"I'm fuzz, sugar, and discussing Melville for money is an 802. You can do time."

"You louse!"

"Better come clean, baby. Unless you want to tell your story down at Alfred Kazin's office, and I don't think he'd be too happy to hear it."

She began to cry. "Don't turn me in, Kaiser," she said. "I needed the money to complete my master's. I've been turned down for a grant. *Twice.* Oh, Christ."

It all poured out—the whole story. Central Park West upbringing, Socialist summer camps, Brandeis. She was every dame you saw waiting in line at the Elgin or the Thalia, or penciling the words "Yes, very true" into the margin of some book on Kant. Only somewhere along the line she had made a wrong turn.

"I needed cash. A girl friend said she knew a married guy whose wife wasn't very profound. He was into Blake. She couldn't hack it. I said sure, for a price I'd talk Blake with him. I was nervous at first. I faked a lot of it. He didn't care. My friend said there were others. Oh, I've been busted before. I got caught reading *Commentary* in a parked car, and I was once stopped and frisked at Tanglewood. Once more and I'm a three-time loser."

"Then take me to Flossie."

She bit her lip and said, "The Hunter College Book Store is a front."

"Yes?"

"Like those bookie joints that have barbershops outside for show. You'll see."

I made a quick call to headquarters

and then said to her, "Okay, sugar. You're off the hook. But don't leave town."

She tilted her face up toward mine gratefully. "I can get you photographs of Dwight Macdonald reading," she said.

"Some other time."

I walked into the Hunter College Book Store. The salesman, a young man with sensitive eyes, came up to me. "Can I help you?" he said.

"I'm looking for a special edition of *Advertisements for Myself*. I understand the author had several thousand gold-leaf copies printed up for friends."

"I'll have to check," he said. "We have a WATS line to Mailer's house."

I fixed him with a look. "Sherry sent me," I said.

"Oh, in that case, go on back," he said. He pressed a button. A wall of books opened, and I walked like a lamb into that bustling pleasure palace known as Flossie's.

Red flecked wallpaper and a Victorian décor set the tone. Pale, nervous girls with black-rimmed glasses and blunt-cut hair lolled around on sofas, riffling Penguin Classics provocatively. A blonde with a big smile winked at me, nodded toward a room upstairs, and said, "Wallace Stevens, eh?" But it wasn't just intellectual experiences—they were peddling emotional ones, too. For fifty bucks, I learned, you could "relate without getting close." For a hundred, a girl would lend you her Bartók records, have dinner, and then let you watch while she had an anxiety attack. For one-fifty, you could listen to FM radio with twins. For three bills, you got the works: A thin Jewish brunette would pretend to pick you up at the Museum of Modern Art, let you read her master's, get you involved in a screaming quarrel at Elaine's over Freud's conception of women, and then fake a suicide of your choosing—the perfect evening, for some guys. Nice racket. Great town, New York.

"Like what you see?" a voice said behind me. I turned and suddenly found myself standing face to face with the business end of a .38. I'm a guy with a strong stomach, but this time it did a back flip. It was Flossie, all right. The voice was the same, but Flossie was a man. His face was hidden by a mask.

"You'll never believe this," he said, "but I don't even have a college degree. I was thrown out for low grades."

"Is that why you wear that mask?"

"I devised a complicated scheme to take over *The New York Review of Books*, but it meant I had to pass for Lionel Trilling. I went to Mexico for an operation. There's a doctor in Juarez who gives people Trilling's features—for a price. Something went wrong. I came out looking like Auden, with Mary McCarthy's voice. That's when I started working the other side of the law."

Quickly, before he could tighten his finger on the trigger, I went into action. Heaving forward, I snapped my elbow across his jaw and grabbed the gun as he fell back. He hit the ground like a ton of bricks. He was still whimpering when the police showed up.

Nice work, Kaiser," Sergeant Holmes said. "When we're through with this guy, the F.B.I. wants to have a talk with him. A little matter involving some gamblers and an annotated copy of Dante's *Inferno*. Take him away, boys."

Later that night, I looked up an old account of mine named Gloria. She was blond. She had graduated *cum laude*. The difference was she majored in physical education. It felt good.

Joyce Carol Oates (1938–)

Where Are You Going, Where Have You Been?

for Bob Dylan

Her name was Connie. She was fifteen and she had a quick, nervous giggling habit of craning her neck to glance into mirrors or checking other people's faces to make sure her own was all right. Her mother, who noticed everything and knew everything and who hadn't much reason any longer to look at her own face, always scolded Connie about it. "Stop gawking at yourself. Who are you? You think you're so pretty?" she would say. Connie would raise her eyebrows at these familiar old complaints and look right through her mother, into a shadowy vision of herself as she was right at that moment: she knew she was pretty and that was everything. Her mother had been pretty once too, if you could believe those old snapshots in the album, but now her looks were gone and that was why she was always after Connie.

"Why don't you keep your room clean like your sister? How've you got your hair fixed—what the hell stinks? Hair spray? You don't see your sister using that junk."

Her sister June was twenty-four and still lived at home. She was a secretary in the high school Connie attended, and if that wasn't bad enough—with her in the same building—she was so plain and chunky and steady that Connie had to hear her praised all the time by her mother and her mother's sisters. June did this, June did that, she saved money and helped clean the house and cooked and Connie couldn't do a thing, her mind was all filled with trashy daydreams. Their father was away at work most of the time and when he came home he wanted supper and he read the newspaper at supper and after supper he went to bed. He didn't bother talking much to them, but around his bent head Connie's mother kept picking at her until Connie wished her mother was dead and she herself was dead and it was all over. "She makes me want to throw up sometimes," she complained to her friends. She had a high, breathless, amused voice that made everything she said sound a little forced, whether it was sincere or not.

There was one good thing: June went places with girl friends of hers, girls who were just as plain and steady as she, and so when Connie wanted to do that her mother had no objections. The father of Connie's best girl friend drove the girls the three miles to town and left them at a shopping plaza so they could walk through the stores or go to a movie, and when he came to pick them up again at eleven he never bothered to ask what they had done.

They must have been familiar sights, walking around the shopping plaza in their shorts and flat ballerina slippers that always scuffed the sidewalk, with charm bracelets jingling on their thin wrists; they would lean together to whisper and laugh secretly if someone passed who amused or interested them. Connie had long dark blond hair that drew anyone's eye to it, and she wore part of it pulled up on her head and puffed out and the rest of it she let fall down her back. She wore a pull-over jersey blouse that looked one way when she was at home and another way when she was away from home. Everything about her had two sides to it, one for home and one for anywhere that was not home: her walk, which could be childlike and bobbing, or languid enough to make anyone think she was hearing music in her head; her mouth, which was pale and smirking most of the time, but bright and pink on these evenings out; her laugh, which was cynical and drawling at home—"Ha, ha, very funny,"—but high-pitched and nervous anywhere else, like the jingling of the charms on her bracelet.

Sometimes they did go shopping or to a movie, but sometimes they went across the highway, ducking fast across the busy road, to a drive-in restaurant where older kids hung out. The restaurant was shaped like a big bottle, though squatter than a real bottle, and on its cap was a revolving figure of a grinning boy holding a hamburger aloft. One night in midsummer they ran across, breathless with daring, and right away someone leaned out a car window and invited them over, but it was just a boy from high school they didn't like. It made them feel good to be able to ignore him. They went up through the maze of parked and cruising cars to the bright-lit, fly-infested restaurant, their faces pleased and expectant as if they were entering a sacred building that loomed up out of the night to give them what haven and blessing they yearned for. They sat at the counter and crossed their legs at the ankles, their thin shoulders rigid with excitement, and listened to the music that made everything so good: the music was always in the background, like music at a church service; it was something to depend upon.

A boy named Eddie came in to talk with them. He sat backwards on his stool, turning himself jerkily around in semicircles and then stopping and turning back again, and after a while he asked Connie if she would like something to eat. She said she would and so she tapped her friend's arm on her way out—her friend pulled her face up into a brave, droll look—and Connie said she would meet her at eleven, across the way. "I just hate to leave her like that," Connie said earnestly, but the boy said that she wouldn't be alone for long. So they went out to his car, and on the way Connie couldn't help but let her eyes wander over the windshields and faces all around her, her face gleaming with a joy that had nothing to do with Eddie or even this place; it might have been the music. She drew her shoulders up and sucked in her breath with the pure pleasure of being alive, and just at that moment she happened to glance at a face just a few feet from hers. It was a boy with shaggy black hair, in a convertible jalopy painted gold. He stared at her and then his lips widened into a grin. Connie slit her eyes at him and turned away, but she couldn't help glancing back and there he was, still watching her. He wagged a finger and laughed and said, "Gonna get you, baby," and Connie turned away again without Eddie noticing anything.

She spent three hours with him, at the restaurant where they ate hamburgers and drank Cokes in wax cups that were always sweating, and then down an alley a mile or so away, and when he left her off at five to eleven only the movie house was still open at the plaza. Her girl friend was there, talking with a boy. When Connie came up, the two girls smiled at each other and Connie said, "How was the movie?" and the girl said, "*You* should know." They rode off with the girl's father, sleepy and pleased, and Connie couldn't help but look back at the darkened shopping plaza with its big empty parking lot and its signs that were faded and ghostly now, and over at the drive-in restaurant where cars were still circling tirelessly. She couldn't hear the music at this distance.

Next morning June asked her how the movie was and Connie said, "So-so."

She and that girl and occasionally another girl went out several times a week, and the rest of the time Connie spent around the house—it was summer vacation—getting in her mother's way and thinking, dreaming about the boys she met. But all the boys fell back and dissolved into a single face that was not even a face but an idea, a feeling, mixed up with the urgent insistent pounding of the music and the humid night air of July. Connie's mother kept dragging her back to the daylight by finding things for her to do or saying suddenly, "What's this about the Pettinger girl?"

And Connie would say nervously, "Oh, her. That dope." She always drew thick clear lines between herself and such girls, and her mother was simple and kind enough to believe it. Her mother was so simple, Connie thought, that it was maybe cruel to fool her so much. Her mother went scuffling around the house in old bedroom slippers and complained over the telephone to one sister about the other, then the other called up and the two of them complained about the third one. If June's name was mentioned her mother's tone was approving, and if Connie's name was mentioned it was disapproving. This did not really mean she disliked Connie, and actually Connie thought that her mother preferred her to June just because she was prettier, but the two of them kept up a pretense of exasperation, a sense that they were tugging and struggling over something of little value to either of them. Sometimes, over coffee, they were almost friends, but something would come up—some vexation that was like a fly buzzing suddenly around their heads—and their faces went hard with contempt.

One Sunday Connie got up at eleven—none of them bothered with church—and washed her hair so that it could dry all day long in the sun. Her parents and sister were going to a barbecue at an aunt's house and Connie said no, she wasn't interested, rolling her eyes to let her mother know just what she thought of it. "Stay home alone then," her mother said sharply. Connie sat out back in a lawn chair and watched them drive away, her father quiet and bald, hunched around so that he could back the car out, her mother with a look that was still angry and not at all softened through the windshield, and in the back seat poor old June, all dressed up as if she didn't know what a barbecue was, with all the running yelling kids and the flies. Connie sat with her eyes closed in the sun, dreaming and dazed with the warmth about her as if this were a kind of love, the caresses of love, and her mind slipped over onto thoughts of the boy she had been with the night before and how nice he had been, how sweet it always was, not the way someone like June would suppose but sweet, gentle, the way it was in movies and promised in songs; and when she opened her eyes she hardly knew where she was, the back yard ran off into weeds and a fence-like line of trees and behind it the sky was perfectly blue and still. The asbestos "ranch house" that was now three years old startled her—it looked small. She shook her head as if to get awake.

It was too hot. She went inside the house and turned on the radio to drown out the quiet. She sat on the edge of her bed, barefoot, and listened for an hour and a half to a program called XYZ Sunday Jamboree, record after record of hard, fast, shrieking songs she sang along with, interspersed by exclamations from "Bobby King": "An' look here, you girls at Napoleon's—Son and Charley want you to pay real close attention to this song coming up!"

And Connie paid close attention herself, bathed in a glow of slow-pulsed joy that seemed to rise mysteriously out of the music itself and lay languidly about the airless little room, breathed in and breathed out with each gentle rise and fall of her chest.

After a while she heard a car coming

up the drive. She sat up at once, startled, because it couldn't be her father so soon. The gravel kept crunching all the way in from the road—the driveway was long—and Connie ran to the window. It was a car she didn't know. It was an open jalopy, painted a bright gold that caught the sunlight opaquely. Her heart began to pound and her fingers snatched at her hair, checking it, and she whispered, "Christ. Christ," wondering how bad she looked. The car came to a stop at the side door and the horn sounded four short taps, as if this were a signal Connie knew.

She went into the kitchen and approached the door slowly, then hung out the screen door, her bare toes curling down off the step. There were two boys in the car and now she recognized the driver: he had shaggy, shabby black hair that looked crazy as a wig and he was grinning at her.

"I ain't late, am I?" he said.

"Who the hell do you think you are?" Connie said.

"Toldja I'd be out, didn't I?"

"I don't even know who you are."

She spoke sullenly, careful to show no interest or pleasure, and he spoke in a fast, bright monotone. Connie looked past him to the other boy, taking her time. He had fair brown hair, with a lock that fell onto his forehead. His sideburns gave him a fierce, embarrassed look, but so far he hadn't even bothered to glance at her. Both boys wore sunglasses. The driver's glasses were metallic and mirrored everything in miniature.

"You wanta come for a ride?" he said.

Connie smirked and let her hair fall loose over one shoulder.

"Don'tcha like my car? New paint job," he said. "Hey."

"What?"

"You're cute."

She pretended to fidget, chasing flies away from the door.

"Don'tcha believe, me, or what?" he said.

"Look, I don't even know who you are," Connie said in disgust.

"Hey, Ellie's got a radio, see. Mine broke down." He lifted his friend's arm and showed her the little transistor radio the boy was holding, and now Connie began to hear the music. It was the same program that was playing inside the house.

"Bobby King?" she said.

"I listen to him all the time. I think he's great."

"He's kind of great," Connie said reluctantly.

"Listen, that guy's *great.* He knows where the action is."

Connie blushed a little, because the glasses made it impossible for her to see just what this boy was looking at. She couldn't decide if she liked him or if he was just a jerk, and so she dawdled in the doorway and wouldn't come down or go back inside. She said, "What's all that stuff painted on your car?"

"Can'tcha read it?" He opened the door very carefully, as if he were afraid it might fall off. He slid out just as carefully, planting his feet firmly on the ground, the tiny metallic world in his glasses slowing down like gelatine hardening, and in the midst of it Connie's bright green blouse. "This here is my name, to begin with," he said. ARNOLD FRIEND was written in tarlike black letters on the side, with a drawing of a round, grinning face that reminded Connie of a pumpkin, except it wore sunglasses. "I wanta introduce myself, I'm Arnold Friend and that's my real name and I'm gonna be your friend, honey, and inside the car's Ellie Oscar, he's kinda shy." Ellie brought his transistor radio up to his shoulder and balanced it there. "Now, these numbers are a secret code, honey," Arnold Friend explained. He read off the numbers 33, 19, 17 and raised his eyebrows at her to see what she thought of that, but she didn't think much of it. The left rear fender had been smashed and around it was written, on the gleaming gold background: DONE BY CRAZY

WOMAN DRIVER. Connie had to laugh at that. Arnold Friend was pleased at her laughter and looked up at her. "Around the other side's a lot more—you wanta come and see them?"

"No."

"Why not?"

"Why should I?"

"Don'tcha wanta see what's on the car? Don'tcha wanta go for a ride?"

"I don't know."

"Why not?"

"I got things to do."

"Like what?"

"Things."

He laughed as if she had said something funny. He slapped his thighs. He was standing in a strange way, leaning back against the car as if he were balancing himself. He wasn't tall, only an inch or so taller than she would be if she came down to him. Connie liked the way he was dressed, which was the way all of them dressed: tight faded jeans stuffed into black, scuffed boots, a belt that pulled his waist in and showed how lean he was, and a white pull-over shirt that was a little soiled and showed the hard small muscles of his arms and shoulders. He looked as if he probably did hard work, lifting and carrying things. Even his neck looked muscular. And his face was a familiar face, somehow: the jaw and chin and cheeks slightly darkened because he hadn't shaved for a day or two, and the nose long and hawklike, sniffing as if she were a treat he was going to gobble up and it was all a joke.

"Connie, you ain't telling the truth. This is your day set aside for a ride with me and you know it," he said, still laughing. The way he straightened and recovered from his fit of laughing showed that it had been all fake.

"How did you know what my name is?" she said suspiciously.

"It's Connie."

"Maybe and maybe not."

"I know my Connie," he said, wagging his finger. Now she remembered him even better, back at the restaurant, and her cheeks warmed at the thought of how she had sucked in her breath just at the moment she passed him—how she must have looked to him. And he had remembered her. "Ellie and I come out here especially for you," he said. "Ellie can sit in back. How about it?"

"Where?"

"Where what?"

"Where're we going?"

He looked at her. He took off the sunglasses and she saw how pale the skin around his eyes was, like holes that were not in shadow but instead in light. His eyes were like chips of broken glass that catch the light in an amiable way. He smiled. It was as if the idea of going for a ride somewhere, to someplace, was a new idea to him.

"Just for a ride, Connie sweetheart."

"I never said my name was Connie." she said.

"But I know what it is. I know your name and all about you, lots of things," Arnold Friend said. He had not moved yet but stood still leaning back against the side of his jalopy. "I took a special interest in you, such a pretty girl, and found out all about you—like I know your parents and sister are gone somewheres and I know where and how long they're going to be gone, and I know who you were with last night, and your best girl friend's name is Betty. Right?"

He spoke in a simple lilting voice, exactly as if he were reciting the words to a song. His smile assured her that everything was fine. In the car Ellie turned up the volume on his radio and did not bother to look around at them.

"Ellie can sit in the back seat," Arnold Friend said. He indicated his friend with a casual jerk of his chin, as if Ellie did not count and she should not bother with him.

"How'd you find out all that stuff?" Connie said.

"Listen: Betty Schultz and Tony Fitch and Jimmy Pettinger and Nancy

Pettinger," he said in a chant. "Raymond Stanley and Bob Hutter—"

"Do you know all those kids?"

"I know everybody."

"Look, you're kidding. You're not from around here."

"Sure."

"But—how come we never saw you before?"

"Sure you saw me before," he said. He looked down at his boots, as if he were a little offended. "You just don't remember."

"I guess I'd remember you," Connie said.

"Yeah?" He looked up at this, beaming. He was pleased. He began to mark time with the music from Ellie's radio, tapping his fists lightly together. Connie looked away from his smile to the car, which was painted so bright it almost hurt her eyes to look at it. She looked at that name, ARNOLD FRIEND. And up at the front fender was an expression that was familiar—MAN THE FLYING SAUCERS. It was an expression kids had used the year before but didn't use this year. She looked at it for a while as if the words meant something to her that she did not yet know.

"What're you thinking about? Huh?" Arnold Friend demanded. "Not worried about your hair blowing around in the car, are you?"

"No."

"Think I maybe can't drive good?"

"How do I know?"

"You're a hard girl to handle. How come?" he said. "Don't you know I'm your friend? Didn't you see me put my sign in the air when you walked by?"

"What sign?"

"My sign." And he drew an X in the air, leaning out toward her. They were maybe ten feet apart. After his hand fell back to his side the X was still in the air, almost visible. Connie let the screen door close and stood perfectly still inside it, listening to the music from her radio and the boy's blend together. She stared at Arnold Friend. He stood there so stiffly relaxed, pretending to be relaxed, with one hand idly on the door handle as if he were keeping himself up that way and had no intention of ever moving again. She recognized most things about him, the tight jeans that showed his thighs and buttocks and the greasy leather boots and the tight shirt, and even that slippery friendly smile of his, that sleepy dreamy smile that all the boys used to get across ideas they didn't want to put into words. She recognized all this and also the singsong way he talked, slightly mocking, kidding, but serious and a little melancholy, and she recognized the way he tapped one fist against the other in homage to the perpetual music behind him. But all these things did not come together.

She said suddenly, "Hey, how old are you?"

His smile faded. She could see then that he wasn't a kid, he was much older—thirty, maybe more. At this knowledge her heart began to pound faster.

"That's a crazy thing to ask. Can'tcha see I'm your own age?"

"Like hell you are."

"Or maybe a coupla years older. I'm eighteen."

"Eighteen?" she said doubtfully.

He grinned to reassure her and lines appeared at the corners of his mouth. His teeth were big and white. He grinned so broadly his eyes became slits and she saw how thick the lashes were, thick and black as if painted with a black tarlike material. Then, abruptly, he seemed to become embarrassed and looked over his shoulder at Ellie. "*Him,* he's crazy," he said. "Ain't he a riot? He's a nut, a real character." Ellie was still listening to the music. His sunglasses told nothing about what he was thinking. He wore a bright orange shirt unbuttoned halfway to show his chest, which was a pale, bluish chest and not muscular like Arnold Friend's. His shirt collar was turned up all around and the very tips of the collar pointed out past his chin as if they were protecting him. He was pressing the transistor radio up against his ear and sat there in a kind of daze, right in the sun.

"He's kinda strange," Connie said.

"Hey, she says you're kinda strange! Kinda strange!" Arnold Friend cried. He pounded on the car to get Ellie's attention. Ellie turned for the first time and Connie saw with shock that he wasn't a kid either—he had a fair, hairless face, cheeks reddened slightly as if the veins grew too close to the surface of his skin, the face of a forty-year-old baby. Connie felt a wave of dizziness rise in her at this sight and she stared at him as if waiting for something to change the shock of the moment, make it all right again. Ellie's lips kept shaping words, mumbling along with the blasting in his ear.

"Maybe you two better go away," Connie said faintly.

"What? How come?" Arnold Friend cried. "We come out here to take you for a ride. It's Sunday." He had the voice of the man on the radio now. It was the same voice, Connie thought. "Don'tcha know it's Sunday all day? And honey, no matter who you were with last night, today you're with Arnold Friend and don't you forget it! Maby you better step out here," he said, and this last was in a different voice. It was a little flatter, as if the heat was finally getting to him.

"No. I got things to do."

"Hey."

"You two better leave."

"We ain't leaving until you come with us."

"Like hell I am—"

"Connie, don't fool around with me. I mean—I mean, don't fool *around*," he said, shaking his head. He laughed incredulously. He placed his sunglasses on top of his head, carefully, as if he were indeed wearing a wig, and brought the stems down behind his ears. Connie stared at him, another wave of dizziness and fear rising in her so that for a moment he wasn't even in focus but was just a blur standing there against his gold car, and she had the idea that he had driven up the driveway all right but had come from nowhere before that and belonged nowhere and that everything about him and even about the music that was so familiar to her was only half real.

"If my father comes and sees you—"

"He ain't coming. He's at a barbecue."

"How do you know that?"

"Aunt Tillie's. Right now they're—uh—they're drinking. Sitting around," he said vaguely, squinting as if he were staring all the way to town and over to Aunt Tillie's back yard. Then the vision seemed to get clear and he nodded energetically. "Yeah. Sitting around. There's your sister in a blue dress, huh? And high heels, the poor sad bitch—nothing like you, sweetheart! And your mother's helping some fat woman with the corn, they're cleaning the corn—husking the corn—"

"What fat woman?" Connie cried.

"How do I know what fat woman, I don't know every goddamn fat woman in the world!" Arnold Friend laughed.

"Oh, that's Mrs. Hornsby. . . . Who invited her?" Connie said. She felt a little lightheaded. Her breath was coming quickly.

"She's too fat. I don't like them fat. I like them the way you are, honey," he said, smiling sleepily at her. They stared at each other for a while through the screen door. He said softly, "Now, what you're going to do is this: you're going to come out that door. You're going to sit up front with me and Ellie's going to sit in the back, the hell with Ellie, right? This isn't Ellie's date. You're my date. I'm your lover, honey."

"What? You're crazy—"

"Yes, I'm your lover. You don't know what that is but you will," he said. "I know that too. I know all about you. But look: it's real nice and you couldn't ask for nobody better than me, or more polite. I always keep my word. I'll tell you how it is, I'm always nice at first, the first time. I'll hold you so tight you won't think you have to try to get away or pretend anything because you'll know you can't. And I'll come inside you where it's all secret and you'll give in to me and you'll love me—"

"Shut up! You're crazy!" Connie said. She backed away from the door. She put her hand up against her ears as if she'd heard something terrible, something not meant for her. "People don't talk like that, you're crazy," she muttered. Her heart was almost too big now for her chest and its pumping made sweat break out all over her. She looked out to see Arnold Friend pause and then take a step toward the porch, lurching. He almost fell. But, like a clever drunken man, he managed to catch his balance. He wobbled in his high boots and grabbed hold of one of the porch posts.

"Honey?" he said. "You still listening?"

"Get the hell out of here!"

"Be nice, honey. Listen."

"I'm going to call the police—"

He wobbled again and out of the side of his mouth came a fast spat curse, an aside not meant for her to hear. But even this "Christ!" sounded forced. Then he began to smile again. She watched this smile come, awkward as if he were smiling from inside a mask. His whole face was a mask, she thought wildly, tanned down to his throat but then running out as if he had plastered make-up on his face but had forgotten about his throat.

"Honey—? Listen, here's how it is. I always tell the truth and I promise you this: I ain't coming in that house after you."

"You better not! I'm going to call the police if you—if you don't—"

"Honey," he said, talking right through her voice, "honey, I'm not coming in there but you are coming out here. You know why?"

She was panting. The kitchen looked like a place she had never seen before, some room she had run inside but that wasn't good enough, wasn't going to help her. The kitchen window had never had a curtain, after three years, and there were dishes in the sink for her to do—probably—and if you ran your hand across the table you'd probably feel something sticky there.

"You listening, honey? Hey?"

"—going to call the police—"

"Soon as you touch the phone I don't need to keep my promise and can come inside. You won't want that."

She rushed forward and tried to lock the door. Her fingers were shaking. "But why lock it," Arnold Friend said gently, talking right into her face. "It's just a screen door. It's just nothing." One of his boots was at a strange angle, as if his foot wasn't in it. It pointed out to the left, bent at the ankle. "I mean, anybody can break through a screen door and glass and wood and iron or anything else if he needs to, anybody at all, and especially Arnold Friend. If the place got lit up with a fire, honey, you'd come runnin' out into my arms, right into my arms an' safe at home—like you knew I was your lover and'd stopped fooling around. I don't mind a nice shy girl but I don't like no fooling around." Part of those words were spoken with a slight rhythmic lilt, and Connie somehow recognized them—the echo of a song from last year, about a girl rushing into her boy friend's arms and coming home again—

Connie stood barefoot on the linoleum floor, staring at him. "What do you want?" she whispered.

"I want you," he said.

"What?"

"Seen you that night and thought, that's the one, yes sir. I never needed to look anymore."

"But my father's coming back. He's coming to get me. I had to wash my hair first—" She spoke in a dry, rapid voice, hardly raising it for him to hear.

"No, your daddy is not coming and yes, you had to wash your hair and you washed it for me. It's nice and shining and all for me. I thank you sweetheart," he said with a mock bow, but again he almost lost his balance. He had to bend and adjust his boots. Evidently his feet did not go all the way down; the boots must have been stuffed with something so that he would seem taller. Connie stared out at him and behind him at Ellie in the car, who seemed to be looking off toward Connie's right, into nothing. This Ellie said, pulling the words out of the air one after another as if he were just discovering them, "You want me to pull out the phone?"

"Shut your mouth and keep it shut," Arnold Friend said, his face red from bending over or maybe from embarrassment because Connie had seen his boots. "This ain't none of your business."

"What—what are you doing? What do you want?" Connie said. "If I call the police they'll get you, they'll arrest you—"

"Promise was not to come in unless you touch that phone, and I'll keep that promise," he said. He resumed his erect position and tried to force his shoulders back. He sounded like a hero in a movie, declaring something important. But he spoke too loudly and it was as if he were speaking to someone behind Connie. "I ain't made plans for coming in that house where I don't belong but just for you to come out to me, the way you should. Don't you know who I am?"

"You're crazy," she whispered. She backed away from the door but did not want to go into another part of the house, as if this would give him permission to come through the door. "What do you . . . you're crazy, you. . . ."

"Huh? What're you saying, honey?"

Her eyes darted everywhere in the kitchen. She could not remember what it was, this room.

"This is how it is, honey: you come out and we'll drive away, have a nice ride. But if you don't come out we're gonna wait till your people come home and then they're all going to get it."

"You want that telephone pulled out?" Ellie said. He held the radio away from his ear and grimaced, as if without the radio the air was too much for him.

"I toldja shut up, Ellie," Arnold Friend said, "you're deaf, get a hearing aid, right? Fix yourself up. This little girl's no trouble and's gonna be nice to me, so Ellie keep to yourself, this ain't your date—right? Don't hem in on me, don't hog, don't crush, don't bird dog, don't trail me," he said in a rapid, meaningless voice, as if he were running through all the expressions he'd learned but was no longer sure which of them was in style, then rushing on to new ones, making them up with his eyes closed. "Don't crawl under my fence, don't squeeze in my chipmunk hole, don't sniff my glue, suck my popsicle, keep your own greasy fingers on yourself!" He shaded his eyes and peered in at Connie, who was backed against the kitchen table. "Don't mind him, honey, he's just a creep. He's a dope. Right? I'm the boy for you and like I said, you come out here nice like a lady and give me your hand, and nobody else gets hurt, I mean, your nice old baldheaded daddy and your mummy and your sister in her high heels. Because listen: why bring them in this?"

"Leave me alone," Connie whispered.

"Hey, you know that old woman down the road, the one with the chickens and stuff—you know her?"

"She's dead!"

"Dead? What? You know her?" Arnold Friend said.

"She's dead—"

"Don't you like her?"

"She's dead—she's—she isn't here any more—"

"But don't you like her, I mean, you got something against her? Some grudge or something?" Then his voice dipped as if he were conscious of a rudeness. He touched the sunglasses perched up on top of his head as if to make sure they were still there. "Now, you be a good girl."

"What are you going to do?"

"Just two things, or maybe three," Arnold Friend said. "But I promise it won't last long and you'll like me the way you get to like people you're close to. You will. It's all over for you here, so come on out. You don't want your people in any trouble, do you?"

She turned and bumped against a chair or something, hurting her leg, but she ran into the back room and picked up the telephone. Something roared in her ear, a tiny roaring, and she was so sick with fear that she could do nothing but listen to it—the telephone was clammy and very heavy and her fingers groped down to the dial but were too weak to touch it. She began to scream into the phone, into the roaring. She cried out, she cried for her mother, she felt her breath start jerking back and forth in her lungs as if it were some thing Arnold Friend was stabbing her with again and again with no tenderness. A noisy sorrowful wailing rose all about her and she was locked inside it the way she was locked inside this house.

After a while she could hear again. She was sitting on the floor with her wet back against the wall.

Arnold Friend was saying from the door, "That's a good girl. Put the phone back."

She kicked the phone away from her.

"No, honey. Pick it up. Put it back right."

She picked it up and put it back. The dial tone stopped.

"That's a good girl. Now, you come outside."

She was hollow with what had been fear but what was now just an emptiness. All that screaming had blasted it out of her. She sat, one leg cramped under her, and deep inside her brain was something like a pinpoint of light that kept going and would not let her relax. She thought, I'm not going to see my mother again. She thought, I'm not going to sleep in my bed again. Her bright green blouse was all wet.

Arnold Friend said, in a gentle-loud voice that was like a stage voice, "The place where you came from ain't there any more, and where you had in mind to go is cancelled out. This place you are now—inside your daddy's house—is nothing but a cardboard box I can knock down any time. You know that and always did know it. You hear me?"

She thought, I have got to think. I have got to know what to do.

"We'll go out to a nice field, out in the country here where it smells so nice and it's sunny," Arnold Friend said. "I'll have my arms tight around you so you won't need to try to get away and I'll show you what love is like, what it does. The hell with this house! It looks solid all right," he said. He ran a fingernail down the screen and the noise did not make Connie shiver, as it would have the day before. "Now, put your hand on your heart, honey. Feel that? That feels solid too but we know better. Be nice to me, be sweet like you can because what else is there for a girl like you but to be sweet and pretty and give in?—and get away before her people come back?"

She felt her pounding heart. Her hand seemed to enclose it. She thought for the first time in her life that it was nothing that was hers, that belonged to her, but just a pounding, living thing inside this body that wasn't really hers either.

"You don't want them to get hurt," Arnold Friend went on. "Now, get up, honey. Get up all by yourself."

She stood.

"Now, turn this way. That's right. Come over here to me.—Ellie, put that away, didn't I tell you? You dope. You miserable creepy dope," Arnold Friend said. His words were not angry but only part of an incantation. The incantation was kindly. "Now, come out through the kitchen to me, honey, and let's see a smile, try it, you're a brave, sweet little girl and now they're eating corn and hot dogs cooked to bursting over an outdoor fire, and they don't know one thing about you and never did and honey, you're better than them because not a one of them would have done this for you."

Connie felt the linoleum under her feet; it was cool. She brushed her hair back out of her eyes. Arnold Friend let go of the post tentatively and opened his arms for her, his elbows pointing in toward each other and his wrists limp, to show that this was an embarrassed embrace and a little mocking, he didn't want to make her self-conscious.

She put out her hand against the screen. She watched herself push the door slowly open as if she were back safe somewhere in the other doorway, watching this body and this head of long hair moving out into the sunlight where Arnold Friend waited.

"My sweet little blue-eyed girl," he said in a half-sung sigh that had nothing to do with her brown eyes but was taken up just the same by the vast sunlit reaches of the land behind him and on all sides of him—so much land that Connie had never seen before and did not recognize except to know that she was going to it.

James Alan McPherson (1943–   )

Of Cabbages and Kings

I

Claude Sheats had been in the Brotherhood all his life and then he had tried to get out. Some of his people and most of his friends were still in the Brotherhood and were still very good members but Claude was no longer a good member because he had tried to get out after over twenty years. To get away from the Brotherhood and all his friends who were still active in it he moved to Washington Square, and took to reading about being militant. But, living there, he developed a craving for whiteness the way a nicely broke-in virgin craves sex. In spite of this he maintained a steady black girl, whom he saw at least twice a month to keep up appearances and once he took both of us with him when he visited his uncle in Harlem who was still in the Brotherhood.

"She's a nice girl, Claude," his uncle's wife had told him that night because the girl, besides being attractive, had some very positive ideas about the Brotherhood. Her name was Marie, she worked as a secretary in my office and it was on her suggestion that I had moved in with Claude Sheats.

"I'm glad to see you don't waste your time on hippies," the uncle had said. "All our young men are selling out these days."

The uncle was the kind of fellow who had played his cards right. He was much older than his wife, and I had the impression, that night, that he must have given her time to experience enough and to become bored enough before he overwhelmed her with his success. He wore glasses and combed his hair back and had that oily kind of composure that made me think of a waiter waiting to be tipped. He was very proud of his English, I observed, and how he always ended his words with just the right sound. He must have felt superior to people who didn't. He must have felt superior to Claude because he was still with the Brotherhood and Claude had tried to get out.

Claude did not like him and always seemed to feel guilty whenever we visited his uncle's house. "Don't mention any of my girls to him," he told me after our first visit.

"Why would I do that?" I said.

"He'll try to psych you into telling him."

"Why should he suspect you? He never comes over to the apartment."

"He just likes to know what I'm doing. I don't want him to know about my girls."

"I won't say anything," I promised.

He was almost twenty-three and had no steady girls, except for Marie. He was well built, so that he had no trouble in the Village area. It was like going to the market for him. During my first days in the apartment the process had seemed like a game. And once, when he was going out, I said: "Bring back two."

Half an hour later he came back with two girls. He got their drinks and then he called me into his room to meet them.

"This is Doris," he said, pointing to the smaller one, "and I forgot your name," he said to the big blonde.

"Jane," she said.

"This is Howard," he told her.

"Hi," I said. Neither one of them smiled. The big blonde in white pants sat on the big bed and the little one sat on a chair near the window. He had given them his worst bourbon.

"Excuse me a minute," Claude said to the girls. "I want to talk to Howard for a minute." He put on a record before we went outside into the hall between our rooms. He was always extremely polite and gentle, and very soft-spoken in spite of his size.

"Listen," he said to me outside, "you can have the blonde."

"What can I do with that amazon?"

"I don't care. Just get her out of the room."

"She's dirty," I said.

"So you can give her a bath."

"It wouldn't help much."

"Well just take her out and talk to her," he told me. "Remember, you asked for her."

We went back in. "Where you from?" I said to the amazon.

"Brighton."

"What school?"

"No. I just got here."

"From where?"

"*Brighton!*"

That's not so far," I said.

"*England*," she said. She looked very bored. Claude Sheats looked at me.

"How did you find Washington Square so fast?"

"I got friends."

She was very superior about it all and seemed to look at us with the same slightly patient irritation of a professional theater critic waiting for a late performance to begin. The little one sat on the chair, her legs crossed, looking up at the ceiling. Her white pants were dirty too. They looked as though they would have been very relieved if we had taken off our clothes and danced for them around the room and across the bed, and made hungry sounds in our throats with our mouths slightly opened.

I said that I had to go out to the drugstore and would be back very soon; but once outside, I walked a whole hour in one direction and then I walked back. I passed them a block away from our apartment. They were walking fast and did not slow down or speak when I passed them.

Claude Sheats was drinking heavily when I came into the apartment.

"What the hell are you trying to pull?" he said.

"I couldn't find a drugstore open."

He got up from the living room table and walked toward me. "You should have asked me," he said. "I got more than enough."

"I wanted some mouthwash too," I said.

He fumed a while longer, and then told me how I had ruined his evening because the amazon would not leave the room to wait for me and the little one would not do anything with the amazon around. He suddenly thought about going down and bringing them back; and he went out for a while. But he came back without them, saying that they had been picked up again.

"When a man looks out for you, you got to look out for him," he warned me.

"I'm sorry."

"A hell of a lot of good *that* does. And that's the last time I look out for *you,* baby," he said. "From now on it's *me* all the way."

"Thanks," I said.

"If she was too much for you I could of taken the amazon."

"It didn't matter that much," I said.

"You could of had Doris if you couldn't handle the amazon."

"They were both too much," I told him.

But Claude Sheats did not answer. He just looked at me.

II

After two months of living with him I concluded that Claude hated whites as much as he loved them. And he hated himself with the very same passion. He hated the country and his place in it and he loved the country and his place in it. He loved the Brotherhood and all that being in it had taught him and he still believed in what he had been taught, even after he had left it and did not have to believe in anything.

"This Man is going *down*, Howard," he would announce with conviction.

"Why?" I would ask.

"Because it's the Black Man's time to rule again. They had five thousand years, now we get five thousand years."

"What if I don't *want* to rule?" I asked. "What happens if I don't want to take over?"

He looked at me with pity in his face. "You go down with the rest of the country."

"I guess I wouldn't mind much anyway," I said. "It would be a hell of a place with nobody to hate."

But I could never get him to smile about it the way I tried to smile about it. He was always serious. And, once, when I questioned the mysticism in the teachings of the Brotherhood, Claude almost attacked me. "Another man might kill you for saying that," he had said. "Another man might not let you get away with saying something like that." He was quite deadly and he stood over me with an air of patient superiority. And because he could afford to be generous and forgiving, being one of the saved, he sat down at the table with me under the single light bulb and began to teach me. He told me the stories about how it was in the beginning before the whites took over, and about all the little secret significances of black, and about the subtle infiltration of white superiority into everyday objects.

"You've never seen me eat white bread or white sugar, have you?"

"No," I said. He used brown bread and brown sugar.

"Or use bleached flour or white rice?"

"No."

"You know why, don't you?" He waited expectantly.

"No," I finally said. "I don't know why."

He was visibly shocked, so much so that he dropped that line of instruction and began to draw on a pad before him on the living room table. He moved his big shoulders over the yellow pad to conceal his drawings and looked across the table at me. "Now I'm going to tell you something that white men have paid thousands of dollars to learn," he said. "Men have been killed for telling this but I'm telling you for nothing. I'm warning you not to repeat it because if the whites find out you know, you could be killed too."

"You know me," I said. "I wouldn't repeat any secrets."

He gave me a long thoughtful look.

I gave him back a long, eager, honest look.

Then he leaned across the table and whispered: "Kennedy isn't buried in this country. He was the only President who never had his coffin opened during the funeral. The body was in state all that time and they never opened the coffin once. You know why?"

"No."

"Because he's not *in it!* They buried an empty coffin. Kennedy was a Thirty-third Degree Mason. His body is in Jerusalem right now."

"How do you know?" I asked.

"If I told you it would put your life in danger."

"Did his family know about it?"

"No. His lodge kept it secret."

"No one knew?"

"I'm telling you, *no!*"

"Then how did you find out?"

He sighed, more from tolerance than from boredom with my inability to comprehend the mysticism of pure reality in its most unadulterated form. Of course I could not believe him and we argued about it, back and forth, but to absolutely cap all my uncertainties he drew the thirty-three degree circle, showed me the secret signs that men had died to learn, and spoke about the time when our black ancestors chased an evil genius out of their kingdom and across a desert and onto an island somewhere in the sea; from which, hundreds of years later, this same evil genius sent forth a perfected breed of white-skinned and evil creatures who, through trickery, managed to enslave for five thousand years the onetime Black Masters of the world. He further explained the significance of the East and why all the saved must go there once during their lifetimes, and possibly be buried there, as Kennedy had been.

It was dark and late at night, and the glaring bulb cast his great shadow into the corners so that there was the sense of some outraged spirit, fuming in the halls and dark places of our closets, waiting to extract some terrible and justifiable revenge from him for disclosing to me, an unbeliever, the closest-kept of secrets. But I was aware of them only for an instant, and then I did not believe him again.

The most convincing thing about it all was that he was very intelligent and had an orderly, well regimented life-style, and yet *he* had no trouble with believing. He believed in the certainty of statistical surveys, which was his work; the nutritional value of wheat germ sprinkled on eggs; the sensuality of gin; and the dangers inherent in smoking. He was stylish in that he did not believe in God, but he was extremely moral and warm and kind; and I wanted sometimes to embrace him for his kindness and bigness and gentle manners. He lived his life so carefully that no matter what he said, I could not help but believe him sometimes. But I did not want to, because I knew that once I started I could not stop; and then there would be no purpose to my own beliefs and no real conviction or direction in my own efforts to achieve when always in the back of my regular thoughts, there would be a sense of futility and a fear of the unknown all about me. So, for the sake of necessity, I chose not to believe him.

He felt that the country was doomed and that the safe thing to do was to make enough money as soon as possible and escape to the Far East. He forecast summer riots in certain Northern cities and warned me, religiously, to avoid all implicating ties with whites so that I might have a chance to be saved when that time came. And I asked him about *his* ties, and the girls, and how it was never a movie date with coffee afterwards but always his room and the cover-all blanket of Motown sounds late into the night.

"A man has different reasons for doing certain things," he had said.

He never seemed to be comfortable with any of the girls. He never seemed to be in control. And after my third month in the apartment I had concluded that he used his virility as a tool and forged, for however long it lasted, a little area of superiority which could never, it seemed, extend itself beyond the certain confines of his room, no matter how late into the night the records played. I could see him fighting to extend the area, as if an increase in the number of girls he saw could compensate for what he had lost in duration. He saw many girls: curious students, unexpected bus-stop pickups, and assorted other one-nighters. And his rationalizations allowed him to believe that each one was an actual conquest, a physical affirmation of a psychological victory over all he hated and loved and hated in the little world of his room.

But then he seemed to have no happiness, even in this. Even here I sensed some intimations of defeat. After each girl, Claude would almost immediately come out of his room, as if there was no need for aftertalk; as if, after it was over, he felt a brooding, silent emptiness that quickly intensified into nervousness and instantaneous shyness and embarrassment so that the cold which sets in after that kind of emotional drain came in very sharp against his skin, and he could not bear to have her there any longer. And when the girl had gone, he would come into my room to talk. These were the times when he was most like a little boy; and these were the times when he really began to trust me.

"That bitch called me everything but the son of God," he would chuckle. And I would put aside my papers brought home from the office, smile at him, and listen.

He would always eat or drink afterwards and in those early days I was glad for his companionship and the return of his trust, and sometimes we drank and talked until dawn. During these times he would tell me more subtleties about the Man and would repredict the fall of the country. Once, he warned me, in a fatherly way, about reading life from books before experiencing it; and another night he advised me on how to schedule girls so that one could run them without being run in return. These were usually good times of good-natured arguments and predictions; but as we drank more often he tended to grow more excited and quick-tempered, especially after he had just entertained. Sometimes he would seethe hate, and every drink he took gave life to increasingly bitter condemnations of the present system and our place in it. There were actually flying saucers, he told me once, piloted by things from other places in the universe which would eventually destroy the country for what it had done to the black man. He had run into his room, on that occasion, and had brought out a book by a man who maintained that the government was deliberately withholding from the public overwhelming evidence of flying saucers and strange creatures from other galaxies that walked among us every day. Claude emphasized the fact that the writer was a Ph.D. who must know what he was talking about, and insisted that the politicians withheld the information because they knew that their time was almost up and if they made it public the black man would know that he had outside friends who would help him take over the world again. Nothing I said could make him reconsider the slightest bit of his information.

"What are we going to use for weapons when we take over?" I asked him once.

"We've got atomic bombs stockpiled and waiting for the day."

"How can you believe that crap?"

He did not answer, but said instead: "You are the living example of what the Man has done to my people."

"I just try to think things out for myself," I said.

"You can't think. The handkerchief over your head is too big."

I smiled.

"I know," he continued. "I know all there is to know about whites because I've been studying them all my life."

I smiled some more.

"I ought to know," he said slowly. "I have supernatural powers."

"I'm tired," I told him. "I want to go to sleep now."

Claude started to leave the room, then he turned. "Listen," he said at the door. He pointed his finger at me to emphasize the gravity of his pronouncement. "I predict that within the next week something is going to happen to this country that will hurt it even more than Kennedy's assassination."

"Goodnight," I said as he closed the door.

He opened it again. "Remember that I predicted it when it happens," he said. For the first time I noticed that he had been deadly serious all along.

Two days later several astronauts burned to death in Florida. He raced into my room hot with the news.

"Do you believe me *now?*" he said. "Just two days and look what happened."

I tried to explain, as much to myself as to him, that in any week of the year something unfortunate was bound to occur. But he insisted that this was only part of a divine plan to bring the country to its knees. He said that he intended to send a letter off right away to Jeanne Dixon in D.C. to let her know that she was not alone because he also had the same power. Then he thought that he had better not because the FBI knew that he had been active in the Brotherhood before he got out.

At first it was good fun believing that someone important cared enough to watch us. And sometimes when the telephone was dead a long time before the dial tone sounded, I would knock on his door and together we would run through our telephone conversations for that day to see if either of us had said anything implicating or suspect, just in case they were listening. This feeling of persecution brought us closer together and soon the instruction sessions began to go on almost every night. At this point I could not help but believe him a little. And he began to trust me again, like a tolerable little brother, and even confided that the summer riots would break out simultaneously in Harlem and Watts during the second week in August. For some reason, something very difficult to put into words, I spent three hot August nights on the streets of Harlem, waiting for the riot to start.

In the seventh month of our living together, he began to introduce me to his girls again when they came in. Most of them came only once, but all of them received the same mechanical treatment. He only discriminated with liquor, the quality of which improved with the attractiveness or reluctance of the girl: gin for slow starters, bourbon for momentary strangers, and the scotch he reserved for those he hoped would come again. There was first the trek into his room, his own trip out for the ice and glasses while classical music was played within; then after a while the classical piece would be replaced by several Motowns. Finally, there was her trip to the bathroom, his calling a cab in the hall, and the sound of both their feet on the stairs as he walked her down to the cab. Then he would come to my room in his red bathrobe, glass in hand, for the aftertalk.

Then in the ninth month the trouble started. It would be very easy to pick out one incident, one day, one area of misunderstanding in that month and say: "That was where it began." It would be easy, but not accurate. It might have been one instance or a combination of many. It might have been the girl who came into the living room, when I was going over the proposed blueprints for a new settlement house, and who lingered too long outside his room in conversation because her father was a builder somewhere. Or it might have been nothing at all. But after that time he warned me about being too friendly with his company.

Another night, when I was leaving the bathroom in my shorts, he came out of his room with a girl who smiled.

"Hi," she said to me.

I nodded hello as I ducked back into the bathroom.

When he had walked her down to the door he came to my room and knocked. He did not have a drink.

"Why didn't you speak to my company?" he demanded.

"I was in my shorts."

"She felt bad about it. She asked what the hell was wrong with you. What could I tell her—'He got problems'?"

"I'm sorry," I said. "But I didn't want to stop in my shorts."

"I see through you, Howard," he said. "You're just jealous of me and try to insult my girls to get to me."

"Why should I be jealous of you?"

"Because I'm a man and you're not."

"What makes a man anyway?" I said. "Your fried eggs and wheat germ? Why should I be jealous of you *or* what you bring in?"

"Some people don't need a reason. You're a black devil and you'll get yours. I predict that you'll get yours."

"Look," I told him, "I'm sorry about the girl. Tell her I'm sorry when you see her again."

"You treated her so bad she probably won't come back."

I said nothing more and he stood there silently for a long time before he turned to leave the room. But at the door he turned again and said: "I see through you, Howard. You're a black devil."

It should have ended there and it might have with anyone else. I took great pains to speak to his girls after that, even though he tried to get them into the room as quickly as possible. But a week later he accused me of walking about in his room after he had gone out, some two weeks before.

"I swear I wasn't in your room," I protested.

"I saw your shadow on the blinds from across the street at the bus stop," he insisted.

"I've *never* been in your room when you weren't there," I told him.

"I *saw* you!"

We went into his room and I tried to explain how, even if he could see the window from the bus stop, the big lamp next to the window prevented any shadow from being cast on the blinds. But he was convinced in his mind that at every opportunity I plundered his closets and drawers. He had no respect for simple logic in these matters, no sense of the absurdity of his accusations, and the affair finally ended with my confessing that I might have done it without actually knowing; and if I had, I would not do it again.

But what had been a gesture for peace on my part became a vindication for him, proof that I *was* a black devil, capable of lying and lying until he confronted me with the inescapable truth of the situation. And so he persisted in creating situations from which, if he insisted on a point long enough and with enough self-righteousness, he could draw my inevitable confession.

And I confessed eagerly, goaded on by the necessity of maintaining peace. I confessed to mixing white sugar crystals in with his own brown crystals so that he could use it and violate the teachings of the Brotherhood; I confessed to cleaning the bathroom all the time merely because I wanted to make him feel guilty for not having ever cleaned it. I confessed to telling the faithful Marie, who brought a surprise dinner over for him, that he was working late at his office in order to implicate him with the girls who worked there. I confessed to leaving my papers about the house so that his company could ask about them and develop an interest in me. And I pleaded guilty to a record of other little infamies, which multiplied into countless others, and again subdivided into hundreds of little subtleties until my every movement was a threat to him. If I had a girlfriend to dinner, we should eat in my room instead of at the table because he had to use the bathroom a lot and, besides not wanting to seem as if he were making a pass at my girl by walking through the room so often, he was genuinely embarrassed to be seen going to the bathroom.

If I protested he would fly into a tantrum and shake his big finger at me vigorously. And so I retreated, step by step, into my room, from which I emerged only to go to the bathroom or kitchen or out of the house. I tried to stay out on nights when he had company. But he had company so often that I could not always help being in my room after he had walked her to the door. Then he would knock on my door for his talk. He might offer me a drink, and if I refused, he would go to his room for a while and then come back. He would pace about for a while, like a big little boy who wants to ask for money over his allowance. At these times my mind would move feverishly over all our contacts for as far back as I could make it reach, searching and attempting to pull out that one incident which would surely be the point of his attack. But it was never any use; it might have been anything.

"Howard, I got something on my chest and I might as well get it off."

"What is it?" I asked from my bed.

"You been acting strange lately. Haven't been talking to me. If you got something on your chest, get if off now."

"I have nothing on my chest," I said.

"Then why don't you talk?"

I did not answer.

"You hardly speak to me in the kitchen. If you have something against me, tell me now."

"I have nothing against you."

"Why don't you talk, then?" He looked directly at me. "If a man doesn't talk, you think *something's* wrong!"

"I've been nervous lately, that's all. I got problems and I don't want to talk."

"Everybody's got problems. That's no reason for going around making a man feel guilty."

"For God's sake, I don't want to talk."

"I know what's wrong with you. Your conscience is bothering you. You're so evil that your conscience is giving you trouble. You got everybody fooled but *me*. I know you're a black devil."

"I'm a black devil," I said. "Now will you let me sleep?"

He went to the door. "You dish it out but you can't take it," he said. "That's *your* trouble."

"I'm a black devil," I said.

I lay there, after he left, hating myself but thankful that he hadn't called me into his room for the fatherly talk as he had done another time. That was the worst. He had come to the door and said: "Come out of there, I want to talk to you." He had walked ahead of me into his room and had sat down in his big leather chair next to the lamp with his legs spread wide and his big hands in his lap. He had said: "Don't be afraid. I'm not going to hurt you. Sit down. I'm not going to argue. What are you so nervous about? Have a drink," in his kindest, most fatherly way, and that had been the worst of all. That was the time he had told me to eat in my room. Now I could hear him pacing about in the hall and I knew that it was not over for the night. I began to pray that I could sleep before he came and that he would not be able to wake me, no matter what he did. I did not care what he did as long as I did not have to face him. I resolved to confess to anything he accused me of if it would make him leave sooner. I was about to go out into the hall for my confession when the door was kicked open and he charged into the room.

"You black son-of-a-bitch!" he said. "I ought to *kill* you." He stood over the bed in the dark room and shook his big fist over me. And I lay there hating the overpowering cowardice in me, which kept my body still and my eyes closed, and hoping that he would kill all of it when his heavy fist landed.

"First you insult a man's company, then you ignore him. I been *good* to you. I let you live here, I let you eat my uncle's food, and I taught you things. But you're a ungrateful motherfucker. I ought to *kill* you right now!"

And I still lay there, as he went on, not hearing him, with nothing in me but a loud throbbing which pulsed through the length of my body and made the sheets move with its pounding. I lay there secure and safe in cowardice for as long as I looked up at him with my eyes big and my body twitching and my mind screaming out to him that it was all right, and I thanked him, because now I truly believed in the new five thousand years of Black Rule.

It is night again. I am in bed again, and I can hear the new blonde girl closing the bathroom door. I know that in a minute he will come out in his red robe and call a cab. His muffled voice through my closed door will seem very tired, but just as kind and patient to the dispatcher as it is to everyone, and as it was to me in those old times. I am afraid because when they came up the stairs earlier they caught me working at the living room table with my back to them. I had not expected him back so soon; but then I should have known that he would not go out. I had turned around in the chair and she smiled and said hello and I said "Hi" before he hurried her into the room. I *did* speak and I know that she heard. But I also know that I must have done something wrong; if not to her, then to him earlier today or yesterday or last week, because he glared at me before following her into the room and he almost paused to say something when he came out to get the glasses and ice. I wish that I could remember just where it was. But it does not matter. I *am* guilty and he knows it.

Now that he knows about me I am afraid. I could move away from the apartment and hide my guilt from him, but I know that he would find me. The brainwashed part of my mind tells me to call the police while he is still busy with her, but what could I charge him with when I know that he is only trying to help me. I could move the big, ragged yellow chair in front of the door, but that would not stop him, and it might make him impatient with me. Even if I pretended to be asleep and ignored him, it would not help when he comes. He has not bothered to knock for weeks.

In the black shadows over my bed and in the corners I can sense the outraged spirits who help him when they hover about his arms as he gestures, with his lessons, above my bed. I am determined now to lie here and take it. It is the price I must pay for all the black secrets I have learned, and all the evil I have learned about myself. I *am* jealous of him, of his learning, of his girls. I am not the same handkerchief-head I was nine months ago. I have Marie to thank for that, and Claude, and the spirits. They know about me, and perhaps it is they who make him do it and he cannot help himself. I believe in the spirits now, just as I believe most of the time that I am a black devil.

They are going down to the cab now.

I will not ever blame him for it. He is helping me. But I blame the girls. I blame them for not staying on afterwards, and for letting all the good nice happy love talk cut off automatically after it is over. *I* need to have them there, after it is over. And he needs it; he needs it much more and much longer than they could ever need what he does for them. He should be able to teach them, as he has taught me. And he should have their appreciation, as he has mine. I blame them. I blame them for letting him try and try and never get just a little of the love there is left in the world.

I can hear him coming back from the cab.

Drama

Tennessee Williams (1914–   )

The Glass Menagerie

THE CHARACTERS

AMANDA WINGFIELD *(the mother)*

A little woman of great but confused vitality clinging frantically to another time and place. Her characterization must be carefully created, not copied from type. She is not paranoiac, but her life is paranoia. There is much to admire in Amanda, and as much to love and pity as there is to laugh at. Certainly she has endurance and a kind of heroism, and though her foolishness makes her unwittingly cruel at times, there is tenderness in her slight person.

LAURA WINGFIELD *(her daughter)*

Amanda, having failed to establish contact with reality, continues to live vitally in her illusions, but Laura's situation is even graver. A childhood illness has left her crippled, one leg slightly shorter than the other, and held in a brace. This defect need not be more than suggested on the stage. Stemming from this, Laura's separation increases till she is like a piece of her own glass collection, too exquisitely fragile to move from the shelf.

TOM WINGFIELD *(her son)*

And the narrator of the play. A poet with a job in a warehouse. His nature is not remorseless, but to escape from a trap he has to act without pity.

JIM O'CONNOR *(the gentleman caller)*

A nice, ordinary, young man.

SCENE

AN ALLEY IN ST. LOUIS

PART I. Preparation for a Gentleman Caller.

PART II. The Gentleman calls.

Time: Now and the Past.

Scene I

The Wingfield apartment is in the rear of the building, one of those vast hive-like conglomerations of cellular living-units that flower as warty growths in overcrowded urban centers of lower middle-class population and are symptomatic of the impulse of this largest and fundamentally enslaved section of American society to avoid fluidity and differentiation and to exist and function as one interfused mass of automatism.

The apartment faces an alley and is entered by a fire-escape, a structure whose name is a touch of accidental poetic truth, for all of these huge buildings are always burning with the slow and implacable fires of human desperation. The fire-escape is included in the set—that is, the landing of it and steps descending from it.

The scene is memory and is therefore nonrealistic. Memory takes a lot of poetic license. It omits some details; others are exaggerated, according to the emotional value of the articles it touches, for memory is seated predominantly in the heart. The interior is therefore rather dim and poetic.

At the rise of the curtain, the audience is faced with the dark, grim rear wall of the Wingfield tenement. This building, which runs parallel to the footlights, is flanked on both sides by dark, narrow alleys which run into murky canyons of tangled clotheslines, garbage cans and the sinister latticework of neighboring fire-escapes. It is up and down these side alleys that exterior entrances and exits are made, during the play. At the end of TOM'S *opening commentary, the dark tenement wall slowly reveals (by means of a transparency) the interior of the ground floor Wingfield apartment.*

Downstage is the living room, which also serves as a sleeping room for LAURA, *the sofa unfolding to make her bed. Upstage, center, and divided by a wide arch or second proscenium with transparent faded portieres (or second curtain), is the dining room. In an old-fashioned what-not in the living room are seen scores of transparent glass animals. A blown-up photograph of the father hangs on the wall of the living room, facing the audience, to the left of the archway. It is the face of a very handsome young man in a doughboy's First World War cap. He is gallantly smiling, ineluctably smiling, as if to say, "I will be smiling forever."*

The audience hears and sees the opening scene in the dining room through both the transparent fourth wall of the building and the transparent gauze portieres of the diningroom arch. It is during this revealing scene that the fourth wall slowly ascends, out of sight. This transparent exterior wall is not brought down again until the very end of the play, during TOM'S *final speech.*

The narrator is an undisguised convention of the play. He takes whatever license with dramatic convention as is convenient to his purposes.

TOM *enters dressed as a merchant sailor from alley, stage left, and strolls across the front of the stage to the fire-escape. There he stops and lights a cigarette. He addresses the audience.*

TOM

Yes, I have tricks in my pocket, I have things up my sleeve. But I am the opposite of a stage magician. He gives you illusion that has the appearance of truth. I give you truth in the pleasant disguise of illusion.

To begin with, I turn back time. I reverse it to that quaint period, the thirties, when the huge middle class of America was matriculating in a school for the blind. Their eyes had failed them, or they had failed their eyes, and so they were having their fingers pressed forcibly down on the fiery Braille alphabet of a dissolving economy.

In Spain there was revolution. Here there was only shouting and confusion.

In Spain there was Guernica. Here there were disturbances of labor, sometimes pretty violent, in otherwise peaceful cities such as Chicago, Cleveland, Saint Louis . . .

This is the social background of the play.

(MUSIC.)

The play is memory.

Being a memory play, it is dimly lighted, it is sentimental, it is not realistic.

In memory everything seems to happen to music. That explains the fiddle in the wings.

I am the narrator of the play, and also a character in it.

The other characters are my mother, Amanda, my sister, Laura, and a gentleman caller who appears in the final scenes.

He is the most realistic character in the play, being an emissary from a world of reality that we were somehow set apart from.

But since I have a poet's weakness for symbols, I am using this character also as a symbol; he is the long delayed but always expected something that we live for.

There is a fifth character in the play who doesn't appear except in this larger-than-life-size photograph over the mantel.

This is our father who left us a long time ago.

He was a telephone man who fell in love with long distances; he gave up his job with the telephone company and skipped the light fantastic out of town . . .

The last we heard of him was a picture post-card from Mazatlan, on the Pacific coast of Mexico, containing a message of two words—

"Hello— Good-bye!" and no address.

I think the rest of the play will explain itself. . . .

(AMANDA'S *voice becomes audible through the portieres.*)

(LEGEND ON SCREEN: "OU SONT LES NEIGES.")

(*He divides the portieres and enters the upstage area.*)

(AMANDA *and* LAURA *are seated at a drop-leaf table. Eating is indicated by gestures without food or utensils.* AMANDA *faces the audience.* TOM *and* LAURA *are seated in profile.*)

(*The interior has lit up softly and through the scrim we see* AMANDA *and* LAURA *seated at the table in the upstage area.*)

AMANDA

(*Calling*)

Tom?

TOM

Yes, Mother.

AMANDA

We can't say grace until you come to the table!

TOM

Coming, Mother. (*He bows slightly and withdraws, reappearing a few moments later in his place at the table.*)

AMANDA

(*To her son*)

Honey, don't *push* with your *fingers.* If you have to push with something, the thing to push with is a crust of bread. And chew—chew! Animals have sections in their stomachs which enable them to digest food without mastication, but human beings are supposed to chew their food before they swallow it down. Eat food leisurely, son, and really enjoy it. A well-cooked meal has lots of delicate flavors that have to be held in the mouth for appreciation. So chew your food and give your salivary glands a chance to function!

(TOM *deliberately lays his imaginary fork down and pushes his chair back from the table.*)

TOM

I haven't enjoyed one bite of this dinner because of your constant directions on how to eat it. It's you that make me rush through meals with your hawk-like attention to every bite I take. Sickening—spoils my appetite—all this discussion of—animals' secretion—salivary glands—mastication!

AMANDA
(*Lightly*)
Temperament like a Metropolitan star! (*He rises and crosses downstage*) You're not excused from the table.

TOM
I'm getting a cigarette.

AMANDA
You smoke too much.
(LAURA *rises.*)

LAURA
I'll bring in the blanc mange.
(*He remains standing with his cigarette by the portieres during the following.*)

AMANDA
(*Rising*)
No, sister, no, sister—you be the lady this time and I'll be the darky.

LAURA
I'm already up.

AMANDA
Resume your seat, little sister—I want you to stay fresh and pretty—for gentlemen callers!

LAURA
I'm not expecting any gentlemen callers.

AMANDA
(*Crossing out to kitchenette. Airily*)
Sometimes they come when they are least expected! Why, I remember one Sunday afternoon in Blue Mountain—
(*Enters kitchenette.*)

TOM
I know what's coming!

LAURA
Yes. But let her tell it.

TOM
Again?

LAURA
She loves to tell it.
(AMANDA *returns with bowl of dessert.*)

AMANDA
One Sunday afternoon in Blue Mountain—your mother received—*seventeen!*—gentlemen callers! Why, sometimes there weren't chairs enough to accommodate them all. We had to send the nigger over to bring in folding chairs from the parish house.

TOM
(*Remaining at portieres*)
How did you entertain those gentlemen callers?

AMANDA
I understood the art of conversation!

TOM
I bet you could talk.

AMANDA
Girls in those days *knew* how to talk, I can tell you.

TOM
Yes?
(IMAGE: AMANDA AS A GIRL ON A PORCH, GREETING CALLERS.)

AMANDA
They knew how to entertain their gentlemen callers. It wasn't enough for a girl to be possessed of a pretty face and a graceful figure—although I wasn't slighted in either respect. She also needed to have a nimble wit and a tongue to meet all occasions.

TOM
What did you talk about?

AMANDA
Things of importance going on in the world! Never anything coarse or common or vulgar. (*She addresses* TOM *as though he were seated in the vacant chair at the table though he remains by portieres. He plays this scene as though he held the book.*) My callers were gentlemen—all! Among my callers were

some of the most prominent young planters of the Mississippi Delta—planters and sons of planters!

(TOM *motions for music and a spot of light on* AMANDA.)

(*Her eyes lift, her face glows, her voice becomes rich and elegiac.*)

(SCREEN LEGEND: "OU SONT LES NEIGES.")

There was young Champ Laughlin who later became vice-president of the Delta Planters Bank.

Hadley Stevenson who was drowned in Moon Lake and left his widow one hundred and fifty thousand in Government bonds.

There were the Cutrere brothers, Wesley and Bates. Bates was one of my bright particular beaux! He got in a quarrel with that wild Wainwright boy. They shot it out on the floor of Moon Lake Casino. Bates was shot through the stomach. Died in the ambulance on his way to Memphis. His widow was also well-provided for, came into eight or ten thousand acres, that's all. She married him on the rebound—never loved her—carried my picture on him the night he died!

And there was that boy that every girl in the Delta had set her cap for! That beautiful, brilliant young Fitzhugh boy from Greene County!

TOM

What did he leave his widow?

AMANDA

He never married! Gracious, you talk as though all of my old admirers had turned up their toes to the daisies!

TOM

Isn't this the first you've mentioned that still survives?

AMANDA

That Fitzhugh boy went North and made a fortune—came to be known as the Wolf of Wall Street! He had the Midas touch, whatever he touched turned to gold!

And I could have been Mrs. Duncan J. Fitzhugh, mind you! But—I picked your *father!*

LAURA

(*Rising*)

Mother, let me clear the table.

AMANDA

No, dear, you go in front and study your typewriter chart. Or practice your shorthand a little. Stay fresh and pretty! —It's almost time for our gentlemen callers to start arriving. (*She flounces girlishly toward the kitchenette*) How many do you suppose we're going to entertain this afternoon?

(TOM *throws down the paper and jumps up with a groan.*)

LAURA

(*Alone in the dining room*)

I don't believe we're going to receive any, Mother.

AMANDA

(*Reappearing, airily*)

What? No one—not one? You must be joking! (LAURA *nervously echoes her laugh. She slips in a fugitive manner through the half-open portieres and draws them gently behind her. A shaft of very clear light is thrown on her face against the faded tapestry of the curtains.* MUSIC: "THE GLASS MENAGERIE" UNDER FAINTLY. *Lightly*) Not one gentleman caller? It can't be true! There must be a flood, there must have been a tornado!

LAURA

It isn't a flood, it's not a tornado, Mother. I'm just not popular like you were in Blue Mountain. . . . (TOM *utters another groan.* LAURA *glances at him with a faint, apologetic smile. Her voice catching a little*) Mother's afraid I'm going to be an old maid.

THE SCENE DIMS OUT WITH "GLASS MENAGERIE" MUSIC

Scene II

"Laura, Haven't You Ever Liked Some Boy?"
On the dark stage the screen is lighted with the image of blue roses.
Gradually LAURA'S *figure becomes apparent and the screen goes out.*
The music subsides.
LAURA *is seated in the delicate ivory chair at the small clawfoot table.*
She wears a dress of soft violet material for a kimono—her hair tied back from her forehead with a ribbon.
She is washing and polishing her collection of glass.
AMANDA *appears on the fire-escape steps. At the sound of her ascent,* LAURA *catches her breath, thrusts the bowl of ornaments away and seats herself stiffly before the diagram of the typewriter keyboard as though it held her spellbound.*
Something has happened to AMANDA. *It is written in her face as she climbs to the landing: a look that is grim and hopeless and a little absurd.*
She has on one of those cheap or imitation velvety-looking cloth coats with imitation fur collar. Her hat is five or six years old, one of those dreadful cloche hats that were worn in the late twenties and she is clasping an enormous black patent-leather pocketbook with nickel clasps and initials. This is her full-dress outfit, the one she usually wears to the D.A.R.
Before entering she looks through the door.
She purses her lips, opens her eyes very wide, rolls them upward and shakes her head. Then she slowly lets herself in the door. Seeing her mother's expression LAURA *touches her lips with a nervous gesture.*

LAURA

Hello, Mother, I was— (*She makes a nervous gesture toward the chart on the wall.* AMANDA *leans against the shut door and stares at* LAURA *with a martyred look.*)

AMANDA

Deception? Deception? (*She slowly removes her hat and gloves, continuing the sweet suffering stare. She lets the hat and gloves fall on the floor—a bit of acting.*)

LAURA

(*Shakily*)

How was the D.A.R. meeting? (AMANDA *slowly opens her purse and removes a dainty white handkerchief which she shakes out delicately and delicately touches to her lips and nostrils*) Didn't you go to the D.A.R. meeting, Mother?

AMANDA

(*Faintly, almost inaudibly*)

—No.—No. (*Then more forcibly*) I did not have the strength—to go to the D.A.R. In fact, I did not have the courage! I wanted to find a hole in the ground and hide myself in it forever! (*She crosses slowly to the wall and removes the diagram of the typewriter keyboard. She holds it in front of her for a second, staring at it sweetly and sorrowfully—then bites her lips and tears it in two pieces.*)

LAURA

(*Faintly*)

Why did you do that, Mother? (AMANDA *repeats the same procedure with the chart of the Gregg Alphabet*) Why are you—

AMANDA

Why? Why? How old are you, Laura?

LAURA

Mother, you know my age.

AMANDA

I thought that you were an adult; it seems that I was mistaken. (*She crosses slowly to the sofa and sinks down and stares at* LAURA.)

LAURA

Please don't stare at me, Mother.

(AMANDA *closes her eyes and lowers her head. Count ten.*)

AMANDA

What are we going to do, what is going to become of us, what is the future?

(*Count ten.*)

LAURA

Has something happened, Mother? (AMANDA *draws a long breath and takes out the handkerchief again. Dabbing process*) Mother has—something happened?

AMANDA

I'll be all right in a minute, I'm just bewildered—(*Count five*)—by life. . . .

LAURA

Mother, I wish that you would tell me what's happened!

AMANDA

As you know, I was supposed to be inducted into my office at the D.A.R. this afternoon. (IMAGE: A SWARM OF TYPEWRITERS) But I stopped off at Rubicam's business college to speak to your teachers about your having a cold and ask them what progress they thought you were making down there.

LAURA

Oh. . . .

AMANDA

I went to the typing instructor and introduced myself as your mother. She didn't know who you were. Wingfield, she said. We don't have any such student enrolled at the school!

I assured her she did, that you had been going to classes since early in January.

"I wonder," she said, "if you could be talking about that terribly shy little girl who dropped out of school after only a few days' attendance?"

"No," I said, "Laura, my daughter, has been going to school every day for the past six weeks!"

"Excuse me," she said. She took the attendance book out and there was your name, unmistakably printed, and all the dates you were absent until they decided that you had dropped out of school.

I still said, "No, there must have been some mistake! There must have been some mix-up in the records!"

And she said, "No—I remember her perfectly now. Her hands shook so that she couldn't hit the right keys! The first time we gave a speed-test, she broke down completely—was sick at the stomach and almost had to be carried into the wash-room! After that morning she never showed up any more. We phoned the house but never got any answer—while I was working at Famous and Barr, I suppose, demonstrating those —Oh!

I felt so weak I could barely keep on my feet!

I had to sit down while they got me a glass of water!

Fifty dollars' tuition, all of our plans —my hopes and ambitions for you— just gone up the spout, just gone up the spout like that.

(LAURA *draws a long breath and gets awkwardly to her feet. She crosses to the victrola and winds it up.*)

What are you doing?

LAURA

Oh! (*She releases the handle and returns to her seat.*)

AMANDA

Laura, where have you been going when you've gone out pretending that you were going to business college?

LAURA

I've just been going out walking.

AMANDA

That's not true.

LAURA

It is. I just went walking.

AMANDA

Walking? Walking? In winter? Deliberately courting pneumonia in that light coat? Where did you walk to, Laura?

LAURA

All sorts of places—mostly in the park.

AMANDA

Even after you'd started catching that cold?

LAURA

It was the lesser of two evils, Mother. (IMAGE: WINTER SCENE IN PARK) I couldn't go back up. I—threw up—on the floor!

AMANDA

From half past seven till after five every day you mean to tell me you walked around in the park, because you wanted to make me think that you were still going to Rubicam's Business College?

LAURA

It wasn't as bad as it sounds. I went inside places to get warmed up.

AMANDA

Inside where?

LAURA

I went in the art museum and the bird-houses at the Zoo. I visited the penguins every day! Sometimes I did without lunch and went to the movies. Lately I've been spending most of my afternoons in the Jewel-box, that big glass house where they raise the tropical flowers.

AMANDA

You did all this to deceive me, just for deception? (LAURA *looks down*) Why?

LAURA

Mother, when you're disappointed, you get that awful suffering look on your face, like the picture of Jesus' mother in the museum!

AMANDA

Hush!

LAURA

I couldn't face it.

(*Pause. A whisper of strings.*)

(LEGEND: "THE CRUST OF HUMILITY.")

AMANDA

(*Hopelessly fingering the huge pocketbook*)

So what are we going to do the rest of our lives? Stay home and watch the parades go by? Amuse ourselves with the glass menagerie, darling? Eternally play those worn-out phonograph records your father left as a painful reminder of him?

We won't have a business career—we've given that up because it gave us nervous indigestion! (*Laughs wearily*) What is there left but dependency all our lives? I know so well what becomes of unmarried women who aren't prepared to occupy a position. I've seen such pitiful cases in the South—barely tolerated spinsters living upon the grudging patronage of sister's husband or brother's wife!—stuck away in some little mouse-trap of a room—encouraged by one in-law to visit another—little birdlike women without any nest—eating the crust of humility all their life!

Is that the future that we've mapped out for ourselves?

I swear it's the only alternative I can think of!

It isn't a very pleasant alternative, is it?

Of course—some girls *do marry.*

(LAURA *twists her hands nervously.*)

Haven't you ever liked some boy?

LAURA

Yes. I liked one once. (*Rises*) I came across his picture a while ago.

AMANDA

(*With some interest*)

He gave you his picture?

LAURA

No, it's in the year-book.

AMANDA

(*Disappointed*)

Oh—a high-school boy.

(SCREEN IMAGE: JIM AS HIGH-SCHOOL HERO BEARING A SILVER CUP.)

LAURA

Yes. His name was Jim. (LAURA *lifts the heavy annual from the claw-foot table*) Here he is in *The Pirates of Penzance.*

AMANDA

(*Absently*)

The what?

LAURA

The operetta the senior class put on. He had a wonderful voice and we sat across the aisle from each other Mondays, Wednesdays and Fridays in the Aud. Here he is with the silver cup for debating! See his grin?

AMANDA

(*Absently*)

He must have had a jolly disposition.

LAURA

He used to call me—Blue Roses.

(IMAGE: BLUE ROSES.)

AMANDA

Why did he call you such a name as that?

LAURA

When I had that attack of pleurosis—he asked me what was the matter when I came back. I said pleurosis—he thought that I said Blue Roses! So that's what he always called me after that. Whenever he saw me, he'd holler, "Hello, Blue Roses!" I didn't care for the girl that he went out with. Emily Meisenbach. Emily was the best-dressed girl at Soldan. She never struck me, though, as being sincere . . . It says in the Personal Section—they're engaged. That's—six years ago! They must be married by now.

AMANDA

Girls that aren't cut out for business careers usually wind up married to some nice man. (*Gets up with a spark of revival*) Sister, that's what you'll do!

(LAURA *utters a startled, doubtful laugh. She reaches quickly for a piece of glass.*)

LAURA

But, Mother—

AMANDA

Yes? (*Crossing to photograph.*)

LAURA

(*In a tone of frightened apology*)

I'm—crippled!

(IMAGE: SCREEN.)

AMANDA

Nonsense! Laura, I've told you never, never to use that word. Why, you're not crippled, you just have a little defect—hardly noticeable, even! When people have some slight disadvantage like that, they cultivate other things to make up for it—develop charm—and vivacity—and—*charm!* That's all you have to do! (*She turns again to the photograph*) One thing your father had *plenty of*—was *charm!*

(TOM *motions to the fiddle in the wings.*)

THE SCENE FADES OUT WITH MUSIC

Scene III

LEGEND ON SCREEN: "AFTER THE FIASCO—" TOM *speaks from the fire-escape landing.*

TOM

After the fiasco at Rubicam's Business College, the idea of getting a gentleman caller for Laura began to play a more and more important part in Mother's calculations.

It became an obsession. Like some archetype of the universal unconscious, the image of the gentleman caller haunted our small apartment. . . .

(IMAGE: YOUNG MAN AT DOOR WITH FLOWERS.)

An evening at home rarely passed without some allusion to this image, this spectre, this hope. . . .

Even when he wasn't mentioned, his presence hung in Mother's preoccupied look and in my sister's frightened, apologetic manner—hung like a sentence passed upon the Wingfields!

Mother was a woman of action as well as words.

She began to take logical steps in the planned direction.

Late that winter and in the early spring—realizing that extra money would be needed to properly feather the nest and plume the bird—she conducted a vigorous campaign on the telephone, roping in subscribers to one of those magazines for matrons called *The Homemaker's Companion*, the type of journal that features the serialized sublimations of ladies of letters who think in terms of delicate cup-like breasts, slim, tapering waists, rich, creamy thighs, eyes like wood-smoke in autumn, fingers that soothe and caress like strains of music, bodies as powerful as Etruscan sculpture.

(SCREEN IMAGE: GLAMOR MAGAZINE COVER.)

(AMANDA *enters with phone on long extension cord. She is spotted in the dim stage.*)

AMANDA

Ida Scott? This is Amanda Wingfield!

We *missed* you at the D.A.R. last Monday!

I said to myself: She's probably suffering with that sinus condition! How is that sinus condition?

Horrors! Heaven have mercy!—You're a Christian martyr, yes, that's what you are, a Christian martyr!

Well, I just now happened to notice that your subscription to the *Companion's* about to expire! Yes, it expires with the next issue, honey!—just when that wonderful new serial by Bessie Mae Hopper is getting off to such an exciting start. Oh, honey, it's something that you can't miss! You remember how *Gone With the Wind* took everybody by storm? You simply couldn't go out if you hadn't read it. All everybody *talked* was Scarlett O'Hara. Well, this book is a book that critics already compare to *Gone With the Wind*. It's the *Gone With the Wind* of the post-World War generation!—What?— Burning?— Oh, honey, don't let them burn, go take a look in the oven and I'll hold the wire! Heavens—I think she's hung up!

DIM OUT

(LEGEND ON SCREEN: "YOU THINK I'M IN LOVE WITH CONTINENTAL SHOEMAKERS?")

(*Before the stage is lighted, the violent voices of* TOM *and* AMANDA *are heard.*)

(*They are quarreling behind the portieres. In front of them stands* LAURA *with clenched hands and panicky expression.*)

(*A clear pool of light on her figure throughout this scene.*)

TOM

What in Christ's name am I—

AMANDA

(*Shrilly*)

Don't you use that—

TOM

Supposed to do!

AMANDA

Expression! Not in my—

TOM

Ohhh!

AMANDA

Presence! Have you gone out of your senses?

TOM

I have, that's true, *driven* out!

AMANDA

What is the matter with you, you—big—big—IDIOT!

TOM

Look!—I've got *no thing,* no single thing—

AMANDA

Lower your voice!

TOM

In my life here that I can call my OWN! Everything is—

AMANDA

Stop that shouting!

TOM

Yesterday you confiscated my books! You had the nerve to—

AMANDA

I took that horrible novel back to the library—yes! That hideous book by that insane Mr. Lawrence. (TOM *laughs wildly*) I cannot control the output of diseased minds or people who cater to them— (TOM *laughs still more wildly*) BUT I WON'T ALLOW SUCH FILTH BROUGHT INTO MY HOUSE! No, no, no, no, no!

TOM

House, house! Who pays rent on it, who makes a slave of himself to—

AMANDA

(*Fairly screeching*)

Don't you DARE to—

TOM

No, no, *I* mustn't say things! *I've* got to just—

AMANDA

Let me tell you—

TOM

I don't want to hear any more! (*He tears the portieres open. The upstage area is lit with a turgid smoky red glow.*)

(AMANDA'*s hair is in metal curlers and she wears a very old bathrobe, much too large for her slight figure, a relic of the faithless Mr. Wingfield.*)

(*An upright typewriter and a wild disarray of manuscripts is on the drop-leaf table. The quarrel was probably precipitated by* AMANDA'*s interruption of his creative labor. A chair lying overthrown on the floor.*)

(*Their gesticulating shadows are cast on the ceiling by the fiery glow.*)

AMANDA

You *will* hear more, you—

TOM

No, I won't hear more, I'm going out!

AMANDA

You come right back in—

TOM

Out, out, out! Because I'm—

AMANDA

Come back here, Tom Wingfield! I'm not through talking to you!

TOM

Oh, go—

LAURA

(*Desperately*)

—Tom!

AMANDA

You're going to listen, and no more insolence from you! I'm at the end of my patience!

(*He comes back toward her.*)

TOM

What do you think I'm at? Aren't I supposed to have any patience to reach the end of, Mother? I know, I know. It seems unimportant to you, what I'm *doing*—what I *want* to do—having a little *difference* between them! You don't think that—

AMANDA

I think you've been doing things that you're ashamed of. That's why you act like this. I don't believe that you go every night to the movies. Nobody goes to the movies night after night. Nobody in their right minds goes to the movies as often as you pretend to. People don't go to the movies at nearly midnight, and movies don't let out at two A.M. Come in stumbling. Muttering to yourself like a maniac! You get three hours' sleep and then go to work. Oh, I can picture the way you're doing down there. Moping, doping, because you're in no condition.

TOM
(*Wildly*)
No, I'm in no condition!

AMANDA
What right have you got to jeopardize your job? Jeopardize the security of us all? How do you think we'd manage if you were—

TOM
Listen! You think I'm crazy *about* the *warehouse?* (*He bends fiercely toward her slight figure*) You think I'm in love with the Continental Shoemakers? You think I want to spend fifty-five *years* down there in that—*celotex interior!* with—*fluorescent—tubes!* Look! I'd rather somebody picked up a crowbar and battered out my brains—than go back mornings! I *go!* Every time you come in yelling that God damn *"Rise and Shine!" "Rise and Shine!"* I say to myself, "How *lucky dead* people are!" But I get up. I *go!* For sixty-five dollars a month I give up all that I dream of doing and being *ever!* And you say self —*self's* all I ever think of. Why, listen, if self is what I thought of, Mother, I'd be where he is—GONE! (*Pointing to father's picture*) As far as the system of transportation reaches! (*He starts past her. She grabs his arm*) Don't grab at me, Mother!

AMANDA
Where are you going?

TOM
I'm going to the *movies!*

AMANDA
I don't believe that lie!

TOM
(*Crouching toward her, overtowering her tiny figure. She backs away, gasping*)
I'm going to opium dens! Yes, opium dens, dens of vice and criminals' hangouts, Mother. I've joined the Hogan gang, I'm a hired assassin, I carry a tommy-gun in a violin case! I run a string of cat-houses in the Valley! They call me Killer, Killer Wingfield, I'm leading a double-life, a simple, honest warehouse worker by day, by night a dynamic *czar* of the *underworld, Mother.* I go to gambling casinos, I spin away fortunes on the roulette table! I wear a patch over one eye and a false mustache, sometimes I put on green whiskers. On those occasions they call me—*El Diablo!* Oh, I could tell you things to make you sleepless! My enemies plan to dynamite this place. They're going to blow us all sky-high some night! I'll be glad, very happy, and so will you! You'll go up, up on a broomstick, over Blue Mountain with seventeen gentlemen callers! You ugly—babbling old—*witch. . . .* (*He goes through a series of violent, clumsy movements, seizing his overcoat, lunging to the door, pulling it fiercely open. The women watch him, aghast. His arm catches in the sleeve of the coat as he struggles to pull it on. For a moment he is pinioned by the bulky garment. With an outraged groan he tears the coat off again, splitting the shoulder of it, and hurls it across the room. It strikes against the shelf of* LAURA's *glass collection, there is a tinkle of shattering glass.* LAURA *cries out as if wounded.*)

(MUSIC. LEGEND: "THE GLASS MENAGERIE.")

LAURA
(*Shrilly*)
My glass!—menagerie. . . . (*She covers her face and turns away.*)

(*But* AMANDA *is still stunned and*

stupefied by the "ugly witch" so that she barely notices this occurrence. Now she recovers her speech.)

AMANDA
(In an awful voice)
I won't speak to you—until you apologize! *(She crosses through portieres and draws them together behind her.* TOM *is left with* LAURA. LAURA *clings weakly to the mantel with her face averted.* TOM *stares at her stupidly for a moment. Then he crosses to shelf. Drops awkwardly on his knees to collect the fallen glass, glancing at* LAURA *as if he would speak but couldn't.)*

"The Glass Menagerie" steals in as

THE SCENE DIMS OUT

Scene IV

The interior is dark. Faint light in the alley.
A deep-voiced bell in a church is tolling the hour of five as the scene commences. TOM *appears at the top of the alley. After each solemn boom of the bell in the tower, he shakes a little noise-maker or rattle as if to express the tiny spasm of man in contrast to the sustained power and dignity of the Almighty. This and the unsteadiness of his advance make it evident that he has been drinking.*
As he climbs the few steps to the fire-escape landing light steals up inside. LAURA *appears in night-dress, observing* TOM'S *empty bed in the front room.*
TOM *fishes in his pockets for door-key, removing a motley assortment of articles in the search, including a perfect shower of movie-ticket stubs and an empty bottle. At last he finds the key, but just as he is about to insert it, it slips from his fingers. He strikes a match and crouches below the door.*

TOM
(Bitterly)
One crack—and it falls through!
(LAURA *opens the door.)*

LAURA
Tom! Tom, what are you doing?

TOM
Looking for a door-key.

LAURA
Where have you been all this time?

TOM
I have been to the movies.

LAURA
All this time at the movies?

TOM
There was a very long program. There was a Garbo picture and a Mickey Mouse and a travelogue and a newsreel and a preview of coming attractions. And there was an organ solo and a collection for the milk-fund—simultaneously—which ended up in a terrible fight between a fat lady and an usher!

LAURA
(Innocently)
Did you have to stay through everything?

TOM
Of course! And, oh, I forgot! There was a big stage show! The headliner on this stage show was Malvolio the Magician. He performed wonderful tricks, many of them, such as pouring water back and forth between pitchers. First it turned to wine and then it turned to beer and then it turned to whiskey. I know it was whiskey it finally turned into because he needed somebody to come up out of the audience to help him, and I came up—both shows! It was Kentucky Straight Bourbon. A very generous fellow, he gave souvenirs. *(He pulls from his back pocket a shimmering rainbow-colored scarf)* He gave me

this. This is his magic scarf. You can have it, Laura. You wave it over a canary cage and you get a bowl of gold-fish. You wave it over the gold-fish bowl and they fly away canaries. . . . But the wonderfullest trick of all was the coffin trick. We nailed him into a coffin and he got out of the coffin without removing one nail. (*He has come inside*) There is a trick that would come in handy for me—get me out of this 2 by 4 situation! (*Flops onto bed and starts removing shoes.*)

LAURA

Tom—Shhh!

TOM

What're you shushing me for?

LAURA

You'll wake up Mother.

TOM

Goody, goody! Pay 'er back for all those "Rise an' Shines." (*Lies down, groaning*) You know it don't take much intelligence to get yourself into a nailed-up coffin, Laura. But who in hell ever got himself out of one without removing one nail?

(*As if in answer, the father's grinning photograph lights up.*)

SCENE DIMS OUT

(*Immediately following: The church bell is heard striking six. At the sixth stroke the alarm clock goes off in* AMANDA'S *room, and after a few moments we hear her calling: "Rise and Shine! Rise and Shine! Laura, go tell your brother to rise and shine!"*)

TOM

(*Sitting up slowly*)

I'll rise—but I won't shine.

(*The light increases.*)

AMANDA

Laura, tell your brother his coffee is ready.

(LAURA *slips into front room.*)

LAURA

Tom!—It's nearly seven. Don't make Mother nervous. (*He stares at her stupidly. Beseechingly*) Tom, speak to Mother this morning. Make up with her, apologize, speak to her!

TOM

She won't to me. It's her that started not speaking.

LAURA

If you just say you're sorry she'll start speaking.

TOM

Her not speaking—is that such a tragedy?

LAURA

Please—please!

AMANDA

(*Calling from kitchenette*)

Laura, are you going to do what I asked you to do, or do I have to get dressed and go out myself?

LAURA

Going, going—soon as I get on my coat! (*She pulls on a shapeless felt hat with nervous, jerky movement, pleadingly glancing at* TOM. *Rushes awkwardly for coat. The coat is one of* AMANDA'S, *inaccurately made-over, the sleeves too short for* LAURA) Butter and what else?

AMANDA

(*Entering upstage*)

Just butter. Tell them to charge it.

LAURA

Mother, they make such faces when I do that.

AMANDA

Sticks and stones can break our bones, but the expression on Mr. Garfinkel's face won't harm us! Tell your brother his coffee is getting cold.

LAURA

(*At door*)

Do what I asked you, will you, will you, Tom?

(*He looks sullenly away.*)

AMANDA

Laura, go now or just don't go at all!

LAURA

(*Rushing out*)

Going—going! (*A second later she cries out.* TOM *springs up and crosses to door.* AMANDA *rushes anxiously in.* TOM *opens the door.*)

TOM

Laura?

LAURA

I'm all right. I slipped, but I'm all right.

AMANDA

(*Peering anxiously after her*)

If anyone breaks a leg on those fire-escape steps, the landlord ought to be sued for every cent he possesses! (*She shuts door. Remembers she isn't speaking and returns to other room*)

(*As* TOM *enters listlessly for his coffee, she turns her back to him and stands rigidly facing the window on the gloomy gray vault of the areaway. Its lights on her face with its aged but childish features is cruelly sharp, satirical as a Daumier print.*)

(MUSIC UNDER: "AVE MARIA.")

(TOM *glances sheepishly but sullenly at her averted figure and slumps at the table. The coffee is scalding hot; he sips it and gasps and spits it back in the cup. At his gasp,* AMANDA *catches her breath and half turns. Then catches herself and turns back to window.*)

(TOM *blows on his coffee, glancing sidewise at his mother. She clears her throat.* TOM *clears his. He starts to rise. Sinks back down again, scratches his head, clears his throat again.* AMANDA *coughs.* TOM *raises his cup in both hands to blow on it, his eyes staring over the rim of it at his mother for several moments. Then he slowly sets the cup down and awkwardly and hesitantly rises from the chair.*)

TOM

(*Hoarsely*)

Mother. I—I apologize, Mother. (AMANDA *draws a quick, shuddering breath. Her face works grotesquely. She breaks into childlike tears*) I'm sorry for what I said, for everything that I said, I didn't mean it.

AMANDA

(*Sobbingly*)

My devotion has made me a witch and so I make myself hateful to my children!

TOM

No, you *don't.*

AMANDA

I worry so much, don't sleep, it makes me nervous!

TOM

(*Gently*)

I understand that.

AMANDA

I've had to put up a solitary battle all these years. But you're my right-hand bower! Don't fall down, don't fail!

TOM

(*Gently*)

I try, Mother.

AMANDA

(*With great enthusiasm*)

Try and you will SUCCEED! (*The notion makes her breathless.*) Why, you —you're just *full* of natural endowments! Both of my children—they're *unusual* children! Don't you think I know it? I'm so—*proud!* Happy and—feel I've—so much to be thankful for but— Promise me one thing, Son!

TOM

What, Mother?

AMANDA

Promise, son, you'll—never be a drunkard!

TOM

(*Turns to her grinning*)

I will never be a drunkard, Mother.

AMANDA

That's what frightened me so, that you'd be drinking! Eat a bowl of Purina!

TOM

Just coffee, Mother.

AMANDA

Shredded wheat biscuit?

TOM

No. No, Mother, just coffee.

AMANDA

You can't put in a day's work on an empty stomach. You've got ten minutes —don't gulp! Drinking too-hot liquids makes cancer of the stomach. . . . Put cream in.

TOM

No, thank you.

AMANDA

To cool it.

TOM

No! No, thank you, I want it black.

AMANDA

I know, but it's not good for you. We have to do all that we can to build ourselves up. In these trying times we live in, all that we have to cling tŏ is—each other. . . . That's why it's so important to— Tom, I— I sent out your sister so I could discuss something with you. If you hadn't spoken I would have spoken to you. (*Sits down.*)

TOM

(*Gently*)

What is it, Mother, that you want to discuss?

AMANDA

Laura!

(TOM *puts his cup down slowly.*)
(LEGEND ON SCREEN: "LAURA.")
(MUSIC: "THE GLASS MENAGERIE.")

TOM

—Oh.—Laura . . .

AMANDA

(*Touching his sleeve*)

You know how Laura is. So quiet but —still water runs deep! She notices things and I think she—broods about them. (TOM *looks up*) A few days ago I came in and she was crying.

TOM

What about?

AMANDA

You.

TOM

Me?

AMANDA

She has an idea that you're not happy here.

TOM

What gave her that idea?

AMANDA

What gives her any idea? However, you do act strangely. I—I'm not criticizing, understand *that!* I know your ambitions do not lie in the warehouse, that like everybody in the whole wide world —you've had to—make sacrifices, but— Tom—Tom—life's not easy, it calls for —Spartan endurance! There's so many things in my heart that I cannot describe to you! I've never told you but I—*loved* your father. . . .

TOM

(*Gently*)

I know that, Mother.

AMANDA

And you—when I see you taking after his ways! Staying out late—and—well, you *had* been drinking the night you were in that—terrifying condition! Laura says that you hate the apartment and that you go out nights to get away from it! Is that true, Tom?

TOM

No. You say there's so much in your heart that you can't describe to me. That's true of me, too. There's so much in my heart that I can't describe to *you!* So let's respect each other's—

AMANDA

But, why—*why*, Tom—are you always so *restless?* Where do you *go* to, nights?

TOM

I—go to the movies.

AMANDA

Why do you go to the movies so much, Tom?

TOM

I go to the movies because—I like adventure. Adventure is something I don't have much of at work, so I go to the movies.

AMANDA

But, Tom, you go to the movies *entirely* too *much!*

TOM

I like a lot of adventure.

(AMANDA *looks baffled, then hurt. As the familiar inquisition resumes he becomes hard and impatient again.* AMANDA *slips back into her querulous attitude toward him.*)

(IMAGE ON SCREEN: SAILING VESSEL WITH JOLLY ROGER.)

AMANDA

Most young men find adventure in their careers.

TOM

Then most young men are not employed in a warehouse.

AMANDA

The world is full of young men employed in warehouses and offices and factories.

TOM

Do all of them find adventure in their careers?

AMANDA

They do or they do without it! Not everybody has a craze for adventure.

TOM

Man is by instinct a lover, a hunter, a fighter, and none of those instincts are given much play at the warehouse!

AMANDA

Man is by instinct! Don't quote instinct to me! Instinct is something that people have got away from! It belongs to animals! Christian adults don't want it!

TOM

What do Christian adults want, then, Mother?

AMANDA

Superior things! Things of the mind and the spirit! Only animals have to satisfy instincts! Surely your aims are somewhat higher than theirs! Than monkeys—pigs—

TOM

I reckon they're not.

AMANDA

You're joking. However, that isn't what I wanted to discuss.

TOM

(*Rising*)

I haven't much time.

AMANDA

(*Pushing his shoulders*)

Sit down.

TOM

You want me to punch in red at the warehouse, Mother?

AMANDA

You have five minutes. I want to talk about Laura.

(LEGEND: "PLANS AND PROVISIONS.")

TOM

All right! What about Laura?

AMANDA

We have to be making some plans and provisions for her. She's older than you, two years, and nothing has happened. She just drifts along doing nothing. It frightens me terribly how she just drifts along.

TOM

I guess she's the type that people call home girls.

AMANDA

There's no such type, and if there is, it's a pity! That is unless the home is hers, with a husband!

TOM

What?

AMANDA

Oh, I see the handwriting on the wall as plain as I see the nose in front of my face! It's terrifying!

More and more you remind me of your father! He was out all hours without explanation!—Then *left! Good-bye!*

And me with the bag to hold. I saw that letter you got from the Merchant Marine. I know what you're dreaming of. I'm not standing here blindfolded.

Very well, then. Then *do* it!

But not till there's somebody to take your place.

TOM

What do you mean?

AMANDA

I mean that as soon as Laura has got somebody to take care of her, married, a home of her own, independent—why, then you'll be free to go wherever you please, on land, on sea, whichever way the wind blows you!

But until that time you've got to look out for your sister. I don't say me because I'm old and don't matter! I say for your sister because she's young and dependent.

I put her in business college—a dismal failure! Frightened her so it made her sick at the stomach.

I took her over to the Young People's League at the church. Another fiasco. She spoke to nobody, nobody spoke to her. Now all she does is fool with those pieces of glass and play those worn-out records. What kind of a life is that for a girl to lead?

TOM

What can I do about it?

AMANDA

Overcome selfishness!

Self, self, self is all that you ever think of!

(TOM *springs up and crosses to get his coat. It is ugly and bulky. He pulls on a cap with earmuffs.*)

Where is your muffler? Put your wool muffler on!

(*He snatches it angrily from the closet and tosses it around his neck and pulls both ends tight.*)

Tom! I haven't said what I had in mind to ask you.

TOM

I'm too late to—

AMANDA

(*Catching his arm—very importunately. Then shyly*)

Down at the warehouse, aren't there some—nice young men?

TOM

No!

AMANDA

There *must* be—*some* . . .

TOM

Mother—

(*Gesture.*)

AMANDA

Find out one that's clean-living—doesn't drink and—ask him out for sister!

TOM

What?

AMANDA

For *sister!* To *meet!* Get *acquainted!*

TOM

(*Stamping to door*)

Oh, my *go-osh!*

AMANDA

Will you? (*He opens door. Imploringly*) Will you? (*He starts down*) Will you? *Will* you, dear?

TOM

(*Calling back*)

YES!

(AMANDA *closes the door hesitantly and with a troubled but faintly hopeful expression.*)

SCREEN IMAGE: GLAMOR MAGAZINE COVER.

Spot AMANDA *at phone.*

AMANDA

Ella Cartwright? This is Amanda Wingfield!

How are you, honey?

How is that kidney condition?

(*Count five.*)

Horrors!

(*Count five.*)

You're a Christian martyr, yes, honey, that's what you are, a Christian martyr!

Well, I just now happened to notice in my little red book that your subscription to the *Companion* has just run out! I knew that you wouldn't want to miss out on the wonderful serial starting in this new issue. It's by Bessie Mae Hopper, the first thing she's written since *Honeymoon for Three.*

Wasn't that a strange and interesting story? Well, this one is even lovelier, I believe. It has a sophisticated, society background. It's all about the horsey set on Long Island!

FADE OUT

Scene V

LEGEND ON SCREEN: "ANNUNCIATION." *Fade with music.*

It is early dusk of a spring evening. Supper has just been finished in the Wingfield apartment. AMANDA *and* LAURA *in light-colored dresses are removing dishes from the table, in the upstage area, which is shadowy, their movements formalized almost as a dance or ritual, their moving forms as pale and silent as moths.*

TOM, *in white shirt and trousers, rises from the table and crosses toward the fire-escape.*

AMANDA

(*As he passes her*)

Son, will you do me a favor?

TOM

What?

AMANDA

Comb your hair! You look so pretty when your hair is combed! (TOM *slouches on sofa with evening paper. Enormous caption "Franco Triumphs"*) There is only one respect in which I would like you to emulate your father.

TOM

What respect is that?

AMANDA

The care he always took of his appearance. He never allowed himself to look untidy. (*He throws down the paper and crosses to fire-escape*) Where are you going?

TOM

I'm going out to smoke.

AMANDA

You smoke too much. A pack a day at fifteen cents a pack. How much would that amount to in a month? Thirty times fifteen is how much, Tom? Figure it out and you will be astounded at what you could save. Enough to give you a night-school course in accounting at Washington U! Just think what a wonderful thing that would be for you, Son!

(TOM *is unmoved by the thought.*)

TOM

I'd rather smoke. *He steps out on landing, letting the screen door slam.*)

AMANDA

(*Sharply*)

I know! That's the tragedy of it. . . . (*Alone, she turns to look at her husband's picture.*)

(DANCE MUSIC: "ALL THE WORLD IS WAITING FOR THE SUNRISE!")

TOM

(*To the audience*)

Across the alley from us was the Paradise Dance Hall. On evenings in spring the windows and doors were open and the music came outdoors. Sometimes the lights were turned out except for a large glass sphere that hung from the ceiling. It would turn slowly about and filter the dusk with delicate rainbow colors. Then the orchestra played a waltz or a tango, something that had a slow and sensuous rhythm. Couples would come outside, to the relative privacy of the alley. You could see them kissing behind ash-pits and telephone poles.

This was the compensation for lives that passed like mine, without any change or adventure.

Adventure and change were imminent in this year. They were waiting around the corner for all these kids.

Suspended in the mist over Berchtesgaden, caught in the folds of Chamberlain's umbrella—

In Spain there was Guernica!

But here there was only hot swing music and liquor, dance halls, bars, and movies, and sex that hung in the gloom like a chandelier and flooded the world with brief, deceptive rainbows. . . .

All the world was waiting for bombardments!

(AMANDA *turns from the picture and comes outside.*)

AMANDA

(*Sighing*)

A fire-escape landing's a poor excuse for a porch. (*She spreads a newspaper on a step and sits down, gracefully and demurely as if she were settling into a swing on a Mississippi veranda*) What are you looking at?

TOM

The moon.

AMANDA

Is there a moon this evening?

TOM

It's rising over Garfinkel's Delicatessen.

AMANDA

So it is! A little silver slipper of a moon. Have you made a wish on it yet?

TOM

Um-hum.

AMANDA

What did you wish for?

TOM

That's a secret.

AMANDA

A secret, huh? Well, I won't tell mine either. I will be just as mysterious as you.

TOM

I bet I can guess what yours is.

AMANDA

Is my head so transparent?

TOM

You're not a sphinx.

AMANDA

No, I don't have secrets. I'll tell you what I wished for on the moon. Success and happiness for my precious children! I wish for that whenever there's a moon, and when there isn't a moon, I wish for it, too.

TOM

I thought perhaps you wished for a gentleman caller.

AMANDA

Why do you say that?

TOM

Don't you remember asking me to fetch one?

AMANDA

I remember suggesting that it would be nice for your sister if you brought home some nice young man from the warehouse. I think that I've made that suggestion more than once.

TOM

Yes, you have made it repeatedly.

AMANDA

Well?

TOM

We are going to have one.

AMANDA

What?

TOM

A gentleman caller!

(THE ANNUNCIATION IS CELEBRATED WITH MUSIC.)

(AMANDA *rises.*)

(IMAGE ON SCREEN: CALLER WITH BOUQUET.)

AMANDA

You mean you have asked some nice young man to come over?

TOM

Yep. I've asked him to dinner.

AMANDA

You really did?

TOM

I did!

AMANDA

You did, and did he—*accept?*

TOM

He did!

AMANDA

Well, well—well, well! That's—lovely!

TOM

I thought that you would be pleased.

AMANDA

It's definite, then?

TOM

Very definite.

AMANDA

Soon?

TOM

Very soon.

AMANDA

For heaven's sake, stop putting on and tell me some things will you?

TOM

What things do you want me to tell you?

AMANDA

Naturally I would like to know when he's *coming!*

TOM

He's coming tomorrow.

AMANDA

Tomorrow?

TOM

Yep. Tomorrow.

AMANDA

But, Tom!

TOM

Yes, Mother?

AMANDA

Tomorrow gives me no time!

TOM

Time for what?

AMANDA

Preparations! Why didn't you phone me at once, as soon as you asked him, the minute that he accepted? Then, don't you see, I could have been getting ready!

TOM

You don't have to make any fuss.

AMANDA

Oh, Tom, Tom, Tom, of course I have to make a fuss! I want things nice, not sloppy! Not thrown together. I'll certainly have to do some fast thinking, won't I?

TOM

I don't see why you have to think at all.

AMANDA

You just don't know. We can't have a gentleman caller in a pig-sty! All my wedding silver has to be polished, the monogrammed table linen ought to be laundered! The windows have to be washed and fresh curtains put up. And how about clothes? We have to *wear* something, don't we?

TOM

Mother, this boy is no one to make a fuss over!

AMANDA

Do you realize he's the first young man we've introduced to your sister?

It's terrible, dreadful, disgraceful that poor little sister has never received a single gentleman caller! Tom, come inside! (*She opens the screen door.*)

TOM

What for?

AMANDA

I want to ask you some things.

TOM

If you're going to make such a fuss, I'll call it off, I'll tell him not to come!

AMANDA

You certainly won't do anything of the kind. Nothing offends people worse than broken engagements. It simply means I'll have to work like a Turk! We won't be brilliant, but we will pass inspection. Come on inside. (TOM *follows, groaning*) Sit down.

TOM

Any particular place you would like me to sit?

AMANDA

Thank heavens I've got that new sofa! I'm also making payments on a floor lamp I'll have sent out! And put the chintz covers on, they'll brighten things up! Of course I'd hoped to have these walls re-papered. . . . What is the young man's name?

TOM

His name is O'Connor.

AMANDA

That, of course, means fish—tomorrow is Friday! I'll have that salmon loaf—with Durkee's dressing! What does he do? He works at the warehouse?

TOM

Of course! How else would I—

AMANDA

Tom, he—doesn't drink?

TOM

Why do you ask me that?

AMANDA

Your father *did!*

TOM

Don't get started on that!

AMANDA

He *does* drink, then?

TOM

Not that I know of!

AMANDA

Make sure, be certain! The last thing I want for my daughter's a boy who drinks!

TOM

Aren't you being a little bit premature? Mr. O'Connor has not yet appeared on the scene!

AMANDA

But will tomorrow. To meet your sister, and what do I know about his character? Nothing! Old maids are better off than wives of drunkards!

TOM

Oh, my God!

AMANDA

Be still!

TOM

(*Leaning forward to whisper*)

Lots of fellows meet girls whom they don't marry!

AMANDA

Oh, talk sensibly, Tom—and don't be sarcastic! (*She has gotten a hairbrush.*)

TOM

What are you doing?

AMANDA

I'm brushing that cow-lick down!

What is this young man's position at the warehouse?

TOM

(*Submitting grimly to the brush and the interrogation*)

This young man's position is that of a shipping clerk, Mother.

AMANDA

Sounds to me like a fairly responsible job, the sort of a job *you* would be in if you just had more *get-up*.

What is his salary? Have you any idea?

TOM

I would judge it to be approximately eighty-five dollars a month.

AMANDA

Well—not princely, but—

TOM

Twenty more than I make.

AMANDA

Yes, how well I know! But for a family man, eighty-five dollars a month is not much more than you can just get by on. . . .

TOM

Yes, but Mr. O'Connor is not a family man.

AMANDA

He might be, mightn't he? Some time in the future?

TOM

I see. Plans and provisions.

AMANDA

You are the only young man that I know of who ignores the fact that the future becomes the present, the present the past, and the past turns into everlasting regret if you don't plan for it!

TOM

I will think that over and see what I can make of it.

AMANDA

Don't be supercilious with your mother! Tell me some more about this —what do you call him?

TOM

James D. O'Connor. The D. is for Delaney.

AMANDA

Irish on *both* sides! *Gracious!* And doesn't drink?

TOM

Shall I call him up and ask him right this minute?

AMANDA

The only way to find out about those things is to make discreet inquiries at the proper moment. When I was a girl in Blue Mountain and it was suspected that a young man drank, the girl whose attentions he had been receiving, if any girl *was*, would sometimes speak to the minister of his church, or rather her father would if her father was living, and sort of feel him out on the young man's character. That is the way such things are discreetly handled to keep a young woman from making a tragic mistake!

TOM

Then how did you happen to make a tragic mistake?

AMANDA

That innocent look of your father's had everyone fooled!

He *smiled*—the world was *enchanted!*

No girl can do worse than put herself at the mercy of a handsome appearance!

I hope that Mr. O'Connor is not too good-looking.

TOM

No, he's not too good-looking. He's covered with freckles and hasn't too much of a nose.

AMANDA

He's not right-down homely, though?

TOM

Not right-down homely. Just medium homely, I'd say.

AMANDA

Character's what to look for in a man.

TOM

That's what I've always said, Mother.

AMANDA

You've never said anything of the kind and I suspect you would never give it a thought.

TOM

Don't be so suspicious of me.

AMANDA

At least I hope he's the type that's up and coming.

TOM

I think he really goes in for self-improvement.

AMANDA

What reason have you to think so?

TOM

He goes to night school.

AMANDA

(*Beaming*)

Splendid! What does he do, I mean study?

TOM

Radio engineering and public speaking!

AMANDA

Then he has visions of being advanced in the world!

Any young man who studies public speaking is aiming to have an executive job some day!

And radio engineering? A thing for the future!

Both of these facts are very illuminating. Those are the sort of things that a mother should know concerning any young man who comes to call on her daughter. Seriously or—not.

TOM

One little warning. He doesn't know about Laura. I didn't let on that we had dark ulterior motives. I just said, why don't you come and have dinner with us? He said okay and that was the whole conversation.

AMANDA

I bet it was! You're eloquent as an oyster.

However, he'll know about Laura when he gets here. When he sees how lovely and sweet and pretty she is, he'll thank his lucky stars he was asked to dinner.

TOM

Mother, you mustn't expect too much of Laura.

AMANDA

What do you mean?

TOM

Laura seems all those things to you and me because she's ours and we love her. We don't even notice she's crippled any more.

AMANDA

Don't say crippled! You know that I never allow that word to be used!

TOM

But face facts, Mother. She is and—that's not all—

AMANDA

What do you mean "not all"?

TOM

Laura is very different from other girls.

AMANDA

I think the difference is all to her advantage.

TOM

Not quite all—in the eyes of others—strangers—she's terribly shy and lives in a world of her own and those things make her seem a little peculiar to people outside the house.

AMANDA

Don't say peculiar.

TOM

Face the facts. She is.

(THE DANCE-HALL MUSIC CHANGES TO A TANGO THAT HAS A MINOR AND SOMEWHAT OMINOUS TONE.)

AMANDA

In what way is she peculiar—may I ask?

TOM

(*Gently*)

She lives in a world of her own—a world of—little glass ornaments, Mother. . . . (*Gets up.* AMANDA *remains holding brush, looking at him, troubled*) She plays old phonograph records and—that's about all— (*He glances at himself in the mirror and crosses to door.*)

AMANDA

(*Sharply*)

Where are you going?

TOM

I'm going to the movies. (*Out screen door.*)

AMANDA

Not to the movies, every night to the movies! (*Follows quickly to screen door*) I don't believe you always go to the movies! (*He is gone.* AMANDA *looks worriedly after him for a moment. Then vitality and optimism return and she turns from the door. Crossing to portieres*) Laura! Laura! (LAURA *answers from kitchenette.*)

LAURA

Yes, Mother.

AMANDA

Let those dishes go and come in front! (LAURA *appears with dish towel. Gaily*) Laura, come here and make a wish on the moon!

(SCREEN IMAGE: MOON.)

LAURA

(*Entering*)

Moon—moon?

AMANDA

A little silver slipper of a moon.

Look over your left shoulder, Laura, and make a wish!

(LAURA *looks faintly puzzled as if called out of sleep.* AMANDA *seizes her shoulders and turns her at an angle by the door.*)

Now!

Now, darling, *wish!*

LAURA

What shall I wish for, Mother?

AMANDA

(*Her voice trembling and her eyes suddenly filling with tears*)

Happiness! Good fortune!

(*The violin rises and the stage dims out.*)

CURTAIN

Scene VI

IMAGE: HIGH SCHOOL HERO.

And so the following evening I brought Jim home to dinner. I had known Jim slightly in high school. In high school Jim was a hero. He had tremendous Irish good nature and vitality with the scrubbed and polished look of white chinaware. He seemed to move in a continual spotlight. He was a star in basketball, captain of the debating club, president of the senior class and the glee club and he sang the male lead in the annual light operas. He was always running or bounding, never just walking. He seemed always at the point of defeating the law of gravity. He was shooting with such velocity through his adolescence that you would logically expect him to arrive at nothing short of the White House by the time he was thirty. But Jim apparently ran into more interference after his graduation from Soldan.

His speed had definitely slowed. Six years after he left high school he was holding a job that wasn't much better than mine.

(IMAGE: CLERK.)

He was the only one at the warehouse with whom I was on friendly terms. I was valuable to him as someone who could remember his former glory, who had seen him win basketball games and the silver cup in debating. He knew of my secret practice of retiring to a cabinet of the wash-room to work on poems when business was slack in the warehouse. He called me Shakespeare. And while the other boys in the warehouse regarded me with suspicious hostility, Jim took a humorous attitude toward me. Gradually his attitude affected the others, their hostility wore off and they also began to smile at me as people smile at an oddly fashioned dog who trots across their path at some distance.

I knew that Jim and Laura had known each other at Soldan, and I had heard Laura speak admiringly of his voice. I didn't know if Jim remembered her or not. In high school Laura had been as unobtrusive as Jim had been astonishing. If he did remember Laura, it was not as my sister, for when I asked him to dinner, he grinned and said, "You know, Shakespeare, I never though of you as having folks!"

He was about to discover that I did. . . .

(LIGHT UP STAGE.)

(LEGEND ON SCREEN: "THE ACCENT OF A COMING FOOT.")

(*Friday evening. It is about five o'clock of a late spring evening which comes "scattering poems in the sky."*)

(*A delicate lemony light is in the Wingfield apartment.*)

(AMANDA *has worked like a Turk in preparation for the gentleman caller. The results are astonishing. The new floor lamp with its rose-silk shade is in place, a colored paper lantern conceals the broken light fixture in the ceiling, new billowing white curtains are at the windows, chintz covers are on chairs and sofa, a pair of new sofa pillows make their initial appearance.*)

(*Open boxes and tissue paper are scattered on the floor.*)

(LAURA *stands in the middle with lifted arms while* AMANDA *crouches before her, adjusting the hem of the new dress, devout and ritualistic. The dress is colored and designed by memory. The arrangement of* LAURA's *hair is changed; it is softer and more becoming. A fragile, unearthly prettiness has come out in* LAURA: *she is like a piece of translucent glass touched by light, given a momentary radiance, not actual, not lasting.*)

AMANDA

(*Impatiently*)

Why are you trembling?

LAURA

Mother, you've made me so nervous!

AMANDA

How have I made you nervous?

LAURA

By all this fuss! You make it seem so important!

AMANDA

I don't understand you, Laura. You couldn't be satisfied with just sitting home, and yet whenever I try to arrange something for you, you seem to resist it.

(*She gets up.*)

Now take a look at yourself.

No, wait! Wait just a moment—I have an idea!

LAURA

What is it now?

(AMANDA *produces two powder puffs which she wraps in handkerchiefs and stuffs in* LAURA'S *bosom.*)

LAURA

Mother, what are you doing?

AMANDA

They call them "Gay Deceivers"!

LAURA

I won't wear them!

AMANDA

You will!

LAURA

Why should I?

AMANDA

Because, to be painfully honest, your chest is flat.

LAURA

You make it seem like we were setting a trap.

AMANDA

All pretty girls are a trap, a pretty trap, and men expect them to be.

(LEGEND: "A PRETTY TRAP.")

Now look at yourself, young lady. This is the prettiest you will ever be! I've got to fix myself now! You're going to be surprised by your mother's appearance! (*She crosses through portieres, humming gaily.*)

(LAURA *moves slowly to the long mirror and stares solemnly at herself.*)

(*A wind blows the white curtains inward in a slow, graceful motion and with a faint, sorrowful sighing.*)

AMANDA

(*Off stage*)

It isn't dark enough yet. (*She turns slowly before the mirror with a troubled look.*)

(LEGEND ON SCREEN: "THIS IS MY SISTER: CELEBRATE HER WITH STRINGS!" MUSIC.)

AMANDA

(*Laughing, off*)

I'm going to show you something. I'm going to make a spectacular appearance!

LAURA

What is it, Mother?

AMANDA

Possess your soul in patience—you will see!

Something I've resurrected from that old trunk! Styles haven't changed so terribly much after all. . . .

(*She parts the portieres.*)

Now just look at your mother!

(*She wears a girlish frock of yellowed voile with a blue silk sash. She carries a bunch of jonquils —the legend of her youth is nearly revived. Feverishly.*)

This is the dress in which I led the cotillion. Won the cakewalk twice at Sunset Hill, wore one spring to the Governor's ball in Jackson!

See how I sashayed around the ballroom, Laura?

(*She raises her skirt and does a mincing step around the room.*)

I wore it on Sundays for my gentlemen callers! I had it on the day I met your father—

I had malaria fever all that spring. The change of climate from East Tennessee to the Delta—weakened resistance—I had a little temperature all the time—not enough to be serious— just enough to make me restless and giddy!—Invitations poured in—parties all over the Delta!—"Stay in bed," said Mother, "you have fever!"—but I just wouldn't.—I took quinine but kept on going, going!—Evenings, dances!— Afternoons, long, long rides! Picnics— lovely!—So lovely, that country in May. —All lacy with dogwood, literally flooded with jonquils!—That was the spring I had the craze for jonquils. Jonquils became an absolute obsession. Mother said, "Honey, there's no more room for jonquils." And still I kept on bringing in more jonquils. Whenever, wherever I saw them, I'd say, "Stop! Stop! I see jonquils!" I made the young men help me gather the jonquils! It was a joke, Amanda and her jonquils! Finally there were no more vases to hold them, every available space was filled with jonquils. No vases to hold them? All right, I'll hold them myself! And then I—(*She stops in front of the picture.* MUSIC) met your father!

Malaria fever and jonquils and then —this—boy. . . .

(*She switches on the rose-colored lamp.*)

I hope they get here before it starts to rain.

(*She crosses upstage and places the jonquils in bowl on table.*)

I gave your brother a little extra change so he and Mr. O'Connor could take the service car home.

LAURA

(*With altered look*)

What did you say his name was?

AMANDA

O'Connor.

LAURA

What is his first name?

AMANDA

I don't remember. Oh, yes, I do. It was—Jim!

(LAURA *sways slightly and catches hold of a chair.*)

(LEGEND ON SCREEN: "NOT JIM!")

LAURA

(*Faintly*)

Not—Jim!

AMANDA

Yes, that was it, it was Jim! I've never known a Jim that wasn't nice!

(MUSIC: OMINOUS.)

LAURA

Are you sure his name is Jim O'Connor?

AMANDA

Yes. Why?

LAURA

Is he the one that Tom used to know in high school?

AMANDA

He didn't say so. I think he just got to know him at the warehouse.

LAURA

There was a Jim O'Connor we both knew in high school—(*Then, with effort*) If that is the one that Tom is bringing to dinner—you'll have to excuse me, I won't come to the table.

AMANDA

What sort of nonsense is this?

LAURA

You asked me once if I'd ever liked a boy. Don't you remember I showed you this boy's picture?

AMANDA

You mean the boy you showed me in the year book?

LAURA

Yes, that boy.

AMANDA

Laura, Laura, were you in love with that boy?

LAURA

I don't know, Mother. All I know is I couldn't sit at the table if it was him!

AMANDA

It won't be him! It isn't the least bit likely. But whether it is or not, you will come to the table. You will not be excused.

LAURA

I'll have to be, Mother.

AMANDA

I don't intend to humor your silliness, Laura. I've had too much from you and your brother, both!

So just sit down and compose yourself till they come. Tom has forgotten his key so you'll have to let them in, when they arrive.

LAURA
(*Panicky*)
Oh, Mother—*you* answer the door!

AMANDA
(*Lightly*)
I'll be in the kitchen—busy!

LAURA
Oh, Mother, please answer the door, don't make me do it!

AMANDA
(*Crossing into kitchenette*)
I've got to fix the dressing for the salmon. Fuss, fuss—silliness!—over a gentleman caller!

(*Door swings shut.* LAURA *is left alone.*)

(LEGEND: "TERROR!")

(*She utters a low moan and turns off the lamp—sits stiffly on the edge of the sofa, knotting her fingers together.*)

(LEGEND OF SCREEN: "THE OPENING OF A DOOR!")

(TOM *and* JIM *appear on the fire-escape steps and climb to landing. Hearing their approach,* LAURA *rises with a panicky gesture. She retreats to the portieres.*)

(*The doorbell.* LAURA *catches her breath and touches her throat. Low drums.*)

AMANDA
(*Calling*)
Laura, sweetheart! The door!

(LAURA *stares at it without moving.*)

JIM
I think we just beat the rain.

TOM
Uh-huh. (*He rings again, nervously.* JIM *whistles and fishes for a cigarette.*)

AMANDA
(*Very, very gaily*)
Laura, that is your brother and Mr. O'Connor! Will you let them in, darling?

(LAURA *crosses toward kitchenette door.*)

LAURA
(*Breathlessly*)
Mother—you go to the door!

(AMANDA *steps out of kitchenette and stares furiously at* LAURA. *She points imperiously at the door.*)

LAURA
Please, please!

AMANDA
(*In a fierce whisper*)
What is the matter with you, you silly thing?

LAURA
(*Desperately*)
Please, you answer it, *please!*

AMANDA
I told you I wasn't going to humor you, Laura. Why have you chosen this moment to lose your mind?

LAURA
Please, please, please, you go!

AMANDA
You'll have to go to the door because I can't!

LAURA
(*Despairingly*)
I can't either!

AMANDA
Why?

LAURA
I'm *sick!*

AMANDA
I'm sick, too—of your nonsense! Why can't you and your brother be normal people? Fantastic whims and behavior!

(TOM *gives a long ring.*)

Preposterous goings on! Can you give

me one reason—(*Calls out lyrically*) COMING! JUST ONE SECOND!—why you should be afraid to open a door? Now you answer it, Laura!

LAURA

Oh, oh, oh . . . (*She returns through the portieres. Darts to the victrola and winds it frantically and turns it on.*)

AMANDA

Laura Wingfield, you march right to that door!

LAURA

Yes—yes, Mother!

(*A faraway, scratchy rendition of "Dardanella" softens the air and gives her strength to move through it. She slips to the door and draws it cautiously open.*)

(TOM *enters with the caller,* JIM O'CONNOR.)

TOM

Laura, this is Jim. Jim, this is my sister, Laura.

JIM

(*Stepping inside*)

I didn't know that Shakespeare had a sister!

LAURA

(*Retreating stiff and trembling from the door*)

How—how do you do?

JIM

(*Heartily extending his hand*)

Okay!

(LAURA *touches it hesitantly with hers.*)

JIM

Your hand's *cold*, Laura!

LAURA

Yes, well—I've been playing the victrola. . . .

JIM

Must have been playing classical music on it! You ought to play a little hot swing music to warm you up!

LAURA

Excuse me—I haven't finished playing the victrola. . . . (*She turns awkwardly and hurries into the front room. She pauses a second by the victrola. Then catches her breath and darts through the portieres like a frightened deer.*)

JIM

(*Grinning*)

What was the matter?

TOM

Oh—with Laura? Laura is—terribly shy.

JIM

Shy, huh? It's unusual to meet a shy girl nowadays. I don't believe you ever mentioned you had a sister.

TOM

Well, now you know. I have one. Here is the *Post Dispatch*. You want a piece of it?

JIM

Uh-huh.

TOM

What piece? The comics?

JIM

Sports! (*Glances at it*) Ole Dizzy Dean is on his bad behavior.

TOM

(*Disinterest*)

Yeah? (*Lights cigarette and crosses back to fire-escape door.*)

JIM

Where are *you* going?

TOM

I'm going out on the terrace.

JIM

(*Goes after him*)

You know, Shakespeare—I'm going to sell you a bill of goods!

TOM

What goods?

JIM

A course I'm taking.

TOM

Huh?

JIM

In public speaking! You and me, we're not the warehouse type.

TOM

Thanks—that's good news.

But what has public speaking got to do with it?

JIM

It fits you for—executive positions!

TOM

Awww.

JIM

I tell you it's done a helluva lot for me.

(IMAGE: EXECUTIVE AT DESK.)

TOM

In what respect?

JIM

In every! Ask yourself what is the difference between you an' me and men in the office down front? Brains?—No! —Ability?—No! Then what? Just one little thing—

TOM

What is that one little thing?

JIM

Primarily it amounts to—social poise! Being able to square up to people and hold your own on any social level!

AMANDA

(*Off stage*)

Tom?

TOM

Yes, Mother?

AMANDA

Is that you and Mr. O'Connor?

TOM

Yes, Mother.

AMANDA

Well, you just make yourselves comfortable in there.

TOM

Yes, Mother.

AMANDA

Ask Mr. O'Connor if he would like to wash his hands.

JIM

Aw, no—no—thank you—I took care of that at the warehouse. Tom—

TOM

Yes?

JIM

Mr. Mendoza was speaking to me about you.

TOM

Favorably?

JIM

What do you think?

TOM

Well—

JIM

You're going to be out of a job if you don't wake up.

TOM

I am waking up—

JIM

You show no signs.

TOM

The signs are interior.

(IMAGE ON SCREEN: THE SAILING VESSEL WITH JOLLY ROGER AGAIN.)

TOM

I'm planning to change. (*He leans over the rail speaking with quiet exhilaration. The incandescent marquees and signs of the first-run movie houses light his face from across the alley. He looks like a voyager*) I'm right at the point of committing myself to a future that doesn't include the warehouse of Mr. Mendoza or even a night-school course in public speaking.

JIM

What are you gassing about?

TOM

I'm tired of the movies.

JIM

Movies!

TOM

Yes, movies! Look at them—(*A wave toward the marvels of Grand Avenue*) All of those glamorous people—having adventures—hogging it all, gobbling the whole thing up! You know what happens? People go to the *movies* instead of *moving!* Hollywood characters are supposed to have all the adventures for everybody in America, while everybody in America sits in a dark room and watches them have them! Yes, until there's a war. That's when adventure becomes available to the masses! *Everyone's* dish, not only Gable's! Then the people in the dark room come out of the dark room to have some adventures themselves—Goody, goody!—It's our turn now, to go to the South Sea Island—to make a safari—to be exotic, far-off!—But I'm not patient. I don't want to wait until then. I'm tired of the *movies* and I am *about* to *move!*

JIM

(*Incredulously*)

Move?

TOM

Yes.

JIM

When?

TOM

Soon!

JIM

Where? Where?

(THEME THREE MUSIC SEEMS TO ANSWER THE QUESTION, WHILE TOM THINKS IT OVER. HE SEARCHES AMONG HIS POCKETS.)

TOM

I'm starting to boil inside. I know I seem dreamy, but inside—well, I'm boiling!—Whenever I pick up a shoe, I shudder a little thinking how short life is and what I am doing!—Whatever that means, I know it doesn't mean shoes—except as something to wear on a traveler's feet! (*Finds paper*) Look—

JIM

What?

TOM

I'm a member.

JIM

(*Reading*)

The Union of Merchant Seamen.

TOM

I paid my dues this month, instead of the light bill.

JIM

You will regret it when they turn the lights off.

TOM

I won't be here.

JIM

How about your mother?

TOM

I'm like my father. The bastard son of a bastard! See how he grins? And he's been absent going on sixteen years!

JIM

You're just talking, you drip. How does your mother feel about it?

TOM

Shhh!—Here comes Mother! Mother is not acquainted with my plans!

AMANDA

(*Enters portieres*)

Where are you all?

TOM

On the terrace, Mother.

(*They start inside. She advances to them.* TOM *is distinctly shocked at her appearance. Even* JIM *blinks a little. He is making his first contact with girlish Southern vivacity and in spite of the night-school course in public speaking is somewhat thrown off the beam by the unexpected outlay of social charm.*)

(*Certain responses are attempted by* JIM *but are swept aside by*

AMANDA's *gay laughter and chatter.* TOM *is embarrassed but after the first shock* JIM *reacts very warmly. Grins and chuckles, is altogether won over.*)

(IMAGINE: AMANDA AS A GIRL).

AMANDA

(*Coyly smiling, shaking her girlish ringlets*)

Well, well, well, so this is Mr. O'Connor. Introductions entirely unnecessary. I've heard so much about you from my boy. I finally said to him, Tom—good gracious!—why don't you bring this paragon to supper? I'd like to meet this nice young man at the warehouse! —Instead of just hearing him sing your praises so much!

I don't know why my son is so standoffish—that's not Southern behavior!

Let's sit down and—I think we could stand a little more air in here! Tom, leave the door open. I felt a nice fresh breeze a moment ago. Where has it gone to?

Mmm, so warm already! And not quite summer, even. We're going to burn up when summer really gets started.

However, we're having—we're having a very light supper. I think light things are better fo' this time of year. The same as light clothes are. Light clothes an' light food are what warm weather calls fo'. You know our blood gets so thick during th' winter—it takes a while fo' us to *adjust* ou'selves!—when the season changes . . .

It's come so quick this year. I wasn't prepared. All of a sudden—heavens! Already summer!—I ran to the trunk an' pulled out this light dress— Terribly old! Historical almost! But feels so good—so good an' co-ol, y' know. . . .

TOM

Mother—

AMANDA

Yes, honey?

TOM

How about—supper?

AMANDA

Honey, you go ask Sister if supper is ready! You know that Sister is in full charge of supper!

Tell her you hungry boys are waiting for it.

(*To* JIM.)

Have you met Laura?

JIM

She—

AMANDA

Let you in? Oh, good, you've met already! It's rare for a girl as sweet an' pretty as Laura to be domestic! But Laura is, thank heavens, not only pretty but also very domestic. I'm not at all. I never was a bit. I never could make a thing but angel-food cake. Well, in the South we had so many servants. Gone, gone, gone. All vestiges of gracious living! Gone completely! I wasn't prepared for what the future brought me. All of my gentlemen callers were sons of planters and so of course I assumed that I would be married to one and raise my family on a large piece of land with plenty of servants. But man proposes—and woman accepts the proposal!—To vary that old, old saying a little bit—I married no planter! I married a man who worked for the telephone company! —That gallantly smiling gentleman over there! (*Points to the picture*) A telephone man who—fell in love with long-distance!—Now he travels and I don't even know where!—But what am I going on for about my—tribulations?

Tell me yours—I hope you don't have any!

Tom?

TOM

(*Returning*)

Yes, Mother?

AMANDA

Is supper nearly ready?

TOM

It looks to me like supper is on the table.

AMANDA

Let me look— (*She rises prettily and looks through portieres*) Oh, lovely!— But where is Sister?

TOM

Laura is not feeling well and she says that she thinks she'd better not come to the table.

AMANDA

What?— Nonsense!— Laura? Oh, Laura!

LAURA

(*Off stage, faintly*)

Yes, Mother.

AMANDA

You really must come to the table. We won't be seated until you come to the table!

Come in, Mr. O'Connor. You sit over there, and I'll—

Laura? Laura Wingfield!

You're keeping us waiting, honey! We can't say grace until you come to the table!

(*The back door is pushed weakly open and* LAURA *comes in. She is obviously quite faint, her lips trembling, her eyes wide and staring. She moves unsteadily toward the table.*)

(LEGEND: "TERROR!")

(*Outside a summer storm is coming abruptly. The white curtains billow inward at the windows and there is a sorrowful murmur and deep blue dusk.*)

(LAURA *suddenly stumbles—she catches at a chair with a faint moan.*)

TOM

Laura!

AMANDA

Laura!

(*There is a clap of thunder.*)

(LEGEND: "AH!")

(*Despairingly*)

Why, Laura, you *are* sick, darling! Tom, help your sister into the living room, dear!

Sit in the living room, Laura—rest on the sofa.

Well!

(*To the gentleman caller.*)

Standing over the hot stove made her ill!—I told her that it was just too warm this evening, but—

(TOM *comes back in.* LAURA *is on the sofa.*)

Is Laura all right now?

TOM

Yes.

AMANDA

What *is* that? Rain? A nice cool rain has come up!

(*She gives the gentleman caller a frightened look.*)

I think we may—have grace—now . . .

(TOM *looks at her stupidly.*)

Tom, honey—you say grace!

TOM

Oh . . .

"For these and all thy mercies—"

(*They bow their heads,* AMANDA *stealing a nervous glance at* JIM. *In the living room* LAURA, *stretched on the sofa, clenches her hand to her lips, to hold back a shuddering sob.*)

God's Holy Name be praised—

THE SCENE DIMS OUT

Scene VII

A Souvenir.

Half an hour later. Dinner is just being finished in the upstage area which is concealed by the drawn portieres.

As the curtain rises LAURA *is still huddled upon the sofa, her feet drawn under her, her head resting on a pale blue pillow, her eyes wide and mysteriously watchful. The new floor lamp with its share of rose-colored silk gives a soft, becoming light to her face. bringing out the fragile, unearthly prettiness which usually escapes attention. There is a steady murmur of rain, but it is slackening and stops soon after the scene begins; the air becomes pale and luminous as the moon breaks out. A moment after the curtain rises, the lights in both rooms flicker and go out.*

JIM

Hey, there, Mr. Light Bulb!

(AMANDA *laughs nervously.*)

(LEGEND: "SUSPENSION OF A PUBLIC SERVICE.")

AMANDA

Where was Moses when the lights went out? Ha-ha. Do you know the answer to that one, Mr. O'Connor?

JIM

No, Ma'am, what's the answer?

AMANDA

In the dark!

(JIM *laughs appreciatively.*)

Everybody sit still. I'll light the candles. Isn't it lucky we have them on the table? Where's a match? Which of you gentlemen can provide a match?

JIM

Here.

AMANDA

Thank you, sir.

JIM

Not at all, Ma'am!

AMANDA

I guess the fuse has burnt out. Mr. O'Connor, can you tell a burnt-out fuse? I know I can't and Tom is a total loss when it comes to mechanics.

(SOUND: GETTING UP: VOICES RECEDE A LITTLE TO KITCHENETTE.)

Oh, be careful you don't bump into something. We don't want our gentleman caller to break his neck. Now wouldn't that be a fine howdy-do?

JIM

Ha-ha!

Where is the fuse-box?

AMANDA

Right here next to the stove. Can you see anything?

JIM

Just a minute.

AMANDA

Isn't electricity a mysterious thing?

Wasn't it Benjamin Franklin who tied a key to a kite?

We live in such a mysterious universe, don't we? Some people say that science clears up all the mysteries for us. In my opinion it only creates more!

Have you found it yet?

JIM

No, Ma'am. All these fuses look okay to me.

AMANDA

Tom!

TOM

Yes, Mother?

AMANDA

That light bill I gave you several days ago. The one I told you we got the notices about?

(LEGEND: "HA!")

TOM

Oh.—Yeah.

AMANDA

You didn't neglect to pay it by any chance?

TOM

Why, I—

AMANDA

Didn't! I might have known it!

JIM

Shakespeare probably wrote a poem on that light bill, Mrs. Wingfield.

AMANDA

I might have known better than to trust him with it! There's such a high price for negligence in this world!

JIM

Maybe the poem will win a ten-dollar prize.

AMANDA

We'll just have to spend the remainder of the evening in the nineteenth century, before Mr. Edison made the Mazda lamp!

JIM

Candlelight is my favorite kind of light.

AMANDA

That shows you're romantic! But that's no excuse for Tom.

Well, we got through dinner. Very considerate of them to let us get through dinner before they plunged us into everlasting darkness, wasn't it, Mr. O'Connor?

JIM

Ha-ha!

AMANDA

Tom, as a penalty for your carelessness you can help me with the dishes.

JIM

Let me give you a hand.

AMANDA

Indeed you will not!

JIM

I ought to be good for something.

AMANDA

Good for something? (*Her tone is rhapsodic.*)

You? Why, Mr. O'Connor, nobody, *nobody's* given me this much entertainment in years—as you have!

JIM

Aw, now, Mrs. Wingfield!

AMANDA

I'm not exaggerating, not one bit! But Sister is all by her lonesome. You go keep her company in the parlor! I'll give you this lovely old candelabrum that used to be on the altar at the church of the Heavenly Rest. It was melted a little out of shape when the church burnt down. Lightning struck it one spring. Gypsy Jones was holding a revival at the time and he intimated that the church was destroyed because the Episcopalians gave card parties.

JIM

Ha-ha.

AMANDA

And how about you coaxing Sister to drink a little wine? I think it would be good for her! Can you carry both at once?

JIM

Sure. I'm Superman!

AMANDA

Now, Thomas, get into this apron!

(*The door of kitchenette swings closed on* AMANDA's *gay laughter; the flickering light approaches the portieres.*)

(LAURA *sits up nervously as he enters. Her speech at first is low and breathless from the almost intolerable strain of being alone with a stranger.*)

(THE LEGEND: "I DON'T SUPPOSE YOU REMEMBER ME AT ALL!")

(*In her first speeches in this scene, before* JIM's *warmth overcomes her paralyzing shyness,* LAURA's *voice is thin and breathless as though she has just run up a steep flight of stairs.*)

(JIM's *attitude is gently humorous. In playing this scene it should be stressed that while the incident is apparently unimportant, it is to* LAURA *the climax of her secret life.*)

JIM

Hello, there, Laura.

LAURA

(*Faintly*)

Hello. (*She clears her throat.*)

JIM

How are you feeling now? Better?

LAURA

Yes. Yes, thank you.

JIM

This is for you. A little dandelion wine. (*He extends it toward her with extravagant gallantry.*)

LAURA

Thank you.

JIM

Drink it—but don't get drunk!

(*He laughs heartily.* LAURA *takes the glass uncertainly; laughs shyly.*)

Where shall I set the candles?

LAURA

Oh—oh, anywhere . . .

JIM

How about here on the floor? Any objections?

LAURA

No.

JIM

I'll spread a newspaper under to catch the drippings. I like to sit on the floor. Mind if I do?

LAURA

Oh, no.

JIM

Give me a pillow?

LAURA

What?

JIM

A pillow!

LAURA

Oh . . . (*Hands him one quickly.*)

JIM

How about you? Don't you like to sit on the floor?

LAURA

Oh—yes.

JIM

Why don't you, then?

LAURA

I—will.

JIM

Take a pillow! (LAURA *does. Sits on the other side of the candelabrum.* JIM *crosses his legs and smiles engagingly at her*) I can't hardly see you sitting way over there.

LAURA

I can—see you.

JIM

I know, but that's not fair, I'm in the limelight. (LAURA *moves her pillow closer*) Good! Now I can see you! Comfortable?

LAURA

Yes.

JIM

So am I. Comfortable as a cow! Will you have some gum?

LAURA

No, thank you.

JIM

I think that I will indulge, with your permission. (*Musingly unwraps it and holds it up*) Think of the fortune made by the guy that invented the first piece of chewing gum. Amazing, huh? The Wrigley Building is one of the sights of Chicago.—I saw it summer before last when I went up to the Century of Progress. Did you take in the Century of Progress?

LAURA

No, I didn't.

JIM

Well, it was quite a wonderful exposition. What impressed me most was the Hall of Science. Gives you an idea of what the future will be in America, even more wonderful than the present time is! (*Pause. Smiling at her*) Your brother tells me you're shy. Is that right, Laura?

LAURA

I—don't know.

JIM

I judge you to be an old-fashioned type of girl. Well, I think that's a pretty good type to be. Hope you don't think I'm being too personal—do you?

LAURA

(*Hastily, out of embarrassment*)

I believe I *will* take a piece of gum, if you—don't mind. (*Clearing her throat*) Mr. O'Connor, have you—kept up with your singing?

JIM

Singing? Me?

LAURA

Yes. I remember what a beautiful voice you had.

JIM

When did you hear me sing?

(VOICE OFF STAGE IN THE PAUSE.)

VOICE

O blow, ye winds, heigh-ho,
A-roving I will go!
I'm off to my love
With a boxing glove—
Ten thousand miles away!

JIM

You say you've heard me sing?

LAURA

Oh, yes! Yes, very often . . . I—don't suppose—you remember me—at all?

JIM

(*Smiling doubtfully*)

You know I have an idea I've seen you before. I had that idea soon as you opened the door. It seemed almost like I was about to remember your name. But the name that I started to call you—wasn't a name! And so I stopped myself before I said it.

LAURA

Wasn't it—Blue Roses?

JIM

(*Springs up. Grinning*)

Blue Roses!—My gosh, yes—Blue Roses!

That's what I had on my tongue when you opened the door!

Isn't it funny what tricks your memory plays? I didn't connect you with high school somehow or other.

But that's where it was; it was high school. I didn't even know you were Shakespeare's sister!

Gosh, I'm sorry.

LAURA

I didn't expect you to. You—barely knew me!

JIM

But we did have a speaking acquaintance, huh?

LAURA

Yes, we—spoke to each other.

JIM

When did you recognize me?

LAURA

Oh, right away!

JIM

Soon as I came in the door?

LAURA

When I heard your name I thought it was probably you. I knew that Tom used to know you a little in high school. So when you came in the door—

Well, then I was—sure.

JIM

Why didn't you *say* something, then?

LAURA

(*Breathlessly*)

I didn't know what to say, I was—too surprised!

JIM

For goodness' sakes! You know, this sure is funny!

LAURA

Yes! Yes, isn't it, though . . .

JIM

Didn't we have a class in something together?

LAURA

Yes, we did.

JIM

What class was that?

LAURA

It was—singing—Chorus!

JIM

Aw!

LAURA

I sat across the aisle from you in the Aud.

JIM

Aw.

LAURA

Mondays, Wednesdays and Fridays.

JIM

Now I remember—you always came in late.

LAURA

Yes, it was so hard for me, getting upstairs. I had that brace on my leg—it clumped so loud!

JIM

I never heard any clumping.

LAURA

(*Wincing at the recollection*)

To me it sounded like—thunder!

JIM

Well, well, well, I never even noticed.

LAURA

And everybody was seated before I came in. I had to walk in front of all those people. My seat was in the back row. I had to go clumping all the way up the aisle with everyone watching!

JIM

You shouldn't have been selfconscious.

LAURA

I know, but I was. It was always such a relief when the singing started.

JIM

Aw, yes, I've placed you now! I used to call you Blue Roses. How was it that I got started calling you that?

LAURA

I was out of school a little while with pleurosis. When I came back you asked me what was the matter. I said I had pleurosis—you thought I said Blue Roses. That's what you always called me after that!

JIM

I hope you didn't mind.

LAURA

Oh, no—I liked it. You see, I wasn't acquainted with many—people. . . .

JIM

As I remember you sort of stuck by yourself.

LAURA

I—I—never have had much luck at—making friends.

JIM

I don't see why you wouldn't.

LAURA

Well, I—started out badly.

JIM

You mean being—

LAURA

Yes, it sort of—stood between me—

JIM

You shouldn't have let it!

LAURA

I know, but it did, and—

JIM

You were shy with people!

LAURA

I tried not to be but never could—

JIM

Overcome it?

LAURA

No, I—I never could!

JIM

I guess being shy is something you have to work out of kind of gradually.

LAURA

(*Sorrowfully*)

Yes—I guess it—

JIM

Takes time!

LAURA

Yes—

JIM

People are not so dreadful when you know them. That's what you have to remember! And everybody has problems. Not just you, but practically everybody has got some problems.

You think of yourself as having the only problems, as being the only one who is disappointed. But just look around you and you will see lots of people as disappointed as you are. For instance, I hoped when I was going to high school that I would be further along at this time, six years later, than I am now— You remember that wonderful write-up I had in *The Torch?*

LAURA

Yes! (*She rises and crosses to table.*)

JIM

It said I was bound to succeed in anything I went into! (LAURA *returns with the annual*) Holy Jeez! *The Torch!* (*He accepts it reverently. They smile across it with mutual wonder.* LAURA *crouches beside him and they begin to turn through it.* LAURA's *shyness is dissolving in his warmth.*)

LAURA

Here you are in *The Pirates of Penzance!*

JIM

(*Wistfully*)

I sang the baritone lead in that operetta.

LAURA

(*Raptly*)

So—*beautifully!*

JIM

(*Protesting*)

Aw—

LAURA

Yes, yes—beautifully—beautifully!

JIM

You heard me?

LAURA

All three times!

JIM

No!

LAURA

Yes!

JIM

All three performances?

LAURA

(*Looking down*)

Yes.

JIM

Why?

LAURA

I—wanted to ask you to—autograph my program.

JIM

Why didn't you ask me to?

LAURA

You were always surrounded by your own friends so much that I never had a chance to.

JIM

You should have just—

LAURA

Well, I—thought you might think I was—

JIM

Thought I might think you was—what?

LAURA

Oh—

JIM

(*With reflective relish*)

I was beleaguered by females in those days.

LAURA

You were terribly popular!

JIM

Yeah—

LAURA

You had such a—friendly way—

JIM

I was spoiled in high school.

LAURA

Everybody—liked you!

JIM

Including you?

LAURA

I—yes, I—I did, too— (*She gently closes the book in her lap*)

JIM

Well, well, well!—Give me that program, Laura. (*She hands it to him. He signs it with a flourish*) There you are—better late than never!

LAURA

Oh, I—what a—surprise!

JIM

My signature isn't worth very much right now.

But some day—maybe—it will increase in value!

Being disappointed is one thing and being discouraged is something else. I am disappointed but I am not discouraged.

I'm twenty-three years old.

How old are you?

LAURA

I'll be twenty-four in June.

JIM

That's not old age!

LAURA

No, but—

JIM

You finished high school?

LAURA

(*With difficulty*)

I didn't go back.

JIM

You mean you dropped out?

LAURA

I made bad grades in my final examinations. (*She rises and replaces the book and the program. Her voice strained*) How is—Emily Meisenbach getting along?

JIM

Oh, that kraut-head!

LAURA

Why do you call her that?

JIM

That's what she was.

LAURA

You're not still—going with her?

JIM

I never see her.

LAURA

It said in the Personal Section that you were—engaged!

JIM

I know, but I wasn't impressed by that—propaganda!

LAURA

It wasn't—the truth?

JIM

Only in Emily's optimistic opinion!

LAURA

Oh—

(LEGEND: "WHAT HAVE YOU DONE SINCE HIGH SCHOOL?")

(JIM *lights a cigarette and leans indolently back on his elbows smiling at* LAURA *with a warmth and charm which lights her inwardly with altar candles. She remains by the table and turns in her hands a piece of glass to cover her tumult.*)

JIM

(*After several reflective puffs on a cigarette*)

What have you done since high school? (*She seems not to hear him*) Huh? (LAURA *looks up*) I said what have you done since high school, Laura?

LAURA

Nothing much.

JIM

You must have been doing something these six long years.

LAURA

Yes.

JIM

Well, then, such as what?

LAURA

I took a business course at business college—

JIM

How did that work out?

LAURA

Well, not very—well—I had to drop out, it gave me—indigestion—

(JIM *laughs gently.*)

JIM

What are you doing now?

LAURA

I don't do anything—much. Oh, please don't think I sit around doing nothing! My glass collection takes up a good deal of time. Glass is something you have to take good care of.

JIM

What did you say—about glass?

LAURA

Collection I said—I have one— (*She clears her throat and turns away again, acutely shy.*)

JIM

You know what I judge to be the trouble with you?

Inferiority complex! Know what that is? That's what they call it when someone low-rates himself!

I understand it because I had it, too. Although my case was not so aggravated as yours seems to be. I had it until I took up public speaking, developed my voice, and learned that I had an aptitude for science. Before that time I never thought of myself as being outstanding in any way whatsoever!

Now I've never made a regular study of it, but I have a friend who says I can analyze people better than doctors that make a profession of it. I don't claim that to be necessarily true, but I can sure guess a person's psychology, Laura! (*Takes out his gum*) Excuse me, Laura. I always take it out when the flavor is gone. I'll use this scrap of paper to wrap it in. I know how it is to get it stuck on a shoe.

Yep—that's what I judge to be your principal trouble. A lack of confidence in yourself as a person. You don't have the proper amount of faith in yourself. I'm basing that fact on a number of your remarks and also on certain observations I've made. For instance that clumping you thought was so awful in high school. You say that you even dreaded to walk into class. You see what you did? You dropped out of school, you gave up an education because of a clump, which as far as I know was practically non-existent! A little physical defect is what you have. Hardly noticeable even! Magnified thousands of times by imagination!

You know what my strong advice to you is? Think of yourself as *superior* in some way!

LAURA

In what way would I think?

JIM

Why, man alive, Laura! Just look about you a little. What do you see? A world full of common people! All of 'em born and all of 'em going to die!

Which of them has one-tenth of your good points! Or mine! Or anyone else's, as far as that goes—Gosh!

Everybody excels in some one thing. Some in many!

(*Unconsciously glances at himself in the mirror.*)

All you've got to do is discover in *what!*

Take me, for instance.

(*He adjusts his tie at the mirror.*)

My interest happens to lie in electrodynamics. I'm taking a course in radio engineering at night school, Laura, on top of a fairly responsible job at the warehouse. I'm taking that course and studying public speaking.

LAURA

Ohhhh.

JIM

Because I believe in the future of television!

(*Turning back to her.*)

I wish to be ready to go up right along with it. Therefore I'm planning to get in on the ground floor. In fact I've already made the right connections and all that remains is for the industry itself to get under way! Full steam—

(*His eyes are starry.*)

Knowledge — Zzzzzp! *Money* — Zzzzzzp! — *Power!*

That's the cycle democracy is built on!

(*His attitude is convincingly dynamic.* LAURA *stares at him, even her shyness eclipsed in her absolute wonder. He suddenly grins.*)

I guess you think I think a lot of myself!

LAURA

No—o-o-o, I—

JIM

Now how about you? Isn't there something you take more interest in than anything else?

LAURA

Well, I do—as I said—have my—glass collection—

(*A peal of girlish laughter from the kitchen.*)

JIM

I'm not right sure I know what you're talking about.

What kind of glass is it?

LAURA

Little articles of it, they're ornaments mostly!

Most of them are little animals made out of glass, the tiniest little animals in the world. Mother calls them a glass menagerie!

Here's an example of one, if you'd like to see it!

This one is one of the oldest. It's nearly thirteen.

(MUSIC: "THE GLASS MENAGERIE.")

(*He stretches out his hand.*)

Oh, be careful—if you breathe, it breaks!

JIM

I'd better not take it. I'm pretty clumsy with things.

LAURA

Go on, I trust you with him!

(*Places it in his palm*)

There now—you're holding him gently!

Hold him over the light, he loves the light! You see how the light shines through him?

JIM

It sure does shine!

LAURA

I shouldn't be partial, but he is my favorite one.

JIM

What kind of a thing is this one supposed to be?

LAURA

Haven't you noticed the single horn on his forehead?

JIM

A unicorn, huh?

LAURA

Mmm-hmmm!

JIM

Unicorns, aren't they extinct in the modern world?

LAURA

I know!

JIM

Poor little fellow, he must feel sort of lonesome.

LAURA
(*Smiling*)
Well, if he does he doesn't complain about it. He stays on a shelf with some horses that don't have horns and all of them seem to get along nicely together.

JIM
How do you know?

LAURA
(*Lightly*)
I haven't heard any arguments among them!

JIM
(*Grinning*)
No arguments, huh? Well, that's a pretty good sign!
Where shall I set him?

LAURA
Put him on the table. They all like a change of scenery once in a while!

JIM
(*Stretching*)
Well, well, well, well—
Look how big my shadow is when I stretch!

LAURA
Oh, oh, yes—it stretches across the ceiling!

JIM
(*Crossing to door*)
I think it's stopped raining. (*Opens fire-escape door*) Where does the music come from?

LAURA
From the Paradise Dance Hall across the alley.

JIM
How about cutting the rug a little, Miss Wingfield?

LAURA
Oh, I—

JIM
Or is your program filled up? Let me have a look at it. (*Grasps imaginary card*) Why, every dance is taken! I'll just have to scratch some out. (WALTZ MUSIC: "LA GOLONDRINA") Ahhh, a waltz! (*He executes some sweeping turns by himself then holds his arms toward* LAURA.)

LAURA
(*Breathlessly*)
I—can't dance!

JIM
There you go, that inferiority stuff!

LAURA
I've never danced in my life!

JIM
Come on, try!

LAURA
Oh, but I'd step on you!

JIM
I'm not made out of glass.

LAURA
How—how—how do we start?

JIM
Just leave it to me. You hold your arms out a little.

LAURA
Like this?

JIM
A little bit higher. Right. Now don't tighten up, that's the main thing about it—relax.

LAURA
(*Laughing breathlessly*)
It's hard not to.

JIM
Okay.

LAURA
I'm afraid you can't budge me.

JIM
What do you bet I can't. (*He swings her into motion.*)

LAURA
Goodness, yes, you can!

JIM

Let yourself go, now, Laura, just let yourself go.

LAURA

I'm—

JIM

Come on!

LAURA

Trying!

JIM

Not so stiff— Easy does it!

LAURA

I know but I'm—

JIM

Loosen th' backbone! There now, that's a lot better.

LAURA

Am I?

JIM

Lots, lots better! (*He moves her about the room in a clumsy waltz.*)

LAURA

Oh, my!

JIM

Ha-ha!

LAURA

Oh, my goodness!

JIM

Ha-ha-ha! (*They suddenly bump into the table.* JIM *stops*) What did we hit on?

LAURA

Table.

JIM

Did something fall off it? I think—

LAURA

Yes.

JIM

I hope that it wasn't the little glass horse with the horn!

LAURA

Yes.

JIM

Aw, aw, aw. Is it broken?

LAURA

Now it is just like all the other horses.

JIM

It's lost its—

LAURA

Horn!

It doesn't matter. Maybe it's a blessing in disguise.

JIM

You'll never forgive me. I bet that that was your favorite piece of glass.

LAURA

I don't have favorites much. It's no tragedy, freckles. Glass breaks so easily. No matter how careful you are. The traffic jars the shelves and things fall off them.

JIM

Still I'm awfully sorry that I was the cause.

LAURA

(*Smiling*)

I'll just imagine he had an operation.

The horn was removed to make him feel less—freakish!

(*They both laugh.*)

Now he will feel more at home with the other horses, the ones that don't have horns. . .

JIM

Ha-ha, that's very funny!

(*Suddenly serious.*)

I'm glad to see that you have a sense of humor.

You know—you're—well—very different!

Surprisingly different from anyone else I know!

(*His voice becomes soft and hesitant with a genuine feeling.*)

Do you mind me telling you that?

(LAURA *is abashed beyond speech.*)

I mean it in a nice way . . .

(LAURA *nods shyly, looking away.*)

You make me feel sort of—I don't know how to put it!

I'm usually pretty good at expressing things, but—

This is something that I don't know how to say!

(LAURA *touches her throat and clears it—turns the broken unicorn in her hands.*)

(*Even softer.*)

Has anyone ever told you that you were pretty?

(PAUSE: MUSIC.)

(LAURA *looks up slowly, with wonder, and shakes her head.*)

Well, you are! In a very different way from anyone else.

And all the nicer because of the difference, too.

(*His voice becomes low and husky.* LAURA *turns away, nearly faint with the novelty of her emotions.*)

I wish that you were my sister. I'd teach you to have some confidence in yourself. The different people are not like other people, but being different is nothing to be ashamed of. Because other people are not such wonderful people. They're one hundred times one thousand. You're one times one! They walk all over the earth. You just stay here. They're common as—weeds, but—you —well, you're—*Blue Roses!*

(IMAGE ON SCREEN: BLUE ROSES.)

(MUSIC CHANGES.)

LAURA

But blue is wrong for—roses . . .

JIM

It's right for you!—You're—pretty!

LAURA

In what respect am I pretty?

JIM

In all respects—believe me! Your eyes—your hair—are pretty! Your hands are pretty!

(*He catches hold of her hand.*)

You think I'm making this up because I'm invited to dinner and have to be nice. Oh, I could do that! I could put on an act for you, Laura, and say lots of things without being very sincere. But this time I am. I'm talking to you sincerely. I happened to notice you had this inferiority complex that keeps you from feeling comfortable with people. Somebody needs to build your confidence up and make you proud instead of shy and turning away and—blushing—

Somebody—ought to—

Ought to—*kiss* you, Laura!

(*His hand slips slowly up her arm to her shoulder.*)

(MUSIC SWELLS TUMULTOUSLY.)

(*He suddenly turns her about and kisses her on the lips.*)

(*When he releases her,* LAURA *sinks on the sofa with a bright, dazed look.*)

(JIM *backs away and fishes in his pocket for a cigarette.*)

(LEGEND ON SCREEN: "SOUVENIR.")

Stumble-john!

(*He lights the cigarette, avoiding her look.*)

(*There is a peal of girlish laughter from* AMANDA *in the kitchen.*)

(LAURA *slowly raises and opens her hand. It still contains the little broken glass animal. She looks at it with a tender, bewildered expression.*)

Stumble-john!

I shouldn't have done that— That was way off the beam.

You don't smoke, do you?

(*She looks up, smiling, not hearing the question.*)

(*He sits beside her a little gingerly. She looks at him speechlessly—waiting.*)

(*He coughs decorously and moves a little farther aside as he considers the situation and senses her feelings, dimly, with perturbation.*)

(*Gently.*)

Would you—care for a—mint?

(*She doesn't seem to hear him but her look grows brighter even.*)

Peppermint—Life-Saver?

My pocket's a regular drug store—wherever I go . . .

(*He pops a mint in his mouth. Then gulps and decides to make a clean breast of it. He speaks slowly and gingerly.*)

Laura, you know, if I had a sister like you, I'd do the same thing as Tom. I'd bring out fellows and—introduce her to them. The right type of boys of a type to—appreciate her.

Only—well—he made a mistake about me.

Maybe I've got no call to be saying this. That may not have been the idea in having me over. But what if it was?

There's nothing wrong about that. The only trouble is that in my case—I'm not in a situation to—do the right thing.

I can't take down your number and say I'll phone.

I can't call up next week and—ask for a date.

I thought I had better explain the situation in case you—misunderstood it and—hurt your feelings. . . .

(*Pause.*)

(*Slowly, very slowly,* LAURA'S *look changes, her eyes returning slowly from his to the ornament in her palm.*)

(AMANDA *utters another gay laugh in the kitchen.*)

LAURA

(*Faintly*)

You—won't—call again?

JIM

No, Laura, I can't.

(*He rises from the sofa.*)

As I was just explaining, I've—got strings on me.

Laura, I've—been going steady!

I go out all of the time with a girl named Betty. She's a home-girl like you, and Catholic, and Irish, and in a great many ways we—get along fine.

I met her last summer on a moonlight boat trip up the river to Alton, on the *Majestic*.

Well—right away from the start it was—love!

(LEGEND: LOVE!)

(LAURA *sways slightly forward and grips the arm of the sofa. He fails to notice, now enrapt in his own comfortable being.*)

Being in love has made a new man of me!

(*Leaning stiffly forward, clutching the arm of the sofa,* LAURA *struggles visibly with her storm. But* JIM *is oblivious, she is a long way off.*)

The power of love is really pretty tremendous!

Love is something that—changes the whole world, Laura!

(*The storm abates a little and* LAURA *leans back. He notices her again.*)

It happened that Betty's aunt took sick, she got a wire and had to go to Centralia. So Tom—when he asked me to dinner—I naturally just accepted the invitation, not knowing that you—that he—that I—

(*He stops awkwardly.*)

Huh—I'm a stumble-john!

(*He flops back on the sofa.*)

(*The holy candles in the altar of* LAURA'S *face have been snuffed out. There is a look of almost infinite desolation.*)

(JIM *glances at her uneasily.*)

I wish that you would—say something. (*She bites her lip which was trembling and then bravely smiles. She opens her hand again on the broken glass ornament. Then she gently takes his hand and raises it level with her own. She carefully places the unicorn in the palm of his hand, then pushes his fingers closed upon it*) What are you—doing that for? You want me to have him?—Laura? (*She nods*) What for?

LAURA

A—souvenir . . .

(*She rises unsteadily and crouches beside the victrola to wind it up.*)

(LEGEND ON SCREEN: "THINGS

HAVE A WAY OF TURNING OUT SO BADLY!")
(OR IMAGE: "GENTLEMAN CALLER WAVING GOOD-BYE!—GAILY.")
(*At this moment* AMANDA *rushes brightly back in the front room. She bears a pitcher of fruit punch in an old-fashioned cut-glass pitcher and a plate of macaroons. The plate has a gold border and poppies painted on it.*)

AMANDA

Well, well, well! Isn't the air delightful after the shower?

I've made you children a little liquid refreshment.

(*Turns gaily to the gentleman caller*)

Jim, do you know that song about lemonade?

"Lemonade, lemonade
Made in the shade and stirred
with a spade—
Good enough for any old maid!"

JIM

(*Uneasily*)

Ha-ha! No—I never heard it.

AMANDA

Why, Laura! You look so serious!

JIM

We were having a serious conversation.

AMANDA

Good! Now you're better acquainted!

JIM

(*Uncertainly*)

Ha-ha! Yes.

AMANDA

You modern young people are much more serious-minded than my generation. I was so gay as a girl!

JIM

You haven't changed, Mrs. Wingfield.

AMANDA

Tonight I'm rejuvenated! The gaiety of the occasion, Mr. O'Connor!

(*She tosses her head with a peal of laughter. Spills lemonade.*)

Oooo! I'm baptizing myself!

JIM

Here—let me—

AMANDA

(*Setting the pitcher down*)

There now. I discovered we had some maraschino cherries. I dumped them in, juice and all!

JIM

You shouldn't have gone to that trouble, Mrs. Wingfield.

AMANDA

Trouble, trouble? Why, it was loads of fun!

Didn't you hear me cutting up in the kitchen? I bet your ears were burning! I told Tom how outdone with him I was for keeping you to himself so long a time! He should have brought you over much, much sooner! Well, now that you've found your way, I want you to be a very frequent caller! Not just occasional but all the time.

Oh, we're going to have a lot of gay times together! I see them coming!

Mmm, just breathe that air! So fresh, and the moon's so pretty!

I'll skip back out—I know where my place is when young folks are having a—serious conversation!

JIM

Oh, don't go out, Mrs. Wingfield. The fact of the matter is I've got to be going.

AMANDA

Going, now? You're joking! Why, it's only the shank of the evening, Mr. O'Connor!

JIM

Well, you know how it is.

AMANDA

You mean you're a young workingman and have to keep workingmen's hours. We'll let you off early tonight. But only on the condition that next time you stay later.

What's the best night for you? Isn't Saturday night the best night for you workingmen?

JIM

I have a couple of time-clocks to punch, Mrs. Wingfield. One at morning, another one at night!

AMANDA

My, but you *are* ambitious! You work at night, too?

JIM

No, Ma'am, not work but—Betty! (*He crosses deliberately to pick up his hat. The band at the Paradise Dance Hall goes into a tender waltz.*)

AMANDA

Betty? Betty? Who's—Betty!

(*There is an ominous cracking sound in the sky.*)

JIM

Oh, just a girl. The girl I go steady with! (*He smiles charmingly. The sky falls.*)

(LEGEND: "THE SKY FALLS.")

AMANDA

(*A long-drawn exhalation*)

Ohhhh . . . Is it a serious romance, Mr. O'Connor?

JIM

We're going to be married the second Sunday in June.

AMANDA

Ohhhh—how nice!

Tom didn't mention that you were engaged to be married.

JIM

The cat's not out of the bag at the warehouse yet.

You know how they are. They call you Romeo and stuff like that.

(*He stops at the oval mirror to put on his hat. He carefully shapes the brim and the crown to give a discreetly dashing effect.*)

It's been a wonderful evening, Mrs. Wingfield. I guess this is what they mean by Southern hospitality.

AMANDA

It really wasn't anything at all.

JIM

I hope it don't seem like I'm rushing off. But I promised Betty I'd pick her up at the Wabash depot, an' by the time I get my jalopy down there her train'll be in. Some women are pretty upset if you keep 'em waiting.

AMANDA

Yes, I know— The tyranny of women!

(*Extends her hand.*)

Good-bye, Mr. O'Connor.

I wish you luck—and happiness—and success! All three of them, and so does Laura!—Don't you, Laura?

LAURA

Yes!

JIM

(*Taking her hand*)

Good-bye, Laura. I'm certainly going to treasure that souvenir. And don't you forget the good advice I gave you.

(*Raises his voice to a cheery shout.*)

So long, Shakespeare!

Thanks again, ladies— Good night!

(*He grins and ducks jauntily out.*)

(*Still bravely grimacing,* AMANDA *closes the door on the gentleman caller. Then she turns back to the room with a puzzled expression. She and* LAURA *don't dare to face each other.* LAURA *crouches beside the victrola to wind it.*)

AMANDA

(*Faintly*)

Things have a way of turning out so badly.

I don't believe that I would play the victrola.

Well, well—well—

Our gentleman caller was engaged to be married!

Tom!

TOM

(*From back*)

Yes, Mother?

AMANDA

Come in here a minute. I want to tell you something awfully funny.

TOM

(*Enters with macaroon and a glass of the lemonade*)

Has the gentleman caller gotten away already?

AMANDA

The gentleman caller has made an early departure.

What a wonderful joke you played on us!

TOM

How do you mean?

AMANDA

You didn't mention that he was engaged to be married.

TOM

Jim? Engaged?

AMANDA

That's what he just informed us.

TOM

I'll be jiggered! I didn't know about that.

AMANDA

That seems very peculiar.

TOM

What's peculiar about it?

AMANDA

Didn't you call him your best friend down at the warehouse?

TOM

He is, but how did I know?

AMANDA

It seems extremely peculiar that you wouldn't know your best friend was going to be married!

TOM

The warehouse is where I work, not where I know things about people!

AMANDA

You don't know things anywhere! You live in a dream; you manufacture illusions!

(*He crosses to door.*)

Where are you going?

TOM

I'm going to the movies.

AMANDA

That's right, now that you've had us make such fools of ourselves. The effort, the preparations, all the expense! The new floor lamp, the rug, the clothes for Laura! All for what? To entertain some other girl's fiancé!

Go to the movies, go! Don't think about us, a mother deserted, an unmarried sister who's crippled and has no job! Don't let anything interfere with your selfish pleasure!

Just go, go, go—to the movies!

TOM

All right, I will! The more you shout about my selfishness to me the quicker I'll go, and I won't go to the movies!

AMANDA

Go, then! Then go to the moon—you selfish dreamer!

(TOM *smashes his glass on the floor. He plunges out on the fire-escape, slamming the door.* LAURA *screams—cut by door.*)

(*Dance-hall music up.* TOM *goes to the rail and grips it desperately, lifting his face in the chill white moonlight penetrating the narrow abyss of the alley.*)

(LEGEND ON SCREEN: "AND SO GOOD-BYE . . .")

(TOM'S *closing speech is timed with the interior pantomime. The interior scene is played as though viewed through soundproof glass.* AMANDA *appears to be making a comforting speech to* LAURA *who is huddled upon the sofa. Now that we cannot hear the mother's speech, her silliness is gone and she has dignity and tragic beauty.* LAURA'S *dark hair hides her face until at the end of the speech she lifts it to smile at her mother.* AMANDA'S *gestures are slow and graceful, almost dancelike, as she comforts the daughter. At the end of her speech she glances a moment at the father's picture—then withdraws through the portieres. At close of* TOM'S *speech,* LAURA *blows out the candles, ending the play.*)

TOM

I didn't go to the moon, I went much further—for time is the longest distance between two places—

Not long after that I was fired for writing a poem on the lid of a shoe-box.

I left Saint Louis. I descended the steps of this fire-escape for a last time and followed, from then on, in my father's footsteps, attempting to find in motion what was lost in space—

I traveled around a great deal. The cities swept about me like dead leaves, leaves that were brightly colored but torn away from the branches.

I would have stopped, but I was pursued by something.

It always came upon me unawares, taking me altogether by surprise. Perhaps it was a familiar bit of music. Perhaps it was only a piece of transparent glass—

Perhaps I am walking along a street at night, in some strange city, before I have found companions. I pass the lighted window of a shop where perfume is sold. The window is filled with pieces of colored glass, tiny transparent bottles in delicate colors, like bits of a shattered rainbow.

Then all at once my sister touches my shoulder. I turn around and look into her eyes . . .

Oh, Laura, Laura, I tried to leave you behind me, but I am more faithful than I intended to be!

I reach for a cigarette, I cross the street, I run into the movies or a bar, I buy a drink, I speak to the nearest stranger—anything that can blow your candles out!

(LAURA *bends over the candles.*)

—for nowadays the world is lit by lightning! Blow out your candles, Laura —and so good-bye. . . .

(*She blows the candles out.*)

THE SCENE DISSOLVES

Arthur Miller (1915–)

Death of a Salesman

CHARACTERS

WILLY LOMAN	CHARLEY
LINDA	UNCLE BEN
BIFF	HOWARD WAGNER
HAPPY	JENNY
BERNARD	STANLEY
THE WOMAN	MISS FORSYTHE

LETTA

The action takes place in Willy Loman's house and yard and in various places he visits in the New York and Boston of today.

Act One

A melody is heard, played upon a flute. It is small and fine, telling of grass and trees and the horizon. The curtain rises.

Before us is the Salesman's house. We are aware of towering, angular shapes behind it, surrounding it on all sides. Only the blue light of the sky falls upon the house and forestage; the surrounding area shows an angry glow of orange. As more light appears, we see a solid vault of apartment houses around the small, fragile-seeming home. An air of the dream clings to the place, a dream rising out of reality. The kitchen at center seems actual enough, for there is a kitchen table with three chairs, and a refrigerator. But no other fixtures are seen. At the back of the kitchen there is a draped entrance, which leads to the living-room. To the right of the kitchen, on a level raised two feet, is a bedroom furnished only with a brass bedstead and a straight chair. On a shelf over the bed a silver athletic trophy stands. A window opens onto the apartment house at the side.

Behind the kitchen, on a level raised six and a half feet, is the boys' bedroom, at present barely visible. Two beds are dimly seen, and at the back of the room a dormer window. (This bedroom is above the unseen living-room.) At the left a stairway curves up to it from the kitchen.

The entire setting is wholly or, in some places, partially transparent. The roof-line of the house is one-dimensional; under and over it we see the apartment buildings. Before the house lies an apron, curving beyond the forestage into the orchestra. This forward area serves as the back yard as well as the locale of all Willy's imaginings and of his city scenes. Whenever the action is in the present the actors observe the imaginary wall-lines, entering the house only through its door at the left. But in the scenes of the past these boundaries are broken, and characters enter or leave a room by stepping "through" a wall onto the forestage.

From the right, Willy Loman, the Salesman, enters, carrying two large sample cases. The flute plays on. He hears but is not aware of it. He is past sixty years of age, dressed quietly. Even as he crosses the stage to the doorway of the house, his exhaustion is apparent. He unlocks the door, comes into the kitchen, and thankfully lets his burden down, feeling the soreness of his palms. A word-sigh escapes his lips —it might be "Oh, boy, oh boy." He closes the door, then carries his cases out into the living-room, through the draped kitchen doorway.

Linda, his wife, has stirred in her bed at the right. She gets out and puts on a robe, listening. Most often jovial, she has developed an iron repression of her exceptions to Willy's behavior—she more than loves him, she admires him, as though his mercurial nature, his temper, his massive dreams and little cruelties, served her only as sharp reminders of the turbulent longings within him, longings which she shares but lacks the temperament to utter and follow to their end.

LINDA: *{Hearing Willy outside the bedroom, calls with some trepidation}* Willy!

WILLY: It's all right. I came back.

LINDA: Why? What happened? *{Slight pause}* Did something happen, Willy?

WILLY: No, nothing happened.

LINDA: You didn't smash the car, did you?

WILLY: *{With casual irritation}* I said nothing happened. Didn't you hear me?

LINDA: Don't you feel well?

WILLY: I'm tired to the death. *{The flute has faded away. He sits on the bed beside her, a little numb}* I couldn't make it. I just couldn't make it, Linda.

LINDA: *{Very carefully, delicately}* Where were you all day? You look terrible.

WILLY: I got as far as a little above Yonkers. I stopped for a cup of coffee. Maybe it was the coffee.

LINDA: What?

WILLY: *{After a pause}* I suddenly couldn't drive any more. The car kept going off onto the shoulder, y'know?

LINDA: *{Helpfully}* Oh. Maybe it was the steering again. I don't think Angelo knows the Studebaker.

WILLY: No, it's me, it's me. Suddenly I realize I'm goin' sixty miles an hour and I don't remember the last five minutes. I'm—I can't seem to—keep my mind to it.

LINDA: Maybe it's your glasses. You never went for your new glasses.

WILLY: No, I see everything. I came back ten miles an hour. It took me nearly four hours from Yonkers.

LINDA: *{Resigned}* Well, you'll just have to take a rest, Willy, you can't continue this way.

WILLY: I just got back from Florida.

LINDA: But you didn't rest your mind. Your mind is overactive, and the mind is what counts, dear.

WILLY: I'll start out in the morning. Maybe I'll feel better in the morning. *{She is taking off his shoes}* These goddamn arch supports are killing me.

LINDA: Take an aspirin. Should I get you an aspirin? It'll soothe you.

WILLY: *{With wonder}* I was driving along, you understand? And I was fine. I was even observing the scenery. You can imagine, me looking at scenery, on the road every week of my life. But it's so beautiful up there, Linda, the trees are so thick, and the sun is warm. I opened the windshield and just let the warm air bathe over me. And then all of a sudden I'm goin' off the road! I'm tellin' ya, I absolutely forgot I was driving. If I'd've gone the other way over the white line I might've killed somebody. So I went on again—and five minutes later I'm dreamin' again, and I nearly— *{He presses two fingers against* *his eyes}* I have such thoughts, I have such strange thoughts.

LINDA: Willy, dear. Talk to them again. There's no reason why you can't work in New York.

WILLY: They don't need me in New York. I'm the New England man. I'm vital in New England.

LINDA: But you're sixty years old. They can't expect you to keep traveling every week.

WILLY: I'll have to send a wire to Portland. I'm supposed to see Brown and Morrison tomorrow morning at ten o'clock to show the line. Goddammit, I could sell them! *{He starts putting on his jacket}*

LINDA: *{Taking the jacket from him}* Why don't you go down to the place tomorrow and tell Howard you've simply got to work in New York? You're too accommodating, dear.

WILLY: If old man Wagner was alive I'd a been in charge of New York now! That man was a prince, he was a masterful man. But that boy of his, that Howard, he don't appreciate. When I went north the first time, the Wagner Company didn't know where New England was!

LINDA: Why don't you tell those things to Howard, dear?

WILLY: *{Encouraged}* I will, I definitely will. Is there any cheese?

LINDA: I'll make you a sandwich.

WILLY: No, go to sleep. I'll take some milk. I'll be up right away. The boys in?

LINDA: They're sleeping. Happy took Biff on a date tonight.

WILLY: *{Interested}* That so?

LINDA: It was so nice to see them shaving together, one behind the other, in the bathroom. And going out together. You notice? The whole house smells of shaving lotion.

WILLY: Figure it out. Work a lifetime to pay off a house. You finally own it, and there's nobody to live in it.

LINDA: Well, dear, life is a casting off. It's always that way.

WILLY: No, no, some people—some people accomplish something. Did Biff say anything after I went this morning?

LINDA: You shouldn't have criticized him, Willy, especially after he just got off the train. You mustn't lose your temper with him.

WILLY: When the hell did I lose my temper? I simply asked him if he was making any money? Is that a criticism?

LINDA: But, dear, how could he make any money?

WILLY: *{Worried and angered}* There's such an undercurrent in him. He became a moody man. Did he apologize when I left this morning?

LINDA: *He was crestfallen, Willy.* You know how he admires you. I think if he finds himself, then you'll both be happier and not fight any more.

WILLY: How can he find himself on a farm? Is that a life? A farmhand? In the beginning, when he was young, I thought, well, a young man, it's good for him to tramp around, take a lot of different jobs. But it's more than ten years now and he has yet to make thirty-five dollars a week!

LINDA: He's finding himself, Willy.

WILLY: Not finding yourself at the age of thirty-four is a disgrace!

LINDA: Shh!

WILLY: The trouble is he's lazy, god dammit!

LINDA: Willy, please!

WILLY: Biff is a lazy bum!

LINDA: They're sleeping. Get something to eat. Go on down.

WILLY: Why did he come home? I would like to know what brought him home.

LINDA: I don't know. I think he's still lost, Willy. I think he's very lost.

WILLY: Biff Loman is lost. In the greatest country in the world a young man with such—personal attractiveness, gets lost. And such a hard worker. There's one thing about Biff—he's not lazy.

LINDA: Never.

WILLY: *{With pity and resolve}* I'll see him in the morning; I'll have a nice talk with him. I'll get him a job selling. He could be big in no time. My God! Remember how they used to follow him around in high school? When he smiled at one of them their faces lit up. When he walked down the street . . . *{He loses himself in reminiscences}*

LINDA: *{Trying to bring him out of it}* Willy, dear, I got a new kind of American-type cheese today. It's whipped.

WILLY: Why do you get American when I like Swiss?

LINDA: I just thought you'd like a change—

WILLY: I don't want a change! I want Swiss cheese. Why am I always being contradicted?

LINDA: *{With a covering laugh}* I thought it would be a surprise.

WILLY: Why don't you open a window in here, for God's sake?

LINDA: *{With infinite patience}* They're all open, dear.

WILLY: The way they boxed us in here. Bricks and windows, windows and bricks.

LINDA: We should've bought the land next door.

WILLY: The street is lined with cars. There's not a breath of fresh air in the neighborhood. The grass don't grow any more, you can't raise a carrot in the back yard. They should've had a law against apartment houses. Remember those two beautiful elm trees out there? When I and Biff hung the swing between them?

LINDA: Yeah, like being a million miles from the city.

WILLY: They should've arrested the builder for cutting those down. They massacred the neighborhood. *{Lost}* More and more I think of those days, Linda. This time of year it was lilac and wisteria. And then the peonies would come out, and the daffodils. What fragrance in this room!

LINDA: Well, after all, people had to move somewhere.

WILLY: No, there's more people now.

LINDA: I don't think there's more people. I think—

WILLY: There's more people! That's what's ruining this country! Population is getting out of control! The competition is maddening! Smell the stink from that apartment house! And another one on the other side . . . How can they whip cheese? *{On Willy's last line, Biff and Happy raise themselves up in their beds, listening.}*

LINDA: Go down, try it. And be quiet.

WILLY: *{Turning to Linda, guiltily}* You're not worried about me, are you, sweetheart?

BIFF: What's the matter?

HAPPY: Listen!

LINDA: You've got too much on the ball to worry about.

WILLY: You're my foundation and my support, Linda.

LINDA: Just try to relax, dear. You make mountains out of molehills.

WILLY: I won't fight with him any more. If he wants to go back to Texas, let him go.

LINDA: He'll find his way.

WILLY: Sure. Certain men just don't get started till later in life. Like Thomas Edison, I think. Or B. F. Goodrich. One of them was deaf. *{He starts for the bedroom doorway}* I'll put my money on Biff.

LINDA: And, Willy—if it's warm Sunday we'll drive in the country. And we'll open the windshield, and take lunch.

WILLY: No, the windshields don't open on the new cars.

LINDA: But you opened it today.

WILLY: Me? I didn't. *{He stops}* Now isn't that peculiar! Isn't that remarkable—*{He breaks off in amazement and fright as the flute is heard distantly}*

LINDA: What, darling?

WILLY: That is the most remarkable thing.

LINDA: What, dear?

WILLY: I was thinking of the Chevvy *{Slight pause}* Nineteen twenty-eight . . . when I had that red Chevvy—

{Breaks off} That's funny? I coulda sworn I was driving that Chevvy today.

LINDA: Well, that's nothing. Something must've reminded you.

WILLY: Remarkable. Ts. Remember those days? The way Biff used to simonize that car? The dealer refused to believe there was eighty thousand miles on it. *{He shakes his head}* Heh! *{To Linda}* Close your eyes, I'll be right up. *{He walks out of the bedroom}*

HAPPY: *{To Biff}* Jesus, maybe he smashed up the car again!

LINDA: *{Calling after Willy}* Be careful on the stairs, dear! The cheese is on the middle shelf! *{She turns, goes over to the bed, takes his jacket, and goes out of the bedroom}*

{Light has risen on the boys' room. Unseen, Willy is heard talking to himself, "Eighty thousand miles," and a little laugh. Biff gets out of bed, comes downstage a bit, and stands attentively. Biff is two years older than his brother Happy, well built, but in these days bears a worn air and seems less self-assured. He has succeeded less, and his dreams are stronger and less acceptable than Happy's. Happy is tall, powerfully made. Sexuality is like a visible color on him, or a scent that many women have discovered. He, like his brother, is lost, but in a different way, for he has never allowed himself to turn his face toward defeat and is thus more confused and hard-skinned, although seemingly more content.}

HAPPY: *{Getting out of bed}* He's going to get his license taken away if he keeps that up. I'm getting nervous about him, y'know, Biff?

BIFF: His eyes are going.

HAPPY: No, I've driven with him. He sees all right. He just doesn't keep his mind on it. I drove into the city with him last week. He stops at a green light and then it turns red and he goes. *{He laughs}*

BIFFS Maybe he's color-blind.

HAPPY: Pop? Why he's got the finest eye for color in the business. You know that.

BIFF: *{Sitting down on his bed}* I'm going to sleep.

HAPPY: You're not still sour on Dad, are you, Biff?

BIFF: He's all right, I guess.

WILLY: *{Underneath them, in the living-room}* Yes, sir, eighty thousand miles—eighty-two thousand!

BIFF: You smoking?

HAPPY: *{Holding out a pack of cigarettes}* Want one?

BIFF: *{Taking a cigarette}* I can never sleep when I smell it.

WILLY: What a simonizing job, heh!

HAPPY: *{With deep sentiment}* Funny, Biff, y'know? Us sleeping in here again? The old beds. *{He pats his bed affectionately}* All the talk that went across those two beds, huh? Our whole lives.

BIFF: Yeah. Lotta dreams and plans.

HAPPY: *{With a deep and masculine laugh}* About five hundred women would like to know what was said in this room. *{They share a short laugh}*

BIFF: Remember that big Betsy something—what the hell was her name—over on Bushwick Avenue?

HAPPY: *{Combing his hair}* With the collie dog!

BIFF: That's the one. I got you in there, remember?

HAPPY: Yeah, that was my first time—I think. Boy, there was a pig! *{They laugh, almost crudely}* You taught me everything I know about women. Don't forget that.

BIFF: I bet you forgot how bashful you used to be. Especially with girls.

HAPPY: Oh, I still am, Biff.

BIFF: Oh, go on.

HAPPY: I just control it, that's all. I think I got less bashful and you got more so. What happened, Biff? Where's the old humor, the old confidence? *{He shakes Biff's knee. Biff gets up and moves restlessly about the room}* What's the matter?

BIFF: Why does Dad mock me all the time?

HAPPY: He's not mocking you, he—

BIFF: Everything I say there's a twist

of mockery on his face. I can't get near him.

HAPPY: He just wants you to make good, that's all. I wanted to talk to you about Dad for a long time, Biff. Something's—happening to him. He—talks to himself.

BIFF: I noticed that this morning. But he always mumbled.

HAPPY: But not so noticeable. It got so embarrassing I sent him to Florida. And you know something? Most of the time he's talking to you.

BIFF: What's he say about me?

HAPPY: I can't make it out.

BIFF: What's he say about me?

HAPPY: I think the fact that you're not settled, that you're still kind of up in the air.

BIFF: There's one or two other things depressing him, Happy.

HAPPY: What do you mean?

BIFF: Never mind. Just don't lay it all to me.

HAPPY: But I think if you just got started—I mean—is there any future for you out there?

BIFF: I tell ya, Hap, I don't know what the future is. I don't know—what I'm suppose to want.

HAPPY: What do you mean?

BIFF: Well, I spent six or seven years after high school trying to work myself up. Shipping clerk, salesman, business of one kind or another. And it's a measly manner of existence. To get on that subway on the hot mornings in summer. To devote your whole life to keeping stock, or making phone calls, or selling or buying. To suffer fifty weeks of the year for the sake of a two-week vacation, when all you really desire is to be outdoors, with your shirt off. And always to have to get ahead of the next fella. And still—that's how you build a future.

HAPPY: Well, you really enjoy it on a farm? Are you content out there?

BIFF: *{with rising agitation}* Hap, I've had twenty or thirty different kinds of jobs since I left home before the war, and it always turns out the same. I just realized it lately. In Nebraska where I herded cattle, and the Dakotas, and Arizona, and now in Texas. It's why I came home now, I guess, because I realized it. This farm I work on, it's spring there now, see? And they've got about fifteen new colts. There's nothing more inspiring or—beautiful than the sight of a mare and a new colt. And it's cool there now, see? Texas is cool now, and it's spring. And whenever spring comes to where I am, I suddenly get the feeling, my God, I'm not gettin' anywhere! What the hell am I doing, playing around with horses, twenty-eight dollars a week! I'm thirty-four years old, I oughta be makin' my future. That's when I come running home. And now, I get here, and I don't know what to do with myself. *{After a pause}* I've always made a point of not wasting my life, and everytime I come back here I know that all I've done is to waste my life.

HAPPY: You're a poet, you know that, Biff? You're a—you're an idealist!

BIFF: No, I'm mixed up very bad. Maybe I oughta get married. Maybe I oughta get stuck into something. Maybe that's my trouble. I'm like a boy. I'm not married, I'm not in business, I just—I'm like a boy. Are you content, Hap? You're a success, aren't you? Are you content?

HAPPY: Hell, no!

BIFF: Why? You're making money, aren't you?

HAPPY: *{Moving about with energy, expressiveness}* All I can do now is wait for the merchandise manager to die. And suppose I get to be merchandise manager? He's a good friend of mine, and he just built a terrific estate on Long Island. And he lived there about two months and sold it, and now he's building another one. He can't enjoy it once it's finished. And I know that's just what I would do. I don't know what the hell I'm working for. Sometimes I sit in my apartment—all alone. And I think of the rent I'm paying. And it's crazy. But then, it's what I always wanted. My own apartment, a car, and plenty of women. And still, goddammit, I'm lonely.

BIFF: *{With enthusiasm}* Listen, why don't you come out West with me?

HAPPY: You and I, heh?

BIFF: Sure, maybe we could buy a ranch. Raise cattle, use our muscles. Men built like we are should be working out in the open.

HAPPY: *{Avidly}* The Loman Brothers, heh?

BIFF: *{With vast affection}* Sure, we'd be known all over the counties!

HAPPY: *{Enthralled}* That's what I dream about, Biff. Sometimes I want to just rip my clothes off in the middle of the store and outbox that goddam merchandise manager. I mean I can outbox, outrun, and outlift anybody in that store, and I have to take orders from those common, petty sons-of-bitches till I can't stand it any more.

BIFF: I'm tellin' you, kid, if you were with me I'd be happy out there.

HAPPY: *{Enthused}* See, Biff, everybody around me is so false that I'm constantly lowering my ideals . . .

BIFF: Baby, together we'd stand up for one another, we'd have someone to trust.

HAPPY: If I were around you—

BIFF: Hap, the trouble is we weren't brought up to grub for money. I don't know how to do it.

HAPPY: Neither can I!

BIFF: Then let's go!

HAPPY: The only thing is—what can you make out there?

BIFF: But look at your friend. Builds an estate and then hasn't the peace of mind to live in it.

HAPPY: Yeah, but when he walks into the store the waves part in front of him. That's fifty-two thousand dollars a year coming through the revolving door, and I got more in my pinky finger than he's got in his head.

BIFF: Yeah, but you just said—

HAPPY: I gotta show some of those pompous, self-important executives over there that Hap Loman can make the grade. I want to walk into the store the way he walks in. Then I'll go with you, Biff. We'll be together yet, I swear. But take those two we had tonight? Now weren't they gorgeous creatures?

BIFF: Yeah, yeah, most gorgeous I've had in years.

HAPPY: I get that any time I want, Biff. Whenever I feel disgusted. The only trouble is, it gets like bowling or something. I just keep knockin' them over and it doesn't mean anything. You still run around a lot?

BIFF: Naa. I'd like to find a girl—steady, somebody with substance.

HAPPY: That's what I long for.

BIFF: Go on! You'd never come home.

HAPPY: I would! Somebody with character, with resistance! Like Mom, y'know? You're gonna call me a bastard when I tell you this. That girl Charlotte I was with tonight is engaged to be married in five weeks. *{He tries on his new hat}*

BIFF: No kiddin'!

HAPPY: Sure, the guy's in line for the vice-presidency of the store. I don't know what gets into me, maybe I just have an overdeveloped sense of competition or something, but I went and ruined her, and furthermore I can't get rid of her. And he's the third executive I've done that to. Isn't that a crummy characteristic? And to top it all, I go to their weddings! *{Indignantly, but laughing}* Like I'm not supposed to take bribes. Manufacturers offer me a hundred-dollar bill now and then to throw an order their way. You know how honest I am, but it's like this girl, see. I hate myself for it. Because I don't want the girl, and, still, I take it and—I love it!

BIFF: Let's go to sleep.

HAPPY: I guess we didn't settle anything, heh?

BIFF: I just got one idea that I think I'm going to try.

HAPPY: What's that?

BIFF: Remember Bill Oliver?

HAPPY: Sure, Oliver is very big now. You want to work for him again?

BIFF: No, but when I quit he said something to me. He put his arm on my shoulder and he said, "Biff, if you ever need anything, come to me."

HAPPY: I remember that. That sounds good.

BIFF: I think I'll go to see him. If I could get ten thousand or even seven or eight thousand dollars I could buy a beautiful ranch.

HAPPY: I bet he'd back you. 'Cause he thought highly of you, Biff. I mean, they all do. You're well liked, Biff. That's why I say to come back here, and we both have the apartment. And I'm tellin' you, Biff, any babe you want . . .

BIFF: No, with a ranch I could do the work I like and still be something. I just wonder though. I wonder if Oliver still thinks I stole that carton of basketballs.

HAPPY: Oh, he probably forgot that long ago. It's almost ten years. You're too sensitive. Anyway, he didn't really fire you.

BIFF: Well, I think he was going to. I think that's why I quit. I was never sure whether he knew or not. I know he thought the world of me, though. I was the only one he'd let lock up the place.

WILLY: *{Below}* You gonna wash the engine, Biff?

HAPPY: Shh! *{Biff looks at Happy, who is gazing down, listening. Willy is mumbling in the parlor}*

HAPPY: You hear that? *{They listen. Willy laughs warmly}*

BIFF: *{Growing angry}* Doesn't he know Mom can hear that?

WILLY: Don't get your sweater dirty, Biff! *{A look of pain crosses Biff's face}*

HAPPY: Isn't that terrible? Don't leave again, will you? You'll find a job here. You gotta stick around. I don't know what to do about him, it's getting embarrassing.

WILLY: What a simonizing job!

BIFF: Mom's hearing that!

WILLY: No kiddin', Biff, you got a date? Wonderful!

HAPPY: Go on to sleep. But talk to him in the morning, will you?

BIFF: *{Reluctantly getting into bed}* With her in the house. Brother!

HAPPY: *{Getting into bed}* I wish you'd have a good talk with him.

{The light on their room begins to fade.}

BIFF: *{To himself, in bed}* That selfish, stupid . . .

HAPPY: Sh . . . Sleep, Biff.

{Their light is out. Well before they have finished speaking, Willy's form is dimly seen below in the darkened kitchen. He opens the refrigerator, searches in there and takes out a bottle of milk. The apartment houses are fading out, and the entire house and surroundings become covered with leaves. Music insinuates itself as the leaves appear.}

WILLY: Just wanna be careful with those girls, Biff, that's all. Don't make any promises. No promises of any kind. Because a girl, y'know, they always believe what you tell 'em, and you're very young, Biff, you're too young to be talking seriously to girls.

{Light rises on the kitchen. Willy, talking, shuts the refrigerator door and comes downstage to the kitchen table. He pours milk into a glass. He is totally immersed in himself, smiling faintly.}

WILLY: Too young entirely, Biff. You want to watch your schooling first. Then when you're all set, there'll be plenty of girls for a boy like you. *{He smiles broadly at a kitchen chair}* That so? The girls pay for you? *{He laughs}* Boy, you must really be makin' a hit.

{Willy is gradually addressing—physically—a point offstage, speaking through the wall of the kitchen, and his voice has been rising in volume to that of a normal conversation.}

WILLY: I been wondering why you polish the car so careful. Ha! Don't leave the hubcaps, boys. Get the chamois to the hubcabs. Happy, use newspapers on the windows, it's the easiest thing. Show him how to do it, Biff! You see, Happy? Pad it up, use it like a pad.

That's it, that's it, good work. You're doin' all right, Hap. *{He pauses, then nods in approbation for a few seconds, then looks upward}* Biff, first thing we gotta do when we get time is clip that big branch over the house. Afraid it's gonna fall in a storm and hit the roof. Tell you what. We get a rope and sling her around, and then we climb up there with a couple of saws and take her down. Soon as you finish the car, boys, I wanna see ya. I got a surprise for you, boys.

BIFF: *{Offstage}* Whatta ya got, Dad?

WILLY: No, you finish first. Never leave a job till you're finished—remember that. *{Looking toward the "big trees"}* Biff, up in Albany I saw a beautiful hammock. I think I'll buy it next trip, and we'll hang it right between those two elms. Wouldn't that be something? Just swingin' there under those branches. Boy, that would be . . .

{Young Biff and Young Happy appear from the direction Willy was addressing. Happy carries rags and a pail of water. Biff, wearing a sweater with a block "S," carries a football.}

BIFF: *{Pointing in the direction of the car offstage}*. How's that, Pop, professional?

WILLY: Terrific. Terrific job, boys. Good work, Biff.

HAPPY: Where's the surprise, Pop?

WILLY: In the back seat of the car.

HAPPY: Boy! *{He runs off}*

BIFF: What is it, Dad? Tell me, what'd you buy?

WILLY: *{Laughing, cuffs him}* Never mind, something I want you to have.

BIFF: *{Turns and starts off}* What is it, Hap?

HAPPY: *{Offstage}* It's a punching bag!

BIFF: Oh, Pop!

WILLY: It's got Gene Tunney's signature on it!

{Happy runs onstage with a punching bag.}

BIFF: Gee, how'd you know we wanted a punching bag?

WILLY: Well, it's the finest thing for the timing.

HAPPY: *{Lies down on his back and pedals with his feet}* I'm losing weight, you notice, Pop?

WILLY: *{To Happy}* Jumping rope is good too.

BIFF: Did you see the new football I got?

WILLY: *{Examining the ball}* Where'd you get a new ball?

BIFF: The coach told me to practice my passing.

WILLY: That so? And he gave you the ball, heh?

BIFF: Well, I borrowed it from the locker room. *{He laughs confidentially}*

WILLY: *{Laughing with him at the theft}* I want you to return that.

HAPPY: I told you he wouldn't like it!

BIFF: *{Angrily}* Well, I'm bringing it back!

WILLY: *{Stopping the incipient argument, to Happy}* Sure he's gotta practice with a regulation ball, doesn't he? *{To Biff}* Coach'll probably congratulate you on your initiative!

BIFF: Oh, he keeps congratulating my initiative all the time, Pop.

WILLY: That's because he likes you. If somebody else took the ball there'd be an uproar. So what's the report, boys, what's the report?

BIFF: Where'd you go this time, Dad? Gee, we were lonesome for you.

WILLY: *{Pleased, puts an arm around each boy and they come down to the apron}* Lonesome, heh?

BIFF: Missed you every minute.

WILLY: Don't say? Tell you a secret, boys. Don't breathe it to a soul. Someday I'll have my own business, and I'll never have to leave home any more.

HAPPY: Like Uncle Charley, heh?

WILLY: Bigger than Uncle Charley! Because Charley is not liked. He's liked, but he's not—well liked.

BIFF: Where'd you go this time, Dad?

WILLY: Well, I got on the road, and I went north to Providence. Met the Mayor.

BIFF: The Mayor of Providence!

WILLY: He was sitting in the hotel lobby.

BIFF: What'd he say?

WILLY: He said, "Morning!" And I said, "You got a fine city here, Mayor." And then he had coffee with me. And then I went to Waterbury. Waterbury is a fine city. Big clock city, the famous Waterbury clock. Sold a nice bill there. And then Boston—Boston is the cradle of the Revolution. A fine city. And a couple of other towns in Mass., and on to Portland and Bangor and straight home!

BIFF: Gee, I'd love to go with you sometime, Dad.

WILLY: Soon as summer comes.

HAPPY: Promise?

WILLY: You and Hap and I, and I'll show you all the towns. America is full of beautiful towns and fine, upstanding people. And they know me, boys, they know me up and down New England. The finest people. And when I bring you fellas up, there'll be open sesame for all of us, 'cause one thing, boys: I have friends. I can park my car in any street in New England, and the cops protect it like their own. This summer, heh?

BIFF and HAPPY: *{Together}* Yeah! You bet!

WILLY: We'll take our bathing suits.

HAPPY: We'll carry your bags, Pop!

WILLY: Oh, won't that be somethin'! Me comin' into the Boston stores with you boys carryin' my bags. What a sensation! *{Biff is prancing around, practicing passing the ball.}*

WILLY: You nervous, Biff, about the game?

BIFF: Not if you're gonna be there.

WILLY: What do they say about you in school, now that they made you captain?

HAPPY: There's a crowd of girls behind him everytime the classes change.

BIFF: *{Taking Willy's hand}* This Saturday, Pop, this Saturday—just for you, I'm going to break through for a touchdown.

HAPPY: You're supposed to pass.

BIFF: I'm takin' one play for Pop. You watch me, Pop, and when I take off my helmet, that means I'm breakin' out. Then you watch me crash through that line!

WILLY: *{Kisses Biff}* Oh, wait'll I tell this in Boston!

{Bernard enters in knickers. He is younger than Biff, earnest and loyal, a worried boy.}

BERNARD: Biff, where are you. You're supposed to study with me today.

WILLY: Hey, looka Bernard. What're you lookin' so anemic about, Bernard?

BERNARD: He's gotta study, Uncle Willy. He's got Regents next week.

HAPPY: *{Tauntingly, spinning Bernard around}* Let's box, Bernard!

BERNARD: Biff! *{He gets away from Happy}* Listen, Biff, I heard Mr. Birnbaum say that if you don't start studyin' math he's gonna flunk you, and you won't graduate! I heard him!

WILLY: You better study with him, Biff. Go ahead now.

BERNARD: I heard him!

BIFF: Oh, Pop, you didn't see my sneakers! *{He holds up a foot for Willy to look at}*

WILLY: Hey, that's a beautiful job of printing!

BERNARD: *{Wiping his glasses}* Just because he printed University of Virginia on his sneakers doesn't mean they've got to graduate him, Uncle Willy!

WILLY: *{Angrily}* What're you talking about? With scholarships to three universities they're gonna flunk him?

BERNARD: But I heard Mr. Birnbaum say—

WILLY: Don't be a pest, Bernard! *{To his boys}* What an anemic!

BERNARD: Okay, I'm waiting for you in my house, Biff.

{Bernard goes off. The Lomans laugh.}

WILLY: Bernard is not well liked, is he?

BIFF: He's liked, but he's not well liked.

HAPPY: That's right, Pop.

WILLY: That's just what I mean. Bernard can get the best marks in school, y'understand, but when he gets out in the business world, y'understand, you are going to be five times ahead of him. That's why I thank Almighty God you're both built like Adonises. Because the man who makes an appearance in the business world, the man who creates personal interest, is the man who gets ahead. Be liked and you will never want. You take me, for instance. I never have to wait in line to see a buyer. "Willy Loman is here!" That's all they have to know, and I go right through.

BIFF: Did you knock them dead, Pop?

WILLY: Knocked 'em cold in Providence, slaughtered 'em in Boston.

HAPPY: *{On his back, pedaling again}* I'm losing weight, you notice, Pop?

{Linda enters, as of old, a ribbon in her hair, carrying a basket of washing.}

LINDA: *{With youthfuy energy}* Hello, dear!

WILLY: Sweetheart!

LINDA: How'd the Chevvy run?

WILLY: Chevrolet, Linda, is the greatest car ever built. *{To the boys}* Since when do you let your mother carry wash up the stairs?

BIFF: Grab hold there, boy!

HAPPY: Where to, Mom?

LINDA: Hang them up on the line. And you better go down to your friends, Biff. The cellar is full of boys. They don't know what to do with themselves.

BIFF: Ah, when Pop comes home they can wait!

WILLY: *{Laughs appreciatively}* You better go down and tell them what to do, Biff.

BIFF: I think I'll have them sweep out the furnace room.

WILLY: Good work, Biff.

BIFF: *{Goes through wall-line of kitchen to doorway at back and calls down}* Fellas! Everybody sweep out the furnace room! I'll be right down!

VOICES: All right! Okay, Biff!

BIFF: George and Sam and Frank, come out back! We're hangin' up the wash! Come on, Hap, on the double! *{He and Happy carry out the basket}*

LINDA: The way they obey him!

WILLY: Well, that's training, the training. I'm tellin' you, I was sellin' thousands and thousands, but I had to come home.

LINDA: Oh, the whole block'll be at that game. Did you sell anything?

WILLY: I did five hundred gross in Providence and seven hundred gross in Boston.

LINDA: No! Wait a minute, I've got a pencil. *{She pulls pencil and paper out of her apron pocket}* That makes your commission . . . Two hundred—my God! Two hundred and twelve dollars!

WILLY: Well, I didn't figure it yet, but . . .

LINDA: How much did you do?

WILLY: Well, I—I did—about a hundred and eighty gross in Providence. Well, no,—it came to—roughly two hundred gross on the whole trip.

LINDA: *{Without hesitation}* Two hundred gross. That's . . . *{She figures}*

WILLY: The trouble was that three of the stores were half closed for inventory in Boston. Otherwise I woulda broke records.

LINDA: Well, it makes seventy dollars and some pennies. That's very good.

WILLY: What do we owe?

LINDA: Well, on the first there's sixteen dollars on the refrigerator—

WILLY: Why sixteen?

LINDA: Well, the fan belt broke, so it was a dollar eighty.

WILLY: But it's brand new .

LINDA: Well, the man said that's the way it is. Till they work themselves in, y'know.

{They move through the wall-line into the kitchen.}

WILLY: I hope we didn't get stuck on that machine.

LINDA: They got the biggest ads of any of them!

WILLY: I know, it's a fine machine. What else?

LINDA: Well, there's nine-sixty for the washing machine. And for the vacuum cleaner there's three and a half due on the fifteenth. Then the roof, you got twenty-one dollars remaining.

WILLY: It don't leak, does it?

LINDA: No, they did a wonderful job. Then you owe Frank for the carburetor.

WILLY: I'm not going to pay that man! That goddam Chevrolet, they ought to prohibit the manufacture of that car!

LINDA: Well, you owe him three and a half. And odds and ends, comes to around a hundred and twenty dollars by the fifteenth.

WILLY: A hundred and twenty dollars! My God, if business don't pick up I don't know what I'm gonna do!

LINDA: Well, next week you'll do better.

WILLY: Oh, I'll knock 'em dead next week. I'll go to Hartford. I'm very well liked in Hartford. You know, the trouble is, Linda, people don't seem to take to me.

(They move onto the forestage.)

LINDA: Oh, don't be foolish.

WILLY: I know it when I walk in. They seem to laugh at me.

LINDA: Why? Why would they laugh at you? Don't talk that way, Willy.

(Willy moves to the edge of the stage. Linda goes into the kitchen and starts to darn stockings.)

WILLY: I don't know the reason for it, but they just pass me by. I'm not noticed.

LINDA: But you're doing wonderful, dear. You're making seventy to a hundred dollars a week.

WILLY: But I gotta be at it ten, twelve hours a day. Other men—I don't know—they do it easier. I don't know why—I can't stop myself—I talk too much. A man oughta come in with a few words. One thing about Charley. He's a man of few words, and they respect him.

LINDA: You don't talk too much, you're just lively.

WILLY: *(Smiling)* Well, I figure, what the hell, life is short, a couple of jokes. *(To himself)* I joke too much! *(The smile goes)*

LINDA: Why? You're—

WILLY: I'm fat. I'm very—foolish to look at, Linda. I didn't tell you, but Christmas time I happened to be calling on F. H. Stewarts, and a salesman I know, as I was going in to see the buyer I heard him say something about—walrus. And I—I cracked him right across the face. I won't take that. I simply will not take that. But they do laugh at me. I know that.

LINDA: Darling . . .

WILLY: I gotta overcome it. I know I gotta overcome it. I'm not dressing to advantage, maybe.

LINDA: Willy, darling, you're the handsomest man in the world—

WILLY: Oh, no, Linda.

LINDA: To me you are. *(Slight pause)* The handsomest.

(From the darkness is heard the laughter of a woman. Willy doesn't turn to it, but it continues through Linda's lines.)

LINDA: And the boys, Willy. Few men are idolized by their children the way you are.

(Music is heard as behind a scrim, to the left of the house. The Woman, dimly seen, is dressing.)

WILLY: *(With great feeling)* You're the best there is, Linda, you're a pal, you know that? On the road—on the road I want to grab you sometimes and just kiss the life outa you.

(The laughter is loud now, and he moves into a brightening area at the left, where The Woman has come from behind the scrim and is standing, putting on her hat, looking into a "mirror" and laughing.)

WILLY: 'Cause I get so lonely—especially when business is bad and there's nobody to talk to. I get the feeling that I'll never sell anything again, that I won't make a living for you, or a business, a business for the boys. *(He talks through The Woman's subsiding laughter; The Woman primps at the "mirror")* There's so much I want to make for—

THE WOMAN: Me? You didn't make me, Willy. I picked you.

WILLY: *(Pleased)* You picked me?

THE WOMAN: *(Who is quite proper-looking, Willy's age)* I did. I've been sitting at that desk watching all the salesmen go by, day in, day out. But you've got such a sense of humor, and we do have such a good time together, don't we?

WILLY: Sure, sure. *{He takes her in his arms}* Why do you have to go now?

THE WOMAN: It's two o'clock . . .

WILLY: No, come on in! *{He pulls her}*

THE WOMAN: . . . my sisters'll be scandalized. When'll you be back?

WILLY: Oh, two weeks about. Will you come up again?

THE WOMAN: Sure thing. You do make me laugh. It's good for me. *{She squeezes his arm, kisses him}* And I think you're a wonderful man.

WILLY: You picked me, heh?

THE WOMAN: Sure. Because you're so sweet. And such a kidder.

WILLY: Well, I'll see you next time I'm in Boston.

THE WOMAN: I'll put you right through to the buyers.

WILLY: *{Slapping her bottom}* Right. Well, bottoms up!

THE WOMAN: *{Slaps him gently and laughs}* You just kill me, Willy. *{He suddenly grabs her and kisses her roughly}* You kill me. And thanks for the stockings. I love a lot of stockings. Well, good night.

WILLY: Good night. And keep your pores open!

THE WOMAN: Oh, Willy!

{The Woman bursts out laughing, and Linda's laughter blends in. The Woman disappears into the dark. Now the area at the kitchen table brightens. Linda is sitting where she was at the kitchen table, but now is mending a pair of her silk stockings.}

LINDA: You are, Willy. The handsomest man. You've got no reason to feel that—

WILLY: *{Coming out of The Woman's dimming area and going over to Linda}* I'll make it all up to you. Linda, I'll—

LINDA: There's nothing to make up, dear. You're doing fine, better than—

WILLY: *{Noticing her mending}* What's that?

LINDA: Just mending my stockings. They're so expensive—

WILLY: *{Angrily, taking them from her}* I won't have you mending stockings in this house! Now throw them out!

{Linda puts the stockings in her pocket.}

BERNARD: *{Entering on the run}* Where is he? If he doesn't study!

WILLY: *{Moving to the forestage, with great agitation}* You'll give him the answers!

BERNARD: I do, but I can't on a Regents! That's a state exam! They're liable to arrest me!

WILLY: Where is he? I'll whip him, I'll whip him!

LINDA: And he'd better give back that football, Willy, it's not nice.

WILLY: Biff? Where is he? Why is he taking everything?

LINDA: He's too rough with the girls, Willy. All of the mothers are afraid of him!

WILLY: I'll whip him!

BERNARD: He's driving the car without a license!

{The Woman's laugh is heard.}

WILLY: Shut up!

LINDA: All the mothers—

WILLY: Shut up!

BERNARD: *{Backing quietly away and out}* Mr. Birnbaum says he's stuck up.

WILLY: Get outa here!

BERNARD: If he doesn't buckle down he'll flunk math! *{He goes off}*

LINDA: He's right, Willy, you've gotta—

WILLY: *{Exploding at her}* There's nothing the matter with him! You want him to be a worm like Bernard! He's got spirit, personality . . .

{As he speaks, Linda, almost in tears, exits into the living-room. Willy is alone in the kitchen, wilting and staring. The leaves are gone. It is night again, and the apartment houses look down from behind.}

WILLY: Loaded with it. Loaded! What

is he stealing? He's giving it back, isn't he? Why is he stealing? What did I tell him? I never in my life told him anything but decent things.

{Happy in pajamas has come down the stairs; Willy suddenly becomes aware of Happy's presence.}

HAPPY: Let's go now, come on.

WILLY: *{Sitting down at the kitchen table}* Huh! Why did she have to wax the floors herself? Everytime she waxes the floors she keels over. She knows that!

HAPPY: Shh! Take it easy. What brought you back tonight?

WILLY: I got an awful scare. Nearly hit a kid in Yonkers. God! Why didn't I go to Alaska with my brother Ben that time! Ben! That man was a genius, that man was success incarnate! What a mistake! He begged me to go.

HAPPY: Well, there's no use in—

WILLY: You guys! There was a man started with the clothes on his back and ended up with diamond mines!

HAPPY: Boy, some day I'd like to know how he did it.

WILLY: What's the mystery? The man knew what he wanted and went out and got it! Walked into a jungle, and comes out, the age of twenty-one, and he's rich! The world is an oyster, but you don't crack it open on a mattress!

HAPPY: Pop, I told you I'm gonna retire you for life.

WILLY: You'll retire me for life on seventy goddam dollars a week? And your women and your car and your apartment, and you'll retire me for life! Christ's sake, I couldn't get past Yonkers today! Where are you guys, where are you? The woods are burning! I can't drive a car!

{Charley has appeared in the doorway. He is a large man, slow of speech, laconic, immovable. In all he says, despite what he says, there is pity, and, now, trepidation. He has a robe over pajamas, slippers on his feet. He enters the kitchen.}

CHARLEY: Everything all right?

HAPPY: Yeah, Charley, everything's...

WILLY: What's the matter?

CHARLEY: I heard some noise. I thought something happened. Can't we do something about the walls? You sneeze in here, and in my house hats blow off.

HAPPY: Let's go to bed, Dad. Come on.

{Charley signals to Happy to go.}

WILLY: You go ahead, I'm not tired at the moment.

HAPPY: *{To Willy}* Take it easy, huh? *{He exits}*

WILLY: What're you doin' up?

CHARLEY: *{Sitting down at the kitchen table opposite Willy}* Couldn't sleep good. I had a heartburn.

WILLY: Well, you don't know how to eat.

CHARLEY: I eat with my mouth.

WILLY: No, you're ignorant. You gotta know about vitamins and things like that.

CHARLEY: Come on, let's shoot. Tire you out a little.

WILLY: *{Hesitantly]* All right. You got cards?

CHARLEY: *{Taking a deck from his pocket}* Yeah, I got them. Someplace. What is it with those vitamins?

WILLY: *{Dealing}* They build up your bones. Chemistry.

CHARLEY: Yeah, but there's no bones in a heartburn.

WILLY: What are you talkin' about? Do you know the first thing about it?

CHARLEY: Don't get insulted.

WILLY: Don't talk about something you don't know anything about.

{They are playing. Pause.}

CHARLEY: What're you doin' home?

WILLY: A little trouble with the car.

CHARLEY: Oh. *{Pause}* I'd like to take a trip to California.

WILLY: Don't say.

CHARLEY: You want a job?

WILLY: I got a job, I told you that. *{After a slight pause}* What the hell are you offering me a job for?

CHARLEY: Don't get insulted.

WILLY: Don't insult me.

CHARLEY: I don't see no sense in it. You don't have to go on this way.

WILLY: I got a good job. *{Slight pause}* What do you keep comin' in here for?

CHARLEY: You want me to go?

WILLY: *{After a pause, withering}* I can't understand it. He's going back to Texas again. What the hell is that?

CHARLEY: Let him go.

WILLY: I got nothin' to give him, Charley, I'm clean, I'm clean.

CHARLEY: He won't starve. None of them starve. Forget about him.

WILLY: Then what have I got to remember?

CHARLEY: You take it too hard. To hell with it. When a deposit bottle is broken you don't get your nickel back.

WILLY: That's easy enough for you to say.

CHARLEY: That ain't easy for me to say.

WILLY: Did you see the ceiling I put up in the living-room?

CHARLEY: Yeah, that's a piece of work. To put up a ceiling is a mystery to me. How do you do it?

WILLY: What's the difference?

CHARLEY: Well, talk about it.

WILLY: You gonna put up a ceiling?

CHARLEY: How could I put up a ceiling?

WILLY: Then what the hell are you bothering me for?

CHARLEY: You're insulted again.

WILLY: A man who can't handle tools is not a man. You're disgusting.

CHARLEY: Don't call me disgusting, Willy.

{Uncle Ben, carrying a valise and an umbrella, enters the forestage from around the right corner of the house. He is a stolid man, in his sixties, with a mustache and an authoritative air. He is utterly certain of his destiny, and there is an aura of far places about him. He enters exactly as Willy speaks.}

WILLY: I'm getting awfully tired, Ben. *{Ben's music is heard. Ben looks around at everything.}*

CHARLEY: Good, keep playing; you'll sleep better. Did you call me Ben? *{Ben looks at his watch.}*

WILLY: That's funny. For a second there you reminded me of my brother Ben.

BEN: I only have a few minutes. *{He strolls, inspecting the place. Willy and Charley continue playing}*

CHARLEY: You never heard from him again, heh? Since that time?

WILLY: Didn't Linda tell you? Couple of weeks ago we got a letter from his wife in Africa. He died.

CHARLEY: That so.

BEN: *{Chuckling}* So this is Brooklyn, eh?

CHARLEY: Maybe you're in for some of his money.

WILLY: Naa, he had seven sons. There's just one opportunity I had with that man . . .

BEN: I must make a train, William. There are several properties I'm looking at in Alaska.

WILLY: Sure, sure! If I'd gone with him to Alaska that time, everything would've been totally different.

CHARLEY: Go on, you'd froze to death up there.

WILLY: What're you talking about?

BEN: Opportunity is tremendous in Alaska, William. Surprised you're not up there.

WILLY: Sure, tremendous.

CHARLEY: Heh?

WILLY: There was the only man I ever met who knew the answers.

CHARLEY: Who?

BEN: How are you all?

WILLY: *{Taking a pot, smiling}* Fine, fine.

CHARLEY: Pretty sharp tonight.

BEN: Is Mother living with you?

WILLY: No, she died a long time ago.

CHARLEY: Who?

BEN: That's too bad. Fine specimen of a lady, Mother.

WILLY: *{To Charley}* Heh?

BEN: I'd hoped to see the old girl.

CHARLEY: Who died?

BEN: Heard anything from Father, have you?

WILLY: *{Unnerved}* What do you mean, who died?

CHARLEY: *{Taking a pot}* What're you talkin' about?

BEN: *{Looking at his watch}* William, it's half-past eight!

WILLY: *{As though to dispel his confusion he angrily stops Charley's hand}* That's my build!

CHARLEY: I put the ace—

WILLY: If you don't know how to play the game I'm not gonna throw my money away on you!

CHARLEY: *{Rising}* It was my ace, for God's sake!

WILLY: I'm through, I'm through!

BEN: When did Mother die?

WILLY: Long ago. Since the beginning you never knew how to play cards.

CHARLEY: *{Picks up the cards and goes to the door}* All right! Next time I'll bring a deck with five aces.

WILLY: I don't play that kind of game!

CHARLEY: *{Turning to him}* You ought to be ashamed of yourself!

WILLY: Yeah?

CHARLEY: Yeah! *{He goes out}*

WILLY: *{Slamming the door after him}* Ignoramus!

BEN: *{As Willy comes toward him through the wall-line of the kitchen}* So you're William.

WILLY: *{Shaking Ben's hand}* Ben! I've been waiting for you so long! What's the answer? How did you do it?

BEN: Oh, there's a story in that.

{Linda enters the forestage, as of old, carrying the wash basket.}

LINDA: Is this Ben?

BEN: *{Gallantly}* How do you do, my dear.

LINDA: Where've you been all these years? Willy's always wondered why you—

WILLY: *{Pulling Ben away from her impatiently}* Where is Dad? Didn't you follow him? How did you get started?

BEN: Well, I don't know how much you remember.

WILLY: Well, I was just a baby, of course, only three or four years old—

BEN: Three years and eleven months.

WILLY: What a memory, Ben!

BEN: I have many enterprises, William, and I have never kept books.

WILLY: I remember I was sitting under the wagon in—was it Nebraska?

BEN: It was South Dakota, and I gave you a bunch of wild flowers.

WILLY: I remember you walking away down some open road.

BEN: *{Laughing}* I was going to find Father in Alaska.

WILLY: Where is he?

BEN: At that age I had a very faulty view of geography, William. I discovered after a few days that I was heading due south, so instead of Alaska, I ended up in Africa.

LINDA: Africa!

WILLY: The Gold Coast!

BEN: Principally diamond mines.

LINDA: Diamond mines!

BEN: Yes, my dear. But I've only a few minutes—

WILLY: No! Boys! Boys! *{Young Biff and Happy appear}* Listen to this. This is your Uncle Ben, a great man! Tell my boys, Ben!

BEN: Why, boys, when I was seventeen I walked into the jungle, and when I was twenty-one I walked out. *{He laughs}* And by God I was rich.

WILLY: *{To the boys}* You see what I been talking about. The greatest things can happen!

BEN: *{Glancing at his watch}* I have an appointment in Ketchikan Tuesday week.

WILLY: No, Ben! Please tell about Dad. I want my boys to hear. I want them to know the kind of stock they spring from. All I remember is a man with a big beard, and I was in Mamma's lap, sitting around a fire, and some kind of high music.

BEN: His flute. He played the flute.

WILLY: Sure, the flute, that's right!

{New music is heard, a high, rollicking tune.}

BEN: Father was a very great and a very wild-hearted man. We would start in Boston, and he'd toss the whole family into the wagon, and then he'd drive the team right across the country; through Ohio, and Indiana, Michigan, Illinois, and all the Western states. And we'd stop in the towns and sell the flutes he'd made on the way. Great inventor, Father. With one gadget he made more in a week than a man like you could make in a lifetime.

WILLY: That's just the way I'm bringing them up, Ben—rugged, well liked, all-around.

BEN: Yeah? *{To Biff}* Hit that, boy—hard as you can. *{He pounds his stomach}*

BIFF: Oh, no, sir!

BEN: *{Taking boxing stance}* Come on, get to me! *{He laughs}*

WILLY: Go to it, Biff! Go ahead, show him!

BIFF: Okay! *{He cocks his fists and starts in}*

LINDA: *{To Willy}* Why must he fight, dear?

BEN: *{Sparring with Biff}* Good boy! Good boy!

WILLY: How's that, Ben, heh?

HAPPY: Give him the left, Biff!

LINDA: Why are you fighting?

BEN: Good boy! *{Suddenly comes in, trips Biff, and stands over him, the point of his umbrella poised over Biff's eye}*

LINDA: Look out, Biff!

BIFF: Gee!

BEN: *{Patting Biff's knee}* Never fight fair with a stranger, boy. You'll never get out of the jungle that way. *{Taking Linda's hand and bowing}* It was an honor and a pleasure to meet you, Linda.

LINDA: *{Withdrawing her hand coldly, frightened}* Have a nice—trip.

BEN: *{To Willy}* And good luck with your—what do you do?

WILLY: Selling.

BEN: Yes. Well . . . *{He raises his hand in farewell to all}*

WILLY: No, Ben, I don't want you to think . . . *{He takes Ben's arm to show him}* It's Brooklyn, I know, but we hunt too.

BEN: Really, now.

WILLY: Oh, sure, there's snakes and rabbits and—that's why I moved out here. Why, Biff can fell any one of these trees in no time! Boys! Go right over to where they're building the apartment house and get some sand. We're gonna rebuild the entire front stoop right now! Watch this, Ben!

BIFF: Yes, sir! On the double, Hap!

HAPPY: *{As he and Biff run off}* I lost weight, Pop, you notice?

{Charley enters in knickers, even before the boys are gone.}

CHARLEY: Listen, if they steal any more from that building the watchman'll put the cops on them!

LINDA: *{To Willy}* Don't let Biff . . . *{Ben laughs lustily.}*

WILLY: You shoulda seen the lumber they brought home last week. At least a dozen six-by-tens worth all kinds a money.

CHARLEY: Listen, if that watchman—

WILLY: I gave them hell, understand. But I got a couple of fearless characters there.

CHARLEY: Willy, the jails are full of fearless characters.

BEN: *{Clapping Willy on the back, with a laugh at Charley}* And the stock exchange, friend!

WILLY: *{Joining in Ben's laughter}* Where are the rest of your pants?

CHARLEY: My wife bought them.

WILLY: Now all you need is a golf club and you can go upstairs and go to sleep. *{To Ben}* Great athlete! Between him and his son Bernard they can't hammer a nail!

BERNARD: *{Rushing in}* The watchman's chasing Biff!

WILLY: *{Angrily}* Shut up! He's not stealing anything!

LINDA: *{Alarmed, hurrying off left}* Where is he? Biff, dear! *{She exits}*

WILLY: *{Moving toward the left, away from Ben}* There's nothing wrong. What's the matter with you?

BEN: Nervy boy. Good!

WILLY: *{Laughing}* Oh, nerves of

iron, that Biff!

CHARLEY: Don't know what it is. My New England man comes back and he's bleedin', they murdered him up there.

WILLY: It's contacts, Charley, I got important contacts!

CHARLEY: *{Sarcastically}* Glad to hear it, Willy. Come in later, we'll shoot a little casino. I'll take some of your Portland money. *{He laughs at Willy and exits}*

WILLY: *{Turning to Ben}* Business is bad, it's murderous. But not for me, of course.

BEN: I'll stop by on my way back to Africa.

WILLY: *{Longingly}* Can't you stay a few days? You're just what I need, Ben, because I—I have a fine position here, but I—well, Dad left when I was such a baby and I never had a chance to talk to him and I still feel—kind of temporary about myself.

BEN: I'll be late for my train.

{They are at opposite ends of the stage.}

WILLY: Ben, my boys—can't we talk? They'd go into the jaws of hell for me, see, but I—

BEN: William, you're being first-rate with your boys. Outstanding, manly chaps.

WILLY: *{Hanging on to his words}* Oh, Ben, that's good to hear! Because sometimes I'm afraid that I'm not teaching them the right kind of—Ben, how should I teach them?

BEN: *{Giving great weight to each word, and with a certain vicious audacity}* William, when I walked into the jungle, I was seventeen. When I walked out I was twenty-one. And, by God, I was rich! *{He goes off into the darkness around the right corner of the house}*

WILLY: . . . was rich! That's just the spirit I want to imbue them with! To walk into a jungle! I was right! I was right! I was right!

{Ben is gone, but Willy is still speaking to him as Linda, in nightgown and robe, enters the kitchen, glances around for Willy, then goes to the door of the house, looks out and sees him. Comes down to his left. He looks at her.}

LINDA: Willy, dear? Willy?

WILLY: I was right!

LINDA: Did you have some cheese? *{He can't answer}* It's very late, darling. Come to bed, heh?

WILLY: *{Looking straight up}* Gotta break your neck to see a star in this yard.

LINDA: You coming in?

WILLY: Whatever happened to that diamond watch fob? Remember? When Ben came from Africa that time? Didn't he give me a watch fob with a diamond in it?

LINDA: You pawned it, dear. Twelve, thirteen years ago. For Biff's radio correspondence course.

WILLY: Gee, that was a beautiful thing. I'll take a walk.

LINDA: But you're in your slippers.

WILLY: *{Starting to go around the house at the left}* I was right! I was! *{Half to Linda, as he goes, shaking his head}* What a man! There was a man worth talking to. I was right!

LINDA: *{Calling after Willy}* But in your slippers, Willy!

{Willy is almost gone when Biff, in his pajamas, comes down the stairs and enters the kitchen.}

BIFF: What is he doing out there?

LINDA: Sh!

BIFF: God Almighty, Mom, how long has he been doing this?

LINDA: Don't, he'll hear you.

BIFF: What the hell is the matter with him?

LINDA: It'll pass by morning.

BIFF: Shouldn't we do anything?

LINDA: Oh, my dear, you should do a lot of things, but there's nothing to do, so go to sleep.

{Happy comes down the stairs and sits on the steps.}

HAPPY: I never heard him so loud, Mom.

LINDA: Well, come around more often; you'll hear him. *{She sits down at the table and mends the lining of Willy's jacket}*

BIFF: Why didn't you ever write me about this, Mom?

LINDA: How would I write to you? For over three months you had no address.

BIFF: I was on the move. But you know I thought of you all the time. You know that, don't you, pal?

LINDA: I know, dear, I know. But he likes to have a letter. Just to know that there's still a possibility for better things.

BIFF: He's not like this all the time, is he?

LINDA: It's when you come home he's always the worst.

BIFF: When I come home?

LINDA: When you write you're coming, he's all smiles, and talks about the future, and—he's just wonderful. And then the closer you seem to come, the more shaky he gets, and then, by the time you get here, he's arguing, and he seems angry at you. I think it's just that maybe he can't bring himself to—open up to you. Why are you so hateful to each other? Why is that?

BIFF: *{Evasively}* I'm not hateful, Mom.

LINDA: But you no sooner come in the door than you're fighting!

BIFF: I don't know why, I mean to change. I'm tryin', Mom, you understand?

LINDA: Are you home to stay now?

BIFF: I don't know. I want to look around, see what's doin'.

LINDA: Biff, you can't look around all your life, can you?

BIFF: I just can't take hold, Mom. I can't take hold of some kind of life.

LINDA: Biff, a man is not a bird, to come and go with the springtime.

BIFF: Your hair . . . *{He touches her hair}* Your hair got so gray.

LINDA: Oh, it's been gray since you were in high school. I just stopped dyeing it, that's all.

BIFF: Dye it again, will ya? I don't want my pal looking old. *{He smiles}*

LINDA: You're such a boy! You think you can go away for a year and . . . You've got to get it into your head now that one day you'll knock on this door and there'll be strange people here—

BIFF: What are you talking about? You're not even sixty, Mom.

LINDA: But what about your father?

BIFF: *{Lamely}* Well, I meant him too.

HAPPY: He admires Pop.

LINDA: Biff, dear, if you don't have any feeling for him, then you can't have any feeling for me.

BIFF: Sure I can, Mom.

LINDA: No. You can't just come to see me, because I love him. *{With a threat, but only a threat of tears}* He's the dearest man in the world to me, and I won't have anyone making him feel unwanted and low and blue. You've got to make up your mind now, darling, there's no leeway any more. Either he's your father and you pay him that respect, or else you're not to come here. I know he's not easy to get along with—nobody knows that better than me—but . . .

WILLY: *{From the left, with a laugh}* Hey, hey, Biffo!

BIFF: *{Starting to go out after Willy}* What the hell is the matter with him? *{Happy stops him}*

LINDA: Don't—don't go near him!

BIFF: Stop making excuses for him! He always, always wiped the floor with you! Never had an ounce of respect for you.

HAPPY: He's always had respect for—

BIFF: What the hell do you know about it?

HAPPY: *{Surlily}* Just don't call him crazy!

BIFF: He's got no character—Charley wouldn't do this. Not in his own house—spewing out that vomit from his mind.

HAPPY: Charley never had to cope with what he's got to.

BIFF: People are worse off than Willy Loman. Believe me, I've seen them!

LINDA: Then make Charley your father, Biff. You can't do that, can you? I don't say he's a great man. Willy Loman never made a lot of money. His name was never in the paper. He's not the finest character that ever lived. But he's a human being, and a terrible thing is happening to him. So attention must be paid. He's not to be allowed to fall into his grave like an old dog. Attention, attention must be finally paid to such a person. You called him crazy—

BIFF: I didn't mean—

LINDA: No, a lot of people think he's lost his—balance. But you don't have to be very smart to know what his trouble is. The man is exhausted.

HAPPY: Sure!

LINDA: A small man can be just as exhausted as a great man. He works for a company thirty-six years this March, opens up unheard-of territories to their trademark, and now in his old age they take his salary away.

HAPPY: *{Indignantly}* I didn't know that, Mom.

LINDA: You never asked, my dear! Now that you get your spending money someplace else you don't trouble your mind with him.

HAPPY: But I gave you money last—

LINDA: Christmas time, fifty dollars! To fix the hot water it cost ninety-seven fifty! For five weeks he's been on straight commission, like a beginner, an unknown!

BIFF: Those ungrateful bastards!

LINDA: Are they any worse than his sons? When he brought them business, when he was young, they were glad to see him. But now his old friends, the old buyers that loved him so and always found some order to hand him in a pinch—they're all dead, retired. He used to be able to make six, seven calls a day in Boston. Now he takes his valises out of the car and puts them back and takes them out again and he's exhausted. Instead of walking he talks now. He drives seven hundred miles, and when he gets there no one knows him any more, no one welcomes him. And what goes through a man's mind, driving seven hundred miles home without having earned a cent? Why shouldn't he talk to himself? Why? When he has to go to Charley and borrow fifty dollars a week and pretend to me that it's his pay? How long can that go on? How long? You see what I'm sitting here and waiting for? And you tell me he has no character? The man who never worked a day but for your benefit? When does he get the medal for that? Is this his reward—to turn around at the age of sixty-three and find his sons, who he loved better than his life, one a philandering bum—

HAPPY: Mom!

LINDA: That's all you are, my baby! *{To Biff}* And you! What happened to the love you had for him? You were such pals! How you used to talk to him on the phone every night! How lonely he was till he could come home to you!

BIFF: All right, Mom. I'll live here in my room, and I'll get a job. I'll keep away from him, that's all.

LINDA: No, Biff. You can't stay here and fight all the time.

BIFF: He threw me out of this house, remember that.

LINDA: Why did he do that? I never knew why.

BIFF: Because I know he's a fake and he doesn't like anybody around who knows!

LINDA: Why a fake? In what way? What do you mean?

BIFF: Just don't lay it all at my feet. It's between me and him—that's all I have to say. I'll chip in from now on. He'll settle for half my pay check. He'll be all right. I'm going to bed. *{He starts for the stairs}*

LINDA: He won't be all right.

BIFF: *{Turning on the stairs, furiously}* I hate this city and I'll stay here. Now what do you want?

LINDA: He's dying Biff.

{Happy turns quickly to her, shocked.}

BIFF: *{After a pause}* Why is he dying?

LINDA: He's been trying to kill himself.

BIFF: *{With great horror}* How?

LINDA: I live from day to day.

BIFF: What're you talking about?

LINDA: Remember I wrote you that he smashed up the car again? In February?

BIFF: Well?

LINDA: The insurance inspector came. He said that they have evidence. That all these accidents in the last year—weren't—weren't—accidents.

HAPPY: How can they tell that? That's a lie.

LINDA: It seems there's a woman . . . *{She takes a breath as}*

BIFF: *{Sharply but contained}* What woman?

LINDA: *{Simultaneously}* . . . and this woman . . .

LINDA: What?

BIFF: Nothing. Go ahead.

LINDA: What did you say?

BIFF: Nothing. I just said what woman?

HAPPY: What about her?

LINDA: Well, it seems she was walking down the road and saw his car. She says that he wasn't driving fast at all, and that he didn't skid. She says he came to that little bridge, and then deliberately smashed into the railing, and it was only the shallowness of the water that saved him.

BIFF: Oh, no, he probably just fell asleep again.

LINDA: I don't think he fell asleep.

BIFF: Why not?

LINDA: Last month . . . *{With great difficulty}* Oh, boys, it's so hard to say a thing like this! He's just a big stupid man to you, but I tell you there's more good in him than in many other people. *{She chokes, wipes her eyes}* I was looking for a fuse. The lights blew out, and I went down the cellar. And behind the fuse box—it happened to fall out—was a length of rubber pipe—just short.

HAPPY: No kidding?

LINDA: There's a little attachment on the end of it. I knew right away. And sure enough, on the bottom of the water heater there's a new little nipple on the gas pipe.

HAPPY: *{Angrily}* That jerk.

BIFF: Did you have it taken off?

LINDA: I'm—I'm ashamed to. How can I mention it to him? Every day I go down and take away that little rubber pipe. But, when he comes home, I put it back where it was. How can I insult him that way? I don't know what to do. I live from day to day, boys. I tell you, I know every thought in his mind. It sounds so old-fashioned and silly, but I tell you he put his whole life into you and you've turned your backs on him. *{She is bent over in the chair, weeping, her face in her hands}* Biff, I swear to God! Biff, his life is in your hands!

HAPPY: *{To Biff}* How do you like that damned fool!

BIFF: *{Kissing her}* All right, pal, all right. It's all settled now. I've been remiss. I know that, Mom. But now I'll stay, and I swear to you, I'll apply myself. *{Kneeling in front of her, in a fever of self-reproach}* It's just—you see, Mom, I don't fit in business. Not that I won't try. I'll try, and I'll make good.

HAPPY: Sure you will. The trouble with you in business was you never tried to please people.

BIFF: I know, I—

HAPPY: Like when you worked for Harrison's. Bob Harrison said you were tops, and then you go and do some damn fool think like whistling whole songs in the elevator like a comedian.

BIFF: *{Against Happy}* So what? I like to whistle sometimes.

HAPPY: You don't raise a guy to a responsible job who whistles in the elevator!

LINDA: Well, don't argue about it now.

HAPPY: Like when you'd go off and swim in the middle of the day instead of taking the line around.

BIFF: *{His resentment rising}* Well, don't you run off? You take off sometimes, don't you? On a nice summer day?

HAPPY: Yeah, but I cover myself!

LINDA: Boys!

HAPPY: If I'm going to take a fade the boss can call any number where I'm supposed to be and they'll swear to him that I just left. I'll tell you something that I hate to say, Biff, but in the business world some of them think you're crazy.

BIFF: *{Angered}* Screw the business world!

HAPPY: All right, screw it! Great, but cover yourself!

LINDA: Hap, Hap!

BIFF: I don't care what they think! They've laughed at Dad for years, and you know why? Because we don't belong in this nuthouse of a city! We should be mixing cement on some open plain, or—or carpenters. A carpenter is allowed to whistle.

{Willy walks in from the entrance of the house, at left.}

WILLY: Even your grandfather was better than a carpenter. *{Pause. They watch him}* You never grew up. Bernard does not whistle in the elevator, I assure you.

BIFF: *{As though to laugh Willy out of it}* Yeah, but you do, Pop.

WILLY: I never in my life whistled in an elevator! And who in the business world thinks I'm crazy?

BIFF: I didn't mean it like that, Pop. Now don't make a whole thing out of it, will ya?

WILLY: Go back to the West! Be a carpenter, a cowboy, enjoy yourself!

LINDA: Willy, he was just saying—

WILLY: I heard what he said!

HAPPY: *{Trying to quiet Willy}* Hey, Pop, come on now . . .

WILLY: *{Continuing over Happy's line}* They laugh at me, heh? Go to Filene's, go to the Hub, go to Slattery's, Boston. Call out the name Willy Loman and see what happens! Big shot!

BIFF: All right, Pop.

WILLY: Big!

BIFF: All right!

WILLY: Why do you always insult me?

BIFF: I didn't say a word. *{To Linda}* Did I say a word?

LINDA: He didn't say anything, Willy.

WILLY: *{Going to the doorway of the living-room}* All right, good night, good night.

LINDA: Willy, dear, he just decided . . .

WILLY: *{To Biff}* If you get tired hanging around tomorrow, paint the ceiling I put up in the living-room.

BIFF: I'm leaving early tomorrow.

HAPPY: He's going to see Bill Oliver, Pop.

WILLY: *{Interestedly}* Oliver? For what?

BIFF: *{With reserve, but trying, trying}* He always said he'd stake me. I'd like to go into business, so maybe I can take him up on it.

LINDA: Isn't that wonderful?

WILLY: Don't interrupt. What's wonderful about it? There's fifty men in the City of New York who'd stake him. *{To Biff}* Sporting goods?

BIFF: I guess so. I know something about it and—

WILLY: He knows something about it! You know sporting goods better than Spalding, for God's sake! How much is he giving you?

BIFF: I don't know, I didn't even see him yet, but—

WILLY: Then what're you talkin' about?

BIFF: *{Getting angry}* Well, all I said was I'm gonna see him, that's all!

WILLY: *{Turning away}* Ah, you're counting your chickens again.

BIFF: *{Starting left for the stairs}* Oh, Jesus, I'm going to sleep!

WILLY: *{Calling after him}* Don't curse in this house!

BIFF: *{Turning}* Since when did you get so clean?

HAPPY: *{Trying to stop them}* Wait a . . .

WILLY: Don't use that language to me! I won't have it!

HAPPY: *{Grabbing Biff, shouts}* Wait a minute! I got an idea. I got a feasible idea. Come here, Biff, let's talk this over now, let's talk some sense here. When I was down in Florida last time, I thought of a great idea to sell sporting goods. It just came back to me. You and I, Biff—we have a line, the Loman Line. We train a couple of weeks, and put on a couple of exhibitions, see?

WILLY: That's an idea!

HAPPY: Wait! We form two basketball teams, see? Two water-polo teams. We play each other. It's a million dollars' worth of publicity. Two brothers, see? The Loman Brothers. Displays in the Royal Palms—all the hotels. And banners over the ring and the basketball court: "Loman Brothers." Baby, we could sell sporting goods!

WILLY: That is a one-million-dollar idea!

LINDA: Marvelous!

BIFF: I'm in great shape as far as that's concerned.

HAPPY: And the beauty of it is, Biff, it wouldn't be like a business. We'd be out playin' ball again . . .

BIFF: *{Enthused}* Yeah, that's . . .

WILLY: Million-dollar . . .

HAPPY: And you wouldn't get fed up with it, Biff. It'd be the family again. There'd be the old honor, and comradeship, and if you wanted to go off for a swim or somethin'—well, you'd do it! Without some smart cooky gettin' up ahead of you!

WILLY: Lick the world! You guys together could absolutely lick the civilized world.

BIFF: I'll see Oliver tomorrow. Hap, if we could work that out . . .

LINDA: Maybe things are beginning to—

WILLY: *{Wildly enthused, to Linda}* Stop interrupting! *{To Biff}* But don't wear sport jacket and slacks when you see Oliver.

BIFF: No, I'll—

WILLY: A business suit, and talk as little as possible, and don't crack any jokes.

BIFF: He did like me. Always liked me.

LINDA: He loved you!

WILLY: *{To Linda}* Will you stop? *{To Biff}* Walk in very serious. You are not applying for a boy's job. Money is to pass. Be quiet, fine, and serious. Everybody likes a kidder, but nobody lends him money.

HAPPY: I'll try to get some myself, Biff. I'm sure I can.

WILLY: I see great things for you kids. I think your troubles are over. But remember, start big and you'll end big. Ask for fifteen. How much you gonna ask for?

BIFF: Gee, I don't know—

WILLY: And don't say "Gee." "Gee" is a boy's word. A man walking in for fifteen thousand dollars does not say "Gee!"

BIFF: Ten, I think, would be top though.

WILLY: Don't be so modest. You always started too low. Walk in with a big laugh. Don't look worried. Start off with a couple of your good stories to lighten things up. It's not what you say, it's how you say it—because personality always wins the day.

LINDA: Oliver always thought the highest of him—

WILLY: Will you let me talk?

BIFF: Don't yell at her, Pop, will ya?

WILLY: *{Angrily}* I was talking, wasn't I?

BIFF: I don't like you yelling at her all the time, and I'm tellin' you, that's all.

WILLY: What're you, takin' over this house?

LINDA: Willy—

WILLY: *{Turning on her}* Don't take his side all the time, goddammit!

BIFF: *{Furiously}* Stop yelling at her!

WILLY: *{Suddenly pulling on his cheek, beaten down, guilt ridden}* Give my best to Bill Oliver—he may remember me. *{He exits through the living-room doorway}*

LINDA: *{Her voice subdued}* What'd you have to start that for? *{Biff turns away}* You see how sweet he was as soon as you talked hopefully? *{She goes over to Biff}* Come up and say good night to him. Don't let him go to bed that way.

HAPPY: Come on, Biff, let's buck him up.

LINDA: Please, dear. Just say good night. It takes so little to make him happy. Come. *{She goes through the living-room doorway, calling upstairs from within the living-room}* Your pajamas are hanging in the bathroom, Willy!

HAPPY: *{Looking toward where Linda went out}* What a woman! They broke the mold when they made her. You know that, Biff?

BIFF: He's off salary. My God, working on commission!

HAPPY: Well, let's face it: he's no hot-shot selling man. Except that sometimes, you have to admit, he's a sweet personality.

BIFF: *{Deciding}* Lend me ten bucks, will ya? I want to buy some new ties.

HAPPY: I'll take you to a place I know. Beautiful stuff. Wear one of my striped shirts tomorrow.

BIFF: She got gray. Mom got awful old. Gee, I'm gonna go in to Oliver tomorrow and knock him for a—

HAPPY: Come on up. Tell that to Dad. Let's give him a whirl. Come on.

BIFF: *{Steamed up}* You know, with ten thousand bucks, boy!

HAPPY: *{As they go into the living-room}* That's the talk, Biff, that's the first time I've heard the old confidence out of you! *{From within the living-room, fading off}* You're gonna live with me, kid, and any babe you want just say the word . . . *{The last lines are hardly heard. They are mounting the stairs to their parents' bedroom}*

LINDA: *{Entering her bedroom and addressing Willy, who is in the bathroom. She is straightening the bed for him}*. Can you do anything about the shower? It drips.

WILLY: *{From the bathroom}* All of a sudden everything falls to pieces! Goddam plumbing, oughta be sued, those people. I hardly finished putting it in and the thing . . . *{His words rumble off}*

LINDA: I'm just wondering if Oliver will remember him. You think he might?

WILLY: *{Coming out of the bathroom in his pajamas}* Remember him? What's the matter with you, you crazy? If he'd've stayed with Oliver he'd be on top by now! Wait'll Oliver gets a look at him. You don't know the average caliber any more. The average young man today—*{He is getting into bed}*—is got a caliber of zero. Greatest thing in the world for him was to bum around. *{Biff and Happy enter the bedroom. Slight pause.}*

WILLY: *{Stops short, looking at Biff}* Glad to hear it, boy.

HAPPY: He wanted to say good night to you, sport.

WILLY: *{To Biff}* Yeah. Knock him dead, boy. What'd you want to tell me?

BIFF: Just take it easy, Pop. Good night. *{He turns to go}*

WILLY: *{Unable to resist}* And if anything falls off the desk while you're talking to him—like a package or something—don't you pick it up. They have office boys for that.

LINDA: I'll make a big breakfast—

WILLY: Will you let me finish? *{To Biff}* Tell him you were in the business in the West. Not farm work.

BIFF: All right, Dad.

LINDA: I think everything—

WILLY: *{Going right through her speech}* And don't undersell yourself. No less than fifteen thousand dollars.

BIFF: *{Unable to bear him}* Okay. Good night, Mom. *{He starts moving}*

WILLY: Because you got a greatness in you, Biff, remember that. You got all kinds of greatness . . . *{He lies back, exhausted. Biff walks out}*

LINDA: *{Calling after Biff}* Sleep well, darling!

HAPPY: I'm gonna get married, Mom. I wanted to tell you.

LINDA: Go to sleep, dear.

HAPPY: *{Going}* I just wanted to tell you.

WILLY: Keep up the good work. *{Happy exits}* God . . . remember that Ebbets Field game? The championship of the city?

LINDA: Just rest. Should I sing to you?

WILLY: Yeah. Sing to me. *{Linda hums a soft lullaby}* When that team came out—he was the tallest, remember?

LINDA: Oh, yes. And in gold.

{Biff enters the darkened kitchen, takes a cigarette, and leaves the house. He comes downstage into a golden pool of light. He smokes, staring at the night.}

WILLY: Like a young god. Hercules—something like that. And the sun, the sun all around him. Remember how he waved to me? Right up from the field, with the representatives of three colleges standing by? And the buyers I brought, and the cheers when he came out—Loman, Loman, Loman! God Almighty, he'll be great yet. A star like that, magnificent, can never really fade away!

{The light on Willy is fading. The gas heater begins to glow through the kitchen wall, near the stairs, a blue flame beneath red coils.}

LINDA: *{Timidly}* Willy dear, what has he got against you?

WILLY: I'm so tired. Don't talk any more.

{Biff slowly returns to the kitchen. He stops, stares toward the heater.}

LINDA: Will you ask Howard to let you work in New York?

WILLY: First thing in the morning. Everything'll be all right.

{Biff reaches behind the heater and draws out a length of rubber tubing. He is horrified and turns his head toward Willy's room, still dimly lit, from which the strains of Linda's desperate but monotonous humming rise.}

WILLY: *{Staring through the window into the moonlight}* Gee, look at the moon moving between the buildings!

{Biff wraps the tubing around his hand and quickly goes up the stairs.}

CURTAIN

Act Two

Music is heard, gay and bright. The curtain rises as the music fades away. Willy, in shirt sleeves, is sitting at the kitchen table, sipping coffee, his hat in his lap. Linda is filling his cup when she can.

WILLY: Wonderful coffee. Meal in itself.

LINDA: Can I make you some eggs?

WILLY: No. Take a breath.

LINDA: You look so rested, dear.

WILLY: I slept like a dead one. First time in months. Imagine, sleeping till ten on a Tuesday morning. Boys left nice and early, heh?

LINDA: They were out of here by eight o'clock.

WILLY: Good work!

LINDA: It was so thrilling to see them leaving together. I can't get over the shaving lotion in this house!

WILLY: *{Smiling}* Mmm—

LINDA: Biff was very changed this morning. His whole attitude seemed to be hopeful. He couldn't wait to get downtown to see Oliver.

WILLY: He's heading for a change. There's no question, there simply are certain men that take longer to get—solidified. How did he dress?

LINDA: His blue suit. He's so handsome in that suit. He could be a—anything in that suit!

(Willy gets up from the table. Linda holds his jacket for him.)

WILLY: There's no question, no question at all. Gee, on the way home tonight I'd like to buy some seeds.

LINDA: *(Laughing)* That'd be wonderful. But not enough sun gets back there. Nothing'll grow any more.

WILLY: You wait, kid, before it's all over we're gonna get a little place out in the country, and I'll raise some vegetables, a couple of chickens . . .

LINDA: You'll do it yet, dear.

(Willy walks out of his jacket. Linda follows him.)

WILLY: And they'll get married, and come for a weekend. I'd build a little guest house. 'Cause I got so many fine tools, all I'd need would be a little lumber and some peace of mind.

LINDA: *(Joyfully)* I sewed the lining . . .

WILLY: I could build two guest houses, so they'd both come. Did he decide how much he's going to ask Oliver for?

LINDA: *(Getting him into the jacket)*. He didn't mention it, but I imagine ten or fifteen thousand. You going to talk to Howard today?

WILLY: Yeah, I'll put it to him straight and simple. He'll just have to take me off the road.

LINDA: And Willy, don't forget to ask for a little advance, because we've got the insurance premium. It's the grace period now.

WILLY: That's a hundred . . . ?

LINDA: A hundred and eight, sixty-eight. Because we're a little short again.

WILLY: Why are we short?

LINDA: Well, you had the motor job on the car . . .

WILLY: That goddamn Studebaker!

LINDA: And you got one more payment on the refrigerator . . .

WILLY: But it just broke again!

LINDA: Well, it's old, dear.

WILLY: I told you we should've bought a well-advertised machine. Charley bought a General Electric and it's twenty years old and it's still good, that son-of-a-bitch.

LINDA: But, Willy—

WILLY: Whoever heard of a Hastings refrigerator. Once in my life I would like to own something outright before it's broken! I'm always in a race with the junkyard! I just finished paying for the car and it's on its last legs. The refrigerator consumes belts like a goddam maniac. They time those things. They time them so when you finally paid for them, they're used up.

LINDA: *(Buttoning up his jacket as he unbottons it)* All told, about two hundred dollars would carry us, dear. But that includes the last payment on the mortgage. After this payment, Willy, the house belongs to us.

WILLY: It's twenty-five years!

LINDA: Biff was nine years old when we bought it.

WILLY: Well, that's a great thing. To weather a twenty-five-year mortgage is—

LINDA: It's an accomplishment.

WILLY: All the cement, the lumber, the reconstruction I put in this house! There ain't a crack to be found in it any more.

LINDA: Well, it served its purpose.

WILLY: What purpose? Some stranger'll come along, move in, and that's that. If only Biff would take this house, and raise a family . . . *(He starts to go)* Good-by, I'm late.

LINDA: *(Suddenly remembering)* Oh, I forgot! You're supposed to meet them for dinner.

WILLY: Me?

LINDA: At Frank's Chop House on Forty-eighth near Sixth Avenue.

WILLY: Is that so! How about you?

LINDA: No, just the three of you. They're gonna blow you to a big meal!

WILLY: Don't say! Who thought of that?

LINDA: Biff came to me this morning, Willy, and he said, "Tell Dad, we want to blow him to a big meal." Be there six o'clock. You and your two boys are going to have dinner.

WILLY: Gee whiz! That's really somethin'. I'm gonna knock Howard for a loop, kid. I'll get an advance, and I'll come home with a New York job. Goddammit, now I'm gonna do it!

LINDA: Oh, that's the spirit, Willy!

WILLY: I will never get behind a wheel the rest of my life!

LINDA: It's changing, Willy, I can feel it changing!

WILLY: Beyond a question. G'by, I'm late. *{He starts to go again}*

LINDA: *{Calling after him as she runs to the kitchen table for a handkerchief}* You got your glasses?

WILLY: *{Feels for them, then comes back in}* Yeah, yeah, got my glasses.

LINDA: *{Giving him the handkerchief}* And a handkerchief.

WILLY: Yeah, handkerchief.

LINDA: And your saccharine?

WILLY: Yeah, my saccharine.

LINDA: Be careful on the subway stairs.

{She kisses him, and a silk stocking is seen hanging from her hand. Willy notices it.}

WILLY: Will you stop mending stockings? At least while I'm in the house. It gets me nervous. I can't tell you. Please.

{Linda hides the stocking in her hand as she follows Willy across the forestage in front of the house.}

LINDA: Remember, Frank's Chop House.

WILLY: *{Passing the apron}* Maybe beets would grow out there.

LINDA: *{Laughing}* But you tried so many times.

WILLY: Yeah. Well, don't work hard today. *{He disappears around the right corner of the house}*

LINDA: Be careful!

{As Willy vanishes, Linda waves to him. Suddenly the phone rings. She runs across the stage and into the kitchen and lifts it.}

LINDA: Hello? Oh, Biff! I'm so glad you called, I just . . . Yes, sure, I just told him. Yes, he'll be there for dinner at six o'clock, I didn't forget. Listen, I was just dying to tell you. You know that little rubber pipe I told you about? That he connected to the gas heater? I finally decided to go down the cellar this morning and take it away and destroy it. But it's gone! Imagine? He took it away himself, it isn't there! *{She listens}* When? Oh, then you took it. Oh nothing, it's just that I'd hoped he'd taken it away himself. Oh, I'm not worried, darling, because this morning he left in such high spirits, it was like the old days! I'm not afraid any more. Did Mr. Oliver see you? . . . Well, you wait there then. And make a nice impression on him, darling. Just don't perspire too much before you see him. And have a nice time with Dad. He may have big news too! . . . That's right, a New York job. And be sweet to him tonight, dear. Be loving to him. Because he's only a little boat looking for a harbor. *{She is trembling with sorrow and joy}* Oh, that's wonderful, Biff, you'll save his life. Thanks, darling. Just put your arm around him when he comes into the restaurant. Give him a smile. That's the boy . . . Good-by, dear. . . . You got your comb? . . . That's fine. Good-by, Biff dear.

{In the middle of her speech, Howard Wagner, thirty-six, wheels in a small typewriter table on which is a wire-recording machine and proceeds to plug it in. This is on the left forestage. Light slowly fades on Linda as it rises on Howard. Howard is intent on threading the machine and only glances over his shoulder as Willy appears.}

WILLY: Pst! Pst!

HOWARD: Hello, Willy, come in.

WILLY: Like to have a little talk with you, Howard.

HOWARD: Sorry to keep you waiting.

I'll be with you in a minute.

WILLY: What's that, Howard?

HOWARD: Didn't you ever see one of these? Wire recorder.

WILLY: Oh. Can we talk a minute?

HOWARD: Records things. Just got delivered yesterday. Been driving me crazy, the most terrific machine I ever saw in my life. I was up all night with it.

WILLY: What do you do with it?

HOWARD: I bought it for dictation, but you can do anything with it. Listen to this. I had it home last night. Listen to what I picked up. The first one is my daughter. Get this. *{He flicks the switch and "Roll Out the Barrel" is heard being whistled}* Listen to that kid whistle.

WILLY: That is lifelike, isn't it?

HOWARD: Seven years old. Get that tone.

WILLY: Ts, ts. Like to ask a little favor of you . . .

{The whistling breaks off, and the voice of Howard's daughter is heard.}

HIS DAUGHTER: "Now you, Daddy."

HOWARD: She's crazy for me! *{Again the same song is whistled}* That's me! Ha! *{He winks}*

WILLY: You're very good!

{The whistling breaks off again. The machine runs silent for a moment.}

HOWARD: Sh! Get this now, this is my son.

HIS SON: "The capital of Alabama is Montgomery; the capital of Arizona is Phoenix; the capital of Arkansas is Little Rock; the capital of California is Sacramento . . ." *{And on, and on}*

HOWARD: *{Holding up five fingers}* Five years old, Willy!

WILLY: He'll make an announcer some day!

HIS SON: *{Continuing}* "The capital . . ."

HOWARD: Get that—alphabetical order! *{The machine breaks off suddenly}* Wait a minute. The maid kicked the plug out.

WILLY: It certainly is a—

HOWARD: Sh, for God's sake!

HIS SON: "It's nine o'clock, Bulova watch time. So I have to go to sleep."

WILLY: That really is—

HOWARD: Wait a minute! The next is my wife.

{They wait.}

HOWARD'S VOICE: "Go on, say something." *{Pause}* "Well, you gonna talk?"

HIS WIFE: "I can't think of anything."

HOWARD'S VOICE: "Well, talk—it's turning."

HIS WIFE: *{Shyly, beaten}* "Hello." *{Silence}* "Oh, Howard, I can't talk into this . . ."

HOWARD: *{Snapping the machine off}* That was my wife.

WILLY: That is a wonderful machine. Can we—

HOWARD: I tell you, Willy, I'm gonna take my camera, and my bandsaw, and all my hobbies, and out they go. This is the most fascinating relaxation I ever found.

WILLY: I think I'll get one myself.

HOWARD: Sure, they're only a hundred and a half. You can't do without it. Supposing you wanna hear Jack Benny, see? But you can't be at home at that hour. So you tell the maid to turn the radio on when Jack Benny comes on, and this automatically goes on with the radio . . .

WILLY: And when you come home you . . .

HOWARD: You can come home twelve o'clock, one o'clock, any time you like, and you get yourself a Coke and sit yourself down, throw the switch, and there's Jack Benny's program in the middle of the night!

WILLY: I'm definitely going to get one. Because lots of time I'm on the road, and I think to myself, what I must be missing on the radio!

HOWARD: Don't you have a radio in the car?

WILLY: Well, yeah, but who ever thinks of turning it on?

HOWARD: Say, aren't you supposed to be in Boston?

WILLY: That's what I want to talk to you about, Howard. You got a minute?

{He draws a chair in from the wing}

HOWARD: What happened? What're you doing here?

WILLY: Well . . .

HOWARD: You didn't crack up again, did you?

WILLY: Oh, no. No . . .

HOWARD: Geez, you had me worried there for a minute. What's the trouble?

WILLY: Well, tell you the truth, Howard. I've come to the decision that I'd rather not travel any more.

HOWARD: Not travel! Well, what'll you do?

WILLY: Remember, Christmas time, when you had the party here? You said you'd try to think of some spot for me here in town.

HOWARD: With us?

WILLY: Well, sure.

HOWARD: Oh, yeah, yeah. I remember. Well, I couldn't think of anything for you, Willy.

WILLY: I tell ya, Howard. The kids are all grown up, y'know. I don't need much any more. If I could take home—well, sixty-five dollars a week, I could swing it.

HOWARD: Yeah, but Willy, see I—

WILLY: I tell ya why, Howard. Speaking frankly and between the two of us, y'know—I'm just a little tired.

HOWARD: Oh, I could understand that, Willy. But you're a road man, Willy, and we do a road business. We've only got a half-dozen salesmen on the floor here.

WILLY: God knows, Howard, I never asked a favor of any man. But I was with the firm when your father used to carry you in here in his arms.

HOWARD: I know that, Willy, but—

WILLY: Your father came to me the day you were born and asked me what I thought of the name of Howard, may he rest in peace.

HOWARD: I appreciate that, Willy, but there just is no spot here for you. If I had a spot I'd slam you right in, but I just don't have a single solitary spot. *{He looks for his lighter. Willy has picked it up and gives it to him. Pause.}*

WILLY: *{With increasing anger}* Howard, all I need to set my table is fifty dollars a week.

HOWARD: But where am I going to put you, kid?

WILLY: Look, it isn't a question of whether I can sell merchandise, is it?

HOWARD: No, but it's a business, kid, and everybody's gotta pull his own weight.

WILLY: *{Desperately}* Just let me tell you a story, Howard—

HOWARD: 'Cause you gotta admit, business is business.

WILLY: *{Angrily}* Business is definitely business, but just listen for a minute. You don't understand this. When I was a boy—eighteen, nineteen—I was already on the road. And there was a question in my mind as to whether selling had a future for me. Because in those days I had a yearning to go to Alaska. See, there were three gold strikes in one month in Alaska, and I felt like going out. Just for the ride, you might say.

HOWARD: *{Barely interested}* Don't say.

WILLY: Oh, yeah, my father lived many years in Alaska. He was an adventurous man. We've got quite a little streak of self-reliance in our family. I thought I'd go out with my older brother and try to locate him, and maybe settle in the North with the old man. And I was almost decided to go, when I met a salesman in the Parker House. His name was Dave Singleman. And he was eighty-four years old, and he'd drummed merchandise in thirty-one states. And old Dave, he'd go up to his room, y'understand, put on his green velvet slippers—I'll never forget—and pick up his phone and call the buyers, and without ever leaving his room, at the age of eighty-four, he made his living. And when I saw that, I realized that selling was the greatest career a man could want. 'Cause what could be more satisfying than to be able to go, at the age of eighty-four, into twenty or thirty different cities, and pick up a phone, and be remembered and loved and helped by so many different people? Do you know? when he died—and by the way he died the death of a salesman, in his green velvet slippers in the smoker of the New York, New Haven and Hartford, going into Boston—when he died, hundreds of salesmen and buyers were at his funeral. Things were sad on a lotta trains for months after that. *{He stands up. Howard has not looked at him}* In those days there was personality in it, Howard. There was respect, and comradeship, and gratitude in it. Today, it's all cut and dried, and there's no chance for bringing friendship to bear—or personality. You see what I mean? They don't know me any more.

HOWARD: *{Moving away, to the right}* That's just the thing, Willy.

WILLY: If I had forty dollars a week —that's all I'd need. Forty dollars, Howard.

HOWARD: Kid, I can't take blood from a stone, I—

WILLY: *{Desperation is on him now}* Howard, the year Al Smith was nominated, your father came to me and—

HOWARD: *{Starting to go off}* I've got to see some people, kid.

WILLY: *{Stopping him}* I'm talking about your father! There were promises made across this desk! You mustn't tell me you've got people to see—I put thirty-four years into this firm, Howard, and now I can't pay my insurance! You can't eat the orange and throw the peel away—a man is not a piece of fruit! *{After a pause}* Now pay attention. Your father—in 1928 I had a big year. I averaged a hundred and seventy dollars a week in commissions.

HOWARD: *{Impatiently}* Now, Willy, you never averaged—

WILLY: *{Banging his hand on the desk}* I averaged a hundred and seventy dollars a week in the year of 1928; and your father came to me—or rather, I was in the office here—it was right over this desk—and he put his hand on my shoulder—

HOWARD: *{Getting up}* You'll have to excuse me, Willy. I gotta see some people. Pull yourself together. *{Going out}* I'll be back in a little while.

{On Howard's exit, the light on his chair grows very bright and strange.}

WILLY: Pull myself together! What the hell did I say to him? My God, I was yelling at him! How could I! *{Willy breaks off, staring at the light, which occupies the chair, animating it. He approaches this chair, standing across the desk from it}* Frank, Frank, don't you remember what you told me that time? How you put your hand on my shoulder ,and Frank . . . *{He leans on the desk and as he speaks the dead man's name he accidentally switches on the recorder, and instantly}*

HOWARD'S SON: ". . . of New York is Albany. The capital of Ohio is Cincinnati, the capital of Rhode Island is . . ." *{The recitation continues}*

WILLY: *{Leaping away with fright, shouting}* Ha! Howard! Howard! Howard!

HOWARD: *{Rushing in}* What happened?

WILLY: *{Pointing at the machine, which continues nasally, childishly, with the capital cities}* Shut it off! Shut it off!

HOWARD: *{Pulling the plug out}* Look, Willy . . .

WILLY: *{Pressing his hands to his eyes}* I gotta get myself some coffee. I'll get some coffee . . .

{Willy starts to walk out. Howard stops him.}

HOWARD: *{Rolling up the cord}* Willy, look . . .

WILLY: I'll go to Boston.

HOWARD: Willy, you can't go to Boston for us.

WILLY: Why can't I go?

HOWARD: I don't want you to represent us. I've been meaning to tell you for a long time now.

WILLY: Howard, are you firing me?

HOWARD: I think you need a good long rest, Willy.

WILLY: Howard—

HOWARD: And when you feel better, come back, and we'll see if we can work something out.

WILLY: But I gotta earn money, Howard. I'm in no position to—

HOWARD: Where are your sons? Why don't your sons give you a hand?

WILLY: They're working on a very big deal.

HOWARD: This is no time for false pride, Willy. You go to your sons and tell them that you're tired. You've got two great boys, haven't you?

WILLY: Oh, no question, no question, but in the meantime . . .

HOWARD: Then that's that, heh?

WILLY: All right, I'll go to Boston tomorrow.

HOWARD: No, no.

WILLY: I can't throw myself on my sons. I'm not a cripple!

HOWARD: Look, kid, I'm busy this morning.

WILLY: *{Grasping Howard's arm}* Howard, you've got to let me go to Boston!

HOWARD: *{Hard, keeping himself under control}* I've got a line of people to see this morning. Sit down, take five minutes, and pull yourself together, and then go home, will ya? I need the office, Willy. *{He starts to go, turns, remembering the recorder, starts to push off the table holding the recorder}* Oh, yeah. Whenever you can this week, stop by and drop off the samples. You'll feel better, Willy, and then come back and we'll talk. Pull yourself together, kid, there's people outside.

{Howard exits, pushing the table off left. Willy stares into space, exhausted. Now the music is heard—Ben's music—first distantly, then closer, closer. As Willy speaks, Ben enters from the right. He carries valise and umbrella.}

WILLY: Oh, Ben, how did you do it? What is the answer? Did you wind up the Alaska deal already?

BEN: Doesn't take much time if you know what you're doing. Just a short business trip. Boarding ship in an hour. Wanted to say good-by.

WILLY: Ben, I've got to talk to you.

BEN: *{Glancing at his watch}* Haven't the time, William.

WILLY: *{Crossing the apron to Ben}* Ben, nothing's working out. I don't know what to do.

BEN: Now, look here, William. I've bought timberland in Alaska and I need a man to look after things for me.

WILLY: God, timberland! Me and my boys in those grand outdoors!

BEN: You've a new continent at your doorstep, William. Get out of these cities, they're full of talk and time payments and courts of law. Screw on your fists and you can fight for a fortune up there.

WILLY: Yes, yes! Linda, Linda!

{Linda enters, as of old, with the wash.}

LINDA: Oh, you're back?

BEN: I haven't much time.

WILLY: No, wait! Linda, he's got a proposition for me in Alaska.

LINDA: But you've got— *{To Ben}* He's got a beautiful job here.

WILLY: But in Alaska, kid, I could—

LINDA: You're doing well enough, Willy!

BEN: *{To Linda}* Enough for what, dear?

LINDA: *{Frightened of Ben and angry at him}* Don't say those things to him! Enough to be happy right here, right now. *{To Willy, while Ben laughs}* Why must everybody conquer the world? You're well liked, and the boys love you, and someday— *{To Ben}* —why, old man Wagner told him just the other day that if he keeps it up he'll be a member of the firm, didn't he, Willy?

WILLY: Sure, sure. I am building something with this firm, Ben, and if a man is building something he must be on the right track, mustn't he?

BEN: What are you building? Lay your hand on it. Where is it?

WILLY: *{Hesitantly}* That's true, Linda, there's nothing.

LINDA: Why? *{To Ben}* There's a man eighty-four years old—

WILLY: That's right, Ben, that's right. When I look at that man I say, what is there to worry about?

BEN: Bah!

WILLY: It's true, Ben. All he has to do is go into any city, pick up the phone, and he's making his living—and you know why?

BEN: *{Picking up his valise}* I've got to go.

WILLY: *{Holding Ben back}* Look at this boy!

{Biff, in his high school sweater, enters carrying suitcase. Happy carries Biff's shoulder guards, gold helmet, and football pants.}

WILLY: Without a penny to his name, three great universities are begging for him, and from there the sky's the limit, because it's not what you do, Ben. It's who you know and the smile on your face! It's contacts, Ben, contacts! The whole wealth of Alaska passes over the lunch table at the Commodore Hotel, and that's the wonder, the wonder of this country, that a man can end with diamonds here on the basis of being liked! *{He turns to Biff}* And that's why when you get out on that field today it's important. Because thousands of people will be rooting for you and loving you. *{To Ben, who has again begun to leave}* And Ben! when he walks into a business office his name will sound out like a bell and all the doors will open to him! I've seen it, Ben, I've seen it a thousand times! You can't feel it with your hand like timber, but it's there!

BEN: Good-by, William.

WILLY: Ben, am I right? Don't you think I'm right? I value your advice.

BEN: There's a new continent at your doorstep, William. You could walk out rich. Rich! *{He is gone}*

WILLY: We'll do it here, Ben! You hear me? We're gonna do it here!

{Young Bernard rushes in. The gay music of the Boys is heard.}

BERNARD: Oh, gee, I was afraid you left already!

WILLY: Why? What time is it?

BERNARD: It's half-past one!

WILLY: Well, come on, everybody! Ebbets Field next stop! Where's the pennants? *{He rushes through the wall-line of the kitchen and out into the living-room}*

LINDA: *{To Biff}* Did you pack fresh underwear?

BIFF: *{Who has been limbering up}* I want to go!

BERNARD: Biff, I'm carrying your helmet, ain't I?

HAPPY: No, I'm carrying the helmet.

BERNARD: Oh, Biff, you promised me.

HAPPY: I'm carrying the helmet.

BERNARD: How am I going to get in the locker room?

LINDA: Let him carry the shoulder guards. *{She puts her coat and hat on in the kitchen}*

BERNARD: Can I, Biff? 'Cause I told everybody I'm going to be in the locker room.

HAPPY: In Ebbets Field it's the clubhouse.

BFRNARD: I meant the clubhouse. Biff!

HAPPY: Biff!

BIFF: *{Grandly, after a slight pause}* Let him carry the shoulder guards.

HAPPY: *{As he gives Bernard the shoulder guards}* Stay close to us now.

{Willy rushes in with the pennants.}

WILLY: *{Handing them out}* Everybody wave when Biff comes out on the field. *{Happy and Bernard run off}* You set now, boy?

{The music has died away.}

BIFF: Ready to go, Pop. Every muscle is ready.

WILLY: *{At the edge of the apron}* You realize what this means?

BIFF: That's right, Pop.

WILLY: *{Feeling Biff's muscles}*

You're comin' home this afternoon captain of the All-Scholastic Championship Team of the City of New York.

BIFF: I got it, Pop. And remember, pal, when I take off my helmet, that touchdown is for you.

WILLY: Let's go! *{He is starting out, with his arm around Biff, when Charley enters, as of old, in knickers}* I got no room for you, Charley.

CHARLEY: Room? For what?

WILLY: In the car.

CHARLEY: You goin' for a ride? I wanted to shoot some casino.

WILLY: *{Furiously}* Casino! *{Incredulously}* Don't you realize what today is?

LINDA: Oh, he knows, Willy. He's just kidding you.

WILLY: That's nothing to kid about!

CHARLEY: No, Linda, what's goin' on?

LINDA: He's playing in Ebbets Field.

CHARLEY: Baseball in this weather?

WILLY: Don't talk to him. Come on, come on! *{He is pushing them out}*

CHARLEY: Wait a minute, didn't you hear the news?

WILLY: What?

CHARLEY: Don't you listen to the radio? Ebbets Field just blew up.

WILLY: You go to hell! *{Charley laughs. Pushing them out}* Come on, come on! We're late.

CHARLEY: *{As they go}* Knock a homer, Biff, knock a homer!

WILLY: *{The last to leave, turning to Charley}* I don't think that was funny, Charley. This is the greatest day of his life.

CHARLEY: Willy, when are you going to grow up?

WILLY: Yeah, heh? When this game is over, Charley, you'll be laughing out of the other side of your face. They'll be calling him another Red Grange. Twenty-five thousand a year.

CHARLEY: *{Kidding}* Is that so?

WILLY: Yeah, that's so.

CHARLEY: Well, then, I'm sorry, Willy. But tell me something.

WILLY: What?

CHARLEY: Who is Red Grange?

WILLY: Put up your hands. Goddam you, put up your hands!

{Charley, chuckling, shakes his head and walks away, around the left corner of the stage. Willy follows him. The music rises to a mocking frenzy.}

WILLY: Who the hell do you think you are, better than everybody else? You don't know everything, you big, ignorant, stupid . . . Put up your hands! *{Light rises, on the right side of the forestage, on a small table in the reception room of Charley's office. Traffic sounds are heard. Bernard, now mature, sits whistling to himself. A pair of tennis rackets and an overnight bag are on the floor beside him.}*

WILLY: *{Offstage}* What are you walking away for? Don't walk away! If you're going to say something say it to my face! I know you laugh at me behind my back. You'll laugh out of the other side of your goddam face after this game. Touchdown! Touchdown! Eighty thousand people! Touchdown! Right between the goal posts.

{Bernard is a quiet, earnest, but self-assured young man. Willy's voice is coming from right upstage now. Bernard lowers his feet off the table and listens. Jenny, his father's secretary, enters.}

JENNY: *{Distressed}* Say, Bernard, will you go out in the hall?

BERNARD: What is that noise? Who is it?

JENNY: Mr. Loman. He just got off the elevator.

BERNARD: *{Getting up}* Who's he arguing with?

JENNY: Nobody. There's nobody with him. I can't deal with him any more, and your father gets all upset everytime he comes. I've got a lot of typing to do, and your father's waiting to sign it. Will you see him?

WILLY: *{Entering}* Touchdown! Touch— *{He sees Jenny}* Jenny, Jenny, good to see you. How're ya? Workin'? Or still honest?

JENNY: Fine. How've you been feeling?

WILLY: Not much any more, Jenny.

Ha, ha! *{He is surprised to see the rackets}*

BERNARD: Hello, Uncle Willy.

WILLY: *{Almost shocked}* Bernard! Well, look who's here! *{He comes quickly, guiltily, to Bernard and warmly shakes his hand}*

BERNARD: How are you? Good to see you.

WILLY: What are you doing here?

BERNARD: Oh, just stopped by to see Pop. Get off my feet till my train leaves. I'm going to Washington in a few minutes.

WILLY: Is he in?

BERNARD: Yes, he's in his office with the accountant. Sit down.

WILLY: *{Sitting down}* What're you going to do in Washington?

BERNARD: Oh, just a case I've got there, Willy.

WILLY: That so? *{Indicating the rackets}* You going to play tennis there?

BERNARD: I'm staying with a friend who's got a court.

WILLY: Don't say. His own tennis court. Must be fine people, I bet.

BERNARD: They are, very nice. Dad tells me Biff's in town.

WILLY: *{With a big smile}* Yeah, Biff's in. Working on a very big deal, Bernard.

BERNARD: What's Biff doing?

WILLY: Well, he's been doing very big things in the West. But he decided to establish himself here. Very big. We're having dinner. Did I hear your wife had a boy?

BERNARD: That's right. Our second.

WILLY: Two boys! What do you know.

BERNARD: What kind of a deal has Biff got?

WILLY: Well, Bill Oliver—very big sporting-goods man—he wants Biff very badly. Called him in from the West. Long distance, carte blanche, special deliveries. Your friends have their own private tennis court?

BERNARD: You still with the old firm, Willy?

WILLY: *{After a pause}* I'm—I'm overjoyed to see how you made the grade, Bernard, overjoyed. It's an encouraging thing to see a young man really—really— Looks very good for Biff—very— *{He breaks off, then}* Bernard— *{He is so full of emotion, he breaks off again}*

BERNARD: What is it, Willy?

WILLY: *{Small and alone}* What—what's the secret?

BERNARD: What secret?

WILLY: How—how did you? Why didn't he ever catch on?

BERNARD: I wouldn't know that, Willy.

WILLY: *{Confidentially, desperately}* You were his friend, his boyhood friend. There's something I don't understand about it. His life ended after that Ebbets Field game. From the age of seventeen nothing good ever happened to him.

BERNARD: He never trained himself for anything.

WILLY: But he did, he did. After high school he took so many correspondence courses. Radio mechanics; television; God knows what, and never made the slightest mark.

BERNARD: *{Taking off his glasses}* Willy, do you want to talk candidly?

WILLY: *{Rising, faces Bernard}* I regard you as a very brilliant man, Bernard. I value your advice.

BERNARD: Oh, the hell with the advice, Willy. I couldn't advise you. There's just one thing I've always wanted to ask you. When he was supposed to graduate, and the math teacher flunked him—

WILLY: Oh, that son-of-a-bitch ruined his life.

BERNARD: Yeah, but, Willy, all he had to do was go to summer school and make up the subject.

WILLY: That's right, that's right.

BERNARD: Did you tell him not to go to summer school?

WILLY: Me? I begged him to go. I ordered him to go!

BERNARD: Then why wouldn't he go?

WILLY: Why? Why! Bernard, that question has been trailing me like a ghost for the last fifteen years. He flunked the subject, and laid down and died like a hammer hit him!

BERNARD: Take it easy, kid.

WILLY: Let me talk to you—I got nobody to talk to. Bernard, Bernard, was it my fault? Y'see? It keeps going around in my mind, maybe I did something to him. I got nothing to give him.

BERNARD: Don't take it so hard.

WILLY: Why did he lay down? What is the story there? You were his friend!

BERNARD: Willy, I remember, it was June, and our grades came out. And he'd flunked math.

WILLY: That son-of-a-bitch!

BERNARD: No, it wasn't right then. Biff just got very angry, I remember, and he was ready to enroll in summer school.

WILLY: *{Surprised}* He was?

BERNARD: He wasn't beaten by it at all. But then, Willy, he disappeared from the block for almost a month. And I got the idea that he'd gone up to New England to see you. Did he have a talk with you then?

{Willy stares in silence.}

BERNARD: Willy?

WILLY: *{With a strong edge of resentment in his voice}* Yeah, he came to Boston. What about it?

BERNARD: Well, just that when he came back—I'll never forget this, it always mystifies me. Because I'd thought so well of Biff, even though he'd always taken advantage of me. I loved him, Willy, y'know? And he came back after that month and took his sneakers—remember those sneakers with "University of Virginia" printed on them? He was so proud of those, wore them every day. And he took them down in the cellar, and burned them up in the furnace. We had a fist fight. It lasted at least half an hour. Just the two of us, punching each other down the cellar, and crying right through it. I've often thought of how strange it was that I knew he'd given up his life. What happened in Boston, Willy?

{Willy looks at him as at an intruder.}

BERNARD: I just bring it up because you asked me.

WILLY: *{Angrily}* Nothing. What do you mean, "What happened?" What's that got to do with anything?

BERNARD: Well, don't get sore.

WILLY: What are you trying to do, blame it on me? If a boy lays down is that my fault?

BERNARD: Now, Willy, don't get—

WILLY: Well, don't—don't talk to me that way! What does that mean, "What happened?"

{Charley enters. He is in his vest, and he carries a bottle of bourbon.}

CHARLEY: Hey, you're going to miss the train. *{He waves the bottle}*

BERNARD: Yeah, I'm going. *{He takes the bottle}* Thanks, Pop. *{He picks up his rackets and bag}* Good-by, Willy, and don't worry about it. You know, "If at first you don't succeed . . ."

WILLY: Yes, I believe in that.

BERNARD: But sometimes, Willy, it's better for a man just to walk away.

WILLY: Walk away?

BERNARD: That's right.

WILLY: But if you can't walk away?

BERNARD: *{After a slight pause}* I guess that's when it's rough. *{Extending his hand}* Good-by, Willy.

WILLY: *{Shaking Bernard's hand}* Good-by, boy.

CHARLEY: *{An arm on Bernard's shoulder}* How do you like this kid? Gonna argue a case in front of the Supreme Court.

BERNARD: *{Protesting}* Pop!

WILLY: *{Genuinely shocked, pained and happy}* No! The Supreme Court!

BERNARD: I gotta run. 'By, Dad!

CHARLEY. Knock 'em dead, Bernard!

{Bernard goes off.}

WILLY: *{As Charley takes out his wallet}* The Supreme Court! And he didn't even mention it!

CHARLEY: *{Counting out money on the desk}* He don't have to—he's gonna do it.

WILLY: And you never told him what to do, did you? You never took any interest in him.

CHARLEY: My salvation is that I never took any interest in anything. There's some money—fifty dollars. I got an accountant inside.

WILLY: Charley, look . . . *{With difficulty}* I got my insurance to pay. If you can manage it—I need a hundred and ten dollars.

{Charley doesn't reply for a moment; merely stops moving.}

WILLY: I'd draw it from my bank, but Linda would know, and I . . .

CHARLEY: Sit down, Willy.

WILLY: *{Moving toward the chair}* I'm keeping an account of everything, remember. I'll pay every penny back. *{He sits}*

CHARLEY: Now listen to me, Willy.

WILLY: I want you to know I appreciate . . .

CHARLEY: *{Sitting down on the table}* Willy, what're you doin'? What the hell is goin' on in your head?

WILLY: Why? I'm simply . . .

CHARLEY: I offered you a job. You can make fifty dollars a week. And I won't send you on the road.

WILLY: I've got a job.

CHARLEY: Without pay? What kind of a job is a job without pay? *{He rises}* Now, look, kid, enough is enough. I'm no genius but I know when I'm being insulted.

WILLY: Insulted!

CHARLEY: Why don't you want to work for me?

WILLY: What's the matter with you? I've got a job.

CHARLEY: Then what're you walkin' in here every week for?

WILLY: *{Getting up}* Well, if you don't want me to walk in here—

CHARLEY: I am offering you a job.

WILLY: I don't want your goddam job!

CHARLEY: When the hell are you going to grow up?

WILLY: *{Furiously}* You big ignoramus, if you say that to me again I'll rap you one! I don't care how big you are! *{He's ready to fight}*

{Pause.}

CHARLEY: *{Kindly, going to him}* How much do you need, Willy?

WILLY: Charley, I'm strapped, I'm strapped. I don't know what to do. I was just fired.

CHARLEY: Howard fired you?

WILLY: That snotnose. Imagine that? I named him. I named him Howard.

CHARLEY: Willy, when're you gonna realize that them things don't mean anything? You named him Howard, but you can't sell that. The only thing you got in this world is what you can sell. And the funny thing is that you're a salesman, and you don't know that.

WILLY: I've always tried to think otherwise, I guess. I always felt that if a man was impressive, and well liked, that nothing—

CHARLEY: Why must everybody like you? Who liked J. P. Morgan? Was he impressive? In a Turkish bath he'd look like a butcher. But with his pockets on he was very well liked. Now listen, Willy, I know you don't like me, and nobody can say I'm in love with you, but I'll give you a job because—just for the hell of it, put it that way. Now what do you say?

WILLY: I—I just can't work for you, Charley.

CHARLEY: What're you, jealous of me?

WILLY: I can't work for you, that's all, don't ask me why.

CHARLEY: *{Angered, takes out more bills}* You been jealous of me all your life, you damned fool! Here, pay your insurance. *{He puts the money in Willy's hand}*

WILLY: I'm keeping strict accounts.

CHARLEY: I've got some work to do. Take care of yourself. And pay your insurance.

WILLY: *{Moving to the right}* Funny, y'know? After all the highways, and the trains, and the appointments, and the years, you end up worth more dead than alive.

CHARLEY: Willy, nobody's worth nothin' dead. *{After a slight pause}* Did you hear what I said?

{Willy stands still, dreaming.}

CHARLEY: Willy!

WILLY: Apologize to Bernard for me when you see him. I didn't mean to argue with him. He's a fine boy. They're all fine boys, and they'll end up big—all of them. Someday they'll all play tennis together. Wish me luck, Charley. He saw Bill Oliver today.

CHARLEY: Good luck.

WILLY: *{On the verge of tears}* Charley, you're the only friend I got. Isn't that a remarkable thing? *{He goes out}*

CHARLEY: Jesus!

{Charley stares after him a moment and follows. All light blacks out. Suddenly raucous music is heard, and a red glow rises behind the screen at right. Stanley, a young waiter, appears, carrying a table, followed by Happy, who is carrying two chairs}

STANLEY: *{Putting the table down}* That's all right, Mr. Loman. I can handle it myself. *{He turns and takes the chairs from Happy and places them at the table}*

HAPPY: *{Glancing around}* Oh, this is better.

STANLEY: Sure, in the front there you're in the middle of all kinds of noise. Whenever you got a party, Mr. Loman, you just tell me and I'll put you back here. Y'know, there's a lotta people they don't like it private, because when they go out they like to see a lotta action around them because they're sick and tired to stay in the house by theirself. But I know you, you ain't from Hackensack. You know what I mean?

HAPPY: *{Sitting down}* So how's it coming, Stanley?

STANLEY: Ah, it's a dog's life. I only wish during the war they'd a took me in the Army. I coulda been dead by now.

HAPPY: My brother's back, Stanley.

STANLEY: Oh, he come back, heh? From the Far West.

HAPPY: Yeah, big cattle man, my brother. so treat him right. And my father's coming too.

STANLEY: Oh, your father too!

HAPPY: You got a couple of nice lobsters?

STANLEY: Hundred per cent, big.

HAPPY: I want them with the claws.

STANLEY: Don't worry, I don't give you no mice. *{Happy laughs}* How about some wine? It'll put a head on the meal.

HAPPY: No. You remember, Stanley, that recipe I brought you from overseas? With the champagne in it?

STANLEY: Oh, yeah, sure. I still got it tacked up yet in the kitchen. But that'll have to cost a buck apiece anyways.

HAPPY: That's all right.

STANLEY: What'd you, hit a number or somethin'?

HAPPY: No, it's a little celebration. My brother is—I think he pulled off a big deal today. I think we're going into business together.

STANLEY: Great! That's the best for you. Because a family business, you know what I mean?—that's the best.

HAPPY: That's what I think.

STANLEY: 'Cause what's the difference? Somebody steals? It's in the family. Know what I mean? *{Sotto voce}* Like this bartender here. The boss is goin' crazy what kinda leak he's got in the cash register. You put it in but it don't come out.

HAPPY: *{Raising his head}* Sh!

STANLEY: What?

HAPPY: You notice I wasn't lookin' right or left, was I?

STANLEY: No.

HAPPY: And my eyes are closed.

STANLEY: So what's the—?

HAPPY: Strudel's comin'.

STANLEY: *{Catching on, looks around}* Ah, no, there's no—

{He breaks off as a furred, lavishly dressed girl enters and sits at the next table. Both follow her with their eyes.}

STANLEY: Geez, how'd ya know?

HAPPY: I got radar or something. *{Staring directly at her profile}* Oooooooo . . . Stanley.

STANLEY: I think that's for you, Mr. Loman.

HAPPY: Look at that mouth. Oh,

God. And the binoculars.

STANLEY: Geez, you got a life, Mr. Loman.

HAPPY: Wait on her.

STANLEY: *(Going to the girl's table)* Would you like a menu, ma'am?

GIRL: I'm expecting someone, but I'd like a—

HAPPY: Why don't you bring her—excuse me, miss, do you mind? I sell champagne, and I'd like you to try my brand. Bring her a champagne, Stanley.

GIRL: That's awfully nice of you.

HAPPY: Don't mention it. It's all company money. *(He laughs)*

GIRL: That's a charming product to be selling, isn't it?

HAPPY: Oh, gets to be like everything else. Selling is selling y'know.

GIRL: I suppose.

HAPPY: You don't happen to sell, do you?

GIRL: No, I don't sell.

HAPPY: Would you object to a compliment from a stranger? You ought to be on a magazine cover.

GIRL: *(Looking at him a little archly)* I have been.

(Stanley comes in with a glass of champagne.)

HAPPY: What'd I say before, Stanley? You see? She's a cover girl.

STANLEY: Oh, I could see, I could see.

HAPPY: *(To the Girl)* What magazine?

GIRL: Oh, a lot of them. *(She takes the drink)* Thank you.

HAPPY: You know what they say in France, don't you? "Champagne is the drink of the complexion"—Hya, Biff!

(Biff has entered and sits with Happy.)

BIFF: Hello, kid. Sorry I'm late.

HAPPY: I just got here. Uh, Miss—?

GIRL: Forsythe.

HAPPY: Miss Forsythe, this is my brother.

BIFF: Is Dad here?

HAPPY: His name is Biff. You might've heard of him. Great football player.

GIRL: Really? What team?

HAPPY: Are you familiar with football?

GIRL: No, I'm afraid I'm not.

HAPPY: Biff is a quarterback with the New York Giants.

GIRL: Well, that is nice, isn't it? *(She drinks)*

HAPPY: Good health.

GIRL: I'm happy to meet you.

HAPPY: That's my name. Hap. It's really Harold, but at West Point they called me Happy.

GIRL: *(Now really impressed)* Oh, I see. How do you do? *(She turns her profile)*

BIFF: Isn't Dad coming?

HAPPY: You want her?

BIFF: Oh, I could never make that.

HAPPY: I remember the time that idea would never come into your head. Where's the old confidence, Biff?

BIFF: I just saw Oliver—

HAPPY: Wait a minute. I've got to see that old confidence again. Do you want her? She's on call.

BIFF: Oh, no. *(He turns to look at the Girl)*

HAPPY: I'm telling you. Watch this. *(Turning to the girl)* Honey? *(She turns to him)* Are you busy?

GIRL: Well, I am . . . but I could make a phone call.

HAPPY: Do that, will you, honey? And see if you can get a friend. We'll be here for a while. Biff is one of the greatest football players in the country.

GIRL: *(Standing up)* Well, I'm certainly happy to meet you.

HAPPY: Come back soon.

GIRL: I'll try.

HAPPY: Don't try, honey, try hard.

(The Girl exits. Stanley follows, shaking his head in bewildered admiration.)

HAPPY: Isn't that a shame now? A beautiful girl like that? That's why I can't get married. There's not a good woman in a thousand. New York is loaded with them, kid!

BIFF: Hap, look—

HAPPY: I told you she was on call!

BIFF: *(Strangely unnerved)* Cut it out, will ya? I want to say something to you.

HAPPY: Did you see Oliver?

BIFF: I saw him all right. Now look, I want to tell Dad a couple of things and I want you to help me.

HAPPY: What? Is he going to back you?

BIFF: Are you crazy? You're out of your goddam head, you know that?

HAPPY: Why? What happened?

BIFF: *{Breathlessly}* I did a terrible thing today, Hap. It's been the strangest day I ever went through. I'm all numb, I swear.

HAPPY: You mean he wouldn't see you?

BIFF: Well, I waited six hours for him, see? All day. Kept sending my name in. Even tried to date his secretary so she'd get me to him, but no soap.

HAPPY: Because you're not showin' the old confidence, Biff. He remembered you, didn't he?

BIFF: *{Stopping Happy with a gesture}* Finally, about five o'clock, he comes out. Didn't remember who I was or anything. I felt like such an idiot, Hap.

HAPPY: Did you tell him my Florida idea?

BIFF: He walked away. I saw him for one minute. I got so mad I could've torn the walls down! How the hell did I ever get the idea I was a salesman there? I even believed myself that I'd been a salesman for him! And then he gave me one look and—I realized what a ridiculous lie my whole life has been! We've been talking in a dream for fifteen years. I was a shipping clerk.

HAPPY: What'd you do?

BIFF: *{With great tension and wonder}* Well, he left, see. And the secretary went out. I was all alone in the waiting-room. I don't know what came over me, Hap. The next thing I know I'm in his office—paneled walls, everything. I can't explain it. I—Hap, I took his fountain pen.

HAPPY: Geez, did he catch you?

BIFF: I ran out. I ran down all eleven flights. I ran and ran and ran.

HAPPY: That was an awful dumb—what'd you do that for?

BIFF: *{Agonized}* I don't know, I just—wanted to take something, I don't know. You gotta help me, Hap, I'm gonna tell Pop.

HAPPY: You crazy? What for?

BIFF: Hap, he's got to understand that I'm not the man somebody lends that kind of money to. He thinks I've been spiting him all these years and it's eating him up.

HAPPY: That's just it. You tell him something nice.

BIFF: I can't.

HAPPY: Say you got a lunch date with Oliver tomorrow.

BIFF: So what do I do tomorrow?

HAPPY: You leave the house tomorrow and come back at night and say Oliver is thinking it over. And he thinks it over for a couple of weeks, and gradually it fades away and nobody's the worse.

BIFF: But it'll go on forever!

HAPPY: Dad is never so happy as when he's looking forward to something!

{Willy enters.}

HAPPY: Hello, scout!

WILLY: Gee, I haven't been here in years! *{Stanley has followed Willy in and sets a chair for him. Stanley starts off but Happy stops him.}*

HAPPY: Stanley!

{Stanley stands by, waiting for an order.}

BIFF: *{Going to Willy with guilt, as to an invalid}* Sit down, Pop. You want a drink?

WILLY: Sure, I don't mind.

BIFF: Let's get a load on.

WILLY: You look worried.

BIFF: N-no. *{To Stanley}* Scotch all around. Make it doubles.

STANLEY: Doubles, right. *{He goes}*

WILLY: You had a couple already, didn't you?

BIFF: Just a couple, yeah.

WILLY: Well, what happened, boy? *{Nodding affirmatively, with a smile}* Everything go all right?

BIFF: *(Takes a breath, then reaches over and grasps Willy's hand)* Pal . . . *(He is smiling bravely, and Willy is smiling too)* I had an experience today.

HAPPY: Terrific, Pop.

WILLY: That so? What happened?

BIFF: *(High, slightly alcoholic, above the earth)* I'm going to tell you everything from first to last. It's been a strange day. *(Silence. He looks around, composes himself as best he can, but his breath keeps breaking the rhythm of his voice)* I had to wait quite a while for him, and—

WILLY: Oliver?

BIFF: Yeah, Oliver. All day, as a matter of cold fact. And a lot of—instances—facts, Pop, facts about my life came back to me. Who was it, Pop? Who ever said I was a salesman with Oliver?

WILLY: Well, you were.

BIFF: No, Dad, I was a shipping clerk.

WILLY: But you were practically—

BIFF: *(With determination)* Dad, I don't know who said it first, but I was never a salesman for Bill Oliver.

WILLY: What're you talking about?

BIFF: Let's hold on to the facts tonight, Pop. We're not going to get anywhere bullin' around. I was a shipping clerk.

WILLY: *(Angrily)* All right, now listen to me—

BIFF: Why don't you let me finish?

WILLY: I'm not interested in stories about the past or any crap of that kind because the woods are burning, boys, you understand? There's a big blaze going on all around. I was fired today.

BIFF: *(Shocked)* How could you be?

WILLY: I was fired, and I'm looking for a little good news to tell your mother, because the woman has waited and the woman has suffered. The gist of it is that I haven't got a story left in my head, Biff. So don't give me a lecture about facts and aspects. I am not interested. Now what've you got to say to me?

(Stanley enters with three drinks. They wait until he leaves.)

WILLY: Did you see Oliver?

BIFF: Jesus, Dad!

WILLY: You mean you didn't go up there?

HAPPY: Sure he went up there.

BIFF: I did. I—saw him. How could they fire you?

WILLY: *(On the edge of his chair)* What kind of welcome did he give you?

BIFF: He won't even let you work on commission?

WILLY: I'm out! *(Driving)* So tell me, he gave you a warm welcome?

HAPPY: Sure, Pop, sure!

BIFF: *(Driven)* Well, it was kind of—

WILLY: I was wondering if he'd remember you. *(To Happy)* Imagine, man doesn't see him for ten, twelve years and gives him that kind of a welcome!

HAPPY: Damn right!

BIFF: *(Trying to return to the offensive)* Pop, look—

WILLY: You know why he remembered you, don't you? Because you impressed him in those days.

BIFF: Let's talk quietly and get this down to the facts, huh?

WILLY: *(As though Biff had been interrupting)* Well, what happened? It's great news, Biff. Did he take you into his office or'd you talk in the waiting-room?

BIFF: Well, he came in, see, and—

WILLY: *(With a big smile)* What'd he say? Betcha he threw his arm around you.

BIFF: Well, he kinda—

WILLY: He's a fine man. *(To Happy)* Very hard man to see, y'know.

HAPPY: *(Agreeing)* Oh, I know.

WILLY: *(To Biff)* Is that where you had the drinks?

BIFF: Yeah, he gave me a couple of —no, no!

HAPPY: *(Cutting in)* He told him my Florida idea.

WILLY: Don't interrupt. *(To Biff)* How'd he react to the Florida idea?

BIFF: Dad, will you give me a minute to explain?

WILLY: I've been waiting for you to explain since I sat down here! What happened? He took you into his office and what?

BIFF: Well—I talked. And—and he listened, see.

WILLY: Famous for the way he listens, y'know. What was his answer?

BIFF: His answer was— *{He breaks off, suddenly angry}* Dad, you're not letting me tell you what I want to tell you!

WILLY: *{Accusing, angered}* You didn't see him, did you?

BIFF: I did see him!

WILLY: What'd you insult him or something? You insulted him, didn't you?

BIFF: Listen, will you let me out of it, will you let me out of it!

HAPPY: What the hell!

WILLY: Tell me what happened!

BIFF: *{To Happy}* I can't talk to him! *{A single trumpet note jars the ear. The light of green leaves stains the house, which holds the air of night and a dream. Young Bernard enters and knocks on the door of the house.}*

YOUNG BERNARD: *{Frantically}* Mrs. Loman, Mrs. Loman!

HAPPY: Tell him what happened!

BIFF: *{To Happy}* Shut up and leave me alone!

WILLY: No, no! You had to go and flunk math!

BIFF: What math! What're you talking about?

YOUNG BERNARD: Mrs. Loman, Mrs. Loman!

{Linda appears in the house, as of old.}

WILLY: *{Wildly}* Math, math, math!

BIFF: Take it easy, Pop!

YOUNG BERNARD: Mrs. Loman!

WILLY: *{Furiously}* If you hadn't flunked you'd've been set by now!

BIFF: Now, look, I'm gonna tell you what happened, and you're going to listen to me.

YOUNG BERNARD: Mrs. Loman!

BIFF: I waited six hours—

HAPPY: What the hell are you saying?

BIFF: I kept sending in my name but he wouldn't see me. So finally he . . . *{He continues unheard as light fades low on the restaurant}*

YOUNG BERNARD: Biff flunked math!

LINDA: No!

YOUNG BERNARD: Birnbaum flunked him! They won't graduate him!

LINDA: But they have to. He's gotta go to the university. Where is he? Biff! Biff!

YOUNG BERNARD: No, he left. He went to Grand Central.

LINDA: Grand—You mean he went to Boston!

YOUNG BERNARD: Is Uncle Willy in Boston?

LINDA: Oh, maybe Willy can talk to the teacher. Oh, the poor, poor boy! *{Light on house area snaps out.}*

BIFF: *{At the table, now audible, holding up a gold fountain pen}* . . . so I'm washed up with Oliver, you understand? Are you listening to me?

WILLY: *{At a loss}* Yeah, sure. If you hadn't flunked—

BIFF: Flunked what? What're you talking about?

WILLY: Don't blame everything on me! I didn't flunk math—you did! What pen?

HAPPY: That was awful dumb, Biff, a pen like that is worth—

WILLY: *{Seeing the pen for the first time}* You took Oliver's pen?

BIFF: *{Weakening}* Dad, I just explained it to you.

WILLY: You stole Bill Oliver's fountain pen!

BIFF: I didn't exactly steal it! That's just what I've been explaining to you!

HAPPY: He had it in his hand and just then Oliver walked in, so he got nervous and stuck it in his pocket!

WILLY: My God, Biff!

BIFF: I never intended to do it, Dad!

OPERATOR' VOICE: Standish Arms, good evening!

WILLY: *{Shouting}* I'm not in my room!

BIFF: *{Frightened}* Dad, what's the

matter? *{He and Happy stand up}*

OPERATOR: Ringing Mr. Loman for you!

WILLY: I'm not there, stop it!

BIFF: *{Horrified, gets down on one knee before Willy}* Dad, I'll make good, I'll make good. *{Willy tries to get to his feet. Biff holds him down}* Sit down now.

WILLY: No, you're no good, you're no good for anything.

BIFF: I am, Dad, I'll find something else, you understand? Now don't worry about anything. *{He holds up Willy's face}* Talk to me, Dad.

OPERATOR: Mr. Loman does not answer. Shall I page him?

WILLY: *{Attempting to stand, as though to rush and silence the Operator}* No, no, no!

HAPPY: He'll strike something, Pop.

WILLY: No, no . . .

BIFF: *{Desperately, standing over Willy}* Pop, listen! Listen to me! I'm telling you something good. Oliver talked to his partner about the Florida idea. You listening? He—he talked to his partner, and he came to me . . . I'm going to be all right, you hear? Dad, listen to me, he said it was just a question of the amount!

WILLY: Then you . . . got it?

HAPPY: He's gonna be terrific, Pop!

WILLY: *{Trying to stand}* Then you got it, haven't you? You got it! You got it!

BIFF: *{Agonized, holds Willy down}* No, no. Look, Pop, I'm supposed to have lunch with them tomorrow. I'm just telling you this so you'll know that I can still make an impression, Pop. And I'll make good somewhere, but I can't go tomorrow, see?

WILLY: Why not? You simply—

BIFF: But the pen, Pop!

WILLY: You give it to him and tell him it was an oversight!

HAPPY: Sure, have lunch tomorrow!

BIFF: I can't say that—

WILLY: You were doing a crossword puzzle and accidentally used his pen!

BIFF: Listen, kid, I took those balls years ago, now I walk in with his fountain pen? That clinches it, don't you see? I can't face him like that! I'll try elsewhere.

PAGE'S VOICE: Paging Mr. Loman!

WILLY: Don't you want to be anything?

BIFF: Pop, how can I go back?

WILLY: You don't want to be anything, is that what's behind it?

BIFF: *{Now angry at Willy for not crediting his sympathy}* Don't take it that way! You think it was easy walking into that office after what I'd done to him? A team of horses couldn't have dragged me back to Bill Oliver!

WILLY: Then why'd you go?

BIFF: Why did I go? Why did I go? Look at you! Look at what's become of you!

{Off left, The Woman laughs.}

WILLY: Biff, you're going to go to the lunch tomorrow, or—

BIFF: I can't go. I've got no appointment!

HAPPY: Biff, for . . . !

WILLY: Are you spiting me?

BIFF: Don't take it that way! Goddammit!

WILLY: *{Strikes Biff and falters away from the table}* You rotten little louse! Are you spiting me?

THE WOMAN: Someone's at the door, Willy!

BIFF: I'm no good, can't you see what I am?

HAPPY: *{Separating them}* Hey, you're in a restaurant! Now cut it out, both of you! *{The girls enter}* Hello, girls, sit down.

{The Woman laughs, off left.}

MISS FORSYTHE: I guess we might as well. This is Letta.

THE WOMAN: Willy, are you going to wake up?

BIFF: *{Ignoring Willy}* How're ya, miss, sit down. What do you drink?

MISS FORSYTHE: Letta might not be able to stay long.

LETTA: I gotta get up very early tomorrow. I got jury duty. I'm so excited! Were you fellows ever on a jury?

BIFF: No, but I been in front of them! *{The girls laugh}* This is my father.

LETTA: Isn't he cute? Sit down with us, Pop.

HAPPY: Sit him down, Biff!

BIFF: *{Going to him}* Come on, slugger, drink us under the table. To hell with it! Come on, sit down, pal!

{On Biff's last insistence, Willy is about to sit.}

THE WOMAN: *{Now urgently}* Willy, are you going to answer the door!

{The Woman's call pulls Willy back. He starts right, befuddled.}

BIFF: Hey, where are you going?

WILLY: Open the door.

BIFF: The door?

WILLY: The washroom . . . the door . . . where's the door?

BIFF: *{Leading Willy to the left}* Just go straight down.

{Willy moves left.}

THE WOMAN: Willy, Willy, are you going to get up, get up, get up, get up?

{Willy exits left.}

LETTA: I think it's sweet you bring your daddy along.

MISS FORSYTHE: Oh, he isn't really your father!

BIFF: *{At left, turning to her resentfully}* Miss Forsythe, you've just seen a prince walk by. A fine, troubled prince. A hardworking, unappreciated prince. A pal, you understand? A good companion. Always for his boys.

LETTA: That's so sweet.

HAPPY: Well, girls, what's the program? We're wasting time. Come on, Biff. Gather round. Where would you like to go?

BIFF: Why don't you do something for him?

HAPPY: Me!

BIFF: Don't you give a damn for him, Hap?

HAPPY: What're you talking about? I'm the one who—

BIFF: I sense it, you don't give a good goddam about him. *{He takes the rolled-up hose from his pocket and puts it on the table in front of Happy}* Look what I found in the cellar, for Christ's sake. How can you bear to let it go on?

HAPPY: Me? Who goes away? Who runs off and—

BIFF: Yeah, but he doesn't mean anything to you. You could help him—I can't! Don't you understand what I'm talking about? He's going to kill himself, don't you know that?

HAPPY: Don't I know it! Me!

BIFF: Hap, help him! Jesus . . . help him . . . Help me, help me, I can't bear to look at his face! *{Ready to weep, he hurries out, up right}*

HAPPY: *{Staring after him}* Where are you going?

MISS FORSYTHE: What's he so mad about?

HAPPY: Come on, girls, we'll catch up with him.

MISS FORSYTHE: *{As Happy pushes her out}* Say, I don't like that temper of his!

HAPPY: He's just a little overstrung, he'll be all right!

WILLY: *{Off left, as The Woman laughs}* Don't answer! Don't answer!

LETTA: Don't you want to tell your father—

HAPPY: No, that's not my father. He's just a guy. Come on, we'll catch Biff, and, honey, we're going to paint this town! Stanley, where's the check! Hey, Stanley!

{They exit. Stanley looks toward left.}

STANLEY: *{Calling to Happy indignantly}* Mr. Loman! Mr. Loman!

{Stanley picks up a chair and follows them off. Knocking is heard off left. The Woman enters, laughing. Willy follows her. She is in a black slip; he is buttoning his shirt. Raw, sensuous music accompanies their speech.}

WILLY: Will you stop laughing? Will you stop?

THE WOMAN: Aren't you going to answer the door? He'll wake the whole hotel.

WILLY: I'm not expecting anybody.

THE WOMAN: Whyn't you have another drink, honey, and stop being so damn self-centered?

WILLY: I'm so lonely.

THE WOMAN: You know you ruined me, Willy? From now on, whenever you come to the office, I'll see that you go right through to the buyers. No waiting at my desk any more, Willy. You ruined me.

WILLY: That's nice of you to say that.

THE WOMAN: Gee, you are self-centered! Why so sad? You are the saddest, self-centeredest soul I ever did see-saw. *{She laughs. He kisses her}* Come on inside drummer boy. It's silly to be dressing in the middle of the night. *{As knocking is heard}* Aren't you going to answer the door?

WILLY: They're knocking on the wrong door.

THE WOMAN: But I felt the knocking. And he heard us talking in here. Maybe the hotel's on fire!

WILLY: *{His terror rising}* It's a mistake.

THE WOMAN: Then tell him to go away!

WILLY: There's nobody there.

THE WOMAN: It's getting on my nerves, Willy. There's somebody standing out there and it's getting on my nerves!

WILLY: *{Pushing her away from him}* All right, stay in the bathroom here, and don't come out. I think there's a law in Massachusetts about it, so don't come out. It may be that new room clerk. He looked very mean. So don't come out. It's a mistake, there's no fire.

{The knocking is heard again. He takes a few steps away from her, and she vanishes into the wing. The light follows him, and now he is facing Young Biff, who carries a suitcase. Biff steps toward him. The music is gone.}

BIFF: Why didn't you answer?

WILLY: Biff! What are you doing in Boston?

BIFF: Why didn't you answer? I've been knocking for five minutes, I called you on the phone—

WILLY: I just heard you. I was in the bathroom and had the door shut. Did anything happen home?

BIFF: Dad—I let you down.

WILLY: What do you mean?

BIFF: Dad . . .

WILLY: Biffo, what's this about? *{Putting his arm around Biff}* Come on, let's go downstairs and get you a malted.

BIFF: Dad, I flunked math.

WILLY: Not for the term?

BIFF: The term. I haven't got enough credits to graduate.

WILLY: You mean to say Bernard wouldn't give you the answers?

BIFF: He did, he tried, but I only got a sixty-one.

WILLY: And they wouldn't give you four points?

BIFF: Birnbaum refused absolutely. I begged him, Pop, but he won't give me those points. You gotta talk to him before they close the school. Because if he saw the kind of man you are, and you just talked to him in your way, I'm sure he'd come through for me. The class came right before practice, see, and I didn't go enough. Would you talk to him? He'd like you, Pop. You know the way you could talk.

WILLY: You're on. We'll drive right back.

BIFF: Oh, Dad, good work! I'm sure he'll change it for you!

WILLY: Go downstairs and tell the clerk I'm checkin' out Go right down.

BIFF: Yes, sir! See, the reason he hates me, Pop—one day he was late for class so I got up at the blackboard and imitated him. I crossed my eyes and talked with a lithp.

WILLY: *{Laughing}* You did? The kids like it?

BIFF: They nearly died laughing.

WILLY: Yeah? What'd you do?

BIFF: The thquare root of thixty two is . . . *{Willy bursts out laughing; Biff joins him}* And in the middle of it he walked in!

{Willy laughs and The Woman joins in offstage.}

WILLY: *{Without hesitation}* Hurry downstairs and—

BIFF: Somebody in there?

WILLY: No, that was next door.

{The Woman laughs offstage.}

BIFF: Somebody got in your bathroom!

WILLY: No, it's the next room, there's a party—

THE WOMAN: *{Enters, laughing. She lisps this}* Can I come in? There's something in the bathtub, Willy, and it's moving!

{Willy looks at Biff, who is staring open-mouthed and horrified at The Woman.}

WILLY: Ah—you better go back to your room. They must be finished painting by now. They're painting her room so I let her take a shower here. Go back, go back . . . *{He pushes her}*

THE WOMAN: *{Resisting}* But I've got to get dressed, Willy, I can't—

WILLY: Get out of here! Go back, go back . . . *{Suddenly striving for the ordinary}* This is Miss Francis, Biff, she's a buyer. They're painting her room. Go back, Miss Francis, go back . . .

THE WOMAN: But my clothes, I can't go out naked in the hall!

WILLY: *{Pushing her offstage}* Get outa here! Go back, go back!

{Biff slowly sits down on his suitcase as the argument continues offstage.}

THE WOMAN: Where's my stockings? You promised me stockings, Willy!

WILLY: I have no stockings here!

THE WOMAN: You had two boxes of size nine sheers for me, and I want them!

WILLY: Here, for God's sake, will you get outa here!

THE WOMAN: *{Enters holding a box of stockings}* I just hope there's nobody in the hall. That's all I hope. *{To Biff}* Are you football or baseball?

BIFF: Football.

THE WOMAN: *{Angry, humiliated}* That's me too. G'night. *{She snatches her clothes from Willy, and walks out}*

WILLY: *{After a pause}* Well, better get going. I want to get to the school first thing in the morning. Get my suits out of the closet. I'll get my valises. *{Biff doesn't move}* What's the matter? *{Biff remains motionless, tears falling}* She's a buyer. Buys for J. H. Simmons. She lives down the hall—they're painting. You don't imagine— *{He breaks off. After a pause}* Now listen, pal, she's just a buyer. She sees merchandise in her room and they have to keep it looking just so . . . *{Pause, Assuming command}* All right, get my suits. *{Biff doesn't move}* Now stop crying and do as I say. I gave you an order. Biff, I gave you an order! Is that what you do when I give you an order? How dare you cry! *{Putting his arm around Biff}* Now look, Biff, when you grow up you'll understand about these things. You mustn't—you mustn't overemphasize a thing like this. I'll see Birnbaum first thing in the morning.

BIFF: Never mind.

WILLY: *{Getting down beside Biff}* Never mind! He's going to give you those points. I'll see to it.

BIFF: He wouldn't listen to you.

WILLY: He certainly will listen to me. You need those points for the U. of Virginia.

BIFF: I'm not going there.

WILLY: Heh? If I can't get him to change that mark you'll make it up in summer school. You've got all summer to—

BIFF: *{His weeping breaking from him}* Dad . . .

WILLY: *{Infected by it}* Oh, my boy . . .

BIFF: Dad . . .

WILLY: She's nothing to me, Biff. I was lonely, I was terribly lonely.

BIFF: You—you gave her Mama's stockings! *{His tears break through and he rises to go}*

WILLY: *{Grabbing for Biff}* I gave you an order!

BIFF: Don't touch me, you—liar!

WILLY: Apologize for that!

BIFF: You fake! You phony little fake! You fake! *{Overcome, he turns quickly and weeping fully goes out with his suitcase. Willy is left on the floor on his knees}*

WILLY: I gave you an order! Biff, come back here or I'll beat you! Come back here! I'll whip you!

{Stanley comes quickly in from the right and stands in front of Willy.}

WILLY: *{Shouts at Stanley}* I gave you an order . . .

STANLEY: Hey, let's pick it up, pick it up, Mr. Loman. *{He helps Willy to his feet}* Your boys left with the chippies. They said they'll see you home.

{A second waiter watches some distance away.}

WILLY: But we were supposed to have dinner together.

{Music is heard, Willy's theme.}

STANLEY: Can you make it?

WILLY: I'll—sure, I can make it. *{Suddenly concerned about his clothes}* Do I—I look all right?

STANLEY: Sure, you look all right. *{He flicks a speck off Willy's lapel}*

WILLY: Here—here's a dollar.

STANLEY: Oh, your son paid me. It's all right.

WILLY: *{Putting it in Stanley's hand}* No, take it. You're a good boy.

STANLEY: Oh, no, you don't have to . . .

WILLY: Here—here's some more, I don't need it any more. *{After a slight pause}* Tell me—is there a seed store in the neighborhood?

STANLEY: Seeds? You mean like to plant?

{As Willy turns, Stanley slips the money back into his jacket pocket.}

WILLY: Yes. Carrots, peas . . .

STANLEY: Well, there's hardware stores on Sixth Avenue, but it may be too late now.

WILLY: *{Anxiously}* Oh, I'd better hurry. I've got to get some seeds. *{He starts off to the right}* I've got to get some seeds, right away. Nothing's planted. I don't have a thing in the ground.

{Willy hurries out as the light goes down. Stanley moves over to the right after him, watches him off. The other waiter has been staring at Willy.}

STANLEY: *{To the waiter}* Well, whatta you looking at?

{The waiter picks up the chairs and moves off right. Stanley takes the table and follows him. The light fades on this area. There is a long pause, the sound of the flute coming over. The light gradually rises on the kitchen, which is empty. Happy appears at the door of the house, followed by Biff. Happy is carrying a large bunch of long-stemmed roses. He enters the kitchen, looks around for Linda. Not seeing her, he turns to Biff, who is just outside the house door, and makes a gesture with his hands, indicating "Not here, I guess." He looks into the living-room and freezes. Inside, Linda, unseen, is seated, Willy's coat on her lap. She rises ominously and quietly and moves toward Happy, who backs up into the kitchen, afraid.}

HAPPY: Hey, what're you doing up? *{Linda says nothing but moves toward him implacably}* Where's Pop? *{He keeps backing to the right, and now Linda is in full view in the doorway to the living-room}* Is he sleeping?

LINDA: Where were you?

HAPPY: *{Trying to laugh it off}* We met two girls, Mom, very fine types. Here, we brought you some flowers. *{Offering them to her}* Put them in your room, Ma.

{She knocks them to the floor at Biff's feet. He has now come inside and closed the door behind him. She stares at Biff, silent.}

HAPPY: Now what'd you do that for? Mom, I want you to have some flowers—

LINDA: *{Cutting Happy off, violently to Biff}* Don't you care whether he lives or dies?

HAPPY: *{Going to the stairs}* Come upstairs, Biff.

BIFF: *{With a flare of disgust, to Happy}* Go away from me! *{To Linda}* What do you mean, lives or dies? Nobody's dying around here, pal.

LINDA: Get out of my sight! Get out of here!

BIFF: I wanna see the boss.

LINDA: You're not going near him!

BIFF: Where is he? *{He moves into the living-room and Linda follows}*

LINDA: *{Shouting after Biff}* You invite him for dinner. He looks forward to it all day—*{Biff appears in his parents' bedroom, looks around, and exits}* —and then you desert him there. There's no stranger you'd do that to!

HAPPY: Why? He had a swell time with us. Listen, when I—*{Linda comes back into the kitchen}*—desert him I hope I don't outlive the day!

LINDA: Get out of here!

HAPPY: Now look, Mom . . .

LINDA: Did you have to go to women tonight? You and your lousy rotten whores!

{Biff re-enters the kitchen.}

HAPPY: Mom, all we did was follow Biff around trying to cheer him up! *{To Biff}* Boy, what a night you gave me!

LINDA: Get out of here, both of you, and don't come back! I don't want you tormenting him any more. Go on now, get your things together!. *{To Biff}* You can sleep in his apartment. *{She starts to pick up the flowers and stops herself}* Pick up this stuff, I'm not your maid any more. Pick it up, you bum, you!

{Happy turns his back to her in refusal. Biff slowly moves over and gets down on his knees, picking up the flowers.}

LINDA: You're a pair of animals! Not one, not another living soul would have had the cruelty to walk out on that man in a restaurant!

BIFF: *{Not looking at her}* Is that what he said?

LINDA: He didn't have to say anything. He was so humiliated he nearly limped when he came in.

HAPPY: But, Mom, he had a great time with us—

BIFF: *{Cutting him off violently}* Shut up!

{Without another word, Happy goes upstairs.}

LINDA: You! You didn't even go in to see if he was all right!

BIFF: *{Still on the floor in front of Linda, the flowers in his hand; with self-loathing}* No. Didn't. Didn't do a damned thing. How do you like that, heh? Left him babbling in a toilet.

LINDA: You louse. You . . .

BIFF: Now you hit it on the nose! *{He gets up, throws the flowers in the wastebasket}* The scum of the earth, and you're looking at him!

LINDA: Get out of here!

BIFF: I gotta talk to the boss, Mom. Where is he?

LINDA: You're not going near him. Get out of this house!

BIFF: *{With absolute assurance, determination}* No. We're gonna have an abrupt conversation, him and me.

LINDA: You're not talking to him!

{Hammering is heard from outside the house, off right. Biff turns toward the noise.}

LINDA: *{Suddenly pleading}* Will you please leave him alone?

BIFF: What's he doing out there?

LINDA: He's planting the garden!

BIFF: *{Quietly}* Now? Oh, my God!

{Biff moves outside, Linda following. The light dies down on them and comes up on the center of the apron as Willy walks into it. He is carrying a flashlight, a hoe, and a handful of seed packets. He raps the top of the hoe sharply to fix it firmly, and then moves to the left, measuring off the distance with his foot. He holds the flashlight to look at the seed packets, reading off the instructions. He is in the blue of night.}

WILLY: Carrots . . . quarter-inch apart. Rows . . . one-foot rows. *{He measures it off}* One foot. *{He puts down a package and measures off}* Beets. *{He puts down another package and measures again}* Lettuce. *{He reads the package, puts it down}* One foot—*{He breaks off as Ben appears at the right and moves slowly down to him}* What a proposition, ts, ts. Terrific, terrific. 'Cause she's suffered, Ben, the woman has suffered. You understand me? A man can't go out the way he came in,

Ben, a man has got to add up to something. You can't, you can't—*{Ben moves toward him as though to interrupt}* You gotta consider, now. Don't answer so quick. Remember, it's a guaranteed twenty-thousand-dollar proposition. Now look, Ben, I want you to go through the ins and outs of this thing with me. I've got nobody to talk to, Ben, and the woman has suffered, you hear me?

BEN: *{Standing still, considering}* What's the proposition?

WILLY: It's twenty thousand dollars on the barrelhead. Guaranteed, gilt-edged, you understand?

BEN: You don't want to make a fool of yourself. They might not honor the policy.

WILLY: How can they dare refuse? Didn't I work like a coolie to meet every premium on the nose? And now they don't pay off? Impossible!

BEN: It's called a cowardly thing, William.

WILLY: Why? Does it take more guts to stand here the rest of my life ringing up a zero?

BEN: *{Yielding}* That's a point, William. *{He moves, thinking, turns}* And twenty thousand—that *is* something one can feel with the hand, it is there.

WILLY: *{Now assured, with rising power}* Oh, Ben, that's the whole beauty of it! I see it like a diamond, shining in the dark, hard and rough, that I can pick up and touch in my hand. Not like —like an appointment! This would not be another damned-fool appointment, Ben, and it changes all the aspects. Because he thinks I'm nothing, see, and so he spites me. But the funeral—*{Straightening up}* Ben, that funeral will be massive! They'll come from Maine, Massachusetts, Vermont, New Hampshire! All the old-timers with the strange license plates—that boy will be thunderstruck, Ben, because he never realized—I am known! Rhode Island, New York, New Jersey—I am known, Ben, and he'll see it with his eyes once and for all. He'll see what I am, Ben! He's in for a shock, that boy!

BEN: *{Coming down to the edge of the garden}* He'll call you a coward.

WILLY: *{Suddenly fearful}* No, that would be terrible.

BEN: Yes. And a damned fool.

WILLY: No, no, he mustn't. I won't have that! *{He is broken and desperate}*

BEN: He'll hate you, William.

{The gay music of the Boys is heard.}

WILLY: Oh, Ben, how do we get back to all the great times? Used to be so full of light, and comradeship, the sleigh-riding in winter, and the ruddiness on his cheeks. And always some kind of good news coming up, always something nice coming up ahead. And never even let me carry the valises in the house, and simonizing, simonizing that little red car! Why, why can't I give him something and not have him hate me?

BEN: Let me think about it. *{He glances at his watch}* I still have a little time. Remarkable proposition, but you've got to be sure you're not making a fool of yourself.

{Ben drifts off upstage and goes out of sight. Biff comes down from the left.}

WILLY: *{Suddenly conscious of Biff, turns and looks up at him, then begins picking up the packages of seeds in confusion}* Where the hell is that seed? *{Indignantly}* You can't see nothing out here! They boxed in the whole goddam neighborhood!

BIFF: There are people all around here. Don't you realize that?

WILLY: I'm busy. Don't bother me.

BIFF: *{Taking the hoe from Willy}* I'm saying good-by to you, Pop. *{Willy looks at him, silent, unable to move}* I'm not coming back any more.

WILLY: You're not going to see Oliver tomorrow?

BIFF: I've got no appointment, Dad.

WILLY: He put his arm around you, and you've got no appointment?

BIFF: Pop, get this now, will you? Everytime I've left it's been a fight that sent me out of here. Today I realized something about myself and I tried to explain it to you and I—I think I'm just not smart enough to make any sense out of it for you. To hell with whose fault it is or anything like that. *{He takes Willy's arm}* Let's just wrap it up, heh? Come on in, we'll tell Mom. *{He gently tries to pull Willy to left}*

WILLY: *{Frozen, immobile, with guilt in his voice}* No, I didn't want to see her.

BIFF: Come on! *{He pulls again, and Willy tries to pull away}*

WILLY: *{Highly nervous}* No, no, I don't want to see her.

BIFF: *{Tries to look into Willy's face, as if to find the answer there}* Why don't you want to see her?

WILLY: *{More harshly now}* Don't bother me, will you?

BIFF: What do you mean, you don't want to see her? You don't want them calling you yellow, do you? This isn't your fault; it's me, I'm a bum. Now come inside. *{Willy strains to get away}* Did you hear what I said to you?

{Willy pulls away and quickly goes by himself into the house. Biff follows.}

LINDA: *{To Willy}* Did you plant, dear?

BIFF: *{At the door, to Linda}* All right, we had it out. I'm going and I'm not writing any more.

LINDA: *{Going to Willy in the kitchen}* I think that's the best way, dear. 'Cause there's no use drawing it out, you'll just never get along.

{Willy doesn't respond.}

BIFF: People ask where I am and what I'm doing, you don't know, and you don't care. That way it'll be off your mind and you can start brightening up again. All right? That clears it, doesn't it? *{Willy is silent, and Biff goes to him}* You gonna wish me luck, scout? *{He extends his hand}* What do you say?

LINDA: Shake his hand, Willy.

WILLY: *{Turning to her, seething with hurt}* There's no necessity to mention the pen at all, y'know.

BIFF: *{Gently}* I've got no appointment, Dad.

WILLY: *{Erupting fiercely}* He put his arm around . . . ?

BIFF: Dad, you're never going to see what I am, so what's the use of arguing? If I strike oil I'll send you a check. Meanwhile, forget I'm alive.

WILLY: *{To Linda}* Spite, see?

BIFF: Shake hands, Dad.

WILLY: Not my hand.

BIFF: I was hoping not to go this way.

WILLY: Well, this is the way you're going. Good-by.

{Biff looks at him a moment, then turns sharply and goes to the stairs.}

WILLY: *{Stops him with}* May you rot in hell if you leave this house!

BIFF: *{Turning}* Exactly what is it that you want from me?

WILLY: I want you to know, on the train, in the mountains, in the valleys, wherever you go, that you cut down your life for spite!

BIFF: No, no.

WILLY: Spite, spite, is the word of your undoing! And when you're down and out, remember what did it. When you're rotting somewhere beside the railroad tracks, remember, and don't you dare blame it on me!

BIFF: I'm not blaming it on you!

WILLY: I won't take the rap for this, you hear?

{Happy comes down the stairs and stands on the bottom step, watching.}

BIFF: That's just what I'm telling you!

WILLY: *{Sinking down into a chair at the table, with full accusation}* You're trying to put a knife in me—don't think I don't know what you're doing!

BIFF: All right, phony! Then let's lay it on the line. *{He whips the rubber tube out of his pocket and puts it on the table}*

HAPPY: You crazy—

LINDA: Biff! *{She moves to grab the*

hose, but Biff holds it down with his hand)

BIFF: Leave it there! Don't move it!

WILLY: *(Not looking at it)* What is that?

BIFF: You know goddam well what that is.

WILLY: *(Caged, wanting to escape)* I never saw that.

BIFF: You saw it. The mice didn't bring it into the cellar! What is this supposed to do, make a hero out of you? This supposed to make me sorry for you?

WILLY: Never heard of it.

BIFF: There'll be no pity for you, you hear it? No pity!

WILLY: *(To Linda)* You hear the spite!

BIFF: No, you're going to hear the truth—what you are and what I am!

LINDA: Stop it!

WILLY: Spite!

HAPPY: *(Coming down toward Biff)* You cut it now!

BIFF: *(To Happy)* The man don't know who we are! The man is gonna know! *(To Willy)* We never told the truth for ten minutes in this house!

HAPPY: We always told the truth!

BIFF: *(Turning on him)* You big blow, are you the assistant buyer? You're one of the two assistants to the assistant, aren't you?

HAPPY: Well, I'm practically—

BIFF: You're practically full of it! We all are! And I'm through with it! *(To Willy)* Now hear this, Willy, this is me.

WILLY: I know you!

BIFF: You know why I had no address for three months? I stole a suit in Kansas City and I was in jail. *(To Linda, who is sobbing)* Stop crying, I'm through with it. *(Linda turns away from them, her hands covering her face.)*

WILLY: I suppose that's my fault!

BIFF: I stole myself out of every good job since high school!

WILLY: And whose fault is that?

BIFF: And I never got anywhere because you blew me so full of hot air I could never stand taking orders from anybody! That's whose fault it is!

WILLY: I hear that!

LINDA: Don't, Biff!

BIFF: It's goddam time you heard that! I had to be boss big shot in two weeks, and I'm through with it!

WILLY: Then hang yourself! For spite, hang yourself!

BIFF: No! Nobody's hanging himself, Willy! I ran down eleven flights with a pen in my hand today. And suddenly I stopped, you hear me? And in the middle of that office building, do you hear this? I stopped in the middle of that building and I saw—the sky. I saw the things that I love in this world. The work and the food and time to sit and smoke. And I looked at the pen and said to myself, what the hell am I grabbing this for? Why am I trying to become what I don't want to be? What am I doing in an office, making a contemptuous, begging fool of myself, when all I want is out there, waiting for me the minute I say I know who I am! Why can't I say that, Willy? *(He tries to make Willy face him, but Willy pulls away and moves to the left)*

WILLY: *(With hatred, threateningly)* The door of your life is wide open!

BIFF: Pop, I'm a dime a dozen, and so are you!

WILLY: *(Turning on him now in an uncontrolled outburst)* I am not a dime a dozen! I am Willy Loman, and you are Biff Loman!

(Biff starts for Willy, but is blocked by Happy. In his fury, Biff seems on the verge of attacking his father.)

BIFF: I am not a leader of men, Willy, and neither are you. You were never anything but a hard-working drummer who landed in the ash can like all the rest of them! I'm one dollar an hour, Willy! I tried seven states and couldn't raise it. A buck an hour! Do you gather my meaning? I'm not bringing home any prizes any more, and you're going to stop waiting for me to bring them home!

WILLY: *{Directly to Biff}* You vengeful, spiteful mutt!

{Biff breaks from Happy. Willy, in fright, starts up the stairs. Biff grabs him.}

BIFF: *{At the peak of his fury}* Pop, I'm nothing! I'm nothing, Pop. Can't you understand that? There's no spite in it any more. I'm just what I am, that's all.

{Biff's fury has spent itself, and he breaks down, sobbing, holding on to Willy, who dumbly fumbles for Biff's face.}

WILLY: *{Astonished}* What're you doing? What're you doing? *{To Linda}* Why is he crying?

BIFF: *{Crying, broken}* Will you let me go, for Christ's sake? Will you take that phony dream and burn it before something happens? *{Struggling to contain himself, he pulls away and moves to the stairs}* I'll go in the morning. Put him—put him to bed. *{Exhausted, Biff moves up the stairs to his room}*

WILLY: *{After a long pause, astonished, elevated}* Isn't that—isn't that remarkable? Biff—he likes me!

LINDA: He loves you, Willy.

HAPPY: *{Deeply moved}* Always did, Pop.

WILLY: Oh, Biff! *{Staring wildly}* He cried! Cried to me. *{He is choking with his love, and now cries out his promise}* That boy—that boy is going to be magnificent!

{Ben appears in the light just outside the kitchen.}

BEN: Yes outstanding, with twenty thousand behind him.

LINDA: *{Sensing the racing of his mind, fearfully, carefully}* Now come to bed, Willy. It's all settled now.

WILLY: *{Finding it difficult not to rush out of the house}* Yes, we'll sleep. Come on. Go to sleep, Hap.

BEN: And it does take a great kind of a man to crack the jungle.

{In accents of dread, Ben's idyllic music starts up.}

HAPPY: *{His arm around Linda}* I'm getting married, Pop, don't forget it. I'm changing everything. I'm gonna run that department before the year is up. You'll see, Mom. *{He kisses her}*

BEN: The jungle is dark but full of diamonds, Willy.

{Willy turns, moves, listening to Ben.}

LINDA: Be good. You're both good boys, just act that way, that's all.

HAPPY: 'Night, Pop. *{He goes upstairs}*

LINDA: *{To Willy}* Come, dear.

BEN: *{With greater force}* One must go in to fetch a diamond out.

WILLY: *{To Linda, as he moves slowly along the edge of the kitchen, toward the door}* I just want to get settled down, Linda. Let me sit alone for a little.

LINDA: *{Almost uttering her fear}* I want you upstairs.

WILLY: *{Taking her in his arms}* In a few minutes, Linda. I couldn't sleep right now. Go on, you look awful tired. *{He kisses her}*

BEN: Not like an appointment at all. A diamond is rough and hard to the touch.

WILLY: Go on now. I'll be right up.

LINDA: I think this is the only way, Willy.

WILLY: Sure, it's the best thing.

BEN: Best thing!

WILLY: The only way. Everything is gonna be—go on, kid, get to bed. You look so tired.

LINDA: Come right up.

WILLY: Two minutes.

{Linda goes into the living-room, then reappears in her bedroom. Willy moves just outside the kitchen door.}

WILLY: Loves me. *{Wonderingly}* Always loved me. Isn't that a remarkable thing? Ben, he'll worship me for it!

BEN: *{With promise}* It's dark there, but full of diamonds.

WILLY: Can you imagine that magnificence with twenty thousand dollars in his pocket?

LINDA: *{Calling from her room}* Willy! Come up!

WILLY: *{Calling into the kitchen}* Yes! Yes. Coming! It's very smart, you realize that, don't you, sweetheart? Even Ben sees it. I gotta go, baby. 'By! 'By! *{Going over to Ben, almost dancing}* Imagine? When the mail comes he'll be ahead of Bernard again!

BEN: A perfect proposition all around.

WILLY: Did you see how he cried to me? Oh, if I could kiss him, Ben!

BEN: Time, William, time!

WILLY: Oh, Ben, I always knew one way or another we were gonna make it, Biff and I!

BEN: *{Looking at his watch}* The boat. We'll be late. *{He moves slowly off into the darkness}*

WILLY: *{Elegiacally, turning to the house}* Now when you kick off, boy, I want a seventy-yard boot, and get right down the field under the ball, and when you hit, hit low and hard, because it's important, boy. *{He swings around and faces the audience}* There's all kinds of important people in the stands, and the first thing you know . . . *{Suddenly realizing he is alone}* Ben, Ben, where do I . . . ? *{He makes a sudden movement of search}* Ben, how do I . . . ?

LINDA: *{Calling}* Willy, you coming up?

WILLY: *{Uttering a gasp of fear, whirling about as if to quiet her}* Sh! *{He turns around as if to find his way; sounds, faces, voices seem to be swarming in upon him and he flicks at them, crying}* Sh! Sh! *{Suddenly music, faint and high, stops him. It rises in intensity, almost to an unbearable scream. He goes up and down on his toes, and rushes off around the house}* Shhh!

LINDA: Willy?

{There is no answer. Linda waits. Biff gets up off his bed. He is still in his clothes. Happy sits up. Bill stands listening.}

LINDA: *{With real fear}* Willy, answer me! Willy!

{There is the sound of a car starting and moving away at full speed.}

LINDA: No!

BIFF: *{Rushing down the stairs}* Pop! *{As the car speeds off, the music crashes down in a frenzy of sound, which becomes the soft pulsation of a single cello string. Biff slowly returns to his bedroom. He and Happy gravely don their jackets. Linda slowly walks out of her room. The music has developed into a death march. The leaves of day are appearing over everything. Charley and Bernard, somberly dressed, appear and knock on the kitchen door. Biff and Happy slowly descend the stairs to the kitchen as Charley and Bernard enter. All stop a moment when Linda, in clothes of mourning, bearing a little bunch of roses, comes through the draped doorway into the kitchen. She goes to Charley and takes his arm. Now all move toward the audience, through the wall-line of the kitchen. At the limit of the apron, Linda lays down the flowers, kneels, and sits back on her heels. All stare down at the grave.}*

REQUIEM

CHARLEY: It's getting dark, Linda.

{Linda doesn't react. She stares at the grave.}

BIFF: How about it, Mom? Better get some rest, heh? They'll be closing the gate soon.

{Linda makes no move. Pause.}

HAPPY: *{Deeply angered}* He had no right to do that. There was no necessity for it. We would've helped him.

CHARLEY: *{Grunting}* Hmmm.

BIFF: Come along, Mom.

LINDA: Why didn't anybody come?

CHARLEY: It was a very nice funeral.

LINDA: But where were all the people he knew? Maybe they blame him.

CHARLEY: Naa. It's a rough world, Linda. They wouldn't blame him.

LINDA: I can't understand it. At this time especially. First time in thirty-five years we were just about free and clear. He only needed a little salary. He was even finished with the dentist.

CHARLEY: No man only needs a little salary.

LINDA: I can't understand it.

BIFF: There were a lot of nice days. When he'd come home from a trip; or on Sundays, making the stoop; finishing the cellar; putting on the new porch; when he built the extra bathroom; and put up the garage. You know something, Charley, there's more of him in that front stoop than in all the sales he ever made.

CHARLEY: Yeah, he was a happy man with a batch of cement.

LINDA: He was so wonderful with his hands.

BIFF: He had the wrong dreams. All, all, wrong.

HAPPY: *{Almost ready to fight Biff}* Don't say that!

BIFF: He never knew who he was.

CHARLEY: *{Stopping Happy's movement and reply. To Biff}* Nobody dast blame this man. You don't understand: Willy was a salesman. And for a salesman, there is no rock bottom to the life. He don't put a bolt to a nut, he don't tell you the law or give you medicine. He's the man way out there in the blue riding on a smile and a shoeshine. And when they start not smiling back—that's an earthquake. And then you get yourself a couple of spots on your hat, and you're finished. Nobody dast blame this man. A salesman is got to dream, boy. It comes with the territory.

BIFF: Charley, the man didn't know who he was.

HAPPY: *{Infuriated}* Don't say that!

BIFF: Why don't you come with me, Happy?

HAPPY: I'm not licked that easily. I'm staying right in this city, and I'm gonna beat this racket! *{He looks at Biff, his chin set}* The Loman Brothers!

BIFF: I know who I am, kid.

HAPPY: All right, boy. I'm gonna show you and everybody else that Willy Loman did not die in vain. He had a good dream. It's the only dream you can have —to come out number-one man. He fought it out here, and this is where I'm gonna win it for him.

BIFF: *{With a hopeless glance at Happy, bends toward his mother}* Let's go, Mom.

LINDA: I'll be with you in a minute. Go on, Charley. *{He hesitates}* I want to, just for a minute. I never had a chance to say good-by.

{Charley moves away, followed by Happy. Biff remains a slight distance up and left of Linda. She sits there, summoning herself. The flute begins, not far away, playing behind her speech.}

LINDA: Forgive me, dear. I can't cry. I don't know what it is, but I can't cry. I don't understand it. Why did you ever do that? Help me, Willy, I can't cry. It seems to me that you're just on another trip. I keep expecting you. Willy, dear, I can't cry. Why did you do it? I search and search and I search, and I can't understand it, Willy. I made the last payment on the house today. Today, dear. And there'll be nobody home. *{A sob rises in her throat}* We're free and clear. *{Sobbing more fully, released}* We're free. *{Biff comes slowly toward her}* We're free . . . We're free . . . *{Biff lifts her to her feet and moves up light with her in his arms. Linda sobs quietly. Bernard and Charley come together and follow them, followed by Happy. Only the music of the flute is left on the darkening stage as over the house the hard towers of the apartment buildings rise into sharp focus, and}*

THE CURTAIN FALLS

Samuel Beckett (1906–   )

Act Without Words, I

A Mime for One Player

Desert. Dazzling light.

The man is flung backwards on stage from right wing. He falls, gets up immediately, dusts himself, turns aside, reflects.

Whistle from right wing.

He reflects, goes out right.

Immediately flung back on stage he falls, gets up immediately, dusts himself, turns aside, reflects.

Whistle from left wing.

He reflects, goes out left.

Immediately flung back on stage he falls, gets up immediately, dusts himself, turns aside, reflects.

Whistle from left wing.

He reflects, goes towards left wing, hesitates, thinks better of it, halts, turns aside, reflects.

A little tree descends from flies, lands. It has a single bough some three yards from ground and at its summit a meager tuft of palms casting at its foot a circle of shadow.

He continues to reflect.

Whistle from above.

He turns, sees tree, reflects, goes to it, sits down in its shadow, looks at his hands.

A pair of tailor's scissors descends from flies, comes to rest before tree, a yard from ground.

He continues to look at his hands.

Whistle from above.

He looks up, sees scissors, takes them and starts to trim his nails.

The palms close like a parasol, the shadow disappears.

He drops scissors, reflects.

A tiny carafe, to which is attached a huge label inscribed WATER, descends from flies, comes to rest some three yards from ground.

He continues to reflect.

Whistle from above.

He looks up, sees carafe, reflects, gets up, goes and stands under it, tries in vain to reach it, renounces, turns aside, reflects.

A big cube descends from flies, lands.

He continues to reflect.

Whistle from above.

He turns, sees cube, looks at it, at carafe, reflects, goes to cube, takes it up, carries it over and sets it down under carafe, tests its stability, gets up on it, tries in vain to reach carafe, renounces, gets down, carries cube back to its place, turns aside, reflects.

A second smaller cube descends from flies, lands.

He continues to reflect.

Whistle from above.

He turns, sees second cube, looks at it, at carafe, goes to second cube, takes it up, carries it over and sets it down under carafe, tests its stability, gets up on it, tries in vain to reach carafe, renounces, gets down, takes up second cube to carry it back to its place, hesitates, thinks better of it, sets it down, goes to big cube, takes it up, carries it over and puts it on small one, tests their stability, gets up on them, the cubes collapse, he falls, gets up immediately, brushes himself, reflects.

He takes up small cube, puts it on big one, tests their stability, gets up on them and is about to reach carafe when it is pulled up a little way and comes to rest beyond his reach.

He gets down, reflects, carries cubes back to their place, one by one, turns aside, reflects.

A third still smaller cube descends from flies, lands.

He continues to reflect.

Whistle from above.

He turns, sees third cube, looks at it, reflects, turns aside, reflects.

The third cube is pulled up and disappears in flies.

Beside carafe a rope descends from flies, with knots to facilitate ascent.

He continues to reflect.

Whistle from above.

He turns, sees rope, reflects, goes to it, climbs up it and is about to reach carafe when rope is let out and deposits him back on ground.

He reflects, looks around for scissors, sees them, goes and picks them up, returns to rope and starts to cut it with scissors.

The rope is pulled up, lifts him off ground, he hangs on, succeeds in cutting rope, falls back on ground, drops scissors, falls, gets up again immediately, brushes himself, reflects.

The rope is pulled up quickly and disappears in flies.

With length of rope in his possession he makes a lasso with which he tries to lasso carafe.

The carafe is pulled up quickly and disappears in flies.

He turns aside, reflects.

He goes with lasso in his hand to tree, looks at bough, turns and looks at cubes, looks again at bough, drops lasso, goes to cubes, takes up small one, carries it over and sets it down under bough, goes back for big one, takes it up and carries it over under bough, makes to put it on small one, hesitates, thinks better of it, sets it down, takes up small one and puts it on big one, tests their stability, turns aside and stoops to pick up lasso.

The bough folds down against trunk.

He straightens up with lasso in his hand, turns and sees what has happened.

He drops lasso, turns aside, reflects.

He carries back cubes to their place, one by one, goes back for lasso, carries it over to cubes and lays it in a neat coil on small one.

He turns aside, reflects.

Whistle from right wing.

He reflects, goes out right.

Immediately flung back on stage he falls, gets up immediately, brushes himself, turns aside, reflects.

Whistle from left wing.

He does not move.

He looks at his hands, looks around for scissors, sees them, goes and picks them up, starts to trim his nails, stops, reflects, runs his finger along blade of scissors, goes and lays them on small cube, turns aside, opens his collar, frees his neck and fingers it.

The small cube is pulled up and disappears in flies, carrying away rope and scissors.

He turns to take scissors, sees what has happened.

He turns aside, reflects.

He goes and sits down on big cube.

The big cube is pulled from under him. He falls. The big cube is pulled up and disappears in flies.

He remains lying on his side, his face towards auditorium, staring before him.

The carafe descends from flies and comes to rest a few feet from his body.

He does not move.

Whistle from above.

He does not move.

The carafe descends further, dangles and plays about his face.

He does not move.

The carafe is pulled up and disappears in flies.

The bough returns to horizontal, the palms open, the shadow returns.

Whistle from above.

He does not move.

The tree is pulled up and disappears in flies.

He looks at his hands.

CURTAIN

Poetry

Edith Sitwell (1887–1964)

Dirge for the New Sunrise

(Fifteen minutes past eight o'clock,
on the morning of Monday,
the 6th of August, 1945.)

Bound to my heart as Ixion to the
 wheel,
Nailed to my heart as the Thief upon
 the Cross,
I hang between our Christ and the gap
 where the world was lost

And watch the phantom Sun in Famine
 Street—
The ghost of the heart of man . . . red
 Cain, 5
And the more murderous brain
Of Man, still redder Nero that
 conceived the death
Of his mother Earth, and tore
Her womb, to know the place where he
 was conceived.

But no eyes grieved— 10
For none were left for tears:
They were blinded as the years
Since Christ was born. Mother or
 Murderer, you have given or taken
 life—
Now all is one!
There was a morning when the holy
 Light 15
Was young . . . The beautiful First
 Creature came
To our water-springs, and thought us
 without blame.

Our hearts seemed safe in our breasts
 and sang to the Light—
The marrow in the bone
We dreamed was safe . . . the blood in
 the veins, the sap in the tree 20
Were springs of Deity.
But I saw the little Ant-men as they ran
Carrying the world's weight of the
 world's filth
And the filth in the heart of Man—
Compressed till those lusts and greeds
 had a greater heat than that of the
 Sun. 25

And the ray from that heat came
 soundless, shook the sky
As if in search for food, and squeezed
 the stems
Of all that grows on the earth till they
 were dry—
And drank the marrow of the bone:
The eyes that saw, the lips that kissed,
 are gone— 30
Or black as thunder lie and grin at the
 murdered Sun.

The living blind and seeing Dead
 together lie
As if in love . . . There was no more
 hating then,
And no more love: Gone is the heart of
 Man.

Marianne Moore (1887–1972)

Poetry

I, too, dislike it: there are things that are important beyond all this
fiddle.
Reading it, however, with a perfect contempt for it, one discovers in
it after all, a place for the genuine.
Hands that can grasp, eyes
that can dilate, hair that can rise 5
if it must, these things are important not because a

high-sounding interpretation can be put upon them but because they
are
useful. When they become so derivative as to become unintelligible,
the same thing may be said for all of us, that we
do not admire what 10
we cannot understand: the bat
holding on upside down or in quest of something to

eat, elephants pushing, a wild horse taking a roll, a tireless wolf under
a tree, the immovable critic twitching his skin like a horse that feels
a flea, the base-
ball fan, the statistician— 15
nor is it valid
to discriminate against 'business documents and

school-books'; all these phenomena are important. One must make a
distinction
however: when dragged into prominence by half poets, the result is
not poetry,
nor till the poets among us can be 20
'literalists of
the imagination'—above
insolence and triviality and can present

for inspection, 'imaginary gardens with real toads in them', shall we
have
it. In the meantime, if you demand on the one hand, 25
the raw material of poetry in
all its rawness and
that which is on the other hand
genuine, you are interested in poetry.

The Steeple-Jack

Dürer would have seen a reason for living
in a town like this, with eight stranded whales
to look at; with the sweet sea air coming into your house
on a fine day, from water etched
with waves as formal as the scales
on a fish. 5

One by one in two's and three's, the seagulls keep
flying back and forth over the town clock,
or sailing around the light house without moving their wings—
rising steadily with a slight 10
quiver of the body—or flock
mewing where

a sea the purple of the peacock's neck is
paled to greenish azure as Dürer changed
the pine green of the Tyrol to peacock blue and guinea 15
gray. You can see a twenty-five-
pound lobster; and fish nets arranged
to dry. The

whirlwind fife-and-drum of the storm bends the salt
marsh grass, disturbs stars in the sky and the 20
star on the steeple; it is a privilege to see so
much confusion. Disguised by what
might seem the opposite, the sea-
side flowers and

trees are favored by the fog so that you have 25
the tropics at first hand: the trumpet vine,
foxglove, giant snapdragon, a salpiglossis that has
spots and stripes; morning-glories, gourds,
or moon-vines trained on fishing twine
at the back door: 30

cattails, flags, blueberries and spiderwort,
striped grass, lichens, sunflowers, asters, daisies—
yellow and crab-claw ragged sailors with green bracts—toad-plant,
petunias, ferns; pink lilies, blue
ones, tigers; poppies, black sweet-peas. 35
The climate

is not right for the banyan, frangipani, or
jack-fruit trees; or for exotic serpent
life. Ring lizard and snakeskin for the foot, if you see fit;
but here they've cats, not cobras, to 40
keep down the rats. The diffident
little newt

with white pin-dots on black horizontal spaced-
out bands lives here; yet there is nothing that
ambition can buy or take away. The college student 45
named Ambrose sits on the hillside
with his not-native books and hat
and sees boats

at sea progress white and rigid as if in
a groove. Liking an elegance of which 50
the source is not bravado, he knows by heart the antique
sugar-bowl shaped summerhouse of
interlacing slats, and the pitch
of the church

spire, not true, from which a man in scarlet lets 55
down a rope as a spider spins a thread;
he might be part of a novel, but on the sidewalk a
sign says C. J. Poole, Steeple Jack,
in black and white; and one in red
and white says 60

Danger. The church portico has four fluted
columns, each a single piece of stone, made
modester by whitewash. This would be a fit haven for
waifs, children, animals, prisoners,
and presidents who have repaid 65
sin-driven

senators by not thinking about them. The
place has a schoolhouse, a post-office in a
store, fish-houses, hen-houses, a three masted schooner on
the stocks. The hero, the student, 70
the steeple jack, each in his way,
is at home.

It could not be dangerous to be living
in a town like this, of simple people,
who have a steeple-jack placing danger signs by the church 75
while he is gilding the solid-
pointed star, which on a steeple
stands for hope.

Langston Hughes (1902–1967)

Theme for English B

The instructor said,

Go home and write
a page tonight.
And let that page come out of you—
Then, it will be true.

I wonder if it's that simple? 5

I am twenty-two, colored, born in Winston-Salem.
I went to school there, then Durham, then here
to this college on the hill above Harlem.
I am the only colored student in my class. 10
The steps from the hill lead down into Harlem,
through a park, then I cross St. Nicholas,
Eighth Avenue, Seventh, and I come to the Y,
the Harlem Branch Y, where I take the elevator
up to my room, sit down, and write this page: 15

It's not easy to know what is true for you or me
at twenty-two, my age. But I guess I'm what
I feel and see and hear, Harlem, I hear you:
hear you, here me—we two—you, me, talk on this page.
(I hear New York, too) Me—who? 20
Well, I like to eat, sleep, drink, and be in love.
I like to work, read, learn, and understand life.
I like a pipe for a Christmas present,
or records—Bessie, bop, or Bach.
I guess being colored doesn't make me *not* like 25
the same things other folks like who are other races.
So will my page be colored that I write?

Being me, it will not be white.
But it will be
a part of you, instructor. 30
You are white—
yet a part of me, as I am a part of you.
That's American.
Sometimes perhaps you don't want to be a part of me.
Nor do I often want to be a part of you. 35
But we are, that's true!

As I learn from you,
I guess you learn from me—
although you're older—and white—
and somewhat more free. 40

This is my page for English B.

The Negro Speaks of Rivers

(To W. E. B. DuBois)

I've known rivers:
I've known rivers ancient as the world and older than the flow of human blood in human veins.

My soul has grown deep like the rivers.

I bathed in the Euphrates when dawns were young.
I built my hut near the Congo and it lulled me to sleep.
I looked up the Nile and raised the pyramids above it.
I heard the singing of the Mississippi when Abe Lincoln went down to New Orleans, and I've seen its muddy bosom turn all golden in the sunset.

I've known rivers:
Ancient, dusky rivers.

My soul has grown deep like the rivers.

Dinner Guest: Me

I know I am
The Negro Problem
Being wined and dined,
Answering the usual questions
That come to white mind
Which seeks demurely
To probe in polite way
The why and wherewithal
Of darkness U.S.A.—
Wondering how things got this way
In current democratic night,
Murmuring gently

Over *fraises du bois*,
"I'm so ashamed of being white."

The lobster is delicious,
The wine divine,
And center of attention
At the damask table, mine.
To be a Problem on
Park Avenue at eight
Is not so bad.
Solutions to the Problem,
Of course, wait.

Harlem

What happens to a dream deferred?

Does it dry up
like a raisin in the sun?
Or fester like a sore—
And then run? 5
Does it stink like rotten meat?
Or crust and sugar over—
like a syrupy sweet?

Maybe it just sags
like a heavy load. 10

Or does it explode?

Richard Eberhart (1904–)

The Fury of Aerial Bombardment

You would think the fury of aerial bombardment
Would rouse God to relent; the infinite spaces
Are still silent. He looks on shock-pried faces.
History, even, does not know what is meant.

You would feel that after so many centuries 5
God would give man to repent; yet he can kill
As Cain could, but with multitudinous will,
No farther advanced than in his ancient furies.

Was man made stupid to see his own stupidity?
Is God by definition indifferent, beyond us all? 10
Is the eternal truth man's fighting soul
Wherein the Beast ravens in its own avidity?

Of Van Wettering I speak, and Averill,
Names on a list, whose faces I do not recall
But they are gone to early death, who late in school 15
Distinguished the belt feed lever from the belt holding pawl.

On Shooting Particles Beyond the World

"White Sands, N.M., Dec. 18 (U. P.). 'We first throw a little something into the skies,' Zwicky said. 'Then a little more, then a shipload of instruments, then ourselves.'"

On this day man's disgust is known
Incipient before but now full blown
With minor wars of major consequence,
Duly building empirical delusions.

Now this little creature in a rage 5
Like new-born infant screaming
 compleat angler
Objects to the whole globe itself
And with a vicious lunge he throws

Metal particles beyond the orbit of
 mankind.
Beethoven shaking his fist at death, 10
A giant dignity in human terms,
Is nothing to this imbecile metal fury.

The world is too much for him. The
 green
Of earth is not enough, love's deities,
Peaceful intercourse, happiness of
 nations, 15
The wild animals dazzled on the desert.

If the maniac would only realize
The comforts of his padded cell
He would have penetrated the
Impenetrability of the spiritual. 20
It is not intelligent to go too far.
How he frets that he can't go too!
But his particles would maim a star,
His free-floating bombards rock the
 moon.

Good Boy! We pat the baby to
 eructate, 25
We pat him then for eructation.
Good Boy Man! Your innards are put
 out,
From now all space will be your
 vomitorium.

The atom bomb accepted this world,
Its hatred of man blew death in his
 face. 30
But not content, he'll send slugs
 beyond,
His particles of intellect will spit on the
 sun.

Not God he'll catch, in the mystery of
 space.
He flaunts his own out-cast state
As he throws his imperfections outward
 bound 35
And his shout that gives a hissing
 sound.

John Betjeman (1906–)

In Westminster Abbey

Let me take this other glove off
  As the *vox humana* swells,
And the beauteous fields of Eden
  Bask beneath the Abbey bells.
Here, where England's statesmen lie, 5
Listen to a lady's cry.

Gracious Lord, oh bomb the Germans.
  Spare their women for Thy Sake,
And if that is not too easy
  We will pardon Thy Mistake. 10
But, gracious Lord, whate'er shall be,
Don't let anyone bomb me.

Keep our Empire undismembered
  Guide our Forces by Thy Hand,
Gallant blacks from far Jamaica, 15
  Honduras and Togoland;
Protect them Lord in all their fights,
And, even more, protect the whites.

Think of what our Nation stands for,
  Books from Boots' and country
    lanes, 20
Free speech, free passes, class
    distinction,
  Democracy and proper drains.
Lord, put beneath Thy special care
One-eighty-nine Cadogan Square.

Although dear Lord I am a sinner, 25
  I have done no major crime;
Now I'll come to Evening Service
  Whensoever I have the time.
So, Lord, reserve for me a crown,
And do not let my shares go down. 30

I will labour for Thy Kingdom,
  Help our lads to win the war,
Send white feathers to the cowards
  Join the Women's Army Corps,
Then wash the Steps around Thy
    Throne 35
In the Eternal Safety Zone.

Now I feel a little better,
  What a treat to hear Thy Word,
Where the bones of leading statesmen,
  Have so often been interr'd. 40
And now, dear Lord, I cannot wait
Because I have a luncheon date.

Theodore Roethke (1908–1963)

Open House

My secrets cry aloud.
I have no need for tongue.
My heart keeps open house,
My doors are widely swung.
An epic of the eyes 5
My love, with no disguise.

My truths are all foreknown,
This anguish self-revealed.
I'm naked to the bone,
With nakedness my shield, 10
Myself is what I wear:
I keep the spirit spare.

The anger will endure,
The deed will speak the truth
In language strict and pure. 15
I stop the lying mouth:
Rage warps my clearest cry
To witless agony.

My Papa's Waltz

The whiskey on your breath
Could make a small boy dizzy;
But I hung on like death:
Such waltzing was not easy.

We romped until the pans 5
Slid from the kitchen shelf;
My mother's countenance
Could not unfrown itself.

The hand that held my wrist
Was battered on one knuckle; 10
At every step you missed
My right ear scraped a buckle.

You beat time on my head
With a palm caked hard by dirt,
Then waltzed me off to bed 15
Still clinging to your shirt.

Highway: Michigan

Here from the field's edge we survey
The progress of the jaded. Mile
On mile of traffic from the town
Rides by, for at the end of day
The time of workers is their own. 5

They jockey for position on
The strip reserved for passing only.
The drivers from production lines
Hold to advantage dearly won.
They toy with death and traffic
fines. 10

Acceleration is their need:
A mania keeps them on the move
Until the toughest nerves are frayed.
They are the prisoners of speed
Who flee in what their hands have
made. 15
The pavement smokes when two cars
meet
And steel rips through conflicting steel.
We shiver at the siren's blast.
One driver, pinned beneath the seat,
Escapes from the machine at last. 20

Lull

(November, 1939)

The winds of hatred blow
Cold, cold across the flesh
And chill the anxious heart;
Intricate phobia grow
From each malignant wish 5
To spoil collective life.
Now each man stands apart.
We watch opinion drift,
Think of our separate skins,
On well-upholstered bums 10
The generals cough and shift
Playing with painted pins.
The arbitrators wait;
The newsmen suck their thumbs.
The mind is quick to turn 15
Away from simple faith
To the cant and fury of
Fools who will never learn;
Reason embraces death,
While out of frightened eyes 20
Still stares the wish to love.

Ballad of the Clairvoyant Widow

A kindly Widow Lady, who lived upon a hill,
Climbed to her attic window and gazed across the sill.

"Oh tell me, Widow Lady, what is it that you see,
As you look across my city, in God's country?"

"I see ten million windows, I see ten thousand streets, 5
I see the traffic doing miraculous feats.

The lawyers all are cunning, the business men are fat,
Their wives go out on Sunday beneath the latest hat.

The kids play cops and robbers, the kids play mumbley-peg,
Some learn the art of thieving, and some grow up to beg; 10

The rich can play at polo, the poor can do the shag,
Professors are condoning the cultural lag.

I see a banker's mansion with twenty wood-grate fires,
Alone, his wife is grieving for what her heart desires.

Next door there is a love-nest of plaster board and tin, 15
The rats soon will be leaving, the snow will come in."

"Clairvoyant Widow Lady, with an eye like a telescope,
Do you see any sign or semblance of that thing called 'Hope'?"

"I see the river harbor, alive with men and ships,
A surgeon guides a scalpel with thumb and finger-tips. 20

I see grandpa surviving a series of seven strokes,
The unemployed are telling stale unemployment jokes.

The gulls ride on the water, the gulls have come and gone,
The men on rail and roadway keep moving on and on.

The salmon climb the rivers, the rivers nudge the sea, 25
The green comes up forever in the fields of our country."

Ben Belitt (1911–)

Xerox

The original man lies down to be copied
face down on glass. He thinks what it is
to be other than he was, while the pilot light
goes garnet, a salamander's eye
blinks in the camera's cave, green burns like the skin 5
of the water seen by a surfacing swimmer,
and the moving and shaking begin.

What must it be, to be many? thinks the singular
man. Underneath, in the banked fluorescence, the rollers
are ready. A tarpaulin falls. A humming of flanges 10
arises, a sound like rail meeting rail
when power slams out of the fuses. A wick explodes
in the gases—and under the whole of his length
the eye of the holocaust passes.

And all that was lonely, essential, unique 15
as a fingerprint, is doubled. Substance and essence,
the mirror and the figure that printed the mirror,
the deluge that blackened creation and the hovering pigeon
with the leaf's taste in its beak,
are joined. The indivisible sleeper is troubled; 20
What does it mean to be legion?

"The final tragedy is that even my wildest fantasies are ordinary."

he cries in the hell of the copied. The rapists, the lovers,
the stealers of blessings, the corrupt and derivative
devils, whirl over the vacant emulsion.
The comedian peers from the brink and unsteadily copies 25
its laughter. The agonist prints its convulsion.
Like turns to like, while the seminal man on the glass
stares at his semblance and calls from the pit of the ink:

Forgive our duplicity. We are human
and heterogeneous. Give us our imitations! 30
Heart copies heart with a valentine's
arrows and laces. The Athenian dream and the adulterers paired
in the storm tell us the mirrors are misted. The whole of our art
is to double our witness, and wait. And the original man on the plate
stands and steps down, unassisted. 35

Karl Shapiro (1913–   )

Hollywood

Farthest from any war, unique in time
Like Athens or Baghdad, this city lies
Between dry purple mountains and the sea.
The air is clear and famous, every day
Bright as a postcard, bringing bungalows 5
    And sights. The broad nights advertise
For love and music and astronomy.

Heart of a continent, the hearts converge
On open boulevards where palms are nursed
With flare-pots like a grove, on villa roads 10
Where castles cultivated like a style
Breed fabulous metaphors in foreign stone,
    And on enormous movie lots
Where history repeats its vivid blunders.

Alice and Cinderella are most real. 15
Here may the tourist, quite sincere at last,
Rest from his dream of travels. All is new,
No ruins claim his awe, and permanence,
Despised like customs, fails at every turn.
    Here where the eccentric thrives, 20
Laughter and love are leading industries.

Luck is another. Here the body-guard,
The parasite, the scholar are well paid,
The quack erects his alabaster office,
The moron and the genius are enshrined, 25
And the mystic makes a fortune quietly;
    Here all superlatives come true
And beauty is marketed like a basic food.

O can we understand it? Is it ours,
A crude whim of a beginning people, 30
A private orgy in a secluded spot?
Or alien like the word *harem,* or true
Like hideous Pittsburgh or depraved Atlanta?
    Is adolescence just as vile
As this its architecture and its talk? 35

Or are they parvenus, like boys and girls?
Or ours and happy, cleverest of all?

Yes. Yes. Though glamorous to the ignorant
This is the simplest city, a new school.
What is more nearly ours? If soul can mean 40
  The civilization of the brain,
This is a soul, a possibly proud Florence.

The Conscientious Objector

The gates clanged and they walked you into jail
More tense than felons but relieved to find
The hostile world shut out, the flags that dripped
From every mother's windowpane, obscene
The bloodlust sweating from the public heart, 5
The dog authority slavering at your throat.
A sense of quiet, of pulling down the blind
Possessed you. Punishment you felt was clean.

The decks, the catwalks, and the narrow light
Composed a ship. This was a mutinous crew 10
Troubling the captains for plain decencies,
A *Mayflower* brim with pilgrims headed out
To establish new theocracies to west,
A Noah's ark coasting the topmost seas
Ten miles above the sodomites and fish. 15
These inmates loved the only living doves.

Like all men hunted from the world you made
A good community, voyaging the storm
To no safe Plymouth or green Ararat;
Trouble or calm, the men with Bibles prayed, 20
The gaunt politicals constructed our hate.
The opposite of all armies, you were best
Opposing uniformity and yourselves;
Prison and personality were your fate.

You suffered not so physically but knew 25
Maltreatment, hunger, ennui of the mind.
Well might the soldier kissing the hot beach
Erupting in his face damn all your kind.
Yet you who saved neither yourselves nor us
Are equally with those who shed the blood 30
The heroes of our cause. Your conscience is
What we come back to in the armistice.

University

To hurt the Negro and avoid the Jew
Is the curriculum. In mid-September
The entering boys, identified by hats,
Wander in a maze of mannered brick
  Where boxwood and magnolia brood 5
  And columns with imperious stance
  Like rows of anti-bellum girls
    Eye them, outlanders.

In whited cells, on lawns equipped for peace,
Under the arch, and lofty banister, 10
Equals shake hands, unequals blankly pass;
The exemplary weather whispers, "Quiet, quiet"
  And visitors on tiptoe leave
  For the raw North, the unfinished West,
  As the young, detecting an advantage, 15
    Practice a face.

Where, on their separate hill, the colleges,
Like manor houses of an older law,
Gaze down embankments on a land in fee,
The Deans, dry spinsters over family plate, 20
  Ring out the English name like coin,
  Humor the snob and lure the lout.
  Within the precincts of this world
    Poise is a club.

But on the neighboring range, misty and high, 25
The past is absolute: some luckless race
Dull with inbreeding and conformity
Wears out its heart, and comes barefoot and bad
  For charity or jail. The scholar
  Sanctions their obsolete disease; 30
  The gentleman revolts with shame
  At his ancestor.

  And the true nobleman, once a democrat,
Sleeps on his private mountain. He was one
Whose thought was shapely and whose dream was broad; 35
This school he held his art and epitaph.
  But now it takes from him his name,
  Falls open like a dishonest look,
  And shows us, rotted and endowed,
    Its senile pleasure. 40

Drug Store

I do remember an apothecary,
And hereabouts 'a dwells—

It baffles the foreigner like an idiom,
And he is right to adopt it as a form
Less serious than the living-room or bar; 5
For it disestablishes the café,
Is a collective, and on basic country.

Not that it praises hygiene and corrupts
The ice-cream parlor and the tobacconist's
Is it a center; but that the attractive symbols 10
Watch over puberty and leer
Like rubber bottles waiting for sick-use.

Youth comes to jingle nickels and crack wise;
The baseball scores are his, the magazines
Devoted to lust, the jazz, the Coca-Cola, 15
The lending-library of love's latest.
He is the customer; he is heroized.

And every nook and cranny of the flesh
Is spoken to by packages with wiles,
"Buy me, buy me," they whimper and cajole; 20
The hectic range of lipstick pouts,
Revealing the wicked and the simple mouth.

With scarcely any evasion in their eye
They smoke, undress their girls, exact a stance;
But only for a moment. The clock goes round; 25
Crude fellowships are made and lost;
They slump in booths like rags, not even drunk.

The Humanities Building

All the bad Bauhaus comes to a head
In this gray slab, this domino, this plinth
Standing among the olives or the old oak trees,
As the case may be and whatever the clime.
No bells, no murals, no gargoyles,
But rearing like a fort, with slits of eyes
Suspicious in the aggregate, its tons
Of concrete—glaciers of no known color—
Gaze down upon us. St. Thomas More,
Behold the Humanities Building!
On the top floor
Are one and a half professors of Greek,

Kicked upstairs but with the finest view,
Two philosophers, and assorted Slavics;
Then stacks of languages coming down,
Mainly the mother tongue and its dissident children
(History has a building all its own),
To the bottom level with its secretaries,
Advisers, blue-green photographic light
Of many precious copying machines;
All is bathed in cool fluorescence
From top to bottom, justly distributed:
Light, Innovation, Progress, Equity—
Though in my cell I hope and pray
Not to be confronted by
A student with a gun or a nervous breakdown,
Or a girl who closes the door as she comes in.

The Old Guard sits in judgment and wears ties,
Eying the New in proletarian drag,
And the Assistant with one lowered eyelid
Plots against Tenure, dreaming of getting it,

And in the lobby, under the bulletin boards,
The Baudelairean forest of posters
For Transcendental Meditation, Audubon Group,
"The Hunchback of Notre Dame," Scientology,
Arab Students Co-op, "Case of the Curious Bride,"
Two students munch upon a single sandwich.

Robert E. Hayden (1913–   )

Frederick Douglass

When it is finally ours, this freedom, this liberty, this beautiful
and terrible thing, needful to man as air,
usable as earth; when it belongs at last to all,
when it is truly instinct, brain matter, diastole, systole,
reflex action; when it is finally won; when it is more
than the gaudy mumbo jumbo of politicians:
this man, this Douglass, this former slave, this Negro
beaten to his knees, exiled, visioning a world
where none is lonely, none hunted, alien,
this man, superb in love and logic, this man   10
shall be remembered. Oh, not with statutes' rhetoric,
not with legends and poems and wreaths of bronze alone,
but with the lives grown out of his life, the lives
fleshing his dream of the beautiful, needful thing.

Runagate Runagate

I.

Runs falls rises stumbles on from darkness into darkness
and the darkness thickened with shapes of terror
and the hunters pursuing and the hounds pursuing
and the night cold and the night long and the river
to cross and the jack-muh-lanterns beckoning beckoning 5
and blackness ahead and when shall I reach that somewhere
morning and keep on going and never turn back and keep on going

Runagate
Runagate 10
Runagate

Many thousands rise and go
many thousands crossing over

O mythic North
O star-shaped yonder Bible city

15

Some go weeping and some rejoicing
some in coffins and some in carriages
some in silks and some in shackles

Rise and go or fare you well

No more auction block for me 20
no more driver's lash for me

If you see my Pompey, 30 yrs of age,
new breeches, plain stockings, negro shoes;
if you see my Anna, likely young mulatto
branded E on the right cheek, R on the left, 25
catch them if you can and notify subscriber.
Catch them if you can, but it won't be easy.
They'll dart underground when you try to catch them,
plunge into quicksand, whirlpools, mazes,
turn into scorpions when you try to catch them.

30

And before I'll be a slave
I'll be buried in my grave

North star and bonanza gold
I'm bound for the freedom, freedom-bound
and oh Susyanna don't you cry for me

35

Runagate
Runagate

II.

Rises from their anguish and their power,

Harriet Tubman,

woman of earth, whipscarred,
a summoning, a shining 40

Mean to be free

And this was the way of it, brethren brethren,
way we journeyed from Can't to Can.
Moon so bright and no place to hide,
the cry up and the patterollers riding, 45
hound dogs belling in bladed air.
And fears starts a-murbling, Never make it,
we'll never make it. *Hush that now.*
and she's turned upon us, levelled pistol
glinting in the moonlight: 50
Dead folks can't jaybird-talk, she says;
you keep on going now or die, she says.

Wanted Harriet Tubman alias The General
alias Moses Stealer of Slaves

In league with Garrison Alcott Emerson 55
Garrett Douglass Thoreau John Brown

Armed and known to be Dangerous

Wanted Reward Dead or Alive

Tell me, Ezekiel, oh tell me do you see
mailed Jehovah coming to deliver me? 60

Hoot-owl calling in the ghosted air,
five times calling to the hants in the air.
Shadow of a face in the scary leaves,
shadow of a voice in the talking leaves:

come ride-a my train 65

Oh that train, ghost-story train
through swamp and savanna movering movering,
over trestles of dew, through caves of the wish,
Midnight Special on a sabre track movering movering,
first stop Mercy and the last Hallelujah. 70

Come ride-a my train

Mean mean mean to be free.

"Summertime and the Living . . ."

Nobody planted roses, he recalls,
but sunflowers gangled there sometimes,
tough-stalked and bold
and like the vivid children there unplanned.
There circus-poster horses curveted 5
in trees of heaven
above the quarrels and shattered glass,
and he was bareback rider of them all.

No roses there in summer—
oh, never roses except when people died— 10
and no vacations for his elders,
so harshened after each unrelenting day
that they were shouting-angry.
But summer was, they said, the poor folks' time
of year. And he remembers 15
how they would sit on broken steps amid

The fevered tossings of the dusk, the dark,
wafting hearsay with funeral-parlor fans
or making evening solemn by
their quietness. Feels their Mosaic eyes 20
upon him, though the florist roses
that only sorrow could afford
long since have bidden them Godspeed.

Oh, summer summer summertime—

Then grim street preachers shook 25
their tambourines and Bibles in the face
of tolerant wickedness;
then Elks parades and big splendiferous
Jack Johnson in his diamond limousine
set the ghetto burgeoning 30
with fantasies
of Ethiopia spreading her gorgeous wings.

Tour 5

The road winds down through autumn hills
in blazonry of farewell scarlet
and recessional gold,
past cedar groves, through static villages
whose names are all that's left 5
of Choctaw, Chickasaw.

We stop a moment in a town
watched over by Confederate sentinels,
buy gas and ask directions of a rawboned man
whose eyes revile us as the enemy. 10

Shrill gorgon silence breathes behind
his taut civility
and in the ever-tautening air,
dark for us despite its Indian summer glow.
We drive on, following the route 15
of highwaymen and phantoms,

Of slaves and armies.
Children, wordless and remote,
wave at us from kindling porches.
And now the land is flat for miles, 20
the landscape lush, metallic, flayed,
its brightness harsh as bloodstained swords.

Randall Jarrell (1914–1965)

A Camp in the Prussian Forest

I walk beside the prisoners to the road.
Load on puffed load,
Their corpses, stacked like sodden
wood,
Lie barred or galled with blood

By the charred warehouse. No one
comes today 5
In the old way
To knock the fillings from their teeth;
The dark, coned, common wreath

Is plaited for their grave—a kind of
grief.
The living leaf 10
Clings to the planted profitable
Pine if it is able;

The boughs sigh, mile on green, calm,
breathing mile,
From this dead file
The planners ruled for them. . . . One
year 15
They sent a million here:

Here men were drunk like water, burnt
like wood.
The fat of good
And evil, the breast's star of hope
Were rendered into soap. 20

I paint the star I sawed from yellow
pine—
And plant the sign
In soil that does not yet refuse
Its usual Jews

Their first asylum. But the white,
dwarfed star— 25
This dead white star—
Hides nothing, pays for nothing; smoke
Fouls it, a yellow joke,

The needles of the wreath are chalked
with ash, 30
A filmy trash
Litters the black woods with the death
Of men; and one last breath

Curls from the monstrous chimney.
. . . I laugh aloud
Again and again; 35
The star laughs from its rotting shroud
Of flesh. O star of men!

Paul Freeman. "Concentration Camp," *The New York Times Book Review,* May 29, 1966.

The Death of the Ball Turret Gunner

From my mother's sleep I fell into the State,
And I hunched in its belly till my wet fur froze.
Six miles from earth, loosed from its dream of life,
I woke to black flak and the nightmare fighters.
When I died they washed me out of the turret with a hose. 5

A Girl in a Library

An object among dreams, you sit here with your shoes off
and curl your legs up under you; your eyes
Close for a moment, your face moves toward sleep . . .
You are very human.
But my mind, gone out in tenderness, 5
Shrinks from its object with a thoughtful sigh.
This is a waist the spirit breaks its arm on.
The gods themselves, against you, struggle in vain.
This broad low strong-boned brow; these heavy eyes;
These calves, grown muscular with certainties; 10
This nose, three medium-sized pink strawberries
—But I exaggerate. In a little you will leave:
I'll hear, half squeal, half shriek, your laugh of greeting—
Then, *decrescendo,* bars of that strange speech
In which each sound sets out to seek each other, 15
Murders its own father, marries its own mother,
And ends as one grand transcendental vowel.

(Yet for all I know, the Egyptian Helen spoke so.)
As I look, the world contracts around you:
I see Brünnhilde has brown braids and glasses 20
She used for studying; Salome straight brown bangs,
A calf's brown eyes, and sturdy light-brown limbs
Dusted with cinnamon, an apple-dumpling's . . .
Many a beast has gnawn a leg off and got free,

Many a dolphin curved up from Necessity— 25
The trap has closed about you, and you sleep.
If someone questioned you, *What doest thou here?*
You'd knit your brows like an orangoutang
(But not so sadly; not so thoughtfully)
And answer with a pure heart, guilelessly: 30
I'm studying. . . .
If only you were not!
Assignments,
recipes,
the *Official Rulebook* 35
Of Basketball—ah, let them go; you needn't mind.
The soul has no assignments, neither cooks
Nor referees: it wastes its time.
It wastes its time.
Here in this enclave there are centuries 40
For you to waste: the short and narrow stream
Of Life meanders into a thousand valleys
Of all that was, or might have been, or is to be.
The books, just leafed through, whisper endlessly . . .
Yet it is hard. One sees in your blurred eyes 45
The "uneasy half-soul" Kipling saw in dogs'.
One sees it, in the glass, in one's own eyes.
In rooms alone, in galleries, in libraries,
In tears, in searchings of the heart, in staggering joys
We memorize once more our old creation, 50
Humanity: with what yawns the unwilling
Flesh puts on its spirit, O my sister!

So many dreams! And not one troubles
Your sleep of life? no self stares shadowily
From these worn hexahedrons, beckoning 55
With false smiles, tears? . . .
Meanwhile Tatyana
Larina (gray eyes nickel with the moonlight
That falls through the willows onto Lensky's tomb;
Now young and shy, now old and cold and sure) 60
Asks, smiling: "But what is she dreaming of, fat thing?"
I answer: She's not fat. She isn't dreaming.
She purrs or laps or runs, all in her sleep;
Believes, awake, that she is beautiful;
She never dreams. 65
Those sunrise-colored clouds
Around man's head—that inconceivable enchantment
From which, at sunset, we come back to life
To find our graves dug, families dead, selves dying:
Of all this, Tanya, she is innocent. 70
For nineteen years she's faced reality:
They look alike already.
They say, man wouldn't be
The best thing in this world—and isn't he?—

If he were not too good for it. But she 75
—She's good enough for it.

And yet sometimes
Her sturdy form, in its pink strapless formal,
Is as if bathed in moonlight—modulated
Into a form of joy, a Lydian mode; 80
This Wooden Mean's a kind, furred animal
That speaks, in the Wild of things, delighting riddles
To the soul that listens, trusting . . .

Poor senseless Life:
When, in the last light sleep of dawn, the messenger 85
Comes with his message, you will not awake.
He'll give his feathery whistle, shake you hard,
You'll look with wide eyes at the dewy yard
And dream, with calm slow factuality:
"Today's Commencement. My bachelor's degree 90
In Home Ec., my doctorate of philosophy
In Phys. Ed.

[Tanya, they won't even *scan*]
Are waiting for me. . . ."

Oh, Tatyana, 95
The Angel comes: better to squawk like a chicken
Than to say with truth, "But I'm a *good* girl,"
And Meet his Challenge with a last firm strange
Uncomprehending smile; and —then, then!—see
The blind date that has stood you up; your life. 100
(For all this, if it isn't, perhaps, life,
Has yet, at least, a language of its own
Different from the books'; worse than the books'.)
And yet, the ways we miss our lives are life.
Yet . . . yet . . . 105

to have one's life add up to *yet!*
You sigh a shuddering sigh. Tatyana murmurs,
"Don't cry, little peasant"; leaves us with a swift
"Good-bye, good-bye . . . Ah, don't think ill of me . . ."
Your eyes open: you sit here thoughtlessly. 110
I love you—and yet—and yet—I love you.

Don't cry, little peasant. Sit and dream.
One comes, a finger's width beneath your skin,
To the braided maidens singing as they spin;
There sound the shepherd's pipe, the watchman's rattle 115
Across the short dark distance of the years.
I am a thought of yours: and yet, you do not think . . .
The firelight of a long, blind, dreaming story
Lingers upon your lips; and I have seen
Firm, fixed forever in your closing eyes, 120
The Corn King beckoning to his Spring Queen.

The Old and the New Masters

About suffering, about adoration, the old masters
Disagree. When someone suffers, no one else eats
Or walks or opens the window—no one breathes
As the sufferers watch the sufferer. 5
In *St. Sebastian Mourned by St. Irene*
The flame of one torch is the only light.
All the eyes except the maidservant's (she weeps
And covers them with a cloth) are fixed on the shaft
Set in his chest like a column; St. Irene's 10
Hands are spread in the gesture of the Madonna,
Revealing, accepting, what she does not understand
Her hands say: "Lo! Behold!"
Beside her a monk's hooded head is bowed, his hands
Are put together in the work of mourning. 15
It is as if they were still looking at the lance
Piercing the side of Christ, nailed on his cross.
The same nails pierce all their hands and feet, the same
Thin blood, mixed with water, trickles from their sides.
The taste of vinegar is on every tongue 20
That gasps, "My God, my God, why hast Thou forsaken me?"
They watch, they are, the one thing in the world.

So, earlier, everything is pointed
In Van der Goes' *Nativity,* toward the naked
Shining baby, like the needle of a compass.
The different orders and sizes of the world:

The angels like Little People, perched in the rafters
Or hovering in mid-air like hummingbirds;
The shepherds, so big and crude, so plainly adoring;
The medium-sized donor, his little family, 30
And their big patron saints; the Virgin who kneels
Before her child in worship; the Magi out in the hills
With their camels—they ask directions, and have pointed out
By a man kneeling, the true way; the ox
And the donkey, two heads in the manger 35
So much greater than a human head, who also adore;
Even the offerings, a sheaf of wheat,
A jar and a glass of flowers, are absolutely still
In natural concentration, as they take their part
In the salvation of the natural world.

The time of the world concentrates 40
On this one instant; far off in the rocks
You can see Mary and Joseph and their donkey
Coming to Bethlehem; on the grassy hillside
Where their flocks are grazing, the shepherds gesticulate
In wonder at the star; and so many hundreds 45
Of years in the future, the donor, his wife,
And their children are kneeling, looking: everything
That was or will be in the world is fixed
On its small, helpless, human center.

After a while the masters show the crucifixion 50
In one corner of the canvas: the men come to see
What is important, see that it is not important.
The new masters paint a subject as they please,
And Veronese is prosecuted by the Inquisition
For the dogs playing at the feet of Christ, 55
The earth is a plant among galaxies.
Later Christ disappears, the dogs disappear: in abstract
Understanding, without adoration, the last master puts
Colors on canvas, a picture of the universe
In which a bright spot somewhere in the corner 60
Is the small radioactive planet men called Earth.

Gunner

Did they send me away from my cat and my wife
To a doctor who poked me and counted my teeth,
To a line on a plain, to a stove in a tent?
Did I nod in the flies of the schools?

And the fighters rolled into the tracer like rabbits, 5
The blood froze over my splints like a scab—
Did I snore, all still and grey in the turret,
Till the palms rose out of the sea with my death?

And the world ends here, in the sand of a grave,
All my wars over? . . . It was easy as that! 10
Has my wife a pension of so many mice?
Did the medals go home to my cat?

Henry Reed (1914–)

Lessons of the War

To Alan Michell

Vixi duellis nuper idoneus
Et militavi non sine gloria

1. NAMING OF PARTS

Today we have naming of parts. Yesterday,
We had daily cleaning. And tomorrow morning,
We shall have what to do after firing. But today,
Today we have naming of parts. Japonica
Glistens like coral in all of the neighbouring gardens, 5
And today we have naming of parts.

This is the lower sling swivel. And this
Is the upper sling swivel, whose use you will see,
When you are given your slings. And this is the piling swivel,
Which in your case you have not got. The branches 10
Hold in the gardens their silent, eloquent gestures,
Which in our case we have not got.

This is the safety-catch, which is always released
With an easy flick of the thumb. And please do not let me
See anyone using his finger. You can do it quite easy 15
If you have any strength in your thumb. The blossoms
Are fragile and motionless, never letting anyone see
Any of them using their finger.

And this you can see is the bolt. The purpose of this
Is to open the breech, as you see. We can slide it 20
Rapidly backwards and forwards: we call this
Easing the spring. And rapidly backwards and forwards
The early bees are assaulting and fumbling the flowers:
They call it easing the Spring.

They call it easing the Spring: it is perfectly easy 25
If you have any strength in your thumb: like the bolt,
And the breech, and the cocking-piece, and the point of balance,
Which in our case we have not got; and the almond-blossom
Silent in all of the gardens and the bees going backwards and forwards,
For today we have naming of parts. 30

Dylan Thomas (1914–1953)

A Refusal to Mourn the Death, by Fire, of a Child in London

Never until the mankind making
Bird beast and flower
Fathering and all humbling darkness
Tells with silence the last light breaking
And the still hour 5
Is come of the sea tumbling in harness

And I must enter again the round
Zion of the water bead
And the synagogue of the ear of corn
Shall I let pray the shadow of a
sound 10
Or sow my salt seed
In the least valley of sackcloth to mourn

The majesty and burning of the child's
death.

I shall not murder
The mankind of her going with a grave
truth 15
Nor blaspheme down the stations of the
breath
With any further
Elegy of innocence and youth.

Deep with the first dead lies London's
daughter,
Robed in the long friends, 20
The grains beyond age, the dark veins
of her mother
Secret by the unmourning water
Of the riding Thames.
After the first death, there is no other.

Fern Hill

Now as I was young and easy under the
apple boughs
About the lilting house and happy as
the grass was green,
The night above the dingle starry,
Time let me hail and climb
Golden in the heydays of his eyes, 5
And honoured among wagons I was
prince of the apple towns
And once below a time I lordly had the
trees and leaves
Trail with daisies and barley
Down the rivers of the windfall light.

And as I was green and carefree,
famous among the barns 10
About the happy yard and singing as
the farm was home,
In the sun that is young once only,
Time let me play and be
Golden in the mercy of his means,
And green and golden I was huntsman
and herdsman, the calves 15
Sang to my horn, the foxes on the hills
barked clear and cold,
And the sabbath rang slowly
In the pebbles of the holy streams.

All the sun long it was running, it was
lovely, the hay-
Fields high as the house, the tunes from
the chimneys, it was air 20

and playing, lovely and watery
And fire green as grass.
And nightly under the simple stars
As I rode to sleep the owls were bearing the farm away,
All the moon long I heard, blessed among stables, the night-jars 25
Flying with the ricks, and the horses
Flashing into the dark.

And then to awake, and the farm, like a wanderer white
With the dew, come back, the cock on his shoulder: it was all
Shining, it was Adam and maiden, 30
The sky gathered again
And the sun grew round that very day.
So it must have been after the birth of the simple light
In the first, spinning place, the spellbound horses walking warm
Out of the whinnying green stable 35
On to the fields of praise.

And honoured among foxes and pheasants by the gay house
Under the new made clouds and happy as the heart was long,
In the sun born over and over,
I ran my heedless ways, 40
My wishes raced through the house-high hay
And nothing I cared, at my sky blue trades, that time allows
In all his tuneful turning so few and such morning songs
Before the children green and golden
Follow him out of grace, 45

Nothing I cared, in the lamb white days, that time would take me
Up to the swallow thronged loft by the shadow of my hand,
In the moon that is always rising,
Nor that riding to sleep
I should hear him fly with the high fields 50
And wake to the farm forever fled from the childless land.
Oh as I was young and easy in the mercy of his means,
Time held me green and dying
Though I sang in my chains like the sea.

Among Those Killed in the Dawn Raid Was a Man Aged One Hundred

When the morning was waking over the war
He put on his clothes and stepped out and he died,
The locks yawned loose and a blast blew them wide,
He dropped where he loved on the burst pavement stone
And the funeral grains of the slaughtered floor. 5
Tell his street on its back he stopped a sun
And the craters of his eyes grew springshoots and fire
When all the keys shot from the locks, and rang.
Dig no more for the chains of his grey haired heart.
The heavenly ambulance drawn by a wound 10
Assembling waits for the spades' ring on the cage.
O keep his bones away from that common cart,
The morning is flying on the wings of his age
And a hundred storks perch on the sun's right hand.

In My Craft or Sullen Art

In my craft or sullen art
Exercised in the still night
When only the moon rages
And the lovers lie abed
With all their griefs in their arms, 5
I labour by singing light
Not for ambition or bread
Or the strut and trade of charms
On the ivory stages
But for the common wages 10
Of their most secret heart.

Not for the proud man apart
From the raging moon I write
On these spindrift pages
Not for the towering dead 15
With their nightingales and psalms
But for the lovers, their arms
Round the griefs of the ages,
Who pay no praise or wages
Nor heed my craft or art. 20

John Ciardi (1916–   )

Elegy for G. B. Shaw

"If I survive this, I shall be immortal."

Administrators of minutes into hours,
Hours into ash, and ash to its own wedding
At the edge of fire and air—here's time at last
To make an ash of Shaw, who in his time
Survived his times, retired, and for a hobby 5
Bred fire to fire as one breeds guinea pigs.

In time, one can imagine, schoolchildren
Will confuse him as a contemporary of Socrates.
For a time, the fact is, he confused us:
We half believed he really had lived forever. 10
Sometimes, perhaps, a man can. That is to say,
Civilization is one man at a time,

And that forever, and he was that man.
For this we will not forgive him. Neither
The ape in me nor the ape in you, tenants 15
Of the flag-flying tree and drinkers of blood in season.
We meant to resemble the agonies of statues:
He left us only a treadmill in a cage.

Consider his crimes: He would not commit our diet.
He opened our tombs. He sold his medals for cash. 20
His laughter blew out our anthems. He wiped his nose
On the flags we die for—a crazy Irishman
Who looked like a goat and would not be serious.
But when we are finished, he will be our times.

And all times will be nothing in his eye. 25
All marshals, kings, and presidents we obey.
His presence in men's minds is contempt of court,
Of congress, and of flags. So must we pray
That he be born again, anarch and rare,
The race we are not in the race we are. 30

On a Photo of Sgt. Ciardi a Year Later

The sgt. stands so fluently in leather,
So poster-holstered and so newsreel-jawed
As death's costumed and fashionable brother,
My civil memory is overawed.

Behind him see the circuses of doom 5
Dance a finale chorus on the sun.
He leans on gunsights, doesn't give a damn
For dice or stripes, and waits to see the fun.

The cameraman whose ornate public eye
Invented that fine bravura look of calm 10
At murderous clocks hung ticking in the sky
Palmed the deception off without a qualm.

Even the camera, focused and exact
To a two dimensional conclusion,
Uttered its formula of physical fact 15
Only to lend data to illusion.

The camera always lies. By a law of perception
The obvious surface is always an optical ruse.
The leather was living tissue in its own dimension,
The holsters held benzedrine tablets, the guns were no use. 20

The careful slouch and dangling cigarette
Were always superstitious as Amen.
The shadow under the shadow is never caught;
The camera photographs the cameraman.

Chorus

They were singing Old MacDonald in the schoolbus
With a *peep peep* here and a *peep peep* there after
Margie Littenach had been delivered to the right mailbox
And the gears had gnashed their teeth uphill to the Cliff House
Where the driver, shifting gears, honked at the countergirls, 5

And the tourists turned from panorama all smiles
To remember schooldays, long curls, hooky, and how

The view had always stretched for miles and miles
Where the gentle cumulus puffed small in gentle weather
Putting a cottonfluff roof on the green world leaning down hill 10
To the bluelevelfield of sea, and all together
With an *oink oink* here and a *moo moo* there the children
Were singing Old MacDonald in the schoolbus

When a bolt fell from the compound interest problem,
A rod broke in the third chapter of the Civicsbook 15
Where the country had no money for inspection in the first place
and
Momentum had no brakes, but with a *honk honk* here
And a *honk honk* there went sidewise over tirescreech
Downturning in round air away from panorama where 20
Even the tourists could tell sea didn't measure each
Stone falling, or button, or bolt, or Caroline Helmhold,
Nor anywhere its multitudinous self incarnadine, but only swallowed
What books, belts, lunchpails, pity
Spilled over the touristfaredge of the world and Old MacDonald 25

Peter Viereck (1916–)

Kilroy

Also Ulysses once—that other war.
(Is it because we find his scrawl
Today on every ivy door
That we forget his ancient role?)
Also was there—he did it for the wages— 5
When a Cathay-drunk Genoese set sail.
Whenever "longen folk to goon on pilgrimages,"
Kilroy is there;
he tells The Miller's Tale.

At times he seems a paranoiac king 10
Who stamps his crest on walls and says "My Own!"
But in the end he fades like a lost tune,
Tossed here and there, whom all the breezes sing.

"Kilroy was here"; these words sound wanly gay,
Haughty yet tired with long marching. 15
He is Orestes—guilty of what crime?—

"Kilroy" first appeared in *Terror & Decorum*, out of print, recipient of Pulitzer Prize for poetry in 1949. Reprinted in Peter Viereck's *New and Selected Poems*, Bobbs-Merrill Co., N.Y.C., 1967.

For whom the Furies still are searching;
When they arrive, they find their prey
(Leaving his name to mock them) went away. 20
Sometimes he does not flee from them in time:
"Kilroy was—"
with his blood a dying man
Wrote half the phrase out in Bataan.

Kilroy, beware. "HOME" is the final trap 25
That lurks for you in many a wily shape:
In pipe-and-slippers plus a Loyal Hound
Or fooling around, just fooling around.
Kind to the old (their warm Penelope)
But fierce to boys, 30
Thus "home" becomes that sea,
Horribly disguised, where you were always drowned—
(How could suburban Crete condone
The yarns you would have V-mailed from the sun?)—
And folksy fishes sip Icarian tea.

One stab of hopeless wings imprinted your 35
Exultant Kilroy-signature
Upon sheer sky for all the world to stare:
"I was there! I was there! I was there!"

God is like Kilroy. He, too, sees it all;
That's how He knows of every sparrow's fall; 40
That's why we prayed each time the tightropes cracked
On which our loveliest clowns contrived their act,
The G. I. Faustus who was
everywhere
Strolled home again. "What was it like outside?" 45
Asked Can't, with his good neighbors Ought and But
And pale Perhaps and grave-eyed Better Not;
For "Kilroy" means: the world is very wide.
He was there, he was there, he was there!

And in the suburbs Can't sat down and cried. 50

"Fresh, spirited American troops, flushed with victory, are bringing in thousands of hungry, ragged, battle-weary prisoners . . ." (News item)

Gwendolyn Brooks (1917–   )

The Chicago Defender Sends a Man to Little Rock

Fall, 1957

In Little Rock the people bear
Babes, and comb and part their hair
And watch the want ads, put repair
To roof and latch. While wheat toast burns
A woman waters multiferns. 5

Time upholds or overturns
The many, tight, and small concerns.

In Little Rock the people sing
Sunday hymns like anything,
Through Sunday pomp and polishing. 10

And after testament and tunes,
Some soften Sunday afternoons
With lemon tea and Lorna Doones.

I forecast
and I believe 15
Come Christmas Little Rock will cleave
To Christmas tree and trifle, weave,
From laugh and tinsel, texture fast.

In Little Rock is baseball; Barcarolle.
That hotness in July . . . the uniformed figures raw and implacable
And not intellectual, 20
Battling the hotness or clawing the suffering dust.
The Open Air Concert, on the special twilight green . . .
When Beethoven is brutal or whispers to lady-like air.
Blanket-sitters are solemn, as Johann troubles to lean 25
To tell them what to mean. . . .

There is love, too, in Little Rock. Soft women softly
Opening themselves in kindness,
Or, pitying one's blindness,
Awaiting one's pleasure 30
In azure
Glory with anguished rose at the root . . .
To wash away old semi-discomfitures.

They re-teach purple and unsullen blue.
The wispy soils go. And uncertain 35
Half-havings have they clarified to sures.
In Little Rock they know
Not answering the telephone is a way of rejecting life,
That it is our business to be bothered, is our business
To cherish bores or boredom, be polite 40
To lies and love and many-faceted fuzziness.

I scratch my head, massage the hate-I-had.
I blink across my prim and pencilled pad.
The saga I was sent for is not down.
Because there is a puzzle in this town. 45
The biggest News I do not dare
Telegraph to the Editor's chair:
"They are like people everywhere."

The angry Editor would reply
In hundred harryings of Why. 50

And true, they are hurling spittle, rock,
Garbage and fruit in Little Rock.
And I saw coiling storm a-writhe
On bright madonnas. And a scythe
Of men harassing brownish girls. 55
(The bows and barrettes in the curls
And braids declined away from joy.)

I saw a bleeding brownish boy. . . .

The lariat lynch-wish I deplored.

The loveliest lynchee was our Lord. 60

the preacher: ruminates behind the sermon

I think it must be lonely to be God.
Nobody loves a master. No. Despite
The bright hosannas, bright dear-Lords, and bright
Determined reverence of Sunday eyes.

Picture Jehovah striding through the hall 5
Of His importance, creatures running out
From servant-corners to acclaim, to shout
Appreciation of His merit's glare.

But who walks with Him?—dares to take His arm,
To slap Him on the shoulder, tweak His ear, 10
Buy Him a Coca-Cola or a beer,
Pooh-pooh His politics, call Him a fool?

Perhaps—who knows?—He tires of looking down.
Those eyes are never lifted. Never straight.
Perhaps sometimes He tires of being great 15
In solitude. Without a hand to hold.

my dreams, my works, must wait till after hell

I hold my honey and I store my bread
In little jars and cabinets of my will.
I label clearly, and each latch and lid
I bid, Be firm till I return from hell.
I am very hungry. I am incomplete. 5
And none can tell when I may dine again.
No man can give me any word but Wait,
The puny light. I keep eyes pointed in;
Hoping that, when the devil days of my hurt
Drag out to their last dregs and I resume 10
On such legs as are left me, in such heart
As I can manage, remember to go home,
My taste will not have turned insensitive
To honey and bread old purity could love.

Robert Lowell (1917–1977)

Fall 1961

Back and forth, back and forth
goes the tock, tock, tock
of the orange, bland, ambassadorial
face of the moon
on the grandfather clock. 5

All autumn, the chafe and jar
of nuclear war;
we have talked our extinction to death.
I swim like a minnow
behind my studio window. 10

Our end drifts nearer,
the moon lifts,
radiant with terror.
The state
is a diver under a glass bell. 15

A father's no shield
for his child.
We are like a lot of wild
spiders crying together,
but without tears. 20

Nature holds up a mirror.
One swallow makes a summer.
It's easy to tick
off the minutes,
but the clockhands stick. 25

Back and forth!
Back and forth, back and forth—
my one point of rest
is the orange and black oriole's
swinging nest!

The Quaker Graveyard in Nantucket

(For Warren Winslow, Dead at Sea)

Let man have dominion over the fishes of the sea and the fowls of the air and the beasts and the whole earth, and every creature that moveth upon the earth.

I

A brackish reach of shoal off Madaket,—
The sea was still breaking violently and night
Had steamed into our North Atlantic Fleet,
When the drowned sailor clutched the drag-net. Light
Flashed from his matted head and marble feet, 5
He grappled at the net
With the coiled, hurdling muscles of his thighs:
The corpse was bloodless, a botch of reds and whites,
Its open staring eyes
Were lusterless dead-lights 10
Or cabin-windows on a stranded hulk
Heavy with sand. We weight the body, close
Its eyes and heave it seaward whence it came,
Where the heel-headed dogfish barks its nose
On Ahab's void and forehead; and the name 15
Is blocked in yellow chalk.
Sailors, who pitch this portent at the sea
Where dreadnaughts shall confess
Its hell-bent deity,
When you were powerless 20
To sand-bag the Atlantic bulwark, faced
By the earth-shaker, green, unwearied, chaste
In his steel scales: ask for no Orphean lute
To pluck life back. The guns of the steeled fleet
Recoil and then repeat 25
The hoarse salute.

II

Whenever winds are moving and their breadth
Heaves at the roped-in bulwarks of this pier,
The terns and sea-gulls tremble at your death
In these home waters. Sailor, can you hear 30
The Pequod's sea wings, beating landward, fall
Headlong and break on our Atlantic wall
Off 'Sconset, where the yawning S-boats splash

The bellbuoy, with ballooning spinnakers,
As the entangled, screeching mainsheet clears 35
The blocks: off Madaket, where lubbers lash
The heavy surf and throw their long lead squids
For blue-fish? Sea-gulls blink their heavy lids
Seaward. The winds' wings beat upon the stones,
Cousin, and scream for you and the claws rush 40
At the sea's throat and wring it in the slush
Of this old Quaker graveyard where the bones
Cry out in the long night for the hurt beast
Bobbing by Ahab's whaleboats in the East.

III

All you recovered from Poseidon died 45
With you, my cousin, and the harrowed brine
Is fruitless on the blue beard of the god,
Stretching beyond us to the castles in Spain,
Nantucket's westward haven. To Cape Cod
Guns, cradled on the tide, 50
Blast the eelgrass about a waterclock
Of bilge and backwash, roil the salt and sand
Lashing earth's scaffold, rock
Our warships on the hand
Of the great God, where time's contrition blues 55
Whatever it was these Quaker sailors lost
In the mad scramble of their lives. They died
When time was open-eyed,
Wooden and childish; only bones abide
There, in the nowhere, where their boats were tossed 60
Sky-high, where mariners had fabled news
Of IS, the whited monster. What it cost
Them is their secret. In the sperm-whale's slick
I see the Quakers drown and hear their cry:
"If God himself had not been on our side, 65
If God himself had not been on our side,
When the Atlantic rose against us, why,
Then it had swallowed us up quick."

IV

This is the end of the whaleroad and the whale
Who spewed Nantucket bones on the thrashed swell 70
And stirred the troubled waters to whirlpools
To send the Pequod packing off to hell:
This is the end of them, three-quarters fools,
Snatching at straws to sail
Seaward and seaward on the turntail whale, 75
Spouting out blood and water as it rolls,
Sick as a dog to these Atlantic shoals:
Clamavimus, O depths. Let the sea-gulls wail

For water, for the deep where the high tide
Mutters to its hurt self, mutters and ebbs. 80
Waves wallow in their wash, go out and out,
Leave only the death-rattle of the crabs,
The beach increasing, its enormous snout
Sucking the ocean's side.
This is the end of running on the waves; 85
We are poured out like water. Who will dance
The mast-lashed master of Leviathans
Up from this field of Quakers in their unstoned graves?

V

When the whale's viscera go and the roll
Of its corruption overruns this world 90
Beyond tree-swept Nantucket and Wood's Hole
And Martha's Vineyard, Sailor, will your sword
Whistle and fall and sink into the fat?
In the great ash-pit of Jehoshaphat
The bones cry for the blood of the white whale, 95
The fat flukes arch and whack about its ears,
The death-lance churns into the sanctuary, tears
The gun-blue swingle, heaving like a flail,
And hacks the coiling life out: it works and drags
And rips the sperm-whale's midriff into rags, 100
Gobbets of blubber spill to wind and weather,
Sailor, and gulls go round the stoven timbers
Where the morning stars sing out together
And thunder shakes the white surf and dismembers
The red flag hammered in the mast-head. Hide, 105
Our steel, Jonas Messias, in Thy side.

VI
OUR LADY OF WALSINGHAM

There once the penitents took off their shoes
And then walked barefoot the remaining mile;
And the small trees, a stream and hedgerows file
Slowly along the munching English lane, 110
Like cows to the old shrine, until you lose
Track of your dragging pain.
The stream flows down under the druid tree,
Shiloh's whirlpools gurgle and make glad
The castle of God. Sailor, you were glad 115
And whistled Sion by that stream. But see:

Our Lady too small for her canopy,
Sits near the altar. There's no comeliness
At all or charm in that expressionless
Face with its heavy eyelids. As before, 120

This face, for centuries a memory,
Non est species, neque decor,
Expressionless, expresses God: it goes
Past castled Sion. She knows what God knows,
No Calvary's Cross nor crib at Bethlehem 125
Now, and the world shall come to Walsingham.

VII

The empty winds are creaking and the oak
Splatters and splatters on the cenotaph,
The boughs are trembling and a gaff
Bobs on the untimely stroke 130
Of the greased wash exploding on a shoal-bell
In the old mouth of the Atlantic. It's well;
Atlantic, you are fouled with the blue sailors,
Sea-monsters, upward angel, downward fish:
Unmarried and corroding, spare of flesh 135
Mart once of supercilious, wing'd clippers,
Atlantic, where your bell-trap guts its spoil
You could cut the brackish winds with a knife
Here in Nantucket, and cast up the time
When the Lord God formed man from the sea's slime 140
And breathed into his face the breath of life,
And blue-lung'd combers lumbered to the kill.
The Lord survives the rainbow of His will.

Mr. Edwards and the Spider

I saw the spiders marching through the air,
Swimming from tree to tree that mildewed day
  In latter August when the hay
  Came creaking to the barn. But where
    The wind is westerly, 5
Where gnarled November makes the spiders fly
Into the apparitions of the sky,
They purpose nothing but their ease and die
Urgently beating east to sunrise and the sea;

What are we in the hands of the great God? 10
It was in vain you set up thorn and briar
  In battle array against the fire
  And treason crackling in your blood;
    For the wild thorns grow tame
And will do nothing to oppose the flame; 15
Your lacerations tell the losing game
You play against a sickness past your cure.

How will the hands be strong? How will the heart endure?
A very little thing, a little worm,
Or hourglass-blazoned spider, it is said, 20
Can kill a tiger. Will the dead
Hold up his mirror and affirm
To the four winds the smell
And flash of his authority? It's well
If God who holds you to the pit of hell, 25
Much as one holds a spider, will destroy,
Baffle and dissipate your soul. As a small boy

On Windsor Marsh, I saw the spider die
When thrown into the bowels of fierce fire:
There's no long struggle, no desire 30
To get up on its feet and fly—
It stretches out its feet
And dies. This is the sinner's last retreat;
Yes, and no strength exerted on the heat
Then sinews the abolished will, when sick 35
And full of burning, it will whistle on a brick.

But who can plumb the sinking of that soul?
Josiah Hawley, picture yourself cast
Into a brick-kiln where the blast
Fans your quick vitals to a coal— 40
If measured by a glass,
How long would it seem burning! Let there pass
A minute, ten, ten trillion; but the blaze
Is infinite, eternal: this is death,
To die and know it. This is the Black Widow, death. 45

Lawrence Ferlinghetti (1919–   )

Dada would have liked a day like this

Dada would have liked a day like this
with its various very realistic
unrealities
each about to become
too real for its locality 5
which is never quite remote enough
to be Bohemia
Dada would have loved a day like this
with its light-bulb sun

which shines so differently 10
for different people
but which still shines the same
on everyone
and on everything
such as 15
a bird on a bench about to sing
a plane in a gilded cloud
a dishpan hand
waving at a window
or a phone about to ring 20
or a mouth about to give up
smoking
or a new newspaper
with its new news story
of a cancerous dancer 25
Yes Dada would have died for a day like this
with its sweet street carnival
and its too real funeral
just passing thru it
with its real dead dancer 30
so beautiful and dumb
in her shroud
and her last lover lost
in the unlonely crowd
and its dancer's darling baby 35
about to say Dada
and its passing priest
about to pray
Dada
and offer his so transcendental 40
apologies
Yes Dada would have loved a day like this
with its not so accidental
analogies

Howard Nemerov (1920–)

Boom!

SEES BOOM IN RELIGION, TOO

Atlantic City, June 23, 1957 (AP).—*President Eisenhower's pastor said tonight that Americans are living in a period of "unprecedented religious activity" caused partially by paid vacations, the eight-hour day and modern conveniences.*

"These fruits of material progress," said the Rev. Edward L. R. Elson of the National Presbyterian Church, Washington, "have provided the leisure, the energy, and the means for a level of human and spiritual values never before reached."

Here at the Vespasian-Carlton, it's just one
religious activity after another; the sky
is constantly being crossed by cruciform
airplanes, in which nobody disbelieves
for a second, and the tide, the tide 5
of spiritual progress and prosperity
miraculously keeps rising, to a level
never before attained. The churches are full,
the beaches are full, and the filling-stations
are full, God's great ocean is full 10
of paid vacationers praying an eight-hour day
to the human and spiritual values, the fruits,
the leisure, the energy, and the means, Lord,
the means for the level, the unprecedented level,
and the modern conveniences, which also are full. 15
Never before, O Lord, have the prayers and praises
from belfry and phonebooth, from ballpark and barbecue
the sacrifices, so endlessly ascended.

It was not thus when Job in Palestine
sat in the dust and cried, cried bitterly; 20
when Damien kissed the lepers on their wounds
it was not thus; it was not thus
when Francis worked a fourteen-hour day
strictly for the birds; when Dante took
a week's vacation without pay and it rained 25
part of the time, O Lord, it was not thus.

But now the gears mesh and the tires burn
and the ice chatters in the shaker and the priest
in the pulpit, and Thy Name, O Lord,
is kept before the public, while the fruits 30
ripen and religion booms and the level rises
and every modern convenience runneth over,
that it may never be with us as it hath been
with Athens and Karnak and Nagasaki,
nor Thy sun for one instant refrain from shining 35
on the rainbow Buick by the breezeway
or the Chris Craft with the uplift life raft;
that we may continue to be the just folks we are,
plain people with ordinary superliners and
disposable diaperliners, people of the stop'n'shop 40
'n' pray as you go, of hotel, motel, boatel,
the humble pilgrims of no deposit no return
and please adjust thy clothing, who will give to Thee,
if Thee will keep us going, our annual
Miss Universe, for Thy Name's Sake, Amen. 45

Richard Wilbur (1921–   )

Advice to a Prophet

When you come, as you soon must, to the streets of our city,
Mad-eyed from stating the obvious,
Not proclaiming our fall but begging us
In God's name to have self-pity,

Spare us all word of the weapons, their force and range, 5
The long numbers that rocket the mind;
Our slow, unreckoning hearts will be left behind,
Unable to fear what is too strange.

Nor shall you scare us with talk of the death of the race.
How should we dream of this place without us?—
The sun mere fire, the leaves untroubled about us,
A stone look on the stone's face?

Speak of the world's own change. Though we cannot conceive
Of an undreamt thing, we know to our cost
How the dreamt cloud crumbles, the vines are blackened by frost, 15
How the view alters. We could believe,

If you told us so, that the white-tailed deer will slip
Into perfect shade, grown perfectly shy,
The lark avoid the reaches of our eye,
The jack-pine lose its knuckled grip 20

On the cold ledge, and every torrent burn
As Xanthus once, its gliding trout
Stunned in a twinkling. What should we be without
The dolphin's arc, the dove's return,

These things in which we have seen ourselves and spoken? 25
Ask us, prophet, how we shall call
Our natures forth when that live tongue is all
Dispelled, that glass obscured or broken

In which we have said the rose of our love and the clean
Horse of our courage, in which beheld 30
The singing locust of the soul unshelled,
And all we mean or wish to mean.

Ask us, ask us whether with the worldless rose
Our hearts shall fail us; come demanding
Whether there shall be lofty or long standing 35
When the bronze annals of the oak-tree close.

The Writer

In her room at the prow of the house
Where light breaks, and the windows are tossed with linden,
My daughter is writing a story.

I pause in the stairwell, hearing
From her shut door a commotion of typewriter-keys 5
Like a chain hauled over a gunwale.

Young as she is, the stuff
Of her life is a great cargo, and some of it heavy:
I wish her a lucky passage.

But now it is she who pauses, 10
As if to reject my thought and its easy figure.
A stillness greatens, in which

The whole house seems to be thinking,
And then she is at it again with a bunched clamor
Of strokes, and again is silent. 15

I remember the dazed starling
Which was trapped in that very room, two years ago;
How we stole in, lifted a sash

And retreated, not to affright it;
And how for a helpless hour, through the crack of the door, 20
We watched the sleek, wild, dark

And iridescent creature
Batter against the brilliance, drop like a glove
To the hard floor, or the desk-top,

And wait then, humped and bloody, 25
For the wits to try it again; and how our spirits
Rose when, suddenly sure,

It lifted off from a chair-back,
Beating a smooth course for the right window
And clearing the sill of the world. 30

It is always a matter, my darling,
Of life or death, as I had forgotten. I wish
What I wished you before, but harder.

Philip Larkin (1922–   )

Church Going

Once I am sure there's nothing going on
I step inside, letting the door thud shut.
Another church: matting, seats, and stone,
And little books; sprawlings of flowers, cut
For Sunday, brownish now; some brass and stuff 5
Up at the holy end; the small neat organ;
And a tense, musty, unignorable silence,
Brewed God knows how long. Hatless, I take off
My cycle-clips in awkward reverence,

Move forward, run my hand around the font. 10
From where I stand, the roof looks almost new—
Cleaned, or restored? Someone would know: I don't.
Mounting the lectern, I peruse a few
Hectoring large-scale verses, and pronounce
"Here endeth" much more loudly than I'd meant. 15
The echoes snigger briefly. Back at the door
I sign the book, donate an Irish sixpence,
Reflect the place was not worth stopping for.

Yet stop I did: in fact I often do,
And always end much at a loss like this, 20
Wondering what to look for; wondering, too,
When churches fall completely out of use
What we shall turn them into, if we shall keep
A few cathedrals chronically on show,
Their parchment, plate and pyx in locked cases, 25
And let the rest rent-free to rain and sheep.
Shall we avoid them as unlucky places?

Or after dark, will dubious women come
To make their children touch a particular stone;
Pick simples for a cancer; or on some 30
Advised night see walking a dead one?
Power of some sort or another will go on
In games, in riddles, seemingly at random;
But superstition, like belief, must die,
And what remains when disbelief has gone? 35
Grass, weedy pavement, brambles, buttress, sky,

A shape less recognizable each week,
A purpose more obscure. I wonder who
Will be the last, the very last, to seek

This place for what it was; one of the crew 40
That tap and jot and know what rood-lofts were?
Some ruin-bibber, randy for antique,
Or Christmas-addict, counting on a whiff
Of gown-and-bands and organ-pipes and myrrh?
Or will he be my representative, 45

Bored, uninformed, knowing the ghostly silt
Dispersed, yet tending to this cross of ground
Through suburb scrub because it held unspilt
So long and equably what since is found
Only in separation—marriage, and birth, 50
And death, and thoughts of these—for which was built
This special shell? For, though I've no idea
What this accoutred frowsty barn is worth,
It pleases me to stand in silence here;

A serious house on serious earth it is, 55
In whose blent air all our compulsions meet,
Are recognized, and robed as destinies.
And that much never can be obsolete,
Since someone will forever be surprising
A hunger in himself to be more serious, 60
And gravitating with it to this ground,
Which, he once heard, was proper to grow wise in,
If only that so many dead lie round.

MCMXIV

Those long uneven lines
Standing as patiently
As if they were stretched outside
The Oval or Villa Park,
The crowns of hats, the sun 5
On moustached archaic faces
Grinning as if it were all
An August Bank Holiday lark;

And the shut shops, the bleached
Established names on the sunblinds, 10
The farthings and sovereigns,
And dark-clothed children at play
Called after kings and queens,
The tin advertisements
For cocoa and twist, and the pubs 15
Wide open all day;

And the countryside not caring:
The place-names all hazed over
With flowering grasses, and fields
Shadowing Domesday lines 20
Under wheat's restless silence;
The differently-dressed servants
With tiny rooms in huge houses,
The dust behind limousines;

Never such innocence, 25
Never before or since,
As changed itself to past
Without a word—the men
Leaving the gardens tidy,
The thousands of marriages 30
Lasting a little while longer:
Never such innocence again.

I Remember, I Remember

Coming up England by a different line
For once, early in the cold new year,
We stopped, and, watching men with number-plates
Sprint down the platform to familiar gates,
"Why, Coventry!" I exclaimed, "I was born here." 5

I leant far out, and squinnied for a sign
That this was still the town that had been "mine"
So long, but found I wasn't even clear
Which side was which. From where those cycle-crates
Were standing, had we annually departed 10

For all those family hols? . . . A whistle went:
Things moved. I sat back, staring at my boots.
"Was that," my friend smiled, "where you 'have your roots'?"
No, only where my childhood was unspent,
I wanted to retort, just where I started: 15

By now I've got the whole place clearly charted.
Or garden, first: where I did not invent
Blinding theologies of flowers and fruits,
And wasn't spoken to by an old hat.
And here we have that splendid family 20

I never ran to when I got depressed,
The boys all biceps and the girls all chest,
Their comic Ford, their farm where I could be
"Really myself." I'll show you, come to that,
The bracken where I never trembling sat, 25

Determined to go through with it; where she
Lay back, and "all became a burning mist."
And, in those offices, my doggerel
Was not set up in blunt ten-point, nor read
By a distinguished cousin of the mayor, 30

Who didn't call and tell my father *There*
Before us, had we the gift to see ahead—
"You look as if you wished the place in Hell,"
My friend said, "judging from your face." "Oh well,
I suppose it's not the place's fault," I said, 35
"Nothing, like something, happens anywhere."

Reasons for Attendance

The trumpet's voice, loud and authoritative,
Draws me a moment to the lighted glass
To watch the dancers—all under twenty-five—
Shifting intently, face to flushed face,
Solemnly on the beat of happiness. 5

—Or so I fancy, sensing the smoke and sweat,
The wonderful feel of girls. Why be out here?
But then, why be in there? Sex, yes, but what
Is sex? Surely, to think the lion's share
Of happiness is found by couples—sheer 10
Inaccuracy, as far as I'm concerned.
What calls me is that lifted, rough-tongued bell
(Art, if you like) whose individual sound
Insists I too am individual.
It speaks; I hear; others may hear as well; 15

But not for me, nor I for them; and so
With happiness. Therefore I stay outside,
Believing this; and they maul to and fro,
Believing that; and both are satisfied,
If no one has misjudged himself. Or lied. 20

Anthony Hecht (1923–)

The Dover Bitch
A Criticism of Life

So there stood Matthew Arnold and this girl
With the cliffs of England crumbling away behind them,
And he said to her, "Try to be true to me,
And I'll do the same for you, for things are bad
All over, etc., etc." 5
Well now, I knew this girl. It's true she had read
Sophocles in a fairly good translation
And caught that bitter allusion to the sea,
But all the time he was talking she had in mind
The notion of what his whiskers would feel like 10
On the back of her neck. She told me later on
That after a while she got to looking out
At the lights across the channel, and really felt sad,
Thinking of all the wine and enormous beds
And blandishments in French and the perfumes. 15
And then she got really angry. To have been brought
All the way down from London, and then be addressed
As a sort of mournful cosmic last resort
Is really tough on a girl, and she was pretty.

Anyway, she watched him pace the room 20
And finger his watch-chain and seem to sweat a bit,
And then she said one or two unprintable things.
But you mustn't judge her by that. What I mean to say is,
She's really all right. I still see her once in a while
And she always treats me right. We have a drink 25
And I give her a good time, and perhaps it's a year
Before I see her again, but there she is,
Running to fat, but dependable as they come.
And sometimes I bring her a bottle of *Nuit d'Amour.*

"More Light! More Light!"

Composed in the Tower before his execution
These moving verses, and being brought at that time

Painfully to the stake, submitted, declaring thus:
"I implore my God to witness that I have made no crime"

Nor was he forsaken of courage, but the death was horrible, 5
The sack of gunpowder failing to ignite.
His legs were blistered sticks on which the black sap
Bubbled and burst as he howled for the Kindly Light.

And that was but one, and by no means one of the worst;
Permitted at least his pitiful dignity; 10
And such as were made prayers in the names of Christ,
That shall judge all men, for his soul's tranquillity.

We move now to outside a German wood.
Three men are there commanded to dig a hole
In which the two Jews are ordered to lie down 15
And be buried alive by the third, who is a Pole.

Not light from the shrine at Weimar beyond the hill
Nor light from heaven appeared. But he did refuse.
A Lüger settled back deeply in its glove.
He was ordered to change places with the Jews. 20

Much casual death had drained away their souls.
The thick dirt mounted toward the quivering chin.
When only the head was exposed the order came
To dig him out again and to get back in.

No light, no light in the blue Polish eye. 25
When he finished a riding boot packed down the earth.
The Lüger hovered lightly in its glove.
He was shot in the belly and in three hours bled to death.

No prayers or incense rose up in those hours
Which grew to be years, and every day came mute 30
Thousands sifting down through the crisp air
And settled upon his eyes in a black soot.

Ruth Ann Lief (1923–)

Eve's Daughters

The old masters of subordination, were they right?
Superior by testicle to this weak vessel with plentiful hair?
When Nora got liberated, where did she go, you want to know.
Where? Here and there like her captors to register title
On erasable slate to traits flesh was heir to. Did she learn 5
More than an embrace is an embrace, and when the cords
Strained with intolerable rage in her neck
Drink and sex were ways, thinking was another?
And of course she poetastered, Mr. Pope.
Her plight was intricate, implicit with sins 10
Perpetuate in her and her mother. On the whole
Little help from the men, who had a tendency
To trace the causes of her malady to a curable
Itch in the crotch, with which she was more seldom
Afflicted than her doctors. Oh well, in another hundred years 15
She should be human. Then what shall we do for difference

Sailing for Oblivion

This is no world for old girls.
The thread of generation snaps and stings their womb.
Umbilicals shrivel in their scrapbooks.
They are due from gynecology to pass
Into the hands of the internist soon. 5
What will he find to keep his interest in the species
Alive?

Inoperable clots. Daughter begotten
Prodigal of promise (is she honest?
Madam, do you really want to hear?) 10
Son come a cropper, supervised
By prognoses of fear.
Last egg spermed by elderly sire
Poses possible malignancy.

Starting with the head, then the heart— 15
The tender parts—the slender teeth have eaten
And the permanent now gnaw with all reasonable speed
Intestine, gizzard, et cetera.
Will it profit (bright little teeth
Flashing in lightless nest of consumption)— 20
Will it get all the protein it needs?

There are parent study groups
In the schools of the world,
But there are no good places
For the old girls. . . . 25

September

This is no touch-and-go
Tear on the talcummed cheek,
Resistant rivulets in the oiled dust
Of a parched city. This means, this rain,
To irritate the root, hugging the canal 5
Of nostalgia to a bed of pain:
No post-coital reverie
Of damages sustained
Through investments of lust—
Though that too, intermixed 10
With what I must, remembering
Those teens roaring the climax of being,
Forever receding, now admit
As intimation that, stirred and spurred,
I left the future far behind me. 15

What acned image of stick-thin mannequins—
Slim heels, pin legs, sheer shifts,
Cloche-matted curls, umbrellas bent
To the wind, eternal flapping flappers
Hastening through half-light to their hims, 20
Elongated in the wet Elysées—
What picture of suspended destinies
Toe-clinging the brink of instants did I
Devise to fix the dream of becoming
Beyond the fitful fall of days, 25
The unreached rendezvous, the free
Peripeteia of potential?
How often in the arms of lover fate,
The dastard undoer of purpose, did I
Eat sadness like salad in the green world 30
And feel my protein liver swirl
In the brown gorge of central earth

Down the root which dying, dying,
Emptied that Parisian rue,
The inky trees insouciant, 35
And left the lamp posts frosting mist
And silvering rococo windows
Of inconclusive trysts?

It hurts no more or less today,
The scene cleansed of thou and me,
The climate of hopes eroded well 40
Before they were entertained, nor way
In routeless future which has passed
To make quietus with this rain.

Louis Simpson (1923–)

Walt Whitman at Bear Mountain

*... life which does not give the
preference to any other life, of any
previous period, which therefore
prefers its own existence ...*
—Ortega y Gasset

Neither on horseback nor seated,
But like himself, squarely on two feet,
The poet of death and lilacs
Loafs by the footpath. Even the bronze
looks alive
Where it is folded like cloth. And he
seems friendly. 5

"Where is the Mississippi panorama
And the girl who played the piano?
Where are you, Walt?
The Open Road goes to the used-car lot.

"Where is the nation you promised? 10
These houses built of wood sustain
Colossal snows,
And the light above the street is sick to
death.

"As for the people—see how they
neglect you!
Only a poet pauses to read the
inscription." 15

"I am here," he answered.
"It seems you have found me out.
Yet, I did not warn you that it was
Myself
I advertised? Were my words not
sufficiently plain?

"I gave no prescriptions, 20
And those who have taken my moods
for prophecies
Mistake the matter."
Then, vastly amused—"Why do you
reproach me?
I freely confess I am wholly
disreputable.
Yet I am happy, because you have
found me out." 25

A crocodile in wrinkled metal
loafing . . .

Then all the realtors,
Pickpockets, salesmen, and the actors
performing
Official scenarios,
Turned a deaf ear, for they had
contracted 30
American dreams.

But the man who keeps a store on a
lonely road,
And the housewife who knows she's
dumb.
And the earth, are relieved.

All that grave weight of America 35
Cancelled! Like Greece and Rome.
The future in ruins!
The castles, the prisons, the cathedrals
Unbuilding, and roses
Blossoming from the stones that are not
there . . . 40

The clouds are lifting from the high
Sierras.
The Bay mists clearing;
And the angel in the gate, the flowering
plum,
Dances like Italy, imagining red.

My Father in the Night Commanding No

My father in the night commanding No
Has work to do. Smoke issues from his lips;
He reads in silence.
The frogs are croaking and the streetlamps glow.

And then my mother winds the gramophone; 5
The Birds of Lammermoor begins to shriek—
Or reads a story
About a prince, a castle and a dragon.

The moon is glittering above the hill.
I stand before the gateposts of the King— 10
So runs the story—
Of Thule, at midnight when the mice are still.

And I have been in Thule! It has come true—
The journey and the danger of the world,
All that there is 15
To bear and to enjoy, endure and do.

Landscapes, seascapes . . . where have I been led?
The names of cities—Paris, Venice, Rome—
Held out their arms.
A feathered god, seductive, went ahead. 20

Here is my house. Under a red rose tree
A child is swinging; another gravely plays.
They are not surprised
That I am here; they were expecting me.

And yet my father sits and reads in silence, 25
My mother sheds a tear, the moon is still,
And the dark wind
Is murmuring that nothing ever happens.

Beyond his jurisdiction as I move
Do I not prove him wrong? And yet, it's true 30
They will not change
There, on the stage of terror and of love.

The actors in that playhouse always sit
In fixed positions—father, mother, child
With painted eyes. 35
How sad it is to be a little puppet!

Their heads are wooden. And you once pretended
To understand them! Shake them as you will,
They cannot speak.
Do what you will, the comedy is ended. 40

Father, why did you work? Why did you weep,
Mother, Was the story so important?
"Listen!" the wind
Said to the children, and they fell asleep.

James Dickey (1923–)

The Heaven of Animals

Here they are. The soft eyes open.
If they have lived in a wood
It is a wood.
If they have lived on plains
It is grass rolling 5
Under their feet forever.

Having no souls, they have come,
Anyway, beyond their knowing.
Their instincts wholly bloom
And they rise. 10
The soft eyes open.

To match them, the landscape flowers,
Outdoing, desperately
Outdoing what is required:
The richest wood, 15
The deepest field.

For some of these,
It could not be the place
It is, without blood.
These hunt, as they have done, 20
But with claws and teeth grown perfect,

More deadly than they can believe.
They stalk more silently,
And crouch on the limbs of trees,
And their descent 25
Upon the bright backs of their prey

May take years
In a sovereign floating of joy.
And those that are hunted
Know this as their life, 30
Their reward: to walk

Under such trees in full knowledge
Of what is in glory above them,
And to feel no fear,
But acceptance, compliance. 35
Fulfilling themselves without pain

At the cycle's center,
They tremble, they walk
Under the tree,
They fall, they are torn, 40
They rise, they walk again.

Allen Ginsberg (1926–)

A Supermarket in California

What thoughts I have of you tonight, Walt Whitman, for I walked down the side-streets under the trees with a headache self-conscious looking at the full moon.
In my hungry fatigue, and shopping for images, I went into the neon fruit supermarket, dreaming of your enumerations!
What peaches and what penumbras! Whole families shopping at night! Aisles full of husbands! Wives in the avocados, babies in the tomatoes!—and you, Garcia Lorca, what were you doing down by the watermelons? 5

I saw you, Walt Whitman, childless, lonely old grubber, poking among the meats in the refrigerator and eyeing the grocery boys.
I heard you asking questions of each: Who killed the pork chops? What price bananas? Are you my Angel? 10
I wandered in and out of the brilliant stacks of cans following you, and followed in my imagination by the store detective.
We strode down the open corridors together in our solitary fancy tasting artichokes, possessing every frozen delicacy, and never passing the cashier. 15

Where are we going, Walt Whitman? The doors close in an hour. Which way does your beard point tonight?
(I touch your book and dream of our odyssey in the supermarket and feel absurd.)
Will we walk all night through solitary streets? The trees add shade to shade, lights out in the houses, we'll both be lonely. 20

Will we stroll dreaming of the lost America of love past blue automobiles in driveways, home to our silent cottage?
Ah, dear father, graybeard, lonely old courage-teacher, what America did you have when Charon quit poling his ferry and you got out on a smoking bank and stood watching the boat disappear on the black waters of Lethe? 25

America

America I've given you all and now I'm nothing.
America two dollars and twenty-seven cents January 17, 1956.
I can't stand my own mind.
America when will we end the human war?
Go fuck yourself with your atom bomb 5
I don't feel good don't bother me.
I won't write my poem till I'm in my right mind.
America when will you be angelic?
When will you take off your clothes?
When will you look at yourself through the grave? 10
When will you be worthy of your million Trotskyites?
America why are your libraries full of tears?
America when will you send your eggs to India?
I'm sick of your insane demands.
When can I go into the supermarket and buy what I need with my good looks? 15
America after all it is you and I who are perfect not the next world.
Your machinery is too much for me.
You made me want to be a saint.
There must be some other way to settle this argument.
Burroughs is in Tangiers I don't think he'll come back it's sinister. 20
Are you being sinister or is this some form of practical joke?
I'm trying to come to the point.
I refuse to give up my obsession.
America stop pushing I know what I'm doing.
America the plum blossoms are falling. 25
I haven't read the newspapers for months, everyday somebody goes on trial for murder.
America I feel sentimental about the Wobblies.
America I used to be a communist when I was a kid I'm not sorry.
I smoke marijuana every chance I get.
I sit in my house for days on end and stare at the roses in the closet. 30
When I go to Chinatown I get drunk and never get laid.
My mind is made up there's going to be trouble.
You should have seen me reading Marx.
My psychoanalyst thinks I'm perfectly right.
I won't say the Lord's Prayer. 35
I have mystical visions and cosmic vibrations.
America I still haven't told you what you did to Uncle Max after he came over from Russia.

I'm addressing you.
Are you going to let our emotional life be run by Time Magazine?
I'm obsessed by Time Magazine. 40
I read it every week.
Its cover stares at me every time I slink past the corner candystore.
I read it in the basement of the Berkeley Public Library.
It's always telling me about responsibility. Businessmen are serious. Movie producers are serious. Everybody's serious but me. 45

It occurs to me that I am America.
I am talking to myself again.

Asia is rising against me.
I haven't got a chinaman's chance.
I'd better consider my national resources. 50
My national resources consist of two joints of marijuana millions of genitals an unpublishable private literature that goes 1400 miles an hour and twentyfivethousand mental institutions.
I say nothing about my prisons nor the millions of underprivileged who live in my flowerpots under the light of five hundred suns.
I have abolished the whorehouses of France, Tangiers is the next to go.
My ambition is to be President despite the fact that I'm a Catholic.

America how can I write a holy litany in your silly mood? 55
I will continue like Henry Ford my strophes are as individual as his automobiles more so they're all different sexes.
America I will sell you strophes $2500 apiece $500 down on your old strophe
America free Tom Mooney
America save the Spanish Loyalists
America Sacco & Vanzetti must not die 60
America I am the Scottsboro boys.
America when I was seven momma took me to Communist Cell meetings they sold us garbanzos a handful per ticket a ticket costs a nickel and the speeches were free everybody was angelic and sentimental about the workers it was all so sincere you have no idea what a good thing the party was in 1935 Scott Nearing was a grand old man a real mensch Mother Bloor made me cry I once saw Israel Amter plain. Everybody must have been a spy.
America you don't really want to go to war.
America it's them bad Russians.
Them Russians them Russians and them Chinamen. And them Russians. 65
The Russia wants to eat us alive. The Russia's power mad. She wants to take our cars from out our garages.
Her wants to grab Chicago. Her needs a Red Reader's Digest. Her wants our auto plants in Siberia. Him big bureaucracy running our fillingstations.
That no good. Ugh. Him make Indians learn read. Him need big black niggers. Hah. Her make us all work sixteen hours a day. Help.
America this is quite serious.
America this is the impression I get from looking in the television set. 70
America is this correct?
I'd better get right down to the job.
It's true I don't want to join the Army or turn lathes in precision parts factories, I'm nearsighted and psychopathic anyway.
America I'm putting my queer shoulder to the wheel.

Sunflower Sutra

I walked on the banks of the tincan banana dock and sat down under the huge shade of a Southern Pacific locomotive to look at the sunset over the box house hills and cry.

Jack Kerouac sat beside me on a busted rusty iron pole, companion, we thought the same thoughts of the soul, bleak and blue and sad-eyed, surrounded by the gnarled steel roots of trees of machinery.

The oily water on the river mirrored the red sky, sun sank on top of final Frisco peaks, no fish in that stream, no hermit in those mounts, just ourselves rheumy-eyed and hungover like old bums on the riverbank, tired and wily.

Look at the Sunflower, he said, there was a dead gray shadow against the sky, big as a man, sitting dry on top of a pile of ancient sawdust—

—I rushed up enchanted—it was my first sunflower, memories of Blake—my visions—Harlem

and Hells of the Eastern rivers, bridges clanking Joes Greasy Sandwiches, dead baby carriages, black treadless tires forgotten and unretreaded, the poem of the riverbank, condoms & pots, steel knives, nothing stainless, only the dank muck and the razor sharp artifacts passing into the past—

and the gray Sunflower poised against the sunset, cracky bleak and dusty with the smut and smog and smoke of olden locomotives in its eye—

corolla of bleary spikes pushed down and broken like a battered crown, seeds fallen out of its face, soon-to-be-toothless mouth of sunny air, sunrays obliterated on its hairy head like a dried wire spiderweb,

leaves stuck out like arms out of the stem, gestures from the sawdust root, broke pieces of plaster fallen out of the black twigs, a dead fly in its ear,

Unholy battered old thing you were, my sunflower O my soul, I loved you then!

The grime was no man's grime but death and human locomotives,

all that dress of dust, that veil of darkened railroad skin, that smog of cheek, that eyelid of black mis'ry, that sooty hand or phallus or protuberance of artificial worse-than-dirt—industrial—modern—all that civilization spotting your crazy golden crown—

and those blear thoughts of death and dusty loveless eyes and ends and withered roots below, in the home-pile of sand and sawdust, rubber dollar bills, skin of machinery, the guts and innards of the weeping coughing car, the empty lonely tincans with their rusty tongues slack, what more could I name, the smoked ashes of some cock cigar, the cunts of wheelbarrows and the milky breasts of cars, worn-out asses out of chairs & sphincters of dynamos—all these

entangled in your mummied roots—and you there standing before me in the sunset, all your glory in your form!

A perfect beauty of a sunflower! a perfect excellent lovely sunflower existence! a sweet natural eye to the new hip moon, woke up alive and excited grasping in the sunset shadow sunrise golden monthly breeze!

How many flies buzzed round you innocent of your grime, while you cursed the heavens of the railroad and your flower soul?

Poor dead flower? when did you forget you were a flower? when did you look at your skin and decide you were an impotent dirty old locomotive? the ghost of a locomotive? the specter and shade of a once powerful mad American locomotive?

You were never no locomotive, Sunflower, you were a sunflower!

And you Locomotive, you are a locomotive, forget me not!
So I grabbed up that skeleton thick sunflower and stuck it at my side like a scepter.
and deliver my sermon to my soul, and Jack's soul too, and anyone who'll listen,
—We're not our skin of grime, we're not our dread bleak dusty imageless locomotive, we're all beautiful golden sunflowers inside, we're blessed by our own seed & golden hairy naked accomplishment—bodies growing into mad black formal sunflowers in the sunset, spied on by our eyes under the shadow of the mad locomotive riverbank sunset Frisko hilly tincan evening sitdown vision.

Robert Bly (1926–)

Watching Television

Sounds are heard too high for ears,
From the body cells there is an answering bay;
Soon the inner streets fill with a chorus of barks.

We see the landing craft coming in,
The black car sliding to a stop, 5
The Puritan killer loosening his guns.

Wild dogs tear off noses and eyes
And run off with them down the street—
The body tears off its own arms and throws them into the air.

The detective draws fifty-five million people into his revolver, 10
Who sleep restlessly as in an air raid in London;
Their backs become curved in the sloping dark.

The filaments of the soul slowly separate:
The spirit breaks, a puff of dust floats up,
Like a house in Nebraska that suddenly explodes. 15

Those Being Eaten By America

The cry of those being eaten by America,
Others pale and soft being stored for later eating

And Jefferson
Who saw hope in new oats

The wild houses go on 5
With long hair growing from between their toes
The feet at night get up
And run down the long white roads by themselves

The dams reverse themselves and want to go stand alone in the desert

Ministers who dive headfirst into the earth 10
The pale flesh
Spreading guiltily into new literatures

That is why these poems are so sad
The long dead running over the fields

The mass sinking down 15
The light in children's faces fading at six or seven

The world will soon break up into small colonies of the saved

Counting Small-Boned Bodies

Let's count the bodies over again.

If we could only make the bodies smaller,
The size of skulls,
We could make a whole plain white with skulls in the moonlight!

If we could only make the bodies smaller, 5
Maybe we could get
A whole year's kill in front of us on a desk!

If we could only make the bodies smaller,
We could fit
A body into a finger-ring, for a keepsake forever. 10

W. D. Snodgrass (1926–)

The Campus on the Hill

Up the reputable walks of old established trees
They stalk, children of the *nouveaux riches*; chimes
Of the tall Clock Tower drench their heads in blessing:
"I don't wanna play at your house;
I don't like you any more." 5
My house stands opposite, on the other hill,
Among meadows, with the orchard fences down and falling;
Deer come almost to the door.
You cannot see it, even in this clearest morning.
White birds hang in the air between 10
Over the garbage landfill and those homes thereto adjacent,
Hovering slowly, turning, settling down
Like the flakes sifting imperceptibly onto the little town
In a waterball of glass.
And yet, this morning, beyond this quiet scene, 15
The floating birds, the backyards of the poor,
Beyond the shopping plaza, the dead canal, the hillside
  lying tilted in the air,
Tomorrow has broken out today:
Riot in Algeria, in Cyprus, in Alabama; 20
Aged in wrong, the empires are declining,
And China gathers soundlessly, like evidence.
What shall I say to the young on such a morning?—
Mind is the one salvation?—also grammar?—
No; my little ones lean not toward revolt. They 25
Are the Whites, the vaguely furiously driven, who resist
Their souls with such passivity
As would make Quakers swear. All day, dear Lord, all day
They wear their godhead lightly.
They look out from their hill and say, 30
To themselves, "We have nowhere to go but down;
The great destination is to stay."
Surely the nations will be reasonable;
They look at the world—don't they?—the world's way?
The clock just now has nothing more to say. 35

April Inventory

The green catalpa tree has turned
All white; the cherry blooms once more.
In one whole year I haven't learned
A blessed thing they pay you for.
The blossoms snow down in my hair; 5
The trees and I will soon be bare.

The trees have more than I to spare.
The sleek, expensive girls I teach,
Younger and pinker every year,
Bloom gradually out of reach. 10
The pear tree lets its petals drop
Like dandruff on a tabletop.

The girls have grown so young by now
I have to nudge myself to stare.
This year they smile and mind me how 15
My teeth are falling with my hair.
In thirty years I may not get
Younger, shrewder, or out of debt.

The tenth time, just a year ago,
I made myself a little list 20
Of all the things I'd ought to know,
Then told my parents, analyst,
And everyone who's trusted me
I'd be substantial, presently.

I haven't read one book about 25
A book or memorized one plot.
Or found a mind I did not doubt.
I learned one date. And then forgot.
And one by one the solid scholars
Get the degrees, the jobs, the dollars. 30

And smile above their starchy collars.
I taught my classes Whitehead's notions;
One lovely girl, a song of Mahler's.
Lacking a source-book or promotions,
I showed one child the colors of 35
A luna moth and how to love.

I taught myself to name my name,
To bark back, loosen love and crying;
To ease my woman so she came,
To ease an old man who was dying. 40
I have not learned how often I
Can win, can love, but choose to die.

I have not learned there is a lie
Love shall be blonder, slimmer, younger;
That my equivocating eye 45
Loves only by my body's hunger;
That I have forces, true to feel,
Or that the lovely world is real.

While scholars speak authority
And wear their ulcers on their sleeves, 50
My eyes in spectacles shall see
These trees procure and spend their leaves.
There is a value underneath
The gold and silver in my teeth.

Though trees turn bare and girls turn wives, 55
We shall afford our costly seasons;
There is a gentleness survives
That will outspeak and has its reasons.
There is a loveliness exists,
Preserves us, not for specialists. 60

Charles Tomlinson (1927–)

Poem

Upended, it crouches on broken limbs
About to run forward. No longer
threatened
But surprised into this vigilance
It gapes enmity from its hollowed core.

Moist woodflesh, softened to a paste 5
Of marl and white splinter, dangles
Wherever overhead the torn root
Casts up its wounds in a ragged orchis.

The seasons strip, but do not tame you.
I grant you become more smooth 10
As you are emptied and where the
heart shreds
The gap mouths a more practiced silence.

You would impress, but merely startle.
Your accomplice
Twilight is dragging its shadows here
Deliberate and unsocial: I leave you 15
To your own meaning, yourself alone.

Return to Hinton

Written on the author's return to Hinton Blewett from the United States

Ten years
and will you be
a footnote, merely,
England
of the Bible 5
open at Genesis
on the parlour table?
"God
saw the light
that it was good." 10
It falls
athwart the book
through window-lace
whose shadow
decorates the sheets 15
of "The Bridal March"—
a square of white
above the keyboard
and below
a text which is a prayer. 20
The television box
is one,
the mullions and flagged floor
of the kitchen
through an open door 25
witness a second
world in which
beside the hob
the enormous kettles'
blackened bellies ride— 30
as much the tokens of an order as
the burnished brass.
You live
between the two
and, ballasted against 35
the merely new, the tide
and shift of time
you wear
your widow's silk
your hair 40
plaited, as it has been
throughout those years
whose rime it bears.
A tractor
mounts the ramp of stones 45
into the yard:
a son surveys
the scenes
that occupied a father's days.
Proud of his machine, 50
will he transmit
that more than bread
that leaves you undisquieted?
This house
is poorer by a death 55
than last I saw it
yet
who may judge
as poverty that
sadness without bitterness 60
those sudden tears
that your composure
clears, admonishes?
Your qualities
are like the land 65
—inherited:
but you
have earned
your right to them
have given 70
grief its due
and, on despair,
have closed your door
as the gravestones tell you to.
Speak 75
your composure and you share
the accent of their rhymes
express
won readiness
in a worn dress 80
of chapel gospel.
Death's
not the enemy
of you nor of your kind:
a surer death 85
creeps after me
out of that generous
rich and nervous land

where, buried by
the soft oppression of
prosperity, 90
locality's mere grist
to build
the even bed
of roads that will not rest
until they lead 95
into a common future
rational
and secure
that we must speed
by means that are not either. 100
Narrow
your farm-bred certainties
I do not hold:
I share
your certain enemy. 105
For we who write
the verse you do not read
already plead your cause
before
that cold tribunal 110
while you're unaware
they hold their session.
Our language is our land
that we'll
not waste or sell 115
against a promised mess
of pottage that we may not
taste.
For who has known
the seasons' sweet succession
and would still 120
exchange them for a whim, a wish
or swim into
a mill-race for an unglimpsed
fish?

James Wright (1927–1980)

The Revelation

Stress of his anger set me back
To musing over time and space.
The apple branches dripping black
Divided light across his face.
Towering beneath the broken tree, 5
He seemed a stony shade to me.
He spoke no language I could hear
For long with my distracted ear.

Between his lips and my delight
In blowing wind, a bird-song rose. 10
And soon in fierce, blockading light
The planet's shadow hid his face.
And all that strongly molded bone
Of chest and shoulder soon were gone,
Devoured among the soiled shade. 15
Assured his angry voice was dead,

And satisfied his judging eyes
Had given over plaguing me,
I stood to let the darkness rise—
My darkness, gathering in the tree, 20
The field, the swollen shock of hay,
Bank of the creek half washed away.
Lost in my self, and unaware
Of love, I took the evening air.
I blighted, for a moment's length, 25
My father out of sight and sound;
Prayed to annihilate his strength,
The proud legs planted on the ground.

Why should I hear his angry cry
Or bear the damning of his eye? 30
Anger for anger I could give,
And murder for my right to live.
The moon rose. Lucidly the moon
Ran skimming shadows off the trees,
To strip all shadow but its own 35
Down to the perfect mindlessness.
Yet suddenly the moon light caught
My father's fingers reaching out,
The strong arm begging me for love,
Loneliness I knew nothing of. 40

And weeping in the nakedness
Of moonlight and of agony,
His blue eyes lost their barrenness
And bore a blossom out to me

And as I ran to give it back, 45
The apple branches, dripping black,
Trembled across the lunar air
And dropped white petals on his hair.

Complaint

She's gone. She was my love, my moon or more.
She chased the chickens out and swept the floor,
Emptied the bones and nut-shells after feasts,
And smacked the kids for leaping up like beasts.
Now morbid boys have grown past awkwardness; 5
The girls let stitches out, dress after dress,
To free some swinging body's riding space
And form the new child's unimagined face.
Yet, while vague nephews, spitting on their curls,
Amble to pester winds and blowsy girls, 10
What arm will sweep the room, what hand will hold
New snow against the milk to keep it cold?
And who will dump the garbage, feed the hogs,
And pitch the chickens' heads to hungry dogs?
Not my lost hag who dumbly bore such pain: 15
Childbirth and midnight sassafras and rain.
New snow against her face and hands she bore,
And now lies down, who was my moon or more.

Two Poems About President Harding

One: His Death

In Marion, the honey locust trees are falling.
Everybody in town remembers the white hair,
The campaign of a lost summer, the front porch
Open to the public, and the vaguely stunned smile
Of a lucky man. 5

"Neighbor, I want to be helpful," he said once.
Later, "You think I'm honest, don't you?"
Weeping drunk.

I am drunk this evening in 1961,
In a jog for my countryman, 10
Who died of crab meat on the way back from Alaska.
Everyone knows that joke.

How many honey locusts have fallen,
Pitched rootlong into the open graves of strip mines,
Since the First World War ended 15
And Wilson the gaunt deacon jogged sullenly
Into silence?
Tonight,
The cancerous ghosts of old con men
Shed their leaves. 20
For a proud man,
Lost between the turnpike near Cleveland
And the chiropractors' signs looming among dead mulberry trees,
There is no place left to go
But home. 25

"Warren lacks mentality," one of his friends said.
Yet he was beautiful, he was the snowfall
Turned to white stallions standing still
Under dark elm trees.

He died in public. He claimed the secret right 30
To be ashamed.

Two: His Tomb in Ohio

. . . he died of a busted gut.
—Mencken, on Bryan

A hundred slag piles north of us,
At the mercy of the moon and rain,
He lies in his ridiculous
Tomb, our fellow citizen. 35
No, I have never seen that place,
Where many shadows of faceless thieves
Chuckle and stumble and embrace
On beer cans, stogie butts, and graves.

One holiday, one rainy week 40
After the country fell apart,
Hoover and Coolidge came to speak
And snivel about his broken heart.
His grave, a huge absurdity,
Embarrassed cops and visitors. 45
Hoover and Coolidge crept away
By night, and women closed their doors.

Now junkmen call their children in
Before they catch their death of cold;
Young lovers let the moon begin 50
Its quick spring; and the day grows old;
The mean one-legger who rakes up leaves
Has chased the loafers out of the park;
Minnegan Leonard half-believes 55
In God, and the poolroom goes dark;

America goes on, goes on
Laughing, and Harding was a fool.
Even his big pretentious stone
Lays him bare to ridicule. 60
I know it. But don't look at me.
By God, I didn't start this mess.
Whatever moon and rain may be,
The hearts of men are merciless.

Eisenhower's Visit to Franco, 1959

. . . we die of cold, and not
of darkness.—Unamuno

The American hero must triumph over
The forces of darkness.
He has flown through the very light of
heaven
And come down in the slow dusk
Of Spain. 5

Franco stands in a shining circle of
police.
His arms open in welcome.
He promises all dark things
Will be hunted down.

State police yawn in the prisons. 10
Antonio Machado follows the moon
Down a road of white dust,
To a cave of silent children
Under the Pyrenees.
Wine darkens in stone jars in
villages. 15
Wine sleeps in the mouths of old men,
it is a dark red color.

Smiles glitter in Madrid.
Eisenhower has touched hands with
Franco, embracing
In a glare of photographers.
Clean new bombers from America
muffle their engines 20
And glide down now.

Their wings shine in the searchlights
Of bare fields,
In Spain.

Bink Noll (1927–)

The Lock

remembers the first door, on which
it was the first bolt shot forward
and declares "You are somewhat bad,
Mankind." And I say "These are mine."

She calls down "Have you locked the door?" 5
Habit, same as owning a moat:
"Have you filled the moat?"

Two or three
bad men pollute the neighborhood—
pillage, arson, mutilation, rape— 10
and round us the stagnant moat.

And the stranger locked out who could
help himself to fruit and a drink,
nap on the couch, walk off with a spoon.
Of course I've locked the door. 15

Originally published by *The Virginia Quarterly Review*, September 1971. Used by permission of Bink Noll.

But think:
those raised floors—pavillions sideless
and grass-roofed—where villages sleep
without knowing they own so much
that Want prowls forward through the murk. 20
O Happy Savages!

But we
northern men for ten thousand years
have bred attack into the dogs
that sleep by our fires, leap and SNAP! 25
like the more recent, more certain lock.

O Efficacious Lock! your wedge,
your spring, your admirable wards,
your keyhold and my key and this,
your inside bolt, and all is safe. 30
Stranger Want does not hear your snap
but expects you, your counter force,
my door stubborn as a policeman
with prudence on its side, and law.

Philip Levine (1928–)

They Feed They Lion

Out of burlap sacks, out of bearing butter,
Out of black bean and wet slate bread,
Out of the acids of rage, the candor of tar,
Out of creosote, gasoline, drive shafts, wooden dollies,
They Lion grow. 5
Out of the gray hills
Of industrial barns, out of rain, out of bus ride,
West Virginia to Kiss My Ass, out of buried aunties,
Mothers hardening like pounded stumps, out of stumps,
Out of the bones' need to sharpen and the muscles' to stretch, 10
They Lion grow.
Earth is eating trees, fence posts,
Gutter cars, earth is calling in her little ones,
"Come home, Come home!" From pig balls,
From the ferocity of pig driven to holiness, 15
From the furred ear and the full jowl come
The repose of the hung belly, from the purpose
They Lion grow.

From the sweet glues of the trotters
Come the sweet kinks of the fist, from the full flower 20
Of the hams the thorax of caves,
From "Bow Down" come "Rise Up,"
Come they Lion from the reeds of shovels,
The grained arm that pulls the hands,
They Lion grow. 25
From my five arms and all my hands,
From all my white sins forgiven, they feed,
From my car passing under the stars,
They Lion, from my children inherit,
From the oak turned to a wall, they Lion, 30
From the sack and they belly opened
And all that was hidden burning on the oil-stained earth
They feed they Lion and he comes.

Coming Home, Detroit, 1968

A winter Tuesday, the city pouring fire,
Ford Rouge sulfurs the sun, Cadillac, Lincoln,
Chevy gray. The fat stacks
of breweries hold their tongues. Rags,
papers, hands, the stems of birches 5
dirtied with words.
Near the freeway
you stop and wonder what came off,
recall the snowstorm where you lost it all,
the wolverine, the northern bear, the wolf 10
caught out, ice and steel raining
from the foundries in a shower
of human breath. On sleds in the false sun
the new material rests. One brown child
stares and stares into your frozen eyes 15
until the lights change and you go
forward to work. The charred faces, the eyes
boarded up, the rubble of innards, the cry
of wet smoke hanging in your throat,
the twisted river stopped at the color of iron. 20
We burn this city every day.

Donald Hall (1928–   )

The Body Politic

I shot my friend to save my country's
  life,
And when the happy bullet struck him
  dead,
I was saluted by the drum and fife
Corps of a high school, while the traitor
  bled.

I never thought until I pulled the
  trigger 5
But that I did the difficult and good.
I thought republics stood for something
  bigger,
For the mind of man, as Plato said they
  stood.

So when I heard the duty they assigned,
Shooting my friend seemed only
  sanity; 10
To keep disorder from the state of mind
Was mental rectitude, it seemed to me.

The audience dispersed. I felt
  depressed.
I went to where my orders issued from,
But the right number on the street was
  just 15
A vacant lot. Oh, boy, had I been
  dumb!

I tried to find the true address, but
  where?
Nobody told me what I had to know,
And secretaries sent me here and there
To other secretaries, just for show. 20

Poor Fred. His presence will be greatly
  missed
By children and by cronies by the score.
The State (I learn too late) does not
  exist;
Man lives by love, and not by
  metaphor.

Anne Sexton (1928–1974)

Cinderella

You always read about it:
the plumber with twelve children
who wins the Irish Sweepstakes.
From toilets to riches.
That story. 5

Or the nursemaid
some luscious sweet from Denmark
who captures the oldest son's heart.
From diapers to Dior
That story. 10

Or a milkman who serves the wealthy,
eggs, cream, butter, yogurt, milk,

the white truck like an ambulance
who goes into real estate
and makes a pile. 15
From homogenized to martinis at lunch.

Or the charwoman
who is on the bus when it cracks up
and collects enough from the insurance.
From mops to Bonwit Teller. 20
That story.

Once
the wife of a rich man was on her deathbed
and she said to her daughter Cinderella:
Be devout. Be good. Then I will smile 25
down from heaven in the seam of a cloud.
The man took another wife who had
two daughters, pretty enough
but with hearts like blackjacks.
Cinderella was their maid. 30
She slept on the sooty hearth each night
and walked around looking like Al Jolson.
Her father brought presents home from town,
jewels and gowns for the other women
but the twig of a tree for Cinderella. 35
She planted that twig on her mother's grave
and it grew to a tree where a white dove sat.
Whenever she wished for anything the dove
would drop it like an egg upon the ground.
The bird is important, my dears, so heed him. 40

Next came the ball, as you all know.
It was a marriage market.
The prince was looking for a wife.
All but Cinderella were preparing
and gussying up for the big event. 45
Cinderella begged to go too.
Her stepmother threw a dish of lentils
into the cinders and said: Pick them
up in an hour and you shall go.
The white dove brought all his friends; 50
all the warm wings of the fatherland came,
and picked up the lentils in a jiffy.
No, Cinderella, said the stepmother,
you have no clothes and cannot dance.
That's the way with stepmothers. 55

Cinderella went to the tree at the grave
and cried forth like a gospel singer:
Mama! Mama! My turtledove,
send me to the prince's ball!
The bird dropped down a golden dress 60

and delicate little gold slippers.
Rather a large package for a simple bird.
So she went. Which is no surprise.
Her stepmother and sisters didn't
recognize her without her cinder face 65
and the prince took her hand on the spot
and danced with no other the whole day.

As nightfall came she thought she'd better
get home. The prince walked her home
and she disappeared into the pigeon house 70
and although the prince took an axe and broke
it open she was gone. Back to her cinders.
These events repeated themselves for three days.
However on the third day the prince
covered the palace steps with cobbler's wax 75
and Cinderella's gold shoe stuck upon it.

Now he would find whom the shoe fit
and find his strange dancing girl for keeps.
He went to their house and the two sisters
were delighted because they had lovely feet. 80
The eldest went into a room to try the slipper on
but her big toe got in the way so she simply
sliced it off and put on the slipper.
The prince rode away with her until the white dove
told him to look at the blood pouring forth. 85
That is the way with amputations.
They don't just heal up like a wish.
The other sister cut off her heel
but the blood told as blood will.
The prince was getting tired. 90
He began to feel like a shoe salesman.
But he gave it one last try.
This time Cinderella fit into the shoe
like a love letter into its envelope.

At the wedding ceremony 95
the two sisters came to curry favor
and the white dove pecked their eyes out.
Two hollow spots were left
like soup spoons.

Cinderella and the prince 100
lived, they say, happily ever after,
like two dolls in a museum case
never bothered by diapers or dust,
never arguing over the timing of an egg,
never telling the same story twice, 105

never getting a middle-aged spread,
their darling smiles pasted on for eternity.
Regular Bobbsey Twins.
That story.

The Wedding Night

There was this time in Boston
before spring was ready—a short
celebration—
and then it was over.
I walked down Marlborough Street the
day you left me
under branches as tedious as leather, 5
under branches as stiff as driver's
gloves.
I said, (but only because you were gone)
"Magnolia blossoms have rather a
southern sound,
so unlike Boston anyhow,"
and whatever it was that happened, all
that pink, 10
and for so short a time,
was unbelievable, was pinned on.

The magnolias had sat once, each in a
pink dress,
looking, of course, at the ceiling.
For weeks the buds had been as sure-
bodied 15
as the twelve-year-old flower girl I was
at Aunt Edna's wedding.
Will they bend, I had asked,
as I walked under them toward you,
bend two to a branch, 20
cheek, forehead, shoulder to the floor?
I could see that none were clumsy.
I could see that each was tight and firm.
Not one of them had trickled blood—
waiting as polished as gull beaks, 25
as closed as all that.

I stood under them for nights,
hesitating,
and then drove away in my car.
Yet one night in the April night
someone (someone!) kicked each bud
open— 30
to disprove, to mock, to puncture!
The next day they were all hot-colored,
moist, not flawed in fact.
Then they no longer huddled.
They forgot how to hide. 35
Tense as they had been,
they were flags, gaudy, chafing in the
wind.
There was such abandonment in all
that!
Such entertainment
in their flaring up. 40

After that, well—
like faces in a parade,
I could not tell the difference between
losing you
and losing them.
They dropped separately after the
celebration, 45
handpicked,
one after the other like artichoke leaves.
After that I walked to my car
awkwardly
over the painful bare remains on the
brick sidewalk,
knowing that someone had, in one
night, 50
passed roughly through,
and before it was time.

The Addict

Sleepmonger,
deathmonger,
with capsules in my palms each night,
eight at a time from sweet
pharmaceutical bottles
I make arrangements for a pint-sized
journey. 5
I'm the queen of this condition.
I'm an expert on making the trip
and now they say I'm an addict.
Now they ask why.
Why! 10

Don't they know
that I promised to die!
I'm keeping in practice.
I'm merely staying in shape.
The pills are a mother, but better, 15
every color and as good as sour balls.
I'm on a diet from death.

Yes, I admit
it has gotten to be a bit of a habit—
blows eight at a time, socked in the
eye, 20
hauled away by the pink, the orange,
the green and the white goodnights.
I'm becoming something of a chemical
mixture
That's it! 25

My supply
of tablets
has got to last for years and years.
I like them more than I like me.
Stubborn as hell, they won't let go. 30

It's a kind of marriage.
It's a kind of war
where I plant bombs inside
of myself.

Yes 35
I try
to kill myself in small amounts,
an innocuous occupation.
Actually I'm hung up on it.
But remember I don't make too much
noise. 40
And frankly no one has to lug me out

and I don't stand there in my winding
sheet.
I'm a little buttercup in my yellow
nightie
eating my eight loaves in a row
and in a certain order as in 45
the laying on of hands
or the black sacrament.

It's a ceremony
but like any other sport
it's full of rules. 50
It's like a musical tennis match where
my mouth keeps catching the ball.
Then I lie on my altar
elevated by the eight chemical kisses.

What a lay me down this is 55
with two pink, two orange,
two green, two white goodnights.
Fee-fi-fo-fum—
Now I'm borrowed.
Now I'm numb. 60

All My Pretty Ones

All my pretty ones?
Did you say all? O hell-kite! All?
What! all my pretty chickens and their dam
At one fell swoop? . . .
I cannot but remember such things were,
That were most precious to me. MACBETH

Father, this year's jinx rides us apart
where you followed our mother to her cold slumber,
a second shock boiling its stone to your heart,
leaving me here to shuffle and disencumber
you from the residence you could not afford: 5
a gold key, your half of a woollen mill,
twenty suits from Dunne's, an English Ford,
the love and legal verbiage of another will,
boxes of pictures of people I do not know.
I touch their cardboard faces. They must go. 10

But the eyes, as thick as wood in this album,
hold me. I stop here, where a small boy
waits in a ruffled dress for someone to come . . .
for this soldier who holds his bugle like a toy
or for this velvet lady who cannot smile. 15
Is this your father's father, this commodore
in a mailman suit? My father, time meanwhile
has made it unimportant who you are looking for..
I'll never know what these faces are all about.
I lock them into their book and throw them out. 20

This is the yellow scrapbook that you began
the year I was born; as crackling now and wrinkly
as tobacco leaves: clippings where Hoover outran
the Democrats, wriggling his dry finger at me
and Prohibition; news where the *Hindenburg* went 25
down and recent years where you went flush
on war. This year, solvent but sick, you meant
to marry that pretty widow in a one-month rush.
But before you had that second chance, I cried
on your fat shoulder. Three days later you died. 30

These are the snapshots of marriage, stopped in places.
Side by side at the rail toward Nassau now;
here, with the winner's cup at the speedboat races,
here, in tails at the Cotillion, you take a bow.

here, by our kennel of dogs with their pink eyes, 35
running like show-bred pigs in their chain-link pep;
here, at the horseshow where my sister wins a prize;
and here, standing like a duke among groups of men.
Now I fold you down, my drunkard, my navigator,
my first lost keeper, to love or look at later. 40

I hold a five-year diary that my mother kept
for three years, telling all she does not say
of your alcoholic tendency. You overslept,
she writes. My God, father, each Christmas Day
with your blood, will I drink down your glass 45
of wine? The diary of your hurly-burly years
goes to my shelf to wait for my age to pass.
Only in this hoarded span will love persevere.
Whether you are pretty or not, I outlive you,
bend down my strange face to yours and forgive you. 50

Thom Gunn (1929–)

On the Move

'Man, you gotta Go.'

The blue jay scuffling in the bushes follows
Some hidden purpose, and the gust of birds
That spurts across the field, the wheeling swallows,
Have nested in the trees and undergrowth.
Seeking their instinct, or their poise, or both, 5
One moves with an uncertain violence
Under the dust thrown by a baffled sense
Or the dull thunder of approximate words.

On motorcycles, up the road, they come:
Small, black, as flies hanging in heat, the Boys, 10
Until the distance throws them forth, their hum
Bulges to thunder held by calf and thigh.
In goggles, donned impersonality,
In gleaming jackets trophied with the dust,
They strap in doubt—by hiding it, robust— 15
And almost hear a meaning in their noise.

Exact conclusion of their hardiness
Has no shape yet, but from known whereabouts
They ride, direction where the tires press.
They scare a flight of birds across the field: 20
Much that is natural, to the will must yield.
Men manufacture both machine and soul,
And use what they imperfectly control
To dare a future from the taken routes.

It is a part solution, after all. 25
One is not necessarily discord
On earth; or damned because, half animal,
One lacks direct instinct, because one wakes
Afloat on movement that divides and breaks.
One joins the movement in a valueless world, 30
Choosing it, till, both hurler and the hurled,
One moves as well, always toward, toward.

A minute holds them, who have come to go:
The self-defined, astride the created will
They burst away; the towns they travel through 35
Are home for neither bird nor holiness,
For birds and saints complete their purposes.
At worse, one is in motion; and at best,
Reaching no absolute, in which to rest,
One is always nearer by not keeping still. 40

Raymond R. Patterson (1929–)

At That Moment

(For Malcolm X)

When they shot Malcolm Little down
On the stage of the Audubon Ballroom,
When his life ran out through bullet holes
(Like the people running out when the murder began)
His blood soaked the floor
One drop found a crack through the stark
Pounding thunder—slipped under the stage and began
Its journey: burrowed through concrete into the cellar,
Dropped down darkness, exploding like quicksilver
Pellets of light, panicking rats, paralyzing cockroaches—
Tunneled through rubble and wrecks of foundations,
The rocks that buttress the bowels of the city, flowed
Into pipes and powerlines, the mains and cables of the city:
A thousand fiery seeds.
At that moment,
Those who drank water where he entered . . .
Those who cooked food where he passed . . .
Those who burned light while he listened . . .
Those who were talking as he went, knew he was water
Running out of faucets, gas running out of jets, power
Running out of sockets, meaning running along taut wires—
To the hungers of their living. It is said
Whole slums of clotted Harlem plumbing groaned
And sundered free that day, and disconnected gas and light

Went on and on and on. . . .
They rushed his riddled body on a stretcher
To the hospital. But the police were too late.
It had already happened.

Adrienne Rich (1929–)

Toward the Solstice

The thirtieth of November.
Snow is starting to fall.
A peculiar silence is spreading
over the fields, the maple grove.
It is the thirtieth of May, 5
rain pours on ancient bushes, runs
down the youngest blade of grass.
I am trying to hold in one steady glance
all the parts of my life.
A spring torrent races 10
on this old slanting roof,
the slanted field below
thickens with winter's first whiteness.
Thistles dried to sticks in last year's wind
stand nakedly in the green, 15
stand sullenly in the slowly whitening,
field.

My brain glows
more violently, more avidly
the quieter, the thicker 20
the quilt of crystals settles,
the louder, more relentlessly
the torrent beats itself out
on the old boards and shingles.
It is the thirtieth of May, 25
the thirtieth of November,
a beginning or an end,
we are moving into the solstice
and there is so much here
I still do not understand. 30
If I could make sense of how
my life is still tangled
with dead weeds, thistles,
enormous burdocks, burdens
slowly shifting under 35
this first fall of snow,

beaten by this early, racking rain
calling all new life to declare itself strong
or die,
if I could know 40
in what language to address
the spirits that claim a place
beneath these low and simple ceilings,
tenants that neither speak nor stir
yet dwell in mute insistence 45
till I can feel utterly ghosted in this house.

If history is a spider-thread
spun over and over though brushed away
it seems I might some twilight
or dawn in the hushed country light 50
discern its greyness stretching
from molding or doorframe, out
into the empty dooryard
and following it climb
the path into the pinewoods, 55
tracing from tree to tree
in the failing light, in the slowly
lucidifying day
its constant, purposive trail,
till I reach whatever cellar hole 60
filling with snowflakes or lichen,
whatever fallen shack
or unremembered clearing
I am meant to have found
and there, under the first or last 65
star, trusting to instinct
the words would come to mind
I have failed or forgotten to say
year after year, winter
after summer, the right rune 70
to ease the hold of the past
upon the rest of my life
and ease my hold on the past.
If some rite of separation
is still unaccomplished 75
between myself and the long-gone
tenants of this house,
between myself and my childhood,
and the childhood of my children,
it is I who have neglected 80
to perform the needed acts,
set water in corners, light and eucalyptus
in front of mirrors,
or merely pause and listen
to my own pulse vibrating 85
lightly as falling snow,
relentlessly as the rainstorm,

and hear what it has been saying.
It seems I am still waiting
for them to make some clear demand 90
some articulate sound or gesture,
for release to come from anywhere
but from inside myself.

A decade of cutting away
dead flesh, cauterizing 95
old scars ripped open over and over
and still it is not enough.
A decade of performing
the loving humdrum acts
of attention to this house 100
transplanting lilac suckers,
washing panes, scrubbing
wood-smoke from splitting paint,
sweeping stairs, brushing the thread
of the spider aside, 105
and so much yet undone,
a woman's work, the solstice nearing,
and my hand still suspended
as if above a letter
I long and dread to close. 110

Jon Silkin (1930–)

Furnished Lives

I have been walking today
Where the sour children of London's poor sleep
Pressed close to the unfrosted glare
Torment lying closed in to tenement,
Of the clay fire; I 5
Have watched their whispering souls fly straight to God:

"O Lord, please give to us
A dinner-service, austere, yet gay: like snow
When swans are on it; Bird
Unfold your wings until like a white smile 10
You fill this mid-white room."
I have balanced myself on this meagre Strand where

Each man and woman turn
On the deliberate hour of the cock,
As if two new risen souls,
Through the cragged landscape of each other's eyes. 15
But where lover upon lover
Should meet—where sheet, and pillow, and eiderdown

Should frolic and crisp,
As dolphins on the stylized crown of the sea 20
Their pale cerements lie.
They tread with chocolate souls and paper hands;
They walk into that room
Your gay and daffodil smile has never seen:

Not to love's pleasant feast 25
They go, in the mutations of the night,
But to their humiliations
Paled as a swan's dead feather scorched in the sun.
I have been walking today
Among the newly paper-crowned, among those 30

Whose casual, paper body
Is crushed between fate's fingers and the platter;
But Sir, their perpetual fire
Was not stubbed out, folded on brass or stone
Extinguished in the dark, 35
But burns with the drear dampness of cut flowers.

I cannot hear their piped
Cry. These souls have no players. They have resigned
The vivid performance of their world.
And your world, Lord, 40
Has now become
Like a dumb winter show, held in one room,

Which must now reek of age
Before you have retouched its lips with such straight fire
As through your stony earth 45
Burns with ferocious tears in the world's eyes:
Church-stone, door-knocker and polished railway lines
Move in their separate dumb way
So why not these lives;
I ask you often, but you never say? 50

Gregory Corso (1930–   )

Marriage

Should I get married? Should I be good?
Astound the girl next door with my velvet suit and faustus hood?
Don't take her to movies but to cemeteries
tell all about werewolf bathtubs and forked clarinets 5
then desire her and kiss her and all the preliminaries
and she going just so far and I understanding why
not getting angry saying You must feel! It's beautiful to feel!
Instead take her in my arms lean against an old crooked tombstone
and woo her the entire night the constellations in the sky— 10

When she introduces me to her parents
back straightened, hair finally combed, strangled by a tie,
should I sit knees together on their 3rd degree sofa
and not ask Where's the bathroom?
How else to feel other than I am, 15
often thinking Flash Gordon soap—
O how terrible it must be for a young man
seated before a family and the family thinking
We never saw him before! He wants our Mary Lou!
After tea and homemade cookies they ask What do you do for a living? 20

Should I tell them? Would they like me then?
Say All right get married, we're losing a daughter
but we're gaining a son—
And should I then ask Where's the bathroom?

O God, and the wedding! All her family and her friends 25
and only a handful of mine all scroungy and bearded
just wait to get at the drinks and food—
And the priest! he looking at me as if I masturbated
asking me Do you take this woman for your lawful wedded wife?
And I trembling what to say say Pie Glue! 30
I kiss the bride all those corny men slapping me on the back
She's all yours, boy! Ha-ha-ha!
And in their eyes you could see some obscene honeymoon going on—

Then all that absurd rice and clanky cans and shoes
Niagara Falls! Hordes of us! Husbands! Wives! Flowers! Chocolates! 35

All streaming into cozy hotels
All going to do the same thing tonight
The indifferent clerk he knowing what was going to happen
The lobby zombies they knowing what
The whistling elevator man he knowing

The winking bellboy knowing 40
Everybody knowing! I'd be almost inclined not to do anything!
Stay up all night! Stare that hotel clerk in the eye!
Screaming: I deny honeymoon! I deny honeymoon!
running rampant into those almost climactic suites
yelling Radio belly? Cat shovel! 45
O I'd live in Niagara forever! in a dark cave beneath the Falls
I'd sit there the Mad Honeymooner
devising ways to break marriages, a scourge of bigamy
a saint of divorce—

But I should get married I should be good 50
How nice it'd be to come home to her
and sit by the fireplace and she in the kitchen
aproned young and lovely wanting my baby
and so happy about me she burns the roast beef
and comes crying to me and I get up from my big papa chair 55
saying Christmas teeth! Radiant brains! Apple deaf!
God what a husband I'd make! Yes, I should get married!
So much to do! like sneaking into Mr Jones' house late at night
and cover his golf clubs with 1920 Norwegian books
Like hanging a picture of Rimbaud on the lawnmower 60
like pasting Tannu Tuva postage stamps all over the picket fence
like when Mrs Kindhead comes to collect for the Community Chest
grab her and tell her There are unfavorable omens in the sky!
And when the mayor comes to get my vote tell him
When are you going to stop killing whales! 65
And when the milkman comes leave him a note in the bottle
Penguin dust, bring me penguin dust, I want penguin dust—

Yet if I should get married and it's Connecticut and snow
and she gives birth to a child and I am sleepless, worn,
up for nights, head bowed against a quiet window, the past behind me, 70
finding myself in the most common of situations a trembling man
knowledged with responsibility not twig-smear nor Roman coin soup—
O what would that be like!
Surely I'd give it for a nipple a rubber Tacitus
For a rattle a bag of broken Bach records 75
Tack Della Francesca all over its crib
Sew the Greek alphabet on its bib
And build for its playpen a roofless Parthenon

No, I doubt I'd be that kind of father
not rural not snow no quiet window 80
but hot smelly tight New York City
seven flights up roaches and rats in the walls
a fat Reichian wife screeching over potatoes Get a job!
And five nose running brats in love with Batman
And the neighbors all toothless and dry haired 85
like those hag masses of the 18th century
all wanting to come in and watch TV
The landlord wants his rent

Grocery store Blue Cross Gas & Electric Knights of Columbus
Impossible to lie back and dream Telephone snow, ghost parking— 90
No! I should not get married I should never get married!
But—imagine If I were married to a beautiful sophisticated woman
tall and pale wearing an elegant black dress and long black gloves
holding a cigarette holder in one hand and a highball in the other
and we lived high up in a penthouse with a huge window 95
from which we could see all of New York and ever farther on clear days
No, can't imagine myself married to that pleasant prison dream—

O but what about love? I forget love
not that I am incapable of love
it's just that I see love as odd as wearing shoes— 100
I never wanted to marry a girl who was like my mother
And Ingrid Bergman was always impossible
And there's maybe a girl now but she's already married
And I don't like men and—
but there's got to be somebody! 105
Because what if I'm 60 years old and not married,
all alone in a furnished room with pee stains on my underwear
and everybody else is married! All the universe married but me!

Ah, yet well I know that were a woman possible as I am possible
then marriage would be possible— 110
Like SHE in her lonely alien gaud waiting her Egyptian lover
so I wait—bereft of 2,000 years and the bath of life.

1960

Ted Hughes (1930–)

The Hawk in the Rain

I drown in the drumming ploughland, I drag up
Heel after heel from the swallowing of the earth's mouth,
From clay that clutches my each step to the ankle
With the habit of the dogged grave, but the hawk

Effortlessly at height hangs his still eye. 5
His wings hold all creation in a weightless quiet,
Steady as a hallucination in the streaming air.
While banging wind kills these stubborn hedges,

Thumbs my eyes, throws my breath, tackles my heart,
And rain hacks my head to the bone, the hawk hangs 10
The diamond point of will that polestars
The sea drowner's endurance: and I,

Bloodily grabbed dazed last-moment-counting
Morsel in the earth's mouth, strain towards the master-
Fulcrum of violence where the hawk hangs still. 15
That maybe in his own time meets the weather

Coming the wrong way, suffers the air, hurled upside down,
Fall from his eye, the ponderous shires crash on him,
The horizon trap him; the round angelic eye
Smashed, mixed his heart's blood with the mire of the land. 20

The Jaguar

The apes yawn and adore their fleas in the sun.
The parrots shriek as if they were on fire, or strut
Like cheap tarts to attract the stroller with the nut.
Fatigued with indolence, tiger and lion

Lie still as the sun. The boa-constrictor's coil 5
Is a fossil. Cage after cage seems empty, or
Stinks of sleepers from the breathing straw.
It might be painted on a nursery wall.

But who runs like the rest past these arrives
At a cage where the crowd stands, stares, mesmerized, 10
As a child at a dream, at a jaguar hurrying enraged
Through prison darkness after the drills of his eyes

On a short fierce fuse. Not in boredom—
The eye satisfied to be blind in fire,
By the bang of blood in the brain deaf the ear— 15
He spins from the bars, but there's no cage to him

More than to the visionary his cell:
His stride is wildernesses of freedom:
The world rolls under the long thrust of his heel.
Over the cage floor the horizons come. 20

Crow's First Lesson

God tried to teach Crow how to talk.
"Love," said God. "Say, Love."
Crow gaped, and the white shark crashed into the sea
And went rolling downwards, discovering its own depth.

"No, no," said God. "Say Love. Now try it. LOVE." 5
Crow gaped, and a bluefly, a tsetse, a mosquito
Zoomed out and down
To their sundry flesh-pots.

"A final try," said God. "Now, LOVE."
Crow convulsed, gaped, retched and 10
Man's bodiless prodigious head
Bulbed out onto the earth, with swivelling eyes,
Jabbering protest —

And Crow retched again, before God could stop him.
And woman's vulva dropped over man's neck and tightened. 15
The two struggled together on the grass.
God struggled to part them, cursed, wept—

Crow flew guiltily off.

Crow's Theology

Crow realized God loved him—
Otherwise, he would have dropped dead.
So that was proved.
Crow reclined, marvelling, on his heart-beat.

And he realized that God spoke Crow— 5
Just existing was His revelation.

But what
Loved the stones and spoke stone?
They seemed to exist too. 10
And what spoke that strange silence
After his clamour of caws faded?

And what loved the shot-pellets
That dribbled from those strung-up mummifying crows?
What spoke the silence of lead?

Crow realized there were two Gods— 15

One of them much bigger than the other
Loving his enemies
And having all the weapons.

Barry Spacks (1931–   )

Freshmen

My freshmen
settle in. Achilles
sulks; Pascal consults
his watch; and true
Cordelia—with her just-washed hair, 5
stern-hearted princess, ready to defend
the meticulous garden of truths in her
high-school notebook—
uncaps her ballpoint pen.

And the corridors drum:
give us a flourish, fluorescence of light,
for the teachers come, 10
green and seasoned, bearers
of the Word, who differ
like its letters; there are some
so wise their eyes
are birdbites; one 15

a mad, grinning gent with a golden
tooth, God knows
he might be Pan, or the sub-
custodian; another
is a walking podium, dense
with his mystery—high 20

priests and attachés
of the ministry; kindly
old women, like unfashionable watering
places;
and the assuming young, rolled tight as
a City
umbrella; 25

thought-salesmen with samples cases,
and saints upon whom
merely to gaze is like Sunday—
their rapt, bright,
cat-licked faces! 30

And the freshmen wait;
wait bristling, acned, glowing like a
brand,
or easy, chatting, munching, muscles
lax,
each in his chosen corner, and in each
a chosen corner. 35

Full of certainties and reasons,
or uncertainties and reasons.
full of reasons as a conch contains the
sea,
they wait: for the term's first bell;
for another mismatched wrestle through
the year; 40

for a teacher who's religious in his art,
a wizard of a sort, to call the roll
and from mere names
cause people
to appear. 45

The best look like the swinging door
to the opera just before
the Marx Brothers break through.
The worst—debased,
on the back row, 50

as far as one can go
from speech—
are walls where childish scribbling's
been erased;
are stones
to teach. 55

And I am paid to ask them questions:
Dare man proceed by need alone?
Did Esau like
his pottage?
Is any heart in order after Belsen? 60

And when one stops to think, I'll catch
his heel,
put scissors to him, excavate his chest!
Watch, freshmen, for my words about
the past

can make you turn your back. I wait to
  throw,
most foul, most foul, the future in your
  face. 65

John Updike (1932–)

Energy: A Villanelle

The log gives back, in burning, solar fire
  green leaves imbibed and processed one by one;
nothing is lost but, still, the cost grows higher.

The ocean's tons of tide, to turn, require
  no more than time and moon; it's cosmic fun.
The log gives back, in burning, solar fire.

All microörganisms must expire
  and quite a few became petroleum;
nothing is lost but, still, the cost grows higher.

The oil rigs in Bahrain imply a buyer
  who counts no cost, when all is said and done.
The logs give back, in burning, solar fire

but Good Gulf gives it faster; every tire
  is by the fiery heavens lightly spun.
Nothing is lost but, still, the cost grows higher.

So guzzle gas, the leaden night draws nigher
  when cinders mark where stood the blazing sun.
The logs give back, in burning, solar fire;
nothing is lost but, still, the cost grows higher.

Sylvia Plath (1932–1963)

Daddy

You do not do, you do not do
Any more, black shoe
In which I have lived like a foot
For thirty years, poor and white,
Barely daring to breathe or Achoo. 5

Daddy, I have had to kill you.
You died before I had time—
Marble-heavy, a bag full of God,
Ghastly statue with one grey toe
Big as a Frisco seal 10

And a head in the freakish Atlantic
Where it pours bean green over blue
In the waters off beautiful Nauset.
I used to pray to recover you.
Ach, du. 15

In the German tongue, in the Polish
town
Scraped flat by the roller
Of wars, wars, wars.
But the name of the town is common.
My Polack friend 20

Says there are a dozen or two
So I never could tell where you
Put your foot, your root,
I never could talk to you.
The tongue stuck in my jaw. 25

It stuck in a barb wire snare.
Ich, ich, ich, ich,
I could hardly speak.
I thought every German was you.
And the language obscene 30

An engine, an engine
Chuffing me off like a Jew.
A Jew to Dachau, Auschwitz, Belsen.
I began to talk like a Jew.
I think I may well be a Jew. 35

The snows of the Tyrol, the clear beer
of Vienna
Are not very pure or true.
With my gypsy ancestress and my
weird luck
And my Taroc pack and my Taroc pack
I may be a bit of a Jew. 40

I have always been scared of *you*,
With your Luftwaffe, your
gobbledygoo.
And your neat moustache
And your Aryan eye, bright blue.
Panzer-man, panzer-man, O You— 45

Not God but a swastika
So black no sky could squeak through.
Every woman adores a Fascist,
The boot in the face, the brute
Brute heart of a brute like you. 50

You stand at the blackboard, daddy,
In the picture I have of you,
A cleft in your chin instead of your foot
But no less a devil for that, no not
Any less the black man who 55

Bit my pretty red heart in two.
I was ten when they buried you.
At twenty I tried to die
And get back, back, back to you.
I thought even the bones would do. 60

But they pulled me out of the sack,
And they stuck me together with glue.
And then I knew what to do.
I made a model of you,
A man in black with a Meinkampf
look 65

And a love of the race and the screw.
And I said I do, I do.

So daddy, I'm finally through.
The black telephone's off at the root,
The voices just can't worm through. 70

If I've killed one man, I've killed two—
The vampire who said he was you
And drank my blood for a year,
Seven years, if you want to know.
Daddy, you can lie back now. 75

There's a stake in your fat black heart
And the villagers never liked you
They are dancing and stamping on you.
They always *knew* it was you.
Daddy, daddy, you bastard, I'm
through. 80

The Applicant

First, are you our sort of a person?
Do you wear
A glass eye, false teeth or a crutch,
A brace or a hook,
Rubber breasts or a rubber crotch, 5

Stitches to show something missing?
No, no? Then
How can we give you a thing?
Stop crying.
Open your hand.
Empty? Empty. Here is a hand 10

To fill it and willing
To bring teacups and roll away
headaches
And do whatever you tell it.
Will you marry it?
It is guaranteed 15

To thumb shut your eyes at the end
And dissolve of sorrow.
We make new stock from the salt.
I notice you are stark naked.
How about this suit— 20

Black and stiff, but not a bad fit.
Will you marry it?
It is waterproof, shatterproof, proof
Against fire and bombs through the roof.
Believe me, they'll bury you in it. 25

Now your head, excuse me, is empty.
I have the ticket for that.
Come here, sweetie, out of the closet.
Well, what do you think of *that*?
Naked as paper to start 30

But in twenty-five years she'll be silver,
In fifty, gold
A living doll, everywhere you look.
It can sew, it can cook,
It can talk, talk, talk. 35

It works, there is nothing wrong with it.
You have a hole, it's a poultice.
You have an eye, it's an image.
My boy, it's your last resort.
Will you marry it, marry it, marry it. 40

JULES FEIFFER
EVERY GENERATION MUST RAISE ITS CHILDREN DIFFERENTLY.
THE WAY I RAISED YOU, MY SON, IS THE WAY OTHERS OF MY GENERATION RAISED THEIR CHILDREN.
TRUE, WE MADE MISTAKES. AND PROFITING FROM THOSE MISTAKES YOUR GENERATION HAS GONE ON TO RAISE ITS CHILDREN.
AND OUT OF YOUR MISTAKES WILL YET ANOTHER GENERATION LEARN. AND SO IT GOES-
OUT OF MISTAKES COMES KNOWLEDGE. OUT OF KNOWLEDGE COMES PROGRESS. IT IS LIFE FEEDING UPON LIFE.
AND IT IS WITHIN THIS PERSPECTIVE THAT I ASK OF YOU, MY SON, WHAT WERE MY MISTAKES?
NONE, MOMMA.
NONE? SURELY, THERE MUST HAVE BEEN ONE.
WELL, THEN- ONE.
ONE?
IS THAT THE THANKS I GET?
©1967 JULES FEIFFER
2-12

A Life

Touch it: it won't shrink like an eyeball,
This egg-shaped bailiwick, clear as a tear.
Here's yesterday, last year—
Palm-spear and lily distinct as flora in the vast   5
Windless threadwork of a tapestry.

Flick the glass with your fingernail:
It will ping like a Chinese chime in the slightest air stir
Though nobody in there looks up or bothers to answer.
The inhabitants are light as cork,   10
Every one of them permanently busy.

At their feet, the sea waves bow in single file.
Never trespassing in bad temper:
Stalling in midair,
Short-reined, pawing like paradeground horses.   15
Overhead, the clouds sit tasseled and fancy

As Victorian cushions. This family
Of valentine faces might please a collector:
They ring true, like good china.
Elsewhere the landscape is more frank.   20
The light falls without letup, blindingly.

A woman is dragging her shadow in a circle
About a bald hospital saucer
It resembles the moon, or a sheet of blank paper
And appears to have suffered a sort of private blitzkrieg.   25
She lives quietly

With no attachments, like a foetus in a bottle,
The obsolete house, the sea, flattened to a picture
She has one too many dimensions to enter.
Grief and anger, exorcised,   30
Leave her alone now.

The future is a grey seagull
Tattling in its cat-voice of departure, departure.
Age and terror, like nurses, attend her,
And a drowned man, complaining of the great cold,   35
Crawls up out of the sea.

Lady Lazarus

I have done it again.
One year in every ten
I manage it——

A sort of walking miracle, my skin
Bright as a Nazi lampshade, 5
My right foot

A paperweight,
My face a featureless, fine
Jew linen.

Peel off the napkin 10
O my enemy.
Do I terrify?——

The nose, the eye pits, the full set
of teeth?
The sour breath
Will vanish in a day. 15

Soon, soon the flesh
The grave cave ate will be
At home on me

And I a smiling woman.
I am only thirty. 20
And like the cat I have nine times
to die.

This is Number Three.
What a trash
To annihilate each decade.

What a million filaments. 25
The peanut-crunching crowd
Shoves in to see

Them unwrap me hand and foot——
The big strip tease.
Gentlemen, ladies 30

These are my hands
My knees.
I may be skin and bone,

Nevertheless, I am the same, identical
woman.
The first time it happened I was ten. 35
It was an accident.

The second time I meant
To last it out and not come back at all.
I rocked shut

As a seashell. 40
They had to call and call
And pick the worms off me like
sticky pearls.

Dying
Is an art, like everything else.
I do it exceptionally well. 45

I do it so it feels like hell.
I do it so it feels real.
I guess you could say I've a call.

It's easy enough to do it in a cell.
It's easy enough to do it and stay put 50
It's the theatrical

Come back in broad day
To the same place, the same face,
the same brute
Amused shout:

"A miracle!" 55
That knocks me out.
There is a charge

For the eyeing of my scars, there is a
charge
For the hearing of my heart——
It really goes. 60

And there is a charge, a very large charge
For a word or a touch
Or a bit of blood

Or a piece of my hair or my clothes.
So, so, Herr Doktor. 65
So, Herr Enemy.

I am your opus,
I am your valuable,
The pure gold baby

That melts to a shriek. 70
I turn and burn.
Do not think I underestimate your
great concern.

Ash, ash—
You poke and stir.
Flesh, bone, there is nothing
there—— 75

A cake of soap,
A wedding ring,
A gold filling.

Herr God, Herr Lucifer
Beware 80
Beware.

Out of the ash
I rise with my red hair
And I eat men like air.

Imamu Amiri Baraka (LeRoi Jones) (1934–)

In Memory of Radio

Who has ever stopped to think of the divinity of Lamont Cranston?
(Only Jack Kerouac, that I know of: & me.
The rest of you probably had on WCBS and Kate Smith,
Or something equally unattractive.)

What can I say? 5
It is better to have loved and lost
Than to put linoleum in your living rooms?

Am I a sage or something?
Mandrake's hypnotic gesture of the week?
(Remember, I do not have the healing powers of Oral Roberts . . . 10
I cannot, like F. J. Sheen, tell you how to get saved *& rich!*
I cannot even order you to gaschamber satori like Hitler or Goody Knight

& Love is an evil word.
Turn it backwards/see, what I mean?
An evol word. & besides 15
Who understands it?
I certainly wouldn't like to go out on that kind of limb.

Saturday mornings we listened to *Red Lantern* & his undersea folk.
At 11, *Let's Pretend*/& we did/& I, the poet, still do, Thank God!
What was it he used to say (after the transformation, when he was safe 20
& invisible & the unbelievers couldn't throw stones?) "Heh, heh, heh,
Who knows what evil lurks in the hearts of men? The Shadow knows."

O, yes he does
O, yes he does.
An evil word it is, 25
This Love.

Poem for Half White College Students

Who are you, listening to me, who are you
listening to yourself? Are you white or
black, or does that have anything to do
with it? Can you pop your fingers to no
music, except those wild monkies go on 5
in your head, can you jerk, to no melody,
except finger poppers get it together
when you turn from starchecking to checking
yourself. How do you sound, your words, are they
yours? The ghost you see in the mirror, is it really 10
you, can you swear you are not an imitation greyboy,
can you look right next to you in that chair, and swear,
that the sister you have your hand on is not really
so full of Elizabeth Taylor, Richard Burton is
coming out of her ears. You may even have to be Richard 15
with a white shirt and face, and four million negroes
think you cute, you may have to be Elizabeth Taylor, old lady,
if you want to sit up in your crazy spot dreaming about dresses,
and the sway of certain porters' hips. Check yourself, learn who it is
speaking, when you make some ultrasophisticated point, check yourself, 20
when you find yourself gesturing like Steve McQueen, check it out, ask
in your black heart who it is you are, and is that image black or white,
you might be surprised right out the window, whistling dixie on the way in

Clarence Major (1936–   )

Something Is Eating Me Up Inside

I go in & out a thousand times a day
& the round fat women with black velvet skin
expressions sit out on the
front steps, watching—"where does he go
so much" as if the knowledge could give meaning to 5
a hood from the 20s I look like in
my pocket black shirt button-down collar & black ivy
league. In & out to break the
agony in the pit of skull of fire for a drink a
cigarette bumming it anything the floor is 10
too depressing. I turn around inside the closet to search
the floor for a dime/ a nickel

this is from time & drunks of time again nights when
the pants pockets turned
inside turned 15
out but seriously something is
eating me up inside I don't
believe in anything anymore, science, magic—
in tape worms inside philosophy inside
I go outside 20

maybe inside you but not anybody else but
in the middle of going like
it's an inscrutable (what

ever
that 25
is)
something getting itself in deeper in. In,
time I mean pushing in against
my ear drums my time

—this is what I move full of. 30
slow young strong & sure of nothing myself a gangster
of the sunshine the sun is blood in my guts:
moving me from gin highs to lakesides to sit down
beside reasons for being in
the first place 35
in the second place looking
outward to definitions for definitions like

a formal ending would be unlawful unfair

Dick Allen (1939–   )

Oh, Rousseau, Rousseau

—for David and Susan

Our friends are moving back
  to small lonesome towns,
are building porches back
  on half-ruined dwellings.

Evenings, they watch 5
  cities through their television sets,
grow marijuana in
  their outlandish backyards,

or slowly carpenter
  grandfather clocks— 10
like ancestors turning
  their lives into fixtures.

And I had thought
  the future was space
travel and tubes, 15
  and aphrodisiac culture.

Who could predict
  their faces grown stern,
this strict new religion
  of seasons and walls? 20

As we drive upstate
  into the valleys,
we pass the statues of
  colonial soldiers

whose economic war 25
  seems sensible again.
We stop at a cluttered
  ramshackle store

and spend too much
  for a lovely glass deer, 30
a pink and blue vase,
  uncertainly china.

Lately, I've noticed,
  we are choosing gifts
smaller and smaller 35
  as if we have sensed

or accepted, perhaps,
  a world of miniatures,
each of us one
  microscopic circuit 40

through which the energy
  of life must be routed
if anything is to work,
  find salvation, or fail.

But for reasons beyond us 45
  our friends are scattering
and it may mean, at last,
  our civilization machine—

its unknown job being done—
  may now be deserted 50
and we are finally free
  to begin to go home,

collect green bottles, shop
  at the General Store;
think no more 55
  of strange lives stranger than ours.

Theory of the Alternate Universe

Another world lies tangent to our
  own—
where everything is whackeyed. You
wear purple skirts; you leave
the dustcloth on translucent shelves;
the sun 5
is slightly green.
I sculpture wood and plastic, talk
about the rain.
You take
swigs from bottles of intense
  champagne. 10
To everything there is
"a touch of strange."
When you go out of sight
you're walking down a lamplit street
and in your place 15
the woman I embrace
writes strange lovephrases on my
  cellophane
skin.
The worlds
slide in and out. They look 20
like time-exposure pictures of the moon
passed through eclipse
or our child's bronze
toy of spiral rings
resting at the bottom of the stairs. 25
And there's no stopping this
constant alternation of ourselves—
no steady state.
One moment you
are X, the other you're X-1. 30
Only in your death
when both your bodies lie
stupid and nonplused as iron machines
will you be
like those 35
who live in one world, spend
their lives explaining why they cannot
  change,
hanging portraits in their oval frames.

Dave Smith (1942–   )

The Colors of Our Age: Pink and Black

That year the war went on, nameless, somewhere,
but I felt no war in my heart,
not even the shotgun's ba-bam
at the brown blur of quail.
I abandoned brothers and fathers,
the slow march through marsh
and soybean nap where
at field's end the black shacks
noiselessly squatted under strings
of smoke, I wore flags of pink:
shirts, cufflinks, belt, stitching.
Black pants noosed my ankles
into scuffed buck shoes.
I whistled Be-Bop-A-Lula
below a hat like Gene Vincent's.
My uniform for the light, and girls.

Or one girl, anyway, whose name I licked
like candy, for it was deliciously

pink as her sweater. Celia,
slow, drawling, and honey-haired,
whose lips hold in the deep mind
our malignant innocence, joy,
and the white scar of being.
Among my children, on the first
of October, I sit for supper,
feet bare, tongue numb with smoke,
to help them sort out my history's
hysterical photographs. In pink
hands, they take us up, fearless
as we are funny and otherworldly.

Just beyond our sill two late hummingbirds,
black and white, fight for the feeder's
red and time-stalled one drop.
They dart in, drink, are gone,
and small hands part before me
an age of look-alikes, images
in time like a truce wall
I stare over. The hot, warping
smell of concrete comes, fear
bitter as tear gas rakes
a public parking lot. "Mid-City
Shopping Center, Portsmouth, Va.,"
the magazine says, ink
faded only slightly, paper yellowing.

Everyone is here, centered, in horror
like Lee Oswald's stunned escort.
A 1958 Ford convertible, finned,
top down and furred dice hung,
seems ready to leap in the background.
The black teen-ager, no name given,
glares at the lens in distraction.
Half crouched, he shows no teeth,
is shirtless, finely muscled,
his arms extended like wings.
White sneakers with red stars
make him pigeon-toed, alert.
His fingers spread by his thighs
like Wilt Chamberlain trying
to know without looking what moves.

Three girls lean behind him, Norcom H.S.
stencilled on one. One wears a circle
pin, another a ring and chain.
Their soft chocolate faces appear
glazed, cheeks like Almond Joys.
They face the other side, white,
reared the opposite direction—
barbered heads, ears, necks.

In between, a new shiny hammer
towers like an icon lifted
to its highest trajectory.
A Klan ring sinks into flesh,
third finger, left hand,
cuddling the hammer handle.
This man's shirt is white, soiled,
eagle-shaped, and voluminous. Collar up.

Each detail enters my eye like grit
from long nights without sleep.
I might have been this man, risen,
a small-town hero gone gimpy
with hatred of anyone's black eyes.
I watch the hummingbirds feint
and watch my children dismiss them,
focussing hammer and then a woman
tattooed under the man's scarred
and hairless forearm. The scroll
beneath the woman says *Freedom.*
Above her head, in dark letters
shaped like a school name on
my son's team jacket: *Seoul, 1953.*
When our youngest asks, I try
to answer: A soldier, a war . . .
"Was that black man the enemy?"

I watch the feeder's tiny eye-round
drop, perfect as a breast
under the sweater of a girl
I saw go down, scuttling
like a crab, low, hands no use
against whatever had come to beat
into her silky black curls.
Her eyes were like quick birds
when the hammer nailed
her boyfriend's skull. Sick,
she flew against Penney's wall,
our hands trying to slap her sane.
In the Smarte Shop, acidly,
the mannequins smiled
in disbelief. Then I was
yanked from the light, a door

opened. I fell, as in memory I fall
to a time before that time.
Celia and I had gone to a field,
blanket spread, church done,
no one to see, no one expected.
But the black shack door opened,
the man who'd been wordless,
always, spoke, his words intimate

as a brother's but banging out.
He grinned, he laughed, he wouldn't
stop. I damned his lippy face
but too late. He wiggled
his way inside my head.
He looked out, kept looking
from car window, school mirror,
from face black and tongue
pink as the clothes we wore.

Often enough Celia shrieked for joy,
no place too strange or obscene
for her, a child of the South,
manic for the black inside.
When he fell, she squeezed
my hand, and more, her lips came
fragrant at my ear. I see them
near my face, past the hammer.
But what do they say? Why, now,
do I feel the insuck of breath
as I begin to run—and from her?
Children, I lived there and wish
I could tell you this is only
a moment fading and long past.

But in Richmond, Charlotte, God knows
where else, by the ninth green,
at the end of a flagstone pathway
under pine shadow, a Buick waits
and I wait, heart hammering,
bearing the done and the undone,
unforgiven, wondering in what
year, in what terrible hour,
the summons will at last come.
That elegant card in the hand
below the seamless, sealed face—
when it calls whoever I am
will I stand for once and not run?
Or be whistled back, what I was, hers?

In Utah, supper waiting, I watch my son
slip off, jacketed—time, place,
ancestors of no consequence to him,
no more than pictures a man carries
(unless a dunk-shot inscribed).
For him, we are the irrelevance of age.
Who, then, will tell him of wars,
of faces that gather in his face
like shadows? For Christ's sake,
look, I call to him, or you will
have to wait, somewhere, with us.
There I am, nearest the stranger

whose hammer moves quicker
than the Lord's own hand. I am
only seventeen. I don't smoke.
That's my friend Celia, kissing me.
We don't know what we're doing.
We're wearing pink and black.
She's dead now, I think.

Nikki Giovanni (1943–)

For Saundra

i wanted to write
a poem
that rhymes
but revolution doesn't lend
itself to be-bopping

then my neighbor
who thinks i hate
asked—do you ever write
tree poems—i like trees

so i thought
i'll write a beautiful green tree poem
peeked from my window
to check the image

noticed the school yard was covered
with asphalt
no green—no trees grow
in manhattan

then, well, i thought the sky
i'll do a big blue sky poem
but all the clouds have winged
low since no-Dick was elected

so i thought again
and it occurred to me
maybe i shouldn't write
at all
but clean my gun
and check my kerosene supply

perhaps these are not poetic
times
at all

Ego Tripping
(there may be a reason why)

I was born in the congo
I walked to the fertile crescent and built
the sphinx
I designed a pyramid so tough that a star
that only glows every one hundred years falls 5
into the center giving divine perfect light
I am bad

I sat on the throne
  drinking nectar with allah
I got hot and sent an ice age to europe 10
  to cool my thirst
My oldest daughter is nefertiti
  the tears from my birth pains
  created the nile
I am a beautiful woman 15

I gazed on the forest and burned
  out the sahara desert
  with a packet of goat's meat
  and a change of clothes
I crossed it in two hours 20
I am a gazelle so swift
  so swift you can't catch me

  For a birthday present when he was three
I gave my son hannibal an elephant
  He gave me rome for mother's day 25
My strength flows ever on

My son noah built new/ark and
I stood proudly at the helm
  as we sailed on a soft summer day
I turned myself into myself and was 30
  jesus
  men intone my loving name
  All praises All praises
I am the one who would save

I sowed diamonds in my back yard 35
My bowels deliver uranium
  the filings from my fingernails are
  semi-precious jewels
  On a trip north
I caught a cold and blew 40
My nose giving oil to the arab world
I am so hip even my errors are correct
I sailed west to reach east and had to round off
  the earth as I went
  The hair from my head thinned and gold was laid 45
  across three continents

I am so perfect so divine so ethereal so surreal
I cannot be comprehended
  except by my permission

I mean . . . I . . . can fly 50
  like a bird in the sky . . .

Appendix

Introduction to the Forms of Discourse

Some people read a great deal, others read a moderate amount, and still others read hardly at all. Those who do read — and they number most influential people of any society — do so to be entertained or informed, and occasionally they may be emotionally moved or mentally persuaded as well. In their quest for the enriched life literature can bring, people read both creative and discursive writing, and what they read has traditionally been classified into four categories. These rhetorical divisions, usually called the forms of discourse, are description, narration, exposition, and argumentation. It is useful for anyone who wishes to read or to write well to be familiar with these categories; for by seeing the distinctiveness of each form, as well as the ways in which all the forms work cooperatively with each other to achieve intellectual and emotional communication, the good student can see the methods by which writers achieve their purposes. From such perception, intelligent readers and effective writers are made.

Imaginative description is seldom written for its own sake alone (save, possibly, in such freshman writing assignments as "My Room" or "The Beach at Night"), but, instead, enriches the other forms of discourse. Unlike scientific description (which is a form of exposition), imaginative description is less concerned with the precision and the colorlessness of denotative words and objective truths than with creating a vivid impression of a person, place, or object by a careful selection and orderly presentation of a number of visual and other sensual details. To capture with words the full picture of some subject, the writer draws upon the suggestiveness of connotative language; the vividness of the senses of sight, taste, touch, smell, and hearing; and the truthfulness of memorable comparisons. To organize his picture, the writer often presents his material in some logical spatial arrangement, as from left to right, from top to bottom, or from near to far. Usually in such an organization, the writer establishes a point of view—that is, an angle of vision from which the picture is being viewed—and the logic of that point of view dictates the order in which the parts of the picture come into view. At times, too, the writer may wish to communicate a dominant emotional impression—that is, to emphasize one basic truth about a person or a place—and to do so selects his details and charges his language to insist upon that psychological reality. In the following passage from William Faulkner's story "Delta Autumn," an old man ponders the changes in the land, as well as the changes in his fellow man, since he was young. As he sees one of the few remaining places where man has not brought destruction, he feels the majesty of the land compared to the puniness of man—but with the irony that it is the land that must retreat before the ravages of man. This dominant impression of brooding majesty and ironic destruction, conveyed here through description, is central to the point of "Delta Autumn," which is not only about the loss of the land but also about the consequences of that loss to the dignity and majesty of life itself. The passage reads:

> . . . he watched even the last puny marks of man—cabin, clearing, the small and irregular fields which a year ago were

> jungle and in which the skeleton stalks of this year's cotton stood almost as tall and rank as the old cane had stood, as if man had had to marry his planting to the wilderness in order to conquer it—fall away and vanish. The twin banks marched with wilderness as he remembered it—the tangle of brier and cane impenetrable even to sight twenty feet away, the tall tremendous soaring of oak and gum and ash and hickory which had rung to no axe save the hunter's, had echoed to no machinery save the beat of oldtime steam boats traversing it or to the snarling of launches like their own of people going into it to dwell for a week or two weeks because it was still wilderness. There was some of it left, although now it was two hundred miles from Jefferson when once it had been thirty. He had watched it, not being conquered, destroyed, so much as retreating since its purpose was served now and its time an outmoded time, retreating southward through this inverted-apex, this ∇-shaped section of earth between hills and River until what was left of it seemed now to be gathered and for the time arrested in one tremendous density of brooding and inscrutable impenetrability at the ultimate funneling tip.

Narration, a second form of discourse, ranges from the short anecdote (a simple bit of action told to make a point) to the long novel, but narratives are all organized in a time pattern; they are all interested (unlike most histories and biographies) in action for its own sake rather than as an excuse for analysis and interpretation; and they all gain effectiveness, or lack of it, from the way in which they tease their readers into wanting to answer the question, "What happens next?" Simple narratives tend toward a straightforward sequence of time, while more complex narratives (discussed in detail later in the Appendix) often manipulate their chronology for artistic effectiveness. Where the action of the simple narrative may begin with A, the first event in time, and continue consecutively on to G, the last event in the action, the complex narrative may look more like this: C D E A B F G.

Because narration dramatizes events, depicts the conflicts and motives of people, is easy to follow, and has strong emotional appeal, writers of exposition and argumentation often introduce their ideas and reinforce their points by appropriate bits of narrative. Loren Eiseley, in his essay "The Bird and the Machine," uses numerous incidents to dramatize his quarrel with the purely mechanistic concept of life. One of the most effective of these occurs when Eisely tells of how he once trapped a hawk, separating him from his mate, and then the next day, in compassion, set the bird free on the grass:

> He lay there a long minute, without hope, unmoving, his eyes still fixed on that blue vault above him. . . .
>
> In the next second after that long minute he was gone. Like a flicker of light, he had vanished with my eyes full on him, but without actually seeing even a premonitory wing beat. He was gone straight into that towering emptiness of light and crystal that my eyes could scarcely bear to penetrate. For another long moment there was silence. I could not see him. The light was too intense. Then from far up somewhere a cry came ringing down.
>
> I was young then and had seen little of the world, but when I heard that cry my heart turned over. It was not the cry of the hawk I had captured; for, by shifting my position against the sun, I was now seeing further up. Straight out of the sun's eye, where she must have been soaring restlessly above us for untold hours, hurtled his mate. And from far up, ringing from peak to peak of the summits over us, came a cry of such unutterable and ecstatic joy that it sounds down across the years and tingles among the cups on my quiet breakfast table.

The most common form of discourse—the one by which the practical everyday concerns of life are largely carried on—is exposition. Concerned primarily with ideas rather than with action or sensory impressions, exposition explains the logical relationships of things. When exposition is well written, it reveals the connection of a number of parts to one unified whole. Though exposition may make use of the other forms of discourse, its master is not the clock or the senses but the intellect, and when exposition does employ the devices of narration and description, it does so better to fulfill its primary obligation: to explain, clearly and interestingly, the logical nature of something.

If he is to explain an expository topic well, the writer must think effectively about the logical connections of the parts of his subject before he begins to write, so that he can show with organization and clarity the relationship of each part of his material to the whole subject. In addition he should remember that a good expository paragraph does two further things: it states, or implies, a general concept (often called a topic statement); and it proves, in sufficient detail to make the case, the truth of that topic statement. As in a lawyer's brief, the general statement should be neither too broad to be proved convincingly nor too narrow to lack opportunity for discussion; and the proof itself should be sufficiently detailed to be convincing but not so overly developed as to become repetitious and uninteresting.

Whether he is writing a paragraph, an article, or a book, the writer must never forget the importance of unity, coherence, and emphasis—elements necessary to all good writing but more often lacking in exposition than in description or narration—and if he is writing a work of some length and complexity, he may find it useful to make an outline before he begins. By so doing, he may avoid the temptation to stray from the one subject to which he is committed (a violation of unity); to omit connections between the parts of his subject (a violation of coherence); or to give inadequate space to a major idea or excessive attention to a minor one (a violation of emphasis). Note the way in which the paragraph on page 732 (from Henry David Thoreau's *Civil Disobedience*) clings to one idea (as stated in the topic sentence that opens the passage and that limits the concept to be developed); makes appropriate connections from the paragraph preceding it and between the sentences within the paragraph; and makes emphatic the one idea of the paragraph by adequate development and vivid language. (The editors have underlined the principal connective devices and made, to the sides, editorial comments on these transitions.)

In the paragraph on page 732, Thoreau develops his material by the use of *comparison and contrast,* but this method of development is only one of numerous ways by which topic ideas may be resolved and illuminated. In another paragraph from *Civil Disobedience* Thoreau develops his material by *definition* (technically definition by exclusion) when he tells of all the things that government does not do (and men can do) and thus makes his point that government is merely a recent, useless, and relatively unprincipled tradition:

> This American government,—what is it but a tradition, though a recent one, endeavoring to transmit itself unimpaired to posterity, but each instant losing some of its integrity? It has not the vitality and force of a single living man; for a single man can bend it to his will. It is a sort of wooden gun to the people themselves. But it is not the less necessary for this; for the people must have some complicated machinery or other, and hear its din, to satisfy that idea of government which they have. Governments show thus how successfully men can be imposed on, even impose on themselves, for their own advantage. It is excellent, we must all allow. Yet this government never of itself furthered any enterprise, but by the alacrity with which it got out of its way. *It* does not keep the country free. *It* does not settle the West. *It* does not educate. The character inherent in the American people has done all that has been accomplished; and it would have done somewhat more, if the government had not sometimes got in its way. For government is an expedient by which men would fain succeed in letting one another alone; and, as has been said, when it is most expedient, the governed are most let alone by it. Trade and commerce, if they were not made of india-rubber, would never manage to bounce over the obstacles which legislators are continually putting in their way; and, if one were to judge these men wholly by the effects of their actions and not partly by their intentions, they would deserve to be classed and punished with those mischievous persons who put obstructions on the railroads.

Thomas Henry Huxley uses yet another common method of development of expository material when, in "The Method of Scientific Investigation," he uses an *illustration* to aid him in showing the relationship of scientific thought to everyday reasoning:

> A very trivial circumstance will serve to exemplify this [the similarity between scientific thought and everyday reasoning]. Suppose you go into a fruiterer's shop, wanting an apple. You take up one, and on biting it you find it is sour; you look at it and see that it is hard and green. You take up another one, and that too is

hard, green, and sour. The shopman offers you a third; but before biting it you examine it and find that is is hard and green, and you immediately say that you will not have it, as it must be sour like those that you have already tried.

Nothing can be more simple than that, you think; but if you will take the trouble to analyze and trace out into its logical elements what has been done by the mind, you will be greatly surprised. In the first place you have performed the operation of induction. You found that in two experiences hardness and greenness in apples go together with sourness. It was so in the first case, and it was confirmed by the second. True, it is a very small basis, but still it is enough to make an induction from; you generalize the facts, and you expect to find sourness in apples where you get hardness and greenness. You found upon that a general law that all hard and green apples are sour; and that, so far as it goes, is a perfect induction. Well, having got your natural law in this way, when you are offered another apple which you find is hard and green, you say, "All hard and green apples are sour; this apple is hard and green; therefore this apple is sour." That train of reasoning is what logicians call a syllogism and has all its various parts and terms—its major premise, its minor premise, and its conclusion. And by the help of further reasoning, which if drawn out would have to be exhibited in two or three other syllogisms, you arrive at your final determination, "I will not have that apple."

To these common methods of expository development—by comparison and contrast, by definition, and by illustration—many more could be added, but it is the material that should determine the method of development. The important thing is that ideas, to be of any significance, must be effectively developed. An idea without development is like a tadpole that never grew to be a frog. To put it another way, the secret of good writing—if there is a single secret—is effective development; and the secret of effective development is not only for the writer to have information about his subject but also to have the wisdom to communicate fully and clearly the knowledge that he has.

The last of the conventional forms of discourse is argumentation. Since an effective argument inevitably demands a considerable amount of explanation, argumentation is similar to exposition; but the ultimate aim of argument is less to analyze and explain than it is to convince and persuade. The contrast between the two is clearly illustrated by the difference between Huxley's "The Method of Scientific Investigation," which aims to define and clarify a mode of human thought, and Thoreau's "Civil Disobedience," which aims to persuade Americans that they must not only cease to support the American government but must actively attempt to prevent its orderly functioning.

In fulfilling his purpose, the writer of an argument may follow some of the more useful conventions of argumentation. He may, for instance, begin his essay by defining and limiting the terms and scope of the argument and by considering the past history and present importance of his subject. Next, he will probably make the best case he can for the side of the question to which he is committed. Then he may recognize the most compelling arguments of the opposition in order to refute them as convincingly as he can. Finally, he may summarize his position, and if the topic is appropriate, request a call for action.

The most important aspect of the argument is, of course, the effectiveness with which the writer persuades his audience to agree with his position. In making his case, the writer may appeal to the emotions or the intellect, or he may, in different degrees, make both kinds of appeals. When he flatters his audience, for instance, by telling each of its members that they are honorable men, all honorable men, he is appealing to emotion, not intellect.

One of the great American writers to use emotional appeals was Tom Paine. In the first paper of the *Crisis,* Paine argued effectively for a continuation of the American Revolution; and perhaps because he had relatively few points that were intellectually convincing, he emphasized such emotional appeals as the concept that God was on the American side; as name calling; as threats of physical violence aimed at those Tories who would not change their ways; and as tearful pictures of helpless little children who depended upon the selflessness of their parents for their future freedom and salvation. At the end of his essay Paine

The mass of men serve the state thus, not as men mainly, but as machines, with their bodies. They are the standing army, and the militia, jailers, constables, *posse comitatus,* etc. In most cases there is no free exercise whatever of the judgment or of the moral sense; but they put themselves on a level with wood and earth and stones; and wooden men can perhaps be manufactured that will serve the purpose as well. Such [men] command no more respect than men of straw or a lump of dirt. They have the same sort of worth only as horses and dogs. Yet such [men] as these even are commonly esteemed good citizens. Others [other men]—as most legislators, politicians, lawyers, ministers, and office-holders—serve the state chiefly with their heads; and, as they rarely make any moral distinctions, they are as likely to serve the Devil without *intending* it, as God. A very few [men],—as heroes, patriots, martyrs; reformers in the great sense, and *men*—serve the state with their consciences also, and so necessarily resist it for the most part; and they are commonly treated as enemies by it. A wise man will only be useful as a man, and will not submit to be "clay," and "stop a hole to keep the wind away," but leave that office to his dust at least:—

> "I am too high-born to be propertied,
> To be a secondary at control,
> Or useful serving-man and
> instrument
> To any sovereign state throughout
> the world."

The opening sentence or generalization limiting the development of the paragraph contrasts the way men actually serve the state (as mere machines) with the implied way they might serve the state (as more than machines).

The word "they" is, of course, a pronoun, and since pronouns, by definition, refer backward to an antecedent, ideally a single unambiguous one, they are effective transitional devices.

Soon afterward Thoreau repeats his key word "men" and makes the contrast between what "men" often are, wooden creatures with no more humanity than a machine, and what "men" should be, thinking creatures with a moral sense; and Thoreau constantly uses his key word, or synonyms for it, to insist upon this contrast.

"The state" is another key phrase that is repeated constantly, and it is contrasted, as the master of unthinking men, with real thinking men of conscience who should be master of the state.

The transitional word "thus" (or "it follows therefore") shows the logical connection between this paragraph and the one preceding it.

"In most cases" refers to the key concept of the paragraph (that most men serve the state as mere machines), and that concept is held constantly before the reader.

The word "yet" serves here as a conjunction, in the sense of "nevertheless"; and conjunctions are, of course, joining words whose primary duty is to connect—usually, as with the conjunction "and," in the sense of continuity, but often, as with the conjunction "but," in the sense of contrast, of "on the other hand."

Finally, in his last sentence, Thoreau shifts from his key word, "men" to a logical limitation of that word in defining one basic quality of "a wise man": he will not submit to being dead clay while he is alive, and he will not accept his own murder, for the service of the state, without protest.

VL-226 (REV. 9-82)

MESSAGE MEMO

TO	MSG BY	DATE	TIME

FROM	TEL. NO./EXT.

O PHONED YOU	O RETURNED YOUR CALL	O WISHES TO SEE YOU
O PLEASE CALL	O WILL CALL AGAIN	O STOPPED TO SEE YOU

PLEASE		FOR YOUR	RECOMMEND
O CIRCULATE	O HANDLE	O INFORMATION	O APPROVAL
O SEE ME	O RETURN	O SIGNATURE	O DENIAL
O PREPARE REPLY MY SIGNATURE	O FILE	O ANALYSIS	O WE DISCUSS THIS MATTER

MESSAGE: Things to Print

~~Diet~~ ✓
Diet. 1 ✓
Diet, 2

ADIDAS ✓
COMP 2 ✓
GRADES ✓
HORSE ✓
NY COMPARE ✓

LECTURE

imagines the future if the English were to conquer the American patriots, and the imagery of his vision suggests the extent to which emotional appeals may be carried:

> By perseverance and fortitude we [Americans] have the prospect of a glorious issue; by cowardice and submission, the sad choice of a variety of evils—a ravaged country and depopulated city—habitations without safety, and slavery without hope—our homes turned into barracks and bawdy-houses for Hessians, and a future race to provide for, whose fathers we shall doubt of. Look on this picture and weep over it! and if there yet remains one thoughtless wretch who believes it not, let him suffer it unlamented.

When they have, or think they have, facts and logic on their side, most writers prefer to direct their appeals to the head rather than the heart. Doing so, they tend to argue from one or more particular facts (the evidence) to a general conclusion (argument by induction), or from general premises (major and minor) to a particular conclusion deduced from them (argument by deduction). The first kind of reasoning brings conclusions that are probabilities (the dependableness of the probability varying with the extent of the evidence), while the second kind, when the premises are sound and the reasoning valid, brings logical certainty.

The distinction between these two basic kinds of argument (of which all other types are merely variants) can be seen by comparing Darwin's essay on "Natural Selection" (from his long argument *On The Origin of Species*) with Thoreau's essay "Civil Disobedience." In the first, a scientist, on the basis of the evidence of accumulated observations, argues that over the centuries, changes in the conditions of life have resulted in changes in organic beings; and since some of these changes, according to the evidence of history, have been retained in various species, while other mutations have been eliminated, Darwin theorizes that those modifications that aid the preservation of a species have been retained, while those modifications that are injurious have been destroyed. Darwin summarizes his argument by stating:

> It may metaphorically be said that natural selection is daily and hourly scrutinizing, throughout the world, the slightest variations; rejecting those that are bad, preserving and adding up all that are good; silently and insensibly working, *whenever and wherever opportunity offers,* at the improvement of each organic being in relation to its organic and inorganic conditions of life. We see nothing of these slow changes in progress, until the hand of time has marked the lapse of ages, and then so imperfect is our view into long-past geological ages, that we see only that the forms of life are now different from what they formerly were. . . .

Thoreau, on the other hand, does not pile up evidence based on observation to bring himself to a conclusion. Instead, he argues from a conviction that the American government of his time is morally evil and, therefore, an honorable man cannot support it. Thoreau's argument is based on deduction, and the steps in his logic can be shown by the syllogistic form especially associated with deductive logic.

Major premise:—A morally evil government can be supported only by immoral men.

Minor premise:—The present American government is morally evil.

Conclusion:—Therefore, the present American government can be supported only by immoral men.

By the same kind of logic, Thoreau later attempts to refute the argument that a man must obey the commands of the government if he is to avoid punishment. He does so by claiming that the essential part of a man is not his body but his mind; and the government, in its blindness, imprisons the body (the animal part of man) but leaves the essential quality of a man (his mind) unfettered and unpunished. Syllogistically, Thoreau's argument runs as follows:

> The mind is the essential element in a man.
> Government cannot imprison (and punish) the mind.
> Therefore, government cannot imprison (and punish) the essential part of a man.

Mechanically, the first of Thoreau's arguments is valid (though not necessarily factually accurate), and the second is in-st is valid for the same rea- arble that is put in a hatbox n a barrel is not only in the also in the barrel. Note how argument against support of the American government might be diagramed:

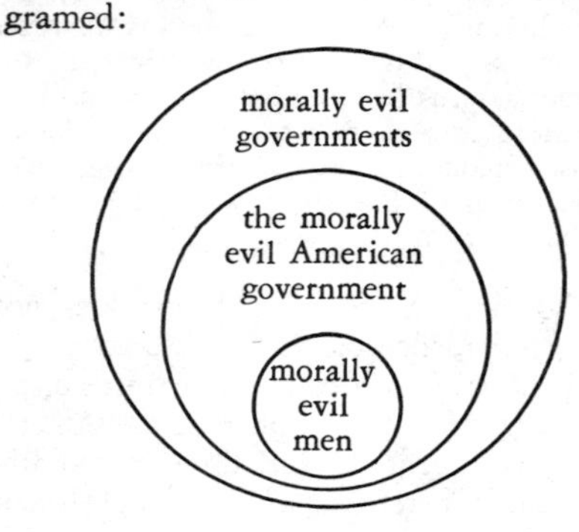

On the other hand, Thoreau's second argument is mechanically invalid (though the conclusion might be truthful), for though there seem three terms in the argument (and there must always be three terms in a valid syllogism), there are actually only two because "the mind" and "the essential element in man" are stated to be the same thing.

The second of Thoreau's arguments could, therefore, be attacked on the basis of the fallibility of its reasoning, but a critic who wished to attack Thoreau's first argument would have to quarrel with his premises, not his reasoning. Thus the minor premise—that "the present American government is morally evil"—might be attacked by defending the morality of both the Mexican War and the institution of slavery. If such an attack on the minor premise seemed weak, the critic might quarrel with the major premise—possibly by claiming, as does the philosopher Thomas Hobbes, that moral men can support immoral governments because even the worst of governments is better than the anarchy unloosed by no government at all.

With all this said, the most important thing yet remains to be noted. That is, that an effective argument is only effective if it persuades as well as convinces its audience. And persuasion, like love, arises from a host of intangibles that go beyond logic. Perhaps most of all, an audience is persuaded by a well-chosen tone—one that is appropriate for that particular audience at that particular time. Thus a modest tone may be effective on most occasions, but it is possible that on other occasions a tone of boldness and certitude may be even more appropriate. At times it may be wise to seem a seeker of truth, and at other times it may be even wiser to assume the posture of one who knows the truth. The mark of the mature writer of argument is the fact that he has the intelligence to recognize the slightest differentiation in tones and the wisdom to use the right one at the right time.

Introduction to the Short Story

The short story may be identified simply as a brief narrative—but not so lacking in development as to be merely an anecdote—that aims at unity of impression. Early, though relatively crude, examples may be found in episodes from the Bible (such as the New Testament parable of The Prodigal Son), *The Arabian Nights* (the tale of Ali Baba), and *The Canterbury Tales* (The Nun's Priest's Tale). Not until the nineteenth century, however, did writers begin to reflect upon the form, and it did not really come of age until Edgar Allan Poe rationalized his own artistic practices into a theory of the short story. For Poe, the short story, in its ideal form, could be read at a single sitting of an hour or so. In that time the author had the opportunity to make one vivid, uninterrupted impression upon the reader. Reviewing Nathaniel Hawthorne's tales, Poe generalized:

> A skillful literary artist has contructed a tale. If wise, he has not fashioned his thoughts to accommodate his incidents; but having conceived, with deliberate care, a certain unique or single *effect* to be wrought out, he then invents such incidents—he then combines such events as may best aid him in establishing this

> preconceived effect. If his very initial sentence tend not to the outbringing of this effect then he has failed in his first step. In the whole composition there should be no word written, of which the tendency, direct or indirect, is not to the one pre-established design. . . . The idea of the tale has been presented unblemished, because undisturbed, and this is an end unattainable by the novel. Undue brevity is just as exceptionable here as in the poem; but undue length is yet more to be avoided.

Though the short story differs, most obviously so in length, from such longer narrative forms as the novel and the *nouvelle,* the short story also has much in common with them. To discuss any form of fiction effectively, one must understand some of the rudiments of setting, plot, character, and theme. At times, setting is relatively unimportant, most especially so when an implied point in the tale is in its universality, in the fact that the action could occur anywhere and the characters live in any epoch. At other times, setting may be extremely important—as, for instance, when the author of a tale of local color wants to capture the language, appearance, and mentality of people who live in a particular place at a specific moment in history; or when the author wishes to capture a mood, as Poe often does in his tales of the supernatural and irrational; or when the writer desires to filter setting through a character's mind so that the time and place reflect the mood of the character as much as actual physical reality; or, finally, when the author conceives of nature as hostile, indifferent, or benign and reflects his philosophical conviction in one dominating impression. In many of the short stories in *The Modern Age,* an understanding of the significance of the setting illuminates much of the meaning of the story. For instance, in Stephen Crane's short story "The Open Boat," the natural setting—vast sky above and endless sea below—illuminates the puniness of man in a world of powerful and mysterious forces he can neither fully comprehend nor efficiently control.

Plot, a second basic element of narrative fiction, may be defined as the writer's dramatic manipulation of the events of his tale for the maximum artistic effect. Usually the writer of a modern short story (or play) will observe the unities of time, place, and action—the narrative will cover a short period of time, will occur in a limited area of space, and will be limited to a single dramatic event—and will tell his story in a straightforward chronological manner. Sometimes, however, the writer may violate the unities of time and place (though seldom, in short fiction, of action) and may choose to violate conventional chronology. Occasionally, especially if the story covers a lengthy period of time, the writer may begin his tale in the middle of the action *(in medias res)* and later on convey the necessary information preceding the initial action by summary exposition or by dramatic flashbacks. Whichever way he chooses to tell his story, the action (as distinct from the plot) covers the chronological sequence of events, from the first event in time until the last; and the reader should see the action clearly before he begins to ponder the significance of any of the author's variations from straightforward chronological narration.

In an effective plot there is a conflict that arouses suspense concerning the victor by pitting two relatively equal powers (an irresistible force meeting an immovable object) in a meaningful struggle. Four major kinds of conflict deserve to be noted. The most obvious is the struggle of man against man, as in Joyce Carol Oates's story "Where Are You Going, Where Have You Been?," in which the young girl Connie and the nightmarish Arnold Friend pit their wills against each other until Connie submits and in so doing abandons the shelter of her home for the embrace of Arnold. A second conflict is man against nature. In Lawrence's "The Horse Dealer's Daughter," Dr. Fergusson rescues Mabel from the pond in which she has attempted suicide, but in doing so (since he cannot swim), he struggles fearfully against the "deep, soft clay" which seems to pull him down, and the "foul earthy water" which he feels is "hideous" and "cold." Still another is the conflict of the individual against society, as in E. M. Forster's "The Machine Stops," in which the youth Kuno violates the laws of his state in order to escape his warm, secure home (or womb) and see and explore the dangerous outer world of nature. Finally, the most common of conflicts is that of man against himself, as revealed in "The Horse Dealer's Daughter" when Doctor Fergusson, at the insistence of the girl whom he has rescued from suicide, must decide between life (and the pains of love) and death (and its chill "freedom") for Mabel (literally) and for himself (symbolically). The latter kind of conflict can be extremely subtle, as well as psychologically illuminating, but some critics have objected to what they consider excesses of this kind of drama (or lack of drama). To one such critic, Henry James responded, in "The Art of Fiction," by proclaiming:

> Mr. Henry Besant does not, to my sense, light up the subject by intimating that a story must, under penalty of not being a story, consist of "adventures." Why of adventures more than of green spectacles? He mentions a category of impossible things, and among them he places "fiction without adventure." . . . And what *is* adventure, when it comes to that, and by what sign is the listening pupil to recognize it? . . . A psychological reason [or conflict] is, to my imagination, an object adorably pictorial; to catch the tint of its complexion—I feel as if that idea might inspire me to Titianesque efforts.

The intelligent student of fiction, of course, recognizes that it is less important to perceive a general area of conflict than it is to see how any conflict manifests itself in a particular situation (one individual with a unique problem that he must attempt to solve). What is more, a single work of fiction may embody a variety of conflicts. "The Machine Stops," for instance, dramatizes the conflict of man against himself (in Kuno's efforts to train his body and his mind to survive without the machine); of man against man (in Kuno's attempt to persuade his mother to approve his rebellion); of man against his society (in Kuno's determination to escape the machine and the people it enslaves and the machine's opposition to anything save conformity and submission); and of man against nature (in Kuno's efforts to breathe without mechanical assistance when he briefly escapes the machine). Finally, it is wise to remember that conflict, especially the climax, or highest intensity of conflict, is usually, in artistically serious stories, more important in illuminating the meaning of the story than in merely satisfying the curiosity of the reader as to the victor in the struggle.

A third fundamental aspect of fiction is character. Though it is critically useful to discuss action and character separately, it is also wise to remember that the two are really merely different sides of the same coin. In "The Art of Fiction," Henry James made this point when he noted:

> What is character but the determination of incident? What is incident but the illustration of character? . . . It is an incident for a women to stand with her hand resting on a table and look out at you in a certain way. . . . At the same time it is an expression of character.

In depicting their characters, authors use various techniques. At times an author may speak directly in his own voice to tell how a character is to be seen—as miserly, generous, or sadistic. Occasionally the author may describe his characters physically and imply a connection between the physical appearance and the internal reality. (In nineteenth-century melodramas it was an easy task to discover the villain because he always wore a mustache.) At other times, the author may illuminate his characters by things they say about themselves or things others say about them. (Of course the reader should be wary about accepting such evidence at face value.) Most often, however, the modern author will illuminate his characters through what they do—for it is action that makes for drama—so that a character who speaks benevolently and acts tyranically may be correctly adjudged to be not only a tyrant but a hypocrite.

Since verisimilitude (or the feeling of believableness) is important to any piece of fiction, characters should be consistent (or consistently inconsistent) in their behavior, and they should act with sufficient motivation. The more complicated the character, the more complex his motivations may be; but the reader should probe what a character thinks and does in order to find the answer to what he ultimately *is*. By continual questioning, the reader can often find in serious fiction, where there is usually more order and reason than in life itself, an illumination not only of the superficial causes, but even of the deepest roots of human action. In such a story as Graham Greene's "The Basement Room," the author suggests, by dramatizing an event of a child's life, a reason for a man's total withdrawal from the realities of existence; and though Greene's explanation may be something of a Freudian oversimplification, he does give a plausible explanation for a profound mystery of human behavior. A psychologist might even be able to suggest an explanation for The Misfit's action in "A Good Man Is Hard to Find," but perhaps Flannery O'Connor's decision to minimize psychological explanations and to emphasize religious choices ultimately makes for a more disturbing story about the inexplicableness of evil than might otherwise have been true.

The perceptive reader not only searches for the reasons characters act as they do, but is also aware that characters may change, at least in small ways, in the course of a short story. A character that develops in the course of the narrative may be called dynamic, while a character that stays the same may be termed static. Sometimes characters develop through changes in, or modifications of, personality traits. More often in modern stories, characters develop through gaining, for a moment at least, greater awareness of the truth about life and about themselves. These delicate, evanescent moments, these "showings forth" of the nature of reality, occur often in the stories of Katherine Mansfield and James Joyce. One of these "epiphanies," as Joyce called these radiant illuminations, occurs in Joyce's story "Araby" when the major character sees clearly the romantic dreams by which he has deluded himself and perceives himself "as a creature driven and derided by vanity; and my eyes burned with anguish and anger."

In developing his characters, an author may, especially in longer fiction, attempt to capture a rounded personality, full of the complexities of a real human being. Such a person is unique, an individual character. If, however, the author desires to satirize a particular category of people —say the conventional businessman or the female flirt—he may draw a flat, uncomplicated, universal type. One of the limitations of short fiction is that it is impossible, because of the brevity of the story, to delineate a fully rounded being. This does not, however, mean that the short-story writer is doomed to depicting only familiar types. What he is confined to is selectivity, the depiction of limited aspects (and possibly only one aspect) of his major characters (one of whom usually dominates the story). Thus, James Joyce, in "Araby," leads toward his epiphany by confining his story to events that arouse his protagonist's daydreams, discontent, and eventual frustrated outbreak. By limiting his events and characters, Joyce focuses sharply; and though he does not capture the wholeness of his protagonist, he depicts one essential part so well that he implies much of the whole. That kind of suggestivity is a major aspect of an effective modern short story.

The last of the fundamental elements of the short story is theme or meaning. Though some escapist works have little or no meaning (horror stories, for instance, may have the sole purpose of arousing a shudder), the theme is, perhaps, the most important aspect of a serious work of art. The reason for this is simply that serious writers want to say something about the nature of man and the purpose (or lack of it) of life itself. To do so, they have chosen a more indirect method of statement than that of the formal essay; but they, like poets, are as concerned as philosophers and scientists with presenting a truth (which is not to be confused with the kind of factual truth that scientists seek) that is important to them. In dramatizing his ideas, the writer may draw upon sociology or history or psychology, and in attempting to persuade his readers toward his own convictions, he may become propagandistic; but the reality of his "truth" is dependent only upon the power with which he creates and populates his world.

Whether the theme of a piece of fiction is extremely simple or exceedingly complex, one of the first duties of the intelligent reader on completing the story is to formulate a hypothesis about the dominant idea (as distinct from subordinate themes) of the work. In doing so, he should remember Poe's injunction that "there should be no word written, of which the tendency, direct or indirect, is not to the one pre-established design."

hat advice in mind, he should test idity of his attempt to state the central idea, and if he finds his tentative theme unable to withstand analysis, he should modify or alter his concept. Doing so, he will continually attempt to sharpen his statement, so that it is not so broad as to be meaningless (" 'The Magic Barrel' is about love."); so partial or so obsessed by the attempt to find a "moral" moral as to distort the uniqueness of the work (" 'Quenby and Ola, Swede and Carl' proves that you shouldn't fool around with somebody else's woman"); or so much a meaningless cliché as to offend intelligence (" 'In Another Country' demonstrates that war is hell").

In justifying the theme of a story, the scholar may find it wise to go beyond the four fundamental elements of fiction. Point of view, or the angle of vision from which a story is told, may well illuminate meaning. (The fact that "The Open Boat" varies the point of view from the limited perceptions of the people in the boat ["None of them knew the color of the sky."] to the broader perception of an objective onlooker of the scene ultimately has thematic implications.)

There are numerous variations in point of view (and one should not confuse this technical element of fiction with the author's attitudes, or "point of view"), but the most important categories are first person, third person, omniscient, and dramatic. In the first-person point of view, the "I" who tells the story may be the major character or an interested observer who may or may not participate in a subordinate way in the action. The writer who uses the first person tends for the most part to limit himself to what his narrator sees and knows about the actions and characters of whom he writes, but since this can often be confining, the author may occasionally go beyond his narrator's first-hand knowledge—as, for instance, when Nick Carraway, the narrator of Fitzgerald's novel *The Great Gatsby,* imagines what might have occurred at certain times. The third-person point of view may be quite limited (as when the author confines himself to the thoughts and perceptions of one character), or it may be extremely broad (as when the author decides to reveal the inward world of all his major characters). The author who writes from the omniscient point of view (which is seldom used in contemporary short fiction) takes a god-like stance, in which he knows all and reveals what he wishes, and at times the omniscient narrator may go beyond revealing the inward worlds of his characters and enter the narrative himself by commenting upon the action and its actors. Directly opposed to the omniscient viewpoint is the dramatic angle of vision, in which the author deliberately refrains from entering the minds of any of his characters and tells his tale as though it were a play taking place before his eyes. Each of these viewpoints, and their variations, has narrative strengths and weaknesses, and often a reader may find his analysis of a story deepened by pondering such problems as what Barthelme may have gained by the particular variation of the first-person viewpoint that he uses in his story "Me and Miss Mandible."

The reader of serious prose fiction, most especially of that of the twentieth century, should also be aware of, though not obsessed by, the significance of symbols in literature. A symbol is something that casts meanings beyond its factual reality—as, for instance, the color white may symbolize purity in one story and sterility in another; or it may, as it does in the whiteness of the whale in *Moby Dick,* suggest a complex range of concepts from the beauty to the horror to the blankness of the whale and nature and divinity. Through the use of symbols the author can achieve indirection (and most modern writers dislike bluntness of any kind); compression (for the symbol implies but does not develop meanings); and genuine emotion (if the artist is very good or very lucky). Almost anything in the story—action, setting, particular objects—may become symbolic if the author wishes to make it so by either hinting or insisting (through imagery, repetition, connotative language, or other artistic devices) that the material means more than it literally does; but it is wise to remember that excessive symbol hunting can be both juvenile and misleading, and that symbolic interpretations of a whole story, or any of its parts, must be defended through evidence of symbolic intentions within the story itself. When a literary symbol, however, does exist and does reinforce the meaning and deepen the emotions inherent in a story, it is myopic to overlook it and folly to insist that those who have better eyesight are imagining the things they see. In "The Basement Room," for instance, Graham Greene makes it clear that the Meccano set that the young boy never uses after his traumatic childhood experience is symbolic of the lack of creativity, the wasted life, that results from the boy's mental wound suffered in childhood; and probing deeper, a good reader should see that the basement room where much of the action takes place is filled with Freudian overtones that indicate that this setting implies more than a mere physical locale. Similarly, some stories are so charged with suggestive meanings that any attempt to understand them without probing the symbolic overtones is doomed. Such a story is D. H. Lawrence's "The Horse Dealer's Daughter," where the atmosphere of heightened meanings pervades all things, from the tone set by the heavy dullness of the beginning, to the imagery surrounding the brackish pond, to the movement from death toward life in the acceptance (reluctant as it may be on the man's part) of the delights, torments, and obligations of love.

The style and tone of any literary work also merit analysis. Though the discussion of the style of a work or of a writer may become almost as complicated as the psychological analysis of a human personality, the most important thing to remember about style is that it is the revelation of individuality, whether of an artist (the Hemingway style), a period (literary style in the fifteenth century), a place (American literary style), or a genre (the style of naturalism). A writer reveals his uniqueness through the peculiar manner of his expression (as opposed to the variety of his thoughts), and though it is as easy to feel the stylistic differences between writers as to sense the differences in the personalities of Arthur Miller and Allen Ginsberg, it is necessary in analyzing literary style to consider such things as the writer's preferences in diction, in figures of speech (such as simile, metaphor, irony, and allusion), in sentence variety and rhythms, and in rhetorical devices for gaining emphasis.

The tone of a particular work is one aspect of the artist's style, and like a man's tone of voice, it suggests the writer's attitude—angry, ironic, humorous, whatever—toward his material. Through the use of connotative words, for instance, the writer may slant his presentation of an action or a character so that his readers are persuaded toward an emotion (possibly of admiration or contempt); and by the manipulation of his audience's feelings the writer implies not only his judgment of his own world and its inhabitants but also his evaluation of the larger universe that his art reflects.

In his fantasy "The Machine Stops," E. M. Forster uses a narrator who seems identical with the author, and the narrator makes Forster's tone clear from the very beginning. In the narrator's "meditation" (to use his word for his apocalyptic vision), each person in the future will live in "a small room . . . like the cell of a bee," and this charged image dramatizes the narrator's attitude, or tone, which implies that the quality of life in the new civilization will be restricted, cramped, and dehumanized. In the room, the "soft radiance" of the light (which owes nothing to natural sunlight), the freshness of the air (which comes elsewhere than from natural ventilation), and the melodious, uninterrupted throbbing (which bears no resemblance to the sounds of life on earth)—all these selective details insist upon the unnaturalness of "life" in this air-conditioned womb.

The attitude of the narrator toward his material is made even more clear by the tone with which he describes his first character. Apparently a typical citizen of this new civilization, she is a "swaddled lump of flesh," and her face—"as white as a fungus"—shows that she is more a parasite than a human being. Later on when this dependent thing hears the noise of something resembling a telephone, the narrator notes: "She knew several thousand people; in certain directions human intercourse had advanced enormously." The sentence, of course, drips with irony, for much more is meant than is said and much of what is meant—as is usually true of irony—is exactly the opposite of what is said. In truth, irony is the dominant aspect of the tone of "The Machine Stops," for more than anything else the story is an attack upon modern "progress," which, Forster says, is leading men to ever greater dependence upon, and worship of, machines, and is contributing to a constant weakening of the links that join man to man and man to nature. By the end of his vision, Forster has used his tone to persuade his audience to fear the machine and to detest life in a civilization lived under the rule of the machine. Obviously, he means his statement to apply to life during the twentieth century even more than to life in some "utopia" of a distant time.

One last note. Ideally, intelligent analysis (which does not mean interminable attention to pedantic minutiae) should deepen the pleasure of reading, just as understanding the logistics of the construction of the Brooklyn Bridge intensifies the awe with which we view the structure. Through effective reading, the reader becomes a lesser creator, for in probing a work of art, he not only opens intercourse with the great and original minds of all times but he challenges the depths of his own mind. There is joy in that.

An Analysis of "The Basement Room"

Transcendental meditation, gestalt, Erhard's sensitivity training, neo-Freudianism, the new feminism—all of these, as well as numerous other psychological modes and social trends—have made the theories of Dr. Sigmund Freud less revered than they once were. Whatever their ultimate scientific validity may be, however, Freud's ideas—with their vocabulary asserting the esoteric mysteries of the id, the ego, the libido, the subconscious, and the Oedipal and Electra complexes; with their biological pessimism; and with their emphasis on the many ways in which unconscious forces betray reason—have shown many creative artists how to dramatize the dark terrain of man's psyche. Graham Greene, in his story "The Basement Room," uses Freudian concepts to illuminate his perception that the source of a wasted life may be a traumatic, but buried, childhood experience. Greene indicates the Freudian—but universal—theme of the story when he intrudes, as author, into his narrative to quote: "In the lost childhood of Judas/Christ was betrayed." (The original quotation, from the poem "Germinal" by George W. Russell, or "A.E.," had less universal implications in its use of the word "boyhood" rather than "childhood," and read more fully:

> In ancient shadows and twilight
> Where childhood had strayed,
> The world's great sorrows were born
> And its heroes were made.
> In the lost boyhood of Judas
> Christ was betrayed.)

To make his point, Greene interweaves two related narratives concerned with love, life, and death. One of these dramatizes the rather sordid sexual triangle of Baines, his wife, and his mistress, Emmy; the other narrates the discovery by the seven-year-old child, Philip Lane, through his involuntary participation in Baines's drama, of what "life" is like. Both narratives are concerned with death, one physical, the other, emotional; both illuminate man's need for love and the way in which life becomes twisted when that need is denied or frustrated; and both reach their climax when Baines makes his silent plea (which Greene illuminates through the extended image of a telegrapher unable to make contact) that Philip care for Baines enough to remain silent about the facts of Mrs. Baines's death.

The more important of the narratives thematically is that of Philip's initiation into, and rejection of, "life." On the surface the event, which really is the beginning and the end of Philip's life, seems unimportant, or so the author, from his omniscient stance, intrudes to tell the reader: "In a week he had forgotten it." The event, however, is buried in the later man's subconscious, so that, beyond reason, it "conditioned his career, the long austerity of his life." Even on Philip's deathbed, sixty years later, the memory of the incident recurs, and the meaning of the woman Emmy, who "belonged to a world of which he knew nothing at all," makes the old man wonder, "Who is she? Who is she?"

For Philip, whether as a seven-year-old, mature adult, or dying man, this dominant incident in his life begins when his parents go for a holiday and leave him alone with the butler and his wife. After his parents have left, Philip immediately sets his feet on the basement stairs, to think "This is life"; when he goes upstairs toward his nursery he comes "into a wash of sunlight on a parquet floor, the gleam of mirrors dusted and polished and beautified by Mrs. Baines." In imagery and action the world upstairs is associated with childhood, wealth, order, and death (note Mrs. Baines's "shrouding" of the furniture), while the world of the basement is identified with disorder, servitude, human passion, and life.

In the world of the basement Philip is drawn into the marital conflict of Baines and his wife. Before his initiation into the basement room is done, Philip has had a "larger dose of life than he had bargained for." The tension is too much for the child to handle and he thrusts the events of that day and night out of his memory, to the subconscious "basement" self. Yet the memories remain, so that the child never really completes the psychological journey to manhood. Instead, he remains internally a child, full of fear, dominated by ego, and unable to grow. The Meccano set, with which Mrs. Baines tries to bribe him, remains forever linked to the childhood terror. The set, a collection of wires and wheels, bolts and screws, with which children construct toy cars and bridges and buildings, symbolically becomes associated with the retreat from life itself, so that, "He never opened his Meccano set again . . . never created anything, died, the old dilettante, sixty years later with nothing to show rather than preserve the memory of Mrs. Baines's malicious voice . . ."

In drawing his three major characters Greene uses symbolic language and dramatic tension to suggest his theme. Mrs. Baines is a thin, twisted, domineering woman who lives a joyless, dusty life, full of bitterness. When she talks to Philip, it is to command or to whine; and when she looks at him, it is "with . . . hateful peevish eyes . . . getting everything in order, meticulous and loveless and doing her duty." With her stale breath and black dresses, she is to Philip more witch than woman—a creature to fear and to flee. In truth she is the antithesis of love and life, and Greene makes this point often in symbolic imagery: "she was the frozen blocks of earth he had seen one winter in a graveyard . . . ; she was the flowers gone bad and smelling. . . . You had to endure her when she was there and forget about her quickly when she was away, suppress the thought of her, ram it down deep."

Baines, on the other hand, is an easy-going man, for whom Philip has mixed feelings of love, pity, and responsibility. With a liking for beer, sausages, and the simple joys of life, Baines has numerous memories of Africa (much like his creator, Graham Greene, who spent considerable time in Africa, and, as a matter of fact, "conceived ["The Basement Room"] on a cargo steamer on the way home from Liberia to relieve the tedium of the voyage."). In these recollections, Baines remembers the affection of the Negroes, and recalls that he himself was then a man of authority in a strange exotic world. Baines's tales of African adventure are tales of life and love—vastly different from the lovelessness of his life after his marriage to Mrs. Baines—and it is the need for love that leads Baines to his affair with Emmy. With her he can be masculine and tender, and for him Emmy is love itself. When Philip watches Baines and Emmy at tea, with the two quarreling over Baines's gift of second-hand cosmetics, there is love in the battle, the involvement of two people who care for each other, and the scene is one that Philip "would never escape. . . . In a week he had forgotten it, but it conditioned his career, the long austerity of his life; when he was dying he said: 'Who is she?' "

Philip Lane is the seven-year-old child torn between love of Baines and fear of Mrs. Baines. In dramatizing the tension of the conflict within Philip, Greene presents him as a child full of insecurity—thus the terrors of the nightmares that visit him in sleep—and largely free of previous experience. Without meaningful parental influence, Philip, on his parents' departure, feels free ("He could go anywhere") for the first time in his life. Like the Freudianly suggestive empty rooms of his home, Philip is at an age to receive the events and emotions that fill a lived-in life as furniture fills an empty room. Like a blank page, his mind is etched forever. What is most imprinted there is the choice Philip must make between Baines and Mrs. Baines at the climax of the story. At that point, Philip has returned home with a suspicious policeman who is questioning Baines about the details of the fall and death of Mrs. Baines. In order for Philip to go upstairs and to bed he must go past—or so he fears—the fallen body of Mrs. Baines. To do so would take courage, but through such bravery, he would protect Baines. He had already made that choice once, when awakened in the middle of the night he screamed a warning to Mr. Baines that his wife had returned home. On that occasion Mrs. Baines had returned and driven herself in fury toward him, so that he was left with a nightmare and "hadn't any more courage left for ever; he'd spent it all, had been allowed no time to let it grow." Now, Philip is asked to make that same choice again—and in that decision to choose love and life over bitterness and death. Philip does not know the meaning of his choice, but he has learned forever the reality of fear. Out of fear, Philip betrays Baines and in so doing "exorcised himself from life, from love, from Baines with a merciless egotism." In his betrayal, Philip eliminates the world of the "completely disinherited," to which Emmy belongs; the world of Africa, to which Baines so often alludes and with which he is so much identified, with its paradoxical innocence and corruption, its darkness and its love; and all other worlds that differ from the nursery and the upperclass, the familiar and the known. The rest of Philip's life—or what passes as life—is lived as "a whole prolonged retreat from life, from care, from human relationships. . . ."

The meaning of the story is clear, and it reiterates Greene's comment, made in his essay on Charles Dickens in *The Last Childhood*, that Greene is "inclined to believe" that "the creative writer perceives his world once and for all in childhood and adolescence, and his whole career is an effort to illustrate his private world in terms of the great public world we all share." The artistry of the story, however, lies not in its theme, or in its debt to Greene's biography or his reading in Freud, but in the way in which Greene weaves the elements of plot, character, setting, and imagery together to make a timeless point. The Platonic doctrine that all knowledge is simply recollection suggests that concept, as does William Wordsworth's poetic line "The child is father of the man." Philosophers, psychologists, poets, dramatists, and fiction writers will continue to illuminate that truth—some well, some poorly. Graham Greene makes the reader believe in his tale and his "truth," and in that is his art.

Introduction to Drama

A play is meant to be seen, not read. Why then do we bother reading plays? Apart from the impossibility of seeing all the plays now in print—the cost alone would be staggering—there is profit as well as pleasure in reading plays. The profit comes from studying the play's literary values, many of the same values discussed in the section on fiction in this book. The pleasure depends to some extent on one's ability to imagine the play on a stage with actors speaking the lines that appear in print. The decision to produce a play—that is, actually put it on the stage—begins with a reading. Dramatic potential can be gleaned by a skilled reader from a text alone; but the fact that most plays do not succeed, either financially or esthetically, indicates that regardless of how expert the reader is, the text of a play is not the final test. Only the stage, with its actors, its sets, its lighting, and a director who develops and coordinates the whole, can provide the final testing ground.

Drama, therefore, is the only literary form that requires more than a writer and a reader. When the story writer finishes his short story or novel, he is finished. He will receive his rewards or punishments from his readers; nothing stands in the way. But when a modern playwright finishes the text of a play, he has just begun his job. Then comes the equally difficult task of putting it into production, of having many people interpret and shape the text, of changing it, of making numerous revisions before it reaches its audience. The differences between the first finished version of a play and its opening-night version can be enormous. What we do when we read a play, therefore, is second best. The ideal is to see a play, then read it, then study it.

Playwriting requires a special literary skill. A fine poet or novelist is not necessarily a good playwright. Shelley, Henry James, Thomas Wolfe, Ernest Hemingway—to mention a few—all tried their hands at playwriting and failed. James, in particular, tried again and again to mount a successful play but never did. The detailed reasons for these failures are not our business here. They merely indicate that drama demands a gift for constructing plots and a felicity in dialogue peculiar to itself as a distinct literary genre.

The essence of successful drama, ancient or modern, as Aristotle observed long ago, is action, an action that brings a protagonist in conflict with the world, with destiny, or with himself. The conflict may be external (one person against another, one group against another), or it may be internal (one person debating with himself). In classical tragedy—*Oedipus Rex,* for example—the conflict is largely internal. Although Oedipus debates with Tiresias, who warns him of his destructive course, the conflict takes place within Oedipus himself as he draws nearer and nearer to his own doom, sees that he is doing so, yet chooses, with dramatic irony, to ignore clear warnings. Because classical tragedy usually does not reveal physical conflict on the stage, the focus is on the internal struggle.

Shakespearean tragedy similarly portrays much of its conflict internally. Macbeth, Lear, Hamlet, and Othello all must resolve conflicts within themselves that arise from the drama of struggles without. We feel the tension of Hamlet's pursuit of Claudius, but the enigma of Hamlet is locked within himself, and this enigma carries much of the dramatic impact. Hamlet's "To be or not to be" speech remains a dramatic highlight precisely because it expounds a purely internal conflict. Indeed, the purpose of the soliloquy—that is, the speech given by one character when he is alone on stage—is to get inside the character's mind, to project his thoughts in dramatic utterance. And more often than not the thoughts thus projected center about some conflict.

Modern drama, while rarely using the soliloquy, has its own devices for articulating conflict. *The Hairy Ape,* in its third scene, dramatizes a traumatic moment in the life of Yank, when Mildred shudders at the sight of him, which leads him to question the meaning of the worth of his life. The psychological tension between the need to believe in something—or, as O'Neill puts it, to "belong" to something—and the inability of Yank to find anything in which he can place his faith make for the conflict within Yank. That internal conflict is made dramatic by a series of events, some of them realistically believable (for instance, the scene with the IWW), some of them believable only as surrealistic projections on the stage of the internal conflict within Yank (for instance, the scene in which Yank bumps into the men of wealth but makes no impression on them) and some of them absurd save as symbolic communication (for instance, the last scene of the play in which Yank enters the cage of the ape to greet his "brother").

The action of a particular play dictates its structure. A play generally unfolds its action in such a way that the audience, despite the best playbill in the world, will not understand it until the characters on stage explain not only who they are but the situation in which they find themselves.

That which explains what has gone on before the opening of the play is called the exposition. The best kind of exposition does not call attention to itself. It comes out in dialogue and action that are appropriate to the tone of the play. Take, for example, the opening scene in *Major Barbara.* Lady Britomart Undershaft is discussing family finances with her son Stephen, a reluctant discussant. She asks for his help with the girls:

> STEPHEN: But the girls are all right. They are engaged.
> LADY BRITOMART: *{Complacently}* Yes: I have made a very good match for Sarah. Charles Lomax will be a millionaire at thirty-five. But that is ten years ahead; and in the meantime his trustees cannot under the terms of his father's will allow him more than £ 800 a year.
> STEPHEN: But the will says also that if he increases his income by his own exertions, they may double the increase.
> LADY BRITOMART: Charles Lomax's exertions are much more likely to decrease his income than to increase it. Sarah will have to find at least another £ 800 a year for the next ten years; and even then they will be as poor as church mice. And what about Barbara? I thought Barbara was going to make the most brilliant career of all of you. And what does she do? Joins the Salvation Army; discharges her maid; lives on a pound a week; and walks in one evening with a professor of Greek whom she has picked up in the street, and who pretends to be a Salvationist, and actually plays the big drum for her in public because he has fallen head over ears in love with her.

What the audience has learned from the brief exchange is not only the identification of the leading characters but also the chief topic with which the play deals: money. Lady Britomart wants money for her children and for herself. Barbara thinks she wants to live on one pound a week but soon finds that when money runs out there is no salvation for anyone. Even her philosopher husband, after accepting a job with Undershaft, says:

> I think all power is spiritual: these cannons will not go off by themselves. I have tried to make spiritual power by teaching Greek. But the world can never be really touched by a dead language and a dead civilization. . . .

So he turns to the business of making guns and, of course, money. Undershaft, on the other hand, suffers no illusions about the money. It saves souls, he says, from the seven deadly sins: "Food, clothing, firing, rent, taxes, respectability and children. Nothing can lift those seven millstones from Man's neck but money; and the spirit cannot soar until the millstones are lifted." And in the final moment, at least according to one critical interpretation, it is Undershaft who triumphs.

Not all plays are constructed like *Major Barbara,* where there is a considerable amount of important exposition and it is revealed early in the play. In *The Hairy Ape* there is no need for exposition, for the real "life" of Yank actually begins at the time of his traumatic awakening to the vision of himself as others may see him, as a hairy ape, rather than as he sees himself, an essential source of vitality and power.

The psychological revelations of *The Hairy Ape* are not sought in Tennesse Williams' *The Glass Menagerie.* Instead the audience is moved by various artistic devices that emphasize the fact that this is a "memory" play: the poetic passages with which the play begins and ends, the recurring musical theme, the shades of lighting from soft purple to harsh white, the transparent gauze veil behind which the opening scene is played, and the symbolic glass menagerie. Even more the audience is held by a gradually increasing interest in the characters, the environment, and the themes of the play. Set in the 1930s, the drama illuminates a milieu in which the great depression was the prevailing American problem, and the rising surge of fascism was the dominant international reality. These facts, and the tensions consequent upon them, are never far from the surface of *The Glass Menagerie,* but they serve primarily as complementary reflections of the truth illustrated by the drama of the Wingfield family. That truth is simple: in this Darwinistic world the strong survive and the weak perish. Christ, in the imagery of the play, becomes only a greater magician, and his magic is a fraud; the gentleman caller of whom we dream brings not salvation but only greater despair. There is no salvation and no escape.

The conflict of the play, then, is less that between individuals (though the quarrels of Tom Wingfield and his mother are both humorous and pathetic) than between images and concepts: between visions of light and images of darkness, between the Christian faith and the Darwinian fact, between the urge for peace and static beauty and the drive toward adventure and continual change. At the end of the play when the heroine, Laura, blows her "candles" out and the stage—the world—is left in darkness, the victor in this conflict is memorably apparent.

In the last analysis the mystery of dramatic success eludes solution. No single technique, whether it be Shaw's skill in creating reversal of attitudes in *Major Barbara*; Miller's movement back and forth in time, between past memories and present realities, in *Death of a Salesman*; or Williams' use of a Darwinian action complemented by antireligious imagery in *The Glass Menagerie*, provides an infallible clue to the mystery. But certainly the stage illusion is woven by the actors, costumes, sound effects, lighting, and sets. All of these are manipulated by a director inspired by the latent possibilities of the playwright's text, and this complex manipulation is responsible for creating in the spectators the illusion of a living action in which (despite theatrical artifice and paradoxically because of that artifice) they participate.

An Analysis of "The Skin of Our Teeth"

Thornton Wilder won his second Pulitzer Prize for drama with *The Skin of Our Teeth,* which was first performed in New Haven Connecticut, on October 15, 1942, and had its New York opening on November 18 of the same year. The roles of Sabina and Mr. and Mrs. Antrobus were played respectively by Tallulah Bankhead, Fredric March, and Florence Eldridge, and the opening-night audience must have been aware from the very beginning of the play that it was in for an unusual evening. The opening scene was of a news broadcast, and in it pertinent lantern slides were flashed on the theater curtain. The first slide was of the sun rising above the horizon, and of this slide the news broadcaster commented: "The sun rose this morning at 6:32 A.M. This gratifying event was first reported by Mrs. Dorothy Stetson of Freeport, Long Island, who promptly telephoned the Mayor. The Society for Affirming the End of the World at once went into a special session and postponed the arrival of that event for TWENTY-FOUR HOURS. All honor to Mrs. Stetson for her public spirit."

Eccentric though such an opening may have seemed, it wasn't long before the audience was not only aware of its perfect relevance—for the play is concerned basically with the survival of man and his universe—but was also aware that the opening was only one of many playwriting eccentricities through which Wilder made his own dramatic points and at the same time spoofed conventional dramatic form. Among these eccentricities are scenery that seems always ready to fall, and when it does, falls upward instead of down; a dinosaur and a mammoth who are apparently the family pets of the Antrobus family; two characters named Homer and Moses who sing Greek and Jewish songs; a character who is the baby of the Antrobus family and at the beginning of the play is "only four thousand years old"; and another character, Sabina, who at one point refuses to play a sexual scene because she's afraid it will offend a friend of hers in the audience, and at another interrupts the play to tell the audience of her disgust with it: "I can't invent any words for this play, and I'm glad I can't. I hate this play and every word in it. As for me, I don't understand a single word of it, anyway—all about the troubles the human race has gone through, there's a subject for you. Besides, the author hasn't made up his silly mind as to whether we're all living back in caves or in New Jersey today, and that's the way it is all the way through." The reason for such dramatic idiosyncrasy was Wilder's unhappiness with the conventional box-set, picture-window staging that dominated nineteenth- and twentieth-century drama and that emphasized a particular time and place—partially doing so by an elaborate use of scenery—in an attempt to achieve verisimilitude. Because he was "unable to lend credence to such childish attempts to be 'real'" and because he felt that such a technique produced plays in which "the characters are all dead from the start," Wilder began to write plays in which he tried "to capture not verisimilitude but reality."

To put it simply, the eccentricity of *The Skin of Our Teeth* is an example of controlled chaos in art, an aspect that probably, as much as anything else, led to a senseless furor, shortly after the play opened, in which the play was charged with being plagiarized from Joyce's highly unintelligible *Finnegans Wake.* (Wilder suggested, quite seriously, that he thought he was more indebted to *Hellzapoppin* than to *Finnegans Wake.*) Undoubtedly the dominating singularity of the play is the one that disgusts Sabina—the dislocation of time and space. The cause for this dislocation is, of course, Wilder's insistence upon the universal, but that does not alleviate a confusion in which the first act seems to be taking place in both modern New Jersey and in the time of the ice age; in which the second act seems to be set both at a modern convention meeting in Atlantic City and in the days of the flood and Noah's Ark; and in which the third act is set after a war—any war—while at the end of the act the hours of the night (named for such philosophers as Aristotle and Spinoza) pass by in their eternal wisdom, their eternal orbits, cycle upon cycle upon cycle. In insisting upon this dislocation of time and space, Wilder affirms his belief that the external events of most men's lives make what he calls "repetitive patterns," and this concept dramatically affirms his belief, as he once stated it, that "Literature is the orchestration of platitudes." The duty of the dramatist is to use an individual experience to indicate a general truth. To fuse the two truths is the obligation of the worthwhile dramatist, because, as Wilder says, "The theatre is admirably fitted to tell both truths. It has one foot planted firmly in the particular, since each actor before us (even when he wears a mask!) is indubitably a living breathing 'one'; yet it tends and strains to exhibit a general truth. . . . It is through the theatre's power to raise the exhibited individual action into the realm of idea and type and universal that it is able to evoke our belief."

The conflict of *The Skin of Our Teeth* is the eternal one of man for survival. The conflict has two facets: that of man with his environment and that of man with the evil in himself. The conflict is seen through the struggle for survival of the Antrobus family and their servant Sabina, or in biblical, and universal, terms, the family of man as embodied in the figures of Adam, Eve, Cain, and Lilith. The first facet of the conflict dominates the first act, and it is of man against an ever hostile environment. Constantly through the first act the family is trying to gain warmth, and at the end of the act Sabina is pleading with the audience to pass up their seats in order to fuel the fire that will "save the human race." Constantly, too, in this act there are telegraph reports from the office of Mr. Antrobus to his home. These reports expand the specific conflict against the cold and ice to a general one of man with his external environment, for the reports bring news of how Mr. Antrobus is engaged in works that will aid human survival, of how he has invented the wheel and formulated the alphabet and the multiplication table. When he comes home from the office, however, Mr. Antrobus brings with him some characters that suggest the need of man in life for more than mere animal survival. What Mr. Antrobus brings home are a doctor, Judge Moses, and the nine sisters called the Muses. Mrs. Antrobus calls the whole horde tramps, especially objecting to the Muses—"That's the end," she says, "A singing troupe!"—but Mr. Antrobus insists on giving shelter to the entire group. As he says to Mrs. Antrobus,

"I don't want any coffee if I can't drink it with some good people."

Apparently the opening-night audience—as well as later ones—contributed enough fuel to save the race, for the Antrobuses, as typical representatives of the human race, survive into the second act. By this time the couple have been married five thousand years, and in the act Mr. Antrobus and his charming wife—"every inch a mammal"—are at Atlantic City for the convention of the "Ancient and Honorable Order of Mammals, Subdivision Humans." The basic conflict of the action is still over survival, but now there is a perfect fusion between the two possible causes for the destruction of man. Destruction by the environment overshadows the act, for thunder and lightning intermittently occur, and a weather indicator rises straight up from the orchestra pit. One black disk on the indicator indicates bad weather; two, storm; three, hurricane; and four, the end of the world. As the act progresses the disks multiply, and at the end they indicate the end of the world. At that time, in the midst of thunder and lightning, Mr. Antrobus—like Noah before him—hurries his family, and the animals of the earth, two by two, into a boat. A Cassandra-like fortune teller, who has earlier in the act foretold the future doom of man, watches the Antrobuses depart; and as they do, she mutters, "They're safe. George Antrobus! Think it over! A new world to make—think it over!'

As important as the conflict with the environment is the conflict within man, for the carnival, convention atmosphere suggests the evil that God ended when he caused the flood to cover the earth. This kind of evil now exists in Mr. Antrobus, for he has been elected President of the Mammals and has caught what the fortune teller calls the "great man" dizziness. In his speech to the convention Mr. Antrobus shows how far he has degenerated in his humanity, for he ends his speech with the Dionysian injunction: "I give you the watchword for the future: Enjoy yourselves." In pursuit of this aim Mr. Antrobus begins an affair with Sabina—who in this act has become Miss Atlantic City, 1942, and who dreams of taking Mr. Antrobus "away from that wife of his. Then I'll take every man away from his wife. I'll turn the whole earth upside down." The affair is going well, and Mr. Antrobus is pretty well convinced of the truth, evil though it is, of the philosophy that Sabina espouses: ". . . everybody in the world except a few people like you and me are just people of straw . . . there's a kind of secret society at the top of the world,—like you and me,—that know this. The world was made for us." However, before Mr. Antrobus—and the human race—are doomed, Mrs. Antrobus, the maternal preserver of family ties, appears. To her husband she shows the essential Sabina, vulgar and common, in his own daughter, Gladys. At the same time, Mr. Antrobus becomes reawakened to the potential Cain in his son Henry. The realization of the evil strains in his children leads him to forsake Sabina, to proclaim, "I . . . I have to go and see what I can do about this." In leaving Sabina and her philosophy of selfishness, Mr. Antrobus preserves the human race again—at least into the third act.

In the last act the essential conflict is of man against himself, but that conflict also has two facets. One is of man against man; the other is the internal one of man within himself. The first facet is dramatized by the quarrel within the family of man as implied in the conflict between Mr. Antrobus and his son Henry. The two have returned from the war—any war—with hatred for each other in their hearts, each still desirous of totally destroying the other. The reason for this hatred is, as Sabina proclaims, that Mr. Antrobus has discovered during the war that "the enemy is *Henry;* Henry *is* the enemy. Everybody knows that." Why Henry is the enemy is revealed by the omnipresent allusion to him, from the first act on, as not only Henry but Cain. As Henrycain or Cainhenry—one word in either spelling—Henry stands for two kinds of evil, either of which has the potential of destroying the world. The first facet of his evil is his opposition to his father's desire to build a better world for all. What Henry wants is a better world for Henry; and the conflict between father and son, within the family of man, will never end, as Mr. Antrobus says, "as long as you [Henry] mix up your idea of liberty with your idea of hogging everything for yourself." Henry, however, also suggests a second kind of conflict. He cannot stand authority, and this inability to control, to discipline, himself leads to violent acts and violent results for which even Henry is sorry. Thus Henry advances upon his father ready to kill, screaming, "Let me get my hands on his throat." At this point Sabina interrupts the action, saying that the scene must not be played because at the previous night's performance Henry had almost strangled his father. The two men, the two actors, then halt and Henry apologizes, saying, "I don't know what comes over me." Mr. Antrobus does, however, for Henry is the spoiled child, perhaps made so by the father, but no matter where the fault lies the conclusion is the same: "How can you make a world for people to live in, unless you've first put order in yourself?" The answer is, you cannot; and at the end of the play Henry, "brooding and unreconciled," as the stage directions note, reappears at the edge of the scene, and in him reappears the most important threat—especially so today when man has largely conquered his environment—to the survival of man.

Little remains to be said, but one cannot leave the play without commenting upon the voices of the night that appear at the end of the last act. The appearance of the voices is foreshadowed at the beginning of the third act when the stage manager interrupts the action to explain that a number of the actors have suddenly been taken ill. These actors were to have played the voices—"a kind of poetic effect of the author," says the stage manager—and since there are no understudies for these minor roles, it is necessary that there be a short rehearsal with some volunteers who have agreed to play the voices. While the rehearsal is taking place, it is suggested that the audience smoke in the lobby, or chat quietly in their seats, or even watch the rehearsal. For the latter, the stage manager explains that each of the voices is a philosopher. To this, one of the volunteers adds that "just like the hours and stars go by over our heads at night, in the same way the ideas and thoughts of the great men are in the air around us all the time and they're working on us, even when we don't know it." At the end of the play, then, the voices reappear—nine o'clock, Spinoza; ten o'clock, Plato; eleven o'clock, Aristotle; and twelve o'clock, the Bible. Spinoza asserts the need of the wise to search for the good in man; Plato, the need of man to establish order in himself; Aristotle, the energy of God and man (the one greater, the other lesser), so that man through energy, by work, best reflects God; and the Bible, the creation of the universe: "And the Lord said let there be light and there was light."

The play ends, or almost ends, upon this religious note, and what that note implies is an optimistic, theological commonplace. That is, that God created the universe, but he left it up to man to make his own destiny. That destiny may be an earthly paradise—achieved by man's constant working toward the betterment of existence—or it may be man's own destruction. Whatever the result, God is not the cause. He may know the final answer, but He does not predestine it; man makes his own fate, and in the making of that fate is his glory or his shame.

What that fate may be is still undecided, for at the end of the play Sabina reappears voicing again her first lines of the play, "Oh, oh, oh. Six o'clock and the master not home yet." Then Sabina comes down to the footlights and addresses the audience: "This is where you came in. We have to go on for ages and ages yet. You go home."

The end of the play does undoubtedly suggest that man's fate is still in doubt, but an audience seeing the play does not really believe the assertion. Perhaps the reason is that there is too much stage trickery constantly going on in the play and too much homespun Pollyanna philosophy being mouthed in the course of the action. Because of these qualities, Wilder leaves his audience not basically disturbed, as it should be, but complacent and consoled. Perhaps this is why Wilder was so popular in Germany shortly after World War II. It was a psychological necessity for the Germans to feel that the evil they had lived with was but part of a continual cycle, for if they could feel so, they could live with themselves. It was also necessary for them to feel that soon life would go on as it had before—and Wilder told them that, too. Finally Wilder told them, and us too, that man has been left to make his own destiny, either to survive and even prevail, or to work his own destruction.

Perhaps, however, what man needs—and what the greatest playwrights give him—is less consolation and ego satisfaction and more realization of his human weakness and potential depravity. That is what the great tragic playwrights give us in their greatest works, and the lack of this in Wilder's plays makes them best described as amusements—well done, but, nevertheless, amusements. They should be judged on that basis, and on that level they are successful art.

Introduction to Poetry

Poetry is difficult to define. William Wordsworth said it was "the spontaneous overflow of powerful feelings recollected in tranquility." Edgar Allan Poe called it "the rhythmical creation of beauty." And Robert Frost, in apparent desperation, said that "Poetry is what poets write." Regardless of the precise or "poetical" definition, however, most people, at one time or another, do read poetry, and one derives more pleasure from his reading if he understands the nature of poetry and the skills that go into its creation. Poetry is an art—it has form and meaning that enable it to survive. However casual and spontaneous a poem may seem, it has not just "happened." Milton referred to his great epic *Paradise Lost* as "unpremeditated verse"; but obviously he did not simply toss off twelve books of distinguished poetry. Milton meant that divine inspiration rather than pure intellect had moved him to write. But whether divine inspiration or rationality or both are the sources of great poetry, the poetic work is language molded into a form, and one that edifies and delights.

Traditionally, poetry has been categorized as epic (which celebrates a figure of heroic proportions doing deeds that illuminate the history and character of a nation); as dramatic (which tells or implies a story involving dramatic tensions); and as lyric (which melodiously emphasizes the personal emotions of the poet). But whatever type of poetry we read, it is the language of the poem that first attracts us. Technical details such as meter and rhyme are important parts of poetry; yet long before we learn about these we must concentrate on what words mean, what they suggest, and how they are used in their poetic context. It is possible, of course, to know the dictionary definition of each word and yet fail to understand a poem; but not to know what the words mean is a guarantee of such failure.

Consider the poor student who guesses at the meaning of "bootless" in Shakespeare's line "And trouble deaf Heaven with my bootless cries." The word in question obviously does not mean "shoeless"; yet the "cries" are not ordinary "cries" and the adjective that tells about them cannot be guessed at or ignored. In this particular context, "bootless" means "fruitless" and therefore describes the frustration of the supplication to Heaven.

Or take these lines from "The Eve of St. Agnes" by John Keats:

> Full on this casement shone the wintry moon,
> And threw warm gules on Madeline's fair breast

The intended sensuality of the scene is lost unless one knows that the "warm gules" are the red shades of light caused by the moon's rays passing through the stained-glass casement windows. In the same poem we learn that the Beadsman's fingers were numb "while he told/ His rosary . . ." We know the usual meaning of "told," but in this context the usual meaning is wrong. The Beadsman, who is paid to recite prayers for the dead, is not telling his rosary anything; he is instead "telling" or "numbering" his prayers.

Examples of the importance of meaning are endless, and they exist in prose as well as in poetry. Most students, however, are uninhibited by prose, which they see and read almost daily, but avoid poetry, partly because in addition to looking strange on the page, a poem uses language in unusual and challenging ways. One of the notable characteristics of poetry is, for example, compression. Prose paraphrases of good poems are usually longer than the poems themselves; for good poetry distills experience and emotion. One word does the work of several, and a single phrase condenses a whole train of thought.

Compression is achieved by a number of devices, one of which is metaphor. T. S. Eliot's J. Alfred Prufrock describes his genteel, meaningless existence in metaphoric language: "I have measured out my life with coffee spoons." Because everything about Prufrock (except his thoughts and dreams) is small and trivial, coffee spoons are appropriate measuring devices. His life has dribbled away in actions no more distinguished than sugaring coffee. Much as Prufrock longs for it, there is no epic role for him to play among the "tea and cakes and ices." Prufrock's awareness of his own inconsequence and his longing to escape from human sentience and suffering are expressed in his wish to be "a pair of ragged claws," merely a crab on the ocean floor. "Coffee spoons" and "ragged claws" say in four words what would take hundreds of words in prose.

In "To an Athlete Dying Young," Housman describes fame as a "garland briefer than a girl's." Two ideas are compressed in this one phrase: Fame is slighter and more fragile than a garland, and fame is less enduring than a floral wreath. In the same poem the runner is "chaired" through town, that is, carried in triumph on his comrades' shoulders. This same athlete, however, is "carried shoulder-high" by the pallbearers after his early death. The ironical parallel between victory and death is thus economically expressed.

An even greater degree of compression is achieved in the sustained metaphor of Emily Dickinson's "I Like to See It Lap the Miles." Here a train is seen as a rambunctious, playful, yet threatening horse. It laps, licks, feeds, steps, peers, crawls, complains, neighs—but finally, "punctual as a star," it stops at "its own stable door." The star, usually symbolic of a distant goal, has no such romantic connotations here. It is instead an astronomical phenomenon of dependability and accuracy. The poem then concerns itself with the relationship of the manmade and the godlike, and the underlying irony that something man devised should ever compete with cosmic "punctuality."

In Whitman's lyrical tribute to intuitive knowledge, "When I Heard the Learn'd Astronomer," he has the persona of the poem (that is, the character that the poet creates for the purposes of his poem) leave the lecture of "the learn'd astronomer" out of disgust with the superficiality of the factual knowledge the astronomer purveys. Then, in the open air, the persona looks up in "perfect silence at the stars." In these terms the stars express, symbolically, exalted height and eternal beauty, but even more they suggest the existence of a transcendent mystery beyond the perception of such "learned" scientists as the astronomer.

A symbol may be any object from man's perceptual reality—a star, a road, a rose—that suggests and comes to stand for something that is not palpable in the real world—a goal, a choice, a rare beauty. In each stanza of "In Time of 'The Breaking of Nations' " by Thomas Hardy, something eternal is symbolized—man working the earth; the home fire; the young lovers. Each represents something permanent or continual that will be present long after "War's annals . . . fade." At the time of World War I, Hardy expressed, symbolically, the hope that despite the wracking of nations, the old patterns of work, home, and love would endure.

A metaphor is an implied comparison. Two dissimilar things are compared on the basis of one or more features they have in common. In "A Narrow Fellow in the Grass," Emily Dickinson calls the straightened body of the snake a "spotted shaft." Like an arrow, the snake is tapered, assumes direction, and moves swiftly. When the snake uncoils, she calls it "a whiplash/ Unbraiding"; and when it contracts muscularly for movement, she says it "wrinkled, and was gone." Here the snake's appearance and movement are described by an implied comparison with leather and fabric. In the same poem the observer, using simile, reports, "The grass divides as with a comb." A simile is a direct comparison using "like" or "as." "My luve is like a red, red rose," writes Robert Burns. Like the metaphor, a simile suggests the similarity in things that appear dissimilar and compresses into a single figure several ideas. In "Fern Hill," Dylan Thomas describes a boy who was "happy as the grass was green." Logically, happiness has nothing to do with the color of grass. In the poem, however, the simile stresses the eternal color of grass and the lastingly intense quality of a boy's happiness.

Just as words may be used figuratively or connotatively, they may be used to evoke images, to present imaginatively an appeal to one of our senses. In "The Love Song of J. Alfred Prufrock," the mood of the evening is set by being compared to "a patient etherized upon a table." This kinesthetic image suggests a state of suspended animation, of immobility, of something deathlike. Later in the poem a visual image intensifies the gloom:

> The yellow fog that rubs its back upon
> the window-panes,
> The yellow smoke that rubs its muzzle on
> the window-panes. . . .

Metaphorically these lines suggest the catlike stealth of the fog. We can visualize its disagreeable assault upon city buildings. In addition we respond to the tactile suggestion of dampness, slime, and industrial grit, and the noiseless advance of the fog and smoke creates an auditory image that strikes us as ominous.

Auditory images are forcibly assisted by the sounds of words in themselves. In "A Prayer for My Daughter" by William Butler Yeats, a father hears a storm and imagines the years to come:

> Dancing to a frenzied drum,
> Out of the murderous innocence of the
> sea.

The generally low vowels, the heavy, thudding *"d's"* in "*d*ancing," "frenzie*d*," "*d*rum," and "mur*d*erous," and the recurrent nasal consonants in "da*n*cing," "fre*n*zied dru*m*," and "*m*urderous i*nn*ocence" reinforce the auditory image of the storm and suggest the tumultuous crisis of the father's thoughts. The ponderous, snarling sounds also strengthen the threat to innocence, beauty, and graciousness implicit in human nature as it aproaches the dangers of a chaotic future.

Thomas Hardy's "Darkling Thrush" offers a variety of images that create the bleakness of a winter landscape. The frost is "spectre-gray"; the sun is the "weakening eye of day." These grim visual images cause us not only to "see" the thin light and shrouded surfaces but to "feel" the bitter cold. The thermal image of cold is intensified by the lines that close the first stanza:

> And all mankind that haunted nigh
> Had sought their household fires.

Hardy next transfers to the century just completed the features of this winter landscape, as though they were the "Century's corpse outleant." The era is dead and buried and with it, seemingly, all the hopes and promises men believed it contained. The wind sings its "death-lament," and the pulse of life seems frozen eternally. Suddenly, the silence is broken by a sound that possibly offers hope: the song of an "aged thrush" in "blast-be-ruffled plume." Ironically, however, there is still nothing to sing about, and even if there were, even if—contrary to what we know—the bird had divine insight, man himself remains "unaware" of the "cause for carolings/ Of such ecstatic sound." Hardy, therefore, uses language imaginatively to affect our sensory perceptions; that is, he evokes images. But these images do not stand in isolation. They serve to heighten the irony, the intellectual wit of the poem. The poem works on two levels: the sensory and the intellectual.

A comparable use of figurative language and irony is found in Wilfred Owen's "Arms and the Boy." By personifying items in the arsenal of the modern world, Owen makes vivid the latent hostility of weapons and the vulnerability of young flesh. The steel of the bayonet is "cold" and "keen with hunger of blood"; it is "Blue with all malice" and "famishing for flesh." The bulletheads, "blind," that is, indiscriminating, as they are, "long to nuzzle in the hearts of lads." The cartridges, like predators, have sharp "teeth." The personified weapons are thus endowed with malignant purpose, and by implication the boy who is to embrace them will fondle them with naïve admiration and anticipation. The advice to allow him to do so, of course, is given as a warning and hence is meant ironically: If the boy embraces these "arms," he will embrace death. Yet, to compound the irony, the weapons are the only real defense the boy has. He has teeth, but they are meant "for laughing round an apple." His fingers lack claws, and, God-created though he is, he has "no talons at his heels/ Nor antlers through the thickness of his curls." We infer that what God intended for him was not battle, for which he needs artificial means, but happiness in a Garden of Eden where an apple was once his symbolic downfall. The allusion in the final stanza of the poem to the fateful apple underscores man's propensity for disobeying the will of his creator.

Another poetic allusion occurs when J. Alfred Prufrock says, "I have heard the mermaids singing each to each." The sirens of legend sang to lure men to their destruction, and for a moment Prufrock stands ready to be moved by some overwhelming passion. He concludes, however, that they will not sing to him. His death will be as undramatic as his life. He personifies death as an "Eternal Footman," decorous, prosaic, and obsequious.

In addition to meaning, of course, poetry has sound and movement. No one who remembers his elementary school days can forget the pupil who, falling into the predominant meter of a poem, read it so mechanically that he destroyed it forever. It is difficult, for example, to read the opening line of Poe's "The Raven" without smiling: "Ońce ŭpón ă ḿidnĭght d́reăry, whíle Ĭ pónderĕd, wéak ănd wéarў." There is nothing amusing about the meaning of the line, but there is something funny about the metrical possibilities. The consistent pattern of trochaic feet (metrical units in which the first syllable receives strong stress, the second a weak stress as in "midnight") tempts one into a singsong. When the meter is perfectly regular, one must be careful not to be swept along oblivious to the meaning of the lines. Or take Byron's "The Destruction of the Sennacherib":

> The Assyrian came down like the wolf on the fold,
> And his cohorts were gleaming in purple and gold,

Here the meter, which is anapestic (that is, every third syllable is stressed: "Ănd hĭs cóhŏrts"), nearly overwhelms the lines.

These examples illustrate a feature that some people think of as the most essential, or at least most characteristic, feature of poetry: metrical pattern. Although it is true that most poems have meter, metrical regularity is usually not as pronounced as it is in the aforementioned examples. Meter exists as a part of the total fabric of a poem; and, even though it may be isolated for study, its function can be understood only in relation to other poetic elements.

In Housman's poem "To an Athlete Dying Young," the basic meter is iambic: every other syllable, beginning with the second, is stressed. The iambic pattern is unbroken until the third stanza. There, the speaker addresses the dead athlete directly with the epithet "Smart lad." These two equally stressed syllables form the metrical foot we call a "spondee." When such a substitute foot obtrudes upon the basic meter, it metrically calls attention to the words or syllables so stressed.

In "The Second Coming" by William Butler Yeats, the meter is also basically iambic, but the first line begins with substitute feet: "Túrnĭng ănd túrnĭng ĭn thĕ wídĕnĭng gýre." Here a dactyl (a stressed syllable followed by two unstressed ones), followed by a trochaic and then a pyrrhic foot (a metrical unit of two unstressed syllables), makes for strong initial stresses that simulate the impulse, and lightly accented syllables that simulate the spinning. The final line of the poem also illustrates the contribution of metrical irregularity to total effect. The line "Slóuchĕs tówărd Béthlĕhĕm tŏ bĕ bórn" slouches much in the manner of the beast who comes to destroy. The breakdown of rhythm in this line ramifies the falling apart of "things" feared in the first stanza.

A poem written in free verse lacks both metrical pattern and rhyme scheme. In W. H. Auden's "Musée des Beaux Arts," for example, the very absence of the poetic artifices of meter and rhyme enables Auden to establish a casual conversational tone, a manner of offhand observation, which ironically underplays the tragic topic of human mortality. The understatement, assisted by natural speech rhythms, heightens the terror of the scene in Brueghel's painting by adopting the very detachment and indifference that characterize the world's reaction to individual suffering. How well such "Old Masters" as Brueghel understood that human suffering must be done in isolation!

An Analysis of "Anthem for Doomed Youth"

Although no poetic analysis, however accurate and complete, is a substitute for the poem itself, the following analysis of Wilfred Owen's "Anthem for Doomed Youth" is intended to illustrate some of the characteristics that have been discussed.

Anthem for Doomed Youth

What passing-bells for these who die as cattle?
Only the monstrous anger of the guns.
Only the stuttering rifles' rapid rattle
Can patter out their hasty orisons.
No mockeries for them; no prayers nor bells,
Nor any voice of mourning save the choirs,—
The shrill, demented choirs of wailing shells;
And bugles calling for them from sad shires.

What candles may be held to speed them all?
Not in the hands of boys, but in their eyes
Shall shine the holy glimmers of goodbyes.
The pallor of girls' brows shall be their pall;
Their flowers the tenderness of patient minds,
And each slow dusk, a drawing-down of blinds.

A quick reading of this poem indicates that it is about the inhumanity of war. Young men die on the battlefield, and no one formally mourns them. Although inspired by the events of World War I, the poem just as easily could have been written about any war since the invention of the rifle. The idea is not new; the poetic expression of the idea, however, is unique.

Wilfred Owen chose as his form the sonnet, a poem of fourteen lines in a basic meter of iambic pentameter. The rhyme scheme is that of an English (as opposed to an Italian, or Petrarchan) sonnet; that is, the first and third lines rhyme in each four-line unit or quatrain. The poem also ends, as English sonnets do, with a rhymed couplet, a two-line rhyme. A special form of the lyric, the sonnet is well suited for brief expressions of joy or grief, love or hate, for which the restraint of a prescribed form is appropriate.

The sonnet is organized around two related questions, the first in line one, the second in line nine. The first question explicitly compares the youths who die to cattle. By implication, of course, these youths are led to slaughter as a herd would be, dumbly, not knowing they will die. The only mourning sound is the "monstrous anger of the guns." In the absence of human voices and sentiments, the guns are personified as outraged. We feel the bitter irony that the guns, actually the unwitting instruments of this slaughter, alone commemorate the deaths audibly.

In the third line the alliterative "*r*'s" and "*t*'s" in "stuttering rifles' rapid rattle" simulate onomatopoetically the sound described by the words. This quick, light (perhaps because distant) sound "patters out" mechanically the prayers of the dying. Again, it is the sound of weapons rather than human utterance we are made aware of. The irony of these lines is strengthened by the linking in rhyme of the key words "guns" and "orisons."

The next four lines particularize the answer to the opening question and develop an unexpected irony. Since "prayers" or "bells" for the dead in a public display of sorrow would be inapt for "cattle" and mere hypocrisy in the official realm that sanctioned the battle in which the youth were "doomed," they are mourned by "shrill, demented choirs of wailing shells" rather than by the solemn harmony of human voices in a church. The instruments of death are again personified as agents, here not only mad ("demented") but paradoxically lamenting ("wailing"). These "voices" are joined by bugle calls coming from the localities bereaved by the death of their young men, the "sad shires." The repeated "*s*'s" here suggest the hush of these villages. Ironically, the bugle still summons young men to battle. The rhyme of "bells" and "shells" not only unifies the quatrain but stresses the military "music" that accompanies the dying.

The second question of the sonnet, in line nine, turns attention to the specifically human response: what "candles," what memorial services will "speed" or help the dead men on their way? In an inversion of normal word order that places the subject ("the holy glimmers of goodbyes") in an emphatic position at the end of the two-line sentence, the speaker predicts again no formal ostentation of sorrow for the dead but something more touching, meaningful, and sacred: the tears in the eyes of boys, or, with a less literalistic reading of the verb "shall shine," perhaps a light or a radiance that signifies remembrance. Notably, Owen does not paint the hackneyed picture of the mothers' grief but directs attention to the boys and girls who survive their only slightly older brothers and friends, for they are members of a depleted generation and their remembrance is the most poignant. The "pallor of girls' brows" is expressive, of course, of the unblemished white of young skin, but the word "pallor" also suggests the fading of healthy color under oppressive conditions of sadness or sickness. The pining, the silent mourning of maidens, then, shall be the "pall" for the doomed youth. The obvious play on the words "pallor" and "pall" draws together the meanings of the words. The dictionary meaning of a pall is either a coffin or a square of heavy cloth placed over the coffin. Of these two meanings, the second seems metaphorically more apt to the context. The coffins of the dead will be, in effect, not adorned literally. But a third dictionary meaning of "pall" is "something that covers or conceals; *esp:* an overspreading element that produces an effect of gloom." The paleness of the girls, then, will silently express their mourning, just as their "flowers," presumably laid memorially on the soldiers' graves, will express the "tenderness of patient minds." It is interesting that the words that describe in these lines a wordless mourning are characterized by low vowels, an absence of abrupt stop consonants, and a predominance of sibilants, aspirates, and liquids. The last line of the sonnet illustrates the influence of metrical variation upon pace. The spondee "slow dusk" brings together three equally stressed monosyllables: "each slow dusk" slows the line to suggest the tedious passage of time for those who remain alive and who at evening shut out the dusk by a "drawing-down of blinds." The drawing-down of blinds may also be understood metaphorically as a shutting out of light once the light, here suggesting hope, has vanished. It in this sense reminds us of the eternal darkness of the buried and at the same time the despair of the living. The repeated "*d*'s" weight the line to assist the notion of heaviness and hopelessness.

The implicit irony of the sonnet is clear. No human ceremony marks the death throes on the battlefield. The men who ostensibly fought for human values die without even completing their prayers. The sound of mourning comes from weapons, not from human voices. The grief of the survivors is expressed in personal suffering, not formal tributes.

Selective Glossary of Literary Terms*

AESTHETIC DISTANCE—critical or creative disinterestedness; the ability to regard an artistic object without prejudice or preconception; the power to objectify fully in artistic form the emotion or experience which requires expression.

ALLEGORY—a literary mode in which characters, events, and settings are of interest not only in themselves but in their power to imply a set of meanings over and beyond themselves. This second level of meanings may be religious, political, or philosophical. Characters are frequently personifications of abstract qualities or conditions of being. Thus Gulliver is the credulous traveller through whose eyes Jonathan Swift

* Cross-references are shown in italics; so also are a number of literary terms not given entries of their own.

ironically surveys the follies and vices of mankind; Christian, the hero of John Bunyan's *Pilgrim's Progress,* allegorically undertakes the journey from religious indifference to spiritual dedication. *The Faerie Queene* by Edmund Spenser, the most complex, ambitious allegory in the English language, sustains the adventures of its characters, on the level of *chivalric romance,* for the sake of illustrating specific Christian virtues and the obstacles to their attainment. Mr. and Mrs. Antrobus in *The Skin of Our Teeth* are obviously Mr. and Mrs. Everyman, beset by difficulties over the ages but bravely and miraculously coping and surviving against all odds.

ALLITERATION—the repetition of initial consonant or vowel sounds to effect a reinforcement of meaning or mood, as in Emily Dickinson's phrase "horrid, hooting," which suggests in its very sound the hollow "complaining" of the train in "I Like to See It Lap the Miles."

ALLUSION—an indirect reference to a literary, mythical, or historical context. When T. S. Eliot's Prufrock confesses he has seen his head "brought in upon a platter," he alludes to St. John the Baptist, to whom he bears no resemblance: "I am no prophet."

AMBIGUITY—a term which designates the presence of more than one meaning in a word or a more extended literary passage. Although the term may be applied to unintentionally imprecise expression, functional ambiguity in literature is a device to gain compression and multiplicity of meaning. Wilfred Owen intends ambiguity in "Arms and The Boy" (the word "arms" in the title, for example, is deliberately ambiguous). Although the advice in the poem seems to be ironic (the "arms" would seem to be the vulnerable boy's worst enemy), a further *irony* lies in the possibility of an equally possible, more cynical interpretation: the boy in his innocence, lacking "claws" and "teeth" as natural means of defense, would do well to embrace artificial means against his enemies.

ANAPEST—a metric foot of two unaccented syllables followed by one accented syllable (◡◡/).

ANTAGONIST—a term designating the one opposed to the *hero* or *protagonist* in dramatic conflict.

ANTICLIMAX—the arranging of material in order of decreasing emphasis or interest; a rhetorical weakness unless used deliberately for humorous effect, in which case the effect is *bathetic* (from the noun "bathos").

ANTIHERO—As rather loosely distinguished from a *hero,* the antihero is a protagonist, of relatively modern origin, whose thoughts and actions—whose very being—seems ironically to mock the idea of the heroic. (In common usage the *hero,* or *heroine,* of a tale is the *protagonist*—that is the major character of the narrative—and thus, paradoxically, an antihero may often be described quite accurately as a "hero.")

ANTITHESIS—a rhetorical device in which strongly contrasting terms or ideas are structurally balanced against each other for emphasis or *paradox,* as in Robert Frost's description in "Two Tramps in Mud Time": "The sun was warm but the wind was chill. . . ."

APOSTROPHE—direct address to a person or a personified entity, usually absent, as though present. In "Kilroy" the poet addresses that "G. I. Faustus who was everywhere" when he warns: "Kilroy, beware. 'HOME' is the final trap/that lurks for you in many a wily shape. . . ."

ARCHETYPE—A critical term used by the psychologist Carl G. Jung (and popularized by such archetypal critics as Northrop Frye), archetypes, according to Jung, are "racial memories" deep in the "collective unconscious" of all men—as, for instance, the memories of the jungle that came to Yank at the end of *The Hairy Ape.* These archetypes may manifest themselves in dreams and *myths*, and literary artists who draw upon such materials have the potential of stirring readers and audiences beyond their rational existence, deep down into their bones and their unconscious being.

ASSONANCE—the repetition of similar vowel sounds within a poetic line (or lines) or at the end of a line in place of end rime. See Dylan Thomas's "Fern Hill": "Now as I was yOUng and Easy Under the Apple boughs/ About the lilting h*ou*se and h*A*ppy *A*s the gr*A*ss was grEen. . . ."

ATMOSPHERE—the dominant mood, often descriptively established, of a literary work; for example, Joyce Carol Oates creates an atmosphere at once sensuous and foreboding in her story "Where Are You Going, Where Have You Been?"

BALLAD—a form of narrative originating among people with little or no literary sophistication, intended to be sung or recited and dealing generally with a single strong emotion or elemental situation, such as betrayal, heroism, love, heartbreak, or untimely death. The characters, sometimes legendary, are simply characterized, perhaps merely by an epithet, and the action is adumbrated rather than detailed. The narrator may leap over some steps in the action and linger descriptively at points of emotional crisis. The literary ballad, written deliberately to simulate the folk ballad, borrows its form and devices (incremental repetition, use of dialogue and the supernatural) but yields a meaning which transcends the story it tells. (See Theodore Roethke, "Ballad of the Clairvoyant Widow.")

BLANK VERSE—unrhymed *iambic pentameter.* It was put to best use in Elizabethan drama and in epic poetry by John Milton in *Paradise Lost.* Since then it has been used in idylls, lyrics, and an occasional play, such as T. S. Eliot's *The Cocktail Party.* Stephen Spender employs it in his poem "The Express."

BURLESQUE—exaggeration, often preposterous, for comic or satiric effect. In "The Love Song of J. Alfred Prufrock" Prufrock sees himself as a burlesque Hamlet. Although he wrestles with a decision, his problem, unlike Hamlet's, is "no great matter." One of the most renowned burlesques is Cervantes's *Don Quixote,* in which the form of the medieval romance encompasses the ridiculous tilting of the celebrated Don. Often burlesque employs a deliberately inappropriate style, as in *The Importance of Being Earnest,* where, for all their glossy manners and affectations, the upper classes deal with nothing more important than cucumber sandwiches and where being earnest substitutes for being sensible.

CARICATURE—a deliberate distortion, in drawing or in writing, which exaggerates specific features of a person or animal for satiric purposes. Max Beerbohm's "Self-Caricature 1897" highlights the playboy dandy of the turn-of-the-century to the exclusion of other realistic features. Emily Dickinson caricatures gentlewomen in "What Soft, Cherubic Creatures."

CATHARSIS—the purgation of strong feeling aroused by a dramatic situation through identification with its characters, a process alleged to take place with the resolution of conflict.

CLICHÉ—an overworked, consequently stale, expression; a stereotype. In "I Paint What I See," E. B. White balances Rivera's assertion antithetically with Nelson Rockefeller's "I know what I like" to suggest the discrepancy between a fresh vision in the painter and a hackneyed reaction in the millionaire.

CLIMAX—the arrangement of elements in ascending order of importance; the culmination of episodes in a story or novel; the point of greatest emotional intensity. In drama, a "turning point" in the action which reverses the course of the protagonist and makes his destiny clear.

COMEDY—as opposed to tragedy, that form of drama in which *conflict* is resolved short of death, and the continuance of life is insured by the temporary removal or overcoming of obstacles for its chief characters. Modern comedy frequently suggests that all is not well that ends well; the mere preservation of life is not synonymous with its renewal. Such "comedy" may seem sadder than tragedy.

COMPLICATION—in the action of a story or drama, the embroiling of characters in an increasingly complex fabric of *conflict,* leading up to the climax and resolved in the *dénouement.*

CONCEIT—originally synonymous with "idea" or "conception," the term has come to designate an elaborate, contrived, or intellectually ingenious metaphor, a farfetched comparison of unlike things. In "Freshmen" Barry Spacks describes the look of alert apprehension in the "best" students by comparing it to "the swinging door/ to the opera just before/ the Marx Brothers break through." This "conceit" presupposes subtlety of perception as well as specialized cinematic experience in the reader. The "conceits" of the so-called metaphysical poets as a rule are more detailed and sustained than those of modern poets.

CONNOTATION—as opposed to the *denotation* of a word, the suggestions a word makes or the associations it evokes; the emotional charge of a word as distinct from its dictionary definition. Gwendolyn Brooks in "The Chicago Defender Sends a Man to Little Rock" writes: "they are hurling spittle." The word "spittle" denotes "saliva," but conjures up repellent connotations of disease, senility, or sheer vulgarity.

CONSONANCE—at the end of poetic lines, half rime or slant rime; stressed syllables of the same final consonant but unlike vowel sounds, a device common in the poetry of Emily Dickinson, who rhymes "pearl" with "alcohol" in "I Taste a Liquor Never Brewed." Within a line consonance contributes sound effects which may reinforce meaning. In the line "Where all's accustomed, ceremonious" the consonance of the nasal *m*'s and *n* lends a measure, weight, and continuity to Yeats's meaning in "A Prayer for My Daughter."

COUPLET—two successive rhymed lines of identical meter.

DACTYL—a metric foot of one accented syllable followed by two unaccented syllables (/ ◡◡).

DECORUM—appropriateness or propriety in the treatment of literary subjects; the avoidance of the incongruous, incredible, or obscene.

DENOTATION—the literal or dictionary meaning of a word.

DENOUEMENT—that point in the action of a play or narrative at which everything in the plot is made clear and explained. In *Major Barbara,* for example, the dénouement begins when Undershaft explains his ideas on society and convinces Barbara, who has previously preached Christian salvation, to join him in the munitions business.

DEUS EX MACHINA—literally, "god from the machine"; metaphorically, any arbitrary action from outside the main action which resolves dramatic problems. The term originated with the Greek theatre, especially with the plays of Euripides, where the actors who played gods were lowered onto the stage by a crane or machine. Their role was to set situations right. In modern times such devices as the arrival of the cavalry to rescue beleaguered forces just in the nick of time, or the discovery of a birthmark which identifies the protagonist as a prince instead of a pauper, are instances of this artificial device. Often regarded as the failure of a writer to control his plot, this device is burlesqued in *Tom Jones.*

DRAMATIC MONOLOGUE—a lyric poem in which one character only speaks and reveals himself and his inner thoughts. Robert Browning brought the form into popular acclaim, and several twentieth-century poets, including T. S. Eliot in "The Love Song of J. Alfred Prufrock," have used it.

ELEGY—a dignified, meditative poem occasioned by the thought of death or the death of a particular person, for example, Walt Whitman's "When Lilacs Last in the Dooryard Bloom'd" or John Ciardi's "Elegy for G. B. Shaw."

EMPATHY—"feeling into"; in the reading of literature, the involuntary identification of the reader with fictitious characters; the vicarious "living" of their created lives.

END-STOPPED LINES—poetic lines in which the completion of syntax and meaning coincide with the end of the line.

ENJAMBEMENT—a device by which the syntax and meaning of one poetic line is carried to the succeeding line, or lines, without a break.

EPIC—a lengthy narrative poem concerning characters of heroic proportions in an action which has worldly or universal significance. The epic style is elevated and characterized by formal rhetorical devices such as the invocation of the Muse, the roll call of heroes past and present, extended *similes, apostrophes,* and *antitheses.* Beginning at a crucial point midway in the total action to be narrated, the epic author works forward and backward in time, incorporating accounts of battles, councils, and single combats between great contestants that are tangential to the main action. Gods as well as men take part in these actions, and the outcome affects not only the epic hero but his people, his nation, or mankind itself, as Adam's fall does in John Milton's *Paradise Lost.* Milton, like Virgil in *The Aeneid,* patterned his epic upon those of his famous Greek predecessor Homer: *The Iliad* and *The Odyssey.*

EPIGRAM—a pointed saying, characterized by elegance, terseness, and wit.

EPILOGUE—a section appended to a literary work; in drama, a short speech delivered by a performer directly to the audience at the conclusion of the play.

EULOGY—a piece, written or oral, in praise of a person or thing.

EUPHEMISM—an innocuous term substituted for a socially offensive one, such as "passing away" for "dying" or "perspiring" for "sweating."

EXPOSITION—that material in a story or play which gives information antecedent to the action proper but essential to understanding the present action or fictional situation. In *Major Barbara,* for instance, the history of the Undershaft lineage is vital to understanding either the action or the meaning of the play.

EXPRESSIONISM—a movement of late-nineteenth-century and early-twentieth-century artists who proposed to objectify inner states of feeling in unconventional ways. By saying he has measured out his life in coffee spoons, T. S. Eliot's Prufrock presents directly, in an image of triviality, the tedium and inconsequence of his days and hours.

FABLE—a short tale with a moral, didactic in nature, and frequently endowing animals with human attributes to show men's absurdities and vices. Aesop's well-known beast fables gain political dimension in the modern fable *Animal Farm* by George Orwell.

FALLING ACTION—the resolution of dramatic action after the climax.

FIGURE OF SPEECH—a word or words used to give forceful, imaginative expression to something other than their literal meaning. Words so used undergo either a shift in meaning (as when Sylvia Plath metaphorically calls her father a "black shoe") or a shift for the sake of rhetorical emphasis, as in *apostrophe* and *antithesis.*

FLASHBACK—a break in narrative sequence for the sake of recounting what has happened prior to the present action. Willy Loman's dramatized memories of early days with his sons are flashbacks in Arthur Miller's *Death of a Salesman.*

FOOT—a metrical unit such as the *iamb* (◡/), *trochee* (/◡), *anapest* (◡◡/), and *dactyl* (/◡◡).

FORESHADOWING—the preparation of expectations for what is to come in a story or drama by means of setting; speeches which appear significant only in the light of later developments; images or symbols which adumbrate central ideas or future crises.

FREE VERSE—verse which relies for its effects on devices other than meter and rhyme.

GENRE—a literary type, as well as a subdivision of such kinds; for example, the novel is a genre distinct from the fable or the short story, as the picaresque novel is a genre distinct from the historical novel.

GOTHIC—a term applied to elements in a literary work which introduce the supernatural (rather than the spiritual), the extravagant, the grotesque, or the exotic for the sake of creating atmosphere. The stories of Edgar Allan Poe and the cartoons of Charles Addams (for quite different purposes) employ Gothic features: live burial, torture chambers, predatory birds, ghosts, clanking chains, cobwebs, hanging moss, castles, monsters, fiends, and hags. The term Gothic originally designated the barbaric and crude as opposed to the classical in art, architecture, and literature.

HEROIC COUPLET—two successive lines of rhymed iambic pentameter.

HUBRIS—the *tragic flaw* of many classical protagonists: the excessive pride which goes before their fall.

HYPERBOLE—an exaggeration, for rhetorical effect, which proposes a literal impossibility or improbability; for example, "I'll die if I don't pass English."

IAMB—a poetic foot in which an unaccented syllable is followed by an accented one. The following line is written in iambs and consists of four iambic feet:

I líke to sée it láp the míles.

Technically the line is, therefore, written in iambic (◡/) tetrameter (four feet to the line).

IMAGERY—the use of verbal sensory appeals to stimulate the imagination and at times to suggest by indirection the major elements in the intellectual content of a literary work. The most common of the sensory appeals is visual, but the other senses—hearing, taste, touch and smell, as well as the sense of movement—are often used effectively, sometimes in complexly mingled fashions, by the sophisticated writer. Figures of speech such as the simile and the metaphor often make vivid use of images, and individual images may be made symbolic by artistic manipulation (often through repetition) in the course of a literary work. In Housman's "Loveliest of Trees" the cherry tree "Wearing white for Eastertide" makes a memorable image which ultimately goes beyond the white color to the concept of purity and then to the yearly resurrection of nature.

IMPRESSIONISM—a literary term drawn from a school of nineteenth-century French painting (Claude Monet was among its leaders) which attempted to demonstrate, through its depiction of the changing effects of light, that even in the external world "objective reality" was varied. In literature the term is associated with the concept that subjective reality is more "true" than objective facts. Thus the author may emphasize (as James Joyce often does) the inward world of his characters to the neglect of the external environment, or he may (as Eugene O'Neill often does) use distortions of reality (the sailor's quarters in a ship may be made to seem like a cage for animals) to communicate "truths" that realistic treatment cannot capture. In his poem "On a Photo of Sgt. Ciardi a Year Later" John Ciardi espouses the impressionistic credo when he writes: "The camera always lies. By a law of perception/ The obvious surface is always an optical ruse."

INEVITABILITY—the mood created by an author to dramatize the concept that lives are predestined and events are fated. For the ancient Greek playwrights the inevitability of dramatic actions often sprang from a concept of man's relationship to the gods; thus Oedipus, in Sophocles' play *Oedipus Rex,* tries to elude the fulfillment of the prophesy of the Oracle (that Oedipus would kill his own father and marry his own mother) and succeeds only in exposing his own flaw of *hubris* (or excessive pride). In modern drama, as in O'Neill's plays *Desire Under the Elms* and *Mourning Becomes Electra,* the feeling of the inevitability of events flows from inward compulsions of the characters (often based on such Freudian concepts as the Oedipal complex) which cannot be successfully resisted.

INFORMAL ESSAY—a short literary composition. As contrasted to the formal essay, the informal (or personal or familiar) essay is subjective and individualistic, disposed more toward the illumination of personal feelings and opinions than toward the teaching of facts and the expounding of ideas. Though the distinction between the formal and informal essay is often imprecise, Huxley's "The Method of Scientific Investigation" exemplifies the formal essay while George Orwell's "Shooting an Elephant" is undoubtedly informal.

INVOCATION—an author's plea to the gods (most especially the Greek muses) to bring him inspiration, divine powers, in the creation of his art. The epic poem customarily begins with an invocation to Calliope, the muse of epic poetry.

IRONY—a literary device which especially involves contrast in meaning and indirection in technique. Two significant forms of irony are the irony of words and the irony of events. The first especially involves a contrast between what is said and what is meant; the second usually involves a contrast between what one expects to result from an action and what actually occurs. A simple example of verbal irony may be seen in the title of T. S. Eliot's poem

"The Love Song of J. Alfred Prufrock" (for the poem mocks Prufrock's capacity for both life and love); an example of the irony of events may be seen in *The Glass Menagerie* (where the Wingfield family seeks a gentleman caller for the heroine, Laura, but when he arrives, he ultimately brings not salvation, but only greater despair).

LYRIC—in Greek poetry, a poem to be sung to the accompaniment of a lyre, but now a short poem with strong musical and subjective elements.

MELODRAMA—a type of play, most popular in the late nineteenth century, which exploits extreme (and improbable) situations involving simple black and white characters (villains and heroes) to come to a resolution in which evil is overcome and virtue triumphantly prevails.

METAPHOR—Among the most common forms of figurative language, the metaphor implies a comparison, without the use of like or as, between two dissimilar objects by stating that the two are identical. By asserting the identity of the two, a literal impossibility, the writer forces the audience to probe for a way in which the assertion may be valid in respect to some essential similarity between the objects compared. A simple metaphor is the statement, "America is an insane asylum."

METER—in English poetry, the basic rhythmic pattern of stressed (/) and unstressed (◡) syllables in a line of verse. The most common metrical patterns are *iambic* (◡/), *trochaic* (/◡), *anapestic* (◡◡/), and *dactylic* (/◡◡). Most poetry, especially modern poetry, makes use of considerable metrical variation in order to avoid monotonous regularity.

MOTIVATION—the reasons, largely psychological, that a character acts in certain ways in particular situations. When a character acts in ways inappropriate to the personality he has established, his actions become implausible and the narrative becomes unbelievable.

MYTH—in the traditional sense, a fictitious narrative usually involving supernatural beings; revealing popular ideas about the mysteries of natural phenomena and their explanation; and dramatically symbolizing some of the more profound beliefs of a particular culture. These primitive legends have, for such writers as Sigmund Freud and Carl Jung, been seen as similar to dreams in that they may be used as sources for symbolic revelations of the deeper truths of individuals and civilizations. Carl Jung's theory of *archetypal* memories posits a racial "collective unconscious," a common mental inheritance, that "remembers" at the deepest level of being such repeated racial experiences and events as those of birth and death. These ideas have been used by such critics as Leslie Fiedler and Northrop Frye to serve as the foundation of a critical system involving archetypes (what Jung calls "primordial images") in literature. Modern poets and novelists such as T. S. Eliot and James Joyce have made much use of myth in such primary works of the twentieth century as *The Wasteland* and *Ulysses.*

NATURALISM—Sometimes defined as "realism on all fours," naturalism emphasizes the physical, brute, instinctive nature of man (the "natural" man) rather than the mental abilities (such as the skill of reading) and spiritual aspirations (toward morality) which differentiate man from a purely animal being. The generally acknowledged "father" of realism was the French writer Émile Zola, and in *Le roman expérimental* ("The Experimental Novel") he insisted that the novelist should be, like the scientist, a dispassionate observer whose "experiments" revealed the "law" by which men's actions and lives were determined by heredity and environment. These kinds of determinism—biological determinism, which implies man is what he must be because of his genes, and environmental determinism, which insists that a man is what he is because of where he is nurtured—are, perhaps, the dominant traits of naturalism. Its other qualities often include a tendency towards great detail (in an effort to tell the whole truth); towards the depiction of lower life (in an attempt to depict the animal source of man); towards presenting an unplotted "slice of life" (in an effort to suggest the purposeless chaos of existence); and towards implying a Darwinistic, evolutionary philosophy (in an effort to dramatize the thesis that force is the ultimate law in a world dominated by the struggle for survival).

ODE—A formal lyric characterized by extended length, elevated language, exalted emotion, and a serious and dignified theme, the ode was originally a precise choral form (divided, in the Pindaric ode, into strophe, antistrophe, and epode) and was used in such Greek dramas as *Oedipus Rex;* now the ode, when written at all, is usually an intellectual, introspective meditation, not conceived for public performance but to aid self understanding.

ONOMATOPEIA—the use of words whose very sound ("buzz," "bang") implies their meanings. In the hands of a subtle poet individual lines or even complete stanzas may so manipulate sound as to imply the event by the sound itself; note, for instance, how Matthew Arnold, at the end of the first stanza of "Dover Beach," captures by his manipulation of sound the movement of water against shore.

PARADOX—a statement which seems on superficial examination to be either absurd or contradictory but which on closer inspection reveals its own validity. Like *irony,* paradox implies contrast, and some critics (especially among those categorized as New Critics) see irony and paradox (as well as indirection generally) as the particular language appropriate to poetry (as opposed to the factual, explicit language appropriate to science).

PARODY—a humorous mockery, usually by exaggerated stylistic and thematic imitation, of another piece of work. Anthony Hecht's "The Dover Bitch" is in part a parody of Matthew Arnold's "Dover Beach."

PATHETIC FALLACY—a phrase first used by John Ruskin to categorize that tendency of impassioned writers to ascribe human emotions to inanimate objects. In his *Modern Painters* (1856), Ruskin quotes the passage:

> They rowed her in across the rolling foam—
> The cruel, crawling foam.

Then Ruskin comments:

> The foam is not cruel, neither does it crawl. The state of mind which attributes to it these characters of a living creature is one in which the reason is unhinged by grief. All violent feelings have the same effect. They produce in us a falseness in all our impressions of external things, which I would generally characterize as the "pathetic fallacy."

PERSONA—in one sense the character or characters (personae) in a work, most especially a play. In a second sense the voice (or mask) through which the author speaks in a particular artistic work. Thus Mark Twain uses Huckleberry Finn as his persona in *The Adventures of Huckleberry Finn,* but Mark Twain is obviously not Huckleberry Finn even though Twain may have drawn upon his own experiences and emotions to give *verisimilitude* to his narrative.

PERSONIFICATION—a figure of speech in which non-human objects and ideas are treated as if they possessed human attributes. Edna St. Vincent Millay in "Justice Denied in Massachusetts" personifies death in the lines:

> Let us sit here, sit still,
> Here in the sitting-room until we die;
> At the step of Death on the walk,
> rise and so; . . .

PICARESQUE NOVEL—an episodic narrative, realistic in its language and details, in which the central figure (or picaro) wanders from place to place and undergoes a series of adventures which in large part satirize the follies of various social classes, most especially the bourgeoisie. Originating in Spain as a burlesque of chivalric romances (as was Cervantes' *Don Quixote),* the form, with considerable modification, has been employed effectively by novelists as diverse as Daniel Defoe *(Moll Flanders),* Mark Twain *(The Adventures of Huckleberry Finn),* and Saul Bellow *(The Adventures of Augie March).*

PLOT—a series of causally related events (the second arising from the first, the third from the second) with a clearly discernible beginning, middle, and end and involving a *conflict* of forces which ultimately comes to a *climax*. The plot may differ from the action of a story, for the plot is the author's arrangement of events to gain the highest dramatic effect (often ignoring chronological sequence), while the *action* is the chronological ordering of the events. In his *Poetics,* Aristotle insists on the necessity of *unity* in plot; thus by his test no event in the plot can be omitted or rearranged without altering the whole.

POINT OF VIEW—the angle of vision from which a story is told. The basic points of view are the first person and the third person. In the first person the story is told by "I," and "I" may be the major actor in the story, a minor participant, or merely someone who observes what occurs or narrates what he has heard from others. The third person narrator ("he"), may be omniscient (that is, he knows everything about all his characters, including their thoughts, and tells anything which he desires); may have selective omniscience (in which case the author limits what his narrator knows); or may merely see, like an audience at a play, what takes place before his eyes (the objective or dramatic point of view). The particular point of view of any story may be highly complex, for in any story there may be considerable overlapping in point of view, and there are innumerable variations of both the first and third person angles of vision.

PUN (or PARONOMASIA)—word play in which differences in meaning in a single word, or similarities in sound between two words with different meanings are manipulated for humorous or thematic effects. That the pun is not always the lowest form of humor is proved by one of the greatest of punsters, Shakespeare, as, for instance, in his play upon the word "dust" in the following lines: "Golden lads and girls all must/ As chimney sweepers, come to dust."

QUATRAIN—a *stanza* of four lines of either rhymed or unrhymed verse.

REALISM—Historically a mode of writing especially associated with the nineteenth century, realism may generally be defined as a literary mode which emphasizes fact or reality and rejects the impractical or visionary. William Dean Howells, sometimes called the "Father" of American realism, defined the mode as "nothing more and nothing less than the truthful treatment of materials"; in his own realistic credo he insisted upon the primacy of the ordinary and the commonplace and upon the duty of the realist "to front the every-day world and catch the charm of its work-worn, care-worn, brave, kindly face." Realists such as John W. De Forest, W. D. Howells, and Henry James often satirize the excesses of romantic overstatement and idealization, and they generally avoid the tendency of naturalists towards deterministic philosophies. In their treatment of ordinary materials, the realists tend towards precision and understatement, towards simple, even colloquial, expression, and towards minimizing of rhetorical language and symbolic suggestion.

RHYME—the repetition of similar patterns of sound (cat: rat) in verse. The most common place where rhyme occurs is at the end of a poetic line (end rhyme), but internal rhyme (in which the rhyming syllable or syllables come after the beginning and before the end of a line) is common, and beginning rhyme (in which the rhyming syllable or syllables occur at the beginning of a line) is occasionally practiced. Masculine (or single) rhyme is the correspondence of final syllables (time: crime; decay: portray); feminine (or double) rhyme is the correspondence of the last two syllables (lending: bending); and polysyllabic rhyme is the correspondence of three or more syllables (Victorian: Praetorian). Approximate rhyme (or *slant* or *half rhyme)* occurs when the similarity of sounds is imperfect (steel: tell). The *rhyme scheme* of a poem is the pattern of the end rhymes in the work. A common pattern for a Petrarchan sonnet is as follows: abbaabbacdcdcd; the repetition of the various letters indicates the pattern of repetition in the rhyme scheme.

RHYTHM—the general quality of the rise and fall of emphasis which exists with relative looseness in prose and relative rigidity in poetry. Broader in concept than meter, rhythm is, nevertheless, closely associated with *meter* in verse, save that the regularity of metrical stresses is not the sole determinant of the rhythm of a poem. In *free verse,* which lacks metrical symmetry, rhythm exists but it is less rigidly organized than in metrical poetry.

RISING ACTION—that part of the action of a dramatic narrative which proceeds from the *complication* (in which opposition to the protagonist first becomes evident in the plot) through the development of the *conflict* to the *climax* (in which the dramatic tension is at its height). The falling action follows the climax and leads ultimately to the *dénouement.*

ROMANTICISM—in English and American literature a movement of the late eighteenth century which was in large part a revolt against neo-classic formalism as well as a reaction against artistic, political, and religious orthodoxy. Often used as a term in contrast to *realism* or *classicism,* romanticism in art emphasizes the individualistic, the spontaneous, the emotional, and the imaginative, but the vagueness of the term, the imprecision of its definition, has led some scholars such as Professor A. O. Lovejoy to complain that the confusion over the meaning of romanticism is a literary "scandal" and to insist that the varied, and often conflicting, senses of the term imply that there is no such thing as "romanticism" but only a diversity of "romanticisms." Be that as it may, certain characteristics in art are generally recognized as "romantic" (though the possession of any one or more of them does not mean that the writer possessing these characteristics is necessarily a "romantic" writer). Among these qualities is a tendency towards introspection; the worship of nature; an interest in the foreign, the mysterious, and the exotic; a tendency to adulate childhood and the "natural" in any form; an obsession with, and a quest for, absolute truth; an enthusiasm for unique, experimental styles; and a fondness for *symbols* which emphasize and yet illuminate the mystery of existence. Among modern writers whose art, as well as their lives, exemplify important aspects of romanticism are Dylan Thomas and F. Scott Fitzgerald. Though few writers can be said to be wholly romantic (or *realistic* or *naturalistic*)—Hemingway, with different parts of himself, is all three—it can be said that the art of most writers is such that they can be conveniently categorized; it is important to remember, however, that the art, not the label, is what matters most.

RUN-ON-LINE—as opposed to an *end-stopped* line, a run-on or *enjambed* line is a poetic line in which there is no pause, either in sense or grammatic structure, from one line to the succeeding one.

SATIRE—a humorous indictment of human vices, frailties, and foibles, usually with the intent of reforming either man or society or both. Among classical Roman writers Horace mocked, with relative gentleness, the vices of his society, while Juvenal was more bitter and personal in his attacks upon the frailties and foibles of man; the most common differentiation of satire, into Horatian and Juvenalian, springs from this distinction. "The Machine Stops," in its indictment of various tendencies of modern technology, would properly be classified as Horatian satire.

SENTIMENTALISM—generally emotional self-indulgence stemming from a disproportion between an emotional response and the cause for that reaction. In another sense sentimentalism refers to a general philosophic outlook which denies the existence of evil and simplifies man into a creature that is essentially virtuous and benevolent.

SETTING—the physical details—most especially as to place and time—which illuminate the external (and sometimes the internal) background in which a story takes place. Often the setting of a story is extremely important in illuminating aspects of meaning in a narrative, and occasionally the primacy of setting in a story (such as Poe's "Fall of the House of Usher") may lead critics to refer to it as a story of setting.

SIMILE—a comparison, usually by the use of "like" or "as," between two essentially dissimilar things. The following simile, from D. H. Lawrence's "Wedding Morn," makes an effective comparison:

The morning breaks like pomegranate
In a shining crack of red;

In addition, however, the simile suggests the sexual psychology and imagery of the poem as a whole. In doing so, the simile becomes not only ornamentative but functional.

SONNET—characteristically a fourteen line poem written in *iambic pentameter.* The most common kinds of sonnets are *Petrarchan* (or Italian) and *Shakespearean* (or English). The former takes its name from a great fourteenth-century Italian sonnet writer, and is characterized by a rhyme scheme in which the first eight lines (or *octet)* are regularly rhymed abbaabba; the last six lines (or *sestet)* are usually rhymed cde cde, but common variants of the sestet are such rhyme schemes as cd cd cd, cde edc, and cde dce. Typically the pattern of thought of the Petrarchan sonnet corresponds to the twofold division of the rhyme, so that the octet poses a question or suggests a psychological dilemma and the sestet asserts a possible resolution. The Shakespearean sonnet takes its name from the greatest practitioner of this modified form of the Petrarchan sonnet. In it the rhyme scheme is abab cdcd efef gg, that is, three quatrains followed by a rhymed couplet. Often the pattern of thought follows the fourfold pattern of the rhyme, with possibly the first three parts of the poem being three different images making a single thematic point and the whole summarized epigrammatically by the end couplet. A common practise, however, is to break the pattern of thought into a twofold one similar to the pattern of the Petrarchan sonnet, with the division being between the first eight lines and the last six. In addition to these common forms of the sonnet, a third form, irregular, is often practised. The variants in rhyme and meter in the irregular sonnet are innumerable, and twelve, sixteen, and twenty line sonnets are not unknown. Numerous writers have also written *sonnet sequences,* in which a series of sonnets are linked to each other by their treatment of a unified topic. Among the most celebrated sonnet sequences are Mrs. Elizabeth Barrett Browning's "Sonnets from the Portuguese," W. H. Auden's "The Quest," and Dylan Thomas's "Altarwise by Owl-light."

SPONDEE—in poetry, two long or accented syllables in succession.

STANZA—a poetic unit, usually similar in pattern to other such units in a single poem, and comparable, when short, to a prose sentence or, when long, to a prose paragraph. Among the more common stanzaic forms are the *couplet* (two lines), *terza rima* (three lines), *quatrain* (four lines), *rime royal* (seven lines), *ottava rima* (eight lines), and *Spenserian* (nine lines).

STREAM-OF-CONSCIOUSNESS—a type of psychological *realism* which uses the mind as the dominant force behind the form of the work. In using the technique the author attempts to capture the flux of a character's thought, often chaotic and disconnected, as it flows from different levels of consciousness and unconsciousness. Among the great novels to use this fictional technique are James Joyce's *Ulysses* and William Faulkner's *The Sound and the Fury.*

STYLE—When used in reference to literary style (as distinct from, say, a painting style or a life style), style is the use of language in all its variety—from diction to sentence patterns to imagery to symbolism—in a way that best expresses the artistic intent and the unique individuality of a particular author. There are, of course, an infinite number of styles, some of them named after authors *(Miltonic, Ciceronian, Euphuistic),* some after literary periods *(neoclassic, naturalistic),* some after particular professions *(journalistic, legalistic),* but these categories, though convenient, are only the beginning of saying anything truly intelligent about a particular writer's style.

SUSPENSE—the uncertainty and anxiety, especially appropriate to drama and fiction, which teases the reader or audience into excited anticipation of what will occur next.

SYMBOLISM—the conscious use in literature of things (events, images, objects) which are not only themselves but also stand for things (that is, become symbols that symbolize concepts) that extend beyond themselves. In his practise of symbolism, the symbolist may use natural symbols (the ebb and flow of the tide to suggest the ebb and flow of life), conventional symbols (white as suggestive of purity), Freudian symbols (a gun as symbolic of masculine sexuality), or private symbols (which he or a select circle of friends may alone know). Often the symbolist, by his use of symbols, attempts to suggest an unseen reality, an absolute truth, behind what he may conceive to be the veil of appearances. This attempt to hint rather than to state, to imply mysteries rather than assert facts, is to be found in many of the great writers of the *Symbolist Movement* (among them Rimbaud, Mallarmé, and Valéry) which flourished in France in the latter part of the nineteenth century.

THEME—generally speaking, the central meaning, either directly or indirectly expressed by the author, in a serious literary work. On occasions the dominant theme of a work is obvious; on others, it is elusive. In either case it is probably true that all else in a serious work—setting, plot, character, tone, whatever—will help to illuminate theme.

TONE—the emotional coloring of a piece of writing which suggests the author's attitude towards his material—tender, passionate, ironic—much as the tone of voice of a speaker implies part of the total meaning of what he says.

TRAGEDY—As distinct from *comedy,* tragedy uses dignified language to deal with a subject of high importance; dramatizes characters of some importance whose fate is of more than mere personal significance; and ends with the destruction, either physically or spiritually, of the hero. Aristotle in his *Poetics* insisted that the hero of a tragedy should not be either evil or stupid; thus his downfall arises through a *tragic flaw (hamartia)* in himself with which the audience can sympathize. The ultimate effect of tragedy, according to Aristotle, is to arouse the emotions of pity and fear in order to effect a *catharsis* in the audience—that is, to produce in them a purgation, or possibly a purification, of their emotions. For Aristotle, *Oedipus Rex* is the perfect example of tragedy. In our time few dramatists have attempted to write classical tragedy, and some critics have claimed that such art is inappropriate to the temper of man and society in the modern age.

UNITY—that quality in literature by which the variety of the parts in a work is directed towards a single effect, so that all parts of the whole serve a function, and no part seems unnecessary or out of place. Aristotle insisted in his *Poetics* that a play should have unity of action, and Renaissance critics extended his theory to a deification of the *unities* of time (the action of the play should cover no more than twenty-four hours), place (the action should be set in one locale), and action (there should be only one narrative line). Partly as a reaction to such limitations, some critics and artists (among them Coleridge and Emerson) preached the doctrine of organic unity (or organic form), by which the work of art was compared to a living thing which grows from within itself rather than is shaped by rigid man-made laws.

VERISIMILITUDE—the feeling of truth achieved in a literary work by the use of details that are, or seem to be, drawn from reality.

Index